MICHAEL CONNELLY

Three Great Novels: The Thrillers

Also by Michael Connelly

The Black Echo

The Black Ice

The Concrete Blonde

The Last Coyote

Trunk Music

Michael Connelly

Three Great Novels: The Thrillers

The Poet
Blood Work
Void Moon

ORION

This omnibus edition first published in Great Britain in 2002 by Orion,
an imprint of the Orion Publishing Group Ltd.

A CIP catalogue record for this book is available from the British Library.
ISBN 0 75285 354 6 (hardback) 0 75285 355 4 (trade paperback)

Typeset by Deltatype Ltd, Birkenhead, Merseyside
Printed and bound in Great Britain by
Clays Ltd, St Ives plc.

The Orion Publishing Group Ltd
Orion House
5 Upper Saint Martin's Lane
London, WC2H 9EA

Contents

The Poet

This is for Philip Spitzer and Joel Gotler.
Great advisors and agents, but most of all great friends.

1

Death is my beat. I make my living from it. I forge my professional reputation on it. I treat it with the passion and precision of an undertaker – somber and sympathetic about it when I'm with the bereaved, a skilled craftsman with it when I'm alone. I've always thought the secret of dealing with death was to keep it at arm's length. That's the rule. Don't let it breathe in your face.

But my rule didn't protect me. When the two detectives came for me and told me about Sean, a cold numbness quickly enveloped me. It was like I was on the other side of the aquarium window. I moved as if underwater – back and forth, back and forth – and looked out at the rest of the world through the glass. From the backseat of their car I could see my eyes in the rearview mirror, flashing each time we passed beneath a streetlight. I recognized the thousand-yard stare I had seen in the eyes of fresh widows I had interviewed over the years.

I knew only one of the two detectives. Harold Wexler. I had met him a few months earlier when I stopped into the Pints Of for a drink with Sean. They worked CAPs together on the Denver PD. I remember Sean called him Wex. Cops always use nicknames for each other. Wexler's is Wex, Sean's, Mac. It's some kind of tribal bonding thing. Some of the names aren't complimentary but the cops don't complain. I know one down in Colorado Springs named Scoto whom most other cops call Scroto. Some even go all the way and call him Scrotum, but my guess is that you have to be a close friend to get away with that.

Wexler was built like a small bull, powerful but squat. A voice slowly cured over the years by cigarette smoke and whiskey. A hatchet face that always seemed red the times I saw him. I remember he drank Jim Beam over ice. I'm always interested in what cops drink. It tells a lot about them. When they're taking it straight like that, I always think that maybe they've seen too many things too many times that most people never see even once. Sean was drinking Lite beer that night, but he was young. Even though he was the supe of the CAPs unit, he was at least ten years younger than Wexler. Maybe in ten years he would have been taking his medicine cold and straight like Wexler. But now I'll never know.

I spent most of the drive out from Denver thinking about that night at the Pints Of. Not that anything important had happened. It was just drinks with my brother at the cop bar. And it was the last good time between us, before Theresa Lofton came up. That memory put me back in the aquarium.

But during the moments that reality was able to punch through the glass and into my heart, I was seized by a feeling of failure and grief. It was the first real tearing of the soul I had experienced in my thirty-four years. That included the death of my sister. I was too young then to properly grieve for Sarah or even to understand the pain of a life unfulfilled. I grieved now because I had not even known Sean was so close to the edge. He was Lite beer while all the other cops I knew were whiskey on the rocks.

Of course, I also recognized how self-pitying this kind of grief was. The truth was that for a long time we hadn't listened much to each other. We had taken different paths. And each time I acknowledged this truth the cycle of my grief would begin again.

My brother once told me the theory of the limit. He said every homicide cop had a limit but the limit was unknown until it was reached. He was talking about dead bodies. Sean believed that there were just so many that a cop could look at. It was a different number for every person. Some hit it early. Some put in twenty in homicide and never got close. But there was a number. And when it came up, that was it. You transferred to records, you turned in your badge, you did something. Because you just couldn't look at another one. And if you did, if you exceeded your limit, well, then you were in trouble. You might end up sucking down a bullet. That's what Sean said.

I realized that the other one, Ray St. Louis, had said something to me.

He turned around in his seat to look back at me. He was much larger than Wexler. Even in the dim light of the car I could make out the rough texture of his pockmarked face. I didn't know him but I'd heard him referred to by other cops and I knew they called him Big Dog. I had thought that he and Wexler made the perfect Mutt and Jeff team when I first saw them waiting for me in the lobby at the *Rocky*. It was like they had stepped out of a late-night movie. Long, dark overcoats, hats. The whole scene should have been in black and white.

'You hear me, Jack. We'll break it to her. That's our job, but we'd just like you to be there to sort of help us out, maybe stay with her if it gets rough. You know, if she needs to be with somebody. Okay?'

'Okay.'

'Good, Jack.'

We were going to Sean's house. Not the apartment he split with four other cops in Denver so in accordance with city regs he was a Denver resident. His house in Boulder where his wife, Riley, would answer our knock. I knew nobody was going to be breaking anything to her. She'd know what the news was the moment she opened the door and saw the three of us standing there without Sean. Any cop's wife would know. They spend their lives dreading and preparing for that day. Every time there's a knock on the door they expect it to be death's messengers standing there when they open it. This time it would be.

'You know, she's going to know,' I told them.

'Probably,' Wexler said. 'They always do.'

I realized they were counting on Riley knowing the score as soon as she opened the door. It would make their job easier.

I dropped my chin to my chest and brought my fingers up beneath my glasses to pinch the bridge of my nose. I realized I had become a character in one of my own stories – exhibiting the details of grief and loss I worked so hard to get so I could make a thirty-inch newspaper story seem meaningful. Now I was one of the details in this story.

A sense of shame descended on me as I thought of all the calls I had made to a widow or parent of a dead child. Or brother of a suicide. Yes, I had even made those. I don't think there was any kind of death that I hadn't written about, that hadn't brought me around as the intruder into somebody's pain.

How do you feel? Trusty words for a reporter. Always the first question. If not so direct, then carefully camouflaged in words meant to impart sympathy and understanding – feelings I didn't actually have. I carried a reminder of this callousness. A thin white scar running along my left cheek just above the line of my beard. It was from the diamond engagement ring of a woman whose fiancé had been killed in an avalanche near Breckenridge. I asked her the old standby and she responded with a backhand across my face. At the time I was new to the job and thought I had been wronged. Now I wear the scar like a badge.

'You better pull over,' I said. 'I'm going to be sick.'

Wexler jerked the car into the freeway's breakdown lane. We skidded a little on the black ice but then he got control. Before the car had completely stopped I tried desperately to open the door but the handle wouldn't work. It was a detective car, I realized, and the passengers who most often rode in the back were suspects and prisoners. The back doors had security locks controlled from the front.

'The door,' I managed to strangle out.

The car finally jerked to a stop as Wexler disengaged the security lock. I opened the door, leaned out and vomited into the dirty slush. Three great heaves from the gut. For a half a minute I didn't move, waiting for more, but that was it. I was empty. I thought about the backseat of the car. For prisoners and suspects. And I guessed that I was both now. Suspect as a brother. A prisoner of my own pride. The sentence, of course, would now be life.

Those thoughts quickly slipped away with the relief the physical exorcism brought. I gingerly stepped out of the car and walked to the edge of the asphalt where the light from the passing cars reflected in moving rainbows on the petroleum-exhaust glaze on the February snow. It looked as if we had stopped alongside a grazing meadow but I didn't know where. I hadn't been paying attention to how far along to Boulder we were. I took off my gloves and glasses and put them in the pockets of my coat. Then I reached down and dug beneath the spoiled surface to where the snow was white and pure. I took up two handfuls of the cold, clean powder and pressed it to my face, rubbing my skin until it stung.

'You okay?' St. Louis asked.

He had come up behind me with his stupid question. It was up there with *How do you feel?* I ignored it.

'Let's go,' I said.

We got back in and Wexler wordlessly pulled the car back onto the freeway. I saw a sign for the Broomfield exit and knew we were about halfway there. Growing up in Boulder, I had made the thirty-mile run between there and Denver a thousand times but the stretch seemed like alien territory to me now.

For the first time I thought of my parents and how they would deal with this. Stoicly, I decided. They handled everything that way. They never discussed it. They moved on. They'd done it with Sarah. Now they'd do it with Sean.

'Why'd he do it?' I asked after a few minutes.

Wexler and St. Louis said nothing.

'I'm his brother. We're twins, for Christ's sake.'

'You're also a reporter,' St. Louis said. 'We picked you up because we want Riley to be with family if she needs it. You're the only–'

'My brother fucking killed himself!'

I said it too loud. It had a quality of hysteria to it that I knew never worked with cops. You start yelling and they have a way of shutting down, going cold. I continued in a subdued voice.

'I think I am entitled to know what happened and why. I'm not writing a fucking story. Jesus, you guys are . . .'

I shook my head and didn't finish. If I tried I thought I would lose it again. I gazed out the window and could see the lights of Boulder coming up. So many more than when I was a kid.

'We don't know why,' Wexler finally said after a half minute. 'Okay? All I can say is that it happens. Sometimes cops get tired of all the shit that comes down the pipe. Mac might've gotten tired, that's all. Who knows? But they're working on it. And when they know, I'll know. And I'll tell you. That's a promise.'

'Who's working it?'

'The park services turned it over to our department. SIU is handling it.'

'What do you mean Special Investigations? They don't handle cop suicides.'

'Normally, they don't. We do. CAPs. But this time it's just that they're not going to let us investigate our own. Conflict of interest, you know.'

CAPs, I thought. Crimes Against Persons. Homicide, assault, rape, suicide. I wondered who would be listed in the reports as the person against whom this crime had been committed. Riley? Me? My parents? My brother?

'It was because of Theresa Lofton, wasn't it?' I asked, though it wasn't really a question. I didn't feel I needed their confirmation or denial. I was just saying out loud what I believed to be the obvious.

'We don't know, Jack,' St. Louis said. 'Let's leave it at that for now.'

The death of Theresa Lofton was the kind of murder that gave people pause.

Not just in Denver, but everywhere. It made anybody who heard or read about it stop for at least a moment to consider the violent images it conjured in the mind, the twist it caused in the gut.

Most homicides are little murders. That's what we call them in the newspaper business. Their effect on others is limited, their grasp on the imagination is short-lived. They get a few paragraphs on the inside pages. Buried in the paper the way the victims are buried in the ground.

But when an attractive college student is found in two pieces in a theretofore peaceful place like Washington Park, there usually isn't enough space in the paper for all the inches of copy it will generate. Theresa Lofton's was no little murder. It was a magnet that pulled at reporters from across the country. Theresa Lofton was the girl in two pieces. That was the catchy thing about this one. And so they descended on Denver from places like New York and Chicago and Los Angeles, television, tabloid and newspaper reporters alike. For a week, they stayed at hotels with good room service, roamed the city and the University of Denver campus, asked meaningless questions and got meaningless answers. Some staked out the day care center where Lofton had worked part-time or went up to Butte, where she had come from. Wherever they went they learned the same thing, that Theresa Lofton fit that most exclusive media image of all, the All-American Girl.

The Theresa Lofton murder was inevitably compared to the Black Dahlia case of fifty years ago in Los Angeles. In that case, a not so All-American Girl was found severed at the midriff in an empty lot. A tabloid television show dubbed Theresa Lofton the White Dahlia, playing on the fact that she had been found on a snow-covered field near Denver's Lake Grasmere.

And so the story fed on itself. It burned as hot as a trash-can fire for almost two weeks. But nobody was arrested and there were other crimes, other fires for the national media to warm itself by. Updates on the Lofton case dropped back into the inside pages of the Colorado papers. They became briefs for the digest pages. And Theresa Lofton finally took her spot among the little murders. She was buried.

All the while, the police in general, and my brother in particular, remained virtually mute, refusing even to confirm the detail that the victim had been found in two parts. That report had come only by accident from a photographer at the *Rocky* named Iggy Gomez. He had been in the park looking for wild art – the feature photos that fill the pages on a slow news day – when he happened upon the crime scene ahead of any other reporters or photographers. The cops had made the callouts to the coroner's and crime scene offices by landline since they knew the *Rocky* and the *Post* monitored their radio frequencies. Gomez took shots of two stretchers being used to remove two body bags. He called the city desk and said the cops were working a two-bagger and from the looks of the size of the bags the victims were probably children.

Later, a cop shop reporter for the *Rocky* named Van Jackson got a source in the coroner's office to confirm the grim fact that a victim had come into the morgue in two parts. The next morning's story in the *Rocky* served as the siren call to the media across the country.

My brother and his CAPs team worked as if they felt no obligation to talk to the public at all. Each day, the Denver Police Department media office put out a scant few lines in a press release, announcing that the investigation was continuing and that there had been no arrests. When cornered, the brass vowed that the case would not be investigated in the media, though that in itself was a laughable statement. Left with little information from authorities, the media did what it always does in such cases. It investigated the case on its own, numbing the reading and television-watching public with assorted details about the victim's life that actually had nothing to do with anything.

Still, almost nothing leaked from the department and little was known outside headquarters on Delaware Street; and after a couple of weeks the media onslaught was over, strangled by the lack of its lifeblood, information.

I didn't write about Theresa Lofton. But I wanted to. It wasn't the kind of story that comes along often in this place and any reporter would have wanted a piece of it. But at first, Van Jackson worked it with Laura Fitzgibbons, the university beat reporter. I had to bide my time. I knew that as long as the cops didn't clear it, I'd get my shot at it. So when Jackson asked me in the early days of the case if I could get anything from my brother, even off the record, I told him I would try, but I didn't try. I wanted the story and I wasn't going to help Jackson stay on it by feeding him from my source.

In late January, when the case was a month old and had dropped out of the news, I made my move. And my mistake.

One morning I went in to see Greg Glenn, the city editor, and told him I'd like to do a take out on the Lofton case. That was my specialty, my beat. Long takes on the notable murders of the Rocky Mountain Empire. To use a newspaper cliché, my expertise was going behind the headlines to bring you the real story. So I went to Glenn and reminded him I had an in. It was my brother's case, I said, and he'd only talk to me about it. Glenn didn't hesitate to consider the time and effort Jackson had already put on the story. I knew that he wouldn't. All he cared about was getting a story the *Post* didn't have. I walked out of the office with the assignment.

My mistake was that I told Glenn I had the in before I had talked to my brother. The next day I walked the two blocks from the *Rocky* to the cop shop and met him for lunch in the cafeteria. I told him about my assignment. Sean told me to turn around.

'Go back, Jack. I can't help you.'

'What are you talking about? It's your case.'

'It's my case but I'm not cooperating with you or anybody else who wants to write about it. I've given the basic details, that's all I'm required to do, that's where it stays.'

He looked off across the cafeteria. He had an annoying habit of not looking at you when you disagreed with him. When we were little, I would jump on him when he did it and punch him on the back. I couldn't do that anymore, though many times I wanted to.

'Sean, this is a good story. You have –'

'I don't have to do anything and I don't give a shit what kind of story it is.

This one is bad, Jack. Okay? I can't stop thinking about it. And I'm not going to help you sell newspapers with it.'

'C'mon, man, I'm a writer. Look at me. I don't care if it sells papers or not. The story is the thing. I don't give a shit about the paper. You know how I feel about that.'

He finally turned back to me.

'Now you know how I feel about this case,' he said.

I was silent a moment and took out a cigarette. I was down to maybe half a pack a day back then and could have skipped it but I knew it bothered him. So I smoked when I wanted to work on him.

'This isn't a smoking section, Jack.'

'Then turn me in. At least you'll be arresting *somebody*.'

'Why are you such an asshole when you don't get what you want?'

'Why are you? You aren't going to clear it, are you? That's what this is all about. You don't want me digging around and writing about your failure. You're giving up.'

'Jack, don't try the below-the-belt shit. You know it's never worked.'

He was right. It never had.

'Then what? You just want to keep this little horror story for yourself? That it?'

'Yeah, something like that. You could say that.'

In the car with Wexler and St. Louis I sat with my arms crossed. It was comforting. Almost as if I were holding myself together. The more I thought about my brother the more the whole thing made no sense to me. I knew the Lofton case had weighed on him but not to the point that he'd want to take his own life. Not Sean.

'Did he use his gun?'

Wexler looked at me in the mirror. Studied me, I thought. I wondered if he knew what had come between my brother and me.

'Yes.'

It hit me then. I just didn't see it. All the times that we'd had together coming to that. I didn't care about the Lofton case. What they were saying couldn't be.

'Not Sean.'

St. Louis turned around to look at me.

'What's that?'

'He wouldn't have done it, that's all.'

'Look, Jack, he –'

'He didn't get tired of the shit coming down the pipe. He loved it. You ask Riley. You ask anybody on the – Wex, you knew him the best and you know it's bullshit. He loved the hunt. That's what he called it. He wouldn't have traded it for anything. He probably could have been the assistant fucking chief by now but he didn't want it. He wanted to work homicides. He stayed in CAPs.'

Wexler didn't reply. We were in Boulder now, on Baseline heading toward Cascade. I was falling through the silence of the car. The impact of what they were telling me Sean had done was settling on me and leaving me as cold and dirty as the snow back on the side of the freeway.

'What about a note or something?' I said. 'What –'

'There was a note. We think it was a note.'

I noticed St. Louis glance over at Wexler and give him a look that said, you're saying too much.

'What? What did it say?'

There was a long silence, then Wexler ignored St. Louis.

'Out of space,' he said. 'Out of time.'

' "Out of space. Out of time." Just like that?'

'Just like that. That's all it said.'

The smile on Riley's face lasted maybe three seconds. Then it was instantly replaced by a look of horror out of that painting by Munch. The brain is an amazing computer. Three seconds to look at three faces at your door and to know your husband isn't coming home. IBM could never match that. Her mouth formed into a horrible black hole from which an unintelligible sound came, then the inevitable useless word: 'No!'

'Riley,' Wexler tried. 'Let's sit down a minute.'

'No, oh God, no!'

'Riley . . .'

She retreated from the door, moving like a cornered animal, first darting one way and then the opposite, as if maybe she thought she could change things if she could elude us. She went around the corner into the living room. When we followed we found her collapsed on the middle of the couch in an almost catatonic state, not too dissimilar from my own. The tears were just starting to come to her eyes. Wexler sat next to her on the couch. Big Dog and I stood by, silent as cowards.

'Is he dead?' she asked, knowing the answer but realizing she had to get it over with.

Wexler nodded.

'How?'

Wexler looked down and hesitated a moment. He looked over at me and then back at Riley.

'He did it himself, Riley. I'm sorry.'

She didn't believe it, just as I hadn't. But Wexler had a way of telling the story and after a while she stopped protesting. That was when she looked at me for the first time, tears rolling. Her face had an imploring look, as if she were asking me if we were sharing the same nightmare and couldn't I do something about it. Couldn't I wake her up? Couldn't I tell these two characters from a black and white how wrong they were? I went to the couch, sat next to her and hugged her. That's what I was there for. I'd seen this scene often enough to know what I was supposed to do.

'I'll stay,' I whispered. 'As long as you like.'

She didn't answer. She turned from my arms to Wexler.

'Where did it happen?'

'Estes Park. By the lake.'

'No, he wouldn't go – what was he doing up there?'

'He got a call. Somebody said they might have some information about one of his cases. He was going up to meet them for coffee at the Stanley. Then after he . . . he drove out to the lake. We don't know why he went there. He was found in his car by a ranger who heard the shot.'

'What case?' I asked.

'Look, Jack, I don't want to get into –'

'*What case?*' I yelled, this time not caring about the inflection of my voice. 'It was Lofton, wasn't it?'

Wexler gave one short nod and St. Louis walked away shaking his head.

'Who was he meeting?'

'That's it, Jack. We're not going to get into that with you.'

'I'm his brother. This is his wife.'

'It's all under investigation but if you're looking for doubts, there aren't any. We were up there. He killed himself. He used his own gun, he left a note and we got GSR on his hands. I wish he didn't do it. But he did.'

2

In the winter in Colorado the earth comes out in frozen chunks when they dig through the frost line with the backhoe to open up a grave. My brother was buried in Green Mountain Memorial Park in Boulder, a spot not more than a mile from the house where we grew up. As kids we were driven by the cemetery on our way to summer camp hikes in Chautauqua Park. I don't think we ever once looked at the stones as we passed and thought of the confines of the cemetery as our own final destination, but now that was what it was to be for Sean.

Green Mountain stood over the cemetery like a huge altar, making the small gathering at his grave seem even smaller. Riley, of course, was there, along with her parents and mine, Wexler and St. Louis, a couple dozen or so other cops, a few high school friends that neither Sean nor I nor Riley had stayed in touch with and me. It wasn't the official police burial with all the fanfare and colors. That ritual was reserved for those who fell in the line of duty. Though it could be argued that it was still a line-of-duty death, it wasn't considered one by the department. So Sean didn't get the Show and most of the Denver police force stayed away. Suicide is believed to be contagious by many in the thin blue line.

I was one of the pallbearers. I took the front along with my father. Two cops I didn't know before that day, but who were on Sean's CAPs team, took the middle, and Wexler and St. Louis were on the back. St. Louis was too tall and Wexler too short. Mutt and Jeff. It gave the coffin an uneven cant at the back as we carried it. I think it must have looked odd. My mind wandered as we struggled with the weight and I thought of Sean's body pitching around inside it.

I didn't say much to my parents that day, though I rode with them in the limousine with Riley and her parents. We had not talked of anything meaningful in many years and even Sean's death could not penetrate the barrier. After my sister's death twenty years before, something in them changed toward me. It seemed that I, as the survivor of the accident, was suspect for having done just that. Survived. I am also sure that since that time I have continued to disappoint them in the choices I have made. I think of these as small disappointments accruing over time like interest in a bank account until it was enough for them to comfortably retire on. We are strangers. I see them only on the required holidays. And so there was nothing that I could say to them that would matter and there was nothing they could say to me. Aside from the occasional hurt-animal sound of Riley crying, the inside of the limo was as quiet as the inside of Sean's casket.

After the funeral I took two weeks of vacation and the one week of bereavement leave the paper allowed and drove by myself up into the Rockies. The mountains have never lost their glory for me. It's mountains where I heal the fastest.

Headed west on the 70, I drove through the Loveland Pass and over the peaks to Grand Junction. I did it slowly, taking three days. I stopped to ski; sometimes I just stopped on the turnouts to think. After Grand Junction I diverted south and made it to Telluride the next day. I kept the Cherokee in four-wheel drive the whole way. I stayed in Silverton because the rooms were cheaper and skied every day for a week. I spent the nights drinking Jagermeister in my room or near the fireplace of whatever ski lodge I stopped in. I tried to exhaust my body with the hope that my mind would follow. But I couldn't succeed. It was all Sean. Out of space. Out of time. His last message was a riddle my mind could not put aside.

For some reason my brother's noble calling had betrayed him. It had killed him. The grief that this simple conclusion brought me would not ebb, even when I was gliding down the slopes, the wind cutting in behind my sunglasses and pulling tears from my eyes.

I no longer questioned the official conclusion but it had not been Wexler and St. Louis who had convinced me. I did that on my own. It was the erosion of my resolve by time and by facts. As each day went by, the horror of what he had done was somehow easier to believe and even accept. And then there was Riley. On the day after that first night she had told me something that even Wexler and St. Louis hadn't known yet. Sean had been going once a week to see a psychologist. Of course, there were counseling services available to him through the department, but he had chosen this secret path because he didn't want his position to be undermined by rumors.

I came to realize he was seeing the therapist at the same time I went to him wanting to write about Lofton. I thought maybe he was trying to spare me the same anguish that the case had brought him. I liked the thought that that was what he was doing and I tried to hold on to that idea during those days up in the mountains.

In front of the hotel room mirror one night after too many drinks, I contemplated shaving my beard off and cutting my hair short like Sean's had been. We were identical twins – same hazel eyes, light brown hair, lanky build – but not many people realized that. We had always gone to great lengths to forge separate identities. Sean wore contacts and pumped iron to put muscle on his frame. I wore glasses, had had a beard since college, and hadn't picked up the weights since high school basketball. I also had the scar from that woman's ring in Breckenridge. My battle scar.

Sean went into the service after high school and then the cops, keeping the crew cut as he went. He later got a CU degree while going part-time. He needed it to get ahead in the department. I bummed around for a couple of years, lived in New York and Paris, and then went the full-time college route. I wanted to be a writer, ended up in the newspaper business. In the back of my mind I told myself it was just a temporary stop. I'd been telling myself that for ten years now, maybe longer.

That night in the hotel room, I looked at myself in the mirror for a long time but I didn't shave off my beard or cut my hair. I kept thinking about Sean under the frozen ground and I had a crushed feeling in my stomach. I decided that when my time came I wanted to be burned. I didn't want to be down there under the ice.

What hooked me deepest was the message. The official police line was this: After my brother left the Stanley Hotel and drove up through Estes Park to Bear Lake, he parked his department car and for a while left the engine running, the heat on. When the heat had fogged the windshield he reached up and wrote his message there with a gloved finger. He wrote it backward so you could read it from outside the car. His last words to a world that included two parents, a wife and a twin brother.

Out of space. Out of time.

I couldn't understand. Time for what? Space for what? He had come to some desperate conclusion, yet he never tested us on it. He had not reached out to me, nor to my parents or Riley. Was it up to us to reach for him, not even knowing of his secret injuries? In my solitude on the road, I concluded that it was not. He should have reached. He should have tried. By not doing so he had robbed us of the chance to rescue him. And in not doing so he had left us unable to be rescued from our own grief and guilt. I realized that much of my grief was actually anger. I was mad at him, my twin, for what he had done to me.

But it's hard to hold a grudge against the dead. I couldn't stay angry with Sean. And the only way to alleviate the anger was to doubt the story. And so the cycle would begin again. Denial, acceptance, anger. Denial, acceptance, anger.

On my last day in Telluride I called Wexler. I could tell he didn't like hearing from me.

'Did you find the informant, the one from the Stanley?'

'No, Jack, no luck. I told you I'd let you know about that.'

'I know. I just still have questions. Don't you?'

'Let it go, Jack. We'll all be better off when we can put this behind us.'

'What about SIU? They already put it behind? Case closed?'

'Pretty much. I haven't talked to them this week.'

'Then why are you still trying to find the informant?'

'I've got questions, just like you. Just loose ends.'

'You changed your mind about Sean?'

'No. I just want to put everything in order. I'd like to know what he talked about with the informant, if they even talked. The Lofton case is still open, you know. I wouldn't mind nailing that one for Sean.'

I noticed he was no longer calling him Mac. Sean had left the clique.

*

The following Monday I went back to work at the *Rocky Mountain News.* As I entered the newsroom I felt several eyes upon me. But this was not unusual. I often thought they watched me when I came in. I had a gig every reporter in the newsroom wanted. No daily grind, no daily deadlines. I was free to roam the entire Rocky Mountain region and write about one thing. Murder. Everybody likes a good murder story. Some weeks I'd take apart a shooting in the projects, telling the tale of the shooter and the victim and their fateful collision. Some weeks I'd write about a society murder out in Cherry Hill or a bar shooting in Leadville. Highbrow and lowbrow, little murder and big murder. My brother was right, it sold papers if you told it right. And I got to tell it. I got to take my time and tell it right.

Stacked on my desk next to the computer was a foot-high pile of newspapers. This was my main source material for stories. I subscribed to every daily, weekly and monthly newspaper published from Pueblo north to Bozeman. I scoured these for small stories on killings that I could turn into long take outs. There were always a lot to choose from. The Rocky Mountain Empire had a violent streak that had been there since the gold rush. Not as much violence as Los Angeles or Miami or New York, not even close. But I was never short of source material. I was always looking for something new or different about the crime or the investigation, an element of gee whiz or a heart-tugging sadness. It was my job to exploit those elements.

But on this morning I wasn't looking for a story idea. I began looking through the stack for back issues of the *Rocky* and our competition, the *Post.* Suicides are not normal fare for newspapers unless there are unusual circumstances. My brother's death qualified. I thought there was a good chance there had been a story.

I was right. Though the *Rocky* had not published a story, probably in deference to me, the *Post* had run a six-inch story on the bottom of one of the local pages the morning after Sean died.

DPD INVESTIGATOR TAKES LIFE IN NATIONAL PARK

> A veteran Denver Police detective who was in charge of the investigation into the slaying of University of Denver student Theresa Lofton was found dead of an apparent self-inflicted gunshot wound Thursday in the Rocky Mountain National Park, officials said.
>
> Sean McEvoy, 34, was found in his unmarked DPD car, which was parked in a lot at Bear Lake near the Estes Park entrance to the rugged mountain park.
>
> The body of the detective was discovered by a park ranger who heard a shot about 5 P.M. and went to the parking lot to investigate.
>
> Park services officials have asked the DPD to investigate the death and the department's Special Investigations Unit is handling the matter. Detective Robert Scalari, who is heading the investigation, said preliminary indications were that the death was a suicide.
>
> Scalari said a note was found at the scene but he refused to disclose its

contents. He said it was believed that McEvoy was despondent over job difficulties, but also refused to discuss what problems he was having.

McEvoy, who grew up and still lived in Boulder, was married but had no children. He was a twelve-year veteran of the police department who rose quickly through the ranks to an assignment on the Crimes Against Persons unit, which handles investigations of all violent crimes in the city.

McEvoy was currently head of the unit and had most recently directed the investigation into the death of Lofton, 19, who was found strangled and mutilated three months ago in Washington Park.

Scalari refused to comment on whether the Lofton case, which remains unsolved, was cited in McEvoy's note or was one of the job difficulties he may have been suffering.

Scalari said it wasn't known why McEvoy went to Estes Park before killing himself. He said the investigation of the death is continuing.

I read the story twice. It contained nothing that I didn't already know but it held a strange fascination for me. Maybe that was because I believed I knew or had the beginnings of an idea why Sean had gone to Estes Park and driven all the way up to Bear Lake. It was a reason I didn't want to think about, though. I clipped the article, put it in a manila file and slid it into a desk drawer.

My computer beeped and a message printed across the top of the screen. It was a summons from the city editor. I was back at work.

Greg Glenn's office was at the back of the newsroom. One wall was glass, enabling him to look out across the rows of pods where the reporters worked and through the windows along the west wall to the mountain line when it wasn't hidden by smog.

Glenn was a good editor who prized a good read more than anything else about a story. That's what I liked about him. In this business editors are of two schools. Some like facts and cram them into a story until it is so overburdened that practically no one will read it to the end. And some like words and never let the facts get in the way. Glenn liked me because I could write and he pretty much let me choose what I wrote about. He never hustled me for copy and never badly dinged up what I turned in. I had long realized that should he ever leave the paper or be demoted or promoted out of the newsroom, all of this most likely would change. City editors made their own nests. If he were gone, I'd probably find myself back on the daily cop beat, writing briefs off the police log. Doing little murders.

I sat down in the cushioned seat in front of his desk as he finished up a phone call. Glenn was about five years older than me. When I'd first started at the *Rocky* ten years earlier, he was one of the hot shot writers like I was now. But eventually he made the move into management. Now he wore a suit every day, had one of those little statues on his desk of a Bronco football player with a bobbing head, spent more time on the phone than on any other activity in his life and always paid careful attention to the political winds blowing out of the corporate home office in Cincinnati. He was a forty-year-old guy with a paunch, a wife, two kids and a good salary that wasn't good enough to buy a house in the neighborhood his wife wanted to live in. He told me all of this once over a beer at the Wynkoop, the only night I'd seen him out in the past four years.

Tacked across one wall of Glenn's office were the last seven days of front pages. Each day, the first thing he did was take the seven-day-old edition down and tack up the latest front page. I guess he did this to keep track of the news and the continuity of our coverage. Or maybe, because he never got bylines as a writer anymore, putting the pages up was a way of reminding himself that he was in charge. Glenn hung up and looked up at me.

'Thanks for coming in,' he said. 'I just wanted to tell you again that I'm sorry about your brother. And if you feel like you want some more time, it's no problem. We'll work something out.'

'Thanks. But I'm back.'

He nodded but made no move to dismiss me. I knew there was something more to the summons.

'Well, to business then. Do you have anything going at the moment? As far as I remember, you were looking for your next project when . . . when it happened. I figure if you are back, then maybe it would be good for you to get busy with something. You know, dive back in.'

It was in that moment that I knew what I would do next. Oh, it had been there all right. But it hadn't come to the surface, not until Glenn asked that question. Then, of course, it was obvious.

'I'm going to write about my brother,' I said.

I don't know if that was what Glenn was hoping I would say, but I think it was. I think he had had his eye on a story ever since he'd heard the cops had met me down in the lobby and told me what my brother had done. He was probably smart enough to know he didn't have to suggest the story, that it would come to me on its own. He just had to ask the simple question.

Anyway, I took the bait. And all things in my life changed after that. As clearly as you can chart anyone's life in retrospect, mine changed with that one sentence, in that one moment when I told Glenn what I would do. I thought I knew something about death then. I thought I knew about evil. But I didn't know anything.

3

William Gladden's eyes scanned the happy faces as they moved past him. It was like a giant vending machine. Take your pick. Don't like him? Here comes another. Will she do?

This time none would do. Besides, their parents were too close by. He'd have to wait for the one time one of them made a mistake, walked out on the pier or over to the snack window for cotton candy, leaving their precious one all alone.

Gladden loved the carousel on the Santa Monica Pier. He didn't love it because it was an original, and, according to the story in the display case, it took six years to hand-paint the galloping horses and restore it to its original condition. He didn't love it because it had been featured in lots of movies that he had seen over the years, especially while in Raiford. And he didn't love it because it brought to mind memories of riding with his Best Pal on the merry-go-round at the Sarasota County Fair. He loved it because of the children who rode on it. Innocence and abandonment to pure happiness played on each one's face as it circled again and again to the accompaniment of the calliope. Since arriving from Phoenix he had been coming here. Every day. He knew it might take some time but one day it would eventually pay off and he would be able to fill his order.

As he watched the collage of colors his mind jumped backward as it had so often since Raiford. He remembered his Best Pal. He remembered the black-dark closet with only the band of light at the bottom. He huddled on the floor near the light, near the air. He could see his feet coming that way. Each step. He wished he were older, taller, so that he could reach the top shelf. If only he were, he would have a surprise waiting for his Best Pal.

Gladden came back. He looked around. The ride had ended and the last of the children were making their way to waiting parents on the other side of the gate. There was a line of more children ready to run to the carousel and pick their horse. He looked again for a dark-haired girl with smooth brown skin but saw none. Then he noticed the woman who took the tickets from the children staring at him. Their eyes met and Gladden looked away. He adjusted the strap of his duffel bag. The weight of the camera and the books inside it had pulled it down on his shoulder. He made a note to leave the books in the car next time. He took a last look at the carousel and headed for one of the doors that exited onto the pier.

When he got to the door he casually looked back at the woman. The children screamed as they ran to the wooden horses. Some with parents, most alone. The woman taking tickets had already forgotten about him. He was safe.

4

Laurie Prine looked up from her terminal and smiled when I walked in. I was hoping she'd be there. I came around the counter and pulled an extra chair away from an empty desk and sat down next to hers. It looked like a slow moment at the *Rocky* library.

'Oh no,' she said cheerfully. 'When you come in and sit down, I know it's going to be a long one.'

She was referring to the extensive search requests I usually made in preparation for stories. A lot of the crime stories I wrote spiraled into wide-ranging law enforcement issues. I always needed to know what else had been written about the subject and where.

'Sorry,' I said, a feigned contrition. 'This one might keep you with Lex and Nex the rest of the day.'

'You mean, *if* I can get to it. What do you need?'

She was attractive in an understated way. She had dark hair I had never seen in anything other than a braid, brown eyes behind the steel-rimmed glasses and full lips that were never painted. She pulled a yellow legal pad over in front of her, adjusted her glasses and picked up a pen, ready to take down the list of things I wanted. Lexis and Nexis were computer databases that carried most major and not so major newspapers in the country, as well as court rulings and a whole host of other parking lots on the information highway. If you were trying to see how much had been written on a specific subject or particular story, the Lexis/Nexis network was the place to start.

'Police suicide,' I said. 'I want to find out everything I can about it.'

Her face stiffened. I guessed she suspected the search was for personal reasons. The computer time is expensive and the company strictly forbids its use for personal reasons.

'Don't worry, I'm on a story. Glenn just okayed the assignment.'

She nodded but I wondered if she believed me. I assumed she would check with Glenn. Her eyes returned to her yellow pad.

'What I'm looking for is any national statistics on occurrence, any stats on the rate of cop suicide compared to other jobs and the population as a whole, and any mention of think tanks or government agencies that might have studied this. Uh, let's see, what else . . . oh, and anything anecdotal.'

'Anecdotal?'

'You know, any clips on cop suicides that have run. Let's go back five years. I'm looking for examples.'

'Like your . . .'

She realized what she was saying.

'Yes, like my brother.'

'It's a shame.'

She didn't say anything more. I let the silence hang between us for a few moments and then asked her how long she thought the computer search would take. My requests were often given a low priority since I was not a deadline writer.

'Well, it's really a shotgun search, nothing specific. I'm going to have to spend some time on it and you know I'll get pulled when the dailies start coming in. But I'll try. How about late this afternoon, that be okay?'

'Perfect.'

As I went back into the newsroom I checked the overhead clock and saw it was half past eleven. The timing was good for what I needed to do. At my desk I made a call to a source at the cop shop.

'Hey, Skipper, you going to be there?'

'When?'

'During lunch. I might need something. I probably will.'

'Shit. Okay. I'm here. Hey, when'd you get back?'

'Today. Talk to you.'

I hung up, then I put on my long coat and headed out of the newsroom. I walked the two blocks over to the Denver Police Department headquarters, flipped my press pass at the front counter to a cop who didn't bother to look up from his *Post* and went on up to the SIU offices on the fourth floor.

'I've got one question,' Detective Robert Scalari said after I told him what I wanted. 'Are you here as a brother or as a reporter?'

'Both.'

'Sit down.'

Scalari leaned across his desk, maybe, I guessed, so I could appreciate the intricate hair-weaving job he had done to hide his bald spot.

'Listen, Jack,' he said. 'I have a problem with that.'

'What problem?'

'Look, if you were coming to me as a brother who wanted to know why, that would be one thing and I would probably tell you what I know. But if what I tell you is going to end up in the *Rocky Mountain News,* I'm not interested. I've got too much respect for your brother to let what happened to him help sell newspapers. Even if you don't.'

We were alone in a small office with four desks in it. Scalari's words made me angry but I swallowed it back. I leaned toward him so he could see my healthy, full head of hair.

'Let me ask you something, Detective Scalari. Was my brother murdered?'

'No, he wasn't.'

'You are sure it was suicide, right?'

'That is correct.'

'And the case is closed?'

'Right again.'

I leaned back away from him.

'Then that really bothers me.'

'Why is that?'

'Because you're trying to have it both ways. You're telling me the case is closed, yet I can't look at the records. If it is closed, then I should be allowed to look at the case because he was my brother. And if it's closed, that means that, as a reporter, I can't compromise an ongoing investigation by looking at the records, either.'

I let him digest that for a few moments.

'So,' I finally continued, 'going by your own logic, there is no reason why I shouldn't be able to look at the records.'

Scalari looked at me. I could see the anger working behind his cheeks now.

'Listen to me, Jack, there are things in that file better left not known, and certainly not published.'

'I think I'm a better judge of that, Detective Scalari. He was my brother. My twin. I'm not going to hurt him. I'm just trying to make sense of something for myself. If I then write about it, it will be to finally put it in the ground with him. Okay?'

We sat there staring at each other for a long moment. It was his turn and I waited him out.

'I can't help you,' he said finally. 'Even if I wanted to. It's closed. Case is closed. The file went to records for processing. You want it, go see them.'

I stood up.

'Thanks for telling me at the beginning of the conversation.'

I walked out without saying another word. I had known Scalari would blow me off. I went to him because I had to go through the motions and because I wanted to see if I could learn the location of the file.

I went down the stairs that mostly only cops used and into the office of the department's administrative captain. It was fifteen minutes past twelve so the desk in the reception area was empty. I walked past it, knocked on the door and heard a voice tell me to enter.

Inside, Captain Forest Grolon sat behind his desk. He was such a large man that the standard issue desk looked like child's furniture. He was a dark-complected black man with a shaven head. He stood to shake my hand and I was reminded that he topped out above six and a half feet. I figured a scale would have to have 300 on its dial if it were going to take his full measure. I shook his hand and smiled. He had been a source of mine since I was on the daily police beat six years earlier and he was a patrol sergeant. We had both risen through the ranks since then.

'Jack, how's it going? You say you're just back?'

'Yeah, I took some time. I'm okay.'

He didn't mention my brother. He had been one of the few at the funeral and that made it clear how he felt. He sat back down and I took one of the chairs in front of his desk.

Grolon's job had little to do with policing the city. He was in the business end of the department. He was in charge of the annual budget, hiring and training. Firing, too. It had little to do with police work but it was all part of his plan. Grolon wanted to be police chief one day and was gathering a wide variety of experience so when the time came he'd look best for the job. Part of that plan was also to keep contacts in the local media. When the time was right, he'd count on me for a positive profile in the *Rocky*. And I would come through. In the meantime, I could count on him for things as well.

'So what am I missing lunch for?' he said gruffly, which was part of the routine we played. I knew that Grolon preferred meeting me at lunch when his adjutant was out and there was less chance that he would be seen with me.

'You're not missing lunch. You're just getting it late. I want to see the file on my brother. Scalari said he already sent it to get filmed. I thought maybe you could pull it and let me look at it real quick.'

'Why do you want to do that, Jack? Whyn't you let sleeping dogs lie?'

'I've gotta look, Captain. I'm not quoting from it. I just want to look at it. You get it now and I'll be done with it before the microfilm folks even get back from lunch. Nobody will know. Except you and me. And I'll remember it.'

Ten minutes later, Grolon handed me the file. It was as thin as the year-round residents phone book for Aspen. I don't know why but I had expected something thicker, heavier, as if the size of the investigative file bore some resemblance to the significance of the death.

Inside on top was an envelope marked PHOTOS which I put to the side of the desk without opening. Next there was an autopsy report and several standard reports that were paper-clipped together.

I had studied autopsy reports often enough to know that I could skip the pages of endless description of body glands, organs and general condition and go to the last pages, where conclusions were written. And there were no surprises here. Cause of death was a gunshot wound to the head. The word suicide was circled below it. Blood scans for commonly used drugs showed traces of dextromethorphan hydrobromide. Following this entry a lab tech's notes said 'cough suppressant – glove box.' It meant that other than a shot or two of cough syrup from a bottle kept in the car, my brother was stone cold sober when he put the gun in his mouth.

The forensic analysis report contained a subreport labeled GSR, which I knew meant gunshot residue. It stated that a neutron activation analysis of leather gloves worn by the victim found particles of burned gunpowder on the right glove, indicating he had used that hand to fire the weapon. GSR and gas burns were also found in the victim's throat. The conclusion was that the barrel had been in Sean's mouth when the gun discharged.

Next in the packet was an evidence inventory and I saw nothing unusual here. After this I found the witness statement. The witness was Park Ranger Stephen Pena, who was assigned to a one-ranger substation and information booth at Bear Lake.

> Witness stated he did not have a view of the parking area while working in the booth. At approx. 4:58 P.M. witness heard a muffled report he identified from experience as a gunshot. He identified the origin as the parking lot and immediately went to investigate the possibility of illegal

hunting. At this time there was only one vehicle in the lot and through the partially fogged windows he saw the victim slumped back in the driver's seat. Witness ran to the vehicle but could not open the door because it was locked. Looking closely through the fogged windows he determined that the victim appeared to be deceased because of the massive damage to the rear of the head. Witness then returned to the park booth where he immediately notified authorities and his supervisors. He then returned to the victim's car to await the arrival of authorities.

Witness states that the victim's vehicle was within his sight no more than five seconds after he heard the shot. The car was parked approx. 50 yards from the nearest forest cover or structure. It is believed by the witness to have been impossible for someone to have left the victim's car after the shooting and gotten to the cover without the witness seeing him.

I returned the statement sheet to its place in the packet and glanced through the other reports. There was a page titled Case Report that detailed my brother's last day. He reported to work at 7:30 A.M., had lunch with Wexler at noon and signed out at 2 P.M. to go to the Stanley. He did not tell Wexler or anyone else whom he was going to see.

Attempts by investigators to determine if Sean had actually gone to the Stanley were unsuccessful. All waitresses and busboys in the hotel's restaurant were interviewed and none recalled my brother.

There was a one-page report in the file summarizing Scalari's interview with Sean's psychologist. Somehow, maybe through Riley, he had found out that Sean was seeing the Denver therapist. Dr Colin Dorschner, according to Scalari's report, said Sean was suffering from acute depression brought about by job stress, in particular his failure to close the Lofton case. What was not contained in the interview summary was whether Scalari ever asked Dorschner if he had thought my brother was suicidal. I wondered if Scalari had even asked that question.

The last sheaf of papers in the package was the investigating officer's final report. The last paragraph was Scalari's summary and conclusion.

Based upon physical evidence and the eyewitness account of the death of Detective Sean McEvoy, I/O concludes that the victim died of a self-inflicted gunshot wound after writing a message on the inside of the fogged windshield. The victim was known by colleagues, including I/O, and his wife and psychologist Colin Dorschner to be emotionally burdened by his unsuccessful efforts to clear by arrest the Dec. 19 homicide of Theresa Lofton (case no. 832). It is believed at this time that this disturbance may have led him to take his own life. DPD psychological consultant Dr Armand Griggs said in an interview (2/22) that the message – Out of space – Out of time – written on the windshield could be considered a suicide-style farewell consistent with the victim's state of mind.

At this time, there is no evidence conflicting with the conclusion of suicide.

Clipping the reports back together, I realized there was only one thing left that I hadn't looked at.

Grolon had decided to go to the cafeteria to pick up a sandwich to go. I was left alone in his office. Probably five minutes passed in stillness while I considered the envelope. I knew that if I looked at the photographs they would become the lasting image in my mind of my brother. I did not want that. But I also knew that I needed to see the photos to know for sure about his death, to help disperse any last doubts.

I opened the envelope quickly so as to not change my mind. As I slid the stack of 8 × 10 color prints out, the first image that greeted me was an establishing shot. My brother's detective car, a white Chevy Caprice, alone at the end of the parking lot. I could see the ranger shack up a low hill from it. The lot had been freshly plowed, a four-foot embankment of snow around the edges.

The next photo was a close-up of the windshield from the outside. The message was barely legible, as the steam had dissipated from the glass. But it was there and through the glass I could also see Sean. His head was snapped back, his jaw up. I went to the next photo and I was inside the car with him. Taken from the passenger side front, his whole body visible. Blood had worked its way like a thick necklace around his neck from the back and then down over the sweater. His heavy snow coat was open. There was spatter on the roof and back side window. The gun was on the seat next to his right thigh.

The rest of the photos were mostly close-ups from various angles. But they did not have the effect on me I thought they would. The sterile lighting robbed my brother of his humanity. He looked like a mannequin. But I found nothing about them as upsetting as the fact that I had once more convinced myself that Sean had indeed taken his own life. I admitted to myself then that I had secretly come with a hope and that it was gone now.

Grolon came back in then. He looked at me with curious eyes. I stood up and placed the file on his desk as he maneuvered around it to his seat. He opened a brown paper bag and removed a plastic-wrapped egg salad sandwich.

'You okay?'

'I'm fine.'

'You want half?'

'No.'

'Well, how do you feel?'

I smiled at the question because I had asked the same thing so many times. It must have thrown him off. He frowned.

'See this?' I said, pointing to the scar on my face. 'I got that for asking somebody that same thing once.'

'Sorry.'

'Don't be. I wasn't.'

5

After viewing the file on my brother's death I wanted the details of the Theresa Lofton case. If I was going to write about what my brother did, I had to know what he knew. I had to understand what he had come to understand. Only this time Grolon couldn't help me. The active homicide files were kept under lock and Grolon would see more of a risk than a benefit in attempting to get the Lofton file for me.

After I checked the CAPs squad room and found it emptied for lunch, the first place I looked for Wexler was the Satire. It was a favored place for cops to eat – and drink – at lunch. I saw him there in one of the rear booths. The only problem was, he was with St. Louis. They didn't see me and I debated whether it would be better just to withdraw and try later to get to Wexler alone. But then Wexler's eyes stopped on me. I walked over. I could see by their ketchup-smeared plates that they had finished eating. Wexler had what looked like a Jim Beam and ice on the table in front of him.

'Would ya look at this?' Wexler said good-naturedly.

I slid into the wide booth next to St. Louis. I chose his side so I would be looking at Wexler.

'What is this?' St. Louis mildly protested.

'It's the press,' I said. 'Howzit going?'

'Don't answer,' St. Louis said quickly to Wexler. 'He wants something he can't have.'

'Of course I do,' I said. 'What else is new?'

'Nothing is new, Jack,' Wexler said. 'Is what Big Dog says true? You want something you can't have?'

It was a dance. Friendly patter designed to ferret out the basic nut of information without specifically asking for it and confronting it. It went with the nicknames cops used. I had danced like this many times and I was good at it. They were finesse moves. Like practicing the three-man weave in high school basketball. Keep your eyes open for the ball, watch the other two men at once. I was always the finesse player. Sean was the strength. He was football. I was basketball.

'Not exactly,' I said. 'But I am back on the job again, boys.'

'Oh, here we go,' St. Louis whined. 'Hold on to your hats.'

'So, what's happening on the Lofton case?' I asked Wexler, ignoring St. Louis.

'Whoa there, Jack, are you talking to us as a reporter now?' Wexler asked.

'I'm only talking to you. And that's right, as a reporter.'

'Then no comment on Lofton.'

'So the answer is nothing is happening.'

'I said no comment.'

'Look, I want to see what you've got. The case is almost three months old now. It's going into the dead case file soon if it isn't already there and you know it. I just want to see the file. I want to know what hooked Sean so deep.'

'You're forgetting something. Your brother was ruled a suicide. Case closed. It doesn't matter what hooked him about Lofton. Besides, it's not known as fact that it had anything to do with what he did. It's collateral at best. But we'll never know.'

'Cut the crap. I just saw the file on Sean.' Wexler's eyebrows raised a subliminal amount, I thought. 'It's all there. Sean was fucked up over this case. He was seeing a shrink, he was spending all of his time on it. So don't tell me we'll never know.'

'Look, kid, we –'

'Did you ever call Sean that?' I interrupted.

'What?'

'Kid. Did you ever call him kid?'

Wexler looked confused.

'Nope.'

'Then don't call me it, either.'

Wexler raised his arms in a hands-off manner.

'Why can't I see the file? You're not going anywhere with it.'

'Who says?'

'I do. You're afraid of it, man. You saw what it did to Sean and you don't want it to happen to you. So the case is stuck in a drawer somewhere. It's got dust on it. I guarantee it.'

'You know, Jack, you're seriously full of shit. And if you weren't your brother's brother, I'd throw you outta here on your ass. You're getting me pissed. I don't like being pissed.'

'Yeah? Then imagine how I'm feeling. The thing of it is, I am his brother and I think that cuts me in.'

St. Louis gave a smirking type of laugh meant to belittle me.

'Hey, Big Dog, isn't it about time you went out and watered a fire hydrant or something?' I said.

Wexler burst out with the start of a laugh but quickly contained it. But St. Louis's face turned red.

'Listen, you little fuck,' he said. 'I'll put you –'

'All right, boys,' Wexler intervened. 'All right. Listen, Ray, why don't you go outside and have a smoke? Let me talk to Jackie, straighten him out, and I'll be out.'

I got out of the booth so St. Louis could slide out. He gave me the dead man's stare as he went by. I slid back in.

'Drink up, Wex. No sense acting like there isn't any Beam on the table.'

Wexler grinned and took a pull from his glass.

'You know, twins or not, you're a lot like your brother. You don't give up on things easy. And you can be a smart-ass. You get rid of that beard and the hippie hair and you could pass for him. You'd have to do something about that scar, too.'

'Look, what about the file?'

'What about it?'

'You owe it to him to let me see it.'

'I don't follow, Jack.'

'Yes, you do. I can't put it behind me until I've looked it all over. I'm just trying to understand.'

'You're also trying to write about it.'

'Writing does for me what you got in that glass does for you. If I can write about it, I can understand it. And I can put it in the ground. That's all I want to do.'

Wexler looked away from me and picked up the check the waitress had left. Then he downed the rest of his drink and slid out of the booth. Standing, he looked down at me and let out a heavy breath redolent of bourbon.

'Come back to the office,' he said. 'I'll give you one hour.'

He held his finger up and repeated himself in case I was confused.

'One hour.'

In the CAPs squad room I used the desk my brother had used. No one had taken it yet. Maybe it was a bad-luck desk now. Wexler was standing at a wall of file cabinets looking through an open drawer. St. Louis was nowhere to be seen, apparently choosing to have nothing to do with this. Wexler finally stepped away from the drawer with two thick files. He placed them in front of me.

'This everything?'

'Everything. You got an hour.'

'C'mon, there's five inches of paper here,' I tried. 'Let me take it home and I'll bring it –'

'See, just like your brother. One hour, McEvoy. Set your watch, because those go back in the drawer in one hour. Make that fifty-nine minutes. You're wasting time.'

I stopped belaboring the point and opened the top file.

Theresa Lofton had been a beautiful young woman who came to the university to study for an education degree. She wanted to be a first-grade teacher.

She was in her first year and lived in a campus dorm. She carried a full curriculum as well as working part-time in the day care center at the university's married-housing dorm.

Lofton was believed to have been abducted on or near the campus on a Wednesday, the day after classes ended for the Christmas break. Most students had already left for the holiday. Theresa was still in Denver for two reasons. She had her job; the day care center didn't close for the holidays until the end of the week. And there was also the problem of her car. She was waiting for a new clutch to be put into the old Beetle so she could make the drive home.

Her abduction was not reported because her roommate and all her friends had already gone home for the holidays. No one knew she was missing. When she didn't show up for work at the day care center on Thursday morning, the manager thought she had simply gone home to Montana early, not completing the week because she wasn't due to return to the job after the Christmas break. It would not be the first time a student pulled this kind of stunt, especially once finals were over and the holiday break beckoned. The manager made no inquiry or report to authorities.

Her body was found Friday morning in Washington Park. The investigators traced her last known movements back to noon on Wednesday when she called the mechanic from the day care center – he remembered children's voices in the background – and he told her the car was ready. She said she would pick it up after work, first stopping at the bank. She did neither. She said good-bye to the day care center manager at noon and went out the door. She was not seen alive again. Except, of course, by her killer.

I only had to look at the photos in the file to realize how the case could have grabbed Sean and put a leash around his heart. They were before-and-after photos. A portrait shot of her, probably for the high school yearbook. A fresh-faced young girl with a whole life ahead of her. She had dark wavy hair and crystal-blue eyes. Each reflected a small star of light, the flash of the camera. There was also a candid of her, in shorts and a tank top. She was smiling, carrying a cardboard box away from a car. The muscles of her slender, tan arms were taut. It looked as though it was a slight strain for her to stand still with the heavy box for the photographer. I turned it over and read in what I guessed was a parent's scrawl: 'Terri's first day on campus! Denver, Colo.'

The other pictures were taken after. There were more of these and I was struck by the number. Why did the cops need so many? Each one seemed like some kind of a terrible invasion, even though the girl was already dead. Theresa Lofton's eyes had lost their brilliance in these photographs. They were open but dull, webbed in a milky caul.

The photos showed the victim lying in about two feet of brush and snow on a slight incline. The news stories had been correct. She was in two pieces. A scarf was tightly wrapped around her neck and her eyes were sufficiently wide and bugged to suggest this was how she died. But the killer apparently had more work to do afterward. The body had been hacked apart at the midriff, the bottom half then placed over the top half in a horrific tableau suggesting that she was performing a sex act on herself.

I realized that Wexler was at the other desk watching me as I looked at the gallery of ghastly photos. I tried not to show my disgust. Or my fascination. I knew now what my brother was protecting me from. I had never seen anything so horrible. I finally looked at Wexler.

'Jesus.'

'Yeah.'

'The stuff the tabs said about it being like the Black Dahlia in L.A., it was close, wasn't it?'

'Yeah. Mac bought a book about it. He called some old horse in the LAPD, too. There were some similarities. The chop job. But that one was fifty years ago.'

'Maybe somebody got the idea from that.'

'Maybe. He thought of that.'

I returned the photos to the envelope and looked back at Wexler.

'Was she a lesbian?'

'No, not as far as we could tell. She had a boyfriend back up in Butte. Good kid. We cleared him. Your brother thought the same thing for a while. Because of what the killer did, you know, with the parts of the body. He thought maybe somebody was getting back at her for being a lezzie. Maybe making some kind of sick statement about something. He never got anywhere with it.'

I nodded.

'You've got forty-five minutes left.'

'You know, that's the first time I've heard you call him "Mac" in a long time.'

'Don't worry about it. Make that forty-four minutes.'

The autopsy report was pretty much anticlimactic after the photos. I noticed that the time of death was set on the first day of Lofton's disappearance. She had been dead more than forty hours when her body was found.

Most of the summary reports dealt with dead ends. Routine investigations of the victim's family, boyfriend, friends on campus, coworkers and even parents of children she cared for, turned up nothing. Almost all were cleared through alibis or other investigative means.

The conclusions in the reports were that Theresa Lofton had not known her killer, that her path had somehow intersected with his, that it had simply been bad luck. The unknown killer was always referred to as a male, though there was no positive proof of this. The victim had not been sexually assaulted. But most violent murderers and mutilators of women were men, and it was believed it would have taken a physically strong person to cut through the body's bone and gristle. No cutting weapon was ever found.

Though the body had nearly completely bled out, there were indications of postmortem lividity, which meant some time had passed between the victim's death and the mutilation. Possibly, according to the report, as long as two or three hours.

Another peculiarity was the timing of when the body was left in the park. It was discovered approximately forty hours after investigators believed Theresa Lofton had been killed. Yet the park was a popular running and walking spot. It was unlikely that the body could have been in place in the open park field for that long without being noticed, even though an early snow considerably cut down on the number of people who passed through. In fact, the report concluded that the body had been in place no more than three hours when it was spotted after dawn by an early morning jogger.

So where was it all that time? The investigators couldn't answer that question. But they had a clue.

The fibers analysis report listed numerous foreign hairs and cotton fibers that had been found on the body and combed out of the hair. These would primarily be used to match a suspect to the victim, once a suspect became known. One particular section of the report had been circled. This section dealt with the recovery of a specific fiber – kapok – found on the body in large quantity. Thirty-three kapok seed hairs had been removed from the body. The number suggested direct contact with the source. The report said that while similar to cotton, kapok fibers were uncommon and primarily found in materials requiring buoyancy, such as boat cushions, life vests and some sleeping bags. I wondered why this section had been circled on the report and asked Wexler.

'Sean thought the kapok fibers were the key to where the body had been during the missing hours. You know, if we found a spot where we found that fiber, which isn't all that common, then we'd have the crime scene. But we never found it.'

Because the reports were in chronological order I could see how theories were considered and discarded. And I could sense a growing desperation in the investigation. It was going nowhere. It was clear that my brother believed Theresa Lofton had crossed paths with a serial killer, the toughest criminal to track. There was a return report from the FBI's National Center for the Analysis of Violent Crime containing a psychological profile of the killer. My brother had also kept a copy in the file of a seventeen-page checklist survey of aspects of the crime he had sent to the bureau's Violent Criminal Apprehension Program. But the VICAP computer's response to the survey was negative. The Lofton killing did not match any other killings across the country in enough details to warrant further attention from the FBI.

The profile the bureau had forwarded was produced by an agent listed on the report as Rachel Walling. It contained a host of generalities that were largely worthless to the investigation because while the characterizations were in depth and possibly even on target, they did not necessarily help the detectives winnow down the millions of men who might qualify as suspects. The profile projected that the killer was most likely a white male, twenty to thirty years old, with unresolved feelings of inadequacy and anger toward women, hence the gross mutilation of the victim's body. He was probably raised by a domineering mother and his father probably was not present in the household or was absorbed in earning a living and forfeited child rearing and development to the mother. The profile classified the killer as 'organized' in his methodology and warned that his seemingly successful completion of the crime and escape from detection could lead him to try further crimes of a similar nature.

The last reports in the first file were investigative summaries of interviews, tips that were checked out and other details from the case that might have meant nothing at the moment they were typed up but could be pivotal later. Through these reports I could chart Sean's growing attachment to Theresa

Lofton. In the initial pages she was always referred to as the victim, sometimes Lofton. Later on, he began referring to her as Theresa. And in the last reports, those filed in February before his death, he called her Terri, probably having picked up the diminutive name from her family and friends, or maybe from the back of the photo of her first day on campus. The happy day.

With ten minutes left I closed the file and opened the other one. This one was thinner and seemed to be filled with a hodgepodge of investigative loose ends. There were several letters from citizens offering theories on the killing. One letter was from a medium who said Theresa Lofton's living spirit was circling somewhere above the ozone layer in a high-frequency sound belt. She spoke in a voice so fast that it sounded like a chirp to the untrained ear, but the medium could decipher the chirping and was willing to ask her questions if Sean wanted to. There was no indication from the file that he did.

A supplemental report noted that Theresa's bank and auto repair shop were within walking distance of the campus. Three times detectives walked the routes between her dorm room, the day care center, the bank and the repair shop but came across no witnesses who remembered seeing Theresa on the Wednesday after classes ended. Despite this, my brother's theory – outlined in another supplemental – was that Lofton had been abducted sometime after calling her mechanic from the day care center but before she got to the bank to get money to pay him.

The file also contained a chronological record of the activity of the investigators assigned to the case. Initially, four members of the CAPs squad worked the case full-time. But as little headway was made and more cases came up, the investigative effort was winnowed down to Sean and Wexler. Then just Sean. He wouldn't let it go.

The last entry in the chronological record was made on the day he died. It was just one line: 'Mar. 13 – RUSHER at Stanley. P/R info on Terri.'

'Time.'

I looked up and Wexler was pointing to his watch. I closed the file without protest.

'What's P-slash-R mean?'

'Person Reporting. It meant he got a call.'

'Who is Rusher?'

'We don't know. There's a couple people in the phone book with that name. We called them, they didn't know what the fuck we were talking about. I ran something on NCIC but with just a last name didn't get anything to work with. Bottom line is, we don't know who it was or is. We don't even know if it's a man or woman. We don't know if Sean actually met anybody or not. We found nobody at the Stanley who saw him.'

'Why would he go to meet this person without telling you or leaving some kind of record about who it was? Why'd he go alone?'

'Who knows? We've gotten so many calls on that case, you could spend all day just writing notes. And maybe he didn't know. Maybe all he knew was that someone wanted to talk to him. Your brother was so caught up on this one, he would have gone to meet anybody who said they knew something. I'll let you in on a little secret. It's something that's not in there because he didn't want people around here thinking he was loony. But he went to see that psychic – the medium – that's mentioned in there.'

'What did he get?'

'Nothing. Just some bullshit about the killer being out there wanting to do it again. I mean, it was like – yeah, no kidding, thanks for the tip. Anyway, that's off the record, the psychic stuff. I don't want people thinking Mac was a flake.'

I didn't bother to say anything about the stupidity of what he had just said. My brother had killed himself and yet Wexler was engaged in trying to limit the damage his image might suffer if it was known he had consulted a psychic.

'It doesn't go past this room,' I said instead. After a few moments of silence I said, 'So what's your theory on what happened that day, Wex? Off the record, I mean.'

'My theory? My theory is he went out there and whoever it was who'd called him didn't show. It was another dead end for him and it tipped the scale. He drove up to that lake and he did what he did . . . Are you going to write a story about him?'

'I don't know. I think so.'

'Look, I don't know how to say this but here goes. He was your brother but he was my friend. I might've even known him better than you. Leave it alone. Just let it go.'

I told him I would think about it but it was only to placate him. I had already decided. I left then, checking my watch to make sure I had enough time to get out to Estes Park before dark.

6

I didn't get to the parking lot at Bear Lake until after five. I realized it was just as it had been for my brother, deserted. The lake was frozen and the temperature was dropping quickly. The sky was already purple and going dark. It wasn't much of a draw for locals or tourists this late in the day.

As I drove through the lot I thought about why he had picked this place to come. As far as I knew it had nothing to do with the Lofton case. But I thought I knew why. I parked where he had parked and just sat there thinking.

There was a light on in the ceiling of the overhang above the front of the ranger shack. I decided to get out and see if Pena, the witness, was there. Then another thought struck me. I slid over to the passenger side of the Tempo. I took a couple of deep breaths, then opened the door and started running for the woods where they grew closest to the car. As I ran I counted by thousands out loud. I was at eleven thousand by the time I had gotten over the snowbank and reached the cover.

Standing there in the woods, a foot deep in snow without boots on, I bent over and put my hands on my knees as I caught my breath. There was no way a shooter could have gotten into the woods to hide if Pena had been out of the shack as quickly as he had reported. I finally stopped gulping the air and headed toward the ranger's shack, debating how to approach him. As a reporter or a brother?

It was Pena behind the window. I could see the nameplate on his uniform. He was locking a desk when I looked through the window. He was calling it a day.

'Can I help you, sir? I'm closing up.'

'Yes, I was wondering if I could ask you a few questions.'

He came out, eyeing me suspiciously because I obviously wasn't dressed for a hike in the snow. I had on jeans and Reeboks, a corduroy shirt beneath a thick woolen sweater. I had left my long coat in the car and I was very cold.

'My name is Jack McEvoy.'

I waited a moment to see if it registered. It didn't. He had probably only seen the name written in reports he had to sign, or in the newspaper. Its pronunciation – Mac-a-voy – didn't jibe with its spelling.

'My brother . . . he was the one you found a couple weeks ago.'

I pointed toward the lot.

'Oh,' he said, understanding. 'In the car. The officer.'

'Uh, I've been with the police all day, looking at the reports and stuff. I just wanted to come out and take a look. It's hard, you know . . . to accept it.'

He nodded and tried to hide a quick glance at his watch.

'I just have a few quick questions. You were inside there when you heard it? The shot?'

I spoke quickly, not giving him the chance to stop me.

'Yes,' he said. He looked like he was trying to decide something and then he did. He continued. 'I was locking up just like tonight, 'bout to go home. I heard it. It was one of those things, I kinda knew what it was. I don't know why. Really what I thought was that it might be poachers after the deer. I came out pretty quick and the first place I looked was the lot. I saw his car. Could see him in there. All the windows were fogged up pretty good but I could see him. He was behind the wheel. Something about the way he was leaning back, I knew what happened . . . Sorry it was your brother.'

I nodded and studied the ranger's shack. Just a small office and storage room. I realized that five seconds was probably a long estimate from the time Pena heard the shot until he saw the lot.

'There was no pain,' Pena said.

'What?'

'If it's something you want to know. There was no physical pain, I don't think. I ran to the car. He was dead. It was instant.'

'The police reports said you couldn't get to him. The doors were locked.'

'Yeah, I tried the door. But I could tell he was gone. I came back up here to make the calls.'

'How long do you think he was parked there before he did it?'

'I don't know. Like I told the police, I don't have a view of the lot. I'd been in the shed – I got a heater in there – oh, I'd say at least a half hour before I heard the shot. He could have been parked there the whole time. Thinking about it, I guess.'

I nodded.

'You didn't see him out on the lake, did you? You know, before the shot.'

'On the lake? No. Nobody was on the lake.'

I stood there trying to think of something else.

'Did they come up with any reason why?' Pena asked. 'Like I said, I know he was an officer.'

I shook my head no. I didn't want to get into it with this stranger. I thanked him and started back to the lot while he locked the shack door. The Tempo was the only car in the plowed lot. I thought of something and turned back.

'How often do they plow?'

Pena stepped away from the door.

'After every snow.'

I nodded and thought of something else.

'Where do you park?'

'We've got an equipment yard a half mile down the road. I park there and walk up the trail in the morning, down at quitting time.'

'You want a ride?'

'Nah. Thanks, though. The trail will get me there quicker.'

The whole way back to Boulder I thought of the last time I had been to Bear Lake. It was also winter then. But the lake wasn't frozen, not all the way. And when I left that time, I felt just as cold and alone. And guilty.

Riley looked as if she had aged ten years since I had seen her at the funeral. Even so, I was immediately struck when she opened the door by what I hadn't realized before. Theresa Lofton looked like a nineteen-year-old Riley McEvoy. I wondered if Scalari or anybody else had asked the shrinks about that.

She asked me in. She knew she looked bad. After she opened the door she casually raised her hand to the side of her face to hide it. She tried a feeble smile. We went into the kitchen and she asked if I wanted her to make coffee but I said I wasn't staying long. I sat down at the kitchen table. It seemed that whenever I visited we would gather around the kitchen table. Even with Sean gone that hadn't changed.

'I wanted to tell you that I'm going to write about Sean.'

She was silent for a long time and she didn't look at me. She got up and started emptying the dishwasher. I waited.

'Do you have to?' she finally asked.

'Yes . . . I think so.'

She said nothing.

'I'm going to call the psychologist, Dorschner. I don't know if he'll talk to me, but now that Sean's gone I don't see why not. But, uh, he might call you for permission . . .'

'Don't worry, Jack, I won't try to stop you.'

I nodded my thanks but I noted the edge to her words.

'I was with the cops today and I went up to the lake.'

'I don't want to hear about it, Jack. If you have to write about it that's your choice. Do what you have to do. But my choice is that I don't want to hear about it. And if you do write about Sean, I won't read that, either. I have to do what *I* have to do.'

I nodded and said, 'I understand. There is one thing I need to ask, though. Then I'll leave you out of it.'

'What do you mean, leave me out of it?' she asked angrily. 'I wish I could be left out of it. But I'm in it. For the rest of my life I'm in it. You want to write about it? You think that's a way to get rid of it? What do *I* do, Jack?'

I looked down at the floor. I wanted to go but didn't know how to exit. Her pain and anger radiated toward me like heat from a closed oven.

'You want to know about that girl,' she said in a low, calmer voice. 'That's what all the detectives asked about.'

'Yes. Why did this one . . . ?'

I didn't know how to phrase the question.

'Why did it make him forget about everything good in his life? The answer is I don't know. I don't goddamn know.'

I could see anger and tears welling in her eyes again. It was as if her husband had deserted her for another woman. And here I was, as close a flesh and blood approximation of Sean as she would ever see now. No wonder she was venting her anger and pain at me.

'Did he talk about the case at home?' I asked.

'Not especially. He told me about cases from time to time. This one didn't seem that different except for what happened to her. He told me what the killer did to her. He told me how he had to look at her. After, I mean. I know it bothered him but a lot of things bothered him. A lot of cases. He didn't want anybody to get away. He always said that.'

'But this time he went to see that doctor.'

'He'd had dreams and I told him he should go. I made him go.'

'What were the dreams?'

'That he was there. You know, when it happened to her. He dreamed he saw it but couldn't do anything to stop it.'

Her comment made me think of another death a long time ago. Sarah. Falling through the ice. I remembered the helpless feeling of watching and being unable to do anything. I looked at Riley.

'You know why Sean went up there?'

'No.'

'Was it because of Sarah?'

'I said I don't know.'

'That was before we knew you. But that was where she died. An accident . . .'

'I know, Jack. But I don't know what it had to do with anything. Not now.'

I didn't, either. It was one of many confusing thoughts but I couldn't let it go.

Before heading back to Denver I drove over to the cemetery. I don't know what I was doing. It was dark and there had been two snows since the funeral. It took me fifteen minutes just to find the spot where Sean was in the ground. There was no stone yet. I found it by finding the one next to it. My sister's.

On Sean's there were a couple of pots of frozen flowers and a plastic sign sticking out of the snow with his name on it. There were no flowers on Sarah's. I looked at Sean's spot for a while. It was a clear night and the moonlight was enough for me to see. My breath came out in clouds.

'How come, Sean?' I asked out loud. 'How come?'

I realized what I was doing and looked around. I was the only one in the cemetery. The only one alive. I thought about what Riley had said about Sean not wanting anybody to get away. And I thought about how I didn't even care about such things, as long as it made a good thirty-inch story. How had we separated so completely? My brother and I. My twin. I didn't know. It just made me feel sad. Made me feel like maybe the wrong one was in the ground.

I remembered what Wexler had said that first night when they came for me and told me about my brother. He talked about all the shit coming down the pipe finally being too much for Sean. I still didn't believe it. But I had to believe something. I thought of Riley and the pictures of Theresa Lofton. And I thought of my sister slipping through the ice. I believed then that the girl's murder had infected my brother with the most desperate kind of hopelessness. I believed he became haunted by that hopelessness and the crystal-blue eyes of the girl who had been cut in half. And since he didn't have his brother to turn to, he turned to his sister. He went to the lake that took her. And then he joined her.

I walked out of the cemetery without looking back.

7

Gladden posted himself at a spot along the railing on the other side from where the woman took the tickets from the children. She couldn't see him. But once the great carousel began turning, he was able to study each child. Gladden pushed his fingers through his dyed blond hair and looked around. He was pretty sure everybody else regarded him as just another parent.

The ride was starting again. The calliope was grinding out the strains of a song Gladden could not identify and the horses began their bobbing, counterclockwise turn. Gladden had never actually ridden on the carousel, though he had seen that many of the parents got on with their children. He thought that it might be too risky for him to do it.

He noticed a girl of about five clinging desperately to one of the black stallions. She was leaning forward with her tiny arms wrapped around the candy-striped pole that came up through the painted horse's neck. One side of her little pink shorts had ridden up the inside of her thigh. Her skin was coffee brown. Gladden reached into his duffel and brought out the camera. He amped up the shutter speed to cut down on movement blurring and pointed the camera at the carousel. He focused and waited for the girl to come around again.

It took him two revolutions of the carousel but he believed he got the shot and brought the camera back down. He looked around just to be sure he was cool and he noticed a man leaning on the railing about twenty feet to his right. The man hadn't been there before. And most alarming, he was wearing a sports coat and tie. The man was either a pervert or a policeman. Gladden decided he'd better leave.

Out on the pier the sun was almost blinding. Gladden shoved the camera into the duffel and pulled his mirrored shades out. He decided to walk out further on the pier to where it was crowded. He could lose this guy if he had to. If he was actually being followed. He walked about halfway out, nice and steady, acting cool. Then he stopped along the railing and turned and leaned back against it as if he wanted to catch a few rays. He turned his face up toward the sun but his eyes, behind the mirrors, took in the area of the pier he had just come from.

For a few moments there was nothing. He didn't see the man in the sports coat and tie. Then he saw him, jacket over the arm, sunglasses on, walking along the front of the arcade concession, slowly moving toward Gladden.

'Fuck!' Gladden said out loud.

A woman sitting on a nearby bench with a young boy looked at Gladden with baleful eyes when she and the boy heard the exclamation.

'Sorry,' Gladden said.

He turned and looked around the rest of the pier. He had to think quickly. He knew cops usually worked in pairs while in the field. Where was the other one? It took him thirty seconds but he picked her out of the crowd. A woman about thirty yards behind the man in the tie. She was wearing long pants and a polo shirt. Not as formal as the man. She blended in, except for the two-way radio down at her side. Gladden could see that she was trying to hide it. As he watched, she turned so that her back was to him and began talking into the two-way.

She had just called for backup. Had to be. He had to stay cool but come up with a plan. The man in the tie was maybe twenty yards away. Gladden stepped away from the railing and started walking at a slightly faster pace toward the end of the pier. He did what the woman cop had done. He used his body as a shield and pulled the duffel bag around so that it was in front of him. He unzipped it and reached in and grabbed the camera. Without pulling it out, he turned it over until he found the CLEAR switch and erased the chip. There wasn't much on there. The girl on the carousel, a few kids at the public showers. No big loss.

That done, he again proceeded down the pier. He took his cigarettes out of the bag and, using his body as a shield, turned around and huddled against the wind to light one. When he had the smoke lit, he looked up and saw the two cops were getting closer. He knew they thought they had him bottled. He was going to the dead end of the pier. The woman had caught up to the man and they were talking as they closed in. Probably deciding whether to wait for the backup, Gladden thought.

Gladden quickly walked toward the bait shop and the pier offices. He knew the layout of the end of the pier well. On two occasions during the week he had followed children with their parents from the carousel to the end of the pier. He knew that on the other side of the bait shop were stairs that led to the observation deck on the roof.

As he turned the corner of the shop out of sight of the cops, Gladden ran down the side to the back and then up the steps. He could now look down on the pier in front of the shop. The two cops were there below, talking again. Then the man followed Gladden's path and the woman stayed back. They weren't going to take a chance on letting him slip away. A question suddenly occurred to Gladden. How did they know? A cop in a suit just doesn't happen by the pier. The cops had gone there for a purpose. Him. But how did they know?

He broke away from those thoughts to the situation at hand. He needed a diversion. The man would soon figure out he wasn't with the fishermen at the end of the pier and come up to the observation deck looking for him. He saw the trash can in the corner by the wooden railing. He ran to it and looked in. It was almost empty. He put the duffel bag down, lifted the trash can over his head and with a running start moved to the railing. He threw it out as far as he could, then watched it go over the heads of two fishermen below and down into the water. It made a large splash and he heard a young boy yell, 'Hey!'

'Man in the water!' Gladden yelled. 'Man in the water!'

He then grabbed the duffel bag and quickly moved back to the rear railing of the deck. He looked for the woman cop. She was still there below him but had clearly heard the splash and his yelling. A couple of children ran around the side of the bait shop to see what the yelling and excitement were about. After what seemed to be a physical hesitation, the woman followed the children around the corner of the building to the source of the splash and ensuing commotion. Gladden hooked the duffel over his shoulder and quickly climbed over the railing, lowered himself down and then dropped the final five feet. He started running down the pier toward land.

About halfway to land Gladden saw the two beach cops on bikes. They wore shorts and blue polo shirts. Ridiculous. He'd watched them the day before, amused that they even considered themselves cops. Now he ran right toward them, waving his hands to make them stop.

'Are you the backup?' he yelled when he got to them. 'They're at the end of the pier. The perp's in the water. He jumped. They need your help and they need a boat. They sent me to get you.'

'Go!' one of the cops yelled to his partner.

As one started pedaling away, the other pulled a two-way off his belt and started radioing for a lifeguard boat.

Gladden waved his thanks for their speedy reaction and started walking away. After a few seconds he looked back and saw the second cop pedaling toward the end of the pier. Gladden started his run again.

On the crest of the bridge from the beach up to Ocean Avenue, Gladden looked back and could see the commotion at the end of the pier. He lit another cigarette and took his sunglasses off. Cops are so stupid, he thought. They get what they deserve. He hurried up to the street surface, crossed Ocean and walked down to the Third Street Promenade, where he was sure he could lose himself in the crowds at the popular shopping and dining area. Fuck those cops, he thought. They had their one chance and blew it. That's all they get.

On the promenade he walked down a corridor that led to several small fast-food restaurants. The excitement had left Gladden famished and he went into one of these places for a slice of pizza and a soda. As he waited for the girl to warm up the pizza in the oven, he thought of the girl on the carousel and wished he hadn't cleared the camera. But how could he know he'd so easily slip away?

'I should have known,' he said angrily out loud. Then he looked around to make sure the girl behind the counter hadn't noticed. He studied her for a moment and found her unattractive. She was too old. She could practically have children herself.

As he watched, she used her fingers to gingerly pull the slice of pizza out of the oven and onto a paper plate. She licked her fingers afterward – she had burned them – and put Gladden's meal on the counter. He took it back to his table but didn't eat it. He didn't like other people touching his food.

Gladden wondered how long he would have to wait until it was safe to go back down to the beach and get the car. Good thing it was in an overnight lot. Just in case. No matter what, they must not get to his car. If they got to his car, they would open the trunk and get his computer. If they got that, they would never let him go.

The more he thought about the episode with the cops, the angrier he became. The carousel was now lost to him. He couldn't go back. At least not for a long time. He'd have to put out a message to the others on the network.

He still couldn't figure out how it had happened. His mind bounced along the possibilities, even considering someone on the net, but then the ball stopped on the woman who took the tickets. She must have made the complaint. She was the only one who saw him each of the days. It was her.

He closed his eyes and leaned his head back against the wall. In his mind he was at the carousel, approaching the ticket taker. He had his knife. He was going to teach her a lesson about minding her own business. She thought she could just –

He sensed someone's presence. Someone was looking at him.

Gladden opened his eyes. The two cops from the pier were standing there. The man, drenched in sweat, raised his hand and signaled Gladden to stand up.

'Get up, asshole.'

The two cops said nothing of value to Gladden on the way in. They had taken the duffel bag, searched him, handcuffed him and told him he was under arrest but they refused to say what for. They took his cigarettes and wallet. The camera was the only thing he cared about. Luckily, he hadn't brought his books with him this time.

Gladden considered what was in the wallet. None of it mattered, he decided. The Alabama license identified him as Harold Brisbane. He had gotten it through the network, trading photos for IDs. He had another ID in the car and he'd kiss Harold Brisbane good-bye as soon as he got out of custody.

They didn't get the keys to the car. They were hidden in the wheel well. Gladden had been prepared for the eventuality that he might be popped. He knew he had to keep the cops away from the car. He had learned from experience to take such precautions, to always plan for the worst case scenario. That was what Horace had taught him at Raiford. All those nights together.

In the detective bureau of the Santa Monica Police Department, he was roughly but silently ushered into a small interview room. They sat him down on one of the gray steel chairs and took off one of the cuffs, which they then locked to an iron ring attached by a bolted clamp to the top center of the table. The detectives then walked out and he was left alone for more than an hour.

On the wall he faced there was a mirrored window and Gladden knew he was in a viewing room. He just couldn't figure out for sure whom they would have on the other side of the glass. He saw no way that he could have been tracked from Phoenix or Denver or anywhere else.

At one point he thought he could hear voices from the other side of the glass. They were in there, watching him, looking at him, whispering. He closed his eyes and turned his chin down to his chest so they couldn't see his face. Then suddenly he raised his face with a leering, maniacal grin and he yelled, 'You'll be fucking sorry!'

That ought to put a stutter in the mind of whoever the cops have in there, he thought. That fucking ticket taker, he thought again. He went back to his daydream of revenge against her.

In the ninetieth minute of his cloistering in the room, the door finally opened and the same two cops came in. They took chairs, the woman directly across from him and the man to his left side. The woman put a tape recorder on the table along with the duffel bag. This was nothing, he told himself over and over like a mantra. He'd be kicked loose before the sun was down.

'Sorry to make you wait,' the woman said cordially.

'No problem,' he said. 'Can I have my cigarettes?'

He nodded toward the duffel bag. He didn't really want a smoke, he just wanted to see if the camera was still in there. You couldn't trust the fucking cops. He didn't even need Horace to teach him that. The detective ignored his request and turned on the tape recorder. She then identified herself as Detective Constance Delpy and her partner as Detective Ron Sweetzer. Both were with the Exploited Child Unit.

Gladden was surprised that she seemed to be taking the lead here. She looked to be about five to eight years younger than Sweetzer. She had blond hair kept in an easily managed short style. She was maybe fifteen pounds overweight and that was mostly in her hips and upper arms. Gladden guessed she worked out on the pipes. He also thought she was a lesbian. He could tell these things. He had a sense.

Sweetzer had a washed-out face and a laconic demeanor. He had lost hair in a pattern that left him with a thin strip of growth down the center of his pate. Gladden decided to concentrate on Delpy. She was the one.

Delpy took a card from her pocket and read Gladden his constitutional rights.

'What do I need those for?' he asked when she was done. 'I didn't do anything wrong.'

'Do you understand those rights?'

'What I don't understand is why I'm here.'

'Mr Brisbane, do you under –?'

'Yes.'

'Good. By the way, your driver's license is from Alabama. What are you doing out here?'

'That's my business. I'd like to contact a lawyer now. I'm not answering any questions. Like I said, I do understand those rights you just read.'

He knew that what they wanted was his local address and the location of his car. What they had was nothing. But the fact that he had run would probably be enough for a local judge to find probable cause and give them a warrant to search his premises and car if they knew where those were. He couldn't allow that, no matter what.

'We'll talk about your lawyer in just a moment,' Delpy said. 'But I want to give you the chance to clear this up, maybe even walk out of here without wasting your money on a lawyer.'

She opened the duffel bag and pulled out the camera and the bag of Starburst candy the kids liked so much.

'What is all of this?' she asked.

'Looks pretty evident to me.'

She held the camera up and looked at it as if she had never seen one before.

'What is this used for?'

'Takes pictures.'

'Of children?'

'I'd like a lawyer now.'

'What about this candy? What do you do with that? Do you give that to children?'

'I'd *like* to speak to a lawyer.'

'Fuck the lawyer,' Sweetzer said angrily. 'We've got your ass, Brisbane. You were taking pictures of kids at the showers. Little naked kids with their mothers. You fucking disgust me.'

Gladden cleared his throat and looked at Delpy with dead eyes.

'I don't know anything about that. But I do have a question. I have to ask, where is the crime? You know? I'm not saying I did it, but if I did, I didn't know taking photos of children at the beach was against the law now.'

Gladden shook his head as if confused. Delpy shook her head as if disgusted.

'Detective Delpy, I can assure you that there are numerous legal precedents that have held that observation of acceptable public nudity – in this case, a mother cleaning up a young child at the beach – cannot be transcribed as prurient interest. You see, if the photographer who took such a picture committed a crime, then you'd have to prosecute the mother as well for providing the opportunity. But you probably know all of this. I'm sure one of you spent the last hour and a half consulting the city attorney.'

Sweetzer leaned close to him across the table. Gladden noted the smell of cigarettes and barbecued potato chips on his breath. He guessed Sweetzer had eaten the chips on purpose, just so his breath would be intolerable during the interrogation.

'Listen to me, asshole, we know exactly what you are and what you're doing. I've worked rape, homicide . . . but you guys, you are the lowest form of life there is on the planet. You don't want to talk to us? Fine, no sweat. What we're going to do is take you down to Biscailuz tonight and put you in with the general population. I know some people in there, Brisbane. And I'm going to put out the word. Know what happens to pedophiles in there?'

Gladden turned his head slowly until he was staring calmly into Sweetzer's eyes for the first time.

'Detective, I'm not sure but I think your breath alone might constitute cruel and unusual punishment. If by chance I am ever convicted of taking photographs at the beach, I might make it a point of appeal.'

Sweetzer swung his arm back.

'Ron!'

He froze, looked at Delpy and slowly lowered his arm. Gladden had not even flinched at the threat. He would have welcomed the blow. He knew it would have helped him in court.

'Cute,' Sweetzer said. 'What we've got here is a jailhouse lawyer thinks he knows all the angles. That's nice. Well, you're going to be filing some briefs tonight, if you know what I mean.'

'Can I call a lawyer now,' Gladden said in a bored voice.

He knew what they were doing. They had nothing and they were trying to scare him into making a mistake. But he wouldn't accommodate them because he was too smart for them. And he suspected that deep down they knew he was.

'Look, I'm not going to Biscailuz and we all know it. What have you got? You've got my camera, which, I don't know if you checked, has no pictures in it. And you've got some ticket taker or a lifeguard or somebody else who says I took some photos. But there is no evidence of that other than their word. And if you just had them looking through the mirror at me, then that identification is tainted as well. It wasn't by any stretch of the imagination an unbiased line up.'

He waited but they said nothing. He was in charge now.

'But the bottom line to this whole matter is that whoever you had behind that glass, she or he is a witness to something that wasn't even a crime. How that equates to a night in the county jail, I don't know. But maybe you can explain that to me, Detective Sweetzer, if it isn't too much of a strain on your intelligence.'

Sweetzer stood up, knocking his chair back into the wall. Delpy reached an arm over, this time physically restraining him.

'Take it easy, Ron,' she ordered. 'Sit down. Just sit down.'

Sweetzer did as instructed. Delpy then looked at Gladden.

'If you are going to continue this, I'll have to make that call,' he said. 'Where's the phone, please?'

'You'll get the phone. Right after you're booked. But you can forget the cigarettes. The county jail is a smoke-free facility. We care about your health.'

'Booked on what charge? You can't hold me.'

'Pollution of public waterways, vandalism of city property. Evading a police officer.'

Gladden's eyebrows went up in a questioning look. Delpy smiled at him.

'You forgot something,' she said. 'The trash can you threw into Santa Monica Bay.'

She nodded in victory and turned off the tape recorder.

In the holding cell of the police station Gladden was allowed to make his call. When he held the receiver to his ear he smelled the industrial-strength soap they had given him to wash the ink off his fingers. It served as a reminder to him that he had to get out before the prints went through the national computer. He dialed a number that he had committed to memory the first night he had made it to the coast. Krasner was on the network list.

At first the lawyer's secretary was going to put him off but Gladden said to tell Mr Krasner that the caller was referred by Mr Pederson, the name suggested on the network bulletin board. Krasner came on the line quickly after that.

'Yes, this is Arthur Krasner, what can I do for you?'

'Mr Krasner, my name is Harold Brisbane and I have a problem.'

Gladden then proceeded to tell Krasner in detail what had happened to him. He spoke low into the phone because he was not alone. There were two other men in the holding cell, waiting to be transferred to the county jail at Biscailuz Center. One was lying on the floor asleep, an addict on the nod. The other was sitting on the opposite side of the cell but he was watching Gladden and attempting to listen to him because there was nothing else to do. Gladden thought he might be a plant, a cop posing as a prisoner so he could eavesdrop on his call to the lawyer.

Gladden left nothing out save for his real name. When he was done Krasner was silent for a long time.

'What's that noise?' he finally asked.

'Guy sleeping on the floor in here. Snoring.'

'Harold, you shouldn't be amongst people like that,' Krasner lamented in a patronizing tone Gladden disliked. 'We've got to do something.'

'That's why I'm calling.'

'My fee for my work on this today and tomorrow will be one thousand dollars. That is a generous discount. I offer it to those referrals I receive from . . . Mr Pederson. If my involvement goes further than tomorrow, then we'll have to discuss it. Will it be a problem for you to have the money?'

'No, no problem.'

'What about bail? After my fee, what can you do on bail? It sounds like pledging property is out of the question. Bondsmen need ten percent of the bail fixed by the judge. That amount is their fee. You won't get it back.'

'Yes, forget property. After taking care of your exorbitant fee I can probably go up to five more. That's immediately. I can get more but it might be difficult. I want to keep it to five max and I want to get out as soon as possible.'

Krasner ignored the remark about his fee.

'Is that five thousand?' he asked.

'Yes, of course. Five thousand. What can you do with it?'

Gladden figured Krasner was probably kicking himself over discounting his inflated fee.

'Okay, that means you can handle fifty thousand bail. I think we're in good shape. It's a felony arrest for now. But the fleeing and the pollution are wobblers, meaning they can be filed as either felonies or misdemeanors. I am sure that they will go low on them. It's a bullshit case trumped up by the cops. We just have to get you into court and out on bail.'

'Yes.'

'I think fifty thousand will be high for this matter but it will be part of the horse trading I do with the filing deputy. We'll see how it goes. I take it you do not want to provide an address.'

'That's correct. I need a new one.'

'Then we might have to go the whole fifty. But in the meantime I will see about an address. There may be additional expenses incurred from that. It won't be much. I can prom –'

'Fine. Just do it.'

Gladden looked back at the man on the other side of the cell.

'What about tonight?' he asked quietly. 'I told you, these cops are going to try to get me hurt.'

'I think they are bluffing but –'

'That's easy for you to –'

'*But* I am not taking any chances. Hear me out, Mr Brisbane. I can't get you out tonight but I am going to make some calls. You will be okay. I am going to get you in there with a K-9 jacket.'

'What's that?'

'It's keep-away status in the jail. It's usually reserved for informants or high-power cases. I'll make a call to the jail and inform them that you are an informant in a federal investigation out of Washington.'

'Won't they check?'

'Yes, but it will be too late today. They'll put you in a K-9 jacket and by the time they find out tomorrow it's bogus, you'll be in court and then hopefully free after that.'

'That's a nice scam, Krasner.'

'Yes, but I won't be able to use it again. I think I may have to raise the fee we just discussed a bit to cover the loss.'

'Fuck that. Look, this is the deal. I have access to six grand max. You get me out and whatever's left after the bondsman, you get. It's an incentive deal.'

'That's a deal. Now, one other thing. You also mentioned the need to beat the prints. I need to have an idea about this. So that in clear conscience I will not make any statements before the court that will –'

'I have a history, if that is what you're asking. But I don't think you and I have to go into that.'

'I understand.'

'When will my arraignment be?'

'Late morning. When I make my calls to the jail after we hang up, I'll see to it you are scheduled for the early bus to Santa Monica. It's better to wait in the court hold than Biscailuz.'

'I wouldn't know. My first time here.'

'Uh, Mr Brisbane, I need to bring up my fee and the bail money again. I'm afraid I'll need that in my possession before I go into court tomorrow.'

'You have a wire account?'

'Yes.'

'Give me the number. I'll have it wired in the morning. Will I be able to dial long distance in K-9?'

'No. You'll have to call my office. I'll tell Judy to expect the call. She'll then dial the number you give her on the other line and cross-connect you. It will be no problem. I've done it this way before.'

Krasner gave him his wire account number and Gladden used the memorizing technique Horace had taught him to commit it to memory.

'Mr Krasner, you would be doing yourself a great favor if you destroy the wire records of this transaction and simply carry the fee as paid in cash on your accounts.'

'I understand. Anything else on your mind?'

'Yes. You better put something on the PTL net, tell the others what happened, tell them to stay away from that carousel.'

'Will do.'

After he hung up, Gladden turned his back to the wall and slid down until he was sitting on the floor. He avoided looking at the man across the room. He noticed the snoring had stopped and guessed that maybe the man on the floor might be dead. OD'd. Then the man stirred slightly. For a moment Gladden considered reaching down and pulling the plastic bracelet off the man and replacing it with his own. He'd probably be released in the morning without the cost of a lawyer and $50,000 bail.

It was too risky, he decided. The man sitting across the cell might be a cop and, besides, the one on the floor might be a multiple repeat offender. You never knew when a judge was going to say enough was enough. Gladden decided to take his chances with Krasner. After all, he'd gotten his name off the network board. The lawyer must know what he was doing. Still, the six thousand bothered him. He was being extorted by the judicial system. Six thousand for what? What had he done wrong?

His hand went to his pocket for a cigarette but then he remembered they had been taken away. That brought the anger down on him even heavier. And the self-pity. He was being persecuted by society and for what? His instincts and desires were not of his choosing. Why couldn't they understand that?

Gladden wished he had his laptop with him. He wanted to sign on and talk to those on the network. Those of his kind. He felt lonely in the cell. He thought that he might even start to cry except that the man leaning against the other wall was watching him. He would not cry in front of him.

8

I didn't sleep well after my day with the files. I kept thinking about the photos. First of Theresa, then of my brother. Both of them captured forever in horrible poses, stored away in envelopes. I wanted to go back and steal the photos and burn them. I didn't want anyone ever to see them.

In the morning, after I had made coffee, I turned on my computer and dialed into the *Rocky*'s system to check messages. I ate handfuls of Cheerios from the box as I waited for the connection to be made and my password to be approved. I kept my laptop and printer set up on the dining room table because I most often ate while using them. It beat sitting at the table alone and thinking about how I'd been eating alone for more years than I cared to remember.

My home was small. I'd had the same one-bedroom apartment with the same furniture for nine years. It wasn't a bad place but it was nothing special. Other than Sean, I couldn't remember who the last visitor was. When I was with women, I didn't take them there. There hadn't been many of them, anyway.

I thought when I first moved in I'd only be staying a couple years, that maybe I'd eventually buy a house and get married or have a dog or something. But it hadn't happened and I'm not sure why. The job, I guess. At least that's what I told myself. I concentrated my energy on my work. In each room of the apartment there were stacks of newspapers with my stories in them. I liked to reread them and save them. If I died at home, I knew they'd come in there and find me and mistakenly think I was one of those pack rats I'd written about who die with newspapers stacked to the ceiling and their cash stuffed into the mattress. They wouldn't bother to pick up one of the papers and read my story.

On the computer I had only a couple of messages. The most recent was from Greg Glenn asking how it was going. It had been sent at six-thirty the night before. The timing annoyed me; the guy okayed the assignment Monday morning and on Monday night he wanted to know where I was going with it. 'How's it going?' was editor-speak for 'Where's the story?'

Fuck him, I thought. I sent back a brief reply saying I had spent Monday with the cops and was convinced of my brother's suicide. That out of the way, I would begin exploring the causes and frequency of police suicide.

The previous message on the tube was from Laurie Prine in the library. It had been sent at four-thirty Monday. All it said was, 'Interesting stuff on Nexis. It's on the counter.'

I sent a message back thanking her for the quick search and saying I had unexpectedly been tied up in Boulder but would pick up the search package right away. I thought she had an interest in me, though I had never responded to her on anything other than the professional level. You have to be careful and be sure. You make a wanted advance and you're cool. You make an unwanted advance and you get a personnel complaint. My view is that it's better just to avoid the whole thing.

Next I scrolled through the AP and UPI wires to see if there was anything interesting going on. There was a story about a doctor being shot outside a women's clinic in Colorado Springs. An anti-abortion activist was in custody, but the doctor had not died yet. I made an electronic copy of the story and transferred it to my personal storage basket, but I didn't think I'd ever do anything with it unless the doctor died.

There was a knock on my door and I looked through the peephole before opening it. It was Jane, who lived across the hall and down one. She'd been there about a year and I'd met her when she asked for help moving some furniture around when she was setting up her place. She was impressed when I told her I was a newspaper reporter, not knowing anything about what it was like. We'd gone to the movies twice and dinner once and spent a day skiing at Keystone but these outings were spread over the year she'd been in the building and nothing ever seemed to come of it. I think it was my hesitation, not hers. She was attractive in an outdoorsy sort of way and maybe that was it. I was outdoorsy myself – at least in my mind – and wanted something different from that.

'Hello, Jack. I saw your car in the garage last night so I knew you were back. How was the trip?'

'It was good. It was good to get away.'

'Did you ski?'

'A little bit. I went out to Telluride.'

'Sounds nice. You know, I was going to tell you but you already left, if you're ever going away again, I could take care of your plants or pick up the mail or whatever. Just ask.'

'Oh, thanks. But I don't really have any plants. I end up traveling a lot overnight for the job, so I don't keep any.'

I turned from the door and looked back into the apartment as if to make sure. I guess I should have invited her in for coffee but I didn't.

'You on your way to work?' I asked instead.

'Yeah.'

'Me, too. I better get going. But, listen, once I get settled in, let's do something. A movie or something.'

We both liked DeNiro movies. That was the one thing we had.

'Okay, call me.'

'I will.'

After closing the door I chastised myself again for not inviting her in. In the dining room I shut the computer down and my eyes caught on the inch-thick stack of paper next to the printer. My unfinished novel. I had started it more than a year earlier but it wasn't going anywhere. It was supposed to be about a writer who becomes a quadriplegic in a motorcycle accident. With the money from the legal settlement, he hires a beautiful young woman from the local university to type for him as he orally composes the sentences. But soon he realizes she is editing and rewriting what he tells her before she even types it in. And what dawns on him is that she is the better writer. Soon he sits mute in the room while she writes. He only watches. He wants to kill her, strangle her with his hands. But he can't move his hands to do it. He is in hell.

The stack of pages sat there on the table daring me to try again. I don't know why I didn't shove it into a drawer with the other one I had started and never finished years earlier. But I didn't. I guess I wanted it there where I could see it.

The *Rocky*'s newsroom was deserted when I got there. The morning editor and the early reporter were at the city desk but I didn't see anybody else. Most of the staffers didn't start coming in until nine or later. My first stop was the cafeteria for more coffee and then I swung by the library, where I took a thick computer printout with my name on it off the counter. I checked Laurie Prine's desk to thank her in person but she wasn't in yet, either.

Back at my desk I could see into Greg Glenn's office. He was there, on the phone as usual. I began my usual routine of reading the *Rocky* and the *Post* in tandem. I always enjoyed this, the daily judging of the Denver newspaper war. If you were keeping tabs, exclusive stories always scored the most points. But, generally, the papers covered the same stories and this was the trench war, where the real battle was. I would read our story and then I would read theirs, seeing who wrote it better, who had the best information. I didn't always pull for the *Rocky*. In fact, most times I didn't. I worked with some real assholes and didn't mind seeing their butts kicked by the *Post*. I would never admit this to anyone, though. It was the nature of the business and the competition. We competed with the other newspaper, we competed with each other. That was why I was sure some of them watched me whenever I walked through the newsroom. To some of the younger reporters I was almost a hero, with the kind of story clips, talent and beat to shoot for. To some of the others, I'm sure I was a pathetic hack with an undeservedly cushy beat. A dinosaur. They wanted to shoot at me. But that was okay. I understood this. I'd think the same thing if I were in their position.

The Denver papers were feeders for the bigger dailies in New York and L.A. and Chicago and Washington. I probably should have moved on long ago and had even turned down an offer with the *L.A. Times* a few years back. But not before I used it as leverage with Glenn to get my murder beat. He thought the offer was for a hot shot job covering the cops. I didn't tell him it was a job in a suburban section called the Valley Edition. He offered to create the murder beat for me if I stayed. Sometimes I thought I had made a mistake taking Glenn's offer. Maybe it would be good to start somewhere fresh.

We had done all right in the morning competition. I put the papers aside and picked up the library printout. Laurie Prine had found several stories in the eastern papers analyzing the pathology of police suicides and a handful of smaller spot news reports on specific suicides from around the country. She had the discretion not to print the *Denver Post* report on my brother.

Most of the longer reports examined suicide as a job risk that went with police work. Each started with a particular cop's suicide and then steered the story into a discussion among shrinks and police experts on what made cops eat their guns. All of the stories concluded that there was a causal relationship between police suicide and job stress and a traumatic event in the life of the victim.

The articles were valuable because what experts I would need for my story were named right there. And several pieces mentioned an ongoing FBI-sponsored study on police suicides at the Law Enforcement Foundation in Washington, D.C. I highlighted this, figuring that I could use updated statistics from the bureau or foundation to lend my story freshness and credibility.

The phone rang and it was my mother. We hadn't spoken since the funeral. After a few preliminary questions about my trip and how everybody was doing, she got to the point.

'Riley told me you are going to write about Sean.'

It wasn't a question but I answered as if it was.

'Yes, I am.'

'Why, John?'

She was the only one who called me John.

'Because I have to. I . . . just can't go on now like it didn't happen. I have to at least try to understand.'

'You always took things apart when you were a boy. You remember? All the toys you ruined.'

'What are you talking about, Mom? This is –'

'What I am saying is that when you take things apart you can't always put them back together again. Then what have you got? Nothing, Johnny, you have nothing.'

'Mom, you're not making sense. Look, I have to do this.'

I did not understand why I was so quick to anger when I talked to her.

'Have you thought about anyone else besides yourself? Do you know how putting this in the paper can hurt people?'

'You mean Dad? It might also help him.'

There was a long silence and I imagined her in her kitchen at the table, eyes closed and holding the phone to her ear. My father was probably sitting there, too, afraid to talk to me about it.

'Did you have any idea?' I asked quietly. 'Did either of you?'

'Of course not,' she said sadly. 'No one knew.'

More silence and then she made her last plea.

'Think about it, John. It's better to heal in private.'

'Like with Sarah?'

'What do you mean?'

'You never talked about it . . . you never talked to me.'

'I can't talk about that now.'

'You never can. It's only been twenty years.'

'Don't be sarcastic about something like that.'

'I'm sorry. Look, I'm not trying to be like this.'

'Just think about what I asked you.'

'I will,' I said. 'I'll let you know.'

She hung up as angry with me as I was with her. It bothered me that she didn't want me to write about Sean. It was almost as if she was still protecting and favoring him. He was gone. I was still here.

I straightened up in my seat so I could look over the sound partitions of the pod my desk was in. I could see the newsroom was filling up now. Glenn was out of his office and at the city desk talking with the morning editor about the coverage plan for the abortion-doctor shooting. I slumped back down in my chair so they wouldn't see me and get the idea of assigning me to rewrite. I was always dodging rewrite. They'd send out a bunch of reporters to a crime scene or disaster and these people would call their info back to me. I then had to write up the story on deadline and decide which names went on the byline. It was the newspaper business at its most fast and furious, but I was burned out by it. I just wanted to write my stories about murder and be left alone.

I almost took the printout up to the cafeteria so I'd be out of sight but decided to take my chances. I went back to reading. The most impressive piece had run in the *New York Times* five months earlier. No surprise there. The *Times* was the Holy Grail of journalism. The best. I started reading the piece and then decided to put it down and save it for last. After I had scanned and read through the rest of the material, I went up for another cup of coffee, then started to reread the *Times* article, taking my time with it.

The news peg was the seemingly unrelated suicides of three of New York's finest within a six-week period. The victims didn't know each other but all succumbed to the police blues, as it was called in the article. Two with their guns at home; one hanged himself in a heroin shooting gallery while six stoned hypes watched in dazed horror. The article reported at length on the ongoing police suicide study being conducted jointly by the FBI's Behavioral Science Services in Quantico, Virginia, and the Law Enforcement Foundation. The article quoted the foundation's director, Nathan Ford, and I wrote the name down in my notebook before going on. Ford said the project had studied every reported police suicide in the last five years looking for similarities in causes. He said the bottom line was that it was impossible to determine who might be susceptible to the police blues. But once diagnosed, it could be properly treated if a suffering officer sought help. Ford said the goal of the project was to build a database that could be translated into a protocol that would help police managers spot officers with the police blues before it was too late.

The *Times* article included a sidebar story about a year-old Chicago case where the officer had come forward but still was not saved. As I read, my stomach tightened. The article said Chicago police detective John Brooks had begun therapy sessions with a psychiatrist after a particular homicide case he was assigned to began bothering him. The case was the kidnapping and murder of a twelve-year-old boy named Bobby Smathers. The boy was missing for two days before his remains were found in a snowbank near the Lincoln Park Zoo. He had been strangled. Eight of his fingers were missing.

An autopsy determined that the fingers had been severed before his death. That, and not being able to identify and catch the killer, apparently was too much for Brooks to take.

> Mr Brooks, a highly regarded investigator, took the death of the precocious, brown-eyed boy unusually hard.
>
> After supervisors and colleagues became aware that it was affecting his work, he took a four-week leave and began intensive therapy sessions with Dr Ronald Cantor, whom he was referred to by a Chicago Police Department psychologist.
>
> At the start of these sessions, according to Dr Cantor, Brooks openly spoke of his suicidal feelings and said he was haunted by dreams of the young boy screaming in agony.
>
> After twenty therapy sessions over a four-week period, Dr Cantor approved of the detective's return to his assignment in the homicide unit. Mr Brooks by all accounts functioned properly and continued to handle and solve several new homicide cases. He told friends that his nightmares were gone. Known as 'Jumpin' John' because of his frenetic, go get'em attitude, Mr Brooks even continued his ultimately unsuccessful pursuit of the killer of Bobby Smathers.
>
> But sometime during the cold Chicago winter something apparently changed. On March 13 – which would have been the thirteenth birthday celebrated by the Smathers boy – Mr Brooks sat in his favorite chair in the den where he liked to write poems as a distraction from his job as a homicide detective. He'd taken at least two tablets of Percocet he had left over from treatment of a back injury the year before. He wrote a single line in his poetry notebook. Then he put the barrel of his .38 Special into his mouth and pulled the trigger. He was found by his wife when she came home from work.
>
> The death of Mr Brooks left family and friends bereaved and full of questions. What could they have done? What were the signs they had missed? Cantor shook his head wistfully when asked during an interview if there were answers for these troubling questions.
>
> 'The mind is a funny, unpredictable and sometimes terrible thing,' the soft-spoken psychologist said in his office. 'I thought that John had come very far with me. But, obviously, we did not come far enough.'
>
> Mr Brooks and whatever it was that haunted him remain an enigma. Even his last message is a puzzle. The line he wrote on the pad offered little in the way of insight into what caused him to turn his gun on himself.
>
> 'Through the pale door,' were his last written words. The line was not

original. Mr Brooks borrowed it from Edgar Allan Poe. In his poem 'The Haunted Palace,' which originally appeared in one of Poe's best-known stories, 'The Fall of the House of Usher,' Poe wrote:

> While like a ghastly rapid river,
> Through the pale door
> A hideous throng rush out forever
> And laugh – but smile no more.

The meaning of those words to Mr Brooks is unclear but they certainly carry the melancholy incumbent in his final act.

Meantime, the murder of Bobby Smathers remains an open case. In the homicide unit where Mr Brooks worked and his colleagues still pursue the case, the detectives now say they are seeking justice for two victims.

'Far as I'm concerned, this is a double murder,' said Lawrence Washington, a detective who grew up with Brooks and was partnered with him in the homicide unit. 'Whoever did the boy also did Jumpin' John. You can't convince me any different.'

I straightened up and glanced around the newsroom. No one was looking at me. I looked back down at the printout and read the end of the story again. I was stunned, almost to the same degree as the night Wexler and St. Louis had come for me. I could hear my heart beating, my guts being taken in a cold and crushing grip. I couldn't read anything else but the name of the story. Usher. I had read it in high school and again in college. I knew the story. And I knew the character of the title. Roderick Usher. I opened my notebook and looked at the few notes I had jotted down after leaving Wexler the day before. The name was there. Sean had written it in the chronological record. It was his last entry.

RUSHER

After dialing the editorial library I asked for Laurie Prine.

'Laurie, it's –'

'Jack. Yes, I know.'

'Look, I need an emergency search. I mean, I think it's a search. I'm not sure how to get –'

'What is it, Jack?'

'Edgar Allan Poe. Do we have anything on him?'

'Sure. I'm sure we have lots of biographical abstracts. I could –'

'I mean do we have any of his short stories or works? I'm looking for "The Fall of the House of Usher." And sorry to interrupt.'

'That's okay. Um, I don't know what we would have right here as far as his written works go. Like I said, it's mostly biographical. I can take a look. But, I mean, any bookstore around here is going to sell his stuff if we don't have it.'

'Okay, thanks. I'll just go over to the Tattered Cover.'

I was about to put the phone down when she said my name.

'Yes?'

'I just thought of something. Like if you want to quote a line or something, we have lots of quotations on CD-ROM. I could just plug it in real quick.'

'Okay. Do it.'

She put the phone down for an eternity. I reread the end of the *Times* story again. What I was thinking seemed like a long shot but the coincidences in the way my brother and Brooks had died and in the names of Roderick Usher and RUSHER could not be ignored.

'Okay, Jack,' Laurie said after picking back up. 'I just checked our indexes. We have no books containing Poe's works in whole. I've got the poetry disk in, so let's give it a whirl. What do you want?'

'There is a poem called "The Haunted Palace" that is part of the story "The Fall of the House of Usher." Can you get that?'

She didn't answer. I heard her typing on the computer.

'Okay, yeah, there are selected quotes from the story and the poem. Three screens.'

'Okay, is there a line that goes "Out of space, out of time"?'

'Out of space. Out of time.'

'Right. I don't know the punctuation.'

'Doesn't matter.'

She was typing.

'Uh, no. It's not in –'

'Damn!'

I don't know why I made such an outburst. It immediately bothered me.

'But, Jack, it is a line from another poem.'

'What? By Poe?'

'Yes. It's in a poem called "Dream-Land." You want me to read it? The whole stanza's here.'

'Read it.'

'Okay, I'm not that great at reading poetry but here goes. "By a route obscure and lonely, / Haunted by ill angels only, / Where an Eidolon, named NIGHT, / On a black throne reigns upright, / I have reached these lands but newly, / From an ultimate dim Thule – / From a wild weird clime that lieth, sublime, / Out of SPACE – out of TIME." That's it. But there is an editor's note. It says an Eidolon means a phantom.'

I didn't say anything. I was frozen still.

'Jack?'

'Read it again. Slower, this time.'

I wrote the stanza in my notebook. I could have just asked her to print it out and then gone and picked it up but I didn't want to move. I wanted, for the short moment, to be totally alone with this. I had to be.

'Jack, what is it?' she asked when she was done reading. 'You seem so anxious about this.'

'I don't know yet. I've gotta go.'

I hung up.

In an instant I began to feel overly warm, claustrophobic. As large as the newsroom was, I felt like the walls were closing in. My heart pounded. A vision of my brother in the car flashed through my mind.

Glenn was on the phone when I walked into his office and sat down in front of him. He pointed to the door and nodded like he wanted me to wait outside until he was done. I didn't move. He pointed again and I shook my head.

'Listen, I've got something happening here,' he said into the phone. 'Can I call you back? Great. Yeah.'

He hung up.

'What's –'

'I need to go to Chicago,' I said. 'Today. And then probably to Washington, then maybe Quantico, Virginia. To the FBI.'

Glenn didn't buy it.

'Out of space? Out of time? I mean, come on, Jack, that has got to be a thought that goes through the minds of many people who contemplate or actually do commit suicide. The fact that it's mentioned in a poem written by some morbid guy a hundred and fifty years ago who also wrote another poem this other dead cop quoted, it's not the stuff conspiracies are made of.'

'What about Rusher and Roderick Usher? You think that's a coincidence, too? So now we have a triple coincidence and you say it's not worth checking out.'

'I didn't say it's not worth checking out.' His voice rose a notch to a level signaling indignation. 'Of course, you check it out. Get on the phones, check it out. But I'm not sending you off on a national tour on the basis of what you've got now.'

He swiveled in his chair so he could check his computer for pending messages. There were none. He turned to face me again.

'What's the motive?'

'What?'

'Who'd want to kill your brother and this guy in Chicago? It doesn't make – How come the cops missed this?'

'I don't know.'

'Well, you spent the day with them and the case, where's the hole in the suicide? How could someone have done this and just walked away? How come you came away yesterday convinced that it was suicide? I got your message, you said you were convinced. How come the cops are convinced?'

'I don't have any answers for that yet. That's why I want to go to Chicago and then to the bureau.'

'Look, Jack, you've got a cushy beat here. I can't tell you how many times reporters have come in here saying they wanted it. You –'

'Who?'

'What?'

'Who wants my beat?'

'Never mind. It's not what we're talking about. The point is, you've got it good here and you get to go anywhere in the state you want to go. But for this kind of travel, I've got to be able to justify it with Neff and Neighbors. I also have a newsroom full of reporters who would like to travel every once in a while on a story. I would like them to travel. It helps keep them motivated.

But we're in an economic downturn here and I can't okay every trip that gets proposed.'

I hated these sermons and I wondered if Neff and Neighbors, the managing editor and editor of the paper, even cared whom he sent where as long as they got good stories. This was a good story. Glenn was full of shit and he knew it.

'Okay, I'll just take vacation time and do it myself.'

'You used everything you had after the funeral. Besides you're not going to run around the country saying you're a *Rocky Mountain News* reporter if you're not on an assignment for the *Rocky Mountain News*.'

'What about unpaid leave? You said yesterday that if I wanted more time you'd work something out.'

'I meant time to grieve, not go running across the country. Anyway, you know the rules on unpaid leave. I can't protect your position. You take a leave and you might not have the beat when you come back.'

I wanted to quit right there but I wasn't brave enough and I knew I needed the paper. I needed the institution of the media as my access card to cops, researchers, everybody involved. Without my press card, I'd be just some suicide's brother who could be pushed aside.

'I need more than what you've got now to justify this, Jack,' Glenn said. 'We can't afford an expensive fishing expedition, we need facts. If you had more, I could maybe see going to Chicago. But this foundation and the FBI you could definitely do by phone. If you can't, then maybe I can get somebody from the Washington news bureau to go over there.'

'It's my brother, my fucking story. You're not giving it to anybody.'

He raised his hands in a calming manner. He knew his suggestion was way out of bounds.

'Then work the phones and come back to me with something.'

'Look, don't you see what you're saying? You're saying don't go without the proof. But I need to go to get the proof.'

Back at my desk, I opened up a new computer file and began typing in everything I knew about the deaths of Theresa Lofton and my brother. I put down every detail I could remember from the files. The phone rang but I didn't answer it. I only typed. I knew I needed to start with a base of information. Then I would use it to knock apart the case against my brother. Glenn had finally cut a deal with me. If I got the cops to reopen my brother's case, I'd go to Chicago. He said we'd still have to talk about D.C., but I knew that if I got to Chicago I would get to Washington.

As I typed, the picture of my brother kept coming back to me. Now that sterile, lifeless photo bothered me. For I had believed the impossible. I had let him down and now felt a keener sense of guilt. It was my brother in that car, my twin. It was me.

9

I ended up with four pages of notes which I then synthesized after an hour of study and thought to six lines of shorthand questions I had to find the answers to. I had found that if I looked at the facts of the case from the opposite perspective, believing Sean had been murdered and had not taken his own life, I saw something the cops had possibly missed. Their mistake had been their predisposition to believe and therefore accept that Sean had killed himself. They knew Sean and knew he was burdened by the Theresa Lofton case. Or maybe it was something every cop could believe about every other cop. Maybe they'd all seen too many corpses and the only surprise was that most didn't kill themselves. But when I sifted through the facts with a disbeliever's eye, I saw what they did not see.

I studied the list I had written on a page in my notebook.

Pena:	his hands?
	after – how long?
Wexler/Scalari:	the car?
	heater?
	lock?
Riley:	gloves?

I realized I could handle Riley by phone. I dialed and was about to hang up after six rings when she picked up.

'Riley? It's Jack. You okay? This a bad time?'

'When's a good time?'

It sounded like she had been drinking.

'You want me to come out, Riley? I'm coming out.'

'No, don't, Jack. I'm okay. Just, you know, one of those blue days. I keep thinking about him, you know?'

'Yes. I think about him, too.'

'Then how come you hadn't been around for so long before he went and . . . I'm sorry, I shouldn't bring things up . . .'

I was quiet a moment.

'I don't know, Riles. We sorta had a fight about something. I said some things I shouldn't have. He did, too, I guess. I think we were kind of in a cooling-off period . . . He did it before I could get back with him.'

I realized I hadn't called her Riles in a long time. I wondered if she had noticed.

'What was the fight about, the girl that got cut in two?'

'Why do you say that? Did he tell you about it?'

'No. I just guessed. She had him wrapped around her finger, why not you? That's all I was thinking.'

'Riley, you've got – Look, this isn't good for you to be dwelling on. Try to think about the good things.'

I almost broke down and told her what I was pursuing. I would have liked to give her something to ease her pain. But it was too early.

'It's hard to do that.'

'I know, Riley. I'm sorry. I don't know what to tell you.'

There was a long silence on the line between us. I heard nothing in the background. No music. No TV. I wondered what she was doing in the house alone.

'Mom called me today. You told her what I was doing.'

'Yes. I thought she should know.'

I didn't say anything.

'What did you want, Jack?' she finally asked.

'Just a question. It's kind of out of left field but here it is. Did the cops show you or give you back Sean's gloves?'

'His gloves?'

'The ones he was wearing that day.'

'No. I haven't gotten them. Nobody asked me about them.'

'Well, then, what kind of gloves did Sean have?'

'Leather. Why?'

'Just something I'm playing with. I'll tell you about it later if it amounts to anything. What about the color, black?'

'Yes, black leather. I think they were fur-lined.'

Her description matched the gloves I had seen in the crime scene photographs. It didn't really mean anything one way or the other. Just a point to check, one duck put in the row.

We talked for a few minutes more and I asked if she wanted to have dinner that night because I was coming out to Boulder, but she said no. After that we hung up. I was worried about her and hoped the conversation – just the human contact – would raise her spirits. I contemplated dropping by her place anyway, after I was done with everything else.

As I passed through Boulder I could see snow clouds forming along the tops of the Flatirons. I knew from growing up out there how fast it could come down once the clouds moved in. I hoped the company Tempo I was driving had chains in the trunk but knew it was unlikely.

At Bear Lake I found Pena standing outside the ranger shack talking with a group of cross-country skiers who were passing through. While I waited I walked out to the lake. I saw a few spots where people had cleared away the snow down to the ice. I tentatively walked out on the frozen lake and looked down into one of these blue-black portals and imagined the depths below. I felt a slight tremor at my center. Twenty years earlier my sister had slipped through the ice and died in this lake. Now my brother had died in his car not fifty yards away. Looking down at the black ice I remembered hearing somewhere that some of the lake fish get frozen in the winter but when the thaw comes in spring they wake up and just snap out of it. I wondered if it was true and thought it was too bad people weren't the same way.

'It's you again.'

I turned around and saw Pena.

'Yes, I'm sorry to bother you. I have just a few more questions.'

'No bother. I wish I could have done something before, you know? Maybe had seen him before, when he first pulled in, seen if he needed help. I don't know.'

We had started walking back toward the shack.

'I don't know what anybody could have done,' I said, just to be saying something.

'So, what are your questions?'

I took out my notebook.

'Uh, first off, when you ran to the car, did you see his hands? Like where they were?'

He walked without speaking. I think he was envisioning the incident in his mind.

'You know,' he finally said, 'I think I did look at his hands. Because when I ran up and saw it was just him, I immediately figured he had shot himself. So I'm pretty sure I looked at his hands to see if he was holding the gun.'

'Was he?'

'No. I saw it on the seat next to him. It fell on the seat.'

'Do you remember if he was wearing gloves when you looked in?'

'Gloves . . . gloves,' he said, as if he was trying to prompt an answer from his memory banks. After another long pause he said, 'I don't know. I'm not getting a picture in my mind. What do the police say?'

'Well, I'm just trying to see if you remember.'

'Well, I'm not getting anything, sorry.'

'If the police wanted to, would you let them hypnotize you? To see if they could bring it out that way?'

'Hypnotize me? They do that sort of stuff?'

'Sometimes. If it's important.'

'Well, if it was important, I guess I'd do it.'

We were standing in front of the shack now. I was looking at the Tempo parked in the same place my brother had parked.

'The other thing I wanted to ask about was the timing. The police reports say that you had the car in sight within five seconds of hearing the shot. And with only five seconds there is no way anybody could make it from the car and into the woods without being seen.'

'Right. No way. Would've seen 'em.'

'Okay, then what about after?'

'After what?'

'After you ran to the car and saw the man was shot. You told me the other day you ran back to the shack here and made two calls. That right?'

'Yes, nine one one and my supe.'

'So you were inside the shack here and couldn't see the car, right?'

'Right.'

'How long?'

Pena nodded, seeing what I was getting at.

'But that doesn't matter because he was alone in the car.'

'I know but humor me. How long?'

He shrugged his shoulders as if to say what the hell and fell silent again. He walked into the shack and made a motion with his hand like lifting up the phone.

'I got through on nine one one right away. That was pretty quick. They took my name and stuff and that took some time. Then I called in and asked for Doug Paquin, that's my boss. I said it was an emergency and they put me through right away. He got on and I told him what happened and he told me to go out and watch the vehicle until the police came. That was it. I went back out.'

I considered all of that and figured that he had probably been out of sight of the Caprice for at least thirty seconds.

'On the car, when you first ran out, did you check all the doors to see if any were unlocked?'

'Just on the driver's side. But they were all locked.'

'How do you know?'

'When the cops got out here they tried them all and they were locked. They had to use one of those slim jim things to pop the lock.'

I nodded and said, 'What about the backseat? You said yesterday that the windows were fogged. Did you put your face up to the glass and look directly into the backseat? Down at the floor?'

Pena understood now what I was asking about. He thought for a moment and shook his head in the negative.

'No, I didn't look directly into the back. I just thought it was the one guy, is all.'

'Did the cops ask you these questions?'

'No, not really. I see what you're driving at, though.'

I nodded.

'One last thing. When you called it in, did you say it was a suicide or just that it was a shooting?'

'I . . . Yeah, I said somebody up here went and shot hisself. Just like that. They got a tape, I 'spect.'

'Probably. Thanks a lot.'

I started back to my car as the first flurries started floating down. Pena called after me.

'What about the hypnotizing?'

'They'll call you if they want to do it.'

Before getting in the car I checked the trunk. There were no chains.

On my way back through Boulder I stopped at a bookstore called, appropriately enough, The Rue Morgue and picked up a thick volume containing the complete stories and poems of Edgar Allan Poe. My intention was to start reading it that night. As I drove back to Denver I worked on trying to put Pena's answers into the theory I was working on. And no matter how I moved his answers around, there was nothing that derailed my new belief.

When I got to the DPD, I was told up in the SIU office that Scalari was out of the building, so I went to homicide and found Wexler behind his desk. I didn't see St. Louis around.

'Shit,' Wexler said. 'You here to bust my chops again?'

'No,' I said. 'You going to bust mine?'

'Depends on what you're going to ask me.'

'Where's my brother's car? It back in service yet?'

'What is this, Jack? Can't you even conceive of the possibility that we know how to run an investigation?'

He angrily threw the pen he was holding into a trash can in the corner of the room. He then realized what he had done and went and picked it out.

'Look, I'm not trying to show you up or cause you any problems,' I said in an even tone. 'I'm just trying to settle all my questions and the more I try the more questions I have.'

'Like what?'

I told him about my visit with Pena and I could see him getting angry. Blood rushed into his face and there was a slight tremor along his left jawline.

'Look, you guys closed the case,' I said. 'There is nothing wrong with me talking to Pena. Besides, you or Scalari or somebody missed something. The car was out of his sight for more than half a minute while he was calling it in.'

'So fucking what?'

'You guys were only concerned with the time prior to his seeing the car. Five seconds, so nobody could've run away. Case closed, suicide. But Pena told me the windows were fogged. They had to have been for someone to have written the note. Pena didn't look in the back, onto the floor. Then he leaves for at least thirty seconds. Somebody could've been lying down in the back, got out while he was making the calls and run into the woods. It could have happened easily.'

'Are you fucked in the head? What about the note? What about the GSR on the glove?'

'Anybody could have written on the windshield. And the glove with the residue could have been worn by the killer. Then he took it off and put it on Sean. Thirty seconds is a long time. It might've been longer. It probably was longer. He made two calls, Wex.'

'It's too iffy. The killer would be relying too much on Pena taking that much time.'

'Maybe not. Maybe he figured he'd either have enough time or he'd just take out Pena. The way you guys handled this thing, you would have just said Sean killed him and then himself.'

'That's bullshit, Jack. I loved your brother like he was my own fucking brother. You think I want to believe he swallowed the goddamn bullet?'

'Let me ask you something. Where were you when you found out about Sean?'

'Right here at the desk. Why?'

'Who told you? You get a call?'

'Yeah, I got a call. It was the captain. Parks called the watch captain. He called our captain.'

'What did he tell you? His exact words.'

Wexler hesitated a moment as he remembered.

'I don't remember. He just said that Mac was dead.'

'He said it like that or did he say Mac had killed himself?'

'I don't know what he said. He might've. What's the point?'

'The ranger out there who called it in said Sean shot himself. That started the whole thing rolling. You all went out there expecting a suicide and that's what you found. The parts of the puzzle fit into the picture you brought with you. Everybody around here knew what the Lofton case was doing to him. You see what I'm saying? You were all predisposed to believe it. You even got me believing it on the ride out to Boulder that night.'

'That's all bullshit, Jack. And I don't have the time. There's no proof of what you're saying and I don't have time for theories from somebody who can't face the facts.'

I was silent a moment, letting him cool down.

'Then where's the car, Wex? If you're so sure, show me the car. I know how I can prove it to you.'

Wexler paused himself. I guessed he was contemplating whether he should get involved. If he showed me the car, he was admitting that I had at least put a small doubt in his own mind.

'It's still in the yard,' he finally said. 'I see it every goddamn day when I come in.'

'Is it still in the same condition as the day it was found?'

'Yeah, yeah, still the same. It's sealed. Every day I come in I get to see his blood all over the window.'

'Let's go look at it, Wex. I think there's a way to convince you. One way or the other.'

The snow flurries had made it over from Boulder. In the police yard Wexler got the key from the fleet manager. He also checked an inventory list to see if anyone had taken the keys or been inside the car other than the investigators. No one had. The car would be in the same condition as it was when it was towed in.

'They've been waiting for a requisition from the chief's office to clean it up. They have to send it out. You know there are companies that specialize in cleaning houses and cars and stuff after somebody's been killed in them? Some fuckin' job.'

I think Wexler was talking so much because he was nervous now. We approached the car and stood there looking at it. The snow was swirling around us in a current. The blood sprayed on the inside back window had dried to a dark brown.

'It's going to stink when we open it,' Wexler said. 'Christ, I can't believe I'm doing this. This is going no further until you tell me what is going on.'

I nodded.

'Okay. There are two things I want to look at. I want to see if the heat switch is on high and if the security lock on the rear doors is on or off.'

'What for?'

'The windows were fogged and it was cold but it wasn't that cold. I saw in the pictures that Sean was dressed warmly. He had his jacket on. He wouldn't need the heat on high. How else do windows get fogged when you're parked with the engine off?'

'I don't –'

'Think about surveillances, Wex. What causes fogging? My brother once told me about the stakeout you two blew 'cause the windows fogged up and you missed the guy coming out of his house.'

'Talking. It was the week after the Super Bowl and we were talking about the fucking Broncos losing again and the hot air fogged everything up.'

'Yeah. And last I knew, my brother didn't talk to himself. So if the heat is on low and the windows are fogged enough to write on them, I think it means there was someone with him. They were talking.'

'That's a long shot that doesn't prove anything either way. What about the lock?'

I gave him the theory: 'Somebody is with Sean. Somehow he gets Sean's gun. Maybe he comes with his own gun and disarms Sean. He also tells him to hand over his gloves. Sean does. The guy puts the gloves on and then kills Sean with his own gun. He then jumps over the seat into the back where he hides down on the floor. He waits until Pena comes and goes, then he leans back over the seat, writes the note on the windshield and puts the gloves back on Sean's hands – now you've got the GSR on Sean. Then the doer gets out the back door, locks it and splits into the cover of the trees. No footprints, 'cause the lot's been plowed. He's gone by the time Pena comes back out to watch the car like he's told to do by his supervisor.'

Wexler was silent a long time while catching up.

'Okay, it's a theory,' he finally said. 'Now prove it.'

'You know my brother. You worked with him. What was the routine with the security lock? Always keep it on. Right? That way no mistakes with prisoners. No slip-ups. If you take a nonprisoner you can always disengage it for them. Like you did on the night you came for me. When I got sick, the lock was on. Remember? You had to switch it off so I could open the door to puke.'

Wexler said nothing but in his face I saw that I'd struck home. If the security lock was off in the Caprice it wouldn't be rock-solid proof of anything. But he would know in the way he knew my brother that Sean hadn't been alone in the car.

He finally said, 'You can't tell by looking at it. It's just a button. Somebody will have to get in the back and see if they can get out.'

'Open it. I'll get in.'

Wexler unlocked the door, flipped the electric locks and I opened the rear passenger side door. The sickly sweet smell of dried blood hit me. I stepped into the car and closed the door.

For a long moment I didn't move. I had seen the photos but they didn't prepare me for being in the car. The sickly smell, the dried blood sprayed over the window, the roof and the driver's headrest. My brother's blood. I felt the cloying grip of nausea in my throat. I quickly looked over the seat to the dashboard and the heater control panel. Then, through the right window, I looked out at Wexler. For a moment our eyes met and I wondered if I really wanted the security lock to be off. The thought occurred to me that it might be easier to just let it go, but I quickly ran it from my mind. I knew if I let this go I would be haunted for the rest of my life.

I reached over and hit the passenger lock switch for my door. I pulled the door handle and the door swung open. I stepped out and looked at Wexler. Snow was starting to stick to his hair and shoulders.

'And the heater's off. It couldn't have fogged the windows. I think Sean had somebody in the car with him. They were talking. Then whoever the bastard was killed him.'

Wexler looked as if he had seen a ghost. It was all clicking in his mind. It was more than just a theory now and he knew it. It looked as though he might start to cry.

'Goddammit,' he said.

'Look, we all missed it.'

'No, it's different. A cop never lets his partner down like that. What good are we if we can't watch out for our own? A fucking reporter . . .'

He didn't finish but I think I knew what he was feeling. He felt as though he had somehow betrayed Sean. I knew that was how he felt because it was the same for me.

'It's not done with yet,' I said. 'We can still make up for believing the wrong thing.'

He still looked forlorn. I wasn't the one who could comfort him. That would have to come from within.

'All that's lost is a little time, Wex,' I said anyway. 'Let's go back inside. It's getting cold out here.'

My brother's house was dark when I went there to tell Riley. I paused before knocking, wondering at how absurd it was that I believed the news I was bringing might in some way cheer her. Good news, Riley, Sean didn't kill himself like we all thought, he was murdered by some nut who has probably done it before and probably will again.

I knocked anyway. It wasn't late. I imagined that she was sitting in there in the dark, or maybe in one of the back bedrooms which emitted no light. The lantern light came on above me and she opened up before I had to knock a second time.

'Jack.'

'Riley. I was wondering if I could come in and talk to you.'

I knew she didn't know yet. I had made a deal with Wexler. I would tell her in person. He didn't care. He was too busy reopening the investigation, drawing up lists of likely suspects, getting Sean's car inspected again for prints and other evidence. I hadn't told him anything about Chicago. I'd kept that to myself and I wasn't sure why. Was it the story? Did I want the story just for myself? That was the easy answer and I used it to soothe my uneasiness at not telling him everything. But in the deeper folds of my mind I believed it was something else. Something maybe I didn't want to bring out into the light to view.

'Come in,' Riley said. 'Is something wrong?'

'Not really.'

I walked in behind her and she led the way to the kitchen, where she turned on the light over the table. She was wearing blue jeans, heavy wool socks and a Colorado Buffaloes sweatshirt.

'There's just been some new developments about Sean and I wanted to tell you. You know, instead of on the phone.'

We both took chairs at the table. The circles under her eyes hadn't disappeared and she had done nothing with makeup to hide them. I felt her gloom descending on me and I looked away from her face. I thought I had escaped but it was impossible here. Her pain invaded every space in the house and was contagious.

'Were you asleep?'

'No, I was reading. What is it, Jack?'

I told her. But unlike Wexler, I told her everything. About Chicago, about the poems, about what I wanted to do now. She nodded occasionally during the story but showed nothing else. No tears, no questions. All of that would come when I was done.

'So that's the story,' I said. 'I came to tell you. I'm going to Chicago as soon as I can.'

After a long silence she spoke.

'It's funny, I feel so guilty.'

I could see tears in her eyes but they didn't fall. She probably didn't have enough left for that.

'Guilty? About what?'

'All of this time. I've been so angry at him. You know, for what he'd done. Like he had done it to me, not himself. I started hating him, hating his memory. Now, you . . . now this.'

'We were all like that. It was the only way to live with it.'

'Have you told Millie and Tom?'

My parents. She never felt comfortable addressing them any other way.

'Not yet. I will, though.'

'Why didn't you tell Wexler about Chicago?'

'I don't know. I wanted a head start, I guess. They'll find out about it tomorrow.'

'Jack, if what you're saying is true, they should know everything. I don't want whoever did this to get away just so you can pursue a story.'

'Look, Riley,' I said, trying to keep calm, 'whoever did this had already gotten away until I came along. I just want to get to the cops in Chicago before Wexler. One day.'

We were silent a moment before I spoke again.

'And make no mistake. I want the story, that's true. But it's about more than just the story. It's about me and Sean.'

She nodded and I let the silence hang between us. I didn't know how to explain to her my motives. My skill in life was putting words together in a coherent and interesting narrative but inside I had no words for this. Not yet. I knew she needed to hear more from me and I tried to give her what she needed, an explanation I didn't quite understand myself.

'I remember when we graduated from high school we both pretty much knew what we wanted to do. I was going to write books and be famous or rich or both. Sean was going to be chief of detectives at DPD and solve all of the mysteries of the city . . . Neither of us quite made it. Sean was closest, though.'

She tried a smile at my memory but it didn't quite go with the rest of her face and so she put it aside.

'Anyway,' I continued, 'at the end of that summer I was leaving for Paris to go write the great American novel. And he was waiting to go into the service. We made this deal when we said good-bye. It was pretty corny. The deal was that when I got rich I would buy him a Porsche with ski racks. Like Redford had in *Downhill Racer*. That's it. That's all he wanted. He'd get to choose the model. But I'd have to pay. I told him it was a bad deal for me because he had nothing to trade. But then he said he did. He said that if anything ever happened to me – you know, like I got killed or hurt or robbed or anything – he'd find out who did it. He'd make sure nobody got away with it. And, you know, even back then I believed it. I believed he could do it. And something about it was a comfort.'

The story didn't seem to make much sense the way I had told it. I wasn't sure what the point was.

'But that was his promise, not yours,' Riley said.

'Yes, I know.' I was quiet for a few moments while she watched me. 'It's just that . . . I don't know, I just can't sit back and watch and wait. I've got to be out there. I've got to . . .'

There were no words to explain it.

'Do something?'

'I guess. I don't know. I can't really talk about it, Riley. I just have to do it. I'm going to Chicago.'

10

Gladden and five other men were ushered into a glass-enclosed seating area in the corner of the huge courtroom. There was a foot-wide slot that ran the length of the glass enclosure at face height through which the arraignment proceedings in the courtroom could be heard and the defendants could answer questions from their attorneys or the judge.

Gladden was disheveled from a night of no sleep. He had been in a single cell but the noise of the jail kept him awake and reminded him too much of Raiford. He looked around the courtroom and didn't see anyone he recognized. This included the cops, Delpy and Sweetzer. He also didn't see any television or still cameras. He took this as a sign that his true identity had not yet been discovered. He was encouraged by this. A man with curly red hair and thick glasses made his way around the attorneys' tables to the glass booth. He was short and had to raise his chin as if standing in tall water for his mouth to reach the slot in the glass.

'Mr Brisbane?' he asked, looking expectantly at the men who had just been ushered in.

Gladden walked over and looked down through the opening.

'Krasner?'

'Yes, how are you?'

He reached his hand up and through the slot. Gladden shook it reluctantly. He didn't like being touched by anyone, unless it was a child. He didn't answer Krasner's question. It was the wrong thing to ask someone who had spent the night in county jail.

'You talk to the prosecutor yet?' he asked instead.

'Yes, I did. We had quite a conversation. Your bad luck is continuing in that the deputy DA assigned the case is a woman who I have had some dealings with before. She is a ballbuster and the arresting officers have informed her of the, uh, situation as they saw it at the pier.'

'So she's going to go balls to the wall against me.'

'Right. However, this judge is okay. We're all right there. He's the only one in the building, I think, who wasn't a prosecutor before being elected.'

'Well, hurray for me. Did you get the money?'

'Yes, that happened just as you said. So we're set. One question, do you want to enter a plea today or continue it?'

'What does it matter?'

'Not a great deal. In arguing for bail it might just move the judge an inch or so our way if, you know, psychologically he knows you've already denied the charges and are readying for a fight.'

'Okay, not guilty. Just get me out of here.'

Santa Monica municipal judge Harold Nyberg called the name Harold Brisbane and Gladden went back to the slot. Krasner came back around the tables and stood by the slot so he could confer, if needed, with his client. Krasner announced himself as did deputy district attorney Tamara Feinstock. After Krasner waived a lengthy reading of the charges, he told the judge that his client pleaded not guilty. Judge Nyberg hesitated a moment. It was apparent that entering a plea so early in a case was unusual.

'Are you sure that Mr Brisbane wishes to enter a plea today?'

'Yes, Your Honor. He wants to move quickly because he is absolutely one hundred percent not guilty of these allegations.'

'I see . . .' The judge hesitated while he read something in front of him. So far, he had not even looked over in Gladden's direction. 'Well, then I take it you do not wish to waive your ten days.'

'A moment, Your Honor,' Krasner said, then he turned to Gladden and whispered. 'You have a right to a preliminary hearing on the charges within ten court days. You can waive and he'll schedule a hearing to then set the prelim. If you don't waive, he'll set the prelim now. Ten days from now. If you don't waive, it's another sign that you're going to fight, that you aren't looking for a handout from the DA. It might help on the bail.'

'Don't waive.'

Krasner turned back to the judge.

'Thank you, Your Honor. We don't waive. My client does not believe these charges will survive a preliminary hearing and, therefore, urges the court to schedule it as soon as possible so he can put this –'

'Mr Krasner, Ms Feinstock may not object to your added comments, but I do. This is an arraignment court. You're not arguing your case here.'

'Yes, Your Honor.'

The judge turned and studied a calendar hanging on the far wall, above one of the clerks' desks. He chose the date ten court days away and ordered a preliminary hearing in Division 110. Krasner opened an appointment book and wrote it down. Gladden saw the prosecutor doing the same. She was young but unattractive. So far, she had said nothing during the three-minute hearing.

'Okay,' the judge said. 'Anything on bail?'

'Yes, Your Honor,' Feinstock said, standing for the first time. 'The people urge the court to depart from the bail schedule and set an amount of two hundred and fifty thousand dollars.'

Judge Nyberg looked up from his papers at Feinstock and then over at Gladden for the first time. It was as if he was trying to determine upon physical inspection of the defendant why he was worth such a high bail for what seemed like so lowly a set of charges.

'Why is that, Ms Feinstock?' he asked. 'I don't have anything before me that suggests a deviation.'

'We believe the defendant is a flight risk, Your Honor. He refused to provide the arresting officers with a local address or even a license plate number of a car. His driver's license was issued in Alabama and we have not verified it as a legitimate issuance. So, basically, we don't know if Harold Brisbane is even his real name. We don't know who he is or where he lives, if he has a job or family, and until we do, he is considered a flight risk.'

'Your Honor,' Krasner jumped in. 'Ms Feinstock is misstating the facts. My client's name is known to police. He provided a legitimate Alabama driver's license of which there was no mention of a problem. Mr Brisbane has just arrived in the area from Mobile seeking work and does not yet have a permanent address. When he does, he will be glad to provide it to authorities. In the meantime, he can be contacted if needed through my office and has agreed to check in twice daily with me or any representative of the court Your Honor chooses. As Your Honor knows, a deviation from the bail schedule should be based on a defendant's propensity for flight. Not having a permanent address is in no way an acknowledgment of flight. To the contrary, Mr Brisbane has entered a plea and waived any delays in this case. He clearly wishes to attack these charges and clear his name as soon as possible.'

'Calling your office is fine, but what about the address?' the judge asked. 'Where's he going to be? You seem to have left out of your dissertation any mention of the apparent fact that this man already fled from police prior to his arrest.'

'Your Honor, we challenge that charge. These officers were in plainclothes and at no time identified themselves as police officers. My client was carrying a rather expensive piece of camera equipment – with which, by the way, he earns his living – and feared he was about to become the victim of a robbery. That is why he ran from those people.'

'That's all very interesting,' the judge said. 'What about an address?'

'Mr Brisbane has a room at the Holiday Inn on Pico Boulevard. From there he is endeavoring to find work. He is a freelance photographer and graphic arts designer and is confident of his prospects. He isn't going anywhere. As I said before, he is going to fight these –'

'Yes, Mr Krasner, as you said before. What kind of bail are you looking for here?'

'Well, sir, a quarter million dollars for a charge of throwing a trash can into the ocean is utterly incomprehensible. I think a modest bail of five to ten thousand dollars is more in line with the charges. My client has limited funds. If he uses them all to make bail, he will not have the money on which to live or pay counsel.'

'You left out the evading and vandalism.'

'Your Honor, as I said, he ran from them but he had no earthly idea that they were police officers. He thought –'

'Again, Mr Krasner, save your arguments for the proper venue.'

'I'm sorry, Your Honor, but look at the charges. It is clear this is going to be a misdemeanor case, and the bail should be set accordingly.'

'Anything else?'

'Submitted.'

'Ms Feinstock.'

'Yes, Your Honor. Again, the people urge the court to consider a departure from the bail schedule. The two main charges against Mr Brisbane are felonies and will remain as such. Despite Mr Krasner's assurances, the people still are not convinced the defendant is not a flight risk or that his name is even Harold Brisbane. My detectives tell me that the defendant has dyed hair and that it was dyed at the time the photograph for this driver's license was issued. This is consistent with an attempt to hide identity. We are hoping to borrow the Los Angeles Police Department's fingerprint identification computer today and see if we can get a –'

'Your Honor,' Krasner interjected. 'I have to object here on the basis that –'

'Mr Krasner,' the judge intoned, 'you had your turn.'

'In addition,' Feinstock said, 'Mr Brisbane's arrest came as a result of other suspicious activities which he was involved in. Namely –'

'Objection!'

'– the photographing of young children – some of them unclothed – without their knowledge or the knowledge or consent of their parents. The incident for which –'

'Your Honor!'

'– the charges before you have arisen occurred when Mr Brisbane attempted to elude the officers investigating a complaint against him.'

'Your Honor,' Krasner said loudly. 'There are no outstanding charges against my client. All the district attorney is trying to do is prejudice this man before the court. It is highly improper and unethical. If Mr Brisbane did these things, then where are the charges?'

Silence filled the cavernous courtroom. Krasner's outburst had even served to make the other attorneys whispering to their clients hold their tongues. The gaze of the judge slowly moved from Feinstock to Krasner to Gladden before he finally looked back at the prosecutor and continued.

'Ms Feinstock, are there currently any other charges against this man being considered by your office at this time? And I mean *right* at this time.'

Feinstock hesitated and then grudgingly said, 'No other information has been presented for filing but the police, as I said, are continuing their investigation into the defendant's true identity and activities.'

The judge looked down at the papers in front of him again and began to write. Krasner opened his mouth to add something but then reconsidered. It was clear by the judge's demeanor that he had already made the decision.

'The bail schedule calls for bail to be set at ten thousand dollars,' Judge Nyberg said. 'I am going to make a slight departure and set bail at fifty thousand dollars. Mr Krasner, I will be glad to reconsider this at a later date if at that time your client has assuaged the district attorney's concerns about identity and address, etcetera.'

'Yes, Your Honor. Thank you.'

The judge called the next case. Feinstock closed the file she had in front of her, put it on the stack to her right, and took another off the stack to her left and opened it. Krasner turned to Gladden with a slight smile on his face.

'Sorry, I thought he might go twenty-five. The beauty of it is she's probably happy. She asked for a quarter probably hoping for a dime or a nickel. She got the nickel.'

'Never mind that. Just how long until I'm out of here?'

'Sit tight. I'll have you out in an hour.'

11

The edge of Lake Michigan was frozen, the ice left jagged and treacherous and beautiful after a storm. The upper floors of the Sears Tower were gone, swallowed whole by the grayish white shroud that hung over the city. I saw all of this while coming in on the Stevenson Expressway. It was late morning and I guessed it would be snowing again before day's end. I had thought it was cold in Denver until I landed at Midway.

It was three years since I had been back to Chicago. And despite the cold, I missed the place. I had gone to J-school at Medill in the early eighties and learned to truly love the city. After, I had hoped to stay and get on with one of the local papers but the *Tribune* and *Sun-Times* both took passes, the interview editors telling me to go out and get some experience and then come back with my clips. It was a bitter disappointment. Not the rejection as much as having to leave the city. Of course, I could've stayed on at the City News Bureau, where I worked during school, but that wasn't the kind of experience those editors were looking for, and I didn't like the idea of working for a wire service that paid you like you were a student needing clips more than money. So I went home and got the job at the *Rocky.* A lot of years went by. At first I went to Chicago at least twice a year to see friends and visit favorite bars but that tapered off over the years. The last time had been three years ago. My friend Larry Bernard had just landed at the *Tribune* after going out and getting the same experience they had told me to get. I went up to see him and I hadn't been back since. I guess I had the clips now for a paper like the *Tribune,* but I had never gotten around to sending them to Chicago.

The cab dropped me at the Hyatt across the river from the *Tribune.* I couldn't check in until three, so I left my bag with the bellman and went to the pay phones. After fumbling with the phone book I called the number for CPD's Area Three Violent Crimes and asked for Detective Lawrence Washington. When he answered, I hung up. I just wanted to locate him, make sure he was there. My experience with cops as a reporter had always been not to make appointments. If you did, all you were doing was giving them a specific place to avoid and the exact time to avoid it. Most didn't like talking to reporters, the majority didn't like even being seen with reporters. And the few that did you had to be cautious of. So you had to sneak up on them. It was a game.

I checked my watch after hanging up. Almost noon. I had twenty hours left. My flight to Dulles left at eight the next morning.

Outside the hotel I grabbed a cab and told the driver to turn up the heat and take me to Belmont and Western by way of Lincoln Park. On the way I'd take in the spot where the Smathers boy had been found. It was a year since his body had been discovered. My thought was that the spot, if I could find it, would look almost exactly as it did on that day.

I opened my satchel, booted the computer and pulled up the *Tribune* clips I'd downloaded the night before in the *Rocky*'s library. I scrolled through the stories on the Smathers case until I found the paragraph describing the discovery of the body by a zoo docent cutting through the park on the way from his girlfriend's apartment. The boy had been found in a snow-covered clearing where the Italian-American League's bocce tournaments were held in the summer. The story said the clearing off Clark near Wisconsin was within sight of the red barn, which was part of the city's farm in the zoo.

Traffic was light and we were in the park within ten minutes. I told the driver to cut over to Clark and to pull to the side when we got to Wisconsin.

The snow on the field was fresh and there were only a few tracks across it. It also stood about three inches high on the boards of the benches along the walkway. This area of the park seemed completely deserted. I got out of the cab and walked into the clearing, not expecting anything but in a way expecting something. I didn't know exactly what. Maybe just a feeling. Halfway across I came upon a grouping of tracks in the snow that cut across my intended path from left to right. I crossed these and came upon another grouping heading right to left, the party having headed back the way it had come. Kids, I thought. Maybe going to the zoo. If it was open. I looked toward the red barn and that was when I noticed the flowers at the base of a towering oak twenty yards away.

I walked toward the tree and instinctively knew what I was seeing. A one-year anniversary noted with flowers. When I got to the tree I saw that the flowers – bright red roses splashed like blood on the snow – were fake, made of wood shavings. In the cleft made by the first branching of the tree's trunk I saw that someone had propped a small studio photo of a smiling boy, his elbows on a table and his hands propped against his cheeks. He wore a red jacket and white shirt with a very small blue bow tie. The family had been here, I guessed. I wondered why they hadn't placed their memorial at the boy's grave.

I looked around. The lagoons near the barn were iced over and there were a couple of skaters. No one else. I looked over to Clark Street and saw the cab waiting. Across the street from it a brick tower rose. I saw that the sign on the awning out front said HEMINGWAY HOUSE. It was the place the zoo docent had come from before finding the small boy's body.

I looked back at the photo propped in the tree's cleft and without any hesitation reached up and took it down. It was sealed in plastic like a driver's license to protect it from the elements. On the back of it was written the boy's name but nothing else. I slid the photo into the pocket of my long coat. I knew that someday I might need it to run with the story.

The cab felt as welcome and warm to me as a living room with a fireplace. I began scrolling through the *Tribune* stories while we drove on to Area Three.

The major facts of the case were as horrifying as those in the Theresa Lofton killing. The boy had been lured from a fenced recreation center at a Division Street elementary school. He and two others had gone out to make snowballs. When the teacher noticed they were missing from the classroom, she went out and rounded the boys up. But by then Bobby Smathers was gone. The two twelve-year-old witnesses proved unable to tell police investigators what happened. According to them, Bobby Smathers simply disappeared. They looked up from their work in the snow and didn't see him. They suspected he was hiding and waiting to ambush them, so they didn't go looking.

Bobby was found a day later in the snowbank near the bocce clearing in Lincoln Park. Weeks of full-time investigation headed by Detective John Brooks, who caught the case as lead investigator, never got any closer than the explanation of the two twelve-year-olds: Bobby Smathers had simply disappeared that day at the school.

As I reviewed the stories I looked for similarities to Lofton. There were few. She was a white female adult and he a black male child. As far different in terms of prey as would seem possible. But both were missing for more than twenty-four hours before being found and the mutilated bodies of both victims were found in city parks. Lastly, both had been at children's centers on their last day. The boy at his school, the woman at the day care center where she worked. I didn't know the significance of these connections but they were all I had.

The Area Three headquarters was an orange-brick fortress. It was a two-story sprawling building that also housed the Cook County First Municipal District Court. There was a steady stream of citizens going in and out of the smoked-glass doors. I pushed through the doors to a lobby where the floor was wet with melted snow. The front counter was made of matching brick. Somebody could drive a car through the glass doors and they still wouldn't get to the cops behind the counter. The citizens standing in front of it were another matter.

I looked at the stairs to my right. I knew from memory that they led to the detective bureau and was tempted to ignore procedure and head up. But I decided against it. You break even the mundane rules with the cops and they can get testy. I stepped up to one of the cops behind the counter. He eyed the computer bag slung over my shoulder.

'You moving in with us, are you?'

'No, this is just a computer,' I said. 'Detective Lawrence Washington. I'd like to speak with him.'

'And you are?'

'My name's Jack McEvoy. He doesn't know me.'

'You have an appointment?'

'No. It's about the Smathers case. You can tell him that.'

The cop's eyebrows climbed an inch up his forehead.

'Tell you what, open up the bag and let's check the computer while I make the call.'

I did what he asked, opening up the computer the way they used to make me do at airports. I turned it on, turned it off and put it away. The cop watched with the phone to his ear while talking to someone I assumed was a secretary. I figured that mentioning Smathers would at least get me through the preliminary round.

'Got a citizen down here to see Larry Legs about the kid.'

He listened a few moments and then hung up.

'Second floor. Up the stairs, to your left, go down the hall, last door. Says Homicide. He's the black guy.'

'Thanks.'

As I headed up the stairs I thought about how the cop had simply referred to Smathers as 'the kid' and whoever he had spoken to had understood what he meant. It told me a lot about the case, more than what had been in the newspapers. Cops try their best to depersonalize their cases. They are like serial killers in that way. If the victim is not a person who lived and breathed and hurt, he can't haunt you. Calling a victim 'the kid' is the opposite of that practice. It told me that a year later the case still had a strong hold on Area Three.

The homicide squad room was about the size of half a tennis court and had dark green industrial carpet. There were three work pods consisting of five desks each. Two pairs of desks faced each other and the fifth, the sergeant's desk, was pushed in at the end. Along the wall to my left were row after row of file cabinets with locking bars running through the pull handles. Along the far wall, behind the work pods, were two offices with glass windows looking out on the squad room. One was the lieutenant's office. The other looked like an interview room. There was a table in there and I could see a man and a woman in the room eating sandwiches off deli paper unwrapped and used as place mats. Besides those two there were three others at desks in the room and a secretary sat behind a desk near the door.

'You want to see Larry?' she said to me.

I nodded and she pointed to the man sitting at a desk on the far side of the room. He was alone in the pod. I headed over. He didn't look up from his paperwork, even when I got to him.

'It snowing out there yet?' he asked.

'Not yet. But it's going to.'

'It always does. I'm Washington, whaddaya need?'

I looked at the two detectives in the other pods. Nobody even glanced at me.

'Well, I wanted to talk to you alone, if I could. It's about the Smathers kid. I have some information on it.'

I could tell without looking at them that this made the others look over at me. Washington, too, finally put down his pen and looked up at me. He looked like he was in his thirties but already there was a dusting of gray in his shortcropped hair. Still, he was in good shape. I could tell that before he even stood up. He also looked sharp. He wore a dark brown suit with a white shirt and striped tie. The suit jacket could barely contain his massive chest.

'You want to talk to me alone? Whaddaya got?'

'Well, that's what I want to talk to you alone about.'

'You're not one of these guys wants to confess, are you?'

I smiled.

'What if I was? Maybe I'd be the real thing.'

'That'd be the day. All right, let's go in the room. But I hope you're not going to waste my time – what'd you say your name was?'

'Jack McEvoy.'

'Okay, Jack, if I kick those people outta there and you waste my time, they and me aren't going to be too happy about it.'

'I don't think it will be a problem.'

He stood up now and I could see that he was shorter than I had thought. He had the lower half of another man's body. Short, stubby legs beneath a wide and strong upper torso. Thus the name the desk cop had used, Larry Legs. No matter how sharply he dressed this oddness in his physique would always betray him.

'Something wrong?' he asked when he came around to me.

'Uh, no. I was . . . Jack McEvoy.'

I put down the laptop and held out my hand but Washington didn't take it.

'Let's go into the room, Jack.'

'Sure.'

He had traded the snub of my stare for one of his own. It was okay. I walked behind him over to the door of the room where the man and woman were eating their lunch. He glanced back once, looking down at the satchel I carried.

'Whaddaya got in there?'

'Computer. A couple things to show you if you're interested.'

He opened the door and the man and woman looked up.

'Sorry, folks, picnic's over,' Washington said.

'Can you give us ten, Legs?' the man asked before getting up.

'Can't do it. Got a customer here.'

They rewrapped what was left of their sandwiches and left the room without a further word. The man gave me a stare that I interpreted to be annoyance. I didn't care. Washington signaled me in and I put my computer case down on the table next to a folded cardboard sign with the no-smoking symbol on it. We sat down on opposite sides of the table. The room smelled like stale smoke and Italian salad dressing.

'Now, what can I do for you?' Washington asked.

I gathered my thoughts and tried to appear calm. I was never comfortable dealing with cops, even though their world fascinated me. I always felt that they might suspect something about me. Something bad. Some telling flaw in me.

'I'm not sure where to begin. I'm from Denver. I just got in this morning. I'm a reporter and I came across –'

'Wait a minute, wait a minute. You're a reporter? What kind of reporter?'

I could see a slight pulse of anger beneath the dark skin of his upper left jaw. I was prepared for this.

'Newspaper reporter. I work for the *Rocky Mountain News.* Just hear me out and then if you want to throw me out, that's fine. But I don't think you will.'

'Look, man, I've heard about every pitch in the world from guys like you. I don't have the time. I don't –'

'What if John Brooks was murdered?'

I watched his face for any sign that he might already believe this. There was nothing. He gave nothing away.

'Your partner,' I said. 'I think he might have been murdered.'

Washington shook his head.

'Now, I've heard everything. By who? Who killed him?'

'By the same person who killed my brother.' I stalled a moment and looked at him until I had his full attention. 'He was a homicide cop. He worked in Denver. He was killed about a month ago. They thought at first it was a suicide, too. I started looking into it and I ended up here. I'm a reporter but this isn't really about that. It's about my brother. And it's about your partner.'

Washington creased his brow into a dark V and just stared at me for a long moment. I waited him out. He was at the cliff. He either went over with me or he threw me out. He broke the stare and leaned back. Out of his inside coat pocket he took a pack of cigarettes and lit one. He pulled a steel trash can over from the corner so he could use it for ashes. I wondered how many times he had heard people tell him that smoking would stunt his growth. He cocked his head when he exhaled so that the blue smoke went up and hovered against the ceiling. He leaned forward across the table.

'I don't know if you are some nut or not. Let me see some ID.'

We were going over the cliff. I took out my wallet and gave him my driver's license, press card and DPD police pass. He eyed them all closely but I knew he had already decided to listen to the story. There was something about Brooks's death that made Washington want to listen to a story from a reporter he didn't even know.

'Okay,' he said as he handed the IDs back. 'So you're legit. It still doesn't mean I have to believe a word you say.'

'No. But I think you believe it already.'

'Look, you going to tell your story or not? Don't you think if there was something not right that I'd be on the fucking thing like . . . like – What do you know about it, anyway?'

'Not much. Just what was in the papers.'

Washington stubbed the cigarette out on the side of the trash can and then dropped the butt in.

'Hey, Jack, tell your story. Otherwise, do me a big favor and just get the fuck out of here.'

I didn't need my notes. I told the story with every detail because I knew each one of them. It took a half hour during which Washington smoked two more cigarettes but never asked a question. Each time he kept the cigarette in his mouth, so the smoke curled up and hid his eyes. But I knew. Just like with Wexler. I was confirming something that he had felt inside his guts all along.

'You want Wexler's number?' I asked at the end. 'He'll tell you everything I just said is legit.'

'No, I'll get it if I need it.'

'You have any questions?'

'No, not at the moment.'

He just stared at me.

'Then what's next?'

'I'm going to check this out. Where you going to be?'

'The Hyatt down by the river.'

'Okay, I'll call you.'

'Detective Washington, that's not good enough.'

'How do you mean?'

'I mean, I came here to get information, not just to give it and then go back to my room. I want to ask you about Brooks.'

'Look, kid, we didn't have any kind of deal like that. You came here, you told the story. There was no –'

'Look, don't patronize me by calling me "kid" like I'm some kind of hick from the sticks. I've given you something and I want something back. That's why I came.'

'I don't have anything for you now, Jack.'

'That's bullshit. You can sit there and lie, Larry Legs, but I know you've got something. I need it.'

'What, to make a big story that'll bring the rest of the jackals like you out?'

I was the one who leaned forward this time.

'I told you, this isn't about a story.'

I leaned back and we both looked at each other. I wanted a cigarette but didn't have any and I didn't want to ask him for one. The silence was punctuated when one of the detectives I had seen in the homicide room opened the door and looked in.

'Everything okay?' he asked.

'Get the fuck out of here, Rezzo,' Washington said. After the door was closed, he said, 'Nosy prick. You know what they're thinking, don't you? They're thinking maybe you're in here coppin' to doin' the kid. It's the year anniversary, you know. Weird things happen. Wait till they hear this story.'

I thought of the photo of the boy in my pocket.

'I went by there on the way over,' I said. 'There's flowers.'

'They're always there,' Washington said. 'The family goes by there all the time.'

I nodded and for the first time felt guilty about taking the photo. I didn't say anything. I just waited for Washington. He seemed to ease up some. His face became softer, relaxed.

'Look, Jack, I gotta do some checking. And some thinking. If I tell you I'll call you, I'm gonna call you. Go back to the hotel, get a massage, whatever. I'll call you one way or the other in a couple hours.'

I nodded reluctantly and he stood up. He held his arm across the table, his right hand out. I shook it.

'Pretty good work. For a reporter, I mean.'

I picked up my computer and left. The squad room was more crowded now and a lot of them watched me go. I guess I had been in there long enough for them to know I wasn't a crackpot. Outside it was colder and the snow was beginning to come down hard. It took me fifteen minutes to flag down a cab.

On the ride back I asked the driver to swing by Wisconsin and Clark and I jumped out and ran across the snow to the tree. I put the photo of Bobby Smathers back where I'd found it.

12

Larry Legs kept me twisting in the wind the rest of the afternoon. At five I tried calling him but couldn't locate him at Area Three or Eleven-Twenty-One, as the department's headquarters was known. The secretary in the homicide office refused to disclose his whereabouts or to page him. At six I was resigned to being blown off when there was a knock on my door. It was him.

'Hey, Jack,' he said without stepping in. 'Let's take a ride.'

Washington had his car parked in the valet lane in the hotel drive-up. On the dash he had placed a Police Business card so there was no problem. We got in and pulled out. He crossed the river and started north on Michigan Avenue. The snow had not abated as far as I could tell and there were drifts along both sides of the road. Many of the cars on the road had a three-inch frosting on their horizontal surfaces. I could see my breath in Washington's car and the heater was on high.

'Guess you get a lot of snow where you come from, Jack.'

'Yeah.'

He was just making conversation. I was anxious to see what he really had to say but thought it better to wait, to let him tell me at his speed. I could always pull the reporter act and ask questions later.

He turned west on Division and headed away from the lake. The sparkle of the Miracle Mile and the Gold Coast soon disappeared and the buildings began to get a little more seedy and in need of repair and upkeep. I thought maybe we were heading toward the school Bobby Smathers had disappeared from but Washington didn't say.

It was completely dark now. We went under the El and soon passed a school. Washington pointed at it.

'That's where the kid went. There's the yard. Just like that, he was gone.' He snapped his fingers. 'I staked it all day yesterday. You know, a year since the disappearance. Just in case something happened or the guy, the doer, came back by.'

'Anything?'

Washington shook his head and dropped into a brooding silence.

But we didn't stop. If Washington wanted me to see the school, the view had been quick. We kept heading west and eventually came upon a series of brick towers that somehow looked abandoned in some way. I knew what they were. The projects. They were dimly lit monoliths against the blue-black sky. They had assuredly taken on the appearance of those that were housed within. They were cold and despairing, the have-nots of the city skyline.

'What are we doing?' I asked.

'You know what this place is?'

'Yeah. I went to school here – I mean in Chicago. Everybody knows Cabrini-Green. What about it?'

'I grew up here. So did Jumpin' John Brooks.'

Immediately, I thought of the odds. First of just surviving in such a place, next of surviving and *then* becoming a cop.

'Vertical ghettos, each one of them. Me and John used to say it was the only time when you had to take the elevator up when you were going to hell.'

I just nodded. This was out of my realm completely.

'And that's only if the elevators were working,' he added.

I realized that I never considered that Brooks might be a black man. There was no photo in the computer printouts and no reason to mention race in the stories. I had just assumed he was white and it was an assumption I would have to analyze later. At the moment, I was trying to figure out what Washington was trying to tell me by taking me here.

Washington pulled into a lot next to one of the buildings. There were a couple of dumpsters coated with decades of graffiti slogans. There was a rusted basketball backboard but the rim was long gone. He put the car in park but left it running. I didn't know if that was to keep the heat flowing or to allow us a quick getaway if needed. I saw a small group of teenagers in long coats, their faces as dark as the sky, scurry from the building closest to us, then cross a frozen courtyard and hustle into one of the other buildings.

'At this point you're wondering what the hell you're doing here,' Washington said then. 'That's okay, I understand. A white boy like you.'

Again I said nothing. I was letting him run out his line.

'See that one, third on the right. That was our building. I was on fourteen with my grand-auntie and John lived with his mother on twelve, one below us. They didn't have no thirteen, already enough bad luck 'round here. Neither of us had fathers. At least ones that showed up.'

I thought he wanted me to say something but I didn't know what. I had no earthly idea what kind of struggle the two friends must have had to make it out of the tombstone of a building he had pointed at. I remained mute.

'We were friends for life. Hell, he ended up marrying my first girlfriend, Edna. Then on the department, after we both made homicide and trained with senior detectives for a few years, we asked to be partnered. And damn, it got approved. Story about us in the *Sun-Times* once. They stuck us in Three because it included this place. They figured it was part of our expertise. A lot of our cases come outta here. But it's still on rotation. So we just happened to be the ones catching on the day that boy turned up without no fingers. Shit, the call came in right at eight. Ten minutes before and it would've gone to night shift.'

He was silent for a while, probably thinking about what kind of difference it would have made if the call had gone to somebody else.

'Sometimes at night when we'd been workin' a case or on a stake or something, me'n John would drive out here after shift, park right where we are now and just look the place over.'

It occurred to me then what the message was. Larry Legs knew Jumpin' John hadn't pulled the trigger on himself because he had known the exact struggle Brooks had experienced coming out of a place like this. Brooks had fought his way out of hell and he wasn't about to go back by his own hand. That was the message.

'This is how you knew, isn't it?'

Washington looked across the seat at me and nodded once.

'It was just one of those things you know, that's all. He didn't do it. I told them that in MIU but they just wanted to get it the fuck away from them.'

'So all you had was your gut. There was nothing out of line anywhere else?'

'There was one thing but it wasn't enough for them. I mean they had the handwriting, his history with the shrink, all that in place. It fit too nicely for them. He was a suicide before they zipped up the bag and took him away. Cut and dried.'

'What was the one thing?'

'The two shots.'

'What do you mean?'

'Let's get out of here. Let's get some food.'

He put the car in drive and made a large circle in the lot and then out onto the street. We headed north on streets I had never been on. I had an idea where we were going, though. After five minutes of this I was tired of waiting for the next part of the story.

'What about the two shots?'

'He fired two shots, right?'

'Did he? It wasn't in the papers.'

'They never put out all the details on anything. But I was there at the house. Edna called me after she found him. I got there ahead of MIU. There was one shot in the floor and one shot in the mouth. The official explanation was that the first shot was supposed to be him seeing if he could do it or something, like a practice. Gettin' the courage up. Then the second time was when he went ahead and did it. It didn't make sense. Not to me.'

'Why not? What did you think the two shots were for?'

'I think the first one went in the mouth. The second one was for gunshot residue. The perp wrapped John's hand around the gun and fired it into the floor. John's hand gets GSR on it. The case goes suicide. End of story.'

'But nobody agreed with you.'

'Not until today. Not until you turn up with this Edgar Allan Poe thing. I went to Major Investigations to tell them what you've got. I reminded them of the problems with the suicide. My problems. They are going to reopen it and take another look. Tomorrow A.M. we've got a start-up meeting over at Eleven-Twenty-One. The MIU chief is going to get me detached and put on the squad.'

'That's great.'

I watched out the window and was silent for a while. I was excited. Things were falling into place. I now had the presumed self-inflicted deaths of two cops in two different cities being reinvestigated as possible murders and possibly connected. That was a story. A damn good one. And it was something I could use as a wedge in Washington to get into the foundation records and even the FBI. That is, if I got there first. If Chicago or Denver went to the bureau first, I'd likely be squeezed out because they wouldn't need me anymore.

'Why?' I said out loud.

'Why what?'

'Why is somebody doing this? *What* exactly are they doing?'

Washington didn't answer. He just drove through the cold night.

We had dinner in a booth in the back of the Slammer, a cop bar near Area Three. Both of us ordered the special, roast turkey and gravy, good cold-weather food. As we ate, Washington gave me a rundown on the MIU plan. He told me everything was off the record and that if I wanted to write anything, I had to get it from the lieutenant who would eventually head up the squad. I had no problem with that. The squad was going to exist because of me. The lieutenant would have to talk to me.

Washington kept both elbows on the table while he ate. It looked like he was guarding his food. He spoke with his mouth full at times but that was because he was excited. So was I. I was also wary of protecting my place in the investigation, in the story.

'We'll start off with Denver,' Washington said. 'We'll work together, get our ducks lined up and then see what happens. Hey, did you talk to Wexler? He was mad at you, boy.'

'How come?'

'Why you think? You didn't tell him about Poe, Brooks, Chicago. I think you lost a source there, Jack.'

'Maybe. They got anything new there?'

'Yeah, the ranger.'

'What about him?'

'They did the hypnosis thing. Took him back to that day. He said your brother was wearing only one glove when he looked in the window of the car for the gun. Then that glove, with the GSR, somehow gets back on the hand. Wexler said they've got no doubts about it now.'

I nodded more to myself than to Washington.

'You and Denver, you'll have to go to the FBI, won't you? You're talking about crimes connected across state lines.'

'We'll see. You gotta remember, the locals here never get much excited about working with the G. We go to them and we get bigfooted. Every time, right up the ass. But you're right, it's probably the only way. If this is what I think it is, and what you think it is, the bureau will eventually have to run the show.'

I didn't tell Washington I was going to the FBI myself. I knew I had to get there first. I pushed my plate aside, looked at Washington and shook my head. This story was incredible.

'What's your feeling on this? What are we talking about?'

'Only a few possibilities,' Washington said. 'One, we're talking about one guy, somebody out there killing people, then doubling back and taking out the lead cop working the case.'

I nodded. I was with him.

'Second, the first killings are unrelated and our doer just comes into town, waits for a case he likes or sees on the TV and goes after the cop who heads up the investigation.'

'Yeah.'

'And third is we have two killers. In both cities one does the first killing and the second comes in and does the second, takes out the cop. Of the three, I don't like this one. Too many questions. Do they know each other? Are they working together? It gets pretty far out there.'

'They would have to know each other. How else would the second guy know where the first one has been?'

'Exactly. So we are concentrating on possibilities one and two. We haven't decided whether Denver is coming here and we'll send some people there but we've got to look at the boy and the college kid. Look for any connection and if we find one we go from there.'

I nodded. I was thinking of the first possibility. One person, one killer doing all of this.

'If it is just one guy, who is the real target?' I asked, more to myself than Washington. 'Is it the first victim or the cop?'

Washington put the V back in his brow.

'Maybe,' I said, 'we've got somebody who wants to kill cops. That's his objective, okay? So he uses the first killing – Smathers, Lofton – to draw out his prey. The cop.'

I looked around the table. Saying it out loud, though I had been thinking it since I was on the plane, sent a chill through me.

'Spooky, huh?' Washington asked.

'Yeah. Real spooky.'

'And you know why? Because if this is the case, there's got to be others. Every time a cop supposedly kills himself the investigation is quick and quiet. No department wants that kind of story. So they go through the motions quick and then that's it. So there's gotta be more of them out there. If the first possibility is the correct one, then this guy didn't begin with Brooks and end with your brother. There's more. I'd bet on it.'

He pushed his plate away. He was finished.

A half hour later he dropped me at the front of the Hyatt. The wind off the lake was chilling. I didn't want to stand outside but Washington said he wasn't coming up to the room. He gave me a business card.

'I got my home and beeper on there. Call me.'

'I will.'

'Okay then, Jack.' He put his hand out and I took it. 'And thanks, man.'

'For what?'

'For making believers out of them. I owe you one for that. So does Jumpin' John.'

13

Gladden stared at the bright blue screen for several seconds before starting. It was an exercise he routinely followed to help clear his mind of the pressures and the hatred. But this time it was hard. He was full of rage.

He shook it off and pulled the computer onto his lap. He cleared the screen and rolled the ball with his thumb until the arrow moved from window to window on the screen and stopped on the TERMINAL icon. He clicked the ENTER button and then chose the program he wanted. He clicked on DIAL and then waited while listening to the harsh screech of the computer's uplink. It was like birth, he thought, every time. The horrible screech of the newly born. After the connection was complete, the welcome template appeared on the screen.

WELCOME TO THE PTL CLUB

After a few seconds the screen moved up and there was a coded prompt for Gladden's first password. He entered the letters, waited while they were acknowledged, then entered the second password when he got the prompt. In a moment his entry was approved and the warning template appeared on the screen.

PRAISE THE LORD!

RULES OF THE ROAD

1. NEVER EVER USE A REAL NAME
2. NEVER PROVIDE SYSTEMS NUMBERS TO ACQUAINTANCES
3. NEVER AGREE TO MEET ANOTHER USER
4. BE AWARE THAT OTHER USERS MAY BE FOREIGN BODIES
5. SYSOP RESERVES THE RIGHT TO DELETE ANY USER
6. MESSAGE BOARDS MAY NOT BE USED FOR DISCUSSION OF ANY ILLEGAL ACTIVITIES – THIS IS FORBIDDEN!
7. PTL NETWORK IS NOT RESPONSIBLE FOR CONTENT
8. PRESS ANY KEY TO CONTINUE

Gladden pressed ENTER and the computer informed him he had a private message waiting to be read. He lightly touched the appropriate keys and the message from the systems operator filled the top half of the laptop's screen.

THANKS FOR THE WARNING. HOPE ALL IS WELL AND MOST SORRY TO HEAR OF YOU IN HARM'S WAY. ALL IS WELL ON THIS END. IF YOU ARE READING THIS THEN I ASSUME YOU ARE OUT AND ABOUT. BRAVO! GOOD LUCK AND STAY IN TOUCH WITH YOURSELF AND OTHERS. (HEH, HEH)

PTL

Gladden typed in an R and hit ENTER and a reply message template appeared on the screen. He typed out a message to the sender of the first message.

NOT TO WORRY ABOUT ME. ALL IS TAKEN CARE OF. YOURS TRULY IS NOW OUT AND ABOUT..PTL

That done, Gladden typed in commands so that he could move to the main bulletin board directory. Finally, the screen filled with the directory of message boards. Each board was listed with the number of active messages available to be read.

1. General Forum	89	6. All's fair	51
2. B + 9	46	7. Musings & Whinings	76
3. B − 9	23	8. Legal Beagles	24
4. G + 9	12	9. Services by city	56
5. G − 9	6	10. Barter Board	91

He quickly typed in the necessary commands to move to the Musings & Whinings board. It was one of the most popular boards. He'd already read through most of the files and had contributed a few himself. The writers were all ranting about how unfair life was to them. How maybe in a different time their tastes and instincts would be accepted as normal. It was more whining than musing, Gladden had always thought. He called up the file marked Eidolon and began reading it again.

I think they will know about me soon. My time in the light of public fascination and fear is near. I am ready. Each one of my kind eventually assumes the mantle. Anonymity will be lost. I will be given a name, a designation not reflective of who I am nor of my many skills, but simply determined by its ability to fit nicely into a tabloid newspaper headline and stimulate the masses to thoughts of fear. We study what we fear. Fear sells newspapers and television shows. Soon it will be my turn to sell.

I will be hunted soon and I will be notorious. But they won't find me. Never. That's what they won't realize. That I have always been ready for them.

I have decided it is time to tell my story. I want to tell it. I will input all that I have, all that I am. Through these windows you will see me live and die. My laptop Boswell makes no judgments, cringes not at a single word. Who better to hear my confession than Laptop Boswell? Who more accurate a biographer than Laptop Boswell? I will begin to tell you all now. Turn on your flashlights. I will live and die here in the dark.

Man is sometimes extraordinarily, passionately, in love with suffering.

I didn't write that first but I wish that I had. But it doesn't matter because I believe it. My suffering is my passion, my religion. It never leaves me. It guides me. It is me. I can see that now. I think what is meant by those words is that our pain is the pathway upon which we make our life's travels and choices. It paves the way, so to speak, for all that we do and become. Therefore, we embrace it. We study it and, for all its harshness, we love it. We have no choice.

I have a great feeling of clarity about this, of complete understanding. I can turn and look back on my path and see how the pain made all my choices. I look forward and can see where it will take me. I don't really walk along the path any more. It moves beneath me, carrying me, like a great ribbon through time. It carried me here.

My pain is the rock upon which I make my stand. I am the perpetrator. The Eidolon. True identity is pain. My pain. Until death do we part.

Drive safely, dear friends.

He read it again and felt deeply moved by it. It touched his true heart.

He went back to the main menu and switched into the Barter Board to see if there were any new customers. There weren't. He typed the G command for good-bye. He then turned off the computer and folded it closed.

Gladden wished the cops hadn't taken his camera. He couldn't risk going to claim it and he could barely afford to buy another one with the money he had left. But he knew that without a camera he could not fill orders and there would be no more money. The anger building inside him felt like razors moving through his blood, cutting him from inside. He decided to wire more money out from Florida, then go shopping for another camera.

He went to the window and looked out at the cars slowly moving along Sunset. It was an endless moving parking lot. All that smoking steel, he thought. All that flesh. Where was it going? He wondered how many of them in those cars were like himself. How many had the urges and how many felt the razors? How many had the courage to follow through? Again the anger pushed through his thoughts. It was something palpable inside him now, a black flower spreading its petals in his throat, choking him.

He went to the phone and dialed the number Krasner had given him. Sweetzer picked up after four rings.

'Busy, Sweetzer?'

'Who's this?'

'It's me. How are the kids?'

'What – who is this?'

His instincts told Gladden to hang up right then. Don't deal with their kind. But he was so curious.

'You have my camera,' he said.

There was a short moment of silence.

'Mr Brisbane, and how are you?'

'Fine, Detective, thank you.'

'Yes, we have your camera and you are entitled to have that back since you require it to make a living. Do you want to make an appointment to pick it up?'

Gladden closed his eyes and squeezed the phone until he thought he would crush it. They knew. If they didn't they would have told him to forget the camera. But they knew something. And they wanted him to come in. The question was how much did they know? Gladden wanted to scream but a higher thought was to keep cool with Sweetzer. No false moves, he told himself.

'I'll have to think about that.'

'Well, it looks like a nice camera. I'm not sure how it works but I wouldn't mind having it. It's here if you want –'

'Fuck you, Sweetzer.'

The anger overtook him. Gladden spoke the words through a clenched jaw.

'Look, Brisbane, I was doing my job. If you got a problem with that come see me and we'll do something about that. If you want your fucking camera then you can come and get that, too. But I'm not going to stay on the line while you –'

'You got kids, Sweetzer?'

The line was silent for a long moment but Gladden knew the detective was there.

'What did you say?'

'You heard me.'

'Are you threatening my family, you motherfucking son of a bitch?'

Now Gladden was silent for a moment. Then a low sound started deep in his throat and grew into a maniacal laugh. He let it out uncontrolled until it was all he could hear and think about. Then, suddenly, he slammed the receiver down on the phone and cut the laughter off like a knife in the throat. He had an ugly grimace across his face and he shouted to the empty room through clenched teeth.

'Fuck you!'

Gladden opened his laptop again and accessed the photo directory. The computer's screen was state of the art for a laptop model but the graphics chip still wasn't nearly the quality he'd have on a stationary PC. But the images were clear enough and he was able to make do. He went through the file photo by photo. It was a macabre collection of the dead and the living. Somehow, he was able to find solace in the photos, a sense that he had control over things in his life.

Still, he was saddened by what he saw before him and what he had done. These little sacrifices. Offered up so that he could salve his wounds. He knew how selfish it was, how grotesquely warped it was. And the fact that he turned these sacrifices into money tore away his comfort, turned it into the self-loathing and disgust that always came. Sweetzer and the others were right. He deserved to be hunted.

He rolled onto his back and looked at the water-stained ceiling. Tears filled his eyes. He closed them and tried to sleep, tried to forget. But his Best Pal was there in the darkness behind his eyelids. As always, he was there. His face set, a horrible slash for lips.

Gladden opened his eyes and looked at the door. There had been a knock. He quickly sat up as he heard the metal scrape of a key going into the outside knob. He realized his mistake. Sweetzer had had a trace on the line. They knew he would call!

The door to the room swung open. A small black woman in a white uniform stood in the doorway with two towels draped over her arm.

'Housekeeping,' she said. 'I am sorry I'm so late today but it's been a busy day. Tomorrow I'll do your room first.'

Gladden exhaled and noticed that he had neglected to put the DO NOT DISTURB sign on the outside knob.

'It's okay,' he said, quickly getting up to stop her entrance into the room. 'Just the towels today, anyway.'

As he took the towels he noticed embroidered on her uniform the name Evangeline. She had a lovely face and he immediately felt sorry that this was her job, cleaning up after others.

'Thank you, Evangeline.'

He noticed her eyes go past him into the room and fall down to the bed. It was still made. He hadn't pulled the covers down the night before. Then she looked back at him and nodded with what he guessed was a smile.

'That'd be all you need?'

'Yes, Evangeline.'

'Have a nice day.'

Gladden closed the door and turned around. There on the bed was the open laptop computer. On the screen was one of the photographs. He moved to the bed and studied it without moving the computer. Then he moved back to the door, opened it and stood under the door frame where she had been. He looked at the computer. He could tell. The boy on the ground and what else could that be against the perfect white canvas of snow but blood.

He quickly went to the computer and hit the emergency kill button he had programmed himself. The door was still open. Gladden tried to think. Jesus, he thought, what a mistake.

He walked to the door and stepped out. Evangeline was down the walkway standing next to a housekeeping cart. She looked back at him, her face revealing nothing. But Gladden knew he had to be sure. He could not risk everything on reading this woman's face.

'Evangeline,' he said. 'I changed my mind. The room could probably use a going-over. I need toilet paper and soap, anyway.'

She put down the clipboard she had been writing on and stooped to get toilet paper and soap out of the cart. As Gladden watched he put his hands in his pockets. He noticed she was chewing gum and clicking it. An insulting thing to do in front of someone else. It was like he was invisible. He was nothing.

When Evangeline approached him with the items from the cart, he made no move to take his hands from his pockets. He took a step back to allow her to go into the room. After she stepped in, Gladden walked down to the cart and looked at the clipboard she had placed on top. After room 112 was the notation 'Just Towels.'

Gladden looked around as he headed back to the room. The motel was a courtyard design with two floors of about twenty-four rooms each. He saw another housekeeping cart on the upper floor across the way. It was parked in front of an open door but there was no sign of the maid. The pool at the center of the courtyard was empty of guests. Too cold. He saw no one else anywhere.

He stepped into the room and closed the door as Evangeline came out of the bathroom holding the bag from the trash can.

'Sir, we have to keep the door open when we're working inside a room. Those are the rules.'

He blocked her way to the door.

'Did you see the photograph?'

'What? Sir, I have to open the –'

'Did you see the photo on the computer? On the bed?'

He pointed to the laptop and watched her eyes. She looked confused but didn't turn.

'What photo?'

She turned to look at the sagging bed and then back to him with a look of confusion and growing annoyance on her face.

'I didn't take anything. You call Mr Barrs right now if you think I took somethin'. I'm an honest lady. He can have one of the other girls search me. I don't got your photo. I don't even know what picture you mean.'

Gladden looked at her a moment and then smiled.

'You know, Evangeline, I think maybe you are an honest lady. But I have to be sure. You understand.'

14

The Law Enforcement Foundation was on Ninth Street in Washington, D.C., a few blocks from the Justice Department and FBI headquarters. It was a large building and I assumed other agencies and foundations funded from the public trough were housed here as well. Once I was in through the heavy doors I checked the directory and took the elevator to the third floor.

It looked like the LEF had the entire third floor. From the elevator I was greeted by a large reception desk behind which sat a large woman. In the news business we call them deception desks because the women they hire to sit behind them rarely let you go where you want to go or see whom you want to see. I told her I wanted to speak to Dr Ford, the foundation director quoted in the *New York Times* article about police suicides. Ford was the keeper of the database to which I had to get access.

'He's at lunch. Do you have an appointment?'

I told her I had no appointment and put one of my cards down in front of her. I looked at my watch. Quarter to one.

'Oh, well, a reporter,' she said as if the profession were synonymous with convict. 'That's entirely different. You have to go through the public affairs office before it is even decided that you may speak to Dr Ford.'

'I see. You think there's anybody in public affairs or are they out to lunch, too?'

She picked up the phone and made a call.

'Michael? Are you there or are you on lunch? I have a man here who says he is from the *Rocky Mountain News* in – No, he first asked to see Dr Ford.'

She listened a few moments and then said okay and hung up.

'Michael Warren will see you. He says he has a one-thirty appointment so you'd better hurry.'

'Hurry where?'

'Room three oh three. Go down the hall behind me, take your first right and then it's the first door on the right.'

As I made the trek I kept thinking that the name Michael Warren was familiar but couldn't place it. The door to 303 opened as I was reaching for it. A man of about forty was about to step out when he saw me and stopped.

'Are you the one from the *Rocky*?'

'Yes.'

'I was beginning to wonder if you took a wrong turn. Come on in. I only have a few minutes. I'm Mike Warren. Michael if you use my name in print, though I prefer you don't use it and talk to the staff here instead. Hopefully I can help you with that.'

Once he was behind his cluttered desk I introduced myself and we shook hands. He told me to take a seat. There were newspapers stacked on one side of the desk. On the other side were photos of a wife and two children, angled so that Warren could see them as well as his visitors. There was a computer on a low table to his left and a photo of Warren shaking the president's hand on the wall above it. Warren was clean shaven and wore a white shirt with a maroon tie. The collar was frayed a bit where his afternoon whiskers rubbed against it. His jacket was draped over the back of his chair. His skin was very pale and set off by dark sharp eyes and straight black hair.

'So what's up? Are you in the Scripps D.C. bureau?'

He was talking about the parent company. It maintained a bureau of reporters that fed Washington stories to all papers in the chain. It was the office Greg Glenn had suggested I go through earlier in the week.

'No, I'm out from Denver.'

'Well, what can I do you for?'

'I need to talk to Nathan Ford or maybe whoever is directly handling the police suicide study.'

'Police suicide. That's an FBI project. Oline Fredrick's the researcher handling that with them.'

'Yes, I know the FBI is involved.'

'Let's see.' He picked up the desk phone but then put it back down. 'You know, you didn't call ahead on this, did you? I don't recognize the name.'

'No, I just got into town. It's a breaking story, you could say.'

'Breaking story? Police suicide? That doesn't sound like deadline stuff. Why the hurry?'

Then it struck me who he was.

'Did you used to work for the *L.A. Times*? The Washington bureau? You that Michael Warren?'

He smiled because he, or his name, had been recognized.

'Yes, how'd you know?'

'The *Post-Times* wire. I've been scrolling it for years. I recognized the name. You covered Justice, right? Did good stuff.'

'Until a year ago. I quit and came here.'

I nodded. There was always a moment of uneasy silence when I crossed paths with somebody who had left the life and was now on the other side of the line. Usually, they were burnouts, reporters who grew tired of the always-on-deadline and always-need-to-produce life. I once read a book about a reporter written by a reporter who described the life as always running in front of a thresher. I thought it was the most accurate description I'd read. Sometimes people got tired of running in front of the machine, sometimes they got pulled in and were left shredded. Sometimes they managed to get out from in front of it. They used their expertise in the business to seek the steadiness of a job as a person who handled the media rather than was part of it. This is what Warren had done and somehow I felt sorry for him. He had been damn good. I hoped he didn't feel the same regret.

'You miss it?'

I had to ask him, just to be polite.

'Not yet. Every now and then a good story comes along and I wish I was in there with everybody else, looking for the odd angle. But it can run you ragged.'

He was lying and I think he knew I knew it. He wanted to go back.

'Yeah, I'm beginning to feel it some myself.'

I returned the lie, just to make him feel better, if that was possible.

'So what about police suicides? What's your angle?'

He looked at his watch.

'Well, it wasn't a breaking story until a couple days ago. Now it is. I know you only have a few minutes but I can explain it pretty quickly. I just . . . I don't want to be insulting but I'd like for you to promise me what I say here is in confidence. It's my story and when it's ready, I'm going to break it.'

He nodded.

'Don't worry, I understand completely. I won't discuss whatever it is you are going to tell me with any other journalist unless that other journalist specifically asks about the same thing. I may *have* to talk about it with other people here at the foundation or in law enforcement, for that matter. I can't make any promise in that regard until I know what we are talking about.'

'That's fair.'

I felt myself trusting him. Maybe because it is always easy to trust somebody who has done what you have done. I also think I liked telling what I'd learned to somebody who would know its value as a story. It was a form of bragging and I wasn't above it. I started.

'At the start of this week I began working on a story about police suicide. I know, it's been done before. But I had a new angle. My brother was a cop and a month ago he supposedly committed suicide. I –'

'Oh, Jesus, I am sorry.'

'Thank you, but I didn't bring it up for that reason. I decided to write about it because I wanted to understand what he had done, what the police in Denver said he had done. I went through the routine, pulled clips on a Nexis search and, naturally, I came up with a couple references to the foundation's study.'

He tried to surreptitiously look at his watch and I decided to get his attention.

'To make a long story short, in trying to find out why he killed himself I found out he didn't.'

I looked at him. I had his attention.

'What do you mean, he didn't?'

'My investigation has so far determined that my brother's suicide was a carefully disguised murder. Someone killed him. The case has been reopened. I have also linked it to a supposed cop suicide last year in Chicago. That one also has been reopened. I just came in from there this morning. The cops in Chicago and Denver and I think that somebody might be moving around the country killing cops and making it look like suicide. The key to finding the other cases may be in the information collected for the foundation's study.

Don't you have all the records on cop suicides for the whole country over the last five years?'

We sat in silence for a few moments. Warren just stared at me.

'I think you better tell me the long story,' he finally said. 'No, wait.'

He held up his hand like a crossing guard signaling stop, picked up the phone with the other and pushed a speed-dial number.

'Drex? Mike. Listen, I know this is late but I'm not going to make it. Something's come up over here . . . No . . . We'll have to reschedule. I'll talk to you tomorrow. Thanks, bye.'

He put down the phone and looked at me.

'It was just a lunch. Now tell me this story of yours.'

A half hour later, after he had made some calls to set up a meeting, Warren led me through the labyrinth of the foundation's hallways to a room marked 383. It was a conference room and already seated there were Dr Nathan Ford and Oline Fredrick. The introductions were quick and Warren and I sat down.

Fredrick looked like she was in her mid-twenties with curly blond hair and an uninterested air about her. I immediately paid more attention to Ford. Warren had prepped me. He said any decisions would be made by Ford. The foundation director was a small man in a dark suit but he had a presence that commanded the room. He wore glasses with thick black frames and rose-tinted lenses. He had a full beard of uniform gray that perfectly matched his hair. He didn't moved his head as much as he did his eyes when he followed our movements as we entered and took seats around the large oval table. He had his elbows on the table and his hands clasped together in front of him.

'Why don't we get started,' he said once the introductions were over.

'What I'd like to do is just have Jack tell you both what he told me a little while ago,' Warren said. 'And then we'll go from there. Jack, you mind going over it again?'

'Not at all.'

'I'm going to take some notes this time.'

I told the story in pretty much the same detail as I had with Warren. Every now and then I would remember something new and not necessarily significant but I would throw that in anyway. I knew I needed to impress Ford because he would be the one to decide whether or not I got Oline Fredrick's help.

The only interruption during the telling came from Fredrick. When I spoke of my brother's death, she mentioned that the protocol from the DPD on the case had been received the week before. I told her she could now toss it in the trash can. When I was finished reciting the story, I looked at Warren and raised my hands.

'Anything I missed?'

'I don't think so.'

We both looked at Ford then and waited. He hadn't moved much during the telling. Now he raised his clasped hands and gently bumped them repeatedly against his chin as he thought. I wondered what kind of doctor he was. What do you have to be to run a foundation? More politician than doctor, I thought.

'It's a very interesting story,' he said quietly. 'I can see why you are excited. I can see why Mr Warren is excited. He was a reporter for most of his adult life and I think the excitement of the story remains in his blood sometimes, possibly to the detriment of his current profession.'

He didn't look at Warren as he delivered this blow. His eyes stayed on me.

'What I don't understand, and therefore the reason I don't seem to share the same excitement as you two, is what this has to do with the foundation. I'm not clear on that, Mr McEvoy.'

'Well, Dr Ford,' Warren began, 'Jack has to –'

'No,' Ford cut him off. 'Let Mr McEvoy tell me.'

I tried to think in precise terms. Ford didn't want a lot of bullshit. He just wanted to know how he would benefit from this.

'I assume the suicide project is on a computer.'

'That is correct,' Ford said. 'Most of our studies are collated on computer. We rely on the great number of police departments out there for our field research. Reports come in – the protocol Ms Fredrick mentioned earlier. They are entered on the computer. But that means nothing. It is the skilled researcher who must digest these facts and tell us what they mean. On this study, the researcher is joined by FBI experts in reviewing the raw data.'

'I understand all of that,' I said. 'What I am saying is that you have a huge databank of incidents of police suicide.'

'Going back five, six years, I believe. The work was started before Oline came on board.'

'I need to go into your computer.'

'Why?'

'If we're right – and I'm not just talking about me. The detectives in Chicago and in Denver are thinking this way, too. We've got two cases that are connected. The –'

'Seemingly connected.'

'Right, seemingly connected. If they are, then the chances are that there are others. We're talking about a serial killer. Maybe there's a lot, maybe a few and maybe none. But I want to check and you've got the data right here. All the reported suicides in the last six years. I want to get inside your computer and look for the ones that might be the fakes, that might be our guy.'

'How do you propose doing that?' Fredrick said. 'We've got several hundred cases on file.'

'The protocol that police departments fill out and send in, does it include the victim's rank and position in the department?'

'Yes.'

'Then we first look at all homicide detectives who killed themselves. The theory I'm working with is that this person is killing homicide cops. Maybe it's a hunted-turns-on-the-hunter sort of thing. I don't know the psychology of it, but that's where I'd start. With homicide cops. Once we have that breakout, we look at each case. We need the notes. The suicide notes. From –'

'That's not on computer,' Fredrick said. 'In each incidence, if we even have a copy of the note, it's in the hard-copy protocols in file storage. The notes themselves aren't part of the study unless they have some allusion to the pathology of the victim.'

'But you've kept the hard copies?'

'Yes, all of them. In file storage.'

'Then we go to them,' Warren chimed in excitedly.

His intrusion brought silence. Eventually, everyone's eyes were drawn to Ford's.

'One question,' the director finally said. 'Does the FBI know about this?'

'At the moment, I can't say for sure,' I said. 'I know it is the intention of the Chicago and Denver police to retrace my steps and then, once they are satisfied that I am on the right path, they are going to call in the bureau. It will go from there.'

Ford nodded and said, 'Mr McEvoy, could you step out and wait in the reception area for me? I want to talk to Ms Fredrick and Mr Warren privately before making any decision on this matter.'

'No problem.' I stood up and headed to the door, where I hesitated and looked at Ford. 'I hope . . . I mean . . . I hope we can do this. Anyway, thanks.'

Michael Warren's face told the story before he said anything. I was sitting on a lumpy vinyl-covered couch in the reception area when he came down the hallway with downcast eyes. When he saw me he just shook his head.

'Let's go back to my office,' he said.

I followed silently behind him and took the same seat I had before. He looked as dejected as I felt.

'Why?' I asked.

'Because he's an asshole,' he whispered. 'Because the Justice Department punches our ticket and the FBI is the Justice Department. It's their study – they commissioned it. He's not going to let you walk through it without telling them first. He's not ever going to do anything that might knock the gravy train off the tracks. You said the wrong thing in there, Jack. You should have said the FBI was made aware of this and took a pass.'

'He wouldn't have believed that.'

'The point is, he could've said he did. If it ever blew up on him that he was helping a reporter to information before the bureau, he could have just put it on you and said he thought the bureau passed.'

'So what now? I can't just drop this.'

I wasn't really asking him. I was asking myself.

'You got any sources in the bureau? Because I guarantee he's in his office calling the bureau right now. Probably going right to Bob Backus.'

'Who's that?'

'One of the big shots down there. The suicide project belongs to his team.'

'I think I know that name.'

'You probably know Bob Backus Sr. His father. He was some kind of supercop the bureau brought in years ago to help set up the Behavioral

Science Services and the Violent Criminal Apprehension Program. I guess Bobby Jr. is trying to fill his shoes. The point is, as soon as Ford's off the phone with him, Backus will shut this thing down. Your only way in will be through the bureau.'

I couldn't think. I was totally backed into a corner. I stood up and started pacing in the small office.

'Jesus Christ, I can't believe this. This is my story . . . and I'm getting pushed out of it by some dopey guy in a beard who thinks he's J. Edgar Hoover.'

'Nah, Nat Ford doesn't wear dresses.'

'It's not really that damn funny.'

'I know. I'm sorry.'

I sat back down. He made no move to dismiss me, even though our business was done. It finally occurred to me what it was he expected me to do. I just wasn't sure about how to ask. I'd never worked in Washington and didn't know how it worked. I decided to do it the Denver way. To be blunt.

'You can get into the computer anyway, right?'

I nodded at the terminal to his left. He looked over at me for a moment before responding.

'No fucking way. I'm no Deep Throat, Jack. This isn't about anything other than a crime story. That's the bottom line. You just want to get there ahead of the FBI.'

'You're a reporter.'

'Former reporter. I work here now and I'm not going to jeopardize my –'

'You know it's a story that has to be told. If Ford's in there on the phone with the FBI, they'll be out here by tomorrow and the story will be gone. You know how hard it was to get stuff from them. You were there. This ends completely right here or is published as some half-assed story in a year or maybe longer with more conjecture than facts. That's if you don't get me on that computer.'

'I said no.'

'Look, you're right. All it is is a story that I want. The big scoop. But I deserve it. You know I do. The FBI wouldn't be coming around if it wasn't for me. But I'm getting shut out . . . Think about it. Think if it was you. Think if it was your brother that this happened to.'

'I have and I just said no.'

I stood up.

'Well, if you change your –'

'I won't.'

'Look, when I leave here, I'm going to check in at the Hilton. The one where Reagan got shot.'

That's all I said as I left him there and he didn't say another word.

15

Passing the time in my room at the Hilton I updated my computer files on what little I had learned at the foundation and then called Greg Glenn to fill him in on everything that had transpired in Chicago and Washington. When I was done, he whistled loudly and I pictured him leaning back in the chair, thinking of the possibilities.

It was a fact that I already had a good story, but I was unhappy. I wanted to stay on the leading edge of it. I didn't want to have to rely on the FBI and other investigators to tell me what they felt like telling me. I wanted to investigate. I had written countless stories about murder investigations but each time I was always an outsider looking in. This time I was inside and wanted to stay there. I was riding the front of the wave. I realized that my excitement must be the same as Sean felt when he was on a case. In the hunt, as he called it.

'You there, Jack?'

'What? Yeah, I was just thinking of something else.'

'When can we do the story?'

'Depends. Tomorrow's Friday. Give me till tomorrow. I have this feeling about the foundation guy. But if I don't hear anything by mid-morning tomorrow I'll try the FBI. I've got a name of a guy. If that doesn't get me anywhere I'll come back and write the story Saturday for Sunday.'

Sunday was the biggest circulation day. I knew Glenn would want to go big with it on a Sunday.

'Well,' he said, 'even if we have to settle for that, what you've got is a hell of a lot. You've got a nationwide investigation of a serial killer of cops who's been operating with impunity for who knows how long. This will –'

'It's not that strong. Nothing is confirmed. Right now it's a two-*state* investigation into the *possibility* of a cop killer.'

'It's still damn good. And once the FBI is in, it's nationwide. We'll have the *New York Times*, the *Post*, all of them following our ass.'

Following *my* ass, I felt like saying but didn't. Glenn's words revealed the real truth behind most journalism. There wasn't much that was altruistic about it anymore. It wasn't about public service and the people's right to know. It was about competition, kicking ass and taking names, what paper had the story and which one was left behind. And which one got the Pulitzer at the end of the year. It was a dim view but after as many years as I had been at it, my view pretty much wasn't anything else but cynical.

Still, I'd be lying if I said I didn't savor the idea of busting out a national story and watching everybody follow. I just didn't like talking about it out loud like Glenn. And there was Sean, too. I was not losing sight of that. I wanted the man who did this to him. I wanted that more than anything.

I promised Glenn I'd call if anything developed and hung up. I paced around the room for a while and I have to admit I was thinking about the possibilities, too. I was thinking about the profile this story could give me. It could definitely get me out of Denver if I wanted it to. Maybe to one of the big three. L.A., New York, Washington. To Chicago or Miami, at the least. Then beyond that, I even began to think about a publishing deal. True crime was a major market.

I shook it off, embarrassed. It's lucky no one else knows what our most secret thoughts are. We'd all be seen for the cunning, self-aggrandizing fools we are.

I needed to get out of the room but couldn't leave because of the phone. I turned on the TV and it was just a bunch of competing talk shows serving up the usual daily selection of white trash stories. Children of strippers on one channel, porno stars whose spouses were jealous on another and men who thought women should be kept in line with occasional beatings on a third. I turned it off and thought of an idea. All I had to do was leave the room, I decided. It would guarantee that Warren would call because I wouldn't be there to take the call. It worked every time. I just hoped he would leave a message.

The hotel was on Connecticut Avenue near Dupont Circle. I walked toward the circle and stopped into Mystery Books to buy a book called *Multiple Wounds* by Alan Russell. I'd read a good review of it somewhere and figured reading would take my mind off things.

Before going back into the Hilton I spent a few minutes walking around the outside of the hotel looking for the spot where Hinckley had waited with a gun for Reagan. I remembered the pictures of the chaos vividly but I couldn't find the spot. It made me think the hotel had made some renovations, maybe so that the spot didn't become a tourist destination.

As a police reporter I was a tourist of the macabre. I moved from murder to murder, horror to horror without blinking an eye. Supposedly. As I walked back in through the lobby toward the bank of elevators I thought about what this said about me. Maybe something was wrong with me. Why was the spot where Hinckley waited important to me?

'Jack?'

I turned around at the elevators. It was Michael Warren.

'Hey.'

'I called your room . . . I thought you might be around.'

'I was just taking a walk. I was beginning to give up on you.'

I said it with a smile and a lot of hope. This moment would determine a lot of things for me. He was no longer in the suit he had on at his office. It was blue jeans and a sweater. He had a long tweed coat over his arm. He was following the pattern of a confidential source, coming in person rather than leaving a possible phone record.

'You want to go up to the room or talk down here?'

He moved toward the elevator saying, 'Your room.'

We didn't speak in the elevator of anything of consequence. I looked at his clothes again and said, 'You've already been home.'

'I live off Connecticut on the other side of the beltway. Maryland. Wasn't that far.'

I knew that was a toll call and that was why he hadn't called first. I also figured that the hotel was on the way from his house to the foundation. I was beginning to feel the small tick of excitement in my chest. Warren was going to turn.

There was a damp smell in the hallway that seemed to be the same in every hotel I had ever been in. I got out my card key and let him into my room. My computer was still open on the little desk and my long coat and the one tie I had brought with me were thrown across the bed. Otherwise, the room was neat. He threw his coat on the bed and we took the only chairs in the room.

'So what's going on?' I asked.

'I did a search.'

He started to take a folded paper out of his back pocket.

'I have access to main computer files,' he said. 'Before I left for the day, I went in and searched the field reports for victims who were homicide detectives. There were only thirteen. I have names, departments and dates of death here on a printout.'

He offered me the unfolded page and I took it from him as gently as if it were a sheet of gold.

'Thank you,' I said. 'Will there be a record of your search?'

'I don't really know. But I don't think so. It's a pretty wide-open system. I don't know if there's a security trace option or not.'

'Thank you,' I said again. I didn't know what else to say.

'Anyway, that was the easy part,' he said. 'Going through the protocols in file storage, that's going to take some time . . . I wanted to know if you'd want to help. You'd probably know better than me which ones were important.'

'When?'

'Tonight. It's the only time. The place will be closed up but I have a key to file storage because sometimes I have to dig out old things for media requests. If we don't do it tonight the hard-copy files may be gone tomorrow. I have a feeling the FBI isn't going to like them sitting up here, especially knowing you asked for them. They'll come and grab them first thing tomorrow.'

'Is that what Ford said?'

'Not exactly. I heard it through Oline. He talked to Rachel Walling, not Backus. He said she's –'

'Wait a minute. Rachel Walling?'

I knew the name. It took a moment but then I remembered she was the profiler who had signed the VICAP survey Sean had submitted on Theresa Lofton.

'Yes, Rachel Walling. She's a profiler down there. Why?'

'Nothing. The name's familiar.'

'She works for Backus. Sort of the liaison between the center and the foundation on the suicide project. Anyway, Oline says she told Ford she's going to take a look at all of this. She might even want to talk to you.'

'If I don't talk to her first.' I stood up. 'Let's go.'

'Listen, one thing.' He stood up. 'I didn't do this, okay? You use these files as an investigative tool only. You never publish a story that says you had access to foundation files. You never admit that you even saw a file. It could be my job. Do you agree?'

'Absolutely.'

'Then say it.'

'I agree. To all of it.'

We headed toward the door.

'It's funny,' he said. 'All those years procuring sources. I never really realized what they were risking for me. Now I do. It's kind of scary.'

I just looked at him and nodded. I was afraid if I said anything he'd change his mind and go home.

On the way to the foundation in his car, he added a few more ground rules.

'I am not to be a named source in your story, okay?'

'Okay.'

'And any information from me cannot be attributed to a "foundation source," either. Just a "source familiar with the investigation," okay? That gives me some cover.'

'Okay.'

'What you're looking for here are names that might be connected to your guy. If you find them, fine, but later on you don't have to report on how you got them. Do you understand?'

'Yeah, we've been over this. You're safe, Mike. I don't give up sources. Ever. All I'll do is use what we get here to get other confirmation. It'll be the blueprint. It's no problem.'

He was quiet for a few moments before doubts must have crept into his mind.

'He's going to know it's me, anyway.'

'Then why don't we stop? I don't want to jeopardize your job. I'll just wait for the bureau.'

I didn't want to do that but I had to give him the option. I wasn't that far gone yet that I'd talk a guy into losing his job just to get information for a story. I didn't want that on my conscience. There was enough there already.

'You can forget the FBI as long as it's Walling's case.'

'You know her? She tough?'

'Yeah, one of those as hard as nails with fingernail polish on. I tried shooting the shit with her once. She just shut me down. From what I hear from Oline, she got divorced or something a while back. I guess she's still in her "men are pigs" mode and it's looking permanent to me.'

I held up saying anything. Warren had to make a decision and I couldn't help.

'Don't worry about Ford,' he finally said. 'He may think it's me but he won't be able to do anything about it. I'll deny. So, unless you break the agreement, he'll have nothing but his suspicions.'

'You've got nothing to worry about with me.'

He found a spot on Constitution a half block from the foundation and parked. Our breath was coming out in thick clouds when we got out. I was nervous, whether or not he thought his job was in danger. I think we both were.

There was no guard to be fooled. No staff members working overtime to surprise us. We got in the front door with Warren's key and he knew right where we were going.

The file storage room was about the size of a double-wide garage and was taken up by rows of eight-foot steel shelves stacked with manila files with different-colored tabs.

'How're we going to do this?' I whispered.

He took the folded printout from his pocket.

'There's a section on the suicide study. We look up these names, take the protocols to my office and copy the pages we need. I left the copier on when I left. Won't even have to warm it up. And you don't have to whisper. There's nobody here.'

I noticed he said 'we' one too many times but I didn't say anything about it. He led me down one of the aisles, his finger out and pointing as he read the program headings printed on the shelves. Eventually, he found the heading for the suicide study. The files had red tabs on them.

'These here,' Warren said, raising his hand to point.

The files were thin, yet they took up three complete shelves. Oline Fredrick had been right, there were hundreds. Each red tag protruding from a file was a death. There was a lot of misery on the shelves. Now I had to hope that a few of them didn't belong there. Warren handed me the printout and I scanned the thirteen names.

'Out of all of these files only thirteen were homicide cops?'

'Yeah. The project has accumulated data on over sixteen hundred suicides. About three hundred a year. But most are street cops. Homicide dicks see the bodies but I guess for them the misery is over by the time they get there. They're usually the best and the brightest and the toughest. Seems like less of them eat the gun than the cops out on the beat. So I only came up with thirteen. Your brother and Brooks in Chicago also came up but I figured you have that stuff.'

I just nodded.

'They should be alphabetical,' he said. 'Read me the names on the list and I'll pull the files. And give me your notebook.'

It took less than five minutes to pull the files. Warren tore blank pages from my notebook and marked the spots in the stacks so they could be slipped back in quickly when we were done. It was intense work. It wasn't meeting a source like Deep Throat in a parking garage to help take down a president but my adrenaline was flowing anyway.

Still, the same rules applied. A source, no matter what his information is, has a reason, a motive, for putting himself on the line for you. I looked at Warren and couldn't see the true motive. It was a good story but it wasn't his story. He got nothing from helping other than knowing he had helped. Was that enough? I didn't know but I decided that at the same time that we were entering this sacred bond of reporter and secret source, I had to keep him at arm's length. Until I knew the true motive.

Files in hand, we walked quickly down two hallways until we got to room 303. Warren suddenly stopped and I almost rammed into him from behind. The door to his office was open two inches. He pointed to it and shook his head, signaling that he hadn't left it that way. I raised and dropped my shoulders, signaling back that it was his call. He leaned an ear toward the crack and listened. I heard something, too. It sounded like the crunching of papers, then a swishing sound. I felt a cold finger moving over my scalp. Warren turned back to me with a curious look on his face when suddenly the door swung inward and open.

It was like dominoes. Warren made a startled move, followed by me and then the small Asian man who stood there in the doorway with a feather duster in one hand and a trash bag in the other. We all took a moment to get our normal breathing going again.

'Sorry, mister,' the Asian man said. 'I clean your office.'

'Oh, yeah,' Warren said, smiling. 'That's fine. That's good.'

'You leff copy machine on.'

With that, he carried his goods down the hallway and used a key attached by a chain to his belt to get into the next office down. I looked at Warren and smiled.

'You're right, you're no Deep Throat.'

'You're no Robert Redford. Let's go.'

He told me to close the door, then turned the compact photocopy machine back on and moved around behind his desk, files in hand. I sat in the same chair I had been in earlier in the day.

'Okay,' he said. 'Let's start going through them. There should be a synopsis section in each protocol. Any kind of note or other significant detail should be there. If you think it fits, copy it.'

We started going through the files. As much as I liked him, I didn't like the idea of letting him decide in half of the cases if they fit into my theory. I wanted to look at all of them.

'Remember,' I said, 'we're looking for any kind of flowery language that might sound like literature or a poem or whatever.'

He closed the file he was looking at and dropped it on the stack.

'What?'

'You don't trust me to do this.'

'No. I just . . . I want to make sure we're both on the same wavelength about this, that's all.'

'Look, this is ridiculous,' he said. 'Let's just copy them all and get out of here. You can take them to your hotel and go through them there. It's quicker and safer. You don't need me.'

I nodded and realized it was the way we should have done it all along. For the next fifteen minutes he operated the copier while I took the protocols from the files and replaced them after they were copied. It was a slow machine, not made for heavy use.

When we were done he turned off the machine and told me to wait in the office.

'I forgot about the cleaners. It might be better if I just take these back to storage, then come get you.'

'Okay.'

I started looking through the copied protocols while he was gone but was too nervous to concentrate on them. I felt like running out the door with the copies and getting away before anything could go wrong. I looked around his office to try to pass the time. I picked up the photo of Warren's family. A pretty, petite wife and two kids, a boy and a girl. Both of preschool age in the photo. The door opened while the frame was still in my hand. It was Warren and I felt embarrassed. He paid no notice.

'Okay, we're ready.'

And like two spies we snuck out under cover of darkness.

Warren was silent almost all the way back to the hotel. I think it was because his involvement was over and he knew it. I was the reporter. He was the source. It was my story. I felt his jealousy and desire. For the story. For the job. For what he'd once been and had.

'Why'd you really quit, man?' I asked.

This time he dropped the bullshit.

'My wife, family. I was never home. One crisis after another, you know. I had to cover them all. Finally, I had to make a choice. Some days I think I made the right one. Some days I don't. This is one of those that I don't. This is a hell of a story, Jack.'

Now I was silent for a while. Warren drove into the hotel's main entrance and headed around the circle to the doors. He pointed through the windshield to the right side of the hotel.

'See down there? That's where Reagan got it. I was there. Fuckin' five feet from Hinckley while we were waiting. He even asked me what time it was. Almost no other reporters were out there. Back then, most of them didn't bother staking his exits. But they did after that.'

'Wow.'

'Yeah, that was a highlight.'

I looked over at him and nodded seriously and then we both laughed. We both knew the secret. Only in a reporter's world would it be a highlight. We both knew that probably the only thing better than witnessing a presidential assassination attempt as a reporter was witnessing a successful assassination. Just as long as you didn't catch a bullet in the crossfire.

He pulled over at the door and I got out and leaned my head back into the car.

'You're showing your true identity there, pal.'
He smiled.
'Maybe.'

16

Each of the thirteen files was thin, containing the five-page protocol questionnaire supplied by the FBI and the foundation, and usually just a few more pages of ancillary notes or testimonials to the pressures of the job from colleagues of the deceased.

Most of the stories were the same. Job stress, alcohol, marital difficulty, depression. A basic formula for the police blues. But depression was the key ingredient. In almost all of the files depression of one sort or another was reported as attacking the victim from inside the job. However, only a handful mentioned that the victims were troubled by any specific case, unsolved or otherwise, that they had been assigned to investigate.

I did a quick read-through of the conclusion segment of each of the protocols and quickly eliminated several of the cases from my investigation because of varying factors ranging from the suicides being witnessed by others to their taking place under circumstances precluding a setup.

The remaining eight cases were going to be more difficult to whittle down because each, at least in the summary remarks, seemed to fit. In each of these cases there was some mention of specific cases burdening the victim. The burden of an unsolved case and the quotes from Poe were really all I had as far as a pattern went. So I stayed with it and made it the standard by which I judged whether these eight remaining cases could be part of a series of false suicides.

Following this as my own protocol led to the dropping of two more cases when I found references to the suicide notes. In each, the victim wrote to a specific person, a mother in one, a wife in the other, and asked for forgiveness and understanding. The notes contained nothing resembling a line of poetry or, actually, any kind of literature. I dropped them and then I had six.

Reading one of the remaining files I came across the victim's suicide note – one line, like those left by my brother and Brooks – in an addendum containing the investigator's report. Reading the words sent a chilling, electric surge through me. For I knew them.

I am haunted by ill angels

I quickly opened my notebook to the page where I had written the stanza from 'Dream-Land' that Laurie Prine had read to me from the CD-ROM.

By a route obscure and lonely,
Haunted by ill angels only,
Where an Eidolon, named NIGHT,
On a black throne reins upright,
I have reached these lands but newly,
From an ultimate dim Thule –
From a wild weird clime that lieth, sublime,
Out of SPACE – out of TIME

I had it cold. My brother and Morris Kotite, an Albuquerque detective who supposedly killed himself with a shot to the chest and another to the temple, left suicide notes that quoted the same stanza of poetry. It was a lock.

But these feelings of vindication and excitement quickly gave way to a deep, growing rage. I was angry at what had happened to my brother and to these other men. I was angry at the living cops for not seeing this sooner and my mind flashed to what Wexler had said when I had convinced him of my brother's murder. A fucking reporter, he had said. Now I knew his anger. But most of all, I realized, my anger was for the one who had done this and for how little I knew about him. In his own words, the killer was an Eidolon. I was chasing a phantom.

It took me an hour to get through the remaining five cases. I took notes on three of them and dropped the other two. One was rejected when I noticed the death occurred on the same day John Brooks was killed in Chicago. It seemed unlikely, given the planning each of the killings must have involved, that two could be carried out on one day.

The other case was rejected because the victim's suicide had been attributed, among other things, to his despair over a heinous kidnap-murder of a young girl on Long Island, New York. It initially appeared, though the victim had left no note, that the suicide would generally fit my pattern and require further scrutiny, but I learned when I read the report to the end that this detective had actually cleared the kidnap-murder with the arrest of a suspect. This was outside the pattern and, of course, didn't fit with the theory that Larry Washington had floated in Chicago and that I subscribed to, that the same person was killing both the first victim and the homicide cop.

The final three that held my interest – in addition to the Kotite case – included Garland Petry, a Dallas detective who put one shot into his chest and then another into his face. He left a note that read, 'Sadly, I know I am shorn of my strength.' Of course, I hadn't known Petry. But I had never heard a cop use the word 'shorn' before. The line he had supposedly written had a literary feel to it. I just didn't think it would have come from the hand and mind of a suicidal cop.

The second of the cases was also a one-liner. Clifford Beltran, a detective with the Sarasota County Sheriff's Department in Florida, had supposedly killed himself three years earlier – it was the oldest of the cases – leaving behind a note that said simply, 'Lord help my poor soul.' Again, it was a conglomeration of words that sounded odd to me in the mouth of a cop, any cop. It was just a hunch but I included Beltran on my list.

Lastly, the third case was included on my list even though there was no mention of a note in the suicide of John P. McCafferty, homicide detective with the Baltimore police. I put McCafferty on the list because his death eerily resembled the death of John Brooks. McCafferty had supposedly fired one shot into the floor of his apartment before firing the second and fatal shot into his throat. I remembered Lawrence Washington's belief that this was a way of getting gunshot residue on the victim's hands.

Four names. I studied them and the rest of the notes I had taken for a while and then pulled the book on Poe I had bought in Boulder out of my flight bag.

It was a thick book with everything that Poe had supposedly ever written. I checked the contents page and noted there were seventy-six pages containing his poetry. I realized that my long night was going to get longer. I ordered an eight-cup pot of coffee from room service and asked them to bring some aspirin as well for the headache I felt sure I would get from the caffeine binge. I then started reading.

I'm not one who has ever been afraid of aloneness or the dark. I've lived by myself for ten years, I've even camped alone in the national parks and I've walked through deserted, burned-out buildings to get to a story. I've sat in dark cars on darker streets waiting to confront candidates and mobsters, or to meet timid sources. While the mobsters certainly put fear in me, the fact that I was out there by myself in the dark never did. But I have to say that Poe's words put a chill in me that night. Maybe it was being alone in a hotel room in a city I didn't know. Maybe it was being surrounded by the documents of death and murder, or that I felt the presence of my dead brother somehow near. And maybe also it was just the knowledge of how some of the words I was reading were now being used. Whatever it was, I put a scare on myself that didn't lift as I read, even when I turned the television on to provide the comforting hum of background noise.

Propped against the pillows on the bed, I read with the lights on either side of me turned on and bright. But, still, I bolted upright when a sudden sharp sound of laughter shot down the hallway outside my room. I had just settled back into the comfort of the shell my body had formed in the pillows and was reading a poem titled 'An Enigma' when the phone rang and jolted me again with its double ring so foreign to the sound of my phone at home. It was half past midnight and I assumed it was Greg Glenn in Denver, two hours behind.

But as I reached for the phone I knew I was wrong. I hadn't told Glenn where I had checked in.

The caller was Michael Warren.

'Just wanted to check in – I figured you'd be up – and see what you came up with.'

Again I felt uneasy about his self-involvement, his many questions. It was unlike any other source that had ever provided me with information on the sly. But I couldn't just get rid of him, given the risk he had taken.

'I'm still going through it all,' I said. 'Sitting here reading the poetry of Edgar Allan Poe. I'm scaring myself shitless.'

He laughed politely.

'But does any of it look good – as far as the suicides go?'

Just then I realized something.

'Hey, where are you calling from?'

'Home. Why?'

'Didn't you say you live up in Maryland?'

'Yeah. Why?'

'Then this is a toll call, right? It will be a record on your bill that you called me here, man. Didn't you think about that?'

I couldn't believe his carelessness, especially in light of his own warnings about the FBI and Agent Walling.

'Oh, shit, I . . . I don't really think I care. Nobody's going to pull my records. It's not like I passed on defense secrets, for crying out loud.'

'I don't know. You know'em better than me.'

'So never mind that, what have you got?'

'I told you I'm still looking. I've got a couple names that might be good. A few names.'

'Well, then, good. I'm glad it was worth the risk.'

I nodded but realized he couldn't see me do this.

'Yeah, well, like I said before, thanks. I gotta get back to it now. I'm fading and want to get it done.'

'Then I'll leave you to it. Maybe tomorrow, when you get a chance, give me a call to let me know what's going on.'

'I don't know if that will be a good idea, Michael. I think we better lay low.'

'Well, whatever you think. I guess I'll be reading all about it, eventually, anyway. You have a deadline yet?'

'Nope. Haven't even talked about it.'

'Nice editor. Anyway, go back to it. Happy hunting.'

Soon I was back in the embrace of the words of the poet. Dead a hundred and fifty years but reaching from the grave to grip me. Poe was a master of mood and pace. The mood was gloom and the pace often frenetic. I found myself identifying the words and phrases with my own life. 'I dwelt alone / In a world of moan,' Poe wrote. 'And my soul was a stagnant tide.' Cutting words that seemed, at least at that moment, to fit me.

I read on and soon felt myself gripped by an empathic hold of the poet's own melancholy when I read the stanzas of 'The Lake.'

But when the Night had thrown her pall
Upon that spot, as upon all,
And the mystic wind went by
Murmuring in melody –

Then – ah then I would awake
To the terror of the lone lake

Poe had captured my own dread and fitful memory. My nightmare. He had reached across a century and a half to me and put a cold finger on my chest.

Death was in that poisonous wave,
And in its gulf a fitting grave

I finished reading the last poem at three o'clock in the morning. I had found only one more correlation between the poetry and the suicide notes. The line attributed in the reports to Dallas detective Garland Petry – 'Sadly, I know I am shorn of my strength' – was taken from a poem entitled 'For Annie.'

But I found no match of the last words attributed to Beltran, the Sarasota detective, with any poem that Edgar Allan Poe had written. I began to wonder if through my fatigue I had simply missed it but knew that I had read too carefully, despite the lateness of the hour. There simply wasn't a match. 'Lord help my poor soul.' That was the line. I now thought that it had been the last true prayer of a suicidal man. I scratched Beltran from the list, thinking that his words of misery were truly his.

I studied my notes while fending off sleep and decided that the McCafferty case of Baltimore and the Brooks case of Chicago were too similar to be ignored. I knew then what I would do in the morning. I would go to Baltimore to find out more.

That night my dream came back. The only recurring nightmare of my entire life. As always, I dreamed I was walking across a vast frozen lake, the ice blue-black beneath my feet. In all directions I was equal distances from nowhere, all horizons were a blinding, burning white. I put my head down and walked. I hesitated when I heard a girl's voice, a call for help. I looked around but she was not there. I turned and headed on. A step. Two. Then the hand came up through the ice and gripped me. It pulled me toward the growing hole. Was it pulling me down or trying to pull its way out? I never knew. In all the times I'd had the dream I never knew.

All I saw was the hand and slender arm, reaching up from the black water. I knew the hand was death. I woke up.

The lights and the television were still on. I sat up and looked around, not comprehending at first and then remembering where I was and what I was doing. I waited for the chill to pass and then got up. I flicked the TV off and went to the minibar, broke the seal and opened the door. I selected a small bottle of Amaretto and sipped it without a glass. I checked it off on the little list they give you. Six dollars. I studied the list and the exorbitant prices just to give myself something to do.

Eventually, I felt the liquor start to warm me. I sat on the bed and checked the clock. It was quarter to five. I needed to go back. I needed sleep. I got under the covers and pulled the book off the bed table. I turned to 'The Lake' and read it again. My eyes kept returning to the two lines.

Death was in that poisonous wave,
And in its gulf a fitting grave

Eventually, troubled thoughts gave way to exhaustion. I put the book down and collapsed back into my bed's shell. I slept the sleep of the dead after that.

17

It was against Gladden's instincts to stay in the city but he couldn't leave just yet. There were things he had to do. The wired-funds transfer would land at the Wells Fargo branch in a few hours and he had to get a replacement camera. That was a priority and that couldn't be done if he was on the road, running to Fresno or someplace. So he had to stay in L.A.

He looked up at the mirror over the bed and studied his image. He had black hair now. He hadn't shaved since Wednesday and already the whiskers were coming in thick. He reached to the bed table for the glasses and put them on. He had dumped the colored contacts in the trash can at the In N Out where he'd eaten dinner the night before. He looked back up at the mirror and smiled at his new image. He was a new man.

He glanced over at the television. A woman was performing fellatio on one man while another was having sex with her in the position instinctively favored by dogs. The sound was turned down but he knew what the sound would be if it wasn't. The TV had been on all night. The porno movies that came with the price of the room did little in the way of arousing him because the performers were all too old and looked world-weary. They were disgusting. But he kept the TV on. It helped him remember that everyone had unholy desires.

He looked back to his book and began to read the poem by Poe again. He knew it by heart after so many years and so many readings. But, still, he liked to see the words on the page and hold the book in his hands. He somehow found it comforting.

In visions of the dark night
I have dreamed of joy departed –
But a waking dream of life and light
Hath left me broken-hearted

Gladden sat up and put the book down when he heard a car pull to a stop outside his room. He walked to the curtains and peeked through at the parking lot. The sun hurt his eyes. The car was just somebody checking in. A man and a woman, they both looked drunk already and it wasn't yet noon.

Gladden knew it was time to go out. He first needed to get a newspaper to see if there was a story about Evangeline. About himself. Then to the bank.

Then to find the camera. Maybe, if there was time, he'd go searching after that.

He knew that the more he stayed inside, the better his chances were of avoiding detection. But he also felt confident that he had covered his tracks sufficiently. He had changed motels twice since leaving the Hollywood Star Motel. The first room, in Culver City, he used only to dye his hair. He cleaned up, wiped the place down and left. He then drove to the Valley and checked into the dump in which he sat now, the Bon Soir Motel on Ventura Boulevard in Studio City. Forty bucks a night, three channels of adult films included.

He was registered under the name Richard Kidwell. It was the name on his last ID. He'd have to get on the net and trade for a few more. And he realized that would require him to set up a mail drop to receive the IDs and that was another reason to stay in L.A. At least for a while. He added the mail drop to his list of things to do.

As he pulled on his pants he glanced at the television. A woman with a rubber penis held to her abdomen with straps that went around her pelvis was having sex with another woman. Gladden tied his shoes, turned the TV off and left the room.

Gladden cringed at the sight of the sun. He strode across the parking lot to the motel office. He wore a white T-shirt with a picture of Pluto on it. The dog was his favorite cartoon animal. In the past, wearing the shirt had helped soothe the fears of the children. It always seemed to work.

Behind the glass window of the office sat a frumpy-looking woman with a tattoo on what had been at one time the upper curve of her left breast. Her skin was sagging now and the tattoo was so old and misshapen it was hard to tell it wasn't a bruise. She had on a large blond wig, bright pink lipstick and enough makeup on her cheeks to frost a cupcake or pass for a TV evangelist. She was the one who had checked him in the day before. He put a dollar bill in the pass-through slot and asked for three quarters, two dimes and a nickel. He didn't know how much the papers cost in L.A. In the other cities they had ranged from a quarter to fifty cents.

'Sorry, babe, I don't have change,' she said in a voice that begged for another cigarette.

'Ah shit,' Gladden said angrily. He shook his head. There was no service in this world anymore. 'What about in your purse? I don't want to have to walk down the fuckin' street for a paper.'

'Let me check. And watch that mouth. You don't have to get so testy.'

He watched her get up. She wore a short black tube skirt that embarrassingly displayed a network of varicose veins running down the back of her thighs. He realized he had no idea how old she was, a used-up thirty or an over-the-hill forty-five. It seemed that when she bent over to get her purse out of a lower file drawer, she was intentionally giving him the view. She came up with the purse and dug around in it for change. While the large black bag swallowed her hand like an animal she looked at him through the glass with appraising eyes.

'See anything you like?' she asked.

'No, not really,' Gladden replied. 'You got the change?'

She pulled her hand out of the maw of the bag and looked at the change. 'You don't have to be so rude. Besides, I only got seventy-one cents.'

'I'll take it.'

He shoved the dollar through.

'You sure? Six of it is pennies.'

'Yes, I'm sure. There's the money.'

She dropped the change into the slot and he had a difficult time getting it all up because his fingernails were bitten away to nothing.

'You're in room six, right?' she said, looking at an occupancy list. 'Checked in a single. Still by yourself?'

'What, now is this twenty questions?'

'Just checking. What are you doin' in there alone, anyhow? I hope you're not jerkin' off on the bedspread.'

She smirked. She had gotten him back. His anger boiled up and he lost it. He knew he should keep calm, not leave an impression, but he couldn't hold back.

'Now who's being rude, hmmm? You know what you are, you are fucking disgusting. Those veins running up your ass look like the road map to hell, lady.'

'Hey! You watch your –'

'Or what? You kicking me out?'

'Just watch what you say.'

Gladden got the last coin up, a dime, and turned to walk away without replying. Out on the street, he went to the newspaper box and bought the morning edition.

Safely back inside the dark confines of his room, Gladden dug through the newspaper until he found the Metro section. The story would be here, he knew. He quickly scanned through the eight pages of the section and found nothing about the motel murder case. Disappointed, he guessed that maybe the death of a black maid wasn't news in this town.

He tossed the paper down on the bed. But as soon as it landed a photograph on the front page of the section caught his attention. It was a shot of a young boy on his way down a sliding board. He picked the section back up and read the caption that went with the photo. It said that swing sets and other children's amusements had finally been replaced at MacArthur Park following the long period of their removal while a subway station construction project caused the closure of most of the park.

Gladden looked at the photo again. The boy on the slide was identified as seven-year-old Miguel Arax. Gladden wasn't familiar with the area where the new park was located but he assumed that a subway station would be approved only for a low-income area. That meant most of the children would be poor and with dark brown skin like the boy in the photo. He decided that he would go to the park later, after taking care of his chores and getting situated. It was always easier with the poor ones. They needed and wanted so much.

Situated, Gladden thought. He knew then that getting situated was his real priority. He couldn't stay in this motel or any other, no matter how well he had covered his tracks. It wasn't safe. The stakes were constantly rising and they would be looking for him soon. It was a feeling not based on anything other than his gut instinct. They would be looking soon and he needed to find a safe place.

He put the paper aside and went to the phone. The smoke-cured voice that answered after he dialed zero was unmistakable.

'This is, uh, Richard . . . in six. I just wanted to say I'm sorry about what happened earlier. I was rude and I apologize.'

She didn't say anything and he pressed on.

'Anyway, you were right, it's getting pretty lonely in here and I was wondering if that offer you sort of made before was still out there.'

'What offer?'

She was going to make it difficult.

'You know, you asked if I saw anything I liked. Well, I did, actually.'

'I don't know. You were pretty testy. I don't like testy. Whatcha got in mind?'

'I don't know. But I've got a hundred bucks to make sure it's a good time.'

She was silent a moment.

'Well, I get outta this dump at four. Then I got the whole weekend. I could come over.'

Gladden smiled but kept it out of his voice.

'Can't wait.'

'Then I'm sorry, too. About being rude and the things I said.'

'That's nice to hear. See you soon – oh, you still there?'

'Sure, baby.'

'What's your name?'

'Darlene.'

'Well, Darlene, I can't wait till four.'

She laughed and hung up. Gladden wasn't laughing.

18

In the morning I had to wait until ten before Laurie Prine was at her desk in Denver. By then I was anxious to get on with the day but hers was just starting and I had to go through the greeting and questions about where I was and what I was doing before finally getting to the point.

'When you did that run on police suicides for me, would that have included the *Baltimore Sun?*'

'Yep.'

I assumed it would have but had to check. I also knew that computer searches sometimes missed things.

'Okay, then can you run a search of the *Sun* using just the name John McCafferty.'

I spelled it for her.

'Sure. How far back?'

'I don't know, five years would be good.'

'When do you need it by?'

'Last night.'

'I guess that means you're going to hold.'

'It does.'

I listened to the tapping of keys as she conducted the search. I pulled the Poe book onto my lap and reread some of the poems while I waited. With daylight coming through the curtains, the words did not have the same hold on me as the night before.

'Okay – whoa – we've got a lot of hits here, Jack. Twenty-eight. Anything in particular you're looking for?'

'Uh, no. What's the most recent?'

I knew that she could scan the hits by having just the headlines print out on her screen.

'Okay, last one. "Detective fired for part in former partner's death." '

'That's weird,' I said. 'This should have come up in the first search you did. Can you read me some of that?'

I heard her tap a few keys and then wait for the story to be printed on her screen.

'Okay, here goes. "A Baltimore police detective was fired Monday for altering a crime scene and attempting to make it appear that his longtime partner had not killed himself last spring. The action was taken by a departmental Board of Rights panel against Detective Daniel Bledsoe after a two-day closed hearing. Bledsoe could not be reached for comment but a fellow officer who represented him during the hearing said that the highly decorated detective was being treated with undue harshness by a department he had served well for twenty-two years. According to police officials, Bledsoe's partner, Detective John McCafferty, died of a self-inflicted gunshot wound on May 8. His body was found by his wife, Susan, who first called Bledsoe. Bledsoe, officials said, went to his partner's apartment, destroyed a note he found in the dead detective's shirt pocket and altered other aspects of the crime scene to make it appear that McCafferty had been killed by an intruder who had grabbed the detective's gun. Police said" – Do you want me to keep reading, Jack?'

'Yeah, go ahead.'

' "Police said Bledsoe went so far as to fire an additional shot into McCafferty's body, striking him in the upper leg. Bledsoe then told Susan McCafferty to call 911 and he left the apartment, feigning surprise when he was later informed that his partner was dead. In killing himself, McCafferty had apparently already fired one shot into the floor of his home before placing the gun in his mouth and firing the fatal shot. Investigators contend that Bledsoe attempted to make the death appear to be a murder because Susan McCafferty stood to receive a higher amount of death, health and pension benefits if it could be proved her husband had not killed himself. However, the scheme unraveled when suspicious investigators interviewed Susan McCafferty at length on the day her husband died. She eventually admitted to what she had watched Bledsoe do." Am I reading too fast? Are you taking notes?'

'No, it's fine. Keep going.'

'Okay. "Bledsoe refused to acknowledge any part in the scheme during the investigation and declined to testify in his behalf during the Board of Rights hearing. Jerry Liebling, Bledsoe's fellow detective and defense representative during the hearing, said Bledsoe did what any loyal partner would do for a fallen comrade. 'All he did was try to make things a little better for the widow,' Liebling said. 'But the department has gone too far. He tried to do the good thing and now he's lost his job, his career, his livelihood. What kind of message does this send to the rank and file?' Other officers contacted Monday expressed similar feelings. But ranking officials said that Bledsoe had been treated fairly and cited the department's decision not to file criminal charges against Bledsoe or Susan McCafferty as a sign of compassion for the two. McCafferty and Bledsoe had been partners for seven years and handled some of the higher-profile murders in the city during that time. One of those killings was attributed in part to McCafferty's death. Police said that McCafferty's depression over the unsolved killing of Polly Amherst, a first-grade teacher who was abducted from campus at the private Hopkins School, sexually mutilated and strangled, led him to thoughts of killing himself. McCafferty was also struggling with a drinking problem. 'So now the department hasn't lost one fine investigator,' Liebling said after Monday's hearing, 'it has lost two. They'll never find two guys that were as good as

Bledsoe and McCafferty. The department really blew it today.' " That's it, Jack.'

'Okay. Uh, I'm going to need you to send that to my computer basket. I have my laptop. I can get it.'

'Okay. What about the other stories?'

'Can you go back to the headlines? Are any of them about McCafferty's death or are they all stories on cases?'

She took a half minute to scroll through the headlines.

'It looks like they are all about cases. There are quite a few on the schoolteacher. Nothing else on the suicide. And you know what, the reason that story I just read didn't come up on my search on Monday was because the word "suicide" was never in it. That was the keyword I plugged in.'

I'd already figured that out. I asked her to ship the stories on the teacher to my computer basket, thanked her and hung up.

I called the main detective bureau of the Baltimore Police Department and asked for Jerry Liebling.

'Liebling, autos.'

'Detective Liebling, my name is Jack McEvoy and I'm wondering if you can help me. I'm trying to reach Dan Bledsoe.'

'That would be in regard to what?'

'I'd rather talk to him about it.'

'I'm sorry I can't help you and I've got another call.'

'Look, I know what he tried to do for McCafferty. I want to tell him something that I think will help him. That's really all I can say. But if you don't help me, you are missing a chance to help him. I can give you my number. Why don't you call him and give it to him. Let him decide.'

There was a long silence and I suddenly thought I had been talking to a dead line.

'Hello?'

'Yeah, I'm here. Look, if Dan wants to talk to you he'll talk to you. You call him. He's in the book.'

'What, the phone book?'

'That's right. I gotta go.'

He hung up. I felt foolish. I never even considered the phone book because I never knew a cop who put his name in it. I dialed information for Baltimore again and gave the former detective's name.

'I have no listing for a Daniel Bledsoe,' the operator said. 'I have Bledsoe Insurance and Bledsoe Investigations.'

'Okay, give me those and can I get the addresses, please?'

'Actually, they are separate listings and numbers but the same address in Fells Point.'

He gave me the information and I called the investigations number. A woman answered, 'Bledsoe Investigations.'

'Yes, can I speak to Dan?'

'I'm sorry, he's unavailable.'

'Do you know if he'll be in later today?'

'He's in now. He's just on the line. This is his service. When he's out or on his line it rings through. But I know he's there. He checked for messages not ten minutes ago. But I don't know for how long. I don't keep his schedule.'

Fells Point is a spit of land east of Baltimore's Inner Harbor. The tourist shops and hotels give way to funkier pubs and shops and then old brick factories and Little Italy. On some streets the asphalt has worn off the underlying brick and when the wind is right there is the damp tang of the sea or the smell of the sugar factory just across the inlet. Bledsoe Investigations and Insurance was in a one-story brick building at Caroline and Fleet.

It was a few minutes after one. On the door of his small street-front office was a plastic clock face with adjustable hands and the words BE BACK AT. The clock was set at one. I looked around, saw no one making a run for the door to beat the deadline and decided to wait for him anyway. I had nowhere else to go.

I walked down to the market on Fleet, bought a Coke and went back to my car. From the driver's seat I could see the door to Bledsoe's office. I watched it for twenty minutes until I saw a man with jet-black hair, a middle-age paunch peeking through his jacket and a slight limp walk up, unlock the door and go in. I got out with my computer satchel and headed for him.

Bledsoe's office looked as though it had once been a doctor's office, though I could not figure out why a doctor would have hung a shingle out in this working district. There was a little entry room with a sliding window and counter behind which I imagined a receptionist at one time sat. The window, glazed like a shower door, was closed. I had heard a buzz when I had opened the door but no one responded to it. I stood there a few moments looking around. There was an old couch and a coffee table. Not much room for anything else. A variety of magazines were fanned across the table, none of them fresher than six months old. I was about to call out a hello or knock on the door to the inner sanctum when I heard a toilet flush somewhere on the other side of the sliding window. Then I saw a blurred figure move behind the glass and the door to the left opened. The man with the black hair stood there. I noticed now that he had a mustache as thin as a freeway on a map traveling over his lip.

'Yes, can I help you?'

'Daniel Bledsoe?'

'That's right.'

'My name's Jack McEvoy. I'd like to ask you about John McCafferty. I think we both might be able to help each other.'

'John McCafferty was a long time ago.'

He was eyeing the computer satchel.

'It's just a computer,' I said. 'Can we sit down someplace?'

'Uh, sure. Why not?'

I followed through the door and down a short hallway that had three more doors lined along the right side. He opened the first one and we stepped into an office of cheap faux maple paneling. His state license was framed on the wall as well as some photos from his days as a cop. The whole thing seemed about as cheesy as his mustache but I was determined to play it out. The thing I know about cops, and I guessed that it extended to former cops, was that looks were deceiving. I knew some in Colorado who would still be wearing pale blue polyester leisure suits if they made them anymore. But nevertheless they were some of the best and brightest and toughest of their departments. I suspected it was that way with Bledsoe. He took a seat behind a desk with a black Formica top. It had been a poor choice when he'd bought it at the secondhand office furniture store. I could plainly see the dust buildup on the shiny surface. I sat across from Bledsoe in the only other chair. He accurately registered my impressions.

'Place used to be an abortion clinic. Guy went away for doing third-trimester jobs. I took it over and don't care about the dust and looks. I get a lot of my work over the phone, selling policies to cops. And I usually go to clients, the ones that want an investigation. They don't come to me. The people that do come here usually just leave flowers out by the door. Memorials, I guess. I figure they must be working off old phone books or something. Why don't you tell me what you're looking for here.'

I told him about my brother and then about John Brooks in Chicago. I watched his face fill with skepticism as I talked. It told me I was maybe ten seconds from being thrown out the door.

'What is this?' he said. 'Who sent you here?'

'Nobody. But it's my guess that I'm maybe a day or so ahead of the FBI. But they'll be coming. I just thought you'd maybe talk to me first. I know what it's like, you see. My brother and me, we were twins. I've always heard that longtime partners, especially on homicide, become like brothers. Like twins.'

I held up for a few moments. I had played everything but my ace and I had to wait for the right moment. Bledsoe seemed to cool down a little. His anger was maybe giving way to confusion.

'So what do you want from me?'

'The note. I want to know what McCafferty said in the note.'

'There was no note. I never said there was a note.'

'But his wife said there was.'

'Then go talk to her.'

'No, I think I'd rather talk to you. Let me tell you something. The doer on these cases somehow gets the victims to write out a line or two as a suicide note. I don't know how he does it or why they oblige him, but they do. And every time the line is from a poem. A poem by the same writer. Edgar Allan Poe.'

I reached down to my computer satchel and unzipped it. I pulled out the thick book of Poe's works. I put it on the desk so that he could see it.

'I think your partner was murdered. You came in and it looked like a suicide because that was how it was supposed to look. That note you destroyed, I'd bet you your partner's pension that it's a line from a poem that's in that book.'

Bledsoe looked from me to the book and then back at me again.

'You apparently thought you owed him enough to risk your job to make his widow's life a little easier.'

'Yeah, look what it got me. A piece-of-shit office with a piece-of-shit license on the wall. I sit in a room where they used to cut babies out of women. It's not very noble.'

'Look, everybody on the force knew there was something noble about what you did, else you wouldn't be selling any insurance. You did what you did for your partner. You should follow through, now.'

Bledsoe turned his head and looked at one of the photos on the wall. It was him and another man, arms around each other's neck, smiling with abandon. It looked like it had been taken in a bar somewhere during the good days.

' "The fever called living is conquered at last," ' he said, without looking away from the photo.

I slapped my hand down on the book. The sound scared us both.

'Got it,' I said and picked up the book. I had bent the pages of the poems where the killer's quotes had been taken. I found the page with the poem 'For Annie' on it, scanned until I knew I was right, then put the book on the desk and turned it so he could read it.

'First stanza,' I said.

Bledsoe leaned over to read the poem.

Thank Heaven! the crisis –
The danger is past,
And the lingering illness
Is over at last –
And the fever called 'Living'
Is conquered at last.

19

As I hurried through the lobby of the Hilton at four, I envisioned Greg Glenn slowly making his way out from behind his desk and heading toward the daily news meeting in the metro conference room. I needed to talk to him and I knew that if I didn't snag him first he'd be holed up in that meeting and the weekend meeting that followed for the next two hours.

As I approached the elevators I saw a woman stepping through the open doors of the one available car and quickly followed her in. She had already pushed the 12 button. I moved to the rear of the car and checked my watch again. I thought I was going to make it. The editors' meetings never seemed to get off on time.

The woman had moved to the right side of the car and we had settled into the slightly uncomfortable silence that always comes when strangers are enclosed in an elevator. In the polished-brass trim on the door I could see her face. Her eyes watched the lights over the doors that marked our ascent. She was very attractive and I found it hard to turn away from the reflection, even though I feared she would turn her eyes and catch me. I imagined that she knew I was watching her. I've always believed that beautiful women know and understand they are always being watched.

When the elevator opened on twelve I waited for her to step out first. She turned to the left and headed down the hall. I turned right and headed to my room, stopping myself from taking a backward glance at her. As I approached my door, pulling the card key out of my shirt pocket, I heard light steps on the hallway carpet. I turned and it was her. She smiled.

'Wrong way.'

'Yeah,' I said and smiled. 'After a while it's all a maze.'

Dumb thing to say, I thought as I opened the door and she passed behind me. As I entered the room, I felt a hand suddenly grip the back of my jacket collar and I was shoved into the room. As this happened another hand went up under my jacket and grabbed onto my belt. I was slammed facedown onto the bed. I managed to hold on to the computer bag, not wanting to drop a two-thousand-dollar piece of equipment, but then it was roughly yanked out of my grasp.

'FBI! You're under arrest. Don't move!'

While one hand stayed on the back of my neck and held me facedown, the other then patted my body in a search.

'What the fuck is this?' I managed to say in a voice muffled by the mattress.

Just as suddenly as they had gripped me, the hands were gone.

'Okay, up. Let's go.'

I turned and raised myself until I was seated on the bed. I looked up. It was the woman from the elevator. My mouth dropped open a little. Something about being handled so easily by her, and her alone, burned me deeply and anger flushed my cheeks.

'Don't worry. I've done it to bigger and badder men than you.'

'You better have an ID or you're going to need a lawyer.'

She pulled a wallet out of her coat pocket and flipped it open in front of my face.

'You're the one who needs the lawyer. Now, I want you to take the chair from the desk, put it in the corner and sit there while I go through this place. It won't take long.'

She had what looked like a legitimate FBI badge and ID. It said Special Agent Rachel Walling. Once I read that I began to get an idea of what was going on.

'C'mon, chop, chop. In the corner you go.'

'Let's see the search warrant.'

'You have a choice,' she said sternly. 'Go to the corner or I take you into the bathroom and cuff you to the drain trap under the sink. Make it.'

I stood up and dragged the chair into the corner and sat down.

'I still want to see the fuckin' warrant.'

'Are you aware that your use of coarse language is a rather lame attempt to reestablish your sense of male superiority?'

'Jesus. Are you aware that you are full of shit? Where's the warrant?'

'I don't need a warrant. You invited me in and allowed me to search, then I arrested you after I found the stolen property.'

She stepped back to the door, her eyes on me, and closed it.

'I didn't invite you anywhere. You try that shit and you'll crash and burn. Do you believe any judge is going to believe I was stupid enough to invite a search *if* I had stolen property in here?'

She looked at me and smiled sweetly.

'Mr McEvoy, I am five feet five and weigh one hundred and fifteen pounds. That's with my gun on. Do you think a judge will believe your version of what happened? Would you even want to reveal what I just did to you in open court?'

I looked away from her and out the window. The maid had opened the curtains. The sky was beginning to lose the light.

'I didn't think so,' she said. 'Now, you want to save me some time? Where are the protocols you copied?'

'In the computer bag. I committed no crime in getting them and just having them is not a crime.'

I had to be careful of what I said. I didn't know if Michael Warren had already been found out or not. She was going through the satchel. She pulled out the Poe book, looked at it quizzically and threw it on the bed. She then pulled out my notebook and the sheaf of copies of the protocols. Warren had been right. She was a beautiful woman. A hard shell but beautiful just the same. About my age, maybe a year or two older, her hair was brown and falling to just above her shoulders. Sharp green eyes and the strong aura of confidence. That was what was most attractive about her. Though at the moment I think I hated her, the attraction was not lost on me.

'Breaking and entering is a crime,' she said. 'It came under my jurisdiction when it was determined that the documents stolen belonged to the bureau.'

'I didn't break into anything and I didn't steal anything. What this is is harassment. I've always heard that you bureau people get upset when somebody else does your job for you.'

She was leaning over the bed looking through the papers. She straightened up, reached into her pocket and pulled out a clear plastic evidence bag with a single sheet of paper in it. She held it up for me to look at. I recognized it as having been torn from a reporter's notebook. There were six lines written on it in black ink.

Pena: his hands?
after – how long?
Wexler/Scalari: the car?
heater?
lock?
Riley: gloves?

I recognized my own handwriting and then it all tumbled together. Warren had torn sheets from my notebook to mark the spots of the files we had pulled. He had torn a page with old notes on it and somehow had left it behind when he returned the files. Walling must have seen the recognition in my face.

'Sloppy work. After we get the handwriting analyzed and compared, I think it'll be a slam dunk. What do you think?'

I couldn't even manage a *fuck you* this time.

'I'm seizing your computer, this book and your notebooks as possible evidence. If we don't need any of it, you'll get it back. Okay, we're going to go now. My car's right out front. The one thing I'm willing to do for you to show I'm not such a mean girl is take you down without the cuffs. We've got a long ride down to Virginia, though we might beat some of the traffic if we get going now. Are you going to behave? One false move, as they say, and I'll put you in the back with the cuffs on as tight as a wedding ring.'

I just nodded and stood up. I was in a daze. I couldn't meet her eyes. I walked toward the door with my head down.

'Hey, what do you say?' she said to me.

I mumbled my thanks and I heard her soft laughter behind me.

She was wrong. We didn't beat the traffic. It was Friday evening. More people were trying to get out of the city than most nights and we crawled along with them as we crossed the city to get to a freeway. For a half hour neither of us spoke, except when she cursed at a traffic snarl or a red light. I was in the front seat, thinking the whole time. I had to make a call to Glenn as soon as possible. They had to get me a lawyer. A good one. I saw that the only way out was to reveal a source I had promised I would never reveal. I considered the possibility that if I called Warren he would come forward and confirm that I hadn't broken into the foundation. But I discarded it. I had made a covenant with him. I had to honor it.

When we finally made it south of Georgetown the traffic opened up a little bit and she seemed to relax, or at least remember I was in the car with her. I saw her reach into the ashtray and pull out a white card. She put the dome light on and held the card on the top of the steering wheel so she could read it while she drove.

'You have a pen?'

'What?'

'A pen. I thought all reporters carried pens.'

'Yes. I have a pen.'

'Good. I'm going to read you your constitutional rights.'

'What rights? You've already violated most of them.'

She proceeded to read from the card and then asked if I understood them. I mumbled that I did and she handed me the card.

'Okay, good. I want you to take your pen and sign and date the back of that.'

I did as instructed and handed the card back. She blew on the ink until it dried and then put the card in her pocket.

'There,' she said. 'Now we can talk. Unless you want to call your lawyer. How'd you get into the foundation?'

'I didn't break in. That's all I can say till I talk to a lawyer.'

'You saw the evidence. Are you going to say that's not yours?'

'It can be explained . . . Look, all I'm saying is I did nothing illegal to get those copies. I can't say anything more without revealing . . .'

I didn't finish. I'd said enough.

'The old can't-reveal-my-sources trick. Where were you all day today, Mr McEvoy? I've been waiting since noon.'

'I was in Baltimore.'

'Doing what?'

'That's my business. You have the originals on those protocols, you can figure it out.'

'The McCafferty case. You know, interfering with a federal investigation can get you charged with additional crimes.'

I gave her my best fake laugh.

'Yeah, right,' I said sarcastically. 'What federal investigation? You'd still be down there in your office counting suicides if I hadn't talked to Ford yesterday. But that's the bureau's way, right? If it's a good idea, oh that's *our* idea. If it's a good case, yeah, *we* made that case. Meantime, it's hear no evil, see no evil and a lot of shit goes by unnoticed.'

'Jesus, who died and made you the expert?'

'My brother.'

She didn't see that coming and it shut her down for a few minutes. It also seemed to have the effect of breaking through the shell she surrounded herself with.

'I'm sorry about that,' she finally said.

'So am I.'

All the anger about what had happened to Sean welled up inside of me but I swallowed it back. She was a stranger and I couldn't share something so profoundly personal with her. I shoved it back and thought of something else to say.

'You know, you might've known him. You signed the VICAP survey and the profile he got from the bureau on his case.'

'Yes, I know. But we never spoke.'

'How about if you answer a question now?'

'Maybe. Go ahead.'

'How did you find me?'

I was wondering if Warren had somehow put her on to me. If I could determine that he had, then all bets were off and I wasn't going to go to jail protecting the person who had set me up in the first place.

'That was the easy part,' she said. 'I had your name and pedigree from Dr Ford at the foundation. He called me after your little meeting yesterday and I came up this morning. I thought it might be wise to safeguard those files and sure enough I was right. Just a little late. You do quick work. Once I found the page from a reporter's notebook, it was pretty easy to figure out you'd been there.'

'I didn't break in there.'

'Well, everyone associated with the project denies talking to you. In fact, Dr Ford specifically remembers telling you that you could not have access to the files until the bureau signed off on it. And funny thing, here you are with the files.'

'And how'd you know I was at the Hilton? Was that written on a piece of paper for you, too?'

'Bluffed your city editor like he was a copy boy. I told him I had important information for you and he told me where you were.'

I smiled but turned and looked out the window so she wouldn't see it. She had just made a mistake that was as telling as if she had said outright that Warren had revealed where I was.

'They don't call them copy boys anymore,' I said. 'It's politically incorrect.'

'Copy person?'

'Close enough.'

With a straight face I looked over at her for the first time while in the car. I felt myself making a comeback. The confidence she had so expertly stomped into the bedspread in the hotel room was getting a second life. Now I was playing her.

'I thought you people always worked in twos,' I said.

We were stopping at another red light. I could see the freeway entrance up ahead. I had to make my move.

'Usually,' she said. 'But today was busy, a lot of people out, and, actually, when I left Quantico, I thought I was just going up to the foundation to talk to Oline and Dr Ford and to pull the records. I wasn't counting on a custody arrest.'

Her show was falling apart quickly. I was seeing it now. No cuffs. No partner. Me in the front seat. And I knew that Greg Glenn didn't know where I was staying in D.C. I hadn't told him and I hadn't made the reservation through the *Rocky*'s travel office because there hadn't been time.

My computer satchel was on the seat between us. On top of it she had stacked the copies of the protocol files, the Poe book and my notebook. I reached over and pulled it all onto my lap.

'What are you doing?' she asked.

'I'm getting out of here.' I tossed the protocols onto her lap. 'You can keep those. I've got all the information I need.'

I pulled the door handle and opened the door.

'Don't you fucking move!'

I looked at her and smiled.

'Are you aware that your use of coarse language is a lame attempt to reestablish your superiority? Look, it was a nice play but you ran out of the right answers. I'll just catch a cab back to the hotel. I've got a story to write.'

I got out of the car with my things and stepped onto the sidewalk. I looked around and saw a convenience store with a phone out front and started walking that way. Next I saw her car cut into the parking lot and park in my path. She jerked it to a stop and jumped out.

'You're making a mistake,' she said, coming quickly toward me.

'What mistake? You made the mistake. What was that charade all about?'

She just looked at me. She was speechless.

'Okay, I'll tell you what it was,' I said. 'It was a scam.'

'Scam? Why would I scam you?'

'Information. You wanted to know what I had. Let me guess, once you had what you wanted, you were going to come in and say, "Oh gee, sorry, your source just copped. Never mind, you're free to go and sorry about the little misunderstanding." Well, you better go back down to Quantico and practice your act.'

I walked around her and headed to the pay phone. I picked the receiver off the hook and the phone was dead. I didn't let on, though. She was watching me. I dialed information.

'I need a cab company,' I said to a nonexistent operator.

I dropped a quarter in the slot and dialed a number. I then read the address off the phone and asked for a cab. When I hung up and turned around, Agent Walling was standing there very close. She reached past me and picked up the phone. After holding it to her ear for a second she smiled slightly and hung it back up. She pointed to the side of the box to where the receiver cable was attached. It was severed, the wires tied together in a knot.

'Your act could use some polish, too.'

'Fine. Just leave me alone.'

I turned away and started looking through the store windows to see if there was another phone inside. There wasn't.

'Look, what did you want me to do?' she asked my back. 'I need to know what you know.'

I whipped around on her.

'Then why didn't you just ask? Why'd you have to . . . try to humiliate me?'

'You are a reporter, Jack. Are you going to tell me you were just going to open up your files and share with me?'

'Maybe.'

'Yeah, right. That'll be the day, when one of you people do that. Look at Warren. He's not even a reporter anymore and he was acting like one. It's in the blood.'

'Hey, you know, speaking of blood, there's more at stake here than a story, okay? You don't know what I would have done if you had approached me like a human being.'

'Okay,' she said softly. 'Maybe I don't. I'll grant you that.'

We did a little pacing in opposite directions until she spoke.

'So what do we do? Here we are, you found me out, and now you have a choice. I need to know what you know. Are you going to tell me or are you going to take your ball and go home? You do that and we both lose out. So does your brother.'

She had skillfully backed me into a corner and I knew it. On principle I should have walked off. But I couldn't. Despite everything, I liked her. I silently walked to the car, got in and then looked at her through the windshield. She nodded once and came around to the driver's side. After getting in she turned to me and held out her hand.

'Rachel Walling.'

I took it and shook it.

'Jack McEvoy.'

'I know. Nice to meet you.'

'Likewise.'

20

As a show of good faith Rachel Walling went first – after extracting a promise from me that the conversation was off the record until her team supervisor decided how much cooperation, if any, the bureau would give me. I didn't mind making the promise because I knew I was holding the high hand. I already had a story and the bureau would likely not want a story published yet. I figured that gave me a lot of leverage, whether Agent Walling realized it yet or not.

For a half hour while we moved slowly south on the freeway toward Quantico she told me what the bureau had been doing for the last twenty-eight hours. Nathan Ford of the Law Enforcement Foundation had called her at three o'clock Thursday to inform her of my visit to the foundation, the findings of my own investigation to that point and my request to see the suicide files. Walling concurred with his decision to rebuff me and then consulted with Bob Backus, her immediate supervisor. Backus gave her the go-ahead to drop the profiling work she had been assigned and proceed with a priority investigation of the claims I had made in my meeting with Ford. At this time, the bureau had not yet heard from anyone from the Denver or Chicago police departments. Walling started her work on the Behavioral Science Services computer, which had a direct tie to the foundation computer.

'Basically, I did the same search Michael Warren did for you,' she said. 'In fact, I was on-line in Quantico when he went in and did it. I just ID'ed the user and literally watched him do it on my laptop. I guessed right then that you had turned him as a source and he was doing the search for you. This became a problem of containment, as you can imagine. I didn't need to go up to the city today because we have hard copies of all the protocols at Quantico. But I had to see what you were doing. I got a second confirmation that Warren was leaking to you and that you had copies of the protocols when I found your notebook page left in the files.'

I shook my head.

'What's going to happen to Warren?'

'After I told Ford, we confronted him this morning. He admitted what he had done, even told me what hotel you were at. Ford asked for his resignation and Warren gave it.'

'Shit.'

I felt a pang of guilt, yet I was not overwrought by what had happened. For

I wasn't sure if Warren hadn't somehow engineered his own dismissal. Maybe it was a self-derailment. At least, that's what I told myself. It was easier to handle that way.

'By the way,' she said, 'where did I go wrong with my act?'

'My editor didn't know where I was staying. Only Warren knew.'

She was quiet for a few moments until I prompted her to continue the chronology of her investigation. She told me that on Thursday afternoon when she ran the computer search she'd come up with the same thirteen names of dead homicide detectives that Warren had gotten for me, plus my brother and John Brooks of Chicago. She then pulled the hard copies of the protocols and looked for ties, keying on the suicide notes as I had told Ford I wanted to do. She had the aid of a bureau cryptologist and the FBI cipher computer, which had a database that made the *Rocky*'s look like a comic book.

'Including your brother and Brooks, we came up with a total of five direct connections through the notes,' she said.

'So in about three hours you did what it took me all week to do. How'd you get McCafferty without the note in the file?'

She took her foot off the gas and looked over at me. Only for a moment, then she took the car back up to speed.

'We didn't count McCafferty. There are agents from the Baltimore field office on that now.'

This was puzzling because I had five cases, including McCafferty.

'Then what five have you got?'

'Uh, let me think . . .'

'Okay, my brother and Brooks, that's two.'

I was opening my notebook as I said this.

'Right.'

Reading my notes, I said, 'You got Kotite in Albuquerque? "Haunted by ill angels"?'

'Right. We have him. There was one in –'

'Dallas. Garland Petry. "Sadly, I know I am shorn of my strength." From "For Annie." '

'Yeah, got that.'

'And then I had McCafferty. Who'd you have?'

'Uh, something or other from Florida. It was an old one. He was a sheriff's deputy. I need my notes.'

'Wait a minute.' I flipped through a few pages of my notebook and found it. 'Clifford Beltran, Sarasota County Sheriff's Department. He –'

'That's it.'

'But wait a minute. I've got his note as "Lord help my poor soul." I read all the poems. That wasn't in any of them.'

'You're right. We found it somewhere else.'

'Where? One of the short stories?'

'No. They were his last words. Poe's last words. "Lord help my poor soul." '

I nodded. It wasn't a poem but it fit. So now there were six. I was quiet a moment, almost in respect to the new man added to the list. I looked down at my notes. Beltran had been dead three years. A long time for a murder to go unnoticed.

'Was Poe a suicide?'

'No, though I suppose his lifestyle might be considered a long suicide. He was a womanizer and a heavy drinker. He died at forty, apparently after a lengthy drinking bout in Baltimore.'

I nodded, thinking about the killer, the phantom, and wondering if he drew corollaries to Poe's life.

'Jack, what about McCafferty?' she asked. 'We had him as a possible but no note according to the protocol. What did you get?'

Now I had another problem. Bledsoe. He had revealed something to me that he had not revealed to anyone before. I didn't feel I could just turn around and give it to the FBI.

'I've gotta make a call first before I can tell you.'

'Oh, Jesus, Jack. You're going to pull that shit after all I just told you? I thought we had a deal.'

'We do. I just have to make a call first and clear something with a source. Get me to a phone and I'll do it right then. I don't think it will be a problem. Anyway, the bottom line is McCafferty is on the list. There was a note.'

I looked through my notebook again and then read from it.

' "The fever called living is conquered at last." That was the note. It's from "For Annie." Just like Petry in Dallas.'

I looked over at her and could tell she was still upset.

'Look, Rachel – can I call you that? – I'm not going to hold back on you. I'll make the call. Your agents from the field office probably already got this anyway.'

'Probably,' she said, in a voice that seemed to say, *Anything you can get we can get better.*

'Okay, so go on, then. What happened after you came up with the list of five?'

She told me that at six o'clock Thursday evening she and Backus had convened a meeting of BSS and Critical Incident Unit agents to discuss her preliminary findings. After she trotted out the five names she had and explained the connections, her boss, Backus, became agitated and ordered a full-scale priority investigation. Waller was named lead agent, reporting to him. Other BSS and CIU agents were assigned to victimology and profiling tasks, and VICAP liaison agents from local field offices in the five cities where the deaths occurred were scrambled to immediately begin gathering and shipping data on the deaths involved. The team had literally worked through the night.

'The Poet.'

'What?'

'We're calling him the Poet. Every task force investigation gets a code name.'

'Jesus,' I said. 'The tabloids are going to love that. I can see the headlines. "The Poet Kills without Rhyme or Reason." You guys are asking for it.'

'The tabs will never know about it. Backus is determined to get this guy before he's spooked by any press leaks.'

There was silence while I thought of how to answer that.

'Aren't you forgetting something?' I finally asked.

'Jack, I know you're a reporter and you're the one who started this whole thing. But you've got to understand, if you start a media firestorm about this guy, we'll never get him. He'll get spooked and go back underneath his rock. We'll lose our chance.'

'Well, I'm not on the public payroll. What I am, though, is paid to report and write stories ... The FBI *cannot* tell me what and when to write.'

'You can't use anything I just told you.'

'I know it. I agreed and I'll keep my word. I don't need to use it. I already had it. Most of it. All except for Beltran and all I have to do is read the bio section of this book and I'll find his last words ... I don't need the FBI's information or permission for this story.'

That brought the silence back. I could tell she was steaming but I had to stand my ground. I had to play my cards as shrewdly as I could. In this kind of game you don't get a second deal. After a few minutes of this I started seeing the freeway signs for Quantico. We were close.

'Look,' I said. 'We will talk about the story later. I'm not going to run off and start writing. My editor and I will calmly talk about it and I will let you know what we are going to do. Is that okay?'

'That's fine, Jack. I hope you're thinking about your brother when you have that discussion. I'm sure your editor won't be.'

'Look, do me a favor. Don't talk to me about my brother and my motives. Because you don't know a thing about me or him or what I'm thinking about.'

'Fine.'

We drove a few miles in solid silence. My anger wore off a bit and I began wondering if I'd been too harsh. Her goal was to capture this person they now called the Poet. It was mine, too.

'Look, I'm sorry about the speech,' I said. 'I still think we can help each other. We can cooperate and maybe catch this guy.'

'I don't know,' she replied. 'I don't see the point in cooperating when what I say is just going to show up in the newspapers and then the TV and then the tabloids. You're right, I don't know what you're thinking. I don't know you and I don't think I can trust you.'

She didn't say another word until we got to the gatehouse at Quantico.

21

It was dark and I couldn't see the grounds well as we drove in. The FBI Academy and the research center were located in the heart of a U.S. Marine base. It consisted of three sprawling brick buildings connected by glassed walkways and atriums. Agent Walling pulled into a lot marked for FBI agents only and parked.

She continued her silence as we got out. It was getting to me. I did not want her unhappy with me or thinking of me as self-serving.

'Look, my main priority is obviously to get this guy,' I tried. 'Let me just use a phone. I'll call my source and my editor and we'll work something out. Okay?'

'Sure,' she said grudgingly.

One word and I was happy just to have finally leveraged something out of her. We went into the center building and took a series of hallways to a set of stairs which we took down to the National Center for the Analysis of Violent Crime. It was the basement. She led me past a reception area into a large room that didn't look much different from a newsroom. There were two rows of desks and work spaces with sound partitions between them and a row of private offices running down the right side. She stepped back and pointed me into one of the private offices. I assumed it was hers, though it was austere and impersonal. The only photo I saw anywhere was the one of the president on the rear wall.

'Why don't you sit there and use the phone,' she said. 'I'm going to find out where Bob is and see what's been going on. And don't worry, the phone's not tapped.'

As I noted the sarcasm in her voice I saw her eyes scan the desk, making sure I would not be left alone with any important documents lying about. Satisfied there was nothing, she left. I sat behind the desk and opened my notebook to the numbers Dan Bledsoe had given me. I got him at home.

'It's Jack McEvoy. From today.'

'Right, yeah.'

'Listen, I got picked up by the FBI after I got back into D.C. They're doing a major deal on this guy and they've connected up five cases. But they don't have McCafferty yet because of no note. I can give it to them and they'll go from there. But I wanted to check with you first about it. They'll probably come talk to you if I tell them. They'll probably come even if I don't.'

While he thought about this my eyes scanned the desk as Walling had done. It was very clean, taken up mostly by a monthly calendar that also served as a blotter. I noted that she had just come back from a vacation, the date blocks for the prior week having 'vac' written in each one. There were abbreviated notations in the blocks for other dates of the month but they were indecipherable to me.

'Give it to 'em,' Bledsoe said.

'You sure?'

'Sure. If the bureau comes out and says Johnny Mac was murdered, then his wife gets the bread. That's all I wanted in the first place, so tell 'em. They're not going to do anything to me. They can't. What's done is done. I already heard from a friend that they were up here going through records today.'

'Okay, man, thanks.'

'You going to get a piece of it?'

'I don't know. I'm working on it.'

'It's your case. Hang in there. But don't trust the G, Jack. They'll use you and what you got and then leave you on the sidewalk like dog shit.'

I thanked him for the advice and as I hung up a man in the standard-issue gray FBI suit walked by the open door of the office, noticed me behind the desk and stopped. He stepped in, a curious look on his face.

'Excuse me, what are you doing in here?'

'Waiting for Agent Walling.'

He was a large man with a sharp and ruddy face and short, black hair.

'And you are?'

'My name is Jack McEvoy. She –'

'Just don't sit behind the desk.'

He made a twirling motion with his hand, indicating I should come around to the front of the desk and take one of the chairs there. Rather than argue the point I followed his instructions. He thanked me and left the office. The episode served as a reminder to me of why I never liked dealing with FBI agents. In general, they all carried anal-retentive genes. More than most.

After I was sure he was gone I reached across the desk to Walling's phone and punched in Greg Glenn's direct number. It was shortly after five in Denver and I knew he would be busy supervising deadline, but I had no choice of when I could call.

'Jack, can you call back?'

'No. I've got to talk to you.'

'Okay, hurry. We had another clinic shooting and we're bending deadline.'

I quickly brought him up to date on what I had and what had happened with the FBI. He seemed to forget all about the clinic shooting and the deadline, repeatedly saying that what I had was fantastic and was going to be a fantastic story. I left out the part about Warren losing his job and Walling's attempt to scam me. I told him where I was and what I wanted to do. He approved it.

'We're probably going to need the whole news hole for this clinic stuff anyway,' he said. 'At least the next couple of days. It's going crazy here. I could use you on rewrite.'

'Sorry.'

'Yeah. Well, you go ahead and play it out and see what you get, then let me know. This is going to be great, Jack.'

'I hope so.'

Glenn started talking about the possibilities again in terms of journalism awards and kicking the competition's ass, breaking a national story. While I listened, Walling stepped into the office with a man I assumed was Bob Backus. He also wore a gray suit but had the air of the man in charge. He looked like he was in his mid- to late thirties and was still in good shape. He had a pleasant look on his face, short-cropped brown hair and piercing blue eyes. I held one finger up to signal I was almost done. I cut in on Glenn.

'Greg, I gotta go.'

'Okay, well let me know. And one thing, Jack.'

'What?'

'Get me some art.'

'Right.'

As I hung up, I thought that might be a little too hopeful on his part. Getting a photographer in on this would be a long shot. I had to worry about getting myself in first.

'Jack, this is Bob Backus, assistant special agent in charge. He leads my team. Bob, Jack McEvoy of the *Rocky Mountain News*.'

We shook hands and Backus had a vise for a grip. That was as standard FBI macho as the suit. As he spoke he reached down absentmindedly to the desk and straightened the calendar.

'Always glad to meet one of our friends in the Fourth Estate. Especially one that doesn't come from inside the beltway.'

I just nodded. It was bullshit and everybody there knew it.

'Jack, why don't we go over to the Boardroom and get a cup of coffee,' Backus said. 'It's been a long day. I'll show you around a little on the way.'

As we went upstairs Backus said nothing of consequence other than to express condolences about my brother. After the three of us were seated with our coffee at one of the tables in the cafeteria called the Boardroom, he got down to business.

'Jack, we are off the record,' Backus said. 'Everything that you see or hear while in Quantico is off the record. Are we clear on that?'

'Yes. For the time being.'

'Okay. If you want to talk about changing that agreement, talk to me or Rachel and we'll hash it out. Would you be willing to sign an agreement to that effect?'

'Sure. But I'm going to be the one who writes it.'

Backus nodded as if I had scored a point in a debate final.

'Fair enough.' He moved his coffee cup to the side, brushed some unseen impurity off his palms and leaned across the table toward me. 'Jack, we've got a status meeting in fifteen minutes. As I am sure Rachel has told you, we are going full speed. We'd be criminally negligent, in my opinion, if we proceeded with this investigation in any other way. I've got my entire team on it, eight other BSS agents on loan, two techs assigned full-time and six field offices involved. I can't remember when we've had that kind of commitment to an investigation before.'

'I'm glad to hear that . . . Bob.'

He didn't seem to flinch at my use of his first name. It had been a small test. He was seemingly treating me as an equal, calling me by my first name often. I decided to see what would happen if I did the same. So far, so good.

'You have done some very fine work,' Backus continued. 'What you have done has given us a solid blueprint. It's a start and I want to tell you we're already more than twenty-four solid hours into it.'

Behind Backus I saw the agent who had spoken to me in Walling's office sit down at another table with a cup of coffee and a sandwich. He watched us as he began to eat.

'We are talking about a tremendous amount of resources being committed to the investigation,' Backus said. 'But right now our number one priority is one of containment.'

It was going exactly the way I had expected and I had to struggle to keep a look on my face that did not give away that I knew I held sway over the FBI and the investigation. I had leverage. I was an insider.

'You don't want me to write about it,' I said quietly.

'Yes, that's exactly right. Not yet, at least. We know that you have enough, even without what you've learned from us, to write a hell of a story. It's an explosive story, Jack. If you write about it out there in Denver it is going to attract attention. Overnight it will be on the network and in every newspaper. Then "Hard Copy" and the rest of the TV tabloids. Anybody who doesn't have his head in the sand is going to know about it. And, Jack, plain and simple, we can't have that. Once the offender knows we know about him, he could disappear. If he is smart, and we already know he is damn smart, he will disappear. We'll never get him then. You don't want that. We're talking about the person who killed your brother. You don't want that, do you?'

I nodded that I understood the dilemma and was silent a moment as I composed my reply. I looked from Backus to Walling and then back to Backus.

'My paper has already invested a lot of time and money,' I said. 'I've got the story down cold. Just so you understand, I could write a story tonight that says authorities are conducting a nationwide investigation into the likelihood that a serial killer of cops has been operating for as long as three years without detection.'

'As I said, you've done very good work and nobody's arguing what kind of story this is.'

'So then what are you proposing? I just kill it and walk away, wait for you to hold a press conference one day when, and *if*, you get this guy?'

Backus cleared his throat and leaned back. I glanced over at Walling but her face showed nothing.

'I won't sugarcoat it,' Backus said. 'But, yes, I want you to sit on the story for a little while.'

'Until when? What's "a little while"?'

Backus looked around the cafeteria as if he had never been there. He answered without looking at me.

'Until we get this person.'

I whistled low.

'And what would I get for sitting on the story? What would the *Rocky Mountain News* get?'

'First and foremost, you'd be helping us catch your brother's killer. If that is not enough for you, I'm sure we could work out some sort of exclusivity agreement on the arrest of the suspect.'

No one spoke for a long moment because it was clear the ball was in my court. I weighed my words carefully before finally leaning forward across the table and speaking.

'Well, Bob, as I think you know, this is one of those rare occasions when you guys don't hold all the cards and can't call all of the shots. This is my investigation, you see? I started it and I'm not just going to drop out. I'm not going to go back to Denver and sit behind my desk and wait for the phone to ring. I'm in and if you don't keep me in, then I go back to write the story. It will be in the paper Sunday morning. It's our best circulation day.'

'You'd do that to your own brother?' Walling said, the words tight with anger. 'Don't you give a shit?'

'Rachel, please,' Backus said. 'It's a good point. What we –'

'I give a shit,' I said. 'I was the only one who did. So don't try to lay any guilt on me. My brother stays dead whether you find this guy or not and whether I write the story or not.'

'Okay, Jack, we're not questioning your motives here,' Backus said, his hands raised in a calming gesture. 'We seem to have gotten into an adversarial stance and I don't want that. Why don't you clearly tell me what you want. I'm sure we are going to work this out right here. Before the coffee even gets cold.'

'It's simple,' I said quickly. 'Put me on the investigation. Complete access as an observer. I won't write a word until we either get the son of a bitch or give up.'

'That's blackmail,' Walling said.

'No, it's the agreement I'm offering to make,' I responded. 'It's actually a concession because I have the story now. Having to sit on it is against my instincts and against what I do.'

I looked at Backus. Walling was angry but I knew it didn't matter. Backus would make the call.

'I don't think we can do that, Jack,' he finally said. 'It's against bureau regulations to bring somebody in like that. It could be dangerous to you as well.'

'I don't care about that. Any of it. That's the deal. Take it or leave it. Call whoever you've got to call. But that's the deal.'

Backus pulled his cup in front of him and looked down into the still steaming blackness. He hadn't even sipped it.

'This proposal is well above my level of authority,' he said. 'I'll have to get back to you.'

'When?'

'I'll make the call right now.'

'What about the status conference?'

'They can't start without me. Why don't both of you wait here. This shouldn't take long.'

Backus stood up and carefully slid his chair into the table.

'Just so we're clear,' I said before he turned away, 'if allowed into this as an observer, with two exceptions I will not write about the case until we have an arrest or you determine it is fruitless and focus your primary efforts on other cases.'

'What are the exceptions?' Backus asked.

'One is if you ask me to write about it. There may come a time that you'll want to flush this guy out with a story. I'll write it then. The other exception is if the story leaks. If this shows up in any other paper or on TV, all bets are off. Immediately. If I even get wind that somebody else is about to break it, I'll break it myself first. This is my goddamn story.'

Backus looked at me and nodded.

'I won't be long.'

After he had left, Walling looked at me and quietly said, 'If that had been me, I would have called your bluff.'

'That was no bluff,' I said. 'That was for real.'

'If that's true, that you'd trade catching the guy who killed your brother for a story, then that makes me feel very sad for you. I'm going to get more coffee.'

She got up then and left me. As I watched her walk back to the concession counter my mind wandered over what she had said and then came to rest on the lines by Poe that I had read the night before and that would not leave my memory.

I dwelt alone
In a world of moan
And my soul was a stagnant tide

22

When I entered the conference room with Backus and Walling, there were few seats in the room without agents in them. The status meeting was set up with agents sitting around the long table and then an outside layer of sitters on chairs lining the walls. Backus pointed to a chair on the outer rim and signaled me to sit. He and Walling then went to the two remaining slots at the center of the table. The chairs had apparently been exclusively reserved for them. I felt a lot of eyes on me as the stranger but I reached down to the floor and fiddled with my computer satchel, acting like I was looking for something so I did not have to meet any of their stares.

Backus had taken the deal. Or rather, whoever he had called had taken the deal. I was along for the ride, with Agent Walling assigned to baby-sit – as she called it. I had written out and signed an agreement stating that I would not write about the investigation until its fruition or disbanding, or in the event of the occurrence of either of the exceptions I had mentioned earlier. I had asked Backus about a photographer joining me and he said that wasn't part of the deal. But he did agree to consider specific requests for photography. It was the best I could do for Glenn.

After Backus and Walling were settled in their seats and interest in me lagged, I looked about. There were a dozen other men and three women in the room, including Walling. Most of the men were in shirtsleeves and appeared to have been at whatever they were doing for a while. There were a lot of Styrofoam cups, a lot of paperwork on laps and on the table. A woman was making her way around the room handing out a sheaf of papers to each agent. I noticed one of the agents was the sharp-faced man I had encountered in Walling's office and then had seen again in the cafeteria. When Walling had gone to refill her coffee cup, I had seen him get up from his meal and go to the food counters to talk to her. I couldn't hear what was said but I could tell she had dismissed him and he didn't seem too happy about it.

'Okay, people,' Backus said. 'Let's get this going if we can. It's been a long day and they're probably only going to get longer from here.'

The murmur of conversation abruptly halted. As smoothly as possible I reached down to my computer bag and slid out a notebook. I opened it to a fresh page and got ready to take notes.

'First of all, a short announcement,' Backus said. 'The new man you see seated against the wall is Jack McEvoy. He is a reporter for the *Rocky*

Mountain News and he plans to be with us until this is over. It is his fine work that resulted in this task force being formed. He discovered our Poet. He has agreed not to write about our investigation until we have the offender in custody. I want all of you to extend him every courtesy. He has the special agent in charge's blessing to be here.'

I felt the eyes on me again and I sat frozen with my notebook and pen in hand, as if I had been caught at a crime scene with blood on my hands.

'If he's not going to write, how come he's got the notebook out?'

I looked toward the familiar voice and saw it was the sharp-faced man from Walling's office who had asked the question.

'He needs to take notes, so that when he does write he has the facts,' Walling said, unexpectedly coming to my defense.

'That'll be the day one of them reports the facts,' the agent threw back at her.

'Gordon, let's not make Mr McEvoy uncomfortable,' Backus said, smiling. 'I trust he will do a good job. The special agent in charge trusts that he will. And, in fact, he has done an excellent job up until now so we are going to give him both the benefit of the doubt and our cooperation.'

I watched the one called Gordon shake his head in dismay, his face darkening. At least I was getting clues right away about whom to steer clear of. The next came when the woman with the handouts passed by me without giving me anything.

'This will be our last group meeting,' Backus said. 'Tomorrow most of us separate and the OC for this investigation will move to Denver, site of the latest case. Rachel will remain case agent and coordinator. Brass and Brad will stay here to do the collating and all that good stuff. I want hard-copy reports from all agents by eighteen hundred eastern to Denver and Quantico every day. For now use the fax of the Denver field office. The number should be on the printout you just received. We'll set up our own lines and we'll get those numbers to you as soon as we do. Now, let's go over what we've got. It's very important that we're all on the same wavelength. I don't want anything to slip through the cracks on this one. We've had enough of that already.'

'We better not screw up,' Gordon said sarcastically. 'We've also got the press watching us.'

A few people laughed but Backus cut it off.

'All right, all right, Gordon, you've made your disagreement loud and clear. I'm going to yield to Brass for a few minutes and she'll go over what we've got so far.'

A woman across the table from Backus cleared her throat. She spread three pages of what looked like computer printouts in front of her on the table and stood up.

'Okay,' she said. 'We have six dead detectives in six states. We also have six unsolved homicides that the detectives had been working individually at the time of their own death. The bottom line is we don't feel comfortable yet making a firm commitment to whether we have one or two offenders out there – or possibly even more, though this seems unlikely. Our hunch, however, is that we are dealing with one but at the moment I don't have a lot backing that up. What we do feel comfortable with is that the deaths of the six detectives are certainly linked and therefore most likely the work of one hand. For the moment our emphasis is on this offender. The one we are calling the Poet. Beyond that, we only have the theory of linkage to the other cases. We'll talk about them later. First, let's start with the detectives. Take a look at the first PVR in your package for a few seconds and then I'll point out some things.'

I looked at everyone studying the handout and felt annoyed at being left out. I decided that after the meeting I would talk to Backus about it. I looked over at Gordon and saw him looking at me. He winked at me and then turned his face to the reports in front of him. I then saw Walling get up and come around the table to my side of the room. She handed me a copy of the printout. I nodded my thanks but she had already headed back to her spot. I noticed that as she walked back she glanced at Gordon and their eyes locked in a long stare.

I looked at the pages in my hands. The first sheet was just an organizational structure with the names of the agents involved and their assignments. There were also the phone and fax numbers for the field offices in Denver, Baltimore, Tampa, Chicago, Dallas and Albuquerque. I ran my eyes down the list of agents and found only one Gordon. Gordon Thorson. I saw that his assignment simply read 'Quantico – Go.'

Next I looked for Brass on the list and guessed easily enough that she was Brasilia Doran, assigned on the sheet as 'victim coordinator/ profiling.' Other assignments to agents were listed. There were handwriting and cryptology assignments but most were just noted as cities of assignment followed by a victim's name. Apparently two BSS agents would go to each city where the Poet had been to coordinate investigations of those cases with agents from the city's field office and local police.

I turned the page to the next sheet, which was the one everybody else was reading.

PRELIMINARY VICTIMOLOGY REPORT
– THE POET, BSS95–17

Vict#

1. Clifford Beltran, Sarasota County Sheriff's Dept., homicide.
   WM, DOB 3-14-34, DOD 4-1-92
   Weapon: S&W 12 gauge shotgun
   one shot – head
   POD: residence. No witness
2. John Brooks, Chicago Police Dept., homicide, Area 3.
   BM, DOB 7-21-54, DOD 10-30-93
   Weapon: service, Glock 19
   two shots, one impact – head
   POD: residence. No witness
3. Garland Petry, Dallas Police Dept., homicide.
   WM, DOB 11-11-51, DOD 3-28-94

Weapon: service, Beretta 38
two shots, two impacts – chest and head
POD: residence. No witness

4. Morris Kotite, Albuquerque Police Dept., homicide.
HM, DOB 9-14-56, DOD 9-24-94
Weapon: service, S&W 38
two shots, one impact – head
POD: car. No witness
5. Sean McEvoy, Denver Police Dept., homicide.
WM, DOB 5-21-61, DOD 2-10-95
Weapon: service, S&W 38
one shot – head
POD: car. No witness

The first thing I noticed was that they didn't have McCafferty on the list yet. He'd be number two. I then realized that the eyes of many of those in the room were falling on me again as people read to the last name and apparently realized who I was. I kept my eyes on the page in front of me, staring at the notes under my brother's name. His life had been reduced to short descriptions and dates. Brasilia Doran finally rescued me from the moment.

'Okay, FYI, these were printed up before the sixth case was confirmed,' she said. 'If you want to put it on your sheet now, it will be between Beltran and Brooks. The name is John McCafferty, a homicide detective with the Baltimore Police Department. We'll get more details later. Anyway, as you can see, not a lot of things are consistent through these cases. The weapons used differ, places of death differ, and we have three whites, one black and one Hispanic as victims . . . The additional case, McCafferty, is a white male, forty-seven years old.

'But there are limited common denominators to the physical scene and evidence. Each victim was a male homicide detective who was killed by a fatal head shot and there were no eyewitnesses to these shootings. From there we get into the two key commonalities that we want to exploit. We have a reference to Edgar Allan Poe in each case. That's one. The second key is that each victim was believed by his colleagues to have been obsessive about a particular homicide case – two of them to the point that they had sought counseling.

'If you turn to the next page . . .'

The sound of pages turning whispered through the room. I could feel a grim fascination settling over everyone. It was a surreal moment for me. I felt like maybe a screenwriter does when he finally sees his movie on the screen. Before, all of this was something hidden in my notebooks and computer and head as part of the far realm of possibility. But here was a room crowded with investigators openly talking about it, looking at printouts, confirming the existence of this horror.

The next page contained the suicide notes, all the quotes from Poe's poems that I had found and written down the night before.

'This is where the cases irrefutably come together,' Doran said. 'Our Poet likes Edgar Allan Poe. We don't know why yet, but it's something we'll be working on here at Quantico while you people go traveling. I am going to defer to Brad for a moment to have him tell you a little about this.'

The agent sitting directly next to Doran stood up and took up the lead. I flipped to the front page of the package and found an Agent Bradley Hazelton listed. Brass and Brad. What a team, I thought. Hazelton, a gangly man with acne-scarred cheeks, poked his glasses back on his nose before speaking.

'Um, what we've got here are that the six quotes in these cases – that's including the Baltimore case – come from three of Poe's poems as well as his own last reported words. We are looking at these to determine if we can get some kind of common fix on what the poems were about and how they may relate to this offender. We're looking for anything there. It seems pretty clear that this is where the offender's playing with us and where he is taking the most risk. I don't think we'd be here today or Mr McEvoy would have found a connection among these cases if our guy didn't decide to quote Edgar Allan Poe. So, then, these poems are his signature. We'll be trying to find out why he chose Poe as opposed to, say, Walt Whitman but I –'

'I'll tell you why,' said an agent sitting at the far end of the table. 'Poe was a morbid asshole and so is our guy.'

A few people laughed.

'Uh, yes, probably that's correct in a general sense,' Hazelton said, oblivious that the comment was made to lighten everyone up. 'Nevertheless, Brass and I will be working on this and if you have any ideas, I'd like to hear them. As for right now, a couple things to throw out. Poe is credited with being the father of detective fiction with the publication of *The Murders in the Rue Morgue,* which is basically a mystery story. So we may have an offender out there who is looking at this as some kind of mystery puzzle. He simply likes to taunt us with his own sort of mystery, by using Poe's words as clues. Also, I've started reading through some of the established criticism and analysis of Poe's work and found something interesting. One of the poems that our guy used is called "The Haunted Palace." This poem was contained within a short story called "The Fall of the House of Usher." I'm sure you've all heard of it or read it. Anyway, the standard analysis of this poem is that while at face value it serves as a description of the house of Usher, it is also a disguised or subconscious description of the story's focal character, Roderick Usher. And that name, you know if you were at last night's briefing, came up in the death of victim number six. I'm sorry, that's Sean McEvoy. He's not just a number.'

He looked over at me and nodded and I nodded back.

'The description in the poem . . . hold on.' Hazelton was looking through his notes, then found what he needed, pushed his glasses back again and continued. 'Okay, we've got, "Banners yellow, glorious, golden; / On its roof did float and flow," and then later on we have, "Along the ramparts plumed and pallid." Okay, and then a few lines later we have mention of "two luminous windows" blah, blah, blah. Anyway, what this translates to as far as a description goes is that of a reclusive white male with blond hair, perhaps long or curly blond hair, and eyeglasses. There's your start on the physical profile.'

There was a roll of laughter through the room and Hazelton seemed to take it personally.

'It's in the books,' he protested. 'I'm serious and I think it's a place to start.'

'Wait a minute, wait a minute,' said a voice from the outer rim. A man stood up so he'd have the attention of the whole room. He was older than most of the other agents and carried the no-nonsense air of a veteran. 'What are we talking about here? Yellow banners flowing – what is this shit? This Poe stuff is great, it'll probably help that kid over there sell a lot of papers, but nothing's convinced me in the last twenty hours that I've been here that there's some mope out there on the street who somehow some way got the drop on five, six veteran dicks and put their own weapons in their mouths. I'm having a hard time seeing it, is what I'm saying. Whaddaya got on that?'

There was the hum of agreeing comments and nods in the room. I heard someone call the agent who had started the ball rolling 'Smitty' and I saw a Chuck Smith listed on the front page of the packet. He was heading to Dallas.

Brass Doran stood up to address the issue.

'We know that's the rub,' she said. 'Methodology is what we are least prepared to discuss at this point. But the Poe correlation is definitive in my judgment and Bob agrees. So what's our alternative? Do we say this is impossible and drop it? No, we act as if other lives may be at stake because they may very well be. The questions you have will, hopefully, be answered as we go. But I agree it is something we need to be considering and it is always healthy to be skeptical. It's a question of control. How does the Poet get control of these men?'

She turned her head and scanned the room. Smitty was silent now.

'Brass,' Backus said. 'Let's go on to the first victims.'

'Okay, folks, next page.'

The page we turned to contained information on the murders that had obsessed the detectives the Poet killed. These were called secondary victims on the report, even though in each city they had actually died first. I noticed that once again the sheet was not up to date. Polly Amherst, the woman whose murder had obsessed John McCafferty in Baltimore, had not yet made the list.

SECONDARY VICTIMOLOGY – PRELIMINARY

1. Gabriel Ortiz, Sarasota, FL
   student
   HM, DOB 6-1-82, DOD 2-14-92
   Ligature strangulation, molestation
   (kapok fiber)
2. Robert Smathers, Chicago
   student
   BM, DOB 8-11-81, DOD 8-15-93

Manual strangulation, mutilation antemortem

3. Althea Granadine, Dallas
   student
   BF, DOB 10-10-84, DOD 1-4-94
   Multiple stabbing, chest, mutilation antemortem
4. Manuela Cortez, Albuquerque, NM
   housekeeper
   HF, DOB 4-11-46, DOD 8-16-94
   Multiple blunt force, mutilation postmortem
   (kapok fiber)
5. Theresa Lofton, Denver, CO
   student, day care employee
   WF, DOB 7-4-75, DOD 12-16-94
   Ligature strangulation, mutilation postmortem
   (kapok fiber)

'Okay, once again we are missing one,' Doran said. 'Baltimore. I understand the case was not a child, but a teacher. Polly Amherst. Ligature strangulation and postmortem mutilation.'

She waited a beat in case people were writing notes.

'We are still in the process of having files and data faxed in on these cases,' she continued. 'This was just put together for the meeting. But, preliminarily, what we are looking at as far as these secondary cases go is a commonality involving children. Three victims were children, two worked directly with children and the last one, Manuela Cortez, was a housekeeper who was abducted and murdered at some point while going to the school her employer's children attended to walk them home. The extrapolation is that the intended targets in this chain were children but in half the cases perhaps something went wrong, the stalking pattern was somehow interrupted by the adult victims, and they were eliminated.'

'What is to be made from the mutilation?' an agent on the outer rim asked. 'Some of it's post and with the kids . . . it wasn't.'

'We're not sure, but a guess at this time is that it might be part of his cloaking. By using differing methodology and pathology he has been able to camouflage himself. On this page these cases may look similar but the more complete the analysis the more different they are. It is as if six different men with differing pathologies killed these victims. In fact, all the cases were submitted on VICAP questionnaires by the local agencies but none drew matches to the others. Remember, the questionnaire is now up to eighteen pages.

'Bottom line, I think this offender's read up on us. I think he knew how to do things differently enough with each of these victims so that our trusty computer never scored a match. The only mistake he made was the kapok fibers. That is how we have him.'

An agent on the outer rim raised his hand and Doran nodded at him.

'If there were three incidents of kapok fiber being recovered, why didn't we get a match on the VICAP computer if all cases were entered like you said?'

'Human error. In the first case, the Ortiz boy, kapok was indigenous to the area and dismissed. It wasn't put on the questionnaire. In the Albuquerque case, the fibers were not identified until after a VICAP survey was submitted. Once they were identified as kapok, the survey was not updated. An oversight. We missed the match. We only got that from the field office today. Only in the Denver case was the kapok seen as significant enough to include on the VICAP request.'

There was a groan from several of the agents and I felt my own heart sink a bit. The possibility of confirming that there was a serial killer at work as early as the Albuquerque case had been missed. What if it hadn't been missed, I wondered. Maybe Sean would be alive.

'That brings us to the big question,' Doran said. 'How many killers have we got? One who does the first string and another who does the detectives? Or just one? One who does them all. For the moment, based primarily on the logistical improbabilities associated with two killers, we are pursuing a theory of linkage. Our assumption is that in each city the two deaths are linked.'

'What's the pathology?' Smitty asked.

'We're only guessing now. The obvious one is that he sees killing the detective as a way of covering his tracks, ensuring his escape. But we have another theory as well. That is that the first homicide was committed by the offender in order to draw a homicide detective into the frame. In other words, the first kill is bait, presented in such a horrific fashion as to attract a homicide detective's obsession. We are assuming that the Poet then stalked each one of these officers and learned their habits and routines. That enabled him to get close and carry out the eventual murder without detection.'

This silenced the room. I got the feeling that many of the agents, though surely veterans of numerous investigations of serial killings, had never before encountered a predator like the one they were calling the Poet.

'Of course,' Brass said, 'all we have is theory for the time being . . .'

Backus stood up.

'Thank you, Brass,' he said, then addressing the room added, 'Quickly now, because I want to do some profiling and get this wrapped up, Gordon, you had something for us.'

'Yes, real quick,' Thorson said, standing up and moving to an easel with a large drawing pad on it. 'The map in your package is outdated because of the Baltimore connection. So if I can have your attention up here for a moment.'

He quickly drew the outline of the United States with a thick black marker. Then, with a red marker, he began to draw the Poet's trail. Starting in Florida, which he had drawn proportionately small compared to the rest of the country, the line went up to Baltimore then over to Chicago then down to Dallas then up to Albuquerque and finally up further to Denver. He picked up the black marker again and wrote the dates of the killings in each of the cities.

'It's pretty self-explanatory,' Thorson said. 'Our man is heading west and he's obviously pissed off at homicide cops about something.'

He raised his hand and waved it over the western half of the country he had drawn.

'We'll look for the next hits out here unless we get lucky and get him first.'

Looking at the terminus of the red line Thorson had drawn gave me a strange feeling about what was ahead. Where was the Poet? Who was next?

'Why don't we just let him get to California, so he can be among his own kind? End of problem.'

Everyone laughed at the joke from one of the agents seated in the outer rim. The humor emboldened Hazelton.

'Hey, Gordo,' he said, reaching back to the easel and tapping a pencil on the small rendering of Florida. 'I hope this map wasn't some kind of Freudian slip on your part.'

That brought the loudest laughter of the meeting and Thorson's face reddened, though he smiled at the joke at his expense. I saw Rachel Walling's face light up with delight.

'Very funny, Hazel,' Thorson loudly retorted. 'Why don't you go back to analyzing the poems. You're good at that.'

The laughter dried up quickly and I suspected that Thorson had taunted Hazelton with a barb that was more personal than witty.

'Okay, if I can continue,' Thorson said, 'FYI, tonight we'll be alerting all the FOs, particularly in the West, to be on watch for something like this. It would help us a lot if we could get an early notice on the next one and get our lab into one of the scenes. We'll have a go team ready. But right now we are relying on the locals for everything. Bob?'

Backus cleared his throat to continue the discussion.

'If nobody has anything else, we come to profiling. What can we say about this offender? I would like to put something on the alert Gordon sends out.'

Then came a procession of thrown-out observations, a lot of them free-form non sequiturs, some of them even bringing laughter. I could see there was a lot of camaraderie among the agents. There was also some strife, as exhibited by the play between Thorson and Walling and then Thorson and Hazelton. Nevertheless, I got the feeling that these people had sat around the table in this room doing this before. Sadly, many times before.

The profile that emerged would be of small use in catching the Poet. The generalities the agents threw into the ring were primarily interior descriptions. Anger. Isolation. Above-average education and intelligence. How do you identify these things among the masses, I thought. No chance.

Occasionally, Backus would step in and throw out a question to get the discussion back on course.

'If you subscribe to Brass's last theory, why homicide cops?'

'You answer that and you've got him in a box. That's the mystery. This poetry stuff is the diversion.'

'Rich or poor?'

'He's got money. He has to. Wherever he goes, he's not staying long. No job – killing is his job.'

'He's gotta have a bank account or rich parents, something. And he's got wheels and he needs money to put gas in the tank.'

The session went on for another twenty minutes with Doran taking notes for the preliminary profile. Then Backus ended it and told everyone to take the rest of the night off before traveling in the morning.

As the meeting broke up, a few people came up to me and introduced themselves, expressed condolences for my brother and admiration for my investigation. But it was only a few and they included Hazelton and Doran. After a few minutes of this I was left alone and was looking about for Walling when Gordon Thorson approached. He held his hand out and after hesitating, I shook it.

'Didn't mean to give you a hard time,' he said smiling warmly.

'That's okay. It was fine.'

He had a tight grip and after the standard two-second shake I tried to pull away but he wouldn't let go. Instead, he pulled my hand toward him and leaned forward so that only I would hear what he had to say next.

'It's good that your brother isn't around to see this,' he whispered. 'If I did what you did to get on this case, I'd be ashamed. I couldn't live with myself.'

He straightened up, always continuing the smile. I just looked at him and inexplicably nodded. He dropped my hand and stepped away. I felt humiliated in that I had not defended myself. I had stupidly just nodded my head.

'What was that about?'

I turned. It was Rachel Walling.

'Uh, nothing. He just . . . nothing.'

'Whatever he said, forget it. He can be an asshole.'

I nodded.

'Yeah, I was getting that idea.'

'C'mon, let's go back to the Boardroom. I'm starved.'

In the hallway she told me the travel plans.

'We're leaving early tomorrow. It's better if you stay here tonight instead of going all the way back to the Hilton. The visitor dorms mostly clear out on Fridays. We can put you in one of those and have the Hilton just clear your room and send your stuff to Denver. Will that be a problem?'

'Uh, no. I guess . . .'

I was still thinking about Thorson.

'Fuck him.'

'What?'

'That guy, Thorson, he *is* an asshole.'

'Forget about him. We're leaving tomorrow and he's staying here. What about the Hilton?'

'Yeah, fine. I've got my computer and everything else that's important already with me.'

'I'll see about getting you a fresh shirt in the morning.'

'Oh, my car. I've got a rental in the Hilton's garage.'

'Where are the keys?'

I pulled them out of my pocket.

'Give them to me. We'll take care of it.'

23

In the early hours, when dawn was still only a hint around the curtains, Gladden moved about Darlene's apartment, too nervous to sleep, too excited to want to. He paced through the small rooms, thinking, planning, waiting. He looked in on Darlene in the bedroom, watched her on the bed for a few moments and then returned to the living room.

Unframed posters from old porno movies were taped to the walls and the place was filled with bric-a-brac souvenirs of a worthless life. There was a nicotine veneer on everything. Gladden was a smoker but still found it disgusting. The place was a mess.

He paused in front of one of the posters, from a film called *Inside Darlene.* She had told him she'd been a star in the early eighties before video revolutionized the business and she started looking old, the wear and tear of the life showing around her eyes and mouth. She'd pointed with a wistful smile to the posters where the air-brushed photos showed her body and face smooth and unlined. She was billed simply as Darlene. No last name needed. He wondered what it was like living in a place where the images of your former glorious self mocked your present self from the walls.

He turned away and noticed her purse on the card table in the dining room and looked through it. It was full of makeup, mostly, and empty cigarette packages and matchbooks. There was a small spray can for repelling attackers and her wallet. She had seven dollars. He looked at her license and discovered for the first time what her full name was.

'Darlene Kugel,' he said out loud. 'Pleased to meet you.'

He took the money and put everything else back in the purse. Seven dollars wasn't much but it was seven dollars. The man at the digiTime dealership had made him pay in advance to order the camera. Gladden was now down to a few hundred dollars and he figured seven more couldn't hurt.

He put his money worries aside and began to pace again. He had a problem of timing. The camera had to be shipped from New York. It wouldn't be in until Wednesday. Five more days. He knew that to be safe he'd have to wait it out right here in Darlene's apartment. And he knew he could do it.

He decided to make a list for the store. Darlene's shelves were almost empty except for tuna fish and he hated that shit. He'd have to go out, get supplies, and then dig in until Wednesday. He wouldn't need much. Spring water – Darlene apparently drank tap water. Also Fruit Loops, maybe some Chef Boyardee.

He heard a car drive by outside. He moved toward the door to listen and finally he heard the sound he had been waiting for. The newspaper hitting the ground. Darlene had told him the tenant in the apartment next door got the paper. Gladden was proud of himself for having thought to ask. He went to the window now and peered through the blinds to the street. Dawn was coming up gray and misty. He saw no activity outside.

After turning the two locks, Gladden opened the door and stepped out into the crisp morning air. He looked around and saw the folded newspaper on the sidewalk in front of the apartment next door. No lights were on behind the apartment's doors. Gladden quickly walked to the newspaper, picked it up and returned to the apartment he had come from.

On the couch he quickly went to the Metro section of the paper and flipped through the eight pages. There was no story. Nothing on the maid. He tossed the section aside and picked up the front section.

He turned the section over and there it was at last, his own photo at the bottom right corner of the front page. It was the mug shot from the Santa Monica arrest. He pulled his eyes away from his own image and started reading the story. He was overjoyed. He had made the front page again. After so many years. His face flushed as he read.

MOTEL MURDER SUSPECT ESCAPED THE LAW IN FLORIDA

By Keisha Russell, Times Staff Writer

A Florida man who authorities said escaped justice as a child molester in Florida has been identified as the suspect in the brutal mutilation murder of a Hollywood motel maid, Los Angeles police said Friday.

William Gladden, 29, is being sought in the death of Evangeline Crowder, whose body was found in Gladden's room at the Hollywood Star Motel. The 19-year-old victim's body had been cut into pieces and placed in three drawers of a bureau in the room.

The body was discovered after Gladden checked out of the motel. A motel employee who was looking for the missing maid entered the room and saw blood seeping from the bureau, police said. Crowder was the mother of an infant boy.

Gladden was registered at the hotel under the name Bryce Kidder. But police said that analysis of a fingerprint found in the room identified the suspect as Gladden.

Gladden was sentenced to 70 years in prison after a highly publicized child molestation trial in Tampa, Fla., seven years ago.

However, after serving only two years in prison, he was released when his conviction was overturned on appeal. Key evidence – photos of nude children – was ruled illegally obtained by authorities. After the legal setback, prosecutors allowed Gladden to plead guilty to lesser charges. He was released on probation for time already served in prison.

In another irony, police have also learned that Gladden was arrested in Santa Monica three days before the motel murder was discovered. He was taken into custody on a variety of minor charges stemming from a complaint that he was taking photos of children being washed at beach showers and at the carousel on the pier. However, he was arraigned and released on bail before his true identity was learned.

– Continued, page 14A

Gladden had to open the section and follow the story to an inside page. There he saw another photograph of himself staring out at the reader. This was of the thin-faced and red-haired twenty-one-year-old he had been before the persecution had begun in Florida. And there was another story about him as well. He quickly finished reading the first story.

– Continued from 1A

Police said they have not determined a motive for Crowder's slaying. Though the motel room where Gladden had stayed for nearly a week had been meticulously wiped clean of fingerprints, LAPD detective Ed Thomas said Gladden made one mistake that led to his identification. That was leaving a single fingerprint behind on the underside of the toilet's flush handle.

'It was a lucky break,' Thomas said. 'That one print was all we needed.'

The print was fed into the department's Automated Fingerprint Identification System, part of a nationwide computer network of fingerprint data. A match was found to Gladden's fingerprints, which were on file with the Florida Department of Law Enforcement computer.

According to Thomas, Gladden has been wanted on probation violation for nearly four years. The violation was filed when he stopped regular visits to a probation officer in Florida and disappeared.

In the Santa Monica case, detectives arrested Gladden on Sunday after a chase from the carousel at the pier where they observed him watching young children on the popular ride.

While attempting to run from police, he threw a trash can off the pier into the bay. He was finally captured in a restaurant on the Third Street Promenade.

Gladden, who had used the name Harold Brisbane when arrested, was charged with pollution of public waterways, vandalism of city property and evading a police officer. However, the district attorney's office declined to file any charges relating to his alleged photographing of children, citing insufficient evidence of a crime.

SMPD detective Constance Delpy said she and her partner began watching the carousel ride after receiving a complaint from an employee who had described Gladden as loitering near children and taking pictures out on the beach of nude children being washed at the showers by their parents.

Though Gladden was fingerprinted upon his arrest, Santa Monica does not have its own fingerprint computer and relies on use of a Department of Justice computer and other departments, including the LAPD, to run prints on the AFIS network. The process usually takes days because departments run their own prints as priorities.

In this case, the Santa Monica prints taken of the man originally identified as Brisbane were not run by the LAPD until Tuesday. By then, Gladden – who had spent Sunday night in the county jail – had bailed out by posting a $50,000 bond.

The LAPD then also identified Gladden late Thursday through the print taken from the motel room.

Detectives involved in the two cases were left to wonder about the sequence of events and how they allegedly took a murderous turn.

'There is always second-guessing when things like this happen,' said Delpy of the SMPD Exploited Child Unit. 'What could we have done better to keep him locked up? I don't know. Sometimes you win and sometimes you lose.'

Thomas said the real crime was in Florida where Gladden was allowed to go free.

'Here you have a man, an obvious pedophile, and the system lets him go,' Thomas said. 'When the system doesn't work, it always seems to be a case like this, where somebody innocent pays the price.'

Gladden quickly went on to the other story. He felt a weird sense of elation as he read about himself. He reveled in the glory of it.

SUSPECT DID AN 'END RUN AROUND JUSTICE' IN FLORIDA
By Keisha Russell, Times Staff Writer

A gifted jailhouse lawyer, according to authorities, William Gladden used his prison-learned wiles to subvert the justice system and then disappear – until this week.

Gladden worked at the Little Ducks Childcare Center in Tampa eight years ago when he was arrested and charged with molesting as many as 11 children over a three-year period.

The arrest spawned a highly publicized trial resulting in his conviction on twenty-eight of the charges two years later. By all accounts, the key evidence leading to the convictions was a cache of Polaroid pictures of nine of the young victims. In the photos, the children were seen in various stages of undress in a closet at the now defunct childcare center.

The telling thing about the pictures, however, was not that some of the children were nude, but the looks on their faces, according to Charles Hounchell, the former Hillsborough County prosecutor who was assigned to the case.

'All the kids were scared,' Hounchell said Friday in a telephone interview from Tampa where he is now in private practice. 'These kids didn't like what was being done and it showed. It really went to the truth of the case. What their faces said in the photos matched the things they told the counselors.'

But at trial, the photos were more important than the counselors and what the children had told them. Despite objections from Gladden that the photos had been discovered during an illegal search of his apartment by a police officer whose son was one of the alleged molestation victims, the judge allowed the photos into evidence.

Jurors said afterward that they relied almost exclusively on the photos to convict Gladden because the two counselors who dealt with the children had been discredited by the attorney representing Gladden for their alleged methods of leading the children into voicing accusations against Gladden.

After his conviction, Gladden was sentenced to 70 years' imprisonment to be served at the Union Correctional Institute at Raiford.

In the prison, Gladden, who already had a degree in English literature, studied poetry, psychology and the law. It appears that it is in the law that he excelled. The convicted molester quickly learned the skills of a jailhouse lawyer, according to Hounchell, and helped other inmates with appellate briefs while composing his own.

Among his more celebrated 'clients' in the prison's sexual offender ward were Donel Forks, the so-called pillowcase rapist of Orlando, former Miami surfing champion Alan Jannine and Las Vegas stage hypnotist Horace Gomble. All three are serving time for multiple rape convictions and Gladden was unsuccessful in his attempts to win them freedom or new trials with appeals he wrote while serving time with them.

But within a year of his imprisonment, Hounchell said, Gladden filed a thoroughly researched appeal of his own conviction which challenged once again the search that led to the discovery of the incriminating photos.

Hounchell explained that Raymond Gomez, the officer who found the photos, had gone to Gladden's home in a rage after his five-year-old son revealed that he had been molested by a man who worked at the boy's childcare center.

Receiving no answer after knocking, the off-duty officer said he found the door unlocked and entered. Gomez later testified in a hearing on the matter that he found the photos spread out on a bedspread. He quickly extricated himself from the house and reported his knowledge to detectives who then obtained a search warrant.

Gladden was arrested after the detectives went back later that day with the warrant and found the photos hidden in a closet. Gladden maintained at trial that the door was not unlocked when he had left his apartment and the photos were not on display. Regardless of whether the door was unlocked and the photos left out, he argued, the search by Gomez was a clear breach of his constitutional rights to protection from unlawful search and seizure.

However, the trial judge ruled that Gomez was acting as a father, not a police officer, when he entered the apartment. The accidental discovery of the key evidence was therefore not a breach of the Constitution.

An appeals court later sided with Gladden, saying that Gomez had knowledge through his police training of search and seizure laws and should have known better than to enter the premises without authority. The Florida Supreme Court later refused to reverse the appeals court, clearing the way for a new trial without the use of the photos as evidence.

Faced with the difficult task of winning a case without key evidence the first jury said was vital, authorities allowed Gladden to plead guilty to one count of lewd behavior with a child.

The maximum sentence for such a crime is five years in prison and five years of consecutive probation. By that point, Gladden had served 33 months in prison and had earned an equal amount in good-behavior gain time. At his sentencing, he received the maximum penalty but still walked out of court a free man on probation.

'It was an end run around justice,' Hounchell, the prosecutor, recalled. 'We knew he did it but we couldn't use the evidence we had in our hands. After that sentencing, it was hard for me to look at those parents and their children. Because I knew this guy would be out there and that he'd probably want to do it again.'

Within a year of his release, Gladden disappeared and a warrant was issued for probation violation. He resurfaced this week in southern California with what authorities here called deadly consequences.

Gladden read the story completely through a second time. He was fascinated by its thoroughness and the credit it gave him. He also liked how, if you read between the lines, it questioned the story of the cop Gomez. That liar, Gladden thought. He broke in and he ruined the case. Served him right. He was almost tempted to pick up the phone and call the reporter to thank her for the story but decided against it. Too risky. He thought of Hounchell, the young prosecutor.

'End run,' he said aloud. Then he yelled it out, 'End run!'

His mind raced and filled with joy. There was so much they didn't know and already he was on the front page. They would certainly learn soon. They would know. His moment of glory was coming. Soon now.

Gladden got up and went into the bedroom to prepare to go to the store. He thought it would be best to go early. He looked at Darlene again. Bending over the bed he touched her wrist and tried to lift her arm. Full rigor mortis had set in. He looked at her face. The jaw muscles were already contracting, pulling her lips back into an ugly grin. Her eyes appeared to be staring at their own reflection in the mirror over the bed.

He reached over and pulled the wig off her head. Her real hair was reddish brown and short, unattractive. He noticed some of the blood had gotten on the lower fringe of blond curls and he took the wig into the bathroom to wash it off and to get himself ready. Afterward, he returned to the bedroom and gathered the things from the closet he would need to go to the store. Glancing back at the body as he was leaving the room, Gladden realized he had never asked her what the tattoo was supposed to be. Now it was too late.

Before closing the door and leaving the room he turned the air conditioner on high. In the living room, as he changed clothes, he made a mental note to pick up some more incense at the store. He decided he would use the seven dollars he had taken from her purse. She was creating the problem, he thought, she should pay to fix it.

24

Saturday morning we took a helicopter from Quantico to National and boarded a small bureau jet bound for Colorado. It was where my brother had died. It was where the freshest trail was. It was me, Backus, Walling and a forensic specialist named Thompson I recognized from the meeting the evening before.

Beneath my jacket I was wearing a light blue pullover shirt with the FBI seal on the left breast. Walling had knocked on the door of my dorm that morning and presented it to me with a smile. It was a nice gesture but I couldn't wait to get to Denver so I could change into my own clothes. Still, it beat wearing the same shirt I had already worn for two days.

The ride was smooth. I sat in the back, three rows behind Backus and Walling. Thompson sat behind them. I passed the time by reading the biographical note on Poe in the book I had bought and typing notes into my laptop.

About halfway across the country, Rachel got up from her spot and came back to visit me. She'd dressed in jeans, a green corduroy shirt and black hiking boots. As she moved into the seat next to me she hooked her hair back behind her ear and it helped frame her face. She was beautiful and I realized that in less than twenty-four hours I had gone from hating her to wanting her.

'What're you thinking about all alone back here?'

'Nothing much. My brother, I guess. If we get this guy I guess maybe I'll find out how it happened. It's still hard to believe.'

'Were you close to him?'

'Most of the time.' I didn't have to think about it. 'But in the last few months, no . . . It had happened before. It was kind of cyclical. We'd get along and then we'd get sick of each other.'

'Was he older or younger?'

'Older.'

'How much older?'

'Three minutes. We were twins.'

'I didn't know.'

I nodded and she frowned as if the thought that we had been twins made the loss all the more hurtful. Maybe it had.

'I didn't catch that in the reports.'

'Probably not important.'

'Well, it helps explains why you . . . I've always wondered about twins.'

'You mean like did I get a psychic message from him the night he was killed? The answer is no. That kind of stuff never happened with us. Or, if it did, I never recognized it and he never said anything about it.'

She nodded and I looked back out the window for a few seconds. I felt good being with her, despite the rocky start of the day before. But I was beginning to suspect that Rachel Walling could put her worst enemy at ease.

I tried asking her questions about herself to turn it around. She mentioned the marriage I already knew about from Warren but she didn't say much about her former husband. She said she had gone to Georgetown to study psychology and was recruited in her last year by the bureau. After becoming an agent in the New York field office, she had gone back to school at night at Columbia for a law degree. She freely admitted that being a woman plus having a law degree put her on the bureau's fast track. The BSS was a plum assignment.

'Your folks must be very proud of you,' I said.

She shook her head.

'No?'

'My mother left when I was young. I haven't seen her in a long time. She doesn't know anything about me.'

'Your father?'

'My dad died when I was very young.'

I knew I had strayed beyond the bounds of routine conversation. But my instinct as a journalist was always to ask the next question, the one they don't expect. I also sensed that she wanted to say more but wouldn't unless I asked.

'What happened?'

'He was a policeman. We lived in Baltimore. He killed himself.'

'Oh, man. Rachel, I'm sorry. I shouldn't have –'

'No, it's okay. I wanted you to know that. I think it has everything to do with what I am and what I'm doing. Maybe it's that way with your brother and this story. That's why I wanted to tell you that if I was harsh with you yesterday, I'm sorry.'

'Don't worry about it.'

'Thanks.'

We were silent for a few moments but I sensed the subject wasn't closed yet.

'The suicide study with the foundation, is that . . . ?'

'Yes, that's why I started it.'

Another void of silence followed but I was not uncomfortable and I don't think she was either. Eventually she got up and went to a storage area at the back of the cabin and got everybody sodas. When Backus was through joking about what a fine stewardess she made she sat down with me again. As the conversation began again I tried to move the subject away from the memory of her father.

'Do you ever regret not being a practicing shrink?' I asked. 'Isn't that what you first went to school for?'

'Not at all. This is more satisfying. I've probably had more firsthand experience with sociopaths than most shrinks have in a lifetime.'

'And that's only the agents you work with.'

Her laugh came easily.

'Boy, if you only knew.'

Maybe it was only the fact that she was a woman, but I sensed she was different from the other agents I had known and dealt with over the years. She wasn't as sharp around the edges. She was a listener, not a teller, a thinker, not a reactor. I was beginning to feel I could tell her what I was thinking at any given time and not worry about the consequences.

'Like Thorson,' I said. 'He seems like he's got his top screwed on a little too tight.'

'Definitely,' she said and then an uneasy smile and shake of the head followed.

'What's with him, anyway?'

'He's angry.'

'At what?'

'A lot of things. He's got a lot of baggage. Including me. He was my husband.'

It didn't really surprise me. There had been the visible tension between them. My initial impression of Thorson was that he could be poster boy for the Men Are Pigs Society. No wonder Walling had a dim view of the other side.

'Sorry I brought him up, then,' I said. 'I'm batting a thousand here.'

She smiled.

'That's okay. He leaves that impression on a lot of people.'

'Must be hard to have to work with him. How come you're both in the same unit?'

'We're not exactly. He's in Critical Incident Response. I float between Behavioral Science and CIR. We only have to work together at times like these. We used to be partners before we married. We both worked on the VICAP program and spent a lot of time on the road together. Then we just came apart.'

She drank some of her Coke and I didn't ask any more questions. I couldn't ask any of the right ones so I decided to cool it for a while. But she continued on unbidden.

'When we divorced I left the VICAP team, started handling mostly BSS research projects, profiles and an occasional case. He switched over to Critical Response. But we still have our little meetings in the cafeteria and on cases like this.'

'Then why don't you transfer all the way out?'

'Because, like I said, assignment to the national center is a plum. I don't want to leave and neither does he. It's either that or he just stays around to spite me. Bob Backus talked to us once and said he thought it would be better if one of us transferred out, but neither of us will blink. They can't move Gordon because he's got seniority. He's been there since the center started. If they move me the unit loses one of only three females and they know I'll make a beef about it.'

'What could you do?'

'Just say I'm being moved because I'm the woman. Maybe talk to the *Post.* The center is one of the bureau's bright spots. When we come to town to help the local cops we're heroes, Jack. The media laps it up and the bureau doesn't want to dim that. So Gordon and I get to keep making dirty faces at each other across the table.'

The plane pushed over into a descent and through the window I could look up ahead. On the far west horizon were the familiar Rockies. We were almost there.

'Were you involved in the interviews of Bundy and Manson, people like that?'

I had heard or read somewhere about the BSS project to interview all known serial rapists and killers in prisons across the country. From the interviews came the psychological data bank the BSS used to create profiles of other killers. The interview project had taken years and I remembered something about it having taken its toll on the agents who faced these men.

'That was a trip,' she said. 'Me, Gordon, Bob, we were all part of that. I still get a letter from Charlie every now and then. Usually around Christmas. As a criminal he was most effective in manipulation of his female followers. So I think he thinks that if he is going to get anybody to sympathize with him at the bureau, it will be a woman. Me.'

I saw the logic and nodded.

'And the rapists,' she said. 'A lot of the same pathology as the killers. They were some sweet guys, I tell you. I could just feel them sizing me up when I'd go in. I could tell they were trying to figure out how much time they'd have before the guard could get in. You know, whether they could take me before help came in. It really showed their pathology. They only thought in terms of help coming to save me, not that I might be able to defend myself. Save myself. They simply looked at all women as victims. As prey.'

'You mean you talked to these people alone? No separation?'

'The interviews were informal, usually in a lawyer room. No separation but usually a hack hole. The protocol –'

'Hack hole?'

'A window one of the guards could watch through. The protocol called for two agents in all the interviews but in practice there were just too many of these guys. So most of the time, we'd go to a prison and split up. It was quicker that way. The interview rooms were always monitored but every now and then I'd get this creepy chill from some of those guys. Like I was alone. But I couldn't look up to see if the hack was watching because then the subject would look up and if he saw the hack wasn't looking, then . . . you know.'

'Shit.'

'Well, for some of the more violent offenders, my partner and I would do it together. Gordon or Bob or whoever was with me. But it was always faster when we split up and did separate interviews.'

I imagined that if you spent a couple years doing those interviews you'd come away with some psychological baggage of your own. I wondered if that was what she had meant when she had talked about her marriage to Thorson.

'Did you wear the same clothes?' she asked.

'What?'

'You and your brother. You know, like you see some twins do.'

'Oh, the matching stuff. No, thank God. My parents never pulled any of that with us.'

'So who was the black sheep of the family? You or him?'

'Me, definitely. Sean was the saint and I was the sinner.'

'And what are your sins?'

I looked at her.

'Too many to recount here.'

'Really? Then what was the most saintly thing he ever did?'

As the smile dropped off my face at the memory that would be her answer, the plane banked sharply to the left, came out of it and started to climb. Rachel immediately forgot her question and leaned into the aisle so she could look toward the front. Presently I saw Backus coming down the aisle, his hands grabbing the bulkhead for balance. He signaled to Thompson to follow him and they both made their way back to us.

'What is it?' Rachel asked.

'We're diverting,' Backus said. 'I just got a call from Quantico. This morning the field office in Phoenix responded to our alert. One week ago a homicide detective was found dead in his home. It was supposed to be a suicide but something was wrong. They've ruled it a homicide. Looks like the Poet made a mistake.'

'Phoenix?'

'Yes, the freshest trail.' He looked at his watch. 'And we have to hurry. He's to be buried in four hours and I want to have a look at the body first.'

25

Two government cars and four agents from the field office met us after the jet landed at Sky Harbor International in Phoenix. It was a warm day, compared to where we had come from, and we took our jackets off and carried them with our computer bags and overnighters. Thompson also carried a toolbox which contained his equipment. I rode with Walling and two agents named Matuzak and Mize, white guys who looked like they had less than ten years' experience combined. It was clear by their deferential treatment of Walling that they held the BSS unit in high esteem. They had either been briefed on the fact that I was a reporter or judged by my beard and hair that I was not an agent despite the FBI seal on my shirt. They paid little attention to me.

'Where are we going?' Walling asked as our gray nondescript Ford followed the gray nondescript Ford carrying Backus and Thompson out of the airport.

'Scottsdale Funeral Home,' Mize said. He was in the front passenger seat while Matuzak drove. He looked at his watch. 'Funeral is at two. Your man is probably going to have less than a half hour with the body before they'll have to suit him up and put him in the box for the show.'

'Was it open casket?'

'Yeah, last night,' Matuzak said. 'He's already been embalmed and made up. I don't know what you're expecting.'

'We're not expecting anything. We just want to look. I assume Agent Backus is being briefed up ahead of us. Do you two care to fill us in?'

'*That's* Robert Backus?' Mize said. 'He looks so young.'

'Robert Backus Junior.'

'Oh.' Mize made a face that seemed to show that he understood why such a young man was running the show. 'Figures.'

'You don't know what you're talking about,' Rachel said. 'He's got the name but he's also the hardest-working and most thorough agent I've ever worked with. He earned the position he has. It probably would have been easier for him, in fact, if he had a name like Mize. Now can one of you fill us in on what's going on?'

I saw Matuzak study her in the mirror. He then looked over at me and Rachel registered this.

'He's fine,' she said. 'He's got approval from the top to be here. He knows everything we do. You have a problem with that?'

'Not if you don't,' Matuzak said. 'John, you tell it.'

Mize cleared his throat.

'Not a lot to fill in. We don't have a lot because we weren't invited in. But what we do know is they found this guy, name's William Orsulak, they found him in his house on Monday. Homicide cop. They figured he'd been dead at least three days. He was off Friday 'cause of comp time and the last anybody remembered seeing him was Thursday night at a bar they all go to.'

'Who found him?'

'Somebody from the squad when he didn't show Monday. He was divorced, lived alone. Anyway, they apparently spent all week on the fence. You know, suicide or murder? Eventually, they went with murder. That was yesterday. Apparently there were too many problems with the suicide.'

'What do you know about the scene?'

'I hate to tell you this Agent Walling, but you'd learn just as much as me by picking up one of the local papers. Like I said, Phoenix police didn't invite us to the dance so we don't know what they have. After we got the wire from Quantico this morning, Jamie Fox, he's up in the lead car with Agent Backus, took a look at it while working a little OT doing paperwork. It seemed to fit with what you people were working on and he made the call. Then me and Bob got called out, but like I said, we don't know what's what for sure.'

'Fine.' She sounded put out. I knew she wanted to be up in the lead car. 'I'm sure we'll get it at the funeral home. What about the locals?'

'They're meeting us.'

We parked in the back of the Scottsdale Funeral Home on Camelback Road. The lot was already crowded, though the funeral was still two hours away. There were several men milling about or leaning on cars. Detectives. I could tell. Probably waiting to hear what the FBI had to say. I saw one TV truck with the dish on top parked at the far end of the lot.

Walling and I got out and joined Backus and Thompson and we were led to a rear door of the mortuary. Inside we stepped into a large room with white tile running up to the ceiling. There were two stainless-steel tables for bodies in the center with overhead spray hoses, and stainless-steel counters and equipment against three walls. A group of five men were in the room and as they moved to greet us I could see the body on the far table. I assumed it to be Orsulak, though there was no obvious sign of damage from a gunshot to the head. The body was naked and someone had taken a yard-long length of paper towel from the roll on the counter and placed it across the dead cop's waist to cover the genitals. The suit Orsulak would wear to the grave was on a hanger on a hook on the far wall.

Handshakes were passed all around between us and the living cops. Thompson was directed to the body and he carried his case over and went to work examining it.

'I don't think you'll get anything we don't already have,' said the one called Grayson, who was in charge of the investigation for the locals. He was a stocky man with an assured and good-natured demeanor. He was deeply tanned, as were the other locals.

'We don't, either,' said Walling, quick with the politically correct response. 'You've been over him. Now he's been washed and readied.'

'But we need to go through the motions,' Backus said.

'Why don't you folks tell us what you're working?' Grayson asked. 'Maybe we can make some sense out of this.'

'Fair enough,' Backus said.

As Backus gave an abbreviated report on the Poet investigation, I watched Thompson do his work. He was at home with the body, not timid about touching, probing, squeezing. He spent a good amount of time running gloved fingers through the dead man's gray-white hair and then carefully brushed it back in place with a comb from his own pocket. He then made a careful study of the mouth and throat, using a lighted magnifying glass. At one point he put the magnifier aside and pulled a camera from the toolbox. He took a photo of the throat, the flash drawing the attention of the cops assembled in the room.

'Just documentary photos, gentlemen,' Thompson said, not even looking up from his work.

Next he began studying the extremities of the body, first the right arm and hand, then the left. He used the magnifier again when he studied the left palm and fingers. Then he took two photos of the palm and two of the index finger. The cops in the room didn't seem to make much of this, seemingly accepting his earlier statement that the photos were routine. But because I had noticed that he had not taken photos of the right hand, I knew he had found something of possible significance on the left. Thompson returned the camera to the box after placing the four new Polaroids it had spit out on the counter. He then continued his search of the body but took no more photos. He interrupted Backus to ask for help in turning the body over, then the head-to-foot search began again. I could see a patch of a dark, waxy material in the back of the dead man's head and I assumed this to be where the exit wound was. Thompson didn't bother taking a Polaroid of this.

Thompson finished with the body at about the same time Backus finished his briefing and I wondered if it hadn't been planned that way.

'Anything?' Backus asked.

'Nothing of note, I don't think,' Thompson said. 'I'd like to review the autopsy if I could. Was the report brought along?'

'As requested,' Grayson said. 'Here's a copy of everything.'

He handed a file to him and Thompson stepped back with it to a counter where he opened it and began scanning pages.

'So, I've told you what I know, gentlemen,' Backus said. 'Now I'd like to hear what it was about this case that dissuaded you from calling it suicide.'

'Well, I don't think I was entirely dissuaded until I heard your story,' Grayson said. 'Now I think this Poet fucker – excuse me, Agent Walling – is our guy. Anyway, we raised the question and then decided to go with a classification of homicide because of three reasons. One, when we found Bill, his hair was parted the wrong way. For twenty years he's been coming in the office, his part is on the left. We find him dead and the part's on the right. That was a little thing but there were two others and they add up. Next was the forensics. We had a guy swab the mouth for GSR so we could make a determination if the gun was in his mouth or held a few inches outside or what. We got the GSR but we also got some gun oil and a third substance that we haven't been able to identify properly. Until we could explain it I wasn't comfortable going suicide on this.'

'What can you tell me about the substance?' Thompson asked.

'Some kind of animal-fat extract. There's pulverized silicon in it, too. It's in the forensic report that you've got in that file, too.'

I thought I saw Thompson glance at Backus and then away, a tacit admission of knowledge.

'You know it?' Grayson asked, seeming to catch the same impression.

'Not offhand,' Thompson said. 'I'll get the specifics from the report and have the lab in Quantico run it on the computer. I'll let you know.'

'What was the third reason?' Backus asked, quickly leaving the subject.

'The third reason came from Jim Beam, Orsulak's old partner. He's retired now.'

'That's his name, Jim Beam?' Walling asked.

'Yeah, the Beamer. He called me up from Tucson after he heard about Bill and asked if we'd recovered the slug. I said sure, we dug it out of the wall behind his head. Then he asked me if it was gold.'

'Gold?' Backus asked. 'Real gold?'

'Yes. A golden bullet. I told him no, it was a lead slug like all the others in his clip. Like the one we dug out of the floor, too. We'd figured that the floor shot was the first one, a get-up-the-courage shot. But then Beamer told me it was no suicide, that it was murder.'

'And how did he know this?'

'He and Orsulak went back a lot of years and he knew that Orsulak occasionally . . . hell, there probably isn't a single cop who hasn't thought about it at one time or another.'

'Killing himself,' Walling said, a statement, not a question.

'Right. And Jim Beam tells me that one time Orsulak showed him this golden bullet that he got from somewhere, he didn't know, a mail-order catalog or something. And he says to Beamer, "This is my golden parachute. When I can't take it no more, this one's for me." So what Beam was saying was no golden bullet, no suicide.'

'Did you find the golden bullet?' Walling asked.

'Yeah, we found it. After we talked to Beam we found it. It was in the drawer right next to his bed. Like it was kept nearby in case he ever needed it.'

'So that convinced you.'

'In totality, all three things leaned it way over toward homicide. Murder. But like I said, I wasn't convinced of anything until you walked in here and told your story. Now I got a hard-on for this Poet the size of – sorry for the offense, Agent Walling.'

'None taken. We all have a hard-on for him. Was there a suicide note?'

'Yes, and that's the thing that made it so hard for us to call it a homicide. There was a note and damn if it wasn't in Bill's writing.'

Walling nodded that what he had just said was no surprise.

'What did the note say?'

'It didn't make a whole lot of sense. It was like a poem. It said – well, hold on here. Agent Thomas, let me borrow that file a sec.'

'Thompson,' Thompson said as he handed it over.

'Sorry.'

Grayson looked through some pages until he found what he wanted. He read out loud.

' "Mountains toppling evermore / Into seas without a shore." That was it.'

Walling and Backus looked at me. I opened the book and started paging through the poems.

'I remember the line but I'm not sure where.'

I went to the poems that the Poet had already used and started reading quickly. I found it in 'Dream-Land,' the poem used twice before, including the note left on my brother's windshield.

'I got it,' I said.

I held the book out so Rachel could read the poem. The others crowded around her as well.

'Son of a bitch,' Grayson muttered.

'Can you give us a rundown on how you think it happened?' Rachel asked him.

'Uh, sure. Our theory is whoever this doer was, he came in and surprised Bill in his sleep. With Bill's own gun. He made him get up and get dressed. That's when Bill parted his hair wrong. I mean, he didn't know what was going to happen or maybe he did. Either way, he leaves us a little sign. From there he's taken out into the living room, put in the chair and the doer makes him write out that note on a piece of paper torn outta his own notebook he keeps in his coat pocket. Then he pops him. One in the mouth. Puts the gun in Bill's hand, puts the slug into the floor and you've got gunshot residue on the hand. The doer's outta there and we don't find poor Bill for three days.'

Grayson looked over his shoulder at the body, noticed it was being unattended and looked at his watch.

'Hey, where's the guy?' he said. 'Somebody go get him and tell him we're through. You're through with the body, right?'

'Yes,' Thompson said.

'We have to get him ready.'

'Detective Grayson,' Walling said. 'Was there a specific case that Detective Orsulak was currently pursuing?'

'Oh, yeah, there was a case. The Little Joaquin case. Eight-year-old kid abducted last month. All they found of him was his head.'

Mention of the case and its brutality brought a moment of silence in the room where the dead were prepared. Before that moment I had no doubt that Orsulak's death was related to the others, but after hearing of the crime against the boy I felt an unwavering certainty and the anger that was becoming so familiar to me foaming in my guts.

'I assume everyone is going to the funeral?' Backus said.

'That's right.'

'Can we arrange a time to meet again? We would like to see the reports on the boy, Joaquin, as well.'

They set the meeting for nine o'clock Sunday morning at the Phoenix Police Department. Grayson apparently felt that if it was on his turf he might be better able to hang on to a piece of it. But I had a feeling that the Big G was about to move in and sweep him aside like a tidal wave hitting a lifeguard stand.

'One last thing, the press,' Walling said. 'I saw a TV truck outside.'

'Yeah, they've been all over this, especially when they . . .'

He didn't finish.

'When they what?'

'Well, somebody sort of put it out on the police frequency that we were meeting the FBI here.'

Rachel groaned and Grayson nodded as if he expected it.

'Look, this absolutely has to be contained,' Rachel said. 'If any of what we just told you men gets out, the Poet will go under. We'll never catch the man who did that.'

She nodded at the corpse and a few of the cops turned to make sure it was still there. The undertaker had just stepped into the room and was lifting the hanger containing Orsulak's last suit. He was looking at the assemblage of investigators, waiting for them to leave so that he could be alone with the body.

'We're about out of here, George,' Grayson said. 'You can start.'

Backus said, 'Tell the media that the FBI's interest was purely routine and that you will continue to handle the investigation as a suspected homicide. Don't act like you are sure of anything.'

As we were walking back through the lot to the government cars, a young woman with bleached-blond hair and a grim look on her face came up to us with a microphone, a cameraman in tow. Holding the mike to her own mouth she asked, 'Why is the FBI here today?'

She turned the microphone and pointed it directly under my chin for the response. I opened my mouth but nothing came out. I had no idea why I was chosen but then realized it was the shirt I wore. The FBI seal on the breast pocket apparently assured her that she was talking to the bureau.

'I'll answer that,' Backus said quickly and the microphone went to his chin. 'We came at the request of the Phoenix Police Department to make a routine examination of the body and to hear details of the case. It is expected that our involvement ends here and further questions should go to the police. We have no further comment, thank you.'

'But are you convinced that Detective Orsulak was the victim of foul play?' the reporter persisted.

'I'm sorry,' Backus said. 'You'll have to refer your questions to the Phoenix police.'

'And your name is?'

'I'd rather keep my name out of it, thank you.'

He brushed by her and got into one of the cars. I followed Walling to the other. In a few minutes we were out of there and driving back toward Phoenix.

'Are you worried?' Rachel asked.

'About what?'

'The exclusivity of your story.'

'I'm getting there. But I'm hoping she's like most TV reporters.'

'And how are they?'

'Sourceless and senseless. If she is, then I'll be okay.'

26

The field office was in the federal courthouse on Washington Street, just a few blocks from the police department where we would meet with the locals the next day. As we followed Mize and Matuzak down a polished corridor to a conference room, I sensed anxiety in Rachel and I thought I knew what it was. By traveling with me, she had been unable to be in the other car when Thompson filled Backus in on what he had learned from the body.

The conference room was far smaller than the one we had used in Quantico. When we entered, Backus and Thompson were already seated at the table and Backus held a phone to his ear. He covered the mouthpiece when we entered and said, 'Guys, I'm going to need to talk to my people alone for a few minutes. Uh, what you could do is get us some cars if you can. We'll also need to reserve rooms somewhere. Six rooms, it looks like.'

Matuzak and Mize looked like they had just gotten word that they were demoted. They nodded glumly and left the room. I didn't know where that left me, if I was invited or excluded, since I really wasn't one of Backus's people.

'Jack, Rachel, have a seat,' Backus said. 'Let me finish up and I'll have James bring you up to date.'

We took seats and watched and listened to the one-sided phone conversation. It was clear Backus was listening to messages and responding to them. Not all seemed to have something to do with the Poet investigation.

'Okay, what about Gordon and Carter?' he said after the messages were apparently finished with. 'What's the ETA? That late? Damn. Okay, listen, three things. Call Denver and have them go to the evidence in the McEvoy case. Tell them to check the insides of the gloves for blood. If they find blood, tell them to start exhumation proceedings ... Right, right. If it's a problem call me right away. Also, tell them to see if the police took GSR swabs from the mouth of the victim and if they did, have it all sent to Quantico. That goes for all the cases. The third thing is James Thompson will be FedExing to the lab from out here. We need substance identification ASAP. Same with Denver, if it comes. What else? When's the conference call with Brass? Okay, we'll talk then.'

He hung up and looked at us. I wanted to ask what he meant by exhumation but Rachel spoke first.

'Six rooms? Is Gordon coming out here?'

'He and Carter are coming here.'

'Bob, why? You know –'

'We need them, Rachel. We are hitting critical mass on this investigation and things are moving. At the most, we are now ten days behind this offender. We need more bodies to make the moves we're going to have to make. It's that simple and that's more than enough said about it. Now, Jack, did you have something to say?'

'That exhumation you are talking about . . .'

'We'll talk about that in a few minutes. It will become clear. James, tell them what you found on the body.'

From his pocket Thompson pulled four Polaroid photos and spread them on the table in front of Rachel and me.

'This is the left palm and index finger. The two on the left were taken with the one-to-one. The other two are ten times magnified.'

'Perforations,' Rachel said.

'Right.'

I didn't see them until she had said it, but then I recognized the tiny punch holes in the lines of the skin. Three in the palm, two in the tip of the index finger.

'What is it?' I asked.

'On the surface it looks like nothing more than pinpricks,' Thompson said. 'But there is no scabbing or closing of the wounds. They occurred close to time of death. Shortly before or possibly after, though there wouldn't be much of a point to it after.'

'Point to what?'

'Jack, we're looking for ways this could have been done,' Backus said. 'How could veteran, tough cops be taken like this? Control is what we are talking about. It's one of the keys.'

I waved a hand toward the photos.

'And what does this tell you?'

'That and other things may indicate hypnosis was involved.'

'You're saying this guy hypnotized my brother and these others into putting a gun in their mouths and pulling the trigger?'

'No, I don't think it's that simple. You have to remember that it is quite difficult to use hypnotic suggestion to override the self-preservation instinct in an individual's mind. Most experts say it's flatly impossible. But if a person is susceptible to hypnotism, that person can be controlled to varying extents. He can be made docile, manageable. It's only a possibility at this point. But we have five perforations on this victim's hand. A standard method of testing for hypnotic trance would be to prick the skin with a pin after placing the suggestion that there will be no pain. If the patient reacts, the hypnosis is not working. If he shows no signs of feeling the pain, he is under trance conditions.'

'And controllable,' Thompson added.

'You want to look at my brother's hand.'

'Yes, Jack,' Backus said. 'We'll need an exhumation order. I believe the files said he was married. Will his widow allow this?'

'I don't know.'

'We may need your help on that.'

I just nodded. Things were getting stranger all the time.

'What were the other things? You said the perforations and other things may indicate hypnosis was involved.'

'The autopsies,' Rachel answered. 'None of the victims' blood screens came out totally clean. Each one had something in his blood. Your brother –'

'Cough syrup,' I said defensively. 'From the car's glove box.'

'Right. It ranges from over-the-counter things like cough syrup to prescription drugs. One of them had Percocet, which had been prescribed for a back injury eighteen months earlier. I think that was the Chicago case. Another one – I think it was Petry in Dallas – had codeine in his blood. It came from prescription Tylenol with codeine. The prescription bottle was in his medicine cabinet.'

'Okay, so what's it mean?'

'Well, individually it meant nothing at the time of each of these deaths. Whatever came up on the blood screen in each case was explained by the victim's access to it. I mean, it's reasonable to believe that if someone was going to kill himself, he might take a couple of the Percocets from the old prescription bottle to calm himself. So these things were dismissed.'

'But now they mean something.'

'Possibly,' she said. 'The finding of the perforations suggests hypnosis. If you add to that the introduction of some chemical suppressor into the blood, then you begin to see how these men may have been controlled.'

'Cough syrup?'

'It could possibly enhance a subject's susceptibility to hypnosis. Codeine is a tested enhancer. Over-the-counter cough medications don't have codeine in them anymore but some of the replacement ingredients could still act as similar enhancers.'

'Have you known this all along?'

'No, it was just something that had no context until now.'

'Has it come up before? How do you know so much?'

'Hypnosis is used fairly often as a law enforcement tool,' Backus said. 'It's also come up on the other side before.'

'There was one case several years ago,' Rachel said. 'There was a man, a Las Vegas nightclub kind of guy who did hypnotism as his act. He was also a pedophile. And what he'd do is, when he'd do shows at county fairs and so forth, he'd get close to kids. He had a children's act, a matinee, and he'd tell the audience he needed a young volunteer. The parents would practically throw their kids at him. He'd pick the lucky one and say he had to go backstage to prepare the child while some other act was going on. He'd hypnotize the kid back there, rape her and then through hypnotic suggestion, wipe the memory. Then he'd trot the kid onstage, do his act and then take her out of the trance. He used codeine as an enhancer. Put it in their Cokes.'

'I remember,' Thompson said, nodding. 'Harry the Hypnotic.'

'No, it was Horace the Hypnotist,' Rachel said. 'He was one of our interviews on the rape project. At Raiford down in Florida.'

'Wait a minute,' I said. 'Could he –'

'No, this is not him. He'd still be in prison in Florida. He got something like a twenty-five-year bid. This was only six, seven years ago. He's still inside. He's got to be.'

'I'll have it checked anyway,' Backus said. 'To be sure. But, regardless, you see the possibility we're looking at here, Jack? I'd like you to call your sister-in-law. It would be better if she heard it from you. Tell her how important it is.'

I nodded.

'Okay, Jack, we appreciate it. Now, why don't we take a break here and see what there is to eat in this town? We've got the conference call with the other FOs in an hour and twenty minutes.'

'What about the other thing?' I said.

'What thing?' Backus asked.

'The substance in that detective's mouth. It looked like you guys knew what that was.'

'No. I just made arrangements to send the swab they took back east and then, hopefully, we'll know.'

He was lying and I knew it but I let it go. Everybody stood up and headed into the hallway. I told them I wasn't hungry and needed to find a place to buy some clothes. I said I'd find a cab if there were no stores within walking distance.

'I think I'll go with Jack,' Rachel said.

I didn't know if she really wanted to or her job was just to watch me, make sure I didn't run off and write a story. I raised my hand in an I-don't-care attitude.

With directions from Matuzak we started walking toward a mall called Arizona Center. It was a beautiful day and the walk was a nice break from the intensity of recent days. Rachel and I talked about Phoenix – it was her first visit, too – and eventually I steered the conversation back to my last question to Backus.

'He was lying, so was Thompson.'

'You mean about the oral swabs.'

'Right.'

'I think Bob just doesn't want you to know more than you need to. I'm not talking about as a reporter. I mean, as a brother.'

'If there is something new, I want to know it. The deal was I'd be on the inside. Not on the inside sometimes and then on the outside – like with this hypnosis crap – other times.'

She stopped and turned to me.

'I will tell you, if you want to know, Jack. If it's what we think and all the killings follow a pattern, then it's not going to be very pleasant for you to dwell on.'

I looked in the direction we were headed. The mall was in sight. A sandstone-colored edifice with welcoming open-air walkways.

'Tell me,' I said.

'Nothing is for sure until the swab is analyzed. But it sounds like the substance Grayson described was something we've seen before. You see, some repeat offenders are smart. They know about leaving evidence behind. Evidence like semen. So they use condoms. But if it's a lubricated condom the lubricant can be left behind. Detected. Sometimes it's accidental . . . and sometimes they want us to know what they did.'

I looked at her and almost released an audible groan.

'You're saying the Poet . . . had sex with him?'

'Possibly. But to be frank, we've suspected it from the start. Serial killers . . . Jack, it's almost always about sexual gratification. It's about power and control and these are components of sexual gratification.'

'There wouldn't have been time.'

'What do you mean?'

'With my brother. The ranger was right there. There couldn't have . . .' I stopped, realizing that there only wasn't time afterward. 'Jesus . . . Oh, man.'

'That was what Bob had hoped not to have to tell you.'

I turned away and looked up at the blue sky. The only imperfection was the slash of the twin contrails of a jet long out of the picture.

'I don't get it. Why is this guy doing this?'

'We may never know that, Jack.' She put a comforting hand on my shoulder. 'These people that we hunt . . . sometimes there is no explanation. That's the very hardest part, coming up with the motivation, understanding what drives them to do what they do. We have a saying about it. We say these people are from the moon. Sometimes it is the only way to describe it when we don't have the answers. Trying to figure these people out is like putting a shattered mirror back together. There is no way to explain the behavior of some humans, so we simply say they are not humans. We say they are from the moon. And on the particular moon where the Poet comes from, these instincts that he is following are normal and natural. He is following those instincts, creating scenes that give him satisfaction. It's our job to chart the Poet's moon and then we'll be better able to find him and send him back.'

All I could do was take it all in and nod. There was no comfort in her words. All I knew was that, if given the chance, I wanted to send the Poet back to the moon. I wanted to do it myself.

'C'mon,' she said. 'Try to forget about that for now. Let's go get you some new things. We can't have those reporters thinking you're one of us anymore.'

She smiled and I returned it weakly and let her push me toward the mall.

27

We met back in the conference room of the field office at six-thirty. Backus was there, trying to work out the logistics with the phone, along with Thompson, Matuzak, Mize and three agents I hadn't been introduced to. I put my shopping bag under the conference table. It contained two new shirts, a pair of pants and a package of underwear and socks. I immediately wished I had changed into one of the new shirts because the unintroduced agents studied me and my FBI shirt with grim looks that suggested I had committed some kind of sacrilege by trying to impersonate an agent. Backus told whoever he was talking with to call him back when it was set up and then hung up.

'Okay,' he said. 'We start the full meeting as soon as they have the phones set up. Meantime, let's talk about Phoenix. Beginning tomorrow I want to start a ground-zero investigation of both the detective and the boy. Both cases, from the top. What I'd like – Oh, I'm sorry. Rachel, Jack, this is Vince Pool, SAC Phoenix. He's going to give us whatever we need.'

Pool, who looked like he had twenty-five years on the job, the most of anyone in the room, nodded at us and said nothing. Backus didn't bother to introduce the other men.

'We have the meeting with the locals tomorrow at oh nine hundred,' Backus said.

'I think we'll be able to brush them aside gently,' Pool said.

'Well, we don't want any animosity. These are the fellows who knew Orsulak the best. They'll be good sources. I think we have to bring them into this but remain firmly in control.'

'No problem.'

'This one may be our best chance. It's fresh. We've got to hope the offender made a mistake and between these two deaths, the boy and the detective, we can find it. I'd like to see –'

The phone on the table buzzed and Backus picked up the receiver and said hello.

'Hold on.'

He pushed a button on the phone and hung up the receiver.

'Brass, you there?'

'Here, boss.'

'Okay, let's run down the list, see who've we got.'

Agents from six cities announced their presence on the speaker.

'Okay, good. I want this to be as informal as possible. Why don't we go round-robin to see what people have. Brass, I'd like to finish up with you. So Florida. Is that you, Ted?'

'Uh, yes sir, with Steve, here. We are just getting our feet wet on this and hope to have more by tomorrow. But there are some anomalies here that we think are already worth noting.'

'Go ahead.'

'Uh, this is the first, or believed to be the first, of the Poet's stops. Clifford Beltran. The second incident – in Baltimore – did not take place until nearly ten months later. That is the longest interval we have as well. This leads us to possibly question the randomness of this first kill.'

'You think the Poet knew Beltran?' Rachel asked.

'It's possible. At the moment, though, it's just a hunch we are working. There are a few other things that when thrown into the stew are worth taking a look at in support, however. First, this is the only one with a shotgun. We checked the autopsy file today and they weren't pretty pictures. Total obliteration with both barrels. We all know the symbolic pathology of that.'

'Overkill,' Backus said. 'Suggesting knowledge or acquaintance of the victim.'

'Right. Next we have the weapon itself. According to reports, it was an old Smith and Wesson that Beltran kept in a closet, on a top shelf out of sight. This information is attributed in the reports to his sister. Beltran had never married and lived in the house he grew up in. We haven't talked to the sister ourselves. The point is, if this was a suicide, yeah, fine, he went to the closet and got out the shotgun. But now we come along and say this was no suicide.'

'How did the Poet know the shotgun was up there on the shelf?' Rachel said.

'Riiiiiight . . . How did he know?'

'Good one, Ted, Steve,' Backus said. 'I like it. What else?'

'The last thing is kind of sticky. Is the reporter there?'

Everyone in the room looked at me.

'Yes,' Backus said. 'But we are still off the record. You can say what you were going to say. Right, Jack?'

I nodded and then realized they wouldn't see this in all the other cities.

'That's right,' I said. 'We're off the record.'

'Okay, well, this is more speculation at this time and we're not sure how it fits but we have this. On the autopsy of the first victim, the boy, Gabriel Ortiz, the coroner concluded, based on examination of the anal glands and muscles, that the boy was the victim of long-term molestation. If the boy's killer was also his abuser over a period of time, then this does not fit with our pattern of random selection and acquisition of victims. So that seems unlikely to us.

'However, looking at it from Beltran's point of view three years ago of not having the benefit of our knowledge, something here doesn't fit. He had this one case, knew nothing about the others we know about now. When the autopsy came back concluding the boy was the victim of long-term molestation, it stands to reason that Beltran should have jumped all over that and looked for the abuser as suspect numero uno.'

'He didn't?'

'No. He headed a team of three detectives and he directed almost all investigative work toward the park where the boy had been abducted after school. I got this off the record from one of the guys on the team. He said he suggested a wider focus looking into the boy's background but Beltran turned him down.

'Now the good stuff. My source at the sheriff's tells me Beltran specifically asked for the investigation. He wanted it. After he supposedly offed himself, my source did some checking and it turns out Beltran had known the kid through a local social services program called Best Pals, which puts fatherless boys with adults. Like a Big Brother program. Beltran was a cop, so he had no trouble going through the screening process. He was the boy's Best Pal. I'm sure you can all take it from there.'

'You think perhaps Beltran was the boy's molester?' Backus asked.

'It's possible. I think that's what my source was driving at but he won't put it on the line. Everybody's dead. It was written off. They're not going to go public with a story like that. Not with one of their own and sheriff being an elective office.'

I watched Backus nod his head.

'That's to be expected.'

There was silence for a few moments.

'Ted, Steve, this is all very interesting,' Backus said. 'But how does it fit? Is it just an interesting offshoot or are you seeing something there?'

'We're not sure ourselves. But if you say Beltran was a molester, a pedophile no less, and add that he was put down with a shotgun that somebody knew was on the top shelf of the closet because he knew Beltran, then we are getting into an area I think we should explore further.'

'I agree. Tell us, what else did your source know about Beltran and Best Pals?'

'He said he was told that Beltran had been with Best Pals for a long time. He'd been with a lot of boys, we assume.'

'And that is where you will pursue this, correct?'

'We'll hit it hard in the morning. Nothing we can do with it tonight.'

Backus nodded and put a finger to his mouth in a contemplative gesture.

'Brass?' Backus said. 'What do you think of all of this? How would that play with the psychopathology?'

'Children are a string all through this. So are homicide cops. We just don't have a handle yet on what this guy is all about. I think this is something that should be pursued vigorously.'

'Ted, Steve, do you need more bodies?' Backus asked.

'I think we're set. We've got everybody in the Tampa FO wanting in on this. So what we need, we can take from there.'

'Excellent. By the way, have you talked to the boy's mother about her son's relationship with Beltran?'

'We are still trying to track her as well as Beltran's sister. Remember, it's been three years. Hopefully, we'll get to them tomorrow after Best Pals.'

'Okay, then, how about Baltimore? Sheila?'

'Yes, sir. We spent most of the day re-covering the ground of the locals. We talked to Bledsoe. The theory he had on the Polly Amherst case from the start was that they were looking for a molester. Amherst was a teacher. Bledsoe said he and McCafferty always thought that she might've stumbled onto a molester on the school grounds, was abducted, strangled and then butchered as a means of disguising the true motivation of the crime.'

'Why did it have to be a molester?' Rachel asked. 'Could she have stumbled onto a burglar, a drug deal, anything else?'

'Polly Amherst had third-period recess watch on the day she disappeared. The locals interviewed every child who had been in the yard. A lot of conflicting stories but a handful of the kids remember a man at the fence. He had stringy blond hair and glasses. He was white. Sounds like Brad wasn't too far off with his description of Roderick Usher. They also said this man had a camera. That was about the extent of the description.'

'Okay, Sheila, what else?' Backus asked.

'The one piece of physical evidence recovered with the body was a strand of hair. Bleached blond. Natural color is reddish brown. That's about it for now. We are going to work with Bledsoe again tomorrow.'

'Okay. Chicago's next.'

The rest of the reports contained nothing noteworthy in terms of identifying or adding to the growing database on the Poet. The agents were mostly covering ground the locals had already trod and they were finding nothing new. Even the report from Denver contained mostly old information. But at the end, the agent on the line said that an examination of the gloves worn by my brother was conducted and a single blood spot was found in the fur lining of the right-hand glove. The agent asked whether I was still willing to call Riley and ask her to allow an exhumation. I didn't answer because I was in a daze thinking about what the indication of hypnotism meant my brother's last moments were like. Asked again, I said I would call in the morning.

As an afterthought the agent concluded his report by saying he had shipped the GSR swabs from my brother's mouth to the lab in Quantico.

'They run a pretty good ship here, boss, and I don't think we'll get more than what they found.'

'Which was?' Backus asked, careful not to look at me.

'Just the GSR. Nothing else.'

I didn't know what I felt when I heard those words. I guess there was relief but it was no proof that anything did or did not happen. Sean was still dead and I was still haunted by thoughts of what his last moments and thoughts had been. I tried to shove it aside and concentrate on the conference call. Backus had asked Brass to update everyone on the victimology and I had missed most of the report.

'So we are discounting any correlation,' she was saying. 'Aside from the possibilities mentioned earlier in Florida, I'm saying they are picked at random. They didn't know each other, they never worked together and the paths of all six never crossed. We've found out that four of them went to some kind of bureau-sponsored homicide seminar at Quantico four years ago, but the other two didn't and we don't know if the four who did go ever even met or talked to each other at the seminar. All of this doesn't include Orsulak in Phoenix. We haven't had time yet to do a track on him.'

'So if there is no correlation, we are to assume they are chosen by the offender simply because they take the bait?' Rachel asked.

'I think that's correct.'

'So he must stand by and watch and see his prey for the first time after the bait kill.'

'Again, correct. All of these bait cases received heavy local media attention. He could've seen each of the detectives for the first time on TV or in a newspaper photo.'

'No physically archetypal attraction involved?'

'No. He simply takes whoever gets the case. The lead detective becomes the prey. Now, that is not to say that after that selection, he may not find that one or more of these subjects were more attractive or fulfilling to his fantasy. That can always happen.'

'What fantasy?' I asked, struggling just to keep up with what Brass was saying.

'Is that Jack? Well, Jack, we don't know what fantasy. That's the point. We are coming at it from the wrong direction. We don't know the fantasy that motivates this killer and what we are seeing and guessing about are the parts. We may never know what rocks his world. He's down from the moon, Jack. The only way we'll really ever know is if he decides to tell us someday.'

I nodded and thought of another question. I waited until it was clear no one else had anything.

'Uh, Agent Brass – I mean, Doran?'

'Yes?'

'You might've already said this, but what about the poems? Do you have any more of an idea how they fit?'

'Well, they are obviously being used in exhibition. We noted this yesterday. This is his signature, and though he obviously wants to elude capture, at the same time his psychology is such that he just has to leave a little something that says, *Hey, I was here.* This is where the poems come in. As for the poems themselves the correlation is that they all are or can be read as being about death. There is also the theme that death is a portal to other things, other places. "Through the pale door," I believe, is one of the quotes he used. What it may be is that the Poet may believe he is sending these men he has killed to a better world. He is transforming them. It's something to think about when we consider the pathology of this individual. But once again, we come back to the instability of all our conjectures. It's kind of like we are looking through a full trash can to try to find out what somebody ate for dinner last night. We don't know what this man is doing and we won't until we have him.'

'Brass? Bob again. What are you reading on the planning of these crimes?'

'I'll let Brad answer that.'

'This is Brad. Uh, we're calling this guy a modified traveler. Yes, he is using the whole country as his canvas but he is staying put for weeks and sometimes months at a time. This is unusual in our prior profiling. The Poet is not a hit-and-run killer. He hits and then he stays around for a while. We are to expect that during this period the hunter watches the hunted. He must come to know his victim's routines and nuances. Possibly, he even strikes up a passing acquaintance. That's something to look for. A new friend or acquaintance in each detective's life. Maybe a new neighbor or guy at the local bar. The situation in Denver also suggests that he may come at them as a source, someone with information. He may be using a combination of these approaches.'

'Which leads to the next step,' Backus said. 'After contact.'

'Power,' Hazelton said. 'After he gets close enough to these victims, how does he take control? Well, we assume he has some kind of weapon that initially allows him to take theirs, but there is something more. How does he get six, now seven, homicide detectives to write out lines of poetry? How does he avoid a struggle in every one of these cases? At the moment, we are exploring the possibility of hypnosis combined with chemical enhancers taken from the victims themselves. All but one of these incidents occurred in the victim's home. The McEvoy case is the anomaly. Setting it aside and looking at the others, there is probably no one among us who has an empty medicine cabinet. And there probably isn't a cabinet among the bunch that doesn't have some prescription or store-bought medication that wouldn't serve as an enhancer. Obviously some things work better than others. But the point is, if this scenario is correct, the Poet is using the things made available to him by the victims. We are looking at this hard. That's it, for now.'

'Okay, then,' Backus said. 'Any other questions?'

The room and phone speaker remained silent.

'Okay, people,' he said, leaning forward, his hands on the table and his mouth close to the phone speaker. 'Your best work. We really need it this time.'

Rachel and I followed Backus and Thompson to the Hyatt where Matuzak had reserved rooms. I had to check in and pay for my room while Backus checked in and got keys for the other five, which the government would pay for. Still, I got the discount the hotel regularly gave the FBI. It must have been the shirt.

Rachel and Thompson were waiting in the lobby lounge where we had decided on a drink before dinner. When Backus gave her one of the keys, I heard him say that she was in room 321 and I committed it to memory. I was four doors away in room 317 and I was already thinking about the night ahead, about closing that gap.

After a half hour of small talk Backus stood up and said he was going to his room to review the day's reports before heading out to the airport to pick up Thorson and Carter. He turned down an offer to join us for dinner and headed toward the elevator. A few minutes later, Thompson split, too, saying he wanted to read through the autopsy report on Orsulak in detail.

'Just you and me, Jack,' Rachel said when Thompson was out of earshot. 'What do you feel like eating?'

'I'm not sure. What about you?'

'Haven't thought about it. I know what I want to do first though . . . That's take a hot bath.'

We agreed to meet in an hour for dinner. We rode the elevator up to our floor in a silence couched in sexual tension.

In my room, I tried to take my mind off Rachel by connecting my computer to the phone line and checking my messages in Denver. There was only one, from Greg Glenn asking where I was. I answered it but doubted that he would see it until he came back into work on Monday. I then sent a message to Laurie Prine asking her to search for any stories on Horace the Hypnotist that might have run in the Florida newspapers in the last seven years. I asked her to ship any hits she got to my computer basket but said it was no hurry.

After that I showered and changed into my new clothes for my dinner with Rachel. I was ready twenty minutes early and I thought about going down and seeing if there was a drugstore nearby. But then I thought about the impression it would give Rachel if things worked out and I came to her bed, a condom already in my pocket. I decided against the drugstore. I decided to play things as they came.

'Did you see CNN?'

'No,' I said. I was standing in the doorway of her room. She went back to the bed and sat down to put her shoes on. She looked refreshed and was wearing a cream-colored shirt with black jeans. The TV was still on but it was a story about the clinic shootings in Colorado. I didn't think that was what she was talking about.

'What did it say?'

'We were on. You, me and Bob coming out of the funeral home. Somehow they got Bob's name and put it on the screen.'

'Did it say he was BSS?'

'No, just FBI. But it doesn't matter. CNN must've taken the feed off the local channel. Wherever he is, if our guy saw it, we could have a problem.'

'How come? It's not that unusual for the FBI to take a look at cases like this. The bureau's always sticking its nose in.'

'The problem is it plays to the Poet. We see it in almost all of the cases. One concept of the gratification these kinds of killers seek is seeing their work on TV and in the papers. In a way it allows them to relive the fantasy of the incident. Part of that infatuation with the media extends to the pursuers. I get the feeling that this guy, the Poet, knows more about us than we do about him. If I'm right, then he's probably read books on serial killers. The commercial dreck and even some of the more serious work. He may know names. Bob's father is in many of them. Bob himself is in some. So am I. Our names, photos, our words. If he saw that on CNN and recognized us, then he'll assume we are right behind him. We may lose him now. He might go under.'

Ambivalence won the night. Unable to decide what or where we wanted to eat, we settled for the hotel's restaurant. The food was okay but we shared a bottle of Buehler cabernet that was perfect. I told her not to worry about the government per diem because the newspaper was paying. She ordered cherries jubilee for dessert after I told her that.

'I get the feeling that you'd be happy if there were no free media in the world,' I told her when we were slowing down on the dessert. The implications of the CNN report had dominated the conversation during dinner.

'Not at all. I respect the media as a necessity in a free society. I don't respect the irresponsibility that you see more often than you don't.'

'What was irresponsible about that report?'

'That one was marginal but it bothers me that they used our images without bothering to ask what the ramifications could be. I just wish that sometimes the media would concentrate on the larger picture or story, rather than go for the immediate gratification every time.'

'Not every time. I didn't blow you people off and say I'm writing my story. I went long-term. I went for the larger story.'

'Oh, very noble, coming from somebody who extorted his way into the investigation.'

She was smiling and so was I.

'Hey,' I protested.

'Can we talk about something else? I'm tired of all of this. God, I'd love to just be able to lie back and forget about it for a while.'

There it was again. Her choice of words, the way she looked at me as she said them. Was I reading it correctly or only reading what I wanted to read?

'Okay, forget about the Poet,' I said. 'Let's talk about you.'

'Me? What about me?'

'This stuff going on with Thorson is like a TV sitcom.'

'That's private.'

'Not when you guys are staring daggers across the room all the time and you're trying to get Backus to take him off the case.'

'I don't want him off the case. I just want him off my back and I don't want him out here. He always finds a way to sneak in and try to take over. You watch.'

'How long were you married?'

'Fifteen glorious months.'

'When did it end?'

'Long time ago, three years.'

'That's a long time for hostilities to linger.'

'I don't want to talk about this.'

But I sensed she did. I let a little time go by. The waiter came and refilled our coffee cups.

'What happened?' I asked softly. 'You don't deserve to be unhappy like that.'

She reached up and tugged gently on my beard, the first time she had touched me since ramming my face into the bed back in Washington.

'You're sweet.' She shook her head. 'It was just the wrong thing for both of us. Sometimes, I don't even know what we saw in each other. It just didn't work.'

'How come?'

'Just because. It was a just-because type of thing. Like I said, we both had a lot of baggage. His was heavier. He'd worn a mask and I didn't see all the rage behind it until it was too late. I got out as soon as I could.'

'What was he angry about?'

'A lot of things. He carries a lot of anger. From other women, relationships. I was his second failed marriage. The job. Sometimes it came out like a blowtorch.'

'Did he ever hurt you?'

'No. I didn't stay long enough for him to try. Of course, all men deny the woman's intuition, but I think if I stayed it would have come to that. It was the natural course of things. I still try to stay away from him.'

'And he still has something for you.'

'You're crazy if you think that.'

'There's something there.'

'The only thing he has for me is a desire to see me unhappy. He wants to get back at me for being the cause of his bad marriage, his bad life, everything.'

'How's a guy like that keep his job?'

'Like I said, he's got a mask. He's good at hiding it. You saw him at the meeting. He was contained. You also have to understand something about the FBI. They don't go looking to bust their agents. As long as he did the work, it didn't matter what I felt or said.'

'You complained about him?'

'Not directly. That would've been cutting my own throat. I've got an enviable position in the BSS but make no mistake, the bureau's a man's world. And you don't go to the boss to complain about things you *think* your ex-husband might do. I'd probably end up on the bank squad in Salt Lake City if I tried that.'

'So what can you do?'

'Not much. Indirectly, I've dropped enough hints on Backus for him to know what's going on. As you can tell by what you heard today, he's not going to do anything about it. I have to assume that Gordon's dropping hints in his other ear. If I were Bob, I'd just sit back like he's doing and wait for one of us to fuck up. The first one to do it gets shipped out.'

'And what would constitute a fuck-up?'

'I don't know. With the bureau you never know. But he's got to be more careful with me than him. Prevailing factors, you know. He's got to have his shit together if he's going to try to move a woman out of the unit. So, that's my edge.'

I nodded. We had come to a natural end to that branch of the conversation. But I didn't want her to go back to her room. I wanted to be with her.

'You're a pretty good interviewer, Jack. Pretty sly.'

'What?'

'We've spent the whole time talking about me and the bureau. What about you?'

'What about me? Never married, never divorced. I don't even have plants at home. I sit behind a computer all day. It's not in the same league as you and Thorson.'

She smiled and then giggled a bit girlishly.

'Yes, we are a pair. Were. Do you feel any better after the meeting today, about what they found in Denver?'

'You mean what they didn't find? I don't know. I guess it's better that it looks like he didn't have to go through that. There still is nothing to feel better about, though.'

'Did you call your sister-in-law?'

'No, not yet. I'll do it in the morning. Seems like something that should be discussed in daylight.'

'I've never spent a lot of time with the families of the victims,' she said. 'The bureau always gets called in later.'

'I have ... I'm the master of interviewing the fresh widow, the now childless mother, father of the dead bride. You name it, I've interviewed it.'

We were quiet a long moment. The waiter came by with his coffeepot but we both passed. I asked for the check. I knew it wasn't going to happen with her tonight. I had lost the nerve to pursue it because I didn't want to risk her rejection. My pattern had always been the same. When I didn't care whether a woman rejected me, I always took the chance. When I did care and knew rejection would cut me, I always held back.

'What are you thinking about?' she asked.

'Nothing,' I lied. 'My brother, I guess.'

'Why don't you tell that story?'

'What story?'

'The other day. You were about to tell me something good about him. The nicest thing he ever did for you. What made him a saint.'

I looked across the table at her. I knew the story instantly but thought about it before speaking. I could've easily lied and told her the nicest thing he did was just love me but I trusted her. We trust the things we find beautiful, the things we want. And maybe I wanted to confess to somebody after so many years.

'The nicest thing he ever did was not blame me.'

'For what?'

'Our sister died when we were kids. It was my fault. He knew. He was the only one who really knew. And her. But he never blamed me and he never told anyone. In fact, he took on half the guilt. That was the nicest thing.'

She leaned forward across the table with a pained look on her face. I think she would have made a good, sympathetic psychologist if she had followed that path.

'What happened, Jack?'

'She fell through the ice at the lake. The same place where Sean's body was found. She was bigger than me, older. We'd gone out there with our parents. We had a camper and my folks were making lunch or something. Me and Sean were outside and Sarah was watching us. I ran out on the frozen lake. Sarah ran out after me to stop me from going too far out, to where the ice was thin. Only she was older and bigger and heavier and she fell through. I started screaming. Sean started screaming. My father and some other people there tried but they couldn't get to her in time . . .'

I drank from my coffee cup but it was empty. I looked at her and continued.

'Anyway, everybody was asking what happened, you know, and I couldn't . . . I couldn't talk. And he – Sean – said we had both been out on the ice and then when Sarah came out it cracked and she fell through. It was a lie and I don't know if my parents ever believed it. I don't think they did. But he did it for me. It was like he was willing to share the guilt with me, make it easier by half.'

I stared into my empty cup. Rachel said nothing.

'You might've made it big as a shrink. That's a story I've never told anyone.'

'Well, I think telling it might've just been something you felt you owed your brother. Maybe a way of thanking him.'

The waiter placed a check on our table and thanked us. I opened my wallet and put a credit card down on top of it. I can think of a better way to thank him, I thought.

After we stepped off the elevator I became nearly paralyzed with fear. I couldn't bring myself to act on my desire. We moved to her door first. She pulled the card key from her pocket and looked up at me. I hesitated, said nothing.

'Well,' she said after a long moment. 'I guess we start early tomorrow. Do you eat breakfast?'

'Just coffee, usually.'

'Okay, well, I'll call you and maybe if there's time we can grab a cup.'

I nodded, too overrun with the embarrassment of my failure and cowardice to say anything.

'Good night, Jack.'

' 'Night,' I managed to say before walking off down the hall.

I sat on the edge of the bed watching CNN for a half hour, hoping to see the report she had mentioned or anything to take my mind off the disastrous end of the night. Why is it, I wondered, that it is the ones who mean so much that are the hardest to reach out to? Some deep instinct told me that the moment in the hall had been the time, the right moment. And I had ignored it. I had run from it. And now I feared that my failure would haunt me forever. Because that instinct might never come back.

I don't think I heard the first knock. Because the one that raised me from my dark reverie was very loud and surely not the first effort. It had the urgency of a third or fourth knock. Jarred by the intrusion, I quickly turned off the TV and went to the door, opening it without looking through the peephole. It was her.

'Rachel.'

'Hi.'

'Hi.'

'I, uh, thought I'd give you a chance to redeem yourself. That is, if you wanted to.'

I looked at her and a dozen responses went through my mind, all engineered to neatly put the ball back in her court and make her make the move. But the instinct came back and I knew what she wanted and what I needed to do.

I stepped toward her and put an arm behind her back and kissed her. Then I pulled her into the room and closed the door.

'Thank you,' I whispered.

Almost nothing was said after that. She hit the light switch, then led me to the bed. She put her arms around my neck and pulled me down into a long, deep kiss. We fumbled with each other's clothes and then decided wordlessly to just take off our own. It was faster.

'Do you have something?' she whispered. 'You know, to use?'

Crestfallen by the consequences of my inaction earlier, I shook my head no and was about to offer to go to the drugstore, a trip that I knew would destroy the moment.

'I think I might,' she said.

She pulled her purse onto the bed and I heard the zipper of an interior pocket opening. She then pressed the plastic condom package into my palm.

'Always keep one for emergencies,' she said with a smile in her voice.

We made love after that. Slowly, smiling in the shadows of the room. I think of it now as a wonderful moment, perhaps the most erotic and passionate hour of my life. In reality, though, when I strip the gauze from the memory, I know it was a nervous hour with both of us seemingly too eager and willing to please the other and perhaps thereby robbing ourselves of some of the true enjoyment of the moment. My sense of Rachel was that she was craving the intimacy of the act, not as much the sensual pleasure as the closeness with another human being. It was that way for me as well, but I also found a deep carnal desire for her body. She had wide and dark areolas on small breasts, a lovely rounded stomach with soft hair below it. As we found each other's rhythm her face flushed and became warm. She was beautiful and I told her so. But this seemed only to embarrass her and she pulled me down into an embrace so that I could not see her face. My face in her hair, I smelled the scent of apples.

Afterward, she rolled onto her stomach and I lightly rubbed her back.

'I want to be with you after this,' I said.

She didn't answer but that was okay. I knew that what we had just shared was genuine. She slowly pulled herself up into a sitting position.

'What is it?'

'I can't stay. I want to but I can't. I should be in my own room in the morning in case Bob calls. He'll want to talk before the meeting with the locals and he said he'd call.'

Disappointed, I wordlessly watched her dress. She moved about in the darkness skillfully, knowing her way. When she was finished, she bent down and lightly kissed me on the lips.

'Go to sleep.'

'I will. You, too.'

But after she was gone I couldn't sleep. I felt too good. I felt reaffirmed and filled with an unexplainable joy. Every day you fight death with life and what is more vital in life than the physical act of love? My brother and all that had happened seemed far away.

I rolled to the side of the bed and picked up the phone. Full of myself, I wanted to tell her these thoughts. But after eight rings she didn't pick up and the operator answered.

'Are you sure that was Rachel Walling's room?'

'Yes, sir. Three twenty-one. Would you like to leave a message?'

'No, thanks.'

I sat up and turned on the light. I turned on the television with the remote and flipped back and forth for a few minutes, not really watching. I tried her number again and still no answer.

Getting dressed, I told myself I wanted a Coke. I took change off the bureau and my key and went down the hall to the alcove where the vending machines were. On my way back I stopped by 321 and listened at the door. I heard nothing. I lightly knocked and waited, knocked again. She didn't answer.

At my door I fumbled to use the key and turn the knob while holding the can of Coke. Finally, I put the can down on the rug and was opening the door when I heard footsteps and turned to see a man coming down the hallway toward me. The hall lights were dimmed because of the hour and the bright lights from the elevator alcove cast the approaching man in silhouette. He was a large man and in his hand I saw he carried something. A bag maybe. He was ten feet away.

'Hiya, sport.'

Thorson. His voice, though recognizable, spooked me and I think he saw it in my face. I heard him chuckle as he passed by me.

'Pleasant dreams.'

I said nothing. I picked up the can and moved into my room slowly, continuing to watch Thorson move down the hall. He passed by 321 without hesitation and stopped at a room further down the hallway. As he was opening it with a key he looked back down the hall at me. Our eyes locked for a moment, then I slipped wordlessly into my room.

28

Gladden wished he had asked Darlene where the remote control was before he had killed her. It annoyed him to have to get up to switch channels. Every one of the Los Angeles television channels had picked up on the *Times* story. He'd had to sit right in front of the box, though, and manually change the channel to try to catch all the reports. He had seen what Detective Thomas looked like. He had been interviewed by all of the channels.

He lay on the couch, now too excited to sleep. He wanted to change the channel to CNN but didn't want to get up again. He was on some cable channel on the nether reaches of the list. A woman with a French accent was preparing crêpes filled with yogurt. Gladden didn't know whether it was a dessert or a breakfast but it was making him hungry and he considered opening another can of ravioli. He decided against it. He knew he had to conserve his supplies. Still four days to go.

'Where's the fucking remote, Darlene?' he called out.

He got up and switched the channel, then turned out the lights and returned to the couch. With the monologue of the CNN anchors as a calming background, he thought about the work ahead, his plans. They knew about him now and he had to be more careful than ever.

He fell into a doze, his eyes drooping and the TV noise lulling him finally to sleep. But just as he was about to drop off, his ears picked up on a report from Phoenix about the murder of a police detective. Gladden opened his eyes.

29

In the morning Rachel called me before I was out of bed. I squinted at the clock and saw it was seven-thirty. I didn't ask why she hadn't answered either the phone or her door the night before. I'd already spent a good part of the night brooding about it and decided she had probably been taking a shower during the times I phoned or knocked.

'You up?'

'I am now.'

'Good. Call your sister-in-law.'

'Right. I will.'

'You want to get coffee? How long till you're ready?'

'I have to make the call and get a shower. An hour?'

'You're on your own then, Jack.'

'Okay, a half hour. You've already been up?'

'No.'

'Well, don't you have to take a shower?'

'I don't take an hour to get ready, even on a day off.'

'Okay, okay. A half hour.'

As I got up I found the torn condom package on the floor. I picked it up and committed the brand to memory since it obviously was the one she preferred, then threw it in the bathroom trash can.

I was almost hoping Riley wouldn't be home because I didn't know exactly how to ask her to let people dig up her husband's body or how she would react. But I knew that at five till nine on a Sunday morning there wasn't much chance that she would be anywhere else. As far as I knew, her only appearances in church in recent years were at Sean's funeral and her wedding before that.

She answered on the second ring with a voice that seemed more cheerful than I'd heard in the last month. At first I wasn't even sure it was her.

'Riles?'

'Jack, where are you? I was worried.'

'I'm in Phoenix. Why are you worried?'

'Well, you know, I didn't know what was going on.'

'I'm sorry I didn't call. Everything's okay. I'm with the FBI. I can't say a lot but they are looking into Sean's death. His and some others.'

I looked out the window and saw the lines of a mountain on the horizon.

The tourist pamphlet that came with the room said it was called Camelback Mountain and the name fit. I didn't know if I was saying too much. But it wasn't like Riley was going to go sell the story to the *National Enquirer.*

'Uh, something's come up on the case. They think there might've been some evidence missed on Sean ... Uh, they want to ... Riley, they need to take him out of the ground to look at him again.'

There was no response. I waited a long time.

'Riley?'

'Jack, why?'

'It will help the case. The investigation.'

'But what do they want? Are ... are they going to cut him open again?'

She said the last part in a desperate whisper and I realized how I had bungled the job of telling her.

'Oh, no. Not at all. Uh, all they want to do is look at his hands. Nothing else. You have to give them permission. Otherwise, they have to go through courts and it's a long mess.'

'His hands? Why Jack?'

'It's a long story. I'm not really supposed to tell you but I'll tell you this. They think the guy ... whoever did this, he tried to hypnotize Sean. They want to look at his hands to see if there are pinpricks, you know. That's the test somebody might have given to see if Sean was really hypnotized.'

There was more silence.

'There was something else,' I said. 'Did Sean have a cough or a cold? You know, back on the day it happened.'

'Yes,' she said after a moment's hesitation. 'He was sick and I told him not to go in that day. I was sick, too, and I told him to stay home with me. Jack, you know what?'

'What?'

'I must've felt sick because I was pregnant. I found out Wednesday.'

It caught me off guard. I hesitated.

'Oh, Riley,' I finally said. 'That's wonderful. Did you tell the folks?'

'Yes, they know. They're very happy. It's like a miracle child because I didn't know and we hadn't really been trying.'

'It's great news.'

I didn't know how to get back to the other conversation we had been having. Finally, I just bull-rushed her to the point.

'I've got to go now, Riles. What can I tell them?'

Rachel was in the lobby when I stepped out of the elevator. She had both her computer bag and her overnighter with her.

'You checked out?' I asked, not understanding.

'FBI rules of the road. Never leave anything in the room because you never know when you'll have to fly. We get a break today, I'm not going to have time to come back and pack my things.'

I nodded. It was too late for me to pack and I had almost nothing to pack anyway.

'Did you call her?'

'Yes. She said fine. She said do it. For what it's worth, she also said he was sick. The cough syrup was his. And I figured out why Sean was killed in his car and not at home like the others.'

'Why?'

'His wife, Riley, was home because she was sick, too. My brother would have done everything he could not to take this guy back to his house. Not with her there.'

I nodded sadly at my brother's last and maybe bravest act.

'I think you're right, Jack. It fits. But listen, there's been a development. Bob's just got word and called me from the FO. He's delaying the meeting with the locals. We got a fax from the Poet.'

The mood of the conference room was decidedly somber. Only the agents from Quantico were taking part. Backus, Thompson, Thorson and an agent named Carter who had been at the first status meeting I had attended back at Quantico. I noticed Rachel and Thorson exchange contemptuous looks as we entered. I focused on Backus. He seemed lost in thought. He had his portable computer open on the table in front of him but he wasn't looking at it. He looked fresh in a different gray suit. A bemused smile spread on his face and he looked at me.

'Jack, you get to see firsthand now why we were concerned about containing this story. A five-second video bite was all it took and the offender knows we are on his trail.'

I nodded.

'I don't think he should be here for this,' Thorson said.

'A deal is a deal, Gordon. He certainly had nothing to do with the CNN story.'

'Still, I think it's not –'

'Can it, Gordon,' Rachel said. 'It doesn't matter what you think.'

'Okay, let's halt hostilities and concentrate on the problem,' Backus said. 'I've got copies here.'

He opened a file and passed copies of the fax across the table. I got my own copy. There was silence in the room as we all read.

> Dear Bob Backus, FBI agent,
> And hello to you, sir. I caught the news and saw you in Phoenix, you sly one. No comments to dim bulb reporters do not fool me. I know your face, Bob. You are coming for me and I anxiously await your arrival. But be careful, my friend Bob! Not so close! After all, look what happened to poor Orsulak and those others. They put Orsulak in the ground today, the end of a good job. But an FBI man of such stature as yours, now that would be a noble hunt. Heh, heh.
>
> Not to worry, Bob. You are safe. My next intended has been anointed. I've made my choice and I have him in sight, even as you read these words.
>
> Are you huddled with your masses now? Wondering what makes your opponent tick? It's a terrible mystery, isn't it? Bothers like a pinprick in the palm I suspect. I offer you one clue. (What are friends for?) I am the rotten

apple of my Best Pal's eye, who am I? When you know the answer, Bob, say it over and over again. Then you'll get it. You'll know. You're a pro and I'm sure you are up to the challenge. I'm counting on you, Bob!

I dwell alone in the world of moan, Bob, and my work has just begun. And Bob? May the best man win.

I cannot sign my correspondence for you haven't given me my name yet. What is it, Bob? I'll watch for you on television and I'll wait to hear my name. Until then I will close with this: Short and Tall – I killed them all!

Drive carefully!

I read the fax twice and each time it gave me the same chill. I knew what they meant now. About the moon. The letter was the voice of a man from someplace else. Not here. Not this planet.

'Everybody in agreement on authenticity?' Backus asked.

'There are several authenticators,' Rachel said. 'The pinprick. The quote from Poe. What about the reference to Best Pal? Has Florida been informed about this?'

'Yes. The Best Pals angle obviously becomes the priority. They're dropping everything else for the time being.'

'What does Brass say?'

'That it obviously confirms the linkage theory. There are references here to both strings, the detectives and the others. She and Brad were right. One offender. She's now going with the Florida killings as our model. Everything that follows is just a repetition of the initial crime sequence. He's repeating the ritual.'

'In other words, find out why he killed Beltran and you know why he killed the rest.'

'Right. Brass and Brad have been talking to Florida all morning. Hopefully, it won't take long to get some answers and put the model together.'

Everybody seemed to brood over this for a few moments.

'We're going to stay here?' Rachel asked.

'I think it's best,' Backus said. 'The answers may be in Florida but it's static. History. We're still closest to him here.'

'It says he's already chosen his next intended,' I said. 'Is that the next cop, you think?'

'That's exactly what I think,' Backus said somberly. 'So we've run out of time. As we sit here talking, he is watching another man, another cop, somewhere. And if we don't find out where that is, we're going to have another dead man on our hands.'

He pounded a fist on the table.

'We've got to make a break, people, we've got to do something. We have to find that man before it is too late!'

He said it with force and conviction. He was marshaling his troops. He had asked for their best work before. He needed it to be even better now.

'Bob,' Rachel said. 'The fax makes reference to Orsulak's funeral being *today*. When did this come in and where did it go to?'

'Gordon has that.'

Thorson cleared his throat and spoke without looking at Rachel or me.

'It came to a fax line at Quantico that is assigned to academy business,' Thorson said. 'Needless to say, its sender used a masking option on the sender ID. Nothing there. It arrived at three thirty-eight this morning. That's eastern time. I had Hazelton chase down the sequence. A fax call came into the general Quantico number, the operator recognized the fax beep and switched the call to the wire room. She couldn't tell where or who it was going to because all she had was the beep. So she took a guess and switched it to an academy fax and it was there in the basket until this morning when it was finally noticed and brought down to the center.'

'We're lucky it's not still sitting there unnoticed,' Backus added.

'Right,' Thorson said. 'Anyway, Hazelton took the original to the lab and came up with something. Their take is that it wasn't a fax-to-fax transmission. It came from an inboard fax.'

'A computer,' I said.

'With a fax modem. And since we know this guy is a traveler, it's not likely that he's lugging around an Apple Mac on his back. The speculation is he has a laptop computer with a fax modem. Most likely a cellular modem. It would give him the most freedom.'

Everyone digested this for a few moments. I wasn't sure of its significance. It seemed to me that a lot of the information they had amassed during the investigation was useless until they had a suspect in custody. Then it might be used to build a case against him for trial. But until then, it wasn't much help in catching him.

'All right, so he has state-of-the-art computer equipment,' Rachel finally said. 'What do we have in place for the next fax?'

'We'll be standing by to trace any fax calls to the general line,' Thorson said. 'At best we'll get the originating cell. No closer.'

'What's that mean?' I asked.

Thorson seemed reluctant to answer any question from me. Rachel stepped in when he didn't.

'It means if he's on a cellular we can't make a trace to a direct number or location. We'll get the city and the originating cell where the call came from. Probably at best that will knock it down to a search area of more than a hundred thousand people.'

'But we'll have the city,' Backus said. 'We'll be able to go to the locals and look for cases that may serve as bait cases. It would only have to be a homicide committed in the last week. Just since Orsulak.'

He looked at Thorson.

'Gordon, I want another flag sent to all FOs. Tell them to check with the locals on any recent homicides. We're talking about all the whodunits in general, but child cases in particular and anything with unusual MO or violent assault on the corpse, before or after death. Get that out by this afternoon. Request acknowledgment from SACs by eighteen hundred tomorrow. I don't want it to fall through the cracks.'

'Got it.'

'Also, FYI, Brass suggested one other thing as well,' Backus added. 'And that's that the bit in the fax about his next target being selected could be a bluff. A design to make us react and scramble while the offender is actually slipping away, going under. Remember, it was the chief fear that we had about publicity.'

'I disagree,' Rachel said. 'Reading this, I see a braggart, someone who thinks he's better than us and wants to toy with us. I take him at his word. There's a cop out there somewhere and he's in the sights.'

'I tend to think that way, too,' Backus said. 'I think Brass does as well but felt the need to put the other possibility on the table.'

'So, then, what's our strategy now?'

'Simple,' Backus said. 'We find this guy and arrest him before he hurts anybody else.'

Backus smiled and everyone but Thorson followed suit.

'Actually, I think that until something else breaks, we stay put and redouble our efforts here. And let's keep this fax to ourselves. Meantime, we're ready to move if something develops. We hope for another fax from our guy and Brass is working up another alert for the field offices. I'll tell her to stress its importance to the FOs in the Pacific time zone.'

He scanned the room and nodded. He was finished.

'Need I say it again?' he asked. 'Your best work. We really need it now more than ever.'

30

The meeting with the locals didn't get under way until almost eleven. It was short and sweet. It was the kind of situation where the suitor asks the bride-to-be's father for approval of the marriage. Most of the time it doesn't really matter what the old man says. It's going to happen. In carefully chosen, friendly words Backus told the locals that the Big G was in town and was now running the show. There was a little bit of posturing and disagreement on some particulars but they rolled over with the empty promises Backus made.

During this meeting, I continued to avoid eye contact with Thorson. While driving over from the federal building Rachel had explained to me the reason for the morning's tensions between her and Thorson. The night before she had run into her former husband in the hotel hallway while leaving my room. Her disheveled appearance probably told him all he needed to know. I groaned when I heard, thinking about how it complicated things. She seemed to be unconcerned and viewed the situation as amusing.

At the end of the meeting with the locals, Backus divided assignments. Rachel and Thompson were given the Orsulak crime scene. I was to ride with them. Mize and Matuzak were to start backtracking on the interviews the locals had conducted of Orsulak's friends and to try to reconstruct the dead detective's movements on his last day. Thorson and Carter were given the Little Joaquin case and assigned to re-cover the ground trod by the locals. Grayson would act as liaison to the Phoenix cops, and Backus, of course, would run the show from the field office, maintaining contact on other developments in the case in Quantico and the other cities.

Orsulak had lived in a small yellow ranch house with stucco walls in South Phoenix. It was a marginal neighborhood. I counted three junk cars parked on gravel lawns and two Sunday morning garage sales in full swing on the block.

Rachel used the key she had gotten from Grayson to cut through an evidence sticker spread across the front doorjamb and then unlocked the door. Before pushing it open she turned to me.

'Remember, they didn't find him for three and a half days. Are you up to this?'

'Course.'

For some reason I was embarrassed that she had asked me this in front of

Thompson, who smiled as if I were a rookie. That annoyed me, too, even though in actuality I was less than a rookie.

We were three steps in before the odor engulfed me. As a reporter I had seen plenty of bodies, but I'd never had the pleasure of entering a closed structure where a body had rotted for three days before discovery. The putrid odor was almost palpable. It was like the ghost of William Orsulak, haunting the place and all who dared enter. Rachel left the front door open to help air the place out some.

'What are you looking for?' I asked once I was reasonably assured that I had control of my throat.

'Inside, I don't know,' Rachel replied. 'It's already been gone over by the locals, his friends . . .'

She went to the dining room table in the room to the right of the door and put down and opened a file she had been carrying. She began leafing through the pages. It was part of the package the local cops had turned over to the agents.

'Have a look around,' she said. 'It looks like they were pretty thorough, but you might come up with something. Just don't touch anything.'

'Right.'

I left her there and started slowly to look about. My eyes first caught on the easy chair in the living room. It was a dark green but the headrest was stained darker with blood. It had flowed down the back into the seat of the chair. Orsulak's blood.

On the floor in front of the chair and near the wall behind it, chalk circles outlined two holes where bullets had been retrieved. Thompson knelt here and opened his toolbox. He began probing the bullet holes with a thin steel pick. I left him there and walked further into the house.

There were two bedrooms, Orsulak's and an extra that seemed dusty and unused. There were photos of two teenaged boys on the bureau in the bedroom the detective had used, but I guessed his kids never used the other, they never came to visit. I moved slowly through these rooms and the hallway bathroom but I saw nothing that I thought mattered to the investigation. I secretly hoped I would come upon something that would help and that would impress Rachel, but I came up empty.

When I stepped back into the living room I saw neither Rachel nor Thompson.

'Rachel?'

No answer.

I walked through the dining room to the kitchen but it was empty. I went through the laundry room, opened a door and glanced into the dark garage but saw no one there either. Coming back into the kitchen I saw the door ajar and glanced through the window over the sink. I saw movement in the tall brush at the rear of the backyard. Rachel was walking, with her head down, through the brush, Thompson behind her.

The yard was cleared for maybe twenty yards going back. A seven-foot-high plank fence ran down both sides. But at the back there was no fence line and the dirt yard dropped down into a dry creek bed where there was a lot of brush. Rachel and Thompson were on a trail moving through the brush away from the house.

'Thanks for waiting,' I said when I caught up. 'What are you doing?'

'What do you think, Jack?' Rachel said. 'Did the Poet just park in the driveway, knock on the door and pop Orsulak after being invited in?'

'I don't know. I doubt it.'

'I do, too. No, he watched him. Maybe for days. But the locals canvassed the neighborhood and no neighbor saw a car that didn't belong. Nobody saw anything out of the routine.'

'So you think he came in through here?'

'It's a possibility.'

She studied the ground as we walked. She was looking for anything. A footprint in the mud, a broken twig. She stopped a few times to bend and look at pieces of debris alongside the trail. A cigarette box, an empty soft drink bottle. She didn't touch any of it. It could be collected later if necessary.

The trail took us under a stanchion holding up high-tension power lines and into a stand of heavy brush at the back end of a trailer park. We reached a high point and looked down into the park. It was not well kept and many of the units had crudely fashioned add-ons like porches and toolsheds. On some of the units the porches had been enclosed with plastic sheeting and were being used as additional bedrooms and living spaces. An aura of crowded poverty emanated from the thirty or so dwellings jammed together on the lot like toothpicks in a box.

'Well, shall we?' Rachel asked, as if we were going for high tea.

'Ladies first,' Thompson said.

Several of the inhabitants of the park were sitting on door stoops and old couches set in front of their units. They were mostly Latinos and a few blacks. Maybe some Indians. They watched us emerge from the brush with no real interest, which showed they recognized us as cops. We showed the same lack of interest in them as we started walking along the narrow lane between rows of trailers.

'What are we doing?' I asked.

'Just having a look,' Rachel answered. 'We can ask questions later. If we take it slow and calm, they'll know we're not here to kick ass. It might help.'

Her eyes never stopped scanning the park and every trailer we passed as we walked. I realized that it was the first time I had seen her at work in the field. This wasn't sitting around a table trying to interpret facts. This was the gathering time. I found myself watching her more than anything else.

'He watched Orsulak,' Rachel said, more to herself than to either Thompson or me. 'And once he knew where he lived, he started planning. How to get in and how to get out. He had to have a getaway route and a getaway car, and it would not have been smart to park it anywhere on Orsulak's street.'

We were coming down the main street, as narrow as it was, to the front of the park and the entrance off a city street.

'So he parked somewhere over here and walked through.'

The first trailer at the entrance had a sign on the door that said OFFICE. A larger sign, attached to an iron framework on top of the trailer, said SUNSHINE ACRES MOBILE HOME PARK.

'Sunshine Acres?' Thompson asked. 'More like Sunshine Half Acre.'

'Not much of a park, either,' I added.

Rachel was off on her own, not listening. She walked past the steps to the office door and out to the city street. It was four lanes and we were in an industrial area. Directly across from the trailer park was a U-Store-It and on either side of that were warehouses. I watched Rachel look around and take in the surroundings. Her eyes held on the one streetlight, which was a half block away. I knew what she was thinking. That it would be dark here at night.

She walked alongside the curb, her eyes scanning the asphalt, looking for something, anything, maybe a cigarette butt or a piece of luck. Thompson stood with me, kicking at the ground with one foot. I couldn't take my eyes off Rachel. I saw her stop and look down and bite her lip for a moment. I walked over.

Glimmering like a cache of diamonds against the curb was a pile of shattered safety glass. She toed her shoe through the glass stones.

The trailer park's manager was already about three shots into the day when we opened the door and stepped into the cramped space advertised outside as an office. It was clear the place was also the man's home. He was sitting in a green corduroy La-Z-Boy chair with the feet extension up. Its sides were scarred by cat scratches but it was still the nicest piece of furniture he had. Other than the television. That was a new-looking Panasonic with a built-in VCR. He was watching a home-shopping show and it took him a long time to pull his eyes off the tube to have a look at us. The device being sold sliced and chopped vegetables without all the mess and setup time of a food processor.

'You the manager?' Rachel asked.

'That should be obvious, shouldn't it, Officer?'

A wise guy, I thought. He was about sixty and he wore green fatigues and a white sleeveless T-shirt with burn holes on the chest through which a crop of gray chest hair protruded. He was balding and had a drinker's red face. He was white, the only white person I had seen so far in the park.

'It's Agent,' she said, showing him the inside of her badge wallet.

'FBI? What's the G care about a little car break-in? See, I read a lot. I know you people call yourselves the G. I like that.'

Rachel looked at me and Thompson and then back at the man. I felt the small tingling of anxiousness.

'How do you know about the car break-in?' Rachel asked.

'I seen you out there. I got eyes. You was lookin' at the glass. I swept it up into a pile. Street cleaners only come 'round here maybe once a month. More in the summer when it's dusty out.'

'No. I mean, how did you even know there was a car burglary?'

''Cause I sleep back there in the back room. I heard 'em break the window. I saw them messing about inside that car.'

'When was this?'

'Let's see, that'd be Thursday last. I was wondering when the guy'd report it. But I didn't think no FBI agent would be coming out. How 'bout you two, you with the G, too?'

'Never mind that, Mr – what is your name, sir?'

'Adkins.'

'Okay, Mr Adkins, do you know whose car got broken into?'

'Nope, never saw him. I just heard the window and saw the kids.'

'What about a plate?'

'Nope.'

'You didn't call the police?'

'Don't have no phone. I could use Thibedoux's over to lot three but it was the middle of the night and I knew those cops wouldn't come running on a car rob'ry. Not here. They got too much to do.'

'So you never at any point saw the owner of the car and he never knocked on the door to see if maybe you heard the break-in or saw anybody?'

'That's right.'

'What about the kids who broke in?' Thompson asked, robbing Rachel of the payoff question. 'You know them, Mr Atkins?'

'Adkins. With a D, no T, Mr G.'

Adkins laughed at his command of the alphabet.

'Mr Adkins,' Thompson said, correcting himself. 'Well, do you?'

'Do I what?'

'Know who the kids were.'

'No, I don't know who they were.'

His eyes strayed past us to the television. On the program they were now selling a glove with small rubber bristles on the palm for grooming pets.

'I know what else you could use that for,' Adkins said. He made a masturbation motion with his hand and winked and smiled at Thompson. 'That's what they're really selling that for, you know.'

Rachel stepped over to the TV and turned it off. Adkins didn't protest. She straightened up and looked at him.

'We're investigating the murder of a police officer. We'd like your attention. We have reason to believe the car you saw burglarized belonged to a suspect. We are not interested in prosecuting the boys who broke into the car, but we need to speak to them. You were lying just then, Mr Adkins. I saw it in your eyes. The boys came from this park.'

'No, I –'

'Let me finish. Yes, you were lying to us. But we're going to give you another chance. You can tell us the truth now or we'll go back and get more agents and police and we'll go through this dump you call a trailer park like an army laying siege. You think we'll find any stolen property in those tin cans? You think we might run across some people wanted on warrant? How about some illegals? What about safety code violations? We passed one back there, I saw the extension cord going out the door into the shed. They've got somebody living in there, don't they? And I bet you and your employer charge extra for that. Or maybe just you do. What's your employer going to say when he finds out? What's he going to say when the receivables go down because the people who are supposed to be paying you rent cannot because they've been deported or they're in lock-up on warrant holds for not paying child support? What about you, Mr *Ad*-kins? You want me to run the serial number off that television on the computer?'

'The TV's mine. Bought it fair and square. Know what you are, FBI lady? Fucking Bitch Investigator.'

Rachel ignored the comment, though I thought Thompson turned away to hide a smile.

'Fair and square from who?'

'Never mind. It was those Tyrell brothers, okay? They're the ones what robbed that car. Now if they come in here and beat the shit outta me, I'm suing you. Got that?'

With directions from Adkins we arrived at a trailer four units in from the main entrance. Word had spread that the law was in the park. There were more people on stoops and sitting on the outdoor couches. When we got to Number 4, the Tyrell brothers were waiting for us.

They were sitting on an old glider beneath a blue canvas awning extending from the side of a double-wide trailer. Next to the door of the trailer were a washer and dryer set beneath a blue canvas cover to keep the rain off. The two brothers were teenagers, maybe a year apart and of mixed race, black and white. Rachel stepped to the edge of the shade provided by the awning. Thompson took a spot about five feet to her left.

'Guys,' Rachel said and got no response. 'Your mother home?'

'Nah, she not, Officer,' the older one said.

He looked at the brother with slow eyes. The brother started rocking the glider back and forth with his leg.

'You know,' Rachel said, 'we know you're smart. We don't want any trouble with you. Don't want to give you any trouble. We promised Mr Adkins that when we went in there to ask where your trailer was.'

'Adkins, shit,' the younger one said.

'We're here about the car that was parked out on the road last week.'

'Didn't see it.'

'No, we didn't see it.'

Rachel walked over close to the older one and bent down to talk directly into his ear.

'Come on now,' she said softly. 'This is one of those times your mother told you about. Think now. Use your head. Remember what she told you. You don't want trouble for her or for yourselves. You want us to go away and leave you alone. And there's only one way we're going to do that.'

When Rachel walked into the squad room at the field office, she carried the plastic bag like a trophy. She set it down on Matuzak's desk and a handful of agents gathered around to look. Backus came in and looked down at it as if he were looking at the Holy Grail. Then he looked up at Rachel with excitement plain in his eyes.

'Grayson checked with the PD,' he said. 'No record of any break-in reported at that spot. Not on that day, not on that week. You'd think a legal citizen who gets his car broken into would make a report.'

Rachel nodded.

'You'd think.'

Backus nodded to Matuzak, who picked the evidence bag up off the table.

'You know what to do?'

'Yes.'

'Bring us back some luck. We need it.'

What the bag contained was a car stereo stolen from a late-model Ford Mustang, white or yellow depending on which of the Tyrell brothers had better eyesight in the dark.

It was all we got from them but the feeling, the hope, was that it was enough. Rachel and Thompson had interviewed them separately and then switched sides and interviewed them again, but the radio was all the Tyrell brothers could give. They said they never saw the driver who left the Mustang at the curb in front of Sunshine Acres and they took nothing but the stereo in a quick smash-and-grab. They never bothered to open the trunk. They never looked at the plate to see if the car was even registered in Arizona.

While Rachel spent the rest of the afternoon doing paperwork and preparing an addendum on the car to be transmitted to all field offices, Matuzak fed the serial number of the stereo to the Automotive ID unit at Washington, D.C., headquarters, then gave the stereo itself to a lab tech for processing. Thompson had taken prints of the Tyrell brothers for elimination purposes.

The lab got no usable prints off the stereo other than those left by the Tyrells. But the serial number was not a dead end. It came back to a 1994 pale yellow Mustang registered to Hertz Corporation. Matuzak and Mize then headed to Sky Harbor International to continue tracing the car.

The mood of the agents in the field office was upbeat. Rachel had delivered. There was no guarantee that the Mustang had been driven by the Poet. But the time of its being parked outside Sunshine Acres matched the time period in which Orsulak had been killed. And there was the fact that the break-in by the brothers had never been reported to the police. It added up to a viable lead and, more so, it gave them a little more knowledge about how the Poet operated. It was an important gain. They felt like I felt. That the Poet was an enigma, a phantom somewhere out there in the darkness. Coming up with a lead like the car stereo seemed to make the possibility of catching him more believable. We were closer and we were coming.

For most of the afternoon I stayed out of the way and simply watched Rachel work. I was fascinated by her skill, amazed at how she had come up with the stereo and how she had talked to Adkins and the Tyrells. At one point in the office she noticed my gaze and asked what I was doing.

'Nothing, just watching.'

'You like watching me?'

'You are good at what you do. It's always interesting to watch somebody like that.'

'Thank you. I just got lucky.'

'I have a feeling you get lucky a lot.'

'I think in this business you make your own luck.'

At the end of the day, after Backus had picked up and read a copy of the alert she had transmitted, I watched his eyes narrow into two black marbles.

'I wonder if that choice of car was intentional?' he asked. 'A pale yellow Mustang.'

'Why's that?' I asked.

I saw Rachel nodding. She knew the answer.

'The Bible,' Backus said. ' "Behold a pale horse: and his name that sat on him was Death." '

' "And Hell followed with him," ' Rachel finished.

We made love again Sunday night and she seemed even more giving and needing of the intimacy. In the end, if either of us was holding back, it was me. While I wanted nothing more in the world at that moment than to surrender to the feelings I had for her, a low whisper in the back of my mind found just enough volume to question her motives. Perhaps it was a testament to my own precarious self-confidence, but I couldn't help but listen to the voice when it suggested that perhaps her aim was just as much to hurt her ex-husband as to please me and herself. The thought made me feel guilty and insincere.

When we held each other afterward, she whispered that this time she was going to stay until dawn.

31

The phone pulled me out of a sound sleep. I looked around the strange confines of the room, getting my bearings, and my eyes fell on Rachel's.

'You better get it,' she said calmly. 'It's your room.'

She didn't seem to have nearly the same difficulty I had coming awake. In fact, for a moment I had the feeling she had already been awake and was watching me when the phone rang. I lifted the receiver on what I guessed was the ninth or tenth ring. At the same time I saw that the clock on the bed table said it was seven-fifteen.

'Yes?'

'Put Walling on the line.'

I froze. There was something reminiscent about the voice but I didn't place it in my jumbled mind. Then a thought occurred to me that Rachel shouldn't be in my room.

'You got the wrong room. She's in –'

'Don't fuck with me, reporter. Put her on.'

I covered the phone with my hand and turned to Rachel.

'It's Thorson. He says he knows you're there – here.'

'Give it to me,' she said angrily and jerked the phone out of my hand. 'What do you want?'

There was a period of silence. He must've said two or three sentences to her.

'Where did it come from?'

More silence.

'Why are you calling me?' she asked, the anger back in her voice. 'Go ahead and tell him, if that's what you want. If you want him to know. It says as much about you as me. I'm sure he'd like to know that you're some kind of Peeping Tom.'

She handed me the phone and I hung it up. She pulled a pillow over her face and moaned. I pulled it off her face.

'What is it?'

'I've got bad news for you, Jack.'

'What?'

'In this morning's edition of the *Los Angeles Times* there was a story about the Poet. I'm sorry. I've got to bring you into the FO for a meeting with Bob.'

I was silent for a moment, confused.

'How'd they . . .'

'We don't know. That's what we're going to talk about.'

'How much did they have, did he say?'

'No. But apparently it was enough.'

'I knew I should have written this yesterday. Damn it! Once it was clear that this guy knew about you people, there was no reason not to write it.'

'You made a deal and stuck to it. You had to, Jack. Look, let's wait on this until we get to the office and talk about what they had.'

'I've got to call my editor.'

'You can do that later. Bob's apparently already in and waiting for us. I guess he doesn't sleep.'

The phone rang again. She jerked the phone out of the cradle.

'What is it?' she said in a voice painted with annoyance. Then in a softer tone, she said, 'Hold on.'

She smiled sheepishly and handed me the phone. She then lightly kissed me on the cheek, whispered that she was going to her room to get ready and started to get dressed. I put the phone to my ear.

'Hello?'

'It's Greg Glenn. Who was that?'

'Uh, that was an FBI agent. We've got a meeting. I guess you've heard about the *L.A. Times.*'

'You're damn right I have.'

The sinking sensation in my chest was growing. Glenn went on.

'They've got a story on the killer in the paper. *Our* killer, Jack. They're calling him the Poet. You told me we had the exclusive on this and we were protected.'

'We were.'

It was all I could manage to say. As Rachel finished throwing her clothes on she watched me with sympathetic eyes.

'Not anymore. You've got to come back this morning and write ours for tomorrow. Whatever you've got. And you better have more than they've got. We could've had this in the paper, Jack, but you convinced me. Now we're playing catch-up on our own story, goddammit.'

'All right!' I said sharply just to shut him up.

'And I hope I don't find out that you've extended your stay in Phoenix just because you found some babe to bang down there.'

'Fuck you, Greg. Do you have the story there or not?'

'Of course I do. It's a great story. A great read. But it's in the wrong paper!'

'Just read it to me. No, wait a minute. I gotta go to this meeting. Have somebody in the library –'

'Don't you listen, Jack? You aren't going to any meeting. I want you on the next plane back here to write this for tomorrow.'

I watched Rachel blow a kiss at me and then go out the door.

'I understand. You'll have it for tomorrow. But I can write it here and ship it.'

'No. This is a hands-on story. I want to work this one right here with you.'

'Let me go to this meeting and call you back.'

'Why?'

'There's a new development,' I lied. 'I don't know what it is and I have to go to find out. Let me go and I'll call you. Meantime, have the library take the *Times* story off their wire and ship it to my basket. I'll call it up here. I gotta go.'

I hung up before he could protest. I quickly got dressed and headed out the door with my computer bag. I was in a daze. I didn't know how this could have happened. But a thought was pushing through.

Thorson.

We each grabbed two cups to go from a hospitality stand in the lobby and then headed to the federal building. She had packed all her things again. I had forgotten.

We didn't talk until we had finished our first cups. I imagined we had completely different dilemmas and different thoughts going through our minds.

'Are you going back to Denver?' she asked.

'I don't know yet.'

'How bad was it?'

'It was bad. Last time he'll ever listen to one of my promises.'

'I don't understand how it could've happened. They would have had to call Bob Backus for comment.'

'Maybe they did.'

'No, he would have told you. He would have kept his deal. He's second-generation bureau. I've never seen anyone toe the line like that man.'

'Well, I hope he keeps the deal now. Because I'm writing today.'

'What did the story say?'

'I don't know. I should have it as soon as I can hook up to a phone.'

We were at the courthouse. She pulled into the garage for federal employees.

Only Backus and Thorson were in the conference room.

The meeting began with Backus expressing his regret that the story had leaked before I could write it. It seemed legitimate to me and I regretted impugning his integrity with my comment earlier to Rachel.

'Do you have it? I can get it on my computer if I can use the phone line.'

'By all means. I've been waiting for someone from the L.A. field office to fax it. The only reason I know about it is because Brass tells me we're already getting calls from other media into Quantico.'

I plugged in and turned on my computer and dialed into the *Rocky* system. I didn't bother to read any of my messages. I went right to my personal basket and looked at the files. I noticed there were two new ones: POETCOP and HYPSTORIES. I remembered then that I had asked Laurie Prine for stories on hypnosis and Horace the Hypnotist but I'd have to look at those files later. I called up POETCOPY and got a shock that I should have seen coming before I had even read the first line of the story.

'Damn it!'

'What?' Rachel asked.

'It was written by Warren. He resigns from the Law Enforcement Foundation and then turns around and uses *my* story to get back with the *Times*.'

'Reporters,' Thorson said with unhidden joy. 'Just can't trust them.'

I ignored him but it was hard. I was angry about what had happened. At Warren and at myself. I should have seen it coming.

'Read it, Jack,' Backus said.

I did.

FBI, POLICE SEEK SERIAL COP KILLER

The Hunted Turns on the Hunters

By Michael Warren, Special to the Times

> The FBI has begun a manhunt for a serial killer who has claimed as many as seven homicide detectives as his victims in a nationwide rampage begun as long as three years ago.
>
> Dubbed the 'Poet' because he has left notes containing lines of poetry from the work of Edgar Allan Poe at each murder scene, the suspect has attempted to disguise the deaths of his victims as suicides.
>
> And for as long as three years his victims were counted as such until the similarities of the crimes, including the quotes from Poe, were discovered last week, according to a source close to the investigation.
>
> That discovery prompted the FBI to act quickly in its efforts to identify and capture the Poet. Dozens of FBI agents and police in seven cities are carrying out the investigation under the direction of the FBI's Behavioral Science Services. The investigation currently has its most intense focus on Phoenix, where the latest death attributed to the Poet occurred, the source said.
>
> The source, who talked to the *Times* on the condition of anonymity, declined to disclose how the activities of the Poet were discovered but said that a joint study by the FBI and the Law Enforcement Foundation of police suicides in the last six years provided key information.

The story went on to list the names of the victims and some of the details of each case. It then included a few paragraphs on the BSS unit as filler and ended with a wrap-up quote from the unnamed source saying that the FBI had little to go on in terms of knowing who or where the Poet was.

By the time I was done reading it, my cheeks were hot with anger. There is nothing worse than living by the letter of an agreement when one of the people you made the deal with doesn't. The story was weak, in my opinion, a lot of words around a few facts and all attributed to an anonymous source. Warren didn't even mention the fax or, more importantly, the bait murders. I knew that what I would write that day would be the definitive piece on the Poet. But that didn't move the anger back in my throat much. For whatever the shortcomings of the story were, it was still clear that Warren had talked to somebody in the bureau. And I couldn't help but think that that person was sitting at the conference room table with me.

'We had a deal,' I said, looking up from the computer. 'Somebody gave this to this guy. He knew what I had when I came in to him on Thursday, but he went to somebody in the bureau for the rest. Probably someone on the task force. Probably somebody –'

'That may be true, Jack, but –'

'He already had this because of you,' Thorson interrupted. 'You only have yourself to blame.'

'Wrong,' I said, glaring back at him. 'I gave him most of it but not the Poet. The offender wasn't even called that when I was with Warren. That came from the task force. And that blows our deal. Somebody's talking who shouldn't be talking. The story's out. I have to go write what I know today for tomorrow.'

A small measure of silence passed through the room.

'Jack,' Backus said, 'I know this won't do you much good now but I want you to know that when I get some time and space on this thing, I am going to find out who the leak was and that person won't be working for me anymore, and maybe not even the bureau.'

'You're right. It doesn't do me much good.'

'I need to ask a favor, nonetheless.'

I looked at Backus, wondering if he was actually foolish enough to try again to persuade me to hold off on writing a story every TV station and paper in the country would be running anyway that night and the next day.

'What is it?'

'When you write this . . . I want you to please keep in mind that we still need to get this man. You have information that could irreparably harm our chances of doing that. I'm talking about specific things. Details of the profile. Details about the possible hypnosis, the condoms. If you print those, Jack, and they are repeated on TV or in a newspaper he has access to, then he will change his routine. See what I'm saying? It will only make it harder for us.'

I nodded but then looked at him with a hard stare.

'You're not going to tell me what to write.'

'I know that. I'm asking you to think about your brother, about us, and be *careful* of what you write. I trust you, Jack. Implicitly.'

I thought about that for a long moment and then nodded again.

'Bob, I made a deal with you and came out on the short end. If you want me to protect you now, there's got to be a new deal. You're going to have reporters coming out of the woodwork today. But I want you to refer all calls to public affairs in Quantico. I talk to and quote from you exclusively. Also, I get the fax from the Poet exclusively. You give me that and I won't mention the details of the profile or the hypnosis in my story.'

'That's a deal,' Backus said.

He said it so quickly that I started to think he knew exactly what I had been going to say, that he had known all along that I was going to suggest the new deal.

'But one thing, Jack,' Backus said. 'Let's agree on holding back one line from the fax. If we start getting confessions, we'll be able to use the hold-back line to weed out the phonies.'

'No problem,' I said.

'I'll be here. I'll tell the front that your calls can come through. No one else from the press.'

'There will be a lot of those calls.'

'My intention was to let public affairs handle it anyway.'

'If the statement they put out includes the origination of the case, tell them not to use my name. Just say inquiries from the *Rocky Mountain News* started it rolling.'

Backus nodded.

'One last thing,' I said and then paused a moment. 'I'm still concerned about the leak. If I find out the *L.A. Times* or any other media outlet also got the Poet fax today, then I'll put everything I know into the next story. The profile, everything. Okay?'

'Understood.'

'You weasel,' Thorson said angrily. 'You think you can just come in here and dictate what –'

'Fuck you, Thorson,' I said. 'I've been wanting to say that to you since Quantico. Fuck you, okay? If I was betting, I'd say you were the leak, so don't tell me anything about being a weas –'

'FUCK YOU!' Thorson roared as he stood up to challenge me.

But quickly Backus was up and putting a hand on his shoulder. He gently pushed him back down into his seat. Rachel watched the whole thing, a small, thin smile on her face.

'Easy, Gordon,' Backus soothed. 'Easy. Nobody's accusing anyone of anything. Let's keep things cool. Everybody's a little hot and bothered today but it's no reason why we can't cool down. Jack, that's a dangerous accusation. If you have something to back it up, let's hear it. If not, you'd best leave things like that unsaid.'

I said nothing. I only had my gut instinct that Thorson had leaked the story to fuck me over because of some paranoia about reporters in general and my relationship with Rachel in particular. It wasn't the kind of thing to bring up for discussion. Everybody eventually took their seats and just stared at each other.

'That was entertaining as hell, fellas, but I'd like to do some work today,' Rachel finally said.

'And I have to go,' I said. 'What line do you want to hold back on the fax?'

'The riddle,' Backus answered. 'Don't mention Best Pals.'

I thought a moment. It was one of the better lines.

'Fine. No problem.'

I stood up and so did Rachel.

'I'll give you a ride back to the hotel.'

'Is it that bad, getting scooped like that?' she asked as we were headed back to the hotel.

'It's bad. I guess it's like with you guys, the ones that get away. I hope Backus busts Thorson for this. The asshole.'

'It will be hard for him to prove anything. It's just going to be suspicion.'

'If you told Backus about us and told him that Thorson knew, then he'd believe it.'

'I can't. If I told Backus about us I'd be the one who'd go down.'

After some silence she changed the subject back to the story.

'You'll have so much more than he had.'

'What? Who?'

'I'm talking about Warren. You'll have the better story.'

'First with the story, first with the glory. That's an old newspaper saying. But it's true. In most stories, the one that's there first is always the one who gets the credit, even if the first story is full of holes and bullshit. Even if it's a stolen story.'

'Is that what it's about? Getting credit? Just being first, even if you don't have it right?'

I looked over at her and tried to smile.

'Yeah, sometimes. Most times. Pretty noble job, huh?'

She didn't answer. We drove in silence for a while. I wished that she would say something about us and what we had or didn't have but she didn't. We were getting close to the hotel now.

'What if I can't convince him to let me stay here and I have to go back to Denver? What happens to us?'

She didn't answer for a while.

'I don't know, Jack. What do you want to happen?'

'I don't know but I don't want it to just end like this. I thought . . .'

I didn't know how to say what I wanted to tell her.

'I don't want it to end like this, either.'

She drove to the front of the hotel to drop me off. She said she had to get back. A guy in a red jacket with gold braid on the shoulders opened the door for me, robbing us of any privacy. I wanted to kiss her but something about the situation and being in the G car made it seem inappropriate and awkward.

'I'll see you when I can,' I said. 'As soon as I can.'

'Good,' she said, smiling. 'Good-bye, Jack. Good luck with the story. Call me at the field office and let me know if you are writing from here. Maybe we can get together tonight.'

That was a better reason than any I had come up with for staying in Phoenix. She reached over and touched my beard like she had done once before. And just before I got out of the car she told me to wait. She took a card out of her purse and wrote a number on the back of it, then she gave it to me.

'That's my pager number in case something happens. It's on the satellite, so you can beep me wherever I am.'

'In the whole world?'

'The whole world. Until the satellite falls.'

32

Gladden looked at the words on the screen. They were beautiful, as if written by the unseen hand of God. So right. So knowledgeable. He read them again.

> They know about me now and I am ready. I await them. I am prepared to take my place in the pantheon of faces. I feel as I did as a child when I waited for the closet door to be opened so that I could receive him. The line of light at the bottom. My beacon. I watched the light and the shadows each of his footfalls made. Then I knew he was there and that I would have his love. The apple of his eye.
>
> We are what they make us and yet they turn from us. We are cast off. We become nomads in the world of the moan. My rejection is my pain and motivation. I carry with me the vengeance of all the children. I am the Eidolon. I am called the predator, the one to watch for in your midst. I am the cucoloris, the blur of light and dark. My story is not one of deprivation and abuse. I welcomed the touch. I can admit it. Can you? I wanted, craved, welcomed the touch. It was only the rejection – when my bones grew too large – that cut me so deeply and forced on me the life of a wanderer. I am the cast off. And the children must stay forever young.

He looked up when the phone rang. It was on the counter in the kitchen and he stared at it as it rang. It was the first call she had gotten. The machine picked up after three rings and her taped message played. Gladden had written it out on a piece of paper and made her read it three times before it was recorded on the fourth. Stupid woman, he thought as he listened now. She wasn't much of an actress – at least with her clothes on.

'Hello, this is Darlene, I . . . I can't take your call right now. I've had to go out of town because of an emergency. I will be checking messages – uh, messages and will call you as soon as I can.'

She sounded nervous and Gladden worried that because of the repeat of the one word that a caller would know she was reading. He listened as a male voice left an angry message after the beep.

'Darlene, goddammit! You better call me as soon as you get this. You left me in a big lurch over here. You shoulda called and you just might not have a job to come back to, girl, goddammit!'

Gladden thought it had worked. He got up and erased the message. Her boss, he assumed. But he wouldn't be getting a callback from Darlene.

He noticed the smell as he stood in the kitchen doorway. He grabbed his matches off his cigarettes on the living room coffee table and went into the bedroom. He studied the body for a few moments. The face was a pale green but darker since the last time he had checked. Bloody fluid was draining from the mouth and nose, as the body purged itself of decomposition fluids. He had read about these purges in one of the books he had successfully petitioned to receive before the warden at Raiford. *Forensic Pathology.* Gladden wished he had the camera so he could document the changes in Darlene.

He lit four more sticks of jasmine incense, placing them in ashtrays at the four corners of the bed.

This time, after he had left and closed the bedroom door, he laid a wet towel along the threshold, hoping it would prevent the odor from spreading into the area of the apartment where he was living. He still had two days to go.

33

I talked Greg Glenn into letting me write from Phoenix. For the rest of the morning I stayed in my room making calls, gathering comments from players in the story ranging from Wexler in Denver to Bledsoe in Baltimore. I wrote for five straight hours after that and the only disturbances I had all day were calls from Glenn himself, nervously asking how I was doing. An hour before the five o'clock deadline in Denver, I filed two stories to the metro desk.

My nerves were jangling by the time I shipped the stories and I had a headache that was almost off the scale. I had been through a pot and a half of room service coffee and a full pack of Marlboros – the most I had smoked in one sitting in years. Pacing the room and waiting for Greg Glenn's callback, I made a quick call to room service again, explained that I couldn't leave my room because I was expecting an important call, and ordered a bottle of aspirin from the hotel's lobby shop.

After it arrived I downed three tablets with mineral water from the minibar and almost immediately started feeling better. Next I called my mother and Riley and alerted them that my stories would be in the next day's paper. I also told them there was a chance that reporters from other media outlets might try to contact them now that the story was out and to be prepared. Both said they didn't want to talk to any reporters and I said that was fine, not missing the irony that I was one myself.

Lastly, I realized I had forgotten to call Rachel to tell her I was still in town. I called the Phoenix field office of the FBI but was told by the agent who answered that she was gone.

'What do you mean "gone"? Is she still in Phoenix?'

'I'm not at liberty to say.'

'Can I speak with Agent Backus then?'

'He's gone, too. Who may I ask is calling?'

I hung up and dialed the hotel's front desk and asked for her room. I was told she had checked out. So had Backus. So had Thorson, Carter and Thompson.

'Son of a bitch,' I said after hanging up.

There had been a break. Had to be. For all of them to have checked out, there had to have been a major breakthrough in the investigation. And I realized I had been left behind, that my moment on the inside was surely over now. I got up and paced the room some more, wondering where they would have gone and what could have made them move so quickly. Then I remembered the card Rachel had given me. I dug it out of my pocket and punched the paging number into the phone.

Ten minutes surely seemed enough time to bounce my message off the satellite and then down to her, wherever she was. But ten minutes came and went and the phone didn't ring. Another ten minutes passed and then a half hour. Not even Greg Glenn called. I even picked up the phone to make sure I hadn't broken it.

Restless, but tired of pacing and waiting, I fired up the laptop and logged into the *Rocky* again. I called up my messages but there were none of any importance. I switched to my personal basket, scrolled the files and called up the one labeled HYPSTORIES. The file contained several stories on Horace Gomble, one after the other in chronological order. I began to read from the oldest story forward, my memory of the hypnotist coming back as I went.

It was a colorful history. A physician and researcher for the CIA in the early sixties, Gomble later was a practicing psychiatrist in Beverly Hills who specialized in hypnotherapy. He parlayed his skill and expertise in the hypnotic arts, as he called them, into a nightclub act as Horace the Hypnotist. First it was just appearances on open-mike nights at the clubs in Los Angeles but the act became immensely popular and he started taking it to Las Vegas for weeklong gigs on the strip. Soon Gomble wasn't a practicing shrink anymore. He was a full-time entertainer appearing on the stages of the nicest palaces on the Las Vegas strip. By the mid-seventies his name was on the billing with Sinatra's at Caesar's, albeit in smaller letters. He made four appearances on Carson's show, the last time putting his host in a hypnotic trance and eliciting from him his true thoughts on his other guests that evening. Because of Carson's caustic comments, the studio audience thought it was a gag. But it wasn't. After Carson saw the tape, he canceled the airing of the show and put Horace the Hypnotist on his blacklist. The cancellation made news in the entertainment trade papers and was a knife in the heart of Gomble's career. He never made another network television appearance until his arrest.

His shot at TV gone, Gomble's shtick got old, even in Vegas, and his stages moved further and further away from the strip. Soon he was on the road, working comedy clubs and cabarets, then finally it was the strip club and county fair circuit. His fall from fame was complete. His arrest in Orlando at the Orange County Fair was the exclamation mark at the end of that fall.

According to the trial stories, Gomble was charged with assaulting young girls whom he had chosen as volunteer assistants for matinee performances at the county fair. Prosecutors said he followed a routine of seeking a girl ten to twelve years old from the audience and then taking her backstage to prepare. Once in his private dressing room, he gave the intended victim a Coke laced with codeine and sodium pentothal – a quantity of both was seized during his arrest – and told her he must see if she could be hypnotized before the performance started. With the drugs acting as hypnotic enhancers, the girl was placed in a trance and then assaulted by Gomble. Prosecutors said the molestation primarily involved fellatio and masturbation, actions difficult to prove through physical evidence. Afterward, Gomble repressed memory of the event in the victim's mind with hypnotic suggestion.

It was unknown how many girls were victimized by Gomble. He was not discovered until a psychologist treating a thirteen-year-old girl with behavioral problems brought out her assault by Gomble during a hypnotherapy session. A police investigation was launched and Gomble was eventually charged with attacks on four girls.

At trial the defense's contention was that the events as described by the victims and police simply did not happen. Gomble presented no fewer than six highly qualified experts in hypnotism who testified that the human mind, while in a hypnotic trance, could not be persuaded or forced under any circumstances to do or even say anything that would endanger the person or be morally repugnant to them. And Gomble's attorney never missed a chance to remind the jury that there was no physical evidence of molestation.

But the prosecution won the case with essentially one witness. He was Gomble's former CIA supervisor, who testified that Gomble's research in the early sixties included experimentation with hypnosis and the use of drug combinations to create a 'hypnotic override' of the brain's moral and safety inhibitions. It was mind control, and the former CIA supervisor said codeine and sodium pentothal were both among the drugs Gomble had used with positive results in his studies.

A jury took two days to convict Gomble of four counts of sexual assault of a child. He was sentenced to eighty-five years in prison to be served at the Union Correctional Institute in Raiford. One of the stories in the file said he had appealed the conviction on the basis of incompetent counsel but his plea was rejected all the way up to the Florida supreme court.

As I reached the bottom of the computer file I noticed the last story was only a few days old. I found this curious because Gomble had been convicted seven years earlier. This story also had come from the *L.A. Times* instead of the *Orlando Sentinel,* which all the previous ones had come from.

Curious, I started reading it and at first believed Laurie Prine had simply made a mistake. It happens often enough. I thought she had shipped me a story unrelated to my request and that somebody else at the *Rocky* had probably asked for.

It was a report on a suspect in the murder of a Hollywood motel maid. I was about to stop reading but then I came across Horace Gomble's name. The story said the suspect in the maid's killing had served time at Raiford with Gomble and even helped him with some undescribed jailhouse legal work. I reread the lines as an idea spun in my mind and then finally couldn't be contained.

Once more I called Rachel's pager after disconnecting the laptop. This time my fingers were shaking as I punched out the number and I could hardly keep still afterward. I paced the room again, staring at the phone. Finally, as if the power of my stare had caused it, the phone rang and I grabbed it up before it had even stopped its first sounding.

'Rachel, I think I've got something.'

'Just hope it isn't syphilis, Jack.'

It was Greg Glenn.

'I thought it was somebody else. Listen, I'm waiting on a call. It's very important and when it comes I should take it.'

'Forget it, Jack. We're pushing the envelope. You ready?'

I looked at my watch. It was ten minutes past the first deadline.

'Okay, I'm ready. The faster the better.'

'Okay, first off, good work, Jack. This . . . well, it doesn't make up entirely for not being first, but it's a much better read and much better information.'

'Okay, so what needs to be fixed?' I asked quickly.

I didn't care about his compliment/criticism parlay. I just wanted to be done by the time Rachel answered my page. Because there was only one phone line into the room I couldn't use my laptop to connect with the *Rocky* and view the actual edited version of the story. Instead I called up the original version on the laptop and Glenn read off the changes he had made.

'I want to make the lead a little tighter and stronger, go right out with the fax a little harder. I fiddled around with it and this is what I've got. "A cryptic note from a serial killer who apparently preys on randomly selected children, women and homicide detectives was being analyzed by FBI agents Monday as the latest twist in the investigation of the slayer they have dubbed the Poet." What do you think?'

'Fine.'

He had changed the word 'studied' to 'analyzed.' It wasn't worth protesting. We spent the next ten minutes fine-tuning the main story, going back and forth on nitpicks. He didn't make too many significant changes and with deadline breathing on his neck he didn't have the time to do a lot, anyway. In the end, I thought some of the changes were good and some were made simply for change's sake, a practice all newspaper editors I've worked with seem to share. The second story was a short, first-person account of how my search for understanding of my brother's suicide uncovered the trail of the Poet. It was an understated tooting of the *Rocky*'s horn. Glenn didn't mess with it. When we were done he had me hold on the line while he shipped the stories to the copy desk.

'I think maybe we should keep this line open in case they come up with something on the rim,' Glenn said.

'Who's got it?'

'Brown has the main and Bayer has the side. I'll do the back reading myself.'

I was in good hands. Brown and Bayer were two of the best of the rim rats.

'So, what are you planning for tomorrow?' Glenn asked while we were waiting. 'I know it's early but we also have to talk about the weekend.'

'I haven't thought about that stuff yet.'

'You've got to have a follow, Jack. Something. We don't go out front this big with something and then come back flat-footed the next day. There's gotta be a follow. And for this weekend, I'd like a scene setter. You know, inside the FBI hunt for a serial killer, maybe get into the personalities of the people you've been dealing with. We'll need art, too.'

'I know, I know,' I said. 'I just haven't thought about all of that yet.'

I didn't want to tell him about my latest discovery and the new theory I was brewing. Information like that in an editor's hands was dangerous. The next thing you knew it would be on the daily news budget – practically the same as being written in granite – that I'd have a follow linking the Poet to Horace the Hypnotist. I decided I would wait and talk to Rachel before I told Glenn about that.

'What about the bureau? They going to let you back inside?'

'Good question,' I said. 'I doubt it. I kind of got the sayonara when I left today. In fact, I don't even know where they are. I think they blew town. Something's happening.'

'Shit, Jack. I thought you –'

'Don't worry, Greg, I'll find out where they went. And when I do, I've still got some leverage with them and there are a few things I didn't have room for in the stories today. One way or the other, I'll have something tomorrow. I just don't know what, yet. After that, I'll do the scene setter. But don't count on any art. These people don't like having their pictures taken.'

After a few more minutes Glenn got an all clear from the copy desk and the story was shipped to composing. Glenn said he was going to baby-sit it to production to make sure nothing went wrong. But I was finished for the night. He told me to have a nice dinner on the company expense account and call him in the morning. I told him I would.

As I contemplated whether to page Rachel for a third time, the phone rang.

'Hiya, sport.'

I recognized the sarcasm dripping off the voice.

'Thorson.'

'You got it.'

'What do you want?'

'I'm just letting you know that Agent Walling is tied up and she won't be calling you back any time soon. So do us and yourself a favor and stop calling the pager. It gets annoying.'

'Where is she?'

'That's really none of your business now, is it? You shot your wad, so to speak. You got your story. Now you're on your own.'

'You're in L.A.'

'Message delivered, signing off.'

'Wait! Listen, Thorson, I think I've got something. Let me talk to Backus.'

'No, sir, you aren't talking to anyone on this investigation anymore. You are out, McEvoy. Remember that. All media inquiries on this investigation are now being handled by public affairs at Washington headquarters.'

Anger was balling like a fist inside me. My jaw was clenched tight but I managed to take a shot at him.

'Does that include Michael Warren's inquiries, Thorson? Or does he have a direct line to you?'

'You're wrong about that, fuckhead. I'm no leak. You kind of people make me sick. I've got more respect for some of the scumbags I've put in stir than I have for you.'

'Fuck you, too.'

'See what I mean? You people have no respect whatso –'

'Fuck that, Thorson. Let me talk to Rachel or Backus. I've got a lead they should have.'

'You have something, you give it to me. They're busy.'

It galled me to tell him anything at all but I swallowed back the anger and did what I thought was the right thing.

'I have a name. It could be the guy. William Gladden. He's a pedophile from Florida but he's in L.A. At least he was. He –'

'I know who he is and what he is.'

'You do?'

'Past experience.'

Then I remembered. The prison interviews.

'The rape project? Rachel told me about that. He was one of the subjects?'

'Yes. So forget him, he's not the guy. Thought you were going to be the hero and solve it, didn't you?'

'How do you know he's not the guy? He fits and there's the possibility he learned hypnotism from Horace Gomble. If you know about Gladden, then you know about Gomble. It all fits. They're looking for Gladden in L.A. He cut up a motel maid. Don't you see? The maid could be the bait murder. The detective – his name is Ed Thomas – could be the intended victim he was talking about in the fax. Let me –'

'You're wrong,' Thorson interrupted loudly. 'We already checked this guy out. You're not the first to come up with him, McEvoy. You're not that special. We checked Gladden out and he's not our guy, okay? We're not stupid. Now drop it and go the fuck back to Denver. When we get the real guy, you'll know.'

'How do you mean you checked Gladden out?'

'I'm not going into it. We're busy and you're no longer inside. You're out and you're staying out. Just don't call the pager anymore. Like I said, it gets annoying.'

He hung up before I could say another word. I slammed the phone into its cradle and it bounced down to the floor. I was tempted to page Rachel again immediately but thought better of it. What could she be doing, I wondered, that would have made her ask Thorson to call me instead of calling me herself? A crushing feeling began to form in my chest and many thoughts went through my mind. Had she merely been baby-sitting me while I was on the case with them? Watching me while I watched them? Had everything just been an act for her?

I broke away from it. There was no way to know the answers until I spoke to her. I had to guard against letting my impressions of Thorson's comments speak for her. Instead, I began to analyze what Thorson had told me. He said Rachel could not call me. She was tied up. What could that mean? Did they have a suspect in custody and she, as lead investigator, was conducting the interrogation? Was the suspect under surveillance? If so, she might be in a car and away from a telephone.

Or by asking Thorson to call me was she sending me a message, communicating something she didn't have the guts to tell me herself?

The nuances of the situation were unreadable to me. I gave up on a deeper meaning and thought about the surface. I thought about Thorson's reaction to my mention of William Gladden. He'd showed no surprise at the name and seemed to easily dismiss it. But in replaying the conversation in my mind, I realized that whether I was right or wrong about Gladden, Thorson would have played it the same way. If I was right, he would have wanted to deflect me. If I was wrong, he would not have missed the opportunity to let me know.

The next thought I focused on was the possibility that I was right about Gladden and that the bureau had somehow made a mistake in dismissing him as a suspect. If this was the case, the detective in Los Angeles could be in danger and not even know it.

It took me two calls to the Los Angeles Police Department to get a number for Detective Thomas at the Hollywood Division. But when I called the number it went unanswered and kicked over to the station's front desk. The officer who answered told me Thomas was unavailable. He would not tell me why or when the detective would be available. I decided not to leave a message.

I paced the room for a few minutes after hanging up and wrestled with thoughts about what to do. I came to the same conclusion from every angle I tried. There was only one way of learning the answers to the questions I had about Gladden and I knew that was to go to Los Angeles. To go to Detective Thomas. I had nothing to lose. My stories were filed and I was off the case. I made some calls and booked the next Southwest flight from Phoenix to Burbank. The airline agent told me Burbank was just as close to Hollywood as L.A. International.

The front-desk clerk was the same man who had checked all of us in on Saturday.

'You're leaving on the fly, too, I see.'

I nodded, realizing he was talking about the FBI agents.

'Yes,' I said. 'They got a head start, though.'

He smiled.

'I saw you on TV the other night.'

At first perplexed, I then realized what he meant. The scene out at the funeral home. Me in the FBI shirt. I knew then that the clerk thought I was an FBI agent. I didn't bother to correct him.

'The boss man wasn't too happy about that,' I said.

'Well, you people must get that a lot when you swoop into town like that. Anyway, I hope you catch him.'

'Yeah, we do, too.'

He went about processing my bill. He asked if I had any room charges and I told him about the room service and the items I had taken from the bar.

'Listen,' I said. 'I guess you also have to charge me for a pillowcase. I had to buy clothes here and didn't have any luggage and . . .'

I held up the pillowcase in which I had packed my few belongings and he chuckled at my predicament. But figuring what to charge me caused confusion and finally he just told me it was on the house.

'I understand you people have to move quickly,' he said. 'The others didn't even have time to check out. Just blew out of town like a Texas tornado, I guess.'

'Well,' I said smiling. 'I hope they at least paid.'

'Oh, yes. Agent Backus called from the airport and said just to keep it on the credit card and send him the receipts. But that's no problem. We aim to please.'

I just looked at him, thinking. Deciding.

'I'm going to be catching up with them tonight,' I finally said. 'You want me to take the receipts?'

He looked up at me from the paperwork in front of him. I could see his hesitation. I held my hand up in a not-to-worry fashion.

'It's all right. It was just a thought. I'll see them tonight and thought it might speed things along. You know, save the postage.'

I didn't know what I was saying but I was already lacking confidence in my decision and wanted to back away.

'Well,' the clerk said, 'I don't really see the harm in it. I've got their paperwork in an envelope ready to go. I guess I can trust you as much as the mailman.'

He smiled and now I smiled back.

'The same guy signs our checks, right?'

'Uncle Sam,' he said brightly. 'Be right back.'

He disappeared into a back office and I looked around the front desk and lobby, halfway expecting Thorson and Backus and Walling to jump out from behind the columns and scream, 'See? We can't trust your kind!'

But nobody jumped out from anywhere and soon the clerk was back with a manila envelope he handed across the counter to me with my own hotel bill.

'Thanks,' I said. 'They'll appreciate it.'

'No problem,' the clerk said. 'Thank you for choosing to stay with us, Agent McEvoy.'

I nodded and shoved the envelope into my computer bag like a thief, then headed to the door.

34

The plane was climbing toward thirty thousand feet before I had a chance to open the envelope. There were several pages of bills. One itemized breakdown for each agent's room. This was what I counted on and I immediately was pulled to the bill with Thorson's name on it and began to study the phone charges.

The bill showed no calls to the Maryland area code, 301, where Warren lived. However, there was a call to the 213 area code. Los Angeles. I knew it was not inconceivable that Warren had gone to L.A. to pitch his story to his former editors. He then could have written it from there. The call had been made at 12:41 A.M. Sunday, just an hour or so after Thorson had apparently checked into the hotel in Phoenix.

After using my Visa card to pop the air phone from the seatback in front of me, I slid the credit card through and punched in the number listed on the hotel bill. The call was answered immediately by a woman who said, 'New Otani Hotel, may I help you?'

Momentarily confused, I recovered before she hung up and asked for the room of Michael Warren. I was connected but there was no answer. I realized it was too early for him to be in his room. I depressed the receiver button and called information to get the number of the *Los Angeles Times.* When I called that number I asked for the newsroom and then asked for Warren. I was connected.

'Warren,' I said.

It was a statement, a fact. A verdict. For Thorson as well as Warren.

'Yes, can I help you?'

He didn't know who it was.

'I just wanted to say fuck you, Warren. And to let you know, someday I'm going to write about all this and what you did is going in the book.'

I didn't know exactly what I was saying. I only knew that I felt the need to threaten him and had nothing to do it with. Only words.

'McEvoy? Is this McEvoy?' He paused to inject a sarcastic laugh. 'What book? I've already got my agent on the street with a proposal. What've you got? Huh? What've you got? Hey, Jack, do you even have an agent?'

He waited for an answer and I only had rage. I was silent.

'Yeah, I thought so,' Warren said. 'Look, Jack, you're a nice guy and all, and I'm sorry how this worked out. I really am. But I was in a jam and I just couldn't take that job anymore. This was my ticket out. I took it.'

'You fucking asshole! It was my story.'

I said it too loud. Though I was by myself in a row of three seats, a man across the aisle looked at me angrily. He was seated with an elderly woman who I guessed was his mother and who had never heard such language. I turned away toward the window. There was only blackness out there. I put my hand over my other ear so I could hear Warren's reply above the steady thrum of the plane. His voice was low and steady.

'The story belongs to whoever writes it, Jack. Remember that. Whoever writes it, it's their story. You want to go up against me, that's fine. Then write the fuckin' story instead of calling me up and whining about it. Go ahead, kick my ass. Try it. I'm right here and I'll see you on the front page.'

Everything he had just said was dead right and I knew it the moment he said it. I felt embarrassed that I had even called, and as angry with myself as I was with Warren and Thorson. But I couldn't let it go.

'Well, don't count on getting anything from your source anymore,' I said. 'I'm going to put Thorson in the ground. I got him by the balls. I know he called you late Saturday at the hotel. I got him.'

'I don't know what you're talking about and I don't talk about sources. With anyone.'

'You don't need to. He's mine. Cut and dried. You want to call him after this, you might want to try the bank squad in Salt Lake City. That's where he'll be.'

Using Rachel's reference to a Siberian assignment did not dull the anger much. My jaw was still clenched as I waited for his reply.

'Good night, Jack,' he said finally. 'All I can say is get over it and get a fucking life.'

'Wait a minute, Warren. Answer one question for me.'

There was a pleading whine to my voice that I hated. When he didn't reply I pushed on.

'The page from my notebook that you left in the file room at the foundation, did you leave it on purpose? Was it a setup from the start?'

'That's two questions,' he said and I could hear the smile in his voice. 'I gotta go.'

He hung up.

Ten minutes later, as the plane began to level off, I finally began to smooth out inside, too. Largely with the help of a strong Bloody Mary. The fact that I could now back up my accusation against Thorson with some evidence also served to mollify me. The truth was, I couldn't blame Warren. He had used me, but that's what reporters do. Who knew that better than me?

However, I could blame Thorson and I did. I didn't know how or when I was going to do it but I was going to make sure Thorson's hotel bill and the significance of the phone call came to the attention of Bob Backus. I was going to see Thorson go down.

After I finished the drink, I went back to the bills, which I had stuffed into the seat pocket. With nothing more than idle curiosity at that point, I began with Thorson's and studied the calls he had made before and after the call to Warren.

He had made only three long distance calls during his two-day stay in Phoenix, all of them within a half hour's time. There was the call to Warren at 12:41 A.M., Sunday, a call placed four minutes before to a number with a 703 area code, and a call to a 904 area number at 12:56 A.M. I assumed the 703 number was to the FBI center in Virginia, but because I had nothing else to do, I used the phone again. I keyed in the number and it was answered immediately.

'FBI, Quantico.'

I hung up. I had been right. Next I called the third number, not even knowing where the 904 area code was. After three rings the call was answered with a high-pitched squeal – the language only computers know. I listened until the electronic wail ended. Its mating call unanswered, the computer disconnected me.

Puzzled, I called information for the 904 area and asked the operator what the largest city in the zone was. Jacksonville, I was told. I then asked if the zone included the town of Raiford and was told that it did. I thanked her and hung up.

I knew from the library stories on Horace Gomble that the Union Correctional Institute was located in Raiford. UCI was where Horace Gomble was currently incarcerated and where William Gladden had once been imprisoned. I wondered if Thorson's call to a computer in the 904 area code zone had any connection to the prison or Gladden or Gomble.

One more time I called information for the 904 area. This time I asked for the general number for UCI in Raiford. The exchange prefix I got was 431, the same as the number Thorson had called from his hotel room. I leaned back and brooded about this. Why had he called the prison? Could he have made a direct connection with a prison computer in order to check on Gomble's status there or to look at a file on Gladden? I recalled Backus saying he would have Gomble's status at the prison checked. Possibly, he had given the assignment to Thorson after he picked him up at the airport Saturday night.

I thought of one other possibility for the call. Thorson had told me less than an hour earlier that Gladden had been checked out and dropped as a suspect. Perhaps his call was in some way part of that check. But what part, I couldn't guess. The only thing that seemed clear to me was that I had not been made privy to everything the agents had been doing. I'd been in their midst, but on some things I had simply been kept in the dark.

The other hotel bills provided no surprises. The bills for Carter's and Thompson's rooms were clean. No calls. Backus, according to his bill, had called the same Quantico number at about midnight on both Saturday and Sunday. Curious, I called the number from the plane. It was answered immediately.

'Quantico, Operations Board.'

I hung up without saying anything. I was satisfied that Backus had called Quantico as Thorson had done to return or check messages or take care of other bureau business.

Lastly, I was down to Rachel's bill and an odd feeling of trepidation suddenly came over me. It was a sense I didn't have as I had studied the other bills. This time I felt like a suspicious husband checking on his wife's affairs. There was a voyeuristic thrill to it as well as a sense of guilt.

She'd made four calls from her room. All were to Quantico exchanges and twice she had called the same number as Backus. The Operations Board. I called one of the new numbers she had called and a machine answered the call with her voice.

'This is FBI Special Agent Rachel Walling. I am not available at the moment but if you leave your name and a brief message I will return your call as soon as possible. Thank you.'

She had checked her own office line for messages. I keyed in the last number, which she had called on Sunday evening at 6:10 and a female voice answered.

'Profiling, Doran.'

I disconnected the call without speaking and felt bad about it. I liked Brass, but not enough to possibly tip her off to the fact that I was checking out the calls her fellow agents had made.

Done with the hotel bills, I folded them and put them back in my computer bag, then I snapped the air phone back into its cradle.

35

By the time I pulled up in front of the LAPD's Hollywood Division it was nearly eight-thirty. I didn't know what to expect as I looked at the brick fortress on Wilcox Street. I didn't know whether Thomas would still be there this late, but I hoped that because he was the lead detective working a fresh case – the motel maid killing – that he was still on the clock, preferably behind the bricks working the phones instead of out on the street looking for Gladden.

Inside the front door was a lobby of gray linoleum, two green vinyl couches and the front counter, behind which three uniformed officers sat. There was an entry to a hallway on the left and on the wall above it a sign that said DETECTIVE BUREAU above an arrow pointing down the hall. I glanced at the only desk officer not on a phone and nodded as if I was making my nightly visit. I got to about three feet from the hallway when he stopped me.

'Hold on there, partner. Can I help you?'

I turned back to him and pointed up to the sign.

'I need to go to the detective bureau.'

'What for?'

I walked over to the counter so our conversation would not be heard by everyone in the station.

'I want to see Detective Thomas.'

I took out my press identification.

'Denver,' the cop said, in case I had forgotten where I was from. 'Let me see if he's back there. He expecting you?'

'Not that I know of.'

'What's Denver got to do with – yeah, Ed Thomas back there? Got one here from Denver to see him.'

He listened for a few moments, creased his brow at whatever information he was being given and then hung up.

'Okay. Go on down the hall. Second door on the left.'

I thanked him and headed down the hallway. Along both walls were dozens of framed black-and-white publicity shots of entertainers interspersed among photos of police softball teams and officers killed in the line of duty. The door I was told to go to was marked HOMICIDE. I knocked, waited a beat for a reply and then opened the door and stepped in when I didn't get one.

Rachel was sitting behind one of the six desks in the room. The others were empty.

'Hello, Jack.'

I nodded. I wasn't that surprised to see her.

'What are you doing here?'

'That should be obvious, since you've obviously been waiting for me. Where's Thomas?'

'He's safe.'

'Why all the lies?'

'What lies?'

'Thorson said Gladden was not a suspect. He said he was checked out and dropped. That's why I came out. I thought he was either wrong or lying. Why didn't you call me, Rachel? This whole thing –'

'Jack, I was busy with Thomas and I knew if I called anyway, I'd have to lie to you and I didn't want to.'

'So, you just had Thorson do it. Great. Thanks. That makes it better.'

'Stop being a baby. I had more to worry about than your feelings. I'm sorry. Look, I'm here, aren't I? Why do you think that is?'

I hiked my shoulders.

'I knew you'd come no matter what Gordon told you,' she said. 'I know you, Jack. All I had to do was call the airlines. Once I knew your ETA, all I had to do was wait. I only hope that Gladden wasn't out there watching the place. You were on TV with us. That means he probably thinks you are an agent. If he saw you come in here he'll know we're running a setup.'

'But if he was out there and close enough to see me, then you'd have him now, right? Because you've got a twenty-four-hour watch for him on the outside of this place.'

She smiled thinly. I had guessed right.

She picked a two-way radio up off the desk and called her command post. I recognized the voice that came back. It was Backus. She told him she was coming in with a visitor. She then ended the call and stood up.

'Let's go.'

'Where?'

'The command post. Not too far.'

Her voice was curt, clipped. It was cold toward me and I found it hard to believe that I had made love to this woman less than twenty-four hours earlier. It was as if I was a stranger to her now. I kept quiet as we walked through a back hallway of the station and to an employee parking lot in the rear where she had a car waiting.

'I've got a car out front,' I said.

'Well, you'll have to leave it for now. Unless you want to stay on your own and keep doing the cowboy shit.'

'Look, Rachel, if I hadn't been lied to this might not have happened. I might not even have come.'

'Sure.'

She got in and started the car and then unlocked my door. It always annoyed me when people did that to me but I didn't say anything when I got in. She headed out of the lot and up toward Sunset Boulevard with a heavy foot on the gas. She didn't speak until a red light forced her to stop the car.

'How did you know that name, Jack?' she asked.

'What name?' I replied, though I knew.

'Gladden, Jack. William Gladden.'

'I did my homework. How did you people come up with it?'

'I can't tell you.'

'Rachel . . . Look, this is me, okay? We made, uh . . .' I couldn't say it out loud for fear it would sound like a lie. 'I thought there was something between us, Rachel. Now you're acting like I'm some kind of leper or something. I don't . . . Look, is it information you want? I'll tell you all I know. I figured it out from the newspapers. Big story on this guy Gladden in the *L.A. Times* on Saturday. Okay? The story said he knew Horace the Hypnotist in Raiford. I just put two and two together. It wasn't hard.'

'Okay, Jack.'

'Now you.'

Silence.

'Rachel?'

'Are we off the record?'

'You know you don't have to ask me that.'

She hesitated a moment and then seemed to relent. She began.

'We arrived at Gladden through two separate leads that just happened to click at the same time. That gives us a high sense of reliability that he's our man. First, the car. Automotive ID traced the stereo serial number to a car which, in turn, was traced to Hertz. You remember this?'

'Yes.'

'Well, Matuzak and Mize went down to the airport and traced the car. Some snowbirds from Chicago had already rerented it. They had to go up to Sedona to get it back. It's been processed. Nothing usable from it. The stereo and window had been replaced. But not by Hertz. Hertz never knew about the break-in. Whoever had the car when the break-in occurred replaced the window and the stereo on their own. Anyway, the rental records put the car in the hands of an N. H. Breedlove for five days this month, including the day Orsulak was killed. This Breedlove turned it in the day after. Matuzak put the name on the computer and got a hit on the ID net. Nathan H. Breedlove was an AKA turned up during the investigation of William Gladden in Florida seven years ago. It was a name used by a man who had placed ads in the papers in Tampa offering his services as a children's photographer. He molested the kids when left alone with them, took dirty pictures. He wore disguises. The Tampa police were looking for this Breedlove at the same time the Gladden case broke. The molestations at the child care center. The investigators always believed Gladden was Breedlove but they never made a case because of the disguises. Besides, they didn't press it because they thought he'd be going away to prison for a long time on the other case.

'Anyway, once we had Gladden's name from the ID net's alias data bank, from there we picked up the wanted that LAPD put out on NCIC last week. And here we are.'

'It seems . . .'

'Too easy? Well, sometimes you make your own luck.'

'You said that before.'

'Because it's true.'

'Why would he use an alias that he must've known was on file somewhere?'

'A lot of these people find comfort in tradition. Plus, he's a cocky son of a bitch. We know that from the fax.'

'But he used a whole new alias when he was arrested by Santa Monica police last week. Why would he –'

'I'm only telling you what we know, Jack. If he's as smart as we think he is, then he probably has several ID packages. They wouldn't be hard to come by. We have the Phoenix field office working on a subpoena for Hertz. We want Breedlove's complete renting history going back three years. He's a Hertz Gold customer no less. Again it shows how smart he is. Most airports, you get off the plane, walk to the Gold lot and your name is on the board. You go to your car and the keys are in it. Most of the time you don't even have to talk to any clerks. You just get in your car, show your license at the gate and you are out of there.'

'Okay, what about the other thing? You said there were two leads to Gladden.'

'The Best Pals. Ted Vincent and Steve Raffa in Florida finally got hold of Beltran's records with the organization this morning. He'd been Best Pal to nine young boys over the years. The second one he sponsored, this is going back something like sixteen years, was Gladden.'

'Jesus.'

'Yeah. It's all starting to fall together.'

I was silent for a few moments as I considered all of the information she had revealed. The investigation was advancing at exponentially increasing speed. It was seat-belt time.

'How come the field office out here didn't pick up on this guy? He's been in the paper.'

'Good question. Bob's going to have a heart-to-heart with the SAC about that. Gordon's flag landed last night. Somebody should've seen it and put two and two together. But we did it ourselves first.'

A typical bureaucratic snafu. I wondered how much sooner they'd have been on to Gladden if someone in the L.A. office had been a little more alert.

'You know Gladden, don't you?' I said.

'Yes. We had him during the rapist interviews. I told you about that. Seven years ago. He and Gomble, among others at that hellhole in Florida. I think our team – Gordon, Bob, me – spent a week down there, we had so many candidates for interviews.'

I was tempted to bring up Thorson's call to the prison's computer but thought better of it. It was enough just to get her to talk to me again like a human. Telling her I had rifled through the hotel bills was no way to ensure that she would continue. This dilemma also created a problem in regard to nailing Thorson. For the time being I would have to sit on his hotel phone records as well.

'You think there is any connection between Gomble supposedly using hypnotism and what you are seeing on the Poet cases?' I said instead. 'Think maybe Gomble taught him his secret?'

'Possibly.'

She had regressed to the one-word reply.

'Possibly,' I repeated, a thin line of sarcasm in it.

'Eventually, I'll go to Florida to talk to Gomble again. And I'm going to ask him that. Until I get an answer one way or the other, it's possibly. Okay, Jack?'

We pulled into an alley that ran behind a row of old motels and shops. She finally slowed down to the point where I let go of the armrest.

'But you can't go to Florida now, can you?' I asked.

'That's up to Bob. But we're close to Gladden here. For the time being I think Bob wants to put everything we have into L.A. Gladden's here. Or he's close. We can all feel it. We've got to get him. Once we have him, then I'll worry about the other things, the psychological motivation. We'll need to go to Florida then.'

'Why then? To add data to the serial killer studies?'

'No. I mean, yes, there's that, but primarily we'll go for the prosecution. Guy like this, he's got to go the insanity route. It's his only choice. So that means we'll have to build a case on his psychology. One that shows he knew what he was doing and he knew right from wrong. The same old thing.'

Prosecution of the Poet in a courtroom had never entered my mind. I realized that I had assumed that he would not be taken alive. And this assumption, I knew, was based on my own desire that he not be allowed to live after this.

'What's the matter, Jack, you don't want a trial? You want us to kill him where we find him?'

I looked over at her. The lights from a passing window flicked across her face and for a moment I saw her eyes.

'I hadn't thought about it.'

'Sure you have. Would you like to kill him, Jack? If you had a moment with him and there were no consequences, could you do it? Do you think that would make up for things?'

I didn't like discussing this subject with her. I sensed more than just a passing interest from her.

'I don't know,' I finally answered. 'Could you kill him? Have you ever killed anyone, Rachel?'

'Given the chance, I'd kill him in a heartbeat.'

'Why?'

'Because I've known the others. I've looked in their eyes and know what's back there in the darkness. If I could kill them all I think I would.'

I waited for her to continue but she didn't. She pulled the car to a stop next to two other matching Caprices behind one of the old motels.

'You didn't answer the second question.'

'No, I've never killed anyone.'

We went in through a back door into a hallway painted in two tones; dingy lime to about eye level, dingy white the rest of the way up. Rachel went to the first door on the left and knocked and we were let in. It was a motel room, one that would have passed as a kitchenette in the sixties, when it was last refurbished. Backus and Thorson were there waiting, sitting at an old Formica table against the wall. There were two phones on the table that looked as if they had just been added to the room. There was also a three-foot-high aluminum trunk standing on one end with its lid open to reveal a bank of three video monitors. Wires ran out the back of the trunk, along the floor and out the window, which was opened just enough to allow them through.

'Jack, I can't say I'm happy to see you,' Backus said.

But he said it with a wry smile on his face and he stood up and shook my hand.

'Sorry,' I said, not really knowing why. Then, looking at Thorson, I added, 'I didn't mean to blunder into your setup but I was given some bad information.'

The thought of the phone records went through my mind again but I dismissed it. It was not the right time.

'Well,' Backus said, 'I have to admit we were trying a little misdirection there. We just thought it would be best if we could work this out without any distractions.'

'I'll try not to be a distraction.'

'You already are,' Thorson said.

I ignored him and kept my eyes on Backus.

'Have a seat,' he said.

Rachel and I took the two remaining chairs at the table.

'I assume you know what is happening,' Backus said.

'I assume you're watching Thomas.'

I turned so I could see the video monitors and for the first time studied the view each one had. The top monitor showed a hallway not unlike the one outside the room we were in. Several doors going down both sides. All of them closed and with numbers on them. The next tube showed the exterior of a motel front. In the blue-gray haze of the video I could just make out the words on the sign above the door. HOTEL MARK TWAIN. The bottom monitor showed an alley-side view of what I assumed was the same hotel.

'Is this where we are?' I asked, pointing at the display.

'No,' Backus said. 'That is where Detective Thomas is. We're about a block away.'

'Doesn't look very nice. What are they paying these days in this town?'

'It is not his home. But the detectives at Hollywood Station often use the hotel to stash witnesses or sleep over if they're working twenty-hour days on a case. Detective Thomas chose to stay there rather than at home. He has a wife and three children at home.'

'Well, that answers my next question. I'm glad you told him he was being used as bait.'

'You seem measurably more cynical than when we last met this morning, Jack.'

'I guess that's because I am.'

I looked away from him and checked out the video setup again. Backus spoke to my back.

'We have three-point camera surveillance beamed to a mobile dish on our roof here. We also have the field office's critical response unit and LAPD's top surveillance squad watching Thomas around the clock. No one can get near him. Even at the station. He's perfectly safe.'

'Wait until it's over and then tell me that.'

'I will. But in the meantime, you have to step aside, Jack.'

I turned back to him, my best puzzled look on my face.

'You understand what I'm telling you,' Backus said, not buying the face. 'We are at the most critical stage. He is in our sights and, frankly, Jack, you have to get out of the way.'

'I am out of the way and I'll stay out of the way. The same deal, nothing I see goes into the paper until you okay it. But I'm not going back to Denver to wait. I'm too close, too . . . This means too much. You've got to let me back inside.'

'This could take weeks. Remember the fax. All it said was that he had his next man in sight. It didn't say when it would happen. There was no time frame. We have no idea when he'll try to hit Thomas.'

I shook my head.

'I don't care. Whatever it takes, I want to be part of the investigation. I've kept up my end of the deal.'

An uneasy silence settled over the room, during which Backus stood up and began pacing on the carpet behind my chair. I looked over at Rachel. She was looking down at the table in a contemplative way. I threw my last chip into the pile.

'I have to write a story tomorrow, Bob. My editor's expecting it. If you don't want it written, bring me in. That's the only way I can convince him to back off. That's the bottom line.'

Thorson made a derisive sound and shook his head.

'This is trouble,' he said. 'Bob, you give in to this guy again and where does it end?'

'The only time there's been trouble,' I said, 'is when I've been lied to or kept out of the investigation, which, by the way, I started.'

Backus looked over at Rachel.

'What do you think?'

'Don't ask her,' Thorson interjected. 'I can tell you right now what she's going to say.'

'If you have something to say about me, say it,' Rachel demanded.

'All right, enough,' Backus said, holding his hands out like a referee. 'You two don't quit, do you? Jack, you're in. For the time being. Same deal as before. That means no story tomorrow. Understood?'

I nodded. I looked over at Thorson, who had already stood up and was heading out the door, defeated.

36

The Wilcox Hotel, as I learned it was called, had room for one more – especially when the night clerk learned I was with the government people already staying there and was willing to pay the top price, thirty-five dollars a night. It was the only hotel I'd ever checked into where I felt a nervous sense of foreboding about giving the man behind the front counter my credit card number. This one looked like he was halfway through a bottle on this shift alone. It also appeared as though he had decided on the last four successive mornings that he wasn't quite ready for a shave yet. He never looked at me during the entire check-in process – which took an unusually long five minutes as he hunted for a pen and then accepted a loan of one from me.

'What're you people doin', anyway?' he said as he slid a key with the stamped room number almost worn off it across the equally worn Formica counter.

'They didn't tell you?' I asked, feigning surprise.

'Nope. I'm just checkin' people in is all.'

'It's a credit card fraud investigation. A lot of it going on around here.'

'Oh.'

'By the way, which room is Agent Walling in?'

It took him a half minute to interpret his own records.

'That'd be seventeen.'

My room was small and when I sat on the edge of the bed it sank at least a half foot, the other side rising by an equal amount with the accompanying protest of old springs. It was a ground-floor room with spare but neat furnishings and the stale smell of cigarettes. The yellowed blinds were up and I could see a metal grate over the one window. If there was a fire, I'd be trapped like a lobster in a cage if I didn't get out the door fast enough.

I took the travel-size toothpaste tube and folding toothbrush I had bought out of the pillowcase and went into the bathroom. I could still taste the Bloody Mary from the plane and wanted to get rid of it. I also wanted to be ready for all eventualities with Rachel.

The bathrooms in old hotel rooms are always the most depressing. This one was slightly larger than the phone booths I used to see at every gas station when I was growing up. Sink, toilet and portable shower stall all complete with matching rust stains were set in a crowded configuration. If you were ever sitting on the toilet when somebody came in, you'd lose your kneecaps. When I was finished and had returned to the comparative spaciousness of the room, I looked at the bed and knew I didn't want to sit back down there. I didn't even want to sleep there. I decided to risk leaving the computer and my pillowcase full of clothes and left the room.

My light knock on the door of room seventeen was answered so quickly I thought Rachel had been waiting on the other side. She quickly ushered me in.

'Bob's room is across the hall,' she whispered by way of explanation. 'What is it?'

I didn't answer. We looked at each other for a long moment, each waiting for the other to act. I finally did, stepping close to her and pulling her into a long kiss. She seemed as into it as I was and this quickly calmed many of the worries I had allowed to simmer in my brain. She broke the kiss off and strongly pulled me into an embrace. Over her shoulder I surveyed her room. It was bigger than mine and the furniture was maybe a decade newer but it wasn't any less depressing. Her computer was on the bed and there were some papers spread over the worn yellow spread where a thousand people had lain and fucked and farted and fought.

'Funny,' she whispered, 'I just left you this morning and I found myself already missing you.'

'Same here.'

'Jack, I'm sorry, but I don't want to make love on that bed, in this room or in this hotel.'

'That's okay,' I said nobly, though I regretted the words as I spoke them. 'I understand. Looks like you got a luxury suite compared to mine.'

'We'll have to wait but then we'll make up for it.'

'Yeah. Why are we staying here, anyway?'

'Bob wants to be close. So we can move if they spot him.'

I nodded.

'Well, can we leave for a little while? Want to get a drink? There's got to be someplace around.'

'Probably no better than this. Let's just stay and talk.'

She went to the bed and cleared the papers and the computer, then sat back against the headboard, propped on a pillow. I sat in the room's one chair, its cushion scarred by an ancient knife slash repaired with tape.

'What do you want to talk about, Rachel?'

'I don't know. You're the reporter. I thought you'd ask the questions.' She smiled.

'About the case?'

'About anything.'

I looked at her for a long moment. I decided to start with something simple and then see how far I could go from there.

'What's this Thomas guy like?'

'He's fine. For a local. Not overly cooperative, but not an asshole.'

'What do you mean not overly cooperative? He's letting you use him as human bait, isn't that enough?'

'I guess. Maybe it's me. I never seem to get along with the locals.'

I moved from the chair onto the bed with her.

'So what? It's not your job to get along with anybody.'

'That's right,' she said, smiling again. 'You know, there's a soda machine in the lobby.'

'You want something?'

'No, but you said something about getting a drink.'

'I was thinking of something stronger. It's all right, though. I'm happy.'

She reached over and did her finger drag through my beard. I caught her hand as she dropped it away and held it for a moment.

'Do you think the intensity of what we're doing and what we're involved with is causing this?' I asked.

'As opposed to what?'

'I don't know. I'm just asking.'

'I know what you're saying,' she said after a long moment. 'I have to admit I've never made love with anybody thirty-six hours after the first time I'd ever seen him in my life.'

She smiled and it sent a beautiful thrill through me.

'Me neither.'

She leaned toward me and we kissed again. I turned and we rolled into a from-here-to-eternity kiss. Only our beach was the old bedspread in a ratty old hotel room three decades past its prime. But all of that didn't matter anymore. Soon I was moving my kisses down her neck and then we made love.

We couldn't both fit in the bathroom or the shower so she went first. As she showered I lay in bed thinking about her and wishing for a smoke.

It was hard to tell because of the sound of the shower but at one point I thought I heard a light knock on the door. Alerted, I sat up on the edge of the bed and started pulling on my pants as I stared at the door. I listened but heard nothing again. Then, I distinctly saw the doorknob move, or thought I did. I got up and moved to the door, pulling up my pants, and tilted my head to the jamb to listen. I heard nothing. There was a peephole but I was reluctant to look through it. The light was on in the room and if I looked through the peephole I would block it, possibly letting whoever was out there know that someone was looking at him.

Rachel cut the shower off at that point. After a few moments of no noticeable sound from the hallway I moved to the peephole and looked. There was nothing out there.

'What are you doing?'

I turned. Rachel stood by the bed, attempting to show modesty with the tiny towel that came with the room.

'I thought I heard someone knock.'

'Who was it?'

'I don't know. There was no one there when I looked. Maybe it was nothing. All right if I take a shower?'

'Sure.'

I stepped out of my pants and while walking past her stopped. She dropped her towel, exposing her body. She was beautiful to me. I stepped over and we held each other for a long moment.

'Be right back,' I finally said and then headed into the shower.

Rachel was dressed and waiting when I came out. I looked at my watch, which I had left on the bed table, and saw it was eleven. There was a battered old television in the room but I decided not to suggest watching the news. I realized I hadn't eaten dinner but still wasn't hungry.

'I'm not tired,' she said.

'Neither am I.'

'Maybe we could find a place for a drink after all.'

After I dressed, we quietly left the room. She looked out first to make sure Backus or Thorson or anybody else wasn't lurking about. We encountered no one in the hallway or the lobby and outside the street seemed deserted and dark. We walked south to Sunset.

'You got your gun?' I asked, half kidding and half serious.

'Always. Besides, we've got our people around. They probably saw us leave.'

'Really? I thought they were just keeping an eye on Thomas.'

'They are. But they should have a good idea who is on the street at any given time. If they're doing their job.'

I turned and walked backward for a few steps, staring back up the street at the green neon sign for the Mark Twain. I surveyed the street, the cars parked along both sides. Again, I saw no shadows or silhouettes of the watchers.

'How many are out there?'

'Should be five. Two on foot in fixed positions. Two in cars, stationary. One car roving. All the time.'

I turned back around and pulled the collar of my jacket up. It was colder outside than I had expected. Our breath came out in thin clouds, mingled together and then disappeared.

When we got to Sunset I looked both ways and saw a neon sign over an archway a block to the west that said CAT & FIDDLE BAR. I pointed that way and Rachel started walking. We were silent until we got there.

Going through the archway we entered an outdoor garden with several tables below green canvas umbrellas but they were all empty. Past these and through the windows on the other side we could see what looked like a lively and warm bar. We went in, found an empty booth on the opposite side from the dartboards and sat down. It was an English-style pub. When the barmaid came around Rachel told me to go first and I ordered a black and tan. Rachel then did the same.

We looked around the place and small-talked until our drinks arrived. We clinked glasses and drank. I watched her. I didn't think she'd ever had a black and tan before.

'The Harp is heavier. It always stays at the bottom, the Guinness on top.'

She smiled.

'When you said black and tan, I thought that was a brand that you knew. But it's good. I like it but it's strong.'

'One thing the Irish know is how to make a beer. The English have to give them that.'

'Two of these and you'll have to call for backup to get me back.'

'I doubt it.'

We lapsed into a comfortable silence. There was a fireplace in the rear wall and the warmth from its fully engulfed fire extended across the room.

'Is your real name John?'

I nodded.

'I'm not Irish but I always thought Sean was Irish for John.'

'Yes, it's the Gaelic version. Since we were twins my parents decided ... actually my mother.'

'I think it's nice.'

After a few more drinks from my glass I started asking questions about the case.

'So, tell me about Gladden.'

'There isn't a whole lot to tell yet.'

'Well, you met him. Interviewed him. You must have a feel for him.'

'He wasn't exactly cooperative. His appeal was still pending and he didn't trust us not to use what he said to disrupt that. We all took turns trying to get him to open up. Finally, I think it was Bob's idea, he agreed to talk to us in the third person. As if the perpetrator of the crimes he was convicted of was somebody else.'

'Bundy did that, too, right?'

I remembered that from a book I had read.

'Yes. And others as well. It was just a device to assure them that we were not there to make cases against them. Most of these men have tremendous egos. They wanted to talk to us but they had to be convinced they were safe from legal reprisals. Gladden was like that. Especially since he knew he had a valid appeal still pending.'

'It must be a rare thing that you have a prior relationship, no matter how small, with an active serial killer.'

'Yes. But I have a feeling that if any one of the people we interviewed was set loose like William Gladden, we'd end up hunting for them as well. These people don't get better, Jack, and they don't get rehabbed. They are what they are.'

She said it like a warning, the second such intimation she had made. I thought about it a few moments, wondering if there was more she was trying to tell me. Or, I thought, was she really warning herself?

'So what did he say? Did he tell you about Beltran or Best Pals?'

'Of course not, or I would have remembered when I saw Beltran's name on the victim list. Gladden didn't mention names. But he did give the usual abuse excuse. Said that he was assaulted sexually as a child. Repeatedly. He was at the same age as the children he later victimized in Tampa. You see, that's the cycle. It's a pattern we often see. They become fixated on themselves at the point in their own lives when they were ... ruined.'

I nodded but didn't say anything, hoping she would continue.

'For a three-year period,' she said, 'from ages nine to twelve. The episodes were frequent and included oral and anal penetration. He didn't tell us who the abuser was other than to say it was a nonrelative. According to Gladden, he never told his mother because he feared this man. The man threatened him. He was a figure of some authority in his life. Bob made some follow-up calls about it but never got anywhere with it. Gladden wasn't specific enough for him to track it. Gladden was in his twenties by then and the period of abuse had been years earlier. There would've been statute-of-limitations problems even if we had pursued it. We couldn't even find his mother to ask her about it. She left Tampa after his arrest and all the publicity. We, of course, can now surmise that the abuser was Beltran.'

I nodded. I had finished my beer but Rachel was nursing hers. She didn't like it. I signaled the barmaid and ordered an Amstel Light for her. I said I'd finish her black and tan.

'So how did it end? The abuse, I mean.'

'That's the irony you so often see. It ended when he became too old for Beltran. Beltran rejected him and went on to his next victim. All the boys he sponsored through Best Pals are being located and will be interviewed. I'll bet they all were abused by him. He's the evil seed to all of this, Jack. Make sure you get that across in whatever you write about this. Beltran got what he deserved.'

'You sound like you sympathize with Gladden.'

Wrong thing to say. I saw the anger flare in her eyes.

'You are damn right I sympathize. It doesn't mean I condone a single thing he's done or that I wouldn't drop him with a bullet if I got the chance. But he didn't invent the monster that is inside of him. It was created by someone else.'

'Okay, I wasn't trying to suggest –'

The barmaid came with Rachel's beer and saved me from walking down the wrong path any further. I pulled Rachel's black and tan across the table and took a long drink, hoping we were past my misstep.

'So, aside from what he told you,' I asked, 'what was your take on Gladden? Did he seem to have the smarts that everyone around here is attributing to him?'

She seemed to compose her thoughts before answering.

'William Gladden knew his sexual appetite was legally, socially and culturally unacceptable. He was clearly burdened by this, I think. I believe he was at war within himself, attempting to understand his urges and desires. He wanted to tell us his story, whether it was third person or not, and I think he believed that by telling us about himself he would in some way help himself as well as maybe somebody else down the road. If you look at these dilemmas he had, I think it shows a highly intellectual being. I mean, most of these people I interviewed were like animals. Machines. They did what they did . . . almost by instinct or programming, as if they had to. And they did it without much thought. Gladden was different. So, yes, I think he is as smart as we are saying he is, maybe smarter.'

'It's strange what you just said. You know, that he was burdened. Doesn't sound like the guy we're chasing now. The one we're chasing seems to have about as much of a conscience about what he is doing as Hitler had.'

'You're right. But we've seen ample evidence of these types of predators changing, evolving. Without treatment, whether it was drug therapy or not, it is not without precedent that someone with William Gladden's background could evolve into someone like the Poet. Bottom line is, people change. After the interviews he was in prison another long year before winning his appeal and copping the deal that got him out. Pedophiles are treated the most harshly in prison society. Because of that they tend to band together in knots – just as in free society. That's why you have Gladden being the acquaintance of Gomble as well as other pedophiles in Raiford. I guess what I am saying is that I am not surprised that the man I interviewed so many years ago became the man we call the Poet today. I can see it happening.'

A loud burst of laughter and applause broke out near one of the dartboards and distracted me. It looked like the night's champion had been crowned.

'Enough about Gladden for now,' Rachel said when I looked back at her. 'It's depressing as hell.'

'Okay.'

'What about you?'

'I'm depressed, too.'

'No. I mean, what about *you.* You talk to your editor yet, tell him you're back inside?'

'No, not yet. I'll have to call in the morning and tell him there's no follow coming from me, but that I'm back inside.'

'How will he take that?'

'Not well. He'll want a follow anyway. The story's moving like a locomotive now. The national media's on it and you've got to keep throwing stories into the fire to make the big train move. But what the hell. He's got other reporters. He can put one of them on it and see what they get. Which won't be much. Then Michael Warren will probably crack another exclusive in the *L.A. Times* and I'll really be in the doghouse.'

'You are a cynical man.'

'I'm a realist.'

'Don't worry about Warren. Gor – whoever leaked to him before isn't going to do it again. It would be risking too much with Bob.'

'Freudian slip there, right? Anyway, we'll see.'

'How did you get so cynical, Jack? I thought only those rundown middle-aged cops were like that.'

'I was born with it, I guess.'

'I bet.'

It seemed even colder on the walk back. I wanted to put my arm around her but I knew she wouldn't allow it. There were eyes on the street and I didn't try. As we got close to the hotel I remembered a story and told her.

'You know how when you're in high school and there's always this grapevine that passes information on about who likes whom and who's got a crush on whom? Remember?'

'Yes, I remember.'

'Well, there was this girl and I had a thing, a crush on her. And I was . . . I can't remember how but the word went out on the grapevine, you know? And when that happened what you usually did was wait and see how the person responded. It was one of those things where I knew that she knew that I had this desire for her and she knew I knew she knew. Understand?'

'Yes.'

'But the thing was I had no confidence and I was . . . I don't know. One day I was in the gym, sitting in the bleachers. I think I was in there early for a basketball game or something and it was filling up with people. Then she comes in, she's with a friend, and they're walking along the bleachers looking for a place to sit. It was one of those do-or-die moments and she looks right at me and waves . . . And I froze. And . . . then . . . I turned and looked behind me to see if she was waving to somebody else.'

'Jack, you fool!' Rachel said, smiling and not taking the story to heart as I had done for so long. 'What did she do?'

'When I turned back around she had looked away, embarrassed. See, I had embarrassed her by setting the whole thing into motion and then turning away . . . snubbing her . . . She started going out with somebody else after that. Ended up marrying him. It took me a long time to get over her.'

We took the last steps to the hotel door silently. I opened the door for Rachel and looked at her with a pained, embarrassed smile. The story could still do that to me all these years later.

'So that's the story,' I said. 'It proves I've been a cynical fool all along.'

'Everybody has stories from growing up like that,' she said in a voice that seemed to dismiss the whole thing.

We crossed the lobby and the night man looked up and nodded. It seemed as if his whiskers had grown even longer in the few hours since I had first seen him. At the stairs Rachel stopped and in a whispered voice designed to leave the night man out of earshot told me not to come up.

'I think we should go to our own rooms.'

'I can still walk you up.'

'No, that's okay.'

She looked back at the front desk. The night man had his head down and was reading a gossip tabloid. Rachel turned back to me, gave me a silent kiss on the cheek and whispered good night. I watched her go up the stairs.

I knew I wouldn't be able to sleep. Too many thoughts. I had made love to a beautiful woman and spent the evening falling in love with her. I wasn't sure what love was but I knew acceptance was part of it. That's what I sensed from Rachel. It was a quality that had been a rarity in my life and I found its nearness thrilling and disquieting in the same instant.

As I stepped out to the front of the hotel to smoke a cigarette the feeling of disquiet grew and then infected my mind with other thoughts. The ghost story intruded and my embarrassment and thoughts of what might have been still grabbed me so many years after that day on the bleachers. I marveled at the hold of some memories and at how well and precisely they can be relived. I hadn't told Rachel everything about the high school girl. I hadn't told her the ending, that the girl was Riley and that the boy she went out with and then married was my brother. I didn't know why I had left that part out.

I was out of cigarettes. I stepped back into the lobby to ask the night man where I could get a pack. He told me to go back to the Cat & Fiddle. I saw he had an open pack of Camels on the counter next to his stack of tabloids but he didn't offer me any and I didn't ask for one.

As I walked Sunset alone I thought about Rachel again and became preoccupied with something I had noticed during our lovemaking. Each of the three times we had been together in bed she had been fully giving of herself, yet I would say she was decidedly passive. She deferred control to me. I waited for the small nuances of change on the second and third times we made love, even hesitating in my own movements and choices in order to allow her to take the lead, but she never did. Even at the sacred moment when I entered her, it was my hand fumbling at the door. Three times. No woman that I had been with before on that number of occasions had done the same.

There was nothing wrong with this and it did not bother me in the least, but still I found it to be a curiosity. For her passivity in these horizontal moments was diametrically opposed to her demeanor in our vertical moments. When we were away from the bed she certainly exercised or sought to exercise her control. It was the sort of subtle contradiction that I believed made her so enthralling to me.

As I stopped to cross Sunset to the bar, my peripheral vision picked up movement to the far left as I glanced back to check traffic. My eyes followed the movement and I saw the form of a person ducking back into the shadowed doorway of a closed shop. A chill raced through me but I didn't move. I watched the spot where I had seen the movement for several seconds. The doorway was maybe twenty yards from me. I felt sure it had been a man and he was probably still there, possibly watching me from the darkness while I watched for him.

I took four quick, determined steps toward the doorway but then stopped dead. It had been a bluff but when no one ran from the doorway, I had only bluffed myself. I felt my heartbeat rising. I knew it might only be a homeless man looking for a spot to sleep. I knew there might be a hundred explanations. But just the same I was scared. Maybe it was a transient. Maybe it was the Poet. In a split second a myriad of possibilities took over my mind. I was on TV. The Poet saw TV. The Poet had made his choice. The dark doorway was on the path between me and the Wilcox Hotel. I could not go back. I quickly turned and stepped into the street to cross to the bar.

The blast of a car horn greeted me and I jumped back. I had not been in any danger. The car that sped past trailing the laughter of teenagers was two lanes away but maybe they had seen my face, seen the look, and known I was easy prey for a scare.

I ordered another black and tan at the bar along with a basket of chicken wings, and got directions to the cigarette machine. I noticed the unsteadiness of my hands as I lit the match after finally getting a cigarette into my mouth. Now what, I thought as I exhaled the stream of blue smoke toward my reflection in the mirror behind the bar.

I stayed until last call at two and then left the Cat & Fiddle with the exodus of die-hards. There was safety in numbers, I had decided. By loitering behind the crowd, I was able to identify a group of three drunks walking east toward Wilcox and fell in a few yards behind them. We passed the doorway in question from the other side of Sunset and as I looked across the four lanes I could not tell if the darkened alcove was empty. But I didn't linger. At Wilcox I broke away from my escort and trotted across Sunset and up to the hotel. I didn't breathe normally until I entered the lobby and saw the familiar, safe face of the night man.

Despite the lateness of the hour and the heavy beer I had filled myself with, the scare I had submitted myself to robbed me of any fatigue. I could not sleep. In my room I undressed, got into bed and turned off the light but I knew as I was doing it that it was fruitless. After ten minutes I faced the facts of my situation and turned on the light.

I needed a distraction. A trick that would allow my mind to rest easily and for me to sleep. I did what I had done on countless prior occasions of similar necessity. I pulled my computer up onto the bed. I booted it, plugged the room's phone line into the modem outlet and dialed long distance into the *Rocky*'s net. I had no messages and wasn't really expecting any but the motions of doing it began to calm me. I scrolled the wires a little bit and came across my own story, in abbreviated form, on the AP national wire. It would hit the ground tomorrow and burst like a shell. Editors from New York to here in L.A. would know my byline. I hoped.

After signing off and shutting down the connection, I played a few hands of computer solitaire but became bored with losing. Looking for something else to distract me, I reached into the computer bag for the hotel receipts from Phoenix but couldn't find them. I checked every pocket of the bag but the folded sheaf of papers wasn't there. I quickly grabbed the pillowcase and frisked it like a suspect but there were only clothes.

'Shit,' I said out loud.

I closed my eyes and tried to envision what I had done with the pages on the plane. A sense of dread came over me as I remembered at one point stuffing them into the seat pocket. But then I recalled that, after talking to Warren, I had retrieved them to make the other calls. I conjured a vision of putting the pages back into the computer bag as the plane was on final approach. I was sure I had not left them on the plane.

The alternative to this, I knew, was that someone had been in my room and taken them. I paced around a little bit, not sure what I could do. I had had what could be construed as stolen property stolen from me. Who could I complain to?

Angrily, I opened the door and walked down the hallway to the front desk.

The night man was looking at a magazine called *High Society* which had a cover photo of a nude woman skillfully using her arms and hands to strategically cover enough of her body to allow the magazine to be sold on the newsstand.

'Hey, did you see anybody go down to my room?'

He hiked his shoulders and shook his head.

'Nobody?'

'On'y ones I seen around was that lady that was with you, and you. Tha's it.'

I looked at him for a moment, waiting for more, but he had said his piece.

'Okay.'

I went back to my room, studying the keyhole for signs of a pick before going inside. I couldn't tell. The keyhole was worn and scratched but it could have been that way for years. I wouldn't know how to identify a picked lock if my life depended on it but I looked anyway. I was mad.

I was tempted to call Rachel and tell her about the burglary of my room but my dilemma was that I couldn't tell her about what had been taken in the burglary. I didn't want her to know what I had done. The memory of that day on the bleachers and other lessons learned since went through my mind. I got undressed and got back into bed.

Sleep eventually came but not before I had visions of Thorson in my room going through my things. When it finally came, the anger had not left me.

37

I was awakened by a sharp banging on my door. I opened my eyes and saw light bleeding brightly around the curtains. The sun was already well up and I realized I should have been also. I pulled on my pants and was still buttoning a shirt as I opened the door without looking through the peephole. It wasn't Rachel.

''Morning, sport. Rise and shine. You're with me today and we've got to get going.'

I stared blankly at him. Thorson reached over and knocked on the open door.

'Hello? Anyone home?'

'What do you mean I'm with you?'

'Just like it sounds. Your girlfriend has some things she has to do alone. Agent Backus has assigned you to be with me today.'

My face must have shown my thoughts on the prospect of spending the day with Thorson.

'I'm not exactly thrilled to pieces myself,' he said to me. 'But I do what I'm told. Now, if you just want to stay in bed all day, that'd be no skin off my back. I'd just tell –'

'I'm getting dressed. Give me a few minutes.'

'You've got five minutes. I'll meet you in the alley at the car. If you're not there you're on your own.'

After he was gone I looked at my watch on the bed table. It was eight-thirty, not as late as I had thought. I took ten minutes instead of five. I held my head under the shower and thought about being with Thorson for the day, dreading every moment of it. But most of all I thought about Rachel and wondered what assignment Backus had given her and why it didn't include me.

After leaving my room I went up to her door and knocked but got no answer. I listened at the door for a few moments and heard nothing. She was gone.

Thorson was leaning on the trunk of one of the cars when I got out to the alley.

'You're late.'

'Yeah. Sorry. Where's Rachel?'

'Sorry, sport, talk to Backus. He seems to be your bureau rabbi.'

'Look, Thorson, my name isn't sport, okay? If you don't want to call me by my name, just don't call me anything. I'm late because I had to call my editor and tell him there was no story coming. He wasn't happy.'

I went to the passenger door and he went around to the driver's side. I had to wait for him to unlock it and it seemed like he took forever to notice I was waiting.

'I don't really give a shit how your editor was this morning,' he said over the car before sliding in.

Inside the car, I saw two containers of coffee sitting on the dashboard, steam from them fogging the windshield. I looked at them the way a junkie looks at the spoon held to the candle but didn't say anything. I assumed they were part of some game Thorson was going to try to play.

'One of those is yours, sp – uh, Jack. You want cream or sugar, check the glove box.'

He started the car. I looked at him and then back at the coffee. Thorson reached over and took one of the containers and opened it. He took a small sip, like a swimmer dipping a toe into the water to test the temperature.

'Ahh,' he said. 'I take mine hot and black. Just like my women.'

He looked over and winked in a man-to-man gesture.

'Go ahead, Jack, take the coffee. I don't want it to spill when I move the car.'

I took the container and opened it. Thorson started driving. I took a small sip, but I did it more like the Czar's official food taster. It was good and the caffeine hit came quickly.

'Thanks,' I said.

'No problem. Can't get started without the stuff myself. So what happened, bad night?'

'You could say that.'

'Not me. I can sleep anywhere, even a dump like that. I slept fine.'

'Didn't do any sleepwalking, did you?'

'Sleepwalking? What do you mean?'

'Look, Thorson, thanks for the coffee and all but I know it was you who called Warren and I know it was you who was in my room last night.'

Thorson pulled to a stop at a curb marked for deliveries only. He threw the car into park and looked at me.

'What did you say? What're you saying?'

'You heard what I said. You were in there. I might not have the proof now but if Warren comes up with anything ahead of me, I'll go to Backus anyway and tell him what I saw.'

'Listen, sport, see that coffee? That was my peace offering. If you want to throw it in my face, fine. But I don't know what the fuck you are talking about and for the last time, I don't talk to reporters. Period. I'm only talking to you now because you have special dispensation. That's it.'

He jammed the car into drive and lurched out into traffic, prompting an angry rebuke from the horn of another driver. Hot coffee slopped onto my hand but I kept silent about it. We drove in silence for several minutes, entering a canyon of concrete and glass and steel. Wilshire Boulevard. We were heading toward the towers of downtown. The coffee no longer tasted good to me and I put the cap back on it.

'Where are we going?' I finally asked.

'To see Gladden's lawyer. After that we're going out to Santa Monica, talk to the dynamic duo that had this dirtbag in their hands and let him go.'

'I read the *Times* story. They didn't know who they had. You can't really blame them.'

'Yeah, that's right, nobody's ever to blame.'

I had completely succeeded in taking Thorson's offering of goodwill and flushing it down the toilet. He had turned sullen and bitter. His usual self as far as I could tell, yet it was still my fault.

'Look,' I said, putting my coffee on the floor and holding my hands in an I-give-up gesture, 'I'm sorry, okay? If I'm wrong about you and Warren and everything else, I'm sorry. I was just looking at things the way they seem to me. If I'm wrong, I'm wrong.'

He said nothing and the silence became oppressive. I felt like the ball was still in my court, that there was more I needed to say.

'I'll drop it, okay?' I lied. 'And I'm sorry about . . . if you're upset about me and Rachel. Things just happened.'

'Tell you what, Jack, you can keep your apology. I don't care about you and I don't care about Rachel. She thinks I do and I'm sure she's told you that. But she's wrong. And if I were you, I'd watch my ass with her. There's always something else going on with her. Remember I told you that.'

'Sure.'

But I drop-kicked that stuff as soon as he said it. I wasn't going to let his bitterness infect my thoughts about Rachel.

'You ever heard of the Painted Desert, Jack?'

I looked at him, my eyes squinted in confusion.

'Yeah, I've heard of it.'

'Been there?'

'No.'

'Well, if you're with Rachel, then you're there now. She's the Painted Desert. Beautiful to look at, yeah. But, man, once you're there, she's desolate. There's nothing there past the beauty, Jack, and it gets cold at night in the desert.'

I wanted to hit him with some kind of comeback that would be the verbal equivalent of a roundhouse punch. But the depth of his acid and anger stunned me into silence.

'She can play you,' he continued. 'Or play *with* you. Like a toy. One minute she wants to share it, the next she doesn't. She disappears on you.'

I still said nothing. I turned and looked out the window so I wouldn't even have him in my peripheral vision. In a couple of minutes he said we were there and he pulled into the parking garage of one of the downtown office buildings.

After consulting a directory in the lobby of the Fuentes Law Center, we silently rode the elevator up to the seventh floor. To the right we found a door with a mahogany plaque set to the side of it that announced the law offices of Krasner & Peacock. Inside, Thorson placed his opened badge and ID wallet on the counter in front of the receptionist and asked to see Krasner.

'I'm sorry,' she said, 'Mr Krasner is in court this morning.'

'Are you sure?'

'Of course I'm sure. He's in arraignments. He won't be back until after lunch.'

'Down here? Which courthouse?'

'Down here. The CCB.'

We left the car where it was and walked to the Criminal Courts Building. Arraignments were held on the fifth floor in a huge, marble-walled courtroom heavily crowded with lawyers, the accused and the families of the accused. Thorson approached a deputy marshal sitting behind a desk at the first row of the gallery and asked her which of the lawyers milling about was Arthur Krasner. She pointed to a short man with thinning red hair and a red face who was standing near the court railing talking with another man in a suit, undoubtedly another lawyer. Thorson headed toward him, mumbling something about his looking like a Jewish leprechaun.

'Mr Krasner?' Thorson said, not waiting for a lull in the conversation the two men were having.

'Yes?'

'Can I have a word with you out in the hallway?'

'Who are you?'

'I can explain in the hallway.'

'You can explain now or you can go out to the hallway by yourself.'

Thorson opened his wallet, Krasner looked at the badge and read the ID, and I watched his small porcine eyes move back and forth as he thought.

'That's right, I think you know what it's about,' Thorson said. Looking at the other lawyer, he said, 'Will you excuse us now?'

In the hallway Krasner had regained some of his lawyerly bluff.

'All right, I have an arraignment in there in five minutes. What's this about?'

'I thought we were past that,' Thorson said. 'It's about one of your clients, William Gladden.'

'Never heard of him.'

He made a move to go past Thorson to the courtroom door. Thorson nonchalantly reached out and put a hand on the other man's chest, stopping him dead.

'Please,' Krasner said. 'You have no right to touch me. Don't touch me.'

'You know who we're talking about, Mr Krasner. You are in serious trouble for hiding this man's true identity from the court and the police.'

'No, you are wrong. I had no idea who he was. I took the case at face value. Who he turned out to be was not my concern. And there is not one scintilla of evidence or even a suggestion that I knew otherwise.'

'Never mind the bullshit, Counselor. You can save it for the judge in there. Where is Gladden?'

'I have no idea and even if I did I –'

'You wouldn't say? That's the wrong attitude, Mr Krasner. Let me tell you something, I've gone over the record of your representation of Mr Gladden and things don't look good, if you know what I mean. Not kosher is what I am saying. This could be a problem for you.'

'I don't know what you're talking about.'

'How did he come to call you after his arrest?'

'I don't know. I didn't ask.'

'Was it a referral?'

'Yes, I think so.'

'From who?'

'I don't know. I said I didn't ask.'

'Are you a pedophile, Mr Krasner? Is it little girls or little boys that turn you on? Or maybe both?'

'What?'

Little by little Thorson had backed him up against the marble wall of the hallway with his verbal assault. Krasner was beginning to look spent. He was holding his briefcase in front of his body now, almost as a shield. But it wasn't thick enough.

'You know what I'm talking about,' Thorson said, bearing down on him. 'Of all the lawyers in this town, why'd Gladden call you?'

'I told you,' Krasner yelled, drawing looks from everyone passing in the hall. He continued in a whisper. 'I don't know why he chose me. He just did. I'm in the book. It's a free country.'

Thorson hesitated, allowing Krasner to say more but the lawyer didn't take the bait.

'I looked at the records yesterday,' Thorson said. 'You had him out two hours and fifteen minutes after bail was set. How did you make the bond? The answer is you already had the money from him, didn't you? So the real question is, how'd you get the money from him if he spent the night in jail?'

'Wire transfer. Nothing illegal. We talked the night before about my fee and what the bond might be and he had it wired the following morning. I had nothing to do with it. I . . . You can't stand here and slander me in this way.'

'I can do whatever I want to do. You fucking disgust me. I checked you out with the locals, Krasner. I know about you.'

'What are you talking about?'

'If you don't know now, you're going to know soon enough. They're coming for you, little man. You put this guy back on the street and look what he did. Look what he fucking did.'

'I didn't know!' Krasner said in a whine that pleaded for forgiveness.

'Sure, nobody ever knows. You have a phone?'

'What?'

'A phone. A telephone.'

Thorson slapped an open hand against Krasner's briefcase, a move that made the little man jump as if shocked with a cattle prod.

'Yes, yes, I have a phone. You don't have to –'

'Good. Get it out, call your receptionist and tell her to pull the wire transfer records from your file. Tell her I'll be there in fifteen minutes for a copy of it.'

'You can't take – I have an attorney/client relationship with this individual that I must protect no matter what he's done. I –'

Thorson slapped a backhand off the briefcase again, which shut Krasner up in mid-sentence. I could see Thorson received a genuine sense of accomplishment from pushing the little lawyer around.

'Make the call, Krasner, and I'll tell the locals you helped out. Make the call or the next person to die is on you. Because now you do know who and what we're talking about here.'

Krasner slowly nodded and began opening his briefcase.

'That's it, Counselor,' Thorson said. 'Now you see the light.'

As Krasner called his receptionist and issued the order in a shaky voice, Thorson stood silently watching. I had never seen or heard of anyone using the bad cop routine without the good cop counterpart and still so expertly finesse the information needed from a source. I wasn't sure if I admired Thorson's skill or was appalled by it. But he had turned the posturing bluff artist into a shaking mess. As Krasner was folding the phone closed, Thorson asked what the amount of the wire transfer had been.

'Six thousand dollars even.'

'Five for bail and one for you. How come you didn't squeeze him?'

'He said it was all he could afford. I believed him. May I go now?'

There was a resigned and defeated look on Krasner's face. Before Thorson answered his question the door to the courtroom opened and a bailiff leaned out.

'Artie, you're up.'

'Okay, Jerry.'

Without waiting for further comment from Thorson, Krasner began moving toward the door again. And once again Thorson stopped him with a hand on the chest. This time Krasner made no protest about being touched. He simply stopped, leaving his eyes staring dead ahead.

'Artie – can I call you Artie? – you better do some soul-searching. That is if you have one. You know more than you've said here. A lot more. And the more time you waste, the more there's a chance that a life will be wasted. Think about that and give me a call.'

He reached over and slid a business card into the handkerchief pocket of Krasner's suit coat, then patted it gently.

'My local number is written on the back. Call me. If I get what I need from somewhere else and find out you had the same information, I will be merciless, Counselor. Fucking merciless.'

Thorson then stepped back so the lawyer could slowly make his way back into the courtroom.

*

We were back out on the sidewalk before Thorson spoke to me.

'Think he got the message?'

'Yeah, he got it. I'd stay by the phone. He's gonna call.'

'We'll see.'

'Can I ask you something?'

'What?'

'Did you really check him out with the locals?'

Thorson smiled by way of an answer.

'The part about him being a pedophile. How do you know that?'

'Just takin' a shot. Pedophiles are networkers. They like to surround themselves with their own kind. They have phone nets, computer nets, a whole support system. They view it as them against society. The misunderstood minority, that kind of bullshit. So I figured maybe he got Krasner's name on a referral list somewhere. It was worth the shot. The way I read Krasner, I think it hit him. He wouldn't have given up the wire records if it didn't.'

'Maybe. Maybe he was telling the truth about not knowing who Gladden was. Maybe he just has a conscience and doesn't want to see anybody else hurt.'

'I take it you don't know that many lawyers.'

Ten minutes later we were waiting for the elevator outside the Krasner & Peacock law offices, Thorson looking at the wire transfer receipt for the sum of $6,000.

'It's a bank out of Jacksonville,' he said without looking up. 'We'll have to get Rach on it.'

I noticed his use of the diminutive of her name. There was something intimate about it.

'Why her?' I asked.

''Cause she's in Florida.'

He looked up from the receipt at me. He was smiling.

'Didn't I tell you?'

'No, you didn't tell me.'

'Yeah, Backus sent her out this morning. She went to see Horace the Hypnotist and work with the Florida team. Tell you what, let's stop in the lobby and use the phone, see if I can get somebody to get this account number to her.'

38

Very little was said between us on the way out from down town to Santa Monica. I was thinking about Rachel in Florida. I couldn't understand why Backus would send her when the front line seemed to be out here. There were two possibilities, I decided. One was that Rachel was being disciplined for some reason, possibly me, and taken off the front line. The other was that there was some new break to the case I didn't know about and was purposely not being told. Either choice was a bad one, but I found myself secretly choosing the first.

Thorson seemed lost in thought during most of the drive, or perhaps just tired of being around me. But when we parked out front of the Santa Monica Police Department, he answered the question I had before I even asked it.

'We just need to pick up the property they took from Gladden when he was arrested. We want to consolidate it all.'

'And they're going to let you do that?'

I knew how small departments, in fact, all departments, tended to react to being bigfooted by the Big G.

'We'll see.'

At the front counter of the detective bureau, we were told that Constance Delpy was in court but her partner, Ron Sweetzer, would be with us shortly. Shortly to Sweetzer turned out to be ten minutes. A period of time that didn't sit well with Thorson. I got the idea that the FBI, in the embodiment of Gordon Thorson at least, didn't appreciate having to wait for anybody, especially a small-town gold badge.

When Sweetzer finally appeared, he stood behind the counter and asked how he could help us. He gave me a second glance, probably computing how my beard and clothes did not jibe with his image of the FBI. He said nothing and made no movement that could have been translated as an invitation back to his office. Thorson responded in kind with short sentences and his own brand of rudeness. He took a folded white page from his inside pocket and spread it on the counter.

'That's the property inventory from the arrest of William Gladden, AKA Harold Brisbane. I'm here to accept custody of the property.'

'What are you talking about?' Sweetzer said.

'I'm talking about what I just said. The FBI has entered the case and is heading the nationwide investigation of William Gladden. We need to have some experts look over what you've got here.'

'Wait a minute, Mr Agent. We've got our own experts and we've got a case against this guy. We're not turning over the evidence to anybody. Not without a court order or the DA's approval.'

Thorson took a deep breath but he seemed to me to be going through an act he had performed countless times before. The bully who comes into town and picks on the little guy.

'First of all,' he said, 'you know and I know your case is for shit. And secondly, we're not talking about evidence, anyway. You've got a camera, a bag of candy. That's not evidence of anything. He's charged with fleeing an officer, vandalism and polluting a waterway. Where's the camera come into it?'

Sweetzer started to say something, then stopped, apparently stymied for a reply.

'Just wait here, please?'

Sweetzer started away from the counter.

'I don't have all day, Detective,' Thorson said after him. 'I'm trying to catch this guy. Too bad he's still on the loose.'

Sweetzer angrily swung around.

'What's that supposed to mean? What the *fuck* does that mean?'

Thorson held his hands up in a no-harm gesture.

'Means exactly what you think it means. Now go ahead, get your CO. I'll talk to him now.'

Sweetzer left and in two minutes returned with a man ten years older, thirty pounds heavier and twice as angry.

'What's the problem here?' he said in a short, clipped voice.

'There's no problem, Captain.'

'It's Lieutenant.'

'Oh, well, Lieutenant, your man here seems confused. I've explained that the FBI has stepped into the investigation of William Gladden and is working hand in hand with the Los Angeles police and other departments across the country. The bureau also extends that hand to Santa Monica. But Detective Sweetzer seems to think that by holding on to the property seized from Mr Gladden, he is helping the investigation and eventual capture of Mr Gladden. In reality, he is impeding our efforts. I'm surprised, frankly, to be treated this way. I've got a member of the national media with me and I didn't expect that he'd see something like this.'

Thorson gestured toward me and Sweetzer and his lieutenant studied me. I felt myself getting angry at being used. The lieutenant looked from me back to Thorson.

'What we don't understand is why you need to take this property. I've looked at the inventory. It's a camera, a pair of sunglasses, a duffel bag and a bag of candy, that's it. No film, no pictures. Why does the FBI have to take this from us?'

'Have you submitted candy samples to a chemical analysis lab?'

The lieutenant looked at Sweetzer, who shook his head slightly as if it were some kind of a secret signal.

'We will do that, Lieutenant,' Thorson said. 'To determine if the candy was in any way doctored. And the camera. You are not aware of this but there have been some photos recovered in our investigation. I cannot go into the content of these photos but suffice it to say they are of a highly illegal nature. But the point is, analysis of these photos shows an imperfection in the lens of the camera with which these photos were taken. It's like a fingerprint on every photo. We can match those photos to a camera. But we need the camera to do it. If you allow us to take it and we make a match, we will be able to prove this man took the photos. There will then be additional charges when we catch him. It will also help us determine exactly what this man has been up to. This is why we request that you turn this property over. Really, gentlemen, we want the same thing.'

The lieutenant didn't say anything for a long moment. Then he turned and started away from the counter. To Sweetzer, he said, 'Make sure you get a chain-of-evidence receipt.'

Sweetzer's face fell and he followed the lieutenant away from the counter, not protesting but whispering something about not getting the explanation Thorson had just made before dragging the lieutenant into it. After both of them had turned a corner back into the bureau, I moved up next to Thorson at the counter so I could whisper.

'Next time you're going to use me like that, give me some warning,' I said. 'I don't appreciate it at all.'

Thorson smirked.

'The good investigator uses any and all tools available to him. You were available.'

'Is that true about photos being recovered and camera analysis?'

'Sounded good, didn't it?'

The only way Sweetzer could salvage any kind of pride from the transaction was to leave us waiting at the counter for another ten minutes. Finally, he came out with a cardboard box and slid it across the counter. He then told Thorson to sign a property receipt. Thorson started to open the box first. Sweetzer put his hand on the lid to stop him.

'It's all there,' Sweetzer said. 'Just sign the receipt so I can get back to work. I'm busy.'

Thorson, having won the war, gave him the last battle and signed the receipt.

'I trust you. It's all in here.'

'You know, I used to want to be an FBI agent.'

'Well, don't feel bad about it. Lot of people fail the test.'

Sweetzer's face flushed pink.

'It wasn't that,' he said. 'I just decided that I liked being a human too much.'

Thorson raised his hand and pointed a finger like a gun.

'Good one,' he said. 'Have a nice day, Detective Sweetzer.'

'Hey,' Sweetzer said, 'if you fellows over there at the bureau need anything else, and I mean anything at all, be sure to hesitate to call.'

On the way back to the car I couldn't resist.

'I guess you never heard that you supposedly can catch more flies with sugar than with lemon.'

'Why waste the sugar on flies?' he replied.

He didn't open the property box until we were in the car. After he removed the lid I saw there were the items already discussed wrapped in plastic bags and a sealed envelope marked CONFIDENTIAL: FBI EYES ONLY. Thorson ripped open the envelope and from it took out a photograph. It was a Polaroid, probably taken with a jail booking camera. It was a close-up shot of a man's buttocks, hands grasping and spreading them to afford a clear, deep view of the anus. Thorson studied it a moment and then tossed it over the seat into the back.

'That's strange,' he said. 'I wonder why Sweetzer included a picture of his mother?'

I gave a short laugh and said, 'There's the most telling example of interagency cooperation I've ever seen.'

But Thorson ignored the comment or didn't hear it. His face turned somber and from the box he pulled a plastic bag containing the camera. I watched him stare at it intently. He turned it in his hands, studying it. I saw his face grow dark.

'Those fucking assholes,' he said slowly. 'They've been sitting on this all this time.'

I looked at the camera. There was something odd about its bulky shape. It looked like a Polaroid but had a standard-looking 35mm lens on it.

'What is it? What's wrong?'

'Know what this is?'

'No, what?'

Thorson didn't answer. He pressed a button to turn the camera on. Then he studied the computerized display on the back.

'No pictures,' he said.

'What is it?'

He didn't answer. He put the camera back in the box, closed it and started the car.

Thorson drove the car down the street from the police station like a fire engine heading to a four-alarm. He pulled into a gas station on Pico Boulevard and jumped out while the car was still jerking in response to his skidding stop. He ran to the phone and punched in a long distance number without putting in any coins. While he waited for a response he took out a pen and a small notebook. I saw him write something down after saying a few words into the phone. When he keyed in another long distance number without putting in coins, I guessed he had gotten directory assistance for a toll-free 800 number.

I was tempted to get out of the car and go up to him so that I could hear his conversation but decided to wait. In a minute or so I saw him writing information into his notebook. While he did that I looked at the evidence box Sweetzer had given him. I wanted to open it and look at the camera again but thought this might anger Thorson.

'You mind telling me what's going on?' I asked as soon as he was behind the wheel again.

'Sure I mind, but you're going to find out anyway.' He opened the box and lifted out the camera again. 'Know what this is?'

'You asked that. A camera.'

'Right, but what kind of camera is what's important.'

As he turned it in his hands I saw the manufacturer's symbol imprinted on the front. A large lowercase *d* in pale blue. I knew it was the symbol of the computer manufacturer called digiTime. Printed beneath the corporate symbol was *Digishot 200.*

'This is a digital camera, Jack. That hillbilly Sweetzer didn't know what the fuck he had. We just have to hope we're not too late.'

'You're losing me. I guess I'm just a hillbilly, too, but can you –'

'You know what a digital camera is?'

'Yeah, it doesn't use film. They've been experimenting with them at the paper.'

'Right, no film. The image the camera shoots is captured on a microchip instead. The image can then be put into a computer, edited, blown up, whatever, then printed. Depending on your equipment – and this is top-of-the-line equipment, comes with a Nikon lens – you can come up with high-resolution photographs. As good as the real thing.'

I had seen prints taken on digital at the *Rocky.* Thorson was correct in his assessment.

'So what's it mean?'

'Two things. Remember what I told you about pedophiles? The networking they do?'

'Right.'

'Okay, we pretty much know Gladden has a computer because of the fax, right?'

'Right.'

'And now we know he had a digital camera. With the digital camera, his computer and the same modem he used to send the fax, he could send a photo anywhere he wanted to in the world, to anybody who had a phone and a computer and the software to receive it.'

It hit me then in a split second.

'He's sending people pictures of kids?'

'No, he's *selling* them pictures of kids. That's my guess. The questions we had about how he lives and gets money? About this account in Jacksonville he wired money from? This is the answer. The Poet makes his money selling pictures of kids, maybe even the kids he killed. Who knows, maybe even the cops he killed.'

'There are people who would . . .'

I didn't finish. I knew the question was stupid.

'If there is one thing I know from this job it's that there is an appetite and therefore a market for anything and everything,' Thorson said. 'Your darkest thought is not unique. The worst thing you can possibly imagine, whatever it is, no matter how bad, there is a market for it . . . I gotta make another call, get this list of dealers split up.'

'What was the second thing?'

'What?'

'You said there were two things significant about –'

'It's a break. It's a big fucking break. That is, if we're not too late because Santa Monica's been sitting on the goddamn camera. If Gladden's income, his traveling money, comes from selling photos to other pedophiles, shipping them through the Internet or some private bulletin board, then he lost his main tool last week when the cops took this away.'

He tapped the top of the cardboard box on the seat between us.

'He's got to replace it,' I said.

'You got it.'

'You're going to go to the digiTime dealers.'

'You're a smart guy, sport. How come you became a reporter?'

This time I didn't protest the use of his name for me. There wasn't the same malice as when he had called me by it before.

'I called the digiTime 800 number and got eight dealers who sell the digiShot 200 in L.A. I figure he's got to go for the same model. He'd already have all the other equipment. I've got to make that call to split these up. You got a quarter, Jack? I'm out.'

I gave him the quarter and he jumped out of the car and went back to the phone. I imagined he was calling Backus, gleefully telling him about the break and splitting up the list. I sat there thinking that Rachel should have been the one standing there on the phone. In a few minutes, Thorson was back.

'We're checking out three of them. All over here on the west side. Bob's giving the other five to Carter and some guys from the FO.'

'Do you have to order these cameras or do they keep them in stock?'

Thorson pulled back into the traffic and headed east on Pico. He referred to one of the addresses he had written down in his notebook as he talked and drove.

'Some places keep them in stock,' he said. 'If they don't they can get 'em pretty quick. That's what the digiTime operator said.'

'Then what are we doing? It's been a week. He would've got one by now.'

'Maybe, maybe not. We're playing a hunch. This is not a cheap piece of equipment. You buy it in a kit with the downloading and editing software and the serial cable to connect it to your computer, the leather case and flash and all the extras, you're getting up well over a grand. Probably fifteen hundred. But . . .'

He raised his finger to make the point.

'What if you already have all the extras and all you want is the camera? No cable. No software. None of that stuff. What if you just shelled out six grand for bail and a lawyer and you're hurting for cash and not only don't need all those extras but can't afford them?'

'You special-order just a camera and save a lot of money.'

'That's right. That's my hunch. I think that if making bail came close to busting our friend Gladden just like that shyster lawyer said it did, then he'd be looking to save a dollar here and there. If he replaced the camera, I'm betting he made the special order.'

He was juiced and it was contagious. I had caught his excitement and was beginning to look at Thorson in perhaps a truer light. I knew these were the moments he lived for. Moments of understanding and clarity. Of knowing he was close.

'McEvoy, we are on a roll,' he suddenly said. 'I think you might be good luck after all. Just make it good enough that we're not too late.'

I nodded my agreement.

We drove for a few minutes in silence before I questioned him again.

'How do you know so much about digital cameras?'

'It's come up before and it's becoming more prevalent. At Quantico we have a unit now that does nothing but computer crime. Internet crime. A lot of what they do bleeds over into pornography, child crimes. They put out bureau-wide briefings to keep people current. I try to keep current.'

I nodded.

'There was this old lady – a schoolteacher, no less – up near Cornell in New York checks the download file in her home computer one day and sees a new entry she doesn't recognize. She prints it out and what she gets is a murky black-and-white but clearly identifiable picture of a boy of about ten copping some old guy's joint. She calls the locals and they figure out it got to her computer by mistake. Her Internet address is just a number and they figure the sender transposed a couple digits or something. Anyway, the routing history of the file is right there and they trace it back to some gimp, a pedophile with a nice long record. Out here in fact, he was from L.A. Anyway, they do the search-and-bust and take him down pretty neat. The first digital bust. The guy had something like five hundred different photos in his computer. Christ, he needed a double hard drive. I'm talking about kids of every age, persuasion, doing things normal grownups don't even do . . . Anyway, good case. He got life, no parole. He had a digiShot, though that might've been a 100 model. They put the story out last year in the FBI *Bulletin*.'

'How come the picture the teacher got was so murky?'

'She didn't have the printer for it. You know, you need a nice colorgraphics printer and high-gloss paper. She had neither.'

The first two stops were dead ends. One store hadn't sold a digiShot in two weeks and the other had sold two in the last week. However, those two cameras had gone to a well-known Los Angeles artist whose collage portraits made of Polaroid photos were celebrated and displayed in museums around the world. He now wanted to dabble in a newer photographic medium and was going digital. Thorson didn't even bother writing down notes for further follow-up.

The last stop on our list was a street-front shop called Data Imaging Answers on Pico, two blocks from the Westwood Pavilion shopping center.

After pulling to the curb in a no-parking zone out front, Thorson smiled and said, 'This is it. This is the one.'

'How do you know?' I asked.

'Walk-in store on a busy street. The other two were more like mail-order offices, not storefronts. Gladden would have wanted the storefront. More visual stimulation. People passing outside, people coming in and out, more distractions. It would be better for him. He doesn't want to be remembered.'

It was a small store with two desks in the showroom and several unopened boxes stacked about. There were two circular counters with computer terminals and video equipment on display along with stacks of computer equipment catalogs. A balding man wearing thick glasses with black frames was sitting at one of the desks and looked up as we entered. There was no one at the other desk and it looked unused.

'Are you the manager?' Thorson inquired.

'Not only that, I'm the owner.' The man stood up with proprietary pride and smiled as we approached his desk. 'Not only that, I am the number one employee.'

When we didn't join in his guffaw he asked what he could do for us.

Thorson showed him the inside of his badge wallet.

'FBI?'

It seemed incomprehensible to him.

'Yes. You sell the digiShot 200, correct?'

'Yes, we do. Top-of-the-line digital camera. But I'm out of stock at the moment. Sold my last one last week.'

I felt my guts seize. We were too late.

'I can have one in three or four days. In fact, seein' that it's the FBI I might get them to ship two-day. No charge extra, of course.'

He smiled and nodded but his eyes had a quizzical look behind the thick glasses. He was nervous dealing with the FBI, especially not knowing what it was all about.

'And your name is?'

'Olin Coombs. I'm the owner.'

'Yes, you said that. Okay, Mr Coombs, I'm not interested in buying anything. Do you have the name of the person who bought your last digiShot?'

'Uh . . .' He creased his brow, probably wondering if he should ask if it was legal for the FBI to ask for such information. 'Of course I keep records. I can get that for you.'

Coombs sat down and opened a drawer in his desk. He looked through a hanging file until he found what he was looking for, pulled out a sheet of paper and laid it flat on the desk. He then turned it around so Thorson didn't have to read it upside down. Thorson leaned over, studied the document and I saw his head make a slight turn to the right and then back. Looking at the receipt, it looked to me as if numerous pieces of equipment had been purchased along with the digiShot camera.

'This isn't what I'm looking for,' Thorson said. 'I'm looking for a man that we believe wanted to purchase a digiShot camera only. This is the only one you've sold in the last week?'

'Yes – uh, no. It's the only one with delivery. We've sold two others but they had to be ordered.'

'And they haven't been delivered yet?'

'No. Tomorrow. I'm expecting a truck in the morning.'

'Either of those two just order the camera?'

'The camera?'

'You know, none of the other stuff. The software, the cable, the whole kit.'

'Oh, yes. Uh, as a matter of fact, there is . . .'

His words trailed off as he opened the drawer again and pulled out a clipboard with several pink forms on it. He started peeling them back and reading.

'I have a Mr Childs. Just wanted the camera, nothing else. Paid cash in advance. Nine ninety-five plus California sales tax. Came to –'

'Did he leave a number or address?'

I stopped breathing. We had him. This had to be Gladden. The irony of the name he had given was not lost on me. I felt a chill roll across my back.

'No, no number or address,' Coombs said. 'I wrote a note to myself. It says Mr Wilton Childs will call to check on the equipment's arrival. I told him to call tomorrow.'

'Then he'll come pick it up?'

'Yes, if it's here by then he'll come pick it up. Like I said, we don't have an address so we can't deliver it.'

'Do you remember what he looked like, Mr Coombs?'

'Looked like? Uh, well, yes I suppose so.'

'Can you describe him?'

'He was a white fellow, I remember that. He . . .'

'Blond hair?'

'Uh, no. It was dark. And he was growing a beard, I remember that.'

'How old?'

'About twenty-five or perhaps thirty.'

That was good enough for Thorson. It was in the ballpark and the rest of the information fit. He pointed at the empty desk.

'Anybody using that desk?'

'Not at the moment. Business is not so good.'

'Then is it all right if we do?'

39

There was a discernible electric buzz in the air as everyone gathered around a table in the conference room with the million-dollar view. After being brought up to speed by a phone call from Thorson, Backus had decided to move his operation command post from the Wilcox Hotel to the FBI offices in Westwood. We gathered on the seventeenth floor of the federal building in a conference room with a panoramic view of the city. I could see Catalina Island floating out in a golden ocean reflecting the spectacular burnt-orange-and-red start of another sunset.

It was four-thirty Pacific time and the meeting had been scheduled late to give Rachel as much time as possible to obtain and execute a search warrant for records of Gladden's bank account in Jacksonville.

In the conference room, Backus was joined by Thorson, Carter, Thompson, six agents I hadn't been introduced to but who I assumed were locals, and me. Quantico and all the field offices involved in the investigation were also on the conference line. And even these unseen people seemed excited. Brass Doran kept saying over the speaker, 'Are we ready to start yet?'

Finally, Backus, sitting at the center of the table, closest to the speakerphone, called everyone to order. Behind him, on an easel, was a crude top-view diagram of the Data Imaging Answers store and the block of Pico Boulevard where it was located.

'Okay, people, things are happening,' he said. 'This is what we worked for. So let's talk about it and then let's do it and let's do it right.'

He stood up. Maybe the moment was getting to him as well.

'We have a priority one lead we're working and we want to hear from Rachel and Brass. First, though, I'm going to have Gordon give the rundown on what we've got set up for tomorrow.'

As Thorson told the captive audience about our day's work and discoveries, my mind wandered. I thought of Rachel somewhere in Jacksonville, twenty-five hundred miles from her investigation and listening to a man she didn't like and probably even despised talk about the major break he had made. I wanted to talk to her and try in some way to console her, but not with twenty-five people listening. I wanted to ask Backus where she was so I could call afterward but knew I couldn't do that, either. Then I remembered the pager. I would do that later.

'We are shifting our critical incident team off Thomas,' Thorson said. 'The LAPD surveillance team is doubling up and will stay with Thomas. We are redirecting our people to be used in a twofold plan to facilitate the arrest of this offender. First off, we now have caller ID on the phones at Data Imaging. We will have a mobile receiver and LED readout to monitor incoming calls on both lines and the field office is providing all available hands for response teams. We're going to trace this subject's call when he checks in to see if his product is in and try to hold him at the phone until our people can get there. If they do, standard felony arrest procedures will follow. Any questions so far?'

'Air support?' an agent asked.

'We're working on it. I'm told we can count on one bird but we are going for two. All right then, step two is if we are unable to effect capture of the subject through caller ID. At Digital Imaging Answers – let's call it DIA for short – I'll be inside with Coombs, the owner. If we get the call from this guy, he will be told that the camera he ordered is ready for pickup. We'll try to press for a pickup time but not too hard, just keeping it natural.

'If the subject slips through the first net, the plan is to set up on him once he comes to the store. The store's been wired – sound and video. If he comes in, I'll just give him his camera and send him on his way, another satisfied customer. The felony arrest will take place at the time Don Sample, he's our critical team leader, thinks is appropriate and gives the word. Obviously, that will be the first controlled setting our man takes us to. We hope that will be his car. But you all know the procedures for other contingencies. Questions?'

'Why not prone his ass right there in the store?'

'We feel we need Coombs to be there so as not to spook the subject. He bought the camera from Coombs, Coombs should be there. I don't want to try to take this guy down that close to a civilian. Also, it's a small store and we may be pressing it having even one agent in there. You put more in and it's going to look suspicious to this guy. So why don't we just give him the camera and take him down out there on the street, where we can control things a little better?'

With Thorson, Backus and Sample handing off to each other, they outlined the plan in more detail. Coombs would be in the store with Thorson to handle the daily business and real customers throughout the day. But when the outside surveillance teams reported the approach of any customer even remotely matching Gladden's description, Thorson would remain up front to handle the transaction while Coombs excused himself, retreated to a small rear storage room and locked himself in. Another agent, posing as a customer, would enter through the front door as backup after Gladden entered. The interior of the store would be monitored by a video setup. The exterior would be monitored by roving and stationary agents ready to deal with all contingencies once Gladden was identified. Additionally, a female agent in a Los Angeles parking enforcement uniform and car would continuously patrol the block where DIA was located.

'I don't think I need to remind everybody just how dangerous this individual is,' Backus said when the briefing was done. 'Everybody pack some extra common sense tomorrow. Watch out for yourself and your partner. Questions?'

I waited a beat to see if there were any questions from agents. When there weren't, I spoke up.

'What if the digiShot doesn't come in tomorrow like Mr Coombs said it was supposed to?'

'Oh, yes, good point,' Backus said. 'We're not taking any chances. The Internet group at Quantico has one of these cameras and it's coming out tonight on a plane. We'll use that whether the one he really ordered comes in or not. Ours will be wired with a homer just in case, God forbid, he gets by us. We'll be able to track him. Anything else?'

'Has any thought been given to not taking him down?'

It was Rachel's voice on the speakerphone.

'How do you mean?'

'Just playing devil's advocate, it looks like we've got this pretty well buttoned down. This could be a rare opportunity for us to watch a serial killer and observe his hunting and victim acquisition patterns. It could be invaluable to our studies.'

Her question set off a debate among the agents over the plan.

'And risk the chance that we lose him and he kills some kid or another cop?' Thorson responded. 'No thanks – especially with the Fourth Estate here watching.'

Almost everybody came down on Thorson's side of it, the feeling being that a monster like Gladden, though a worthy research subject, should be studied only in the closed setting of a prison cell. The risks of his potential escape far outweighed the riches that might be gained by watching him at work in an open environment.

'Look, people, the plan has been set,' Backus finally said, closing the subject. 'We've considered the alternatives that have been suggested and I feel that going at him in the way we have outlined is the best and safest plan. So let's move on. Rachel, what have you got for us?'

I watched the body language of the agents in the room change as their attention went from Backus and Thorson to the white phone positioned at the center of the table. People seemed to lean toward it. Backus, still standing, leaned down with his palms on the tabletop.

'Let me start with the bank,' Rachel said. 'I just got these records about ninety minutes ago, so there hasn't been a lot of time. But, preliminarily, it looks like we have withdrawals wired to three of our cities, Chicago, Denver and L.A. The dates look good. He got money in those cities within days, just before or after, the bait murders in each. There are two wires to L.A. One coincides with the bail last week, and then on Saturday there was another transfer of twelve hundred. He picked the money up at the same bank. A Wells Fargo on Ventura Boulevard in Sherman Oaks. I was thinking this might be another way of taking him if he doesn't show up tomorrow for his camera. We could watch the account and intercept him next time he gets money. Only problem with that is that he's running low on funds. After pulling out that twelve hundred, he's down to about two hundred in the account.'

'But he's going to try to make some more with the new camera,' Thorson said.

'Going on to the deposits,' Rachel continued. 'These are very interesting but I just haven't had the time to really . . . uh, in the last two years there has been about forty-five thousand dollars wired to the account. Deposits coming from all over the place. Maine, Texas, California – several from California, New York. There doesn't seem to be a correlating pattern to our killings. Also, I found one overlap. Last November one there were wire deposits made from New York and Texas on the same day.'

'He's obviously not making the deposits,' Backus said. 'Or at least not all of them.'

'Those are payments,' Brass said over the conference line. 'From selling the photos. Payments wired in directly by the buyers.'

'Exactly,' Rachel said.

'Will we . . . can we trace back these wires and get to these purchasers?' Thompson asked.

'Uh,' Rachel replied when no one else did. 'We can try. I mean, we can trace them back but I wouldn't count on much. If you have cash, you can walk into almost any bank in the country and make a wire transfer as long as you have the destination account number and you pay the service charge. You have to give bare-bones sender's information but you don't have to show ID. People buying child pornography and possibly – probably – much worse are likely to use false names.'

'True.'

'What else, Rachel?' Backus asked. 'Anything else from the subpoena?'

'There is a P.O. box for the account mail. It's local and it's probably a mail drop. I'll be checking it out in the morning.'

'Okay. Do you want to report on Horace Gomble or save that until you've put your thoughts together?'

'No, I'll tell you the high points, which weren't many. My old pal Horace was not too happy to see me again. We sparred for a while and then his ego got the better of him. He acknowledged that he and Gladden had discussed the practice of hypnosis when they were cellmates. He admitted finally that he traded lessons for Gladden's legal work on his appeal. But he would go no further than that. I sensed . . . I don't know.'

'What, Rachel?'

'I don't know, some kind of appreciation for what Gladden was doing.'

'You told him?'

'No, I didn't tell him, but it was obvious to him that I was there for a reason. Still, it seemed like he knew something more. Maybe Gladden told him before he left Raiford what he planned to do. Told him about Beltran. I don't know. He also might've seen CNN today – if they have cable in the dorm. They picked up Jack McEvoy's story big time. I saw it at the airport. Of course, nothing in it links the Poet to Gladden, but Gomble could have figured it out. CNN used the tape from Phoenix again. If he saw that and then I showed up, he'd know what it was about without me saying a word.'

It had been the first I'd heard about any response to my story. In fact, I had totally forgotten about it because of the events of the day.

'Any chance Gladden and Gomble have been communicating?' Backus asked.

'I don't think so,' Rachel said. 'I checked with the hacks. Gomble's mail is still filtered. Coming in and out. He's managed to work his way up to trustee status, works in the prison's receiving shop. I guess there is always the possibility that incoming shipments might contain some kind of message but it seems doubtful. I also doubt Gomble would want to risk his position. He's got it pretty nice after seven years in. Nice job with a little office. He's supposedly in charge of supplying the prison canteen. In that society, that would make him a power. He's got a single cell now and his own TV. I don't see the reason to communicate with a wanted man like Gladden and risk all of that.'

'Okay, Rachel,' Backus said. 'Anything else?'

'That's it, Bob.'

Everyone was silent for a few moments, digesting what had been said so far.

'That brings us finally to the model,' Backus said. 'Brass?'

Again all eyes went to the phone on the table.

'Yes, Bob. The profile is coming together and Brad is adding some of the new details even as we speak. This is what we think we have. We might have a – this could be a situation where the offender went back to the man who set him on the path, who abused him and thereby nurtured the aberrant fantasies he later felt compelled to act upon as an adult.

'It's a play on the patricide model we have all seen before. We are almost solely focusing on the Florida cases. What we see here is the offender, in effect, seeking out his replacement. That is, the boy, Gabriel Ortiz, who currently held the attentions of Clifford Beltran, the father figure who abused him and then discarded him. It is the feeling of rejection the offender encountered that may motivate everything.

'Gladden killed the object of his abuser's current affection and then came back around and killed the abuser himself. It looks to me like an exorcism, if you will, the cathartic rush of eliminating the cause of all that was wrong in his life.'

There was a long period of quiet while I thought Backus and the others waited to see if Brass would continue. Backus finally spoke up.

'And then, what you're saying is, he repeats the crime over and over.'

'Correct,' Brass said. 'He is killing Beltran, his abuser, over and over. It is how he gains his peace. But, of course, the peace doesn't last long. He has to go back out and kill again. These other victims – the detectives – are innocents. They did nothing other than their jobs to be chosen by him.'

'What about the bait cases in the other cities?' Thorson asked. 'They don't all fit the archetype of the first boy.'

'I don't think the bait cases would be as important anymore,' Brass said. 'What is important is that he draws out a detective, a good detective, a formidable foe. This way the stakes are high and the purging he needs is there. As far as the bait cases go, they may have simply evolved into a means to the end. He uses the children to make money. The photos.'

As high as the group had been with the prospect of a major break or even conclusion to the investigation coming the following day, a gloom now descended over everyone. It was the gloom of knowing what horrors there were out there in the world. This was just one case. There would always be others. Always.

'Keep working it, Brass,' Backus finally said. 'I'd like you to send a psychopathologic report as soon as possible.'

'Will do. Oh, and one other thing. This is good.'

'Then go ahead.'

'I just pulled the hard file on Gladden that was put together after some of you visited him six years ago for the rapist profile data project. There's really nothing here that wasn't on the computer already. But there is a photograph.'

'Right,' Rachel said. 'I remember. The hacks let us go into the block after lockdown to take a picture of them, Gladden and Gomble, in their cell together.'

'Yes, that's what this is. And in the photograph there are three bookshelves situated over the toilet. I would assume these were shared shelves, both men's books. But anyway, the spines of these books are clearly visible. Most are law books that I am assuming Gladden must have used while working on his own appeal and for other inmates. Also, there is *Forensic Pathology* by DiMaio and DiMaio, *Techniques of Crime Scene Investigation* by Fisher, and *Psycho-Pathologic Profiling* by Robert Backus Sr. I'm familiar with these books and I think Gladden could have learned enough from these, particularly the book by Bob's father, to possibly know how to make each of the bait killings and crime scenes different enough from each other so that a VICAP hit could be avoided.'

'Shit,' Thorson said. 'What the fu – what was he doing with those books?'

'I assume by law the prison had to allow him access to them so that he could properly prepare his appeal,' Doran replied. 'Remember, he was pro se. He was certified in court as his own attorney.'

'Okay, good work, Brass,' Backus said. 'That's a help.'

'It's not all, either. There were two other books of note on the shelf. *Edgar Allan Poe, the Poems* and *The Complete Works of Edgar Allan Poe.*'

Backus whistled his delight.

'Now, that's really starting to tie things up,' he said. 'I assume we can find all the quotes in these books?'

'Yes. One of these is the book Jack McEvoy used already to verify the quotes.'

'Right. Okay, can you shoot us out a copy of that photo?'

'Will do, boss.'

The excitement in the room and coming over the phone lines seemed almost palpable. It was all coming together, all the pieces. And tomorrow the agents were going to go out and get this son of a bitch.

'I love the smell of napalm in the morning,' Thorson said. 'Smells like . . .'

'Victory!' shouted those in the room and on every phone.

'Okay, folks,' Backus said, clapping his hands twice. 'I think we've covered enough for now. Let's keep sharp. Let's keep this spirit. Tomorrow could be the day. Let's say it *is* the day. And you people listening in the cities, don't stop for one minute. Keep working your end. If we get this guy, we'll still need physical evidence connecting him to the other crimes. We need to place him in every city for trial.'

'If there is a trial,' Thorson said.

I looked at him. The humor he had shown a moment before had now evaporated. His jaw was set. He got up and headed out of the conference room.

I spent the evening alone in my room, filling my computer with notes from the conference meeting and waiting for Rachel to call. I had paged her twice.

Finally, at nine – midnight in Florida – she called.

'I can't sleep and I just wanted to make sure you didn't have another woman with you in there.'

I smiled.

'Not very likely. I've been waiting for you to call. Didn't you get my pages or are you just busy with another man?'

'No, let me check.'

She put the phone down for a few moments.

'Darn, the battery's down. I've got to get another. Sorry.'

'You talking about the pager or the other man?'

'Funny guy.'

'So why can't you sleep?'

'I keep thinking about Thorson in that store tomorrow.'

'And?'

'And I have to admit I'm fucking jealous. If he gets the arrest on this . . . I mean, it's my case and I'm two thousand fucking miles away from it.'

'Maybe it won't happen tomorrow. Maybe you'll be back in time. Even if you're not, it's not going to be him. It's going to be the critical team.'

'I don't know. Gordon's got a way of getting in there. And I have a bad feeling. It's tomorrow.'

'Some people might call that a good feeling, knowing that this guy's going to be taken off the street.'

'I know, I know. Still, why him? I think he and Bob . . . I didn't really get it clear from Bob why he sent me to Florida instead of someone else, instead of Gordon. He took the case away from me and I just let him.'

'Maybe Thorson told him about you and me.'

'I was thinking that. He would, too. But I don't see Bob doing what he did and not talking to me about it, not telling me why first. He's not that way. He doesn't take a side until he hears both sides.'

'I'm sorry, Rachel. But look, everybody knows it's your case. And it was your break with that Hertz car that brought everybody to L.A.'

'Thanks, Jack. But it was just one of the breaks. And it doesn't matter.

Making the arrest is like what you said about getting the story first. Doesn't really matter what's happened before.'

I knew I wasn't going to be able to make her feel better about the situation. She had brooded over it all night and there weren't enough words for me to change her mind. I decided to change the subject.

'Anyway, that was good stuff you got today. It seems like everything is coming together. We haven't even caught the guy and so much is known about him.'

'I guess. After hearing everything Brass said, do you have sympathy for him, Jack? For Gladden?'

'The man who killed my brother? Nope. No sympathy at all.'

'I didn't think so.'

'But you still do.'

She took a long time answering.

'I think of a little child that could have been a lot of different things until that man did what he did. Beltran set the child on the path. He's the real monster in all of this. Like I said before, if anybody got what he deserved, it was him.'

'Okay, Rachel.'

She started laughing.

'Sorry, I guess I'm finally getting tired. I didn't mean to be so intense all of a sudden.'

'It's okay. I know what you meant. There is a means to every end. A root to any cause. Sometimes the root is more evil than the cause, though it's the cause that is usually the most vilified.'

'You have a way with words, Jack.'

'I'd rather have my way with you.'

'You have that, too.'

I laughed and thanked her. Then we were silent for a few moments, the line open between us, stretching two thousand miles. I felt comfortable. No need to talk.

'I don't know how close they'll let you get tomorrow,' she said. 'But be careful.'

'I will. You too. When will you be back?'

'I hope by tomorrow afternoon. I told them to have the jet ready by twelve. I'm going to check out Gladden's mail drop and then get on the plane.'

'Okay. Why don't you try to go to sleep now?'

'Okay. I wish I was with you.'

'Me, too.'

I thought she was about to hang up but she didn't.

'Did you talk about me with Gordon today?'

I thought about his comment, calling her the Painted Desert.

'No. We had a pretty busy day.'

I don't think she believed me and I felt bad about lying.

'I'll see you, Jack.'

'Okay, Rachel.'

*

I thought about the phone conversation for a while after hanging up. Our conversation made me feel kind of sad and I couldn't pinpoint the true reason. After a while, I got up and left the room. It was raining. From the doorway of the hotel I checked the street and saw no one hiding, no one waiting for me. I shrugged off the fears of the night before and stepped out.

Walking close to the buildings to avoid as much of the rain as I could, I went to the Cat & Fiddle and ordered a beer at the bar. The place was crowded despite the rain. My hair was wet and in the mirror behind the bar I saw dark circles cut under my eyes. I touched my beard the way Rachel had caressed it. When I was done with the black and tan I ordered another.

40

The incense had long burned away by Wednesday morning. Gladden moved about the apartment with a T-shirt tied around his head, covering his mouth and nose, making him look like a bank robber from the Old West. He had sprinkled perfume he had found in the bathroom on the shirt and around the apartment, like a priest with holy water, but just like holy water, it didn't help him much. The smell was still everywhere, haunting him. But he didn't care anymore. He had made it through. It was time to leave. Time to change.

In the bathroom, he once again used a pink plastic razor he had found on the bathtub ledge to shave. He then took a long, hot and then cold, shower and afterward moved about the apartment naked, letting the air dry his body. He had taken a mirror off the wall of the bedroom earlier and propped it up against the living room wall. He now practiced walking in front of it again, back and forth, back and forth, watching his hips.

When he was satisfied he had it down, he went into the bedroom. The processed air chilled his naked body and the smell nearly made him convulse. But he stood his ground and looked down at her. She was gone now. The body on the bed was bloated and had lost all recognizable values. The eyes were coated in a milky caul. Bloody decomposition fluids had purged from everywhere, even the scalp. And the bugs had her now. He couldn't see them but he could hear them. They were there. He knew. It was in the books.

As he closed the door he thought he heard a whisper and he looked back in. It was nothing. Just the bugs. He closed the door and put the towel back in place.

41

The man we believed to be William Gladden called Data Imaging Answers at 11:05 on Wednesday morning, identifying himself as Wilton Childs and inquiring about the digiShot camera he had ordered. Thorson took the call and, according to plan, asked if Childs could call back in five or ten minutes. Thorson explained that a shipment of merchandise had just been delivered and he hadn't had a chance to look through it all. Childs said he would call back.

Meantime, Backus monitored the caller ID display and quickly gave the number Childs/Gladden had called from to an AT&T operator standing by on the law enforcement request desk. The operator punched the number into her computer and reported that it belonged to a pay phone on Ventura Boulevard in Studio City before Thorson had even hung up.

One of the roving two-car teams of FBI agents was on the 101 freeway in Sherman Oaks, about five minutes away from the pay phone with good traffic. They gassed it down to the Vineland Boulevard exit without use of sirens, exited to Ventura Boulevard and took positions within sight of the pay phone, which was on a wall outside the office of a $40-a-night motel, porno movies included. No one was at the phone by the time they got there but they waited. Meantime, another roving team was en route from Hollywood as backup and a helicopter was circling on standby over Van Nuys, ready to move over the scene when the ground agents moved in.

The agents in place waited. And so did I, in a car with Backus and Carter a block from Data Imaging. Carter turned the car on, ready to roll if the word came over the radio that the others had Gladden in sight.

Five minutes passed and then ten. It was all very intense, even sitting blind with Backus and Carter. The backup cars had enough time to take positions a few blocks behind the first team's cars on Ventura. There were now eight agents within a block of the pay phone.

But at 11:33, when the phone on Thorson's desk at Data Imaging rang, the agents in place were still watching an unused pay phone. Backus picked up the two-way.

'We've got a ring here. Anything?'

'Nada. No one's using this phone.'

'Be ready to move.'

Backus put the two-way down and picked up the mobile phone, hitting the preset key for calling the AT&T law enforcement desk. I was leaning over from the backseat, watching him and the video monitor on the transmission hump beneath the dashboard. It was a black-and-white fish-eye view of the whole Digital Imaging showroom. I saw Thorson pick the phone up on the seventh ring. Though both phone lines into the store were tapped, we could only hear Thorson's side of the conversation in the car. Thorson gave the high sign on the video, raising his hand over his head and making a circling motion with his finger. It was the sign that Childs/Gladden was calling again. Backus began the same rundown with caller ID that he had done before.

Not wanting to possibly spook Childs/Gladden, Thorson engaged no delay tactics on the second call. He also had no way of knowing that the call was coming from a different phone this time. For all he knew, agents were moving in on Gladden as he spoke to him.

But they weren't. As Thorson was telling the caller that his digiShot 200 had arrived and was ready for pickup, Backus was learning from the AT&T operator that the new call was being placed from another pay phone at Hollywood Boulevard and Las Palmas Street.

'Shit,' Backus said after hanging up. 'He's in Hollywood. I just pulled everyone out of there.'

Was it by design or luck that Gladden had escaped? No one knew, of course, but it was eerie, sitting there in the car with Backus and Carter. The Poet had kept moving and so far had avoided the net. Backus went through the motions of sending the roving teams to the intersection in Hollywood but I could tell by his voice he knew there wasn't much of a percentage in it. The caller would be gone. The only chance now would be to take him after he came for the camera. If he came.

On the phone in the store, Thorson was delicately attempting to pin the caller down on what time he would be by to pick up his camera but trying to act uninterested about it. Thorson was a good actor, it seemed to me. After a few moments he hung up.

He immediately looked toward the fish-eye lens of the camera and calmly said, 'Talk to me people. What's going on?'

Backus used the mobile phone to call the store and fill Thorson in on the near miss. I watched on the video as Thorson balled his hand into a fist and lightly bounced it once on the desk. I couldn't tell if it was a sign of disappointment that the arrest had not gone down or maybe a sign of thanks that he would now get the chance to come face to face with the Poet.

Most of the next four hours was spent in the car with Backus and Carter. At least I had the backseat so I could stretch. The only break came when they sent me around the corner to a deli on Pico to pick up sandwiches and coffee. I went quickly and missed nothing.

It was a long day, even with the hourly drive-bys Carter made of the store and the arrival of several customers at different times, which always proved to be tense moments until they were identified as real customers, not Gladden.

By four, Backus was already talking over plans for the next day with

Carter, not giving in to the thought that maybe Gladden wasn't coming, that maybe he knew something was amiss and had outsmarted the bureau. He told Carter that he had decided he wanted to open a two-way mike so that he didn't have to use one of the phone lines to communicate with Thorson in the store.

'I want that fixed by tomorrow,' he said.

'You got it,' Carter answered. 'After we close this down, I'll go in with technical and get it all fixed up.'

The car dropped into silence again. I could tell Backus and Carter, the veterans of too many stakeouts to recall, were used to long stretches of silent company. To me, though, it made the time pass all the more slowly. Occasionally I attempted conversation but they never carried it further than a few words.

Shortly after four a car pulled to the curb behind us. I turned around to look and saw it was Rachel. She got out and got into our car next to me.

'Well, well,' Backus said. 'I had a feeling you wouldn't stay away for long, Rachel. Are you sure you covered everything you needed to cover in Florida?'

He was being even but I sensed that he was annoyed that she had rushed back. I think he wanted her in Florida.

'Everything's fine, Bob. Anything happening here?'

'Nope, it's been slow.'

When Backus turned back around, she reached over and squeezed my hand on the seat and made a curious face at me. It took me a few moments to realize why.

'Did you check the mail drop, Rachel?'

She broke her look away from me and looked at the back of Backus's head. He had not turned around and she was sitting directly behind him.

'Yes, Bob, I did,' she said in a voice slightly tinged with exasperation. 'It was a dead end. There was nothing in the box. The owner said that he believed a woman, an older woman, came in every month or so and cleaned it out. He said the only mail that ever came looked like bank statements. I think it was Gladden's mother. She's probably living somewhere around there but I couldn't find a listing and there was nothing from Florida DMV.'

'Maybe you should've stayed a little longer and looked a little harder.'

She was silent a moment. I knew she was still confused by the way Backus was now treating her.

'Maybe,' she said. 'But I think that's something the agents in Florida can handle. I'm the lead agent on this case. Remember, Bob?'

'Yes, I remember.'

The car was silent for a few minutes after that. I spent most of that time staring out my window. When I sensed the tension had dissipated a bit I looked over at Rachel and raised my eyebrows. She raised her hand to reach to my face but then thought better of it and put it down.

'You shaved.'

'Yeah.'

Backus turned around and looked at me, then returned to his normal position.

'I thought something was different,' he said.

'How come?' Rachel asked.

I hiked my shoulders.

'I don't know.'

A voice crackled over the radio.

'Customer.'

Carter picked up the mike and said, 'What've we got?'

'White male, twenties, blond hair, carrying a box. No vehicle observed. He's either going in Data or next door for a haircut. He could use one.'

There was a hair salon directly west of Data Imaging Answers. On the east side was an out-of-business hardware store. The observation agents had been calling out the potential customers all day; most of them ended up going into the salon rather than DIA.

'He's going in.'

I leaned over the seat to look at the monitor and saw the man enter the store with the box. The video frame was a black-and-white image that encompassed the whole showroom. The figure was too grainy and small to be identified as Gladden or not. I held my breath as I had each time a customer had entered. The man walked directly to the desk where Thorson sat. I saw Thorson move his right hand to his midsection, ready to go inside his coat for his weapon if needed.

'Can I help you?' he asked.

'Yes, I have these great monthly planners here.' He started reaching into the box. Thorson started standing. 'I'm selling them to a lot of your neighbors here.'

Thorson grabbed the man's arm to stop him from reaching, then tilted the box down so he could see inside it.

'I'm not interested,' he said after inspecting the contents.

The salesman, slightly taken aback by Thorson grabbing him, recovered and completed the sales pitch.

'Are you sure? Just ten bucks. Something like this'll run you thirty, thirty-five dollars in the office supply store. It's genuine Naugahyde and it's –'

'Not interested. Thank you.'

The salesman turned to Coombs sitting behind the other desk.

'How 'bout you, sir? Let me show you the deluxe mo –'

'We're not interested,' Thorson barked. 'Now if you would please leave the store, we're busy here. There's no soliciting here.'

'Yeah, I can see. Well, have a nice day to you, too.'

The man left the store.

'People,' Thorson said.

He shook his head as he sat down and didn't say anything more. Then he yawned. Watching it made me yawn, then Rachel caught it from me.

'The excitement is getting to Gordo,' Backus commented.

Me, too. I needed a caffeine fix. If I had been in the newsroom, I would have had at least six cups by this time of day. But because of the stakeout, there had been only one run for food and coffee and that had been three hours earlier.

I opened the door.

'I'm going for coffee. You guys want any?'

'You're gonna miss it, Jack,' Backus kidded.

'Yeah, right. Now I know why so many cops get hemorrhoids. Sitting and waiting for nothing.'

I got out, my knees cracking as I straightened my body. Carter and Backus said they'd pass on the coffee. Rachel said she would love some. I was hoping she wouldn't say she'd go with me and she didn't.

'How do you like it?' I asked, though I knew the answer.

'Black,' she said, smiling at my act.

'Okay. Be right back.'

42

Carrying four containers of black coffee in a small cardboard box, I stepped through the door of the Data Imaging Answers store to see Thorson's shocked face. Before he could say anything the phone on his desk started ringing. He picked it up and said, 'I know.'

He held the phone out for me.

'For you, sport.'

It was Backus.

'Jack, get the hell out of there right now!'

'I will. I just wanted to drop off some coffee to these guys. You saw Gordo, he's falling asleep, it's so boring in here.'

'Very funny, Jack, but get out. Our agreement was that you would do things my way and I would protect the story. Now, please, do as – you've got a customer. Tell Thorson. It's a woman.'

I held the phone against my chest and looked at Thorson.

'Customer on the way. But it's a woman.'

I held the receiver back up.

'Okay, I'm out of here,' I said to Backus.

I hung the phone up and took one of the coffee containers out of the box and put it on Thorson's desk. I heard the door open behind me, the sound of traffic going by on Pico getting momentarily louder and then buffered again by the closed glass. Without turning around to look at the customer I went over to the desk where Coombs was sitting.

'Coffee?'

'Thank you very much.'

I put another cup down and reached into the box for packets of sugar and powdered cream and a stirring straw. When I turned around I saw the woman standing in front of Thorson's desk, digging through a big black purse. She had fluffy blond hair in a Dolly Parton cascade. An obvious wig. She wore a white blouse over a short skirt and black stockings. She was tall, even with the high heels. I noticed that when she had opened the door to the shop a strong odor of perfume entered with her.

'Ah,' she said, finding what she was looking for. 'I'm here to pick this up for my boss.'

She placed a folded yellow sheet on the desk in front of Thorson. He looked over at Coombs, an attempt to signal that Coombs should take over this transaction.

'Take it easy, Gordo,' I said.

As I started for the door I looked over at Thorson, expecting him to reply to my repeated use of the nickname Backus had used for him. I saw Thorson looking at the now unfolded sheet she had given him and his eyes fixed on something. I saw his eyes glance at the west wall of the store. I knew he was looking at the camera. At Backus. He then looked up at the woman. I was behind her at this point and could only see Thorson's eyes just over her shoulder. He was rising and I saw his mouth coming open in a silent O. His right arm was coming up and he was reaching inside his jacket. Then I saw her right arm coming up from the bag. When it cleared her torso I saw the knife grasped in her hand.

She brought the knife down well before Thorson had his arm out of his jacket. I heard his strangled cry as the knife plunged into his throat. He started falling back, a spray of arterial blood going up, hitting her in the shoulder as she leaned all the way over the desk reaching for something.

She straightened up and spun around, Thorson's gun in hand.

'Nobody fuckin' move!'

The woman's voice was gone, replaced by the near hysterical and taut voice of the cornered male animal. He aimed the gun at Coombs and then swung it around at me.

'Get away from that door. Get in here!'

I dropped the box with the two coffee containers, raised my hands and moved away from the door, further into the showroom. The man in the dress then wheeled again on Coombs, who shrieked.

'No! Please, they're watching, no!'

'Who's watching? Who?'

'They're watching on the camera!'

'Who?'

'The FBI, Gladden,' I said in as calm a tone as I could muster, which probably wasn't too far removed from the same shriek that Coombs had emitted.

'Can they hear?'

'Yes, they can hear.'

'FBI!' Gladden yelled. 'FBI, you got one dead already. You come in here and you'll get two more.'

He then turned to the display table and aimed Thorson's gun at the video camera with the red light on. He fired three times until he hit it and it flew backward off the table, breaking apart.

'Get over here,' he yelled at me. 'Where are the keys?'

'Keys to what?'

'The goddamn store.'

'Take it easy. I don't work here.'

'Then who does?'

He turned the gun on Coombs.

'In my pocket. The keys are in my pocket.'

'Go lock that front door. You try to run through and I'll shoot you down like the camera.'

'Yes, sir.'

Coombs did as he was told and then Gladden ordered both of us to the back of the showroom and told us to sit on the floor against the door to the rear storage room, blocking anybody from charging through. He then turned over both desks so they would act as blinds and maybe even barriers against bullets from outside the front windows. He crouched down behind the desk where Thorson had been.

I could see Thorson's body from my position. Most of his previously white shirt was soaked in blood. There was no movement and his eyes were half closed and fixed. The handle of a knife still protruded from his throat. I shuddered at the sight, realizing that a moment ago the man was alive and that whether I liked him or not, I knew him. Now he was dead.

The thought occurred to me then that Backus must be panicked. With the video out, he might not know Thorson's status. If he believed Thorson was alive and there was a chance he could be saved, I could expect the critical response team to start coming through with stun grenades and everything else at any moment. If they believed Thorson to be dead, I might as well settle in for what could be a long night.

'You don't work here,' Gladden said to me. 'Who are you? Do I know you?'

I hesitated. Who was I? Did I tell this man the truth?

'You're FBI.'

'No. I'm not FBI. I'm a reporter.'

'A reporter? You came for my story, is that it?'

'If you want to give it. If you want to talk to the FBI, put that phone over there on the floor back on its hook. They'll call on that line.'

He looked over at the phone that had come apart on the floor when he had overturned the desk. Just then it began emitting the sharp tone signaling it was off the hook. He could reach the line without moving out of cover. He dragged the phone over and hung it up. He looked at me.

'I recognize you,' he said. 'You –'

The phone rang and he picked it up.

'Talk,' he commanded.

There was a long silence until he finally responded to whatever had been said.

'Well, well, Agent Backus, good to make your acquaintance again. I have learned a lot about you since we last met in Florida. And Dad, of course. Read his book. I always hoped we would talk again . . . You and I . . . No, you see, that would be impossible because I have these two hostages here. You fuck with me, Bob, and I fuck with them in ways you won't believe when you come in here. You remember Attica? Think about that, Agent Backus. Think about how Dad would handle this. I gotta go.'

He hung up and looked at me. He pulled the wig off and threw it angrily across the showroom.

'How the hell did you get in here, reporter? The FBI doesn't let –'

'You killed my brother. That's what got me in.'

Gladden looked at me a long moment.

'I didn't kill anyone.'

'They've got you cold. No matter what you do to us, they've got you, Gladden. And they're not going to let you out of here. They –'

'All right, shut the fuck up! I don't have to listen to that.'

Gladden picked up the phone and dialed a number.

'Let me talk to Krasner, it's an emergency . . . William Gladden . . . Yeah, that one.'

We looked at each other while he waited for the lawyer to pick up. I tried to show a calm exterior but inside my brain was racing. I didn't see any way out of this without somebody else dying. Gladden didn't seem like the type who could be talked into raising his hands and giving up so he could be strapped into the electric chair or the gas chamber in a few years, depending on which state got the first shot at him.

Krasner apparently came on the line and for the next ten minutes Gladden heatedly reviewed the situation for him, getting angry at whatever course of action Krasner suggested he take. Finally, he slammed the phone down.

'Fuck that.'

I kept quiet. I figured that every minute that went by was in my favor. The FBI had to be formulating something out there. The sharpshooters, the surgical entry team.

The light was dimming outside. I looked through the front plate-glass window and to the plaza shopping center across the street. My eyes followed the roofline but I saw no figures, not even the telltale barrel of a sniper's rifle. Not yet.

I looked away and then quickly back. I realized there was no traffic going by on Pico. They had closed the road. Whatever was going to happen was going to happen soon. I looked over at Coombs, wondering if there was some way of letting him know to brace himself.

Coombs had sweated through his shirt. The knot of his tie, the recipient of all the sweat sliding down his cheeks and neck, was soaked. He looked like someone who had just spent the better part of an hour throwing up. He was sick.

'Gladden, show 'em something. Let Mr Coombs go. He doesn't have anything to do with this.'

'No, I don't think so.'

The phone rang and he picked it up and listened without saying anything. Then he softly placed the receiver down on the hook. The phone rang again in a few moments and he answered and quickly pushed the hold button. He punched the key for picking up the other line and put that on hold as well. Now no one could call in.

'You're fucking up,' I said. 'Let them talk to you, they'll figure something out.'

'Listen, when I want your advice I'll beat it out of you. Now, shut the fuck up!'

'Okay.'

'I said shut up!'

I raised my hands in an I-give-up gesture.

'You fucking media assholes never know what you're talking about anyway. You – what's your name, anyway?'

'Jack McEvoy.'

'You got ID?'

'In my pocket.'

'Throw it over here.'

I slowly pulled my wallet out and slid it across the rug to him. He opened it and looked through the press passes.

'I thought you – Denver? What the fuck you doing in L.A.?'

'I told you. My brother.'

'Yeah, and I told you. I didn't kill anybody.'

'What about him?'

I nodded toward Thorson's still inert body. Gladden looked at the body and then back at me.

'He made the play. I finished it. Rules of the game.'

'The guy's dead. It's no fucking game.'

Gladden raised the gun and pointed it at my face.

'If I say it's a game, then it's a game.'

I said nothing in response.

'Please,' Coombs said. 'Please . . .'

'Please what? Just shut the fuck up. You . . . uh, paperboy, what are you going to write when this is over? Assuming you can still write.'

I thought for at least a minute and he let me.

'I'll tell why if you want me to,' I said finally. 'It's always the most interesting question. Why did you do it? I'd tell that. Is it because of that guy in Florida? Beltran?'

He snorted in derision, more in displeasure that I had mentioned the name, not that I knew it.

'This isn't an interview. And if it is, no fucking comment.'

Gladden looked down at the gun in his hands for what seemed like a long time. I think at that point he felt the futility of the situation pressing down on him. He knew he wasn't going anywhere and I got the sense that he'd known his trail would eventually end in a scene like this. It seemed he was at a weak point and I tried again.

'You should pick up that phone and tell them you want to speak to Rachel Walling,' I said. 'Tell 'em you'll talk to her. She's an agent. You remember her? She came to you at Raiford. She knows all about you, Gladden, and she'd help.'

He shook his head no.

'I had to kill your brother,' he said softly, without looking at me. 'I had to do it.'

I waited and that was all he said.

'Why?'

'The only way to save him.'

'Save him from what?'

'Don't you see?' He looked up at me now, deep pain and anger in his eyes. 'From becoming like me. Look at me! From becoming like me!'

I was about to ask another question when there was the sudden sound of shattering glass. I looked toward the front and saw a dark object about the size of a baseball bounce across the room toward the overturned desk near Gladden. I registered what it was and began to roll and bring my arms up to cradle my head and shield my eyes just as there was a tremendous detonation in the showroom, a blast of light that burned through my closed eyes and a following concussion so strong it sent a pounding energy wave through me like a punch to my whole body.

The rest of the windows shattered and as I completed my roll I opened my eyes enough to get a bead on Gladden. He was squirming on the floor, his eyes wide but not focused and his hands held to his ears. But I could tell he had been too late in recognizing what was happening. I had been able to block at least some of the impact of the concussion grenade. He looked as if he had taken the full brunt of it. I saw the gun lying loose on the floor next to his legs. Without pausing to consider my chances, I quickly crawled toward it.

Gladden sat up as I got to him and we both lunged for the gun, our hands reaching it at the same time. We fought for control and rolled over each other. My thought was to get to the trigger and just start firing. It didn't matter if I hit him, as long as I didn't hit myself. I knew the concussion grenade would be followed by the charge of the agents. If I could empty the gun, it wouldn't matter who had it. It would be over.

I managed to squeeze my left thumb in behind the trigger guard but the only place my right hand could grasp was the end of the barrel. The gun was between our chests, pointing toward our chins. At the moment I judged – hoped – I was out of the line of fire, I squeezed with my left hand while opening my right hand. The gun discharged and I felt a sharp pain as the bullet clipped the webbing between my thumb and palm and the escaping gases scorched my hand. At the same moment I heard Gladden howl. I looked up to his face and saw blood spreading from his nose. What was left of it. The bullet had ripped off the rim of his left nostril and cut a slashing crease up his forehead.

I felt his grip momentarily weaken and in one burst of strength – possibly my last – I wrenched away control of the gun. I was pulling myself away from him, registering the sound of footsteps in glass and unintelligible yells when Gladden made another lunge for the gun in my hands. My thumb was still caught in the trigger guard, all the way past the joint. It was pressed against the trigger and there was no room left for movement. Gladden tried to wrench the gun back and in doing so it discharged once again. Our eyes met at that moment and there was something telling in his. They told me that he had wanted the bullet.

Immediately his grip on the gun relaxed and he fell back away from me. I saw the gaping wound in his chest. His eyes stared at me with the same look of resolve I had seen moments before. Like he knew what was going to happen. He reached to his chest and looked down at the blood pumping into his hand.

Suddenly I was grabbed from behind and pulled away from him. A hand firmly gripped my arm and another carefully removed the gun from my hand. I looked up and saw a man wearing a black helmet and matching black jumpsuit with a large armored vest on the outside. He held some kind of assault weapon and wore a radio headset, a thin black bar curving in front of his mouth. He looked down at me and touched the transmit button at his ear.

'We're all secure here,' he said. 'We've got two down and two walking. Come on in.'

43

There was no pain and that surprised him. The blood, gushing through his fingers and over his hands, was warm and comforting. He had a giddy feeling of having just passed some test. He had made it. Whatever that was. The sound and movement around him were all dulled and in slow motion. He looked about and saw the one who had shot him. Denver. For a moment their eyes locked but then someone got in the way. The man in black bent down over him and did something. Gladden looked down and saw the handcuffs on his wrists. He smiled at the stupidity of it. No handcuffs could hold him where he was going now.

Then he saw her. A woman crouching over the one from Denver. She squeezed his hand. Gladden recognized her. She was one of those who had come to him so many years before in prison. He remembered now.

He was getting cold. His shoulders and neck. His legs, they were numb. He wanted a blanket but no one was looking at him. No one cared. The room was getting brighter, like TV cameras. He was slipping away and knew it.

'This is what it is like,' he whispered but no one seemed to hear.

Except the woman. She turned at the sound of his soft words. Their eyes connected and after a moment Gladden thought he saw the slight nod, the knowledge of recognition.

Recognition of what, he wondered. That I'm dying? That there was purpose to my being here? He turned his head toward her and waited for the life to finish flowing from him. He could rest now. Finally.

He looked at her once more but she was looking down at the man again. Gladden studied him, the man who had killed him, and an odd thought pushed its way through the blood. He seemed too old to have had a brother that young. There must be a mistake somewhere.

Gladden died with his eyes open, staring at the man who had killed him.

44

It was a surrealistic scene. People running around the showroom, yelling, huddled over the dead and the dying. My ears ringing, my hand throbbing. It seemed almost to be in slow motion. At least that is the way it is in my memory. And out of all of this Rachel appeared, stepping through the glass like a guardian angel sent to shepherd me away. She reached down and grabbed my uninjured hand and squeezed it. Her touch was like a code-blue paddle shocking me back from a flat line. I suddenly realized what had happened and what I had done, and I was overcome with the joy of simply surviving. Thoughts of justice and vengeance were far away.

I looked over at Thorson. The paramedics were working on him, one of them sitting astride him, putting all her weight behind the heart massage, the other holding the oxygen mask in place. Still another zipping his prone body into a pressure suit. Backus knelt next to his fallen agent, holding his hand and rubbing his wrist, yelling, 'Breathe, dammit, breathe! Come on, Gordo, breathe!'

But it was not to be. They couldn't bring poor Thorson back from the dead. They all knew it but no one stopped. They kept working on him and when the stretcher and gurney were brought in through the blasted-out front window and he was loaded aboard, the paramedic took her spot straddled on top of him again. Her elbows locked, her hands locked together and pushing up and down, up and down, on his chest. They were wheeled out like that.

I watched Rachel watch the procession with not sad but distant eyes, then her stare fell from her former husband's exit to his killer on the floor next to me.

I looked over at Gladden. He had been cuffed and no one was working on him yet. They were going to let him die. Any thoughts of what they might be able to learn from him went out the window when he drove that knife into Thorson's throat.

I looked at him and thought, in fact, that he already was dead, his eyes staring blankly at the ceiling. But then his mouth moved and he said something I couldn't hear. Then his head slowly turned toward me. At first, his eyes held on Rachel. It lasted only a moment but I saw their eyes lock and some kind of communication pass between them. Recognition maybe. Perhaps he remembered her. Then he slowly turned his eyes until he stared directly at me again. I was looking at his eyes when the life ran out of them.

*

After Rachel walked me out of Data Imaging, I was taken in an ambulance to a hospital called Cedars-Sinai. By the time I arrived, Thorson and Gladden had already been there and had been pronounced dead. In an emergency room suite a doctor looked my hand over, irrigated the wound with something that looked like a piece of a black soda straw and then sewed it shut. He put some kind of balm on the burns and then wrapped bandages around the whole thing.

'The burns are nothing,' he said as he wrapped. 'Don't worry about them. But the wound's going to be tough. On the positive, it's through and through, no bones involved. But on the negative, the bullet chopped through that tendon there and you're going to have restricted thumb movement if you leave it the way it is. I can put you in touch with a specialist who can probably reattach the tendon or make a new one for you. With the surgery and some exercise it should be okay.'

'What about typing?'

'Not for a while.'

'No, I mean as exercise.'

'Yeah, maybe. You'll have to ask your doctor.'

He patted my shoulder and left the room. I was alone for ten minutes, sitting on the examination table, before Backus and Rachel came in. Backus had the washed-out look of a man who has seen all his plans turn to shit.

'How're you doing, Jack?' he asked.

'I'm okay. I'm sorry about Agent Thorson. It was . . .'

'I know. These things . . .'

Nobody spoke for a few moments. I looked at Rachel and our eyes held each other's.

'Are you sure you're all right?'

'Yeah, fine. I won't be typing for a while but . . . I guess I'm the lucky one. What happened to Coombs?'

'He's still in shock at what happened but he's all right.'

I looked at Backus.

'Bob, there was nothing I could do. Something happened. It looked like they suddenly knew who each other was. I don't know. Why didn't Thorson go ahead with the plan? Why didn't he just give him the camera instead of going for his gun?'

'Because he wanted to be the hero,' Rachel said. 'He wanted the arrest. Or the kill.'

'Rachel, we don't know that,' Backus said. 'We never will. The one question that can be answered, though, is why did you go in there in the first place, Jack? Why?'

I looked down at my bandaged hand. With my good hand I touched my cheek.

'I don't know,' I answered. 'I saw Thorson yawn on the monitor and thought . . . I don't know why I did it. He brought me coffee once . . . I was returning the favor. I didn't think Gladden was going to show.'

I lied. But I could not articulate my true motives or emotions. All I knew was that I had a sense that if I went into that store Gladden might come. And I wanted him to see me. Without disguise. I wanted him to see my brother.

'Well,' Backus said after a spell of silence. 'Think you'll be up for spending some time with a stenographer tomorrow? I realize you are hurt but we'd like to get your statement so we can get this all squared away. We'll have to submit something to the local district attorney.'

I nodded.

'Yeah, I'll be there.'

'You know, Jack, when Gladden took out the camera, he took down the sound as well. We don't know what was said in there. So tell me, did Gladden say anything?'

I thought a moment. The memory was still coming back to me.

'First he said he didn't kill anybody. Then he admitted killing Sean. He said he killed my brother.'

Backus arched his eyebrows as if surprised and then nodded.

'Okay, Jack, we'll see you then.' He turned to Rachel. 'You said you'll get him back to the room?'

'Yes, Bob.'

'Okay.'

Backus left the room with his head down and I felt bad. I didn't think he had accepted my explanation and I wondered if he would always blame me for how horribly wrong things had gone.

'What will happen to him?' I asked.

'Well, the first thing is there's a lobby full of media out there and he's got to tell them how this got all fucked up. After that I'm sure the director will want Professional Standards to come out to investigate the planning of this. It's not going to get any better for him.'

'It was Thorson's plan. Can't they just –'

'Bob approved it. If somebody has to take a fall, Gordon isn't around anymore.'

Looking through the open door where Backus had just walked I saw a doctor stop and look in. He carried a stethoscope in his hand and several pens in the pocket of his white jacket.

'Everything okay in here?' he inquired.

'Fine.'

'We're fine,' Rachel added.

She turned away from the door and looked at me.

'You sure?'

I nodded.

'I'm so glad you are okay. That was a foolish thing you did.'

'I just thought he could use the coffee. I didn't ex –'

'I mean going for the gun. Getting it from Gladden.'

I shook my shoulders. Maybe it was foolish, I thought, but maybe it saved my life.

'How did you know, Rachel?'

'Know what?'

'You asked me what would happen if I ever faced him. It was like you knew.'

'I didn't know, Jack. It was just a question.'

She reached up and traced my jawline like she did when I'd had the beard. Then with her finger she tilted my chin up until I was looking at her. She moved in between my legs and pulled me into a deep kiss. It was healing and sensual at the same time. I closed my eyes. My good hand went up under her jacket and I rested it lightly on her breast.

When she pulled away I opened my eyes and over her shoulder I saw the doctor who had poked his head in earlier turning away.

'Peeping Tom,' I said.

'What?'

'That doctor. I think he was watching us.'

'Never mind him. Are you ready to go?'

'Yeah, I'm ready.'

'Did you get a prescription for pain?'

'I'm supposed to get some pills before I sign out.'

'You can't sign out. The media's up there and they'll be all over you.'

'Damn, I forgot. I've got to call in.'

I looked at my watch. It was almost eight in Denver. Greg Glenn was probably there, waiting to hear from me, refusing to release the front page to the printers until he'd heard from me. I figured the latest he could go would be nine. I looked around. There was a phone on the wall above a supplies and equipment counter at the back of the room.

'Could you go tell them I can't sign out up there?' I asked. 'In the meantime I'll just call in at the *Rocky* and tell them I'm still alive.'

Glenn was almost delirious when I got through to him.

'Jack, where the hell you been?'

'I've sort of been tied up. I –'

'Are you okay? The wires say you were shot.'

'I'm okay. I'll be typing one-handed for a while.'

'The wires say the Poet's dead. AP quotes one source who says you . . . uh, killed him.'

'AP's got a good source.'

'Jesus, Jack.'

I didn't reply.

'CNN's been going live from the scene every ten minutes but they don't have shit. There's supposed to be a press conference at the hospital.'

'Right. And if you can get me hooked up with somebody to take some rewrite, I can give you enough of the story for the front page. It will be better than anyone else gets tonight.'

He said nothing in response.

'Greg?'

'Wait a minute, Jack. I have to think. You . . .'

He didn't finish but I waited him out.

'Jack, I'm going to put you on the line with Jackson. Tell what you can to him. He'll also take notes off the press conference if CNN carries it.'

'Wait a minute. I don't want to give anything to Jackson. Just give me a copy messenger or a clerk and I'll dictate the story. It's going to be better than what they put out at the press conference.'

'No, Jack, you can't. It's different now.'

'What are you talking about?'

'You're not covering the story anymore. You are part of it. You killed the guy who killed your brother. You killed the Poet. The story's about you now. You can't write it. I'm putting you on with Jackson. But do me a favor. Stay away from the other reporters out there. Give us a one-day exclusive on our own guy, at least.'

'Look, I've always been part of this story.'

'Yeah, but you didn't shoot anybody. Jack, that's not what reporters do. That's what cops do and you crossed that line. You're off the story. I'm sorry.'

'It was him or me, Greg.'

'I'm sure it was and thank God it was him. But that doesn't change things, Jack.'

I said nothing. In my mind I knew he was right about me not writing it. I just couldn't believe it. It was my story and now it was gone. I was inside still but I was out.

Just as Rachel came back in the room with a clipboard and several forms for me to sign, Jackson came on the line. He told me what a great story it was going to be and started asking questions. I answered them all and told him some things unasked. I signed the forms where Rachel pointed as I talked. The interview was quick. Jackson said he wanted to watch the press conference on CNN so he would have official comment and confirmation to go with my version of events. He asked if I would call back in an hour in case of follow-up questions and I agreed. We then hung up and I was thankful to get off the line.

'Well, now that you just signed away your life and your firstborn son, you're free to go,' Rachel said. 'You sure you don't want to read any of this stuff?'

'Nah, let's go. You get the painkillers? My hand's beginning to hurt again.'

'Yes, right here.'

She pulled a vial out of her coat pocket and handed it to me along with a stack of pink phone message slips, apparently taken at the hospital's front desk.

'What are . . .'

There were calls from news producers at the three networks, 'Nightline' with Ted Koppel, and two of the morning shows, and from reporters at the *New York Times* and the *Washington Post.*

'You're a celebrity, Jack,' Rachel said. 'You went face to face with the devil and survived. People want to ask you how that felt. People always want to know about the devil.'

I shoved the messages into my back pocket.

'You going to call them?'
'Nope. Let's go.'

On the way back to Hollywood I told Rachel I didn't want to spend the night in the Wilcox Hotel. I said I wanted to order room service and then lie in a comfortable bed and watch TV with a remote in my hand, amenities that the Wilcox obviously didn't offer. She saw my point.

After we stopped at the Wilcox so I could get my things and check out, Rachel drove down Sunset Boulevard toward the strip. At the Chateau Marmont she stayed in the car while I went to the desk. I said I wanted a room with a view and didn't care what it cost. They gave me a room with a balcony that cost more than I'd ever spent for a hotel in my life. The balcony was overlooking the Marlboro Man and the rest of the billboards on the strip. I liked looking at the Marlboro Man. Rachel didn't bother getting her own room.

We didn't talk much while we ate our room service dinner. Instead, we maintained the kind of comfortable silence that couples of many years achieve. Afterward, I took a long bath and listened over the bathroom speaker to the CNN report on the shootout at Digital Imaging. There was nothing new. More questions than answers. A good portion of the news conference was focused on Thorson and the ultimate sacrifice he had made. For the first time I thought about Rachel and how she was dealing with this. She had lost her ex-husband. A man she had grown to despise but someone she had shared an intimate relationship with just the same.

When I came out of the bathroom I wore the terrycloth bathrobe the hotel provided. She was lying on the bed, propped against the pillows, and still watching the television.

'The local news is about to start,' she said.

I crawled across the bed and kissed her.

'You okay?'

'Yeah, why?'

'I don't know. Uh, whatever the relationship was that you had with Thorson, I'm sorry. Okay?'

'So am I.'

'I was thinking . . . you want to make love?'

'Yes.'

I turned off the television and the lights. At one point in the dark I tasted tears on her cheeks and she held me tighter than she had ever done before. There was a bittersweet feel to our lovemaking. It was as if two sad and lonely people had crossed paths and had agreed to help heal each other. Afterward, she huddled against my back and I tried to sleep but I couldn't. The demons of the day were still wide awake inside.

'Jack?' she whispered. 'Why did you cry?'

I was silent for a few moments, trying to find the words that would explain an answer.

'I don't know,' I finally said. 'It's hard. All along, I think, I was hoping in a daydreaming sort of way that I would get the chance to . . . Just be glad you've never done what I did today. Just be glad.'

Still later sleep would not come, even after I had taken one of the pills from the hospital. She asked me what my thoughts were.

'I'm thinking about what he said to me at the end. I don't understand what he meant.'

'What did he tell you?'

'He said he killed Sean to save him.'

'From what?'

'From becoming like him. That's what I don't understand.'

'We probably never will. You should just let it go now. It's over.'

'He said something else. At the end. When everyone was there. Did you hear it?'

'I think so.'

'What was it?'

'He said something like, "This is what it's like." That's all.'

'What does it mean?'

'I think he was solving the mystery.'

'Death.'

'He saw it coming. He saw the answers. He said, "This is what it's like." Then he died.'

45

In the morning we found Backus already waiting in the conference room on the seventeenth floor of the federal building. It was another clear day and I could see the top of Catalina rising behind the marine layer of morning fog out on the Santa Monica Bay. It was eight-thirty but Backus had his jacket off and looked as though he had already been at it for several hours. His spot at the meeting table was cluttered with a spread of paperwork, two open laptops and a stack of pink phone message slips. His face was drawn and sad. It looked as though the loss of Thorson would leave a permanent mark on him.

'Rachel, Jack,' he said by means of salutation. It wasn't a good morning and he didn't say that. 'How's the hand?'

'It's okay.'

We had brought containers of coffee with us but I saw he had none. I offered him mine but he said he'd already had too much.

'What have we got?' Rachel asked.

'Did you two check out? I tried to call you this morning, Rachel.'

'Yes,' she said. 'Jack wanted something a little more comfortable. We moved over to the Chateau Marmont.'

'Pretty comfortable.'

'Don't worry. I won't submit it for reimbursement.'

He nodded and I got the idea from the way he looked at her that he knew she hadn't gotten her own room and had nothing to submit anyway. It was the least of his worries, though.

'It's coming together,' he said. 'Another one for the studies, I suppose. These people – if you can call them that – never cease to amaze me. Every one of them, their stories . . . each one of them's a black hole. And there's never enough blood to fill it.'

Rachel pulled out a chair and sat across from him. I sat next to her. We didn't say anything. We knew he wanted to go on. He reached over with a pen and tapped the side of one of the laptops.

'This was his,' he said. 'It was recovered from the trunk of his car last night.'

'A Hertz car?' I asked.

'No. He arrived at Data Imaging in an eighty-four Plymouth registered to a Darlene Kugel, thirty-six, of North Hollywood. We went to her apartment last night, got no response and went in. She was in the bed. Her throat was cut, probably with the same knife he used on Gordon. She'd been dead for days. It looked like he'd burned incense, slopped perfume around to hide the smell.'

'He stayed in there with her body?' Rachel asked.

'Looks like it.'

'Were those her clothes he was wearing?' I asked.

'And the wig.'

'What was he doing dressed like her, anyway?' Rachel asked.

'Don't know and never will now. My guess is he knew everybody was looking for him. Police, the bureau. He thought it was a way to leave her place, get the camera and then maybe get out of town.'

'Probably. What did you get from her place?'

'There was nothing that was of much use inside, but her unit had two parking spaces assigned to it in the garage and we found an eighty-six Pontiac Firebird in one of them. Florida plate, it came back to Gladys Oliveros of Gainesville.'

'His mother?' I asked.

'Yes. Moved there when he went to prison so she'd be close for visits, I guess. Remarried and changed her name. Anyway, we opened the trunk of the Pontiac and found the computer, some other things, including the books Brass found in the picture from the cell. There was an old sleeping bag. There's blood on it and the lab has it. The initial report is that there is kapok in the insulation.'

'It means he put some of his victims in the trunk,' I said.

'Which accounts for the hours they were missing,' Rachel added.

'Wait a minute,' I said. 'If he had his mother's car, what about the car from Hertz in Phoenix? Why would he rent a car if he already had one?'

'Just another way of confusing the trail, Jack. Use mother's to move from city to city, but then he rents one when he moves in for the kill on the cop.'

My confusion over the logic of that theory showed on my face. But Backus dismissed it.

'Anyway, we haven't gotten the Hertz records yet, so let's not get sidetracked. For the moment, the computer is what's important.'

'What's in it?' Rachel asked.

'The office here has a computer unit, works with the group in Quantico. One of the agents, Don Clearmountain, took this last night and broke down the coding by about three this morning. He copied the hard disk to the mainframe here. Anyway, it's full of photographs. Fifty-seven of them.'

Backus used his thumb and forefinger to pinch the bridge of his nose. He had aged since I'd last seen him at the hospital. Aged badly.

'Children?' Rachel asked.

Backus nodded.

'Jesus. The victims?'

'Yes . . . before and after. It's horrible stuff. Truly horrible.'

'And he was transmitting these somewhere? Like we thought?'

'Yes, the computer has a cellular modem as Gordon . . . as he guessed. It, too, is registered out of Gainesville to Oliveros. We just got the records a little while ago.'

He indicated some of the paperwork in front of him.

'There are a lot of calls,' he said. 'All over the place. He was into some kind of net. A network where the users were interested in these kinds of photographs.'

He looked up from the papers at us, his eyes sick but defiant.

'We are tracing them all now. We're going to make a lot of arrests. A lot of people will pay for this. What happened to Gordon will not be for nothing.'

He nodded more to himself than us.

'We can compare the transmissions and the users to the bank deposits I found in Jacksonville,' Rachel said. 'I bet we'll be able to know just how much they paid for the photos and when.'

'Clearmountain and his people are already working on it. They're down the hall in the Group Three offices if you want to stop in.'

'Bob?' I said. 'Did they look at all fifty-seven photos?'

He looked at me a moment before answering.

'I did, Jack. I did.'

'They were only the kids?'

I felt my chest tightening. Whatever I had told myself about being emotionally deadened to my brother and what had happened was a lie.

'No, Jack,' Backus said. 'There are no pictures of those victims. None of the police officers, none of the other adult victims. I guess . . .'

He didn't finish.

'What?' I asked.

'I guess those kinds of photos would not have been profitable to him.'

I looked down at my hands on the table. My right hand was beginning to ache and felt clammy under the white bandages. I felt relief go through me. I think it was relief. What else is it that you feel when you learn that there are no photographs of your murdered brother's body out there all over the country, floating out there on the Internet and ready to be downloaded by any sick individual with a taste for it.

'I think when this gets out about this guy, there'll be a lot of people who'll want to throw a parade for you, Jack,' Backus said. 'Put you in a convertible and drive you down Madison Avenue.'

I looked at him. I didn't know if it was an attempt at humor but I didn't smile.

'Maybe sometimes vengeance is just as good as justice,' he said.

'They're pretty much the same if you ask me.'

After a few moments of silence, Backus changed the subject.

'Jack, we have to get your formal statement. I've got one of the office's stenographers set up for nine-thirty. Are you ready?'

'Ready as I'll ever be.'

'We just want the linear story. From A to B, don't leave any detail out. I thought, Rachel, you'd handle that, ask the questions.'

'Sure, Bob.'

'I'd like to get this wrapped up today and submitted to the DA tomorrow. Maybe we can all go home then.'

'Who's doing the package for the DA?' Rachel asked.

'Carter.'

He looked at his watch.

'Uh, you have a few minutes but why don't you go down the hall and ask for Sally Kimball. She might be ready to go now.'

Dismissed, we stood and headed for the door. I watched Rachel, trying to judge whether she was annoyed at being assigned to taking my statement while the local agents were tracing Gladden's computer records, which seemed at the moment to be the more exciting branch of the investigation. She showed nothing and at the door of the conference room she turned and told Backus she'd be around if he needed anything else.

'Thanks, Rachel,' he said. 'Oh, and Jack, these are for you.'

He held up the stack of pink message slips. I went back to the table and took them.

'And this.'

He raised my computer satchel from the floor next to his seat and handed it across the table to me.

'You left that in the car yesterday.'

'Thanks.'

I studied the stack of pink slips. There must have been a dozen of them.

'You're a popular man,' Backus said. 'Don't let it go to your head.'

'Only if they give me that parade.'

He didn't smile.

While Rachel went to look for the stenographer I stood in the hallway and looked through the messages. They were mostly repeats from the networks but a few print reporters had called, even one from my hometown competition, the *Denver Post.* The tabloids, of both the print and television variety, had left messages. There was also a call from Michael Warren. I noted from the 213 callback number that he was still in town.

The three messages that intrigued me the most weren't from the news media. Dan Bledsoe had called just an hour earlier from Baltimore. And there were two messages from book publishers, one from a senior editor at a New York-based house and one from an assistant to the publisher at another house. I recognized both imprints and felt a mixture of trepidation and thrill course through my chest.

Rachel came up to me then.

'She's going to be a couple minutes. There's an office down here we're going to use. Let's wait there.'

I followed her.

The room was a smaller version of the one we had met Backus in, with a round table and four chairs, a side counter with a phone, and a picture window with a view east toward downtown. I asked Rachel if it would be all right if I used the phone while we waited and she said go ahead. I keyed in the number Bledsoe had left and he picked up after one ring.

'Bledsoe Investigations.'

'It's Jack McEvoy.'

'Jack Mac, how you doing?'

'I'm fine. How are you?'

'A lot better since I heard the news this morning.'

'Well, I'm glad, then.'

'You did good, Jack, putting that guy in the hole. You did real good.'

Then how come I don't feel so good, I thought but didn't say.

'Jack?'

'What?'

'I owe you one, buddy. And Johnny Mac owes you one.'

'No you don't. We're even, Dan. You helped me.'

'Well, just the same, you get back out here one day and we're going to go for crabs at the tavern. It'll go on my tab.'

'Thanks, Dan. I'll be out.'

'Hey, what about this G-girl who's been in the papers and TV? Agent Walling. She's a looker.'

I looked over at Rachel.

'Yeah, she is.'

'I seen the clip on CNN of her walking you out of that store last night. You be careful, young man.'

He managed to get a smile out of me. I hung up and looked at the two messages from the publishers. I was tempted to return the calls but thought better of it. I didn't know much about the publishing industry, but back when I was writing my first novel – the one later left unfinished and hidden in a drawer – I'd done a little research and decided that if I ever finished the book I'd get an agent before I went to the publishers. I had even picked the agent I would seek to represent me. Only I had never finished a book to send to him. I decided I would look up his name and number again and call him later.

Next to consider was the call from Warren. The stenographer still had not arrived in the office so I hit the buttons for the number he had left. An operator answered and when I asked for Warren I saw Rachel immediately look up at me with quizzical eyes. I winked at her as the voice on the line told me Warren was out of the office. I told her my name but left no message or callback number. Warren would have to think about missing the call when he got that.

'Why were you calling him?' Rachel asked after I hung up. 'I thought you two were enemies.'

'I guess we are. I was probably going to tell him to go fuck himself.'

It took me an hour and fifteen minutes to tell my story in full detail to Rachel with the stenographer taking it down. Rachel primarily asked leading questions, designed to move me along through the story in chronological order. When I got to the shooting, her questions were more specific and for the first time she asked what my thoughts were at the time of specific actions.

I told her I went for the gun to simply get it away from Gladden, nothing more. I told her of my idea to empty the weapon once the struggle ensued and how the second shot was not deliberate.

'It was more him pulling the gun than me pulling the trigger, you know? He just tried for it one more time and my thumb was still in the guard. When he pulled, it went off. He kind of killed himself. It was like he knew what was going to happen.'

We went a few more minutes after that, with Rachel asking some follow-up questions. She then told the stenographer she would need the transcript the next morning for inclusion in the charging package that would be submitted to the district attorney.

'What do you mean, "charging package"?' I asked after the stenographer had left the room.

'It's just a term. We call it that whether we are seeking a charge or an indictment or not. Relax. We obviously aren't seeking anything here but a finding of self-defense, justifiable homicide. Don't worry, Jack.'

It was early but we decided to get lunch. Rachel said she'd drop me by the hotel afterward. She had work to do back at the field office but I'd be done for the day. We were walking down the hallway when she noticed the door marked Group Three was open and she looked in. There were two men in the room, both sitting at computers, paperwork on the keyboards and on top of the terminals. I noticed a copy of the same book I had on Edgar Allan Poe on top of one of the agent's monitors. He was the first to notice us.

'Hi, I'm Rachel Walling, how is it going?'

The other looked up then and they said their hellos along with their names. Rachel then introduced me. The agent who had first looked up and had identified himself as Don Clearmountain spoke.

'We're doing good. End of the day we'll have a list of names and addresses. We'll ship them to the nearest FOs and they should have enough for search warrants.'

I visualized teams of agents hitting doors and pulling the pedophiles who had bought digital photos of murdered children out of their beds. It would be a nationwide reckoning. I began to visualize the headlines. The Dead Poet's Society. That's what they'd call these men.

'But I've got something else working here that is really pretty special,' Clearmountain said.

The computer agent had a hacker's smile on his face as he looked at us. It was an invitation and Rachel moved into the room, me right behind her.

'What is it?' she said.

'Well, what we have here are a bunch of numbers that Gladden shipped digital photos to. Then we also have the wire deposit records of the bank in Jacksonville. We collated it and it all fits together pretty well.'

He took a stack of pages off the keyboard of the other agent, looked through it and selected a sheet.

'For example, on December fifth of last year there was a deposit of five hundred dollars made to the account. It was wired from the Minnesota National Bank in St. Paul. The sender was listed as Davis Smith. Probably a false name. The next day, Gladden's cellular modem placed a call to a number we've traced to a fellow named Dante Sherwood in St. Paul. The connection lasted four minutes, about what it takes to transmit and download a photograph. We've got literally dozens of transactions like this. One-day correlations between deposits and transmissions.'

'Great.'

'Now, the question all of this raises is, how did all these buyers know about Gladden and what he had to sell? In other words, where was the marketplace for these photos?'

'And you found it.'

'Yes, we did. The number called most often on the cellular modem. It's a computer bulletin board. It's called the PTL Network.'

Rachel's face showed her surprise.

'Praise The Lord?'

'You wish. Actually, we think it means Pre-Teen Love.'

'Gross.'

'Yeah. It was actually kind of easy to figure out. Not that original and most of these boards use these kinds of euphemisms. It was getting into the network that took us all morning.'

'How'd you do it?'

'We came up with Gladden's passwords.'

'Wait a minute,' Rachel said. 'What happened last night has been all over the news across the whole country. Wouldn't whoever was operating this bulletin board have wiped him out? You know, killed his access and his password before we got in?'

'He should've but he didn't.' Then Clearmountain looked at the other agent and they shared conspiratorial smiles. There was something still not said. 'Maybe the systems operator was sort of tied up and couldn't get to it in time.'

'Okay, tell me the rest,' Rachel said impatiently.

'Well, we tried everything to get in, variations on Gladden's name, DOB, social security, all the usual tricks. Nothing. We were thinking the same thing you were, that he was deleted from the system.'

'But?'

'But then we went to Poe.'

Clearmountain took the heavy book off his monitor and held it up.

'It's a two-password entry system. We got the first one easy. It was Edgar. But then the second, that's where we had trouble. We tried Raven, Eidolon, Usher, everything we could pull out of this book. Then we doubled back and went through Gladden's names and numbers again. Still nothing. Then – bingo! – we nailed it. Joe did while he was having coffee cake.'

Clearmountain pointed to the other agent, Joe Perez, who smiled and took a bow in his seat. For computer cops, I guessed that what he had done was like making a felony arrest for a street cop. He looked as proud as a boy who scores in a hotel room on prom night.

'I was just reading about Poe while taking a break,' Perez explained. 'My eyes get tired looking at a monitor too long.'

'Lucky for us he decided to rest them looking at a book,' Clearmountain said, regaining the narrative. 'Joe, in the biographical section, comes across a reference to Poe having once used an alias to enlist in the army or something. Edgar Perry. We stuck it in and like I said, bingo! We were in.'

Clearmountain turned and exchanged a high five with Perez. They looked like a couple of nerds in heat. Today's FBI, I thought.

'What did you find?'

'There are twelve message boards. Most are for discussion about specific tastes. In other words, girls under twelve, boys under ten, that sort of thing. There is a lawyer referral board. We found Gladden's lawyer, Krasner, listed on it. Then there's also a kind of bio board with a lot of strange shit on it, essays and such. There's a few that have to be by our man. Look at this.'

He looked through the stack of papers again and pulled out a printout. He started reading from it.

'This is from one of them. "I think they know about me. My time in the light of public fascination and fear is near. I am ready." Then further down he goes, "My suffering is my passion, my religion. It never leaves me. It guides me. It is me." It's full of that kind of stuff and the author at one point calls himself Eidolon. So we think it's gotta be him. You BSS people are going to get a lot of stuff for the research banks out of this.'

'Good,' Rachel said. 'What else?'

'Well, one of the boards is a barter board. You know, where people post things to sell or buy.'

'Like photos and IDs?'

'Yup. There's somebody on there selling Alabama DLs. I assume we're going to have to shut that sucker down in a hurry. And there was a file for selling what Gladden had in his computer. Minimum price was five hundred dollars per picture. Three for a grand. You wanted something, you left a message with a computer number. You wired the money to a bank account and your pictures showed up in your computer. On the barter board, this advertiser said he could provide photos to meet specific tastes and desires.'

'Like he was taking orders and then he'd go out and . . .'

'Right.'

'You tell Bob Backus about this yet?'

'Yeah, he was just in here.'

Rachel looked at me.

'That parade is sounding better and better all the time.'

'You're forgetting the neatest part,' Clearmountain said. 'And what parade?'

'It's nothing. What's the neatest part?'

'The bulletin board. We traced the number to a location.'

'And?'

'Union Correctional Institution, Raiford, Florida.'

'Oh, my God! Gomble?'

Clearmountain smiled and nodded.

'That's what Bob Backus thinks. He's going to have somebody check it out. I already called the prison and asked the captain of the day where that line went to. He said it was to the supplies office. And, see, I had noticed that all of Gladden's calls to that number were placed after five P.M. eastern time. The captain told me that the supply office was closed and locked up every day at five. Opens up at eight every morning. I also asked him if there was a computer in that office for keeping track of orders and supplies and such and he said there sure was. I said what about a phone and he said there was one but it wasn't connected to the computer. But believe me, this is not a guy who knows a modem from a hole in the ground. This is a guy who volunteers to go to prison every day. Think about that. I told him to check again on the phone line, like some night after that office is closed up and –'

'Wait a minute. He isn't –'

'Don't worry, he's not going to do anything. I told him not to mess with things until he hears from us. For now, the network should remain on line, after five in the East, that is. I asked him who works in there and he told me Horace Gomble. He's a trustee. I see you are already familiar with him. I guess each night he sticks the phone line into the computer before he locks up and goes back to his cell.'

Rachel canceled lunch with me because of the new developments. She said I'd have to grab a cab back to the hotel and that she'd call me when she could. She said she might be going back to Florida but would let me know. I wanted to stay, too, but fatigue was finally setting in from my sleepless night.

I took the elevator down and was walking through the lobby of the federal building, thinking about calling Greg Glenn and checking my messages, when I heard a familiar voice behind me.

'Hey, hot shot, howzit hanging?'

I turned around and Michael Warren walked up to me.

'Warren. I just tried to call you at the *Times*. They said you were out.'

'I was here. Supposed to be another press conference at two. Thought I'd come early and see what I could dig up.'

'Like another source maybe?'

'I told you, Jack, I'm not talking to you about that.'

'Yeah, well, I'm not talking to you either.'

I turned and started away. He called after me.

'Then why'd you call me? To gloat?'

I looked back at him.

'Something like that. I guess. But you know, Warren, I'm not really mad at you. You went after a story that was given to you and that's cool. I can't blame you. Thorson had his own agenda and you didn't know about that. He used you but we all get used. I'll see you.'

'Wait a minute, Jack. If you're not pissed off, why don't you talk to me?'

'Because we're still competitors.'

'No we're not, man. You're not even on the story anymore. I had the front page of the *Rocky* faxed to me this morning. They gave it to somebody else. Only place your name appears is in the story. No bylines, Jack. You're not on the story. You *are* the story. So why don't we go on the record here and let me ask you a few questions?'

'Like "How do you feel?" Is that what you want to ask?'

'That's one of them, yeah.'

I looked at him a good long moment. No matter how much I didn't like him or what he had done, I couldn't deny the empathy I had for his position. He was doing what I had done so many times before. I looked at my watch and out at the parking circle beyond the lobby. There were none of the waiting cabs I had seen the day before.

'You got a car?'

'Yeah, company car.'

'Give me a ride to the Chateau Marmont. We'll talk on the way.'

'On the record?'

'On the record.'

He turned on a tape recorder and put it on the dashboard. He just wanted the basics from me. He wanted to quote me about what I had done the night before rather than rely on a secondhand source like an FBI spokesman. That was too easy and he was too good a reporter to settle for a spokesman. Whenever possible he went straight to the source. I understood this. I was the same way.

Telling him the story somehow made me feel good. I enjoyed it. It wasn't anything I hadn't already given Jackson at my own paper, so it wasn't like I was revealing company secrets. But Warren had been around at almost the start of the trail and I liked being the one who told him where it had led and how it had ended.

I didn't tell him about the latest developments, about the PTL network and Gomble running it from a prison. That was too good to give away. I planned on writing that one myself, whether it was for the *Rocky* or one of those publishers in New York.

Finally, Warren drove up the short hill to the entrance of the Chateau Marmont. A doorman opened the door but I didn't get out. I looked at Warren.

'Anything else?'

'No, I think I got it. I have to get back to the federal building for the press conference anyway. But this is going to be great.'

'Well, you and the *Rocky* are the only ones that got it. I'm not planning to go to "Hard Copy" unless it's six figures.'

He looked at me, surprised.

'Just kidding, Warren. I'd break into the records room with you at the foundation but, hey, I draw the line at selling my story to the tabs.'

'What about the publishers?'

'I'm working on it. You?'

'I gave up once your first story came out. My agent said the editors he talked to were more interested in you than me. You had the brother, you know? You were obviously on the inside. Only thing I'd be able to sell was one of those quick-and-dirty jobs. I'm not interested. I've got a reputation.'

I nodded and turned to get out of the car.

'Thanks for the ride.'

'Thanks for the story.'

I was out and about to close the door when Warren started to say something but then stopped.

'What is it?'

'I was going . . . ah, hell, look, Jack, about the source on that story. If –'

'Forget it, man, it doesn't matter anymore. Like I said, the guy's dead and you did what any reporter would do.'

'No, wait. That's not what I'm saying . . . I don't give up sources, Jack, but I can tell you who isn't a source. And Thorson wasn't my source, okay? I didn't even know the guy.'

I just nodded, saying nothing. He didn't know that I had seen the hotel phone records and that I knew he was lying. A new Jaguar pulled under the parking overhang and a couple dressed head to toe in black started getting out. I looked back at Warren, wondering what he was trying to do. What scam could he be pulling by lying now?

'That it?'

Warren turned a hand upside down and nodded.

'Yeah, that's it. Being that he's dead and you were there, I thought you might want to know.'

I looked at him for another moment.

'Okay, man,' I said. 'Thanks. I'll see you around.'

I straightened up and closed the door, then bent down to look at Warren through the window and gave a wave. He snapped off a military-style salute and drove away.

46

In my room I connected my computer to the phone line and dialed into the *Rocky*'s computer. I had thirty-six E-mail messages waiting for me. I hadn't checked in two days. Most of the in-house messages were congratulatory, although they weren't explicitly worded as such because the senders probably hesitated to do so, wondering if it was proper to congratulate me for killing the Poet. There were two from Van Jackson asking me where I was and to call and three from Greg Glenn asking the same. The *Rocky* operator had also dumped my phone messages into my E-mail basket and there were several from reporters across the country and from Hollywood production companies. My mother and Riley had also called. There was no doubt I was in demand. I saved all the messages in case I wanted to call back and signed off.

Greg Glenn's direct line rang through to the operator. She said Glenn was in a story meeting and she had standing orders not to ring into the conference room. I left my name and number and hung up.

After waiting fifteen minutes for Glenn to return my call and trying not to think about what Warren had told me at the end of our ride, I got impatient and left the room. I started walking down the strip and eventually stopped at Book Soup, a bookstore I had noticed earlier during the ride with Warren. I went to the mystery section and found a book I had once read which I knew was dedicated to the author's agent. My theory was that this was at least the sign of a good agent. With the name in hand, I next went to the research section and looked up the agent in a book listing literary agencies, their addresses and phone numbers. I committed the phone number to memory, left the store and walked back to the hotel.

The red light on the phone was flashing when I got back to my room and I knew it was probably Glenn, but I decided to call the agent first. It was five o'clock in New York and I didn't know what hours he kept. He answered after two rings. I introduced myself and quickly went into my pitch.

'I wanted to see if I could talk to you about representing me in regard to a, uh, I guess it would be called a true crime book. Do you do true crime?'

'Yes,' he said. 'But rather than discuss this on the phone I would really prefer that you send me a query letter telling me about yourself and the project. Then I can respond.'

'I would but I don't think there is time. I've got publishers and movie people calling me and I have to make some decisions quickly.'

That set the hook. I knew it would.

'Why are they calling you? What's it about?'

'Have you read or seen anything on TV about this killer out in L.A., the Poet?'

'Yes, of course.'

'I'm the one who, uh, shot him. I'm a writer – a reporter. My brother –'

'You're the one?'

'I'm the one.'

Though he was interrupted often by other calls, we talked for twenty minutes about the possible book project and the interest I'd already gotten from the movie production people. He said he worked with an agent in Los Angeles who could handle the interest from that industry. In the meantime, he wanted to know how quickly I could send him a two-page proposal. I told him I'd get it to him within the hour and he gave me the number of his computer's fax modem. He said that if the story was as good as he had seen on TV, he thought that he could have the book sold by the end of the week. I told him the story was better.

'One last thing,' he said. 'How did you get my name?'

'It was in *A Morning for Flamingos.*'

The red light on the phone continued to wink at me but I ignored it after hanging up and went to work on my laptop writing the proposal, trying to consolidate the last two weeks into two pages. It was a difficult process, not helped by having only one usable hand, and I went long, finishing with four pages.

By the time I was done, my hand was beginning to throb even though I had tried not to use it. I took another one of the pills the hospital had given me and had gone back to the computer, proofreading my proposal, when the phone rang.

It was Glenn and he was livid.

'Jack!' he cried out. 'I've been waiting on your call! What the fuck are you doing?'

'I did call! I left a message. I've been sitting here an hour waiting for you to call back.'

'I did, goddammit! You didn't get *my* message?'

'No. You must've called when I went down the hall for a Coke. But I didn't get any –'

'Never mind, never mind. Look, what do we have for tomorrow? I've got Jackson on it here and Sheedy took a plane out this morning. She's going to a press conference at the bureau. But what can you give us that's new? Every paper in the country is following our ass and we need to stay in front of them. What's new? What do you have that they don't have?'

'I don't know,' I lied. 'Not a lot's going on. The bureau people are still tying up the details, I guess . . . I'm still off the story?'

'Look, Jack, I don't see how you can write this. We went over this yesterday. You're too involved. You can't expect me to let –'

'Okay, okay, I was just asking. Um . . . uh, there's a couple things. First, they traced this guy Gladden back to an apartment last night and they found a body there. Another victim. You can start with that. But that might be what the press conference is about. Then, also, tell Jackson to call the field office out here and ask about the computer they found.'

'The computer?'

'Yeah, Gladden had a laptop in his car. They had their computer geeks going over it all night and this morning. I don't know, it might be worth a call. I don't know what they found.'

'Well, what have you been doing?'

'I had to go down there and give a statement. Took all morning. They have to go to the district attorney and ask for a justifiable homicide ruling or something. I came back here when I was done.'

'They're not telling you what's going on?'

'No, I only overheard a couple of agents talking about the body and the thing about the computer, that's all.'

'Okay, well that's a start.'

I was smiling and trying to keep it out of my voice. I didn't care about revealing the discovery of the Poet's last victim. That was probably going to come out anyway. But someone like Jackson calling cold wouldn't be able to even get confirmation that there was a computer, let alone what was in it. The bureau wouldn't put that out until it was good and ready to.

'Sorry that's all I've got, Greg,' I said. 'Tell Jackson I'm sorry. So what's Sheedy going to do besides the press conference?'

Sheedy was an up-and-comer. She had recently been appointed to the go team – reporters who have packed suitcases in their car trunks and are ready to hit the road within minutes of any calamity, disaster or other breaking news story outside of Denver. I had been a go team reporter once. But after covering my third airliner crash and talking to people whose loved ones had been reduced to crispy critters or found in small parts, the job got old and I went back to the cop beat.

'I don't know,' Glenn said. 'She'll hunt around. When are you coming back?'

'They want me to stay around in case the district attorney's office wants to interview me. I think by tomorrow I'll be done.'

'Okay, well, if you hear anything let me know right away. And give them shit down at the front desk for not giving you my message. I'll pass this computer thing on to Jackson. I'll seeya, Jack.'

'Okay. Oh, and Greg? My hand's okay.'

'What?'

'I knew you were concerned. But it's feeling a lot better. It will probably be fine.'

'Jack, I'm sorry. It's been one of those days.'

'Yeah. I know. I'll see you.'

47

The pain pill I had taken was beginning to kick in. The discomfort in my hand was subsiding and a calm current of relaxation was overtaking me. After I hung up with Glenn I connected the phone line back into my computer, engaged the fax program and transmitted the book proposal to the number the literary agent had given me. As I listened to the braying sound of the computers coupling, a thought hit me like a bolt. The calls I had made on the flight out to L.A.

I had been so concerned about proving and exposing Thorson as the leak to Warren, I had paid only passing attention to the other calls on his hotel bill, the calls I had repeated myself on the plane to L.A. One of them had been answered by the high-pitched tone of a computer in Florida, possibly at UCI in Raiford.

I grabbed my computer satchel off the bed, pulled out my notebooks and flipped through both of them but found no notes on the calls I had made on the plane. I remembered then that I had not written notes or the phone numbers down because I had not expected someone to steal the hotel bills from my room.

Clearing my mind of everything else, I tried to review the exact course of events on the plane. The main concern I'd had at the time was the record of the call to Warren that was on Thorson's bill. That had confirmed for me that Thorson was Warren's source. The other calls made from his room – though made within minutes of each other – had held little interest to me at the time.

I had not seen the number that Clearmountain had said was called the most often from Gladden's computer. I thought about calling him and asking for the number but I doubted that he would hand it over to a reporter without seeking approval from Rachel or Backus. And that would tip my hand, something that an instinct told me not to do yet.

I slid my Visa card out of my wallet and turned it over. After reconnecting the phone I dialed the 800 number on the credit card and told the operator I had a billing inquiry. After three minutes of Muzak, another operator came on the line and I asked if it was possible to check on charges added to my credit account as recently as three days earlier. After verifying my identity through my social security number and other details, she said she could check my records on the computer to see if the charges had been posted and I told her what I was looking for.

The calls had just been posted on the Visa billing computer. And the phone numbers I had called were also part of the billing record. In five minutes I had copied all the numbers I had called on the plane into my notebook, thanked the operator and hung up.

Once again I plugged the phone line into my computer. I opened the terminal window, typed in the phone number that had been called from Thorson's room and ran the program. I looked at the bedside clock. It was three here, six in Florida. There was one ring and then a connection. I heard the familiar squeal of computers meeting and then mating. My screen went blank and then a template printed across it.

WELCOME TO THE PTL CLUB

I exhaled, leaned back and felt a surge of electricity go through me. After a few seconds the screen moved up and there was a coded prompt for a user's password. I typed in EDGAR, noticing that my good hand was shaking as I did this. Edgar was approved and followed by a prompt for a second password. I typed in PERRY. In a moment this, too, was approved and followed by a warning template.

PRAISE THE LORD!

RULES OF THE ROAD

1. NEVER EVER USE A REAL NAME
2. NEVER PROVIDE SYSTEMS NUMBERS TO ACQUAINTANCES
3. NEVER AGREE TO MEET ANOTHER USER
4. BE AWARE THAT OTHER USERS MAY BE FOREIGN BODIES
5. SYSOP RESERVES THE RIGHT TO DELETE ANY USER
6. MESSAGE BOARDS MAY NOT BE USED FOR DISCUSSION OF ANY ILLEGAL ACTIVITIES – THIS IS FORBIDDEN!
7. PTL NETWORK IS NOT RESPONSIBLE FOR CONTENT
8. PRESS ANY KEY TO CONTINUE

I hit RETURN and got a table of contents for the various message boards available to users. These were, as Clearmountain had said, a cornucopia of subjects catering to the modern pedophile. I hit the escape key and the computer asked if I wanted to exit PTL. I hit the yes prompt and disconnected. I wasn't interested in exploring the PTL Network at the moment. I was more interested in the fact that Thorson, or whoever had made that call early Sunday morning, knew about the PTL Network and even had access to it at least four days ago.

The call to the PTL board had been placed from Thorson's room so it seemed obvious that he had made the call. But I carefully considered other factors. The call to the PTL board had been made, as I recalled, within minutes of the call from the same room to Warren in Los Angeles. Thorson had vehemently denied being Warren's source on at least three occasions.

Warren twice denied it as well, including after Thorson was dead and it didn't matter anymore if he had been the source. The seed planted by Warren during that second denial just a few hours before weighed on me now. It was blossoming in my mind into a flower of doubt I could not put aside.

If Warren and Thorson were to be believed, who had made the calls from Thorson's room? As the possibilities played through my mind they invariably came back with a dull thud in my chest to one person. Rachel.

It was the fermentation of various and unrelated facts that led me down this path.

First, Rachel had a laptop computer. This, of course, was the weakest piece. Thorson, Backus, everyone possessed or had access to a computer that would have allowed them to make the linkage to the PTL board. But second, Rachel was not in her room late Saturday night when I called and then even knocked. So where was she? Could she have gone to Thorson's room?

I considered the things Thorson had said to me about Rachel. He had called her the Painted Desert. But he had said something else. *She can play with you . . . like a toy. One minute she wants to share it, the next she doesn't. She disappears on you.*

And last, I thought of seeing Thorson in the hallway that night. I knew it had been after midnight by then and roughly near the times of the long distance calls placed from his room. As he had passed me in the hall I noticed he carried something. A small bag or a box. I now remembered the sound of the little zippered pocket opening in Rachel's purse and the condom – the one she carried for emergencies – being placed in my palm. And I thought of a way Rachel could have gotten Thorson out of his own room so that she could use the phone.

A feeling of pure dread began to descend on me now. Warren's flower was in full bloom and was choking me. I stood up to pace a little but felt light-headed. I blamed it on the painkiller and sat back down on the bed. After a few moments' rest, I reconnected the phone and called the hotel in Phoenix, asking for the billing office. A young woman took the call.

'Yes, hello, I stayed at your hotel over the weekend and didn't really look at my bill until I got back. I had a question about a few phone calls I was billed for. I've been meaning to call but keep forgetting. Is there someone I could talk to about that?'

'Yes, sir, I would be glad to help. If you give me your name I can call up your statement.'

'Thanks. It's Gordon Thorson.'

She didn't reply and I froze, thinking maybe she recognized the name from the TV or a newspaper as the agent slain in L.A., but then I heard her begin tapping on a keyboard.

'Yes, Mr Thorson. That was room three twenty-five for two nights. What seems to be the problem?'

I wrote the room number down in my notebook, just to be doing something. Following the journalist's routine of making a record of facts helped calm me.

'You know what? I can't – I'm looking around my desk here for my copy and I seem to have misplaced . . . Darn it! I can't find it now. Uh, I'll have to call you back. But in the meantime maybe you can look it up and have it ready. What I was concerned about was that there were three calls made after midnight on Saturday that I just don't remember making. I have the numbers written down here some – here they are.'

I quickly gave her the three numbers I had gotten from the Visa operator, hoping I'd be able to finesse my way through this.

'Yes, they are on your billing. Are you sure you –'

'What time were they made? See, that's the problem. I don't conduct business in the middle of the night.'

She gave me the times. The call to Quantico was logged at 12:37 A.M., followed by the call to Warren at 12:41 A.M. and then the call to the PTL Network line at 12:56 A.M. I stared at the numbers after writing them down.

'You don't believe you made these?'

'What?'

'I said you don't believe you made these?'

'That's right.'

'Was there anyone else in the room with you?'

That was the point, wasn't it, I thought but didn't say.

'Uh, no,' I said, and then quickly added, 'Can you just double-check those for me and if there is nothing wrong with your machines, I'll be glad to pay. Thank you.'

I hung up and looked at the times I had written in my notebook. They fit. Rachel had stayed in my room until almost midnight. The next morning she told me she had bumped into Thorson while in the hall after leaving. Maybe she had lied to me. Maybe she had done more than bump into him. Maybe she had gone to his room.

With Thorson dead, there was only one way of pursuing this theory outside of going to Rachel, which I couldn't do yet. I picked the phone up once again and called the FBI office in the federal building. The operator, under strict orders to screen calls to Backus, especially from the media, was not going to put me through until I told her I was the one who had killed the Poet and that I had an urgent need to speak to the special agent. Finally, I was put through and Backus picked up.

'Jack, what's the problem?'

'Bob, listen to me, I'm very serious. Are you alone?'

'Jack, what –'

'Just answer the question! Look, I'm sorry, I didn't mean to yell. I've just got – Look, just tell me, are you alone?'

There was a hesitation and his voice was skeptical when it returned.

'Yes. Now what's this about?'

'We've talked about the trust in our relationship. I've trusted you and you've trusted me. I want you to trust me again, Bob, for the next few minutes and just answer my questions without asking me any questions. I will explain it all after. Okay?'

'Jack, I'm very busy here. I don't under –'

'Five minutes, Bob. That's all. It's important.'

'What's your question?'

'What happened to Thorson's things? His clothes and things from his hotel. Who got it after he . . . died?'

'I gathered it all together last night. I don't see what this has to do with anything. His property is nobody's business.'

'Indulge me, Bob. This isn't for a story. It's for me. And for you. I have two questions. First, did you find the hotel receipts, the bills, from Phoenix with his stuff?'

'From Phoenix? No, they weren't there and they weren't supposed to be. We checked out on the fly, never went back. I'm sure the bill is being sent to my office in Quantico. What is on your mind, Jack?'

The first piece clicked into place. If Thorson didn't have the bills, he likely wasn't the one who had taken them from my room. I thought about Rachel again. I couldn't help it. The first night in Hollywood, after we had made love, she got up and took the first shower. Then it was my turn. I envisioned her taking the room key from the pocket of my pants, going downstairs and slipping into my room to conduct a quick search of my things. Maybe she was just looking around. Maybe she knew somehow that I had the hotel bills. Maybe she had called the hotel in Phoenix and had been told.

'Next question,' I said to Backus, ignoring his own question. 'Did you find any condoms with Thorson's things?'

'Look, I don't know what kind of morbid fascination you have with this but I'm not going to go on with it. I'm hanging up now, Jack, and I don't want you –'

'Wait a minute! What morbid fascination? I'm trying to figure out something you people have missed! Did you talk to Clearmountain today about the computer? About the PTL Network?'

'Yes, I've been fully briefed. What's it got to do with a box of condoms?'

I noticed he had inadvertently answered my question about condoms. I had not said anything about a box.

'Did you know that a call was placed to the PTL Network from Thorson's room in Phoenix on Sunday morning?'

'That's preposterous. And how the hell would you know something like that?'

'Because when I checked out of that hotel, the clerk thought I was an FBI agent. Remember? Just like that reporter at the funeral home. He gave me the hotel bills to take to you people out here. He thought it would save the time of mailing them.'

There was a long silence after this confession.

'Are you saying you stole the hotel bills?'

'I'm saying what I just said. They were given to me. And on Thorson's bill there were calls to both Michael Warren and the PTL. And that's funny, since you people supposedly didn't know about the PTL until today.'

'I'm sending someone over to pick up those bills.'

'Don't bother. I don't have them. They were stolen from my room in Hollywood. You've got a fox in the henhouse, Bob.'

'What are you talking about?'

'Tell me about the box of condoms you found in Thorson's things and I'll tell you what I'm talking about.'

I heard him exhale in a tired, I-give-up fashion.

'There was a box of condoms, okay? It wasn't even opened. Now, what's it mean?'

'Where is it now?'

'It's in a sealed cardboard box with the rest of his things. It goes back to Virginia with his body tomorrow morning.'

'Where's this sealed box?'

'Right here with me.'

'I need you to open it, Bob. Look at the condoms, see if there is a price tag or anything that shows where he got them.'

As I listened to the sounds of him tearing cardboard and tape my mind served up my memory of the sight of Thorson coming down the hall with something in his hand.

'I can tell you right now,' Backus said as he was opening the property box, 'they were in a bag from a drugstore.'

I felt my heart leap and next I heard the crinkling sound of a bag opening.

'Okay, I've got it,' Backus said in a voice showing his strained patience. 'Scottsdale Drugs. Open twenty-four hours. Box of twelve condoms, nine ninety-five. You want to know the brand, too, Jack?'

I ignored his sarcasm but his question gave me an idea for later.

'There's a receipt?'

'I just read it to you.'

'What about the date and time of purchase, that on there? Most of these computer registers put it on there.'

Silence. So long I wanted to scream.

'Sunday morning, twelve fifty-four.'

I closed my eyes. While Thorson was buying a box of condoms, of which he wouldn't even use one, someone was in his room making phone calls.

'Okay, Jack, what's it mean?' Backus asked.

'It means everything is a lie.'

I opened my eyes and pulled the phone from my ear. I looked at it like it was some alien thing attached to my hand and slowly dropped it back into its cradle.

Bledsoe was still in his office and answered on the first ring.

'Dan, it's Jack again.'

'Jack Mac, what's up?'

'You know that beer you said you owed me? I thought of something else you can do for me instead.'

'You got it.'

I told him what I needed him to do and he didn't hesitate, even when I told him I needed it done now. He said he couldn't promise results but that he'd get back to me one way or the other as soon as possible.

*

I thought about the first call made while Thorson was out of his room. It had been to the general public line at the Quantico center. It hadn't struck me as odd when I called the number on the plane. But now it did. Why would someone call the general number in the middle of the night? I knew now that the answer could only be that the caller did not want to call a direct number at the center, thereby revealing knowledge of that number. Instead, through her computer, she called the general number and when the operator recognized the fax mating beep, the call was transferred to one of the general fax lines.

I recalled that during the Sunday morning meeting on the fax from the Poet, Thorson had recited the details after getting the rundown from Quantico. The fax had come through on the general number and had been transferred to a fax machine.

Without a word an operator at Quantico switched me to the BSS offices when I called and asked for Agent Brad Hazelton. The phone rang three times and I thought I was too late, that he had gone home for the day, when he finally picked up.

'Brad, it's Jack McEvoy. In Los Angeles.'

'Hey, Jack, how're you doing? Pretty close call for you yesterday.'

'I'm doing okay. I'm sorry about Agent Thorson. I know everybody works very closely together there . . .'

'Well, he was pretty much an asshole but nobody deserves what happened to him. It's pretty awful. Not a lot of smiling faces around here today.'

'I can imagine.'

'So what's going on?'

'Well, it's just a couple of minor points. I'm putting together a chronology of events so that I have this story down straight. You know, if I ever get to write the whole thing.'

I hated lying to this man who had only been friendly to me, but I couldn't afford to tell him the truth because then he certainly wouldn't help me.

'And, anyway, I seem to have misplaced my notes on the fax. You know, the fax the Poet sent to Quantico on Sunday. I remember Gordon said he got the details from either you or Brass. What I wanted to know is the exact time it came in. If you have it.'

'Uh, hold on, Jack.'

He was gone before I could say I would hold. I closed my eyes and spent the next few minutes wondering whether he was actually looking up the information or first checking to see if he could give it to me.

Finally, he came back on the line.

'Sorry, Jack, I had to look through all the papers here. The fax came to machine number two in the academy offices wire room at three thirty-eight Sunday morning.'

I looked at my notes. Subtracting the three-hour time difference, the fax came in at Quantico one minute after the call to the general number had been placed from Thorson's room.

'Okay, Jack?'

'Oh, yeah, thanks. Uh, I had one other question.'

'Shoot – oh, shit, sorry.'

'That's okay. Uh, the question I have is, um . . . Agent Thompson sent back an oral swab from the victim in Phoenix. Orsulak.'

'Yes, Orsulak.'

'Uh, he wanted to identify the substance. He believed it was the lubricant from a condom. The question I had was whether it was identified as coming from a specific brand of condom. Can that be done? Was it done?'

Hazelton didn't answer at first and I almost jumped into the silence. But then he spoke.

'That's a strange question, Jack.'

'Yeah, I know but, uh, the details of the case, and how you people do things, really fascinates me. It's important to have them right – it makes a better story.'

'Hold on another second.'

Again he was gone before I could agree to hold. This time he came back very quickly.

'Yes, I have that information. Do you want to tell me why you really want it?'

Now it was my turn to be silent.

'No,' I finally said, trying the honesty route. 'I'm just trying to work something out, Brad. If it goes the way I think it's going, the FBI's going to be the first to know about it. Believe me.'

Hazelton paused for a moment.

'Okay, Jack, I'll trust you. Besides, Gladden's dead. It's not like I'm giving away trial evidence and there's not much you can prove with this anyway. The substance was narrowed down to being similar to two different brands. Ramses Lubricated and Trojan Golds. Problem is they are two of the most popular brands in the country. It is not what we'd call unequivocal evidence of anything.'

Maybe it wasn't evidence you could take into a courtroom, but Ramses Lubricated was the brand that Rachel had handed me from her purse on Saturday night in my hotel room. I thanked Hazelton without further discussion and hung up.

It was all there and it all seemed to fit. No matter how many ways over the next hour that I tried to destroy my own theory, I couldn't. It was a theory built on a foundation of suspicion and speculation but it worked like a machine, all the parts meshing together. And I had nothing to throw into its gears that could bring it to a grinding halt.

The last part I needed was Bledsoe. I paced the room waiting for his call, the feeling of anxiety churning in my stomach like something that was alive. I went out on the balcony for fresh air but that didn't help. Staring at me was the Marlboro Man, his thirty-foot-high face holding dominion over the Sunset Strip. I went back inside.

Instead of the cigarette I wanted, I decided on a Coke. I left the room, turning the night lock so the door wouldn't close all the way and trotted down the hallway to the vending machines. In spite of the painkiller, my nerves were jangling. But I knew that this intensity would translate to fatigue in a little while if I didn't ante up with a shot of sugar and caffeine. Halfway back to my room, I heard the phone ringing and I ran. I went for the phone before even closing the door, grabbing it on what I thought might be the ninth ring.

'Dan?'

Silence.

'It's Rachel. Who is Dan?'

'Oh.' I could barely catch my breath. 'He's, uh – He's just a friend at the paper. He was supposed to call.'

'What's the matter with you, Jack?'

'I'm out of breath. I was down the hall getting a Coke and I heard the phone.'

'Jesus, it must've been the hundred-yard dash.'

'Something like that. Hold on.'

I went back to the door and closed it, then put my actor's face on as I went back to the phone.

'Rachel?'

'Listen, I just wanted you to know I'm leaving. Bob wants me to go back to Florida and handle this PTL thing.'

'Oh.'

'It will probably be a few days.'

The message light on my phone came on. Bledsoe, I thought, and silently cursed the timing of his call.

'Okay, Rachel.'

'We'll have to get together somewhere afterward. I was thinking of taking a vacation.'

'I thought you just did.'

I remembered the notation on the calendar I had seen on her desk in Quantico. It struck me for the first time that that was when she must have gone to Phoenix to stalk and kill Orsulak.

'I haven't had a real vacation in a long time. I was thinking about Italy maybe. Venice.'

I didn't challenge her on the lie. I remained silent and she lost her patience. My acting wasn't working.

'Jack, what's the matter?'

'Nothing.'

'I don't believe you.'

I hesitated and then said, 'There is one thing that's been kind of bothering me, Rachel.'

'Tell it to me.'

'The other night, our first night together, I called your room after you left. I just wanted to say good night, you know, and tell you how much I enjoyed what we did. And there was no answer. I even went to your door and knocked. No answer. Then the next morning you said you had seen Thorson in the hall. And I don't know, I guess I've been thinking about that.'

'Thinking what, Jack?'

'I don't know, just thinking. I was wondering where you were when I called and when I knocked.'

She was silent for a moment and when she finally spoke her anger crackled through the phone like a fire.

'Jack, you know what you sound like? A jealous high school boy. Like the boy on the bleachers you told me about. Yes, I saw Thorson in the hall and, yes, I'll even admit that he thought I was looking for him, that I wanted him. But that's as far as it went. I can't explain why I didn't get your call, okay? Maybe you called the wrong room and maybe it was when I was taking a shower and thinking about how nice the night had been, too. And maybe I shouldn't have to defend myself or explain myself to you. If you can't deal with your petty jealousies then find a different woman and get a different life.'

'Rachel, look I'm sorry, okay? You asked me what was wrong and I told you.'

'You must have taken too many of those pills the doctor gave you. My advice is that you sleep it off, Jack. I have a plane to catch.'

She hung up.

'Good-bye,' I said into the silence.

48

The sun was going down and the sky was the color of ripe pumpkin with slashes of phosphorescent pink. It was beautiful and even the clutter of billboards up and down the strip looked beautiful to me. I was back out on the balcony, trying to think, trying to figure things out, waiting for Bledsoe to call back. He was the one who had left the message while I talked to Rachel. His message said he was out of the office but would call back.

I looked at the Marlboro Man, his crinkled eyes and stoic chin unchanged by time. He'd always been one of my heroes, an icon, no matter that he was always as shallow as a magazine page or a billboard sign. I remembered being at the dinner table, my position every night always to my father's right. Him always smoking and the ashtray always to the right of his plate. Me learning to smoke by virtue of that. He looked like the Marlboro Man to me, my father. Back then, at least.

Back in the room, I called home and my mother answered. She went into histrionics asking whether I was all right and gently scolded me for not calling sooner. Finally, after I had calmed her and assured her that I was okay, I asked her to put my father on the line. We had not spoken since the funeral – if we had even spoken then.

'Dad?'

'Son. You sure you're okay?'

'I'm fine. You okay?'

'Oh, sure. We were just worried about you, that's all.'

'Well, don't. Everything's fine.'

'It's a crazy thing, isn't it?'

'You mean about Gladden? Yeah.'

'Riley's here with us. She's going to spend a few days.'

'That's good, Dad.'

'Do you want to talk to her?'

'No, I wanted to talk to you.'

That silenced him, maybe made him nervous.

'You in Los Angeles?'

He said it with a hard G.

'Yeah, at least a day or two more. I just . . . I called because I wanted – I've been thinking about things and I wanted to say I'm sorry.'

'Sorry for what, Son?'

'Anything, everything. Sarah, Sean, you name it.' I laughed the way you laugh when something isn't funny, when it's uncomfortable. 'I'm sorry for everything.'

'Jack, you sure you're okay?'

'I'm fine.'

'Well, you don't have to say you're sorry for anything.'

'Yes, I do. I do.'

'Well . . . we're sorry, too, then. I'm sorry.'

I let a little bit of silence underline that.

'Thanks, Dad. I'm gonna go. Tell Mom I said good-bye and tell Riley I said hello.'

'I will. Why don't you come down here when you get back? Spend a couple days, too.'

'I will.'

I hung up. Marlboro Man, I thought. I looked out the open balcony door and saw his eyes peeking over the railing, watching me. My hand was hurting again. So was my head. I knew too much and didn't want to. I took another pill.

At five-thirty Bledsoe finally called. The news he had was not good. It was the final piece, the final tearing of the veil of hope I'd held on to. As I listened to him it felt like the blood was draining from my heart. I was alone again. And what was worse was that the one I had desired had not simply rejected me. She had used and betrayed me in a way I would've thought no woman could do.

'This is what I got, buddy,' Bledsoe said. 'Hang on to your hat, is all I can say.'

'Give it to me.'

'Rachel Walling. Her father was Harvey Walling. I didn't know him. When he was in dicks, I was still in patrol. I talked to one of the old guys from dicks and he said your guy was called Harvey Wallbanger. You know, after the drink. He was sort of an odd duck, loner type.'

'What about his death?'

'I'm getting to that. I had a buddy pull the old file out of archives. Happened nineteen years ago. Funny I don't remember it. I guess I was working with my head down. Anyway, I met my pal over at the Fells Point Tavern. He brought the file. And, first off, this was definitely her old man. Her name's in there. She was the one who found him. He'd shot himself. Temple shot. It went suicide but there were some problems.'

'What?'

'Well, no note for one thing. And for another, he'd worn gloves. It was in the winter, yes, but he did it inside. First thing in the morning. The investigator wrote down in the reports that he didn't like that part of it.'

'Was there gunshot residue on one of the gloves?'

'Yeah, it was there.'

'Was she – was Rachel home when it happened?'

'She said she was upstairs in her bedroom sleeping when she heard the shot. In her king-size bed. She got scared, said she didn't come down for an hour after the shot. Then she found him. This is according to the reports.'

'What about the mother?'

'There was no mother. She'd taken off years before. Rachel was left alone with the father then.'

I thought about that for a few moments. His mention of the size of her bed and something about the way he'd said the last line bothered me.

'What else, Dan? You're not telling me everything.'

'Jack, let me ask you something. Are you involved with this woman? Like I told you, I saw on the CNN how she wal –'

'Look, I'm out of time! What aren't you telling me?'

'Okay, okay, the only other thing noted in the reports that was strange was that his bed was made.'

'What are you talking about?'

'His bed. It was made. The way it had to've worked was he got up, made his bed, got dressed and put on his coat and gloves, like he was going to work, but then instead sat down in the chair and put a bullet through his head. Either that or he stayed up all night thinking about it and then did the job.'

I felt depression and fatigue wash over me in a wave. I slid off the chair to the floor, the phone still held to my ear.

'The guy who worked the case is retired but still around. Mo Friedman. We go back. I was just coming up in dicks when he was near the end. But he was a good man. I just got off the line with him a few minutes ago. Lives up in the Poconos. I asked him about this one and what his take on it was. His unofficial take, I told him.'

'And he said?'

'He said he let it go because either way he figured Harvey Wallbanger got what he had coming.'

'But what did he say his take was?'

'He said that he thought that bed was made because it never was slept in. Never used. He said he thought the father was sleeping with the daughter in the king-size and one morning she drew the line. He didn't know about anything after that, none of this stuff that's been going on lately. Mo's seventy-one years old. He does crossword puzzles. He said he doesn't like watching the news. He didn't know the daughter became an FBI agent.'

I couldn't talk. I couldn't even move.

'Jack, you still there?'

'I gotta go.'

The field office operator said Backus had left for the day. When I asked her to double-check, she put me on hold for five minutes while I was sure she was doing her nails or touching up her makeup. When she came back on she said he was definitely gone and that I could try back in the morning. She hung up before I could say anything else.

Backus was the key. I had to get to him, tell him what I had and play it whatever way he wanted. I decided that if he wasn't at the FO, he might be back at the motel on Wilcox. I had to go there anyway to pick up my car. I threw the strap of my computer bag over my shoulder and headed for the door. I opened it and stopped dead. Backus stood there, fist raised, ready to knock.

'Gladden wasn't the Poet. He was a killer, yes, but not the Poet. I can prove it.'

Backus looked at me as if I had just reported that I had seen the Marlboro Man wink at me.

'Jack, look, you've spent the day making some strange calls. First to me, then to Quantico. I came by because I'm wondering if there's something maybe the doctors overlooked last night. I thought maybe we'd take a ride over to –'

'Look, Bob, I don't blame you for thinking that after what I asked you and Hazelton today. But I had to hold things back until I was sure. Now, I'm sure. Pretty sure. I can explain it now. I was going out the door to find you just now.'

'Then sit down here and tell me what you're talking about. You said that I had a fox in the henhouse. What did you mean?'

'What I meant was here you people are, your job is to identify and catch these people. The serial offenders, as you call them. And there was one in your midst all along.'

Backus let out his breath loudly and shook his head.

'Sit down, Bob, and I'll tell you the story. If you think I'm crazy when I'm done, then you can take me to the hospital. But I know you won't think I'm crazy.'

Backus sat down on the end of the bed and I started spinning the story, recounting the moves and calls I had made through the afternoon. It took me nearly a half hour just to tell that part of it. And just when I was ready to begin telling him my interpretation of the facts I had gathered, he interrupted me with something I had already considered and was ready for.

'You're forgetting one thing. You said Gladden admitted killing your brother. At the end. You said this yourself and I read it in your statement this afternoon. You even said he recognized you.'

'But he was wrong. I was wrong. I never told him Sean's name. I just said my brother. I told him he had killed my brother and he thought one of the kids was my brother. You see? That's why he said what he said, that he killed my brother to save him. I think what he meant was that he killed those kids because he knew that once he'd been with them they'd be fucked up for life. Just like he was fucked up by Beltran. So in his mind he thought that by killing them he was saving them from becoming like he was. He wasn't talking about the cops, just those kids. I don't think he even knew about the cops.

'And as far as him recognizing me, I was on TV. CNN, remember? He could've recognized me from that.'

Backus looked down at the floor and I watched him try to compute this and I saw by the expression on his face that he found it plausible. I was getting through to him.

'Okay,' he said. 'What about Phoenix, the hotel rooms, all of that? Where do you see that going?'

'We were getting close. Rachel knew it and needed some way to either derail the investigation or make sure it pointed only to Gladden when we got him. Even though every cop in the country wanted him dead, she couldn't be sure that would happen.

'So she did three things. First, she sent the fax, the one from the Poet, from her computer to the general number at Quantico. She wrote it in a way that she knew the information it contained would become the definitive link between Gladden and the cop killings. Think back, remember the meeting on the fax? She was the one who said it tied all the cases together.'

Backus nodded but said nothing.

'Next,' I said, 'she thought that if she leaked the story to Warren, it would trigger my story and the rest of the whole media stampede. Gladden would have to see the story somewhere and he'd go underground, knowing that he was being blamed not only for the murders he did commit but the cop killings that came after. So she called up Warren and gave him the story. She must've known that he'd gone to L.A. to peddle the story after he got canned at the foundation. Maybe he had called and left her a message about where he was. You follow all of this?'

'You were so sure it was Gordon.'

'I was. And with good reason. The hotel bills. But the drugstore receipt shows he wasn't even in his room when the calls were made and Warren told me today his source wasn't Thorson. By then he had no reason to lie. Thorson was dead.'

'What was the third thing?'

'I think she made a connection by computer to the PTL Network. I don't know how she already knew about it. Maybe it was a tip to the bureau or something. I'm not sure. But she dialed in. I don't know, maybe that was when she shipped one of those Eidolon files that Clearmountain found. Again, it would be evidence linking Gladden to the Poet murders. She was sealing him up tight in a package. Even if I didn't kill him and he lived to deny everything, the evidence would be there and nobody would believe him, especially in light of the killings he did commit.'

I took a breather so Backus could digest everything said so far.

'All three of the calls she made were from Thorson's room,' I said after a half minute. 'It was just one more buffer. If things went wrong there would be no record of her making the calls. They'd be on Thorson's room. But the box of condoms destroys that. See, you know firsthand about the relationship she had with Thorson. They battled but there was still something there. He still had something for her and she knew it. She used it. So I think if she told him to go get a box of condoms and she'd be waiting for him in his bed, he'd've run out the door to the drugstore like a man with his pants on fire. And I think that's exactly what she did do. Only she didn't wait in his bed. She made those calls. Then when Thorson got back she was gone. Thorson didn't exactly tell me all of that but in so many words he did. When we worked together that day.'

Backus nodded. He looked like a man lost. I thought maybe he saw what was to become of his career now. First his command questioned by the fiasco of the Gladden arrest, and now this. His days as an assistant special agent in charge were numbered.

'It seems so . . .'

He didn't finish and I didn't finish it for him. There was still more for me to tell him but I waited. Backus got up and paced a little. He looked out the balcony door at the Marlboro Man. He didn't seem to have the same fascination with him that I had.

'Tell me about the moon, Jack.'

'What do you mean?'

'The Poet's moon. You've told me the end of the story. What's the beginning? How does a woman end up at the point we are at now?'

He turned from the door and looked at me, a challenge in his eyes. He was looking for something, anything that he could build a case on for not believing. I cleared my throat before beginning.

'That's the hard part,' I said. 'You should ask Brass.'

'I will. But you try it.'

I thought a moment before starting.

'A young girl, I don't know, twelve, thirteen years old. She's abused by her father. Sexually. Her mother either . . . her mother leaves. She either knew what was happening and couldn't stop it or just didn't care. The mother leaves and then the girl is left alone with him. He's a cop. A detective. He threatens her, convinces her she can never tell anyone because he's a detective and he'll find out. He tells her she won't be believed and she believes him.

'So one day she's finally had enough or she'd had enough all along but didn't have the chance or hadn't thought out the right plan. Whatever. But that one day comes and she kills him, makes it look like he did it himself. Suicide. She gets away with it. There's a detective on the case who knows something isn't right but what's he gonna do? He knows the guy had it coming to him. He lets it go.'

Backus was standing in the middle of the room staring at the floor.

'I knew about her father. The official version, I mean.'

'I had a friend find out the details of the unofficial version.'

'What next?'

'What happens next is she blossoms. The power she had in that one moment makes up for a lot of things. She gets past it. Few do, but she makes it. She's a smart girl and she goes on to the university to study psychology, to learn about herself. And then she even gets drafted by the FBI. She's a prize and she moves fast through the bureau until she's in the unit that actually studies people like her father. And like herself. You see, her whole life has been this struggle to understand. And then when her team leader wants to study police suicides he goes to her because he knows the official story about her father. Not the truth. Just the official story. She takes the job, knowing inside that the reason she had been chosen was a sham.'

I stopped there. The more I told of the story the more power I felt. Knowledge of someone's secrets is an intoxicating power. I reveled in my ability to put the story together.

'And so,' Backus whispered then, 'how does it all come apart for her?'

I cleared my throat.

'Things were going good,' I continued. 'She married her partner and things were going good. But then things weren't so good. I don't know if it was pressure from the job, the memories, the breakup of that marriage, maybe all of those things. But she started coming apart. Her husband left her, thinking that she was empty inside. The Painted Desert, he called her, and she hated him for it. And then . . . maybe she remembered the day when she killed her tormentor. Her father. And she remembered the peace that came after . . . the release.'

I looked at him. He had a far-off look in his eyes, maybe envisioning the story as I conjured it from hell.

'One day,' I continued, 'one day a request for a profile comes in. A boy has been killed and mutilated in Florida. The case detective wants a profile of the person who did this. Only she recognizes the detective, knows his name. Beltran. A name from the past. A name maybe brought up in an old interview and she knows that he, too, was a tormentor, an abuser like her father, and that the victim he is calling about was also probably his victim . . .'

'Right,' Backus said, taking up the strand. 'So she goes down to Florida to this man, Beltran, and does it again. Just like with her father. Makes it look like a suicide. She even knew where Beltran kept his shotgun hidden. Gladden had told her that. It was probably an easy thing to get to him. She flies down, goes to him with her bureau credentials and gets inside the house to do it. It brings her peace again. Fills that void. Only thing is it doesn't last. Soon she is empty again and she has to do it again. And then again and again. She follows the killer, Gladden, and kills those who are after him, using him to cover her tracks before she had even made them.'

Backus was staring blankly at some vision as he spoke.

'She knew all the touches, all the moves,' he said. 'Wiping the lubricated condom off inside Orsulak's mouth. The perfect deflection. It was true genius.'

I nodded and took it from there.

'She had seen Gladden's cell and knew there was a photograph in the files that could be found one day,' I said. 'She knew the books about Poe were in the photo. It was all a setup. She followed Gladden around the country. She had a sense. She knew from the cases coming in for profiling which were the ones he did. She had an empathy. She'd follow him. She'd go out and kill the cop that was after him. She made each one look like a suicide, but she had Gladden to put it on if someday someone came along and it unraveled.'

Backus looked at me.
'Someone like you,' he said.
'Yeah. Like me.'

49

Backus said the story was like a sheet hanging on a clothes-line in high wind. Barely held on by a few clothespins, it was ready to fly away.

'We need more, Jack.'

I nodded. He was the expert. Besides, the real trial had already been held in my heart and the verdict was in.

'What are you going to do?' I asked.

'I'm thinking. You had – you were beginning a relationship with her, weren't you?'

'It was that obvious?'

'Yes.'

Then he didn't say anything for a full minute. He paced the room, not really looking at anything, all interior dialogue and thought. Finally, he stopped moving and looked at me.

'Would you wear a wire?'

'What do you mean?'

'You know what I mean. I'll bring her back here, put her alone with you and you draw it out. You might be the only one who could.'

I looked down at the floor. I remembered our last phone conversation and how she had seen through my act.

'I don't know. I don't think I could pull it off.'

'She might be suspicious and check,' Backus said, discarding the idea and searching the floor with his eyes for another. 'Still, you're the one, Jack. You're not an agent and she knows if need be she can take you.'

'Take me where?'

'Take you out.' He snapped his fingers. 'I've got it. You won't have to wear a wire. We'll put you inside the wire.'

'What are you talking about?'

He raised a finger as if to tell me to hold on. He picked up the phone, wedged the receiver into the crook of his neck and carried it with him while he tapped in a number and waited for an answer. The cord was like a leash, containing his pacing to only a few steps in any direction.

'Pack your things,' he said to me while waiting for the call to be picked up.

I got up and slowly began to follow his order, putting my few things in the computer bag and the pillowcase while listening as he asked for Agent Carter and then began issuing directions. He told Carter to call Quantico communications and to relay a message to the bureau jet with Rachel on it. Call the plane back, Backus ordered.

'Just tell them something's come up that cannot be discussed on the air and that I need her back here,' he said into the phone. 'Nothing more than that. Understand?'

Satisfied with Carter's reply, he pressed on.

'Now, before you do that, put me on hold and call the SAC's office. I need the exact address and key combination for the earthquake house. He'll know what I mean. I'll be going there from here. I want you to grab a sound and video tech and two good agents. I'll fill you in there. Call the SAC now.'

I looked at Backus with a curious expression.

'I'm on hold.'

'Earthquake house?'

'Clearmountain told me about it. It's in the hills over the Valley. Top to bottom it's wired. Sound and video. It was damaged in the quake and the real owners just left it, didn't have insurance. The bureau leased it from the bank and used it for a sting on local building and safety inspectors, contractors and repairmen. A lot of fraud involving the funds from the Federal Emergency Management Agency. That's where the bureau came in. Indictments are pending. The sting's been closed down but the bureau's lease isn't up. So it's –'

He held his hand up. Carter had come back on the line. Backus listened for a few moments and nodded his head.

'Right on Mulholland and then the first left. Easy enough. What's your ETA?'

He hung up after telling Carter we'd get there ahead of him and adding that he needed the agent's best work on this.

As Backus drove away from the hotel I made a secret salute to the Marlboro Man. We went east on Sunset to Laurel Canyon Boulevard and then up the winding cut through the mountains.

'How's this going to work?' I asked him. 'How are you going to get Rachel up to this place we're going?'

'You'll leave a message for Rachel on her voice mail at Quantico. You'll tell her you're at a friend's house – somebody you used to know from the paper who moved out here – and leave the number. Then when I talk to Rachel I'll tell her I called her back from Florida because you've been making calls and strange accusations about her but nobody knows where you are. I'll tell her I think you've popped too many pain pills but that we need to bring you in.'

I was feeling increasingly uncomfortable about the prospect of being used as bait and having to face Rachel. I did not know how I'd be able to bring it off.

'Eventually,' Backus continued, 'Rachel will get the message. But she won't call you. Instead, she'll trace the number to the house and she'll go to you, Jack. Alone. For one of two things.'

'What?' I asked, though I already had a pretty good idea.

'To either try to set you straight . . . or to kill you. She'll think you're the only one who knows. She'll need to convince you that you are wrong about these wild-ass ideas. Or she'll need to put you in the ground. My guess is that it will be the ground.'

I nodded. It was my guess, too.

'But we'll be there. Inside with you, close.'

It wasn't comforting.

'I don't know . . .'

'Not to worry, Jack,' Backus said, reaching over and giving me a playful punch on the shoulder. 'You'll be all right and this time we're going to do it right. What you *do* have to worry about is getting her to talk. Get her on the tape, Jack. Get her admitting to just one part of the Poet's story and we've got her for the rest. Get her on tape.'

'I'll try.'

'You'll be fine.'

At Mulholland Drive, Backus turned right as Carter had instructed and we followed the road as it snaked along the mountain crest, offering a view through the darkening haze of the Valley below. We serpentined for nearly a mile until we saw Wrightwood Drive and turned left and descended into a neighborhood of small homes built on steel pylons, their weight hanging out over the mountain's edge, precarious testaments to engineering and the desires of developers to leave their mark on every crest in the city.

'Do you believe people live in these things?' Backus asked.

'Hate to be in one during an earthquake.'

Backus drove slowly, checking the address numbers painted on the curb. I let him do that while I watched between the houses for glimpses of the Valley below. It was approaching dusk and many of the lights were coming on down there. Backus finally stopped the car in front of a house on a bend in the road.

'This is it.'

It was a small, wood-frame structure. From the front the pylons that supported it could not be seen and it seemed to be floating above the deep drop-off to the Valley. We both looked at it for a long moment without making a move to get out.

'What if she knows about the house?'

'Rachel? She won't, Jack. I only know because of Clearmountain. It came up during a bit of gossip. Some of the guys from the FO use the place on occasion, if you know what I mean. When they're with someone they can't bring home.'

I looked over at him and he winked at me.

'Let's check it out,' he said. 'Don't forget your stuff.'

There was a lockbox on the front door. Backus knew the combination and opened it, retrieved the key from the tiny compartment and opened the door.

He entered the house and flicked on the light in an entrance alcove. I followed him in and closed the door. The house was only modestly furnished but I ignored this because my attention was immediately drawn to the rear wall of the living room. The wall was made entirely of thick glass panels offering a spectacular view of the entire Valley sprawling below the house. I crossed the room and gazed out. At the far rim of the Valley I saw the rise of another mountain chain. I stepped close enough to the glass so that I could see my own breath against it and looked down into the dark arroyo directly below. A sense of unease at being at such a precipice licked at me and I stepped back as Backus turned on a lamp behind me.

It was then that I saw the cracks. Three of the five glass panels had fractures spidering through them. I turned to the left and saw the disjointed image of myself and Backus in a mirrored wall that had also been fractured by the earthquake.

'What else happened? Is it safe to be in here?'

'It's safe, Jack. But safety is a relative thing. The next big one could come along and change everything ... As far as other damage, there is a floor below us. Was a floor, I should say. Clearmountain said that is where the damage was. Buckled walls, broken water pipes.'

I put my computer bag and pillowcase down on the floor and turned back to the rear window. My eyes were drawn to the view and I bravely stepped to the glass again. I heard a sharp creaking sound from the direction of the alcove where we had come in. I looked at Backus with alarm.

'Don't worry, they had the pylons checked by an engineer before they even started the sting. The house isn't going anywhere. It just looks like it is and sounds like it is and that's what they wanted for the sting.'

I nodded again but not with a lot of confidence. I looked back at him through the glass.

'The only thing going somewhere is you, Jack.'

I glanced at him in the mirror, not sure what he meant. And there, quadrupled in the broken reflection, I saw the gun in his hand.

'What is this?' I asked.

'This is the end of the line.'

In a rush it came to me. I'd taken a wrong turn and blamed the wrong one. In that moment I also came to the realization that it was the flaw in my own interior that had led me the wrong way. My inability to believe and accept. I had taken Rachel's emotions and looked for the flaw in them instead of the truth.

'You,' I said. 'You are the Poet.'

He didn't answer. Instead he gave a small smile and a nod. I knew then that Rachel's plane hadn't been recalled and that Agent Carter was not coming with a tech and two good agents. I could see the true plan perfectly, right down to the finger Backus must have kept on the phone while he faked the call in my hotel room. I was alone now with the Poet.

'Bob, why? Why you?'

I was so shocked I was still calling him by his first name like a friend would.

'It's a story as old as any of them,' he replied. 'Too old and forgotten to tell you. You don't need to know it now, anyway. Sit down on the chair, Jack.'

He signaled with the gun toward the stuffed chair opposite the couch. Then he aimed the gun back at me. I didn't move.

'The calls,' I said. 'You made the calls from Thorson's room?'

I said it more to be saying something as a stall for time, though in my gut I knew that time was meaningless to me now. No one knew I was here. No one would be coming. Backus laughed in a forced, scoffing manner at my question.

'The luck of chance,' he said. 'That night I checked in for all of us – Carter, Thorson, me. Then I apparently mixed the keys up. I made those calls from my own room, but the bill had Thorson's name on it. I didn't know that, of course, until I took the bills from your room Monday night while you were with Rachel.'

I thought about what Rachel had said about making your own luck. I guessed it applied to serial killers as well.

'How'd you know I had the bills?'

'I didn't. Not for sure. But you called Michael Warren and told him you had his source by the balls. He then called me because I was his source. Even though he said you accused Gordon of being the source, I had to find out what you knew. That was the reason I let you back into the investigation, Jack. I had to figure out what you knew. It wasn't until I went into your room while you were bedding Rachel that I found out it was the hotel bills.'

'Was that you who followed me later, to the bar?'

'That night you were the one with the luck. If you had gone to that doorway to see who was there, this would all have been over right then.

'But then the next day when you didn't come to me and accuse Thorson of breaking into your room, I thought the threat was over. That you were letting it go. Everything proceeded nicely from there – right according to plan – until you called up today and started asking about condoms and phone calls. I knew what you were up to, Jack. I knew I had to move quickly. Now sit down in that chair. I'm not going to ask you again.'

I moved to the chair and sat down. I rubbed my hands down my thighs and felt my hands shaking. My back was now to the rear wall of glass. I had nothing to look at but Backus.

'How'd you know about Gladden?' I asked. 'Gladden and Beltran.'

'I was there. Remember? I was part of the team. While Rachel and Gordon conducted other interviews I had my own little sit-down with William. From what he was willing to say it was not difficult for me to identify Beltran. Then I waited for Gladden to act once he was set free. I knew he'd act out. It was in his nature. I know about that. And so I used him as cover. I knew that if one day my work was discovered, the evidence would lead to him.'

'And the PTL Network?'

'We're talking too much, Jack. I have work to do here.'

Without taking his eyes off me he stooped to the floor, picked up and then emptied the pillowcase. He reached down and felt around in my belongings, his eyes always on me. Unsatisfied, he did the same with my computer bag, until he came up with the vial of pills I had gotten at the hospital. He glanced down quickly at the label, read it and looked back at me with a smile.

'Tylenol with codeine,' he said and smiled. 'This is going to work out nicely. Take one, Jack. Take two, in fact.'

He tossed the vial to me and I instinctively caught it.

'I can't,' I said. 'I took one a couple hours ago. I can't take any for another two hours.'

'Take two, Jack. Now.'

His voice had stayed in a steady monologue but the look in his eyes chilled me. I fumbled with the cap and finally managed to open the vial.

'I need water.'

'No water, Jack. Take the pills.'

I put two of the pills into my mouth and tried to act as if I had swallowed them as I moved them under my tongue.

'Okay.'

'Open wide, Jack.'

I did and he leaned forward to look but he never came close enough for me to take a swing at the gun. He stayed out of reach.

'Know what I think? I think they're under your tongue, Jack. But that's okay because they'll dissolve. It'll just take a little extra time. I've got the –'

There was another creaking sound and he looked around but then quickly back at me.

'I've got the time.'

'You wrote those PTL files. You're the Eidolon.'

'Yes, I am the Eidolon, thank you. And to answer your earlier questions, I learned of the PTL board from Beltran. He was kind enough to be on-line the night I paid my visit to him. So I took his place on the net, so to speak. I used his passwords and later had the systems operator change them to Edgar and Perry. I'm afraid Mr Gomble never knew that he had a . . . fox in the henhouse, to use your turn of phrase.'

I looked at the mirror to my right and in it I could see the reflection of the Valley lights behind me. All those lights, all those people, I thought, and no one to see or help me. I felt the shudder of fear move through me, stronger.

'You have to relax, Jack,' Backus said in a calming monotone. 'That's the key. Are you feeling the codeine yet?'

The pills had broken up under my tongue and filled my mouth with an acrid taste.

'What are you going to do to me?'

'I'm going to do for you what I did for all of them. You wanted to know about the Poet? You are going to know all there is to know. Everything. Firsthand knowledge, Jack. You see, you are the choice. Remember what the fax said? The choice has been made, he's in my sights. That was you, Jack. All along.'

'Backus, you sick fuck! You –'

My outburst jarred some of the debris loose in my mouth and I swallowed it before I could stop. Backus, seemingly knowing what had happened, burst out laughing but then abruptly cut it off. He glared at me and I could see a dim light in his unblinking eyes. I realized then how mad he was and it dawned on me that because Rachel was not the one, the thing that I had believed was part of her misdirection might in actuality be part of the real

Poet's killing pattern. The condoms, the sexual aspects. It could all be part of his killing program.

'What did you do to my brother?'

'That was between him and me. Personal.'

'Tell me.'

He exhaled.

'Nothing, Jack. Nothing. He was the one who wouldn't go along with the program. He was my one failure. But now I have the closest thing to a second chance. I won't fail this time.'

I looked down at the ground. I could feel the effects of the painkillers beginning to move through me. I squeezed my eyes shut and balled my fists but it was too late. The poison was in my blood.

'There's nothing you can do,' Backus said. 'Just relax, Jack, let it take you. Soon it will all be over.'

'You're not going to get away. There's no way Rachel's not going to see this for what it was.'

'You know, Jack, I think you are one hundred percent correct. She'll know. She may already. That's why I'm leaving after this. You are the last chore on my list, then I take my leave.'

I didn't get it.

'Leaving?'

'I'm sure Rachel already has her suspicions. That's why I've had to keep sending her to Florida. But it's only a temporary deflection. Soon enough she'll know. That's why it's time to shed the skin and move on. I've got to be me, Jack.'

His face lit up with the last line. I thought he was about to sing it but he didn't.

'How's it feeling now, Jack? A little light-headed?'

I didn't reply but he knew the answer was yes. I felt like I was beginning to slip into a void of darkness, a boat going over the falls. All the while Backus just watched, talking in his calm monotone, using my name often.

'Let it work itself through you, Jack. Just enjoy these moments. Think about your brother. Think about what you are going to say to him. I think you should tell him what a great investigator you turned out to be. Two in the family, that's something. Think of Sean's face. Smiling. Smiling at you, Jack. Now let your eyes close until you can see him. Go ahead. Nothing's going to happen. You're safe, Jack.'

I couldn't help it. My eyelids were drooping. I tried to look away from him. I stared at the lights in the mirror but the fatigue still grabbed me and took me under. I closed my eyes.

'That's good, Jack. Excellent. Do you see Sean now?'

I nodded, then I felt his hand on my left wrist. He moved it onto the arm of the chair. Then he did the same with my right arm.

'Perfect, Jack. You're a wonderful subject. So cooperative. Now I don't want you to feel any pain. No pain, Jack. No matter what happens here, you will not feel any pain, do you understand that?'

'Yes,' I said.

'I don't want you to move, Jack. In fact, Jack, you cannot move. Your arms are like dead weights. You cannot move them. Isn't that right?'

'Yes,' I said.

My eyes were still closed and my chin was resting on my chest but I was totally aware of my surroundings. It was as if my mind and body had separated. It was as if I was looking down from above at myself in the chair.

'Open your eyes now, Jack.'

I did as I was told and saw Backus standing before me. His gun was holstered under his open jacket and in one hand he now held a long steel needle. This was my chance. The gun was in the holster but I could not move from the chair or reach out to him. My mind could no longer send messages to my body. I sat motionless and could only watch as he matter-of-factly pressed the point of the needle into my unbandaged palm. He repeated the procedure with two of my fingers. I made no move to stop it.

'That's good, Jack. I think you are ready for me now. Remember, arms like dead weights. You just can't move them no matter how much you want to. You can't speak, no matter how much you want to. But keep your eyes open, Jack, you don't want to miss this.'

He stepped back and looked at me with an appraising look.

'Who's best now, Jack?' he asked. 'Who's the better man? Who has won and who has lost?'

My mind filled with revulsion. I couldn't move my arms or speak but still felt the energy wave of absolute fear go screaming through me. I felt tears form in my eyes but they didn't fall. I watched as his hands went to his belt buckle and he said, 'I don't even have to use rubbers anymore, Jack.'

Just as he said that the light in the alcove behind him went out. Then I saw movement in the shadows left behind and heard her voice. Rachel.

'Don't move an inch, Bob. Not even an inch.'

She said it calmly and confidently. Backus froze, his eyes on mine, as if he could see her reflection in them. They were dead eyes. His right hand, shielded from Rachel's view, started moving inside his jacket. I wanted to call out a warning but I could not. At once, I strained every muscle of my body to move just an inch and my left leg kicked out from the chair impotently.

But it was enough. The hold Backus had was losing its grip.

'Rachel!' I yelled just as Backus pulled his gun from his holster and spun around on her.

There was an exchange of shots and Backus was launched backward onto the floor. I heard the shattering of one of the glass panels and the cool evening air rushed into the room as Backus scrambled to cover behind the chair I sat in.

Rachel dipped around the corner, grabbed the lamp and jerked it away from the socket. The house plunged into a darkness only interrupted by the stray light from the Valley below. Backus fired twice more at her, the report of his weapon so close to my head it was deafening. I felt him jerk the chair backward to give him better cover. I was like a man coming out of a deep dream, struggling just to move. As I began to pull myself up, his hand clamped over my shoulder and pulled me back down into the chair. It held me in place.

'Rachel,' Backus called out. 'You shoot and you hit him, you want that? Put the gun down and come out. We'll talk about this.'

'Forget it, Rachel,' I called. 'He'll kill us both. Shoot him! Shoot him!'

Rachel swung around the bullet-pocked wall once more. This time she was low to the ground. The barrel of her gun took a bead on a spot just over my right shoulder but she hesitated. Backus didn't. He fired twice more as Rachel dove back to cover and I saw the corner of the alcove entrance explode in plaster dust and debris.

'Rachel!' I yelled.

I dug the heels of both shoes into the carpet and in one great burst of what strength I could command I shoved the chair back as hard and as quick as I could.

The move surprised Backus. I felt the chair hit him solidly, its impact knocking him away from cover. At that moment Rachel wheeled around the corner of the alcove and the room exploded in the light of another round being fired from her gun.

Behind me I heard a shriek from Backus and then silence. My eyes now adjusted to the dim light, I saw Rachel step out of the alcove and come toward me. She held her gun raised in both hands, her elbows locked. The weapon was pointed past me. I slowly turned as she stepped by. At the precipice, she pointed the gun down toward the darkness into which Backus had fallen. She stood stock still for at least a half a minute before being satisfied that he was gone.

Silence gripped the house. I felt the cool night air against my skin. She finally turned and came to me. Grabbing my arm, she pulled me up until I was standing.

'Come on, Jack,' she said. 'Come out of it. Are you hurt? Are you hit?'

'Sean.'

'What?'

'Nothing. Are you all right?'

'I think so. Are you hit?'

I noticed her looking at the floor behind me and turned around. There was blood on the floor. And shattered glass.

'No, that's not me,' I said. 'You hit him. Or the glass got him.'

I stepped back to the edge with her. There was only blackness below. The only sounds were the breeze through the trees down there and traffic noises filtering up from further down.

'Rachel, I'm sorry,' I said. 'I thought it . . . I thought it was you. I'm sorry.'

'Don't say it, Jack. We'll talk about it later.'

'I thought you were on a plane.'

'After I talked to you I knew something wasn't right. Then Brad Hazelton called and told me what you had called him about. I decided to talk to you before I left. I went to the hotel and saw you leaving with Backus. I don't know why but I followed. I guess it was because Bob had sent me to Florida before when he should have sent Gordon. I didn't trust him anymore.'

'How much did you hear up here?'

'Enough. I just couldn't make a move until he holstered his weapon. I'm sorry you had to go through all of that, Jack.'

She stepped back from the edge but I stayed there, staring into the darkness.

'I didn't ask him about the others. I didn't ask him why.'

'What others?'

'Sean, the others. Beltran got what he deserved. But why Sean? Why the others?'

'There's no explanation, Jack. And if there was, we'll never know it now. My car's down the road a bit. I need to go back and call for backup and a helicopter to search the canyon. To make sure. I better call the hospital, too.'

'Why?'

'To tell them how many of those pills you've taken and to see what we should do about it.'

She started walking toward the entrance alcove.

'Rachel,' I called after her. 'Thanks.'

'Anytime, Jack.'

50

Pretty soon after Rachel left I passed out on the couch. The sound of a close helicopter invaded my dreams but not enough to wake me. Finally, when I awoke on my own, it was three in the morning. I was taken to the thirteenth floor of the federal building and placed in a small interview room. Two dour-faced agents I had never met before asked me questions for the next five hours, going over my story again and again until I was sick of regurgitating it. For this interview they did not have a stenographer sit in the corner of the room with her machine because this time we were talking about one of their own and I had the feeling that they wanted to sculpt my story into the form that could best serve them before putting it down on the record.

Sometime after eight they finally said I could go down to the cafeteria for breakfast before they brought the stenographer in and made a formal record. By then we had been over the story so many times I knew exactly how they wanted me to answer nearly every question. I wasn't hungry but I wanted out of that room and away from them so badly I would have said yes to anything. At least they didn't escort me down to the cafeteria like a prisoner.

I found Rachel sitting there, alone at a table. I bought a coffee and a sugar doughnut that looked like it was three days old and went over.

'Can I sit here?'

'It's a free country.'

'Sometimes I wonder. Those guys, Cooper and Kelley, they've held me in that room up there for five hours.'

'You've got to understand something. You're the messenger, Jack. They know you are going to go out from here and tell the story in newspapers, on TV, probably a book. The whole world will know about the FBI's one bad apple. It doesn't matter how much good we do or how many bad guys we stop, the fact that there was a bad guy among us is going to be a big, big story. You are going to be rich and we are going to have to live with what comes after. That, in a nutshell, is why Cooper and Kelley aren't treating you like a prima donna.'

I studied her for a few moments. It looked like she had eaten a full breakfast. I could see egg yolk smeared on her empty plate.

'Good morning, Rachel,' I said. 'Maybe we can start over.'

That just got her mad.

'Look, Jack, I'm not going to treat you gently, either. Just how do you expect me to react to you now?'

'I don't know. The whole time with those guys I've been answering their questions but doing nothing but thinking about you. About us.'

I studied her face for reaction but got none. She was looking down at her plate.

'Look, I could try to explain to you all the reasons I thought it was you but it wouldn't matter. It all comes down to me, Rachel. Something in me is missing and . . . I couldn't accept what you offered without some suspicion, some kind of cynicism. It was from that small doubt that everything grew and got blown out of proportion . . . Rachel, you have my apology and my promise that if I were given a new chance with you I would work to overcome it, to fill that void. And I promise you that I would succeed.'

Still nothing, not even eye contact. I became resigned. It was over.

'Rachel, can I ask you something?'

'What is it?'

'Your father. And you . . . Did he hurt you?'

'Do you mean did he fuck me?'

I just looked at her, silently.

'That's part of me and my life I don't have to talk to anyone about.'

I turned my coffee cup on the table, staring at it like it was the most interesting thing I'd ever seen. Now I was the one who couldn't look up.

'Well, I've got to get back up there,' I finally said. 'They only gave me fifteen minutes.'

I made a move to stand up.

'Have you told them about me?' she asked.

I stopped.

'About us? No, I've been trying to avoid that.'

'Don't hold back with them, Jack. They already know, anyway.'

'You told them?'

'Yes. There was no point in trying to hide anything from them.'

I nodded.

'What if I tell them and they ask if we still are . . . if we still have a relationship?'

'Tell them the jury's still out.'

I nodded again and stood up. Her use of the word jury reminded me of my own thoughts of the night before when in my mind, as the jury of one, I had reached a verdict about her. I thought it was only appropriate now that she should be weighing the evidence against me.

'Let me know when you reach a verdict.'

I dropped the doughnut into the trash can by the cafeteria door on my way out.

It was almost noon before I was finished with Kelley and Cooper. It was also not until then that I heard about Backus. Walking through the field office I noticed how empty it was. The doors to all the group rooms were open and the desks empty. It was like a detective bureau during a cop's funeral, and in a way it was. I almost walked back to the interrogation room where I had left my inquisitors to ask them what was going on. But I knew they didn't like me and wouldn't tell me anything they didn't want or have to tell me.

As I passed the communications room, I heard the chatter of two-way radio talk. I looked in and saw Rachel sitting alone in the room. She had a microphone console in front of her on a desk. I walked in.

'Hey.'

'Hey.'

'I'm done. They told me I could leave. Where is everyone? What's going on?'

'They're all out looking for him.'

'Backus?'

She nodded.

'I thought . . .' I didn't finish. It was obvious now that he hadn't been found at the bottom of the drop-off. I hadn't asked before because I just assumed that his body had been recovered. 'Jesus. How could he have . . .'

'Survived? Who knows? He was gone by the time they got down there with their flashlights and dogs. There was a tall eucalyptus tree. They found blood in the upper branches. The theory is that he fell into the tree. It broke his fall. The dogs lost his scent on the road further down the hill. The helicopter was pretty much useless except for keeping everybody on the hillside up half the night. Everybody but you. They're still out there. We've put everybody out on the street, the hospitals. So far, nothing.'

'Jesus.'

Backus was still out there. Somewhere. I couldn't believe it.

'I wouldn't worry,' she said. 'The possibility that he would go after you, or me for that matter, is considered very remote. His goal now is escape. Survival.'

'That's not what I meant,' I said, though I guess it was. 'It's just scary. Someone like that out there . . . Have they come up with anything about . . . why?'

'They're working on it. Brass and Brad are on it. But he's going to be a tough one to crack. There was just no sign at all. The wall between his two lives was as thick as a bank vault's door. On some of them we just never get through. The unexplainable ones. All you know is that it was there inside them. The seed. And then one day it metastasized . . . and he began doing what he was probably only fantasizing about before.'

I didn't say anything. I just wanted her to continue, to talk to me.

'They'll start with the father,' she said. 'I heard Brass was going up to New York to see him today. That's one visit I wouldn't want to have to make. Your son follows you into the bureau and turns out to be your worst nightmare. What's that line that Nietzsche said? "Whoever fights monsters . . ." '

' "Should see to it that in the process he does not become a monster." '

'Yeah.'

We were both quiet for a few moments, thinking about that.

'Why aren't you out there?' I finally asked.

'Because I've been assigned to desk duty until I'm cleared on the shooting . . . and my other actions.'

'Isn't that academic? Especially since he isn't even dead.'

'It should be, but there are other factors.'

'Us? Are we one of those factors?'

She nodded.

'You could say my judgment is being questioned. Getting involved with a witness and journalist is not what you'd call standard FBI practice. Then there's this that came in this morning.'

She turned over a sheet of paper and handed it to me. It was a faxed copy of a grainy black-and-white photo. It was a picture of me sitting on a table and Rachel standing between my spread legs, kissing me. It took me a moment to place it and then I realized it was the hospital emergency room suite.

'Remember that doctor you saw looking in on us?' Rachel asked. 'Well, he wasn't a doctor. He was some freelance piece of shit who sold the photo to the *National Enquirer*. Must've snuck in there in his disguise. It will be on the cashier stand at every supermarket in the country by Tuesday. In keeping with their aboveboard journalistic ethics they faxed this over and asked for an interview or at least a comment. What do you think, Jack? How about "fuck you" for a comment? Think they'll print that?'

I put the fax photo down and looked at her.

'I'm sorry, Rachel.'

'You know, that's all you can say now. "Sorry, Rachel. Sorry, Rachel." It doesn't look very good on you, Jack.'

I almost said it again but instead just nodded. I looked at her, brooding for a moment about how I could ever have made the mistake I made. I knew then it had cost me my chance with her. Feeling sorry for myself, my mind ran through all the parts that had made the whole and had convinced me of something my heart should have known was wrong. I was looking for excuses but knew there weren't any.

'Remember that day we met and you took me down to Quantico?'

'Yes, I remember.'

'That was Backus's office you put me in, wasn't it? To make my calls. Why'd you do that? I thought it was your office.'

'I don't have an office. I have a desk and work space. I put you in there so you'd have some privacy. Why?'

'Nothing. It was just one of the parts that seemed . . . to fit so well before. The calendar on the desk, it showed he was on vacation when Orsulak . . . So I thought you lied to me about not having a vacation in so long.'

'We're not going to talk about this now.'

'Then when? If we don't talk about it now we never will. I made a mistake, Rachel. I've got no acceptable excuse. But I want you to know what I knew. I want you to understand what I –'

'I don't care!'

'Maybe you never cared.'

'Don't try to put it on me. You're the one who fucked up. I wasn't the one who –'

'What did you do that night, the first night, after you left my room? I called and you weren't there. I knocked on your door and you weren't there. I went out in the hall and I saw Thorson. He was coming from the drugstore. You sent him didn't you?'

She looked down at the desk for the longest time.

'At least answer that, Rachel.'

'I saw him in the hallway, too,' she said softly. 'Earlier. After I left you. It made me so angry that he was there, that Backus brought him out. It all boiled up. I wanted to hurt him. Humiliate him. I needed . . . something.'

So with a promise that she'd be waiting, she sent him out to the drugstore for a condom. But she was gone when he got back.

'I was in my room when you called and knocked. I didn't answer because I thought it was him. He must've done the same because twice people knocked. Twice they called. I never answered.'

I nodded.

'I'm not proud of what I did to him,' she said. 'Especially now.'

'Everybody has things they're not proud of, Rachel. It doesn't stop them from going on. It shouldn't.'

She didn't say anything.

'I'm going now, Rachel. I hope things work out for you. And I hope you'll call me sometime. I'll be waiting.'

'Good-bye, Jack.'

As I moved away from her I brought my hand up. With one finger I traced the line of her jaw. Our eyes briefly met and held. Then I walked out.

51

He huddled in the dark of the storm-drainage tunnel, resting and concentrating his mind on mastering the pain. Already he knew there was infection. The wound was minor in terms of damage, a through-and-through shot that tore an upper abdominal muscle but little else before leaving, but it was dirty and he could feel the poisons beginning to move through his body, making him want to lie down and sleep.

He looked down the length of the dark tunnel. Only stray light leaking from somewhere up above made it this far down. Lost light. He pushed himself up the slippery wall until he was standing and then he began moving again. One day, he thought as he moved. Make it through the first day and you'll make it through the rest. It was the mantra he repeated in his mind.

In a sense, there was relief. Despite the pain and now the hunger, there was the relief. No more separation. The facade was gone. Backus was gone. Now there was only Eidolon. And Eidolon would triumph. They were nothing before him and could do nothing now to stop him.

'NOTHING!'

His voice echoed down the tunnel into the blackness and disappeared. With one hand clamped over his wound he headed that way.

52

In late spring a city Department of Water and Power inspector, investigating the source of a foul odor that had drawn complaints from the residents living above, found the remains of the body in the tunnels.

The remains of *a* body. It carried his identification and FBI badge and the clothes were his. It was found, what was left of it, laid out on a concrete shelf in an underground intersection of two stormwater drainage culverts. The cause of death was unknown because advanced decomposition – sped along by the damp, fetid surroundings of the drainage culvert – and disturbance of the remains by animals precluded accurate autopsy results. The medical examiner did find what appeared to be a wound channel and a cracked rib in the rotting flesh but no bullet fragments that could conclusively tie the wound to Rachel's gun.

As far as the identification went, it, too, was inconclusive. There was the badge and the ID and the clothing but nothing else that proved that these were indeed the remains of Special Agent Robert Backus Jr. The animals that had attacked the body – if it had truly been animals – had made off with the complete lower mandible and an upper bridge, which precluded a comparison with dental records.

That seemed too convenient to me. And others. Brad Hazelton called me to fill me in on these facts. He said the bureau was officially closing the case but there would be those who would still look for him. Unofficially. He said that some people viewed the discovery in the drainage tunnel as nothing more than a skin Backus had left behind, probably a homeless man he had encountered in the pipes. He said they believed Backus was still out there and so did I.

Brad Hazelton told me that while the official search for Backus might be over, the effort to explore the psychological motivations was continuing. But cracking the nut of Backus's pathology was proving difficult. Agents spent three days in his condominium near Quantico but found nothing remotely indicative of his secret life. No souvenirs of his kills, no clipped newspaper stories, nothing.

There were only little things known, small clues. A perfectionist father who never spared the rod. An obsessive-compulsive fixation on cleanliness – I remembered his desk at Quantico and his straightening of the calendar after I had sat there. An engagement broken off years earlier by a bride-to-be who told Brass Doran that Backus required her to shower immediately before and after they made love. A high school friend who came forward and told Hazelton that once Backus had confided to him that when he wet the bed as a boy, his father would handcuff him to the towel bar in the shower – a story denied by Robert Sr.

But these were only details, not answers. They were fragments of the much larger fabric of personality that they could only guess at. I remembered what Rachel had told me once. That it was like trying to put together a shattered mirror. Each piece reflects a part of the subject. But if the subject moves, so does the reflection.

I have stayed in Los Angeles since it all happened. I had my hand repaired by a Beverly Hills surgeon and it only hurts now at the end of a long day at the computer.

I've rented a small house in the hills and on good days I can see the sun's reflection on the Pacific almost fifteen miles away. On bad days the view is depressing and I keep the blinds closed. Sometimes at night I can hear the coyotes whining and barking at each other in Nichols Canyon. It is warm here and I have not had the desire to return to Colorado. I talk to my mother and father and Riley regularly – more so than when I was there – but I still fear the ghosts back there more than the ones here.

Officially, I am on leave from the *Rocky.* Greg Glenn wants me to come back but I have held off on an answer to him. I have the leverage. I'm now a celebrity journalist – I've been on 'Nightline' and 'Larry King Live' – and Greg wants to keep me on staff. So for now, I am on extended leave without pay while writing my book.

My agent sold the book and film rights to my story for more money than I could make in ten years working at the *Rocky.* But most of the money, when I get it all, will go into a trust fund for Riley's unborn baby. Sean's baby. I don't think I could manage with so much in my own bank account and I don't feel deserving of it anyway. It's blood money. I put aside just enough of the first payment from the publisher for living expenses here in L.A. and the possibility that I might make a trip to Italy after I finished the first draft.

That's where Rachel is. Hazelton told me. When they told her she was being transferred out of the BSS unit, out of Quantico, she took her own leave and went overseas. I've waited to hear from her but there has been no word. I don't think there will be now and I don't think I'll be going to Italy as she once suggested. At night, the ghost that haunts me the most is the thing inside of me that led me to doubt the very thing I wanted most.

53

Death is my beat. I have made my living from it and forged a professional reputation on it. I have profited by it. It has always been around me but never as close as those moments with Gladden and Backus, when it breathed right into my face, put its eye to mine and made a grab for me.

I remember their eyes the most. I can't sleep without first thinking of their eyes. Not for what was in them but for what was missing, what was not there. Behind them was only darkness. An empty despair so intriguing that I find myself fighting sleep to think about it sometimes. And when I think of them I can't help but think of Sean as well. My twin. I wonder if he looked into the eyes of his killer at the end. I wonder if he saw what I saw. An evil as pure and as scarring as a flame. I still mourn for Sean. I always will. And I wonder as I watch and wait for the Eidolon when I'll see that flame again.

Acknowledgments

I would like to thank the following people for their fine work and support.

Many thanks to my editor, Michael Pietsch, for long and hard work as always on this manuscript and to his colleagues at Little, Brown, particularly my friend Tom Rusch, for all of their efforts on my behalf. Once again Betty Power came through with a wonderful job of copyediting and more. Also to my agents, Philip Spitzer and Joel Gotler, who were there when it was only an idea, thanks again.

My wife, Linda, and members of my family provided invaluable help to me by reading the early drafts and showing me where I went wrong – repeatedly. And I am most indebted to my father's brother, the Reverend Donald C. Connelly, for his stories about growing up a twin.

I'd like to thank Michele Brustin and David Percelay for their creative advice and, in matters of research, thanks to Bill Ryan and Richard Whittingham, the fine Chicago writer, along with Rick and Kim Garza.

And lastly I would also like to thank the many booksellers I have come to know in the last few years who have put my stories into the hands of the readers.

Blood Work

This is for Terry Hansen
and Myra McCaleb.

HER LAST THOUGHTS were of Raymond. She would see him soon. He would awaken as he always did, his welcome-home embrace warm and sustaining.

She smiled and Mr Kang, behind the counter, smiled back, thinking her brightness was for him. He smiled at her every night, never knowing that her thoughts and smiles were actually for Raymond, for the moment still to come.

The sound of the bell shaken by the opening door behind her made only a peripheral entry into her thoughts. She had the two dollar bills ready and was handing them across the counter to Mr Kang. But he didn't take them. She then noticed that his eyes were no longer on her but focused on the door. His smile was gone and his mouth was opening slightly as if to form a word that wouldn't quite come.

She felt a hand grip her right shoulder from behind. The coldness of steel pressed against her left temple. A shower of light crashed across her vision. Blinding light. In that moment she saw a glimpse of Raymond's sweet face, then everything turned dark.

1

McCaleb saw her before she saw him. He was coming down the main dock, past the row of millionaires' boats, when he saw the woman standing in the stern of *The Following Sea.* It was half past ten on a Saturday morning and the warm whisper of spring had brought a lot of people out to the San Pedro docks. McCaleb was finishing the walk he took every morning – completely around Cabrillo Marina, out along the rock jetty and back. He was huffing by this part of the walk, but he slowed his pace even more as he approached the boat. His first feeling was annoyance – the woman had boarded his boat uninvited. But as he got closer, he put that aside and wondered who she was and what she wanted.

She wasn't dressed for boating. She had on a loose summer dress that came to mid-thigh. The breeze off the water threatened to lift it and so she kept one hand at her side to keep it down. McCaleb couldn't see her feet yet but he guessed by the taut lines of the muscles he saw in her brown legs that she wasn't wearing boat shoes. She had raised heels on. McCaleb's immediate read was that she was there to make some kind of impression on someone.

McCaleb was dressed to make no impression at all. He had on an old pair of jeans ripped by wear, not for style, and a T-shirt from the Catalina Gold Cup tournament a few summers before. The clothes were spattered with stains – mostly fish blood, some of his own blood, marine polyurethane and engine oil. They had served him as both fishing and work clothes. His plan was to use the weekend to work on the boat and he was dressed accordingly.

He became more self-conscious about his appearance as he drew closer to the boat and could see the woman better. He pulled the foam pads of his portable off his ears and turned off the CD in the middle of Howlin' Wolf singing 'I Ain't Superstitious'.

'Can I help you?' he asked before stepping down into his own boat.

His voice seemed to startle her and she turned away from the sliding door that led into the boat's salon. McCaleb figured she had knocked on the glass and was waiting, expecting him to be inside.

'I'm looking for Terrell McCaleb.'

She was an attractive woman in her early thirties, a good decade or so younger than McCaleb. There was a sense of familiarity about her but he couldn't quite place it. It was one of those déjà vu things. At the same time he felt the stir of recognition, it quickly flitted away and he knew he was mistaken, that he did not know this woman. He remembered faces. And hers was nice enough not to forget.

She had mispronounced the name, saying Mc-*Cal*-ub instead of Mc-*Kay*-Leb, and used the formal first name that no one ever used except the reporters. That's when he began to understand. He knew now what had brought her to the boat. Another lost soul come to the wrong place.

'McCaleb,' he corrected. 'Terry McCaleb.'

'Sorry. I, uh, I thought maybe you were inside. I didn't know if it was okay to walk on the boat and knock.'

'But you did anyway.'

She ignored the reprimand and went on. It was as if what she was doing and what she had to say had been rehearsed.

'I need to talk to you.'

'Well, I'm kind of busy at the moment.'

He pointed to the open bilge hatch she was lucky not to have fallen into and the tools he had left spread out on a drop cloth by the stern transom.

'I've been walking around, looking for this boat, for almost an hour,' she said. 'It won't take long. My name is Graciela Rivers and I wanted –'

'Look, Miss Rivers,' he said, holding his hands up and interrupting. 'I'm really . . . You read about me in the newspaper, right?'

She nodded.

'Well, before you start your story, I have to tell you, you're not the first one to come out here and find me or to get my number and call me. And I'm just going to tell you what I told all of the others. I'm not looking for a job. So if this is about you wanting to hire me or have me help you some way, I'm sorry, but I can't do it. I'm not looking for that kind of work.'

She didn't say anything and he felt a pang of sympathy for her, just as he had for the others who had come to him before her.

'Look, I do know a couple of private investigators I can recommend. Good ones that will work hard and won't rip you off.'

He stepped over to the stern gunwale, picked up the sunglasses he had forgotten to take on his walk and put them on, signaling the end of the conversation. But the gesture and his words went by her.

'The article said you were good. It said you hated it whenever somebody got away.'

He put his hands in his pockets and hiked his shoulders.

'You have to remember something. It was never me alone. I had partners, I had the lab teams, I had the whole bureau behind me. It's a lot different than one guy running around out there on his own. A lot different. I probably couldn't help you even if I wanted to.'

She nodded and he thought that he had gotten through to her and that would be the end of this one. He started thinking about the valve job on one of the boat's engines that he'd planned to complete over the weekend.

But he was wrong about her.

'I think you could help me,' she said. 'Maybe help yourself, too.'

'I don't need the money. I do okay.'

'I'm not talking about money.'

He looked at her for a beat before replying.

'I don't know what you mean by that,' he said, injecting exasperation into his voice. 'But I can't help you. I've got no badge anymore and I'm not a private investigator. It would be illegal for me to act as one or to accept money without a state license. If you read the story in the paper, then you know what happened to me. I'm not even supposed to be driving a car.'

He pointed toward the parking lot beyond the row of docks and the gangway.

'You see the one wrapped up like a Christmas present? That's mine. It's sitting there until I get my doctor's approval to drive again. What kind of investigator would that make me? I'd be taking the bus.'

She ignored his protest and just looked at him with a resolute expression that unnerved him. He didn't know how he was going to get her off the boat.

'I'll go get those names for you.'

He walked around her and slid open the salon door. After going in, he pulled the door shut behind him. He needed the separation. He went to the drawers below the chart table and began looking for his phone book. He hadn't needed it in so long he wasn't sure where it was. He glanced out through the door and watched her step to the stern and lean her hips against the transom as she waited.

There was reflective film on the glass of the door. She couldn't see him watching her. The sense of familiarity came over him again and he tried to place her face. He found her very striking. Dark almond-shaped eyes that seemed both sad and understanding of some secret at the same time. He knew he would easily remember if he had ever met her or even just observed her before. But nothing came. His eyes instinctively went to her hands in search of a ring. There was none. He had been right about her shoes. She wore sandals with two-inch cork heels. Her toenails were painted pink and showed off against her soft brown skin. He wondered if this was how she looked all the time, or if she had dressed to entice him into taking the job.

He found his phone book in the second drawer and quickly looked up the names Jack Lavelle and Tom Kimball. He wrote their names and numbers on an old marine service flier and opened the slider. She was opening her purse as he stepped out. He held up the paper.

'Here are two names. Lavelle is LAPD retired and Kimball was with the bureau. I worked with both and either will do a good job for you. Pick one and call. Make sure you tell him you got his name from me. He'll take care of you.'

She didn't take the names from him. Instead she pulled a photo out of her purse and handed it to him. McCaleb took it without thinking. He realized immediately that this was a mistake. In his hand was a photo of a smiling woman watching a small boy blowing out candles on a birthday cake. McCaleb counted seven candles. At first he thought it was a picture of Rivers a few years younger. But then he realized it wasn't her. The woman in the photo had a rounder face and thinner lips. She wasn't as beautiful as Graciela Rivers. Though both had deep brown eyes, the eyes of the woman in the photo did not have the same intensity as the eyes of the woman now watching him.

'Your sister?'

'Yes. And her son.'

'Which one?'

'What?'

'Which one is dead?'

The question was his second mistake, compounding the first by drawing him further in. He knew the moment he asked it that he should have just insisted that she take the names of the two private detectives and been done with it.

'My sister. Gloria Torres. We called her Glory. That's her son, Raymond.'

He nodded and handed the photo back but she didn't take it. He knew she wanted him to ask what had happened but he was finally putting on the brakes.

'Look, this isn't going to work,' he finally said. 'I know what you're doing. It doesn't work on me.'

'You mean you have no sympathy?'

He hesitated as the anger boiled up in his throat.

'I have sympathy. You read the newspaper story, you know what happened to me. Sympathy was my problem all along.'

He swallowed it back and tried to clear away any ill feeling. He knew she was consumed by horrible frustrations. McCaleb had known hundreds of people like her. Loved ones taken from them without reason. No arrests, no convictions, no closure. Some of them were left zombies, their lives irrevocably changed. Lost souls. Graciela Rivers was one of them now. She had to be or she wouldn't have tracked him down. He knew that no matter what she said to him or how angry he got, she didn't deserve to be hit with his own frustrations as well.

'Look,' he said. 'I just can't do this. I'm sorry.'

He put a hand on her arm to lead her back to the dock step. Her skin was warm. He felt the strong muscle beneath the softness. He offered the photo again but she still refused to take it.

'Look at it again. Please. Just one more time and then I'll leave you alone. Tell me if you feel anything else?'

He shook his head and made a feeble hand gesture as if to say it made no difference to him.

'I was an FBI agent, not a psychic.'

But he made a show of holding the photo up and looking at it anyway. The woman and the boy seemed happy. It was a celebration. Seven candles. McCaleb remembered that his parents were still together when he turned seven. But not much longer. His eyes were drawn to the boy more than the woman. He wondered how the boy would get along now without his mother.

'I'm sorry, Miss Rivers. I really am. But there is nothing I can do for you. Do you want this back or not?'

'I have a double of it. You know, two for the price of one. I thought you'd want to keep that one.'

For the first time he felt the undertow in the emotional current. There was something else at play but he didn't know what. He looked closely at Graciela Rivers and had the sense that if he took another step, asked the obvious question, he would be pulled under.

He couldn't help himself.

'Why would I want to keep it if I'm not going to be able to help you?'

She smiled in a sad sort of way.

'Because she's the woman who saved your life. I thought from time to time you might want to remind yourself of what she looked like, who she was.'

He stared at her for a long moment but he wasn't really looking at Graciela Rivers. He was looking inward, running what she had just said through memory and knowledge and coming up short of its meaning.

'What are you talking about?'

It was all he could manage to ask. He had the sense that control of the conversation and everything else was tilting away from him and sliding across the deck to her. The undertow had him now. It was carrying him out.

She raised her hand but reached past the photo he was still holding out to her. She placed her palm on his chest and ran it down the front of his shirt, her fingers tracing the thick rope of the scar beneath. He let her do it. He stood there frozen and let her do it.

'Your heart,' she said. 'It was my sister's. She was the one who saved your life.'

2

Out of the corner of his eye he could just see the monitor. The screen was grainy silver and black, the heart like an undulating ghost, the rivets and staples that closed off blood vessels showing like black buckshot in his chest.

'Almost there,' a voice said.

It came from behind his right ear. Bonnie Fox. Always calm and comforting, professional. Soon he saw the snaking line of the scope move into the monitor's X-ray field, following the path of the artery and entering the heart. He closed his eyes. He hated the tug, the one they say you won't feel but you always do.

'Okay, you shouldn't feel this,' she said.

'Right.'

'Don't talk.'

Then, there it was. Like the slightest tug on the end of a fishing line, a scrap fish stealing your bait. He opened his eyes and saw the line of the scope, as thin as a fishing line, still deep in the heart.

'Okay, we got it,' she said. 'Coming out now. You did good, Terry.'

He felt her pat his shoulder, though he couldn't turn his head to look at her. The scope was removed and she taped a gauze compress against the incision in his neck. The brace that had held his head at such an uncomfortable angle was unstrapped and he slowly straightened his neck, bringing his hand up to work the stiff muscles. Dr Bonnie Fox's smiling face then hovered above his.

'How you feeling?'

'Can't complain. Now that it's over.'

'I'll see you in a little while. I want to check the blood work and get the tissue over to the lab.'

'I want to talk to you about something.'

'You got it. See you in a bit.'

A few minutes later two nurses wheeled McCaleb's bed out of the cath lab and into an elevator. He hated being treated as an invalid. He could have walked but it was against the rules. After a heart biopsy the patient must be kept horizontal. Hospitals always have rules. Cedars-Sinai seemed to have more than most.

He was taken down to the cardiology unit on the sixth floor. While being wheeled down the east hallway, he passed the rooms of the lucky and the waiting – patients who had received new hearts or were still waiting. They passed one room where McCaleb glanced through the open door and saw a young boy on the bed, his body tied by tubes to a heart-lung machine. A man in a suit sat in the chair on the other side of the bed, his eyes staring at the boy but seeing something else. McCaleb looked away. He knew the score. The kid was running out of time. The machine would only hold him up for so long. Then the man in the suit – the father, McCaleb assumed – would be staring at a casket with the same look.

They were at his room now. He was moved from the gurney onto the bed and left alone. He settled in for the wait. He knew from experience that it could be as long as six hours before Fox showed up, depending on how quickly the blood work was run through the lab and how soon she came by to pick up the report.

He had come prepared. The old leather bag in which he had once carried his computer and the countless case files he had worked on was now stuffed with back issues of magazines he saved for biopsy days.

Two and a half hours later Bonnie Fox came through the door. McCaleb put down the copy of *Boat Restoration* he had been reading.

'Wow, that was fast.'

'It's slow in the lab. How are you feeling?'

'My neck feels like it had somebody's foot on it for a couple hours. You've already been to the lab?'

'Yup.'

'How'd everything come out?'

'It all looks good. No rejection, all the levels look good. I'm very pleased. We might lower your prednisone in another week.'

She spoke as she spread the lab report out on the bed's food table and double-checked the good results. She was referring to the carefully orchestrated mix of drugs that McCaleb took every morning and night. Last he'd counted, he was swallowing eighteen pills in the morning and another sixteen at night. The medicine cabinet on the boat wasn't big enough for all the containers. He had to use one of the storage compartments in the forward berth.

'Good,' he said. 'I'm tired of shaving three times a day.'

Fox folded the report closed and picked the clipboard up off the bed table. Her eyes quickly scanned the checklist of questions he had to answer every time he came in.

'No fever at all?'

'No, I'm clean.'

'And no diarrhea.'

'Nope.'

He knew from her constant drilling and double-checking that fever and diarrhea were the twin harbingers of organ rejection. He took his temperature a minimum of twice a day, along with readings of blood pressure and pulse.

'The vitals look good. Why don't you lean forward?'

She put the clipboard down. With a stethoscope she first warmed with her breath, she listened to his heart at three different spots on his back. Then he lay back and she listened through his chest. She took her own measure of his pulse with two fingers on his neck while she looked at her watch. She was very close to him as she did this. She wore a perfume of orange blossoms, which McCaleb had always associated with older women. And Bonnie Fox was not one of them. He looked up at her, studying her face while she studied her watch.

'Do you ever wonder if we should be doing this?' he asked.

'Don't talk.'

Eventually, she moved her fingers to his wrist and measured the pulse there. After that she pulled the pressure collar off the wall, put it on his arm and took a blood pressure reading, maintaining her silence all the time.

'Good,' she said when she was done.

'Good,' he said.

'Whether we should be doing what?'

It was like her to suddenly continue an interrupted or forgotten bit of conversation. She rarely forgot anything McCaleb said to her. Bonnie Fox was a small woman about McCaleb's age with short hair gone prematurely gray. Her white lab coat hung almost to her ankles because it had been designed for a taller person. Embroidered on the breast pocket was an outline of the cardiopulmonary system, her specialty as a surgeon. She was all business when it came to their meetings. She had an air of confidence and caring, a combination McCaleb had always found rare in physicians – and in the last years there had been many. He returned the confidence and caring. He liked her and trusted her. In his most secret thoughts there had once been a hesitation when he considered he would one day put his life in the hands of this woman. But the hesitation quickly left and caused him only a feeling of guilt. When the time came for the transplant, it had been her smiling face that was the last he had seen as he was put to sleep in pre-op. There had been no hesitation in him by then. And it was her smiling face that welcomed him back to the world with a new heart and new life.

McCaleb took the fact that in the eight weeks since the transplant there had not been a hitch in his recovery as proof his belief in her was valid. In the three years since he had first walked into her office, a bond had developed between them that had gone far beyond the professional. They were good friends now, or so McCaleb believed. They had shared meals a half dozen times and countless spirited debates on everything from genetic cloning to the O. J. Simpson trials – McCaleb had won a hundred bucks from her on the first verdict, easily seeing that her unwavering belief in the justice system had blinded her to the racial realities of the case. She wouldn't bet him on the second.

Whatever the subject, half the time McCaleb found himself taking the opposing opinion just because he liked battling with her. Fox now followed her question with a look that said she was ready for another joust.

'Whether we should be doing *this*,' he said, waving a hand around as if to encompass the whole hospital. 'Taking out organs, putting in new ones.

Sometimes I feel like Frankenstein's monster, other people's parts in me.'

'One other person, one other part. Let's not be so dramatic.'

'But it's the big part, isn't it? You know, when I was with the bureau, we had to qualify on the range every year. You know, shoot at targets. And the best way to qualify was to go for the heart. The circle around the heart on those targets scores more than the head. It's called the ten ring. Highest score.'

'Look, if this is the aren't-we-acting-like-God debate again, I thought we were well past that.'

She shook her head, smiled and looked him over for a few seconds. The smile eventually dropped away.

'What's really wrong?'

'I don't know. I guess I'm feeling guilty.'

'What, about living?'

'I don't know.'

'Don't be ridiculous. We've been through this, too. I have no time for survivor's guilt. Look at the choices here. It's simple. You've got life on one side and then you've got death. Big decision. What is there to be guilty about?'

He raised his hands in surrender. She always put things in their clearest context.

'Typical,' she said, refusing to let him back off. 'You hang around almost two years waiting for a heart, draw your string out and nearly don't even make it, and now you wonder if we should have even given it to you. What's really bothering you, Terry? I don't have time to be bullshitting with you.'

He looked back at her. She had developed a skill at reading him. It was something all the best bureau agents and cops he had known had. He hesitated and then decided to say what was on his mind.

'I guess I want to know how come you didn't tell me that the woman whose heart I got had been murdered.'

She was clearly taken aback. The shock of his statement showed on her face.

'Murdered? What are you talking about?'

'She was murdered.'

'How?'

'I don't know exactly. She got caught in the middle of a robbery in some convenience store up in the Valley. Shot in the head. She died and I got her heart.'

'You're not supposed to know anything about your donor. How do you know this?'

'Because her sister came and saw me on Saturday. She told me the whole thing . . . It sort of changes things, you know?'

Fox sat on the hospital bed and leaned over him. A stern look came over her face.

'First of all, I had no idea where your heart came from. We never do. It came through BOPRA. All we were told was that an organ was available with a blood work match to a recipient we had on call and at the top of our list. That was you. You know how BOPRA works. You watched the film during orientation. We get limited information because it works best that way. I told you exactly what we knew. Female, twenty-six years old, if I remember. Perfect health, perfect blood typing, perfect donor. That's it.'

'Then I'm sorry. I thought maybe you knew and just held that back.'

'I didn't. We didn't. So if we didn't know who and where it came from, how did the sister know who and where it went? How did she find you? This could be some kind of a scam she's –'

'No. It's her. I know.'

'How do you know?'

'The newspaper article last Sunday, that "Whatever Happened to . . ." column in the *Times* Metro section. It said I got the heart on February ninth and that I'd been waiting a long time because my blood type was rare. The sister read it and put it together. She obviously knew when her sister died, knew her heart was donated and knew she also had a rare blood type. She's an ER nurse up at Holy Cross and figured out it was me.'

'It still doesn't mean you have her sister's –'

'She also had the letter I wrote.'

'What letter?'

'The one everybody writes afterward. The anonymous thank you note to the family of your donor. The one the hospital mails. She had mine. I looked at it and it's mine. I remember what I wrote.'

'This is not supposed to happen, Terry. What does she want? Money?'

'No, not money. Don't you see? She wants me to find out who did it. Who killed her sister. The cops never closed it. It's two months later and no arrest. She knows they've given up. Then she sees this story about me in the paper, about what I used to do for the bureau. She figures out I got her sister's heart and thinks maybe I can do what the cops apparently can't. Break the case. She spent an hour walking around the San Pedro marinas looking for my boat Saturday. All she had was the name of the boat from the paper. She came looking for me.'

'This is crazy. Give me this woman's name and I'll –'

'No. I don't want you to do anything to her. Think if you were her and you loved your sister. You'd do what she did, too.'

Fox got off the bed, a wide-eyed look on her face.

'You're not actually thinking of doing this.'

She said it as a statement, a doctor's order. He didn't answer and that in itself was an answer. He could see anger once again working itself into Fox's expression.

'Listen to me. You are in no condition to be doing anything like this. You are sixty days post-transplant surgery and you want to run around playing detective?'

'I'm only thinking about it, okay? I told her I'd think about it. I know the risks. I also know that I'm not an FBI agent anymore. It would be a whole different thing.'

Fox angrily folded her thin arms across her chest.

'You shouldn't even be thinking about it. As your doctor, I am telling you not to do this. That's an order.'

Her voice then changed in tone and softened.

'You have to respect the gift you were given, Terry. This second chance.'

'But that respect goes two ways. If I didn't have her heart, I'd be dead by now. I owe her. It's that –'

'You don't owe her or her family anything more than that note you sent them. That's it. She'd be dead whether you or anybody else got her heart. You are wrong about this.'

He nodded that he understood her point but it wasn't enough for him. He knew that just because something makes sense on an intellectual level, it doesn't play any better in the twists of your guts. She read his thoughts.

'But what?'

'I don't know. It's just that I thought if I ever found out what happened, I would find out it was an accident. That's what I prepared myself for. That's what they tell you in orientation and even you told me when we started. That ninety-nine out of a hundred times it's an accident leading to fatal head injury. Car crash or somebody falls down the steps or dumps their motorcycle. But this is different. It changes things.'

'You keep saying that. How can it be different? The heart is just an organ – a biological pump. It's the same no matter how its original owner dies.'

'An accident I could live with. All that time I was waiting, knowing that somebody had to die for me to live, I was getting myself ready to accept it as an accident. With an accident it's like it was fated or something. But a murder . . . that comes with evil intent attached. It's not happenstance. It means that I'm the benefactor of an act of evil, Doctor, and that's why it's different now.'

Fox was silent for a few moments. She shoved her hands into the side pockets of her lab coat. McCaleb thought that she was finally beginning to see his point.

'That's what my life was about for a long time,' he added quietly. 'I was searching out evil. That was my job. And I was good at it but in the long run it was better than me. It got the best of me. I think – no, I know – that's what took my heart. But now it's like none of that meant anything because here I am, I have this new heart, a new life, this second chance you talk about, and the only reason I have it is because of this evil, hateful thing that someone did.'

He blew out a deep breath before going on.

'She went into that store to get a candy bar for her kid and she ends up – look, it's just different. I can't explain it.'

'You're not making a lot of sense.'

'It's hard for me to put it into the words I want. I just know what I'm feeling. It makes sense to me.'

Fox had a resigned look on her face.

'Look, I know what you're going to want to do. You're going to want to help this lady. But you're not ready. Physically, no way. And emotionally, after hearing what you just said, I don't think you're ready to investigate even a car accident. Remember what I told you about the equilibrium between physical and mental health? One feeds off the other. And I'm scared that what you have going on in your head now is going to affect your physical progress.'

'I understand.'

'No, I don't think you do. You are gambling with your own life here. If this goes south, if you start getting infection or rejection, we're not going to be able to save you, Terry. We waited twenty-two months for that heart you have now. You think another one with matching blood work is going to just pop up because you messed up this one? No chance. I've got a patient down the hall on a machine. He's waiting on a heart that isn't coming. That could be you, Terry. This is your one chance. Do not blow it!'

She reached across the bed and placed her hand on his chest. It reminded him of what Graciela Rivers had done. He felt its warmth there.

'Tell this woman no. Save yourself and tell her no.'

3

The moon was like a balloon being kept aloft by children poking at it with sticks. The masts of dozens of sailboats stood raised beneath it, ready to keep it from falling. McCaleb watched it hover in the black sky until it finally escaped by slipping behind the clouds somewhere out over Catalina. As good a hiding spot as any, he thought, as he looked down at the empty coffee cup in his hand. He missed being able to sit in the stern at the end of the day with an ice-cold beer in one hand and a cigarette in the other. But cigarettes had been part of the problem and were gone for good now. And it would be a few months before the medication therapy would relax enough to allow a dose of alcohol into the mix. For now, if he had just one beer, it might give him what Bonnie Fox called a fatal hangover.

McCaleb got up and went into the boat's salon. First he tried sitting at the galley table but soon got up, turned the TV on and started flipping through the channels without really looking at what was on. He turned the tube off and checked the clutter on the chart table but found there was nothing for him there, either. He moved about the cabin, looking for a distraction from his thoughts. But there was nothing.

He moved down the stairs into the forward passageway and into the head. He took the thermometer from the medicine cabinet, shook it and dipped it under his tongue. It was an old-style glass tube instrument. The electronic thermometer with digital reading display the hospital had provided was still in its box on the cabinet shelf. For some reason he didn't trust it.

Looking at himself in the mirror, he pulled open the collar of his shirt and studied the small wound left by the morning's biopsy. It never got a chance to heal. There had been so many biopsies that the incision was always just about covered with new skin when it was opened up again and the artery probed once more. He knew it would be a permanent mark, like the thirteen-inch scar running down his chest. As he stared at himself, his thoughts drifted to his father. He remembered the permanent marks, the tattoos, left on the old man's neck. The coordinates of a radiation battle that served only to prolong the inevitable.

The temperature reading was normal. He washed the thermometer and put it back, then took the clipboard with the temperature log sheet off the towel hook and wrote the date and time. In the last column, under TEMPERATURE, he drew another dash indicating no change.

After hanging up the board, he leaned into the mirror to look at his eyes. Green flecked with gray, the corneas showing hairline cracks of red. He stepped back and pulled the shirt off. The mirror was small but he could still see the scar, whitish pink and thick, ugly. He did this often, appraised himself. It was because he couldn't get used to the way his body looked now and the way it had so fully betrayed him. Cardiomyopathy. Fox had told him it was a virus that could have been waiting in the walls of his heart for years, only to bloom by happenstance and to be nurtured by stress. The explanation meant little to him. It didn't ease the feeling that the man he had once been was gone now forever. He sometimes felt when he looked at himself he was looking at a stranger, someone beaten down and left fragile by life.

After pulling his shirt back on, he went into the forward berth. It was a triangular-shaped room that followed the shape of the bow. There was a double bunk on the port side and a bank of storage compartments to starboard. He had turned the lower berth into a desk and used the overhead berth for storage of cardboard boxes full of old bureau files. Marked on the side of these boxes were the names of the investigations. They said POET, CODE, ZODIAC, FULL MOON and BREMMER. Two of the boxes were marked VARIOUS UNSUBS. McCaleb had copied most of his files before leaving the bureau. It was against policy but no one stopped him. The files in the boxes came from various cases, open and closed. Some filled whole cartons, some were thin enough to share space in the same boxes. He wasn't sure why he had copied everything. He hadn't opened any of the boxes since he had retired. But at various times he had thought he would write a book or maybe even continue his investigations of the open cases. Largely, though, he just liked the idea of having the files as a physical accounting or proof of what he had done with that part of his life.

McCaleb sat down at the desk and turned on the wall-mounted light. Momentarily, his eyes fell on the FBI badge he had carried for sixteen years. It was now encased in a Lucite block and hanging on the wall above the desk. Tacked to the wall next to it was a photo of a young girl with braces, smiling at the camera. It had been copied from a yearbook many years before. McCaleb frowned at the memory and looked away, his eyes falling to the desk clutter.

There was a handful of bills and receipts scattered on the desk, an accordion file full of medical records, a stack of manila files that were mostly empty, three fliers from competing dry-docking services and the Cabrillo Marina dockage rules book. His checkbook was open and ready to be put to use but he couldn't bring himself to wade into the mundane task of paying bills. Not now. He was restless but it was not because of a paucity of things on his mind. He couldn't stop thinking about the visit from Graciela Rivers and the sudden change it had put him through.

He sorted through the clutter on the desk until he found the newspaper clip that had brought the woman to his boat. He had read it the day it was published, cut it out and then tried to forget about it. But that had been impossible. The story had drawn a procession of victims to his boat. The mother whose teenage daughter's body was found mutilated on the beach down in Redondo; the parents whose son had been hanged in an apartment in West Hollywood. The young husband whose wife had gone clubbing on the Sunset Strip one night and had never come back. All of them zombies, left nearly catatonic by grief and the betrayal of their faith in a God who wouldn't allow such things to happen. McCaleb couldn't comfort them, he couldn't help them. He sent them on their way.

He had agreed to the newspaper interview only because he was in the reporter's debt. When he had been with the bureau, Keisha Russell had always been good to him. She was the kind of reporter who gave some and didn't always take. She had called him on the boat a month earlier to collect on that debt. She'd been assigned the story for the *Times*'s 'Whatever Happened to . . .' column. Since a year earlier she had written a story about McCaleb's wait for a heart, she wanted to update it now that he had finally received the transplant. McCaleb wanted to decline the invitation, knowing it would disrupt the anonymous life he was now living, but Russell had reminded him of all the times she had helped him – either holding back details of an investigation or putting them into a story, depending on what McCaleb thought would be useful. McCaleb felt he had no choice. He always made good on his debts.

On the day the story was published, McCaleb had taken it as his official badge of has-been status. Usually, the column was reserved for updates on hack politicians who had disappeared from the local scene or people whose fifteen minutes of fame had long ago lapsed. Every now and then it featured a washed-up TV star who was selling real estate or had become a painter because it was his true creative calling.

He unfolded the clip now and reread it.

New Heart, New Start for Former FBI Agent
By Keisha Russell
TIMES STAFF WRITER

It used to be that Terrell McCaleb's face was a routine fixture on the nightly newscasts of Los Angeles and his words always found space in the local newspapers. It was not a nice routine for him or the city.

An FBI agent, McCaleb was the bureau's point man in the investigations of the handful of serial killers that plagued Los Angeles and the West in the last decade.

A member of the Investigative Support Unit, McCaleb helped focus the investigations of the local police. Media-savvy and always quotable, he often took the spotlight – a move that sometimes rubbed the locals and his supervisors in Quantico, Va., the wrong way.

But it has been more than two years since he has made even a blip on the public radar screen. These days, McCaleb no longer carries a badge or a gun. He says he doesn't even own a standard-issue navy blue FBI suit anymore.

More often than not he wears old blue jeans and torn T-shirts and can be found restoring his 42-foot fishing boat, *The Following Sea.* McCaleb, who was born in Los Angeles and grew up in Avalon on nearby Catalina Island, currently lives on the boat in a San Pedro marina but plans eventually to moor the vessel in Avalon Harbor.

Recovering from heart transplant surgery, McCaleb says hunting serial killers and rapists is the furthest thing from his mind these days.

McCaleb, 46, says he gave his heart to the bureau – his doctors say severe stress triggered a virus that led to the near-fatal weakening of his original heart – but doesn't miss it.

'When you go through something like this, it changes you more than just physically,' he said in an interview last week. 'It puts things in perspective. Those FBI days seem like a long time ago. I've got a new start now. I don't know exactly what I'm going to do with it but I'm not too worried. I'll find something.'

McCaleb almost didn't get the new start. Because he has a blood type found in less than one percent of the population, his wait for a suitable heart lasted almost two years.

'He really strung it out,' said Dr Bonnie Fox, the surgeon who performed the transplant. 'We probably would have lost him or he would have become too weak to undergo the surgery if we'd had to wait much longer.'

McCaleb is out of the hospital and already physically active after only eight weeks. He says that only on occasion does he think about the adrenaline-pumping investigations that once occupied him.

The former agent's case list reads like a Who's Who of a macabre walk of fame. Among the cases he worked locally were the Nightstalker and Poet investigations and he took key roles in the hunts for the Code Killer, Sunset Strip Strangler and Luther Hatch, who became known after his arrest as the Cemetery Man because of his visits to the graves of his victims.

McCaleb had been a profiler in the unit's Quantico base for several years. He specialized in West Coast cases and was flown to Los Angeles often to assist local police in investigations. Finally, the unit's supervisors decided to create a satellite post here and McCaleb was returned to his native Los Angeles to work out of the FBI field office in Westwood. The move put him closer to many of the investigations in which the FBI was called upon for assistance.

Not all of the investigations were successful and eventually the stress took its toll. McCaleb suffered a heart attack while working late one evening in the local field office. He was found by a night janitor, who was credited with saving the agent's life. Doctors determined McCaleb suffered from advanced cardiomyopathy – a weakening of the heart's muscles – and placed him on a transplant list. As he waited, he was given a disability retirement by the bureau.

He traded his bureau pager for a hospital pager and on Feb. 9 it sounded; a heart from a donor with matching blood was available. After six hours of surgery at Cedars-Sinai Medical Center, the donor's heart was beating in McCaleb's chest.

McCaleb is unsure what he'll do with his new life – other than go fishing. He has had offers from former agents and police detectives to join them as a private investigator or security consultant. But his focus so far has been on restoring *The Following Sea*, a twenty-year-old sport-fishing boat he inherited from his father. The boat was left to deteriorate for six years but now has McCaleb's full-time attention.

'At the moment I'm content to take things a little at a time,' he said. 'I'm not worried too much about what's ahead.'

His regrets are few but like all retired investigators and fishermen, McCaleb laments the ones that got away.

'I wish I had solved all the cases,' he said. 'I hated it when somebody got away. I still do.'

For a moment McCaleb studied the photo they had used with the story. It was an old head shot they had used many times before during his days with the bureau. His eyes stared boldly into the camera.

When Keisha Russell had come around to do the story on him, she had come with a photographer. But McCaleb wouldn't let them take a fresh shot. He told them to use one of the old photos. He didn't want anybody to see the way he looked now.

Not that anyone could tell much, unless he had his shirt off. He was about thirty pounds lighter but that wasn't what he wanted to hide. It was the eyes. He had lost that look – the eyes as piercingly hard as bullets. He didn't want anyone to know he had lost that.

He folded the newspaper clip and put it aside. He tapped his fingers on the desk for a few seconds while brooding over things and then looked at the steel paper spike next to the phone. The number Graciela Rivers had given him was scratched in pencil on the scrap of paper that sat at the top of the stack of notes punctured by the spike.

When he was an agent, he had carried with him a bottomless reservoir of rage for the men he hunted. He had seen firsthand what they had done and he wanted them to pay for the horrible manifestations of their fantasies. Blood debts had to be paid in blood. That was why in the bureau's serial killer unit the agents called what they did 'blood work'. There was no other way to describe it. And so it worked on him, cut at him, every time one didn't pay. Every time one got away.

What happened to Gloria Torres now cut at him. He was alive because she had been taken away by evil. Graciela had told him the story. Gloria had died for no reason other than that she was in the way of somebody and a cash register. It was a simple, stupid and ghastly reason to die. It somehow put McCaleb in debt. To her and her son, to Graciela, even to himself.

He picked up the phone and dialed the number scratched on the paper. It was late but he didn't want to wait and he didn't think she would want him to. She answered in a whisper after only one ring.

'Miss Rivers?'

'Yes.'

'It's Terry McCaleb. You came by my –'

'Yes.'

'Is this a bad time?'

'No.'

'Well, listen, I wanted to tell you that I, uh, have been thinking about things and I promised you I'd call you back no matter what I decided.'

'Yes.'

There was a hopeful tone in just her one word. It touched his heart.

'Well, this is what I think. My, um, my skills, I guess you'd call them, they're not really suited to this kind of crime. From what you described about your sister, we're talking about a random occurrence with a financial motive. A robbery. So it's different from, you know, the kind of cases I worked for the bureau, the serial cases.'

'I understand.'

The hopefulness was bleeding out.

'No, I'm not saying I'm not going to – you know, that I'm not interested. I'm calling because I am going to go see the police tomorrow and ask about this. But –'

'Thank you.'

'– I don't know how successful I'm going to be. That's what I'm trying to say. I don't want to get your hopes up, is what I'm saying. These things . . . I don't know.'

'I understand. Thank you for just being willing to do this. Nobody –'

'Well, I'll take a look at things,' he said, cutting her off. He didn't want her thanking him too much. 'I don't know what kind of help or cooperation I'll get from the L.A. police but I'll do what I can. I owe your sister at least that much. To try.'

She was silent and he told her he needed to get some additional information about her sister as well as the names of the LAPD detectives on the case. They talked for about ten minutes and when he had all of the information he needed written down in a small notebook, an uneasy silence played across the telephone line.

'Well,' he finally said, 'I guess that's it, then. I'll call you if I have any other questions or if anything else comes up.'

'Thank you again.'

'Something tells me I should be thanking you. I'm glad I'll be able to do this. I just hope it helps.'

'Oh, it will. You've got her heart. She'll guide you.'

'Yes,' he said hesitantly, not really understanding what she meant or why he was agreeing. 'I'll call you when I can.'

He hung up and stared at the phone for a few moments, thinking about her last line. Then again he unfolded the newspaper clip with his picture. He studied the eyes for a long time.

Finally, he folded the newspaper clip closed and hid it under some of the paperwork on the desk. He looked up at the girl with the braces and after a few moments nodded. Then he turned off the light.

4

When McCaleb had been with the bureau, the agents he worked with called this part the 'hard tango'. It was the finesse moves they had to make with the locals. It was an ego thing and a territorial thing. One dog doesn't piss in another dog's yard. Not without permission.

There was not a single homicide cop working who did not have a healthy ego. It was an absolute job requirement. To do the job, you had to know in your heart that you were up to the task and that you were better, smarter, stronger, meaner, more skilled and more patient than your adversary. You had to flat-out know that you were going to win. And if you had any doubts about that, then you had to back off and work burglaries or take a patrol shift or do something else.

The problem was that homicide egos were often unchecked to the point that some detectives extended the view they had of their adversaries to those who wanted to help them – fellow investigators, especially FBI agents. No homicide cop on a stalled-out case wants to be told that maybe someone else – particularly a fed from Quantico – might be able to help or could do it better. It had been McCaleb's experience that when a cop finally gave up and put a case into cold storage, he secretly didn't want anyone taking it out and proving him wrong by solving it. As an FBI agent McCaleb was almost never asked into a case or called for advice by the lead detective. It was always the supervisor's idea. The supervisor didn't care about egos or hurt feelings. The supervisor cared about clearing cases and improving statistical reports. And so the bureau would be called and McCaleb would come in and have to do the dance with the lead detective. Sometimes it was the smooth dance of coordinated partners. More often it was the hard tango. Toes got stepped on, egos got bruised. On more than one occasion McCaleb suspected that a detective he was working with was holding back information or was secretly pleased when McCaleb was unsuccessful in helping identify a suspect or bringing closure to a case. It was part of the petty territorial bullshit of the law enforcement world. Sometimes consideration of the victim or the victim's family wasn't even on the plate. It was dessert. And sometimes there was no dessert.

McCaleb was pretty sure he was facing a hard tango with the LAPD. It didn't matter that they had apparently hit the wall with the Gloria Torres investigation and could use the help. It was territorial. And to make matters worse, he wasn't even with the FBI anymore. He was going in naked, without a badge. All he had with him when he arrived at seven-thirty on Tuesday morning at the West Valley Division was his leather bag and a box of doughnuts. He was going to be dancing the hard tango without music.

McCaleb had chosen his arrival time because he knew that most detectives started early so they could get done early. It was the time when he had the best chance of catching the two assigned to the Gloria Torres case in their office. Graciela had given him their names. Arrango and Walters. McCaleb didn't know them, but he had met their commanding officer, Lieutenant Dan Buskirk, a few years earlier on the Code Killer case. But it was a superficial relationship. McCaleb didn't know what Buskirk thought about him. He decided, though, that it would be best to follow protocol and start with Buskirk and then, hopefully, get to Arrango and Walters.

West Valley Division was on Owensmouth Street in Reseda. It seemed to be an odd place for a police station. Most of the LAPD's stations were placed in the tough areas where police attention was needed most. They had concrete walls erected at the entranceways to guard against drive-by shootings. But West Valley was different. There were no barriers. The station was in a bucolic, middle-class, residential setting. There was a library on one side and a public park on the other, plenty of parking at the front curb. Across the street was a row of signature San Fernando Valley ranch houses.

After the cab dropped him off out front, McCaleb entered through the main lobby, threw an easy salute at one of the uniformed officers behind the counter and headed toward the hallway to the left. He showed no hesitation. He knew it led to the detective bureau because most of the city's police divisions were laid out the same way.

The uniform didn't stop him and this encouraged McCaleb. Maybe it was the box of doughnuts but he took it to mean he still had at least some of the *look* – the confident walk of a man carrying a gun and a badge. He was carrying neither.

After entering the detective bureau, he came to another counter. By pressing against it and leaning over, he could look to the left and through the glass window of the small office he knew belonged to the detective lieutenant. It was empty.

'Can I help you?'

He straightened up and looked at the young detective who had approached the counter from a nearby desk. Probably a trainee assigned counter duty. Usually, they used old men from the neighborhood who volunteered their time or cops assigned light duty because of injury or disciplinary action.

'I was hoping to see Lieutenant Buskirk. Is he here?'

'He's in a meeting at Valley bureau. Can I help you with something?'

That meant Buskirk was in Van Nuys at the Valley-wide command office. McCaleb's plan to start with him was out the window. He could now wait for Buskirk or leave and come back. But go where? The library? There wasn't even a nearby coffee shop he could walk to. He decided to take his chances with Arrango and Walters. He wanted to keep moving.

'How about Arrango or Walters in homicide?'

The detective glanced at a plastic wall-mounted board with names going down the left side and rows of boxes to be checked that said IN and OUT as well as VACATION and COURT. But there were no check marks of any kind made after the names Arrango and Walters.

'Let me check,' the frontman said. 'Your name?'

'My name is McCaleb but it won't mean anything to them. Tell them it's about the Gloria Torres case.'

The frontman went back to his desk and punched in three digits on the phone. He spoke in a whisper. McCaleb knew then that as far as the frontman was concerned, he didn't have the *look*. In a half minute the call was done and the frontman didn't bother getting up from the desk.

'Turn around, back down the hall, first door on the right.'

McCaleb nodded, took the box of doughnuts off the counter and followed the instructions. As he approached, he put the leather bag under one arm so he could open the door. But it opened as he was reaching for it. A man in a white shirt and tie stood there. His gun was held in a shoulder harness under his right arm. This was a bad sign. Detectives rarely used their weapons, homicide detectives even less than others. Whenever McCaleb saw a homicide detective with a shoulder harness instead of the more comfortable belt clip, he knew he was dealing with a major ego. He almost sighed out loud.

'Mr McCaleb?'

'That's me.'

'I'm Eddie Arrango, what can I do for you? My guy up front said you're here about Glory Torres?'

They shook hands after McCaleb awkwardly transferred the box of doughnuts to his left hand.

'That's right.'

He was a large man, more in horizontal than vertical proportions. Latino, with a full head of black hair feathered with gray. Mid-forties, with a solid build, no stomach over the belt. It went with the shoulder harness. He took up the whole door and made no move to invite his visitor in.

'Is there a place we can talk about this?'

'Talk about what?'

'I'm going to be looking into her murder.'

So much for finesse, McCaleb thought.

'Oh, shit, here we go,' Arrango said.

He shook his head in annoyance, glanced behind him and then back at McCaleb.

'All right,' he said, 'let's get this over with. You got about ten minutes before I toss you outta here.'

He turned around and McCaleb followed him into a room crowded with desks and detectives. Some of them looked up from their work at McCaleb, the intruder, but most didn't bother. Arrango snapped his fingers to draw the attention of a detective at one of the desks along the far wall. He was on the phone but looked up to see Arrango signal him. The man on the phone nodded and held up one finger. Arrango led the way to an interview room with a small table pushed against one wall and three chairs. It was smaller than a prison cell. He closed the door.

'Have a seat. My partner will be in in a minute.'

McCaleb took the chair opposite the table. This meant Arrango would likely take the chair to McCaleb's right or be forced to squeeze behind him to go to the chair on his left. McCaleb wanted him on the right. It was a small thing, but a routine he had always followed as an agent. Put the subject you are talking to on the right. It means they look at you from the left and engage the side of the brain that is less critical and judgmental. A psychologist at Quantico had once given the tip while teaching a class on techniques of hypnosis and interrogation. McCaleb wasn't sure if it worked but he liked to have any edge he could get. And he thought he might need one with Arrango.

'You want a doughnut?' he asked as Arrango took the chair on his right.

'No, I don't want any of your doughnuts. I just want you on your way and out of *my* way. It's the sister, isn't it? You're working for the goddamn sister. Let me see your ticket. I can't believe she's wasting her money on –'

'I don't have a license, if that's what you mean.'

Arrango drummed his fingers on the scarred table as he thought about this.

'Jesus, you know it's stuffy in here. We shouldn't keep it closed up like this.'

Arrango was a bad actor. He delivered the line as if he were reading it off a chart on the wall. He got up, adjusted the thermostat on the wall by the door and then sat back down. McCaleb knew that he had just turned on a tape recorder as well as a video camera hidden behind the air duct grill over the door.

'First off, you say you are conducting an investigation of the Gloria Torres homicide, is that correct?'

'Well, I haven't really started. I was going to talk to you first and then go from there.'

'But you're working for the victim's sister?'

'Graciela Rivers asked me to look into it, yes.'

'And you have no license in the state of California to operate as a private investigator, true?'

'True.'

The door opened and the man Arrango had signaled earlier stepped into the room. Without turning around and looking at his partner, Arrango held a hand up, fingers spread, signaling him not to interrupt. The man McCaleb assumed was Walters folded his arms and leaned against the wall next to the door.

'Do you understand, sir, that it is a crime in this state to operate as a private investigator without a license? I could arrest you on a misdemeanor right now.'

'It's illegal, not to mention unethical, to take money to conduct a private investigation without the proper license. Yes, I'm aware of that.'

'Wait. You're telling me you're doing this for free?'

'That's right. As a friend of the family.'

McCaleb was quickly growing tired of the bullshit and wanted to get on with what he was there for.

'Look, can we skip all the bullshit and turn off the tape and the camera and just talk for a few minutes? Besides, your partner is leaning against the microphone. You're not picking anything up.'

Walters jumped away from the thermostat just as Arrango turned around to see that McCaleb had been right.

'Why didn't you tell me?' Walters said to his partner.

'Shuddup.'

'Hey, have a doughnut, guys,' McCaleb said. 'I'm here to help.'

Arrango turned back to McCaleb, still a bit flustered.

'How the fuck did you know about the tape?'

'Because you've got the same setup in every detective bureau in the city. And I've been in most of them. I used to be with the bureau. That's how I knew.'

'The FBI?' Walters asked.

'FBI retired. Graciela Rivers is an acquaintance. She asked me to look into this, I said I would. I want to help.'

'What's your name?' Walters asked.

Obviously he was coming to everything late because he had been on the phone. McCaleb stood up and extended his hand. Walters shook it as McCaleb introduced himself. Dennis Walters was younger than Arrango. Pale white skin, slim build. His clothes were loose, baggy, suggesting that his wardrobe had not been updated since he had experienced a dramatic loss in weight. He wore no holster at all that McCaleb could see. He probably kept his gun in his briefcase until he went out on the street. McCaleb's kind of cop. Walters knew it wasn't the gun that made the man. His partner didn't.

'I know you,' he said, pointing a finger at McCaleb. 'You're that guy. The serial guy.'

'What are you talking about?' Arrango said.

'You know, the profilers. The serial killer squad. He was the one they sent out here permanently, since most of the nuts are out here. He worked the Sunset Strip Strangler, what else, the Code Killer, that cemetery guy, a bunch of cases out here.'

He then put his attention back on McCaleb.

'Right?'

McCaleb nodded. Walters snapped his fingers.

'Didn't I read about you recently? Something in the *Slimes*, right?'

Once again McCaleb nodded.

'The "Whatever Happened to . . ." column. Two Sundays back.'

'That's it. Right. You got a heart transplant, right?'

McCaleb nodded. He knew that familiarity bred comfort. Eventually, they would get down to business. Walters remained standing behind Arrango but McCaleb saw his gaze drop to the box on the table.

'You want a doughnut, Detective? I'd hate to see them go to waste. I didn't get breakfast but I'm not going to have one if you guys don't.'

'Don't mind if I do,' Walters said.

As he came forward and opened the box, he glanced anxiously at his partner. Arrango's face was a stone. Walters took out a glazed doughnut. McCaleb took a cinnamon sugar and then Arrango broke and reluctantly took a powdered sugar. They ate silently for a few moments before McCaleb reached into his sports coat and pulled out the stack of napkins he had grabbed at Winchell's. He tossed them onto the table and everyone took one.

'So, the bureau pension's so short you've gotta pick up PI work, huh?' Walters said, his mouth full of doughnut.

'I'm not a PI. The sister's an acquaintance. Like I said, I'm not being paid.'

'An acquaintance?' Arrango said. 'That's the second time you said that. How exactly do you know her?'

'I live on a boat down at the harbor. I met her at the marina one day. She likes boats. We met. She found out what I once did for the bureau and asked me to take a look at this. What's the problem?'

He didn't know exactly why he was shading the truth to the point of lying. Other than that he had immediately taken a disliking to Arrango, he didn't feel he wanted to reveal his true connection to Gloria Torres and Graciela Rivers.

'Well, look,' Arrango said, 'I don't know what she told you about this, but this is a convenience store robbery, FBI man. This isn't Charlie Manson or Ted Bundy or Jeffrey Fucking Dahmer. It's not rocket science. This is some mope with a mask and a gun and the right ratio of balls to brains to use it all to make a couple dollars. This isn't what you're used to seein', is what I'm saying.'

'I know that,' McCaleb said. 'But I told her I'd check into it. It's been what, going on two months now? I thought maybe you guys wouldn't mind a fresh set of eyes on something you can't be spending much time on anymore.'

Walters took the bait.

'Our team's pulled four cases since then and Eddie's been in trial the last two weeks in Van Nuys,' he said. 'As far as Torres goes, it's –'

'Still active,' Arrango said, cutting his partner off.

McCaleb looked from Walters to Arrango.

'Right . . . Sure.'

'And we've got a rule that we don't invite amateurs in on active cases.'

'Amateurs?'

'You got no badge, no private ticket, that says amateur to me.'

McCaleb let the insult go by. He guessed Arrango was just taking his measure anyway. He pushed on.

'That's one of those rules you bring up when it's convenient,' he said. 'But we all know here that I might be able to help you. What you need to know is that I'm not here to show you guys up. Not at all. Anything I come up with, you'll be the first to know. Suspects, leads, anything. It all goes to you. I'd just like a little cooperation, that's all.'

'Cooperation in exactly what form?' Arrango asked. 'Like my partner who talks too much says, we're kind of busy here.'

'Copy me the murder book. Also any video you have. I'm good on crime scenes. That was sort of my specialty. I might be able to help you there. Just copy me what you've got and I'll get out of your way.'

'What you're saying is you think we fucked up. That the answer's sitting there in the book ready to jump out at you 'cause you're a fed and the feds are so much smarter than us.'

McCaleb laughed and shook his head. He was beginning to think he should have counted his losses and left as soon as he saw the macho-man holster. He tried once more.

'No, that's not what I'm saying. I don't know if you missed anything or not. I've worked with LAPD many times. If I was betting, I'd bet you missed nothing. All I'm saying is that I told Graciela Rivers I'd check into things. Let me ask you something, does she call you much?'

'The sister? Too much. Week in and week out and I tell her the same thing every time. No suspects, no leads.'

'You're waiting on something to happen, right? Give it new life.'

'Maybe.'

'Well, this could at least be your way of getting her off your back. If I see what you've got and go back to her and say you boys did what you could, she might back off. She'll believe it from me because she knows me.'

Neither of them said anything.

'What have you got to lose?' McCaleb prodded.

'We'd have to clear any kind of cooperation with the lieutenant,' Arrango said. 'We can't just give out copies of investigative records without his say-so, rules or no rules. In fact, you fucked up there, bro. You should've gone to him before you came to us. You know how the game's played. You didn't follow protocol.'

'I understand that. I asked for him when I got here but they said he was at Valley bureau.'

'Yeah, well, he should be back soon,' Arrango said, checking his watch. 'Tell you what, you say you're good with crime scenes?'

'Yeah. If you got a tape, I'd like to take a look at it.'

Arrango looked at Walters and winked, then he looked back at McCaleb. 'We got better than a crime scene tape. We got the crime.'

He kicked back his chair and stood up.

'Come on,' he said. 'Bring those doughnuts with you.'

5

Arrango opened a drawer in one of the desks crammed into the squad room and took out a videotape. He then led the way out of the homicide squad office, down the hall and then through the half door of the main detective bureau counter. McCaleb could see they were headed for Buskirk's office, which was still empty. McCaleb left the doughnuts on the front counter and followed the others in.

Pushed into one corner of the room was a tall steel cabinet on wheels. It was the kind of setup used in classrooms and roll-call rooms. Arrango opened the two doors and there was a television and a videocassette player inside. He turned the equipment on and shoved in the tape.

'So look at this and tell us something we don't know yet,' he said to McCaleb without looking at him. 'Then maybe we go to bat for you with the lieutenant.'

McCaleb moved until he stood directly in front of the television. Arrango hit the play button and soon the black-and-white image came up on the television screen. McCaleb was looking at the view held by an overhead surveillance camera in a small convenience store. The frame was drawn around the front counter area. It was glass-topped and full of cigars and disposable cameras and batteries and other high-end items. A printed date and timeline ran across the bottom of the screen.

The frame was empty for a few moments and then the top of the gray-haired counterman's head came into view in the lower left corner as he leaned over the cash register.

'That's Chan Ho Kang, the owner,' Arrango said, punching the screen with a finger and leaving a smudge of doughnut grease. 'He's spending his last few seconds on the planet here.'

Kang had the cash drawer open. He broke a roll of quarters against the corner of the counter case and then dumped them into the appropriate section of the drawer. Just as he shoved it closed, a woman entered the frame. A customer. McCaleb recognized her instantly from the photo Graciela Rivers had showed him on the boat.

Gloria Torres smiled as she approached the counter and placed two Hershey's candy bars down on the glass. She then pulled her purse up, opened it and took out her wallet as Mr Kang punched keys on the register.

Gloria looked up, money in hand, when suddenly another figure entered the frame. It was a man with a black ski mask covering his face and wearing what looked like a black jumpsuit. He moved up behind Gloria unnoticed. She was still smiling. McCaleb looked at the time counter, saw it said 22:41:35 and then looked back at what was happening in the store. It gave him a strange feeling to watch the action take place in this surreal black-and-white silence. From behind, the man in the ski mask put his right hand on Gloria's right shoulder and in one continuous move of the left hand put the muzzle of a handgun against her left temple. Without hesitation he pulled the trigger.

'Badda-BING!' Arrango said.

McCaleb felt his chest clench like a fist as he watched the bullet tear into Gloria's skull, a horrifying mist of blood jettisoning from the entry and exit wounds on either side of her head.

'Never knew what hit her,' Walters said quietly.

Gloria jerked forward onto the counter and then bounced backward, collapsing into the shooter as he brought his right arm up around her and across her chest. Stepping backward, Gloria in front of him as a shield, he raised his left hand again and fired a shot at Mr Kang, striking him somewhere in the body. The store owner bounced off the wall behind him and then forward, his upper body crashing down over the counter and cracking the glass. His arms flung out across the counter and his hands grappled for a hold like a man going over a cliff. Finally, he let go, his body flopping to the floor behind the counter.

The shooter let Gloria's body slide to the ground and her upper body fell outside the view of the video frame. Only her hand, as if reaching across the floor, and legs stayed in the picture. The shooter moved toward the counter, quickly leaning over and looking down at Mr Kang on the floor. Kang was reaching into a shelf below the counter, frantically pulling out stacks of brown bags. The shooter just watched him, until finally Kang's arm came out, a black revolver in his hand. The man in the ski mask dispassionately shot Kang in the face before he ever got the chance to raise his gun.

Leaning further over the counter, his feet in the air, the shooter grabbed one of the bullet shells that had ejected and fallen next to Kang's arm. He then straightened up, reached over and took the bills from the open cash register drawer. He looked up at the camera. Despite the mask, it was clear the man winked and said something to the camera, then quickly left the frame to the left.

'He's picking up the other two shells,' Walters said.

'No sound on the camera, right?' McCaleb said.

'Right,' Walters said. 'Whatever he said there, he said to himself.'

'Only one camera in the store?'

'Only one. Kang was cheap. That's what we were told.'

As they continued to watch, the shooter made one more pass through the corner of the screen on his way out.

McCaleb stared blankly at the television, stunned by the harshness of the violence, despite his experience. Two lives spent for the contents of a cash drawer.

'You ain't gonna see that on *America's Favorite Home Videos*,' Arrango said.

McCaleb had dealt with cops like Arrango for years. They acted as though nothing ever got to them. They could look at the worst crime scenes and find the joke. It was part of the survival instinct. Act and talk as if it means nothing to you and you've got a shield. You won't get hurt.

'Can I see it again?' McCaleb said. 'Can you slow it down this time?'

'Wait a minute,' Walters said. 'It's not over.'

'What?'

'The Good Samuel comes in just about now.'

He said it with a Hispanic pronunciation. Sam-*well*.

'The Good Samuel?'

'Good Samaritan. Mexican guy comes in the store, finds them and tries to help. He kept the woman alive but there was nothing he could do for Kang. Then he goes out to the pay phone out front and makes – there he is.'

McCaleb looked back at the screen. The timeline now read 22:42:55 and a dark-haired, dark-complected man in jeans and a T-shirt had entered the picture. He first hesitated on the right side of the screen, apparently looking at Gloria Torres, and then went to the counter and looked over it. Kang's body lay on the floor in a lake of blood. There were wide, ugly bullet wounds in his chest and face. His eyes were open and still. He was obviously dead. The Good Samaritan returned to Gloria. He knelt on the floor and apparently hunched over her upper body, which was off-screen. But almost immediately he was up again and out of the picture.

'He went down the aisles looking for bandages,' Arrango said. 'He actually wrapped her head with masking tape and a Kotex. A supersize.'

The Good Samaritan returned and went to work on Gloria, although all of this was off-screen.

'The camera never picked up a great shot of him,' Arrango said. 'And he didn't stick around. After he made the call to nine one one out front, he split.'

'He never came in later?'

'Nope. We went on the TV news with it. You know, asking for him to come forward because he might've seen something that would help the investigation. But nothing. This guy went up in smoke.'

'Weird.'

On the screen the man stood up, his back still to the camera. As he was moving out of the frame, he glanced to his left and a brief profile of his face was visible. He had a dark mustache. He then disappeared from view.

'He now calls the cops?' McCaleb asked.

'Nine one one,' Walters said. 'He said "ambulance" and they put him through to the Fire Department.'

'Why didn't the guy come in?'

'We got a theory on that,' Arrango said.

'Care to share it?'

'The voice on the nine one one tape had an accent,' Walters said. 'Latino.

We figure the guy was an illegal. He didn't stick around because he was afraid if we talked to him, we'd find out and ship him back.'

McCaleb nodded. It was plausible, especially in L.A., where there were hundreds of thousands of illegals avoiding authorities.

'We put out fliers in the Mexican neighborhoods and went on Channel Thirty-four,' Walters continued. 'Promised he wouldn't be deported if he'd just come in and tell us what he saw, but we got nothing. Happens a lot in those neighborhoods. Hell, the places they come from, they're more scared a' the cops than the bad guys.'

'Too bad,' McCaleb said. 'He was there so soon, he probably saw the shooter's car, maybe got the plate.'

'Maybe,' Walters said. 'But if he got the plate, he didn't bother giving it to us on the tape. He did give a half-ass description of the car – "Black car, like a truck," was how he described it. But he hung up before the girl could ask if he got a plate.'

'Can we watch it again?' McCaleb asked.

'Sure, why not?' Arrango said.

He rewound the tape and they silently watched it again, this time with Arrango using the slow motion button during the shooting. McCaleb's eyes stayed on the shooter for every frame that he was on film. Though the mask hid his expression, there were times that his eyes were clearly seen. Brutal eyes that showed nothing as he gunned down two people. Their color indiscernible because of the black-and-white tape.

'Jesus,' McCaleb said when it was over.

Arrango ejected the tape and turned off the equipment. He turned and looked at McCaleb.

'So, tell us something,' he said. 'You're the expert. Help us out here.'

The challenge was clearly evident in his voice. Put up or shut up. They were back to the territorial thing.

'I'd have to think about it, maybe watch the tape some more.'

'Figures,' Arrango responded dismissively.

'I'll tell you one thing,' McCaleb said, looking only at Arrango. 'This wasn't the first time.'

He pointed at the dead TV tube.

'No hesitation, no panic, the quick in and out . . . the calm handling of the weapon and the kick, the presence of mind to pick up the brass. This guy's done this before. This isn't the first time. And probably not the last. Plus, he'd been in there before. He knew there was a camera – that's why he wore the mask. I mean, it's true that lots of places like that have cameras but he looked right up at this one. He knew *where* it was. That means he'd been in there before. He's either from the neighborhood or he came in earlier to case the place.'

Arrango smirked and Walters looked quickly from McCaleb to his partner. He was about to say something when Arrango held up his hand to silence him. McCaleb knew then that what he had just said had been accurate and that they already knew it.

'What?' he asked. 'How many others?'

Arrango now held both hands up in a hands-off gesture.

'That's it for now,' he said. 'We talk to the lieutenant and we let you know.'

'What is this?' McCaleb protested, finally losing his patience. 'Why show me the tape and stop there? Give me a shot at this. I might help you. What have you got to lose?'

'Oh, I'm sure you can help. But our hands are tied. Let us talk to the lieutenant and we'll get back to you.'

He signaled everybody out of the office. McCaleb thought for a moment about refusing to leave but dismissed it as a bad idea. He walked through the door, Arrango and Walters behind him.

'When will I hear from you?'

'As soon as we know what we can do for you,' Arrango said. 'Give me a number, we'll be in touch.'

6

McCaleb stood outside the station's lobby waiting for the cab to show. He was steaming about how he had allowed Arrango to play him. Guys like Arrango got off on holding something out to a person and then snatching it away. McCaleb had always known people like Arrango – on both sides of the law.

But there was nothing he could have done about it. For now it was Arrango's show. McCaleb wasn't really expecting to hear from him again. He knew that he would have to call him for an answer. That was how the game was played. McCaleb decided he would give it until the next morning before he would call.

When the cab got there, McCaleb got in the back behind the driver. It was a way of discouraging conversation. He checked the name on the dashboard license card and saw it was Russian and unpronounceable. He pulled the small notebook out of his bag and gave the driver the address for the Sherman Market in Canoga Park. They headed north on Reseda Boulevard and then west on Sherman Way until they came to the small market near the intersection of Winnetka Avenue.

The cab pulled into the lot in front of the small store. The place was nondescript, unimpressive, its plate-glass windows plastered with brightly colored sale signs. It looked like a thousand other mini-markets in the city. Except someone had decided that this one was worth robbing and that it was worth killing two people in order to accomplish that goal. Before getting out, McCaleb studied the signs covering the windows. They blocked off a view of the interior. He knew that was probably the reason the shooter had chosen this store. Even if passing motorists glanced over, they wouldn't see what was going on inside.

Finally, he opened the door and got out. He stepped to the driver's window and told the man to wait for him. As he went into the store, he heard the tinkling of a bell from above the door. The cash register counter depicted in the video was set up near the back wall directly across from the door. An old woman stood back behind the counter. She was staring at McCaleb and she looked scared. She was Asian. McCaleb realized who she might be.

Looking around as if he had come in with a purpose other than to gawk, he saw the display racks full of candy and picked out a Hershey's bar. He stepped to the counter and placed it down, noticing that the glass top of the case was still cracked. The full realization that he was in the same spot where Glory Torres had stood and smiled at Mr Kang then hit him. He looked up at the old woman with a pained expression on his face and nodded.

'Anything else?'

'No, just this.'

She rang it up and he paid her. He studied her hesitant movements. She knew he wasn't from the neighborhood or a regular customer. She still was not at ease. She probably never would be.

When she gave him his change, McCaleb noticed that the watch she wore on her wrist had a wide, black rubber wristband and a large face. It was a man's watch and it dwarfed her tiny, seemingly fragile wrist. He had seen the watch before. It had been on Chan Ho Kang's wrist in the surveillance video. McCaleb remembered focusing on the watch as the video depicted the wounded Kang scrambling for purchase on the counter and then finally falling to the floor.

'Are you Mrs Kang?' McCaleb asked.

She stopped what she was doing at the register and looked at him.

'Yes. I know you?'

'No. It's just . . . I heard about what happened here. To your husband. I'm sorry.'

She nodded.

'Yes, thank you.' Then, seemingly needing an explanation or salve for her wounds, she added, 'The only way to keep evil out is to not unlock door. We can't do that. We must have business.'

Now McCaleb nodded. It was probably something her husband had told her when she worried about his operating a cash business in a violent city.

He thanked her and left, the bell ringing overhead again as he went through the door. He got back in the cab and appraised the front of the market again. It made no sense to him. Why this place? He thought of the video. The shooter's hand grabbing the cash. He couldn't have gotten much. McCaleb wished he knew more about the crime, more of the details.

The phone on the wall to the right of the store's windows caught his eye. It was the one the unidentified Good Samaritan had apparently used. He wondered if it had been processed for prints after they realized he wasn't coming forward. Probably not. By then it was too late. It was a long shot anyway.

'Where to?' the driver said, his accent discernible in only two syllables.

McCaleb leaned forward to give the man an address but hesitated. He drummed his fingers on the plastic backing of the front seat and thought for a moment.

'Keep the meter running. I've got to make a couple calls first.'

He got out again and headed to the pay phone, once more taking his notebook out. He looked up a number and charged the call to his card. It was answered right away.

'*Times*, Russell.'

'Did you say *Times* or *Slimes*?'

'Funny, who is this?'
'Keisha, it's Terry McCaleb.'
'Hey, how're you doing, man?'
'I'm fine. I wanted to thank you for that story. I should've called sooner. But it was nice.'
'Hey, you're cool. Nobody else ever calls to thank me for anything.'
'Well, I'm not that cool. I was also calling because I need a favor. You got your terminal on?'
'You really know how to spoil a good thing. Yes, my terminal is on. What's up?'
'Well, I'm looking for something but I'm not sure how to find it. You think you could do one of those key-word searches for me? I'm looking for stories that would be about a robber who shoots people.'
She laughed.
'That's it?' she said. 'You know how often people get shot up in robberies? This is L.A., you know.'
'Yeah, I know, that was stupid. Okay, how about adding in *ski mask*. And maybe only go back about eighteen months. Think that will narrow it?'
'Maybe.'
He heard her keyboard start clicking as she tapped into the newspaper's computerized library of story files. By using key words like *robbery* and *ski mask* and *shooting* she would be able to draw up all stories that had contained those words.
'So what's going on, Terry? I thought you were retired.'
'I am.'
'Doesn't sound like it. This is like the old days. Are you doing some kind of investigation?'
'Sort of. I'm checking something for a friend and the LAPD's being the LAPD. And it's worse when you don't have a badge.'
'What's it about?'
'It's not newsworthy yet, Keisha. If it turns out that way, you'll be the first I let know.'
She blew out her breath in exasperation.
'I hate it when you guys do that,' she protested. 'I mean, why should I help you when you won't let me decide whether something's a story or not? I'm the newspaper reporter, not you.'
'I know, I know. I guess what I'm saying is that I just want to keep this to myself until I see what is what. I'll tell you about it after that. I promise, first crack at it. It probably won't pan out, but I'll tell you one way or the other. Did you get anything?'
'Yes,' she said in a mock pout. 'Six hits in the last eighteen months.'
'Six? What are they?'
'Six stories. I'll read you the headlines and you tell me if you think you want me to call up the stories.'
'Okay.'
'Okay, here goes. "Two Shot in Robbery Attempt", then we have "Man Shot, Robbed at ATM". After that we have "Deputies Seek Help in ATM

Shooting". Let's see, the next three look like one related case. The headlines are "Store Owner, Customer Shot in Robbery", followed by "Second Victim Dies; Was *Times* Employee" – oh, shit, I never heard about that. I'll have to read this one myself – and the last one is "Police Seek Good Samaritan". Those are the six.'

McCaleb thought for a moment. Six stories, three different incidents.

'Could you pull up the first three and read them if they're not too long?'

'Why not.'

He listened as her keyboard started clicking. His eyes wandered out past the cab to Sherman Way. It was a four-lane street, busy even at night. He wondered if Arrango and Walters had been able to come up with any witnesses to the shooter's getaway, anybody besides the Good Samaritan.

McCaleb's eyes moved across the street and in the parking lot of a strip mall he saw a man sitting in a car. The man raised a newspaper just as McCaleb noticed this and his face disappeared. McCaleb checked the car. It was an old beater, foreign make, which dissuaded him from the possibility that maybe Arrango had put a quick tail on him. He dismissed it as Keisha started reading the newspaper story on her computer screen.

'Okay, the first one ran on October eighth last year. It's just a short. "A husband and wife were shot and wounded Thursday by a would-be robber who was then wrestled to the ground and captured by a group of passersby, Inglewood police said Thursday. The couple were walking along Manchester Boulevard at eleven when a man wearing a ski mask approached and –"'

'The guy was captured?'

'That's what it says.'

'Okay, skip that one. I'm looking for unsolveds, I think.'

'Okay, the next story ran Friday, January twenty-fourth. Headline is "Man Shot, Robbed at ATM". No byline. It's another short. "A Lancaster man who was withdrawing cash from an automatic teller machine was fatally shot Wednesday night in what Los Angeles County sheriff's deputies called a senseless killing. James Cordell, thirty, was shot once in the head by an unknown assailant who then took the three hundred dollars he had just withdrawn from the machine. The shooting took place at approximately ten P.M. at a Regional State Bank branch in the eighteen-hundred block of Lancaster Road. Sheriff's detective Jaye Winston said a portion of the shooting was captured on the ATM security camera but not enough to identify the gunman. The one glimpse of the gunman on the camera's tape showed he was wearing a dark knit ski mask over his head. However, Winston said that the tape revealed that there was no confrontation or refusal on Cordell's part to turn over the money. 'It was absolutely cold-blooded,' Winston said. 'This guy just walked up, shot the victim and took the money. It was very cold and brutal. This guy didn't care. He just wanted the money.' Cordell collapsed in front of the well-lighted machine but his body was not found until another customer came approximately fifteen minutes later. Paramedics pronounced him dead at the scene." Okay, that's that one. You ready for the next?'

'I'm ready.'

McCaleb had been jotting down some of the details from the story into his notebook. He underlined the name *Winston* three times. He knew Jaye Winston. He thought Winston would be willing to help him – more so than Arrango and Walters had been. Jaye Winston was not a hard tango. McCaleb felt he had finally caught a break.

Keisha Russell started reading the next story.

'Okay, same thing. No byline. It's short and it ran two days later. "Sheriff's deputies said there were no suspects in the fatal shooting this week of a Lancaster man who was withdrawing money from an automatic teller machine. Detective Jaye Winston said the department wished to speak with any motorists or passersby who were in the area of the eighteen-hundred block of Lancaster Road on Wednesday night and may have seen the assailant before or after the ten-twenty shooting. James Cordell, thirty, was shot once in the head by a robber who wore a ski mask. He died at the scene of the robbery. Three hundred dollars were taken during the robbery. Though part of the incident was captured by the Regional State Bank's security camera, detectives were unable to identify the suspect because of the mask he wore. 'He had to have had it off at one point,' Winston said of the mask. 'He didn't just walk or drive down the street with a mask on. People had to have seen this guy and we want to talk to those people.' " Okay, that's the end.'

McCaleb hadn't taken any notes from the second story. But he was thinking about what Keisha had read and didn't respond.

'Terry, you still there?'

'Yeah. Sorry.'

'Any of it help?'

'I think so. Maybe.'

'And you still won't tell me what it's about?'

'Not yet, Keisha, but thanks. You'll be the first to know.'

He hung up and pulled the business card Arrango had given him out of his shirt pocket. He decided not to wait for Arrango or for the next day. He had a lead he could follow now, whether or not the LAPD cooperated with him. While he was waiting for the call to be answered, he looked across the street. The car with the man reading the newspaper was gone.

The phone was picked up after six rings and he was eventually transferred to Arrango. McCaleb asked if Buskirk was back yet.

'Bad news, amigo,' Arrango said. 'The lieutenant's back all right. But he wants to hold off on turning our book over to you.'

'Yeah, how come?' McCaleb asked, trying to disguise his annoyance.

'Well, I didn't really ask but I think he was pissed that you didn't come in to see him first. I told you that. You should've followed line of command.'

'That was kind of hard to do, being that he wasn't there this morning. And I told you, I did ask for him first. Did you tell him that?'

'Yeah, I told him. I think he was in a bad mood, coming from Valley bureau. He probably got his ass chewed about something so then he chewed mine. That's how it goes sometimes. Right down the food chain. Anyway, look, you're lucky. We showed you the whole thing on tape. You got a good start there. We shouldn't've done that for you.'

'Some start. You know, it's amazing that anything ever gets solved with all the bureaucratic bullshit that goes on. I thought the FBI was unique. We used to call it the Federal Bureau of Inertia. But I guess it's the same all around.'

'Hey, look, we don't need your shit. We have a whole plate full of it here. My boss seems to think I invited you in here and now he's pissed at me. I don't need this. If you want to go away mad, that's your problem. But just go away.'

'I'm gone, Arrango. You won't hear from me until I have your shooter. I'll bring him in for you.'

McCaleb knew it was bullshit grandstanding as soon as he said it. But ever since February ninth he had increasingly found that he had zero tolerance for fools.

Arrango laughed sarcastically in response and said, 'Yeah, right. I'll be waiting for you.'

He hung up.

7

McCaleb held up a finger to the cab driver and made another call. He first thought about Jaye Winston but decided to wait. Instead he called Graciela Rivers at the number she had given him for the nursing station in the emergency room of Holy Cross Medical Center. She agreed to meet him for an early lunch, even though he explained that he hadn't accomplished much. He told her to look for him in the emergency room waiting room at eleven-thirty.

The hospital was in a part of the Valley called Mission Hills. On the way there, McCaleb looked out the window at the passing scenery. It was mostly strip shopping centers and gas stations. The driver was making his way toward the 405 so that he could head north.

McCaleb's knowledge of the Valley had come only through cases. There had been many, most of them falling under his review only on paper and photo prints and videotape from the body dumps along the freeway embankments or the hillsides fringing the northern flats. The Code Killer had hit four times in the Valley before he disappeared like the morning marine layer.

'What are you, police?'

McCaleb looked away from the window and over the seat at the rearview mirror. The driver's eyes were on him.

'What?'

'Are you policeman or something?'

McCaleb shook his head.

'No, I'm no one.'

He looked back out the window as the cab labored up a freeway on-ramp. They passed a woman who was holding a sign asking for money. Another victim waiting to be victimized again.

He sat in the waiting room on a plastic chair across from an injured woman and her husband. The woman had internal pain and kept her arms folded across her midsection. She was hunched over, protecting the hurt. Her husband was being attentive, repeatedly asking how she felt and going to the intake window to ask when she would be taken back for examination. But twice McCaleb heard him quietly ask her, 'What are you going to tell them?'

And each time the woman turned her face away.

At quarter to twelve Graciela Rivers came through the double doors of the ER ward. She suggested that they just go to the hospital cafeteria because she had only an hour. McCaleb didn't mind because his taste for food had still not come back since the transplant. Eating at the hospital would be no different to him than eating at Jozu on Melrose. Most days he didn't care what he ate and sometimes he forgot about meals until a headache reminded him that he needed to refuel.

The cafeteria was almost empty. They took their trays to a table next to a window, which looked out on a huge green lawn surrounding a large white cross.

'This is my one chance to look at daylight,' Graciela said. 'Back in the ER rooms there are no windows. So I always try to get a window.'

McCaleb nodded that he understood.

'Way back when I worked in Quantico, our offices were below ground. The basement. No windows, always damp, freezing in the winter even with the heat on. I never saw the sun. It wears on you after a while.'

'Is that why you moved out here?'

'No. Other reasons. But I did figure I'd get a window. I was wrong. They stuck me in a storage closet at the FO. Seventeen floors up but no windows. I think that's why I live on the boat now. I like having the sky close by.'

'What's the FO?'

'Sorry. Field office. It was in Westwood. In the big federal building near the veterans cemetery.'

She nodded.

'So, did you really grow up on Catalina like the paper said?'

'Until I was sixteen,' he said. 'Then I lived with my mother in Chicago . . . It's funny, I spent all the time I was growing up on that island just wanting to get off it. Now I'm just trying to get back there.'

'What will you do there?'

'I don't know. I've got a mooring over there my father left me. Maybe I won't do anything. Maybe I'll just drop a line and sit in the sun with a beer in my hand.'

He smiled and she smiled back.

'If you already have a mooring, why can't you go now?'

'The boat's not ready. Neither am I yet.'

She nodded.

'It was your father's boat?'

Another detail from the newspaper. He had obviously said too much about himself to Keisha Russell. He didn't like people knowing so much about him so easily.

'He lived on it over there. When he died, it came to me. I let it sit in dry dock for years. Now it needs a lot of work.'

'Did he name it or was that you?'

'His name.'

She frowned and squinted her eyes as if something was sour.

'Why did he call it *The Following Sea* instead of just *Following Sea*? It doesn't make sense with *The* in front of *Following Sea*.'

'No, it makes sense. It doesn't refer to the act of following behind the sea. There is something known as *the* following sea, or *a* following sea.'

'Oh. What is it?'

'A sea is a wave. You know, how you hear on surf reports that the seas are two to four feet or whatever?'

'Right.'

'Okay, well a following sea is the one you have to watch out for. It's the one that comes up behind a vessel. You don't see it coming. It hits you from behind and swamps you. Sinks you. The rule is that if you're running in following seas, you've just got to be moving faster than they are. Stay ahead of them. He named the boat that because it was like a reminder. You know, always watch over your shoulder. It was something he always said to me when I was growing up. Even when I went over town.'

'Over town?'

'When I left the island. He told me always to watch out for the following sea, even on land.'

She smiled.

'Now that I know the story, I like the name. Do you miss him?'

He nodded but offered nothing else. The conversation drifted away and they began to eat their sandwiches. McCaleb hadn't planned on the meeting being about him. After a few bites he started filling her in on the morning's lack of solid accomplishment. He didn't tell her about watching her sister being murdered on the videotape but he told her about his hunch that the Torres-Kang slayings were connected to at least one other incident. He told her how he was further guessing that that other incident might be the ATM robbery and shooting recounted in the stories Keisha Russell had read him.

'What will you do next?' she asked when he was done.

'Take a nap.'

She looked at him curiously.

'I'm beat,' he said. 'I haven't been running around and doing as much thinking as this for a long time. I'm going back to my boat and resting up. Tomorrow I'll start again.'

'I'm sorry.'

'No, you're not,' he said with a smile. 'You were looking for somebody with a reason to get involved in this. I've got the reason and I'm involved, but I've got to take it slow at first. You being a nurse, I hope you understand.'

'I do. I don't want you to hurt yourself. That would make Glory's dying even more . . .'

'I understand.'

They were silent for a few moments before he picked up the conversation again.

'Your take on the LAPD was right on. I think they're in a holding pattern, waiting for something to happen – probably for this guy to hit again. They're definitely not working it. It's a cold case until something happens to warm it up.'

She shook her head.

'They're not working it but they don't want you to have a try at it. That makes a lot of sense.'

'It's a territorial thing. It's the way the game is played.'

'It's not a game.'

'I know.'

He wished he had chosen a better word.

'Then what can you do?'

'Well, in the morning, when I'm fresh, I'll try the Sheriff's Department on this other case, the one I think is connected. I know the lead on it. Jaye Winston. We worked a case once a long time ago. It went well and I'm hoping that will get me in the door. At least further in than I got with the L.A. people.'

She nodded but she wasn't all that good at masking her disappointment.

'Graciela,' he said, 'I don't know if you were expecting somebody to just come in and solve this like turning a key in a lock but it's not realistic to believe that. That's movies. This is real. In all my years in the bureau, most of the cases turned on some little detail, some little thing that was missed or didn't seem important at first. But then it comes back around to being the key to the whole thing. It just takes time to get there sometimes, to find that little detail.'

'I know. I know. It just frustrates me that more wasn't done sooner.'

'Yes, when the . . .'

He was going to say when the blood was fresh.

'What?'

'Nothing. It's just that with most cases the more time goes by, the harder it gets.'

He knew he wasn't helping her any by telling her the reality of the situation. But he wanted her to be prepared for his eventual failure. He had been good in his day but not that good. He now realized that by agreeing to take the case he had only set Graciela Rivers up for disappointment. His selfish dream of redemption would be another painful dose of reality for her.

'Those men just didn't care,' she said.

He studied her downcast eyes. He knew she was talking about Arrango and Walters.

'Well, I do.'

They finished eating in silence. After McCaleb pushed his plate aside, he watched her as she gazed out the window. Even in her white polyester nurse's uniform with her hair pinned back, Graciela Rivers stirred something in him. She had a kind of sadness about her that he wished somehow to soothe. He wondered if it had been there before her sister died. With most people it is. McCaleb had even seen it in the faces of babies – the sadness already there. The events of their lives seemed only to confirm the sadness they already carried.

'Was this where she died?' he asked.

She nodded and looked back at him.

'She was first taken to Northridge, stabilized and then transferred here. I was here when life support was terminated. I was with her.'

He shook his head.

'It must have been very hard.'

'I see people dying every day in the ER. We joke about it to relieve the stress, say they are "Three-D". Definitely Done Dancing. But when it's your own . . . I don't joke about it anymore.'

He watched her face as she shook it off, shifted gears and moved on, away from the trouble spot. Some people have that fifth gear that they can drop into, to get away.

'Tell me about her,' he said.

'What do you mean?'

'That's really why I came. Tell me things about her. It will help me. The better feel that I have for her, the better I'll be at this.'

She was quiet a moment, her mouth curled in a frown as she thought about how to sum her sister up in a few words.

'Is there a kitchen on that boat of yours?' she finally asked.

Her question caught him off guard.

'What?'

'A kitchen. On your boat.'

'Uh, it's actually called a galley.'

'Then galley. Is it big enough to cook real meals?'

'Sure. Why are you asking me about my boat?'

'You want to know my sister?'

'Yes.'

'Then you have to meet her son. Everything that was good about my sister is in Raymond. He's all you have to know.'

McCaleb nodded slowly as he understood.

'So how about I bring Raymond down to your boat tonight and we make you dinner. I already told him about you and about the boat. He wants to see it.'

He thought a moment and said, 'Tell you what. How about we wait until tomorrow. That way I can tell you about how my visit to the Sheriff's Department went. Maybe I'll have something more positive to report.'

'Tomorrow will be fine.'

'And don't worry about cooking dinner. Dinner will be my job.'

'You're turning this all around. I wanted to –'

'I know, I know. But you can save that for one night at your home. You're coming to my home tomorrow and I'll take care of dinner, okay?'

'Okay,' she said, still frowning but realizing he wouldn't be budged. Then she smiled. 'We'll be there.'

Traffic south on the 405 was intense and the cab didn't drop him off at the marina in San Pedro until after two. The cab was not air-conditioned and he caught a slight headache from the mixture of freeway exhaust fumes and the driver's body odor.

After he got inside the boat, he checked his phone machine and found the only message he had was a hang-up call. He felt out of sync because his travels that day had involved more physical activity than he'd had for a long while. His leg muscles were sore and his back was aching. He went down to the head and checked his temperature but there was no fever. Blood pressure and pulse also checked out fine. He logged it all on the clipboard, then went to his stateroom, stripped off his clothes and crawled into the unmade bed.

Despite his physical depletion he had insomnia and lay wide awake on the pillow. His mind churned with the thoughts of the day and images from the video. After an hour of fooling himself, he got up and went up to the salon. He dug the notebook out of the jacket he had draped over a chair and read through the notes he had taken earlier. Nothing stood out but he felt comforted in some way at having started a record of his investigation.

On a fresh page he jotted down some additional thoughts about the video and a couple of questions he wanted to be sure to cover with Jaye Winston the next day. Assuming that the investigators had linked the cases, he wanted to know how solid the connection was and whether the three hundred dollars taken from James Cordell in the first case was actually taken from the victim or from the ATM's cash tray.

He put the notebook aside when he realized he was hungry. He got up, scrambled three egg whites in a skillet, mixed in some Tabasco sauce and salsa and made a sandwich with white toast. After two bites he put on more Tabasco.

When he had cleaned up the galley, he felt the fatigue coming back and finally closing him down. He knew he could sleep now. He took a quick shower, another temperature reading and the evening batch of medications. In the mirror he saw he had what looked like a two-day growth of beard even though he had shaved that morning. It was a side effect of one of the drugs he was taking. Prednisone helped fight organ rejection and stimulated hair growth at the same time. He smiled at his reflection, thinking that the day before he should have told Bonnie Fox that he felt like a werewolf, not Frankenstein's creation. He was getting his monsters mixed up. He went to bed.

His dream was in black and white. They all were now but they had not been before the operation. He didn't know what this meant. He had told Dr Fox about it and she had just shrugged.

In this dream he was in the market. He was a player in the video he had been shown by Arrango and Walters. He was at the counter smiling at Chan Ho Kang. The store owner smiled back in an unfriendly way and said something.

'What?' McCaleb asked.

'You don't deserve it,' Mr Kang said.

McCaleb looked down at the counter at his purchase but before he could see what it was he felt the cold ring of steel against his temple. He quickly turned and there was the masked man with a gun. McCaleb knew in the way knowledge and logic accompany dreams that the man was smiling behind the mask. The robber lowered the gun and fired into McCaleb's chest, his bullet hitting the ten ring – the circle of the heart. The bullet went through McCaleb as if he were a paper target. But the impact forced him backward a step and then in slow motion he was falling. He felt no pain, only a sense of relief. He looked at the killer as he was going down and recognized the eyes watching through the mask. They were his own eyes. Then came the wink.

And he kept falling and falling.

8

The distant booming of empty cargo containers being unloaded from a ship in the nearby Port of Los Angeles woke McCaleb before dawn. As he lay in bed, eyes closed but fully awake, he pictured the process. The crane delicately swinging the container the size of a truck trailer off the ship's deck and into the yard, then the ground man giving the drop sign early and the huge steel box dropping the last three feet and producing a concussion like a sonic boom echoing across the nearby marinas. In McCaleb's vision, the ground man was laughing each time.

'Fucking assholes,' McCaleb said, finally giving up on sleep and sitting up. It was the third time in a month it had happened.

He checked the clock and realized he had slept for more than ten hours. He slowly made his way to the head and took a shower. After he had toweled off, he took the morning reading of vital signs and the prescribed complement of assorted pills and liquid chemicals. He logged it all on the progress chart and then got out his razor. He was about to spread shaving cream across his face when he looked in the mirror and said, 'Fuck it.'

He shaved his neck so he would look neat but left it at that, deciding that to shave two or three times a day for the rest of his life, or for as long as he was on prednisone, wasn't an alternative. He had never had a beard before. The bureau wouldn't have allowed it.

After dressing, he took a tall glass of orange juice, his phone book and the portable phone out to the stern and sat in the fishing chair as the sun came up. Between gulps of juice he constantly checked his watch, waiting for it to hit seven-fifteen, which he believed would be the best time to call Jaye Winston.

The Sheriff's Department homicide offices were in Whittier on the far side of the county. From that location, the squad's detectives handled all killings committed in unincorporated Los Angeles County and the various cities the department contracted with to provide law enforcement services. One of those cities was Palmdale, where James Cordell had been murdered.

Because the homicide squad offices were so distant, McCaleb had decided that it would be foolish to take an hour-long cab ride out there without knowing whether Winston would be in when he arrived. So he had decided on the seven-fifteen call rather than the surprise visit with a box of doughnuts.

'Those assholes.'

McCaleb looked around and saw one of his neighbors, Buddy Lockridge, standing in the cockpit of his sailboat, a forty-two-foot Hunter called the *Double-Down.* Buddy's boat was three slips from *The Following Sea.* He was holding a mug of steaming coffee in his hand. He was in a bathrobe and his hair was standing up on one side. McCaleb didn't have to ask whom Buddy was calling assholes.

'Yeah,' he said. 'Not a good way to start the day.'

'Point is they shouldn't be allowed to do that all through the night,' Buddy said. 'Goddamn nuisance. I mean, you gotta be able to hear that from here to Long Beach.'

McCaleb just nodded.

'I talked to them over there in the harbor master's. You know, told them to make a complaint to the Port Authority but they don't give a shit. I'm thinking of gettin' a little petition going. You going to sign it?'

'I'll sign it.'

McCaleb looked at his watch.

'I know, you think it's a waste of time.'

'No. I just don't know if it will work. The port's a twenty-four-hour operation. They're not going to stop unloading ships at night because a bunch of people on their boats in the marina sign a complaint.'

'Yeah, I know. The assholes . . . I wish one of them boxes would drop on *them* one day. Then they'd get the idea.'

Lockridge was a wharf rat. An aging surfer and beach bum, he lived a low-cost, low-maintenance life on his boat, subsisting mostly on money from odd jobs around the marina like boat sitting and hull scraping. The two had met a year earlier, shortly after Lockridge had moved his boat into the marina. McCaleb had been awakened by a middle-of-the-night harmonica concerto. When he got up and left his boat to investigate, he traced the sound to a drunken Lockridge lying in the cockpit of the *Double-Down.* He was playing a harmonica to a tune only he heard on his earphones. Despite McCaleb's complaint that night, the two had become friends over time. This was largely due to the fact that there were no other live-aboards in that area of the marina. Each was the other's only full-time neighbor. Buddy had kept an eye on *The Following Sea* while McCaleb had been in the hospital. He also often offered McCaleb rides to the grocery store or a nearby mall because he knew Terry wasn't supposed to drive. In turn, McCaleb had Lockridge over for dinner every week or so. They usually talked about their shared interest in the blues, debated sailboats versus power boats and sometimes pulled out McCaleb's old file boxes and theoretically solved some of the cases. Lockridge was always fascinated by the details of McCaleb's stories about the bureau and his investigations.

'I've got to make a phone call now, Bud,' McCaleb now called over. 'I'll talk to you later.'

'Sure. Make your call. Take care of business.'

He waved and disappeared down the hatchway into his boat's cabin.

McCaleb shrugged and made his call after looking up the number he had for Jaye Winston in his book. After a few seconds he was connected.

'Jaye, it's Terry McCaleb. You remember me?'

After a beat, she said, ' 'Course I do. How is it going, Terry? I heard you got the new ticker.'

'Yeah and I'm doing okay. How about you?'

'Same old same old.'

'Well, you think you'll have a few minutes if I swing by this morning? You got a case I want to talk about.'

'You on the private ticket now, Terry?'

'Nah. Just doin' a favor for a friend.'

'Which one is it, the case I mean?'

'James Cordell. The ATM case on January twenty-two.'

Winston made a *hmmph* sound but didn't say anything.

'What?' McCaleb asked.

'Well, it's funny. That case has gone cold on me but now you're the second person to call about it in two days.'

Shit, McCaleb thought. He knew who had called.

'Keisha Russell from the *Times*?'

'Yup.'

'That's on me. I asked her for the clips on Cordell. But I wouldn't tell her why. That's why she called you. Fishing.'

'That's what I thought. I played dumb. So who is the friend who talked you into this?'

McCaleb recounted how he had been asked to look into the murder of Gloria Torres and how that ultimately led him to the Cordell case. He acknowledged that he was getting no help from the LAPD and that Winston was his only alternate route into the case. He left out the fact that his new heart had come from Gloria Torres.

'So did I hit it right?' he asked at the end. 'Are they connected?'

Winston hesitated but then confirmed his assumption. She also said her case was in a holding pattern at the moment, pending new developments.

'Listen, Jaye, I'll be right up front with you. What I'm hoping to do is come out, maybe take a look at the books and whatever else you care to show me, then be able to go back to Graciela Rivers and tell her all that could be done has been done or is being done. I'm not trying to be a hero or to show anybody up.'

Winston didn't say anything.

'What do you think?' McCaleb finally asked. 'You got some time today?'

'Not a lot. Can you hold on?'

'Sure.'

McCaleb was put on hold for a minute. He paced around the deck and looked over the side at the dark water his boat floated on.

'Terry?'

'Yo.'

'Look, I've got court at eleven downtown. That means I have to be out of here by ten. Can you make it before then?'

'Sure. How's nine or nine-fifteen?'
'That'll work.'
'Okay, and thanks.'
'Look, Terry, I owe you one, so I'm doing this. But there's nothing here. It's just some scumbag out there with a gun. This is three-strikes shit, that's all.'
'What do you mean?'
'I've got another call on hold here. We'll talk when you get here.'

Before McCaleb got ready to go, he stepped up onto the dock and walked over to the *Double-Down.* The boat was the marina eye-sore. Lockridge had more possessions than the boat was built to hold. His three surfboards, his two bikes and his Zodiac inflatable were stored on the deck, making the boat look like a floating yard sale.

The hatch was still open but McCaleb saw and heard no activity. He called out and waited. It was bad marina etiquette to step onto a boat uninvited.

Eventually, Buddy Lockridge's head and shoulders came up through the hatch. His hair was combed and he was dressed now.

'Buddy, what do you have going for today?'

'Whaddaya mean? The same thing I've always got going. A big goose egg. What'd you think, I was going to Kinko's to update my résumé?'

'Well, look, I need a driver for the next few days, maybe more. You want to do it, the job's yours. I'm paying ten bucks an hour plus any meals. You'd have to bring a book or something because there will be a lot of sitting around waiting for me.'

Buddy climbed all the way up into the cockpit.

'Where're you drivin' to?'

'I've got to go out to Whittier. I need to leave in fifteen minutes. After that, I don't know.'

'What is it, some kind of investigation?'

McCaleb could see the excitement building in Buddy's eyes. He spent a lot of time reading crime novels and often recounted their plots to McCaleb. This would be the real thing.

'Yeah, I'm looking into something for somebody. But I'm not looking for a partner, Buddy, just a driver.'

'That's okay. I'm in. Whose car?'

'We take yours, I pay for gas. We take my Cherokee, I sit in the back. It's got a passenger side air bag. You decide. Either way is fine with me.'

Driving had been forbidden for McCaleb by Bonnie Fox until at least his ninth month. His chest was still closing. The skin was healed but beneath the scarred exterior the sternum was still open. An impact on a steering wheel or from an air bag could be fatal, even in a low-speed accident.

'Well, I like the Cherokee but let's take mine,' Buddy said. 'I'd feel like too much of a chauffeur with you in the back.'

9

In the summer of 1993 the body of a woman had been found in a large outcropping of sandstone known as Vasquez Rocks in the Antelope Valley in northern Los Angeles County. The body had been there several days. Decomposition prevented determination of sexual assault but it was assumed. The body was clothed but the panties were inside out and the blouse misbuttoned – a clear indication that the woman had not dressed herself or had done so only under severe duress. Cause of death was manual strangulation, the means of death in most sexual homicides.

Sheriff's detective Jaye Winston drew the Vasquez Rocks killing as lead investigator. When the case didn't break quickly with an arrest, Winston settled in for the long haul. Ambitious but not burdened by an unchecked ego, she contacted the FBI for help as one of her first moves. Her request was relayed to the serial killer unit and she eventually filled out a case survey for the unit's Violent Criminal Apprehension Program.

The VICAP survey was the means by which McCaleb first became acquainted with Winston. The case package she had sent to Quantico was forwarded to McCaleb's storage room office at the Los Angeles FO. In typical bureaucratic fashion, the package had gone all the way across the country only to be sent back nearly to its origin for follow-up.

Through the VICAP data base computer – which compares an eighty-question survey about an individual killing with those on file – and study of the crime scene and autopsy photos, McCaleb matched the Vasquez Rocks case to another killing a year earlier in the Sepulveda Pass area of Los Angeles. A similar killing method, the dumping of the clothed body on an embankment, other small details and nuances – all matched up. McCaleb believed they had another serial killer working the L.A. basin. In both of the cases it was determined that the woman had been missing two or three days longer than she had been dead. This meant the killer had held her captive and alive during that period, probably to serve in his ghastly fantasies.

Connecting the cases was only one step. Identifying and capturing the killer were the obvious following steps. However, there was nothing to go on. McCaleb was curious about the lengthy interval between the two murders. The Unknown Subject, as the killer was formally called in FBI documents, had gone eleven months before the urges overtook him and he acted out his fantasies by abducting the second woman. To McCaleb, this meant that the event was so strongly implanted in the killer's mind that his fantasy life could essentially live off it or be fueled by it for almost a year. The bureau's serial killer profiling program showed that this interval would grow shorter and shorter each time and the killer would have to seek fresh prey sooner.

McCaleb worked up a profile for Winston but it wasn't much help and they both knew it. White male, twenty to thirty, with a menial job and existence, the Unknown Subject would also have a prior history of sexual crimes or aberrational behavior. If this history included incarceration for any lengthy periods, it could skew the profiled age span of the subject.

It was the same old story. The VICAP profiles were usually dead-on accurate but they rarely led to the acquisition of a suspect. The profile given to Winston could match hundreds, maybe thousands of men in the Los Angeles area. So after all investigative leads were played out, there was nothing to do but wait. McCaleb made a note of the case on his calendar and went on to other cases.

In March of the following year – eight months from the last murder – McCaleb came across the note, reread the file and gave Winston a call. Nothing much had changed. There still were no leads or suspects. McCaleb urged the sheriff's investigator to begin a surveillance of the two body disposal sites and the graves of the two victims. He explained that the killer was near the end of his cycle. His fantasies would be running dry. The urge to freshly re-create the sensation of power and control over another human would be growing and increasingly hard to control. The fact that the Unknown Subject had apparently dressed the bodies after each of the first two murders was a clear sign of the battle raging inside his mind. One part of him was ashamed of what he had done – he sought in a subconscious way to cover it up by replacing each victim's clothes. This suggested that eight months into the cycle the killer would be engulfed in tremendous psychological turmoil. The urge to act out his fantasy again and the shame the act would bring were the two sides in a battle for control. One way to temporarily placate the urge to kill would be to revisit the sites of his previous crimes in an effort to bring new fuel to the fantasy. McCaleb's hunch was that the killer would return to one of the disposal spots or visit the graves. It would bring him closer to his victims and help him stave off the need to kill again.

Winston was reluctant to instigate a multiple point surveillance operation on the basis of an FBI agent's hunch. But McCaleb had already received approval for himself and two other agents for stake-out duty. He also played upon Winston's professionalism, telling her that if she didn't do it, she would always wonder if the stake-out would have been successful, especially if the Unknown Subject hit again. With that kind of threat to her conscience, Winston went to her lieutenant and counterparts on the LAPD case and a surveillance squad was assembled from all three agencies. While planning the surveillance, Winston learned that by coincidence both of the victims were buried in the same Glendale cemetery, about one hundred yards apart. Hearing that, McCaleb predicted that if the Unknown Subject was going to show, it would be in the cemetery.

He was right. On the fifth night of the surveillance, McCaleb, Winston and two other detectives hiding in a mausoleum with a view of both grave sites watched a man drive into the cemetery in a van, get out and climb over the locked gate. Carrying something under his arm, he walked to the grave of the first victim, stood motionless in front of it for ten minutes and then headed to the grave of the second victim. His actions showed a prior knowledge of the location of the graves. At the second grave, he unrolled what turned out to be a sleeping bag on top of the grave, sat down on it and leaned back against the headstone. The detectives did not disturb the man. They were recording his visit with a night-vision video camera. Before long he opened his pants and began masturbating.

Before he returned to the van, the man had already been identified through its license plates as Luther Hatch, a thirty-eight-year-old gardener from North Hollywood released four years earlier from a nine-year Folsom Prison term for a rape conviction.

The subject was no longer unknown. Hatch became a working suspect. When his years in prison were subtracted from his age, he fit the VICAP profile perfectly. He was watched around the clock for three weeks – including during two more visits to the Glendale cemetery – until finally one night the detectives moved in as he attempted to force a young woman leaving the Sherman Oaks Galleria into his van. In the van, the arresting officers found duct tape and clothesline cut into four-foot lengths. After receiving a search warrant, the investigators tore apart the interior of the van as well as Hatch's apartment. They recovered hair, thread and dried fluid evidence that was linked through DNA and other scientific analysis to the two murder victims. Quickly dubbed 'The Cemetery Man' by the local media, Hatch took his place in the pantheon of multiple murderers who fascinate the public.

McCaleb's expertise and hunches had helped Winston break the case. It was one of the successes they still talked about in Los Angeles and Quantico. On the night they arrested Hatch, the surveillance team went out to celebrate. During a lull in the din, Jaye Winston turned to McCaleb at the bar and said, 'I owe you one. We all do.'

Buddy Lockridge had dressed for his job as Terry McCaleb's driver as if he were going to a nightclub on the Sunset Strip. Head to toe, he was clad in black. He also carried a black leather briefcase. Standing on the dock next to the *Double-Down*, McCaleb stared at the ensemble without speaking for a long moment.

'What's the matter?'

'Nothing, let's go.'

'Is this all right?'

'It's fine but I didn't think you'd get so dressed up for just sitting in a car all day. You going to be comfortable?'

'Sure.'

'Then let's go.'

Lockridge's car was a seven-year-old silver Ford Taurus that was well maintained. On the way out to Whittier, he tried three different times to find out what it was McCaleb was investigating but each time the questions were unanswered. Finally, McCaleb was able to deflect the line of questioning by bringing up their old debate over the merits of sailboats versus power boats. They got to the Sheriff's Department Star Center in a little over an hour. Lockridge slid the Taurus into a spot in the visitors' lot and turned off the ignition.

'I don't know how long I'll be,' McCaleb said. 'I hope you brought something to read or you've got one of your harmonicas on you.'

'You sure you don't want me to go in with you?'

'Look, Bud, this might have been a mistake. I'm not looking for a partner. All I need is somebody to drive me. I spent more than a hundred bucks yesterday on cabs. I figured maybe you could use the money instead, but if you're going to be asking me questions and –'

'Okay, okay,' Lockridge said, cutting in. He held his hands up in surrender. 'I'll just sit here and read my book. No more questions.'

'Good. I'll see you.'

McCaleb entered the homicide squad offices on time for his appointment and Jaye Winston was hovering around the reception area waiting for him. She was an attractive woman a few years older than McCaleb. She had blond hair that was straight and kept midlength. She had a slim build and was dressed in a blue suit with a white blouse. McCaleb had not seen her in almost five years, since the night they had celebrated the arrest of Luther Hatch. They shook hands and Winston led McCaleb to a conference room that had an oval table surrounded by six chairs. There was a smaller table against one wall with a double-pot coffeemaker on it. The room was empty. A thick stack of documents and four videocassettes were sitting on the table.

'You want some coffee?' Winston asked.

'Nah, I'm fine.'

'Then let's get started. I've got twenty minutes.'

They took chairs across the table from each other. Winston pointed at the paper stack and the videos.

'This is all yours. I copied everything after you called this morning.'

'Jeez, you kidding? Thanks.'

With two hands McCaleb pulled the pile toward his chest like a man raking in the pot at the poker table.

'I called Arrango over at L.A.,' Winston said. 'He told me not to work with you but I told him you were the best agent I ever dealt with and that I owed you one. He's pissed but he'll get over it.'

'Is this L.A.'s stuff, too?'

'Yeah, we've copied each other back and forth. I haven't gotten anything from Arrango in a couple weeks but that's probably because there hasn't been anything. I think it's all up to date. Problem is, it's a lot of paper and video and it all adds up to nothing so far.'

McCaleb broke the stack of reports in half and started sorting through them. It became clear that about two-thirds of the work had been generated by sheriff's investigators and the rest by the LAPD. He gestured to the videotapes.

'What are these?'

'You've got both crime scenes there and both shoots. Arrango told me he showed you the market robbery already.'

'Yeah.'

'Well, on ours you get even less. The shooter enters the frame for only a few seconds. Just enough for us to see he was wearing a mask. But anyway, it's there for you to look at if you want.'

'On yours, did the guy take the money from the machine or the victim?'

'The machine, why?'

'I might be able to use that to get some help from the bureau, if I need it. Technically, it means the money was taken from the bank, not the victim. That's a federal offense.'

Winston nodded that she understood.

'So how did you connect these, ballistics?' McCaleb asked, mindful that her time was limited and he wanted as much from her as he could get.

She nodded.

'I was working my case already and then a few weeks later I'm reading the paper and see a story about the other one. Sounded the same. I called L.A. and we got together. When you watch the videos, Terry, you'll see. There's no doubt. Same MO, same gun, same guy. The ballistics only underlined what we already knew.'

McCaleb nodded.

'I wonder why the guy picked up the brass if he knew the lead would be there. What was he using?'

'Nine-millimeter hardballs. Federals. Full metal jacket. Picking up the shells is just good practice. On my case, the shot was through and through and we dug the slug out of a concrete wall. He probably was guessing – maybe hoping – it was too mashed up for a ballistics comparison. So like a good little shooter, he picked up the brass.'

McCaleb nodded, noting the disdain in her voice for her quarry.

'Anyway, it doesn't really matter,' she said. 'Like I said, watch the tapes. We're dealing with one guy here. You don't need ballistics to know it.'

'Did you or the LAPD take it any further than that?'

'What do you mean, Firearms and Ballistics?'

'Yeah. Who has the evidence?'

'We do. The L.A. caseload's a little heavier than over here. We agreed, since our case was first, to hold all of the evidence. I had F and B do the regular routine, you know, look for similars, et cetera, but they drew a blank. Looks like just these two cases. For now.'

McCaleb thought about telling her about the bureau's DRUGFIRE computer but decided the time wasn't right yet. He'd wait until he had reviewed the tapes and the murder books before he started suggesting what she should do.

He noticed Winston check her watch.

'You working this by yourself?' he asked.

'I am now. I caught the lead and Dan Sistrunk partnered it with me. You know him?'

'Uh, was he one of the guys in the mausoleum that night?'

'Right, the Hatch surveillance. He was there. Anyway, we worked this one together and then other things happened. Other cases. It's all mine now. Lucky me.'

McCaleb nodded and smiled. He understood how it went. If a case wasn't solved by the team quickly, one player got stuck with it.

'You going to get any flak for giving me this stuff?'

'No. The captain knows what you did for us on Lisa Mondrian.'

Lisa Mondrian was the woman found in Vasquez Rocks. McCaleb thought it was unusual that Winston had referred to her by name. It was unusual because most cops he knew tried to depersonalize the victims. It made it easier to live with.

'The captain was the lieutenant back then,' Winston was saying. 'He knows we owe you one. We talked and he said give you the stuff. I just wish we could pay you with something better than this. I don't know what you'll be able to do with this, Terry. We've just been waiting.'

Meaning they were waiting for the shooter to strike again and hopefully make a mistake. Unfortunately it often took fresh blood to solve old killings.

'Well, I'll see what I can do with it. At least it's something to keep me busy. What was that you said on the phone about it being three-strikes stuff?'

Winston frowned.

'We're getting more and more like these. Ever since they put in the three-strikes law in Sacramento. I don't know since you've been out of the life if you've followed it. But the law says three felony convictions and you're out. Automatic life without parole.'

'Right. I know about it.'

'Well, with some of these assholes, all that did was make 'em more careful. Now they wipe out witnesses where before they'd just rob. Three strikes was supposed to be some kind of deterrent. You ask me, it just got a lot of people killed like James Cordell and the two in that market.'

'So you think that's what this guy's doing?'

'Looks it to me. You saw one of the tapes. There's no hesitation. This scumbag knew what he was going to do before he even went up to that ATM or into that store. He wanted no witnesses. So that's the hunch I've been following. In my spare time I've been going through the files, looking for stick-up men with two or more falls already under their belts. I think the man in the ski mask is one of them. He used to be a robber. Now he's a robbing murderer. Natural evolution.'

'And no luck yet?'

'With the files, nope. But either I'll find him or he'll find me. He's not the type who's going to suddenly go square. And judging by the fact he's shooting people for a few hundred dollars, he's decided that under no circumstances is he going back to the cage. That's for sure. He's going to do this again. I'm surprised it hasn't happened yet – it's been two months since the last one. But when he does, maybe he'll fuck up just a little and we'll get him. Sooner or later, we will. I guarantee it. My victim had a wife and two little daughters. I'm going to get the piece of shit who did this.'

McCaleb nodded. He liked her outrage-fueled dedication. It was a full turn away from Arrango's view of things. He started gathering up the documents and tapes and told Winston he would be calling her after he looked over all of the material. He told her it might be a few days.

'No sweat,' she said. 'Whatever you can do we can use.'

When McCaleb got back to the Taurus, he found Buddy Lockridge sitting with his back to the driver's-side door and his legs stretched across the front seat. He was idly practicing a blues riff on a harmonica while reading a book opened on his lap. McCaleb opened the passenger door and waited for him to move his legs. As he finally got in, he noticed Buddy had been reading a book titled *Inspector Imanishi Investigates.*

'That was pretty quick,' Buddy said.

'Yeah, there wasn't a lot to say.'

He put the stack of reports and videocassettes on the floor between his feet.

'What's all of that?'

'Just some stuff I have to go through.'

Lockridge leaned over and looked at the top sheet. It was an incident report.

'James Cordell,' he read out loud. 'Who's that?'

'Buddy, I'm beginning to think –'

'I know, I know.'

He took the hint, straightened up and started the car. He asked nothing more about the documents.

'So, where to now?'

'Now we just go back. San Pedro.'

'I thought you said you needed me for a few days. I'll stop asking questions, I promise.'

There was a slight protest in his voice.

'It's not that. I still need you. But right now I need to go back and go through some of this stuff.'

Buddy dejectedly tossed his book onto the dashboard, dropped the harp into the door pocket and put the car into gear.

10

There was more natural light in the salon than down below in the office stateroom. McCaleb decided to work there. He also had a television and video player built into a cabinet topside. He cleared the galley table, wiped it with a sponge and paper towel and then put the stack of reports Winston had given him down on top. He got a legal pad and a sharpened pencil out of the chart table drawer and brought them over as well.

He decided that the best way to do it would be to go through the material chronologically. That meant the Cordell case came first. He went through the stack, separating out the reports regarding the Gloria Torres killing and putting them aside. He then took what was left and separated the reports into small stacks relating to the initial investigation and evidence inventory, follow-up interviews, dead-end leads, miscellaneous reports, fact sheets and weekly summaries.

When he had worked for the bureau, it was his routine to completely clear his desk and spread all the paperwork from a submitted case file across it. The cases came in from police departments all over the West. Some sent thick packages and some just thin files. He always asked for videotapes of the crime scene. Big or small, the packages were all about the same thing. McCaleb was fascinated and repulsed at the same time. He became angry and vengeful as he read, all while alone in his little office, his coat on the door hook, his gun in the drawer. He could tune everything out but what was in front of him. He did his best work at the desk. As a field agent, he was average at best. But at his desk, he was better than most. And he felt a secret thrill in the back of his mind each time he opened one of those packages and the hunt for a new evil began again. He felt that thrill now as he began to read.

James Cordell had a lot going for him. A family, nice home and cars, good health and a job that paid well enough to allow his wife to be a full-time mother to their two daughters. He was an engineer with a private firm contracted by the state to maintain the structural integrity of the aqueduct system that delivered water from the snow melt in the mountains in the central state to the reservoirs that nursed the sprawl of Southern California. He lived in Lancaster in northeast Los Angeles County, which put him within an hour and a half by car of any point on the water line. On the night of

January twenty-second he had been heading home from a long day inspecting the Lone Pine segment of the concrete aqueduct. It was payday and he stopped at the Regional State Bank branch just a mile from his home. His paycheck had been automatically deposited and he needed cash. But he was shot in the head and left for dead at the ATM before the machine finished spitting out his money. His killer was the one who took the crisp twenties when they rolled out of the machine.

The first thing McCaleb realized as he read the initial crime reports was that a sanitized version of events had been given to the media. The circumstances described in the *Times* story Keisha Russell had read to him the day before did not mesh cleanly with the facts in the reports. The story she had read said that Cordell's body was found fifteen minutes after the shooting. According to the crime report, Cordell was found almost immediately by an ATM customer who had pulled into the bank lot just as another vehicle – most likely the shooter's – was speeding out. The witness, identified as James Noone, quickly called for help on a cellular car phone.

Because the call was relayed through a cell transponder, the 911 operator did not have an automatic address read-out of the exact location from which the call had been made. She had to take that information the old-fashioned way – manually – and managed to transpose two numbers of the address Noone had given when she dispatched an emergency medical unit. In his statement, Noone said he had watched helplessly as a paramedic ambulance went screaming by to a location seven blocks away. He had to call and explain himself all over again to a new operator. The paramedics were redirected but Cordell was dead by the time they arrived.

As he read the initial reports, it was hard for McCaleb to make a judgment on whether the delay in the arrival of paramedics was of any consequence. Cordell had suffered a devastating head wound. Even if paramedics had gotten to him ten minutes sooner, it probably would have made no difference. It was unlikely that death could have been avoided.

Still, the 911 screwup was just the type of thing the media loved to run with. So somebody in the Sheriff's Department – probably Jaye Winston's supervisor – had decided to keep that information quiet.

The screwup was a side matter that held little interest for McCaleb. What did interest him was that there was at least a partial witness as well as a vehicle description. According to Noone's statement, he had almost been creamed by a black blur as he had pulled into the bank's lot. He described the exiting vehicle as a black Jeep Cherokee with the newer, smoother styling. He got only a split-second view of the driver, a man he described only as white and with either gray hair or a gray cap on his head.

There were no other witnesses listed in the initial reports. Before moving on to the supplemental reports and the autopsy protocol, McCaleb decided to look at the videos. He turned on the television and VCR and first popped in the tape made from the ATM's surveillance camera.

As with the tape from the Sherman Market, there was a timeline running across the bottom of the frame. The picture was shot through a fish-eye lens that distorted the image. The man McCaleb assumed was James Cordell came into the frame and slid his bank card into the machine. His face was very close to the camera, blocking out a view of almost everything else. It was a design flaw – unless the real purpose of the camera was not to capture robberies but the faces of fraud artists using stolen or gimmick bank cards.

As Cordell typed in his code number, he hesitated and looked over his right shoulder, his head tracking something passing behind him – the Cherokee pulling into the lot. He finished typing in his transaction and a nervous look came across his face. Nobody likes going to an ATM at night, even a well-lighted machine in a low-crime neighborhood. The only machine McCaleb ever used was inside a twenty-four-hour supermarket, where there always was the safety and deterrent of crowds. Cordell took a nervous glance over his left shoulder, nodded at someone off-screen and then looked back at the machine. Nothing about the person he looked at had alarmed him further. The shooter obviously had not pulled on the mask. Despite his outward calm, Cordell's eyes dropped down to the cash slot, his mind probably repeating a silent mantra of *Hurry up! Hurry up!*

Then almost immediately the gun came into the frame, reaching over his shoulder and just kissing his left temple before the trigger was pulled and James Cordell's life was taken. There was the blast of blood misting the camera lens and the man went forward and to his right, apparently going into the wall next to the ATM and then falling backward to the ground.

The shooter then moved into the video frame and grabbed the cash as it was delivered through the slot. At that moment McCaleb paused the picture. On the screen was a full view of the masked shooter. He was in the same dark jumpsuit and mask worn by the shooter in the Gloria Torres tape. As Winston had said, ballistics weren't necessary. They would only be a scientific confirmation of something Winston knew and now McCaleb knew in the gut. It was the same man. Same clothes, same method of operation, same dead eyes behind the mask.

He flicked the button again and the video continued. The shooter grabbed the cash from the machine. As he did this, he seemed to be saying something but his face was not squared to the camera as with the Sherman Market shootings. It was as if he was speaking to himself this time rather than to the camera.

The shooter quickly moved to the left of the screen and stooped to pick up something unseen. The bullet casing. He then darted to the right and disappeared from the screen. McCaleb watched for a few moments. The only figure in the picture was the still form of Cordell on the pavement below the machine. The only movement was the widening pool of blood around his head. Seeking the lower ground, the blood slid into a joint in the pavement and started moving in a line toward the curb.

A minute went by and then a man entered the video screen, crouching over Cordell's body. James Noone. He was bald across the top of his head and wearing thin-framed glasses. He touched the wounded man's neck, then looked around, probably to make sure he was safe himself. He then jumped up and was gone, presumably to make the call on his cell phone. Another half minute went by before Noone returned to the frame to wait for help. As the time went by, Noone swiveled his head back and forth, apparently fearing that the gunman, if not in the car he had seen speeding away, might still be around. Finally, his attention was drawn in the direction of the street. His mouth opened in a silent scream and he waved his arms above his head as he apparently watched the paramedics speed by. He then jumped up and left the screen again.

A few moments later the screen jumped. McCaleb checked the time and saw that it was now seven minutes later. Two paramedics moved quickly into place around Cordell. They checked for pulse and pupil response. They ripped open his shirt and one of the rescuers listened to his chest with a stethoscope. Another quickly arrived with a wheeled stretcher. But one of the first two looked at the man and shook his head. Cordell was dead.

A few moments later the screen went blank.

After pausing a moment, almost in reverence, McCaleb put in the crime scene tape next. This was obviously taken from a hand-held video camera. It started with some environmental shots of the bank property and the street. In the bank lot there were two vehicles: a dusty white Chevy Suburban and a smaller vehicle barely visible on its other side. McCaleb assumed the Suburban was Cordell's. It was large and rugged, dusty from driving the mountain and desert roads alongside the aqueduct. He assumed the other car belonged to the witness, James Noone.

The tape then showed the ATM and panned downward to the blood-stained sidewalk in front of it. Cordell's body was sprawled in the spot where the paramedics had found it and then left it. It was uncovered, the dead man's shirt open, his pale chest exposed.

Over the next several minutes the video jumped in time through various stages of the crime scene. First a criminalist measured and photographed the scene, then coroner's investigators worked on the body, wrapped it in a plastic body bag and removed it on a gurney. Lastly, the criminalist and a latents man moved in to search the crime scene more thoroughly for evidence and fingerprints. There was a segment showing the criminalist using a small metal spike to work the bullet slug out of the wall next to the ATM.

Finally, there was a bonus McCaleb had not been expecting. The camera operator recorded James Noone's first recounting of what he had seen. The witness had been taken to the edge of the bank property and was standing next to a public phone and talking to a uniformed deputy when the cameraman wandered up. Noone was a man of about thirty-five. He appeared – in comparison to the deputy – to be short and compactly built. He now had on a baseball cap. He was agitated, still pumped by what he had witnessed and apparently frustrated by the screwup with the paramedics. The camera had been turned on in mid-conversation.

'All I'm saying is that he had a fighting chance.'

'Yes, sir, I understand. I'm sure it will be one of the things they take a look at.'

'I mean, I think somebody ought to investigate how this could – and the thing is, we're only what, a half mile from the hospital?'

'We're aware of that, Mr Noone,' the deputy said patiently. 'Now if we could just move on for a moment. Could you tell me if you saw anything before you found the body? Anything unusual.'

'Yes, I saw the guy. At least I think I did.'

'What guy is that?'

'The robber. I saw the getaway car.'

'Can you describe that, sir?'

'Sure, black Cherokee. The new kind. Not one of those that look like a shoe box.'

The deputy looked a bit confused but McCaleb understood that Noone was describing a Grand Cherokee model. He had one himself.

'I was pulling in and it came tearing out of here, almost hit me,' Noone said. 'The guy was a real asshole. I blasted my horn at him, then I pull in and find this man here. I called on my cell phone but then it got all fucked up.'

'Yes, sir. Can you refrain from that kind of language? This might be played in court one day.'

'Oh. Sorry.'

'Can we go back to this car? Did you happen to see a license plate?'

'I wasn't even looking.'

'How many people in the vehicle?'

'I think one, the driver.'

'Male or female?'

'Male.'

'Can you describe him for me?'

'Wasn't really looking. I was just trying not to get plowed into, that's all.'

'White? Black? Asian?'

'Oh, he was white. I'm pretty sure about that. But I couldn't identify him or anything like that.'

'What about hair color?'

'It was gray.'

'Gray?'

The deputy said it with surprise. An old robber. It seemed unusual to him.

'I think,' Noone said. 'It was all so quick. I can't be sure.'

'What about a hat?'

'Yeah, it could have been a hat.'

'What do you mean, the gray?'

'Yeah, gray hat, gray hair. I can't be sure.'

'Okay, anything else? Was he wearing glasses?'

'Uh, I either don't remember or didn't see. I really wasn't looking at the guy, you know. Besides, the car had dark windows. The only time I could really see the guy was through the windshield and I only saw that for a second. When he was coming right at me.'

'Okay, Mr Noone. This is a help. We are going to need you to make a formal statement and the detectives will need to talk to you. Is this going to be an inconvenience?'

'Yes, but what are you gonna do? I want to help. I *tried* to help. I don't mind.'

'Thank you, sir, I'm going to have a deputy take you into the Palmdale station. The detectives will talk to you there. They'll be with you as soon as possible and I'll make sure they know you are waiting.'

'Well, okay. What about my wheels?'

'Someone will take you back here when they are done.'

The tape ended there. McCaleb ejected it and thought about what he had seen and heard and read so far. The fact that the Sheriff's Department did not give the black Cherokee to the media was curious. It would be something he would have to ask Jaye Winston about. He made a note of it on the legal pad he had been writing questions on and then started through the remaining reports on Cordell.

The crime scene evidence inventory was a single page that was almost blank. Collected evidence amounted to the slug removed from the wall, a half dozen fingerprints lifted from the ATM and photographs of a tire mark possibly made by the shooter's car. The video from the ATM camera was also listed.

Clipped to the report were photocopies of photos of the tread mark and a freeze frame from the ATM video of the gun in the shooter's hand. An ancillary report from the crime lab stated that it was the technician's opinion that the tire mark had been on the asphalt at least several days and was not useful in the investigation.

A ballistics report identified the bullet as a slightly pancaked nine-millimeter Federal FMJ. Stapled to the report was a photocopy of a page from the autopsy showing a top-view drawing of the skull. The track of the bullet through Cordell's brain was charted on the drawing. The bullet had entered just forward on the left temple, then tumbled on a straight line through the frontal lobe and out through the right temple region. The track of the tumbling bullet had been an inch wide. As McCaleb read it, he realized it was probably a good thing the paramedics were late. If they had managed to save Cordell, it probably would have been for a life on a machine in one of those medical centers that were nothing more than vegetable warehouses.

The ballistics report also contained an enhanced photo of the gun. Though much of the weapon was hidden in the gloved grip of the shooter, the sheriff's firearms experts had identified it as a Heckler & Koch P7, a nine-millimeter pistol with a four-inch barrel and nickel finish.

The weapon identification was a curiosity to McCaleb. The HK P7 was a fairly expensive weapon, about a thousand dollars on the legitimate market, and not the kind of weapon normally seen in street crimes. He guessed that Jaye Winston must have assumed that the gun itself had to have been taken earlier in a robbery or burglary. McCaleb looked through the remaining supplemental reports and sure enough Winston had pulled crime reports from across the county in which an HK P7 of matching description had been reported stolen. It did not appear that she had taken the lead much further than that. It was true that many gun thefts went unreported because the people who lost the weapons shouldn't have had them in the first place. But as Winston had undoubtedly done before, McCaleb scanned the list of reported thefts – only five in the last two years – to see if any names or addresses turned a switch. None did. All five of the burglaries Winston had collected were open cases with no suspects. It was a dead end.

After the burglary list was a report detailing all thefts of black Grand Cherokees in the county during the last year. Winston had apparently believed the shooter's car was also a contradiction – a high-line vehicle used in an economically low-line crime. McCaleb thought it was a good jump to consider the car was probably stolen. There were twenty-four Cherokees on the list but no other reports indicating any follow-up. Maybe, he considered, Winston had simply changed her mind after connecting her shooting to the Torres case. The Good Samaritan had described a getaway vehicle from the market shooting that could be a Cherokee. Since that indicated the shooter had not gotten rid of it, it possibly hadn't been stolen after all.

The autopsy protocol was next and McCaleb flipped through the pages quickly. He knew from experience that ninety percent of any autopsy report was dedicated to the minute description of the procedure, identifying the characteristics of the victim's interior organs and state of health at the time of death. Most of the time it was only the summary that was important to McCaleb. But in the Cordell case even that part of the autopsy was irrelevant because it was obvious. He found the summary anyway and nodded as he read what he already knew. Massive brain damage had led to Cordell's death within minutes of the shooting.

He put the autopsy report aside. The next stack of reports dealt with Winston's three-strike theory. Believing the shooter was an ex-convict facing life without parole for another conviction, Winston had gone to the state parole offices in Van Nuys and Lancaster and pulled files on paroled armed robbers who were Caucasian and had two prior felony convictions on their records. These were people facing third-strike penalties if arrested again under the new law. There were seventy-one of them assigned to the two parole offices geographically nearest the two robbery-shootings.

Winston and other deputies had slowly gone through the list in the weeks since the robberies and murders. According to the reports, they had paid visits to nearly every man on the list. Of the seventy-one, only seven of the men couldn't be found. This indicated they had violated parole and had probably left the area or might still be in the area hiding and possibly were more likely to be committing armed robberies and even murders. Nationwide parole pickup bulletins were issued for all these men on law enforcement computer networks. Of the men who were contacted, initial interviews and investigation cleared almost ninety percent through alibis. The remaining eight had been cleared through other investigative means – chiefly because their physical dimensions did not match those of the shooter's upper body on the video.

Aside from the missing seven men on the list, the three-strikes avenue of investigation was stagnant. Winston was apparently hoping that one of those seven would eventually turn up and be tied to the shooting.

McCaleb moved on to the remaining Cordell reports. There were two follow-up interviews with James Noone at the Star Center. His story never differed in these reports and his recollection of the Cherokee driver never got any better.

There also was a crime scene sketch and four field-interview reports on traffic stops of men driving black Cherokees. They had been stopped in Lancaster and Palmdale within an hour of the ATM shooting by deputies made aware of the Cherokee's use in the crime by a sheriff's radio broadcast. The identification of each driver was run through the computer and they were sent on their way after coming up clean. The reports were forwarded to Winston.

The last item McCaleb read was the most recent summary report filed by Winston. It was short and to the point.

'No new leads or suspects at this time. Investigating officer is waiting at this point for additional information that may lead to the ID of a suspect.'

Winston was at the wall. She was waiting. She needed fresh blood.

McCaleb drummed his fingers on the table and thought about all he had just read. He agreed with the moves Winston had made but he tried to think of what she had missed and what else could be done. He liked her three-strike theory and shared her disappointment at not being able to cull a suspect out of the list of seventy-one. The fact that most of the men were cleared through alibis bothered him. How could so many two-strikes dirtbags be able to perfectly account for their exact whereabouts on two different nights? He had always been suspicious of alibis when he was working cases. He knew it took only one liar to make an alibi.

McCaleb stopped his finger roll on the table as he thought of something. He fanned the stack of Cordell reports across the table. He didn't need to look through them because he knew that what he was thinking of was not in the pile. He had realized that Winston had never geographically cross-referenced her various theories.

He got up and left the boat. Buddy Lockridge was sitting in the cockpit of his boat sewing a rip in a wet suit when McCaleb walked up.

'Hey, you got a job?'

'Guy over on millionaires' row wants me to scrape his Bertram. It's the sixty over there. But if you need a ride, I can do his thing whenever I want. He's a once-a-month weekender.'

'No. I just want to know if you have a *Thomas Brothers* I can borrow. Mine's in my car and I don't want to take the tarp off it to get to it.'

'Yeah, sure. It's in the bull.'

Lockridge reached into his pocket and got his car keys out and tossed them to McCaleb. On his way out to the Taurus McCaleb glanced over at millionaires' row. It was a dock with double-wide, long slips to handle the girth of the larger yachts that moored in Cabrillo Marina. He picked out the Bertram 60. It was a beautiful boat. And he knew it had cost its owner, who probably used it no more than once a month, an easy million and a half.

After retrieving the map book from Lockridge's car, returning the key and then returning to his own boat, McCaleb set to work with the Cordell records. First he went through the reports on thefts of Cherokees and HK P7 pistols. He numbered each reported theft and then charted it by address on the appropriate page of the map book. He then went on to the list of three-strike suspects, using the same procedure to chart the home and job locations of each man as well. Lastly, he charted the locations of the shootings.

It took him almost an hour. But by the time he was done, he felt a sense of cautious excitement. One name from the list of seventy-one clearly stood out as being geographically relevant to the Sherman Market shooting and the theft of an HK P7.

The man's name was Mikail Bolotov, a thirty-year-old Russian émigré who had already served two stints in California prisons for armed robberies. Bolotov lived and worked in Canoga Park. His home was off DeSoto near Sherman Way, a mile or so from the market where Gloria Torres and Chan Ho Kang were murdered. His job was at a clock manufacturing plant located on Winnetka only eight blocks south and two blocks east of the market. Lastly, and this was what excited McCaleb, the Russian also worked only four blocks from a Canoga Park home from which an HK P7 had been stolen during a burglary in December. Reading the burglary report, McCaleb noted that the intruder had taken several presents from beneath a Christmas tree, including a new HK P7 that had been wrapped as a gift from the homeowner to his wife – the perfect LA Christmas gift. The burglar left no fingerprints or other evidence behind.

McCaleb read through the entire parole package and investigator's report. Bolotov had a long record of violence, though no previous suspicion of homicide and no tangles with the law since his last discharge from prison three years before. He routinely made his parole appointments and to outward appearance appeared to be on the straight and narrow.

Bolotov had been interviewed on the Cordell matter at his place of employment by two sheriff's investigators named Ritenbaugh and Aguilar. The interview had taken place two weeks after the Cordell murder but nearly three weeks before the Sherman Market murders. Also, the interview had apparently taken place before Winston had pulled the reports on HK P7 thefts. This, he guessed, was why the significance of Bolotov's geographic location was missed.

During the interview, Bolotov's answers had apparently been sufficient to avoid suspicion and his employer had provided an alibi, reporting that on the night James Cordell was murdered, Bolotov had worked his normal two-to-ten shift. He showed the detectives pay records and time cards reflecting the hours worked. That was enough for Ritenbaugh and Aguilar. Cordell had died at about 10:10 P.M. It would have been physically impossible for Bolotov to get from Canoga Park to Lancaster in ten minutes – even if he had used a helicopter. Ritenbaugh and Aguilar moved on to the next name on the list of three-strike candidates.

'Bullshit,' McCaleb said out loud.

He felt excited. Bolotov was a lead that should be rechecked no matter what his boss or the pay records said. The man was an armed robber by trade, not a clock maker. His geographic proximity to key locations relating to the investigation demanded that another look be taken. McCaleb felt he had at least accomplished something that he could go back to Winston with.

He quickly wrote a few notes on the legal pad and then set it aside. He was exhausted from the work done so far and felt the low pounding of a headache coming on. He looked at his watch and saw that time had sped by without his realizing it. It was two o'clock already. He knew he should eat something but he had no desire for any kind of food in particular. He decided instead to take a nap and went below to the stateroom.

11

Refreshed from an hour-long nap during which he had no dreams that he could remember, McCaleb made himself a sandwich of white bread and processed cheese. He opened a can of Coke to go with it and went back to the galley table to go through the Gloria Torres case.

He started with the surveillance tape from the Sherman Market. He had seen it twice already in the company of Arrango and Walters but decided he needed to watch it again. He put the tape in and watched it on normal speed, then put what was left of his sandwich in the sink. He couldn't eat any more. His insides were clenched too tight.

He rewound the tape and started playing it again, this time on slow-motion play. Gloria's movements seemed languid and relaxed. McCaleb found himself almost ready to return the smile she showed. He wondered what she was thinking. Was the smile for Mr Kang? McCaleb doubted it. It was a secret smile. A smile for something inside. His guess was that she was thinking about her son and he knew then that she had at least been happy in that final conscious moment.

The tape brought no new ideas, just the rekindling of anger toward the shooter. He put in the crime scene tape next and watched the documentation, measuring and quantification of the carnage. Gloria's body, of course, was not there and the blood on the floor where she had dropped was minimal – thanks to the Good Samaritan. But the store owner's corpse was crumpled on the floor behind the counter, blood seemingly surrounding it completely. It made McCaleb think of the old woman he had seen in the store the day before. She stood where her husband had fallen. That took a certain kind of courage, a kind McCaleb didn't think he had.

After turning off the tape, he started through the stack of reports. Arrango and Walters had not produced as much paper as Winston had. McCaleb tried not to take this to mean anything significant but he couldn't help it. In his experience, the size of a murder book reflected not only the depth of the investigation but the commitment of the investigators. McCaleb believed there was a sacred bond between the victim and the investigator. All homicide cops understood this. Some took it straight to the heart. Some less so, simply as a matter of psychological survival. But it was there in all of them. It didn't matter if you had religion, if you believed the soul of the departed watched over you. Even if you believed that all things ended with the final breath, you still spoke for the dead. Your name was whispered on the last breath. But only you heard it. Only you knew it. No other crime came with such a covenant.

McCaleb set aside the thick protocols from the autopsies of Torres and Kang to read last. As with the Cordell file, he knew, the autopsies would provide few salient details beyond what was already obvious. He quickly went through the initial crime reports and next came to a thin sheaf of witness reports. They were statements of people who each had a little part of the whole: a gas station attendant, a passing motorist, a *Times* pressroom employee who worked with Gloria. There were also investigative summaries, supplemental reports, fact sheets, crime scene charts, ballistics reports and a chronological record of the travels and calls made by the detectives on the case. Last in this section of the stack was the transcript of the never-identified Good Samaritan's 911 call made after he stumbled into the shooting's aftermath and tried to save Gloria's life. The transcript was of a man speaking English with difficulty as he hurriedly reported a shooting. But when the operator offered to switch him to a Spanish-speaker, he declined.

CALLER: I must go. I go now. The girl is shot very bad. The man, he run. He drive away. A black car, like a truck.

OPERATOR: Sir, please stay on the line . . . Sir? Sir?

That was it. He was gone. He had mentioned the vehicle but gave no description of the suspect.

Following this statement there was a ballistics report identifying the bullets recovered during surgery on Gloria Torres and the autopsy of Chan Ho Kang as nine-millimeter Federal FMJs. A photo from the store video was analyzed and the weapon was again identified as the HK P7.

It struck McCaleb as he finished an initial reading of the rest of the reports that what was missing from the murder book was a timeline. Unlike the Cordell case, which had only one witness, the Torres case had a variety of minor witnesses and time markers. The detectives apparently had not sat down with all of these and collated them into a timeline. They had not re-created the sequence of incidents that made up the event as a whole.

McCaleb sat back and thought about this for a moment. Why wasn't it there? Would such a timeline or exact sequence of events even be useful? Probably not initially, he decided. In terms of identifying a killer, it would give little help. And at least initially, that's all that mattered. But a sequential analysis of the event should have been done later, after the dust had settled, so to speak. McCaleb had often advised investigators who sent their cases to him to create a timeline. It could be useful breaking alibis, finding holes in witness accounts, in simply giving the investigator a better command and knowledge of exactly what had happened.

McCaleb was fully aware that he was Monday morning quarter-backing. Arrango and Walters didn't have the luxury of coming into a case two months after the fact. Maybe thought of a timeline got lost. They had other concerns and other cases to worry about.

He got up and went to the galley to turn on the coffeemaker. He was feeling fatigued again and had been awake only ninety minutes. McCaleb hadn't been drinking much coffee since the transplant. Dr Fox had told him to avoid caffeine and on the occasion that he had ignored that advice and had a cup, it sometimes caused a fluttering sensation in his chest. But he wanted to keep alert and finish his work. He took the risk.

After the coffee was ready, he poured himself a mug, then overpowered it with milk and sugar. He sat back down and silently chastised himself for looking for reasons to excuse Arrango and Walters. They should have taken the time to work the case thoroughly. McCaleb was angry with himself for having thought anything else.

He took up the legal pad and began to read through the witness reports again, noting down the salient times and a brief summary of what each witness brought to the case. He then overlaid various time notations from the other crime reports. It took him an hour to do this, during which time he refilled his mug three times without really thinking about it. When he was finished, he had constructed a timeline on two pages of the pad. The problem, he realized as he studied his work, was that the sequence was inexact in all but a couple of references and contained outright conflicts, if not impossibilities.

10:01 P.M. – End of B shift, *Los Angeles Times* pressroom, Chatsworth facility. Gloria punches out.

10:10 P.M. – approximate – Gloria leaves with coworker Annette Stapleton. They talk in the parking lot approximately five minutes. Gloria leaves in her blue Honda Civic.

10:29 P.M. – Gloria at the Chevron gas station on Winnetka at Roscoe. Self-service credit card sale: $14.40. Attendant Connor Davis recalls Gloria as a regular nighttime customer who would ask about sports scores because he often had a game on the radio. Time ascribed to credit card records.

10:40 to 10:43 P.M. – approximate – Motorist Ellen Taaffe traveling east on Sherman Way, windows down, hears popping sound as she passes the Sherman Market. Looks, sees nothing wrong. Two cars in the lot. Sale signs in windows of the market prevent viewing into the store. As she looks, she hears another popping sound but again sees nothing unusual. Timing of sounds ascribed by Taaffe to the beginning of KFWB news report cycle which started at 10:40.

10:41:03 P.M. – Unidentified male with Spanish accent calls 911, says a woman has been shot at the Sherman Market and needs help. Does not stay for police. Illegal alien?

10:41:37 P.M. – Gloria Torres is shot to death, according to store's security video time clock.

10:42:55 P.M. – Good Samaritan enters store and helps Gloria, according to security video time clock.

10:43:21 P.M. – Ellen Taaffe uses her car phone to call 911 dispatch to report sound of possible gunfire. She is told the shooting has already been reported. Her name and number are forwarded to detectives.

10:47 P.M. – Paramedics arrive, transport Gloria to Northridge Medical Center. Chan Ho Kang pronounced dead.

10:49 P.M. – First police arrive on scene.

He read it all again. He knew homicide was an inexact science but the timeline bothered him. According to the first homicide investigation report, the actual shooting was determined by the detectives to have occurred during the sixty seconds between 10:40 and 10:41 P.M. In deciding this, the detectives had used the one source of time they knew to be exact and unassailably correct – the time log at the department's emergency dispatch center. The first call reporting the shooting – from the Good Samaritan – had come in at 10:41:03 to a 911 operator. Using that time and the report by motorist Ellen Taaffe about hearing the shots sometime after the start of the KFWB news report led to the conclusion that the shooting had to have been after 10:40 but before 10:41:03, when the Good Samaritan made the call.

This time frame, of course, was in contradiction to the time of 10:41:37 shown on the store's videotape at the start of the shooting.

McCaleb looked through the reports again, hoping he had missed some page on which there was an explanation of this discrepancy. There was nothing. He drummed his fingers on the table for a few moments while he thought about things. He checked his watch and saw it was almost five. It was unlikely any of the investigators would still be around.

Again he studied the timeline he had constructed, searching for an explanation for the anomaly. His eyes held on the second call to the dispatch center. Ellen Taaffe, the motorist who had heard the shooting, had called on her mobile phone at 10:43:21 to report the shooting and was told it had already been reported.

He thought about this. The detectives had used her hearing of the shots to set the murders within the minute of 10:40, the very start of the news program. Yet when she called 911, they already knew about the shooting. Why had she delayed more than two minutes to make the call? And was she ever asked if she saw the Good Samaritan?

McCaleb quickly flipped through the stack of reports until he located the Ellen Taaffe witness statement. It was one page, with her signature beneath a statement typed below a two-inch information block. The statement said nothing about how long she had waited between hearing the shots and calling the 911 dispatch center. The statement did say she believed that there were two cars parked in front of the store but she could not identify the type of vehicles they were or remember if there had been any occupants.

He looked at the information box. It said Taaffe was thirty-five years old and married. She lived in Northridge and was an executive with a headhunting firm. She had been driving home from the movies at Topanga Plaza when she heard the shooting. Her home and work phone numbers were contained in the witness information box. McCaleb went to the phone and dialed the work number. A secretary answered, corrected his pronunciation of *Taaffe* and said he had just caught her on her way out the door.

'This is Ellen Taaffe,' a voice said, rhyming the name with *waif.*

'Yes, hello, Mrs Taaffe. You don't know me. My name is McCaleb. I'm an investigator working on that shooting a couple months ago on Sherman Way. The one you heard and talked to the police about?'

He heard her breath going out in a way that indicated she was being put out by the call.

'I don't understand, I already talked to the detectives. Are you with the police?'

'No, I'm . . . I work for the family of the woman who was killed there. Is this a bad time?'

'Yes, I'm on my way out the door. I'd like to beat the traffic and . . . and, frankly, I don't know what I can tell you. I told everything to the police.'

'This will only take a minute. I just have a few quick questions. This woman had a little boy. I'm just trying to catch the guy who took her away.'

He heard the breath go out again.

'All right, I'll try to help. What are the questions?'

'Okay, one, how long did you wait between hearing the shots and calling nine one one on your car phone?'

'I didn't wait. I called right then. I grew up around guns. My father was a police officer and I went with him to the range sometimes. I knew that what I heard was a gun. I called right away.'

'Well, I'm looking at the police records and they say you thought you heard the shooting around ten-forty but didn't call it in until ten-forty-three. I don't –'

'What they don't tell you in those reports is that I got a tape. I called right away but I got a tape. All the nine one one lines were busy and I was put on hold. I don't know how long. It was aggravating. But when my call finally was put through, they said they already knew about the shooting anyway.'

'How long do you think you were on hold?'

'I just said I'm not sure. Maybe a minute. Maybe more or maybe less. I don't know.'

'Okay. The report says you heard a shot and looked out your window at the store. Then you heard another shot. You saw two cars in the lot. The next question is, did you see anyone outside?'

'No. There was no one there. I told this to the police.'

'It seems like if the inside of the store was lit, you might be able to see if there was anyone in the cars.'

'If there was anyone in either of the cars, I don't remember seeing them.'

'Was one of the cars a sports utility vehicle, like a Cherokee?'

'I don't know. The police already asked that. But my attention was on the store. I looked right past the cars.'

'Would you say they were dark or light colored?'

'I really don't know. I just told you that and I've been over this with the police. They have every –'

'Did you hear a third shot?'

'A third? No, only two.'

'But there were three shots. So you don't know if you heard the first two shots or the last two.'

'That's right.'

He thought about this for a second, deciding that it was probably impossible to decide for sure whether she had heard the first two or last two shots.

'Mrs Taaffe, that's it. Thanks a lot. You've been a help and I'm sorry to have bothered you.'

The brief interview helped answer only the question he had about the delay in her 911 call but it still left the discrepancy between the timing of the Good Samaritan's 911 call and the time on the store's surveillance tape. McCaleb checked his watch again. It was now after five. All the detectives would be gone but he decided to call anyway.

To his surprise he was told when he called West Valley Division that both Arrango and Walters were in and asked which one he wanted. He decided to try Walters, since he had seemed sympathetic to his situation the day before. Walters picked up after three rings.

'It's Terry McCaleb . . . The Gloria Torres thing?'

'Right, right.'

'I guess you heard I got the books from Winston over at the sheriff's.'

'Yeah, we're not too happy about that. We also got a call from the *Slimes* about it, too. Some reporter. That wasn't cool. I don't know who you've been talk –'

'Look, your partner put me in a position where I had to look for information where I could get it. Don't worry about the *Times.* They'll sit on the story because there is no story. Not at the moment.'

'And it best stay that way. Anyway, I'm kind of busy here. What've you got?'

'You got a case?'

'Yeah. They just keep dropping like flies out here in the Big Valley.'

'Well, look, I won't hold you up. I've just got one question maybe you can help me with.'

McCaleb waited. Walters didn't say anything. He seemed different from the day before. McCaleb wondered if Arrango was sitting close by and listening. He decided to press on.

'I just want to know about the timing,' he said. 'The video from the store shows the shooting going down at' – he quickly scanned his timeline – 'let's see, ten forty-one thirty-seven. Then you have the nine one one records and they say the call from the Good Samaritan came in at exactly ten forty-one oh three. See what I'm getting at? How'd the guy call it in thirty-four seconds before the shooting actually happened?'

'Simple, the time on the video was off. It was fast.'

'Oh, okay,' McCaleb said, as if the possibility had not occurred to him. 'You guys checked it out?'

'My partner did.'

'Really? I didn't see any report on it in the book.'

'Look, he made a phone call to the security company, checked it out, no report, okay? The guy who installed that system put it in more than a year ago – right after the first time Mr Kang got robbed. Eddie talked to the guy. He set the camera clock off his own watch back then and hasn't been back in there since. He showed Mr Kang how to set the camera clock in case there was a power outage or something.'

'Okay,' McCaleb said, not sure where this was going.

'So, your guess is as good as mine. Is it showing the original time set off the installer's watch or did the old man set it a few times himself? Either way it doesn't matter. We can't trust it just coming off somebody's watch. Maybe the watch was fast, maybe the camera clock has been gaining a couple seconds every week or two. Who knows? We can't trust it, is what I'm saying. But we can trust the nine-eleven clock. That's the time we know is correct and it's the time we went with.'

McCaleb was silent and Walters seemed to take it as some kind of judgment.

'Look, the camera clock is just a detail that doesn't mean anything anyway,' he said. 'If we worried about every detail that didn't fit, we'd still be working our first case. I'm busy here, man, what else you got?'

'That's it, I guess. You guys never checked the surveillance clock, right? You know, to check the time against the dispatch clock?'

'Nope. We went back a couple days later but there had been a power outage – Santa Anas blew down the line. The time on it was useless to us then.'

'Too bad.'

'Yeah, too bad. I gotta go. Keep in touch. You get something, you call us before Winston or we're not going to be happy with you. All right?'

'I'll call you.'

Walters hung up. McCaleb put the phone down and stared at it for a few moments, wondering what his next move should or would be. He was drawing a blank. But it had always been his practice to go back to the start whenever he hit a stall. The start most often meant the crime scene. But this case was different. He could go back to the actual crime.

He put the video of the Sherman Market murders back in the VCR and watched the tape again in slow motion. He sat there gripping the edges of the table so hard his knuckles and finger joints began to hurt. It wasn't until the third run-through that he picked up on something he had missed earlier and had been there all along.

Chan Ho Kang's watch. The watch his wife now wore. On the video the watch was seen as Kang desperately grasped for purchase on the counter.

McCaleb fished around on the video for a few minutes, backing and forwarding the tape until he froze the image on what he believed was the best view of the watch's face. The best he could do was a clean look at it but the LED readout was not picked up by the video shot from the upper wall. The numbers on the watch – the time – were not readable.

He sat there staring at the frozen image, wondering if he should pursue it.

If he could read the time on the watch, he might be able to triangulate the time of the shooting by using the camera clock and the dispatch clock. It might clear up a loose end. But did it mean anything? Walters had been right about one thing. There are always details that don't add up. Always loose ends. And McCaleb wasn't sure if this one was worth the time it would take to tie it up.

His private debate was interrupted. Living on a boat, he had learned to read the subtle rises and falls of his home, to know whether each was caused by a boat wake out in the fairway or the weight of someone coming on board. McCaleb felt the boat dip slightly and immediately looked over his shoulder and out the sliding door. Graciela Rivers had just stepped onboard and was turning around to help a little boy step on next. Raymond. Dinner. He had completely forgotten.

'Shit,' he said as he quickly turned off the video and got up to go out and greet them.

12

'You forgot, didn't you?'

There was an easy smile on her face.

'No – I mean, I sort of forgot for the last five hours. I got lost in all of this paperwork I've been looking through. I meant to go over to the market and –'

'Well, that's okay. We can do it another –'

'No, no, are you kidding? We're going to have dinner. Is this Raymond?'

'Oh, yes.'

Graciela turned to the boy, who was standing shyly behind her at the stern. He seemed small for his age, with dark hair and eyes, brown skin. He wore shorts and a striped shirt. He carried a sweater in his hands.

'Raymond, this is Mr McCaleb. The man I was telling you about. This is his boat. He lives on it.'

McCaleb stepped forward and leaned down with his hand out. The boy was carrying a toy police car in his right hand and had to transfer it to the other. He then tentatively took McCaleb's hand and they shook. McCaleb felt an unexplainable sadness as he met the boy.

'It's Terry,' he said. 'Nice to meet you, Raymond. I've heard a lot about you.'

'Can you fish off this boat?'

'Sure you can. Someday I'll take you out, if you want.'

'That would be good.'

McCaleb straightened up and smiled at Graciela. She looked lovely. She wore a light summer dress similar to the one she had worn the first time she had come to the boat. It was the kind that the breeze off the water easily pushed against her figure. She, too, carried a sweater. McCaleb was in shorts, sandals and a T-shirt that said Robicheaux's Dock & Baitshop on it. He felt a little embarrassed.

'I'll tell you what,' he said. 'Over there they've got a nice restaurant on top of the marine store. They've got good food and a great view of the sunset. Why don't we have dinner there?'

'Sounds good to me,' Graciela said.

'All I have to do is change real quick and, Raymond, I have an idea. Why don't we drop a line off the stern and you see if you can catch something while I go inside and show Graciela a few things I've been working on?'

The boy's face brightened.

'Okay.'

'Okay, then, we'll fix you up.'

McCaleb left them there and went inside. In the salon he took his lightest rod and reel out of the overhead storage rack, went to the tackle box under the chart table and got out a steel leader already set with a number eight hook and a sinker. He attached the leader to the reel line and then went to the cooler in the galley, where he knew he had some frozen squid. Using a sharp knife, he cut off a piece of squid skirt and drove the hook through it.

He returned to the stern with the rod and reel and handed the rig to Raymond. Crouching behind the boy with his arms coming around him, he gave him a quick lesson on casting the bait into the middle of the fairway. He then told him how to keep his finger on the line and to read it for nibbles.

'You okay now?' he asked when the lesson was completed.

'Uh-huh. Are there fish in here by the boats?'

'Sure, I've seen a school of sheepshead swimming right where your line is.'

'Sheepshead?'

'It's a fish with yellow stripes. Sometimes you can see them moving in the water. You watch for them.'

'Okay.'

'Are you all right now if I go in and get your mother something to drink?'

'She's not my mother.'

'Oh, yes, I – I'm sorry, Raymond. I meant Graciela. You okay?'

'I'm okay.'

'Okay, give a holler if you hook one. And then start reeling!'

He pointed a finger into the boy's side and dragged it up his tiny rib cage. McCaleb's father had done the same thing to him when he was holding a fishing pole, his sides unprotected. Raymond giggled and maneuvered away, never taking his eyes off the spot where his line disappeared into the dark water.

Graciela followed McCaleb into the salon and he closed the slider so the boy would not hear them. His face must have been red from the slip-up with the boy. She read him before he got the chance to apologize.

'That's okay. It's going to happen a lot now.'

He nodded.

'Is he going to stay with you?'

'Yes. I'm the only one but that doesn't matter. I've been around since he was born. For him to lose his mother and then me, I think it would be too much. I want him to stay with me.'

'Where's his father?'

'Who knows.'

McCaleb nodded and decided to step out of that area of questioning.

'You are going to be great for him,' he said. 'You want a glass of wine?'

'*That* would be great.'

'Red or white?'

'Whatever you're having.'

'I can't have any right now. In a couple months.'

'Oh, then I don't want you to open a bottle of wine just for me. I can have –'

'Please, I want to. How about a red? I've got some good red and if I open it, I can at least smell it.'

She smiled.

'I remember Glory was like that when she was pregnant. She used to sit right next to me and say she just wanted to smell the wine I was drinking.'

The smile turned sad.

'She was a good person,' McCaleb said. 'I can tell that by the boy. That's what you wanted me to see.'

She nodded. He went to the galley and got a bottle of red wine out of the sea rack. It was a Sanford pinot noir, one of his favorites. While he was opening it, she came over to the counter. He could smell a light scent of perfume. It was vanilla, he thought. It thrilled him. It wasn't so much being close to her as feeling that something was awakening in him after a long dormancy.

'Do you have children?' she asked then.

'Me, no.'

'Were you ever married?'

'Yes, once.'

He poured her a glass and watched her taste it. She smiled and nodded.

'It's good. How long ago was that?'

'What, when I was married? Let's see, I got married about ten years ago. Lasted three years. She was an agent and we worked together in Quantico. Then, when it didn't work out and we got divorced, we still had to work with each other and it . . . I don't know, we were cool about it but it wasn't a good thing, you know? About the same time my dad was getting sick out here. So I gave them the idea of sending someone from the unit out here permanently. I sold it to them as a cost-cutting move. I mean, I was flying out here all the time anyway. A lot of us were. I figured they ought to have a little outpost or something out here and save some of that dough. They agreed and I got the job.'

Graciela nodded, turned and looked out the slider to check on Raymond. He was staring intently into the water where he hoped the fish were.

'How 'bout you?' McCaleb asked. 'You ever get married?'

'Once, too.'

'Kids?'

'No.'

She was still looking out at Raymond. Her smile was still in place but straining under the conversation. McCaleb was curious about her but decided to let it go.

'By the way, you were good with him,' she said, nodding in Raymond's direction. 'It's a balance. You have to teach them and let them find out for themselves. That was nice with him.'

She looked at him and he shook his shoulders to indicate it was luck. He took her glass and held it up to his nose to savor its aroma and then handed it back to her. He then poured himself the last from the coffee pot and added some milk and sugar. They clicked mug to glass and drank.

'Sorry,' she said. 'I feel so bad drinking this in front of you.'

'Don't. I'm glad you like it.'

Silence filled the salon. Her eyes fell to the stacks of reports and videotapes on the galley table.

'What did you want to show me?'

'Uh, nothing specific. I just didn't want to talk in front of Raymond.'

He checked on the boy through the glass. He was doing fine. His focus was still intently on the line cutting through the incoming tide. McCaleb hoped he would hook something but guessed it was unlikely. Below the marina's beautiful surface the water was fouled with pollutants. Any fish that survived down there was a bottom feeder with the survival skills of a cockroach.

He looked back at Graciela.

'But I wanted to let you know I met with the sheriff's detective this morning. She was a lot cooler about it than the LAPD guys.'

'She?'

'Jaye Winston. She's good. We worked together before. Anyway, she gave me copies of everything on both cases. That's what I spent all day looking through. There's a lot.'

'And?'

He summarized as best he could, trying to be gentle about details relating to her sister. He didn't tell her he had a videotape of her sister's murder there on the boat with them.

'In the bureau we have this thing called doing a full field,' he said at the end of the summary. 'It means leaving nothing untouched, nothing to chance. The bottom line here is that the investigation of your sister's murder was not a full field but at the same time there's nothing that jumps out at me as a gaping hole in what *was* done. There were some mistakes made, maybe some assumptions that were made before all the facts were in but they weren't necessarily wrong anyway. The investigation was thorough enough.'

'Thorough enough,' she repeated, looking down as she talked. McCaleb realized it had been a poor choice of words.

'I mean –'

'So this guy is just going to get away with it,' she said as a statement. 'I guess I should've known this is what you were going to tell me.'

'Well, I'm not telling you that. Winston, over at the sheriff's department – at least she's still actively pursuing this. And I'm not done, either, Graciela. I'm not saying that. I have a stake in this, too.'

'I know. I don't mean to sound unhappy with you. It's not you at all. But I'm frustrated.'

'I understand that. I don't want you to be. Let's go have a nice dinner and we'll talk more later.'

'Okay.'

'You go on out there with Raymond. I've got to change.'

After changing into a clean pair of Dockers and a yellow Hawaiian shirt with flying slices of pineapple on it, McCaleb led them down the docks to the restaurant. He hadn't bothered reeling in Raymond's line. He'd put the rod in one of the gunwale holders and told the boy they'd check on it when they got back.

They ate at the table with Graciela and Raymond on the side that afforded them a view of the sun just starting to set over the forest of sailboat masts. Graciela and McCaleb ordered the grilled swordfish special, while Raymond had fish and chips. McCaleb repeatedly tried to draw Raymond into conversation but was unsuccessful most of the time. He and Graciela mostly talked about the differences between living on a boat and living in a house. McCaleb told Graciela about how peaceful and restoring it was to be on the water.

'And it's even better when you're out there,' he said, pointing in the direction of the Pacific.

'How long before you have your boat ready?' Graciela asked.

'Not long. As soon as I get the second engine back together, it will be ready to run. The rest is all cosmetic. I can do that anytime.'

On the way back after dinner, Raymond walked quickly ahead of them along the seawall, an ice-cream cone in one hand and a flashlight in the other, his blue sweater on, his head bobbing this way and that as he hunted with the light for fiddler crabs scaling the walls. The light was almost gone from the sky now. It would be time for Graciela and Raymond to leave when they got back to the boat. McCaleb felt as though he was already missing them.

When the boy got far enough in front of them, Graciela brought up the case again.

'What else can you do at this point?'

'On the case? For one thing, I have a lead I want to follow, something they might have missed.'

'What?'

He explained the geographic cross-referencing he had done and how he came up with Mikail Bolotov. When he saw her getting excited, he quickly cautioned her against it.

'This guy's got an alibi. It's a lead but it may go nowhere.'

He moved on.

'I also am thinking about going to the bureau to get them involved in the ballistics.'

'How so?'

'This guy could've done this elsewhere. He uses a very expensive gun. The fact that he didn't get rid of it between these two cases means he's hanging on to it and so he might've used it before somewhere else. They have some ballistic evidence – the bullets. The bureau might be able to do something with it if I can get them the material.'

She didn't comment and he wondered if her common sense told her that this was a long shot. He moved on.

'I'm also thinking about going back to a couple of the witnesses and interviewing them a little differently. Especially the man who saw part of the shooting up in the desert. And that's going to take some finesse. I mean, I don't want to step on Winston's toes or make her feel I think she dropped the ball. But I'd like to talk to the guy myself. He's the best witness. I'd like to talk to him and then maybe a couple of the witnesses to when your sister was . . . you know.'

'I didn't know there were witnesses. There were people in the store?'

'No, I don't mean direct witnesses. But there was a woman who drove by and heard shots. There are also a couple of people in the reports that your sister worked with that night over at the *Times*. I'd just like to talk to all of them myself, see if maybe anything changed in their memories about that night.'

'I can probably help you set that up. I know most of her friends.'

'Good.'

They walked along in silence for a few moments. Raymond was still well ahead of them. Graciela finally spoke.

'I wonder if you'd do a favor for me.'

'Sure.'

'Glory used to go see this lady in our neighborhood. Mrs Otero. She also would leave Raymond with her if I wasn't around. But Glory would go by herself sometimes to talk to her about her problems. I was wondering if you would talk to her.'

'Uh . . . I don't . . . you mean, you think she might know something about this or is this, like, to console her?'

'It's possible she might be able to help.'

'How would she be able to . . . ?'

Then it dawned on him.

'Are you talking about a psychic?'

'A spiritualist. Glory trusted Mrs Otero. She said she was in touch with the angels and Glory believed it. And she's been calling and saying she wants to talk to me and, I don't know, I just thought maybe you'd go with me.'

'I don't know. I don't really believe in that sort of stuff, Graciela. I don't know what I'd say to her.'

She just looked at him and it cut him that he thought he saw disapproval in her eyes.

'Graciela . . . I saw too many bad things and bad people to believe in that stuff. How can there be angels out there or up there when people do the kinds of things they do down here?'

She still didn't say anything and he knew her silence was a judgment.

'How 'bout I think about it and let you know?'

'Fine,' she finally said.

'Don't be upset.'

'Look, I'm sorry. I got you involved in this and I know it's a big intrusion. I don't know what I thought. I guess I just thought you'd . . .'

'Look, don't worry about it. I'm doing it now for me as much as you. Okay? Just don't give up hope. Like I said, there's still a few things I'm going to do and Winston isn't going to let this drop, either. Give me a few days. If I get stalled out, maybe then we'll go see Mrs Otero. Okay?'

She nodded but he could tell she was disappointed.

'She was such a good kid,' she said after a while. 'Having Raymond changed everything for her. She straightened up, moved in with me and just got her priorities right. She was going to school in the mornings at Cal State. That's why she had that night job. She was smart. She wanted to get into the other side of the newspaper business. Be a reporter.'

He nodded and kept silent. He knew it was good for her to keep talking like this.

'She would have been good at it. I think. She cared about people. I mean, look at her. She was a volunteer. After the riots she went down to South-Central to help clean up. After the earthquake she came into the hospital to just be in the ER and tell people it would be okay. She was an organ donor. She gave blood – anytime any hospital called and said they needed blood, she came in. That rare blood . . . well, she was rarer. Sometimes I really wish I could've traded places and that it was me who went into that store.'

He reached over and put his arm around her shoulders in a comforting manner.

'Come on,' he said. 'Look at all the people you help at the hospital. And look at Raymond. You're going to be great for him. You can't think about who was more worthy or about switching places. What happened to her shouldn't have happened to anyone.'

'But all I know is Raymond having his own mother would've been better than me.'

There was no way to argue with her. He moved his arm and put his hand on her neck. She wasn't crying but she looked like she might start. He wanted to console her but knew there was only one way he could do that.

They were almost to his dock. Raymond was waiting at the security gate, which was open a couple of inches as usual. The spring return was rusted and the gate never closed on its own.

'We should go,' Graciela said when they caught up to the boy. 'It's getting late and you have school.'

'What about the fishing pole?' Raymond protested.

'Mr McCaleb can take care of that. Now thank him for the fishing and the dinner and the ice cream.'

Raymond put out his little hand and McCaleb shook it again. It was cold and sticky.

'It's Terry. And look, we'll do some real fishing soon. As soon as I get the boat going. We'll take it out then and we'll catch you a big one. I know a spot on the other side of Catalina. This time of year, we'll catch calico bass. Lots of them. We'll go there, okay?'

Raymond nodded silently as if he guessed it would never happen. It sent a shiver of sadness through McCaleb. He looked at Graciela.

'How about Saturday? The boat won't be ready but you guys could come down in the morning and we could fish off the jetty. You could stay over if you want. Plenty of room.'

'Yeah!' Raymond cried.

'Well,' Graciela said, 'let's see how the rest of the week goes.'

McCaleb nodded, realizing the mistake he had just made. Graciela opened the passenger door of her Rabbit convertible and the boy got in. She came over to McCaleb after closing the door.

'Sorry about that,' he said in a low voice. 'I guess I shouldn't have suggested that in front of him.'

'It's all right,' she said. 'I'd like to do it but I might have to juggle some things, so let's wait and see. Unless you need to know for sure right now.'

'No, that's fine. Just let me know.'

She took a step closer to him and held out her hand to shake.

'Thank you very much for tonight,' she said. 'He's quiet most of the time but I think he enjoyed it and I know I did.'

McCaleb took her hand and shook it but then she leaned into him, brought her face up and kissed him on the cheek. As she stepped back, she brought her hand to her mouth.

'Bristly,' she said with a smile. 'Are you growing a beard?'

'Thinking about it.'

This made her laugh for some reason. She walked around the car and he followed so he could hold open the door. When she was in her seat, she looked up at him.

'You know, you should believe in them,' she said.

He looked down at her.

'You mean angels?'

She nodded. He nodded back. She started the car and drove off.

Back at the boat, he went over to the corner of the stern. The fishing pole was still in the slot and the line was still in the water as Raymond had left it. But as he reeled the line in, McCaleb could tell there was no drag on it. When the line finally came out of the water, he saw the hook and weight but no bait. Something down there had cleaned him out.

13

On Thursday morning McCaleb was up before the port stevedores had anything to do with it. The caffeine of the day before had surged through his veins without ebb and kept him from sleep. It fueled disquieting thoughts of the investigation, of the differences between angles and angels and of Graciela and the boy. Eventually, he gave up on sleep and just waited with eyes open for the first light to filter through the blinds.

He was showered and finished measuring vital signs and swallowing pills by six o'clock. He took the stack of investigative reports back up to the table in the salon, put on another pot of coffee and ate a bowl of cereal. In between, he constantly checked his watch and thought about whether to call Vernon Carruthers without talking to Jaye Winston first.

Winston wouldn't be in yet. But three hours ahead at FBI headquarters in Washington, DC, McCaleb's friend Vernon Carruthers would be in his place in the FAT unit of the crime lab. McCaleb knew he shouldn't talk to Carruthers before getting the go-ahead from Winston. It was Winston's case. But the three-hour time difference between L.A. and Washington had him anxious. At his core McCaleb was an impatient man. The urge to get something going and not lose the day was pressing him.

After rinsing out the bowl and leaving it in the sink, he checked his watch once more and decided not to wait. He got out his phone book and called Carruthers on his direct line. He picked up on one ring.

'Vernon, it's Terry.'

'Terrell McCaleb! You here in the city?'

'Nah, still in L.A. How are you, man?'

'How are *you*? I mean, like long time, no hear.'

'I know, I know. But I'm doing okay. Thanks for the cards you sent to the hospital. Tell Marie I said thanks, too. It meant a lot. I know I should've called or written. I'm sorry.'

'Well, we tried calling you but you're unlisted and nobody in the FO seemed to have the new number. Talked to Kate and she didn't even know. All she knew was you gave up your apartment in Westwood. Somebody else in the FO said you were livin' on a boat now. You really cut yourself off from everybody.'

'Well, I just thought it would be best for a while. You know, until I was mobile and everything. But everything's good. How about you?'

'Can't complain. You coming out here anytime soon? You know you still have the room. Haven't rented it out to anybody from Quantico yet. Wouldn't dare.'

McCaleb laughed and told him that unfortunately there were no immediate plans for a trip east. He had known Carruthers for nearly twelve years. McCaleb had worked out of Quantico and Carruthers had worked out of Firearms and Toolmarks in the crime lab up in DC but it seemed that the two were often working the same cases. Whenever Carruthers came down to Quantico for meetings, McCaleb and his then wife, Kate, had put him up in their spare bedroom. It beat the spare accommodations of a room in an academy dorm. In return, whenever McCaleb was in DC, Carruthers and his wife, Marie, had let him bunk in the room that had belonged to their son. He had died years earlier of leukemia when he was twelve. Carruthers had insisted on the trade-off, even though it meant McCaleb was giving up a decent FBI-paid room at the Hilton near Dupont Circle. At first McCaleb felt like an intruder sleeping in the boy's room. But Vernon and Marie made him feel welcome. And the southern cooking and the good company couldn't be touched by the Hilton.

'Well, anytime,' Carruthers said with a returning laugh. 'Anytime.'

'Thanks, man.'

'So by my estimate, it's gotta be barely the crack a' dawn out there. What're you calling so early for?'

'Well, I'm calling on a bit of business.'

'You? Business? I was about to ask you how the wonderful world of retirement was treating you. Are you really living on a goddamned boat?'

'Yeah, I'm on a boat. But I'm not quite into the pasture yet.'

'Well, what's up, then?'

McCaleb told him the story, including the part about his receiving Gloria Torres's heart. McCaleb wanted Carruthers to know everything, unlike the others involved. He knew he could trust him with it and knew he would understand the bond McCaleb had to the victim. Carruthers had a strong empathy for victims, especially the young ones. The trauma of watching his son die over time in front of him had manifested itself in a dedication to his job that surpassed that of even the best field agents McCaleb had known.

Halfway through the telling, the booming sound of a cargo ship being unloaded began echoing across the marina. Carruthers asked what the hell it was and McCaleb told him as he took the phone down into the forward stateroom and closed the door to get away as much as possible from the noise.

'So what you want is for me to take a look at a slug from this?' Carruthers asked when McCaleb was finished. 'I don't know. That Sheriff's Department out there, they've got good people.'

'I know that. I'm not doubting that. I just want a fresh look and, mostly, I want you to put a laser profile through your computer, if you can. You never know. We might hit something. I've got a feeling about this one.'

'You and your feelings. I remember those. All right, then who am I getting the package from? Them or you?'

'I'm going to try to finesse it. Get the Sheriff's Department out here to send in the package. I don't want you doing this off the books. But if you can, I'd like to put some grease on it. This shooter's a repeater. We might save somebody's life if we can get a line on him.'

Carruthers was silent a few moments and McCaleb guessed he was running his schedule through his head.

'This is the thing. Today's Thursday. I need it by Tuesday morning latest and preferably Monday so I have time to do it justice. Next Wednesday I'm flying out to Kansas City to testify. Mob case. They think I'll be out there the rest of the week. So if you want it expedited, *you've* got to expedite it to me. If you do, I'll give it my immediate attention.'

'That's not going to cause major problems?'

' 'Course it is. I'm backed up two months here, what else is new? But just get me the package and I'll take care of it.'

'I'll get it to you. One way or the other by Monday latest.'

'Okay, buddy.'

'Oh, one last thing. Take my number. Like I said, I'm not acting in any official capacity on this thing. By rights, you should communicate with the Sheriff's Department but I'd appreciate a heads-up if you come up with anything unusual.'

'You got it,' he said without hesitation. 'Give me the number. *And* the address. Marie will want that for Christmas cards.'

After McCaleb gave him the information, Carruthers cleared his throat.

'So, you talk to Kate lately?' he asked.

'She called the hospital a couple days after the transplant. But I was still out of it. We didn't talk long.'

'Hmmm. Well, you ought to call her just to let her know you're okay.'

'I don't know. How is she doing?'

'Fine, I guess. Haven't heard anything to the contrary. You should call her.'

'It's better just to leave it alone, I think. We're divorced, remember?'

'Whatever. You're the boss. I'll send her an E-mail just to let her know you're still breathing out there.'

After a few more minutes of catching up, McCaleb clicked off the phone and went back up to the salon for more coffee. He was out of milk so he took it black. It was hair of the dog that bit him but he had to keep the momentum. If things went as he hoped, he would be on the road most of the day.

It was now near seven and almost time to call Winston. He went out onto the deck to take a look at the morning. The marine layer had come in strong and thick and the other boats looked ghostlike in the mist. It would be a few hours before it burned off and anybody got a look at the sun. He looked over at Buddy Lockridge's boat and saw no activity yet.

At 7:10 he sat at the salon table with his legal pad and punched Jaye Winston's number into the cordless phone. He caught her just as she was sitting down at her desk.

'I just walked in,' she said. 'And I didn't expect to hear from you for a couple of days. That was a lot of paper I gave you.'

'Yeah, well, once I got into it, I couldn't put it down, I guess.'

'What did you think?'

McCaleb knew she was asking what he thought of her investigation, asking him to make a judgment.

'I think you run a tight show but I already knew that from before. I liked all the moves you made on this one, Jaye. No complaints from me.'

'But?'

'But I've got a few questions I wrote down here if you've got a few minutes. Maybe a couple of suggestions if you want 'em. A lead or two maybe.'

Winston laughed good-naturedly.

'You federal guys always have questions, always have suggestions, always have new leads.'

'Hey, I'm not federal anymore.'

'Well, I guess it sticks in the blood, then. Go ahead.'

McCaleb looked over the notes he had taken the day before and started right in on the Mikail Bolotov angle.

'First off, Ritenbaugh and Aguilar, you close to them?'

'Don't even know them. They're not in homicide. The captain pulled them out of burglaries and gave them to me for a week. That was when we were running down the three-strikes names. What about them?'

'Well, I think one of the names that they scratched off that list needs a second look.'

'Which one?'

'Mikail Bolotov.'

McCaleb heard the rustling of papers as Winston looked for the report from Ritenbaugh and Aguilar.

'Okay, got it. What are you seeing here? Looks like he's got a solid alibi.'

'Have you ever heard of geographic cross-referencing?'

'What?'

He explained the concept and told her what he had done and how it led to Bolotov. He further explained that Bolotov had been interviewed before the Sherman Market robbery/shooting and therefore the significance of the location of Bolotov's home and employment to the market murders and one of the HK P7 thefts was not as apparent as it was to the other case. When he was done, Winston agreed that the Russian needed to be rechecked but she was not as enthusiastic about the prospect as McCaleb.

'Look, like I said, I don't know those two guys, so I can't vouch for them, but I have to assume they're not fresh off the boat. I have to assume they could handle an interview like this and check out the alibi.'

McCaleb didn't say anything.

'Look, I've got court this week. I can't go check this guy out again.'

'I can.'

Now she didn't say anything.

'I'll be cool,' McCaleb said. 'Just sort of play it by ear.'

'I don't know, Terry. You're a citizen now. This might be going too far.'

'Well, think about it. I've got some other stuff here to talk about.'

'Fine. What else?'

McCaleb knew that if she didn't bring up Bolotov again during the conversation, she was giving him unofficial permission to check the Russian out. She just didn't want to sanction what he was doing.

He glanced down at the legal pad again. He wanted to be careful with what he asked next. He needed to build up to the big questions he had, bring Winston along and not let her think he was second-guessing everything.

'Um, first off, I didn't see anything in there about the bank card in the Cordell case. I know the guy took the money. Did he take the card?'

'No. It was in the machine. It rolled it out but when he didn't take it, the machine automatically swallowed it again. It's a built-in security measure so people don't leave their cards to be taken.'

McCaleb nodded and drew a check mark next to that question on his pad.

'Okay. Next I have a question about the Cherokee. How come you didn't put that out to the media?'

'Well, we did put it out but not right away. On that first day we were still evaluating things and didn't put it into the first press release. I wasn't sure we should put that out because then the guy might see it and just dump the car. A few days later, when nothing was happening and we were hitting the wall, I put out another press release with the Cherokee in it. Trouble is, Cordell was old news and nobody picked it up. A little weekly paper up there in the desert was the only one to run it. I know, it was a screwup. I guess I should've put it all out in the first press release.'

'Not necessarily,' McCaleb said as he drew another check on the pad. 'I can see your reasoning.'

He read through the notes on the page again.

'Couple things . . . In both tapes the shooter says something – after the shots. He's either talking to himself or the camera. There were no reports on that. Was anything done to –'

'There's a guy in the bureau here who has a brother who is deaf. He took the tapes to him to see if he could lip-read them. He couldn't be sure but on the first one – the ATM tape – he thought he said, "Don't forget the cashola" just as he took the money from the machine. On the other tape he was less sure. He thought he might have said either the same thing or possibly something along the lines of "Don't fuck with the" something or other. The last word was least clear to him on both tapes. I guess I never typed up a supp on it. You don't miss a thing, do you?'

'All the time,' McCaleb said. 'Would the lip reader know Russian if that was what this guy was saying?'

'What? Oh, you mean if it was Bolotov. No, I doubt his brother knows Russian.'

McCaleb wrote down the possible translations of what the shooter had said. He then drummed the pen against the pad and wondered if he should take his shot now.

'Do you have anything else?' Winston finally asked.

He decided it wasn't the right moment to bring up Carruthers. At least not directly.

'The gun,' he said.

'I know. I don't like it, either. The P7 is not your routine scumbag's choice of firearm. It had to have been stolen. You saw I pulled reports on stolens. But like with everything else, I hit a wall. It got me nowhere.'

'I think it's a good theory,' McCaleb said. 'To a point, I don't like him keeping it after the first shooting. If it was stolen, I see him throwing that thing as far out into the desert as he can about ten minutes after he takes down Cordell. He then goes and steals another for the next time.'

'No, you can't say that,' Winston said and McCaleb envisioned her shaking her head. 'There is no definitive pattern here. He could have been just as likely to keep the gun because he knew it was valuable. And you have to remember, Cordell was a through-and-through shot. He might have figured the lead wouldn't be found or if it had hit the bank – like it actually did – it would be too mangled for comparison. Remember, he picked up the brass. He probably believed the gun had at least one more use.'

'I guess you're probably right.'

They took a breather, neither one of them talking for a few moments. McCaleb had two more things on his page.

'Next thing,' he began carefully. 'The slugs.'

'What about them?'

'You said yesterday that you're holding the ballistics from both cases.'

'That's right. It's all in evidence lockup. What are you getting at?'

'Have you ever heard of the bureau's DRUGFIRE computer?'

'No.'

'It might work for us. For you. It's a long shot but it's worth a shot.'

'What is it?'

McCaleb told her. DRUGFIRE was an FBI computer program designed along similar lines of computerized storage of latent fingerprint data. It was the brainchild of the crime lab in the early 1980s, when the cocaine wars that broke out in most cities, particularly Miami, were responsible for a jump in murders nationwide. Most of the slayings were by gunfire. The bureau, struggling for a means of tracking related murders and killers across the country, came up with the DRUGFIRE program. The unique characteristics of groove marks found on the spent bullets used in drug murders were read by a laser, coded for computer storage and entered into a data bank. The computer's program operated in much the same way as fingerprint computer systems used by law enforcement agencies across the nation. The system allowed for the quick comparison of coded bullet profiles.

Eventually, the database grew as more ballistic entries were added. The program was also widened, though it kept the name DRUGFIRE, to include all cases referred to the FBI. Whether it was a mob killing in Las Vegas or a gang killing in South Los Angeles or a serial killing in Fort Lauderdale, every gunshot case sent to the FBI for analysis was added to the database. After more than a decade, there were thousands of bullets on file in the computer.

'I've been thinking about this guy,' McCaleb said. 'He hangs on to that gun. Whatever the reason, whether he stole it or not, his hanging on to it is really the only mistake he's made. It makes me think we've got a chance of making a match. Looking at the MO on those tapes, chances are he just didn't start popping people beginning with your case. He's used a gun before – maybe even that particular gun.'

'But I told you, we checked for similars. Nothing on ballistics. We also put out teletypes and a request on the National Crime Index computer. We got blanked.'

'I understand. But this guy's method could be evolving, changing. Maybe what he did with that gun in, say, Phoenix isn't the same as what he did with it here. All I'm saying is that there's a chance that this guy came into town from someplace else. If he did, then he probably used that gun in that other place. And if we're lucky, the data is sitting there in the bureau computer.'

'Maybe,' Winston said.

She went quiet as she brooded over his proposal. McCaleb knew what the considerations were. DRUGFIRE was a long shot and Winston was smart enough to know that. But if she went for it, she would be drawing in federal involvement, not to mention acknowledging that she was taking direction from McCaleb, an outsider with no real standing in the case.

'What do you think?' McCaleb finally asked. 'You only need to send them one bullet. You have, what, four of them from the two cases?'

'I don't know,' she said. 'I'm not so keen on sending our stuff off to Washington. I doubt L.A. will be, either.'

'L.A. doesn't have to know. You're the keeper of the evidence. You can send one bullet if you want. And it could be to DC and back inside a week. Arrango wouldn't have to know it was even sent. I already talked to a guy I know in Firearms and Toolmarks. He said he'd grease this one if we got him the package.'

McCaleb closed his eyes. If there was a point at which she might get outright angry, it was now.

'You already told this guy we'd be doing this?' she asked, annoyance in her voice.

'No, I didn't tell him that. I told him I was dealing with a detective out here who was very thorough and dedicated and would probably want to make sure she left no stone uncovered.'

'Gee, where have I heard that before?'

McCaleb smiled.

'There's another thing,' he said. 'Even if we don't get lucky with this, we'll at least have the gun in the computer. Somewhere down the road, it might match up with something.'

She thought about this for a moment. McCaleb was pretty sure he had painted her into the corner. Like watching the cemetery for Luther Hatch. She had to go for it or she'd wonder about it always.

'Okay, okay,' Winston finally said. 'I'll talk to the captain about it. I'll tell him I want to do this. If he gives the go-ahead, I'll send a package. One bullet – that's all.'

'That's all it takes.'

McCaleb filled her in further on Carruthers's need to get the package by Monday evening and urged her to get in with the captain as soon as possible. This created another silence.

'All I can say is, it's worth the shot, Jaye,' he said by way of reinforcement.

'I know. It's just that . . . well, never mind. Give me your guy's name and his number.'

McCaleb clenched his fist and punched it into the air in front of him. It didn't matter how long a shot it was. They were rolling the dice. It felt good to him to be getting something going.

After he gave Winston the direct number and address for contacting Carruthers, she asked if there was anything else McCaleb wanted to talk about. He looked down at his pad but what he wanted to talk about wasn't written down on it.

'I've got one last thing that's probably going to put you on the spot,' he said.

'Oh, no,' Winston said with a groan. 'Serves me right for answering the phone on a court day. Give it to me, McCaleb. What is it?'

'James Noone.'

'The witness? What about him?'

'He saw the shooter. He saw the shooter's car.'

'Yeah, a lot of good it did us. There's only about a hundred thousand of those Cherokees in southern California and his description of the guy is so vague he can't tell if the guy was wearing a hat or not. He's a witness but just barely.'

'But he saw him. It was during a stress situation. The more stress, the deeper the imprint. Noone would be perfect.'

'Perfect for what?'

'To be hypnotized.'

14

Buddy Lockridge pulled the Taurus into an open spot in the parking lot of Video GraFX Consultants on La Brea Avenue in Hollywood. Lockridge was not dressed Hollywood-cool for his second day as McCaleb's driver. This time he was wearing boat shorts and a Hawaiian shirt with ukuleles and hula girls floating on an ocean blue background. McCaleb told him he didn't think he would be long and got out.

VGC was a business used mostly by the entertainment industry. It rented professional video equipment as well as video editing and dubbing studios. Adult filmmakers, whose product was almost exclusively shot on video, were its main clients but VGC also provided one of the best video-effects and image-enhancing labs in Hollywood.

McCaleb had been inside VGC once before, working on loan to the field office's bank unit. It was the downside of his being transferred from Quantico to the FO outpost; technically he was under the command of the FO's special agent in charge. And whenever the SAC thought things were slow – if they ever were – in the serials unit, he would yank McCaleb out and put him on something else, usually something McCaleb considered menial.

When he had walked into VGC the previous time, he had a videotape from the ceiling camera of a Wells Fargo Bank in Beverly Hills. The bank had been robbed by several masked gunmen who had escaped with $363,000 in cash. It was the group's fourth bank robbery in twelve days. The one lead agents had was on the video. When one of the robbers had reached his arm across the teller's counter to grab the bag she had just stuffed her cash into, his sleeve had caught on the edge of the marble counter and was pulled back. The robber quickly pulled the sleeve forward again but for a split second the form of a tattoo was seen on the inside of his forearm. The image was grainy and had been shot by a camera thirty feet away. After a tech in the field office lab said he could do nothing with it, it was decided not to send the tape to Washington HQ because it would take more than a month to have it analyzed. The robbers were hitting every three days. They seemed agitated in the videos, on the verge of violence. Speed was a necessity.

McCaleb took the tape to Video GraFX. A VGC tech took the frame from the video and in one day enhanced it through pixel redefinition and amplification to the point that the tattoo was identifiable. It was a flying hawk clutching a rifle in one claw and a scythe in the other.

The tattoo broke the case. Its description and a photocopy were teletyped and faxed to sixty field offices across the country. A supervisor in the Butte office then retransmitted the information to the smaller Resident Agency in Coeur d'Alene, Idaho, where an agent recognized the tattoo as the insignia he had seen on a flag flown outside the house of a member of a local group of anti-government extremists. The group had intermittently been under bureau observation and suspicion because of its recent purchases of huge tracts of rural land outside the city. The supervisor of the RA was able to provide the Los Angeles FO with a list of members' names and social security numbers. Agents then began checking hotels and soon found seven members of the group staying at the Airport Hilton. The group was placed under surveillance and the following day watched as they robbed a bank in Willowbrook. Thirty agents were poised in surveillance points outside and ready to go in at the first sign of violence. There wasn't any. The robbers were followed back to their hotel and systematically arrested in their rooms by agents posing as room service waiters and house-keeping staff. One of the robbers eventually cooperated with agents and admitted that the group had been robbing banks in order to raise capital to buy more land in Idaho. The group wanted the land so members could safely sit out the Armageddon their leader promised was coming to the United States.

Now McCaleb was back. As he stepped to the reception counter, he noticed that the letter of thanks under the bureau's seal that he had sent following the bank robbery investigation was framed on the wall behind the receptionist. He leaned over the counter until he could read the name of the man he had sent the letter to.

'Can I help you?' the receptionist asked.

McCaleb pointed at the letter and said, 'I'd like to talk to Tony Banks.'

She asked McCaleb his name, didn't seem to recognize it though it was on the letter that hung on the wall above her, and then put in a call. Shortly after, a man McCaleb recognized as Tony Banks came out to greet him. He didn't recognize McCaleb until he started recounting the bank video story.

'Right, right, I remember. You sent the letter.'

He pointed to the framed letter.

'That's me.'

'So what can I do for you? Another bank job?'

He was eyeing the videotape McCaleb had in his hand.

'Well, I've got another case here. I'm wondering if you could take a look at this tape. There's something on it I want to see if I can get a better look at.'

'Well, let's take a look. Always glad to help out.'

He led McCaleb down a hallway of gray carpet past several doors that he knew from his previous visit were editing booths. Business was good. There were Occupied signs on all of the doors. From behind one of them McCaleb heard muffled cries of passion. Banks looked over his shoulder at him and rolled his eyes.

'It's not real,' he said. 'They're editing a tape.'

McCaleb nodded. Banks had explained the same thing to him when he had been there before.

Banks opened the last door in the hallway. He ducked his head inside to make sure the room was empty, then stepped back and signaled McCaleb inside. There were two chairs set in front of a video editing machine with twin thirty-inch monitors above it. Banks turned on the equipment, pushed a button and the left side cassette cradle opened.

'Now this is going to be pretty graphic,' McCaleb said. 'Somebody gets shot. If you want, you can go outside and I'll just move it to the frame I want you to look at.'

Banks took a moment to think about the offer. He was a thin man of about thirty, with limp hair dyed so blond it was almost white. It was long on the top and shaved around the sides. A Hollywood haircut.

'I've seen graphic,' he said. 'Put it in.'

'None like this, I don't think. There's a difference between graphic real life and the stuff they put in movies.'

'Put it in.'

McCaleb put the tape in the slot and Banks began to play it. McCaleb heard the younger man's breath catch as he watched Gloria Torres get grabbed from behind and the gun placed against her head and fired. McCaleb reached over and put his hand on the pause button. At the right moment, after Chan Ho Kang had been shot and his body had fallen across the counter and then slid back, he pushed the button and froze the frame. Then, by using a dial, he could move the picture backward and forward slowly until he had exactly the image he wanted. He looked at Banks. The man looked as though all of the evil of humanity had just been revealed to him.

'You okay?'

'It's horrible.'

'Yes. It is.'

'How can I help you?'

Taking a pen from his shirt pocket, McCaleb pointed at the screen and tapped it on the watch on Kang's wrist.

'The watch?'

'Yes. I want to know if it is possible to blow this frame up or do something that would let me read the watch. I want to know what time it was at this point of the video.'

'Time? What about this?'

He pointed to the timeline running along the bottom of the screen.

'I can't trust that time. That's why I need the watch.'

Banks leaned forward and began fiddling with the dials on the console that controlled the focus and image amplification.

'This is not the original,' he said.

'The tape? No, why?'

'I'm not getting much amplification. Can you get the original?'

'I don't think so.'

McCaleb looked at the screen. Banks had made the image clearer and larger. The screen was filled with Kang's upper body and outstretched arm. But the face of the watch was still a blurred gray.

'Well, then what I can do, if you want to leave it with me, is work with it a little bit, take it to one of the guys in the lab. Maybe bring it up a little, clarify it a bit more with some pixel redefinition. But this is the best I can do with it on this equipment.'

'You think it's worth doing, even without the original? Will we get anything?'

'I don't know but it's worth a try. They can do some wild stuff back there. You're after him, right? This man on the video?'

He gestured toward the screen, though at the moment the shooter wasn't on it.

'Yeah, I'm after him.'

'Then we'll see what we can do. Can you leave this?'

'Yeah. I mean . . . uh, can you dub off a copy for me so I can have it with me? I might need to show it to somebody else.'

'Sure. Let me go get a tape.'

Banks got up and left the booth. McCaleb sat there staring at the screen. He had watched how Banks had used the equipment. He backed the tape up and amplified a frame showing the masked shooter. It didn't help much. He hit the fast forward for a bit and stopped it on a close-up of Gloria's face. It felt intrusive to be so close at such a moment, to be staring at a woman who had just had her life taken. Her face was in left profile and the one eye that he could see was still open.

McCaleb noticed the three earrings on her left ear. One was a stud, a small silver crescent moon. Next, going down the curve of the ear, was a small hoop that he guessed was silver and last, dangling below the lobe, was a cross. He knew it was the style among young women to have multiple earrings on at least one ear.

While he continued to wait for Banks, he played with the dials once more and backed the tape up until there was a view of Gloria's right side, just as she entered the frame. He could see only one earring on her right ear, another crescent moon.

Banks came back in with a tape and quickly inserted it into the second cassette cradle while he finished rewinding the first tape. It took him about thirty seconds to make a high-speed dub copy. He ejected it, slid it into a box and handed it to McCaleb.

'Thanks,' McCaleb said. 'How long you think before somebody gets a chance to work on it?'

'We're kind of busy. But I'll go look at the job board and see if we can't get someone on it as soon as possible. Maybe by tomorrow or Saturday. Is that okay?'

'It's okay. Thanks, Tony, I appreciate it.'

'No problem. I don't know if I still have your card. You want me to call you?'

In that moment McCaleb decided to continue the deception. He didn't tell Banks that he was no longer an FBI agent. He thought Banks might push the project a little harder if he thought that the job was being done for the bureau.

'Tell you what, let me give you a private number. If you call and I don't pick up, just leave a message and I'll get back to you as soon as I can.'

'Sounds good. I hope we can help.'

'Me too. And, Tony? Do me a favor and don't show the tape to anybody who doesn't need to see it.'

'I won't,' Banks said, his face reddening a bit. McCaleb realized either he had needlessly embarrassed Banks with a request that did not need to be spoken or he had made the request just as Banks was thinking about whom he could show the tape to. McCaleb thought it was the latter.

McCaleb gave him his number, they shook hands and McCaleb went back down the hall on his own. As he passed the door from which he had heard the feigned sounds of passion, he noticed there was only silence now.

As McCaleb opened the door of the Taurus, he heard the radio playing and noticed Lockridge had a harmonica on his thigh, ready to be played if the right tune came along. Buddy closed a book called *Death of a Tenor Man.* He had marked a spot about halfway through.

'What happened to Inspector Fujigama?'

'What?'

'The book you had yesterday.'

'*Inspector Imanishi Investigates.* I finished it.'

'Imanishi then. You're a fast reader.'

'Good books read fast. You read crime novels?'

'Why would I want to read made-up stuff when I've seen the real stuff and can't stand it?'

Buddy started the car. He had to turn the ignition twice before it kicked over.

'It's a much different world. Everything is ordered, good and bad clearly defined, the bad guy always gets what he deserves, the hero shines, no loose ends. It's a refreshing antidote to the real world.'

'Sounds boring.'

'No, it's reassuring. Where to now?'

15

After eating lunch at Musso and Frank's, a place McCaleb loved but hadn't been back to in two years, they drove over the hill from Hollywood to the Valley and got to the building that housed Deltona Clocks at quarter to two. McCaleb had called the business before they set out that morning from the marina and learned that Mikail Bolotov was still working a two-to-ten shift.

Deltona Clocks was a large warehouse structure located behind a small street-front showroom and retail shop. After Lockridge parked the Taurus in front of the retail store, McCaleb reached down to the leather bag on the floor in front of him and removed his gun. It was already snugly held in a canvas holster which he then clipped onto his belt.

'Hey, what are you expecting in there?' Lockridge said after he saw the weapon.

'Nothing. It's more a prop than anything else.'

McCaleb next pulled out an inch-thick sheaf of the sheriff's investigative records and made sure the report on the interview with Bolotov and his employer, a man identified as Arnold Toliver, was on top. He was ready. He looked over at Lockridge.

'Okay, sit tight.'

He noted as he got out of the Taurus that this time Buddy hadn't offered to come in with him. He thought maybe he should carry the gun more often.

Inside the retail shop there were no customers. Cheap clocks of almost every size were on display. Most had an industrial look, as though they were more likely to be found in a classroom or an auto supply store than in somebody's home. On the wall behind the counter at the rear of the space was a display of eight matching clocks showing the time in eight cities around the world. There was a young woman sitting on a folding chair behind the counter. McCaleb thought about how slowly time must pass for her with no customers and all of those clocks.

'How do I find Mr Toliver?' he asked as he came up to the counter.

'Arnold or Randy?'

'Arnold.'

'I have to call back. Who are you with?'

'I'm not here to buy clocks. I'm conducting a follow-up on a Sheriff's Department inquiry of February third.'

He dropped the stack of paperwork on the counter so she could see that they were official forms. He then raised his hands and put them on his hips, carefully allowing his sports coat to open and expose the gun. He watched her eyes as she noticed it. She picked up a telephone that was on the counter and dialed three numbers.

'Arnie, it's Wendy. There's a man from the Sheriff's Department here about an investigation or something.'

McCaleb didn't correct her. He hadn't lied to her and he wouldn't lie to her about who he was and whom he was with. But if she wanted to make incorrect assumptions, then he wasn't going to correct her. After listening to the phone for a few moments, Wendy looked up at McCaleb.

'What investigation?'

McCaleb nodded toward the phone and held his hand out. The young woman hesitated but then handed the phone receiver to him.

'Mr Toliver?' he said into the phone. 'Terry McCaleb. A couple months ago you talked to a couple of sheriff's detectives named Ritenbaugh and Aguilar about an employee named Mikail Bolotov. You remember?'

After a long hesitation Toliver agreed that he had.

'Well, I'm investigating that case now. Ritenbaugh and Aguilar are onto other things. I need to ask you some additional questions about that. Can I come back?'

Again a hesitation.

'Well ... we are awfully busy back here. I –'

'I won't take long, sir. Remember, it's a murder investigation and I'm hoping you'll continue to help us out.'

'Well, I suppose ...'

'You suppose what?'

'Uh, just come on back. The girl will tell you where I'm at.'

Three minutes later McCaleb had walked the length of the building, past several rows of assembly and packaging benches, to an office at the rear next to a loading dock. There was a short flight of stairs up into the office. Next to the door was a window that allowed Toliver to look out across the workbenches as well as the shipping and receiving dock. As he had walked past the benches toward the office, McCaleb had overheard the conversations of the employees. Three different times he heard a language he believed was Russian.

As McCaleb opened the office door, the man he assumed was Toliver hung up the phone and waved him in. He was a skinny man in his sixties, with brown, leathery skin and white hair fringed around the sides of his head. He had a plastic pocket guard in his shirt pocket, jammed with an assortment of pens.

'I've gotta make this quick,' he said. 'I have to check the lading on a truck going out.'

'Fine.' McCaleb looked down at the report on top of the stack he carried. 'Two months ago you told detectives Ritenbaugh and Aguilar that Mikail Bolotov was working the night of January twenty-second.'

'That's right. I remember. Hasn't changed.'

'Are you sure, Mr Toliver?'

'What do you mean, am I sure? Yeah, I'm sure. I looked it up for those two guys. It was in the books. I pulled the time card.'

'Are you saying you based it on what you saw in the pay records or did you actually see Bolotov working that night?'

'He was here. I remembered that. Mikail never missed a day.'

'And you remember him working all the way until ten.'

'His time card showed he –'

'I'm not talking about the time card. I'm talking about you remembering he stayed until ten.'

Toliver didn't answer. McCaleb glanced out the window at the rows of workbenches.

'You've got a lot of people working for you, Mr Toliver. How many work the two-to-ten shift?'

'Eighty-eight at the moment.'

'And then?'

'About the same. What's the point?'

'The point is you gave the man an alibi based on a time card. Do you think it could have been possible that Bolotov left early without being noticed, then had a friend punch him out on the clock?'

Toliver didn't respond.

'Forgetting about Bolotov for a moment, have you ever had that problem before? You know, somebody punching out for somebody else, scamming the company that way?'

'We've been in business here sixteen years, it's happened.'

'Okay.' McCaleb nodded. 'Now, could it have happened with Bolotov? Or do you stand at the time clock every night and make sure nobody punches two cards.'

'Anything's possible. We don't stand at the clock. Most nights my son closes up. I'm already home. He keeps an eye on things.'

McCaleb held his breath for a beat and felt the excitement he had been containing build. Toliver's answer, if it were given in court, would be enough to shred Bolotov's alibi.

'Your son, is that Randy?'

'Yeah, Randy.'

'Can I talk to him?'

'He's in Mexico. We've got another plant in Mexicali. He spends one week a month down there. He'll be back next week.'

'Maybe we can call him?'

'I can try but he's probably out on the floor. That's why he goes down there. To make sure the line is running. Besides, how is he going to remember one night three months ago? We make clocks here, Detective. Every night we make the same clocks. Every day we ship them out. One night is no different from the other.'

McCaleb turned away from him and looked out the window again. He noticed that several of the workers were leaving their posts as new workers were taking their places. He watched the shift change until he picked out the man he believed was Bolotov. There had been no photo in the records and only a spare description. But the man McCaleb was now watching wore a black T-shirt with sleeves stretched tightly around his powerful and tattoo-laced arms. The tattoos were all of one ink – jailhouse blue. It had to be Bolotov.

'That's him, right?'

He nodded in the direction of the man who had taken a seat at a workbench. It appeared to McCaleb that it was Bolotov's job to place the plastic casings around completed clock mechanisms and then stack them in a four-wheeled cart.

'Which?'

Toliver had come up next to McCaleb at the window.

'With the tattoos.'

'Yeah.'

McCaleb nodded and thought for a moment.

'Did you tell Ritenbaugh and Aguilar that the alibi you were giving that man was based on what you saw in the pay records and time cards and not what you or your son actually saw on that night?'

'Yeah, I told them. They said fine. They left and that was that. Now, here you are with these new questions. Why don't you guys get your shit together? It would have been a lot easier for my boy to remember after two or three weeks instead of three months.'

McCaleb was silent as he thought about Ritenbaugh and Aguilar. They had probably had a list of twenty-five names they had to cover in the week they were assigned to the case. It was sloppy work but he understood how it could happen.

'Listen, I've got to go out to the dock,' Toliver said. 'You want to wait until I come back or what?'

'Tell you what, why don't you send Bolotov in here on your way out. I need to talk to him.'

'In here?'

'If you don't mind, Mr Toliver. I am sure you want to help us out and continue to cooperate, don't you?'

He stared at Toliver as a final means of ending his unspoken objection.

'Whatever,' Toliver said as he threw his hands up in a gesture of annoyance and headed toward the door. 'Just don't take all day.'

'Oh, Mr Toliver?'

Toliver stopped at the door and looked back at him.

'I heard a lot of Russian being spoken out there. Where do you get the Russians?'

'They're good workers and they don't complain. They don't mind being paid shit, either. When we advertise for help, we do it in the local Russian paper.'

He went through the door then, leaving it open behind him. McCaleb pulled the two chairs in front of the desk away and turned them so they faced each other from about five feet apart. He sat down on the one closest to the door and waited. He quickly thought about how he would handle the interview and decided to come at Bolotov strong. He wanted to engender a response, get some kind of reaction to which he could register his own feel for the man.

He felt a presence in the room and looked at the door. The man he had guessed was Bolotov stood there. He was about five ten, with black hair and pale white skin. But the bulging arm muscles and tattoos – a snake wrapped around one arm, a spider's web covering the other – made his arms the focal point of his image. McCaleb pointed to the empty chair.

'Have a seat.'

Bolotov moved to the chair and sat down without hesitation. McCaleb saw that the spider web apparently continued under the shirt and then came up both sides of the Russian's neck. A black spider sat in the web just below his right ear.

'What is this?'

'Same as before, Bolotov. My name's McCaleb. The night of January twenty-second. Tell me about it.'

'I told them before. I work here that night. It was not me you look for.'

'So you said. But things are different now. We know things we didn't know then.'

'What things?'

McCaleb got up and locked the door and then retook his seat. It was just a little show, an underlining of his control. Something for Bolotov to think about.

'What things?' he asked again.

'Like the burglary of the house over on Mason, just a few blocks from here. You remember, the one with the Christmas tree and all the presents. That's where you got the gun, wasn't it, Bolotov?'

'No, I am clean on these things.'

'Bullshit. You did the break-in and you got that nice new gun. Then you decided to use it. You used it up in Lancaster and then again around the corner from here at the market. You're a killer, Bolotov. A killer.'

The Russian sat still but McCaleb could see his biceps drawing tight, better defining the artwork on his arms. He pressed on.

'What about February seventh, you have an alibi for that night, too?'

'I don't know that night. I have to –'

'You walked into the Sherman Market and you killed two people that night. You should know it.'

Bolotov suddenly stood up.

'Who are you? You're not cop.'

McCaleb just looked up at him, keeping his seat, hoping not to show the surprise he was feeling.

'Cops are in twos. Who are you?'

'I'm the one who's going to take you down. You did it, Bolotov, and I'm going to prove it.'

'Wha –'

There was an angry knock on the door and McCaleb instinctively turned to look. It was a small mistake but it was all Bolotov needed. McCaleb saw the black blur coming at him in his peripheral vision. Instinctively he began bringing his arms up to protect his chest. He wasn't quick enough. Suddenly he was hit with the impact of the other man's weight and his chair went over with him still in it.

Bolotov had him down on the floor while Toliver or whoever was out there continued to knock angrily on the door. The bigger, stronger man held McCaleb down while he went through his pockets. His hand hit the gun and he tore it off the belt and threw it across the room. Finally he found McCaleb's wallet in the inside pocket of his sports coat. He pulled it out, ripping the pocket, and opened it.

'No badge. See, no cop.'

He read the name off the driver's license, which was held behind a plastic window in the wallet.

'Terr-ell-Mack-Cow-leeb.'

Bolotov then read off the address. McCaleb felt relieved that it was actually the address of the harbormaster's office, where he had a postal box.

'Maybe I pay you a visit one day, yes?'

McCaleb didn't answer or move. He knew there was no chance of overpowering the man. As he was considering his predicament, Bolotov dropped the wallet on his chest and jumped up. He jerked the chair out from beneath McCaleb's hips and raised it over his head. McCaleb raised his arms up to protect his face and head, realizing in the same instant that he was leaving his chest unprotected.

He heard the shatter of glass and looked between his arms to see the chair crashing through the office window. He then watched as Bolotov followed it, leaping with ease through the opening and down to the manufacturing floor. Then he was gone.

McCaleb rolled to his side, folding his arms across his chest and bringing his knees up. He spread a hand flat on his chest, trying to feel the beat. He took two deep breaths and slowly got to his knees and raised himself. The pounding on the door continued, now accompanied by Toliver's panicked demands that McCaleb open up.

McCaleb reached over to unlock the door. He felt a wave of vertigo hit him then. It was like sliding down a twelve-foot trough into the valley of a wave. Toliver burst into the office and started screaming at him but McCaleb didn't understand his words. He put his hands flat on the floor and closed his eyes, trying to steady himself.

'Shit,' was all he managed to whisper.

Buddy Lockridge jumped out of the Taurus when he saw McCaleb approaching. He ran around the front of the car and came to McCaleb's side.

'Jesus, what happened?'

'Nothing. I made a mistake, that's all.'

'You look like shit.'

'I'm okay now. Let's go.'

Lockridge opened the door for him and then went around to the driver's side and got in.

'You sure you're okay?'

'Come on, let's go.'

'Where?'

'Find a phone.'

'There's one right there.'

He pointed to the Jack in the Box restaurant next door. There was a pay phone on the wall near one of the doors. McCaleb got out and slowly walked to the phone. He was careful to keep his eyes on the pavement in front of him, not wanting to set off another slide into vertigo.

He called Jaye Winston's direct line, expecting to leave a message, but she picked up immediately.

'It's Terry. I thought you had court.'

'I do but it's the lunch break. I have to be back at two. I was just about to call you.'

'Why?'

'Because we're going to do it.'

'Do what?'

'Hypnotize Mr Noone. The captain signed off on it and I called Mr Noone. He said sure. He just wants us to do it tonight because he's going out of town – back to Vegas, I guess. He's going to be here at six. You can do it then, right?'

'I'll be there.'

'Then we're set. Why were you calling?'

McCaleb hesitated. What he had to tell her might change the evening's plans but he knew he couldn't delay.

'Can you get a photo of Bolotov by tonight?'

'I already have one. You want to show Noone?'

'Yeah. I just paid Bolotov a little visit and he didn't react too well to it.'

'What happened?'

'Before I could ask him three questions, he jumped me and ran.'

'Are you shitting me?'

'I wish.'

'What about his alibi?'

'It's about as solid as a loaf of bread.'

McCaleb briefly recounted his interview with Toliver and then Bolotov. He told Winston she should put out a wanted notice for Bolotov.

'For what, did you or Toliver make a police report?'

'I didn't but Toliver said he was going to make a report on the window.'

'All right, I'll put out a pickup. Are you all right? You sound punchy.'

'I'm okay. Is this going to change things? Or are we still on for tonight?'

'Far as I'm concerned, we're still on.'

'Okay. See you then.'

'Look, Terry, don't put too much stock in Bolotov, okay?'

'I think he looks good for this.'

'I don't know. Lancaster's a long way from where Bolotov lives. You've got to remember, the guy's a convict. He could have and would have done what he did with you whether he's involved with this or not. Because if he didn't do this, then he did something else.'

'Maybe. But I still like the guy.'

'Well, maybe Noone will make our day and point him out in a six-pack.'

'Now you're talking.'

After hanging up, McCaleb made it back to the Taurus without a problem. Once inside he dug the travel kit he always carried with him out of the leather satchel on the floor. It contained a day's worth of medication and a dozen or so throw-away thermometers called Temp-Strips. He peeled the paper off one and put it in his mouth. While he waited, he signaled Lockridge to start the car. Once the engine had fired, McCaleb reached over to the air-conditioner controls and turned it on.

'You want air?' Lockridge asked.

McCaleb nodded and Lockridge turned the fan up higher.

After three minutes McCaleb took the strip out and checked it. He felt a deep shard of fear cut into him as he looked at the thin red vein stretched past the one-hundred-degree mark.

'Let's go home.'

'You sure?'

'Yes. The marina.'

As Lockridge pointed the car south toward the 101 freeway, McCaleb turned the air vents on his side so that the cool air was flowing right into his face. He opened up another Temp-Strip and put it under his tongue. He tried to calm himself by turning on KFWB on the radio and looking out at the passing street scene. Two minutes later the second temperature reading was better than the first, but he was still running a low-grade fever. His fear eased back some and his throat relaxed. He banged his palms against the dashboard and shook his head, convincing himself in the process that the fever was an aberration. He had been perfect so far. There was no reason for this other than that he had gotten overheated while tangling with Bolotov.

He decided to go back to the boat and take an aspirin and a long nap before preparing for the evening's session with James Noone. The alternative was to call Bonnie Fox. And he knew that such a call would result in his finding himself in a hospital bed for several days of testing and observation. Fox was as thorough at what she did as McCaleb liked to think he was at what he did. She wouldn't hesitate to bring him in. He would lose at least a week lying in bed in Cedars. He would certainly miss his chance at Noone and he would lose the momentum that was the only other thing he had going for him in this investigation.

16

To the uninformed – and this included many cops and agents McCaleb had worked with over the years – hypnosis was often seen as a form of voodoo policework, a second-to-last resort just shy of consulting the local psychic. It was considered emblematic of a stalled or failed investigation. McCaleb firmly believed it was not. He believed it was a credible means of plumbing the depths of the mind. In the instances where he had seen or heard of it going wrong, it was usually at the fault of the hypnotist and not the science.

McCaleb had been surprised when Winston said she was in favor of reinterviewing Noone under hypnotic conditions. She had told him that hypnotism had been suggested a couple of times during the weekly homicide bureau meetings when the stalled Cordell investigation came up. But the suggestion had never been acted on for two reasons. The first was the important one. Hypnosis was a tool used often by police until the early eighties, when California's supreme court ruled that witnesses who had memories refreshed through hypnosis could not testify in criminal proceedings. This meant that every time investigators decided whether to use hypnotism on a witness, they had to weigh whether the possible gain from it was worth losing that person as a witness in court. The debate had stalled the use of hypnotism in the Cordell case, since Winston and her captain were reluctant to lose their only witness.

The second reason was that after the supreme court ruling, the Sheriff's Department stopped training detectives in the use of hypnosis. Consequently, the more than fifteen years since the ruling had seen the natural attrition of the detectives who had the skill. There was no one left in the department who could hypnotize Noone, meaning that they would have to go to an outside hypnotherapist. That would further complicate things and cost money.

When McCaleb had told Winston that he had used hypnotism on bureau cases for more than ten years and would be willing to do it, she had brightened on the suggestion even more. A few hours later she'd had the session approved and set up.

McCaleb arrived at the homicide bureau at the Sheriff's Star Center a half hour early. He told Lockridge that he would be a while and encouraged him to go get dinner.

His fever had been trimmed to less than a half a point during an afternoon nap. He felt rested and ready. He was excited by the prospect of digging a solid lead out of the mind of James Noone and accomplishing something that would drive the case forward.

Jaye Winston met him at the front counter and escorted him to the captain's office, talking quickly all the way.

'I posted a wanted on Bolotov. Had a car go by his apartment but he was already gone. He's split. You obviously hit a nerve.'

'Yeah, maybe when I called him a murderer.'

'I'm still not convinced but it's the best thing we've got going at the moment. Typically, Arrango is not happy about what you did. I have to admit, I didn't say we talked about this beforehand. He thinks you were cowboying.'

'Don't worry about it. I don't care what he thinks.'

'Are you worried about Bolotov? You said he has your address.'

'No. He has the marina but not the boat. It's a big place.'

She opened the door and allowed McCaleb to enter first. There were three men and a woman waiting in the cramped office. McCaleb recognized Arrango and Walters from the LAPD. Winston introduced him to Captain Al Hitchens and the woman, an artist named Donna de Groot. She would be available if needed to work up a composite drawing of the suspect, provided that Noone didn't identify Bolotov outright.

'I'm glad you're early,' Hitchens said. 'Mr Noone is already here. Maybe we can get this going.'

McCaleb nodded and looked at the others in the room. Arrango had the smirk of a nonbeliever on his face. A toothpick protruded a half inch from his tight lips.

'This is too many people,' McCaleb said. 'Too much distraction. I need to get this guy relaxed. That won't happen with an audience like this.'

'We're not all going in,' Hitchens said. 'I'd like you and Jaye to be in the room. You bring Donna in at the appropriate time. We're going to videotape it and we have a monitor set up right here. The rest of us will watch from here. That okay with you?'

He pointed to a monitor on a cart in the corner. McCaleb looked at the screen and saw a man sitting at a table with his arms folded in front of him. It was Noone. Even though he was wearing a baseball hat, McCaleb recognized the man from the crime scene and ATM tapes.

'That's fine.'

McCaleb looked at Winston.

'Did you make up a six-pack with Bolotov?'

'Yes. It's on my desk. We'll show it to him first, in case we get lucky. If he makes the ID there will be no hypnosis, so we can save him for court.'

McCaleb nodded.

'Woulda been real nice,' Arrango began, 'if we had shown Noone the pictures before the bird was flushed.'

He looked at McCaleb. McCaleb thought of a response but decided to keep it to himself.

'Anything in particular you want me to ask him?' he asked instead.

Arrango looked at his partner and winked.

'Yeah, get us the license plate off that getaway vehicle. That'd be nice.'

He smiled brilliantly, the toothpick jutting upward from his lower lip. McCaleb smiled back.

'It's been done before. The victim of a rapist once gave me a complete description of a tattoo on her attacker's arm. Before hypnosis she hadn't even remembered the tattoo.'

'Good, then do it again. Get us a plate. Get us a tattoo. Your pal Bolotov has enough of 'em.'

There had been a clear challenge in his voice. Arrango seemed to insist on putting everything on a personal level, as if McCaleb's desire to bring a multiple killer in was in some way a show of disrespect to him. It was ludicrous but McCaleb had challenged him simply by entering the case.

'Okay, guys,' Hitchens said, cutting it off and trying to diffuse tensions. 'We're just taking a shot at this, that's all. It's worth the shot. Maybe we get something, maybe we don't.'

'Meantime, we lose the guy in court,' Arrango said.

'What court?' McCaleb said. 'You're not going anywhere near court with what you guys have got. This is your last chance, Arrango. I'm your last chance.'

Arrango swiftly stood up. Not to challenge McCaleb physically but to underline his next words.

'Lookit, asshole, I don't need some washed-out fed to tell me how to –'

'Okay, okay, that's it,' Hitchens said, standing up also. 'We're gonna do this thing and do it right now. Jaye, why don't you take Terry into the interview room and get started. The rest of us will wait here.'

Winston guided McCaleb out the door. He looked back over his shoulder at Arrango, whose face had turned dark with anger. Past him McCaleb noticed a quizzical smile on Donna de Groot's face. She had apparently enjoyed the testosterone show.

As they walked through the squad room and past rows of empty desks, McCaleb shook his head with embarrassment.

'Sorry,' he said. 'I can't believe I let him draw me into that.'

'It's okay. Guy's an asshole. It was going to happen sooner or later.'

After stopping by Winston's desk to pick up the file containing the photo lineup, they went down a hallway and Winston stopped outside a closed door. She put her hand on the knob but looked back at McCaleb before turning it.

'Okay, any particular way you want to do this?'

'The main thing is that it works best if only I do the talking once the session begins and I communicate verbally only with him. That way he won't get confused about who I am talking to. So if you and I need to communicate, we can either write notes or point to the door and we can come out here.'

'Fine. Are you all right? You look like shit.'

'I'm fine.'

She opened the door and James Noone looked up from the table.

'Mr Noone, this is Terry McCaleb, the hypnotism expert I told you about,' Winston said. 'He used to work for the FBI. He's going to see if he can't work with you on this.'

McCaleb smiled and reached a hand across the table. They shook.

'Good to meet you, Mr Noone. This shouldn't take long and it should be a relaxing experience. Do you mind if I call you James?'

'No, James is fine.'

McCaleb looked around the room and at the table and chairs. The chairs were standard government issue, with a half inch of foam padding on the seats. He looked at Winston.

'Jaye, you think we can get a more comfortable chair for James? Something with arms maybe? Like the one Captain Hitchens was sitting in.'

'Sure. Hang on a minute.'

'Oh, also, I'm going to need a pair of scissors.'

Winston looked at him quizzically but left without a word. McCaleb took an appraising look around the room. There was an overhead bank of fluorescent lights in the ceiling. No other lighting. The glare from the overheads was magnified by the mirrored window on the left wall. He knew the video camera was set up on the other side of the glass, so he needed to keep Noone in a position facing it.

'Let's see,' he said to Noone. 'I need to get up on the table to get at those lights.'

'No problem.'

Using a chair as a stepladder, McCaleb climbed onto the table and reached up to the light panel. He moved slowly, trying to avoid another bout of vertigo. He opened the panel and began removing the long light tubes, handing them down to Noone and engaging him in small talk, hoping to make the witness feel comfortable with him.

'I hear you're going to Vegas from here? Is that work or play?'

'Uh, work mostly.'

'What do you do?'

'Computer software. I'm designing a new accounting and security system for the El Rio. Still working out the bugs. We'll be running tests for the next week or so.'

'A week in Las Vegas? Boy, I could lose a lot of money there in a week.'

'I don't gamble.'

'That's a good thing.'

He had taken out three of the four bulbs, dropping the room into a dim ambience. He hoped that left enough light for the video. As he got off the table, Winston returned with a chair that actually looked like the one Hitchens had been sitting in.

'You took that from the captain?'

'Best chair in the place.'

'Good.'

He looked at the mirror and winked at the camera behind it. As he did this, he noticed the dark circles beginning to form under his eyes and quickly looked away.

Winston reached into the pocket of the blazer she wore and carefully eased out a pair of scissors. McCaleb took them and put them on the table and then pushed it against the wall below the mirror. He then took the captain's chair and positioned it against the opposite wall. He put two chairs from the table facing the captain's chair but split them apart far enough so as not to block the camera's view of Noone. He directed Noone to the captain's chair and then Winston and he took the remaining seats. McCaleb looked at his watch and noted that it was ten minutes before six.

'Okay,' he said. 'We'll try to do this quick and have you on your way, James. First off, any questions you have for us about what we're trying to do here?'

Noone thought a moment before speaking.

'Well, I guess I don't know much about it. What will happen to me?'

'Nothing will happen to you. All hypnosis really is is an altered state of consciousness. What we want you to do is go through some progressive stages of relaxation until you reach a point where you can easily move through the recesses of your mind to pull out some of the stored information. Kind of like turning through a Rolodex and pulling out the card you need.'

McCaleb waited but Noone asked nothing else.

'Why don't we start with an exercise. I want you to tilt your head back slightly and look up. Try to roll your eyes upward as far as they can go. Maybe you should take off your glasses.'

Noone took off the glasses, folded them and put them in his pocket. He tilted his head back and rolled his eyes up. McCaleb studied him. He was able to roll them upward enough so that a quarter inch of white cornea was visible below each iris. This was a good indicator of receptivity to hypnosis.

'Okay, that's good. Now, I want you to just relax if you can, take long, deep breaths and tell us what you can recall about the incident on the night of January twenty-second. Just recount what you now remember about what you saw.'

For the next ten minutes Noone told the story about coming upon the tail end of the shooting and robbery at the ATM in Lancaster. His story was no different than the versions he had recounted during various interviews since the night it had all happened. He added no new details that McCaleb picked up on and seemed to leave nothing out from his prior tellings. This was unusual and encouraging to McCaleb. The memories of most witnesses begin fading after two months. They forgot details. The fact that Noone seemed to remember every detail led McCaleb to hope the computer programmer's recessed memory might be just as sharp. When Noone had finished recounting the event, McCaleb nodded to Winston, who then leaned toward Noone and handed him the six-pack file.

'James, I want you to open the file and look at the photos. Tell us if any of the men was the man you saw in the speeding car.'

Noone put his glasses back on and took the file but said, 'I don't know. I really didn't get a –'

'I know,' Winston said. 'But take a look.'

Noone opened the file. There was a piece of cardboard inside with squares cut out in two rows of three. In the squares were photos of men. Bolotov's photo was the third on the top row. Noone stared at the six-pack, his eyes moving from photo to photo, and then shook his head.

'I'm sorry. I just didn't see him.'

'That's fine,' McCaleb said quickly before Winston could say something that Noone might interpret as a negative. 'I think we're ready to go on, then.'

He took the file from Noone and tossed it onto the table.

'So why don't you start by just telling us what you do to relax, James?' McCaleb asked.

Noone looked back at him blankly.

'You know, when are you happiest? When are you the most relaxed and at peace? Me, I like to work on my boat and go fishing. I don't even care if I catch anything. I just like having a line in the water. How about you, James? You like shooting baskets, hitting golf balls? What?'

'Um, I don't know. I guess I like being on the computer.'

'But that's not relaxing mentally, James, is it? I'm not talking about something where you have to do a lot of thinking. I mean, what do you do when you want to let it all go. When you're tired of thinking and you just want to go blank for a while.'

'Well . . . I don't know. I like to go to the beach. There's a place I know. I go there.'

'What's it look like?'

'The sand is so white and it's wide. You can rent horses and ride along the edge of the water below the cliffs. The water cuts under the cliffs and it's like a hanging edge. People sit under there in the shade.'

'Okay, that's good. That's real good, James. Now, I want you to close your eyes, rest your arms in your lap and in your mind I want you to think about that spot. Picture in your mind that you are walking on that beach. Just relax and walk along the beach.'

McCaleb was silent for a half minute and simply watched Noone's face. The skin around the corners of his closed eyes began to relax and McCaleb then led him through a set of sensory exercises in which he told him to concentrate on the feel of his socks on his feet, his hands on the fabric of his pants, the glasses on the bridge of his nose, even the hair – what was left of it – on his head.

After five minutes of this, McCaleb went on to muscle exercises, telling Noone to crunch his toes together as hard as possible, hold them that way and then release.

Slowly the focus of the exercises was moved up his body, eventually going to every muscle group. McCaleb then started again at the toes and moved back up. It was a method of exhausting the muscles and making the mind more susceptible to the suggestion of relaxation and rest. McCaleb noticed Noone's breathing going deep and long. Things were going well. He looked at his watch and saw it was now six-thirty.

'Okay, James, now without opening your eyes, I want you to hold your left hand out and up in front of your face. Hold it about a foot from your face.'

Noone responded and McCaleb let him hold his arm up for a good minute, all the while counseling him to relax and keep his thoughts on the beach he was walking on.

'Okay, I now want you to very slowly bring your hand toward your face. Very slowly.'

Noone's hand started to move toward his nose.

'Okay, slower now,' McCaleb said, his words slower and softer than before. 'That's it, James. Slowly. And when your hand touches your face you will be totally relaxed and at that point you will drop into a deep hypnotic state.'

He was silent then as he watched Noone's hand move slowly forward until his palm stopped at his nose. At the moment of contact, his head dipped forward and his shoulders slumped. His hand dropped into his lap. McCaleb looked over at Winston. She raised her eyebrows and nodded at him. McCaleb knew they were only halfway there but things were looking good. He decided to run a little test.

'James, you are totally relaxed now, totally at rest. You are so relaxed that your arms are as light as feathers. They weigh nothing at all.'

He watched him but he didn't move, which was good.

'Okay, now I'm going to take a balloon that's full of helium and tie the string to your left hand. I'm tying it on now. There, the balloon is tied to your wrist, James, and I'm letting go of it.'

Immediately, Noone's left arm began to rise until it was stretched upward, his hand up higher than his head. McCaleb just watched. And after half a minute Noone's arm showed no indication of tiring.

'Okay, James, I have a pair of scissors and I'm going to cut the string.'

McCaleb reached back to the table and lifted the scissors. He opened them and closed them sharply on the imaginary string. Noone's arm dropped back into his lap. McCaleb looked over at Winston and nodded.

'Okay, James, you are very relaxed and nothing is bothering you. I want you to picture in your mind that you're walking on that beach and you come to a garden. The garden is green and lush and beautiful and there are flowers and birds singing. It is so beautiful and peaceful. You've never been in any spot as peaceful as this. Now . . . you walk through the garden and come to a small building with a set of doors. They're elevator doors, James. They're made of wood with gold trim around the edges and they're beautiful. Everything here is beautiful.

'The doors open, James, and you step on the elevator because you know it takes you down to your special room. A room where nobody else can go. Only you can go down there and you are in total peace when you go there.'

McCaleb got up and stood in front of Noone, just a few feet away. Noone showed no outward sign of acknowledging the close presence of another person.

'The elevator buttons show you are on number ten and you have to go down to your room on number one. You push the button, James, and the elevator starts to go down. You are feeling more relaxed as each floor goes by.'

McCaleb raised his arm and held it parallel to the ground and a foot in front of Noone's face. He then began raising it, bringing it back around and then up again. He knew the disturbance the motion would make in the light hitting Noone's eyelids would add to his sense of descent.

'You're going down, James. Deeper and deeper. That's the ninth floor ... now the eighth, and seventh ... You are getting deeper and deeper, more and more relaxed. The sixth floor just went by ... now the fifth ... four ... three ... two ... and one ... The doors open now and you step into your special room. You're there, James, and in perfect peace.'

McCaleb went back to his chair. He then told Noone to enter his room and that the most comfortable chair in the world was waiting for him there. He told him to sit down and just melt into the chair. He told him to imagine a pat of butter melting in a frying pan on very low heat.

'No sizzle, just a slow, slow melting. That's you, James. Just melting into your chair.'

He waited a few moments and then told Noone about the television that was sitting right in front of him.

'You've got the remote control in your hand. And this is a special television with a special remote. You can watch whatever you want to on this TV. You can back the picture up, go forward, zoom in or pull back out. Whatever you want to do with it, you can do. Now, turn it on, James. And what we're going to watch on that special TV right now is what you saw on the night of January twenty-second when you were going to the bank in Lancaster to get some money.'

He waited a beat.

'Turn the TV on, James. Is it on now?'

'Yes,' Noone said, his first words in a half hour.

'Okay, good. Now we're going to go back to that night, James. Now tell us what you saw.'

17

James Noone told his story as if McCaleb and Winston were there riding with him in his car, if not his head.

'I have the blinker on and I'm turning in. Here he comes! Brakes! He's going to – he almost hit me, the asshole! I could've –'

Noone raised his left arm, made a fist and shot his middle finger up, an impotent gesture at the driver of the car that had blasted by him. As he did this, McCaleb looked closely at his face, noting the rapid eye movement behind his closed lids. It was one of the indicators he always looked for, a sign that the subject was deeply into the trance.

'He's gone and I'm pulling in now. I see, I see the man. There is a man on the ground under the light. By the ATM. He's down – I'm getting out and check to see . . . there's blood. He's shot – somebody shot him. Uh, uh, I've got to get somebody – I'm going back to my car for the phone. I can call and get him help. He's shot. There's blood on the . . . it's everywhere.'

'Okay, James, okay,' McCaleb said, interrupting him for the first time. 'That's good. Now what I want you to do is take your special remote and back up the picture on the TV until the point that you first see the car coming out of the bank's parking lot. Can you do that?'

'Yes.'

'Okay, are you there?'

'Yes.'

'Okay, now start it again, only this time run it in slow motion. Very slow, so you can see everything. Are you running it?'

'Yes.'

'Okay, I want you to freeze it when you get the best view of the car coming at you.'

McCaleb waited.

'Okay, I got it.'

'Okay, good. Can you tell us what kind of car it is?'

'Yes. Black Cherokee. It's pretty dusty.'

'Can you tell what year?'

'No, it's the newer kind. The Grand Cherokee.'

'Can you see the side of the Cherokee?'

'Yes.'

'How many doors?'

It was a small test to make sure Noone was reporting what he had seen, not what he had been told. McCaleb remembered from the crime scene tape that the deputy who had first interviewed Noone had told him the newer styling on the Cherokee indicated it was the Grand Cherokee model. McCaleb had to confirm the identification of the vehicle and he knew the Grand Cherokee came only in a four-door model.

'Um, two on the side,' Noone said. 'It's a four-door.'

'Good. Now come around to the front. Do you see any damage to the car. Any dents or noticeable scratches?'

'No.'

'Is there any striping on the car?'

'Mmm, no.'

'How about the bumper? Can you see the front bumper?'

'Yes.'

'Okay, I want you to take your remote and zoom in on that bumper. Can you see the license plate?'

'No.'

'Why not, James?'

'It's covered.'

'What's covering it?'

'Uh, there's a T-shirt on it. It's wrapped around the bumper so it covers the plate. Looks like a T-shirt.'

McCaleb glanced over at Winston and could see the disappointment on her face. He pressed on.

'Okay, James, take your remote and zoom up into the car, can you do that?'

'Okay.'

'How many people are in that Cherokee?'

'One. The driver.'

'All right, zoom in on him. Tell me what you see.'

'Can't really.'

'Why not? What's wrong?'

'The lights. He's got the brights on. The glare is too much, I can't –'

'Okay, James, what I want you to do is take the remote and move the picture. Go back and forth until you have the best view of the driver. Tell me when you have that.'

McCaleb looked back at Winston and she looked back with raised eyebrows. They both knew that they would soon find out if this had been worth it or not.

'Okay,' James said.

'Okay, you're seeing the driver.'

'Yes.'

'Tell us what he looks like. What color is his skin?'

'He's white but he has a hat and the brim is down. He's looking downward and the brim covers his face.'

'All of his face?'

'No. I see his mouth.'

'Does he have a beard or mustache?'
'No.'
'Can you see his teeth?'
'No, his mouth is closed.'
'Can you see his eyes?'
'No. That hat is in the way.'
McCaleb sat back and released his breath in frustration. He couldn't believe this. Noone was a perfect subject. He was in a deep trance and yet they couldn't get from him what they needed, a direct look at the shooter.
'Okay, are you sure this is the best view of him?'
'I'm sure.'
'Can you see any of his hair?'
'Yes.'
'What color is it?'
'Dark, like a dark brown or maybe black.'
'What length, can you tell?'
'It looks short.'
'What about the hat? Describe the hat.'
'It's a baseball hat and it's gray. Washed-out gray.'
'Okay, is there any writing on the hat or a team logo?'
'There's a design, like a symbol.'
'Can you describe it?'
'It's like letters overlapping each other.'
'What letters?'
'It looks like a C with a line cut through. A one or a capital I or a small L. And then there's a circle – I mean an oval – around the whole thing.'
McCaleb was silent for a moment thinking about this.
'James,' he then said, 'if I give you something to draw on, do you think you could open your eyes and draw this design for us?'
'Yes.'
'Okay, I want you to open your eyes.'
McCaleb stood up. Winston had already turned the pad she had on a clipboard to a fresh page. McCaleb took it and her pen and handed both to Noone.
Noone's eyes were open and staring blankly at the pad as he drew. He then handed it back. The drawing was as he had described it, a vertical line slashing down through a large C. This design was then captured in an oval. McCaleb handed the pad back to Winston, who briefly held it up to the mirrored window so those watching on video could see.
'Okay, James, that was good. Now close your eyes and look at the picture of the driver again. You got it?'
'Yes.'
'Can you see either of his ears?'
'One. His right.'
'Is there anything unusual?'
'No.'
'No earring?'

'No.'

'What about below the ear? His neck, can you see his neck?'

'Yes.'

'Anything unusual there? What do you see?'

'Uh, nothing. Uh, his neck. Just his neck.'

'This is his right side?'

'Yes, right.'

'No tattoo on his neck?'

'No. No tattoo.'

McCaleb blew out his breath again. He had just effectively eliminated Bolotov as a suspect after spending the day building him as one.

'Okay,' he said in a resigned voice, 'what about his hands, can you see his hands?'

'On the steering wheel. They're holding the wheel.'

'See anything unusual? Anything on his fingers?'

'No.'

'No rings?'

'No.'

'Is he wearing a watch?'

'A watch, yes.'

'What kind?'

'I can't see. I see the band.'

'What kind of band? What color?'

'It's black.'

'Which wrist is it on, his left or right?'

'His . . . right. His right.'

'Okay, can you see and describe any of his clothing?'

'Just his shirt. It's dark. A dark blue sweatshirt.'

McCaleb tried to think of what else to ask. His disappointment in not being able to come up with a substantial lead so far was crowding his focus. Finally, he thought of something he had passed over.

'The windshield, James. Are there any stickers or anything like that on the glass?'

'Mmm, no. I don't see them.'

'Okay, and take a look at the rearview mirror. Anything on that? Like hanging down or hooked to it?'

'Not that I can see.'

McCaleb now slumped in his chair. This was a disaster. They had lost this man as a potential court witness, eliminated a potential suspect and all they got from it was a detailed description of a baseball cap and a dentless Cherokee. He knew the last step was to take Noone forward to his last view of the Cherokee speeding away, but it was likely that if the front license plate had been covered, so too would be the rear plate.

'Okay, James, let's hit fast forward to the point that the Cherokee is past you and you are shooting the guy the bird.'

'Okay.'

'Zoom in on the license plate, can you see it?'

'It's covered.'

'With what?'

'A towel or a T-shirt. I can't tell. Like the front.'

'Zoom back. Do you see anything unusual about the rear of the car.'

'Mmm, no.'

'Bumper stickers? Or maybe the car dealership's name on the rear?'

'No, nothing like that.'

'Anything on the window? Any stickers?'

McCaleb registered the desperation in his own voice.

'No, nothing.'

McCaleb looked at Winston and shook his head.

'Anything else?'

Winston shook her head.

'Do you want to bring the artist in?'

She shook her head again.

'You sure?'

She shook her head one more time. McCaleb turned his attention back to Noone though he couldn't help but think about how this had been a gamble that had not paid off.

'James, over the next few days I want you to think about what you saw on the night of January twenty-second and if anything new comes to mind, if you remember any other details, I want you to call Detective Winston, okay?'

'Okay.'

'Good. Now I'm going to count backward from five and as I do this, you are going to feel your body rejuvenating and you will become more and more alert until I say, "One," and you become fully alert. You are going to have a high level of energy and feel like you've just had eight hours of sleep. You'll stay awake all the way to Las Vegas but when you go to bed tonight, you won't have any trouble sleeping. Okay on all of that?'

'Okay.'

McCaleb brought him out of the trance and Noone looked at Winston with expectant eyes.

'Welcome back,' McCaleb said. 'How do you feel?'

'Great, I guess. How'd I do?'

'You did fine. You remember what we talked about?'

'Yes, I think so.'

'Good. You should. Remember, if anything else comes to the surface, you call Detective Winston.'

'Right.'

'Well, we don't want to hold you up any further. You've got a long drive ahead of you.'

'No problem, I didn't think I'd get out of here until after seven. You're giving me a head start.'

McCaleb looked at his watch and then back at Noone.

'It's almost seven-thirty right now.'

'What?'

He looked at his watch, surprise showing on his face.

'People in the hypnotic state often lose time,' McCaleb said.

'I thought it was only like ten minutes.'

'That's normal. It's called disturbed time.'

McCaleb stood up and they shook hands and Winston walked him out. McCaleb sat back down and clasped his hands together on top of his head. He was bone tired and wished that *he* could feel like he had just had eight hours' sleep.

The door to the interview room opened and Captain Hitchens stepped in. He had a dour expression on his face that was easy to interpret.

'Well, what do you think?' he asked as he sat down on the table next to the scissors.

'Same as you. It was a bust. We got a better description of the car but it still only narrows it down to ten thousand or so. And we got the hat, which there may even be more of.'

'Cleveland Indians?'

'What? Oh, the CI? Maybe, but I think they have a little Indian guy on their hats.'

'Right, right. Well . . . what about Molotov?'

'Bolotov.'

'Whatever. I guess we've painted him out now.'

'Looks it.'

Hitchens clapped his hands together and after a few uncomfortable moments of silence, Winston came back in and stood there with her hands in the pockets of her blazer.

'Where's Arrango and Walters?' McCaleb asked.

'They left,' she said. 'They weren't impressed.'

McCaleb stood back up and told Hitchens that if he got off the table he'd put it back in place and then put the light bulbs back into the ceiling. Hitchens said not to bother. He told McCaleb that he had done enough – which McCaleb took to mean in more ways than one.

'Then I guess I'll be going,' he said. Pointing at the mirror, he added, 'You think at some point I could get a copy of the tape or the transcript? I'd like to look at it at some point. Might get a few ideas for a follow-up.'

'Well, Jaye can make you a copy. We've got a transfer machine. But as far as any follow-ups go, I don't see much of a need to pursue this. The guy clearly didn't see our shooter's face and the plates were covered. What else is there to say?'

McCaleb didn't answer. They all left after that, Hitchens pushing his chair back toward his office and Winston leading McCaleb into the video room. She grabbed a fresh tape off a shelf and put it in a tape machine already attached to the one that had recorded the hypnotism session.

'Look, I still think it was worth the shot,' McCaleb said as she pushed the buttons that began dubbing one tape onto the other.

'Don't worry, it was. I'm disappointed only in the lack of results and because we lost the Russian, not in the fact that we did it. I don't know what the captain thinks and I don't care about those LAPD guys, that's how I look at it.'

McCaleb nodded. It was nice of her to put it that way and let him off the hook. After all, he had pushed for the use of hypnotism and it hadn't paid off. She could have dumped all the blame on him.

'Well, if Hitchens gives you grief, just put it all on me. Tell him it was all me.'

Winston didn't reply. She popped the dubbed tape out of the machine, slid it into its cardboard sleeve and handed it to McCaleb.

'I'll walk you out,' she said.

'Nah, that's okay. I know the way.'

'Okay, Terry, stay in touch.'

'Sure.' They were out in the hallway before McCaleb remembered something. 'Hey, did you talk to the captain about the DRUGFIRE thing?'

'Oh, yeah, we're going to do it. A package goes out FedEx tomorrow. I called your guy in DC and told him it was coming.'

'Great. You tell Arrango?'

Winston frowned and shook her head.

'Basically, I get the idea that any idea that comes from you, Arrango isn't interested in. I didn't tell him.'

McCaleb nodded, threw a salute her way and headed for the exit. He walked through the parking lot, his eyes scanning for Buddy Lockridge's Taurus. Before he spotted it, another car pulled up alongside him. McCaleb glanced over and saw Arrango looking up at him from the passenger seat.

McCaleb braced himself for the detective's gloating about the lack of success from the session.

'What?' he said.

He kept walking and the car stayed alongside him.

'Nothing,' Arrango said. 'I just wanted to tell you that was a hell of a show in there. Four stars. We'll put a teletype out on the watchband first thing in the morning.'

'That's funny, Arrango.'

'Just making the point that your little session in there cost us a witness, a suspect who probably should have never been a suspect, and didn't get us squat.'

'We got more than we had before. I never said the guy was going to give us the shooter's goddamn address.'

'Yeah, well, we already figured out what the CI on the hat means. Complete Idiots – that's what the shooter probably thinks of us.'

'If he does, he was already thinking that before tonight.'

Arrango didn't have an answer for that.

'You know,' McCaleb said, 'you ought to think about your witness. Ellen Taaffe.'

'To hypnotize like that?'

'That's right.'

Arrango barked a command at Walters to stop the car. He popped his door open and jumped out. He came up close to McCaleb, their faces inches apart. Close enough for McCaleb to smell his breath. He guessed that the detective kept a flask of bourbon in the glove compartment.

'Listen to me, bureau man, you stay the fuck away from my witnesses. You just stay the fuck away from my case.'

He didn't back away when he was done. He just stayed there, his whiskey breath burning McCaleb's nose. McCaleb smiled and nodded slowly as if he had just come into possession of a great secret.

'You're really worried, aren't you?' he said. 'You're worried I'm going to break this. You don't care about the actual case, about the people killed or hurt by this. You just don't want me doing what you can't.'

McCaleb waited for a response but Arrango said nothing.

'Then be worried, Arrango.'

'Yeah? Because you're going to break this one?'

He laughed in a fake way that had far more venom in it than humor.

'Because I'll let you in on a little secret,' McCaleb said. 'You know Gloria Torres? The victim you don't give a shit about? I've got her heart.'

McCaleb tapped his chest and looked back at him.

'I got her heart. I'm alive because she's dead. And that cuts me into this in a big way. So I don't care much about your feelings, Arrango. I couldn't give a fuck about stepping on your toes. You're an asshole and that's fine, be an asshole. I'll put up with that. But I'm not backing out of this till we get this guy. I don't care if it's you, me or somebody else. But I'm in this one for the whole ride.'

They just stared at each other for a long moment and then McCaleb raised his right hand and calmly pushed Arrango away from him.

'I gotta go, Arrango. See you around.'

18

He dreamed of darkness. A moving darkness, like blood in water, with darting images in the periphery that he couldn't grab onto with his eyes until they were gone.

Three times in the night he was awakened by some interior alarm. Sitting up so fast he grew dizzy, he would wait and listen and there would be nothing but the sound of the wind through dozens of masts in the marina. He would get up and check the boat, look out across the marina for Bolotov even though he thought it unlikely the Russian would ever show up. He'd then use the bathroom and check the vitals. Status quo each time and he would return to the dark waters of the same indecipherable dream.

At nine o'clock Friday morning the phone woke him. It was Jaye Winston.

'You awake?'

'Yeah. Just getting a slow start today. What's going on?'

'What's going on is that I just heard from Arrango and he told me something that really bothers me.'

'Oh, yeah? What's that?'

'He told me who you got that new heart from.'

McCaleb rubbed a hand across his face. He had forgotten that he had told Arrango.

'Why does that bother you, Jaye?'

'Because I wish you had told me everything. I don't like secrets, Terry. That asshole calls up and makes *me* feel like an asshole because I'm the last one to know this.'

'What's the difference whether you knew or not?'

'It's kind of a conflict of interest, isn't it?'

'No. It's not a conflict. You ask me, it's an enhancement. It makes me want to get this guy even more than you people. Is there something else that's bothering you? Is this about Noone?'

'No, it's not about that. I told you last night, I stand behind doing it. The captain gave me some grief already today but I still think we had to do it.'

'Good. So do I.'

There was a tentative silence after that. McCaleb still thought there was something else she wanted to say and he waited her out.

'Look, just don't go off cowboying on this, okay?' Winston said.

'What do you mean?'

'I'm not sure. I just don't know what you've got planned. And I don't want to have to worry about what you're up to because of your "enhancement", as you call it.'

'I understand. It's not even a point of contention, Jaye. As I've said all along, if I get something, it goes to you guys. That's still the plan.'

'Okay, then.'

'All right.'

He was putting the phone down when he heard her voice.

'By the way, the bullet went to your man today. He'll get it tomorrow if he works Saturdays. If not, Monday.'

'Good.'

'You'll let me know if he gets something, right?'

'He's going to tell you first. You sent the package.'

'Don't bullshit a bullshitter, Terry. He's your man, he's going to call you. Hopefully, he'll call me real quick after.'

'I'll make sure he does.'

Again he was putting the phone down when he heard her.

'So what are you going to do today?'

He hadn't really thought about it.

'Well . . . I don't know. I'm not sure where to go. I'd like to reinterview the witnesses on the Gloria Torres thing but Arrango pretty much threatened me if I went near them.'

'So what's that leave?'

'I don't know. I was thinking about just hanging around the boat today, maybe take another run through the books and the tapes, see if anything comes up. I was quick on the first read-through, but not thorough.'

'Well, that sounds like a boring day. Almost as bad as mine's going to be.'

'Court again?'

'I wish. Trial's in recess Fridays. That means I get to spend the day doing paper. Catching up. And I better get started. I'll see you, Terry. Remember what you said. You'll call me first with the news.'

'You get the news,' he agreed.

She finally hung up and he flopped back on the bed, the phone clutched to his stomach. After a few minutes of trying to recall the dreams of the night before, he lifted the phone and called information to get the number of the emergency room at Holy Cross.

After calling and asking for Graciela Rivers, he waited nearly a minute before she picked up. Her voice was clipped and urgent. He had obviously called at a bad time. He almost hung up but guessed that she might figure out it was him.

'Hello?'

'I'm sorry. I must've caught you in the middle of something.'

'Who is this?'

'It's Terry.'

'Oh, Terry, hi. No, it's not a bad time. I just thought it might be something about Raymond. I usually don't get calls here.'

'Then I'm sorry I alarmed you.'

'It's okay. Are you sick? You don't sound like you. I didn't even recognize your voice.'

She forced a laugh into the phone. He thought she felt embarrassed that she didn't know his voice.

'I'm lying on my back,' he said. 'You ever do that when you're calling in sick? You know, it makes you sound like you really are sick.'

This time her laugh was legitimate.

'No, I never tried that. I'll have to remember.'

'Sure. It's a good tip. You can use it.'

'So what's up? How are things going?'

'Well, on the case not so good. I thought we had something yesterday but then we hit a bit of a stall. I'm going to rethink things today.'

'Okay.'

'I was calling because I was wondering about tomorrow. You know, whether you were thinking of bringing Raymond down so I could take him out to the rocks.'

'The rocks?'

'The jetty. There's good fishing off there. I walk out most mornings and there's always people there, lines out.'

'Well, Raymond hasn't stopped talking about it since we left the other night. So I was planning on it. As long as it's still all right with you.'

McCaleb hesitated, thinking about Bolotov and wondering if he could possibly be a threat. But he wanted to see Graciela and the boy. He felt a need to see them.

'It sounds like maybe we should do it another time,' she said then.

'No,' he said, the specter of Bolotov disappearing from his mind. 'I was just thinking. I want you to come down. It will be fun. And I could make up for that dinner I was supposed to cook the other night.'

'Then good.'

'And you two should stay over. I've got plenty of room. Two staterooms and the salon table collapses and becomes a third bed.'

'Well, we'll see. I like to keep some constants in Raymond's life. Like his bed.'

'I understand.'

They talked about the arrangements a little further and she agreed to come down to the marina the following morning. After hanging up, he continued to lie in bed with the phone sitting on his stomach. His thoughts were on Graciela. He liked being with her and the thought of spending all of Saturday with her made him smile. Then the thought of Bolotov intruded again. McCaleb carefully considered the situation and decided that Bolotov was not a threat. Most spoken threats were never carried out. Even if Bolotov wanted to, it would be difficult for him to find *The Following Sea.* Lastly, the Russian was no longer a suspect in the murders.

Those thoughts led to the next question: If he was not a suspect, then why had he run? McCaleb thought of Winston's explanation the night before. Bolotov had not been the shooter but he was probably guilty of something. He ran.

McCaleb put it aside, rolled out of bed and finally got up.

After he had gotten one cup of coffee down, McCaleb went down to the office and gathered up all of the reports and the tapes and brought them back up to the salon. He then opened the slider to air out the boat and sat back down and began methodically going through all of the videotapes associated with the case.

Twenty minutes later he was watching the shooting of Gloria Torres for the third time in a row when he heard Buddy Lockridge's voice from behind him.

'What the hell is that?'

McCaleb turned around and saw Lockridge standing in the open door of the salon. He hadn't felt him come aboard. He grabbed the remote and flicked off the television.

'It's a tape. What are you doing here?'

'Reporting for duty.'

McCaleb stared blankly at him.

'You told me yesterday you'd need me this morning.'

'Oh, right. Well, I don't think I'm – I'm just going to work around here today, I think. You going to be around later if something comes up?'

'Prob'ly.'

'Okay, thanks.'

McCaleb waited for him to leave but Lockridge just stood there.

'What?'

'Is that what you're working on?' Lockridge asked, pointing at the tube.

'Yes, Buddy, that's it. But I can't talk to you about it. It's a private matter.'

'That's cool.'

'Then what else?'

'Um, well, when's payday?'

'Payday? What are you talk – oh, you mean for you? Oh, anytime. You need some money?'

'Sort of. I could use some today.'

McCaleb went to the galley counter where he had left his wallet and keys. As he was opening the wallet, he computed that he had used Buddy for no more than eight hours. He took out six twenties and handed the bills to Lockridge. Fanning the money in his hands, Buddy said it was too much.

'Some of it's for gas,' McCaleb explained. 'And the extra is for the hanging around and being on call. That okay?'

'Fine with me. Thanks, Terror.'

McCaleb smiled. Lockridge had been calling him that ever since the night they met and McCaleb had been so mad about the harmonica noise.

Lockridge finally left then and McCaleb got back to work. Nothing struck him as significant during his viewing of the videotapes and he went on to the paperwork. On this read-through time was not a factor and he tried to absorb every detail on every page.

He started backward, beginning with the Kang-Torres case. But as he went through the crime reports and investigative summaries, he found nothing aside from the conflict in the timeline he had constructed earlier that tugged at him as being out of order or needing further investigation. Despite his dislike of Arrango's personality and Walters's complacency, he couldn't find anything wrong or anything that had slipped through.

Finally, he came to the autopsy report and the grainy photocopies of the photos of Gloria Torres's body. He hadn't looked at these before. With good reason. Death photos had always been the way he remembered victims. He saw them in death, not in life. He saw what had been done to them. During the first read-through of the murder book, he had decided that he didn't need to see the photos of Gloria. It wasn't what he wanted or needed to know about her.

But now, grasping for anything, he studied the photos. The poor duplication of them by the photocopier made the details murky and softened the impact. He leafed through them quickly and then came back to the first one. It was Gloria's naked body on the steel table, the photo taken before the autopsy. A long incision, made by the surgeon who took her organs, ran between the breasts and down the sternum. McCaleb held the photo in both hands and looked at her violated body for a long moment, feeling a mixture of sadness and the heat of guilt.

The phone rang, startling him. He grabbed the phone before it could ring again.

'Yes?'

'Terry? It's Dr Fox.'

McCaleb inexplicably turned the photo over on the table.

'Are you there?'

'Yes, hi, how are you?'

'I'm fine. How are you?'

'I'm fine, too, Doc.'

'What are you doing?'

'Doing? I'm just sort of sitting here.'

'Terry, you know what I mean. What did you decide about that woman's request? The sister.'

'I, uh . . .' He turned the photo back over and looked at it. 'I decided I needed to look into it.'

She didn't say anything but he pictured her at her desk closing her eyes and shaking her head.

'I'm sorry,' he said.

'I'm sorry, too,' she said. 'Terry, I really don't think you understand the risks of what you are doing.'

'I think I do, Doctor. I don't think I have a choice, anyway.'

'I don't think I have one, either.'

'What do you mean?'

'I mean I don't think I can continue to be your doctor if this is what you are going to do. You obviously don't value my advice or feel you should follow my instructions. You are choosing this pursuit of yours over your health. I can't be around while you do this.'

'Are you firing me, Doc?'

He laughed uneasily.

'It's not a joke. Maybe that's your problem. You think it's some sort of joke, that you're invincible.'

'No, I don't feel invincible.'

'Well, your words and actions don't match up. On Monday I'll have one of my assistants gather your files and put together two or three cardiologists I can refer you to.'

McCaleb closed his eyes.

'Look, Doc, I . . . I don't know what to say. We've been together a long time. Don't you feel an obligation to see it through?'

'It goes two ways. If I don't hear from you by Monday, I'll have to assume you are going on with this. I'll have your records here at the office ready for you.'

She hung up. McCaleb sat still, the phone still to his ear until it started blaring its hang-up tone.

McCaleb got up and took a walk outside. From the cockpit he surveyed the marina and the parking lot. He saw no sign of Buddy Lockridge or anyone else. The air was still. He leaned over the stern and looked down into the water. It was too dark to see the bottom. He spat into the water and with it went the misgivings he felt over Fox's edict. He decided he would not be swayed.

The photo was there on the table waiting for him when he got back. He picked it up again and studied it once more, this time his eyes traveling up the body to the face. There was some kind of dark salve on the eyes and then he remembered that the eyes had probably been taken along with the internal organs.

He noticed the three small perforations running along the ridge of the left ear and down to the lobe. On the right lobe there was only one.

He was about to put the photo aside when he realized that earlier he had read through a property report listing the items removed from the victim at the hospital and then turned over to the police.

Curious to make sure all details checked out, he went back to the stack of paperwork and dug out the property report. His finger ran down the list of clothing until he got to the subheading of jewelry.

JEWELRY

1. Timex watch
2. Three earrings (2 crescent moon, one silver hoop)
3. Two rings (birthstone, silver)

He thought about this for a long moment, remembering that on the video of the shooting it was clear that Gloria Torres was wearing a total of four earrings. The hoop, the crescent moon and the dangling cross on her left ear. On her right ear there had been only a crescent moon. This accounting did not fit with the property report, which listed only three earrings. Nor did it jibe with the perforation marks clearly visible on Gloria's ears in the evidence photo.

He turned to the television, thinking that he would look at the tape again, but then stopped. He was sure. He did not imagine something like a cross. Somehow it was not accounted for.

A loose end. He tapped his fingers on the property report, trying to think about whether this was a notable detail or not. What had happened to the cross earring? Why wasn't it on the list?

He checked his watch and saw it was ten minutes after twelve. Graciela would be at lunch. He called the hospital and asked to be transferred to the main cafeteria. When a woman answered, he asked if it would be possible for her to go to the nurse seated at the table next to one of the windows and give her a message. When the woman hesitated, McCaleb described Graciela and gave her name. The woman on the phone reluctantly asked what the message was.

'Just tell her to call Dr McCaleb as soon as she can.'

About five minutes later he got the callback.

'Dr McCaleb?'

'Sorry, I had to do that so she would be sure to give you the message.'

'What's up?'

'Well, I'm going through the case files again and I've got a loose end here. The property report says that they took two crescent moon earrings and a hoop earring off your sister's ears at the hospital after she was brought in.'

'Right, they would have needed to remove those for the CAT scan. They wanted to look at the wound track.'

'Okay, what about the cross earring she wore in her left ear? There's nothing on the property report about –'

'She wasn't wearing it that night. I always thought that was weird. Like it was bad luck, because that was her favorite earring. She usually wore it every day.'

'Like a personal signature,' McCaleb said. 'What do you mean, she wasn't wearing it that night?'

'Because when the police gave me her things – you know, her watch and rings and earrings – it wasn't there. She wasn't wearing it.'

'Are you sure? In the video she's wearing it.'

'What video?'

'From the store.'

She was silent a moment.

'No, that can't be. I found it in her jewelry box. I gave it to them at the funeral home so they could, you know, put it on for when she was buried.'

Now McCaleb was silent and then he put it together.

'But wouldn't she have had two of them? I don't know anything about crosses, but don't you buy earrings in pairs?'

'Oh, you're right. I didn't think about that.'

'So the one you found was the extra one?'

He felt a stirring inside that he immediately recognized but hadn't felt in a long time.

'I guess . . .' Graciela said. 'So if she did have one on in the store, what happened to it?'

'That's what I want to find out.'

'But what does it matter anyway?'

He was silent for a few moments thinking about how he should answer. He decided that what he was thinking was too speculative at the moment to share with her.

'It's just a loose end that should be tied up. Let me ask you something, was it the kind of earring that just hooked on or was there a hasp to make sure it didn't fall off easily? You know what I mean? I couldn't tell that from the video.'

'Yes. Um, I think there was like a hook that you sort of clipped after it was on your ear. I don't think it would have fallen off.'

While she was speaking, McCaleb was looking through the stack for the paramedics' report. He ran his finger down the lines of the information box until he found the squad number and names of the two paramedics who had treated and transported Gloria.

'Okay, I'm gonna go,' he said. 'Are we still on for tomorrow?'

'Sure. Um, Terry?'

'What?'

'You saw the video from the store? I mean, all of it? You saw Glory . . .'

'Yes,' he said quietly. 'I had to.'

'Was she . . . was she scared?'

'No, Graciela. It was very quick. She never saw it coming.'

'I guess that's good.'

'I think so . . . Listen, are you going to be all right?'

'I'm fine.'

'Okay then. I'll see you tomorrow.'

The paramedics who had transported Gloria worked out of Fire Station 76. McCaleb called but the crew that had worked the night of January 22nd was off until Sunday. However, the station captain told him that under department policy governing what are called 'crime transports', any property left behind on a stretcher or found anywhere in an ambulance would have been turned over to police custody. This meant that if this had occurred following the transport of Gloria Torres, there would be a property-received report in the murder book. There wasn't. The cross earring remained unaccounted for.

The irony that McCaleb carried inside of him alongside a stranger's heart was the secret belief that he had been the wrong one saved. It should have been someone else. In the days and weeks before he received Glory's heart, he had been prepared for the end. He had accepted it as the way it was to be. He was long past believing in a God – the horrors he had seen and documented had little by little sapped his stores of faith until the only absolute he believed in was that there were no bounds to the evil acts of men. And in those seemingly final days, as his own heart withered and tapped out its final cadences, he did not grasp desperately for his lost faith as a shield or a means of easing the fear of the unknown. Instead, he was accepting of the end, of his own nothingness. He was ready.

It was easy to do. When he had been with the bureau, he was driven and consumed by a mission, a calling. And when he carried it out and was successful, he knew he was making a difference. Better than any heart surgeon, he was saving lives from horrible ends. He was facing off against the worst kinds of evil, the most malignant cancers, and the battle, though always wearing and painful, gave his life its meaning.

That was gone the moment his heart deserted him and he fell to the floor of the field office thinking he had surely been stabbed in the chest. It was still gone two years later when the pager sounded and he was told they had a heart for him.

He had a new heart but it didn't feel like a new life. He was a man on a boat that never left port. It didn't matter what stock quotes about second chances he had used with a newspaper reporter. That existence was not enough for McCaleb. That was the struggle he was facing when Graciela Rivers had stepped down off the dock and into his life.

The quest she had given him had been a way of avoiding his own inner struggle. But now things were suddenly different. The missing cross earring stirred something deep and dormant in him. His long experience had given him true knowledge and instincts about evil. He knew its signs.

This was one of them.

19

McCaleb had been to the sheriff's homicide bureau so often during the week that the receptionist just waved him back without a phone call or escort. Jaye Winston was at her desk, using a three-hole punch on a thin stack of documents which she then slipped over the prongs of an open binder. She snapped it closed and looked up at her visitor.

'You moving in?'

'Feels like it. You get caught up on the paper?'

'Instead of four months behind I'm only two. What's going on? I didn't think I was going to see you today.'

'You still upset about me holding that thing back?'

'Water under the bridge.'

She leaned back in her chair, looked him over and waited for an explanation of why he was there.

'I've sort of come up with something I think bears looking into,' he said.

'Is this about Bolotov again?'

'No, it's something new.'

'Don't become the boy who cried wolf on me, McCaleb.'

She smiled.

'I won't.'

'Then tell me.'

He put his palms down on the desk and leaned over it, so he could speak to her in a confidential tone. There were still plenty of Winston's colleagues around the bureau, working at their desks and trying to get things done before the weekend.

'Arrango and Walters missed something,' McCaleb said. 'So did I on my first go-through. But I picked up on it this morning when I took a second look at the videos and the paperwork. It's something that has to be considered pretty seriously. I think it changes things.'

Winston furrowed her eyebrows and looked at him seriously.

'Quit talking in circles. What did they miss?'

'I'd rather show you than tell you.' He reached down to the floor and opened his leather satchel. He pulled out the copy of the surveillance tape and held it up to her. 'Can we go look at this?'

'I guess so.'

Winston got up and led the way to the video room. She turned the machines on and popped in the tape after looking at it and noting it was not one of the tapes she had given McCaleb on Wednesday.

'What is this?'

'It's the surveillance from the market.'

'Not the one I gave you.'

'It's a copy. I'm having somebody look at the other one.'

'What do you mean? Who?'

'A tech I knew when I was with the bureau. I'm just trying to get some of the images enhanced. Not a big deal.'

'So what are you showing me?'

She had the surveillance tape playing.

'Where's the freeze?'

Winston pointed to a button on the console and McCaleb held his finger over it, waiting for the right moment. On the tape Gloria Torres approached the counter and smiled at Kang. Then came the gunman and the shot that threw her body forward over the counter. McCaleb froze the image and used a pen from his pocket to point at Gloria's left ear.

'It's pretty murky but on a blowup you can see she has three earrings on this ear,' he said. Then tapping the pen at each point on the ear, he added, 'A crescent moon on a stud, a hoop and then dangling from the lobe, a cross.'

'Okay. I can't really see it too well but I'll take your word for it.'

McCaleb hit the freeze button again and the video started playing. He stopped it at the moment Gloria's body rebounded backward, her head turning to the left.

'Right ear,' he said, using the pen again to point. 'Just the matching crescent moon.'

'Okay, what's it mean?'

He ignored the question and hit the replay button. The gun was fired. Gloria was hurled into the counter and then rebounded backward into the shooter. Holding her in front of him, he fired at Mr Kang while stepping backward out of the camera's field of vision and lowering Gloria to the ground.

'The victim is then lowered down out of view of the camera.'

'What, you're saying that was intentional?'

'Exactly.'

'Why?'

He opened the satchel again and drew out the property report and handed it to Winston.

'That's the police property report on the victim's possessions. It was filled out at the hospital. Remember, she was still alive. They took her things there, gave them to a patrol officer. That is his report. What don't you see?'

Winston scanned the page.

'I don't know. It's just a list of – the cross earring?'

'Right. It's not there. He took it.'

'The patrolman?'

'No. The shooter. The shooter took her earring.'

A puzzled look came across Winston's face. She wasn't following the logic.

She hadn't had the same experiences or seen the same things that McCaleb had. She didn't see it for what it was.

'Wait a minute,' she said. 'How do you know he took it? It could have just fallen off and gotten lost.'

'No. I've talked to the victim's sister and I've talked to the hospital and the paramedics.'

He knew this was exaggerating his investigation into this aspect but he needed to pin Winston down. He couldn't give her a way out or a way to any other conclusion than his own conclusion.

'The sister says the earring had a safety hasp. It is unlikely that it fell off. Even if it did, the paramedics didn't find it on the stretcher or in the ambulance, and they didn't find it at the hospital. He took it, Jaye. The shooter. Besides, if it was going to fall off, despite the safety hasp, it probably would have been when he fired the round. You saw the impact on the head. If the earring was going to come loose, it would have been then. Only it didn't. It was taken off.'

'Okay, okay, what if he did take it? I'm not saying I believe it yet, but what are you saying it means?'

'It means everything changes. It means this wasn't about a robbery. She wasn't just an innocent nobody who walked into the wrong place at the wrong time. It means she was a target. She was prey.'

'Oh, come on. She . . . What are you trying to do, turn this into a serial killer or something?'

'I'm not trying to turn it into anything. It is what it is. And it's been that way all along. Only you people – we, I mean – didn't see it for what it was.'

Winston turned away from him and walked toward the corner of the room shaking her head. She then turned back to him.

'Okay, you tell me what you're seeing here. Because I'm just not seeing it. I'd love to go to the LAPD and tell those two jerks that they fucked up but I'm just not seeing what you're seeing.'

'Okay, let's start with the earring itself. Like I said, I talked to the sister. She said Glory Torres wore this particular earring every day. She played around with the others, switched them, used different combinations, but never the cross. It was always there. Every day. It had the obvious religious implications but for lack of a better description, it was also her good luck charm. Okay? You with me so far?'

'So far.'

'Okay, now let's just assume that the shooter took it. Like I said, I talked to the hospital and the fire department, and it hasn't showed up anywhere. So let's assume he took it.'

He opened his hands and held them up, waiting. Winston reluctantly nodded her agreement.

'So then let's look at that from two angles. How? And why? The first one is easy. Remember the video. He shot her and let her rebound off the counter and then fall back into him and then down to the floor, outside the view of the camera. He could take the earring then without being seen.'

'You're forgetting one thing.'

'What's that?'

'The Good Samaritan. He wrapped her head up. Maybe he took it.'

'I thought about that. It's not beyond possibility. But it's less likely than it being the shooter. The Good Samaritan is the random player in this. Why would he take it?'

'I don't know. Why would the shooter?'

'Well, like I said, that's a question. But look at the item that was taken. A religious icon, good luck charm. She wore it every day. It was a personality signature, its personal significance more important than its monetary value.'

He waited a beat. He had just given her the setup. Now came the closing pitch. Winston was fighting on this but McCaleb hadn't lost sight of her skills as an investigator. She would see what he was saying. He was confident he would convince her.

'Someone who knew Gloria would know the significance of the earring. Similarly, someone who was close to her, who had studied her over a period of days or longer could pick up on it as well.'

'You're talking about a stalker.'

McCaleb nodded.

'In the acquisition period. He watches her. Learns her habits, sets his plan. He'd also be looking for something. A token. Something to take and to remember her by.'

'The earring.'

He nodded again. Winston started pacing around the small room, not looking at McCaleb.

'I've got to think about this. I've got . . . let's go someplace where we can sit down.'

She didn't wait for a reply. She opened the door and left the room. McCaleb quickly ejected the tape, grabbed his bag and followed. Winston led him to the meeting room in which they had talked the first day McCaleb had come to see her about the case. The room was empty but smelled like a McDonald's restaurant. Winston hunted around, found the offending trash can under the table and escorted it out into the hallway.

'People aren't supposed to eat in this room,' she said as she closed the door and sat down.

McCaleb took the seat across from her.

'All right, what about my guy? How does James Cordell fit in? First of all, he's a guy. The other's a girl. Plus, there was no sex. This woman wasn't touched.'

'None of that matters,' McCaleb said quickly. He had been anticipating the question. He had done nothing but think about the questions and their possible answers during the drive out with Buddy Lockridge from the marina. 'If I'm right, this would fall into what we called the power kill model. Basically, it's a guy who is doing it because he can get away with it. He gets off on that. It's his way of thumbing his nose at authority and shocking society. He transfers his problems with a particular situation – whether it's a job, self-worth, women in general or his mother in particular or whatever – onto the police. The investigators. From tweaking them, he gets the jolt in self-worth that he needs. He derives a form of power from it. And it can be sexual power, even if there are no obvious or physical sexual manifestations in the actual crime. You remember the Code Killer out here a while back? Or Berkowitz, the Son of Sam killer in New York?'

'Of course.'

'Same thing with both of them. There was no sex in each crime itself but it was all about sex. Look at Berkowitz. He shot people up – men and women – and ran away. But he came back days later and masturbated at the scene. We assumed the Code Killer did the same thing but if he did, our surveillances missed him. What I'm saying is that it doesn't have to be obvious, Jaye, that's all. It's not always the obvious wackos who carve their names in people's skin.'

McCaleb watched Winston closely, leery of talking above her. But she seemed to understand his theory.

'But it's not only that,' McCaleb went on. 'There's another part to this. He gets off on the camera, too.'

'He likes us seeing him do it?'

McCaleb nodded.

'That's the new twist. I think he wants the camera. He wants his work and his accomplishments documented, seen and admired. It increases the danger to him and therefore increases the power reflection on him. The payoff. So to get that situation, what does he do? I think he picks up on a target – he chooses his prey – and then watches them until he has their routine and he knows when it takes them into places of business where the cameras are. The ATM, the market. He wants the camera. He talks to it. He winks at it. The camera is you – the investigator. He's talking to you and getting off on it.'

'Then maybe he doesn't choose the victim,' Winston said. 'Maybe he doesn't care about that. Just the camera. Like Berkowitz. He didn't care who he shot. He just went out shooting.'

'But Berkowitz didn't take souvenirs.'

'The earring?'

McCaleb nodded.

'You see that makes it personal. I think these victims were chosen. Not the other way around.'

'You've thought this all out, haven't you?'

'Not everything. I don't know how he chose them or why. But I've been thinking about it, yeah. The whole hour and a half it took us to get out here. Traffic was bad.'

'Us?'

'I have a driver. I can't drive yet.'

She didn't say anything. McCaleb wished he hadn't mentioned the driver. It was revealing a weakness.

'We have to start over,' McCaleb said. 'Because we thought these people were chosen at random. We thought the locations were chosen, not the victims. But I think it's the other way around. The victims were chosen. They were prey. Specific targets that were acquired, followed, stalked. We've got to background them. There's got to be an intersection. Some commonality. A person, a place . . . a moment in time – something that hooks them either to each other or our unknown subject. We find –'

'Wait a minute, wait a minute.'

McCaleb stopped, realizing his voice had been rising in fervor.

'What souvenir was taken from James Cordell? Are you saying the money he took from the ATM is a token?'

'I don't know what was taken but it wasn't the money. That was just part of the robbery show. The money wasn't a symbolic possession. Besides, he took it from the machine, not Cordell.'

'So then, aren't you jumping the gun?'

'No. I'm sure something was taken.'

'We would have seen it. We have the whole thing on video.'

'Nobody picked up on it with Gloria Torres and that was on video, too.'

Winston turned in her chair.

'I don't know. This still seems like a – let me ask you something. And try not to take it too personal. But isn't it possible that you're just looking for what you always looked for before, when you were with the bureau?'

'You mean, like am I exaggerating? Like I want to get back to what I was doing before and this is my way of doing it?'

Winston hiked her shoulders. She didn't want to say it.

'I didn't go looking for this, Jaye. It's just there. It is what it is. Sure, the earring might mean something else. And it might not mean anything at all. But if there is anything I know about in this world, it is this kind of thing. These people. I know them. I know how they think and I know how they act. I feel it here, Jaye. The evil. It's here.'

Winston looked at him strangely and McCaleb guessed that maybe he shouldn't have been so fervent in his response to her doubts.

'Cordell's truck, the Chevy Suburban, wasn't in the video. Did you process his truck? I didn't see anything in the stack you gave me about –'

'No, it wasn't touched. He left his wallet open on the seat and just took his ATM card to the machine. If the shooter had gone into his truck, he would have taken his wallet. When we saw it still there, we didn't bother.'

McCaleb shook his head and said, 'You are still looking at it from the point of view of a robbery. The decision not to process the truck would have been okay – if it had been a real robbery. But what if it wasn't? He wouldn't have gone into the truck and taken something as obvious as the wallet.'

'Then what?'

'I don't know. Something else. Cordell used his truck a lot. Driving all day along the aqueduct. It would be like a second home to him. There could have been lots of things of a personal nature in there that the shooter could've taken. Photos, things hanging from the rearview, maybe a travel diary, you name it. Where is the truck? Make my day and tell me it's still impounded.'

'No chance. We released it to his wife a couple days after the shooting.'

'It's probably been cleaned out and sold by now.'

'Actually, no. The last time I talked to Cordell's wife – which was only a couple weeks ago – she said something about not knowing what to do with the Suburban. It was too big for her and she said it gave her bad vibes now anyway. She didn't use those words but you know what I mean.'

A charge of excitement went through McCaleb.

'Then we go up there and look at the Suburban and we talk to her and we figure out what was taken.'

'*If* something was taken . . .'

Winston frowned. McCaleb knew what she was facing. She already was dealing with a captain who, after the hypnosis and Bolotov fiascos, probably thought she was being controlled too easily by an outsider. She didn't want to have to go back to the man with McCaleb's new theory unless she was sure it was dead-solid perfect. And McCaleb knew it could never be that. It never was.

'What are you going to do?' he asked. 'It's like I'm in the car and ready to go. Are you getting in with me or staying on the sidewalk?'

It had occurred to him that he was not constrained by such worries or by a job, a role, inertia or anything else. Either Winston could get in the car or McCaleb could drive on without her. She apparently realized the same thing.

'No,' she said. 'The question is what are *you* going to do. You're the one who doesn't have to deal with the bullshit around here like I do. After the hypnosis thing, Hitchens has been –'

'Tell you what, Jaye. I don't care about all of that. I only care about one thing – finding this guy. So look. You sit tight and give me a few days. I'll come in with something. I'll go up to the desert and talk to Cordell's wife and take a look at the truck. I'll find something you can go to the captain with. If I don't, then I'll eat my theory. You can cut me loose and I won't bother you again.'

'Look, it's not that you're both –'

'You know what I mean. You've got court, other cases. The last thing you need is to have to overhaul on an old one. I know how it is. Maybe coming in here today was premature. I should've just gone up there and seen the widow. But since it's your case and you've treated me like a human, I wanted to check with you first. Now, you give me your blessing and a little time and I'll go up on my own. I'll let you know what I get.'

Winston was silent for a long moment, then finally she nodded.

'Okay, you got it.'

20

Lockridge and McCaleb took a succession of freeways from Whittier until they reached the Antelope Valley Freeway, which would finally take them to the northeast corner of the country. Lockridge drove one-handed most of the way, holding a harmonica to his mouth with the other hand. It didn't give McCaleb much of a feeling of safety, but it cut out the meaningless banter.

As they passed Vasquez Rocks, McCaleb studied the formation and pinpointed the spot where the body had been found that eventually led to his knowing Jaye Winston. The slanted and jagged formation caused by tectonic upheaval was beautiful in the afternoon light. The sun was hitting the front rock faces at a low angle and throwing the crevices into deep darkness. It looked beautiful and dangerous at the same time. He wondered if that was what had drawn Luther Hatch to it.

'Ever been there, Vasquez Rocks?' Buddy asked after tucking the harmonica between his legs.

'Yeah.'

'Neat place. It's named after a Mexican desperado who holed up in the crevices about a hundred years ago after robbing a bank or something. So many places to hide in there, they could never find him and he became a legend.'

McCaleb nodded. He liked the story. He thought about how his histories of places were so different. They always involved bodies and blood work. No legends. No heroes.

They made good time on the front of the wave of rush hour and weekend traffic out of the city and it was just past five when they got to Lancaster. They cruised through a subdivision called Desert Flower Estates, looking for the home where James Cordell had lived. McCaleb saw a lot of desert but not many flowers or homes that met his definition of estate. The subdivision was built on land as flat and most days as hot as a frying pan. The homes were Spanish style with red-barrel roofs and arched windows and doors in the front. There were dozens of matching developments scattered through the Antelope Valley. The homes were large and reasonably attractive. They were bought mostly by families escaping the expense and crime and crowding of Los Angeles.

Desert Flower Estates had apparently offered three different design plans to its buyers. Consequently, McCaleb noticed as they drove through, about every third house was the same and sometimes there were even side-by-side duplicates. It reminded him of some of the post-World War II neighborhoods in the San Fernando Valley.

The thought of living in one of the homes he was passing depressed him. And it wasn't because of anything he saw. It was the distance this place was from the ocean and the feeling of renewal the sea gave him. He knew he'd never last in a neighborhood like this. He would dry up and blow away like one of the tumbleweeds they periodically passed on the street.

'This is it,' Buddy said.

He pointed to a number on a mailbox and McCaleb nodded. They pulled in. McCaleb noticed that the white Chevy Suburban he had seen in the crime scene video was parked in the driveway below a basketball rim. There was an open garage with a mini-van parked on one side and the other side cluttered with bikes and boxes, a tool bench and other clutter. Standing up in the back of the garage was a surfboard. It was an old long board and it made McCaleb think that maybe at one time James Cordell had known something about the ocean.

'I don't know how long I'll be,' he said.

'It's going to get hot out here. Maybe I could just go in with you. I won't say anything.'

'It's cooling down, Buddy. But if you get hot, run the air. Drive around a little bit. There's probably kids selling lemonade around here someplace.'

He got out before any debate could begin. He wasn't going to bring Lockridge into the investigation and turn it into amateur hour. On the way up the driveway he stopped and looked into the Suburban. The back was full of tools and there was clutter in the front seats. He felt a charge. He might be in luck. It looked as though the truck had been sitting untouched.

James Cordell's widow was named Amelia. McCaleb knew that from the reports. A woman he assumed to be her opened the arched front door before he reached it. Jaye Winston had said she would call ahead to smooth his way in.

'Mrs Cordell?'

'Yes?'

'My name's Terry McCaleb. Did Detective Winston call about me?'

'Yes, she did.'

'Is this a bad time?'

'As opposed to a good time?'

'Poor choice of words. I'm sorry. Do you have some time that we can talk?'

She was a short woman with brown hair and small features. Her nose was red and McCaleb guessed she either had a cold or had been crying. McCaleb wondered if the call from Jaye Winston had set her off.

She nodded and invited him in, leading the way to a neatly kept living room where she sat on the sofa and he took the chair opposite her. There was a box of tissues on the coffee table between them. The sound of television was coming from another room. It sounded like cartoons were on.

'Is that your partner waiting in the car?' she asked.

'Uh, my driver.'

'Does he want to come in? It might get hot out there.'

'No, he's fine.'

'You're a private investigator?'

'Technically, no. I'm a friend of the family of the woman who was killed in Canoga Park. I don't know what Detective Winston told you, but I used to work for the FBI and so I have some experience in these kinds of things. The Sheriff's Department, as you probably know, and the LAPD have not been able to, uh, advance the investigation very far in recent weeks. I'm trying to do what I can to help.'

She nodded.

'First off, I'm sorry about what happened to your husband and your family.'

She frowned and nodded.

'I know it doesn't matter what a stranger thinks but you do have my sympathy. From what I've read in the sheriff's files, James was a good man.'

She smiled and said, 'Thank you. It's just so funny to hear him called James. Everyone called him Jim or Jimmy. And you are right, he was a good man.'

McCaleb nodded.

'What questions can I answer, Mr McCaleb? I really don't know anything about what happened. That's what was confusing about Jaye's call.'

'Well, first . . .' He reached down to his satchel, opened it and took out the Polaroid that Graciela had given him the day she came to his boat. He handed it across the table to Amelia Cordell. 'Could you look at that and tell me if you recognize the woman or if you think she might be someone your husband could have known.'

She took the photo and stared at it, her face serious and her eyes making small movements as she seemed to study everything about the photo. She shook her head finally.

'No, I don't think so. Is she the one who . . .'

'Yes, she was the victim in the second robbery.'

'Is that her son?'

'Yes.'

'I don't understand. How could my husband have known this woman – are you suggesting that they might have –'

'No. No, I'm not suggesting anything, Mrs Cordell. I'm just trying to cover . . . Look, to be very honest, Mrs Cordell, some things have come up in the investigation to possibly indicate – and I have to stress *possibly* – that there was more here than meets the eye.'

'Meaning what?'

'Meaning that *possibly* robbery was not a motive here. Or not the only motive.'

She stared blankly at him for a moment and McCaleb knew she was still taking things the wrong way.

'Mrs Cordell, I am not in any way trying to suggest that your husband and that woman had any kind of a relationship. What I'm saying is that somewhere, sometime, your husband and that woman crossed the shooter's path. So you see there *is* a relationship. But it is a relationship between the victims and the shooter. It is likely that your husband and the other victims crossed the shooter's line at separate points but I need to cover everything and that is why I show you the photograph. You are sure you don't recognize her?'

'I'm sure.'

'Would your husband have any reason in the weeks before the shooting to have spent any time in Canoga Park?'

'Not that I know of.'

'Would he have had any dealings with the *Los Angeles Times*? More specifically, any reason he would have gone to the newspaper's plant in Chatsworth?'

Again her answer was no.

'Was there any problem at work? Anything that he might have wanted to talk to a reporter about?'

'Like what?'

'I don't know.'

'Was she a reporter?'

'No, but she worked where there were reporters. Maybe their paths crossed with the shooter there.'

'Well, I don't think so. If something was bothering Jimmy, he would have told me. He always did.'

'Okay. I understand.'

McCaleb spent the next fifteen minutes asking Mrs Cordell questions about her husband's daily routine and his activities in the weeks before the shooting. He took three pages of notes but even as he wrote them, they didn't seem helpful. Jimmy Cordell seemed like a man who worked hard and spent most of his off time with his family. In the weeks before his death he had been working exclusively on sections of the aqueduct in the central part of the state and his wife did not believe he had spent any time at all to the south. She did not think he had been down into the Valley or other parts of the city since before Christmas.

McCaleb folded his notebook closed.

'I appreciate your time, Mrs Cordell. The last thing I wanted to ask about is whether or not any of your husband's possessions were missing.'

'His possessions? What do you mean?'

Amelia Cordell led McCaleb out to the Chevy Suburban. They had already discussed her husband's clothing and jewelry. Nothing had been taken, she assured him, just as the ATM video had seemed to attest. That left the Suburban.

'No one's been in it?' he asked as she was unlocking it.

'I drove it home from the sheriff's office. That was actually the only time I ever drove it. Jimmy bought it for work only. He said if we started using it for nonwork driving, he couldn't write everything off. I don't drive it because it's too high up for me to be climbing in and out of all the time.'

McCaleb nodded and leaned into the truck through the open driver's door. The rear seat was folded down and the cargo area was full of surveying equipment, a folding drafting table and other tools. McCaleb quickly dismissed it all. It was equipment, not something of a personal nature.

He concentrated on the front section of the vehicle. A patina of road dust covered everything. Cordell must have been driving in the desert with the windows down. Using one finger, he opened a pocket on the door and saw it was crammed with service station receipts and a small spiral notebook on which Cordell had noted mileage, dates and destinations. McCaleb took the notebook out and flipped through the pages to see if there had been any trips to the west Valley, particularly Chatsworth or Canoga Park. There were none recorded. It appeared Amelia Cordell had been correct about her husband.

He flipped down the driver-side visor and found two folded maps. McCaleb walked them around to the front and opened them on the hood. One was a gas station map of central California and another was a survey map that showed the aqueduct and its many access roads. McCaleb was looking for any unusual notations Cordell might have made on the maps but there were none. He refolded them and put them back.

He now sat in the driver's seat and looked around. He noticed the rearview mirror and asked Amelia Cordell if her husband had ever hung anything off it, knickknacks or otherwise. She said she didn't remember anything.

He checked the glove compartment and the center console. There was more paperwork and several tapes for use in the stereo, an assortment of pens and mechanical pencils, and a pack of opened mail. Cordell liked country music. Nothing seemed amiss. Nothing came to mind.

'Do you know if he had any particular kind of pen or pencil he liked? Like a special pen he might have gotten as a gift or something?'

'I don't think so. Nothing I remember.'

McCaleb took the rubber band off the mail and looked through the envelopes. It appeared to be departmental mail, notices of meetings, reports on problems on the aqueduct that Cordell was to check out. McCaleb put the band back around the stack and placed it back in the glove box. Amelia Cordell watched him silently.

In an open bin between the seats there was a pager and a pair of sunglasses. Cordell had been coming home at night when he stopped at the ATM. That explained why the glasses were not on, but not the beeper.

'Mrs Cordell, do you know why his pager is here? How come he wasn't wearing it?'

She thought a moment and then said, 'He usually didn't keep it on his belt for long rides because he said it was uncomfortable. He said it dug into his kidneys. He forgot it a few times. You know, left it in the car and missed his pages. That's how I know why.'

McCaleb nodded. As he sat there thinking about what to check next, the passenger door was suddenly opened and Buddy Lockridge looked in.

'What's up?'

McCaleb had to squint to look at him because of the sun coming into the car over Buddy's shoulder.

'I'm almost done, Buddy. Why don't you wait in the car?'

'My ass was getting sore.' He looked past McCaleb and nodded at Amelia Cordell. 'Sorry, ma'am.'

McCaleb was annoyed by the intrusion but introduced Lockridge as his associate to Amelia Cordell.

'So what are we looking for?' Buddy asked.

'We? I'm just looking for something that's not here. Why don't you wait in the car?'

'Like something that might've been taken. I see.'

He flipped down the passenger-side visor. McCaleb had already checked it and there was nothing there.

'I got it, Buddy. Why don't you –'

'What went there, a picture?'

He pointed toward the dashboard. McCaleb followed the line of his finger but didn't see anything.

'What are you talking about?'

'There. See the dust? Looks like a picture or something. Maybe he kept a parking pass there until he needed it.'

McCaleb looked again but still didn't see what Lockridge was pointing at and talking about. He shifted to his right and leaned toward Buddy and then turned his head back to look at the dashboard.

Now he saw it.

A coat of driving dust had settled on the clear plastic guard over the display of speedometer and other gauges. On one side of the plastic there was a clearly defined square where there was no dust. Something had been propped on the plastic guard until recently. McCaleb realized how lucky he was. He probably would never have noticed it. It only became apparent when viewed from the passenger side and with the sun coming in at a low angle.

'Mrs Cordell?' McCaleb said. 'Can you walk around and look at this through the other door?'

He waited. Lockridge stepped out of the way so she could look in. McCaleb pointed to the outline on the plastic guard. It was about five inches wide by three inches deep.

'Did your husband keep a picture of you or the kids here?'

She shook her head slowly.

'Boy, I don't really know. He had pictures but I just don't know where he put them. He could have but I don't know. I never drive this. We always take the Caravan – even when just Jim and I would go out. Like I said, I didn't like climbing up there.'

McCaleb nodded.

'Is there anyone he worked with who might know, who might have ridden with him to jobs or to lunch, that sort of thing?'

Driving on the Antelope Valley Freeway back toward the city, they passed a seemingly never-ending line of cars stacked in the lanes going the other way. Commuters heading home or travelers getting out of the city for the weekend. McCaleb barely noticed. He was deep in his own thoughts. He barely even heard Lockridge until he repeated himself twice.

'I'm sorry, what?'

'I said I guess I helped you back there, noticing that.'

'You did, Buddy. I might not have noticed it. But I still wish you had stayed in the car. This is all I'm paying you for, to drive.'

With a double hand gesture McCaleb indicated the car.

'Yeah, well, you might still be back there looking if I had stayed in the car.'

'We'll never know now.'

'So aren't you going to tell me what you found out?'

'Nothing, Buddy. I didn't find out anything.'

He had lied. Amelia Cordell had taken him back inside and allowed him to use her phone to call her husband's office. Buddy had been sent back to the car to wait. Inside, McCaleb talked to James Cordell's supervisor, who gave him the names and numbers of some of the aqueduct maintenance supervisors Cordell would have been working with in early January. McCaleb then called the Lone Pine aqueduct station and talked to Maggie Mason, who was one of those supervisors. She reported that she had joined Cordell for lunch twice in the week before the shooting. Both times Cordell had driven.

Avoiding the leading question, McCaleb had asked her if she had noticed anything of a personal nature on the dashboard of the Suburban. Without hesitation Mason said there had been a photograph of Cordell's family on the dashboard. She said she had even leaned over to get a look at it. She remembered that it was Cordell's wife holding their two little daughters on her lap.

As they were heading home, McCaleb felt a mix of dread and excitement growing inside. Someone, somewhere, had Gloria Torres's earring and James Cordell's family photo. He now knew that the evil of these two killings came together in the form of a person who killed not for money, not out of fear and not for revenge against his victims. This evil went far beyond that. This person killed for pleasure and to fulfill a fantasy that burned like a virus inside his brain.

Evil was everywhere. McCaleb knew that better than most. But he also knew that it could not be confronted in the abstract. It needed to be embodied in flesh and blood and breath, to be a person who could be hunted down and destroyed. McCaleb had that now. He felt his heart rise up in rage, and a horrible joy.

21

The Saturday morning mist came in thick and felt like a gentle hand on the back of his neck. McCaleb had gotten up by seven so that he could get into the laundry in the marina's commons building and use several of the machines at once to get all of the bed clothes cleaned. Then he set about getting the boat cleaned up and ready for overnight guests. But as he worked, he found it hard to concentrate on the chores in front of him.

He had talked to Jaye Winston when he got in from the desert the evening before. When he told her about the photo that was missing from Cordell's Suburban, she grudgingly agreed that McCaleb might be onto a viable new lead. An hour later she called back and said a meeting was set for 8 A.M. Monday at the Star Center. She and her captain and a few other sheriff's detectives would be there. So would Arrango and Walters. So would Maggie Griffin from the FBI. Griffin was the agent who had taken McCaleb's place in the VICAP slot in the L.A. field office. McCaleb only knew her by her reputation which was good.

And that was the problem. First thing Monday morning McCaleb would be on the hot seat, the focus of intense scrutiny. Most, if not all, of those in the meeting at the Star Center would be non-believers. But rather than prepare for the meeting or do what additional investigation he could, McCaleb was going fishing on the jetty with a woman and a little boy. It didn't sit right with him and he kept thinking he should cancel the visit from Graciela and Raymond. In the end, he didn't. It was true that he needed to talk with Graciela, but more than that, he found that he just wanted to be with her. And that was what brought the twin paths of his uneasy thoughts to an intersection: guilt over putting the investigation aside and guilt over his desire for a woman who had come to him for his help.

When he was done with the laundry and the general cleanup, he walked over to the marina center. At the store he bought the makings of the evening's dinner. At the bait shop he bought a bucket of live bait, choosing shrimp and squid, and a small rod-and-reel outfit that he planned to present to Raymond as his own. Back at the boat, he put the rod in one of the gunwale holders and dumped the bait bucket into the live well. He then put away the store items in the galley.

He was finished and the boat was ready by ten. Seeing no sign of Graciela's convertible in the parking lot, he decided to walk over and check with Buddy

Lockridge about his availability on Monday morning. He first went up to the gate and made sure it was propped open so Graciela and the boy could enter the marina, then he went to Lockridge's boat.

Adhering to marina custom, McCaleb did not step onto the *Double-Down.* Instead, he called Lockridge's name and waited on the dock. The boat's main hatch was open so he knew Lockridge was awake and around somewhere. After half a minute, Buddy's disheveled hair, followed by his crumpled face, poked up through the hatch. McCaleb guessed he had spent a good part of the night drinking.

'Yo, Terry.'

'Yo. You okay?'

'Fine as always. What's up, we going somewhere?'

'No, not today. But I need you Monday morning early. Can you drive me out to the Star Center? I mean like we've got to leave by seven.'

Buddy thought a moment to see if it fit with his busy schedule and nodded.

'It's a go.'

'You're going to be all right to drive?'

'You bet. What's going on at the Star Center?'

'Just a meeting. But I've got to be there on time.'

'Don't worry about a thing. We leave at seven. I'll set the alarm.'

'Okay, and one other thing. Keep an eye out around here.'

'You mean the guy from the clock plant?'

'Yeah. I doubt he'll show but you never know. He's got tattoos running up both arms. And they're big arms. You'll know him if you see him.'

'I'll be on the lookout. Looks like you've got a couple visitors right now.'

McCaleb saw that Lockridge was looking past him. He turned and looked back at *The Following Sea.* Graciela was standing in the stern. She was lifting Raymond down into the boat.

'I gotta go, Bud. I'll see you Monday.'

Graciela was wearing faded blue jeans and a Dodgers sweatshirt with her hair up under a matching baseball cap. She had a duffel bag slung over her shoulder and was carrying a grocery bag. Raymond was wearing blue jeans and a Kings hockey sweater. He also had on a baseball cap and carried with him a toy fire truck and an old stuffed animal that looked to McCaleb like a lamb.

McCaleb gave Graciela a tentative hug and shook Raymond's hand after the boy stuck his stuffed animal under his other arm.

'Good to see you guys,' he said. 'Ready to catch some fish today, Raymond?'

The boy seemed too shy to answer. Graciela nudged the boy on the shoulder and he nodded in agreement.

McCaleb took the bags, led them into the boat and gave them the complete tour he had not shown them on their earlier visit. Along the way, he left the grocery bag in the galley and put the duffel bag down on the bed in the main stateroom. He told Graciela it was her room and the sheets were freshly washed. He then showed Raymond the upper bunk in the forward stateroom. McCaleb had moved most of the boxes of files under the desk and the room seemed neat enough for the boy. There was a guard bar on the bunk so that he wouldn't roll out of bed. When McCaleb told him it was called a berth, his face scrunched up in confusion.

'That's what they call beds on boats, Raymond,' he said. 'And they call the bathroom the *head*.'

'How come?'

'You know, I never asked.'

He led them to the head and showed them how to use the foot pedal for flushing. He noticed Graciela looking at the temperature chart on the hook and he told her what it was for. She put her finger on the line from Thursday.

'You had a fever?'

'A slight fever. It went away.'

'What did your doctor say?'

'I didn't tell her yet. It went away and I'm fine.'

She looked at him with a mixture of concern and, he thought, annoyance. He then realized how important it probably was to her that he survive. She didn't want her sister's last gift to be for nothing.

'Don't worry,' he said. 'I'm fine. I was just doing a little too much running around that day. I took a long nap and the fever was gone. I've been okay since.'

He pointed to the slashes on the chart following the one fever reading. Raymond pulled on his pants leg and said, 'Where do you sleep?'

McCaleb glanced briefly at Graciela and turned toward the stairs before she could see his face start to color.

'Come on up, I'll show you.'

When they got back up to the salon, McCaleb explained to Raymond how he could turn the galley table into a single berth. The boy seemed satisfied.

'So let's see what you got,' McCaleb said.

He started going through Graciela's grocery bag and putting things away. Their agreement was that she would make lunch, he would do the same with dinner. She had gone to a deli and it looked like they were going to have submarine sandwiches.

'How'd you know that subs were my favorite?' he asked.

'I didn't,' Graciela said. 'But they're Raymond's, too.'

McCaleb reached over and caught Raymond in the ribs again with a finger and the boy recoiled with a giggle.

'Well, while Graciela makes sandwiches to take with us, why don't you come out and help me with the equipment. We have fish out there waitin' for us!'

'Okay!'

As he ushered the boy out to the stern, he looked back at Graciela and winked. Out on the deck he presented Raymond with the rod and reel he had bought him. When the boy realized the outfit was his to keep, he grabbed onto the pole as if it were a rope being dropped to him by a rescue squad. It made McCaleb feel sad instead of good. He wondered whether the young boy had ever had a man in his life.

McCaleb looked up and saw Graciela standing in the open door to the salon. She also had a sad look on her face, even though she was smiling at them. McCaleb decided they had to break away from such emotions.

'Okay,' he said. 'Bait. We've got to fill a bucket, 'cause I've got a feeling they're going to be biting out there today.'

He got the floating bucket and dipping net out of the compartment next to the live well and then showed Raymond how to dip the net into the well and bring up the bait. He put a couple netfuls of shrimp and squid into the bucket and then turned the chore over to Raymond. He then went inside to get the tackle box and a couple more rods for himself and Graciela to use.

When he was inside and out of earshot of the boy, Graciela came up to him and hugged him.

'That was very nice of you,' she said.

He held her eyes for a few moments before saying anything.

'I think maybe it does more for me than him.'

'He's so excited,' she said. 'I can tell. He can't wait to catch something. I hope he does.'

They walked out along the marina's main dock, past the stores and restaurant, and then crossed a parking lot until they came to the main channel into the city's marinas. There was a crushed-gravel path here and it led them out to the mouth of the channel and the breakwater, a rock jetty that curved out into the Pacific for a hundred yards. They carefully stepped from one huge granite slab to another until they were about halfway out.

'Raymond, this is my secret spot. I think we should try it right here.'

There was no objection. McCaleb put down his equipment and set to work getting ready to fish. The rocks were still wet from the nightly assault of high seas. McCaleb had brought towels and walked about the spot looking for flat rocks that would make good seats. He spread the towels out and told Graciela and Raymond to sit down. He opened the tackle box, took out the tube of sun block and handed it to Graciela. He then started baiting lines. He decided to put the squid on Raymond's rig because he thought it would be the best bait and he wanted the boy to catch the first fish.

Fifteen minutes later they had three lines in the water. McCaleb had taught the boy how to cast his line out, leave the reel open and let the squid swim with it in the current.

'What will I catch?' he inquired, his eyes on his line.

'I don't know, Raymond. A lot of fish out there.'

McCaleb took a rock directly next to Graciela's. The boy was too nervous to sit and wait. He danced with his pole from rock to rock, anxiously waiting and hoping.

'I should've brought a camera,' Graciela whispered.

'Next time,' McCaleb said. 'You see that?'

He was pointing across the water to the horizon. The bluish outline of an island could be seen rising in the far mist.

'Catalina?'

'Yeah. That's it.'

'It's weird. I can't get used to the idea of you having lived on an island.'

'Well, I did.'

'How did your family end up here?'

'They were from Chicago. My father was a ballplayer. Baseball. One spring – it was nineteen fifty – he got a tryout with the Cubs. They used to come out to Catalina for spring training. The Wrigleys owned the Cubs and most of the island. So they came out here.

'My father and my mother were high school sweethearts. They had gotten married and he got this chance to go for the Cubs. He was a shortstop and second baseman. Anyway, he came out here but didn't make the team. But he loved the place. He got a job working for the Wrigleys. And he sent for her.'

His plan was to end the story there but she prompted more out of him.

'Then you came.'

'A little while later.'

'But your parents didn't stay?'

'My mother didn't. She couldn't take the island. She stayed ten years and that was enough. It can be claustrophobic for some people . . . Anyway, they split up. My father stayed and he wanted me with him. I stayed. My mother went back to Chicago.'

She nodded.

'What did your father do for the Wrigleys?'

'A lot of things. He worked on their ranch, then he worked up at the house. They kept a sixty-three-foot Chris-Craft in the harbor. He got a job as a deckhand and eventually he skippered that for them. Finally he got his own boat and put it out for charter. He was also a volunteer fireman.'

He smiled and she smiled back.

'And *The Following Sea* was his boat?'

'His boat, his house, his business, everything. The Wrigleys financed him. He lived on the boat for about twelve years. Until he got so sick they – I mean, me, I was the one – I took him over town to the hospital. He died over here. In Long Beach.'

'I'm sorry.'

'It was a long time ago.'

'Not for you.'

He looked at her.

'It's just that at the end there comes a time when everybody knows. He knew there was no chance and he just wanted to go back over there. To his boat. And the island. I wouldn't do it. I wanted to try everything, every goddamn marvel of science and medicine. And besides, if he was over there, it would be a hassle for me to get out to see him. I'd have to take the ferry. I made him stay in that hospital. He died alone in his room. I was down in San Diego on a case.'

McCaleb looked out across the water. He could see a ferry heading toward the island.

'I just wish I had listened to him.'

She reached her hand over and put it on his forearm.

'There is no sense in being haunted by good intentions.'

He glanced over at Raymond. The boy had settled down and was standing still, looking down at his reel while a steady torrent of line was being pulled out. McCaleb knew that a squid didn't have that kind of pulling power.

'Hey, wait a minute, Raymond. I think you've got something there.'

He put his rod down and went to the boy. He flipped the reel's bail over and the line caught. Almost immediately the pole was pulled down and almost out of the boy's hands. McCaleb grabbed it and held it up.

'You got one!'

'Hey! I got one! I got one!'

'Remember what I told you, Raymond. Pull back, reel down. Pull back, reel down. I'll help you with the pole until we tire that boy out. It feels like a big one. You okay?'

'Yeah!'

With McCaleb doing most of the pulling up on the pole, they began to fight the fish. Meantime, McCaleb directed Graciela to reel in the other lines to avoid a tangle with the live line. McCaleb and the boy fought the fish for about ten minutes. All the while McCaleb could feel through the pole the fight slipping out of it as it tired. Finally, he was able to turn the pole over to Raymond so he could finish the job himself.

McCaleb slipped on a pair of gloves from the tackle box and climbed down the rocks to the water's edge. Just a few inches below the surface he saw the silvery fish weakly struggling against the line. McCaleb kneeled on the rock, getting his shoes and pants wet, and leaned out until he could grab hold of Raymond's line. He tugged the fish forward and brought its mouth up, reached into the water and locked a gloved hand around the tail, just forward of the back fins. He then yanked the fish out of the water and climbed back up the rocks to Raymond.

The fish was shining in the sun like polished metal.

'Barracuda, Raymond,' he said, holding it up. 'Look at those teeth.'

22

The day had gone well. Raymond caught two barracudas and a white bass. The first fish had been the biggest and most exciting, though the second was hooked while they were eating lunch and almost pulled the unattended pole into the water. After they got back in the late afternoon, Graciela insisted that Raymond rest before dinner and took him down to the forward stateroom. McCaleb used the time to spray off the fishing equipment with the stern hose. When Graciela came back up and they were alone, sitting on chairs on the deck, he felt a physical craving for a cold beer that he could just sit back and enjoy.

'That was wonderful,' Graciela said of the outing to the jetty.

'I'm glad. Think you're going to stay for dinner?'

'Of course. He wants to stay over, too. He loves boats. And I think he wants to fish again tomorrow. You've created a monster.'

McCaleb nodded, thinking about the night ahead. A few minutes of easy silence went by while they watched the other activities in the marina. Saturdays were always busy days. McCaleb kept his eyes moving. Having guests made him more alert for the Russian, even though he'd decided the chances of Bolotov showing up were slim. He'd had the upper hand in Toliver's office. If he had wanted to harm McCaleb, he could have done it then. But thoughts of Bolotov brought the case intruding. He remembered a question he'd thought of for Graciela.

'Let me ask you something,' he said. 'You first came to me last Saturday. But the story about me ran a week before that. Why did you wait a week?'

'I didn't really. I didn't see the article. A friend of Glory's from the paper called up and said he saw it and wondered if, you know, you could've been the one who got her heart. Then I went to the library and read the story. I came here the next day.'

He nodded. She decided it was her turn to ask a question.

'Those boxes down there.'

'What boxes?'

'Stacked under the desk. Are they your cases?'

'They're old files.'

'I recognize some of the names written on them. The article mentioned some of them. Luther Hatch, I remember him. And the Code Killer. Why did they call him that?'

'Because he – if it was a he – left messages for us or sent messages to us that always had the same number at the bottom.'

'What did it mean?'

'We never found out. The best people at the bureau and even the encryption people at the National Security Agency couldn't crack it. Personally, I didn't think it meant anything at all. It wasn't a code. It was just another way for the UnSub to tweak us, keep us chasing our tails . . . nine-oh-three, four-seven-two, five-six-eight.'

'That's the code?'

'That's the number. Like I said, I don't think there was any code.'

'Is that what they decided in Washington, too?'

'No. They never gave up on it. They were sure it meant something. They thought it might be the guy's Social Security number. You know, scrambled around. With their computer they printed out every combination and then got all the names from Social Security. Hundreds of thousands. They ran them all through the computers.'

'Looking for what?'

'Criminal records, profile matches . . . it was one big wild-goose chase. The UnSub wasn't on the list.'

'What is UnSub?'

'Unknown subject. That's what we called each one until we caught him. We never caught the Code Killer.'

McCaleb heard the faint sound of a harmonica and looked over at the *Double-Down.* Lockridge was down below practicing 'Spoonful'.

'Was he the only one of your cases where that happened?'

'You mean where the guy was never caught? No. Unfortunately, a lot of them get away. But the Code case was personal, I guess. He sent letters to me. He resented me for some reason.'

'What did he do to the people he . . .'

'The Code Killer was unusual. He killed in many different ways and with no discernible pattern. Men, women, even one small child. He shot, he stabbed, he strangled. There was no handle.'

'Then how did you know it was him each time?'

'He told us. The letters, the code left at the crime scenes. You see, the victims and who they were didn't matter. They were only objects by which he could exercise power and stick it in the face of authority. He was an authority-complex killer. There was another killer, the Poet. He was a traveler, was active across the country a few years ago.'

'I remember. He got away here in L.A., right?'

'Right. He was an authority killer, too. See, you strip away their fantasies and their methods and a lot of these people are very much alike. The Poet got off on watching us flailing around. The Code Killer was the same way. He liked to tweak the cops every chance he got.'

'Then he just stopped?'

'He either died or went to jail for something else. Or he moved somewhere else and started a new routine. But it's not something these guys can just turn off.'

'And what did you do in the Luther Hatch case?'

'Just my job. Look, we should talk about something else, don't you think?'

'I'm sorry.'

'It's okay. I just . . . I don't know, I don't like all of those old stories.'

He had wanted to talk to her about her sister and the latest developments but now it didn't seem like the right time. He let the opportunity pass.

For dinner McCaleb grilled hamburgers and barracuda steaks. Raymond seemed enthusiastic about eating the fish he had caught but then didn't like the strong taste of the barracuda. Neither did Graciela, though McCaleb didn't think it was bad.

The meal was followed with another walk to the ice-cream store and then a walk along the shops on Cabrillo Way. It was dark by the time they got back to the boat. The marina was quiet again. Raymond got the bad news from Graciela.

'Raymond, it's been a long day and I want you to go to sleep,' she said gently. 'If you're good, you can fish some more tomorrow before we leave.'

The boy looked at McCaleb, seeking either confirmation or an appeal.

'She's right, Raymond,' he said. 'In the morning I'll take you back out there. We'll catch some more fish. Okay?'

In a cranky tone the boy agreed and Graciela took him down to his room. His parting request was that he be allowed to take his fishing pole to his room with him. There was no objection to that. McCaleb had secured the hook on one of the pole's eyelets.

McCaleb had two space heaters on the boat and he set them up in each of their rooms. He knew that at night it could get cold on the boat, no matter how many blankets you had on.

'What are you going to use?' Graciela asked him.

'I'll be fine. I'm going to use my sleeping bag. I'll probably be warmer than both of you.'

'You sure?'

'I'm sure.'

He left them down there and went topside to wait for Graciela. He poured the last of the Sanford pinot noir he had opened on her first visit into her glass.

He took that and a can of Coke out to the stern. She joined him after ten minutes.

'It gets cold out here,' she said.

'Yeah. Do you think he'll be all right with that heater?'

'Yes, he's fine. He fell asleep almost as soon as he hit the pillow.'

He handed her the glass of wine and she tapped it against his Coke.

'Thank you,' she said. 'He had a wonderful time today.'

'I'm glad.'

He tapped his Coke against her glass. He knew that at some point he needed to finally talk about the investigation with her but he didn't want to spoil the moment. Once again he put it off.

'Who is that girl in the picture down on your desk?'

'What girl?'

'It looks like a photo from a yearbook or something. It's taped to the wall over the desk in Raymond's room.'

'Oh . . . it's just . . . it's just somebody I always want to remember. Somebody who died.'

'You mean like a case or someone you knew?'

'A case.'

'The Code Killer?'

'No, long before that.'

'What was her name?'

'Aubrey-Lynn.'

'What happened?'

'Something that shouldn't happen to anybody. Let's not talk about it right now.'

'Okay. I'm sorry.'

'It's all right. I should have taken that thing down before Raymond came anyway.'

McCaleb didn't get into the sleeping bag. He just draped it over his body and lay on his back with his hands laced behind his head. He knew he should be tired but he wasn't. Many thoughts raced through his mind, from the mundane to the gut-wrenching. He was thinking about the heater in the boy's berth. He knew it was safe but he worried about it anyway. The talk earlier in the day also resurfaced in a strand of thoughts about his father in the hospital bed. Once more he wished he had brought the old man home to die. He remembered taking the boat out after the ceremony at Descanso Beach and circling Catalina, parceling out the ashes a little at a time so that they lasted until he had come all the way around the island.

But those memories and concerns were only distractions from his thoughts of Graciela. The evening had ended on a wrong note after she had brought up Aubrey-Lynn Showitz. The memory had knocked McCaleb off stride and he stopped talking. He was infatuated with Graciela. He wanted her and had hoped the evening would end with them together. But he had let the grim memories intrude and it spoiled the moment.

He felt the boat gently rise and fall as the tide rolled in. He exhaled loudly, hoping to expel the demons. He readjusted himself on the thin cushion. There was a seam down the middle of the makeshift bed and he couldn't get comfortable. He thought about getting up for some orange juice but worried that if he had a glass, there might not be enough left for Raymond and Graciela in the morning.

Finally, he decided to go down and check the vitals. The old standby for killing time. It would give him something to do, maybe make him tired and finally able to sleep.

He had plugged a night-light into the circuit over the sink in case Raymond had to get up and find the toilet. He decided not to turn on the overhead fixture and stood there in the dim light with the thermometer under his tongue. He looked at his shadowy reflection and saw that the circles beneath his eyes were becoming more pronounced.

He had to lean over the sink and hold the thermometer close to the night-light in order to read it. It looked like he had a slight fever. He took the clipboard off the hook and wrote the date and time and 99 instead of a slash. As he replaced the clipboard, he heard the door of the master stateroom open across the passageway.

He had never closed the door to the head. He looked across the dark hallway and saw Graciela's face peering around the edge of her door. The rest of her body she hid behind the door. They spoke in whispers.

'Are you okay?'

'Yes. You?'

'I'm fine. What are you doing?'

'I couldn't sleep. I was just checking my temperature.'

'Do you have a fever?'

'No . . . I'm fine.'

He nodded as he said it. He became aware he was wearing only his boxer shorts. He folded his arms and raised one hand to rub his chin but he was really just trying to hide the ugly scar on his chest.

They looked at each other in silence for a moment. McCaleb realized he had been holding his hand to his chin too long. He dropped his arms to his sides and watched her as her eyes fell to his chest.

'Graciela . . .'

He didn't finish. She had slowly opened the door and he could see she wore a pink silk sleep shirt cut high on her hips. She was beautiful in it. For a moment they just stood there and looked at each other. Graciela still held the door, as if to steady herself against the boat's slight movements. After another moment she took a step into the hallway and he took a step to meet her. He reached forward and traced his hand gently up her side and then around to her back. With his other hand he caressed her throat and moved to the back of her neck. He pulled her into him.

'Can you do this?' she whispered, her face pressed into his neck.

'Nothing's going to stop me,' he whispered back.

They moved into the stateroom and shut the door. He left his shorts on the floor and crawled onto the bed with her as she unbuttoned the nightshirt. The sheets and blanket already had her smell, the vanilla he had noticed once before. He moved on top of her and she pulled him down into a long kiss. He worked his face down to her chest and kissed her breasts. His nose found the spot just below her neck where she had touched the perfume to her skin. The deep musky vanilla filled him and he moved his lips back up to hers.

Graciela moved her hand in between their bodies and held her warm palm against his chest. He felt her body tense and he opened his eyes. In a whisper she said, 'Wait. Terry, wait.'

He froze and lifted himself up with one arm.

'What is it?' he whispered.

'I don't think . . . It doesn't feel right to me. I'm sorry.'

'What's not right?'

'I'm not sure.'

She turned her body underneath him and he had no choice but to get off her.

'Graciela?'

'It's not you, Terry. It's me. I'm . . . I just don't want to rush. I want to think about things.'

She was on her side, looking away from him.

'Is it because of your sister? Because I have her –'

'No, it's not that . . . Well, maybe a little. I just think we should think about it more.'

She reached back and caressed his cheek.

'I'm sorry. I know it was wrong to invite you in and then do this.'

'It's okay. I don't want you to do something you might be unhappy about later. I'll go back up.'

He made a move to slide toward the foot of the bed but she grabbed his arm.

'No, don't leave. Not yet. Lie here with me. I don't want you to leave yet.'

He moved back up the bed and put his head on the pillow next to hers. It was an odd feeling. Though obviously rejected, he felt no anxiety about it. He felt that the time would come for them and he could wait. McCaleb began wondering how long he could stay with her before having to return to his sleeping bag.

'Tell me about the girl,' she said.

'What?' he replied, confused.

'The girl in the yearbook picture on your desk.'

'It's not a nice story, Graciela. Why do you want to know that story?'

'Because I want to know you.'

That was all she said. But McCaleb understood. He knew that if they were to become lovers, they had to share their secrets. It was part of the ritual. He remembered years before how on the night he first made love to the woman who would become his wife, she had told him that she had been sexually abused as a child. Her sharing of such a carefully held and guarded secret had touched him more deeply than the actual physical act of their making love. He always remembered that moment, cherished it, even after the marriage was over.

'All of this was put together from witnesses and physical evidence . . . and the video,' he began.

'What video?'

'I'll get to that. It was a Florida case. This was before I was sent out here. A whole family . . . abducted. Mother, father, two daughters. The Showitz family. Aubrey-Lynn, the girl in the photo, she was the youngest.'

'How old?'

'She had just turned fifteen on the vacation. They were from the Midwest, a little town in Ohio. And it was their first family vacation. They didn't have a lot of money. The father owned a little auto garage – there was still grease under his nails when they found him.'

McCaleb blew his air out in a short laugh – the kind a person makes when something isn't funny but he wished it were.

'So they were on a cut-rate vacation and they did Disney World and all of that and they eventually got down to Fort Lauderdale, where they stayed in one room in this little shitty motel by the I-95 freeway. They had made the reservation from Ohio and thought because the place was called the Sea Breeze, it was near the ocean.'

His voice caught because he had never spoken the story out loud; every detail about it was pitiful and made him hurt inside.

'Anyway, when they got there, they decided to stay. They were only going to be in town a couple days and they'd lose their deposit if they left for a beach hotel. So they stayed. And on their first night there one of the girls spots this pickup in the lot that was attached to a trailer with an airboat on it. You know what an airboat is?'

'Like with an airplane propeller and it goes in the swamp out there?'

'Right, the Everglades.'

'I saw them on CNN when that plane crashed into the swamp and disappeared.'

'Yeah, same thing. But this girl and her family had never seen one other than on TV or in a magazine and so they were looking it over and a man – the owner – just happens to walk up to them. He's a friendly guy and he tells the family that he'll take 'em on out for a real Florida airboat ride if they want.'

Graciela turned her face into the crook of his neck and pressed a hand against his chest. She knew where the story was going.

'So they said okay. I mean, they were from some town in Ohio with only one high school. They didn't know anything about the real world. So they went ahead and accepted this man's – this stranger's – invitation.'

'And he killed them?'

'All of them,' McCaleb said, nodding in the dark. 'They went out with him and they never came back. The father was found first. A couple nights later his body was found by a frogger working the grass. It wasn't too far from a ramp where they launch those boats. He'd been shot once in the back of the head and dumped off the boat.'

'What about the girls?'

'It took the local sheriffs a couple days to ID the father and trace him to the Sea Breeze. When there was no sign there of the wife and kids, and they weren't back in Ohio, the sheriffs went back out into the 'Glades with helicopters and more airboats. They found the three other bodies about six miles out. The middle of nowhere. A spot the airboaters call the Devil's Keep. The bodies were there. He had done things to all three of them. Then he tied them to concrete blocks and threw them over. While they were alive. They drowned.'

'Oh, God . . .'

'God wasn't anywhere around that day. Decomposition gases eventually made the bodies float to the top, even with the concrete blocks attached.'

After a long moment of silence he continued.

'About that time the bureau was called in and I went down there with another agent, named Walling. There wasn't a whole lot to go on. We worked up a profile – we knew it was somebody very familiar with the 'Glades. Most of it's three feet deep anywhere you stop out there. But the women were dropped in a deep spot. He didn't want them found. He had to have known about that spot. The Devil's Keep. It was like a sinkhole or a meteorite crater. He had to have been out there before to have known about it.'

McCaleb was staring through the darkness at the ceiling, but what he was seeing was his own private and horrible version of the events that took place at the Devil's Keep. It was a vision that was never far from memory, always in the dark reaches of his mind.

'He had stripped them, taken their jewelry, anything that would ID them. But in Aubrey-Lynn's hand, when they pried it open, there was a silver necklace with a crucifix. She had somehow hidden it from him and held on to it. Probably praying to her God until the end.'

McCaleb thought about the story and the hold it had on him. Its resonance still moved through his life all these years later, like the incoming tide that gently lifted the boat in an almost rhythmic pattern. The story was always there. He knew he didn't need to display the photo above his desk like a holy card. He would never be able to forget the face of that girl. He knew that his heart had started to die with that girl's face.

'Did they catch that man?' Graciela asked.

She had just heard the story for the first time and already needed to know someone had paid for the horrible crime. She needed the closure. She didn't understand, as McCaleb did, that it didn't matter. That there was never closure on a story like this.

'No. They never caught him. They went through the registry at the Sea Breeze and ran everybody down. There was one person they never found. He had registered as Earl Hanford but it was a phony. The trail ended there . . . until he sent the video.'

A beat of silence passed.

'It was sent to the sheriff's lead detective. The family had a video camera. They took it with them on the airboat trip. The tape starts with lots of happy scenes and smiles. Disney World, the beach, then some of the 'Glades. Then the killer started taping . . . everything. He wore a black hood over his face so we couldn't ID him. He never showed enough of the boat to help us, either. He knew what he was doing.'

'You watched it?'

McCaleb nodded. He disengaged from Graciela and sat on the side of the bed, his back to her.

'He had a rifle. They did what he wanted. All sorts of things . . . the two sisters . . . together. Other things. And he killed them anyway. He – ah, shit . . .'

He shook his head and rubbed his hands harshly over his face. He felt her warm hand on his back.

'The blocks he tied them to weren't enough to take them right down. They struggled, you know, on the surface. He watched and taped it. It got him aroused. He was masturbating while he watched them drown.'

He heard Graciela crying quietly. He lay back down and put an arm around her.

'The tape was the last we ever heard from him,' he said. 'He's out there somewhere. Another one.'

He looked at her in the darkness, not sure if she could see him.

'That's the story.'

'I'm sorry you have that to carry around.'

'And now you have it. I'm sorry, too.'

She rubbed the tears away from her eyes.

'That's when you stopped believing in angels, isn't it?'

He nodded.

An hour or so before dawn McCaleb got up and went back to his uncomfortable bed in the salon. They had spent the night until that point talking in whispers, holding and kissing, but never making love. Once back in his sleeping bag, sleep still did not come to him. McCaleb's mind kept running over the details of the hours he had just spent with Graciela, the touch of her warm hands on his skin, the softness of her breasts against his lips, the taste of her lips. And during moments when his mind wandered from these sensual memories, he also thought about the story he had told her and the way she had reacted.

In the morning they did not talk about what had happened in the stateroom or what had been said, even when Raymond had gone out to the stern to look into the live well and was out of earshot. Graciela seemed to act as if there had been no rendezvous, consummated or not, and McCaleb acted in kind. The first thing he spoke of while he scrambled eggs for the three of them was the case.

'I want you to do something for me when you get home today,' he said, checking over his shoulder to make sure Raymond was still outside. 'I want you to think about your sister and write down as much as you can about her routines. I mean like places she would go, friends she would see. Anything you can think of she did between the first of the year and the night she went into that store. Also, I want to talk to her friends and boss at the *Times*. It might be better if you set that up.'

'All right. How come?'

'Because things are changing about the case. Remember I asked you about the earring?'

McCaleb told her his belief that it had been the shooter who had taken the earring. He also told her how he had found out late Friday that something of a personal nature had been taken from the victim in the first shooting as well.

'What was it?'

'A photo of his wife and kids.'

'What do you think it means?'

'That maybe these weren't robberies. That maybe this man at the ATM and then your sister were picked for some other reason. There's a chance they might have had some prior interaction with the man who shot them. You know, crossed paths with him somewhere. That's why I want you to do this. The wife of the first victim is doing it for me with her husband. I'll look at the two of them together and see if there are any commonalities.'

Graciela folded her arms and leaned against the galley counter.

'You mean like they did something to this man to cause this?'

'No. I mean that they crossed paths and something about them attracted him to them. There's no valid reason. I think we're looking for a psychopath. There is no telling what caught his eye. Why he chose these two people out of the nine million others who live in this county.'

She slowly shook her head in disbelief.

'What do the police say about all of this?'

'I don't think the LAPD even knows yet. And the sheriff's investigator is not sure whether or not she sees it the way I do. We're all going to talk about it tomorrow morning.'

'What about the man?'

'What man?'

'The store owner. Maybe he was the one who crossed the path. Maybe Glory had nothing to do with it.'

McCaleb shook his head and said, 'No. If he was the target, the shooter would have just gone in and shot him when nobody else was in the store. It was your sister. Your sister and the first man up in Lancaster. There is some connection. We have to find it.'

McCaleb reached into the back pocket of his jeans and pulled out a photo Amelia Cordell had given him. It showed James Cordell in close-up, a bright smile on his face. He showed the photo to Graciela.

'Do you recognize this man? Is he someone that your sister might have known?'

She took the photo from him and studied it but then shook her head.

'Not that I know of. Is he . . . the man from Lancaster?'

McCaleb nodded and took the photo back. He put it in his pocket, then told Graciela to go get Raymond to come inside for his breakfast. As she got to the sliding door, he stopped her.

'Graciela, do you trust me?'

She looked back at him.

'Of course.'

'Then trust me about this. I don't care if the LAPD and the sheriffs don't believe me, but I know what I know. With or without them, I'm going to keep pushing on this.'

She nodded and turned back to the door and the boy out in the stern.

23

The detective bureau at the Sheriff's Department's Star Center was crowded with detectives when McCaleb entered at eight o'clock on Monday morning. However, the receptionist who had let him walk back to homicide on his own just three days earlier told him he had to wait for the captain. This puzzled McCaleb but before he could ask about it, the receptionist was on the phone making a call. As soon as she hung up, McCaleb saw Captain Hitchens emerge from the meeting room he had sat in with Jaye Winston on Friday. He closed the door behind him and headed toward McCaleb. Terry noticed that the blinds over the meeting room's glass window were drawn and closed. Hitchens beckoned him to follow.

'Terry, come on back with me.'

McCaleb followed him to his office and Hitchens told him to have a seat. McCaleb was getting a bad feeling about the overly cordial treatment. Hitchens sat behind his desk, folded his arms and leaned forward on the calendar blotter with a smile on his face.

'So, where have you been?'

McCaleb looked at his watch.

'What do you mean? Jaye Winston set the meeting for eight. It's two minutes after.'

'I mean Sunday, Saturday. Jaye's been calling.'

McCaleb immediately knew what had happened. On Saturday, when he had been cleaning up the boat, he had taken the phone and the answer machine and placed them in a cabinet next to the chart table. He had then forgotten about it. Calls to the boat and messages left while they had been out on the jetty fishing both days would have been missed. The phone and machine were still in the cabinet.

'Damn,' he now said to Hitchens. 'I haven't checked my machine.'

'Well, we were calling. Could've saved you a trip out.'

'The meeting's been canceled? I thought Jaye wanted –'

'The meeting isn't canceled, Terry. It's just that some things have come up and we feel it's better if we conduct the investigation without outside complications.'

McCaleb studied him for a long moment.

'Complications? Is this because of the heart transplant? Jaye told you?'

'She didn't have to tell me. But it's because of a number of things. Look, you came in here and shook things up. Gave us a number of things – good hard leads – to follow. We're going to do that and we're going to be very diligent in our investigation, but at this point I have to draw the line on your involvement. I'm sorry.'

There was something not said, McCaleb thought as the captain spoke. Something was going on he didn't understand or at least know about it. Good hard leads, Hitchens had said. Suddenly, McCaleb understood. If Winston couldn't get through to him during the weekend, then neither could Vernon Carruthers in Washington, DC.

'My FAT guy found something?'

'Fat guy?'

'Firearms and Toolmarks. What did he get, Captain?'

Hitchens raised his hands palm out.

'We're not going to talk about that. I told you, we thank you very much for the jump start. But let us handle it from here. We will let you know what happens and if good things happen, you will be properly credited in our records and with the media.'

'I don't need to be credited. I just need to be part of this.'

'I'm sorry. But we'll take it from here.'

'And Jaye agrees with this?'

'It doesn't matter if she agrees or doesn't agree. Last I checked, I was running the detective bureau here, not Jaye Winston.'

There was enough annoyance in his tone for McCaleb to conclude that Winston had not been in agreement with Hitchens. That was good to know. He might need her. Staring at Hitchens, McCaleb knew he wasn't going to go quietly back to his boat and drop it. No way. The captain had to be smart enough to realize it as well.

'I know what you're thinking. And all I'm saying is don't get yourself in a jam. If we come across you in the field, there's going to be a problem.'

McCaleb nodded.

'Fair enough.'

'You've been warned.'

McCaleb told Lockridge to cruise around the visitors' lot. He wanted to get to a phone quickly but first he wanted to see if he could get an idea who had been in the meeting room Hitchens had come out of. He knew Jaye Winston was obviously in there and probably Arrango and Walters. But following his hunch that Vernon Carruthers had come up with a ballistics match with the DRUGFIRE laser program, he also suspected that someone from the bureau besides Maggie Griffin was in the meeting room.

As they moved slowly through the parking lot, McCaleb checked the rear driver's-side window of each parked car they passed. Finally, in the third lane, he saw what he was looking for.

'Hold it here, Bud,' he said.

They stopped behind a metallic blue Ford LTD. On the rear driver's-side window was the telltale bar-code sticker. It was a bureau car. A laser reader at the garage entrance of the federal building in Westwood scanned the bar code and raised the steel gate to permit entrance after hours.

McCaleb got out and walked up to the car. There were no other exterior markings to help him identify the agent who had driven it. But whoever had been driving the car made it easy for him. Driving east to the meeting against a rising sun, the driver had turned down the windshield visor and left it down. All the FBI agents McCaleb had ever known kept the government gas card assigned to their car clipped to the visor for easy access. This driver was no exception. McCaleb looked at the gas card and got the serial number off it. He went back to Lockridge's car.

'What's with the car?' Buddy asked.

'Nothing. Let's go.'

'Where?'

'Find a phone.'

'Shoulda guessed.'

Five minutes later they were at a service station with a bank of phones on the side wall. Lockridge pulled up to the phones, lowered his window so he would be able to eavesdrop and shut off the car. Before getting out, McCaleb opened his wallet and gave him a twenty-dollar bill.

'Go fill it up. We're going back up to the desert, I think.'

'Shit.'

'You said you were free all day.'

'I am, but who wants to go to the desert? Don't any clues point to the beach, for cryin' out loud?'

McCaleb just laughed at him and got out of the car with his phone book.

At the phone, McCaleb called the field office in Westwood and asked to be transferred to the garage. The call was picked up after twelve rings.

'G'age.'

'Yeah, who's this?'

'Roofs.'

'Oh, okay,' McCaleb said, remembering the man. 'Rufus, this is Convey up on fifteen. I've got a question you might be able to answer for me.'

'Shoot, man.'

The familiarity McCaleb had put in his voice had apparently worked. He remembered Rufus and had never been much impressed with his intelligence. This was reflected in the poor upkeep of the federal fleet.

'I found a gas card on the floor up here and it's supposed to be in somebody's car down there. Who's got card eighty-one? Can you look it up?'

'Uh . . . etty-one?'

'Yes, Roof, eight-one.'

There was a spell of silence while the garage man apparently looked through a log.

'Well, that's Misser Spence. He got that one.'

McCaleb didn't respond. Gilbert Spencer was the second-highest-ranking agent in Los Angeles. Rank notwithstanding, McCaleb had never thought much of him as an investigative team leader. But the fact that he was meeting with Jaye Winston and her captain and who knew who else at the Star Center came as a shock. He began to get a better idea why he had been kicked off the case.

' 'Lo?'

'Uh, yeah, Rufus, thanks a lot. That was eighty-one, right?'

'Yuh. Tha's Agent Spence cah.'

'Okay, I'll get him the card.'

'I don't know. I see his car ain' here right now.'

'Okay, don't worry about it. Thanks, Roof.'

McCaleb hung up the phone and immediately picked it up again. Using his calling card number, he called Vernon Carruthers in Washington. It was just about lunchtime there and he hoped he had not missed him.

'This is Vernon.'

McCaleb blew out a sigh.

'It's Terry.'

'Man, where the hell you been? I tried to give you a damn heads-up on Saturday and you wait two days to call me back.'

'I know, I know. I fucked up. But I hear you got something.'

'Damn tootin'.'

'What, Vernon, what?'

'I gotta be careful. I get the feeling there's a need-to-know list on this and your name's –'

'– not on it. Yeah, I know. I already found that out. But this is my car, Vernon, and nobody's going to drive away without me. So you're going to tell me, what did you find that would bring the assistant special agent in charge of the Los Angeles field office out of his little room and into the field, probably for the first time this year?'

' 'Course I'm going to tell you. I got my twenty-five in. What are they going to do to me? Kick me out and then have to pay me double-time witness fees to testify in all the cases I got lined up?'

'So give it to me then.'

'Well, you really stuck your dick in it this time. I lasered the slug this Winston gal sent me and got an eighty-three percent match on a good-sized frag they dug out of the head of one Donald Kenyon back in November. That's why you got the A-SAC's nuts in an uproar out there.'

McCaleb whistled.

'Damn, not in my ear, man,' Carruthers protested.

'Sorry. Was it a Federal FMJ – the one from Kenyon?'

'No, actually, it was a frangible. A Devastator. You know what that is?'

'That's what Reagan got nailed with at the Hilton, right?'

'Right. Little charge in the tip. Bullet is supposed to fragment. But it didn't with Ronnie. He got lucky. Kenyon wasn't lucky.'

McCaleb tried to think about what this might mean. The same gun, the HK P7, had been used in the three murders, Kenyon, Cordell and Torres. But between Kenyon and Cordell the ammunition had changed from a frangible to a hardball. Why?

'Now, remember,' Carruthers was saying, 'you didn't hear this stuff from me.'

'I know. But tell me something. After you got the match, what did you do, go to Lewin or do some checking first?'

Joel Lewin was Carruthers's by-the-book boss.

'What you're asking is if I got anything to send you, am I right?'

'You're right. I need what you can send me.'

'Already on the way. Put it in priority mail on Saturday before the shit hit the fan around here. I printed out what was on the computer. You got all the internals coming. Should be there t'day or t'morrow. You are going to take me on one hell of a fishing trip for this, man.'

'Absolutely.'

'And you didn't get any of that stuff from me.'

'You're cool, Vernon. You don't even have to say it.'

'I know but it makes me feel better.'

'What else can you tell me?'

'That's about it. It was taken out of my hands. Lewin took over everything and it went high-level from there. I did have to tell them why I put the push on it. So they know you were looking into it. I didn't tell them why.'

McCaleb silently chastised himself for losing his temper and control with Arrango after the hypnotism session. If he hadn't revealed the real motivation behind his investigation, he might still be a part of it. Carruthers had not revealed the secret, but Arrango certainly had.

'You there, Terry?'

'Yeah. Listen, if you pick up anything else about this, give me the heads-up.'

'You got it, man. But answer your fuckin' phone. And watch yourself on this.'

'All the time.'

After McCaleb hung up he turned around and almost walked into Buddy Lockridge.

'Buddy, come on, you gotta give me room. Let's get going.'

They started walking to the car, which was still parked at one of the pumps.

'The desert?'

'Yeah. We go back up and I see Mrs Cordell again. See if she's still talking to me.'

'Why wouldn't – never mind, don't answer that. I'm just the driver.'

'Now you got it.'

On the way up to the desert, Buddy warbled on a B flat harmonica while McCaleb used some self-hypnosis techniques to relax his mind so that he would better recall what he knew of the Donald Kenyon case. It had been the latest in what had seemingly been a long line of embarrassments to the bureau in recent years.

Kenyon had been president of Washington Guaranty, a federally insured savings and loan bank with branches in Los Angeles, Orange and San Diego Counties. Kenyon was a golden-haired and silver-tongued climber who curried favor with deep-pocketed investors through insider stock tips until he ascended to the president's office by the shockingly young age of twenty-nine. He was profiled in every business magazine. He was a man who instilled confidence and trust in his investors and employees and the media. So much so that over the period of three years that he was president, he was able to siphon a staggering $35 million from the institution through bogus loans to bogus companies without so much as raising an eyebrow. It wasn't until Washington Guaranty collapsed after being thoroughly hollowed out and Kenyon disappeared that anyone, including federal auditors and watchdogs, realized what had happened.

The story played in the media for months, if not years, McCaleb remembered. Stories on retirees left with nothing, stories on the ripple effect of businesses failing, stories on alleged sightings of Kenyon in Paris, Zurich, Tahiti and other places.

After five years on the run Kenyon was found by the bureau's fugitive unit in Costa Rica, where he had been living in an opulent compound that included two pools, two tennis courts, a live-in personal trainer and horse-breeding facilities. The thief, now thirty-six, was extradited to Los Angeles to face charges in federal court.

While Kenyon sat in the federal holding facility awaiting trial, an asset and forfeiture squad descended on his trail and worked for six months looking for the money. But less than $2 million was found.

This was the puzzle. Kenyon's defense was that he did not have the money because he didn't take it, he only passed it on under threat of death – his and his entire family's. Through his attorneys he averred that he was blackmailed into setting up corporations, loaning them millions from his S&L and then turning the money over to the blackmailer. But even though he faced the potential of years in a federal penitentiary, Kenyon refused to name the extortionist who had taken the money.

Federal investigators and prosecutors chose not to believe him. Citing his high-flying lifestyle both while running the S&L and on the run, and the fact that he clearly had some of the money – albeit a fraction of the whole – with him in Costa Rica, they settled for prosecuting only Kenyon.

After a four-month trial in a federal courtroom packed each day with a gallery of victims who had lost their life savings in the S&L collapse, Kenyon was convicted of the massive fraud and US District Judge Dorothy Windsor sentenced him to forty-eight years in prison.

What happened next would result in one more bludgeoning of the reputation of the FBI.

After passing sentence, Windsor agreed to a defense request to allow Kenyon time at home with his family to prepare for prison while his attorneys prepared appeal motions. Over the prosecutor's strenuous objection, Windsor gave Kenyon sixty days to get his house in order. He then had to report to prison forthwith, whether an appeal was filed or not. Windsor further ordered that Kenyon wear a monitor bracelet around his ankle to ensure he did not attempt another flight from justice.

Such an order following conviction is not unusual. However, it *is* unusual when the convict has already shown his willingness to flee authorities and the country.

But whether Kenyon had somehow been able to influence a federal judge to get such a ruling and planned to flee once more would never be known. On the Tuesday after Thanksgiving, while Kenyon was enjoying the twenty-first day of his two-month reprieve, someone entered the Beverly Hills home he was renting on Maple Drive. Kenyon was alone, his wife having left to take their two children to school. The intruder confronted Kenyon in the kitchen and marched him at gunpoint into the marble-tiled entry of the house. He then shot Kenyon to death just as his wife's car was pulling into the circular drive out front. The intruder escaped out a back door and through the alley running behind the row of mansions on Maple Drive.

Except for the investigation and pursuit of the killer, the story might have ended there or at least taken on the mundane boredom of a cold trail. But the FBI had Lojacked Kenyon – bureau-speak for having placed him under an illegal surveillance that included listening devices planted in his home, cars and attorney's office. At the moment he was shot, a tech van with four agents in it was parked two blocks away. The murder had been recorded.

The agents, aware of their illegal standing, nevertheless raced to the home and gave pursuit to the intruder. But the gunman escaped while Kenyon was being rushed to Cedars-Sinai Medical Center, only to be declared dead on arrival.

The missing millions Kenyon was convicted of looting from Washington Guaranty were never recovered. But that detail was eclipsed when the actions of the FBI were revealed. Not only was the bureau vilified for undertaking such an illegal operation, it was also publicly castigated for allowing a murder to happen right under its nose, for bumbling the chance to intervene and stop the assassination of Kenyon, not to mention capture the gunman.

McCaleb had viewed all of this from afar. He was already out of the bureau and at the time of Kenyon's murder was preparing himself for his own death. But he remembered reading the *Times*, which was at the forefront of the story. He recalled that the newspaper reported that there were demotions all around for the agents involved and calls from politicians in Washington, DC, for congressional hearings on illegal activities by the bureau. To add insult to injury, he also remembered, Kenyon's widow filed an invasion-of-privacy lawsuit against the bureau, seeking millions in damages.

The question McCaleb now had to answer was whether the intruder who killed Kenyon in November was the man who killed Cordell and Torres two and three months later. And if it was the same man, what could possibly be the connection linking a failed savings and loan president with an aqueduct engineer and a newspaper pressroom worker?

He finally looked around and noticed his surroundings. They were well past Vasquez Rocks now. In a few more minutes they would be at Amelia Cordell's house.

24

As promised, Amelia Cordell had spent a good part of the weekend going through her memory and filling four pages of a legal tablet with what she recalled of her husband's travels in the two months before his death on the twenty-second of January. She had it ready and sitting on the coffee table when McCaleb arrived.

'I appreciate the time you put into this,' he told her.

'Well, maybe it will help. I hope it helps.'

'Me too.'

He nodded and sat in silence for a moment.

'Um, by the way, have you heard from Jaye Winston or anybody else from the Sheriff's Department lately?'

'No, not since Jaye called me on Friday to say it was okay to talk to you.'

McCaleb nodded. He was heartened by the fact that Jaye hadn't called back to rescind the permission. Again it made him think that she wasn't going along with her captain's decision to drop McCaleb from the case.

'And nobody else?'

'No . . . like who?'

'I don't know. I'm just curious about whether, you know, they're following up on the information I've given them.'

McCaleb decided he had better change the subject.

'Mrs Cordell, did your husband have a home office?'

'Yes, he had a small den he used, why?'

'Do you mind if I look around there?'

'Well, no, but I'm not sure what you'll find. He just kept files from work there and he did our bills there.'

'Well, for example, if you have credit card statements for the period of January and December, it might help me isolate where he was at different points.'

'I'm not too sure I want you taking our credit card records.'

'Well, all I can do is assure you that I'm only interested in the billing locations and possibly the items purchased. Not your credit card numbers.'

'I know, I'm sorry. That was silly of me. You're the only one who seems to care anymore about Jim. Why am I suspicious of you?'

It made McCaleb feel uneasy not being totally truthful with the woman and telling her he had lost his official sanction. He stood up so that they could move on and he didn't have to think about it.

The office was small and largely used for storage of skiing equipment and cardboard boxes. But one end of the room was largely taken up by a desk with two drawers and two built-in file cabinets.

'Sorry, it's a mess. And I'm still getting used to doing all the bills. Jim always handled that.'

'Don't worry about that. Do you mind if I just sort of sit and look through things a bit?'

'No, not at all.'

'Um, would it be possible for me to have a glass of water in here?'

'Of course, I'll go get you one.'

She headed to the door but then stopped.

'You don't really want the water, do you? You just want to be left alone and not have me hovering around.'

McCaleb smiled slightly and looked down at the worn green carpet.

'I'll get you the water anyway, but then I'll leave you alone.'

'Thanks, Mrs Cordell.'

'Call me Amelia.'

'Amelia.'

McCaleb spent the next half hour going through the drawers and the paperwork on top of the desk. He worked quickly, knowing that the package from Carruthers was probably waiting for him in his postal box in the harbormaster's office.

At the desk McCaleb took some notes on the legal pad Amelia Cordell had already worked on, and he piled documents and credit card records he wanted to take with him to study later. He made an inventory list of the things he wanted to take so that Amelia Cordell would have a record.

The last drawer he went through was in one of the file cabinets. It was almost empty and had been used by Cordell as the place to file work, insurance and estate planning records. There was a thick file on medical insurance, with billing records dating back to the birth of his daughters and his own treatment for a broken leg. The billing address of one of his treating physicians was in Vail, Colorado, leading McCaleb to guess the bone had been broken in a skiing misadventure.

There was a black binder with a handsome leather slipcover. McCaleb opened it and found that it contained documents relating to the wills of both husband and wife. McCaleb saw nothing unordinary. Each spouse had been the other's beneficiary, with the children following in line in the event of both parents dying. McCaleb didn't spend a lot of time with it.

The last file he looked at was simply labeled WORK and it contained various records, including performance evaluations and various office communications. McCaleb scanned the employment reviews and found that Cordell had apparently been held in high regard by his employers. McCaleb wrote down some of the names of supervisors who signed the reports so he could interview them later. Last he scanned the other correspondence but nothing interested him. There were copies of interoffice memos as well as letters of commendation for Cordell's chairing of the engineering firm's annual blood drive and his volunteer work in a program that provided Thanksgiving meals to the needy. There was also a two-year-old letter from a supervisor praising Cordell for stopping and helping the injured victims of a head-on collision in Lone Pine. Details of what Cordell did were not in the letter. McCaleb put the letters and evaluations back in the file and returned it to the file drawer.

McCaleb stood up and looked around the room. There was nothing else that raised any interest. He then noticed a framed photo on the desk. It was of the Cordell family. He picked it up and studied it for a moment, thinking about how much the bullet had shattered. It made him think of Raymond and Graciela. He envisioned a photo that had the two of them and McCaleb in it, smiling.

He took his empty water glass into the kitchen and left it on the counter. He then stepped into the living room and found Amelia Cordell sitting in the chair she had taken earlier. She was just sitting there. The television was not on, she had no book or newspaper in her hands. She appeared to be just staring at the glass top of the coffee table. McCaleb hesitated in the hallway from the kitchen.

'Mrs Cordell?'

She shifted her eyes to him without moving her head.

'Yes?'

'I'm finished for now.'

He stepped in and placed the receipt on the table.

'These are the things I am taking. I'll get it all back to you in a few days. I'll either mail it or bring it up myself.'

Her eyes were on the list now, trying to read it from three feet away.

'Did you find what you need?'

'I don't know yet. These sorts of things, you never know what is important until it becomes important, if you know what I mean.'

'Not really.'

'Well, I guess I mean details. I'm looking for the telling detail. There used to be a game when I was a kid. I don't remember what it was called but they still might have it around for kids today. You've got a clear plastic tube that stands vertical. There are a bunch of plastic straws running through holes all around the center of it. You load a bunch of marbles into the tube so that they are held up by the straws. The object of the game is to pull a straw out without any marbles dropping. And there always seemed to be one straw that when you pulled it out, everything came down like a landslide. That's what I'm looking for. I've got lots of details. I'm looking for the one that brings the landslide when it's pulled out. Trouble is, you can't tell which one it is until you start pulling.'

She looked at him blankly, the way she had been staring at the coffee table.

'Well, look, I've taken too much of your time. I think I'll be on my way and, like I said, I'll get these things back to you. And I'll call you if anything else comes up. My number is on the inventory list there in case you think of anything else or there is anything I can do for you.'

He nodded and she said good-bye. He turned to head to the door when he thought of something and turned back.

'Oh, I almost forgot. There was a letter in one of the files commending your husband for stopping at an accident up near Lone Pine. Do you remember that?'

'Sure. That was two years ago, November.'

'Do you remember what happened?'

'Just that Jimmy was driving home from up there and he came across the accident. It had just happened and there were people and debris thrown every which way and that. He called for ambulances on his cell phone and stopped to comfort the people. A little boy died right in his arms that night. He had a hard time with that.'

McCaleb nodded.

'That was the kind of man he was, Mr McCaleb.'

All McCaleb could do was nod his head again.

McCaleb had to wait out on the front driveway for ten minutes before Buddy Lockridge finally drove up. He had a Howlin' Wolf tape playing loud on the stereo. McCaleb turned it down after climbing in.

'Where you been?'

'Drivin'. Where to?'

'Well, I was waiting. Back to the marina.'

Buddy made a U-turn and headed back to the freeway.

'Well, you told me I didn't have to just sit in the car. You told me to take a drive, I took a drive. How am I supposed to know how long you're going to be if you don't tell me?'

He was right but McCaleb was still annoyed. He didn't apologize.

'If this thing lasts much longer, I ought to get a cell phone for you to carry.'

'If this lasts much longer, I want a raise.'

McCaleb didn't respond. Lockridge turned the tape back up and pulled a harmonica out of the door pocket. He started playing along to 'Wang Dang Doodle'. McCaleb looked out the window and thought about Amelia Cordell and how one bullet had taken two lives.

25

The package from Carruthers was waiting for McCaleb in his mailbox. It was as thick as a phone book. He took it back to the boat, opened it and spread the documents across the salon table. He found the most recent summary on the Kenyon investigation and began reading, deciding to learn the latest developments and then go back to read from the start.

The investigation of the Donald Kenyon murder was a joint FBI-Beverly Hills police operation. But the case was cold. The lead agents for the bureau, a pair from the special investigation unit in Los Angeles named Nevins and Uhlig, had concluded in the most recent report, filed in December, that Kenyon had likely been executed by a contract killer. There were two theories as to who had employed the assassin. Theory one was that one of the two thousand victims of the savings and loan collapse had been unsatisfied with Kenyon's sentence or possibly feared he would flee justice once again and therefore had engaged the services of a killer. Theory two was that the killer had been in the employ of the silent partner who Kenyon had claimed during the trial had forced him to loot the savings and loan. That partner, whom Kenyon had refused to identify, remained unidentified as well by the bureau, according to this last report.

McCaleb found the outlining of theory two in the report interesting because it indicated that the federal government might now give credence to Kenyon's claim that he had been forced to siphon funds from his savings and loan by a second party. This claim had been derided during Kenyon's trial by the prosecution, which took to referring to this alleged second party as Kenyon's phantom. Now, here was an FBI document which suggested that the phantom might actually exist.

Nevins and Uhlig concluded the summary report with a brief profile of the unknown subject who had contracted the murder. The profile fit both theories one and two: the employer was wealthy, had the ability to hide his or her trail and remain anonymous and had connections to or was even part of traditional organized crime.

Aside from the report breathing life into Kenyon's phantom, the second thing that interested McCaleb was the suggestion that the employer, and therefore the actual killer, was connected to traditional organized crime. Traditional organized crime in FBI parlance meant the Mafia. The tendrils of the Mafia were almost everywhere, but, even so, the mob was not a strong influence in southern California. There was a tremendous amount of organized crime in the area, it just wasn't being perpetrated by the traditional mobsters out of the movies. At any given time there were probably more Asian or Russian mobsters operating in southern California than their counterparts of Italian descent.

McCaleb organized the documents in chronological order and went back to the start. Most were routine summaries and updates on aspects of the investigation that were forwarded to supervisors in Washington. Quickly scanning through the documents, he found a report on the surveillance team's activities the morning of the shooting that he read with fascination.

There had been four agents in the surveillance van at the time of the killing. It was change-of-shift time, eight o'clock on a Tuesday morning. Two agents coming on, two going home. The agent monitoring the bugs took off the headset and passed it to his replacement. However, the replacement was a type A personality who claimed he had once gotten an infestation of head lice from another agent during an earphone exchange. So he took the time to put his own pair of foam cushions on the headset and to then spray the equipment with a disinfectant, all the while fending off insulting barbs from the three other agents. After he finally placed the earphones on his head, he heard silence for nearly a minute, then a muffled exchange of conversation and then finally a shot from Kenyon's house. The sound was muffled because no listening devices had been placed in the entryway of the house, the thinking being that any escape planning Kenyon might do would not be done at the front door. The bugs had been placed in the actual living areas of the house.

The overnight team had not yet left and were continuing the banter in the van. After hearing the shot, the agent on the phones shouted for silence. He listened closely for several seconds while another agent put on a second set of phones. What they both heard was someone in the Kenyon house clearly speak one line near one of the microphones: 'Don't forget the cannoli.'

The two agents on the phones looked at each other and agreed that it had not been Kenyon who had spoken the line. Declaring an emergency, the agents blew their cover and sped to the house, arriving moments after Donna Kenyon had arrived home, opened the front door and found her husband lying on the marble floor, his head bathed in blood. After calling for bureau backup, local police and paramedics, the agents searched the house and the surrounding neighborhood. The gunman was gone.

McCaleb moved on to a transcript of the last hour of tape from Kenyon's home. The tape had been enhanced in the FBI lab but still not every word was captured. There were the sounds of the daughters having breakfast and the normal morning talk between Kenyon and his wife and the girls. Then, at 7:40, the girls and their mother left.

The transcript noted nine minutes of silence before Kenyon made a phone call to the home of his attorney, Stanley LaGrossa.

LAGROSSA: Yes?

KENYON: It's Donald.
LAGROSSA: Donald.
KENYON: Are we still on?
LAGROSSA: Yes, if you are still serious about it.
KENYON: I am. I'll see you at the office then.
LAGROSSA: You know the risks. I'll see you there.

Another eight minutes went by and then a new unknown voice was picked up in the house. Some of the terse conversation was lost as Kenyon and the unknown man moved through the house, in and out of the reach of the listening devices. The conversation had apparently taken place while the delayed earphone exchange was taking place in the bureau tech van.

KENYON: What is –
UNKNOWN: Shut up! Do what I say and your family lives, understand?
KENYON: You can't just walk in here and –
UNKNOWN: I said shut up! Let's go. This way.
KENYON: Don't hurt my family. Please, I . . .
UNKNOWN: (unintelligible)
KENYON: . . . do that. I wouldn't and he knows that. I don't understand this. He . . .
UNKNOWN: Shut up. I don't care.
KENYON: (unintelligible)
UNKNOWN: (unintelligible)

The report noted that two minutes of silence went by and then the final exchange.

UNKNOWN: Okay, look and see who . . .
KENYON: Don't . . . She's got nothing to do with this. She . . .

Then one shot was fired. And moments later microphone 4, which was hidden in a rear den with a door to the rear yard, picked up the unknown man's final words.

UNKNOWN: Don't forget the cannoli.

The door to the den was found open. It had been used as part of the killer's escape route.

McCaleb read the transcript again, captivated by knowing it was a man's last moments and words. He wished he had an audiotape, so that he would have a better feel for what had happened.

The next document he read explained why the investigators suspected mob involvement. It was a cryptology report. The tape from the Kenyon house had been sent to the crime lab for enhancement. The transcript was then sent to cryptology. The analyst given the assignment focused on the killer's last line, spoken after Kenyon was down and seemingly a non sequitur. The line – 'Don't forget the cannoli' – was fed into the cryptology computer to see if it matched any known code, prior usage in bureau reports or literary or entertainment reference. It scored a direct match.

In the movie *The Godfather*, the film that inspired a legion of true-life Mafia hoodlums, a top capo for the Corleone family, Peter Clemenza, is given the assignment of taking a traitorous family soldier out into the New Jersey meadowlands and killing him. On the morning he leaves his home for the hit, his wife tells Clemenza to stop by a bakery for pastry. As the hugely overweight Clemenza lumbers out to a waiting car containing the man he is tasked with killing, his wife calls after him, 'Don't forget the cannoli.'

McCaleb loved the movie and now remembered the line. It so clearly captured the essence of movie mob life – the ruthless and guiltless brutality alongside family values and loyalty. He understood now why the bureau had concluded that the Kenyon killing was in some way mob related. The line had the audacity and bravura of the mob life. He could see a stone-cold killer adopting it as the imprimatur of his work.

'Don't forget the cannoli,' McCaleb said out loud.

He suddenly thought of something and a little jolt of electricity went through him.

'Don't forget the cannoli,' he said again.

He quickly went to his leather bag and dug through it until he found the video from the James Cordell shooting. He went to the television and jammed the tape in and started playing it. After getting his bearings on where in the tape he was, he fast-forwarded to the moment of the shooting and hit play again. His eyes stayed on the masked man's mouth and as the man began to speak on the silent tape, McCaleb spoke with him out loud.

'Don't forget the cannoli.'

He backed the tape up and did it again, saying it again. His words matched the shooter's lips. He was sure it fit. He could feel excitement and adrenaline surging inside of him now. It was a feeling that only came when you had momentum, when you were making your own breaks. When you were getting close to the hidden truth.

He pulled the tape of the Gloria Torres murder out, put it in the player and repeated the process again. The words fit the lips of the shooter once again. There was no doubt.

'Don't forget the cannoli,' McCaleb said aloud again.

He went to the cabinet next to the chart table and got the phone out. He still had not played the messages that had accumulated over the weekend but he was too hyped to do it now. He punched in the number for Jaye Winston.

'Where have you been and don't you ever check your machine?' she asked. 'I've been trying to call you all weekend and all day to explain. It wasn't my –'

'I know. It wasn't you. It was Hitchens. I'm not calling about that anyway. I know what the bureau told you. I know what you've got – the connection to Donald Kenyon. You've got to bring me back in.'

'That's impossible. Hitchens already said I shouldn't even talk to you. How am I going to bring –'

'I can help you.'

'How? With what?'

'Just answer me this, see if I have this right. This morning Gilbert Spencer and a couple of field agents – I'm guessing they were named Nevins and Uhlig – come out and give you the news that the bullet you sent to Washington matched up with Kenyon. Right?'

'So far, but that's no great –'

'I'm not done. Next, he tells you the bureau would like to look into your case and the LAPD case but that initially there seems to be no likely connection other than the weapon. He says, after all, Kenyon is a professional hit and you guys are working two street robberies. Not only that, his shooter used a Devastator on Kenyon and your guy used something else. Federals. That backs the bureau theory that the professional shooter in the Kenyon case discarded his weapon somewhere and the shooter from your two cases then came along and picked it up. End of connection. How am I doing so far?'

'Dead on.'

'Okay, so you asked Spencer for information on the Kenyon killing just so you could do your own cross-checking but that didn't go over so well.'

'He said the Kenyon case was at a – quote – sensitive point and that he would rather us peons be on a need-to-know basis.'

'And Hitchens agreed to that?'

'He went along for the ride.'

'And did anybody serve the cannoli?'

'What?'

McCaleb spent the next five minutes explaining the cannoli connection, reading her the transcript from the bugs in Kenyon's house and the conclusions of the cryptology report. Winston said these were all facts that Gilbert Spencer had not mentioned during the morning meeting. McCaleb knew that he would not have. McCaleb had been in the bureau. He knew how it worked. Given the opportunity, you brush the locals aside and say that the bureau will handle it from here.

'So the cannoli connection makes it clear this wasn't a throw-away gun that our guy happened to pick up,' McCaleb said. 'It's the same shooter on all three. Kenyon, then Cordell, then Torres. Whether the bureau people knew that going in to your meeting, I don't know. But if you copied them the case file and the tapes, they know it now. The question is, how do these three killings fit together?'

Winston was silent for a moment before finally expressing her confusion.

'Man, I have no – well, maybe they don't connect. Look, if it's a contract killer like the bureau says, maybe they were three separate contracts. You know? Maybe there is *no* connection other than the same killer did all three on three separate jobs.'

McCaleb shook his head and said, 'It's possible, I guess, but nothing makes sense. I mean, what did Gloria Torres have that would make her a pro hitter's target? She worked in the print shop at the newspaper.'

'It could have been something she saw. Remember what you said Friday about there being some connection between the two, Torres and Cordell? Well, maybe it's still the same, only the connection is something they saw or something they knew.'

McCaleb nodded.

'What about the icons, the things taken from Cordell and Torres?' he asked, more to himself than to Winston.

'I don't know,' she said. 'Maybe it's a hitter who likes to take souvenirs. Maybe he had to prove to his employer that he had hit the right people. Is there anything in the reports about anything being taken from Kenyon?'

'Not that I have seen yet.'

His mind was a jumble of possibilities. Winston's question made him realize that in his excitement he had called her too soon. He still had a stack of unread Kenyon files. The connection he was looking for might be there.

'Terry?'

'Yeah, sorry, I was just thinking. Look, let me call you back. I've got some more stuff to go through and I might be able –'

'What stuff do you have?'

'I think I've got everything, or almost everything, that Spencer wasn't telling you.'

'I would say that that is going to buy you back into the captain's good graces.'

'Well, don't say anything to him yet. Let me figure out a little more about this and I'll call you.'

'You promise?'

'Yeah.'

'Then say it. I don't want you pulling any bureau bullshit on me.'

'Hey, I'm retired, remember? I promise.'

An hour and a half later McCaleb finished going through the bureau documents. The adrenaline that had jazzed him before had dissipated. He had learned a lot of new information as he read the reports but nothing that hinted at a connection between Kenyon and Cordell and Torres.

The rest of the bureau documents contained a lengthy printout of the names, addresses and investment histories of the two thousand victims of the savings and loan collapse. And neither Cordell nor Torres had been investors.

The bureau had had to consider every victim of the S&L collapse a suspect in the Kenyon shooting. Each name on the investors list was backgrounded and screened for criminal connections and other flags that might elevate it to viable suspect status. A dozen or so investors were raised to that level but then eventually cleared through full field investigations.

The investigation had then shifted its focus toward theory two, that Kenyon's phantom was real and had ordered the hit on the man who had stolen millions for him.

This theory gathered momentum after it was learned that Kenyon had been about to reveal whom he had turned over the stolen S&L funds to. According to a statement from Kenyon's attorney, Stanley LaGrossa, Kenyon had decided to cooperate with the authorities in hopes of getting the US Attorney's office to petition the judge who sentenced him to reduce his penalty. LaGrossa said that on the morning Kenyon was murdered, they had planned to meet to discuss how LaGrossa would go about negotiating his cooperation.

McCaleb flipped back through the reports and reread the short transcript of the phone call Kenyon made to LaGrossa just minutes before the murder. The brief exchange between the lawyer and his client appeared to back up LaGrossa's claim that Kenyon was ready to cooperate.

The bureau theory, outlined in a supplemental report to LaGrossa's statement, was that Kenyon's silent partner either was taking no chances and eliminated Kenyon or he eliminated Kenyon after specifically learning that his partner was planning to cooperate with government investigators. The supplemental report noted that federal agents and prosecutors had not yet been approached by the Kenyon camp with the overture of cooperation. That meant that if there was a leak to the silent partner, it came from Kenyon's people, possibly even LaGrossa himself.

McCaleb got up and poured a glass of orange juice, emptying one of the half-gallon cartons he had bought on Saturday morning. As he drank, he thought about what all of the Kenyon information meant to the investigation. It clouded things for sure. Despite the early jolt of adrenaline, he now realized he was basically back to ground zero, no closer to knowing who killed Gloria Torres and why than he was when he opened the package mailed from Carruthers.

As he rinsed out the glass, he noticed two men coming down the main gangway to the docks. They were dressed in almost matching blue suits. Anybody in a suit stood out on the docks – usually, it was a bank loan officer come to chain down a boat for repossession. But McCaleb knew better this time. He recognized the demeanor. They were coming for him. Vernon Carruthers must have been found out.

Quickly, McCaleb went to the table and gathered up the bureau documents. He then split off the sheaf of pages that listed the names, addresses and other information about the savings and loan collapse. He put that thick packet in one of the overhead cabinets in the kitchen. The rest of the documents he shoved into his leather bag, which he then put into the cabinet under the chart table.

He slid the salon door open and stepped out into the cockpit to greet the two agents. He closed and locked the door behind him.

'Mr McCaleb?' the younger one said. He had a mustache, daring by bureau standards.

'Let me guess, Nevins and Uhlig.'

They didn't look happy about being identified.

'Can we come aboard?'

'Sure.'

The younger one was introduced as Nevins. Uhlig, the senior agent, did most of the talking.

'If you know who we are, then you know why we are here. We don't want this to get any messier than it has to be. Especially taking into account your service to the bureau. So if you give us the stolen files, it can all end right here.'

'Whoa,' McCaleb said, holding his hands up. 'Stolen files?'

'Mr McCaleb,' Uhlig said. 'It has come to our attention that you are in the possession of confidential FBI files. You are no longer an agent. You should not be in possession of these files. As I just said, if you want to make this a problem for you, we can make it a problem for you. But all we really want is the files back.'

McCaleb stepped over and sat on the gunwale. He was trying to think about how they knew and it came back to Carruthers. It was the only way. Vernon must have gotten jammed up in Washington and had to give McCaleb up. But it was unlike his old friend to do that, no matter what pressure they put on him.

He decided to trust his instincts and call the bluff. Nevins and Uhlig knew Carruthers had run the ballistics laser comparison at McCaleb's request. That was no secret. They must have then assumed that Carruthers would have forwarded him copies of the computer files.

'Forget it, guys,' he finally said. 'I don't have any files, stolen or otherwise. You got bad info.'

'Then how'd you know who we were?' Nevins asked.

'Easy. I found out today when you guys went to the sheriff's office and told them to keep me out of the case.'

McCaleb folded his arms and looked past the two agents to Buddy Lockridge's boat. Buddy was sitting in the cockpit, sipping from a can of beer and watching the scene with the two suits on *The Following Sea.*

'Well, we're going to have to take a look around, then, to make sure,' Uhlig said.

'Not without a warrant and I doubt you've got a warrant.'

'We didn't need one after you gave us permission to enter and search.'

Nevins stepped over to the salon door and tried to slide it open. He found it was locked. McCaleb smiled.

'Only way you're getting in there is to break it, Nevins. And that won't look much like permission granted, if you ask me. Besides, you don't want to do that with an uninvolved witness watching.'

Both agents started looking around the marina. Finally, they spotted Lockridge, who held his beer can up as a greeting. McCaleb watched as anger turned Uhlig's jaw rigid.

'Okay, McCaleb,' the senior agent said. 'Keep the files. But I'm telling you right now, smart guy, don't get in the way. The bureau's in the process of taking over the case and the last thing we need is some tin man amateur without a badge or his own heart fucking things up for us.'

McCaleb could feel his own jaw drawing tight.

'Get the fuck off my boat.'

'Sure. We're going.'

They both climbed back up onto the dock. As they headed to the gangway, Nevins turned around and said, 'See you around, Tin Man.'

McCaleb watched them all the way through the gate.

'What was that all about?' Lockridge called over.

McCaleb waved him off while still watching the agents.

'Just some old friends come to pay a visit.'

It was nearly 8 P.M. in the east. McCaleb called Carruthers at his home. His friend said he had already been through the wringer.

'I told them, I said, "Hey, I turned over my information to Lewin. Yes, I put a push on the package at the request of former agent McCaleb, but I did not furnish a copy of the report or any other reports to him." Hey, they don't believe me, then they can shove it. I'm fully vested. They want me out, I'm out. Then they can pay me every time I have to come in to testify on one of my cases. And I got voluminous cases, if you know what I mean.'

He was speaking as if for a third party listening in. And with the bureau, you never knew if there wasn't. McCaleb followed suit.

'Same thing out here. They came around, tried to act like I had reports I don't have and I told them to get off my damn boat.'

'Yeah, you're cool.'

'So are you, Vernon. I'm gonna go. Watch the following sea, man.'

'What's that?'

'Watch your back.'

'Oh. Right. You, too.'

Winston picked up the call on a half ring.

'Where have you been?'

'Busy. Nevins and Uhlig just paid me a little visit. Did you copy them everything you copied to me last week?'

'The files, tapes, Hitchens gave them everything.'

'Yeah, well, they must've made the cannoli connection. They're coming after the case, Jaye. You're going to have to hang on.'

'What are you talking about? The bureau can't just take over a murder investigation.'

'They'll find a way. They won't take it away but they'll take charge. I think they know there's more than the gun connecting the cases. They're assholes but they're smart assholes. I think they figured out the same thing I did once they looked at the tapes you gave them. They know it's the same shooter and that there is something hooking all three of these hits together. They came by to intimidate me, to get me off it. Next it will be you.'

'If they think I'm just going to turn this whole thing over to them and –'

'It's not you. They'll go to Hitchens. And if he doesn't agree to back off, then they go farther up the ladder. I was one of them, remember? I know how it works. The higher you go, the more pressure points.'

'Damn!'

'Welcome to the club.'

'What are you going to do?'

'Me? Tomorrow I'm going back to work. I don't have to answer to the bureau or Hitchens or anybody else. Just myself on this one.'

'Well, you might be the only one with a shot at this. Good luck.'

'Thanks. I could use it.'

26

McCaleb didn't get to the notes and financial records he had taken from Amelia Cordell until the end of the day. Tired from all the desk work, he quickly scanned the notes and came across nothing in the widow's recollections that sparked any interest in him. From the bank statements he quickly determined that Cordell was paid every Wednesday by direct deposit. During the three months for which McCaleb had statements, Cordell had made an ATM withdrawal on every payday at the same bank branch at which he was eventually killed. The significance of this was that it confirmed that, like Gloria Torres's nightly stop at the Sherman Market, Cordell had been following a definable pattern when he had been murdered. It gave more credence to the belief that the shooter had watched his victims – in Cordell's case for a minimum of a week, but probably longer.

McCaleb was glancing through the credit card statements when he felt the boat dip and looked out to see Graciela stepping down into the stern. It was a pleasant surprise.

'Graciela,' he said as he stepped out to the stern. 'What are you doing here?'

'You didn't get my message?'

'No, I – oh, I haven't checked messages.'

'Well, I called and said I was coming down. I wrote up some things about Glory. Like you asked.'

McCaleb almost groaned. More paperwork. Instead, he told her he appreciated her doing the work so quickly after his request.

He noticed that she carried a duffel bag slung over her arm. He took it from her.

'What's in the bag? You didn't write that much, did you?'

She looked at him and smiled.

'My stuff. I'm thinking about staying over again.'

McCaleb felt a little thrill inside, even though he knew that her staying over didn't necessarily mean they would be sleeping together.

'Where's Raymond?'

'With Mrs Otero. She'll also get him to school tomorrow. I'm taking the day off.'

'How come?'

'So I can be your driver.'

'I already have somebody to drive me. You don't have to take –'

'I know but I want to. Besides, I made an appointment for you at the *Times* with Glory's boss. And I want to go with you when you talk to him.'

'Okay, you got the job.'

She smiled and he led her into the salon.

After McCaleb took her bag down to the stateroom and poured her a glass of wine from a new bottle of red, he sat with her in the stern and began going over the case's new developments. As he told her about Kenyon, her eyes widened as she struggled to accept the idea that there was a connection somewhere between her sister and the murdered criminal.

'Nothing obvious comes to mind, right?' he asked.

'No. I have no idea how they could be . . .'

She didn't finish.

McCaleb shook his head and slouched in his deck chair. She opened her purse and took out the notebook in which she had written down her sister's activities. They went over it. Nothing she had written jumped out at McCaleb as being significant. But he told her the information could still be useful as the case continued to evolve.

'It's amazing how much everything has changed,' he said. 'A week ago this was a basic holdup. Now we have possibilities of the motivation being pathological or even being some kind of contract hit. The random possibility is now third.'

Graciela sipped her wine before speaking.

'It makes it harder, doesn't it?' she asked in a soft voice.

'No,' he said. 'It just means we're getting close. You have to open up and let all of the possibilities in. Then sift it out . . . All of this just means we're getting close.'

After they watched the sunset, Graciela drove them to a small Italian restaurant in the Belmont Shores section of Long Beach. McCaleb liked the food and they had the privacy of one of the restaurant's three round booths. During dinner McCaleb had tried to change the subject, sensing that Graciela was still depressed by the turns of the investigation. He told her some lame jokes he remembered from his bureau days but they barely brought a smile.

'It must have been hard when this was your full-time job,' she said as she pushed her half-finished plate of gnocchi aside. 'I mean, just dealing with these kinds of people all the time. It must have been . . .'

She didn't finish. He just nodded. He didn't think they needed to go there again.

'Do you ever think you'll get past it?'

'What, the job?'

'No, what it did to you. Like that story you told me. The Devil's Keep. The whole thing of what happened to you. Can you get past that?'

He thought for a moment. He sensed that a lot was riding on his answer. She was asking about faith and she was deciding something about him. He knew it was important that his answer be honest yet the correct one. For himself he needed to be correct.

'Graciela, all I can tell you is that I hope I can get past it. I want to be restored. To what, I'm not sure. But I've been empty for a long time and I want to be filled. In my mind, it feels too weird to talk about but it's there. I want you to know that. I don't know if it answers what you need to know about me. But I'm hoping and waiting to have what I think you have.'

He wasn't sure if he was making sense. He slid around in the booth until he was right next to her. He leaned over and kissed her high on the cheek. Shielded by the red-checked tablecloth, he put his hand on her knee and ran it softly across the top of her thigh. It was the kind of caress a lover would undertake. But he was desperate to hold on to her, not to lose her, and he lacked confidence in his words. He had to touch her in some way.

'Can we go?' she asked.

He looked at her a moment.

'Where?'

'To the boat.'

He nodded.

Back at the boat Graciela led him to the stateroom and made love to him without hesitation. As they moved in a slow rhythm, McCaleb felt his heart pounding so strong and hard in his chest that the beat seemed to echo in his temples, a throbbing sensation that urged him on. He was sure she also felt it, pulsing against her own chest, the cadence of life.

At the end, a shudder rolled through his body and he pressed his face hard into the crook of her neck. A short, clipped laugh, like a gasp, involuntarily came from his throat and he hoped she would think it was a cough or a grab for breath. He gently lowered more of his weight onto her and buried his face in the soft nest of hair behind her ear. She ran a hand down his back, then all the way up again, leaving it soft and warm on his neck.

'What's so funny?' she whispered.

'Nothing . . . I'm just happy, that's all.'

He pressed his face tighter against her and whispered into her ear, his nose full of her smell, his heart and mind full of hope.

'You are the one bringing me back,' he said. 'You're my chance.'

She brought her arms up around his neck and pulled him tightly down on her. She didn't say a word.

In the dead of night McCaleb awoke. He had been dreaming of swimming underwater with no need to break the surface for air.

He was on his back, his arm against Graciela's naked back. He felt the warmth of the contact. He thought about raising himself to look over her at the clock but he didn't want to break the seam of their touch. As he closed his eyes to return to the dream, the unmistakable sound of the slider upstairs being slowly rolled open brought him awake. He realized that something – a sound – had woken him from the dream. He felt an icicle go through his chest and he became fully alert. Somebody was on the boat.

The Russian, he thought. Bolotov had found him and had come to make good on his threat. But then he quickly dismissed the possibility, returning to his instinctive belief that the Russian would not be that stupid.

He rolled to the edge of the bed and reached down to the remote phone set on the floor. He hit the speed dial combination for Buddy Lockridge's boat and waited for him to answer. He wanted Lockridge to look at *The Following Sea* and tell him if he could see anyone or anything amiss. The thought of Donald Kenyon being marched to his front door and shot with a fragmenting bullet flashed through his mind. And he realized that whoever was up there probably wasn't counting on Graciela's being on the boat. He suddenly knew that no matter what happened in the next few minutes, the intruder must not and would not get to her.

After four rings Lockridge didn't answer and McCaleb knew he couldn't waste any more time. He quickly got out of bed and headed toward the stateroom's closed door, checking the red glowing numerals of the clock and seeing it was ten minutes past three.

As he quietly opened the door, he thought about his gun. It was in the bottom drawer of the chart table. The intruder was closer to it than McCaleb was and possibly had already found it.

He mentally canvased the lower deck, looking for a weapon and coming up with nothing. He had the door all the way open now.

'What is it?' Graciela whispered from behind him.

He quickly and quietly turned around and came to the bed. He put his hand over her mouth and whispered, 'Somebody's on the boat.'

He felt her body go rigid beneath his.

'They don't know about you. I want you to quietly move over the side and lie down on the floor until I come get you.'

She didn't move.

'Do it, Graciela.'

She started to move but then he held her.

'Do you have Mace or any kind of weapon in your purse?'

She shook her head no. He nodded and then pushed her to the side of the bed nearest the wall. He went back to the door.

As McCaleb came quietly up the steps, he could see the slider was half open. There was more light in the salon than below and his vision improved. Suddenly the figure of a man was silhouetted against the exterior light beyond the door. The light seemed to reflect off the figure. McCaleb could not tell if the intruder was staring at him or was turned around, looking out at the marina.

McCaleb knew that the corkscrew he had used to open Graciela's wine earlier was on the galley counter, just to the right at the top of the steps. He could easily get to it. He just had to decide if he would be using it against someone with something better.

He decided there was no choice. As he came to the top stair, he stretched out to reach the corkscrew. The stair creaked and McCaleb saw the silhouette tense. The element of surprise was gone.

'Freeze, asshole!' he yelled as he grabbed the corkscrew and moved toward the dark figure.

The intruder quickly moved to the door, going sideways out through it and using one hand to fling it down its track behind him. Grappling to get the door open, McCaleb lost a few seconds and the intruder was up on the dock and running before he was even out of the boat.

Instinctively, he knew he would not be able to catch the intruder but he leaped up onto the dock and gave full-speed chase anyway, the cool night air hardening his skin, the rough wood of the dock planks biting into his bare feet.

As he ran up the slanted gangway he heard a car engine turn over. He jerked open the gate and ran out into the lot just as a car sped through the exit, its tires squealing as they lost grip on the cold asphalt. McCaleb watched it go. It had been too far away for him to get the plate.

'Shit!'

He closed his eyes and brought his hand up and pinched the bridge of his nose. It was a self-hypnosis technique. He tried to commit as many details of what he had just seen to active memory. Red car, small, foreign, worn-out suspension . . . It occurred to him that the car was familiar. But he couldn't place it yet.

McCaleb bent over and put his hands on his knees as a feeling of nausea hit him and his heart seemed to bounce up into a higher gear. He concentrated on long, deep breaths and eventually he felt the beat slow down.

He felt light hit his closed eyelids. He opened his eyes and looked into the beam of an approaching flashlight. It was the marina's security guard, pulling up in his golf cart.

'Mr McCaleb?' the voice behind the light asked. 'That you?'

It was only then that McCaleb finally realized he was naked.

Nothing was missing, nothing was disturbed. At least as far as McCaleb could tell. Nothing appeared out of order. The contents of his leather bag, which he had left on the galley table, seemed to be as he remembered them. He found the thick sheaf of documents he had shoved into the galley cabinet earlier in the day to be where he had left it. McCaleb inspected the sliding door and found scratches from a screwdriver. He knew how easy it was to pop a sliding door with a screwdriver. He also knew that the pop was always louder outside the structure than inside. He had been lucky. Somehow the pop or something else had woken him.

With the security guard, Shel Newbie, watching, McCaleb finished checking every drawer and cabinet in the salon and found nothing amiss.

'What about below?' Newbie asked.

'Not enough time,' McCaleb said. 'I heard him as soon as he opened the door. I guess I scared him off before he did whatever he was coming to do.'

McCaleb was silent as he thought about the possibility that the intruder had not come to steal anything. He thought about Bolotov again but quickly dismissed it. The figure he had seen move sideways through the sliding door was too small to have been the Russian.

'Can I come up? I could make some coffee.'

McCaleb turned to the stairs. Graciela was there. When he had returned to the stateroom to get dressed, he had told her it would be better if she stayed below. But here she was, wearing her pink nightshirt over a pair of baggy gray sweatpants she had taken from his closet. Her hair was a bit disheveled and she couldn't have looked sexier. He stared at her silently for a moment before finally answering.

'Well, we're about to wrap it up, I think.'

'Should I call Pacific Division?' Newbie asked.

McCaleb shook his head.

'It was probably just some dock punk looking to rip off my Loran or the compass,' he said, though he didn't believe it. 'I don't want to drag the police in. We'll be up all night.'

'You sure?'

'Yeah. Thanks for helping, Shel. I appreciate it.'

'Glad to. I guess I'll go back out then. I'm going to have to write up an incident report. In the morning they might want to make an LAPD report anyway.'

'Yeah, that's fine. I just don't feel like waiting up for them to get over here. That run took it out of me. Tomorrow will be fine.'

'Okay, then.'

Newbie saluted and left. McCaleb waited a few moments and then looked at Graciela, who was still in the stairwell.

'You okay?'

'Yes. Scared is all.'

'Why don't you go back down. I'll be right down.'

She went back to the stateroom. McCaleb closed the slider and worked the lock to see if it was still operable. It was. He reached up to the overhead rod racks and took down the wooden gaff handle. He placed it in the door's track and used it as a wedge to hold the door closed. It would do for the night. But he knew he would have to rethink the boat's security.

When he was finished with the door and reasonably assured of security, McCaleb looked down at his bare feet on the salon's Berber carpet. For the first time he realized that the rug was wet. He then remembered how the marina lights had shone off the body of the intruder as he had stood near the door.

27

On the drive up to the *Times* plant in the Valley, McCaleb sat in the passenger seat of Graciela's Volkswagen and was mostly silent. His mind moved over the activities of the night like an anchor dragging across a sandy bottom, seeking but finding no purchase, nothing to grip.

After he had noticed the wet spot on the carpet, he had retraced the chase to the parking lot and found the dock also was wet. It was a cool, crisp night and too early for the morning moisture to have formed. The intruder had clearly been wet when he had broken into the boat. The shine of light on his body indicated he had probably been wearing a wet suit. The question McCaleb could not answer now was *why?*

Before they had left, McCaleb had gone over to Buddy Lockridge's boat to see if his neighbor was there. He found Buddy, looking disheveled as usual, sitting in the cockpit reading a book called *Hocus.* McCaleb asked him if he had spent the night on the boat and he said he had. When asked why he hadn't answered the phone, Buddy insisted that it was because it hadn't rung. McCaleb let it go, thinking either Lockridge had simply been passed out and hadn't heard his call or McCaleb had pushed the wrong speed-dial button.

He told Lockridge that he didn't need him as a driver for the day, but that he wanted to hire him as a diver.

'You want me to scrape your hull?'

'No. I want you to search the hull. And the bottom. And all the piers around the boat.'

'Search? Search for what?'

'I don't know. You'll know it when you see it.'

'Whatever you say. But I ripped my wet suit again doing that Bertram. As soon as I sew it up, I'll go over and check it out.'

'Thanks. Put it on my tab.'

'You got it. Hey, is your lady friend going to be driving you now?'

He was looking past McCaleb at Graciela standing in the stern of *The Following Sea.* McCaleb looked at her and then back at Lockridge.

'No, Buddy. Just today. She's got to introduce me to some people. That okay?'

'Sure. It's okay.'

In the car McCaleb sipped from the mug of coffee he had brought with him and looked out the window, still bothered by Lockridge not having answered his call for help. They were in the Sepulveda Pass, going over the Santa Monica Mountains. Most of the traffic on the 405 was going the other way.

'What are you thinking about?' Graciela asked.

'Last night, I guess,' he said. 'Trying to figure it out. Buddy is going to take a dive under the boat today, maybe find out what the guy was doing.'

'Well, are you sure you want to see this *Times* guy now? We could reschedule it.'

'No, we're already on our way. It can't hurt to talk to as many people as we can. We still don't know what any of this stuff from yesterday means. Until we do, we should keep plugging away.'

'Sounds good. He said we could talk to some of her friends who worked there, too.'

McCaleb nodded and reached down to the leather bag on the floor. It had grown fat with all the documents and tapes he had accumulated. He had decided to leave nothing from the case behind on the boat, in case of another break-in. And adding to the bag's weight was his gun, a Sig-Sauer P-228. Other than at his interview with Bolotov, he hadn't carried the weapon since he had retired from the bureau. But when Graciela went into the shower, he had removed it from its drawer again and slid the clip into it. He did not chamber a round – following the same safety precaution he had always practiced while with the bureau. He then made room for the pistol in his bag by jettisoning his medical kit. His plan was to be back at the boat before it was time for him to take more pills.

He dug through the stacks of paperwork in the bag until he found his legal pad and he opened it to the timeline he had constructed from the reports in the LAPD murder book. He read the top and found what he wanted.

'Annette Stapleton,' he said.

'What about her?'

'You know her? I want to talk to her.'

'She was Glory's friend. She came over once to meet Raymond. And then she was at the funeral. How do you know about her?'

'Her name is in the LAPD stuff. She and your sister talked in the parking lot that night. I want to talk to her about other nights. You know, see if your sister was worried about anything. The LAPD never spent much time with Stapleton. Remember, they were running the random-holdup angle from the start.'

'Bozos.'

'I don't know. It's hard to blame them. They carry a lot of cases and this one looked the way it was set up to look.'

'Still no excuse.'

McCaleb let it go and turned silent. He didn't particularly feel the need to defend Arrango and Walters anyway. He returned to his thoughts on the events of the night and came to one positive conclusion: he was apparently making enough waves to engage a response from someone, though he didn't know what exactly that response had been.

They got to the *L.A. Times* plant ten minutes before their appointment with Glory's supervisor, a man named Clint Neff. The *Times* plant was a huge property at the corner of Winnetka and Prairie in Chatsworth in the northwest corner of Los Angeles. It was a neighborhood of slick office buildings, warehouses and upper-middle-class neighborhoods. The *Times* building looked as though it were made of smoked glass and white plastic. They stopped at a guard station and had to wait while a man in uniform called in to confirm their appointment before lifting the gate. After they parked, McCaleb took the legal pad from his bag to take in with him. The bag itself had become too cumbersome to lug around. He made sure Graciela locked the car before they left it.

Through automatic sliding doors they stepped into a two-story lobby of black marble and terracotta tile. Their steps echoed on the floor. It was cold and austere, and not unlike the paper's coverage of the community, some critics would say.

A white-haired man in a uniform of matching blue pants and shirt came down a hallway and greeted them. The oval patch above the pocket of his shirt said his name was Clint before he got a chance to say it. A set of professional ear protectors like those worn by ground crews at airports was around his neck. Graciela introduced herself and then McCaleb.

'Miss Rivers, all I can say is that we're all real sorry here,' Neff said. 'Your sister was a good gal. A fine worker and a good friend to us.'

'Thank you. She was.'

'If you want to come back, we can sit down for a minute and I can help you as best I can.'

He led the way back down the hall, walking in front of them and throwing conversation over his shoulder.

'Your sister probably told you, but this is where we print all the papers for the Valley edition and then most of the specials we insert in all the editions. You know, the TV magazine and whatnot.'

'Yes, I know,' Graciela said.

'You know, I don't know what good I'll be to you. I told some of the crew you might want to talk to them, too. They said it would be fine.'

They came to a set of stairs and went up.

'Is Annette Stapleton still on the night shift?' McCaleb asked.

'Uh . . . actually, no,' Neff said. He was winded from the climb. 'Nettie . . . got sorta spooked after what happened with Glory and I don't blame her, a thing like that. So she's on days now.'

Neff headed down another hallway toward a set of double doors.

'She's here today?'

'Sure is. You can talk to her if you – the only thing I ask is that you talk to these folks on their breaks. Like Nettie for example. She goes to the break room at ten-thirty and maybe we'll be done by then, so you can talk with her then.'

'No problem,' McCaleb said.

After a few steps in silence Neff turned around to look at McCaleb.

'So you were an FBI man, is that right?'

'Right.'

'That must've been pretty interesting.'

'Sometimes.'

'How come you quit? You look like a young man to me.'

'I guess it got a little too interesting.'

McCaleb looked at Graciela and winked. She smiled. McCaleb was saved from further personal inquiry by the noise of the pressroom. They came to the thick double doors which barely contained the roar of the presses on the other side. From a dispenser attached to the wall next to the doors, Neff pulled two plastic packages containing disposable foam earplugs and handed them to McCaleb and Graciela.

'Better put these in while we walk through. We're running the whole line right now. Printing the *Book Review.* A million-two copies. Those plugs'll knock about thirty decibels off the sound. You still can't hear yourself think, though.'

As they opened the packages and put in the plugs, Neff pulled his ear protectors up and into place. He opened one of the doors and they walked along the line of presses. The sensory impact was tactile as much as it was auditory. The floor vibrated as if they had just stepped into a minor earthquake. The earplugs did little to soften the high-pitched keening of the presses. A heavy thumping sound provided an underlying bass line. Neff led them to a door and into what was obviously the break room. There were long lunch tables and a variety of vending machines. The free spaces on the walls were taken up with corkboards cluttered with company and union announcements and safety-related warnings. The noise was greatly decreased when the door swung shut. They crossed the room and through another door entered Neff's small office. As Neff pulled his ear set down around his neck again, McCaleb and Graciela pulled their plugs.

'Better hang on to those,' Neff said. 'You go out the way you came in. Depending on when that is, we might be rolling out there.'

McCaleb took the plastic bag out of his pocket and put the plugs in it. Neff took the seat behind his desk and signaled them to two in front of it. The vinyl padding of the seat McCaleb was assigned was smeared with ink. He hesitated before sitting.

'Don't worry,' Neff said, 'it's dry.'

For the next fifteen minutes they talked to Neff about Gloria Torres and got very little usable or salient information. It was clear that Neff liked Glory but it was also clear that his relationship was typical of most supervisor-employee interaction. It was primarily job focused and there was little personal information passed back and forth. When asked if he knew of anything that could have been troubling Glory, Neff shook his head and said he wished he knew something that would help. Any disputes with fellow employees? Same shake of the head.

Out of the blue McCaleb asked him if he knew James Cordell.

'Who's that?' Neff said.

'What about Donald Kenyon?'

'What, that savings and loan guy?' Neff smiled. 'Yeah, we were pals. At the country club. Milken and that guy, Boesky, hung out with us, too.'

McCaleb returned the smile and nodded. It was clear Neff was not going to be of much help. His mind drifted and Graciela asked Neff questions about who Glory's friends were. McCaleb thought about the ink-stained chair upon which he sat. He knew where the ink came from. Probably everyone who sat in the chair before him was someone called in off the press line. It was why they all wore the navy blue uniforms. To hide the ink.

A thought occurred to him. Glory had been on her way home from work when she was killed. But she wasn't in any uniform. She had changed. Here. But there had been nothing in the LAPD report about detectives finding work clothes in her car or checking the contents of a locker.

'Excuse me,' McCaleb said, interrupting Neff as he told Graciela about how skilled her sister was at driving a forklift that loaded huge rolls of newsprint into the presses. 'Is there a locker room? Did Glory have a locker?'

'Sure, we got a locker room. Who wants to get into their automobile covered with ink? We've got complete fa –'

'Would Glory's locker have been cleaned out yet?'

Neff sat back and thought a moment.

'You know, we got another hiring freeze here. We haven't been able to get permission to replace Glory. Since we haven't done that, I doubt we've cleaned out her locker.'

McCaleb felt a little jump. Maybe it was a break.

'Then is there a key? Can we look at it?'

'Uh, sure, I suppose so. I have to go get the master from the maintenance supervisor.'

Neff left them in his office while he went to get the master key and to find Nettie Stapleton. Since Glory's locker was obviously in the women's locker room, Neff had said before leaving that Nettie would escort Graciela in to search its contents. McCaleb would have to wait in the hallway with Neff. This did not sit well with McCaleb. It was not that he didn't think Graciela capable of searching a locker. It was just that he would look at and treat the locker in its entirety, taking in the subtleties of what he saw the way he studied crime scenes and crime scene tapes.

Soon Neff was back with Stapleton and introductions were made. She remembered Graciela and offered seemingly heartfelt condolences. Neff then led the entourage downstairs to the hallway leading to the locker rooms. McCaleb was going to make one last offer, that if the locker room was empty, he be allowed in. But as they approached the door to the women's locker room, he could hear the sound of the showers running. He knew he was going to be left out.

McCaleb had run out of things to ask Neff and was short of small talk. While they waited, he slowly sauntered away from the man so that he could avoid idle conversation and personal questions. There were more bulletin boards affixed to the wall between the locker room doors and he acted as though he was reading some of the posted notices.

Four minutes of silence went by in the hallway. McCaleb had moved from one end of the side-by-side bulletin boards to the other. When Graciela and Nettie finally came out, he was staring at a hand-drawn rendering of a liquid drop on a poster attached to the board. The drop was half shaded in with red, indicating that the employees were halfway toward their goal in an ongoing blood drive. Graciela walked up to him.

'Nothing,' she said. 'Just some clothes, a bottle of perfume and her earphones. There were four pictures of Raymond and one of me taped to the door.'

'Earphones?'

'I mean ear protectors. But nothing else.'

'What kind of clothes?'

McCaleb was still staring at the poster as he spoke.

'A couple of fresh uniforms and a top from home and a pair of jeans.'

'You check all the pockets?'

'Yes. Nothing.'

It hit him then, with the impact of an armor-piercing bullet. He leaned forward and put his hand up against the bulletin board for support.

'Terry, what is it?' Graciela said. 'Are you okay?'

He didn't respond. His thoughts were racing. Graciela put her hand to his forehead to feel for fever. He brushed it aside.

'No, it's not that,' he said.

'Is there a problem?' Neff chimed in.

'No,' McCaleb said, a little too loudly. 'We just have to go. I need to get to the car.'

'Is everything all right?'

'Yes,' McCaleb said, again too loudly. 'I'm sorry, but everything's fine. We just have to go.'

McCaleb nodded his thanks to Annette Stapleton and headed down the hallway toward what he believed was the entrance lobby. Graciela followed and Neff called after them, telling them to take their first left.

28

'What was that about? What's going on?'

McCaleb was walking quickly toward the car. He felt that maintaining velocity would somehow help keep the growing dread he was feeling from entirely overtaking his thoughts. Graciela had to trot to keep up.

'The blood.'

'The blood?'

'They both gave blood. Your sister and Cordell. It was right there in front of me all the – I saw that poster and I remembered I saw a letter at Cordell's house . . . and I just knew. Do you have your keys?'

'Listen, slow down, Terry. Slow down.'

He reluctantly slowed his pace and she came up next to him, digging the car keys out of her purse.

'Now tell me what you are talking about.'

'Open the car and I'll show you.'

They reached the car. She unlocked his door first and started around to her side. He slipped in and reached across to open her door. He then leaned forward and started going through the bag on the floor. It was so jammed with paperwork, he had to pull the gun out and place it on the floor mat just so there was room to look through the documents. Graciela got in the car and started watching.

'You can start it,' he said without turning his attention from his task.

'What are you doing?'

He pulled out the Cordell autopsy.

'I'm looking for – shit, this is just the preliminary report.'

He flipped through the protocol to make sure. It was incomplete.

'No toxicology and blood.'

He shoved the autopsy report back into the bag and then the gun. He straightened up.

'We've got to find a phone. I'll call his wife.'

Graciela started the car.

'Fine,' she said. 'We will – we'll go to my house. But you have to tell me what it is you're thinking, Terry.'

'Okay, just give me a minute to think first.'

He slowed the jumble of thoughts streaming through his mind and tried to analyze the jump he had just made.

'I'm talking about the match,' he said. 'The link.'

'What link?'

'What have we been missing? What have we been looking for? The link between these cases. At first the connection was simply the randomness of crime. That's what the cops thought. That's what I thought when I first started looking at it. We had two holdup victims – no connection other than the killer and the chance crossing of his path with the paths of these individuals. This is L.A., this sort of thing happens all the time. The capital of random violence, right?'

Graciela turned onto Sherman Way. They were just a couple of minutes from her home.

'Right.'

'Wrong. Because then we read more into it. We discover a killer who takes personal icons and this suggests something more involved than random collisions of shooter and victim. This suggests a deeper relationship – the targeting, stalking and acquisition of each victim.'

McCaleb stopped. They were passing the Sherman Market and they both wordlessly looked at the store as they went by. McCaleb waited a moment longer before continuing.

'Then all of a sudden we get another wrinkle, another layer of the onion is peeled back. We get the ballistics and it's a whole new ball game. Now we have another murder and what looks like a professional running through this. A hitter. Why? What could possibly be the connection between your sister, James Cordell and Donald Kenyon?'

Graciela didn't answer. She was coming up on Alabama now and moved the car into the left-turn lane.

'Blood,' he said. 'Blood has got to be the link.'

She pulled into the driveway of her home. She turned the engine off.

'Blood,' she said.

McCaleb stared straight ahead at the closed garage door. He spoke slowly, the dread finally catching up with him.

'All this time I've been thinking, What did she see, what did she know? Whose path could she have crossed that would have gotten her killed? You see, I looked at her life and made a judgment. I decided that she didn't have anything that anyone would want to take, so the reason had to be elsewhere. But I missed it. Missed it completely. Your sister was a good mother, a good sister, good employee and friend. But the one thing she had that made her almost unique was her blood. That made what she had inside her so very valuable . . . to someone.'

He waited a beat. He still didn't look at her.

'Someone like me.'

He heard her breath leaving her body and he felt as though it was the hope going out of him. His hope of redemption.

'You're saying she was . . . taken for her organs. You look at a poster back there and can say that?'

He finally looked over at her.

'I just knew it. That's all.'

He opened his door.

'We call Mrs Cordell. She'll tell us her husband's blood type. It will be AB with CMV negative. Perfect match. Then we get Kenyon's blood. It, too, will match. I'd bet on it.'

He turned his body to get out.

'It doesn't make sense,' she said. 'Because you told me Mr Cordell died right there. At the bank. His heart wasn't taken. His organs. It's not the same. And Kenyon. Kenyon died at his house.'

He got out and then leaned down and looked in at her. She was looking out through the windshield now.

'Cordell and Kenyon didn't work out,' he said. 'The shooter learned from them. He finally got it right with your sister.'

McCaleb shut the door and walked toward the house. It was a while before Graciela caught up to him.

Inside, McCaleb sat down on a sectional couch in the living room and Graciela brought him the phone from the kitchen. He realized he had left Amelia Cordell's number in his bag in the car. He also realized that the car was unlocked and his gun was in the bag as well.

As he stepped back outside and approached the car, his eyes casually swept the street. He was looking for the car from the night before at the marina. He saw nothing that remotely matched and no other cars parked along the curb with occupants inside.

Back in the house again, he sat on the couch and punched Amelia Cordell's number into the phone while Graciela sat down in the far corner of the couch and watched him with a distant look on her face. The phone rang five times before a machine picked up. McCaleb left his name, number and the message that he needed James Cordell's blood type as soon as she could get it to him. He clicked off the phone and looked at Graciela.

'Do you know if she works?' she asked.

'No, she doesn't. She could be anywhere.'

He clicked the phone back on and called his own machine to check for messages. There were nine, the machine having accumulated them unplayed since Saturday. He listened to four messages from Jaye Winston and two from Vernon Carruthers that were outdated by events. There was also Graciela's message that she would be coming to the boat Monday. Of the two remaining messages, the first was from Tony Banks, the video tech. He told McCaleb that he had completed the job on the video he had dropped off. The other message was from Jaye Winston again. She had called that morning to tell McCaleb that his prediction had come true. The bureau was increasing its involvement in the investigations of the murders. Hitchens had not only promised full cooperation but was abdicating lead status to agents Nevins and Uhlig. She was frustrated. McCaleb could easily read it in her voice. But so was he. He clicked off and blew out his breath.

'Now what?' Graciela asked.

'I don't know. I need to confirm this . . . this idea before I take the next step.'

'What about the sheriff's detective? She should have the complete autopsy. She'd know the blood type.'

'No.'

He didn't say anything else by way of explanation. He looked around what he could see of the house from the couch. It was small, neatly furnished and kept. There was a large framed photo of Gloria Torres on the top shelf of a china cabinet in the adjoining dining room.

'Why don't you want to call her?' Graciela asked.

'I'm not sure. I just . . . I want to figure things out a little bit before I talk to her. I think I should wait a little while and see if I hear from Mrs Cordell.'

'What about calling the coroner's office directly?'

'No, I don't think that would work, either.'

What he was leaving unsaid was the fact that if he confirmed his theory, it would mean that anyone who benefited from Glory's death would rightly have to be considered a suspect. That included him. Therefore, he did not want to make any inquiry to authorities that might set that into motion. Not until he was ready with a few more answers with which to defend himself.

'I know!' Graciela suddenly said. 'The computer in the blood lab – I can probably confirm it there. Unless his name's been deleted. But I doubt that. I remember coming across the name of a donor who had been dead four years and he was still on there.'

What she was saying made little sense to McCaleb.

'What are you talking about?' he asked.

She looked at her watch and jumped up from her chair.

'Let me change and then we have to hurry. I'll explain everything on the way.'

She then disappeared down a hallway and McCaleb heard a bedroom door close.

29

They got to Holy Cross shortly before noon. Graciela parked in the front lot and they went into the hospital through the general admissions entrance. She did not want to go through the emergency room, since that was where she worked. She explained on the way over that she had been taking a lot of personal days off with little notice to be with Raymond since Gloria's death. But the patience of her supervisors was wearing thin. She didn't think it would be wise to take the day off on one day's notice and flaunt it by walking through the emergency room. Besides, what they were about to do could get her fired. The fewer people who saw her the better.

Once inside the hospital, Graciela, her nurse's uniform and her familiar face, got them where they needed to go. She was like an ambassador for whom all barriers were lifted. No one stopped them. No one questioned them. They took a staff elevator to the fourth floor, arriving a few minutes past twelve.

Graciela had told McCaleb her plan on the way over. She figured they could count on having fifteen minutes to do what they had to do. That was the maximum – just the time it would take for the blood supplies coordinator to go down to the hospital cafeteria, get her lunch and then bring it back up to the pathology lab. The BSC actually had an hour lunch break but it was routine in that job to eat lunch at your desk because there was no replacement while you were gone. The BSC was a nursing position but because the job did not involve direct patient care, no one filled in the spot when the BSC went on break.

As Graciela expected, they got to the path lab at 12:05 and found the BSC desk empty. McCaleb felt his pulse quicken a little bit as he looked at the flying toasters floating across the screen of the computer sitting on the desk. However, the desk sat in a large open lab station. About ten feet from the computer desk was another desk where a woman in a nurse's uniform sat. Graciela showed nothing but ease with the situation.

'Hey, Patrice, what's the haps?' she said cheerfully.

The woman turned from the files she was dealing with in front of her and smiled. She glanced at McCaleb but then looked back at Graciela.

'Graciela,' she said, drawing each syllable out and overdoing the Latin inflection like a television news anchor. 'Nothing's happening, girl. How 'bout you?'

'Nada. Who's the BSC and where's the BSC?'

'It's Patty Kirk for a few days. She went down to get a sandwich a couple minutes ago.'

'Hmmmm,' Graciela said as if it had just dawned on her. 'Well, I'm going to make a quick connect.'

She came around the counter and headed toward the computer.

'We've got an SCW down in emergency with rare blood. I have a feeling this guy's going to run through everything we got and I want to see what's out there.'

'You could've just called up. I would've run it for you.'

'I know but I'm showing my friend, Terry, how we do things around here. Terry, this is Patrice. Patrice, Terry. He's pre-med, UCLA. I'm seeing if I can't talk him out of it.'

Patrice looked at McCaleb and smiled again, then her eyes studied him in an appraising way. He knew what she was thinking.

'I know, it's kind of late,' he said. 'It's a midlife crisis sort of thing.'

'I should say so. Good luck during residency. I've seen twenty-five-year-olds come out of that looking like they were fifty.'

'I know. I'll be ready.'

They smiled at each other and the conversation was finally over. Patrice went back to her files and McCaleb looked at Graciela, who was seated in front of the computer. The toasters were gone and the screen was awake. There was some sort of template with white boxes on it.

'You can come around,' she said. 'Patrice won't bite you.'

Patrice laughed but didn't say anything. McCaleb came around and stood behind her chair. She looked up at him and winked, knowing that he was blocking any view Patrice had of her. He winked back and smiled. Her coolness was impressive. He looked at his watch and then held his arm down so she could see it was now seven after twelve. She turned her attention to the computer.

'Now, we're looking for type AB blood, okay. So what we do is log on here and connect with BOPRA. That's short for Blood and Organ Procurement and Request Agency. That's the big regional blood bank we deal with. Most hospitals around here do.'

'Right.'

She reached up and ran her finger beneath a small piece of paper taped to the monitor above the screen. There was a six-digit number written on it. McCaleb knew this was the access code. On the drive over Graciela had explained how little security was attached to the BOPRA system. The code to access the computer was changed monthly. But the BSC position at Holy Cross was not a full-time position, meaning that nurses assigned to it were put through on rotation. This rotation was also routinely disrupted because nurses who had colds, viruses and any other maladies that did not require them to miss work but required that they be kept away from patients were often assigned to the BSC desk. Because of the high number of people working in the slot, the BOPRA code was simply taped to the monitor each month when it was changed. In eight years as a nurse, Graciela had worked at two other hospitals in Los Angeles. She had said that this practice was the same at each of those hospitals as well. BOPRA had a security system in place that was circumvented in probably every hospital it served.

Graciela typed in the code number followed by the modem command and McCaleb heard the computer dial and then connect to the BOPRA computer.

'Connecting to the mother station,' Graciela said.

McCaleb looked at his watch. They had eight minutes at the most left. The screen went through some welcome templates before settling on an identification and request checklist. Graciela quickly typed in the needed information and continued to describe what she was doing.

'Now we go to the blood request page. We type in what we are looking for and then . . . hocus pocus, we wait.'

She held her hands in front of the screen and wiggled her fingers.

'Graciela, how's Raymond doing?' Patrice asked from behind them. McCaleb turned and looked back but Patrice was still working with her back to them.

'He's good,' Graciela answered. 'It still breaks my heart but he's doing good.'

'Ah, that's good. You gotta bring him in again.'

'I will but he has school. Maybe spring break.'

The screen started printing out an inventory of the availability of type AB blood and the hospital or blood bank location of each pint. While BOPRA was a blood bank itself, it also served as a coordinating agency for smaller banks and hospitals throughout the West.

'Okay,' Graciela said. 'So now we see that there is a pretty good supply of this around. The doctor wants to have at least six units on standby in case our patient with the sucking chest wound needs more surgery. So we click on the order window and put the hold on six. A hold only lasts twenty-four hours. If it's not updated by this time tomorrow, that blood is up for grabs.'

'Okay,' McCaleb said, acting like the student he was supposed to be.

'I'll have to remember to tell Patty to update this tomorrow.'

'What if you called this up and there was no blood?'

On the drive over she had told him to ask the question if there was anyone else in the nurses' station when they connected to BOPRA.

'Good question,' she said as she began moving the computer mouse. 'This is what we do. We go to this icon with the blood droplet on it. We click and that gets us to the donors file. We wait again.'

A few seconds went by and then the screen began filling with names, addresses, phone numbers and other information.

'These are all blood donors with type AB. It shows where they are, how they can be contacted and this other information shows when they gave blood last. You don't want to keep going to the same person all the time. You try to spread it out and you try to find someone either near to us, so they can just come in here, or near to a blood bank. You want it to be convenient for them.'

As she spoke she ran her finger down the list of names. There were about twenty-five of them, from all over the West. She stopped at her sister's name and tapped the screen with her fingernail. Then she kept going. Her finger reached the bottom without coming across the names James Cordell or Donald Kenyon.

McCaleb loudly let out his breath in disappointment but Graciela raised her finger in a *one-moment* gesture. She then hit the screen up key and a new screen of names appeared. There were maybe fifteen more. The name James Cordell sat on top of the new list. She ran her finger down the screen and found Donald Kenyon's name second from the last.

This time McCaleb's breath caught and he just nodded. Graciela looked up at him, the somber look of confirmation in her eyes. McCaleb leaned close to the screen and read the information that followed the names. Cordell hadn't given blood for nine months and it had been more than six years since Kenyon had spared a drop. McCaleb noticed that the final notation after each name was the letter *D* followed by an asterisk. Other names had one or the other but only a few had the combination of both. McCaleb reached down and tapped the screen below the letter.

'What's that? Deceased?'

'No,' Graciela said in a quiet voice. 'The *D* means donor. Organ donor. They signed papers, put it on their driver's licenses, all of that, so that if the time comes that they come into a hospital and die, they can take the organs.'

She looked at him the whole time she said this and McCaleb found it hard to look back at her. He knew what the confirmation meant.

'And the asterisk?'

'I'm not sure.'

She scrolled the screen until she got back to the legend at the top. She ran her finger along the symbols until she got to the asterisk.

'It means CMV negative,' she said. 'Most people carry a non-threatening blood virus called CMV. It's short for some big word. About a quarter of the population doesn't have it. It's something that has to be known to make a complete blood work match between donors and recipients.'

He nodded. It was information he already knew.

'So that's today's lesson,' Graciela said quietly.

She moved the mouse and McCaleb saw the arrow move to the disconnect icon at the top of the screen. He reached down and grabbed her hand before she could click the mouse button and sign off the BOPRA system.

Graciela looked back up at him, the question on her face. McCaleb looked back at Patrice. He couldn't talk. He looked around and saw a clipboard on the counter with some forms on it and a pencil connected to it with a string. He signaled with his hand to Graciela, pointing to Patrice and then back to her and making a talking sign with his fingers. He then grabbed the clipboard and started to write.

'Hey, uh, Patrice, how's Charlie doing?' Graciela asked.

'Oh, he's fine. Still an asshole.'

'Boy, you guys get along so *gooood*!'

'Yeah, we're real lovebirds.'

McCaleb held the clipboard in front of Graciela. He had written three questions.

1. *Can you print out that list?*
2. *Can you call up your sister's file?*
3. *Who got her organs?*

Graciela hiked her shoulders and mouthed the words *I don't know* to him. She then turned to the computer and went to work. First she printed out the list of type AB donors. Thankfully, the computer was attached to a laser printer which did the job almost silently and Patrice paid no notice. McCaleb quickly folded the list lengthwise and put it in his inside coat pocket. Next, Graciela went back to the original welcome screen and pulled down a window of commands. She clicked the mouse on an icon that showed a red heart. A screen that said ORGAN PROCUREMENT SERVICES appeared and there was another template seeking an access code. Graciela hiked her shoulders, looked up at the code taped above the screen and typed it in again.

Nothing.

The arrow switched to an hourglass and nothing happened. McCaleb looked at his watch. It was 12:15, the end of the window of opportunity they had agreed upon. Patty Kirk would be back any moment and they would be discovered. When she had planned all of this out, Graciela hadn't said anything about how they would explain what they were doing if they were caught.

'I think the computer's freezing,' Graciela said.

Out of frustration she whacked the side of the monitor with an open hand. McCaleb always considered it amazing how many people thought this might help a computer. He was about to tell her not to bother when he heard the wheels of Patrice's chair move. He turned to see her getting up. Maybe she was going to take a shot at the computer also.

'There it goes,' Graciela said.

McCaleb kept his body between Patrice's view and the computer.

'Damned thing,' Patrice said. 'It's always doing that. I'm going to go upstairs to the porch for a Coke and a smoke. See you later, Graciela.'

She smiled at McCaleb.

'And nice to meet you,' she added.

McCaleb smiled.

'Nice to meet you,' he said.

'See you later, Patrice,' Graciela added.

Patrice walked around the counter and out into the hallway. She never looked at the computer screen as she passed. When she was gone, McCaleb looked down at the screen. There was a flashing message across it.

LEVEL 1 ACCESS ONLY
TRY AGAIN

'What's that mean?'

'It means I don't have the code to get into that file. What time is it?'

'Time to go. Sign off.'

She clicked on the disconnect button and McCaleb heard the *chick-chick* sound of the telephone connection being broken.

'What were you doing?' Graciela asked. 'What did you want?'

'I'll tell you later. Let's get out of here.'

She got up, moved the chair back the way she had found it and they hurried around the counter. Out in the hallway they took the first right and headed back toward the elevators. They walked quickly, as if they were thieves. There was a woman coming toward them, carrying a can of Coke and a Styrofoam sandwich box. She was about eighty feet away and she was smiling at Graciela.

'Oh, shit,' McCaleb whispered. 'Is that –'

'Yes. We're cool.'

'No, stall her.'

'Why? We're fine.'

He raised his hand to rub his nose and block his words from traveling to the approaching woman.

'The screen saver. They don't usually come on for at least a minute. She'll know.'

'It doesn't matter. We're not stealing government secrets.'

As it turned out, Graciela didn't have to stall. Patty Kirk stalled herself.

'Graciela, what are you doing here?' she said as they approached. 'I just saw Jane Tompkins in the cafeteria and she was bitchin' about you not coming in again.'

They stopped and Patty Kirk stopped.

'Don't tell her I was here!' Graciela urged.

'Well, what are you doing?'

She raised her hand to signal Graciela's uniform.

'This is my friend, Terry. He's pre-med. UCLA. I told him I would show him around today 'cause he might transfer his residency here. I thought with the pinks on, it would be a lot easier to get around. Terry, this is Patty Kirk.'

They shook hands and smiled. McCaleb asked how she was doing and she said fine. He had visions of those flying toasters finally returning to her computer screen.

Patty Kirk looked back at Graciela and shook her head.

'Janie's going to kill you if she finds out. She thought it was something with Raymond again. You owe me big time for this, girl.'

'I know, I know. Just don't tell her, okay? Everybody is mad at me down there. She's the only friend I've got left.'

They said their good-byes and McCaleb and Graciela moved on to the elevator. When Patty Kirk was out of earshot, Graciela asked if the stall was long enough.

'Depends on what the screensaver is set on. But it's probably okay. Let's get out of here.'

*

Back in the Rabbit, Graciela drove out of the hospital lot and headed to the 405 freeway to go south.

'Where to now?' she asked.

'I'm not sure. We have to get into BOPRA somehow. We need the list of recipients. But I doubt we could just drive up and they'd give them to us. Where is BOPRA anyway?'

'West LA, near the airport. But you are right, you're not going to just go in there and be given a list. The whole system is built on confidentiality. I only found you because somebody told me about that newspaper story.'

'Right,' he said.

He was already past that. His mind was racing and it finally snagged on an idea. They were coming up to the freeway entrance.

'Let's go over the hill. To Cedars. I think I know somebody who will help us.'

30

They first went to Bonnie Fox's office in the Cedars west tower. The waiting room was empty and Fox's receptionist, a woman named Gladys who never smiled, confirmed that the doctor was not in.

'She's up in north and I don't expect her back here today,' Gladys said, maintaining her frown. 'Are you here for your records?'

'No, not quite yet.'

McCaleb thanked her and they left. He knew the translation of what Gladys had told them was that Fox was making her rounds on the sixth floor of the north tower, the hospital. They took the third-floor bridge across to north and then the elevator up to the sixth-floor cardiology and transplant ward. McCaleb was growing tired of lugging the heavy leather bag with him.

McCaleb had been on six often enough not to seem out of place. Graciela, still in her nursing uniform, fit in even better. McCaleb led the way down the hall to the left of the elevators to where the transplant waiting and recovery rooms were located as well as the transplant nursing station. There was a good chance he would find Fox somewhere in the area.

As they made their way down the long hallway, McCaleb looked through the doors that were open. He didn't see Fox but he saw the frail forms of mostly older men on beds. These were the rooms for those who waited, hooked to machines, their time getting close and their chances dimming like the quieting of their hearts. As they passed one room, McCaleb saw the young boy he had seen before. The boy was sitting up on a bed, watching television. He appeared to be alone in the room. The wires and tubes snaked out of the sleeve of his hospital gown and ran to the machines and monitors. After he discerned that Fox was not in the room, McCaleb quickly looked away. The young ones were the hardest to take, to even acknowledge. Their organs so new yet inexplicably failing them, a terrible and sometimes fatal life lesson learned for nothing that they had done. For a moment, McCaleb's mind flashed on the Everglades, the gathering of investigators on airboats at Devil's Keep, the black hole into which disappeared his belief that there is a good and valid reason for everything.

They were in luck. As they made the turn to the nurses' station, McCaleb saw Bonnie Fox leaning over the counter and sliding a patient file out of a vertical rack. As she straightened up, she turned and saw them.

'Terry?'

'Hey, Doc.'

'What's wrong? Are you –'

'No, no, everything's fine.'

He held his hands up in a calming gesture.

'Then what are you doing up here? Your records are at my office.'

She seemed to notice Graciela then and clearly didn't recognize her. This added to the confusion already growing on her face.

'I'm not here about the records,' McCaleb said. 'Is there a room – an empty room – that we can use for a few minutes? We need to talk to you.'

'Terry, I'm in the middle of checking on my patients here. It's not right for you to come in here and expect me to –'

'It's important, Doctor. Very important. Give me five minutes and I'm sure you'll agree. If you don't, we're out of here. I'll go pick up my records and be gone.'

She shook her head in annoyance and turned to look at one of the nurses behind the counter.

'Anne, what do we have open?'

One of the nurses leaned to her left and ran her finger down a clipboard.

'Ten, eighteen, thirty-six, take your pick.'

'I'll be in eighteen, since it's close to Mr Koslow. If he rings, tell him I will be in there in five minutes.'

She looked sternly at McCaleb as she said the last two words.

Walking quickly, Fox led them back down the hallway and into room 618. McCaleb entered last and closed the door behind them. He put the heavy bag down on the floor. Fox leaned her hips against the empty bed, put the patient file down next to her and folded her arms. McCaleb could feel the anger coming from her and directed squarely at him.

'You have five minutes. Who is this?'

'This is Graciela Rivers,' McCaleb said. 'I told you about her.'

Fox studied Graciela with unsparing eyes.

'You're the one who started him on this,' she said. 'You know, he won't listen to me but you're a nurse, you should know better. Look at him. His color, the lines under his eyes. A week ago he was fine. He was perfect, goddammit! I'd already taken his file off my desk and put it away. That's how sure I was about him. Now –'

She gestured toward McCaleb's appearance as proof of her point.

'I only did what I felt I had to do,' Graciela said. 'I had to ask –'

'It's been my choice,' McCaleb interrupted. 'Everything. My choice.'

Fox dismissed their explanations with an annoyed shake of her head. She stepped away from the bed and signaled to McCaleb to sit down.

'Take off your shirt and sit down. Start talking. You're down to about four minutes now.'

'I'm not taking off my shirt, Doctor. I want you to listen to what I have to say, not how many times my heart is beating.'

'Fine. Talk. You want to take me away from patients I need to see, fine. Talk.'

She rapped her knuckles on the patient file on the bed.

'Mr Koslow here, he's in the same boat you were in a couple months ago. I'm trying to keep him alive until *maybe* a heart comes along. Then I've got a thirteen-year-old boy who –'

'Are you going to let me tell you why we're here or not?'

'I can't help it. I am so *angry* at you.'

'Well, listen to this and maybe it will change how you feel.'

'I think that's impossible.'

'Can I tell it or not?'

Fox held her hands up in surrender, pursed her lips and bowed to him. Finally, McCaleb began the story. He took ten minutes to summarize the story of his investigation but that was all right. By the five-minute mark, Fox was so transfixed that she wasn't noticing the time. She let him tell it without a single interruption.

'That's it,' he said when he was done. 'That's why we are here.'

Fox's eyes moved back and forth between them for a few moments while she tried to comprehend what McCaleb had just told her. She then began to move about the small space of the room as she recounted her understanding of the story. She wasn't pacing. It was more as though she needed to make room for the story in her mind and was manifesting that need in small movements back and forth that expanded the personal space around her.

'You are saying that you start off with a person who needs an organ – heart, lung, liver, kidney, whatever. But like you, they are of the rare blood group that is type AB with CMV negative. What that translates to is a long, long, possibly unsuccessful wait because only maybe one in two hundred people are in that group, meaning that likewise, only one in two hundred, let's say, livers, that come along would match this person. So have I got this right? You are saying this person decided to improve his odds by going out and shooting people who are in his group because then their organs would become available for transplant?'

She said it with too much sarcasm and that annoyed McCaleb but rather than object, he just nodded.

'And that he got the names of these people in his group from a list of blood donors in the BOPRA computer?'

'Right.'

'But you don't know how he got it.'

'We don't know for sure. But we do know that BOPRA's security system is highly vulnerable to compromise.'

From his pocket McCaleb took out the list that Graciela had printed at Holy Cross. He unfolded it and handed it to Fox.

'I was able to get that today and I don't know the first thing about hacking into computers.'

Fox took the page and waved it at Graciela.

'But you had her to help.'

'We don't know who this person is or who they had to help them. We have to assume that if this person has the connections and ability to hire a contract killer, then he or she could get into the BOPRA computer. The point is, it could be done.'

McCaleb pointed to the list.

'Right there is all that's needed. Everybody on that list is in the group. He would pick one of the donors. He would pick somebody young, do some research. Kenyon was young and fit. A tennis player, equestrian. Cordell was young and strong. Anybody who watched him over some time would know he was fit. A surfer, skier, mountain biker. They both were perfect.'

'Then why kill them – as some sort of practice?' Fox asked.

'No, not practice. It was the real thing but each time things went wrong. With Kenyon the shooter used a fragmenting bullet that pulped his brain and he was dead before they could even get him to the hospital. The killer refined his method. He switched to a full metal jacket load that was fired across the front of the brain. A fatal injury, yes, but not instantaneous. A man who drove up called it in on a cellular phone. Cordell was alive. But the address got screwed up and the paramedics went to the wrong place. Meantime, time goes by, the victim dies at the scene.'

'And again the organs were never harvested,' Fox said, understanding now.

'I hate that word,' Graciela said, her first words in a long time.

'What?' Fox asked.

'Harvested. I hate that. These organs aren't harvested. They're given. By people who cared about other people. They aren't crops on a farm.'

Fox nodded and looked silently at Graciela, seemingly taking her measure all over again.

'It didn't work with Cordell but it was not because of the method,' McCaleb continued. 'So the shooter just went back to his list of potential donors. He –'

'The list from the BOPRA computer.'

'Right. He goes back to the list and picks Gloria Torres. The process starts again. He watches, knows her routine, also knows she is healthy and will do.'

McCaleb looked at Graciela as he said this, afraid the harshness of it would bring another response. She remained quiet. Fox spoke.

'And so now you want to follow this trail of harvested organs and you think the killer – or the person who hired the killer – will have one of them. Do you realize what this sounds like?'

'I know how it sounds,' McCaleb said quickly before she could build on her doubts. 'But there is no other explanation. We need your help with BOPRA.'

'I don't know.'

'Think about it. What are the odds that it could be just a coincidence that the same man – a contract killer, most likely – just happens to gun down three different people from the exact same one-in-two-hundred blood group? You couldn't figure those odds with a computer. Because it can't be coincidence. It's the blood work. The blood work is the connection. The blood work is the motive.'

Fox walked away from them and to the window. McCaleb followed and stood next to her. The room looked down on Beverly Boulevard. He saw the string of businesses across the street, the mystery bookshop and the deli with the Get Well Soon! sign on the roof. He looked at Fox and it looked as though she was staring at her own reflection in the window.

'I have patients waiting,' she said.

'We need your help.'

'What exactly can I do?'

'I'm not sure. But I think you stand a better chance of getting information out of BOPRA than us.'

'Why don't you just go to the police? They have the best chance. Why are you involving me?'

'I can't go to them. Not yet. I go to them and I'm out of it, off the case. Think about what I just told you. I'm a suspect.'

'That's crazy.'

'I know that. But they won't. Besides, that doesn't matter. This is personal. I owe it to Glory Torres and I owe it to Graciela. I'm not going to sit on the sidelines on this one.'

A small bit of silence slipped by.

'Doctor?'

Graciela had come up behind them. They turned to her.

'You have to help. If you don't, then all of this – everything you do here – means nothing. If you can't protect the integrity of the system you work in, then you have no system.'

The two women stared at each other for a long moment and then Fox smiled sadly and nodded.

'Go to my office and wait for me,' she said. 'I have to see Mr Koslow and one other patient. It will take me a half hour at the most. After that I'll come to the office and make the call.'

31

'The coordinator's office.'

'Glenn Leopold, please, this is Bonnie Fox calling.'

They were in Fox's office with the door closed. Fox had the phone speaker on so McCaleb and Graciela could listen. They had waited for her a half hour before she had come in. Her demeanor was different. She was still going to help but McCaleb noticed that she was more agitated than she had appeared when they had gathered in the empty patient room in the north tower. They had gone over a plan McCaleb came up with while waiting, Fox had taken a couple of notes to refer to and then placed the call.

'Bonnie?'

'Hi, Glenn, how are you?'

'I'm fine. What can I do you for? I've got about ten minutes before a meeting.'

'This shouldn't take long. I've got a slight problem here, Glenn, and I think you might be able to help me.'

'Tell me.'

'I performed a transplant here February ninth – it was BOPRA file number ninety-eight thirty-six – and a complication has come up. What I'd like to do is speak with the surgeons who performed transplants with the donor's other organs.'

There was a brief silence before Leopold's voice came up on the speaker again.

'Uh, let's see . . . I mean, this is kind of unusual. What sort of complication are we talking about, Bonnie?'

'Well, I know you have your meeting. To make it as brief as possible, the recipient's blood group was type AB with CMV negative. The organ we received through BOPRA matched that – according to the protocol. But now – what are we, nine weeks or so post-op – our recipient has developed CMV virus and we are showing rejection in the blood work from the latest biopsy. I am trying to isolate how this has happened.'

More silence.

'Well, I think it would have come up before now if it came in with the heart.'

'That's true but we weren't looking for it before. We assumed based on the protocol that there was no CMV. Don't get me wrong, Glenn, I am not saying it came in with the heart. But I have to find out where it came from and I want to cover everything. Best place to start is with the heart.'

'Are you trying to isolate this, as you say, at the request of attorneys? Because if that's what you are doing, then I think I need to get my –'

'No, no, Glenn, this is just me. I need to know if the virus came in with the organ or there was – is – a problem right here.'

'Well, what blood did you use?'

'That's just it, we only used the patient's own blood. I have the file right here. He stored eight units long before surgery. We only used six.'

'And you are sure you used *his* six?'

Leopold's voice was now showing some agitation. Fox was looking at McCaleb as she answered and he saw how uncomfortable it was for her to be deceitful with the BOPRA organ coordinator.

'All I can say is that we followed procedures and I personally double-checked the bag labels before surgery. They were his labels. I have to assume it was his blood.'

'What do you want from us, Bonnie?'

'A list. What organ went to what patient, and the attending surgeon I can call.'

'I don't know. I think maybe I should –'

'Glenn, listen, it is nothing personal, but my patient is having this problem and I need to check this out for myself. I have to be satisfied myself. I will keep it contained, if that's what you are worried about. No one is talking about lawyers or malpractice. We just need to find out how this happened. For all we know, you are right, it's a blood mix-up. But I am sure you would agree that the place to start with something like this is with the new tissue that's been introduced to the patient.'

McCaleb held his breath. They were at the pivotal point. Fox needed to get the names herself. She couldn't let Leopold say he would check it out himself and get back to her.

'I suppose . . .'

Leopold trailed off and Fox leaned forward, folded her arms on the desk and put her head down. In the silence McCaleb heard a sound from the phone that he identified as computer keys being tapped. He felt a slight charge as he realized that Leopold was probably calling up the file on his computer.

McCaleb stood up and leaned over the desk and gently tapped Fox on the elbow. She looked up at him and he made a circular motion with his hand, signaling her to keep going.

'Glenn?' she said. 'What do you think?'

'I'm looking at it right now . . . Harvest occurred at Holy Cross . . . There is nothing here on the donor profile indicating CMV. Nothing. This person was a long-time blood donor. I think it would have come up before if she –'

'That's probably true but I need to double-check. Even if just for my own peace of mind.'

'I understand.'

More sounds of the computer keyboard being played.

'Let's see, transportation was . . . by MedicAir . . . The liver was transplanted right there with the heart at Cedars. Do you know Dr Spivak? Daniel Spivak?'

'No.'

McCaleb grabbed a legal pad from his bag and started writing.

'Well, he did that one. Let's see, the lungs –'

'I'll call Spivak,' Fox interrupted. 'What's the patient's name?'

'Um . . . really going to have to ask you to keep all of this in the strictest confidence, Bonnie.'

'Absolutely.'

'It was J. B. Dickey.'

McCaleb wrote it down.

'Okay,' Fox said. 'You were on to the lungs.'

'Uh, yes, lungs. No takers without the heart. Your patient got the heart.'

'Right. What about bone marrow transfer?'

'You want everything, I guess. The marrow . . . uh, the marrow we did not do well with. We missed the window. The tissue was flown to San Francisco but by the time MedicAir got up there, they had a weather delay. They were redirected to San Jose but with the delay and the ground traffic and everything, it took too long getting up to St Joseph's. We missed the chance. From what I understand, the patient later expired. As you know, this blood group is tough. That was probably our one chance on that one.'

That brought another measure of silence. McCaleb looked at Graciela. Her eyes were downcast and he couldn't read her. For the first time he considered what she was going through. They were talking about her sister and the people she had helped save. But it was all said in such a clinical manner. Graciela was a nurse and was used to such discussions about patients. But not her sister.

McCaleb wrote 'bone marrow' on the page and then drew a line through the words. He then made the *keep-it-rolling* hand motion to Fox again.

'What about kidneys?' she asked.

'The kidneys . . . The kidneys were split. Let's see what we've got on the kidneys . . .'

Over the next four minutes Leopold went down the list of items mined from the body of Gloria Torres and redistributed to living patients. McCaleb wrote it all down, now keeping his eyes on the legal pad and not wanting to look at Graciela again to see how she was handling having to listen to such a grim inventory.

'That's it,' Leopold finally said.

McCaleb, energized by getting the names but exhausted by the cliff walk it took in getting them, blew his breath out loudly. Too loudly.

'Bonnie?' Leopold said quietly. 'Are you alone? You didn't tell me you were with –'

'No, it's just me, Glenn. I'm alone.'

Silence. Fox threw an angry look at McCaleb, then closed her eyes tightly and waited.

'Well, okay,' Leopold finally said. 'I thought I heard someone else there, that's all, and I have to reiterate that this information is highly confidential in –'

'I know that, Glenn.'

'– nature. I've broken my own rules by giving it to you.'

'I understand.' Fox opened her eyes. 'I will make my inquiries discreetly, Glenn, and . . . I'll let you know what I find.'

'Perfect.'

After a few more exchanges of small talk, the call was ended. Fox pushed the phone's disconnect button and brought her head back down on her folded arms.

'God . . . I can't believe what I just did. I . . . lied to this man. *Lied* to a colleague. When he finds out, he's . . .'

She didn't finish. She just shook her head on the cradle of her arms.

'Doctor,' McCaleb tried. 'You did the right thing. There is no harm to him and he'll probably never know what was done with the information. Tomorrow you can call him and say you isolated the CMV problem and it wasn't from the donor. Tell him you destroyed the notes on the other recipients.'

Fox brought her head up and looked at him.

'It doesn't matter. I was deceitful. I hate having to be deceitful. If he finds out, he'll never trust me again.'

McCaleb just looked at her. He had no answer to that.

'You have to promise me one thing,' Fox said. 'That if your theory proves out, that if you are right, then you get whoever did this. That will be the only way I'll be able to accept this. It will be my only defense.'

McCaleb nodded. He came around the desk and leaned down and hugged Fox.

'Thank you,' Graciela said softly. 'You did good.'

Fox smiled weakly at her and nodded.

'One last thing,' McCaleb said. 'Do you have a copying machine?'

32

The elevator down was packed and silent except for the music piped in, which McCaleb identified as an old Louis Jourdan recording of 'Knock Me a Kiss'.

As they stepped out, McCaleb pointed Graciela in the direction of the doors leading to the tramway that would take her to the parking garage.

'You go that way.'

'Why? Where are you going?'

'I'm just going to take a cab back to the boat.'

'Well, what are you going to do? I want to go with you.'

He pulled her to the side of the busy elevator lobby.

'You've got to go back home to Raymond and your job. In fact, Raymond, he's your job. This is my job. This is what you asked me to do.'

'I know but I want to help.'

'You did help. You are helping. But you've got to go to Raymond. I'm going out through the emergency room. There are always cabs down there.'

She frowned. He could tell by her expression that she knew he was right but it didn't sit well. He reached into his pocket and pulled out the photocopy of the list he had made in Fox's office.

'Here, take this. If something happens to me, you have a copy. Give it to Jaye Winston at the sheriff's office.'

'What do you mean if something happens?'

Her voice was almost shrill and McCaleb immediately regretted his choice of words. He moved her into a little alcove where there were pay phones. No one was using the phones and they had a small measure of privacy. He put the bag on the floor between his feet and leaned forward so his eyes were close to hers.

'Don't worry, nothing is going to happen,' he said. 'It's just that all this work I've done, ever since you came to the boat that day, it all has led to this. The names on this paper. I just think it's better if we both have a copy of it, that's all.'

'Do you really think the killer's name is on there?'

'I don't know. That's what I'm going to think about and work on when I get to the boat.'

'I can help you.'

'I know you can, Graciela. You already have. But right now you have to pull back a little bit and be with Raymond. You don't have to worry. I am going to be on the phone telling you everything that happens. Remember, I'm working for you.'

She tried a half smile.

'No, you're not. All I had to do was tell you about Glory and after that you were doing what your heart told you.'

'Maybe.'

'How about if I take you and just drop you off at the boat?'

'No way. That will take you into rush hour and you'll be driving for two hours. Go now, while you can. Go be with Raymond.'

She finally nodded. Still leaning down into her face, McCaleb brought his hands up to her shoulders and gently pulled her into a kiss.

'Graciela?'

'What?'

'There's something else, too.'

'What is it?'

'I want you to think about this, think about if I'm right. I have to think about this.'

'What do you mean?'

'If I'm right, if somebody killed Glory for something she had inside, then in a way they killed her for me as well. I got a part of her, too. If that's true, then can we . . .'

He didn't finish the question and she didn't say anything for a long moment. Her eyes dropped their focus to his chest.

'I know that,' she finally said. 'But you didn't do anything. You didn't cause this.'

'Well, I want you to think about it and just be sure.'

She nodded.

'It's God's way of making something good out of something so bad.'

McCaleb leaned his forehead against hers. He didn't say anything.

'I know what you told me and I know that story about Aubrey-Lynn. It's all the more reason to believe. I wish you would try.'

He pulled her into an embrace and whispered into her ear.

'Okay, I'll try.'

A man with a thick briefcase stepped into the alcove and went to one of the phones. He glanced at them and did a double take when he saw Graciela's nursing uniform. He obviously believed it was a Cedars nurse engaging in some form of unprofessional conduct. It ended the moment for McCaleb. He broke the embrace and looked into Graciela's face.

'You be careful and say hello to Raymond for me. Tell him I want to go fishing again.'

She smiled and nodded.

'You be careful, too. And call me.'

'I will.'

She leaned forward and kissed him quickly and then headed off in the direction of the parking garage. McCaleb glanced at the man on the phone and then walked away in the opposite direction.

33

There were no taxi cabs waiting at the curb outside the emergency room. McCaleb decided to change his plan. He hadn't eaten anything since breakfast and was growing weak with hunger. He felt a low-grade migraine beginning to throb at the base of his skull and knew if he didn't refuel, it would soon crawl over the top of him and encase his whole head. He decided to call Buddy Lockridge to come get him, then have a turkey and coleslaw sandwich from across the street at Jerry's Deli while he waited. The more he thought about the good sandwiches they made over there, the hungrier he got. Once Buddy arrived, they could drive over to Video GraFX Consultants in Hollywood to pick up the tape and the hard copy of the frame Tony Banks had enhanced for him.

He quickly stepped back into the ER lobby and over to the pay phone alcove. There was a young woman on one of the phones tearfully telling someone about somebody else who was apparently being treated in the ER. McCaleb noticed that one nostril and her lower lip were pierced with silver hoops connected by a chain of safety pins.

'He didn't know me, he didn't know Danny,' she wailed. 'He's totally fucked up and they're also calling the cops.'

Momentarily distracted by the safety pins and wondering what would happen if the woman yawned, McCaleb picked up the phone furthest from her and tried to tune her out. He was about to give up on Lockridge after six rings – on a boat like the *Double-Down*, you can't be more than four rings away – when Buddy finally picked up.

'Yo, Buddy, ready to go to work?'

'Terry?'

Before McCaleb could answer, Lockridge's voice dropped to a whisper.

'Man, where are you at?'

'Cedars. I need you to pick me up. What's the matter?'

'Well, I'll pick you up but I'm not sure you want to come back here.'

'Buddy, listen to me. Skip the bullshit and tell me exactly *what* is going on.'

'I'm not sure, man, but you've got people all over your boat.'

'What people?'

'Well, two of them are those two guys in the suits who were here yesterday.'

Nevins and Uhlig.

'They are *inside* my boat?'

'Yeah, inside. Also, they pulled the cover off your Cherokee and have a tow truck out there. I think they're going to take it. I went over there to see what was going on and they almost put me down on the boards. Showed me their badges and a search warrant and told me to get lost. They weren't nice about it. They're searching the boat.'

'Shit!'

McCaleb looked over and saw that his outburst had drawn the attention of the crying woman. He turned his back toward her.

'Buddy, where are you, up top or below?'

'Below.'

'Can you see my boat right now?'

'Sure. I'm looking out the galley window.'

'How many people you see?'

'Well, some are inside. But altogether I think there are four or five of them over there. And there's a couple more with the Cherokee.'

'Is there a woman?'

'Yeah.'

McCaleb described Jaye Winston as best as he could and Lockridge confirmed that a woman matching the description was on the boat.

'She's in the salon right now. It looked like before when I was looking at her that she was just sort of watching.'

McCaleb nodded. His mind was running over the possibilities of what was happening. Each way he looked at it, things added up the same way. The fact that Nevins and Uhlig knew he had FBI documents would not have engendered such a response – a warrant search with a full team. There was only one other possibility. He had become an official suspect. Accepting this, he thought about how Nevins and Uhlig would conduct an evidentiary search.

'Buddy,' he said, 'have you seen them taking anything off the boat? I'm talking about in plastic bags or brown paper bags, like from Lucky's.'

'Yeah, there's been some bags. They put them up on the dock. But you don't have to worry, Terror.'

'What do you mean?'

'I don't think they're going to find what they're really looking for.'

'What are you –'

'Not on the phone, man. You want me to come get you now?'

McCaleb stopped. What was he saying? What was going on?

'Hang tight,' he finally said. 'I'll call you right back.'

McCaleb hung up and immediately dropped in another quarter. He called his own phone number. No one answered. The machine answered and he heard his own tape-recorded voice telling him to leave a message. After the beep he said, 'Jaye Winston, if you're there, pick up.'

He waited for a beat of silence and was about to say it again when the phone was picked up. He felt a slight sense of relief when he recognized Winston's voice.

'This is Winston.'

'This is McCaleb.'

That was all. He figured he would see how she wanted to play it. He would be better able to judge where he stood by the way she handled the call.

'Uh . . . Terry,' she said. 'How did you – where are you?'

Whatever relief he was feeling now started to slip away. Its replacement was dread. He had given her the opportunity to talk to him obliquely, perhaps in code, acting as though she was talking to a fellow deputy or even Captain Hitchens. But she had used his name.

'Doesn't matter where I am,' he said. 'What are you doing on my boat?'

'Why don't you come here and we'll talk about it?'

'No, I want to talk about it now. I'm a suspect? That's what this is about?'

'Look, Terry, don't make this more complicated than it has to be. Why don't you –'

'Is there an arrest warrant? Just answer me that.'

'No, Terry, there isn't.'

'But I am a suspect.'

'Terry, why didn't you tell me you have a black Cherokee?'

McCaleb was stunned as he suddenly realized how things fit together with him in the middle.

'You never asked. Listen to what you are saying, what you are thinking. Would I get involved in all of this, the investigation, bring the bureau in, all of it, if I was the shooter? Are you serious?'

'You got to our only witness.'

'What?'

'You got to Noone. You got inside the investigation and got to the only witness. You hypnotized him, Terry. Now he's no good to us. The one person who might have been able to make the ID and we lost him. He –'

She stopped as there was a click as another phone was picked up.

'McCaleb? This is Nevins. What's your location?'

'Nevins, I'm not talking to you. You've got your head up your ass. I'm only –'

'Listen to me, I'm trying to be civil. We can do this easy and quiet or we can go big time. You decide, my friend. You have to come in and we'll talk about it and let the chips fall.'

McCaleb's mind quickly went over the facts. Nevins and the others had come to the same conclusion that he had come to. They had made the blood work connection. The fact that McCaleb was a direct beneficiary of the Torres killing made him a suspect. He imagined them running his name on the computer and coming up with the registration of the Cherokee. It was probably the piece that sent them over the top. They got a search warrant and went to the boat.

McCaleb felt the cold hand of fear clasp his neck. The intruder from the night before. It began to dawn on him that it wasn't a question of what he had wanted. It was *what had he planted.* He thought about what Buddy had said moments before about the agents not finding what they were looking for. And the picture was taking form.

'Nevins, I'll come in. But you tell me first, what have you got there? What have you found?'

'No, Terry, we don't play it like that. You come in and then we talk about all of this.'

'I'm hanging up, Nevins. Last chance.'

'Don't go in any post offices, McCaleb. Your picture's going to be on the wall. As soon as we get the package together.'

McCaleb hung up, held his hand on the phone and leaned his forehead against it. He wasn't sure what was going on or what to do. What had they found? What had the intruder hidden in the boat?

'You okay?'

He jerked around and it was the girl with the pierced nose and lip.

'Fine. You?'

'I am now. I just had to talk to somebody.'

'I know the feeling.'

She left the phone alcove then and McCaleb picked up the receiver again and dropped another quarter. Buddy picked up on half a ring.

'All right, listen,' McCaleb said. 'I want you to come get me. But you're not going to be able to just walk out of there.'

'How come? It's a free –'

'Because I just talked to them and they know someone tipped me that they were there. So this is what I want you to do. Take off your shoes and put your keys and wallet inside them. Then get your laundry basket and stick your shoes in it and cover them up with clothes. Then carry the basket out of there and make –'

'I don't have any laundry in the basket, Terry. I did laundry this morning, before any of these people showed up.'

'Fine, Buddy. Take some clothes – clean clothes – and put them in the basket so it looks like you've got dirty clothes. Hide your shoes. Make it look like you are only going over to the laundry. Don't close the hatch on your boat and make sure you are carrying four quarters in your hand. They'll stop you but if you play it right, they'll believe you and let you go. Then get in your car and come get me.'

'They might follow me.'

'No. They probably won't even watch you once they let you go to the laundry. Maybe you should go to the laundry first, then to your car.'

'Okay. So where do I find you?'

McCaleb didn't hesitate. He had grown to trust Lockridge. Besides, he knew he could take precautions at his end.

After hanging up, McCaleb called Tony Banks and told him that he would be coming by. Banks said he would be there.

McCaleb walked into Jerry's Famous Deli and ordered a turkey sandwich with coleslaw and Russian dressing to go. He also ordered a sliced pickle and a can of Coke. After he paid for the sandwich, he took it out and crossed Beverly Boulevard back to Cedars. He had spent so many days and nights in the medical center he knew its layout by rote. He took the elevator to the third floor maternity ward, where he knew of a waiting room that looked out across the helipad to Beverly Boulevard and Jerry's. It was not unusual to see an expectant father wolfing down a deli sandwich in the waiting room. McCaleb knew he could sit up there and eat and wait and watch for Buddy Lockridge.

The sandwich lasted less than five minutes but the wait for Buddy Lockridge went on for an hour with no sighting of Lockridge. McCaleb watched two helicopters come in with deliveries of transplant organs packed in red coolers.

He was about to call the *Double-Down* to see if the agents had held Lockridge up when he finally saw Buddy's familiar Taurus pull up to the front of the deli. McCaleb walked to the window and looked long and far up and down Beverly Boulevard, then checked the sky for anything that looked like a law enforcement helicopter. He left the window and headed to the elevator.

A plastic laundry basket full of clothes was on the back seat of the Taurus. McCaleb got in, looked at it and then over at Lockridge, who was playing some unrecognizable tune on his harp.

'Thanks for coming, Buddy. Any problems?'

Lockridge dropped the harmonica into the door pocket.

'Nah. They stopped me like you said they would and asked their questions. But I played dumb; they let me go. I think it was 'cause I only had the four quarters on me that they let me go. That was a smart move, Terry.'

'We'll see. Who was it who stopped you? The two suits?'

'No, it was two other guys and they were cops, not agents. At least they said so, but they didn't give me their names.'

'Was one a big wide guy, Latino, with maybe a toothpick in his mouth.'

'You got it. That's him.'

Arrango. McCaleb found a little bit of satisfaction in putting one past the pompous jerk.

'So where to?' Buddy asked.

McCaleb had thought about this while he waited. And he knew he had to get to work on the list of transplant recipients. He had to get on it quickly. But before he did that, he wanted to make sure he had all his ducks in a row. He had come to look at investigations as being similar to the extension ladders on fire trucks. You kept extending the reach further, and the further out you went, the more wobbly it was out on the end. You could not neglect the base, the start of the investigation. Every loose detail that could be nailed down had to be put in its exact place. And so, he felt now, he had to finish the timeline. He had to answer the questions that he himself had raised before going on to the end of the ladder. It was his philosophy as well as instinct that told him to do this. He was playing out a hunch that within the contradictions he would find a truth.

'Hollywood,' he told Lockridge.

'That video place we went before?'

'You got it. We go to Hollywood first, then up to the Valley.'

*

Lockridge headed a few short blocks up to Melrose Boulevard before turning east toward Hollywood.

'All right, let's hear it,' McCaleb said. 'What were you talking about on the phone, about them not finding what they were looking for?'

'Check out the laundry basket, man.'

'Why?'

'Just take a look.'

He turned his head toward McCaleb and jerked it in the direction of the backseat. McCaleb unsnapped his seat belt and turned around to reach over the seat. As he did so, he checked the cars behind them. There was lots of traffic but no cars that raised any suspicion.

He dropped his eyes to the basket. It was full of underwear and socks. That had been a nice touch by Buddy. It made it less likely Nevins or anybody else would look through the basket when they stopped him.

'This stuff is clean, right?'

' 'Course. It's on the bottom.'

McCaleb brought his knees up onto the seat and leaned all the way over. He dumped the contents of the laundry basket on the backseat. He heard the dull thud of something heavier than clothes hitting the seat. He moved a pair of loud boxer shorts out of the way and saw a plastic Ziploc bag that contained a pistol.

Silently, McCaleb slid back into his seat, holding the bag containing the gun. He smoothed the plastic, which had been yellowed from within by a film of gun oil, so that he could get a better look at the weapon. He felt a sweat break across the back of his neck. The gun in the bag was an HK P7. And he didn't need any ballistics report to know it was *the* HK P7, the weapon that had killed Kenyon, then Cordell, then Torres. He bent down to look closely at the weapon and saw that the serial number had been burned away with acid. The gun was untraceable.

A tremor rolled through McCaleb's hands as he held the murder weapon. His body slumped against the door and his feelings jumped between the anguish of knowing the history of the object he now held in his hands and despair at the thought of his predicament. Someone was setting McCaleb up and the frame would probably have been all but unbreakable if Buddy Lockridge had not found the gun when he went into the dark waters beneath *The Following Sea.*

'Jesus,' McCaleb said in a whisper.

'Looks pretty mean, don't it?'

'Where exactly was it?'

'It was in a diving bag hanging about six feet below your stern. It was tied off on one of the underside eyelets. If you knew it was there, you could reach under with a gaff and hook the line and bring it up. But you had to know it was there. Otherwise, you wouldn't see it from up above.'

'Did the people doing the search go into the water today?'

'Yeah, one diver. He went down, but by then I'd already checked around like you asked. I beat him to it.'

McCaleb nodded and put the gun down on the floor between his feet.

Staring down at it, he folded his arms across his chest as if protecting himself against a chill. It had been that close. And though he was sitting next to the man who had saved him for the time being, an overwhelming sense of isolation came over him. He felt completely alone. And he felt the flickering onset of something he had only read about before – the fight-or-flight syndrome. He felt an almost violent urge to forget about everything and run. Just cut and run and get as far away from all of this as he could.

'I'm in big trouble, Buddy,' he said.

'I kind of figured that,' his driver replied.

34

McCaleb had composed himself and was resolved by the time they reached Video GraFX Consultants. On the way he had examined the possibility of flight and then quickly discarded it. Fight was the only choice. He knew that he was tethered in place by his heart – to flee was to die, for he needed the carefully set post-op drug therapy to prevent his body from rejecting his new heart. To flee would also mean to leave Graciela and Raymond. And it felt already as if doing that would wither his heart just as quickly.

Lockridge dropped him off out front and waited in a red zone. The door was locked but Tony Banks had told him to ring the delivery buzzer if he arrived after closing. McCaleb pushed the button twice before Banks answered the door himself. He had a manila envelope with him and he handed it through the open door to McCaleb.

'This everything?'

'The tape and the hard copies. Everything is pretty clear.'

McCaleb took the package.

'What do I owe you, Tony?'

'Not a thing. Glad to help.'

McCaleb nodded and was about to head back to the car but stopped and looked back at Banks.

'I've got to tell you something. I'm not with the bureau anymore, Tony. I apologize if I misled you, but –'

'I know you're not with the bureau anymore.'

'You do?'

'I called your old office yesterday when you didn't return my call from Saturday. The number was on that letter you sent, the letter on the wall. I called and they said you hadn't worked there in something like two years.'

McCaleb studied Banks, really taking the young man's measure for the first time, and then held up the package.

'Then why are you giving me this?'

'Because you are after him, the man on that tape.'

McCaleb nodded.

'Then good luck. I hope you get him.'

Banks closed and locked the door then. McCaleb said thanks but by then the door was already closed.

*

The Sherman Market was empty save for a couple of young girls mulling choices at the candy rack and a young man behind the counter. McCaleb had been hoping to see the same older woman who had been there on his first visit, the widow of Chan Ho Kang. He spoke slowly and clearly to the young man, hoping he understood English better than the woman had.

'I am looking for the woman who works here during the daytime.'

The man – he was really no more than a teenager – looked sullenly at McCaleb.

'You don't have to talk like I'm some kind of retard,' he said. 'I speak English. I was born here.'

'Oh,' McCaleb said, taken aback by his clumsiness. 'Sorry about that. It's just that the woman that was here before, she had a hard time understanding me.'

'My mother. She lived her first thirty years in Korea speaking Korean. You try it sometime. Why don't you move over there and try to be understood in twenty years.'

'Look, I'm sorry.'

McCaleb held his hands up wide and palms out. This wasn't going well. He tried again.

'You are Chan Ho Kang's son?'

The boy nodded.

'Who are you?'

'My name is Terry McCaleb. I'm sorry about the loss of your father.'

'What do you want?'

'I am doing some work for the family of the woman that was killed in here that –'

'What work?'

'I am trying to find the killer.'

'My mother doesn't know anything. Leave her alone. She's had enough.'

'Actually, all I want to do is to look at her watch. I was in here the other day and I noticed she's wearing the watch your father was wearing that night.'

The young man stared blankly at him, then glanced away from him to check on the girls at the candy racks.

'Okay, girls, let's go. Make your choices.'

McCaleb looked back at the girls. They didn't look happy about being hurried about such an important decision.

'What about the watch?'

McCaleb looked back at him.

'Well, it's kind of complicated. There are things that don't add up on the police reports. I am trying to figure out why. To do that, I need to know the exact time the man with the gun came in here.'

He pointed at the video camera on the wall behind and above the counterman.

'The police gave me a copy of the tape. On the tape your father's watch is seen. I have had it enhanced. If your mother has not reset the watch since . . . she started wearing it, then there is a way I can get the time I need.'

'You don't need the watch. The time is on the tape. You said you had the tape.'

'The police say the time on the tape is wrong. That's what I'm trying to find out. Will you call your mother for me?'

The girls came over to the counter then. The man didn't answer McCaleb as he silently took their money and gave them change. He watched them walk out before looking back at McCaleb.

'I don't understand this. It makes no sense to me what you want.'

McCaleb blew out his breath.

'I am trying to help you. Do you want the man who killed your father to be caught?'

'Of course. But this watch business . . . what does it have to do with anything?'

'I could explain it all to you if you had about a half hour but –'

'I'm not going anywhere.'

McCaleb looked at him a moment and decided that it was going to be the only way to go. He nodded and told him to wait while he got a photo out of the car.

The young man's name was Steve Kang. Riding in the front passenger seat, he directed Buddy Lockridge into a neighborhood just a few blocks from where Graciela Rivers and Raymond Torres lived.

McCaleb had convinced him with his long version. The young man had then thought enough of McCaleb's theory to put a Be Back Soon sign on the door and lock up. He normally walked to and from the store, but Lockridge's car would save them time.

When they got to his home, Steve Kang led McCaleb inside while Lockridge waited in the car. The house was virtually identical in design to Graciela's and had probably been built in the early fifties by the same developer. Kang told McCaleb to sit in the living room and he then disappeared down a hallway leading to the bedrooms. McCaleb heard muffled talking from the hallway. After a few seconds he realized the conversation was in Korean.

While he waited, he thought about the similarities in the houses and envisioned the two different families grieving on the night of the shooting and the days after.

Steve Kang came back then. He handed McCaleb a remote phone and the watch his father had worn.

'She did not change anything,' he said. 'It's just the way it was that night.'

McCaleb nodded. From the corner of his eye he noticed movement. He looked to his left and saw Steve Kang's mother standing in the hallway, just watching him. He nodded to her but she didn't respond in any way.

McCaleb had brought the hard copy of the enhanced video frame in with him along with his notebook and phone book. He had told Steve Kang what he planned to do but was still uncomfortable carrying it out in front of him. He was about to impersonate a police officer, which was a crime, even if that officer was Eddie Arrango.

From his phone book he got the number for the Central Communications Center in downtown L.A. He'd had the number since his days with the L.A. field office, when he would at times need to coordinate intra-agency activities. The CCC was the dark, cavernous dispatch center four floors below City Hall from which all police and fire department radio communications were transmitted. It was also where the clock was from which the official time of the murders of Gloria Torres and Chan Ho Kang had been set.

On the drive from Hollywood to the market McCaleb had pulled out the Torres file and gotten Arrango's badge number from the homicide report. He now placed the watch Steve Kang had given him on the arm of the couch and dialed the nonemergency number of the CCC. An operator answered in four rings.

'This is Arrango, West Valley homicide,' McCaleb said. 'That's serial one four one one. I'm not on the radio. I just need a ten-twenty for a surveillance commencement. And could you give me the seconds with that, too?'

'Seconds? Why, you're a precise man, Detective Arrango.'

'Precisely.'

'Hold one.'

McCaleb looked down at the watch. As the operator spoke, he noted the watch time was 5:14:42 P.M.

'That's seventeen fourteen thirty-eight.'

'Gotcha,' he said. 'Thanks.'

He hung up and looked at Steve Kang.

'Your father's watch is running four seconds ahead of the CCC clock.'

Kang narrowed his eyes and he came around the side of the couch to look over McCaleb as he wrote numbers down in his notebook, referred back to specific times listed on the timeline he had put together earlier, and then did the math.

They both arrived at the same conclusion at the same time.

'That means . . .'

Steve Kang didn't finish. McCaleb noticed that he glanced over at his mother in the hallway and then back at the time McCaleb had underlined in the notebook.

'That bastard!' he said in a hateful whisper.

'He's more than that,' McCaleb said.

Outside, Buddy Lockridge started the Taurus as soon as he saw McCaleb leave the house. McCaleb jumped in.

'Let's go.'

'We giving the kid a ride back?'

'No, he's got to talk to his mother. Let's go.'

'Okay, okay. Where to?'

'Back to the boat.'

'The boat? You can't go there, Terry. Those people might still be there. Or they might be watching it.'

'It doesn't matter. I have no choice.'

35

Lockridge dropped McCaleb off at the curb on Cabrillo Way, about half a mile from the marina. He walked the rest of the way, keeping to the shadows cast by the small shops that lined the boulevard. The plan was for Buddy to leave his keys in the Taurus and then go to his boat as if everything about his life was routine and normal. If he saw anything unusual, anyone hanging around the marina who wasn't recognizable, he was to flick on the mast light on the *Double-Down.* McCaleb would be able to see the light from a good distance away and he would keep clear.

When the marina came into sight, McCaleb's eyes scanned the points of the dozens of masts. It was dark now and he saw no lights. Things looked good. He glanced around and spotted a pay phone outside a mini-market and went to it to call Lockridge anyway. It also gave him a chance to put the heavy leather bag down for a spell. Buddy picked up the phone right away.

'Is it safe?' McCaleb asked, remembering the line from a movie he had enjoyed some years before.

'Think so,' Buddy said. 'I don't see anyone and nobody grabbed me on the way in. I didn't see anything that looked like an unmarked cop car out in the lot, either.'

'What's my boat look like?'

There was a silence while Buddy took a look.

'It's still there. Looks like they got yellow tape strung between the piers, like you're not supposed to go on it or something.'

'Okay, Bud, I'm coming in. I'm going to go into the laundry first and stick my bag in one of the dryers. If I go to the boat and get jumped by them, you come get the bag and sit on it until I get out. You okay with that?'

'Sure.'

'Okay, listen. If everything goes okay on the boat, I won't be staying long, so I'm going to say this now, thanks for everything, Buddy, you've been a big help.'

'No sweat, man. I don't care about what these bastards are trying to do to you. I know you're cool.'

McCaleb thanked him again and hung up, then picked up his bag and started carrying it under his arm as he headed toward the marina. He first ducked into the laundry and found an empty dryer in which to stow the bag. He then made it all the way to the boat without problem. Before unlocking the slider he took one last look around the marina and saw nothing amiss, nothing that raised an alarm. He noticed the dark form of Buddy Lockridge sitting in the cockpit of the *Double-Down*. He heard a *wah-wah* tremolo from a harmonica and he nodded toward the shadow figure. He then slid open the door.

The boat smelled stuffy and stale but there was still a lingering scent of perfume. He guessed Jaye Winston had left it behind. He didn't turn on a light but rather reached for the flashlight clamped on the underside of the chart table. He flicked it on and held the light down at his side and pointing at the floor. He headed below, knowing he had to move quickly. He just wanted to grab enough clothes, drugs and medical supplies to last him a few days. He figured, one way or the other, it would be all the time he would get.

He opened one of the hallway hatches and got out the large duffel bag. He then went into the master stateroom and gathered the clothes he would need. Doing it surreptitiously by flashlight slowed the process down but finally he had what he needed.

When he was done, he carried the bag across the hallway to the head to gather drugs, medical supplies and his clipboard. He put the open bag on the sink and was about to begin laying in the pharmaceutical boxes and vials when he realized something. When he had crossed the hallway, there had been a light on topside. The galley light. Or maybe one of the overheads in the salon. He momentarily froze and tried to listen for any sound from above while he reviewed his own movements. He was sure he had not put on a light when he had come in.

He listened nearly half a minute but there was nothing. He quietly stepped back into the hallway and looked up the stairway. He stood stock still and listened again while trying to weigh his options. The only way out besides going back up the stairs was the deck hatch in the roof of the forward stateroom. But it would be foolish to think that whoever was topside didn't have that escape route covered.

'Buddy,' he called. 'Is that you?'

The answer came after a long beat of silence.

'No, Terry, it's not Buddy.'

A female voice. McCaleb recognized it.

'Jaye?'

'Why don't you come on up?'

He looked back into the head. The flashlight was inside the duffel bag, illuminating little else but its contents. Otherwise he was in the dark.

'I'm coming up.'

She was sitting on the cushioned swivel chair near the teak coffee table. He had apparently gone right past her in the dark. He slid into the matching chair on the other side of the salon.

'Hello, Jaye. How's it going?'

'I've had better days.'

'Same here. I was going to call you in the morning.'

'Well, I'm here now.'

'And where are your friends?'

'They're not my friends. And they definitely aren't your friends, Terry.'

'Didn't sound like it. So what's going on? How come you're here and they're not?'

'Because every now and then one of us dopey locals turns out to be smarter than the bureau boys.'

McCaleb smiled without humor.

'You knew I'd have to come back for my medicine.'

She returned the smile and nodded.

'They figure you're already halfway to Mexico if you're not there already. But I saw that cabinet full of drugs and knew you had to come back. It was like a leash.'

'So now you get to take me in and get the bust and get the glory.'

'Not necessarily.'

He did not respond at first. He thought about her words, wondering how she was playing this.

'What are you saying, Jaye?'

'I'm saying my gut is telling me one thing, the evidence something else. I usually trust my gut.'

'Me too. What evidence are you talking about? What did you people find in here today?'

'Nothing much, just a baseball hat with the CI logo on it. We figured out it means Catalina Island and it matches the description James Noone gave of the cap the driver of the Cherokee was wearing. Then nothing else – until we opened up the top drawer of that chart table.'

McCaleb looked over at the chart table. He remembered opening the top drawer and checking it after the intruder had been scared off the night before. There was nothing in there amiss or that could hurt him.

'What was in it?'

'In it? Nothing. It was underneath. Taped underneath.'

McCaleb got up and went to the chart drawers. He pulled the top drawer out and turned it over. He ran his finger over the adhesive residue left by pieces of heavy tape. He smiled and shook his head. He thought about how quickly the intruder could have come in, taken a pretaped package and slapped it up under the open drawer.

'Let me guess,' he said. 'It was a plastic –'

'No. Don't say anything. You say anything and it could come back to hurt you. I don't want to hurt you, Terry.'

'I'm not worried about that. Not anymore. So let me guess. Under the drawer was a bag – a Ziploc type of bag. Inside it was the cross earring taken from Gloria Torres and a photograph of James Cordell's family. The one taken from his car.'

Winston nodded. McCaleb returned to his seat.

'You left out Donald Kenyon's cuff link,' she said. 'Sterling silver, in the shape of a dollar sign.'

'I didn't know about that. I bet Nevins and Uhlig and that asshole Arrango put on six inches apiece when they found that bag.'

'They were strutting all right,' she said, nodding. 'It made them very happy.'

'But not you.'

'No. It was too easy.'

They sat in silence for a few moments.

'You know, Terry, you don't seem very concerned that evidence linking you to three murders was found in your boat. Not to mention the obvious motive you have for those murders.' She nodded toward McCaleb's chest. 'No, you look like, at best, you are maybe moderately annoyed. You want to tell me why?'

McCaleb leaned forward, elbows on his knees. This brought his face more fully into the light.

'It was all planted, Jaye. The hat, earring, everything. Last night somebody broke in here. He didn't take anything. So he must've left things. I've got witnesses. I'm being set up. I don't know why, but it's a setup.'

'Well, if you're thinking Bolotov, forget it. He's been in Van Nuys jail since his parole officer picked him up Sunday afternoon.'

'No, I'm not thinking Bolotov. He's in the clear.'

'That sure sounds like a different tune.'

'Events have overtaken the possibility of him being a suspect. Remember, I figured him for that burglary near his work in which the HK P7 was taken. That would have given him the right gun to make him a suspect in Cordell and Torres. But that burglary occurred in December, near Christmas. Now add Kenyon. He was killed with a P7 in November. So it can't be the same gun, even if Bolotov did the burglary. So he's clear. I still don't know why he went ape shit on me and ran, though.'

'Well, like you said, he probably is good for that Christmas burglary. You went in there and spooked him, made it sound like you were going to put a couple of murders on him. He ran. That's all.'

McCaleb nodded.

'What's going to happen to him?'

'His boss is going to drop his complaint in lieu of restitution for the window that was broken. That's it. They'll release him after a hearing today.'

McCaleb nodded again and looked down at the carpet.

'So forget about him, Terry. What else have you got?'

He brought his eyes back up and looked intently back at her.

'I'm close. I'm just one or two steps away from putting this all together. I know who the shooter is now. And I'm just a few days away from knowing who hired him. I've got names, a list of suspects. I know the person we want is on that list. Trust your gut on this one, Jaye. You can hook me up now and bring me in and get the bust, but it's wrong and it won't fit. Eventually, I'll be able to prove it. But in the meantime, we'll miss the chance we've got right now.'

'Who is the shooter?'

McCaleb stood up.

'I have to get my bag. I'll show you.'

'Where's your bag?'

'In a dryer in the marina laundry. I stashed it there. I didn't know what to expect when I came in here.'

She thought a moment.

'Let me go get it,' he said. 'You've still got the pharmacy here. I'm not going anywhere. If you don't trust me, come with me.'

She waved him off.

'All right, go. Get your bag. I'll wait.'

On the way to the laundry McCaleb met Buddy Lockridge, who was holding the leather satchel taken from the laundry.

'Everything okay? You told me to go get this if I saw anybody put the moves on you.'

'Everything's fine, Buddy. I think.'

'I don't know what she's telling you, but she was one of them that was here today.'

'I know. But I think she's on my side.'

McCaleb took the bag from him and headed back to his boat. Inside, he turned on the television, put the Sherman Market tape in the VCR, and started playing it. He fast-forwarded the image and watched the jerking motions of the shooter coming in, shooting Gloria Torres and the market owner, then disappearing. Then the Good Samaritan came in and McCaleb put the tape on normal speed. At the moment the Good Samaritan looked up from his work on Gloria's stricken figure, McCaleb hit the pause button and the image froze.

He pointed at the man on the television screen and looked back at Jaye Winston.

'There. There's your shooter.'

She stared at the tube for a long moment, her face betraying none of her thoughts.

'Okay, tell me, how is that my shooter?'

'The timeline. Arrango and Walters never saw this as anything more than a common robbery and shooting. That's how it looked – who can blame them? But they were sloppy. They never bothered completing or verifying a timeline. They took what they saw at face value. But there was a problem between the time on the store video when the shooting went down and the time on the big clock downtown when the Good Samaritan called it in.'

'Right. You told me. What was the discrepancy, a half minute or so?'

'Thirty-four seconds. According to the store's video, the Good Samaritan called in the shooting thirty-four seconds before it happened.'

'But you said Walters or Arrango said they couldn't verify the accuracy of the video clock. They just assumed it was off because the old man – Mr Kang – probably set it himself.'

'Right, they assumed. I didn't.'

McCaleb backed the tape up to the point that Chan Ho Kang's watch was visible as his arm stretched across the counter. He played with it in slow motion, going back and forth until he had the time strip across the bottom at the right moment. He paused the image again. He then went to the bag and took out the hard copy of the video enhancement.

'Okay, what I did was triangulate the time to get an accurate fix on when exactly this went down. You see the watch?'

She nodded. He handed her the hard copy.

'I had a friend who used to do work for the bureau enhance this image. That's the hard copy. As you can see, the time on the watch and the video match. To the second. Old man Kang must have set the camera clock right off his watch. You with me?'

'I'm with you. The video and the watch match. What does it mean?'

McCaleb held his hand up in a *hold-on* gesture and then got out his notebook and referred to his timeline notes.

'Now we know, according to the Central Communications Center clock downtown, that the Good Samaritan called in the shooting at 10:41:03, which was thirty-four seconds before the shooting took place according to the videotape. Okay?'

'Okay.'

He explained that evening's trip to the store and then to the Kang home, where he had been allowed access to the watch. He told her that the watch's setting had not been disturbed since the murders.

'I then called the CCC and got a time check and compared it to the watch. The watch is running only four seconds ahead of the CCC clock. Therefore, that means the video clock was running only four seconds ahead of CCC at the time of the murders.'

Winston narrowed her eyebrows and leaned forward, trying to follow his explanation.

'That would mean . . .'

She didn't finish.

'It means that there is almost no difference – just four seconds – between the video clock and the CCC clock. So when the Good Samaritan called in the store shooting at ten forty-one oh three on the CCC clock, it was exactly ten forty-one oh seven on the store clock. There was only four seconds difference.'

'But that's impossible,' Winston said, shaking her head. 'There was no shooting at the time. That's thirty seconds too early. Gloria wasn't even in the store yet. She was probably just pulling in.'

McCaleb was silent. He decided to let her make the conclusions without having to be told or prompted. He knew it would have a stronger impact if she came to the same spot he was at on her own.

'So,' she said, 'this guy, this Good Samaritan, had to have called in the shooting before the shooting took place.'

McCaleb nodded. He noted the deepening intensity in her eyes.

'Why would he do that unless . . . he knew. Unless he knew the shooting was going down? He's – damn! – he's got to be the shooter!'

McCaleb nodded once more, but this time he had a satisfied smile on his face. He knew he had her in his car now. And they were about to hit the gas pedal.

36

'Have you hashed this around, figured out how it all plays?'

'A little bit.'

'So then tell me.'

McCaleb was standing in the galley now, pouring himself a glass of orange juice. Winston had passed on a drink but was standing in the galley also. Her adrenaline would not allow her to sit. McCaleb knew that feeling.

'Wait a second,' he said.

He gulped down the orange juice in one tilt.

'Sorry, I messed with my blood sugar today, I think. Ate too late.'

'Are you all right?'

'Fine.'

He put the glass in the sink, turned and leaned against the counter.

'Okay, this is how I see it. You start with Mr X, somebody someplace that we'll assume to be a man for now. This person needs something. A new part. Kidney, liver, maybe bone marrow. Possibly corneas but that might be stretching it. It has to be something worth killing for. Something that he might die without. Or in the case of the cornea, possibly go blind and become non-functioning without.'

'What about a heart?'

'That would be on the list but, see, I got the heart. So scratch the heart unless you are Nevins and Uhlig and Arrango and the rest of them who think I'm Mr X, okay?'

'Okay. Go on.'

'This guy, X, he's got money and access. Enough to be able to contact and hire a shooter.'

'With OC connections.'

'Maybe but not necessarily.'

'What about "Don't forget the cannoli"?'

'I don't know. I've been thinking about that. It's kind of showy for real organized crime, don't you think? Makes me think it's a deflection but for now that's just a guess.'

'All right, never mind for now. Go on with Mr X.'

'Well, besides being able to get to a shooter to do the job, he next has to have access to the computer at BOPRA. He's got to know who has the part that he needs. You know what BOPRA is?'

'I learned today. And I said the same thing about you to Nevins. "How could Terry McCaleb get access to BOPRA?" and he told me how bullshit their computer security is. Their theory is that you hacked in one day when you were at Cedars. You got a list of blood donors of type AB with CMV negative and went from there.'

'Okay. Now follow the same theory but instead of me, it's Mr X and he gets the list and then puts the Good Samaritan on the case.'

McCaleb pointed out into the salon, where the image of the Good Samaritan remained frozen on the television screen. They both looked at it for a few moments before he continued.

'The shooter goes down the list and lo and behold he sees a familiar name. Donald Kenyon. Kenyon is a famous man, mostly for all the enemies he has. He becomes the perfect choice because of that. All those enemies – investors and maybe even some mobster lurking behind the scenes, it makes for good camouflage.'

'So the Good Samaritan picks Kenyon.'

'Right. He picks him and then he watches him until he has his routine. And the routine is pretty simple because Kenyon's got a federal dog collar on and usually doesn't go anywhere outside of his house because of it. But the Good Sam is not discouraged. He gets the household routine down and he knows that for twenty minutes each morning Kenyon is in that house alone when the wife drives the kids to school.'

His throat dry from all the talking, McCaleb rescued the glass from the sink and poured himself another glass of orange juice.

'So he hits during that twenty-minute window,' he continued, after gulping down another half glass. 'And going in, he knows he has to do the job in such a way that Kenyon makes it to the hospital but no further. See, he's got to preserve the organs for transplant. But if he goes too far, Kenyon's dead on arrival and no good to him. So he comes into the house, grabs Kenyon and marches him to the front door. He then holds him there and waits for the wife to come back home from dropping the kids. He makes Kenyon look through the peephole and make sure it is her. Then he pops him and lays him out on the floor, fresh and ready when the wife opens the door.'

'But he doesn't make it to the hospital.'

'No. The plan was good but he fucked up. He used a Devastator in the P7. The wrong bullet for this kind of work. It's a frangible, it explodes and basically pulps Kenyon's brain, destroys all life support system controls. Death is almost instantaneous.'

He stopped there and watched Winston as she evaluated the story. Then he held up a finger, signaling her to wait before commenting. He went to his bag in the salon and pulled out a sheaf of documents, careful to keep his body between the bag and Winston. He didn't want her catching a glimpse of the P7, which was still in there.

At the galley counter he looked through the documents until he found what he needed.

'I'm not supposed to even have this but take a look. This is a transcript of the tape the bureau got from the illegal bugs in the Kenyon house. This is the part where he was hit. They didn't get everything that was said but what is there fits with what I just said.'

Winston stood next to him and read the section he had circled with a pen while riding with Buddy Lockridge on the way to the marina.

UNKNOWN: Okay, look and see who . . .
KENYON: Don't . . . She's got nothing to do with this. She . . .

Winston nodded her head.

'He could have told him to look through the peephole,' she said. 'It obviously was the wife because Kenyon then tried to protect her.'

'Right, and notice that the transcript says that there were two minutes of silence before that last exchange and the gunshot. What else could he have been doing but waiting until she showed up so she would get to the body almost as soon as it happened?'

She nodded again.

'It fits,' she said. 'But what about the bureau people listening? You think the shooter didn't know about them?'

'I'm not sure. It doesn't seem like it. I think he just got lucky. But maybe he thought there was a slim chance the place was bugged. Maybe that's where the cannoli line came from. Just a little misdirection, just in case.'

McCaleb finished his orange juice and put the glass back into the sink.

'Okay, so he blew it,' Winston said. 'And it was back to the drawing board. Or, actually, back to the BOPRA list. And the next name he picked was my guy, James Cordell.'

McCaleb nodded and let her run with it. He knew that the more of the puzzle she fit together herself, the more apt she would be to believe in the whole thing.

'He changes the load, goes from frangible to hardball so that he would have a through-and-through wound with less immediate brain damage.

'He watches Cordell until he has the routine down and then he sets up the shoot in a way similar to Kenyon – the hit occurring almost instantaneous to the arrival of a second party who could get help. In Kenyon's case it was his wife. In Cordell's it was James Noone. The shooter probably stood behind Cordell until he saw Noone's car enter the turn lane to come into the bank. That was when he fired.'

'I think Noone was an accident,' McCaleb said. 'There is no way the shooter could have planned on a witness showing up. He was probably going to shoot Cordell and then call nine one one himself on the pay phone out at the curb – on the crime scene tape you can see the pay phone right there. But Noone came along and that forced him to just get the hell out of there. He probably thought the witness would make the call on the pay phone – a legitimate call for help. The bad break for him was that Noone made the call on a cell phone and the address was messed up, resulting in a terminal delay for Cordell.'

Winston nodded her agreement.

'Cordell was DOA,' she said. 'Another one goes to shit. He goes back to the list and it's Gloria Torres this time. Only this time he's not taking a single chance. He calls the shooting in before it even happens.'

'Right, to get the paramedics rolling. He knew her routine. He was probably standing at that pay phone waiting. When he saw her car pulling in, he made the nine one one call.'

'He then goes in, does the job and splits. Outside he pulls off the mask and the jumpsuit and he becomes our Good Samaritan. He goes in, wraps her up and gets the hell out of there. This time it works. It is perfect.'

'It was a learning process. He learned from the mistakes of the first two, perfected it on the third.'

McCaleb folded his arms and waited for Winston to make the next jump.

'So we have to follow the harvest now,' she said. 'One of the people who received one of the organs will be Mr X. We have to go to BOPRA and get the – wait, you said you had a list of names?'

He nodded.

'From BOPRA?'

'From BOPRA.'

He went back to his bag and found the list Bonnie Fox had given him. He turned around and almost bumped into Winston, who had moved out of the galley. He handed her the sheet.

'There's the list.'

She studied it intently, as if she was expecting to see that one of the names on it would actually be Mr X or in some other way be readily identifiable as him.

'How did you get this?'

'Can't say.'

She looked up at him.

'For the time being I have to protect a source. But it's legit. Those people got organs from Gloria Torres.'

'Are you giving me this?'

'If you are going to do something with it.'

'I will. I'll start tomorrow.'

McCaleb was fully aware of what he was giving her. Of course, it might be the key to his exoneration and the capture of the worst kind of killer. But he was also handing her an E-ticket ride. If she was successful in breaking the case while the bureau and the LAPD were heading down the wrong road, her professional future would have no bounds.

'How are you going to run them down?' he asked.

'Anyway I can. I'll look for money, criminal records, anything that stands out. You know, the usual things, the full background. What are you going to be doing?'

McCaleb glanced over at his bag. It was bulging with documents, tapes and the guns.

'I don't know yet. Will you tell me something? How did this all turn on me? What pointed all you people at me?'

Winston folded the list into a neat square and slid it into the pocket of her blazer.

'The bureau. Nevins told me they got a tip. He wouldn't say from where. The tip was suspect-specific, though. He did tell me that. The source said you killed Glory Torres for her heart. They took it from there. They checked the autopsies of all three victims and found the blood matches. From there it was easy, everything fell into place. I have to admit they had me going. At the time, it all seemed to fit.'

'*How*?' McCaleb asked angrily, his voice rising. 'None of this would have even happened if I hadn't started looking into it. The ballistics match to Kenyon was made because of me. That brought the bureau in. You think that is what a guilty man would do? That's crazy.'

He was angrily pointing at his own chest.

'All of that was considered. We sat around and hashed it out this morning. The theory that emerged was that you had this woman – the sister – who had come to you and you figured she wasn't going to let this go. So you decided you better take the case before somebody else did. You took it and proceeded to sabotage it. You came up with this Bolotov goose chase. You hypnotized the only real witness and now he's lost to us as far as court goes. Yes, the ballistics match was made because of you but maybe that was a surprise, maybe you were expecting it to come up empty since a Devastator had been used the first time.'

McCaleb shook his head. He wouldn't allow himself to see their side of it. He still couldn't believe they had turned the focus on him.

'Look, we weren't sold on it one hundred percent,' Winston said. 'We felt there was enough to get and justify a warrant for the search – and there was. We felt the search was make or break. We would find evidence and go further with it, or we would drop it. But then we find out you drive a black Cherokee and then sitting under that drawer are three very damning pieces of evidence. The only thing that could have been worse for you would have been to find the gun.'

McCaleb thought of the gun sitting in his bag five feet away from them. Again he knew how lucky he had been.

'But like you said, it was too easy.'

'For me it was. The others didn't see it that way. Like I said before, they started strutting. They saw the headlines.'

McCaleb shook his head. The discussion had sapped his strength. He stepped over to the galley table and slid into the booth.

'I am being set up,' he said.

Winston came over.

'I believe you,' she said. 'And whoever he is, he's done a good job of it. Have you thought at all about why it is you that's been set up?'

McCaleb nodded as he drew a design in a spray of sugar that had been spilled on the table.

'When I look at it from the shooter's view, I see why.'

He brushed the sugar off the table with his palm.

'After Kenyon didn't work out and the shooter knew he had to go back to the list, he also knew he was doubling the risk. He knew there was an off chance that the cases might be connected through the blood. He knew he had to lay the groundwork for a deflection. He picked me. If he was in the BOPRA computer, then he knew I was next on the list for a heart. He probably backgrounded me like the others. He knew about the Cherokee I drove and used one himself. He took souvenirs from the victims so that he could plant them, if needed, here. Then it was probably him who made the tip call to Nevins when everything was set.'

McCaleb sat silently for a long moment, brooding about his situation. Then he slowly slid back out of the booth.

'I have to finish packing.'

'Where are you going to go?'

'I'm not sure.'

'I'll need to talk to you tomorrow.'

'I'll be in touch.'

He started down the stairs, his hands gripping the overhead rails.

'Terry.'

He stopped and turned to look back at her.

'I'm taking a big chance. My neck's a mile out there.'

'I know that, Jaye. Thanks.'

With that he disappeared into the darkness below.

37

McCaleb's Cherokee had been impounded during the search earlier in the day. He borrowed Lockridge's Taurus and drove it north on the 405. When he reached the 10 interchange, he went west to the Pacific and then continued north again on the coast highway. He was in no hurry and he was tired of freeways. He'd decided to drive along the ocean and then cut up to the Valley through Topanga Canyon. He knew Topanga was desolate enough for him to be able to tell if he was being followed by Winston. Or anybody else.

It was half past nine by the time he reached the shore and was skirting along the black water intermittently broken by the froth of crashing waves. The night fog was coming in heavy and pushing across the highway, butting into the sheer bluffs that guarded the Palisades. It carried with it the strong scent and feel of the sea and it reminded McCaleb of night fishing with his father when he was a boy. It always scared him when his father throttled down and killed the engines so they could drift in the dark. His breath held tight at the end of the night when the old man turned the key to restart. He had nightmares as a boy about drifting alone in the dark in a dead boat. He never told his father about those dreams. He never told him he didn't want to go night fishing. He always held his fears to himself.

McCaleb looked out to his left to try to find the line where ocean met sky but he couldn't see it. Two shades of darkness blending somewhere out there, the moon hidden in cloud cover. It seemed to fit his mood. He turned on the radio and fished around for some blues but gave up and turned it off. He remembered Buddy's collection of harmonicas and reached into the door pocket for one. He flipped on the overhead light and checked the etching on the top plate. It was a Tombo in the key of C. He wiped it off on his shirt and as he drove, he played with the instrument, mostly producing a cacophony that at times made him laugh out loud at how ugly it was. But every now and then he put together a couple of notes. Buddy had tried to teach him once and he'd gotten to the point where he could play the opening riffs of 'Midnight Rambler'. He tried for that now but couldn't find the chord and what he produced sounded more like a wheezing old man.

When he turned into Topanga Canyon, he put the harmonica down. The road through the canyon was a snake and he'd need both hands on the wheel. Fresh out of distractions, he finally began considering his situation.

He first brooded about Winston and how much he could count on her. He knew she was capable and ambitious. What he didn't know was how well she would stand up to the pressure she would certainly encounter by going against the bureau and the LAPD. He concluded that he was lucky to have her on his side but that he couldn't sit back and wait for her to show up with the case wrapped up in a box. He could only count on himself.

He figured that if Winston did not convince the others, then at best he had two days before they had an indictment from a grand jury and would go to the media with their prize. After that, his chances of working the case would diminish rapidly. He'd be the lead on the six and eleven o'clock news. He'd have no choice but to give up the investigation, get a lawyer and surrender. The priority would then be clearing his name in the courtroom, never mind catching the real shooter and whoever it was who had hired him.

There was a gravel turnout on the road and McCaleb pulled over, put the car in park and looked out at the blackness of the drop-off to his right. Far off he saw the square lights of a house deep in the canyon and he wondered what it would be like to be there. He reached over to the seat next to him for the harmonica but it was gone, slipped over the side during one of the turns of the snaking road.

Three minutes went by and no car passed him. He dropped the car back into drive and continued on his way. Once he crested the mountain, the road straightened out some and dropped down into Woodland Hills. He stayed on Topanga Canyon Boulevard until he reached Sherman Way and then he cut east into Canoga Park. Five minutes later he stopped in front of Graciela's home and watched the windows for a few minutes. He thought about what he would say to her. He wasn't sure what he had started with her but it felt strong and right to him. Before he even opened the door to the car, he was mourning the possibility that it might already be over.

She opened the front door before he reached it and he wondered if she had been watching him sitting in the car.

'Terry? Is everything all right? Why are you driving?'

'I had to.'

'Come in, come in.'

She stepped back and allowed him in. They went to the living room and took the same seats on the sectional sofa that they had taken before. A small color television on a wooden stand played softly in the corner. The ten o'clock news on Channel 5 was just starting. Graciela used a remote to turn it off. McCaleb put his heavy bag down between his feet. He had left the duffel in the car, unwilling to presume that he would be asked to stay.

'Tell me,' she said. 'What is happening?'

'They think it was me. The FBI, LAPD, all of them but one sheriff's detective. They think I killed your sister for her heart.'

McCaleb looked at her face and then glanced away like a guilty man. He winced at the thought of what this must show to her but he knew down deep that he was guilty. He was the beneficiary, even if he had nothing to do with the actual crime. He was alive now because Glory was dead. A question echoed through his mind like the slamming of a dozen doors down a dark hallway. How can I live with this?

'That's ridiculous,' Graciela said angrily. 'How can they think that you –'

'Wait,' he said, cutting her off. 'I have to tell you some things, Graciela. Then you decide what and who to believe.'

'I don't have to hear –'

He held his hand up cutting her off again.

'Just listen to me, okay? Where's Raymond?'

'He's asleep. It's a school night.'

He nodded and leaned forward, elbows on his knees, hands clasped together.

'They searched my boat. While I was with you, they were searching my boat. They had made the same connection we made. The blood work. But they're looking at me for it. They found things on my boat. I wanted to tell you before you heard it from them or saw it on TV or the paper.'

'What things, Terry?'

'Hidden under a drawer. They found your sister's earring. The cross the shooter took.'

He watched her a moment before continuing. Her eyes dropped from his to the glass-topped coffee table as she thought about his words.

'They also found the photo from Cordell's car. And they found a cuff link that was taken from Donald Kenyon. They found all the icons the killer took, Graciela. My source, the sheriff's detective, she tells me they are going to go to a grand jury and indict me. I can't go back to my boat now.'

She glanced at him and then away. She stood up and walked to the window, even though the curtain was closed. She shook her head.

'You want me to leave?' he said to her back.

'No, I don't want you to leave. This makes no sense. How can they – did you tell the detective about the intruder? He's the one who must have done this, who put those things in the drawer. He's the killer. Oh my God! We were that close to my sister's . . .'

She didn't finish. McCaleb got up and went to her, relief coursing through him. She didn't believe it. None of it. He put his arms around her from behind and pushed his face into her hair.

'I'm so glad you believe me,' he whispered.

She turned around in his arms and they kissed for a long moment.

'What can I do to help?' she whispered.

'Just keep believing. And I'll do the rest. Can I stay here? Nobody knows that we're together. They might come here, but I don't think it will be to look for me. It might be just to tell you they think it's me.'

'I want you to stay. As long as you need or want to.'

'I just need a place where I can work. Where I can go through everything again. I get this feeling I missed something. Like the blood work. There's got to be some answers in all of that paper.'

'You can work here. I'll stay home tomorrow and help look through –'

'No. You can't. You can't do anything unusual. I just want you to get up in the morning and take Raymond to school and then go to work. I can do this. This part is my job.'

He held her face in his hands. The weight of his guilt was lessened by her just being there with him and he felt the subtle opening inside of some passage that had long been closed. He wasn't sure where it would lead but knew in his heart he wanted to go there, that he must go there.

'I was just about to go to bed,' she said.

He nodded.

'Are you coming with me?'

'What about Raymond? Shouldn't we –'

'Raymond's asleep. Don't worry about him. For right now let's worry about us.'

38

In the morning, after Graciela and Raymond were gone and the house was quiet, McCaleb opened his leather bag and spread all of the accumulated paperwork in six stacks across the coffee table. While contemplating it all, he drank a glass of orange juice and ate two untoasted blueberry Pop Tarts that he guessed were meant for Raymond. When he was done, he set to work, hoping his involvement in the paper would keep his mind off things beyond his control, mainly Jaye Winston's investigation of the names on the list.

Despite that distraction McCaleb could feel the flow of adrenaline start to kick in. He was looking for the tell. The piece of the puzzle that didn't fit before but would make sense now, that would tell him the story. He had survived in the bureau largely by following gut instincts. He was following one now. He knew that the larger the case file was – the larger the accumulation of facts – the easier it was for the tell to be hidden. He would go hunting for it now, in a sense looking for the perfect red apple in the stack at the grocery store – the one that when pulled brings the whole pile down and bouncing across the floor.

But as jazzed as McCaleb had been at eight-thirty in the morning, his spirits had immolated by late afternoon. In eight hours interrupted only by bologna sandwiches and unanswered calls to Winston, he had reviewed every page of every document he had accumulated in the ten days he had worked the case. And the tell – if it had ever been there – remained hidden. The feelings of paranoia and isolation were creeping back up on him. At one point he realized he was daydreaming about what would be the best place to flee to, the mountains of Canada or the beaches of Mexico.

At four o'clock he called the Star Center once more and was told for the fifth time that Winston was not in. This time, however, the secretary added that she was presumed gone for the day. In earlier calls the secretary had dutifully refused to reveal where Winston was or give him her pager number. For that he would have to speak to the captain and McCaleb declined, knowing the jeopardy he would place Winston in if it was revealed she was not only sympathetic to a suspect but was actually aiding him.

After hanging up, he called his phone on the boat and played back two messages that had come in during the last hour. The first was Buddy Lockridge checking in and the second was a wrong number, a woman saying she wasn't sure if she had the right number but was looking for someone named Luther Hatch. She left a callback number. McCaleb recognized the name Luther Hatch – the suspect in the case in which he had first met Jaye Winston. Once he made that connection, he recognized her voice on the message. She was telling him to call her.

As he punched in the numbers Winston had left, he recognized the exchange – it was the same for the bureau offices in Westwood, where he used to work. The phone was answered immediately.

'This is Winston.'

'This is McCaleb.'

Silence.

'Hey,' she finally said. 'I was wondering if you would get that message.'

'What's up? Can you talk?'

'Not really.'

'Okay, I'll talk, then. Do they know you are helping me?'

'No, obviously.'

'But you're there because they moved the investigation to the bureau, right?'

'Uh-huh.'

'Okay, have you had a chance to run those names down yet?'

'I've been out on it all day.'

'Do you have anything? Do any of them look good?'

'No, there's nothing there.'

McCaleb closed his eyes and cursed silently. Where had he gone wrong? How could this be a dead end? He was confused and his mind was running over the possibilities. He wondered if Winston had had enough time to thoroughly run out the list.

'Is there any place or time I can talk to you about this? I need to ask you some questions.'

'In a little while I probably can. Why don't you give me a number and I'll get back to you?'

McCaleb was silent while he thought about this. But he didn't take long. As Winston had said the night before, her neck was way out there for him. He believed he could trust her. He gave her Graciela's number.

'Call me back as soon as you can.'

'I will.'

'One last thing. Did they go to the grand jury yet?'

'No, not yet.'

'How long before they do?'

'I'll see you tomorrow morning, then. Bye.'

She hung up before she heard him curse out loud. The following morning they were going to seek an indictment against him for murder. And he was sure that obtaining it would be only a formality. Grand juries were always rigged in the prosecution's favor. In McCaleb's case, he knew that all they needed to do was show the Sherman Market tape and then introduce the earring found during the search of his boat. They would be staging press conferences by the afternoon – perfect timing for the six o'clock news.

While he was standing there contemplating his grim future, the phone rang in his hand.

'It's Jaye.'

'Where are you?'

'The federal cafeteria. A pay phone.'

McCaleb immediately envisioned her location, in an alcove with vending machines off to the side of the cafeteria dining room. It was private enough.

'What's going on, Jaye?'

'It's not good. They're putting the finishing touches on the package they're going to take to the DA's office tonight. They'll take it to the grand jury tomorrow morning. They're going to seek one murder charge for Gloria Torres. After that's in the pipeline, they'll take their time before adding on Cordell and Kenyon.'

'Okay,' McCaleb said, not sure how to respond. He decided there was no sense in continuing to curse out loud.

'My advice is that you come in, Terry. You tell them what you told me and convince them. I'll be on your side but right now I'm handcuffed. I have information about the Good Samaritan I shouldn't have. If I reveal it, I'll go into the shitter with you.'

'What about the list? Nothing at all?'

'Look, that much I did talk about with them. So I would have the time to work the list. I came in this morning and told them in order to be ready to counter your defense, we needed to investigate the other recipients of the organs from Gloria Torres. I said I had a source who would slip us the list of names without us having to get a search warrant, etcetera, etcetera, and they said great. They gave me the day. But nothing, Terry. I'm sorry but I checked out every name. I got nothing.'

'Tell me.'

'Well, I don't have the list with me but –'

'Hold on.'

McCaleb walked into Graciela's bedroom, where he had seen the copy of the list he had given her on the bureau. He grabbed it and read the first name to Winston.

'J. B. Dickey – he got the liver.'

'Right, okay, he didn't make it. He got the transplant but there were complications and he died three weeks after surgery.'

'But that doesn't mean it wasn't him.'

'I know that. But I talked to the surgeon at St Joseph's. It was a charity case. The guy was on MediCal and the hospital picked up the rest. This wasn't a guy with money or connections to a hit man, Terry. Come on.'

'Okay, next. Tammy Domike, one of the kidneys.'

'Right. She's a schoolteacher. She's twenty-eight, married to a carpenter and has two kids. She doesn't fit either. It just wasn't –'

'William Farley, the other kidney.'

'Retired Chippie from Bakersfield. He's been in a wheelchair for twelve years – since he took a bullet in the spine during a routine traffic pullover on the grapevine. They never caught the guy, either.'

'California Highway Patrol,' McCaleb mused out loud. 'He could have friends who could have pulled this off for him.'

Winston was silent for a long moment before responding.

'It seems unlikely, Terry. I mean, listen to what you're –'

'I know, I know, never mind. What about the eyes? Christine Foye got the corneas.'

'Right. She sells books for a living and just got out of college. It's not her, either. Look, Terry, we were hoping that one of these people would be some millionaire or a politician or anybody with the juice to do this. Somebody obvious. But it's just not there. I'm sorry.'

'So I'm still the best and only suspect.'

'Unfortunately.'

'Thanks, Jaye, you've been a big help. I've got to go.'

'Wait! And don't get mad at me. I've been the only one who has listened to you. Remember?'

'I know, I'm sorry.'

'Well, there was one other thing, I was thinking. I wasn't going to tell you until I had some time to check it out. I'm going to start on it tomorrow. I'm working on a warrant for information right now.'

'What? Tell me. I need something now.'

'Well, you were only thinking in terms of who got the organs that became available after the death of Gloria Torres, right?'

'Right. Cordell's and Kenyon's were not harvested.'

'I know. I'm not talking about that. But there is always a waiting list, right?'

'Yeah, always. I waited almost two years because of the blood type.'

'Well, maybe someone just wanted to move up the list.'

'Move up?'

'You know, they were like you, waiting, and they knew it would be a long wait. Maybe even a fatal wait. Weren't you told that with your blood type there was no telling when a heart would become available?'

'Yeah, they told me not to get my hopes up.'

'Okay, so maybe our guy is still waiting but by taking out Gloria Torres, he has in effect moved up one notch on the list. Improved his chances.'

McCaleb thought about this. He saw the possibility. He suddenly remembered Bonnie Fox telling him that there was another patient on the ward who was in the same situation McCaleb had been in. He wondered now if she meant literally the same situation, waiting for a heart that was type AB with CMV negative. He thought of the boy he had seen in the hospital bed. Could he be the patient Fox meant?

McCaleb thought about what a parent would be willing to do to save a child. Could it be possible?

'It could work,' he said, his adrenaline returning and the monotonal quality of his voice gone now. 'What you're saying is that it could be somebody still waiting.'

'Right. And I am going to go to BOPRA with a warrant to get all their waiting lists and their blood donor records. It should be interesting to see how they respond.'

McCaleb nodded but his mind was skipping ahead.

'Wait a minute, wait a minute,' he said. 'It's too complicated.'

'What is?'

'The whole thing. If somebody wanted to move up on the list, why take out donors? Why not just knock people off the list?'

'Because that might be too obvious. If two or three people needing heart or liver transplants in a row get hit, it's bound to raise a question somewhere. But by hitting the donors, it's more obscure. No one noticed it until you came along.'

'I guess,' McCaleb said, still not sure he was convinced. 'Then if you're right, it could even mean the shooter's going to hit again. You've got to go down the list of AB donors. You've got to warn them, protect them.'

That possibility brought the excitement back. It was jangling in his veins.

'I know,' Winston said. 'When I get the warrant, I'm going to have to tell Nevins and Uhlig, all of them, what I am doing. That's why you have to come in, Terry. It's the only way. You have to come in with a lawyer and lay this all out, then take your chances. Nevins, Uhlig, these are smart people. They'll see where they went wrong.'

McCaleb didn't respond. He saw the logic in what she was saying but was hesitant to agree because it would be putting his fate in the hands of others. He would rather rely on himself.

'Do you have a lawyer, Terry?'

'No, I don't have a lawyer. Why would I have a lawyer? I haven't done anything wrong.'

He cringed. He had heard countless guilty individuals make the same statement before. Winston probably had, too.

'I meant do you know a lawyer who could help you?' she said. 'If you don't, then I can suggest a few. Michael Haller Jr would be a good choice.'

'I know lawyers in case I need one. I have to think about this.'

'Well, call me. I can bring you in, make sure everything is handled right.'

McCaleb's mind wandered and he was inside a holding cell at the county jail. He had been in the lockup on interviews as a bureau agent. He knew how loud jails were and how dangerous. He knew that innocent or not, he would never surrender himself to that.

'Terry, you there?'

'Yeah, sorry. I was just thinking about something. How can I reach you to arrange this?'

'I'll give you my pager and my home. I'll be here until probably six but after that I'm heading home. Call me anywhere, any time.'

She gave him the numbers and McCaleb wrote them down in his notebook. He then put it away and shook his head.

'I can't believe this. I'm sitting here talking about turning myself in for something I didn't do.'

'I know that. But the truth is a powerful thing. It will work out. Just make

sure you call me, Terry. When you decide.'
'I'll call you.'
He hung up.

39

Bonnie Fox's receptionist, the frowner, told McCaleb that the doctor had been in transplant surgery all afternoon and would probably not be available for another two to three hours. McCaleb almost cursed out loud but instead left Graciela's number and told the frowner to write down that he needed Fox to call back as soon as possible no matter what the hour. He was about to hang up when he thought of something.

'Hey, who is getting the heart?'

'What?'

'You said she was in surgery. Which patient? Was it the boy?'

'I'm sorry, I'm not at liberty to discuss other patients with you,' said the frowner.

'Fine,' he said. 'Then just make sure you tell her to call me.'

McCaleb spent the next fifteen minutes pacing between the living room and kitchen, hoping unrealistically that the phone would ring and Fox would be on the line.

He finally managed to shoehorn the anxiety into a side compartment of his brain and started thinking about the larger problems at hand. McCaleb knew he had to start making decisions, chief of which was to decide whether to get a lawyer. He knew Winston was right; it was the smart move to get legal protection. But McCaleb couldn't bring himself to make the call to Michael Haller Jr or anybody else, to give up on his own skills and rely on another's.

In the living room, there were no documents left on the coffee table. As he had gone through the pages, he had returned them to the leather bag until all that was on the table was the stack of videotapes.

Desperate for a diversion from his thoughts about what exactly Fox had said to him about the other patient, he picked up the videocassette on top of the stack and walked it over to the television. He popped it into the VCR without looking to see which tape it was. It didn't matter. He just wanted something else to think about for a while.

But as he dropped back onto the couch, he immediately ignored the tape that was playing. Michael Haller Jr, he thought. Yes, he would be a good attorney. Not as good as his old man, the legendary Mickey Haller. But the legend was long dead and Junior had taken his place as one of the most visible and successful defense attorneys in Los Angeles. Junior would get him out of this, McCaleb knew. But, of course, that would be after the reputation-destroying media blitz, the looting of his savings and the selling of *The Following Sea.* And even when it was over and he was clear, he would still carry the stigma of suspicion and guilt with him.

Forever.

McCaleb squinted his eyes and wondered what it was he was staring at on the TV. The camera was focused on the legs and feet of someone standing on a table. Then he recognized his own walking boots and placed what he was seeing. The hypnosis session. The camera had been running when McCaleb climbed onto the table to remove some of the overhead lighting tubes. James Noone appeared in the frame and reached up as one of the long fluorescent light tubes was handed down to him.

McCaleb grabbed the TV remote off the arm of the couch and hit the fast forward button. Interested because he had forgotten to review the hypnosis session as he had promised Captain Hitchens he would, McCaleb decided to skip through the preliminaries. He moved the tape past the initial interview and relaxation exercises to the actual questioning of Noone under hypnosis. He wanted to hear James Noone's recounting of the details of the shooting and the killer's getaway.

McCaleb watched with total concentration and quickly found himself suffering the same physical effects of frustration he had felt during the actual session. Noone had been a perfect subject. It was rare that he had hypnotized a witness who could recall such detail. The cutting frustration was that he simply hadn't gotten a good look at the driver and the Cherokee's license plates had been covered.

'Damn,' McCaleb cursed out loud as the taped session drew to a close.

He reached for the remote, deciding to rewind and run the interview again, when he suddenly froze, his finger poised over the remote button.

McCaleb had just seen something that did not fit, something he had missed during the actual session because he was distracted by Winston, who had been sitting in. He rewound the tape but only briefly, then replayed the last few questions that were asked.

On the tape, McCaleb was wrapping it up, asking a scatter of leftover and wishful-thinking questions. They were long shots, thrown at Noone out of frustration. He had asked about any stickers on the Cherokee's windshield. Noone said no and then McCaleb was out of questions. He turned to Winston and asked her, 'Anything else?'

Even though McCaleb had broken his own rules by asking a question of a nonparticipant, Winston followed the rules and did not answer verbally. Instead, she shook her head in the negative.

'You sure?' McCaleb asked.

Again she shook her head no. McCaleb then began bringing Noone out of the trance.

But that was wrong and McCaleb had missed it at the time. Now he came around the coffee table, remote in hand, and leaned closer to the screen. He rewound the tape one more time to watch the sequence again.

'Son of a bitch,' he whispered after the play-through. 'You should've answered me, Noone. You should have answered!'

He punched the eject button and turned to grab another tape. He knocked the short stack across the coffee table and then quickly scrabbled through the plastic cassettes until he found the tape with the label marked Sherman Market. He put the tape into the machine, started playing it on fast forward and then paused the image when the Good Samaritan was on the screen.

The VCR could not hold the image still and McCaleb guessed the machine was an inexpensive model with only two tape heads. He ejected the tape and looked at his watch. It was four-forty. He slapped the remote down on top of the television and went to the kitchen for the phone.

Tony Banks agreed to stay once again after closing at Video GraFX Consultants until McCaleb could get there. Crossing the floor of the Valley on the 101, he initially made good time. Most of the rush-hour traffic was going the other way, the workforce of the city returning to the bedroom communities of the Valley. But when he dipped south on the freeway to go through the Cahuenga Pass into Hollywood, the brake lights were flared for as far as he could see and he got bogged down. He finally pulled Buddy Lockridge's Taurus into the small employee lot at VGC at five after six. Once again, Tony Banks answered the door after McCaleb had pushed the night bell.

'Tony, thanks,' McCaleb said to the man's back as he was led down the hallway once again to one of the tech rooms. 'You are really helping me out here.'

'No problem.'

But McCaleb noted that there wasn't as much enthusiasm in the 'No problem' this time. They entered the same room they had sat in the week before. McCaleb handed Banks the two tapes he had brought with him.

'On each of these tapes there is a man,' he said. 'I want to see if they are the same man.'

'You mean, like, you can't tell.'

'Not for sure. They look different. But I think it's a disguise. I think they're the same man but I want to be sure.'

Banks put the first tape into the player on the left side of the console, turned it on and the Sherman Market robbery and shooting began playing on the corresponding overhead video display tube.

'This guy?' Banks said.

'Right. Freeze it when there's a good look.'

Banks froze the image at the moment the so-called Good Samaritan was looking off camera in right profile.

'How is that? I need the profile. It's hard to do a comparison front-on.'

'You're the boss.'

He handed Banks the second tape, which was placed in the righthand player, and soon the hypnosis session was playing on the right VDT screen.

'Back it up,' McCaleb said. 'I think there's a profile before he sits down.'

Banks reversed the tape.

'What are you doing to him on this?'

'Hypnosis.'

'Really?'

'I thought so at the time. But now I think he was playing me the whole – there.'

Banks paused the tape. James Noone was looking to his right, most likely at the door to the interview room. Banks played with the dials and the computer mouse and expanded the picture, then sharpened it. He did the same with the image on the left screen. He then leaned back and looked at the side-by-side profiles. After a few moments he spoke as he unclipped an infrared pointer from his pocket and turned it on.

'Well, the complexions don't match. One guy looks Mexican.'

'That would be easy. A couple hours in a tanning salon could give him that look.'

Banks played the pointer's red dot along the bridge of the Good Samaritan's nose.

'Look at the slope of the nose,' he said. 'See the double bump?'

'Right.'

The red dot jumped to the left screen and found the same double bump in the slope of James Noone's nose.

'It's an unscientific guess but it looks pretty close to me,' Banks said.

'Me too.'

'You've got different-color eyes but that can be done.'

'Contacts.'

'Right. And here, the expanded jawline on this guy on the right. A dental appliance – you know, like a rubber sleep guard – or even wads of tissue paper like Brando used in *The Godfather* could be used to make that appearance.'

McCaleb nodded, silently noting another possible connection to the gangster movie. Cannoli and now possibly wads of tissue paper as cheek implants.

'And hair is always changeable,' Banks was saying. 'In fact, this guy looks like he's got on a wig.'

Banks ran the red dot along the Good Samaritan's hairline. McCaleb silently chastised himself for seeing this only now. The hairline was a perfect line, the telltale indication of a hairpiece.

'Let's see what else we've got.'

Banks went back to the dials and pulled back on the image. He then used the mouse to delineate a new enhancement area. The Good Samaritan's hands.

'It's like chicks,' Banks said. 'They can put on makeup, wigs, even get their tits done. But they can't do nothing about their hands. Their hands – and sometimes their feet – always give 'em away.'

Once he had the Good Samaritan's hands blown up and in focus, he went to work on the other console until he had an enlargement of Noone's right hand on the opposite screen. Banks stood up so that he was at direct eye level with the screens and leaned to within a few inches of each tube as he studied and compared the hands.

'Okay, here, look.'

McCaleb stood up and looked closely at the screens.

'What?'

'The first one has got a bit of a scar here on the knuckle. You see it, the discoloration?'

McCaleb leaned in close to the image of the Good Samaritan's right hand.

'Wait a sec,' Banks said. He opened a drawer in the console and pulled out a photographer's eyepiece, the kind used to study and magnify negatives on a light table. 'Try this.'

McCaleb held the eyepiece over the knuckle in question and looked through it. He could see a swirl of white scar tissue on the knuckle. Though the whole image was distorted and blurry, he identified the scar as almost being in the shape of a question mark.

'Okay,' he said. 'Let's see the other.'

He took a step to his left and used the eyepiece to locate the same knuckle on James Noone's right hand. The hand was not held in the same posture or at the same angle but the thick white swirl of scar tissue was there. McCaleb held steady and studied the image until he was sure. He then closed his eyes for a moment. It was a lock. The man on each of the VDT screens was the same man.

'Is it there?' Banks asked.

McCaleb handed him the eyepiece.

'It's there. Any chance I can get hard copies of those two screens?'

Banks was looking through the eyepiece at the second screen.

'It's there all right,' he said. 'And yes, I can make hard copies. Let me put the images on a disk and take it back to the printer in the lab. It'll take a few minutes.'

'Thanks, man.'

'I hope it helps.'

'More than you know.'

'What's the guy doing anyway? Dressing up like a Mexican and doing good deeds?'

'Not really. Someday I'll tell you the whole thing.'

Banks let it go and went to work on the console, transferring the video images on the screens to a computer disk. He backed up the videos and transferred the headshots as well.

'Be back in a few minutes,' he said, getting up. 'Unless I have to warm up the machine.'

'Hey, is there a phone I can use while you're gone?'

'In the left drawer there. Hit nine first.'

McCaleb called Winston's home number and got her machine. As he listened to her voice, he hesitated about leaving a message, aware of the consequences to Winston if it was ever proved that she had worked with the subject of a murder investigation. A tape of his voice could do that. But he decided that the discoveries he had made in the last hour made it worth the risk. He didn't want to page Winston because he didn't want to wait around for her to call. He had to move. He hatched a quick plan and left a message after the beep.

'Jaye, it's me. I'll explain all of this when I see you but for now just trust me. I know who the shooter is. It's Noone, Jaye, James Noone. I'm heading to his address now – the address on the witness report. Meet me there if you can. I'll run it all down for you then.'

He hung up and called her pager number. He then punched in her home phone number and hung up. With any luck, he thought, Winston would get the message and soon be heading toward Noone's address to back him up.

McCaleb pulled his leather bag onto his lap and opened the zippered center pouch. The two guns were there, his own Sig-Sauer P-228 and the HK P7 he now knew James Noone had planted under his boat. McCaleb reached into the bag and took his own weapon out. He checked the action and tucked the pistol into the waistband of his jeans at the small of his back. He pulled his jacket down over it.

40

When questioned on the night of James Cordell's murder, James Noone had provided deputies with a single address for both his home and workplace. Until McCaleb got there, the address on Atoll Avenue in North Hollywood defied identification as an apartment or an office. That area of the Valley was a hodgepodge mixture of residential, commercial and even industrial zoning.

He slowly crawled north on the 101, back through the Cahuenga Pass, and finally picked up some speed as he switched to the 134 north. He exited on Victory and drove west until he found Atoll Avenue. The neighborhood he turned into was decidedly industrial. He could smell a bakery and he passed a fenced yard where slabs of jagged granite were stacked and pointing at the sky. There were warehouses without names on them. There was a pool chemical supply wholesaler and an industrial waste recycling center. Just where Atoll dead-ended at an old railroad spur with tall weeds poking up between the rails, McCaleb turned the Taurus down a driveway bordered on both sides by a long row of small, single-garage-bay warehouses. Each unit was a separate small business or storage lockup. Some had the names of businesses painted over the aluminum roll-up doors, some had no identifying marks at all and were either unrented or used anonymously for storage. McCaleb stopped the car in front of the rusting door marked with the address James Noone had given deputies three months before. There were no other markings on the door but the address. He killed the car's engine and got out.

It was a black night. No moon, no stars. The row of warehouses was dark save for a single floodlight down at the entrance. McCaleb looked around. He heard the tinny sound of music – Jimi Hendrix singing *Let me stand next to your fire* – from somewhere seemingly far away. And further down the drive, six warehouses away, the door to one of the garages had been pulled down unevenly until it jammed, offering a three-foot slice of the warehouse's interior that looked like a crooked smile blacker than the sky.

He checked Noone's unit, dropping to a crouch to study the line where the garage door met the concrete pavement. He wasn't sure but there appeared to be a dim light emanating from within the warehouse. He stepped closer and could make out the padlock that attached a steel ring on the door to a matching ring embedded in the concrete.

He stood up and banged the door with an open palm. The noise was loud and he heard it reverberate inside. He stepped back and looked around again. Other than the sound of the music, there was only silence. The air was still. The night wind had not found its way down to the space between the rows of garages.

McCaleb got back in the car, started it and backed it up at an angle so that the headlights were at least partially focused on Noone's garage. He then killed the engine but left the lights on, got out and went to the trunk. After lifting up the trunk mat, he found the jack assembly intact. He removed the jack handle and came around the car to the garage door. He looked up and down the drive once more and then bent down to the padlock.

As a bureau agent, McCaleb had never once been involved in an illegal break-in. He knew that they were a matter of routine but he had somehow avoided the ethical dilemma himself. But he felt no dilemma now as he worked the iron bar into the hasp of the lock. He wasn't carrying the badge anymore and, above that, this was personal. Noone was a killer and, worse yet, he had sought to pin his work on McCaleb. McCaleb didn't give a second thought to Noone's rights to protection from unlawful search and seizure.

Holding the jack handle on the far end for leverage, he slowly began pulling the steel bar in a clockwise motion. The padlock hasp remained strong but the steel ring attached to the door groaned under the pressure and then snapped off, its solder points giving way.

McCaleb straightened up and looked around and listened. Nothing. Just Hendrix covering Bob Dylan's 'All Along the Watchtower'. He quickly moved back to the Taurus and returned the jack handle to the spare-tire kit, pulled the trunk mat back over it and closed the trunk lid.

As he came around the car, he bent over next to the front tire and ran two fingers along the wheel rim, picking up a good amount of black carbon dust that had built up from the brake pads. He stepped over to the garage door and, squatting down by the lock, he smeared the carbon over the break points of the solder so that it would appear as though the ring had been broken off the door some time ago and the break points had been exposed to the elements. He then rubbed the rest of the dirt off his fingers onto one of his black socks.

When he was ready, he gripped the door's pull handle with his right hand. With his left he reached behind him and under his coat. He brought it back gripping his pistol, which he held at shoulder height, pointing skyward. With one move he stood and jerked the door up with him, using its momentum to keep it moving up until it was above his head.

His eyes quickly scanned the dim confines of the garage, his gun now pointed in the direction his eyes moved. The car's headlights illuminated about a third of the room. He could see an unmade cot and a stack of cardboard boxes against the left wall. Scanning right, he saw the outline of a desk and file cabinets. There was a computer on the desk, the monitor's screen apparently on and facing the rear wall, throwing a violet glow against it. McCaleb noticed the six-foot-long light hanging from the ceiling. In the shadowy light his eyes traced the aluminum conduit from the junction box along the ceiling and down the wall to a switch near the cot. He stepped sideways and reached for the switch without looking at it.

A fluorescent bulb blinked once, buzzed and then lit the garage with its severe light. McCaleb could now see that there was no one in the room and there were no closets to be checked. Just the approximately twenty-by-twelve-foot space cluttered with a mishmash of office furniture and equipment and the basic necessities of home – a bed, a chest of drawers, an electric space heater, a double-coil hot plate and a half-size refrigerator. No sink and no bathroom.

McCaleb stepped backward and then around the car. He reached in through the open window and shut off the lights. He then slipped the pistol back into his waistband, this time in the front for easier access. Finally, he stepped into the garage.

If the air had been still outside, then on the inside it seemed stagnant. McCaleb moved slowly around the old steel government desk and looked at the computer. The monitor was lit and a screen saver glowed on the screen. Random numbers of different sizes and colors floated on a sea of purple velvet. McCaleb stared at the screen for a few moments and he felt a tugging inside, almost a coiling of some deep muscle. In his mind the picture of a single red apple bouncing on a dirty linoleum floor appeared and then was gone. A tremble climbed the ladder of his spine.

'Shit,' he whispered.

He looked away from the computer screen, noticing that also on the desk was a collection of books clasped between brass bookends. Most were reference books on accessing and using the Internet. There were two volumes containing Internet addresses and two biographies of well-known computer hackers. There were also three books on crime scene investigation, a manual on homicide investigation, a book on an FBI investigation of a serial killer known as the Poet, and, finally, two books on hypnosis, the last about a man named Horace Gomble. McCaleb knew about Gomble. He had been the subject of more than one investigation by the bureau's serial crimes unit. Gomble was a former Las Vegas entertainer who had used his skills as a hypnotist, along with drug enhancers, to molest a series of young girls at county fairs throughout Florida. As far as McCaleb knew, he was still in prison.

McCaleb moved slowly all the way behind the desk now and sat down in the worn command chair facing the computer. Using a pen from his pocket, he pulled the desk's center drawer open. There was not much in it but a few pens and a plastic CD-ROM case. He used his pen to flip the case over and saw that it was called *Brain Scan.* He read the packaging and saw that the CD offered its user a guided tour of the human brain with detailed graphics and analysis of its workings.

He closed the drawer and used the pen again to open one of the two side drawers. The first one was empty except for an unopened box of Crackerjack. He closed it and below it was a file drawer. In this there were several manila files hanging in green folders hooked on two rails. Bending down to see better, McCaleb read the name on the tab of the first file:

GLORIA TORRES

He dropped the pen to the floor and in the same moment decided not to pick it up and that he didn't care anymore about leaving fingerprints or possibly infecting a crime scene. He pulled the file out and opened it on the desk. It contained photos of Gloria Torres in various clothing at various times of the day. In two of the photos Raymond was with her. In one she was with Graciela.

There were typewritten logs in the file. Surveillance logs. Detailed descriptions of Gloria's movements on a day-to-day basis. He quickly scanned these and saw repeated notations of her nightly stop at Sherman Market on her way home from work.

He closed the file, left it on the desk and reached for the next one in the drawer. He could have guessed the name written on the tab before he saw it:

JAMES CORDELL

He didn't bother opening it. He knew it would contain photos and surveillance notes just like the first one. Instead, he reached down and looked at the next file in line. It was as expected:

DONALD KENYON

He didn't pull that file, either. He used his finger to bend back the tabs on the remaining files so he could read them. As he did this, his heart lurched inside his chest, as if it had somehow come loose inside. He knew the names on the file tabs. Every single one of them.

'It's you,' he whispered.

And in his mind he saw the apples cascading onto the floor and going every which way.

He shoved the file drawer closed and the loud bang echoed off the concrete floor and steel walls, startling him like a shot. He looked out into the night through the open door and listened. He heard nothing, not even the music anymore. Only silence.

His eyes moved to the computer monitor and he studied the numbers moving lazily around on the screen. He knew the computer had been left on for a reason. Not because Noone was coming back; McCaleb knew he was long gone. No, it had been left on for him. McCaleb had been expected here. He knew this now, knew in his heart that Noone had choreographed every move.

McCaleb tapped the space bar and the screen saver disappeared. In its place was a prompt for a password. McCaleb didn't hesitate. He had the sense he was being played like a piano. He typed in numbers in an order he knew by heart.

903472568

He hit the enter key and the computer went to work. In a few moments the password was accepted and the screen flashed to the program manager template, a white screen with various icons spread across the field. McCaleb studied these quickly. Most were for accessing games. There also were icons for accessing America Online and Word for Windows. The last symbol he looked at was a tiny file cabinet and he guessed that was the computer's file manager icon. He found the electronic mouse on the side of the computer and used it to move the computer arrow to the file cabinet. He double-clicked and the screen flashed to the file manager. It was basic computer navigating. In the file manager the listing of files ran down the left side of the screen in a neat column. Choosing one of the files and clicking the arrow on it would bring up the titles of the documents contained in that file in a column on the right side of the screen.

Using the mouse, McCaleb ran the arrow down the files column, studying each one. Most were software files for the operation of various icon programs such as America Online, the Las Vegas Casino game and others. But eventually he came to a file titled CODE. He clicked the mouse and several document titles appeared on the right side of the screen. He read through these quickly and realized they corresponded with the names on the file tabs in the desk drawer.

All except for one document. McCaleb stared at it for a long moment, his finger raised and poised over the mouse button.

MCCALEB.DOC

He clicked the mouse and the document quickly filled the screen. McCaleb began to read it like a man reading his own obituary. The words filled him with dread, for he knew that they unalterably changed his life. They stripped his soul from him, took any meaning from his accomplishments and made a horrible mockery of them.

> Hello Agent McCaleb:
>
> It is you out there, I would hope.
>
> I will assume so. I will assume that you have lived up to that wonderful reputation you carried so nobly.
>
> I wonder? Are you alone? Are you running from them now as a wanted man? But, of course, now you have what you need to save yourself from them. But I am asking about before now, how did it feel to be the hunted one? I wanted you to know that feeling. My feelings . . . A terrible thing to live with fear, no?
>
> Fear never sleeps.
>
> Most of all, what I wanted was a place in your heart, Agent McCaleb. I wanted always to be with you. Cain and Abel, Kennedy and Oswald, darkness and light. Two worthy opponents, chained together through time . . .
>
> I could have killed you. I had that power and opportunity. But it would have been too easy, don't you think? The man on the dock, asking

directions. Your morning walk, the man on the rock jetty with the fishing pole. Do you remember me?

Now you do. I was there. But it would have been too easy, don't you agree? Too easy.

You see, I needed something more than vengeance or the vanquishing of a foe. Those are the goals of fools. I wanted – no. I needed and craved – something different. To test you first by turning you into me. The villain. The hunted one.

Then, when you emerged from that fire, your skin scorched but your body whole, to reveal myself as your most ardent benefactor. Yes, it was me. I followed her. I studied her. I chose her for you. She was my Valentine to you.

You are mine forever, Agent McCaleb. Every breath you take belongs to me. Every beat of that stolen heart is the echo of my voice in your head. Always. Every day.

Remember . . .

Every breath . . .

McCaleb folded his arms across his chest and held himself as though he had been flayed open with a blade. A deep shudder rolled through him and a moan escaped his throat. He pushed the chair back from the desk, away from the horrible message still on the screen, and bent his body forward into the crash position. His plane was going down.

41

His thoughts were blood red and black. He felt as though he were in some permanent void, surrounded by a velvet curtain of black space, his hands forever searching for the seam through which to escape but never finding it. He saw the faces of Graciela Rivers and Raymond as distant images receding into the darkness.

Suddenly, he felt a cold hand on his neck and he jumped, a shriek escaping from his throat like a prisoner going over the wall. He sat up. It was Winston. His reaction had scared her as much as she had scared him.

'Terry? Are you okay?'

'Yes. I mean, no. It's him. Noone is the Code Killer. He killed all of them. The last three for me. He did it until he got it right. He killed Gloria Torres for her heart. For me. So that I would live and be the testament to his glory.'

The coincidence of the name and Noone's purpose suddenly struck McCaleb.

'Wait a minute,' Winston said. 'Slow down. What are you talking about?'

'It's him. It's all here. Check the files, the computer. He killed those others. He then decided to save me. To kill for me.'

He pointed to the computer screen, where the message to McCaleb was still displayed. He waited while she read it but finally couldn't contain himself.

'All the pieces, they were right there. All the time.'

'What pieces?'

'The code. It was so simple. He used every digit but the number one. No one. Get it? I am no one. That's all he was saying.'

'Terry, let's talk about this later. Tell me how you got here? How did you know it was Noone?'

'The tape. The session we did with him.'

'The hypnosis? What about it?'

'Remember how I told you not to speak so the subject would not be confused?'

'Right. You said only you should ask questions of Noone. Anything between us should be signals or written down.'

'But at the end, when I knew it was all going to shit, I got frustrated. I said to you, "Anything else?" and you shook your head no. I asked, "Are you sure?" and you shook your head again. I broke my own rule by speaking to you. The thing is, I asked those questions to you out loud. So Noone should have answered me. If he was in a true hypnotic trance, he should have answered because he would not have known those questions were directed at you. But he didn't answer. It shows cognizance of the situation. He knew, either by the direction of my voice or its inflection, that I was talking to you instead of him. He shouldn't have known that. Not in a true trance. He should have answered every question spoken in that room unless it was specifically addressed to someone else. I never used your name.'

'He was faking.'

'Right. And if he was faking it, then his answers were bogus. It meant he was part of the setup. I had the videos compared before I came here. There are hard copies in my car. James Noone and the Good Samaritan are the same guy. The shooter.'

Winston shook her head as if to signal brain overload. Her eyes scanned the room for a place to sit down. There was only the cot.

'You want to sit here,' McCaleb said, standing up.

'I want to sit down but not in here. We have to back out of here, Terry. I need to call Captain Hitchens and then the others, LAPD and the bureau. I better put out a pickup on Noone, too.'

McCaleb was amazed that she still didn't have all the pieces together.

'Aren't you listening? There is no Noone. He doesn't exist.'

'What do you mean?'

'The name. It goes with everything else. Noone. Break it down and you get *no one.* I am no one. The pieces were there all the time . . .'

He shook his head and dropped back into the chair. He put his face in his hands.

'How am I . . . I can't live with this.'

Again Winston put her hand on his neck but this time he didn't startle.

'Come on, Terry, let's not think about that. Let's go out to the car and wait. I have to get a crime scene crew in here, maybe get some prints so we can ID this guy.'

McCaleb stood up and walked around the desk and out toward the door. He spoke without looking back at her.

'He never left a print anywhere else before. I doubt he started now.'

Two hours later McCaleb was sitting in the Taurus, parked out on Atoll behind the yellow police lines that had been strung between the rows of garage warehouses. A hundred yards down the drive he could see the cluster of activity in and around Noone's brightly lit garage. There were several detectives – some McCaleb recognized from the Code Killer task force, technicians, videographers from at least two of the agencies involved, and a half dozen uniformed officers standing by.

Moths to the flame, he thought. He watched it all with a strange detachment. His thoughts were on other things. Graciela and Raymond. And Noone. He couldn't stop thinking about the man who called himself Noone. He had been in the same room with him. He had been that close.

He needed a drink, wanted the burning taste of whiskey in his throat, but he knew to take that taste would be the same as putting a gun to his head. He knew that despite the pain cutting through him, he would not give Noone, or whoever he was, that satisfaction. He decided in the darkness of the car that he would live. Despite it all he would live.

He didn't notice the men walking down the drive toward him until they were almost to the Taurus. He flicked on the lights and identified them as Nevins and Uhlig and Arrango. He turned the lights off and waited. They opened the doors of the car and got in, Nevins in the front, the other two in the back, with Arrango directly behind McCaleb.

'Got any heat in this thing?' Nevins asked. 'It's getting cold out here.'

McCaleb started the car but waited to turn the heater on until the engine got warm. He looked in the rearview mirror at Arrango. It was too dark to see if he had a toothpick in his mouth.

'Where's Walters?'

'Busy.'

'Okay,' Nevins said. 'Uh, we came down to tell you it looks like we were wrong about you, McCaleb. I'm sorry. We're sorry. Looks like Noone is the guy. You did good work.'

McCaleb only nodded. It was a half-assed apology but he didn't care about that. What he had found out in order to clear his name would be harder to live with than if he had been publicly accused of the murders. Apologies meant nothing to him.

'We know it's been a long night for you and we want to get you on your way. I was thinking we could just kind of get your rundown on how all of this shakes out and then maybe tomorrow you come in and give a formal statement. What do you think?'

'Fine. As far as the formal statement goes, I'll give it to Winston. Not you guys.'

'Fair enough. I can understand that. But for now, why don't you tell us how, in your view, how this whole thing works. Can you do that?'

McCaleb leaned forward and switched on the heater. He composed his thoughts for a few moments before beginning.

'I'll call him Noone because that's all we have and maybe all we'll ever have. It begins with the Code Killer. That was Noone. At that time I was the bureau's point man on the task force. By agreement with the LAPD, I became the media spokesman on the case. I led the briefings, requests for interviews went to me. For ten months my face became synonymous on TV with the Code Killer. And so Noone fixated on me. As we got closer to him, he fixated on me. He sent letters to me. In his mind, I was the nemesis. I was the embodiment of the task force that was hunting him.'

'Aren't you taking a lot of the credit for yourself?' Arrango asked. 'I mean, you weren't the only –'

'Shut up and listen, Arrango. You might learn something.'

McCaleb stared at him in the rearview and Arrango stared back. McCaleb saw Nevins hold a hand up in a calming motion directed at Arrango.

'*He* gave me the credit,' McCaleb said. 'I didn't take it. Eventually, when he knew the risks were too great, he dropped out. The killings stopped. The

Code Killer disappeared. About that same time I went down with . . . with my problems. I needed the transplant and it became news because I had been a face in the news. Noone saw this. He could have easily been aware of this. And he hatched what he would consider his grandest scheme.'

'He decided that rather than kill you, he would save you,' Uhlig said.

McCaleb nodded.

'It would give him the ultimate victory because it would last and last. To simply eliminate me, kill me, would bring only a fleeting sense of fulfillment. But by saving me . . . now there was something unique, something that would get him into the hall of fame. And he'd always have me around as a reminder of how smart and powerful he is. Do you understand?'

'I understand,' Nevins said. 'But that's the psychological side. What I want to know is how he did it? How'd he get the names? How did he know about Kenyon and Cordell and then Torres?'

'His computer. Your techs are going to have to take that thing apart.'

'We've got Bob Clearmountain coming in,' Nevins said. 'You remember him?'

McCaleb nodded. Clearmountain was the L.A. field office's resident computer expert. A hacker extraordinary in his own right.

'Good. Then he'll be able to answer that question better than me. Eventually. My guess is that you'll find a hacking program in that computer. Noone got into BOPRA and from there got the names. He chose his targets based on age, physical fitness and proximity. And he went to work. With Kenyon and Cordell things went wrong. They went right with Torres. That is, according to Noone's view.'

'And he planned all along to lay it on you?'

'All I think is that he wanted me to follow the trail and find out for myself what he had done. He knew that would happen if I became a suspect. Because then I would have to look into it myself. But then that didn't happen at first because the case investigators missed the clues.'

He looked at Arrango in the mirror as he said this. He could see the detective's eyes turn dark with anger. He was about to explode.

'Arrango, the fact is, you treated it as an everyday stop-and-rob with the addition of shots fired, nothing more and nothing less. You missed it. So Noone jump-started the whole thing.'

'How?' Uhlig and Nevins asked in unison.

'My involvement came about because of an article in the *Times*. That article was prompted by a letter from a reader. Whatever name was on that letter, I bet it was Noone.'

He stopped there, waiting for disagreement. None came.

'The letter prompts the article. The article prompts Graciela Rivers. Graciela Rivers prompts me. Like dominoes.'

A thought suddenly occurred to him. He remembered the man in the old foreign car watching from across the street the first time he visited the Sherman Market. He realized the car matched the one he had seen speeding from the marina lot the night he chased the intruder.

'I think Noone was watching me all along,' he said. 'Watching his plan unfold. He knew when it was time to get into my boat and plant the evidence. He knew when to call you.'

He looked at Nevins, whose eyes shifted away and out the windshield.

'You got an anonymous call? What was said?'

'Actually it was an anonymous message. Taken down by the overnight person. It just said, "Check the blood. McCaleb has their blood." That was it.'

'It fits. That was him. Just another move in the game.'

They were silent for a while. The windows were beginning to fog with the heat and their breath.

'Well, I don't know how much of this we'll ever confirm,' Nevins said. 'Certainly a lot of maybes.'

McCaleb nodded. He doubted any of it would ever be confirmed because he doubted Noone would ever be identified or found.

'Okay, then,' Nevins continued. 'I guess we'll be in touch.'

He opened his door and the others followed. Before he got out, Uhlig reached over the seat and tapped McCaleb's shoulder with a harmonica.

'It was on the floor back here,' he said.

As Arrango stepped out onto the asphalt, McCaleb lowered his window and looked up at him.

'You know, you could've busted it. It was all there in the book. It was waiting for you.'

'Fuck you, McCaleb.'

He walked away, following the two agents back toward Noone's garage. McCaleb smiled slightly. He had to admit that in spite of everything he still wasn't above the guilty pleasure of tweaking Arrango.

McCaleb sat in the car for a few more minutes before leaving. It was late, past ten o'clock, and he was wondering where to go. He had not talked to Graciela yet and he looked forward to the task with a mixture of dread and relief, the latter coming from knowing that one way or another their relationship would be clearly defined soon. The problem he had was that he wasn't sure that he wanted to deliver his tidings at night. His news seemed better delivered during the unflinching light of day.

He put his hand on the ignition and took one last look up the drive toward the lighted garage where his life had been so brutally changed. He saw that the light cast from the garage and across the driveway was moving. He guessed that the overhead light had been disturbed somehow and was swinging. Something occurred to him then and he took his hand off the ignition.

McCaleb stepped out of the Taurus and without hesitation ducked under the yellow tape. The uniform officer in charge of entry to the crime scene said nothing. He had probably inferred – wrongly – that McCaleb was a detective, having watched three of the lead investigators walk down and sit in the car with him.

He walked to the periphery of the light and waited until he could catch Jaye Winston's eye. She was standing with a clipboard and writing down descriptions of the warehouse's contents. Every item in the place was being tagged and taken.

When Winston stepped out of the way of one of the technicians, she glanced out into the darkness and McCaleb caught her attention with a wave. She walked out of the garage and over to him. She had a cautious smile on her face.

'I thought you were clear. Why aren't you gone?'

'I'm going. Just wanted to say thanks for everything. You gettin' anything in there?'

She frowned and shook her head.

'You were right. Place is clean. Latents guys haven't even found a smudge. There are prints on the computer but my guess is that they are yours. I don't know how we're going to track this guy. It's like he was never here.'

He signaled her closer when he noticed Arrango step out of the garage and put a cigarette in his mouth.

'I think he made a mistake,' he said quietly. 'Get your best latents man and go to the Star Center. Have him laser the light tubes in the ceiling of the interview room. When I was setting up the hypnosis session, I took down some lights and handed them to Noone. He had to take them from me or he might give himself away. There might be prints.'

Her face brightened and she smiled.

'It's on the tape of the session,' he said. 'You can tell them it was your find.'

'Thanks, Terry.'

She clapped him gently on the shoulder. He nodded and started walking back to the car. She called after him and he looked back.

'Are you all right?'

He nodded.

'I don't know where you are going. But good luck.'

He waved and turned back toward his destination.

42

It seemed that every light was on in Graciela's home and this time McCaleb didn't linger in the car. He knew there was no longer any time to brood over choices. He had to face her and tell her the truth – tell her everything and accept the consequences.

Once again she opened the door before he got there. This woman who cares so much as to watch and wait for me, he thought as he stepped to the door. Now I must crush her heart.

'Terry, where have you been? I've been so worried.'

She rushed from the door and embraced him. He felt his will weaken but not break. He pulled her around to his side and led her back in with his arm around her shoulder, holding her close for what might be the last time.

'Let's go in,' he said. 'I have things to tell you.'

'Are you all right?'

'For now.'

They went to the living room and he sat next to her on the sectional. He held both her hands in his.

'Raymond in bed?'

'Yes. What is it, Terry? What's wrong?'

'It's over. They haven't caught him yet but they know who it is. Hopefully, they'll get him soon. I'm in the clear.'

'Tell me.'

He squeezed her hands. He realized that his were sweating and let hers go. It felt as if he were letting loose a fallen bird that he had nursed back to health. He felt that he would never hold her hands again.

'Remember that night we talked about faith and how hard it is for me to have it?'

She nodded.

'Before I tell you everything, I want you to know that in the last few days – actually, in all the time that I've known you – I have felt something inside of me coming back. It's a faith of some sort. Maybe a belief in something. I don't know. But I do know it was a start, a beginning of something good . . .'

'Was?'

He looked away from her for a moment to try to put the words together. It was hard. He knew he only had this one chance.

He looked back at her.

'But it's so new and so fragile, this change. And I don't know if it can last with what I have to tell you. But I want you to decide. I haven't prayed for anything in a long time. But I'll say a prayer that I see you – and Raymond – on my dock again. Or I'll pick up the phone and I'll hear your voice. I'm going to leave it up to you to decide.'

He leaned into her and kissed her gently on the cheek. She didn't resist.

'Tell me,' she said quietly.

'Graciela, your sister is dead because of me. Because of something I did a long time ago. Because I crossed a line somewhere and allowed my ego to challenge a madman's, Gloria is dead.'

His eyes dropped away from hers. The pain he had just put into them was too much for him to witness.

'Tell me,' she said again, even quieter this time.

And he did. He told her about the man known for the time being only as James Noone. He told her of the trail he had followed to the garage warehouse. He told her what he found there and what was waiting for him on the computer.

She began to cry as he told it, quiet tears that rolled down her cheeks and fell to the denim blouse she wore. He wanted to reach out to her, grab her and hold her close and kiss the tears on her cheeks. But he couldn't. He knew he was out of her world at that moment. He could not enter of his own choice. She would have to invite him back in.

When he was done, they sat quietly for a few moments. Graciela finally reached up and with open palms smeared the tears on her cheeks.

'I must look awful.'

'No, you don't.'

She looked down at the rug through the glass coffee table and a long period of silence passed by.

'What will you do now?' she finally asked.

'I'm not sure but I have a few ideas. I'm going to find him, Graciela.'

'Can't you leave it? Let the police find him?'

McCaleb shook his head.

'I don't think I can. Not now. If I don't find him and face him, I'll never know if I can get past this. I don't know if that makes sense or not.'

She nodded, still looking at the floor, and more silence went by. Finally she looked up at him.

'I want you to go now, Terry. I need to be alone.'

McCaleb nodded and slowly stood up.

'Okay.'

Again he fought an almost overwhelming urge to just touch her. Nothing more. He just wanted to feel her warmth once more. Like on the first day when she had touched him.

'Good-bye, Graciela.'

'Good-bye, Terry.'

He crossed the room and headed toward the door. On his way he glanced at the china cabinet in the living room and saw the framed photo of Gloria

Torres. She was smiling at the camera on that happy day so long ago. It was a smile he knew would always haunt him.

43

After a night of fitful sleep with dreams of being dragged down through deep, dark water, McCaleb rose at dawn. He showered and then made himself a heavy breakfast – an onion and green pepper omelet, microwaved sausage and a half quart of orange juice. When he was done, he still felt hungry and didn't know why. Afterward he went down to the head and took another reading of his vital signs. Everything was fine. At five after seven he called Jaye Winston's office number. She was there and he could tell by her voice that she had worked straight through the night.

'Two things,' McCaleb said. 'When do you want to do this formal statement and when do I get my car back?'

'Well, the Cherokee you can have any time. I just have to call over to release it.'

'Where is it?'

'Right here. Our impound lot.'

'I suppose I have to come get it.'

'Well, you've got to come out here anyway to give me a statement. Why don't you do both at the same time?'

'Okay, when? I want to get this over with. I want to get out of here, take a vacation.'

'Where are you going?'

'I don't know. I just have to get away, try to work all of this poison out. Maybe Vegas.'

'Now that's a *great* place for mental rehabilitation.'

McCaleb ignored her sarcasm.

'I know. So when can we meet?'

'I've got to put the case together ASAP and I need your statement. So anytime this morning would be good for me. I'll just make room for you.'

'Then I'm on my way.'

Buddy Lockridge was sleeping on the cockpit bench. McCaleb rousted him and he woke with a start.

'What is – hey, Terror, you're back, man.'

'Yeah, I'm back.'

'How's my car, man?'

'It's still running. Listen, get up, I've got one more trip to make and I need you to drop me off.'

Lockridge slowly pulled himself up into a sitting position. He had been lying under a sleeping bag. He gathered it around him and rubbed his eyes.

'What time is it?'

'It's seven-thirty.'

'Fuck, man.'

'I know, but this will be the last time.'

'Everything okay?'

'Yeah, everything's fine. I just need you to drop me at the sheriff's office so I can get my car. I need to go by a bank on the way.'

'They're not open this early.'

'They'll be open by the time we get out to Whittier.'

'So if I'm driving you out to pick your car up, who is going to drive it back here?'

'Me. Let's go.'

'But you said you aren't supposed to be driving, man. Especially a car with an air bag.'

'Don't worry about it, Buddy.'

They were on the way a half hour later. McCaleb brought a duffel bag with a change of clothes and everything else he would need for his trip. He also brought a thermos of coffee and two cups. He poured coffee and filled Buddy in on the case and all that had happened while they drove. Buddy asked questions for most of the drive.

'I guess I'll have to buy a paper tomorrow,' he said.

'It will probably be on TV, too.'

'Hey, is it going to be a book? Will I be in it?'

'I don't know. The story will probably hit the news today. I guess it depends on how big a story it is before anybody decides on a book.'

'Do they pay you to use your name like that? In a book, I mean. Or like in a movie?'

'I don't know. I guess you could ask for something. You were an important part. You came up with that missing picture in Cordell's car.'

'That's right, I did.'

Lockridge seemed proud of his part and the prospect of possibly making some money from it.

'And the gun. I found the gun that prick hid under the boat.'

McCaleb frowned.

'You know what, Buddy? If there's ever a book or if any reporters or cops come around, I would like it a lot better if you never mentioned that gun. That would help me a lot.'

Lockridge glanced over at him and then back at the road.

'No problem, then. I won't say a word.'

'Good. Unless I tell you otherwise. And if anybody comes to me about a book, I'll be sure to tell 'em to talk to you.'

'Thanks, man.'

It was after nine by the time they fought through all the traffic to Whittier.

McCaleb had Lockridge stop by a Bank of America branch while he went in and wrote a check for $1,000, taking the cash in twenties and tens.

A few minutes later the Taurus pulled into the Star Center parking lot. McCaleb counted out $250 and handed it to Lockridge.

'What's this for?'

'That's for letting me use the car and for the ride today. Also, I'm going to be away for a few days. Will you keep an eye on the boat for me?'

'Will do, man. Where you going?'

'Not sure yet. And I don't know when I'll be back.'

'That's okay. Two-fifty goes a long way.'

'Remember that woman who visited me? The pretty one?'

'Sure.'

'I'm hoping she'll come by the boat looking for me. Watch for her.'

'Okay. What do I do if she shows up?'

McCaleb thought a moment.

'Just tell her I'm still gone but that I was hoping she'd come by.'

McCaleb opened the car door. Before getting out, he shook Lockridge's hand and told him again that he had been a lot of help.

'Okay, I'm out of here.'

'Sure thing, man, have a good one.'

'Oh, hey, know what? I'll probably be doing a lot of driving. You mind if I borrow one of those harps you got?'

'Take your pick.'

He fished around in the door storage pocket and came out with three harmonicas. McCaleb picked the one he had been playing during the drive the other night along the coast highway.

'That's a good one. You start with the key of C.'

'Thanks, Buddy.'

'You sure took your sweet-ass time,' Winston said as McCaleb walked up to her desk. 'I've been wondering where the hell you've been.'

'I've been dicking around at the impound yard for an hour,' McCaleb responded. 'I can't believe you people. You take my car on a bullshit warrant and *I* have to pay towing and impound fees. A hundred and eighty bucks. There is no justice in this world, Jaye.'

'Look, just be lucky they didn't lose it and you got it back in one piece. Have a seat. I'm not quite ready.'

'Then what're you complaining about me being late for?'

She didn't answer. McCaleb took the chair at the side of her desk and watched as she went through a typed report, apparently proofreading and then initialing the bottom of each page.

'Okay,' she said. 'I was going to use one of the interview rooms. The tape's already set up. Shall we?'

'Wait a sec. What's happened since last night?'

'Oh, that's right. You haven't been around.'

'You get any prints off the light tubes?'

She broke into a smile and nodded.

'Why didn't you tell me?' McCaleb protested. 'What did you get?'

'Everything. Two palms, both thumbs, four fingers. We put it on the box and got a hit. Our boy is local. Name is Daniel Crimmins, thirty-two years old. And you remember that profile you did for the Code Killer task force? Well, you were dead-on, McCaleb. A slam dunk.'

McCaleb was beside himself with energy, though he outwardly tried to remain calm. The last pieces of the puzzle were dropping into place. He tried to recall the suspect's name from the case files but drew a blank.

'Tell me.'

'He was an LAPD academy washout. That was five years ago. As near as we can tell, since then he's had a number of private security jobs. I don't mean tin badge stuff. Computer stuff. He advertised on the Internet, had a web page, sent mailers to businesses. He basically sold computer security. We're hearing that he sometimes got work by hacking into a company's computer and then sending the CEO E-mail telling him how easy it was and why they should hire him to make their system hackproof.'

'BOPRA?'

'You got it. We've got a team over there now but they called in a little while ago. There's an executive who remembers getting E-mail from Crimmins last year. But he blew it off as a prank. He killed the message and never got another one. But it shows that Crimmins was inside BOPRA.'

McCaleb nodded.

'Anybody get his LAPD file yet?'

'Yeah, Arrango. He's being a prick with it, dealing it out on a need-to-know basis. But basically the guy lasted five months. Reason for his termination was – quote – failure to thrive in the collegial atmosphere of the academy. Translation: the guy was an introvert who would never last in a squad car. No partner would take him. So they washed him out. The problem for him was he was second generation. His old man retired up to Blue Heaven ten years ago. Uhlig had someone in the Idaho field office look dad up. He said as far as he knew, his son was currently on the LAPD. He didn't know Danny boy had been a washout because Danny boy didn't tell him. He says he hasn't seen his son in something like five or six years but when they talk on the phone, the boy always has good war stories.'

'Yeah, they're just made up.'

McCaleb saw that it all fit. The authority complex. Crimmins had transferred it from the father to the LAPD after he was washed out. The expulsion from the academy could have provided the psychic break that turned a harmless fantasy life into a deadly pastime. The murders were all on LAPD turf. He was showing the institution that deemed him unworthy just how smart, clever and worthy he was.

It occurred to McCaleb that when he had profiled the Code Killer three years before, he had suggested that dismissed officers and academy washouts be questioned as a priority. As far as he knew, that had been done.

'Wait. This guy should have been questioned back then. Failed law enforcement career was in the profile.'

'He *was* questioned. That's why Arrango is dicking around with the file.

Somehow, Crimmins passed the test. He was interviewed by a team from the task force but he didn't raise an eyebrow or warrant a second look. Still, it must've scared him. He was interviewed four weeks after the last Code killing. Maybe it's the reason he stopped.'

'Probably. Still, it's not going to look very good when it comes out this guy was interviewed and skated.'

'Too fucking bad. I say, let the chips fall. We've got the press conference scheduled for three o'clock.'

McCaleb considered what she had said about the killings stopping after Crimmins had been interviewed. He felt a thrill of satisfaction that it might have been his directive to interview academy washouts that had halted the killings. While he was savoring the thought, Winston opened a file and took a color photo off a stack of them. She handed it to him. It showed Crimmins in his academy uniform. Clean cut, clean shaven, a thin face and hopeful eyes that seemed to betray his confidence. It was as if he knew when the photo was taken that he would not make it, that there would be no graduation photo.

'So it looks like when he was Noone, there was not much of a disguise used,' he said. 'The glasses and something inside his cheeks to make his face look fuller.'

'Right. Probably because he knew he would have direct contact with cops and a full-on disguise would show.'

'Can I keep this?'

'Sure, we'll be giving them out today.'

'What's next? You got addresses?'

'Nothing good. The warehouse you already found was the only thing current. But there's got to be another place. His web page was still operational even after we unplugged the warehouse. It means he's got another computer somewhere. Running as we speak.'

'Can't they just trace the phone line in?'

'He's got an anonymous provider.'

'What's that?'

'Anything going to or from the web page goes through this anonymous provider of Internet access. We can't trace and we can't crack open the provider because of First Amendment bullshit. Besides, the expert over at the bureau, Bob Clearmountain, told me guys like him now use microwaves instead of hardwire phone lines. Makes it harder to trace and locate.'

The technology was beyond McCaleb. He changed the subject.

'You going to ID him at the press conference?'

'Think so. We'll get the photo out, show the hypnotism video, see what it brings. By the way, Keisha Russell at the *Times*. Did you tip her off?'

'I owed her the call. She helped me at the beginning of this thing. I left her a voice mail this morning. Thought I'd give her a head start on it. Sorry.'

'No, that's okay. I like her. I needed to talk to her anyway. Nevins told me what you said last night, about it probably being our guy who sent the letter that prompted the story about you in the *Times*.'

'Right. Did she keep the letter?'

'No. She only remembered it was signed Bob something or other. It was probably him. He had this thing so wired.'

McCaleb suddenly thought of something. Graciela had told him that she had not become aware of the *Times* story on him until a man who claimed he had worked with Glory called and told her of the story. She then went to the library to read it. McCaleb realized that the caller could have been Crimmins setting his plan into motion.

'What is it?' Winston asked.

'Nothing. I was just thinking.'

He decided not to tell Winston his hunch yet. He would check it out himself. It would give him a reason to break his promise not to call Graciela. He could make it an official call.

'So,' Winston said. 'Where do you think he is?'

'Crimmins?' He hesitated. 'In the wind, I guess.'

Winston studied his face a moment.

'I thought you might have an idea.'

He looked away from her and down at the desk.

'Well, the wind doesn't blow forever,' she said, letting it go. 'He's got to come down somewhere.'

'Hope so.'

They were silent then, finished with each other except for the formality of the statement he would have to tape.

'It may be none of my business,' Winston said, 'but how are you going to deal with this?'

'I'm working on it.'

'Well, if you ever need somebody to talk to . . .'

He nodded his thanks.

'Okay, then should we go get this over with?'

An hour later McCaleb was alone in the interview room. He had told his story to Winston and she had left with the tape to get it transcribed. She had given him permission to use the phone that was on the table and told him he had the room for as long as he needed it.

He composed his thoughts for a few moments and then punched in the number for the nursing station in the emergency room at Holy Cross. He asked for Graciela but the woman who answered said Graciela was not there.

'Is she on break?'

'No, she's not here today.'

'Okay, thank you.'

He hung up. He guessed that she had called in sick. He couldn't blame her. Not with the news he had delivered the night before. He punched in her home number. But after five rings the call was picked up by an answering machine. After the beep he fumbled through the message he wanted to leave.

'Uh, Graciela, it's me, Terry, you there?'

He waited a long moment and then continued.

'Um, I just wanted . . . they told me you weren't at work and I, uh, I wanted to say hello and there's a couple of questions I need to ask you about things. Loose ends mostly . . . but it would help to – anyway, I'm gonna go and I'll probably try to call you later on. Um, I'll probably be on the road so you don't have to worry about calling me back.'

He wished he could erase the message and start over. He cursed to himself and hung up, then wondered if the curse had been recorded. He shook his head, got up and left the room.

44

It took him two days to find the picture that Daniel Crimmins as James Noone had drawn during the hypnosis session. McCaleb started at Rosarita Beach and then worked his way south. He found it between La Fonda and Ensenada on a remote stretch of the coast. Playa Grande was a small village on a two-tiered rock flow overlooking the sea. The village mostly consisted of a motel with six small detached bungalows, a pottery store, a small restaurant and market and a Pemex station. There was also a small stable for renting horses to ride down on the beach. The commercial core, if it was big enough to be called that, was at the edge of a cliff overlooking the beach. On the stepped bluff above it was a wide scattering of small houses and trailer homes.

What made McCaleb stop was the stable. He remembered Crimmins describing horses on the beach. He got out of the Cherokee and walked down a steep trail cut through the rock outcroppings to the beach. The wide, white beach was a private enclave about a mile long and enclosed on each end by huge, jagged rock flows into the sea. Near the south end, McCaleb saw the rock overhang that Crimmins had described during the hypnosis session. McCaleb knew that the best and most convincing way to lie is to tell as much truth as possible. So he had taken his subject's description of the place at which he felt most relaxed in the world to be a true description of a place he knew. Now, McCaleb had found it.

He had arrived at Playa Grande through simple deduction and legwork. The description Crimmins had given during the session had obviously been the Pacific Coast. He had said he liked to drive *down* to this place and since McCaleb knew there was no California beach south of L.A. as remote as he had described or with horses on it, that obviously made the destination Mexico. And since Crimmins had said he drove there, that pretty much eliminated Cabo and the other points far south along the Baja peninsula. It took two days to cover the coastline that was left. McCaleb stopped at every village and every time he saw a cutoff from the highway to the beach.

Crimmins had been right. It was a truly beautiful and restful spot. The sand was like sugar and a million years of crashing waves had carved a deep bite into the cliff face, creating the overhang that resembled nothing so much as a rock wave, curled and about to break over the beach.

McCaleb was the only person on the beach to be seen in either direction.

It was a weekday and he guessed that this stretch of sand lay largely unpopulated until the weekends. That was why Crimmins had liked it.

Three horses were on the beach. They milled around an empty feed trough while waiting for customers. There was no need to tie them. The beach was completely enclosed by water and rock. The only way off it was the steep trail back up to the stable.

McCaleb wore a baseball cap and sunglasses as protection against the power of the midday sun. He wore long pants and a windbreaker as well. But, entranced by the beauty of the spot, he remained on the beach long after he determined Daniel Crimmins was nowhere to be seen. After a while a teenager wearing shorts and a sweatshirt with no sleeves came down the trail and approached.

'You would like horse ride?'

'No, *gracias.*'

From the pocket of his coat McCaleb pulled the folded photos Tony Banks had made from the videotapes. He showed them to the boy.

'You seen? This man . . . I want to find.'

The boy stared at the photos and made no indication he understood. Finally he just shook his head.

'No, no find.'

He turned and headed back to the trail. McCaleb returned the photos to his jacket and after a few minutes headed back up the steep incline himself. He stopped twice on the way up but the climb still left him exhausted.

McCaleb ate lobster enchiladas at the restaurant for lunch. It cost him the equivalent of $5 American. He showed the photos a few more times but got no takers. He walked to the Pemex station after lunch and used the pay phone there to check the machine on his boat for messages. There were none. He then called Graciela's number for the fourth time while he had been on the road and once again got her machine. He didn't leave a message this time. If she was ignoring his calls, it was probably because she simply no longer wanted to talk to him.

McCaleb checked into the Playa Grande Motel, paying cash and using a phony name. As an afterthought he showed the photos to the man behind the counter in the small office and got another negative response.

His bungalow had a partial view of the beach below and a wide view of the Pacific. He checked what he could see of the beach and it was still empty except for the horses. He took off his windbreaker and decided to take a nap. It had been a wearying two days of driving bad roads, walking on sand and climbing steep trails.

Before lying down, he opened his duffel bag on the bed, put his toothbrush and toothpaste in the bathroom and then arranged the plastic vials containing his medicines and the box of disposable thermometer strips on the bed table. He took the Sig-Sauer out of the bag and put it on the table as well. It was always a marginal risk taking weapons across the border. But at the crossing, as expected, McCaleb had been simply waved through by the bored Mexican *federales.*

As he dropped off to sleep with his head between two musty pillows, he decided he would try the beach again at sunset. Crimmins had described the sunset during the hypnosis session. Maybe he would be on the beach then. If not, McCaleb decided he would begin looking for Crimmins in the scattered neighborhood above the village. McCaleb was confident he would find him. He felt no doubt that he had found the place Crimmins had described.

He dreamed in colors for the first time in months, his eyes darting under tight eyelids. He was on a runaway horse, a huge Appaloosa the same color as the wet sand, galloping down the beach. He was being chased but his unsteady mount prevented him from turning to see who it was behind him. He only knew that he must run, that if he stopped he would perish. The animal's hooves were throwing great clods of wet sand in the air as it galloped.

The rhythmic cadence of the horse's gallop was replaced by the pounding sound of his own heart. McCaleb came awake and tried to calm his body. After a few moments he decided he should check his temperature.

As he sat up and put his feet down on the carpet, his eyes checked the bed table by habit. He was looking for the clock that was on the table next to his own bed on the boat. But there was no clock here. He looked away and then his eyes darted back to the table as he realized the gun was gone.

McCaleb quickly stood up and looked around the room, an eerie feeling of dislocation coming over him. He knew he had placed the gun on the table before sleeping. Someone had been in the room while he slept. Crimmins. He had no doubt. Crimmins had been in the room.

He hastily checked the windbreaker and duffel bag and found nothing else missing. He scanned the room again and his eyes came across a fishing pole standing in the corner of the room next to the door. He went to the corner and grabbed it. It was the same model rod and reel combination he had bought for Raymond. As he turned it in his hands and studied it, he found the initials RT had been cut into the cork hand grip. Raymond had marked the pole as his. Or someone had marked it for him. Regardless, the message was clear: Crimmins had Raymond.

McCaleb was fully alert now, his chest filling with the constricting ache of dread. He punched his fists into the arms of the windbreaker as he put it on and then left the bungalow after studying the door and finding no sign that the lock had been tampered with. He moved quickly to the motel office, the bell ringing loudly overhead as he shoved the door open. The man who had taken his money stood up from the chair behind the counter, an uneasy smile on his face. He was about to say something when McCaleb, in one unhesitating motion, stepped to the counter, reached over it and grabbed the man by the front of his shirt. He jerked him forward until his body was prone over the top of the counter, the edge of the Formica digging into his substantial gut. McCaleb bent down until he was in the man's face.

'Where is he?'

'*Qué?*'

'The man, the one you gave the key to my room. Where is he?'

'*No habla –*'

McCaleb pulled down on the man's shirt harder and put his forearm on the back of his neck. McCaleb could feel his own strength flagging but pushed down harder.

'*Bullshit, you don't. Where is he*?'

The man sputtered and moaned.

'I don't know,' he finally said. 'Please. I don't know where he is.'

'Was he alone when he came here?'

'Alone, yes.'

'Where does he live?'

'I do not know this. Please. He say he your brother and have surprise for you. I give him the key so he surprise you.'

McCaleb let go and pushed the man back over the counter so hard that he fell backward right into his chair. He held his hands up in a beseeching manner and McCaleb realized he must be truly scaring the man.

'Please.'

'Please, what?'

'Please, I don't want to have trouble.'

'It's too late. How did he know I was here?'

'I call him. He pay me. He come here yesterday and say you might come. He give me phone number. He pay me.'

'And how did you know it was me?'

'He give me picture.'

'All right, give it to me. The number and the picture.'

Without hesitation the man reached to a drawer in front of him. McCaleb quickly reached over and grabbed his wrist and roughly jerked it away from the drawer. He opened the drawer himself and his eyes held on a photograph sitting on top of a clutter of paperwork. It was a photo of McCaleb walking along the rock jetty near the marina with Graciela and Raymond. McCaleb could feel his face turning red as the anger pushed hot blood into the tightened muscles of his jaw. He held the photo up and studied the back. There was a phone number written on the back.

'Please,' the motel man said. 'You take the money. One hundred American dollars. I don't want trouble for you.'

He was reaching into his shirt pocket.

'No,' McCaleb said. 'You keep it. You earned it.'

He yanked the door open then, hitting the overhead bell so hard that the twine it hung from snapped and the bell bounced into the corner of the office.

He went through the gravel parking lot and over to the phone at the Pemex station. He dialed the number on the back of the photograph and listened to a series of clicks on the line as the call went through at least two call-forwarding circuits. McCaleb cursed to himself. He would not be able to trace the number to an address, even if he could get someone in local authority to do it for him.

Finally the call reached the last circuit and started ringing. McCaleb held his breath and waited but the call was not picked up by human or machine. After twelve rings he crashed the receiver down onto its hook but it bounced off and dropped, swinging erratically back and forth beneath the phone. McCaleb stood frozen by anger and the impotence of his position, the light sound of the still-ringing phone buzzing from below.

After a long moment he realized he was staring through the glass pane of the phone booth at the motel parking lot. His Cherokee was there and one other car. A dusty white Caprice with a California plate on the back.

Quickly, he left the booth, crossed the parking lot to the trail and headed down to the beach. The trail cut between rock outcroppings and obscured any view below. McCaleb didn't see the beach until he got to the bottom and made the final turn to the left.

The beach was empty. He walked straight out to the water's edge looking both ways but the sand in both directions was deserted. Even the horses had been taken in for the day. His eyes were eventually drawn to the pocket of deep shadows beneath the rock overhang. He headed that way.

Beneath the overhang the sound of the surf was amplified to a magnitude that sounded like the cheering in a stadium. Moving from the bright light of the open beach into the deep shadows temporarily blinded McCaleb. He stopped, closed his eyes tightly and reopened them. As his focus returned, he saw the outlines of the jagged rock surrounding him. Then from the deepest pocket of the enclave stepped Crimmins. He held the Sig-Sauer in his right hand, the muzzle of the weapon pointing at McCaleb.

'I don't want to hurt you,' he said. 'But you know I will if I have to.'

He spoke loudly so that his voice would carry above the din and echo of waves.

'Where is he, Crimmins? Where is Raymond?'

'Don't you mean, "Where are they?"'

McCaleb had assumed as much but the confirmed knowledge of the terror Graciela and Raymond were feeling at that moment – if they were still alive – cut into him. He took a step toward Crimmins but then stopped when Crimmins raised the aim of the weapon to his chest.

'Easy now. Let's be calm. They are safe and sound, Agent McCaleb. Not to worry about that. Their safety, in fact, is in your hands. Not mine.'

McCaleb made a quick study of Crimmins. He had jet black hair and a mustache now. He was growing a beard or needed a shave. He wore pointed-toe boots, black jeans and a denim cowboy shirt with double pockets and a design seam across the chest. His current look put him somewhere between the Good Samaritan and James Noone.

'What do you want?' McCaleb demanded.

Crimmins ignored the question. He spoke in a calm voice. He was confident he had the upper hand.

'I knew if anyone would come, it would be you. I had to take precautions.'

'I said, what do you want? You want me, is that it?'

Crimmins stared wistfully out past McCaleb and shook his head. McCaleb studied the weapon. He could see the safety was off. But the hammer was not cocked back. It was impossible to tell whether Crimmins had chambered a round.

'My last sunset here,' Crimmins said. 'I have to leave this place now.'

He looked back at McCaleb, smiling as though inviting McCaleb to acknowledge the loss.

'You performed much better than I had anticipated.'

'It wasn't me. It was you, Crimmins. You fucked up. You left your fingerprints for them. You told me about this place.'

Crimmins frowned and nodded, acknowledging the mistakes. A long beat of silence went by.

'I know why you came here,' he finally said.

McCaleb did not reply.

'You want to take from me the gift that I gave you.'

McCaleb felt the bile of hate rising and burning in his throat. He remained silent.

'A vengeful man,' Crimmins said. 'I thought I told you how fleeting the fulfillment of vengeance is.'

'Is that what you learned, killing all of those people? I bet when you closed your eyes at night, the old man was still there, no matter how many you killed. He wouldn't go away, would he? What did he do to you, Crimmins, to fuck you up so bad?'

Crimmins tightened his grip on the gun and McCaleb could see his jaw take on a more pronounced line.

'This is not about that,' he responded angrily. 'It's about you. I want you to live. I want to live. None of it will have been worth it unless you live. Don't you see that? Don't you feel the bond between us? We are tied together now. We are brothers.'

'You're crazy, Crimmins.'

'Whatever I am, it is not of my doing.'

'I don't have time for your excuses. What do you want?'

'I want you to thank me for your life. I want to be left alone. I want time. I need time to move my things and find a new place. You will have to give it to me now.'

'How do I know you even have them? You have a fishing pole. It's nothing.'

'Because you know me. You know I have them.'

He waited and McCaleb said nothing.

'I was there when you called and groveled to her machine, when you pleaded for her to pick up like a pathetic schoolboy.'

McCaleb felt his anger become shaded with embarrassment.

'Where are they?' he yelled.

'They are close.'

'Bullshit. How'd you get them across the border?'

Crimmins smiled and gestured with the gun.

'The same way you took this across. No questions asked going south. I gave your Graciela a choice. She and the boy could ride up in the front and be on their best behavior or they could ride in the trunk. She acted accordingly.'

'You better not have hurt them.'

McCaleb realized how desperate he sounded and wished he hadn't said it.

'Whether that happens depends on you.'

'How?'

'I leave now. And you do not follow. You do not attempt to track me. You get in your car and go back up to your boat. You stay by the phone and I will call you from time to time to make sure you are there and not following me. When I know I am safe from you, I will let the woman and the boy go.'

McCaleb shook his head. He knew it was a lie. Killing Graciela and Raymond would be the final misery Crimmins would joyfully and without guilt bestow on him. The ultimate victory. He knew that no matter what happened after, he couldn't let Crimmins off the beach alive. He had come to Mexico for one reason. He now had to act on it.

Crimmins seemed to know his thoughts and smiled.

'No choice, Agent McCaleb. I walk away from here or they die alone in a black hole. You kill me and no one will find them. Not in time. Starvation, darkness . . . it is an awful thing. Besides, you forget something.'

He held the gun up again and waited a beat for McCaleb to reply but there was nothing.

'I hope you think of me often,' Crimmins said. 'As I shall think of you.'

He started walking toward the light.

'Crimmins,' McCaleb said. 'You have nothing.'

Crimmins turned and his eyes dropped to the gun now in McCaleb's hand. McCaleb took two steps toward him and raised the muzzle of the P7 to his chest.

'You should have checked the duffel bag.'

Crimmins countered by raising the Sig-Sauer to McCaleb's chest.

'Your gun's empty, Crimmins.'

McCaleb saw doubt flick through the other man's eyes. It went by fast but he caught it. He knew then that Crimmins had not checked the gun. He didn't know that it contained a full clip but no round had been chambered.

'But this one isn't.'

They stood there, each man holding the muzzle of his gun a foot from the other's heart. Crimmins looked down at the P7, then up to McCaleb's eyes. He stared intently, as if trying to read something. In that moment McCaleb thought about the photo in the newspaper article. The piercing eyes that showed no mercy. He knew then that he had those eyes again.

Crimmins pulled the trigger of the Sig-Sauer. The hammer snapped on an empty chamber. McCaleb fired the P7 and watched as Crimmins jerked backward and fell flat on his back on the sand, his arms outstretched at ninety-degree angles, his mouth open in surprise.

McCaleb moved over him and quickly grabbed away the Sig-Sauer. He then used his shirt to wipe off the P7 and dropped it on the sand, just out of the dying man's reach.

McCaleb got down on his knees and leaned over Crimmins, careful not to get blood on himself.

'Crimmins, I don't know if I believe in a God, but I'll hear your confession. Tell me where they are. Help me save them. Finish it with something good.'

'Fuck you,' Crimmins said forcefully, his mouth wet with blood. 'They die and that's on you.'

He raised a hand and pointed a finger at McCaleb. He then dropped it to the sand and seemed drained by the outburst. He moved his lips once more but McCaleb couldn't hear him. He bent over closer.

'What did you say?'

'I saved you. I *gave* you life.'

McCaleb stood up then, brushed the sand off his pants and looked down at Crimmins. His eyes were tearing and his mouth was moving as he labored for his final breaths. Their eyes connected and held.

'You're wrong,' McCaleb said. 'I traded you for me. I saved myself.'

45

McCaleb drove along the gravel roads on the bluff over the village of Playa Grande and studied each house and trailer he passed, looking for the telltale sign of a telephone line hookup or a mounted microwave dish. He had all the windows of the car open and each time he came upon a property that fit the search profile, he pulled the car in close, turned it off and listened.

Not many of the properties were connected to the outside world by telephone or airwaves. McCaleb assumed most of the people who lived in so remote a location chose to do so because they didn't want that connection. They were expatriates and recluses, people who wanted to be cut off from the rest of the world. It was another reason Crimmins had chosen the place.

Twice people came out of their homes to ask McCaleb what he wanted. He showed them the photos but got negative responses. He apologized for the intrusion and moved on.

By the time the sun was close to the horizon, he was growing desperate. Without daylight he knew his search would be untenable. He would have to stop at every house or wait until the following morning. That would leave Graciela and Raymond alone somewhere for the night, without food and light, probably no heat, scared, bound or held captive in some way.

He increased his speed and quickly moved through an entire trailer park, stopping only once to show the photos to an old woman sitting on the front porch of a decrepit trailer. She shook her head no at the photos and he moved on.

Finally, after the sun was gone and the sky held the last of the day's light, he passed a crushed-shell drive leading over a small rise and then out of sight. A gate was pulled across it and posted with a No Trespassing sign printed in Spanish and English. McCaleb studied the gate for a few moments and saw that it was tied closed with just a short length of wire through the hasp. He got out, pulled the wire free and pushed the gate open.

Once over the first rise, McCaleb could see that the drive led to a trailer home set on the next rise. The ticking of anticipation began in his chest when he saw the small dish mounted on the flat roof. As he got closer, he could see there was no car parked under the aluminum carport. He also noticed a small Quonset-style storage shed at the back of the property near an old fence. Sitting on top of several of the fence posts were bottles and jars, as if set out for shooting practice.

The sound of the Cherokee's tires turning on the crushed shells obliterated any possibility of a quiet approach. It also robbed McCaleb of the chance to listen until he stopped the car.

He pulled into the carport and stopped. He turned the key off and sat frozen still and listened. There was only silence for two seconds and then he heard it. The sound was muffled by the trailer's aluminum siding, but he heard it. The ringing of a telephone inside the trailer. McCaleb held his breath and listened to it ring over and over until he was sure. He blew out his breath and felt a jolt go through his heart. He knew he had found them.

He got out and approached the trailer's door. The phone kept ringing, at least ten times now since he had stopped the car. He knew it would keep ringing until he got inside and answered it or somebody ventured into the phone booth at the Pemex station and hung up the receiver.

He tried the door and found it locked. Using the ring of keys he had taken from Crimmins's pants, he tried several in the knob until he had the door open. He stepped into the quiet and warm trailer and looked around what seemed to be a small living room. The shades had been drawn and it was dark except for the glow of a computer screen that sat on a table against the wall to the right. McCaleb reached to the wall to the left of the door and found a light switch. He flicked it and the room was illuminated.

It was much like the warehouse he had discovered in LA, crowded with computers and other equipment. There was a small sitting area apparently reserved for relaxation. None of it meant anything to McCaleb. He didn't care anymore. He had come for only two reasons.

He stepped into the trailer and called out.

'Graciela? Raymond?'

He heard nothing in reply. He thought about what Crimmins had said, about them being in a black hole. He turned and looked out the door, his eyes scanning the desolate landscape. He saw the Quonset shed and started that way.

With the heel of his palm he banged on the padlocked door and the noise echoed loudly inside but there was no answer. He fumbled as he got the keys out again and quickly jammed the small key with the Master Lock logo on it into the lock. Finally, he swung the door open and stepped into the darkness. The shed was empty and McCaleb felt a great tearing inside.

He turned and braced himself in the doorway, his eyes downcast as his mind filled with a vision of Graciela and Raymond, their arms around each other, in complete darkness somewhere.

That was when he saw it. On the crushed-shell drive in front of him there was a clear depression pattern crossing the two patterns made by a vehicle's tires. There was a trail across the drive, heading in the direction of the sloping hill's crest. It looked to McCaleb as if there was nothing out that way, yet someone had walked there enough times to leave the trail across the drive.

His strides increased to a full run as he headed in the direction the trail led. He came over the crest and in the drop-off below he saw the flat concrete foundation of a structure that had never been built. He slowed to a walk as he approached, wondering what he had found. Rusted iron rebars and plumbing pipes protruded from the concrete. An old pick and a shovel had been left lying on it. There was a step up onto the slab at the spot where a door obviously was to be placed but never was. McCaleb stepped up and looked around. There were no doors to a basement, nothing he saw that matched what Crimmins had said.

He kicked at one of the brass water pipes and looked down into the four-inch main pipe upon which a toilet was supposed to have been placed. In that moment he knew where they were.

He spun around and his eyes covered the ground around the slab. Noting that the step would be the front of the structure, he concentrated on the ground to the rear, looking for the spot where the plumbing would lead: a septic tank. His eyes immediately picked up an area of dirt and rock that he could tell had recently been turned. He grabbed the shovel and ran.

It took him five minutes to clear the dirt and rock off the top of the tank. He knew they had air; the pipes up to the slab would provide it. But he worked as if they were suffocating below him. As he finally opened the manhole-sized cover of the tank, the sky's dying light swept in and he saw their faces. They were scared but alive. McCaleb felt a great lifting of weight off him as he reached down to them.

He helped them out of the darkness, their eyes crinkled against even the weak early-evening light. Then he held them so tight he thought that he might hurt them. Graciela was crying, her body shaking against his.

'It's all right,' he said. 'It's over now.'

She pulled her head back and looked in his eyes.

'It's over now,' he repeated. 'He won't hurt anybody ever again.'

46

The bilge was a claustrophobic crawl space full of the dizzying fumes of gasoline. McCaleb had an old T-shirt wrapped around his face like a bandit but still the fumes filled his lungs. There were nine bolts that held the fuel filter he was changing in place. He had three in and tightened down. He was struggling with the fourth, angling his face forward in a vain effort to keep the sweat from running into his eyes, when he heard her voice above him.

'Hello? Anybody home?'

McCaleb dropped what he was doing and jerked the shirt from around his face. He crawled to the open hatch and came up. Jaye Winston was standing on the dock waiting for him.

'Jaye. Hey, what's up? Come on aboard.'

'No, I'm on the run. I just wanted to stop by and let you know they found him. I'm on my way down to Mexico.'

McCaleb raised his eyebrows.

'He's not alive. He killed himself.'

'Really?'

'We're dealing with the Baja Judicial Police so nothing is for sure until I get down there, but they found him washed up on the beach in a place called Playa Grande. Down on the coast. Shot himself in the heart. A boy who takes care of horses on the beach found him. That was two days ago. We just got the news.'

McCaleb looked around. He saw a man in a white shirt and tie loitering near the gate to the gangway. Her partner, he assumed.

'Are they sure it was him?'

'They say so. The description is close. Plus they tracked him back to a trailer off the beach. They found computers, photos, all kinds of stuff. Looks like our guy. Plus he left a good-bye note on the computer screen.'

'What did he say?'

'Well, this is all secondhand, but essentially he took responsibility for his actions and said he deserved to die for them. It was short and sweet.'

'They find a weapon?'

'Not yet but they're sweeping the beach with metal detectors today. If they find it, it will probably be our HK P7. The bullet taken during the autopsy was a Federal FMJ. We'll see if we can borrow it for comparison to our cases up here.'

McCaleb nodded.

'So how are they playing it out?'

'Pretty simple. The guy knows we're on to him, gets an attack of remorse, writes his note and goes down to the beach, where he puts one in his heart. The tide took him into the rocks there and the body got hung up. That's why it wasn't carried out to sea. We're going down to have a look at things. And to get prints. Probably won't get gunshot residue because the body was in the water. But one thing's for sure, we're not going to close it unless we're absolutely sure it was Crimmins.'

'Yeah, that's a good idea.'

'I just want to make sure because it just didn't seem like it was heading toward a suicide, know what I mean?'

She was looking at him intently.

'Well . . . you never know.'

She nodded and for the first time she looked away from him. She checked on her partner, who was watching them from a distance that put him well out of earshot.

'How was Vegas, Terry?'

He sat down on the gunwale and put the wrench he had been working with down next to him.

'Uh . . . well, I didn't really go anywhere. I decided that if I didn't get this thing running, it might never happen. I turned off the phone and just worked on the boat. I think it's finally ready to go.'

'Good. I hope you catch a lot of fish.'

'I will. You come over some day, I'll take you out to catch a marlin.'

'I might take you up on that.'

She nodded and took another look around the marina.

'Well, I guess I better go. It's a long drive down there and we're getting a late start.'

'Happy hunting.'

'Thanks.'

She made a move to go but then hesitated and looked back at him.

'I saw your Cherokee up there in the lot. You ought to get it washed, Terry. There's an awful lot of sand on it.'

Their eyes held each other's for a long moment then, the silent transmission clear.

'I'll do that,' McCaleb finally said. 'Thanks.'

47

The Following Sea was cutting south at trolling speed across the low swells toward Catalina. Up on the bridge, McCaleb stood braced against the wheel. He had the forward wind curtain down and the chill air coming up off the surface hit him fully, hardening his skin beneath his clothes. Ahead in the mist the island rose like a huge rock cathedral on the horizon. The outbuildings and some of the taller boats of Avalon were coming into view. He saw the circular terracotta roof of the casino, the town's signature structure, clearly now.

He turned to look astern. The mainland was out of sight, discernible only by the haze of smog that hung over it like a sign warning *Do Not Come Here!* He was happy to be free of it.

He thought about Crimmins for a moment. He had no regrets about the way he had left things in Mexico. There would be no questions about his motives and choices now. But he was protecting more than himself. Graciela and Raymond had spent thirty-six hours with Crimmins. Though he had not physically harmed them, they still needed private time to heal, to put the ordeal behind them. McCaleb couldn't see how bringing more cops and questions into their lives could help with that. Graciela had agreed.

From the bridge he looked down into the cockpit and secretly watched the two of them. Raymond was in the fighting chair, his small hands grasping the trolling set. Graciela stood next to him, holding the chair for support. If McCaleb could, he would have willed a big black marlin onto the line for the boy. But he wasn't worried. There would be plenty of time to catch fish.

Graciela seemed to sense his gaze and she looked up at him. They shared a smile of intimacy. McCaleb could feel his heart seize when she smiled at him that way. It made him so happy that it hurt.

The boat trip was a test. Not only for the boat but for the two of them. That was what she had called it. A test to see if they could overcome the thing between them, the painful knowledge of what had happened and what he had done, of why he was here and others were not. Especially Gloria. They would see if they could put that behind them, too, or at least to the side, to be taken out and looked at only when needed.

It was all McCaleb could hope for. It was all he wanted, just the chance. The fact that it was now in his grasp made his faith in her feel requited, fulfilled. For the first time in a long time he was feeling as though there was purpose.

He looked forward again and checked the boat's course. He could see the bell house up on the hill and next to it the roof of the home where the writer and sportsman Zane Grey had lived. It was a beautiful town and he couldn't wait to be back and to show it to them.

He stole another glance down into the stern. Graciela's hair was tied back against the wind and he studied the lovely lines of the nape of her neck. He had been feeling something almost like faith lately and was confused by where it would lead him now. Confused but not concerned. He knew it was of no real matter. His faith was in Graciela Rivers. He had no doubt as he gazed down at her that he was looking at the rock upon which he would make his stand.

Acknowledgments

Blood Work is a work of fiction but it was inspired by conversations with my friend Terry Hansen, who received a heart transplant on Valentine's Day 1993. I thank him for his openness in discussing the emotional and physical changes such an event brought to his life.

I would also like to thank all those who offered their advice and expertise to me during the writing of this novel. Any mistakes in these pages are my own. Particularly, I would like to thank Linda and Callie for putting up with me; William Gaida, LAPD-retired, for teaching me the art of hypnotic interrogation; and Jim Carter for showing me around boats and Cabrillo Marina. Also, thanks go to Gene Riehl, FBI-retired, Scott Anderson, computer czar, Larry Sulkis, first gunner, and Scott Eyman, the writing guru who helped talk me off the ledge after I spiked 240 pages – on purpose! – and had to start again.

The book and the author were benefitted immensely by the thoughts of those who read it along the way. They include Mary Connelly Lavelle, Susan Connelly and Jane Connelly Davis, Joel Gotler, Brian Lipson, Philip Spitzer, Ed Thomas, Bill Gerber, Melissa Rooker and Clint Eastwood. (Special thanks to Joel for the harmonica riffs.) My editor, Michael Pietsch, did his usual superb job in taking a massive manuscript and making smooth sense of it.

Lastly, once again thanks to the booksellers who help me tell my stories.

Void Moon

To Linda, for the first fifteen.

All around them the cacophony of greed carried on in its most glorious and extreme excess. But it couldn't make a dent in their world.

She broke the connection between their eyes just long enough to look down and find her glass and then raise it from the table. It was empty except for ice and a cherry but that didn't matter. He raised his glass in return, maybe one swallow of beer and foam left in it.

'To the end,' she said.

He smiled and nodded. He loved her and she knew it.

'To the end,' he began and then paused. 'To the place where the desert is ocean.'

She smiled back as they touched glasses. She raised hers to her lips and the cherry rolled into her mouth. She looked at him suggestively as he wiped the beer foam out of his mustache. She loved him. It was them against the whole fucking world and she liked their chances just fine.

Then her smile was gone as she thought about how she had played the whole thing wrong. How she should have known what his reaction would be, how he wouldn't let her go up. She should have waited until after it was over to tell him.

'Max,' she said, very serious now. 'Let me do it. I mean it. One last time.'

'No way. It's me. I go up.'

There was a whoop from the casino floor and it was loud enough to break the barrier surrounding them. She looked out and saw some ten-gallon Texan dancing at the end of one of the craps tables, just below the pulpit that reached out over the casino floor. The Texan had his dial-a-date at his side, a woman with big hair who had been working the casinos since all the way back when Cassie was dealing at the Trop for the first time.

Cassie looked back at Max.

'I can't wait until we're out of this place for good. Let me at least flip you for it.'

Max slowly shook his head.

'Not in the cards. This one's mine.'

Max stood up then and she looked up at him. He was handsome and dark. She liked the little scar under his chin, the way no whiskers ever grew there.

'Guess it's time,' Max said.

He looked out across the casino, his eyes scanning but never stopping and holding on anything until they traveled up the arm of the pulpit. Cassie's eyes followed his. There was a man up there, dressed darkly and staring down like a priest on his congregation.

She tried to smile again but couldn't bring the corners of her mouth up. Something didn't feel right. It was the change of plans. The switch. She realized then how much she wanted to go up and how much she was going to miss the charge it would put in her blood. She knew then it was really about her, not Max. She wasn't being protective of Max. She was being selfish. She wanted that charge one last time.

'Anything happens,' Max said, 'I'll see you when I see you.'

Now she frowned outright. That had never been part of the ritual, a good-bye like that. A negative like that.

'Max, what's wrong? Why are you so nervous?'

Max looked down at her and hiked his shoulders.

''Cause it's the end, I guess.'

He tried a smile, then touched her cheek and leaned down. He kissed her on the cheek and then quickly moved over to her lips. He reached a hand down beneath the table where nobody could see and ran his finger up the inside of her leg, tracing the seam of her jeans. Then, without another word, he turned and left the lounge. He started walking through the casino toward the elevator alcove and she watched him go. He didn't look back. That was part of the ritual. You never looked back.

1

The house on Lookout Mountain Road was set far in from the street and nestled against the steep canyon embankment to the rear. This afforded it a long and flat green lawn running from the wide front porch to the white picket fence that ran along the street line. It was unusual in Laurel Canyon to have such an immense lawn, front or back, and one so flat as well. It was that lawn that would be the key selling point of the property.

The open house had been advertised in the real estate section of the *Times* as starting at two P.M. and lasting until five. Cassie Black pulled to the curb ten minutes before the starting time and saw no cars in the driveway and no indication of any activity in the house. The white Volvo station wagon she knew belonged to the owners that was usually parked outside was gone. She couldn't tell about the other car, the black BMW, because the little single-car garage at the side of the house was closed. But she took the missing Volvo to mean that the owners of the home were out for the day and would not be present during the showing. This was fine. Cassie preferred they not be home. She wasn't sure how she would act if the family was right there in the house as she walked through it.

Cassie remained in the Boxster until two P.M. and then grew concerned, her mind jumping to the conclusion that she had gotten the time wrong or, worse yet, the house had already been sold and the showing canceled. She opened the real estate section on the passenger seat and checked the listing again. She had been correct. She looked at the FOR SALE sign posted in the front lawn and checked the broker's name against the name in the advertisement. They matched. She got her cell phone out of her backpack and tried to call the realty office but couldn't get a connection. This didn't surprise her. She was in Laurel Canyon and it always seemed impossible to get a clear cell transmission in any of L.A.'s hillside neighborhoods.

With nothing to do but wait and control her fears, she studied the house that stood behind the FOR SALE sign. According to the advertisement, it was a California Craftsman bungalow built in 1931. Unlike the newer homes on either side, it was not only set back off the street into the hillside rising behind it, but it also seemed to possess a good deal of character. It was smaller than most of the neighboring homes, its designers obviously putting a premium on the large lawn and the openness of the property. The newer houses in the neighborhood had been built to every lot line, under the philosophy that interior space was premium.

The old bungalow had a long, sloping gray roof from which sprouted two dormer windows. Cassie assumed that one belonged to the bedroom shared by the couple and the other was the girl's room. The sidings were painted a reddish brown. A wide porch ran the length of the front of the house and the front door was a single-light French door. Most days the family lowered a set of blinds over the door's glass but today the blinds over the door and the front picture window were up and Cassie could see into the living room. An overhead light had been left on.

The front yard was definitely the play area. It was always neatly cut and trimmed. Built along the left perimeter was a wooden swing set and jungle gym. Cassie knew that the girl who lived in the house preferred to swing with her back to the house and facing the street. She had often thought about this, wondering if there was something about this habit that could be read as some sort of psychological clue.

The empty swing hung perfectly still. Cassie saw a kick ball and a red wagon sitting motionless in the grass, also waiting for the attention of the girl. Cassie thought the play area might be one of the reasons the family was moving. All things being relative in Los Angeles, Laurel Canyon was a pocket of reasonable safety in the sprawling city. Still, it wasn't desirable in any neighborhood to have your children playing in the front yard so close to the street, the place where harm could befall them, where danger could come to them.

It didn't say anything about this potential problem with the yard in the advertisement. Cassie looked down and read it again.

> BRING ALL OFFERS!
> 1931 Classic Calif. Craftsman
> 2/2, spacious living/dining, huge wooded lot.
> Highly motivated and anxious!
> Reduced and priced to sell!

Cassie had noticed the FOR SALE sign on the property during a routine drive-by three weeks earlier. The sighting had thrown her life into turmoil, which was manifested in insomnia and inattention at work. She had not sold a single car in the three weeks, her longest absence ever from the sales tote board.

Today's showing was the first open house as far as she knew. So the wording of the ad struck her as curious. She wondered why the owners would be so anxious to sell that they would already have reduced the price after only three weeks on the market. That did not seem right.

Three minutes after the open house was scheduled to begin, a car Cassie didn't recognize, a maroon Volvo sedan, pulled into the driveway and stopped. A slim, blond woman in her mid forties got out. She was casually but neatly dressed. She opened the trunk of her car and removed an OPEN HOUSE sign, which she carried toward the curb. Cassie checked her hair in the visor mirror, reached to the back of her head and pulled the wig down tight on her scalp. She got out of the Porsche and approached the woman as she set up the sign.

'Are you Laura LeValley?' Cassie asked, reading the name off the bottom of the FOR SALE sign.

'I sure am. Are you here to look at the house?'

'Yes, I'd like to.'

'Well, let me open it up and we'll go from there. Nice car you've got there. Brand new?'

She pointed to the dealer blank in the front license plate holder of the Porsche. Cassie had taken the plates off in the garage at her home before driving to the open house. It was just a precaution. She wasn't sure if brokers took down plate numbers as a means of tracing leads or backgrounding potential buyers. She didn't want to be traced. It was the same reason she was wearing the wig.

'Uh, yes,' she said. 'New to me but used. It's a year old.'

'Nice.'

The Boxster looked pristine from the outside but was actually a repo with almost thirty thousand miles on it, a convertible top that leaked and a CD player that habitually skipped when the car hit the slightest bump in the road. Cassie's boss, Ray Morales, was letting her use it while he dealt with the owner, allowing the guy until the end of the month to come up with the money before putting the car onto the lot. Cassie expected that they would never see a dime from the guy. He was a deadbeat through and through. She'd looked at the package. He'd made the first six payments, late every time, and then skated on the next six. Ray had made the mistake of taking the guy's paper after he'd gotten no takers from the outside loan companies. That was the tip-off right there. But the guy had talked Ray into taking the paper and turning over the keys. It really bugged Ray that he had been beaten. He'd personally gone out on the rig when they hooked up the Boxster outside the deadbeat's hillside box overlooking Sunset Plaza.

The real estate woman went back to her car and removed a briefcase, then led Cassie up the stone walkway to the front porch.

'Are the owners going to be home?' Cassie asked.

'No, it's better when no one's home. Then people can look where they want, say what they want. No hurt feelings. You know, people's tastes are different. One person will think something is gorgeous. Somebody else will call it hideous.'

Cassie smiled to be polite. They got to the front door and LeValley removed a small white envelope from her briefcase and took out a key. As she opened the door she continued the patter.

'Are you being represented by a broker?'

'No. I'm just kind of in the looking stage at the moment.'

'Well, it helps to know what's on the market. Are you currently in ownership?'

'Excuse me?'

'Do you own now? Are you selling?'

'Oh. No, I rent. I'm looking to buy. Something small like this.'

'Children?'

'Just me.'

LeValley opened the door and called out a hello just to make sure no one was home. When there was no answer, she waved Cassie in first.

'Then this should be perfect. It's just two bedrooms but the living spaces are large and very open. I think it's just darling. You'll see.'

They walked into the house and LeValley put her briefcase down. She then offered her hand and introduced herself again.

'Karen Palty,' Cassie lied as she shook the broker's hand.

LeValley gave a quick description of the attributes and assets of the house. From her briefcase she took out a stack of printed fliers containing information on the house and gave Cassie one as she talked. Cassie nodded occasionally but was barely listening. Instead she was intensely scrutinizing the furnishings and the other belongings of the family who lived in the house. She stole long glances at the photos on the walls and on tables and chests. LeValley told her to go ahead and browse while she set up the sign-in sheet and information packets on the dining room table.

The house was very neatly kept and Cassie wondered how much of that was due to the fact that it was being shown to potential buyers. She moved into a short hallway and then up the stairs that led to two bedrooms and bathroom above. She stepped a few feet into the master bedroom and looked around. The room had a large bay window that looked out on the steep rock hillside at the rear of the house. LeValley called from below, seemingly knowing exactly what Cassie was looking at and thinking.

'Mudslides are not a problem. The hillside out there is extruded granite. It's probably been there for ten thousand years and, believe me, it's not going anywhere. But if you are seriously interested in the property, I would suggest you get a geological survey done. If you buy it, it will help you sleep better at night.'

'Good idea,' Cassie called down.

Cassie had seen enough. She stepped out of the room and crossed the hall to the child's bedroom. This room, too, was neat but cluttered with collections of stuffed animals, Barbie dolls and other toys. There was a drawing easel in one corner holding a crayon drawing of a school bus with several stick figures in the window. The bus had pulled up to a building where a red truck was parked in a garage. A firehouse. The girl was a good artist.

Cassie checked the hall to make sure LeValley had not come up and then stepped over to the easel. She flipped over some of the pages containing prior drawings. One drawing depicted a house with a large green lawn in front of it. There was a FOR SALE sign at the front of the house and a stick figure of a girl stood next to it. A bubble coming from the girl's mouth said *Boo Hoo.* Cassie studied it for a long time before breaking away and looking around the rest of the room.

On the left wall there was a framed movie poster for an animated film called *The Little Mermaid.* There were also large wooden letters spelling the name JODIE SHAW, each letter painted a different color of the rainbow. Cassie stood in the middle of the room and silently tried to take it all in and commit it to memory. Her eyes fell on a photo which stood in a small frame on the girl's white bureau. It showed a smiling girl standing with Mickey Mouse amidst a crowd at Disneyland.

'Their daughter's room.'

Cassie almost jumped at the voice behind her.

She turned. Laura LeValley stood in the doorway. Cassie had not heard her on the steps. She wondered if the broker had been suspicious of her and intentionally sneaked up the stairs to catch her stealing or doing something else.

'Cute kid,' LeValley said, giving off no sign of suspicion. 'I met her when I first took the listing. I think she's six or seven.'

'Five. Almost six.'

'Excuse me?'

Cassie quickly pointed to the photo on the bureau.

'I would guess. I mean, if that photo's recent.'

She turned and raised a hand, taking in the whole of the room.

'I also have a niece who is five. This could be her room.'

She waited but there were no further questions from LeValley. It had been a bad slip and Cassie knew she was lucky to have gotten away with it.

'Well,' LeValley said, 'I want to get you to sign in so we have your name and number. Are there any questions I can answer for you? I even have an offer sheet with me if by any chance you're ready to do that.'

She smiled as she said the last line. Cassie smiled back.

'Not just yet,' she said. 'But I do like the house.'

LeValley headed back to the stairs and down. Cassie moved toward the door to follow. As she stepped into the hallway, she glanced back at the collection of stuffed animals on a shelf above the bed. The girl seemed partial to stuffed dogs. Her eyes then went back to the drawing on the easel.

Down in the living room LeValley handed her a clipboard with a sign-in sheet on it. She wrote the name *Karen Palty*, the name belonging to an old friend from her days dealing blackjack, then made up a phone number with a Hollywood exchange and an address on Nichols Canyon Road. After she handed it back LeValley read the entry.

'Karen, you know, if this house isn't what you are looking for, there are several others in the canyon I'd be more than happy to show you.'

'Okay, that would be fine. Let me think about this one first, though.'

'Oh, sure. You just let me know. Here's my card.'

LeValley offered a business card and Cassie took it. She noticed through the living room's picture window a car pulling to the curb behind the Boxster. Another potential buyer. She decided it was time to ask questions while she still had LeValley alone.

'The ad in the paper said the Shaws were anxious to sell the house. Do you mind me asking how come? I mean, is there something wrong here?'

Halfway through her question Cassie realized she had used the name of the owners. Then she remembered the letters on the wall of the girl's room and knew she was covered if LeValley noticed the slip.

'Oh, no, it has nothing to do with the house at all,' LeValley said. 'He's been transferred and they are anxious to make the move and get settled in their new place. If they sell it quickly they can all move together, rather than him having to commute back and forth from the new location. It's a very long trip.'

Cassie felt she needed to sit down but stood still. She felt a terrible dread engulf her heart. She tried to remain steady by placing her hand on the stone hearth but was sure she was not hiding the impact of the words she had just heard.

It's a very long trip.

'Are you okay?' LeValley asked.

'Fine. I'm fine. I had the flu last week and . . . you know.'

'I know. I had it a few weeks ago. It was awful.'

Cassie turned her face and acted as though she were studying the brickwork of the fireplace.

'How far are they moving?' she asked, as casually as was possible considering the fears welling up inside her.

She closed her eyes and waited, sure that LeValley knew by now she wasn't here because of the house.

'Paris. He works for some kind of clothing import business and they want him working on that end of things for a while. They thought about keeping the house, maybe renting it out. But I think realistically they know that they probably won't be coming back. I mean, it's Paris. Who wouldn't want to live there?'

Cassie opened her eyes and nodded.

'Paris . . .'

LeValley continued in an almost conspiring tone.

'That's also the reason they would be very interested in any kind of an offer. His company will cover him on anything below appraisal value. Anything within reason. So a quick, low bid might really be able to turn this. They want to get over there so they can get the girl into one of those language schools this summer. So she can start learning the language and be fairly integrated by the time school starts.'

Cassie wasn't listening to the sales pitch. She stared into the darkness of the hearth. A thousand fires had burned there and warmed this house. But at the moment the bricks were black and cold. And Cassie felt as though she were staring at the inside of her own heart.

In that moment she knew that all things in her life were changing. For the longest time she had lived day to day, carefully avoiding even a glance at the desperate plan that floated out on the horizon like a dream.

But now she knew that it was time to go to the horizon.

2

On the Monday after the open house Cassie got to Hollywood Porsche at ten as usual and spent the rest of the morning in her small office off the showroom going down her list of call-backs, studying the updated inventory list, answering Internet inquiries, and running a search for a customer looking for a vintage Speedster. Mostly, though, her thoughts remained concentrated on the information she had learned during the open house in Laurel Canyon.

Mondays were always the slowest days in the showroom. Occasionally there were leftover buyers and paperwork from the weekend but as a rule very few first-visit car buyers came in. The dealership was located on Sunset Boulevard a half block from the Cinerama Dome and sometimes it was so slow on Mondays that Ray Morales didn't mind if Cassie walked over and caught a flick in the afternoon, just as long as she had her pager on and could be recalled if things started hopping. Ray was always cutting Cassie a break, starting with giving her the job without her having any valid experience. She knew his motives weren't entirely altruistic. She knew it would only be a matter of time before he came to her to collect the return. She was surprised he hadn't made the move yet; it had been ten months.

Hollywood Porsche sold new and used cars. As the newest person on the six-member sales force, it fell to Cassie to work Monday shifts and to handle all Internet-related business. The latter she didn't mind because she had taken computer courses while at High Desert Institution for Women and had found she enjoyed the work. She had learned that she preferred dealing with customers and salesmen from other dealerships over the Internet rather than in person.

Her search for a Speedster of the quality her customer sought was successful. She located a '58 convertible in pristine condition on a lot in San Jose and arranged to have photos and the particulars overnighted. She then left a message for the customer saying he could come in the next afternoon and look at the photos or she would send them over to his office as soon as she got them.

The one test drive of the day came in shortly before lunch. The customer was one of Ray's so-called Hollywood hard-ons, a name the fleet manager had come up with himself.

Ray religiously scoured the *Hollywood Reporter* and *Daily Variety* for stories on nobodies becoming overnight somebodies. Most often these were writers who were snatched from penniless obscurity and made rich and at least known for the day by a studio deal for a book or screenplay. Once Ray chose a target, he tracked down the writer's address through the Writers Guild or a friend he had in the voter registrar's office. He then had the Sunset Liquor Deli deliver a bottle of Macallan Scotch whisky with his card and a note of congratulations. A little more than half the time it worked. The recipient responded with a call to Ray and then a visit to the showroom. Owning a Porsche was almost a rite of passage in Hollywood, especially for males in their twenties – which all the screenwriters seemed to be. Ray passed these customers on to his salespeople, splitting the commission on any eventual sale, after the cost of the whisky.

The test drive Cassie had on Monday was a writer who had just signed a first-look deal with Paramount for seven figures. Ray, fully aware that Cassie had not sold a car in three weeks, gave the 'up' to her. The writer's name was Joe Michaels and he was interested in a new Carrera cabriolet, an automobile that would price out at close to $100,000 fully loaded. Cassie's commission would cover her draw for a month.

With Joe in the passenger seat, Cassie took Nichols Canyon up to Mulholland Drive and then turned the Porsche east on the snaking road. She was following her routine. For it was up on Mulholland that the car and power and sex all blended in the imagination. It became clear to each customer what she was selling.

The traffic as usual was light. Other than the occasional pack of power bikers, the road was theirs. Cassie put the car through the paces, downshifting and powering into the turns. She glanced at Michaels every now and then, to see if he had the look on his face that said the deal was done.

'You working on a movie right now?' she asked.

'I'm doing rewrite on a cop film.'

That was a good sign, his calling a movie a film. Especially a cop movie. The ones who took themselves too seriously – meaning they had money – called them films.

'Who's in it?'

'It hasn't been cast. That's why I'm doing rewrite. The dialogue sucks.'

To prep for the test drive Cassie had read the story in *Variety* about the first-look deal. It said Michaels was a recent graduate of the USC film school and had made a fifteen-minute film that won some kind of studio-sponsored award. He looked maybe twenty-five years old tops. Cassie wondered where he would get his dialogue from. He didn't look as though he had ever met a cop in his life, let alone any outlaws. The dialogue would probably come from television or other movies, she decided.

'You want to drive now, John?'

'It's Joe.'

Another bingo. She had called him the wrong name on purpose, just to see if he would correct her. That he did meant he was serious and ego-driven, a good combination when it came to selling and buying automobiles that were serious and ego-driven.

'Joe, then.'

She pulled into the overlook above the Hollywood Bowl. She killed the engine, set the brake and got out. She didn't look back at Michaels as she walked to the edge and put a foot up on the guardrail. She leaned over and retied her black Doc Marten work shoe and then looked down at the empty bowl. She was wearing tight black jeans and a sleeveless white T-shirt beneath an unbuttoned blue Oxford dress shirt. She knew she looked good and her radar told her that he was looking at her instead of the car. She ran her fingers through her blond hair, newly cut short so she could wear the wig. She turned abruptly and caught him looking at her. He quickly looked past her, out to the view of downtown in the pastel pink smog.

'So what do you think?' she asked.

'I think I like it,' Michaels said. 'But you have to drive it to know for sure.'

He smiled. She smiled. They were definitely moving on the same plane.

'Then let's do it,' she said, careful to keep the double entendre working.

They got back in the Porsche and Cassie sat in the passenger seat a bit sideways, so she was facing Joe. She watched as he brought his right hand up to the steering column and it searched for the ignition and keys.

'Other side,' she said.

He found the keys in the ignition on the dashboard left of the wheel.

'That's a Porsche tradition,' she said. 'From back when they made cars for racing. It was so you could start with your left hand and have your right already on the gear shift. It's a quick-start ignition.'

Michaels nodded. Cassie knew that little story always scored with them. She didn't even know if it was true – she had gotten it from Ray – but she told it every time. She knew Michaels was imagining himself telling it to some sweet little thing outside any number of pickup joints on the Sunset Strip.

He started the engine and backed the car out and then drove back out onto Mulholland, over-revving all the way. But after a few shifts he picked up on the nuances of the gearbox and was taking the curves smoothly. Cassie watched as he tried not to smile when he hit a straightaway and the speedo hit seventy-five in just a few seconds. But the look came over his face. He couldn't hide it. She knew the look and what it felt like. Some people got it from speed and power, some got it in other ways. She thought about how long it had been since she had felt the hot wire coursing through her own blood.

Cassie looked into her little office to check for pink phone slips on the desk. There were none. She moved on through the showroom, running her finger along the spoiler of a classic whale tail, and past the finance office to the fleet manager's office. Ray Morales looked up from some paperwork as she came in and hooked the keys from the Carrera she had used on the test drive on the appropriate hook on the fleet board. She knew he was waiting to hear how it went. After all, he had invested more than a hundred dollars in Scotch whisky.

'He's going to think about it a couple days,' she said without looking at Ray. 'I'll call him Wednesday.'

As Cassie turned to leave, Ray dropped his pen and pushed his seat back from his desk.

'Shit, Cassie, what is up with you? That guy was a hard-on. How'd you lose him?'

'I didn't say I lost him,' Cassie said, too much protest in her voice. 'I said he's going to think about it. Not everybody buys after the first test drive, Ray. That car's going to run a hundred grand.'

'With these guys they do. With Porsche they do. They don't think, they buy. Cassie, damn, he was primed. I could tell when I had him on the phone. You know what you're doing? I think you're psyching these guys out. You gotta come on to these guys like they're the next Cecil B. DeMille. Don't make 'em feel bad about what they do or what they want.'

Cassie put her hands on her hips in indignation.

'Ray, I don't know what you're talking about. I try to sell the car, I don't try to talk 'em out of it. I don't make them feel bad. And none of these guys even know who Cecil B. De Mille was.'

'Then Spielberg, Lucas, whatever. I don't care. There is an art to this, Cassie. That's what I'm saying and what I've been trying to teach you. It's finesse, it's sex, it's givin' the guy a hard-on. When you first came in here you were doin' that. You were moving, what, five, six cars a month. Now, I don't know what you're doing.'

Cassie looked down at his desk for a moment before answering. She slid her hands into her pockets. She knew he was right.

'Okay, Ray, you're right. I'll work on it. I guess I'm just a little out of focus right now.'

'How come?'

'I'm not sure.'

'You want some time, maybe take a few days?'

'No, I'm cool. But tomorrow I'll be in late. I've got my see-and-pee up in Van Nuys.'

'Right. No problem. How's that going? That lady doesn't call or come around anymore.'

'It's going. You probably won't hear from her unless I fuck up.'

'Good. Keep it that way.'

Something about his tone bothered her but she pushed it aside. She averted her eyes and looked down at the paperwork on his desk. She noticed that there was a fleet report on a stack of paperwork to the side of his work space.

'So we have a truck coming?'

Ray followed her eyes to the report and nodded.

'Next Tuesday. Four Boxsters, three Carreras – two of them cabs.'

'Cool. You know colors yet?'

'The Carreras are white. The Boxsters are coming arctic, white, black and I think yellow.'

He grabbed the report and studied it.

'Yeah, yellow. Be nice to have these locked in before they get here. Meehan already has a contract on one of the cabs.'

'I'll see what I can do.'

He winked at her and smiled.

'Thattagirl.'

There was that tone again. And the wink. She was getting the idea that Ray was finally getting around to wanting to collect on all of his goodwill. He'd probably been waiting for her to hit a drought so she'd feel she had less choice in the matter. She knew he would make his move soon and that she should think about how to handle it. But there were too many other things that were more important on her mind. She left him in the office and headed back to her own.

3

The offices of the California Department of Corrections, Parole and Community Services Division, in Van Nuys, were crowded into a one-story building of gray, precast concrete that stood in the shadow of the Municipal Court building. The nondescript design features of its exterior seemed in step with its purpose: the quiet reintegration of convicts into society.

The interior of the building took its cue from the crowd control philosophy employed at popular amusement parks – although those who waited here weren't always anxious to reach the end of their wait. A maze of roped-off cattle rows folded the long lines of ex-cons back and forth in the waiting rooms and hallways. There were lines of cons waiting to check in, lines waiting for urine tests, lines waiting to see parole agents, lines in all quadrants of the building.

To Cassie Black the parole office was more depressing than prison had been. When she was at High Desert, she was in stasis, like a character in those sci-fi movies where the journey back to earth is so long that the travelers are put into a hibernation-type sleep. That was how Cassie saw it. She was breathing but not living, waiting and surviving on hope that the end of her time would come sooner rather than later. That hope for the future and the warmth of her constant dream of freedom got her past all the depression. But the parole office was that future. It was the harsh reality of getting out. And it was squalid and crowded and inhuman. It smelled of desperation and lost hope, of no future. Most of those surrounding her wouldn't make it. One by one they would go back. It was a fact of the life they had chosen. Few went straight, few made it out alive. And for Cassie, who promised herself she would be one of the few, the monthly immersion into this world always left her profoundly depressed.

By ten o'clock on Tuesday morning she had already been through the check-in line and was nearing the front of the pee line. In her hand she held the plastic cup she would have to squat over and fill while an office trainee, dubbed the *wizard* because of the nature of her monitoring duty, watched to make sure it was her own urine going into the container.

While she waited Cassie didn't look at anybody and didn't talk to anybody. When the line moved and she was jostled she just moved with the flow. She thought about her time in High Desert, about how she could just shut herself down when she needed to and go on autopilot, ride that spaceship back to earth. It was the only way to get through that place. And this one, too.

Cassie squeezed into the cubicle that her parole agent, Thelma Kibble, called an office. She was breathing easy now. She was near the end. Kibble was the last stop on the journey.

'There she is . . . ,' Kibble said. 'Howzit going there, Cassie Black?'

'Fine, Thelma. How about you?'

Kibble was an obese black woman whose age Cassie had never tried to guess. There was always a pleasant expression on her wide face and Cassie truly liked her despite the circumstances of their relationship. Kibble wasn't easy but she was fair. Cassie knew she was lucky that her transfer from Nevada had been assigned to Kibble.

'Can't complain,' Kibble said. 'Can't complain at all.'

Cassie sat in the chair next to the desk, which was stacked on all sides with case files, some of them two inches thick. On the left side of the desk was a vertical file labeled RTC which always drew Cassie's attention. She knew RTC meant *return to custody* and the files located there belonged to the losers, the ones going back. It seemed the vertical file was always full and seeing it was as much a deterrent to Cassie as anything else about the parole process.

Kibble had Cassie's file open in front of her and was filling in the monthly report. This was their ritual; a brief face-to-face visit and Kibble would go down the checklist of questions.

'What's up with the hair?' Kibble asked without looking up from the paperwork.

'Just felt like a change. I wanted it short.'

'Change? What are you, so bored you gotta make changes all'a sudden?'

'No, I just . . .'

She finished by hiking her shoulders, hoping the moment would pass. She should have realized that using the word *change* would raise a flag with a parole agent.

Kibble turned her wrist slightly and checked her watch. It was time to go on.

'Your pee going to be a problem?'

'Nope.'

'Good. Anything you want to talk about?'

'No, not really.'

'How's the job going?'

'It's a job. It's going the way jobs go, I guess.'

Kibble raised her eyebrows and Cassie wished she had just stuck to a one-word answer. Now she had raised another flag.

'You drive them fancy damn cars all the time,' Kibble said. 'Most people that come in here are washin' cars like that. And they ain't complaining.'

'I'm not complaining.'

'Then what?'

'Then nothing. Yes, I drive fancy cars. But I don't own them. I sell them. There's a difference.'

Kibble looked up from the file and studied Cassie for a moment. All around them the cacophony of voices from the rows of cubicles filled the air.

'A'right, what's troubling you, girl? I don't have time for bullshit. I got my hard cases and my soft cases and I'll be damned if I'm gonna have to move you to HC. I don't have time for that.'

She slapped one of the stacks of thick files to make her point.

'You won't want that, neither,' she said.

Cassie knew HC meant High Control. She was on minimum supervision now. A move to HC would mean increased visits to the parole office, daily phone checks and more home visits from Kibble. Parole would simply become an extension of her cell and she knew she couldn't handle that. She quickly held her hands up in a calming gesture.

'I'm sorry, I'm sorry. Nothing's wrong, okay? I'm just having . . . I'm just going through one of those times, you know?'

'No, I don't know. What times you talkin' about? Tell me.'

'I can't. I don't know the words. I feel like . . . it's like every day is like the one before. There is no future because it's all the same.'

'Look, what did I tell you when you first came in here? I told you it would get like this. Repetition breeds routine. Routine's boring but it keeps you from thinking and it keeps you out of trouble. You want to stay out of trouble, don't you, girl?'

'Yes, Thelma. But it's like I got out of lockdown but sometimes I feel like I'm still in lockdown. It's not . . .'

'Not what?'

'I don't know. It's not fair.'

There was a sudden outburst from one of the other cubicles as a convict started protesting loudly. Kibble stood up to look over the partitions of the cubicle. Cassie didn't move. She didn't care. She knew what it was, somebody being taken down and put in a holding cell pending revocation of parole. There were one or two takedowns every time she came in. Nobody ever went back peaceably. Cassie had long ago stopped watching the scenes. She couldn't worry about anyone else in this place but herself.

After a few moments Kibble sat back down and turned her attention back to Cassie, who was hoping that the interruption would make the parole agent forget what they had been talking about.

There was no such luck.

'You see that?' Kibble asked.

'I heard it. That was enough.'

'I hope so. Because any little mess-up and that could be you. You understand that, don't you?'

'Perfectly, Thelma. I know what happens.'

'Good, because this isn't about being *fair*, to use your word. Fair's got nothing to do with it. You're down by law, honey, and you're under thumb. You're scaring me, girl, and you should be scaring yourself. You're only ten months into a two-year tail. This is not good when I hear you getting antsy after just ten months.'

'I know. I'm sorry.'

'Shit, there's people in this room with four – and five – and six-year tails. Some even longer.'

Cassie nodded.

'I know, I know. I'm lucky. It's just that I can't stop myself from thinking about things, you know?'

'No, I don't know.'

Kibble folded her massive arms across her chest and leaned back in her chair. Cassie wondered if the chair could take the weight but it held strong. Kibble looked at her sternly. Cassie knew she had made a mistake trying to open up to her. She was in effect inviting Kibble into her life more than she was already into it. But she decided that since she had already strayed across the line, she might as well go all the way now.

'Thelma, can I just ask you something?'

'That's what I'm here for.'

'Do you know . . . are there any, like international treaties or agreements for parole transfers?'

Kibble closed her eyes.

'What the hell are you talking about?'

'Like if I wanted to live in London or Paris or something?'

Kibble opened her eyes, shook her head and looked astonished. She shifted forward and the chair came down heavily.

'Do I look like a travel agent to you? You are a *con*vict, girl. You understand that? You don't just decide you don't like it here and say, "Oh, I think I'll try Paris now." Are you listening to yourself talking crazy here? We aren't running no Club Med here.'

'Okay, I was just –'

'You got the one transfer from Nevada, which you were lucky to get, thanks to your friend at the dealership. But that's it. You are stuck here, girl. For at least the next fourteen months and maybe even further, the way you're acting now.'

'All right. I just thought I'd –'

'End of story.'

'Okay. End of story.'

Kibble leaned over the desk to write something in Cassie's file.

'I don't know about you,' she said as she wrote. 'You know what I oughta do is I oughta thirty-fifty-six you for a couple days, see if that clears your mind of these silly ass ideas. But –'

'You don't have to do that, Thelma. I –'

'– we're full up right now.'

A 3056 was a parole hold – an order putting a parolee in custody pending a hearing to revoke parole. The PA could then drop the revoke charge at the time of the hearing and the parolee would be set free. Meantime, the revisit to lockdown for a few days would serve as a warning to straighten up. It was the harshest threat Kibble had at her disposal and just the mention of it properly scared Cassie.

'I mean it, Thelma, I'm fine. I'm okay. I was just venting some steam, okay? Please don't do that to me.'

She hoped she had put the proper sound of pleading into her voice.

Kibble shook her head.

'All I know is that you were on my A list, girl. Now I don't know. I think I'm gonna at least have to come around and check up on you one of these days. See what's what with you. I'm telling you, Cassie Black, you better watch yourself with me. I am not fat old Thelma who can't get off her chair. I am *not* someone to fuck with. You think so, you check with these folks.'

She raked the end of her pen along the edges of the RTC files to her left. It made a loud ripping sound.

'They'll tell you I am not someone to be fucked with or fucked over.'

Cassie could only nod. She studied the huge woman across from her for a long moment. She needed some way to defuse this, to get the smile back on Kibble's face or at the very least the deep furrow out of her brow.

'You come around, Thelma, and I have a feeling I'll see you before you see me.'

Kibble looked sharply at her. But Cassie saw the tension slowly change in her face. It had been a gamble but Kibble took the comment in good humor. She even started to chuckle and it made her huge shoulders and then the desk shake.

'We'll see about that,' Kibble said. 'You'd be surprised by me.'

4

Cassie felt a weight lifting off her as she came out of the parole offices. Not simply because the monthly ordeal was over. But because she had caught a glimmer of understanding about herself while inside. In her struggle for an explanation of her feelings to Kibble she had arrived at an essential conclusion. She was marking time and she could do it their way or her own way. The open house in Laurel Canyon was not the cause of this. That was simply an accelerant; it was gasoline on an already burning fire. Her decision was clear now and in that clarity were feelings of both relief and fear. The fire was burning strongly now. Inside she began to feel the slight trickle of melt water from the frozen lake that for so long had been her heart.

She walked between the municipal and county courthouses and through the plaza fronting the LAPD's Van Nuys station. There was a bank of pay phones near the stairs leading up to the police station's second-floor entrance. She picked one up, dropped in a quarter and a dime and punched in a number she had committed to memory more than a year earlier while in High Desert. It had come on a note smuggled to her in a tampon.

After three rings the phone was answered by a man.

'Yes?'

It was more than six years since Cassie had heard the voice but it rang true and recognizable to her. It made her catch her breath.

'Yes?'

'Uh, yes, is this . . . is this D. H. Reilly?'

'No, you have the wrong number.'

'Dog House Reilly? I was calling –'

She looked down and read off the number of the phone she was standing at.

'What kind of crazy name is that? No Dog House here and you've got the wrong number.'

He hung up. Cassie did, too. She then turned around and walked back into the plaza and took a seat on a bench about fifty feet from the pay phones. She shared the bench with a disheveled man who was reading a newspaper so yellowed that it had to be months old.

Cassie waited almost forty minutes. When the phone finally started to ring, she was in the midst of a one-sided conversation with the disheveled man about the quality of the food service in the Van Nuys jail. She got up and trotted to the phones, the man yelling a final complaint at her.

'Sausage like fucking Brillo pads! We were playing hockey in there!'

She grabbed the phone after the sixth ring.

'Leo?'

A pause.

'Don't use my name. How you doing, sweetheart?'

'I'm okay. How are –'

'You know, you been out now like a year, am I right?'

'Uh, actually –'

'And all that time and not even a hello from you. I thought I'd hear from you before now. You're lucky I even remembered that Dog House Reilly schtick.'

'Ten months. I've been out ten months.'

'And how's it been?'

'Okay, I guess. Good, actually.'

'Not if you're calling me.'

'I know.'

There was a long silence then. Cassie could hear traffic noise coming from his end. She guessed he had left the house and found a pay phone somewhere on Ventura Boulevard, probably near the deli he liked to eat at.

'So, you called me first,' Leo prompted.

'Right, yeah. I was thinking . . .'

She paused and thought about everything again. She nodded her head.

'Yeah, I need to get some work, Leo.'

'Don't use my name.'

'Sorry.'

But she smiled. Same old Leo.

'You know me, a classic paranoid.'

'I was just thinking that.'

'All right, so you're looking for something. Give me some parameters? What are we talking about here?'

'Cash. One job.'

'One job?' He seemed surprised and maybe even disappointed. 'How big?'

'Big enough to disappear on. To get a good start.'

'Must not be going too good then.'

'It's just that things are happening. I can't . . .'

She shook her head and didn't finish.

'You sure you're okay?'

'Yes, I'm fine. I feel good, actually. Now that I know.'

'I know what you mean. I remember the time when I decided for good. When I said fuck it, this is what I do. And at the time, hell, I was only boosting air bags out of Chryslers. I've come a long way. We both have.'

Cassie turned and glanced back at the man on the bench. He was continuing his conversation. He hadn't really needed Cassie to be there.

'You know, don't you, that with these parameters, you're probably talking Vegas. I mean, I could send you down to Hollywood Park or one of the

Indian rooms but you're not going to see a lot of cash. You're talking fifteen, twenty a pop down there. But if you give me some time to set something in Vegas I could push the take.'

Cassie thought a moment. She had believed when the bus to High Desert pulled out of Las Vegas six years before that she would never see the place again. But she knew that what Leo was saying was accurate. Vegas was where the big money was.

'Vegas is fine,' she said abruptly. 'Just don't take too long.'

'Who's that talking behind you?'

'Just some old guy. Too much pruno while in lockup.'

'Where are you?'

'I just left the PO.'

Leo laughed.

'Nothing like having to pee in a cup to make you see life's possibilities. Tell you what, I'll keep an eye out for something. I got a heads up about something coming up in the next week or so. You'd be perfect. I'll let you know if it pans out. Where can I reach you?'

She gave him the dealership number. The general number and not her direct line or her cell phone number. She didn't want those numbers written down and in his possession in case he took a bust.

'One other thing,' she said. 'Can you still get passports?'

'I can. Take me two, three weeks 'cause I send out for them, but I can get you one. It will be fucking grade A, too. A passport will run you a grand, a whole book twenty-five hundred. Comes with DL, Visa and Amex. Delta miles on the Amex.'

'Good. I'll want a whole book for me and then a second passport.'

'What do you mean, two? I'm telling you the first one will be perfect. You won't need another with –'

'They're not both for me. I need the second for somebody else. Do you want me to send pictures to the house or do you have a drop?'

Leo told her to send the photos to a mail drop. He gave her the address in Burbank, then asked her who the second passport was for and what names she wanted used in the manufacture of the false documents. She had anticipated the questions and had already picked the names. She offered to send the cash with the photos but Leo told her he could front it for the time being. He said it was an act of good faith, seeing that they were going back into business together.

'So,' he said, returning to the main business at hand. 'You going to be ready for this? Been a long time. People get rusty. If I put you out there, I'll be on the line, you know.'

'I know. You don't have to worry. I'll be ready.'

'Okay, then. I'll be talking to you.'

'Thanks. I'll be seeing you.'

'Oh, and sweetheart?'

'What?'

'I'm glad you're back. It'll be like old times again.'

'No, Leo. Not without Max. It will never be the same again.'

This time Leo didn't protest her use of his name. They both hung up and Cassie walked away from the phones. The man on the bench called after her but she couldn't make out what it was he had said.

She had to walk up to Victory Boulevard to get to the Boxster. It was the closest she had been able to get to the criminal justice complex. Along the way she thought about Max Freeling. She remembered their last moments together; the bar at the Cleo, the beer foam in his mustache, the tiny scar on his chin where no whiskers grew.

Max had made a toast and she repeated it now silently.

To the end. To the place where the desert is ocean.

Thinking about what happened afterward left her depressed and still angry, even after so many years. She decided that before she went to the dealership she would drive by Wonderland Elementary and catch the lunch recess. She knew it was the best way possible to chase the blues away.

When she got to the Boxster she found it had been ticketed after the two hours on the meter expired. She pulled the citation off the windshield and tossed it onto the passenger seat. The car was still registered to the deadbeat it had been repossessed from. So when the ticket went unpaid, the bill from the city would go to him. He could deal with it.

She got in the car and drove off. She took Van Nuys Boulevard south to the 101. The boulevard was lined with new-car dealerships. Sometimes she thought of the Valley as one big parking lot.

She tried listening to a Lucinda Williams compact disc but the stereo was so jumpy that she had to pop it out and just listen to the radio. The song playing was an old one. Roseanne Cash singing about a seven-year ache.

Yeah, Cassie thought. Roseanne knew what she was talking about. Seven years. But the song didn't say anything about what happened after seven years. Did that ache go away then? Cassie didn't think it ever would.

5

In the following days, while she waited for word from Leo, Cassie Black found herself dropping into the rhythm of preparation that was both familiar and comforting to her. But most of all it was exciting, putting a thrill into her life she had not felt in many years.

The preparation was also a solitary time of introspection. She studied her decision repeatedly and from all angles. She found no cracks, no second thoughts, no intruding guilt. The hurdle had been in making the choice. Once decided upon, it only brought her relief and a great sense of freedom. There was the excitement of danger and anticipation in her that the years of incarceration had robbed from her memory. She had forgotten how truly addictive the charge of adrenaline could be. Max had simply called it outlaw juice because he could not put his feelings into words. In those days of preparation she came to realize that the true essence of incarceration was aimed at removing that charge, of washing it from memory. If so, then five years in lockdown had failed her. The charge of outlaw juice was boiling in her blood now, banging through her veins like hot water through frozen winter pipes.

She began by changing her body clock, dramatically shortening her sleeping hours and pushing them well into the morning. She offset the sleep deprivation with a regimen of energy-enhancing vitamins and an occasional late-afternoon nap on her living room couch. Within a week she had dropped from seven to four hours of sleep per night without a noticeable impact on her alertness or productivity.

At night she started taking long drives on the dangerously curving Mulholland Drive so that she could sharpen her sustained alertness. When home she moved about her house without lights on, her eyes adjusting and becoming reacquainted with the contours of night shadows. She knew she would have the option of night-vision goggles when the job came up but she also knew it was good to be prepared for any eventuality.

By day, when she wasn't working at the dealership, she started gathering the equipment she might need and making the tools she would use. After carefully making a list of every conceivable thing that would help her overcome any obstacle on a job, she memorized its contents and destroyed it – such a list in her possession was enough in itself to violate her parole. She then spent an entire day driving to a variety of hardware stores and other businesses, gathering the items on the list and spreading her cash purchases across the entire city so that the various parts to her plan could never be construed as the whole.

She bought screwdrivers, iron files, hacksaw blades and hammers; baling wire, nylon twine and bungee cords. She bought a box of latex gloves, a small tub of earthquake wax, a Swiss Army knife and a painter's putty knife with a three-inch-wide blade. She bought a small acetylene torch and went to three hardware stores before finding a small enough battery-powered and rechargeable drill. She bought rubber-tipped pliers, wire cutters and aluminum shears. She added a Polaroid camera and a man's long-sleeved wet suit top to her purchases. She bought big and small flashlights, a pair of tile worker's knee pads and an electric stun gun. She bought a black leather backpack, a black fanny pack and belt, and several black zipper bags of varying sizes that could be folded and carried inside one of the backpack's pockets. Lastly, in every store she went to she bought a keyed padlock, amassing a collection of seven locks made by seven different manufacturers and thereby containing seven slightly different interior locking mechanisms.

In the small bungalow she rented on Selma near the 101 Freeway in Hollywood, she spread her purchases out on the scarred Formica-topped table in the kitchen and readied her equipment, wearing gloves at all times when she handled each piece.

She used the shears and the torch to make lock picks from the baling wire and hacksaw blades. She made a double set of three picks: a tension spike, a hook and a thin, flat tumbler pick. She put one set in a Ziploc bag and buried it in the garden outside the back door. The other set she put aside with the tools for the job she hoped would be coming from Leo very soon.

She cut half a sleeve off the wet suit and used it to encase the drill, sewing the sound-deadening rubber tightly in place with the nylon twine. From the rest of the wet suit she created a roll-up satchel in which she could quietly carry her custom-made burglary kit.

When her working tools were ready, she rolled them up in the satchel, secured it with a bungee cord and then hid it in the hollow of the Boxster's front right fender, attaching it to the suspension struts with more bungee cords. Her fingerprints were on nothing. If the tool satchel were ever discovered by Thelma Kibble or any other law enforcement officer, Cassie would have a degree of deniability that might keep her out of lockdown. The car was not hers. Without prints on the tools or evidence of her having purchased and made them, it ultimately could not be proved that they belonged to her. They could hold her and sweat her but they would eventually have to let her go.

The seven padlocks Cassie used for practice. She locked them onto a wooden clothing hanger and dropped the keys into a coffee cup in a kitchen cabinet. At night she sat in the dark in her living room and blindly worked the extra set of picks into the padlocks. The nuances of finessing a lock open came back to her slowly. It took her four days to open all seven padlocks. She then hooked them back on the hanger and closed them. She started over, this time wearing latex gloves. At the end of two weeks she was regularly timing herself and she could open all seven locks in twelve minutes with gloves on.

She knew all along that what she was doing was as much mental preparation as anything else. It was getting back into the rhythm, the mind-set. Max, her teacher, had always said the rhythm was the most important preparation. The ritual. She knew it was unlikely she would have to pick a lock on the job Leo would find for her. Most of the hotels in Las Vegas and elsewhere had gone to electronically programmed card keys in the last decade. Subverting electronic protection was another matter altogether. It required inside help or a skill at *soshing* – short for social engineering, meaning the con at the front desk or the finesse moves with the housekeeper.

The prep time brought her close to memories of Max, the man who had been both her mentor and lover. These were bittersweet memories because she could not think of the good times without remembering how they had all ended so badly at the Cleopatra. Even still, she often found herself laughing out loud in the darkness of her house, the hanger full of padlocks on her lap, her hands sweating inside tight latex gloves.

She laughed hardest as she remembered one soshing trick Max had pulled to perfection at the Golden Nugget. They needed to get into a room on the fifth floor. Spying a night service maid's cart outside a room down the hall, Max went into a service alcove and took off all his clothes. He then ruffled his hair and walked down the hall to the maid's cart, cupping his privates in his hands. After startling the woman, he explained he had been sleeping and got up to go to the bathroom and in his sleepy confusion had inadvertently stepped through the wrong door and out of his room, the door closing and locking behind him. Not wanting to prolong her encounter with a naked man, the housekeeper quickly handed him her pass key. They were in.

What made the story so funny in memory to Cassie was that once Max was in the room he had to dress and return the key to the maid in order to complete the trick. But his clothes were hidden down the hall in the alcove. So he put on a set of the mark's clothes. The man they had targeted was slightly shorter than Max and rail thin. He weighed at least fifty pounds less. He was also openly gay and his clothes announced this to the world. Max walked back down the hall to the maid in a flamingo pink shirt open to the navel and black leather pants so tight he couldn't bend his knees.

Each night when she had finished practicing and was ready for sleep, Cassie reburied the second set of picks and put a heavy winter coat on the hanger holding the padlocks. She zipped the coat closed, hiding the locks, and returned it to a hallway closet. Ever aware that Thelma Kibble might make good on her threat to make an unscheduled appearance, she left no outward appearance in her home or activities of what she was planning and preparing for.

But she never saw any sign of Kibble's presence. The parole officer apparently didn't even make a follow-up call to Ray Morales to check on Cassie's behavior and work status. Cassie believed the woman was simply overrun with too many cases. Despite the stern words to Cassie, Kibble probably had dozens of hard cases that were more deserving than Cassie of a field visit.

As Cassie waited for the call from Leo she kept her old routines as well. Each morning she went running at the Hollywood Reservoir, circling the lake and crossing the Mulholland Dam twice. The run was penance for her earlier morning ritual: stopping at the farmers' market on Fairfax for doughnuts and coffee at Bob's. She would take her breakfast in the car, driving up into the hills of Laurel Canyon and stopping, if parking was available, near the fenced playground outside the Wonderland School.

As she ate her glazed doughnuts and gulped steaming black coffee, she watched the children being dropped off by parents and playing in the schoolyard before the morning bell. Her eyes would solemnly scan the fenced playing ground until she found the grouping of the kindergarten girls, usually gathered closely around their teacher – a woman who looked very caring and kind. Cassie's eyes would move into the pack and search out the same face each morning: the girl who wore the backpack with the *Have a Nice Day* smiley face on it. She would watch as the bright yellow backpack bobbed and moved in the crowd. Cassie would not lose sight of the girl until the bell rang and the children were herded inside to the classrooms. Only then would she crumple the doughnut bag and start her car to head to the reservoir to work her body and mind to near exhaustion before the day had barely begun.

6

Fifteen days after Cassie Black made contact with Leo, she got the return call. She was sitting in her office, going over the figures on a trade-in sheet with Ray Morales, when the phone rang. Her mind on the work at hand, she grabbed the phone and punched the line without thinking about it.

'This is Cassie Black, can you hold?'

'Sure.'

She recognized the voice with that one word. She paused as a cold finger slid down her spine, then she hit the hold button. A palpable excitement rose in her chest.

'You okay?' Morales asked.

'Sure, fine. I have to take this, though.'

'Go ahead.'

'I mean alone. It's personal.'

'Oh. Okay.'

Ray looked a little rejected and maybe even annoyed. To him *personal* probably meant a new boyfriend was calling. Cassie had gently rebuffed him two days earlier when he had asked her out to dinner after work. Now that he had finally made his move, he was too late. Cassie was waiting on Leo and wasn't going to complicate things with Ray. If things went the way she was planning, she would be doing him a favor by not getting involved with him. He'd have no secrets to hide when the cops came to talk to him.

Ray said he would be in his office if she wanted to finish going over the trade-in report. He moved out of her small office and closed the door without Cassie's having to ask. She leaned forward to look over the desk at the bottom of the doorjamb. She could tell that Ray was standing just outside the door, hoping to hear her conversation.

'Ray?'

He didn't respond but Cassie watched the feet move away. She clicked the hold button on the phone.

'Hello?'

'What, did you go for a test drive or something?'

'Sorry.'

'Well, I got something for you.'

Cassie didn't respond at first. The trilling of adrenaline in her blood was strong. Outlaw juice. She felt a sense of being at the edge of a cliff. It was time to go over. Now or never. Those people who got in padded barrels and floated over the falls had nothing on this.

Leo spoke into the silence, breaking the spell.

'I'm not sure you're going to like it, though.'

Cassie swallowed back a catch in her throat.

'How come?'

'We'll talk about it when I see you.'

'When and where?'

'Just come here. But make it soon. Either tonight or tomorrow first thing. This has to go down by tomorrow night or we lose it.'

'All right, tonight after work. You still in the same place?'

'Always. One last thing. I'm turning on the memo button on the phone machine here so I have this on tape. Kid, you know I love you but it's been a long time. Don't get insulted, because this is just a precaution. Ever since Linda Tripp and Monica Lewinsky, it's standard operating practice around here. Here goes. Are you currently working with any law enforcement agency at this time?'

'Leo . . .'

'Don't say my name. Just answer the question. I'm sorry but this is a precaution I have to take. People been settin' traps right and left out there.'

'No, Leo, I'm not. If I wanted to set you up I could have done it back before I spent the nickel at High Desert. Everybody and their brother wanted me to make a deal then. But I didn't.'

'You sure didn't and you know I appreciated it. Didn't I take care of you when I could? What about that PI you wanted to hire – that cost me five grand, you know.'

'You took care of me, Leo. I won't forget.'

'I wish you'd forget using my name.'

'Sorry.'

'Okay, good enough. The tape's off. We're good to go. I'll see you in a little while. Take –'

'Did you get the passports?'

A pause.

'Not yet. Next time I'm out I'll make a call to check on that. Okay?'

'Okay, but I need them. Soon.'

'I'll deliver the message. See you soon. Take all usual precautions.'

After she hung up Cassie's eyes traveled up the wall next to the door. Her eyes held on the poster taped on the wall and facing her. It showed a woman in a string bikini walking on a sun-drenched beach. The word TAHITI! was scrawled in the sand behind her, just out of reach of the surf's wash.

'To the place where the desert is ocean,' she said out loud.

7

Cassie drove west on Sunset. She had the top down on the Porsche. She loved the thrum of the engine coming through the seat and the deep, guttural tones she heard on the curves. At Beverly Glen she turned the Boxster north and followed the winding canyon road over the hill and down into the Valley.

Leo Renfro lived in Tarzana in the flats north of Ventura Boulevard on a street fronting the 101 Freeway. His house was a small, postwar ranch house without any real defining design or style. It was like every other house in his neighborhood and that was exactly the way Leo wanted it. Leo had survived by being nondescript, by blending in.

She drove by the house without braking and then up and down the surrounding blocks, studying every parked vehicle she passed and looking for the telltale signs of a surveillance vehicle: vans with mirrored windows, cars with more than one antenna, pickup trucks with camper shells on the back. One vehicle caught her attention. It was a plumbing repair van, according to the sign painted on the side panel. It sat at the curb in front of a house one block from Leo's house. Cassie passed it without stopping but then turned around and headed back, pulling to the curb and parking a half block from the van. She sat there watching the vehicle and looking for movement behind the glass, a shifting of the suspension as people moved around inside, any indication of life within. Nothing happened but Cassie maintained her vigil for almost ten minutes before she saw a man in a blue jumpsuit come out of the house and approach the van. He opened the side door and climbed inside. A few moments later he carefully lowered a heavy pipe-snaking machine to the road. He then got out, closed and locked the van's door, and pushed the machine toward the front door of the house. He seemed legit to Cassie. She restarted the Porsche, made one more circuit through the neighborhood and then returned to Leo's house. She parked at the curb out front and reminded herself not to buy into Leo's constant paranoid sensibility. She remembered all the rules and precautions he used to lay on her and Max before a job. Don't bet black before a job, don't eat chicken before a job, never wear a red hat and so on and so on. It was all *step on a crack, break your mother's back* stuff as far as Cassie had been concerned.

Until that last night at the Cleopatra.

When Cassie got to the front door she looked up at the joists of the roof overhang and saw the old bullet camera was still in place. She was wondering if it still worked and got her answer when Leo answered the door before she knocked. She smiled.

'Guess it still works.'

''Course it does. Had that there goin' on what, eight years now. Person put it there guaranteed it for life and I believed her. Nobody knew her shit better than her.'

He smiled.

'How are you, Cassie? Come on in.'

He stepped back to let her in. Leo Renfro was in his early forties, with a trim, medium build. He had thinning hair that was already gray. It had been gray when Cassie met him almost a decade earlier. He'd told her then that it was from having to grow up too quickly. He'd practically raised Max, his stepbrother, after their mother died in a drunk-driving accident. Leo's father was an unknown but Max's wasn't. He was in Nevada State doing ten to twenty-five for armed robbery.

Cassie stepped into the house and Leo pulled her into a fast, tight bear hug. It felt good to her. It felt comforting, like home.

'Hey, kid,' he said with a somber and loving tone.

'Leo,' she said and then pulled back with a concerned look on her face. 'I can say your name now, right?'

He laughed and pointed toward the back and started leading the way to where she knew he kept his office in a wood-paneled den off the pool.

'You look good, Cassie. Real good. Like the short hair. Is that sort of a butch thing left over from High Desert? What was it I heard they call the lamb choppers up there, the High Dee Hoes?'

He glanced back at her and winked.

'You look good, too, Leo. Still the same.'

He looked back again and they exchanged smiles. It had been years since Cassie had seen him but Leo had barely changed. Maybe a little less hair but still deeply tanned and trim. She assumed he must still be following his regimen of yoga and then morning lap swimming to stay in shape.

In the living room they had to step around a couch that was oddly placed at an angle facing the corner of the room rather than the fireplace. This caused Cassie to look about and she noticed all of the furnishings of the room were positioned strangely, as if the fireplace – the obvious center of the room – were not there.

'Remind me to get your interior designer's number before I leave,' she said. 'What style is this – postmodern break-in?'

'Hey, I know. I just had the place feng-shuied and this is the best I can do with it. For now.'

'Feng what?'

'Feng *shui.* The Chinese art of harmonic placement. Feng shui.'

'Oh.'

She thought she remembered reading about feng shui. Something about it being the latest cottage industry in L.A. among the cosmically enlightened.

'This place is doomed,' Leo was saying. 'Bad vibes in all directions. I feel like Dick Van Dyke – comin' in the door and tripping over the furniture. I should just get out of here. But I've been here so long and I have the pool right here and everything. I don't know what I'm gonna do.'

They came to the office. Leo's desk was at one end, next to the row of sliding glass doors that looked out on the pool. Lined along the opposite wall were dozens of cases of champagne. Seeing the stacks of boxes gave Cassie pause. In the past, the Leo Renfro she knew and had worked for would never have stolen property in his own home. He was a middleman who set capers into motion and arranged for the fencing of the merchandise afterward but he almost never came into physical proximity with it unless it was cash. Seeing the champagne right in his office made Cassie question what she was doing there. Maybe things had changed with Leo since Max. She stood in the doorway to the office as if afraid to enter.

Leo went behind his desk and looked back at her. He didn't sit down. 'What's the matter?'

She gestured toward the lineup of boxes completely covering one wall. There must be fifty cases, she guessed.

'Leo, you never kept the swag in your own house. It's not only dangerous but stupid. You –'

'Relax, would you? It's all totally legit. I bought it – ordered it through the distributor. It's an investment.'

'In what?'

'The future. You watch. The millennium celebration is gonna liquidate all stores of champagne. Around the whole fucking world. What's left will sky-rocket in value and I'll be sitting pretty. Every goddamn restaurant in town will be coming to me. You should see my garage. I'm hoarding five hundred cases of this stuff. Six thousand bottles. I double my wholesale price and take home a couple hundred K minimum. You want to buy in on it? I've got investors.'

She came into the room and looked out through the doors at the glimmering surface of the pool. It was lighted from beneath the surface and glowed like blue neon in the night.

'I can't afford it.'

She could see the automatic vacuum slowly moving across the bottom, the water tube trailing behind it and the debris bag rising, undulating in the water like a ghost.

She could hear the background hiss of the nearby freeway. It was the same at her house in Hollywood. She wondered for a moment if it was a coincidence that they both had places so close to the freeway. Or was it something about thieves. They needed to know the escape route was close.

'You'll be able to buy in after we do this thing here,' Leo said. 'Come on, sit down.'

He sat down and opened the middle desk drawer. He took out a pair of half-cut reading glasses and put them on. There was a manila file waiting on the desk. Leo was all business. He could just as well have been preparing to go over a tax return with a client as the details of a hot prowl burglary. He actually had studied accounting at UCLA until he realized he wanted to manage money that was his, not somebody else's.

Cassie came over and sat down in the padded leather chair at the desk opposite Leo. She looked up at a string of red coins that was hanging from the ceiling directly over the desk. Leo caught her stare and waved up at the coins.

'That's the cure. The remedy.'

'Cure for what?'

'For the feng shui. They're I-Ching coins. They make up for the lack of harmony. That's why I have them hanging right here. Where I do my work is the most important spot in the house.'

He gestured to his desk and the open file.

'Leo, you were always paranoid but I think you're finally wigging out.'

'No. I believe it. And it works. Another thing is the stars. I consult the stars now before making a plan.'

'You're not instilling confidence in me. You mean you're asking some astrologer for a blessing on your moves? Leo, don't you –'

'I don't ask or tell anybody anything. I do it on my own. See?'

He turned and pointed to a row of books held between bookends on the credenza behind him. They all had titles that appeared to be taken from astrological circumstances. One title was *Calendar of Voids* and another book was called *Investing in the Stars.*

'Leo, you used to just quote your Jewish grandfather who said things like "Never pick up a penny that is heads down." What about him?'

'I still believe in him. I believe in it all. The important thing is to believe. Not to hope, but to believe. There is a difference. I believe in these things and so that helps me do what I have to do and accomplish what it is I want to accomplish.'

Cassie thought it was a philosophy that could have come from nowhere else but California.

'That's the beauty of it,' Leo was saying. 'I'm covered from all directions. It's good to have any edge you can get, Cass. Max used to say that, remember?'

Cassie nodded somberly.

'I remember.'

A long pause of uneasy silence and sad memories went by. Cassie looked out at the pool. She remembered swimming with Max one night after they thought Leo was asleep. Then the pool light came on and they were naked.

She finally looked back at Leo.

He had opened the file on the desk. There was a quarter-inch-thick stack of hundred-dollar bills in the file along with a page of neatly printed but indecipherable notes torn from a yellow legal pad. One of Leo's precautions. He always kept notes in a coded language that only he knew. He was studying the notes on the yellow paper.

'Now, where do I begin?' he said to himself.

'How about with the reason you said I won't like this one.'

Leo leaned back in his chair and studied her for a long moment.

'Well,' Cassie finally said, 'are you going to tell me or is it written in the stars somewhere for me to read?'

He ignored the jab.

'This is the deal. It's in Las Vegas, which I already warned you about. It's a lot of cash, I am told. But it's a contract job and –'

'With who?'

'Some people. That's all you need to know. Everybody has a part. Nobody knows everybody else. Not even me. We got a guy watching the mark right now and he's just a voice on the phone that tells me things. I have no idea who he is. He knows me by phone but he doesn't know about you. See? It's safest that way. Different players hold different pieces of the same puzzle. Only nobody sees the whole puzzle, just the piece they hold.'

'That's fine, Leo, but I'm not talking about the bit players. You *know* who it is you're setting this up for, right?'

'Yeah, I know them. I've done business with them in the past. They're good people. In fact, they're investors.'

He pointed to the wall of champagne cases.

'Okay,' Cassie said. 'As long as you vouch for them. What else won't I like about this?'

'What else? The big what else is that it's the Cleo.'

'Jesus Christ!'

'I know, I know.'

He raised his hands as if surrendering in an argument. He then leaned back in his chair and took off his glasses. He put one of the ear hooks in the corner of his mouth and let the glasses dangle.

'Leo, you expect me to go back into that place, let alone Las Vegas, after what happened?'

'I know.'

'I'm never going to set foot in that goddamn place again.'

'I know.'

She got up and stood with her face just inches from one of the sliders. She looked out at the pool again. The vacuum was still moving. Back and forth, back and forth. It reminded her of her own existence.

Leo put his glasses back on and spoke to her in a calming and measured tone.

'Now can I say something?'

She gestured for him to go on though she still didn't look at him.

'Okay, let's remember something here. You called me, I didn't call you. You asked me to set up a job. You said you wanted it big and you wanted it soon. And you wanted it to be cash. Have I got all of that right?'

He waited for an answer but she didn't say anything.

'I'll take your silence as a yes. Well, Cass, this is that job.'

She turned to face him.

'But I didn't say –'

He held up his hand, silencing her.

'Let me finish. All I'm saying is that I brought this to you for consideration. You don't want it, fine. I'll make some calls and I'll go with someone else. But, girl, you were the best I ever knew of on the hot prowl. You are a true artist, if ever I knew one. Even Max would have admitted that. He was the teacher but the student got smarter. So when these guys came to me and told me about this thing, I started thinking it was you all the way. But, hey, I'm not forcing you to do anything. Something else will come down the pipe and I'll call you then. I don't know when that will be, but you'll still be first on my list. You will always be first, Cassie. Always.'

She slowly came back to her chair and sat down.

'You're the artist, Leo. A great bullshit artist. That speech is your way of saying I should do it, isn't it?'

'I didn't say that.'

'You don't have to. It's just that, Leo, you believe in your stars and your I-Ching coins and all your other things. The one thing I have to believe is that that place, that night . . . that there was just a ghost or something in the mix. A jinx. And it was either on us or on that place. For six years I've been saying that it wasn't us, that it was that place. And now you . . . you want me to go back there.'

Leo folded the file closed. Cassie watched the stack of money disappear.

'I only want you to do what you want to do. But I have to make some calls now, Cass. I need to set this up with somebody else tonight because the job has to be tomorrow night. The mark's supposed to check out Thursday morning.'

Cassie nodded and felt this awful sense that if she passed on this job there wouldn't be another. She didn't know if this was because Leo wouldn't trust her or because of something else. It was just a premonition. Her mind flashed on the scene of a beach and the surf coming up and wiping out letters drawn in the sand. They were gone before Cassie could read them but she knew what they spelled. *Take the job.*

'What's my end if I do it?'

Leo looked at her and hesitated.

'You sure you want to know?'

She nodded. He opened the file again and slid the yellow page out from beneath the stack of currency. He spoke while looking down at his notes.

'Okay, this is the deal. We get the first hundred off the top and forty points on the rest. They've been watching this guy. They think he's got about five hundred K, all cash. In a briefcase. That pans out, that comes to two-sixty for us. I'd cut it sixty/forty, you on the big end. Better than a hundred and a half for you. I don't know if it's enough to disappear on permanently but it's a fucking A start and not bad for a night's work.'

He looked up at her.

'Not bad for them, either,' she said. 'Two-forty for doing nothing.'

'Not nothing. They found the mark. That's most important. They also have somebody on the inside who will make things very easy for you.'

He paused for a moment to let the money and the details sink in.

'You interested now?'

Cassie thought a moment.

'You don't know when the next one will be coming, do you?'

'Never do. Right now, this one's all I got. But to be honest, I wouldn't count on the next one being this kind of money. Probably take two, three jobs to put this kind of bread together. This is the big one. This is the one you want.'

He leaned back in his chair, looked over his glasses at her and waited. She knew he had played it just right. He'd let her run out with the line but now was slowly reeling it back in. She was hooked and she knew it. A job with a potential payoff of more than a hundred and fifty thousand dollars didn't come along often. The most she and Max had ever pulled on a caper was sixty thousand dollars they took off an assistant to the sultan of Brunei. It was pocket change to the sultan but she and Max had celebrated until dawn at the Aces and Eights Club in North Vegas.

'All right,' she finally said. 'I'm interested. Let's talk about it.'

8

Leo leaned over the counter where he was working and spoke without looking at his notes or at Cassie.

'The mark is registered under the name Diego Hernandez. He's a pro, a TexMex out of Houston. His game is baccarat. Far as anyone knows he plays clean. He's just good at it. Spends a few days at each casino and moves on, that way he isn't taking too much out of one place and raising eyebrows too high. They tracked him from the Nugget to the Stardust and now the Cleo. Cleaned up every place he went.'

They were in the kitchen of Leo's house. Cassie sat at the kitchen table while Leo stood at the counter and made them peanut butter, honey and banana sandwiches. It was his specialty. He used seven-grain bread.

'Each night he takes his winnings in cash and keeps it all in a briefcase. If he leaves the building he takes the case with him. Locked to his wrist. The only time he doesn't have it with him is when he's down in the casino playing. What he does is take it to the front desk and have them hold it in the vault for him while he's playing, then he picks it up when he goes up to bed. Whenever he's carrying the case he's got a security escort. He doesn't take chances.'

'So what you are saying is that the only time to get it is to go in while he's asleep.'

'Exactly.'

Leo came over to the table and put down two plates with two sandwiches each on them. He then went to the refrigerator and came back with two bottles of Dr Pepper. He sat down and opened the bottles as he talked.

'In the room he probably transfers the cash from the case to the closet safe as an added precaution. That's not for sure but we have to expect it. You want a glass with that?'

'No. What is the safe? I don't remember from before.'

Leo looked down and studied his notes.

'It's a Halsey Executive five-button. Sits on the floor in the closet beneath the clothes rack. Bolted to the floor from the inside. You can't move it. You have to go in and open it – while the guy is right there in the room.'

Cassie nodded and picked up half a sandwich. Leo had cut them into triangles. He always did it that way and she remembered he once got annoyed when she had made a sandwich and cut it lengthwise. She took a bite and immediately smiled.

'*Gawd,*' she said, her mouth full of peanut butter and moving slowly. 'I forgot how good these are, Leo. I remember you makin' them for Max and me after we drove all night to get back here after jobs.'

'Made these sandwiches for him since he was six years old. Always his favorite. It always hits the spot.'

Mentioning Max robbed her of the smile. Cassie turned back to the business at hand.

'The Halsey has a front-mounted keypad. I can do it with one camera – two to be safe if there's time. I'll have to know if the mark's right- or left-handed. I'll get that when I see him on the floor.'

She was primarily talking to herself. Seeing the job in her mind. Then a question for Leo came up.

'You ask your man about the paint?'

Leo nodded.

'Swiss Coffee. The room was painted two months ago but it's a smoking room. Our guy smokes cigars.'

'That'll help with the smell.'

She committed the paint color to memory. She decided she'd pick up a pint and a pump bottle at Laurel Hardware in the morning before leaving.

'I'm also told he's a fat fuck,' Leo said. 'A snorer. Makes it a little easier.'

'Nothing's easy, Leo. Not in Las Vegas.'

That made her think about going back to the Cleopatra again and a foreboding came over her.

'If he's leaving Thursday, why don't we wait and see where he goes and hit him at the new place? Why does it have to be the Cleo?'

'Because we don't know if he's going anywhere else. He might be going back to Texas, for all we know. His briefcase might be full and he's going home. Besides, we have the inside man at the Cleo. Who knows if we'll get lucky like that if he moves on.'

Cassie nodded. She knew Leo had thought about all of this and had decided that hitting the mark at the Cleopatra was the only way.

'I read that the Cleo's for sale,' she said, just to be saying something that would take them away from her thoughts.

'Yeah, three thousand rooms and half of them empty on any given night. Big white elephant is what it is. Seven years old and already for sale. I heard Steve Wynn took a look at it but then took a pass. You know something must be fucked up there if he didn't see a way to turn it around. He touches something, it's gold.'

'Maybe the place never got over the bad publicity – you know, with Max.'

Leo shook his head.

'Old news. The problem is they made that place as cheap as Mother Hubbard's flophouse and now it's falling apart and nobody wants to stay there. Too many other nice places on the Strip for the same dough. You got the Bellagio now, the Venetian. The Mandalay Bay down at the end.'

He was naming places that hadn't even existed the last time Cassie had been to Las Vegas. She finished her first sandwich and immediately moved on to the next after taking a swig of cold soda from the bottle. She went back to laying out the plan, talking with her mouth full.

'Unless things have changed, the Cleo is on magno-cards. That means I have to get over there early tomorrow to work on the maid. I finesse my way into the room, set things up and come back at night through the air-return vent – just like last time.'

She gulped down a mouthful and felt it hit her stomach with a thud.

'I don't know, Leo. They might have changed the design of those ducts after me and Max used them.'

She looked over at him. He was looking over his glasses at her and smiling.

'What?'

'You're not listening to me,' he said. 'I told you the spotter is an inside man. Forget the ducts. And the maid, too. No soshing on this one. You'll have a complete package waiting for you at the VIP desk.'

He looked down at the notes.

'Under the name Turcello. You'll have everything you –'

'Why Turcello? Who's that?'

'That's you. Who cares why? It's just the name the spotter gave me. In the package will be everything you'll need. You'll go in through the front door to the room because you'll have a pass key. And you'll also have a room nearby. So you can set up and watch. Also there'll be a pager. You put it on and you'll get a buzz the minute the mark starts cashing out for the night.'

'A pass key only gets me halfway there. I'll need to change out the deadbolt. It's been so long I can't remember the make. Did you get –'

'Got it right here. Relax. I told you, I've got everything. This isn't amateur hour.'

He referred to his notes.

'The deadbolt is a Smithson Commercial. Same as last time. That a problem?'

'I won't know until I get there. Like you said, when they built that place they went cheap in the places you can't see. They used half gears in all the deadbolts. I guess using halves instead of wholes in three thousand locks saved a nice piece of bread. The question is, did they go back and change them all out after that night with Max?'

'What if they did?'

'Then it's trouble. It means I'll have to take out the whole and cut it in half.'

'In the room?'

'No. I'll have to leave and come back. I'll bring a cutting torch with me and leave it in the trunk. But if I have to go down to use it, I'll have to find a place out of sight. Meantime, the guy could go up to the room and end of story.'

'What about the other room? You could take the gear out of that lock, cut it and then take it into the mark's room.'

Before Cassie could say he was right, Leo shook off the possibility that the locks had been changed.

'I tell you, don't worry about it. That place has been losing money since the day it opened its doors. They wouldn't have gone out and changed three thousand deadbolts because one guy – who wasn't going to be doing it again – finessed a lock. Forget about it.'

'Easy for you to say. You're staying here.'

Leo let that go and reached into the file. He pulled out the stack of money and put it down next to Cassie's plate.

'Our partners are serious people. They know there are equipment costs. That's ten grand there. For camera shopping and whatever else you need.'

'I've already spent close to nine hundred on the basics.'

'Let me ask you something, how up to date are you on all of the cameras and stuff? You know what you want?'

'I'll go see my guy at Hooten's. If he's still there. It's been a long time.'

'Sure has.'

'If he's not, I'll go to Radio Shack. I've kept up. I'll make it work, Leo. Don't worry about that part.'

Leo studied her over his eyeglasses again.

'So what happened, Cass? Why'd you wait so long to call me? I had given up hope of you ever turning up again.'

'I don't know, Leo. I guess at first I just thought I was going to make a run at it, you know?'

Leo nodded.

'The straight and narrow,' he said. 'But it wasn't there for you.'

'One day everything changed.'

'Well, welcome back. We could use you on our side.'

He smiled. Cassie shook her head.

'Leo, this is a one-shot deal. I mean it. I'm not on your team. I'm going to disappear after this.'

She knew the money wouldn't be enough. It would only be a start. But that was all she wanted, the promise of a new start.

Leo nodded and looked down at the yellow page of notes.

'Well, this little caper should get you to wherever it is you want to go.'

'Did you make that call on the passports?'

Leo raised his eyes to hers without raising his face.

'I did. I'm told they're on the way. I'll check the drop later. I like going late, after the counter's closed.'

'Good. Thanks for doing that.'

'No problem. I want you to get to where you want to go, Cassie.'

She picked up the money and stood up.

'I guess I better get it in gear if it's going to be tomorrow. I have to –'

'Wait. One more thing. This is important.'

He pushed his plate aside although his second sandwich was uneaten. From the rear pocket of his pants he pulled an appointment book. It was the size of a checkbook but thicker. He took a rubber band off it and opened it to a page marked with a pink Post-it sticker. Cassie could see it was the current month's calendar. Many of the blocks denoting the days were filled with Leo's printing. Leo ran his finger along the blocks until he found what he was looking for. He spoke without taking his eyes off the page.

'I want you to humor me on something when you're over there.'

'Fine. What?'

'Promise me.'

'I'm not going to promise you anything until I know what you're talking about. What is it, Leo?'

'Okay, this is it. Whatever you do, no matter what happens, don't be in that guy's room between three twenty-two and three thirty-eight in the morning. Okay? That's Wednesday night going into Thursday morning. Write it down if you think you'll forget.'

Cassie felt a bemused, questioning smile come across her face.

'What are you talking about?'

'It's a void moon.'

'A void moon . . .'

'This is my astrological calendar, okay? I work with those books I showed you in the office and I chart things, including the moon.'

'Okay, so you chart the moon. What's a void moon?'

'It's an astrological situation, okay? See, when the moon is moving from one house to another up there in the constellations, it sometimes is in no house at all. When that happens it means it is "void of course" until it finally gets into a house. It's a void moon. And like I said, on Wednesday night going into Thursday morning there's a void moon for those, what, sixteen minutes. It's hanging out there between Cancer and Leo. It's void of course from three twenty-two until three thirty-eight. I worked it all out here.'

He closed the calendar and held it up to her as if it were something sacred.

'And so?'

'And so it's a bad luck time, Cass. Anything can happen under a void moon. Anything wrong. Just don't make your move during that time.'

Cassie studied him for a moment and registered his look as completely sincere. Leo had always been a true believer in whatever it was he chose to believe in.

'It's going to be tough,' she said. 'It all depends on when the guy goes down. I need to go two hours into the sleep pattern. At least two hours to be sure.'

'Then go in after the void. I'm not fucking around here, Cass. You know Lincoln, McKinley and Kennedy were all inaugurated during a void moon? All three of them and look what happened to them. Clinton, too, and he might as well've been shot, what happened with him.'

He nodded very somberly and held the calendar up again as if it were proof of something itself. To Cassie there was something endearing about his fervent belief. Maybe it was because she wasn't sure she believed in anything anymore.

'I mean it,' Leo said. 'You can look this stuff up going back as far as you want.'

Cassie took a step toward the table and reached for the book. But as Leo offered it, she pulled her hand back. She wanted to ask something but wasn't sure she wanted the answer.

Leo read her. He somberly nodded.

'Yeah,' he said. 'I looked it up. That night six years ago with Max, he had a void moon, too.'

She just looked at him.

'Remember what you said before about there being a jinx? It was the void moon, Cass. That was the jinx.'

At the door Leo wished her good luck and said he would see her after the job was completed. Cassie hesitated on the front steps. The discussion of the void moon and Max had put a somber veneer over everything now. She rolled her shoulders as if catching a chill.

'What is it?' Leo asked.

She shook her head as if to dismiss the question and then asked her own.

'Leo, do you think about Max?'

Leo didn't answer at first. He stepped through the open door and looked up at the night sky. The moon was pale and hung like an egg in the sky.

'It will be full in a couple days. Nice and bright.'

He continued to stare for a moment and then looked down at Cassie.

'Not a single day goes by that I don't think about him,' he said. 'Not a day.'

Cassie nodded.

'I still miss him a lot, Leo.'

'Me, too, Cass. So you be careful over there. I don't want to lose you that way, too.'

9

By noon on Wednesday, after making a few last stops for paint and supplies, Cassie Black was crossing the desert, the sun gleaming off the silver skin of the Porsche and heat waves rising off the pavement in front of her. Though the highway was reasonably clear and she was driving a car capable of cruising smoothly at 110 mph or better, she kept the Porsche at a steady two miles under the limit. It was tantamount to holding a thoroughbred race horse at a canter but she had good reason. The moment she had left Los Angeles County she was in violation of her parole. Drawing a traffic stop from the highway patrol could result in her immediate incarceration.

As soon as she crossed the county line she knew that the stakes were high and her life was now at risk. Any interaction with law enforcement would probably result in her returning to lockdown. She had been paroled five years into a seven-to-twelve-year sentence for manslaughter. If she got hooked up she'd be returned to prison for a minimum two years but probably even longer.

She put a Lucinda Williams compact disc in the car stereo and listened to it over and over during the drive. The music rarely skipped badly on the smooth freeways. She liked the outlaw spirit of the songs, the sense of yearning and searching for something the singer put in every song. One of them made Cassie cry each time it came up on the disc. It was about a lost lover who had gone back to Lake Charles to die.

Did an angel whisper in your ear
hold you close and take away all your fear
in those long, last moments

For Cassie the question posed in the song was a ghost that haunted her all the time. She hoped an angel had come to Max.

The sharp-edged outlines of the casino resorts were visible ahead by three and she felt an unmistakable mix of excitement and trepidation. For many years she had believed she would never again see the place where she had grown up, where she had met and lived with Max. She had comfortably reconciled that and put Las Vegas behind her. Returning now made her think of pain and regrets and ghosts. But she also couldn't help but marvel at the genius of the place. If ever something had been made out of nothing, Las Vegas no doubt was it.

As she cruised the Strip she found the changes made in her absence to be remarkable. On every block there rose a new resort, a new testament to greed and excess. She drove by a faux New York skyline, the colossal MGM Grand and the new Bellagio. She saw re-creations of the Eiffel Tower and Venice's Piazza San Marco. They were places and things she had never seen. But now here they were on the Las Vegas Strip. She remembered something Max had once said. 'Everything and everybody will eventually come to Las Vegas. It will take away any reason to go anywhere else.'

Then they went to islands and they knew there was at least one place that couldn't be counterfeited or corrupted.

She came to the Cleopatra and her attention was immediately drawn to the side-by-side Tigris and Euphrates Towers. Her eyes drew along the mirrored glass of the top floor of the Euphrates Tower and held momentarily on one window.

Her eyes dropped to the rising triangular form of the glass atrium that covered the sprawling casino twenty floors below. The reflection of the sun was as sharp as a diamond on the side of the mirrored glass uprising. The complex was set almost a hundred yards off the Strip and the entrance drive took the visitor past a series of reflecting pools at graduated levels and from which fountains rose in a choreographed water dance. Set in the reflecting pools were pure white statues of children at play – all under the benevolent eye of Cleopatra, who sat in a throne at the edge of the highest pool. Behind her, an Egyptian motif was integrated into the modern design of the sand-colored exterior of the hotel and casino.

Cassie drove by and waited with the traffic to turn onto Flamingo and head out into the industrial warrens on the west side of the city. She couldn't help but think about Max. About their times here. About the end. She had not expected such biting pain and regret upon her return. The landscape of Las Vegas was always changing, reinventing itself. She had not expected a place that was essentially just a facade to have such a nostalgic resonance. But it was there and it burned. She had not been with another man since Max and she was sure she never would be. Perhaps, she thought, this pain was all she would ever have. That she should embrace it. But then she remembered there was more. There was the plan out on the horizon.

Hooten's Lighting & Supplies was located in an industrial complex near an elevated section of the freeway. It had been there for almost forty years, though its business had changed markedly over that time. Originally a wholesaler of lighting equipment to the casinos, its business had evolved more into the arena of electronics. It was no longer simply a supplier but a manufacturer as well. HLS now built and sold much of the sophisticated surveillance equipment employed in the casinos in Nevada as well as in gaming rooms on Indian reservation land throughout the West.

What the operators of HLS and the casinos that purchased the equipment were not aware of was that inside the company there was at least one person who made the same technology available – for a price – to those intent on circumventing the casino security systems the company installed.

Cassie parked the Boxster in the fenced rear lot, where the installers parked their trucks at night, and went in through the back door. Once inside she stood still for a moment as her eyes adjusted to the dim interior. When she could see clearly, her attention was drawn to the long counter that ran the length of the right side of the no-frills equipment-and-catalog room. Behind the counter were a half dozen men working with customers or working the phones. Most of them had copies of the thick HLS catalog open in front of them and were writing down orders. Cassie noticed that not much in the place had changed. The same slogan that had been painted along the wall behind the counter seven years ago was still there.

IN GOD WE TRUST
ALL OTHERS WE MONITOR

It took Cassie a few seconds to spot Jersey Paltz. He was working on the phone at the far end of the counter. He had a beard now and more gray hair. But he still had the ponytail and the silver loop earring. It was him.

Paltz hung up just as Cassie stepped up to the counter but he didn't look up at her. He finished writing notes on the top page of an order book. Reading upside down, Cassie could see the order was from the Tropicana. She spoke while he was still writing.

'So, Jersey, too busy to say hello to an old friend?'

Paltz finished the line he was on and then looked up smiling. The smile faltered a little and his face showed the slow register of recognition.

'Cassie Black?'

Cassie nodded and smiled.

'Hey, girl, sure been a long time. When did you . . . uh . . .'

'Ten months ago. I just haven't been around. After High Desert I moved to California. I like it out there. Where I live the temperature only hits trips a few times a year.'

Paltz nodded but there was hesitation there. Cassie could easily read him. He was realizing she wasn't there to make old acquaintances – there had never been anything but a business relationship between them in the first place. She glanced around to make sure their conversation was private and then leaned over the counter, her elbows on his open catalog and order book.

'I need a kit. Full rig, at least three cameras, and one has to be green.'

Paltz put the pencil he'd been using behind his ear and shook his head once without looking directly at her.

'I'm going to need a pair of NVGs and a roll of Conduct-O tape, too,' Cassie added. 'I stopped at Radio Shack on the way over and they don't sell the tape anymore. The rest of the tools I brought with me.'

'Well, that might be a problem,' Paltz said.

'The goggles or the tape?'

'No, all of it. We don't . . . I mean, I just don't get involved in that sort of –'

'Look, Jersey. Don't you think that if I was going to set you up I would've done it six years ago when it could have done me some good? I mean, Max and me, we made you a lot of money back then. You remember that, don't you?'

He nodded his head once, reluctantly.

'It's just that things are different now in this town. You cross a line and they come after you. I mean they really come after you.'

Cassie straightened up.

'You don't have to convince me of that. Or Max.'

'Sorry. I know that.'

He nodded once more and put his hands flat on the counter.

'So what do you think, Jersey? I've got cash and I'm ready to rock and roll.'

She casually swung her backpack under her arm and flipped up the top flap, exposing the stack of hundreds Leo had given her. She knew that loyalty and trust were one thing in the outlaw world, but showing the cash was another.

'I gotta know now 'cause if you're not going to help me I've gotta find somebody else.'

Paltz nodded. She could tell, the money had turned him.

'Tell you what,' he said. 'I might be able to do something for you. What time are we talking about?'

'We're talking right now, Jersey. Tonight. I'm here. I gotta job to do.'

He looked up at her, maintaining his hands-on-the- counter pose. His eyes moved around to make sure they were still talking in private.

'All right . . . I'm working till five. How about Aces and Eights at six?'

'That old dump's still in business?'

'Oh, yeah. Always.'

'I'll see you at six.'

She started to step away from the counter but Paltz made a low whistling sound with his mouth and she turned back to him. Paltz took the pencil off his ear and wrote something on a scratch pad. He tore the page off and handed it to her.

'You'll need to have that with you.'

She took the page and looked at it. It had a price on it.

$8,500

She thought it was high. She had read enough about the current technology to know the costs for what she needed should be in the range of five thousand dollars, including a nice profit for Paltz. Before she could say anything Paltz apparently read her.

'Look,' he whispered, 'you're gonna pay high end for this stuff. What we make here is proprietary. You take a bust with this stuff on you and they'll trace it right back here. Now sellin' it to you ain't illegal per se, but they could get me on an aiding-and-abetting bit. They throw conspiracy charges around now like confetti. On top of that, I'd lose my job. So you gotta pay high to cover my exposure here. Take it or leave it, that's the price.'

She now realized she had made a mistake showing him the cash before they had a deal.

'Okay, fine with me,' she finally said. 'I'm on an expense account.'

'See you at six, then.'

'Yeah, six.'

10

Cassie had two hours to kill before her meeting with Jersey Paltz. She thought about going to the Cleo and picking up the package waiting for her at the front desk but decided against it because it meant she would have to leave to make her meeting and then come back. That would mean two extra trips under the cameras. She didn't want to give the people on the other side of those cameras two extra chances at making her.

Instead she stayed away from the Strip. She first stopped at a nail salon in a strip mall on Flamingo and had the manicurist cut her nails as short as possible. It wasn't very stylish but the manicurist, who was Asian, probably Vietnamese, didn't ask any questions and Cassie tipped her nicely for it.

She then drove east on Flamingo out past UNLV and into the neighborhood where she had lived until she was eleven. On the drive from L.A. she had convinced herself that she wanted to see it one last time.

She passed the 7-Eleven where her father took her to get candy and the bus stop where she was let off after school. On Bloom Street the little house her parents had owned was still painted pink but she could see that some changes had been made in the two decades since they had left it. The swamp cooler on the roof had been changed out with a real air conditioner. The garage had been converted into living space and the backyard was now fenced, just like all the other houses on the block. Cassie wondered who lived there now and whether it was the same family that had bought it at auction after the foreclosure. She had the urge to go knock on the door and see if she could be allowed a quick look at her old room. It seemed that the last time she had ever felt completely safe had been in that room. She knew how nice it would be to have that feeling again. The image of her room as it had been back then made her momentarily think of Jodie Shaw's room and the collection of stuffed dogs on the shelf over the bed. But she quickly dismissed that image and moved back to her own memories.

Staring at the house, she thought about the time she came home from school and saw her mother crying while a man in a uniform tacked a foreclosure notice on the front door. He told her it had to be in public view but as soon as he left her mother tore the papers off the door. She then grabbed Cassie and they got in the Chevette. Her mother drove with reckless abandon toward the Strip, finally pulling to a stop with two wheels up on the curb in front of the Riviera. Yanking Cassie along by the hand, she found

Cassie's father at one of the blackjack tables and shoved the foreclosure papers into his face and down the front of his Hawaiian shirt. Cassie always remembered that shirt. It had topless hula dancers on it, their swaying arms covering their breasts. Her mother cursed her father and called him a coward and other things Cassie could no longer remember, until she was pulled away by casino security men.

Cassie could not remember all of the words but she vividly remembered the scene as through the eyes of a child. Her father just sat on his stool and kept his place at the gambling table. He stared at the woman screaming at him as though she were a complete stranger. A thin smile played on his face. And he never said a word.

Her father didn't come home that night or any of the nights after. Cassie saw him only one more time – when she was dealing blackjack at the Trop. But by then he was deep inside the bottle and didn't recognize her. And she didn't have the courage to introduce herself.

She looked away from the house and again images from the house on Lookout Mountain Road intruded. She thought of the drawing on the easel in Jodie Shaw's bedroom. The little girl in the picture was crying because she was leaving her home behind.

Cassie knew exactly how she felt.

11

Traffic into North Las Vegas was a miserable crawl. By the time Cassie got to the Aces and Eights Club she was fifteen minutes late. But before going in she still took the time to sit in the car and put on the wig she had bought for the Lookout Mountain Road open house. She flipped down the visor and used the mirror to style the wig and then used an eyebrow pencil to darken her eyebrows to match. She added a pair of pink tinted glasses she had bought at a Thrifty drugstore.

The Aces and Eights was a locals bar and up until six years ago Cassie had been a regular. Most of the patrons made their living off the casino trade – legally or otherwise – and if there was anyplace where she might be recognized, even after a six-year absence, it was the Aces and Eights. Cassie had almost told Jersey Paltz to choose another spot for the rendezvous but she'd gone along with his choice so as not to spook him. She also had to admit to herself she was a bit nostalgic. She wanted to see if the old hangout had changed.

After checking herself once more in the mirror, she got out of the Boxster and went inside. She carried her backpack over one shoulder. She saw several men at the bar and could tell by their uniforms or the colors of their dealer's aprons what casinos they worked for. There were a couple of women in short dresses and heels with their pagers and cell phones on the bar – hookers waiting for jobs and not worried about being obvious about it. Nobody cared at the Aces and Eights.

She saw Paltz in a circular booth in the rear corner of the dimly lit bar. He was leaning forward over a bowl of chili. Cassie remembered that the chili was the only thing on the menu that the regulars dared to eat. But she'd never eat it again, here or anywhere else, after having to eat chili every Wednesday for five years in High Desert. She walked up and was sliding into the booth when Paltz began protesting.

'Honey, I'm waiting for –'

'It's me.'

He looked up and recognized her.

'Little early for Halloween, isn't it?'

'I thought there might be people in here who'd remember me.'

'Shit, you haven't been around in six years. In Vegas that's ancient history.

You know, I was just about to give up on you but figured, hey, you haven't been here in six, seven years. You don't know how bad traffic's gotten.'

'I just learned. I thought L.A. was bad but this is . . .'

'Makes L.A. look like the fucking Autobahn. They need about three more freeways here, all the building they been doin' around here.'

Cassie didn't want to talk about traffic or the weather. She got right to the point of the meeting.

'Did you bring me something?'

'First things first.'

Paltz slid around in the booth until he was right next to Cassie and moved his left hand under the table and started patting and feeling her body. Cassie immediately stiffened.

'Always wanted to do this,' Paltz said with a smile. 'Ever since I saw you that first time with Max.'

His breath was chili and onions. Cassie turned away and looked out into the bar.

'You're wasting your time, I'm not –'

She stopped when he brought his hand up her torso to her breasts. She pushed his arm away.

'Okay, okay,' Paltz said. 'You just can't be too careful these days, you know? You got eighty-five bumblebees in that bag?'

She looked out of the booth and across the bar to make sure no one was watching. They were clear. If people were noticing their serious looks, they were dismissing it as a pointed negotiation between a big-haired hooker and a john. No big deal. Even the pat-down could be seen as part of the negotiation; these days a buyer had to be sure of the quality and gender of the product.

'I brought what you told me to bring,' she said. 'Where's the kit?'

'In the truck. You show me what I need again and we'll take a walk.'

'We already did this once,' Cassie protested. 'Move back.'

Paltz slid back to his spot. He scooped some chili into his mouth and took a long pull on a bottle of Miller High Life.

Cassie moved the backpack across her lap and put it down on the seat between them. She pulled the flap back halfway. Her rubber tool satchel was now in the bag. On top of it was the sheaf of currency. Hundred-dollar bills – or bumblebees, as some of the longtime locals called them. It was Vegas slang dating back several years to a time when thousands of counterfeit hundred-dollar chips had flooded the Vegas underworld. They were perfect counterfeits of the black-and-yellow hundred-dollar chips used at the Sands. They were called bumblebees. The fakes were so good that the casino had to change the colors and design of their chips. The Sands was long gone now, demolished and replaced by a new casino. But the underworld code of calling a hundred-dollar bill or chip a bumblebee remained. Anyone who used the term had been around a while.

Cassie made sure Paltz got a good look at the money and then flipped the backpack closed just as a barmaid came to the table.

'Can I get you something?' she asked Cassie.

Paltz answered for her.

'No, she's fine,' he said. 'We're just gonna go outside and then I'll be right back. I'll need another beer then, sweetheart.'

The barmaid walked away and Paltz smiled, knowing that what he had just said would leave the waitress thinking that they were going outside to complete a sexual transaction. This didn't bother Cassie because it played into her cover. But what did annoy her was his calling the waitress 'sweetheart.' It always bothered Cassie when men called women they did not know by endearing names they didn't mean. She bit back on an urge to call Paltz on it and started sliding out of the booth.

'Let's do it,' she said instead.

Once they were out the door Paltz led the way to a van parked at the side of the bar. He unhooked a set of keys from his side belt loop and unlocked the sliding door on the passenger side. The van was parked so that the open door was only a few feet from the side wall of the bar. No one could look into the van without coming right up to it. Cassie understood this to be good and bad. Good if Paltz was going to be legit with her. Bad if this was a rip-off.

Paltz climbed into the van and signaled Cassie to follow. The front cab was partitioned off with a wall of plywood. In the rear of the van two bench seats faced each other across a work area. Various tools hung on hooks protruding from punch boards on the walls and five-gallon buckets contained more tools, equipment and rags. Cassie hesitated in the open door. She was carrying close to ten thousand dollars in cash in her backpack and was being beckoned into a van by a man she had not seen, let alone dealt with, in more than six years.

'Well, you want it or not? I don't have all night and I thought you didn't either.'

Paltz pointed to a medium-sized American Tourister suitcase that was on the floor. He picked it up and sat down on a bench seat with it on his lap. He opened it, raising the lid against his chest so that Cassie could see the equipment displayed in foam cushioning in the case.

Cassie nodded and climbed into the van.

'Close the door,' Paltz said.

She slid the door closed but kept her eyes on Paltz as she did it.

'Let's do this quick,' she said. 'I don't like being here.'

'Relax, I'm not going to bite you.'

'I'm not worried about getting bit.'

Now that she was closer, Cassie looked at the case again. Pieces of electronic surveillance equipment were placed in cutouts so they would not move during transport. Cassie recognized most of the pieces from prior use or from electronics magazines and catalogs. There were pinhole cameras, a microwave transmitter, a receiver and several pieces of related equipment. There was also a pair of night-vision goggles.

Like a door-to-door salesman, Paltz waved his arm in front of the display and started his spiel.

'You want me to go over everything or you think you've got a handle on it?'

'Better show me everything but the NVGs. It's been a while.'

'All right, then, let's go from image capture to picture delivery. First, the cameras.'

He pointed to the upper half of the case. Four small black squares with open circuitry and circular centerpieces were displayed in the foam rubber.

'You've got four chip cameras here – should be enough for any job. When we spoke before you didn't say if you needed color but –'

'I don't need color. I don't need audio. I need clarity. I need to read numbers.'

'That's what I figured. These are all black and white. The first three you see here are your standard pinhole board cameras. When I say standard, I mean Hooten L&S standard. Nobody puts together a better board right now. With these you get four hundred lines resolution from a linear electronic iris. Very clear. Runs four to six hours on a dime battery. How's that work for you, timewise?'

'Should be fine.'

Cassie felt herself getting excited. Keeping up through electronics magazines was one thing, but actually seeing the equipment was dipping the hot wire into her blood. She could feel the blood pounding in her temples.

Paltz went on with his show.

'Okay, then this fourth board is your green camera. It's called the ALI – like Muhammad Ali. That's why we call it the "greatest little camera of all time" in the catalog.'

'Ali?'

'A-L-I. Ambient Light Iris. With this one you have vision with lights on or off. With infrared you sometimes get exposure blooms on your LED screen when lights are on. So we developed this. It operates with what light is in the room and gives you enough picture to see what you have to see – shapes, shadows, movement. Green field of vision, as usual. Tell you what, t'night's supposed to be a full moon. If you –'

'A void moon, too.'

'A what?'

'Never mind. Go on.'

'I was just saying that if you can get some moonlight into the area you are filming, then that'll be all you need for this camera to work.'

'Okay, sounds good.'

Cassie only needed to be able to see enough to confirm the mark's location in the darkness of his room. The ALI seemed to be all she needed.

'Good, then moving on, you can take any of these boards and use them in any of the shells contained here.'

He removed a false smoke detector and showed it to her. There was a small drill hole in the cowling. On the inside he showed her where the board camera would fit, aligning the lens with the drill hole.

'Now if you need a lower angle . . .'

He next removed a phony electric wall socket plate. The board camera could be installed behind the upper socket. He handed it to Cassie and she marveled at how small it was.

'This is great.'

'But a little risky. Guy could try to plug something into it and – bingo – he finds a fucking camera in his room. So if you use this one, put it in a spot where it's not likely the guy will want to plug in his computer or shaver or whatever.'

'Got it.'

'Okay, good. So what you do is connect your cameras to the batteries like so.'

Paltz plugged tiny round batteries into cradles attached by wires to the board cameras.

'Then install. You then have to hook the cameras to the transmitter. This is all going to be short run, right?'

Cassie nodded.

'Right. Eight, ten feet at the most, probably less.'

He pulled out a roll of what looked like Scotch tape and held it up.

'Conduct-O tape. You used to use this, right?'

'Yeah, toward the end . . . on a few jobs.'

Paltz went on with his explanation as though Cassie had said the opposite.

'It's your magic tape, man. It's got two conductors in it, one for video and one for ground. You connect to the camera and then run it to your transmitter. Just remember, keep it short. The longer the run, the more image distortion. You don't want that if you're readin' numbers.'

'Right. I remember.'

Sweat was running out of Paltz's hairline and down both of his cheeks. Cassie didn't think it was warm enough inside the van to create such a response. She watched him raise his arm and wipe his face.

'Something wrong?'

'Nothing,' Paltz said as he reached into the suitcase. 'It's getting toasty in here, that's all. This is a four-channel transmitter.'

He pulled a flat square box about the size of a cell phone out of its place in the foam. It had a six-inch stub antenna.

'This is omnidirectional – it don't matter what angle you place it at. Just get it close to your cameras for the clearest signal. You notice this is not disguised in any way. Since it ain't a camera, you can hide it just about anywhere – under a bed or in a drawer or a closet or wherever. It, too, has a battery – lasts about as long as the cameras. Okay?'

'Got it.'

'Now what this transmitter does is send your captured image to your remote. This little baby.'

He pulled from the case the largest piece of equipment. It looked like a small laptop computer. Or maybe a space-age lunch box. Paltz flipped open a screen and folded up another stub antenna.

'This is your microwave receiver/recorder. You can set this up to two hundred yards from your transmitter, depending on the knockdown, and still pull in a decent picture.'

'What's the knockdown?'

'Nothing you'll probably have to worry about. Water mostly. Tree sap is a killer too. You're not going to be working near a forest, right? Those trees just send a signal into the dirt.'

'There a forest in Las Vegas, Jersey?'

'Not that I know of.'

'Then no forest. No trees, no sap.'

She was getting annoyed with his manner and his nervousness. It was getting contagious. She realized that without any windows in the back of the van she had no idea whether there would be someone waiting outside for them – or for her – when they opened the door. This rendezvous had been a mistake.

'What about the pool?' Paltz asked.

The question took Cassie out of her thoughts. She thought a moment and remembered the pool at the Cleopatra was at ground level.

'No pool.'

'Good. Steel, concrete, all of that is no problem. Just stay inside with it and it should work perfect.'

Paltz started working the buttons on the receiver/recorder. He turned it on and the screen came up full of static snow. He tapped a red button on the right side of the mini-keyboard.

'That's your record there. You can record everything or just watch it. You can quarter the screen and watch up to four cameras at once.'

He hit a series of buttons and the screen split twice. It was still four views of snow.

'We won't get a picture because we don't have the cameras connected. But I've got your four camera freeks already loaded on here and it's good to go.'

'Okay. It's a great kit, Jersey. You got anything else to show me? I gotta go.'

'That's it. Now if you pay me what we agreed on, you can get out of here and I can go back to my chili – though it's gotta be cold by now.'

Cassie pulled her backpack around to her lap.

'You working this one alone, Cassie?'

'Yup,' she answered without thinking.

She pulled open the flap just as Paltz closed the suitcase and raised his other arm, revealing that he was holding a pistol pointed at Cassie's chest.

'What are you doing?'

'Stupid, girl,' he said.

Cassie started to stand but he raised the weapon and nodded her back down with it.

'Look, man, I'm going to pay you. I have it right here. What's the matter with you?'

Paltz switched the gun to his other hand and lowered the suitcase to the floor of the van. He then reached out for the backpack.

'I'll take that.'

He roughly grabbed the backpack out of her hands.

'Jersey, we had a deal. We –'

'Just shut the fuck up.'

Cassie tried to remain calm while she waited for him to go for the money. Without flinching a muscle she took all the weight off her left foot and raised it slightly off the ground. Paltz was sitting directly across from her, his knees a foot apart. She spoke in a calm, measured tone.

'Jersey, what are you doing? Why put the kit together if you were just going to rip me off?'

'I had to make sure you were working this alone. Make sure you didn't go and get a replacement for Max.'

Now Cassie began to feel the rage blooming inside her. This guy had played her. All along he had seen her as a victim. Someone he could rip off if she was alone.

'And you know what?' Paltz said, almost giddy now that he had the bag with the money. 'Now that I think of it, maybe I oughta grab me a blow job for good measure. Get some of that stuff Max was keepin' to himself. I bet five years in stir, you could prob'ly use some practice sucking cock.'

He grinned.

'You're makin' a mistake, Jersey. I'm here alone but I'm working for people. You think I just blew into town and picked a target at random? You jack me and you jack them. They won't like that. So why don't we just make the deal. You take the money, I take the kit. I forget about that gun and what you just did. And what you just said.'

'Bullshit.'

Keeping his eyes on Cassie, Paltz began reaching into the backpack for the money. Immediately there was an electronic snapping sound and Paltz let out a yelp. His hand recoiled from the bag and in the same instant Cassie's left leg shot out and she drove her thick-soled Doc Marten shoe into his crotch. Paltz doubled over with a loud grunt and pulled the trigger on the pistol.

The gun fired and the sound was deafening in her ear. Cassie felt a slight tug on her wig as the bullet tore through her false tresses. She felt the sting of burning gunpowder and discharge gases singe her neck and cheek. She leapt onto Paltz and grabbed the gun with both hands. She turned her body into his until she was almost sitting on his lap. She yanked his gun hand up to her face and bit down viciously on the top of his hand. It wasn't fear that charged her actions. It was rage.

Paltz screamed and let go of the gun. Cassie grabbed it and spun away from him. She pointed the gun – which she quickly looked down at now and determined was a 9 mm Glock – at Paltz's face from two feet away.

'You stupid piece of shit!' she yelled. 'You want to die? You want to fucking die here in this van?'

Paltz was gasping for air and waiting for his testicles to recover. Cassie brought a hand up to her face and ran it along her skin looking for blood. She was sure the shot had missed but had always heard that sometimes you didn't even know it when you'd been clipped.

She took her hand away and looked at it. No blood. She cursed loudly anyway. Paltz's ill-conceived decision to try to jack her complicated everything. She tried to think clearly but her ear was ringing and her neck was tingling with the surface burn.

'Lie down on the floor!' she commanded. 'Get down! Fucking rapist! I oughta shove this gun up your ass!'

'I'm sorry,' Paltz whined. 'I was scared. I –'

'Bullshit! Just get on the floor. Face down. Now!'

Paltz slowly got down to his knees and then onto the floor.

'What are you going to do?' he whimpered.

Cassie stood over him, a foot on either side of his body, leaned down and pressed the muzzle of the gun into the back of his head. She palmed the cock back and the sound of it snapping back made Paltz's shoulders shudder.

'Hey, Jersey, what do you think, you want me to suck your cock now? You think you could get it up for me?'

'Oh, God . . .'

Cassie looked around the van and at the buckets of equipment and tools. She grabbed a plastic snap cuff used for bunching cables out of one of the buckets and told Paltz to put his hands behind his back. He did as ordered and Cassie noticed that one of the terminals from the stun gun had left a burn mark in the top of his hand. She wrapped the plastic strip around his wrists and through the lock, pulling it tight, to the point it was cutting into his skin. She then put the gun down on the floor of the van and grabbed more cuffs to bind Paltz's legs and ankles.

'I hope you had enough chili, asshole. It's going to be a while before seconds.'

'I have to take a piss, Cassie. I drank two beers waitin' for you.'

'I'm not stopping you.'

'Oh, man, Cassie, please don't do this.'

Cassie grabbed a rag out of one of the buckets and abruptly dropped her knees onto his back and leaned over close to his ear.

'Keep in mind that it was you who made the play, asshole. Now I'm going to ask you a question and you better give me a straight answer because it could mean your life. You understand?'

'Yes.'

'When I open this door, is there going to be somebody out there waiting for me? Like one of your buddies you brought in on the jack?'

'No, nobody.'

She picked up the gun and pushed the muzzle hard against his cheek.

'You better be straight. I open the door and see anybody, I'm going to empty this into your fucking head.'

'There's nobody. It was just me.'

'Then open wide.'

'Wha –'

She shoved the rag into his open mouth, cutting him off. She looped two snap cuffs together and wrapped them around his head and across his open mouth, holding the gag in place. Paltz's eyes grew wide as she tightened the cuffs.

'Through your nose, Jersey. Breathe through your nose and you'll be okay.'

Cassie unhooked the van's keys from the belt loop on his pants. She then got off him and went to her backpack, removing and unfolding a black gym bag. She started transferring the camera equipment from Paltz's suitcase to the bag.

'Okay, this is the deal,' she said. 'We're taking your van and I'm gonna go do this thing.'

Paltz tried to protest but his words were mumbles into the gag.

'Good, I'm glad you agree, Jersey.'

Once she had everything transferred, she hooked the backpack over one shoulder and moved to the sliding door. She reached up and turned the van's overhead light off and then opened the door with one hand while holding the gun ready with the other.

It was clear. She climbed out of the van, grabbed the gym bag and then locked and closed the door. She came around to the driver's side, still holding the gun up and ready. The parking lot was crowded with cars but she saw nobody waiting in any of them or watching from nearby.

She unlocked the driver's door and opened it. Before getting in she ejected the Glock's clip and thumbed out the bullets, letting them drop onto the asphalt. She then ejected the last round from the chamber and threw the gun and the clip onto the flat roof of the Aces and Eights.

She got into the van, started it and headed out of the parking lot. She noticed that the dashboard radio had a hole torn in it. The bullet Paltz had fired had gone through the plywood partition and into the radio. It reminded her of the burning sting on her neck and cheek. She turned the overhead light on and checked herself in the mirror. Her skin was red and blotchy. It looked as if it had a poison ivy rash.

She checked her watch next. Paltz's play had put her behind schedule. She turned off the light and drove toward the neon Strip, the glow of which she could see in the distance.

12

Koval Road ran parallel to Las Vegas Boulevard and offered easy access to the parking garages behind the grand resorts fronting the always crowded boulevard, better known as the Strip. Cassie passed by the Koval Suites, the monthly apartment building where she and Max had once kept a safe house, and turned into the multi-level parking garage attached to the Flamingo Casino and Resort. The casino garage was centrally located to the casinos on the mid-Strip, the key being never to park at the target hotel. She parked Paltz's van on the roof of the eight-story garage because she knew there would be fewer cars up there and a lesser chance that her bound and gagged passenger would be discovered. She skipped the elevator in favor of the stairs down to the walkway leading into the casino.

Carrying her black bag over one shoulder and the gym bag down at her side, she went in the rear entrance of the Flamingo and walked through the casino to the front door, stopping briefly along the way in one of the lobby shops to buy a pack of cigarettes, in case she had to set off a fire alarm, and a souvenir pack of playing cards with which to pass the time while waiting for her mark to fall asleep. Once she stepped out the front doors, she crossed Las Vegas Boulevard and then walked the two blocks to the Cleopatra.

Cassie was carried past the reflecting pools on a moving sidewalk that delivered gamblers to the casino entrance. She noted that there was no automatic ride that took gamblers away from the casino after they were done losing their money.

The casino entry walls were lined with hieroglyphics that showed ancient Egyptian figures in headdresses playing cards and throwing dice. Cassie wondered if there was any historic precedent for these depictions but also realized that it was not a necessity because there was no historical precedent for anything about Las Vegas.

Farther past the drawings, the walls were dedicated to Cleo's Club – photographs of the big slots winners over the past year. Cassie noticed that many of the winners posed in front of their winning machines were smiling in a way that suggested they were hiding missing teeth. She wondered how many of the winners used the money to see a dentist and how many dumped it right back into the machines.

When she finally got to the casino floor, she paused and tried to take it all in without raising her face toward the cameras she knew were overhead. A visceral sense of dread took hold of her heart. Not for the job that was ahead this night. But for the memory of the last night she had been in the Cleopatra Casino. It was the night that all things in her life had changed with the permanency of death.

The casino looked no different to her. The same setup, the same interchangeable gamblers chasing desperate dreams. The cacophony of money and machines and human voices of joy and anguish was almost deafening. She composed herself and pressed on, weaving her way through a football field of crowded slot machines and blue felt gaming tables. She was also aware that every move she made was now being recorded from above and kept her head level, if not slightly turned down. She pulled the wide brim of her hat down tight over her brow. The drugstore glasses completed her camouflage. Her scalp was warm and damp under the wig but she knew she had hours to go before there would be any relief from it.

As she passed through the cards and dice gaming aisles she saw many men and a few women in the blue-blazer uniform of casino security. They seemed to be posted at every column and at the end of every row of dealers' tables. She saw signs leading to the lobby and followed. She glanced upward at one point but without raising her chin.

The ceiling rose in a three-story-high glass atrium above the gaming tables. When it first opened its doors seven years before, the Cleopatra had been called the 'Crystal Cathedral of Casinos,' a reference to its borrowing of the atrium and other design elements from a California house of God that was prominent on religious television programming. Below the partial glass ceiling iron standards stretched from wall to wall and held up banks of lights and cameras. The Cleopatra was like no other casino in Las Vegas in that it allowed natural light to enter the gaming room. It also made no effort to hide the cameras that watched over everything. Other casinos favored contained environments of artificial lighting and placement of cameras behind mirrored walls and ceiling globes, even though not a single player below doubted that every move that he or she made – as well as the money on the tables – was being closely watched.

Cassie's eyes were drawn upward to the balcony that extended like two joined arms out and above the crowded gaming tables. The hands of the arms formed a cup – the crow's nest from which a craggy-faced man looked down upon the gaming floor. He had white hair and wore a dark suit, not a blue blazer. She guessed he had to be one of the men in charge, maybe the man himself. She couldn't help but wonder if he had stood in the pulpit six years earlier on the last night she had been in the casino.

Once past the tables Cassie got to the lobby and went to the far end of the long desk, where she saw the sign for INVITED GUESTS AND VIPS. There was no one in line. She approached the counter and a woman wearing some sort of white tunic that was only vaguely Egyptian smiled at her.

'Hello,' Cassie said. 'There is supposed to be a package for me here. The name is Turcello.'

'One moment.'

The woman stepped away from the counter and retreated to a door behind her. Cassie felt her breathing slow as thief's paranoia rose in her chest. If this was all a setup, then now would be the time for the men in blue blazers to come back through that door to get her.

But it was the woman in the tunic who came back out. She carried a large manila envelope bearing the Cleopatra symbol – a line drawing of a woman's face in profile, wearing a headdress of a rising serpent – and handed it to her with a smile.

'Thank you very much,' she said.

'No, thank you,' Cassie said.

She carried the envelope without looking at it to a nearby alcove of pay phones. There was no one using any of them. She went to the phone in the corner and huddled close to it, using her back to shield what she was doing from the view of any person or camera.

She tore open the envelope and dumped the contents on the marble counter under the phone. A black pager with a digital readout slid out of the envelope along with an electronic card key, a photograph and a note torn from a Cleopatra scratch pad. She quickly glanced at the pager and hooked it onto her belt. She then slipped the card key into the back pocket of her black jeans and looked at the note. Four lines were printed on it.

> EUPHRATES PENTHOUSE
> His: 2014
> Yours: 2015
> Return envelope with *all contents* to the VIP desk

She studied the first line and felt a turning in her stomach. She leaned her head against the phone. The penthouse of the Euphrates Tower was familiar to her. It was the place where dreams and hopes had ended for her. It was one thing to come back to Vegas, another to return to the Cleo. But to go back to the penthouse . . . Cassie fought the urge to cut and run. She reminded herself of all that was at stake. She had gone too far to turn around at this point.

She tried to change her thoughts. She looked at the note again and picked up the card key. One key for two rooms meant she was holding a pass key. That explained the last line of instructions on the note. The key had to be returned because all pass keys probably had to be accounted for. If any investigation followed the crime she was about to commit, pass keys would be inventoried.

She slowly crumpled the note in one hand and looked at the photo. It showed a baccarat table where there was only one player: an obese man in a suit with a large stack of chips in front of him. Diego Hernandez. The photo had a date-and-time stamp on the corner – it had been taken that afternoon. It was obvious to Cassie that the photo had come from a casino surveillance camera. The pass key and the photo told Cassie that the spotter Leo's partners had was deeper inside than she had thought.

She committed the image of the fat man to memory and then put the photograph and the crumpled note back into the envelope. She folded it twice and shoved it into a zippered pocket on her backpack. She then headed back to the casino floor.

Without raising her head she scanned the table signs in the casino until she saw the one over the baccarat salon. She took the long way, skirting the edge of the gaming area until she came to the railing that ran along the perimeter of the baccarat salon. She put an elbow and an arm along the railing, nonchalantly leaned back against it and looked out across the casino. Her eyes encountered no one looking at her. She was cool. Slowly she turned, as if noticing the baccarat salon behind her for the first time, and shifted her position so that she was looking into the room.

He was still there. The mark. Diego Hernandez. The man was short but obese, the girth of his stomach making him appear to be sitting away from the table. He was overdressed in a baggy dark suit and tie. As Cassie watched, she noted that he played with an economy of physical movement, his eyes constantly scanning the table but his head not moving. On the table in front of him were several stacks of hundred-dollar chips. Cassie estimated that he had at least ten thousand dollars on the table.

Cassie watched a few deals but never held her eyes on Hernandez for more than a few seconds. At one point he suddenly looked up and out toward the railing. She quickly looked away. When she surreptitiously glanced back, his eyes were back on the table. He apparently had paid little mind to her.

She needed only one thing from Hernandez before going up to the penthouse. She focused her attention squarely on his hands as they moved chips and handled his cards. It took less than a minute for her to decide that he favored his left hand. The clincher was when the right cuff of his suit coat caught on the edge of the table's elbow pad and drew back to expose his watch. Cassie had what she needed. Hernandez was left-handed. She stepped away from the railing and proceeded, head down, in the direction of the elevator alcove of the Euphrates Tower.

As Cassie entered an elevator in the Euphrates Tower, she saw that a card key had to be inserted in the panel before the penthouse button could be engaged – a security measure that had been added since the last time she had been in the hotel. She pulled the pass card from her back pocket and engaged the button. She stayed close to the doors and averted the impulse to look up at the lighted numbers over them, assuming there was a camera somewhere above her. She looked at her watch and saw it was already almost nine o'clock. She needed a minimum of an hour in the room and knew she was now pushing it.

On the twentieth floor Cassie came out of the elevator alcove, looked both ways in the hall and found she might already be riding a piece of luck. There was no housekeeping cart in the hallway. It was apparently after VIP turn-down service. The only thing in the hall was a room service table topped with a white tablecloth and the detritus of a candlelight dinner, including an empty champagne bottle floating upside down in a silver ice bucket.

She went to her right to find room 2015 but as she first passed by the door to room 2001 she gave it a wide berth, moving all the way to the left side of the hallway and averting her eyes from the door and the memory behind it. She said a silent prayer, calling on Max to be with her tonight.

The hallway was dimly lit by wall sconces to the left of every door. She found rooms 2014 and 2015 directly across from each other near the end of the hallway and the emergency exit. That was a good break. In case something went wrong, the stairs were right there. Cassie knocked on the door of room 2014 and also pushed the glowing button to the left of the door frame. She heard a soft chiming sound from the other side of the door and she waited.

As expected, no one answered the door. She took the card key out of her back pocket again, looked up and down the hall once more, and then used it to open the door.

As she stepped into the room she felt the immediate jangling of adrenaline coursing through her veins. It felt like a flooding river inside her, powerful enough to take anything in its path.

13

Cassie used an elbow to close the door and turn on the light switch. She dropped quickly to her knees, putting her hat and the gym bag on the floor and then swinging her backpack down in front of her. From the small front pocket of the backpack she took a pair of latex gloves and pulled them on, making sure they were tight around her fingers and short-cut nails.

She quickly removed and untied the rubber satchel that contained her tools. She unrolled it across the carpet and dragged a finger across the tools, making sure she had everything. She then pulled the Polaroid camera out of the gym bag, got up and began a survey of the suite.

It was a VIP accommodation, the kind given to comped guests of the casino. It was one large living room with double doors leading to the bedroom to the right. The furnishings were plush and Cassie knew that in most of the hotels the VIP suites were refurbished annually to keep them looking pristine and their inhabitants thinking they were among the few who got the privileges of the comped.

She became aware of the heavy odor of cigar in the air – Hernandez was helping her without even knowing it. She moved into the bedroom, for it was where she would do all of her work. She flicked on the light, revealing a large room containing a king-size bed, a bureau and a small writing desk in addition to the floor-to-ceiling television cabinet. She noted that the turn-down maid had already been in the room. The bedcovers had been folded back neatly and there was a foil-wrapped mint on the pillow next to a morning room service checklist to be hung outside the room on the door handle.

There was an alcove to the right with an open door to the bathroom on one side and a double set of louvered doors on the other. Cassie opened these to reveal a wide and deep closet. This action also revealed that when the doors were opened an interior light automatically went on. Cassie bent down and saw the room safe anchored to the floor, partially obscured beneath a sports coat and several long, flowing shirts Hernandez had placed on hangers.

Before touching anything in the closet, Cassie stepped back, aimed the Polaroid and took a photo of the clothes. She then squatted down and took a second photo of a pair of shoes and a pile of dirty clothes lying on the floor of the closet.

Cassie stepped back into the bedroom and put the developing photos on the bed. She then began photographing the entire bedroom, covering every angle of the room with the remaining eight photos in the Polaroid cartridge.

When she was confident she had thoroughly documented all areas of the suite she would possibly be disturbing, she went back to the closet, shoved the clothing to the side and looked down at the safe. The information from Leo's spotter was on the money. It was a Halsey five-number combination safe. The five-digit electronic LED screen said LOCKD but she reached down and checked it anyway. It was locked.

As she backed out of the closet and into the bedroom her eyes moved over the walls and up to the ceiling. There was one smoke detector. It was located on the wall directly over the headboard of the bed. She decided that a second one in so large a room would not seem too unusual. She fixed on a spot on the wall just above the entry to the bathroom/closet alcove. Locating a camera there would give her a full view of the bedroom and it would mean only a short run with the Conduct-O tape into the closet.

Having decided on the installation plan, she went back to searching the suite, looking in drawers and on shelves for any weapons or other protection devices that Hernandez might have brought with him. On a shelf above the wet bar in the living room she found a doorknob alarm – a cheap electronic gizmo that is hooked on a doorknob and sounds an ear-splitting alarm if a clip squeezed into the doorjamb is disturbed.

Cassie knew that the alarm was so painfully loud that most users of the device never checked them before inserting the clip into the doorjamb. Instead, they relied on the red signal light that indicates a battery has juice. She used a small screwdriver to remove one screw and then unsnap the outer casing. With pliers she snipped the conductor and ground wires, then pruned a quarter inch of rubber sleeve off each wire and wound them together, closing the circuit usually closed by the clip when it was slid into the doorjamb.

She turned the device on and the signal light came on, indicating good battery. No alarm sounded although the clip was not in place. She turned it off and returned it to the place she had found it on the wet bar shelf.

Cassie went back to the suite's entrance hallway and sat down on the floor. From her backpack she pulled the pair of knee pads, which she strapped on over her black jeans. She then knelt in front of the door and went to work. She picked the drill up off the tool display, put in a Phillips bit and began removing the screws from the cover plate of the interior door handle and deadbolt. The homemade drill cowling dampened its sound considerably. Cassie figured someone would have to actually be listening on the other side of the door to notice the noise.

When she had the cover plate off she put a penlight in her mouth and pointed it into the interior of the lock apparatus while she used a screwdriver to pop the lock washer off the bolt axle. She then gripped the bolt switch with a pair of rubber-tipped pliers and pulled it out of the apparatus, using both hands. She leaned in and looked closely at the interior mechanism.

Cassie took the light out of her mouth and exhaled in a low whistle of relief. Leo had called it correctly. The lock mechanism relied on a half gear to drive the bolt home. Despite knowing this was a problem six years ago, the managers and security providers of the hotel had chosen to avoid the expense of changing every deadbolt in the 3,000-room hotel. The decision made back then would allow Cassie to stay in the room and complete the installation. If a full gear had been installed in the lock's mechanism, she would have had to remove it and take it someplace – maybe the bathtub in the room across the hall – and cut it with the acetylene torch. It was only at that moment of relief that she realized how lucky she was not to have to use the torch; she had forgotten about it and left it in the trunk of the Boxster back at the Aces and Eights.

Cassie put the penlight back in her mouth. She pushed the screwdriver into the barrel slot and used it to turn the half gear forward, to the right, a quarter turn. She then checked her work with the flashlight and slid the bolt axle back into place. She turned the lock and looked into the doorjamb. The bolt extended outward but came just shy of the receiver plate on the other side of the jamb. By turning the half gear forward she had reduced the number of gear teeth driving the bolt home by half. Therefore it crossed the half-inch space of the doorjamb but did not lock the door. The only way for Hernandez to realize this would be to get down on his knees and look into the doorjamb crack. That was unlikely.

Cassie got up and looked through the peephole to make sure the hall was empty. She then opened the door. The bolt barely scraped the jamb but still made a slight noise. She looked out into the hallway to make sure it was empty and then quickly went back to her tools. She grabbed the steel file and quickly ran it back and forth along the scrape line the bolt had made in the jamb plate. She then dropped the file, checked the hall again and once more closed and reopened the door. There was no scraping sound this time.

After closing the door she went to work on the flip-over lock. She used the drill to remove the four screws that attached the flip-over arm to the doorjamb. Once the arm was removed she changed bits and ran the drill into each of the screw holes to widen them. She dug the tub of earthquake wax out of her bag and used a dab of it on the back of the lock's anchor plate to glue it back into place. She then used more of the quick-drying wax to hold the screws back in place in the loosened screw holes.

Cassie sat back on her heels and looked at the door. There was no outward sign that she had tampered with the locks. Yet with the card key she had in her back pocket she would be able to enter the room despite Hernandez's use of the additional locks and his portable alarm.

The first step toward preparing the suite was completed. Cassie checked her watch and saw that it was almost nine-thirty. She rolled her tool satchel up and carried it along with her black bags into the bedroom. She placed everything down in the middle of the floor and set to work. She removed the Conduct-O tape and the ALI camera, snapping the latter into place inside one of the smoke detector cowling shells. She then connected a battery to it, closed it and removed the adhesive backing. She pulled the chair out from the desk and used it to step up and reach the wall over the entry to the closet and bathroom alcove. She pressed the smoke detector camera onto the wall, about a foot below the ceiling line.

The roll of Conduct-O was as small as a roll of household tape. It was clear, with two thin copper wires imbedded in the adhesive and running the length of the tape. She wrapped one end of the tape on the connector posts and then closed the detector cover. She ran the tape down the wall to the lower alcove ceiling and then ran the tape along the ceiling to the wall over the closet. She then ran it down over the door frame and into the closet, where she ran it straight down to the floor alongside the door and then along the baseboard to a position behind the safe.

Cassie removed the transmitter from one of the bags and put it in place behind the safe, where it was unlikely Hernandez would have reason to look. She cut the Conduct-O tape and wrapped it around one of the transmitter's receiving terminals. Cassie turned on the transmitter and went back out to her equipment. She pulled out the receiver/recorder and opened it on the floor. She turned it on and studied the strip of masking tape Paltz had placed below a line of frequency buttons. She pushed the button marked ALI (1) and a view of the room, herself sitting on the floor, appeared on the monitor screen. The image was clear and took in almost the entire room. The important thing was the bed. She had a full view of the bed. She got up and went to the door and turned off the lights, dropping the room into darkness except for the bleed of exterior light – the spotlights thrown on the Cleopatra's towers at night – from around the curtains.

She came back and looked closely at the screen. The outline of the bed was barely visible in the green-tinged image. It wasn't as good as Paltz had claimed it would be but she knew it would have to do. She got up again and went to the curtains, pulling them open just an inch or so and letting a sliver of light into the center of the room.

The added light was enough. The details of the room took on a more defined look on the screen. Cassie now had to hope that Hernandez wouldn't notice the slight opening in the curtains and close them before going to bed.

Cassie turned the light back on and returned quickly to the closet. She had to first make sure that during the hot prowl she would be able to get into the closet where the safe was without the interior light automatically going on and possibly waking the mark and exposing her. She could not simply loosen the bulb in the ceiling of the closet. Hernandez might notice that and have it replaced or, worse yet, become suspicious. She also needed the light working for the cameras she planned to set inside the closet to record Hernandez opening the safe.

The twin louvered doors to the closet slightly overlapped, with a strip of wood edging on the left door covering the joint between the two doors. This meant she could open the left door without opening the right. But if she attempted to open only the right she would pop the left open a few inches because of the overlapping strip. The problem was that the auto-switch for the light was inside the frame of the left door. A small button dropped out of the top frame when the door was opened just an inch, completing the electric circuit that fed juice to the light.

Cassie went to the desk, opened the drawer and looked for something to write with. She found a pencil with a sharp point and went back to the closet. On the exterior trim of the door frame she drew an up-and-down line at the spot where the auto-switch button was located.

From her tool collection she removed the painter's putty knife. She closed the closet doors and reached up with the flat tool to the spot on the exterior trim marked with pencil. She slid the putty knife in and brought pressure upward against the door frame. With her other hand she opened the left door a few inches and then opened the right all the way, the door swinging free of the overlap trim. She then closed the left side, removed the putty knife and stepped into the closet through the right side.

She had entered the closet without turning on the light. But she knew she had no time to celebrate. She opened the left door again and the closet light went on. She leaned over the front of the safe as if to open it with her left hand. She then looked back to her right and put her finger on the wall on a spot where she believed a camera would have the best view of the combination pad. She marked the spot with the pencil and then went back out to the equipment bag, from which she pulled the wall socket cover and one of the board cameras.

She quickly set the camera inside the fake socket plate, attached a battery and Conduct-O tape to the terminals and used the drill to mount it on the spot on the wall with the center screw. She adjusted the plate so that it was level, then ran the tape down the wall to the baseboard and back around the safe to the transmitter.

Back out of the closet she checked the receiver/recorder. She pushed the camera buttons until she had the socket camera on the screen. The location and focus of the camera was perfect. She was looking right at the combination pad and could read the numbers on it. It was perfect. She felt the stirring of excitement inside but it was quickly cut short by the vibration of the pager against her belly.

Cassie caught her breath and froze. She pulled the pager off her belt and looked at the digital display.

CASHING OUT – ON HIS WAY

'Shit!' she exclaimed in a loud whisper. She threw the pager into the backpack rather than put it back on her belt.

The page changed everything. She abandoned her plan to put a second camera in the closet – this one overhead – and quickly backed out of the closet area. The page meant Hernandez had cashed out and left the baccarat table, but he still had to go to the front desk and retrieve his briefcase. That gave her time to finish.

From the gym bag she removed the Ziploc bag containing the small pump spray bottle of paint and the aerosol can of deodorizer. She stepped back into the closet alcove and looked up at the ceiling while shaking the paint bottle. She then sprayed the paint up onto the Conduct-O tape. It wasn't a perfect match but it was close. She started spraying the paint in a large back and forth arc, covering the tape but most of the ceiling as well. She then followed the tape down the wall to the frame of the closet door. Inside the closet she sprayed the tape line running from the false electric socket down to the baseboard and left it at that. She then grabbed the deodorizer and sprayed healthy bursts into the closet and alcove, then throughout the rest of the suite as she hurriedly moved through it.

After quickly packing her equipment in the two bags, Cassie grabbed the Polaroids off the bed and went back to the closet. Using the photos as a guide, she moved the clothing and shoes back into the same positions they had been in when she first entered the suite. She was careful not to allow the clothing to rub on the rear wall of the closet where there was wet paint.

As she slid the hangers back into place on the clothing bar, something heavy and hard in the pocket of a large sports coat banged against her. She reached into the pocket and brought out a gun. It was a Smith & Wesson 9 mm pistol with a black finish. She ejected the clip and found it was full. She paused even though she knew time was critical. Should she leave it or take it? Should she unload it? Too much was happening for her to think through the possibilities and come up with the right answer. She remembered something Max had always said about the ripple effect.

Remember the ripple effect. If you change something in a room it changes the universe of the job. It creates ripples.

She knew the answer then. You take the gun, the mark may notice and the job is finished. You unload the gun and the mark may notice and it is finished. No action means no ripples, no change in the universe.

She shoved the gun back into the pocket of the jacket and backed out of the closet, checking her work against the Polaroid one last time. Time was up. In her mind she saw Hernandez having already retrieved his briefcase and riding up in the elevator.

She grabbed the two bags, hoisting the straps over her shoulders, and headed out of the bedroom. As she stepped into the living room she glanced backward and froze.

She had left the desk chair pulled out from the desk.

No ripples, she thought, as she quickly moved back into the room and put the chair back in its place. She glanced around and everything now seemed right – she had no time for a Polaroid check of the bedroom. She went back to the living room and to the suite's front door, picking her hat up off the floor.

She turned the light out and looked through the peephole. She saw an empty hallway. She turned her head and listened. She heard no footsteps or any other sound. She put her hat on, then opened the door and stepped out into the hall.

As Cassie pulled the door closed she heard the chime signaling the arrival of an elevator car in the alcove down the hall. She quickly pulled the card key out of her back pocket and crossed to room 2015.

She opened the door and stepped in. She had made it.

14

The hallway was empty but she waited. Cassie stood against the door inside room 2015 and pressed her left eye close to the peephole. Her hat tipped off her head and fell to the floor behind her. She heard voices in the hallway and began to believe she was mistaken, that it was not Hernandez but a couple returning to their room.

But then there he was. His huge form moved into her field of vision and the convex lens of the peephole made Hernandez appear even wider. He bent slightly to insert a card key into the door with one hand, the briefcase held at his side with the other. Trailing just behind him and almost out of view through the peephole was another man. Cassie noted the blue blazer with the Cleopatra insignia on the breast pocket. The security escort. She turned away from the peephole and moved close to the doorjamb so that she could listen.

'You want me to check for you, sir?'

'No, I'm fine. I appreciate it, though.'

'Then good night, sir.'

'Good night.'

Cassie heard the door across the hall opening. She switched back to the peephole. The security man was gone and Hernandez was moving into the open doorway. He suddenly stopped and stepped back into the hall.

'Oh, Martin?'

Cassie felt her heart skip a beat. *What did he see, what did I miss?* She tried to quickly review her hurried exit from room 2014 but she could not think of anything. She looked down at the two bags at her feet and started running an inventory through her mind. But she had barely begun when Hernandez began to speak and she moved her ear to the doorjamb.

'I almost forgot. This is it for me. I'll be leaving tomorrow. Can you hold on a second? I'd like to give you something for watching out for me these last few days.'

Martin's voice returned, very close to Cassie's door.

'That's not necessary, Mr Hernandez. You can just thank Mr Grimaldi. He wants all our guests to feel secure and, besides, it's against house policy for me to accept –'

'Who's gonna know? Vincent Grimaldi won't unless you tell him. Hold on a second.'

There was the sound of a door closing and Cassie returned to the visual.

The security man called Martin stood in the hallway, his hands clasped in front of him. He looked up and down the hall, as if worried somebody – maybe the Vincent Grimaldi who was mentioned – would see him taking a gratuity. He then turned and looked right at the peephole through which Cassie was watching him. She froze. She thought that if she moved away he might see a change in the light behind the glass and then know he was being watched.

The door behind Martin opened and Hernandez appeared.

'You know, if you don't mind, come in here and check this out,' Hernandez said. 'There are fumes or something in here.'

Cassie pressed against the door harder and balled her hands into fists. She watched as Martin entered the room, leaving the door open behind him.

She could only see a door-wide slice of the suite. Hernandez and Martin both walked out of sight to the left and then after a few moments crossed her field of vision in the direction of the bedroom. Cassie heard talking and moved to the doorjamb and listened but could not make out what was being said. She moved back to the peephole and in a few moments Martin, followed by Hernandez, appeared again and headed toward the door. Their discussion became clearer as they got closer to Cassie's position.

'. . . in the smoking rooms,' Martin was saying. 'It's pretty much industrial-strength stuff that they use. See, you can't open the windows. No hotel in Vegas has windows that open. Too many jumpers.'

'Well, I guess it's been building up. This is my third day. I've smoked a few in here.'

He guffawed.

'Yes, sir,' Martin said. 'But if it is going to bother you I could check with the desk and see about moving you into another suite. I'm sure we'd have something available.'

Nooooo, Cassie felt like yelling. But it was Hernandez himself who rescued her.

'No, that's not necessary. I'll just have to light one up and see which one is stronger.'

He laughed again and this time Martin joined him.

'Okay, good night, sir. Have a good trip home.'

'I will. Oh, and here. Almost forgot.'

Hernandez held out his hand and Martin raised his. Cassie heard the click of casino chips being dropped into the security man's hand. There must have been a lot of them and they were of high value. Martin's exclamation of thanks came through the door loud and clear.

'Mr Hernandez, thank you! *Thank you!*'

'No, thank you, Martin. Have a good one.'

'With this I'll have more than one!'

Hernandez laughed and closed his door after hooking a DO NOT DISTURB sign on the handle. Martin disappeared from Cassie's point of view. She heard Hernandez turn the deadbolt and then there was the metallic click of the flip-over lock being slapped closed. She stood motionless and not breathing for five seconds. Nothing happened. She knew her work on the door had gone unnoticed.

Cassie turned and leaned against the door and then slid down to the floor. She quickly unzipped the black gym bag and pulled out the receiver/recorder. She opened the screen and raised the antenna, then quickly hit the button that put the view from the bedroom smoke detector camera on the screen.

The bedroom became visible, though the screen was largely in shadow because the only light came from the slight break in the curtains.

She waited.

The door opened and the light came on. Hernandez stepped into the room, the briefcase still at his side. Cassie leaned in close to the screen and saw that the case was attached to his wrist with a handcuff. It put a little shiver of excitement in her. Leo's spotter knew how to pick them.

Hernandez was smoking a fresh cigar and blowing clouds of smoke toward the ceiling while he stood in the center of the room and looked around, never once looking up at the camera. He then stepped beneath the camera and into the alcove leading to the closet and the bathroom.

Cassie switched screens to the closet cam and waited. The screen wasn't completely dark. Light from the bedroom slashed through the slats. In a moment she saw Hernandez's legs through the slats and then the door opened. Cassie hit the record button in case Hernandez opened the safe.

But he didn't. He apparently rustled through his clothes, though Cassie couldn't see this because of the camera angle, then stepped out of the closet. Cassie thought of the gun and retraced her actions with it. She was sure she had returned it to its place in the jacket pocket exactly the way she had found it.

She returned to the bedroom cam and just caught a glimpse of Hernandez going through the door to the living room. She immediately lamented not setting up a camera in the living room. But she just as immediately dismissed the regret as Monday morning quarterbacking. The fact was that if she had installed a camera there, she might not have had the time to install the bedroom or closet cameras, which were necessities.

Getting up quickly, Cassie moved with the receiver/recorder to the table in her suite. Spread on the table were tourist magazines, hotel information and room service folders, a pad and pencil, and a bottle of chardonnay from Robert Long Vineyards with a generic welcome card on it. She pushed everything aside so she would have room to work.

She checked the screen again and saw Hernandez was back in the bedroom. He had placed the briefcase on the bed while he worked a key into the cuff and detached it from his wrist. Once free of the encumbrance he reached over and picked up the foil-wrapped mint that had been left on the pillow as part of the turn-down service. He ate it in one bite, returned the cigar to his mouth and then turned toward the closet alcove, reaching into the inside pockets of his suit coat and removing thick sheaves of money as he approached.

Cassie switched screens to the closet camera and hit the record button. This was it. All her work had been to put her in this position.

On the screen the light came on in the closet and Hernandez's big left arm followed by part of the upper portion of his body dropped into the picture. He reached down to the combination and started tapping the numbers. But before he was done his right arm swung through the picture and he put his hand on the top of the safe to support himself.

SHIT NO! Cassie wanted to yell. But instead she brought a clenched fist up to her mouth.

Hernandez opened the safe's door, dropped to one knee and reached inside. He brought out a two-inch stack of currency and placed it on top of the safe, then put down the equally thick stack he had just removed from his pocket. He reached into the side pockets of his jacket and took out two more wads of cash. He combined all of the currency into one thick stack he could barely hold in one hand. He hefted it. Cassie could not see his face because of the angle of the camera but she knew he was smiling.

Hernandez put the cash into the safe and closed it, then got up and closed the closet door, extinguishing the overhead light.

As Cassie watched she wondered about the briefcase. It appeared that it was too large to fit into the safe. But why hadn't Hernandez taken the cash that must be in it and placed it in the safe?

She switched to the bedroom camera but there was no sign of Hernandez. The briefcase was lying flat on the bed. Her question about the case and Hernandez's decision not to put its contents into the safe did not hold her attention long. There was a more important question she had to answer. She switched the receiver/recorder to the playback program and began watching the recording of the closet camera. She grabbed the hotel pad and pencil and hit the slow-motion button just as Hernandez's hand dipped into the picture.

'Come on, baby.'

The numbers could clearly be seen on the screen. Hernandez's finger hit 4–3–5 but then his right arm, reaching for support on the safe, swung through the frame and obscured the final two numbers. Cassie reversed the recording and replayed it with the same result. She was short the final two numbers of the combination.

'Son of a bitch!'

She got up from the table and paced across the room to the curtains. She pulled them open and looked out, the view going across the Strip to the dark outlines of the mountains far from the city of neon. She looked up and saw the moon.

She knew she couldn't go in with just three numbers and hopes of trying various combinations of the final two to open the safe. The Halsey safes had built-in tampering devices. If three successive erroneous combinations were entered on the keypad, the locking mechanism would freeze. It would then take a visit from security and an electronic device called a D-Lock to open the safe. The D-Lock was usually kept under lock in the hotel manager's safe.

There was only one alternative, Cassie decided. A fire drill.

15

Cassie watched the screen and waited. The alarm was blaring in the hallway and she could smell the smoke. But Hernandez showed no sign of moving from his room. He was fully clothed and lying propped on a pile of pillows on the bed. He was watching the television but the angle of the smoke detector camera prevented Cassie from seeing what was on the screen.

She dialed his room and watched as Hernandez lazily reached for the extension on the bedside table.

'Yes?'

'Mr Hernandez, this is hotel security. We have an alarm and a report of smoke on your floor. We are going to need you to evacuate immediately.'

'A fire? I heard the alarm.'

He sat up abruptly.

'We're not sure yet, sir. We have people coming up. But other guests are reporting smoke on the twentieth floor. Please, sir, gather your valuables and evacuate down the emergency stairs until we can evaluate what is happening.'

'Okay, bye.'

As Hernandez jumped up from the bed Cassie was surprised at the big man's agility and speed. As he was putting his shoes on, Cassie switched screens to the closet camera and hit the record button. She waited.

In a few moments the door opened and this time Hernandez knelt in front of the safe instead of leaning over it. He reached to the combination pad and hit the buttons, in full sight of the camera. Cassie could tell the last number was 2 and wrote it on the hotel pad.

As Hernandez quickly pulled the money from the safe and started stuffing his pockets, Cassie blew out her breath excitedly and hit the playback program on the receiver/recorder. She once more played the opening of the safe in slow motion.

This time she got it. She wrote the last missing number down on the pad.

4–3–5–1–2

She took no time to celebrate. She switched back to the live feed from the bedroom cam. Hernandez was standing at the desk, locking the briefcase onto his wrist. Cassie picked up the phone and called his room. Hernandez grabbed the phone quickly.

'Yes?'

'Mr Hernandez, this is security. We have isolated the problem and there is no risk. You do not have to evacuate your room.'

'What was it?'

'We think someone left a cigarette on a room service cart near a smoke detector. It set off the alarm.'

'Well, can you turn it off now?'

'We're working on it, sir. Sorry for the incon –'

'Did Vincent tell you to call my room?'

Cassie was momentarily taken aback.

'Excuse me?'

'Vincent Grimaldi.'

'Uh, no sir. We're just following standard practice. Good night, sir.'

She hung up. It was the second time in the past half hour that the name Vincent Grimaldi had been mentioned. Cassie was sure she had heard it before. As she was thinking about it, the alarm from out in the hallway was finally turned off.

She went to the suite's door and listened at the jamb. She heard men talking from far down the hall. She could not make out the words but she assumed they had found the cigarette she had left burning on a room service cart under a smoke detector.

Now all she needed was for Hernandez to go to sleep.

She switched the receiver back to the bedroom cam and saw Hernandez had stripped to boxer shorts and a T-shirt. He was back on the bed watching television. All the lights were off except for the glow from the television. Cassie checked her watch; it was almost midnight. She thought about the name Hernandez and the security escort had used. Vincent Grimaldi. It had a resonance but she couldn't place it.

Cassie picked up the phone, dialed the hotel operator and asked to be connected to Vincent Grimaldi. A moment later the connection had been made and the call was picked up after one ring.

'Security,' a man's voice said. 'Mr Grimaldi's office.'

'Oh,' Cassie said. 'I think I have the wrong number. I wanted to see about getting a line of credit in the casino. Does Mr Grimaldi handle that?'

The man at the other end of the line chuckled.

'Well, you could say he's in charge of all of that but he doesn't handle applications. He runs the casino, ma'am. He's the director of all casino operations. So what you need to do is just go down to the casino and apply for credit at the big cashier's station next to the Sphinx. They'll take care of you.'

'Okay, I'll do that. Thanks.'

Cassie hung up as she now remembered the name Vincent Grimaldi and who he was. Six years earlier, his name had been in all of the papers in the days following Max's last caper. He had been part of the cover-up.

She remembered that at the time Grimaldi was identified as the chief of casino security at the Cleo. In the six years since, he had moved up the ladder to director. Maybe it was what had happened with Max that had sent him on his way.

Hernandez's having dropped Grimaldi's name did not seem unusual to Cassie. It seemed legit for a high-rolling, comped guest of the casino to know the casino's director by name. Cassie tried to dismiss the whole thing but remained troubled by the memories the name Vincent Grimaldi conjured in her mind.

Needing a distraction, she put the receiver/recorder on the floor next to the chair where she sat, then opened the front pocket of her backpack and took out the deck of cards she had bought at the Flamingo. She removed the jokers from the deck and put them back into the box and off to the side.

She began running through her old warm-up routine – one-handed deck cuts followed by spread and rolls and then up-and-down shuffling. The shuffling felt clumsy through the latex gloves and at one point the cards exploded in her hands, several falling to the floor. She stripped off the gloves and picked the cards up. She then began dealing blackjack to five nonexistent players at the table and to herself, the house.

As she played she went through the dealer's patter in her head as she turned cards over. *Man with an axe, boy meets girl, jack takes five . . .*

But soon her mind traveled and she remembered the first time she met Max. She would always remember it as the random collision of matching souls. Something that didn't happen often in the world, something that surely would never happen to her again.

She had been dealing Caribbean poker at the Trop on a slow midnight shift and he had taken the number two seat. She had one other player, an old Asian man in the seven seat. Max was a beautiful man. He had a presence and Cassie couldn't help watch the way he handled his cards, cupping them and opening them in a tight spread, then quickly laying them flat and making his bet.

But he bet recklessly and soon it became apparent that he wasn't a schooled gambler. He lost money but didn't seem to mind. After a dozen hands Cassie surmised that he wasn't at the table to gamble. He was there to watch the other player. Max was on a con of some sort and that made him all the more intriguing.

When she went on break she waited near the cashier's window and watched Max watch the Asian gambler. Eventually, the mark slid off his stool and called it a night. After a few moments, Max followed suit and started trailing the Asian. He turned off after watching the Asian step onto an elevator.

And that's when Cassie made her move. She walked right up to him.

'I want in,' she said.

Nonplussed, Max just looked at her.

'I don't know what it is you're doing but I want to learn it. I want you to teach me. I want in.'

He looked at her for a few more minutes and then a small smile curved his mouth.

'My name's Max. You want to get a drink or is that against the rules for the dealers here?'

'It's against the rules but I just quit the rules.'

Now his smile widened into a grin.

As she dealt the cards on the table Cassie periodically checked the screen on the receiver/recorder. When she checked at one o'clock the glow of the television still lit the room. But Hernandez was sprawled across the bed and under the covers with his face turned away from the screen. She noticed that the light from the screen was steady. There was no flickering from changing images. She knew that he was asleep and the pay movie he had been watching was over. On the television screen was probably just a blue screen or the unchanging movie menu.

She checked her watch. She figured that by two forty-five Hernandez would be in the deepest part of the sleep cycle. She decided she would go in at three. That would leave plenty of time for her to be in and out before Leo's void moon began.

She slid the playing cards back into their box and returned it to her bag. She decided to do something she knew put her at unneeded risk and that Max would have never done. But she felt she needed to do it. For Max and for herself.

16

Cassie made her way through the still crowded casino to the cocktail lounge off the hotel lobby. It was crowded here as well but the table she wanted was empty. She sat down and looked out across the gaming room but no longer was really seeing it. She was remembering Max and the run they had had, how the *Sun* and the *Review-Journal* had called them the 'high-roller robbers' and the Las Vegas Casino Association had put a reward up for their arrest and conviction. She remembered how after a while it hadn't even been about the money. It was about the charge it put in their blood. She remembered how they could stay up the rest of the night making love after a job was finished.

'Can I help you?'

Cassie looked up at the cocktail waitress.

'Yes. A Coke with a cherry in it and whatever you have on draft.'

The waitress put down napkins, one in front of Cassie and the other opposite her spot at the small round table. She smiled in a world-weary sort of way.

'Is somebody coming or is the second drink to keep the hitters away?'

Cassie smiled back and nodded.

'I just want to be alone tonight.'

'I don't blame you. It's a mean crowd tonight. Must be the moon.'

Cassie looked up at her.

'The moon?'

'It's full. Didn't you see it? It's burning brighter than any of the neon they've got around here. A full moon always adds an edge to things around here. I've been here long enough. I've seen it.'

She nodded as if to cut off any debate on the subject. Cassie nodded back. The waitress left then and Cassie tried to ignore what she had said and concentrate her thoughts on remembering the night six years before when she had sat in the same spot at the same bar. But no matter how hard she thought of Max's beautiful face she could only focus on the bad that followed. She still marveled at how a moment of wonderful joy then could be the same moment that incited so much pain and dread and guilt now.

She was pulled out of her reverie by the cocktail waitress, who was putting the drinks down on the napkins. The woman put down a piece of paper and left. Cassie turned it over and saw she owed four dollars. She pulled a ten from her pocket and put it down.

Cassie watched the bubbles floating up through the beer and forming a half-inch layer of foam at the top of the glass. She remembered the foam in Max's mustache that night. She knew deep inside that what she was going to do this night was as much about Max as about anything else. She had come to believe that somehow there would be a lightening of her guilt, a redemption for all that had gone before if she did this thing right. It was a crazy thought but it was one she had secretly grabbed on to and now seemed to have placed as high as all others. The thought was that if she did this right she could reach back across the tide of time and make up for things, even for just a moment.

She picked up her Coke and looked around to make sure no one was watching. She caught a woman staring at her but then quickly realized that she was looking at her own face in the mirrored wall at the back of the lounge. Because of the wig and the hat and the glasses she had momentarily not realized who she was looking at.

She quickly looked away. She picked up her glass, reached across the table and tapped it lightly on Max's glass of beer.

'To the end,' she said quietly. 'To the place where the desert is ocean.'

She took a sip and tasted the small hint of cherry. She then put her drink down and got up from the table. She left the lounge and walked back through the casino to the elevators.

She followed the ritual. She didn't look back.

17

At 3:05 A.M. Cassie Black opened the door to room 2015, looked both ways, and came out into the hallway with the desk chair. Her disguise was now gone. She wore black jeans and a tight black sleeveless T-shirt. Around her waist was the small fanny pack with the tools she would need. She placed the chair beneath the wall sconce next to the door of room 2014 and stepped up on it. After licking her gloved fingers she reached over the lip of the sconce and turned the light bulb until it went out. She then moved the chair to a spot below the sconce next to 2015 and turned that bulb out as well. She returned the chair to her room and came back to the hallway with an empty black pillow case and the night-vision goggles hanging from a strap around her neck.

She closed her door against the flip-over lock so it would not close all the way and then stepped across to Hernandez's door. She unhooked the DO NOT DISTURB sign and lowered it to the floor. She raised the card key, checked the time on her watch, and then slid the card through the electronic reader. The little green light on the door handle's face plate glowed. She silently turned the handle and began pushing the door open.

There was a slight click and then the earthquake wax made a sucking sound as it gave way and the flip-over lock came off the doorjamb. Cassie's fingers came through the opening crack and grasped it before it could fall or rattle against the door. At the same moment she heard the clip from Hernandez's electronic alarm fall from the doorjamb, the alarm silenced by Cassie's tampering. She swung herself around the door and then carefully and silently pushed it closed. She unhooked the flip-over bar and placed it down on the carpet. She stood up and held still a moment as her eyes adjusted to the darkness of the suite and she felt the rush run through her. It had been a long time but she remembered the feeling well. The adrenaline was searing through her blood. She felt its soft and welcome finger move down her spine. It seemed as though all the fine blond hair on her arms was standing with the electric current.

Finally, she moved into the suite and scanned the living room. She found it empty as expected and focused her attention on the double doors leading to the bedroom. One of them had been left open and from the room beyond came the sound of deep and heavy snoring. Leo had been on the money again, Cassie thought. Hernandez was a snorer. It was like having an early-warning system built into the caper.

Cassie went through the open door and stepped into the blue glow of the bedroom. She saw that she had been right, the television had reverted to the blue menu screen after the movie Hernandez had been watching had ended. It cast enough light into the room that she decided she would not need to use the goggles.

Cassie could see the shape of Hernandez's great, round body slowly rising and falling in the blue light. His snoring was deep and resonant. Cassie wondered if he was married and if his wife could even sleep in the same room with him.

Beyond him on the bed table the numbers of the clock glowed red. She had plenty of time. Next to the clock she saw Hernandez's watch and wallet – and the gun. Hernandez had apparently removed it from the jacket in the closet to keep it at the ready. She moved around the bed to approach the bed table. Hernandez groaned and started to move. She froze.

Hernandez lifted his head and dropped it, opened his mouth and closed it, and then adjusted the position of his body. He was lying on his back, covered to the neck with the bedspread. The bedsprings protested under the redistribution of his weight but then he finally found comfort and stopped moving.

After a long moment of remaining still, Cassie took the last three steps to the bed table and reached for the gun. She slowly unfolded the pillowcase and put it inside. She put the wallet in next and picked up the watch. She turned it over in her hand, careful to prevent its metal band from chinking. She ran her thumb over the wrist plate and found it to be smooth stainless steel. There was no variation in the feel as there should have been from the Rolex seal stamped on the plate. The watch was a counterfeit. She silently put it back down on the bed table and slowly backed away from the bed.

She had to fight the urge to immediately go to the safe, grab the cash and run. But she knew she had to retrieve the cameras. The equipment was proprietary. It could be traced to Hooten L&S. If it could be traced there it could possibly be traced to Jersey Paltz. From him the trail could lead back to her and Leo.

She pulled the chair away from the desk, positioned it under the smoke detector camera and slowly stepped up onto it. She opened the casing and with a small pair of wire snips taken from the pack on her belt she cut the connection to the Conduct-O tape. She then carefully closed the cover and pulled the smoke detector off the wall, its adhesive strip making a *snick* sound as it came free. She turned on the chair and looked down at the bed. Hernandez didn't move.

Climbing down, Cassie almost shouted when she caught a glimpse of herself in the full-length mirror on the back of one of the doors and mistook it for someone else in the room. She shoved the smoke detector into the pillowcase and put the chair back in its place. Turning her back to the bed she brought her wrist in close to her chest and pressed the illumination button on her watch. It was now 3:11 and she had only the closet and safe remaining.

From the fanny pack she removed the painter's putty knife. She clicked on the night-vision glasses and pulled them up in front of her eyes. She spotted the pencil mark on the door frame and slid the blade of the tool into the crack. Following the same procedure as before, she opened the closet without the interior light being activated. Once she was inside and the doors were closed, she carefully and silently slid Hernandez's clothes to one side, then stepped up onto the safe and reached to the bulb overhead. She unscrewed it and left it on the shelf next to the extra pillow.

She crouched on the floor and used a screwdriver to remove the electric socket plate containing the second camera. She snipped the tape as well. Last came the transmitter. She reached behind the safe, grasped the antenna and pulled it out of its hiding place. She cut the tape connections and secured it in the pillowcase with the rest of the equipment.

Now the safe. She took a deep breath, reached to the keypad and carefully typed in the combination of 4–3–5–1–2 she had committed to memory. The safe came open, making a soft *phump* sound like that of a can of fresh tennis balls being opened. She froze and waited, her left ear next to the door slats. Hernandez's snoring continued uninterrupted.

Cassie carefully pulled the safe's door open all the way, then shifted her position so that her body mass was between the opening and the bedroom behind her. She pulled the goggles down around her neck and took the small penlight from the pack. She reached it into the safe before turning it on.

The light illuminated the thick stack of currency she had watched Hernandez put together. Next to the money was a keychain with four keys on it. And nothing else.

Cassie flicked the light out and sat still for a moment thinking about this. Where were the contents of the briefcase? Where was the half million dollars in cash Leo's partners had promised?

She reached back into the safe and grabbed the stack of money, bringing it out and spreading it on her lap. She flicked the light on for a second and saw the currency appeared to be all one-hundred-dollar bills. Her rough estimate was that she had close to a hundred thousand dollars in her lap. A lot of money to be sure – more than she had ever had or stolen. But it wasn't as much as she expected and had been told to expect. Something was wrong. *Where was the briefcase?*

She realized she had not seen it while moving through the other rooms. She would now have to go back into the suite and find it. Perhaps Hernandez had grown lazy and decided not to open the case and transfer its contents to the closet safe. Perhaps, with his gun and his door alarm, he believed he and the case were safe.

Cassie put the stack of cash into the pillowcase, closed the safe and stood up. She carefully wrapped the loose end of the pillowcase around her right hand, drawing it tight so that the contents would not rustle against each other. She pushed open the right door and was stepping out of the closet and into the blue glow of the room when the phone on the bed table rang.

Cassie jerked herself back into the closet and silently pulled the door closed.

The phone rang a second time and she heard Hernandez stirring. She realized she had made a mistake. Rather than having retreated to the closet she should have moved, gotten out of there with what she had, and retreated to the room across the hall.

Now she was stuck. It was probably going to be security on the phone – they had discovered that someone had entered the room across the hall!

The bedsprings sighed as Hernandez moved on the bed. He answered the phone on the fourth ring.

'Hello?' he said in a scratchy voice.

Cassie just closed her eyes and listened. She was helpless.

'The fuck you doing?' Hernandez said angrily. 'What time is it?'

Cassie opened her eyes. She remembered the gun and wallet. If Hernandez put on the light he would surely see them missing and then come directly to the closet to check the safe.

'Three hours' difference, you moron.'

Cassie reached into the pack and wrapped her fingers around the stun gun. While it was still inside the pack she switched it on, then carefully and quietly pulled it out. She realized as soon as she had it out that the red light indicating that the device was on was not on. She flicked the switch off and on again but didn't get the light. The device was dead. She realized she hadn't turned it off after hiding it in her backpack for her meeting with Jersey Paltz. Leaving it on and the jolt that had been delivered to Paltz had sapped the stored charge. It was useless.

She looked through the door slats and in the blue light saw the hulking form of Hernandez sitting on the side of the bed. She then lowered the pillowcase to the floor and reached inside it.

'Yeah, well, call me then. I don't care how nervous he is, what am I going to do about it at a quarter after three in the goddamn morning?'

She pulled the gun out.

'Yeah, yeah, later. Good-bye.'

Cassie heard him slam down the phone.

'Fuck!' he called out.

The blue glow from the television was extinguished, dropping the closet into complete darkness. Cassie heard the bedsprings move as Hernandez tried to get comfortable and return to sleep. She was pulling the goggles up into place when Hernandez let out another expletive.

'Fuck!'

A light in the bedroom was turned on. Cassie heard the bed protesting and then heavy footfalls on the carpet, coming closer. Hernandez was coming toward the closet. She slowly backed as far into the closet as she could and raised the gun in a two-handed, elbow-locked grip. She told herself that she would not shoot. She would only back him off until she could escape.

Hernandez's wide shadow eclipsed the light coming through the slats. Cassie braced herself.

But then the shadow was gone and the closet doors didn't open. Cassie dropped her aim and took a step toward the door. In a few moments she heard the toilet seat bang against the tank, then came the sound of Hernandez urinating. She lowered the gun all the way and fought the urge to cut and run, to grab the pillowcase and go for the door. She could be on the stairs before Hernandez figured out what was going on. And she would have the gun. He could do nothing but call security. This time of night it would be a skeleton crew. She'd be out of the hotel before anyone could react.

But she stayed in the closet and waited. She knew the best escape was the undetected escape. But that wasn't her reason. The briefcase was the reason. She wanted that case. She needed it.

After the toilet was flushed another long period passed and then Hernandez finally walked back past her viewing point and got back into the bed. The light went out without his noticing that the wallet and gun were missing from the bed table.

Cassie slowly moved down to the floor and sat with her knees up and her back against the safe. She brought her wrist up and pressed the button that lighted the face of her watch. It was now 3:20 and she felt a searing sense of loss. She folded her arms on her knees and put her head down. She knew she wasn't going to leave the closet until well after the void moon began. She couldn't risk it.

Cassie thought about Leo. She wondered if he was awake this late and if he was thinking about the void moon, if he was checking his watch. He had called it a bad luck time. But to Cassie, the bad luck had come before the void moon had started. It was that phone call to Hernandez. That was the bad luck. She would have to tell Leo that. Explain it. Surely he would understand. And if he didn't, Cassie would make him.

18

At 3:46 A.M. Cassie Black opened her eyes in the bedroom closet of the man she was trying to steal from. That man had finally started to snore again and Cassie knew it was time to make her final move. She slowly stood up and pushed the closet door open. She pulled the goggles up over her eyes and looked at the bed. She could see Hernandez under the covers with his head propped up on two pillows. If he opened his eyes he would be staring right at her, but his deep breathing and the guttural pitch of his snoring indicated he was down deep into sleep. It didn't matter to Cassie anymore if he awoke. She was tired of waiting. It was time for her to find the briefcase and get out of the suite and out of Las Vegas for good.

She stooped down and massaged her left calf. It had cramped up while she waited. When she was ready she wrapped the pillowcase around her hand and again slowly pushed the closet door all the way open.

For a moment Cassie stood motionless in the bedroom and studied the sleeping hulk on the bed. It was always the strangest part of a job, to observe the mark sleeping. It was like knowing a secret you weren't supposed to know. She began a sweeping look around the room in search of the briefcase but it was nowhere in sight.

She backed into the alcove and checked the bathroom. Nothing. She came back into the bedroom, got down on the floor and reached the penlight under the bed. She flicked it on, revealing the space to be empty save for an assortment of dust balls and a room service menu.

Cassie got up and went into the living room, where she surveyed every square foot of the room but found nothing that even hinted at the location of the briefcase. She started panicking and thinking about her decision earlier to go down to the bar for a cherry Coke and to rekindle memories of her last moments with Max. During that time had Hernandez possibly gotten up from bed, left the suite and stashed the briefcase, only to return and go right back to sleep? It seemed ludicrous, except for the fact that she could not find the briefcase.

Suddenly she remembered the safe. Hernandez's keys had inexplicably been inside it. Cassie tried to determine what this could mean and quickly came to a conclusion. The keychain held keys that opened the briefcase and the handcuffs. To put those keys in the safe rather than to take measures safeguarding the case and its contents would be done only if those measures *had* been taken in some other way. If Hernandez had not left the suite, how else other than with use of the safe could he safeguard the case?

Cassie moved back into the bedroom and surveyed the bed. She visualized what she had seen through the peephole when Hernandez had opened the door. The briefcase had been attached to his right hand. She came around the right side of the bed and gently pressed her hands down on the rumpled bedcovers, careful to stay away from formations created by Hernandez's body. She didn't breathe as she did this. It was the closest she had ever come to a mark. It was too close and every one of her senses was focused on the bed and the huge body that snored beneath the covers.

Her hand eventually came down on something flat and hard and she knew she had found the briefcase. She slowly began lifting the bedspread until she had uncovered the case and the handcuff link to Hernandez's right wrist.

Realizing she needed the keys to remove the case, she went back to the closet and reopened the safe. As she did this she noticed that she had left the gun sitting on top of the safe. She grabbed it, opened the safe and carefully removed the keys. In the green vision of the goggles she studied them. There were four keys and Cassie had had enough experience with handcuffs to know the little key with a round barrel went to the handcuffs. She detached it from the others so that she could work with it without causing the others to jangle and left the closet once more for the bedroom.

Hernandez hadn't moved. Cassie put the gun down on the bed and silently worked the key into the cuff attached to the steel handle of the case. She turned it and the cuff came open with a metallic clicking sound. She started to remove it just as Hernandez, possibly alerted by the sound, began to stir.

Cassie quietly removed the handcuff and straightened up, taking the briefcase off the bed. She reached down and grabbed the gun. Hernandez let out a sigh and started kicking his legs beneath the covers. He was waking up.

Cassie raised the gun. She told herself she could do it if she had to. She could blame it on the bad timing of a phone call, on the void moon or on simple fate. It didn't matter. But she could do what she needed to do. She held the gun straight out and pointed it dead center at the moving mass on the bed.

○ ◐

19

The first thing Jack Karch noticed as he walked through the Cleopatra Casino was that the crow's nest was empty. He knew Vincent Grimaldi wouldn't be up there right now because he knew exactly where Grimaldi was. But the custom and practice of the casino since the day it opened had been always to have somebody up in the nest. That was twenty-four hours a day, seven days a week. If it wasn't Grimaldi, then it was usually somebody else. Karch knew it was all imagery. Sleight of hand. The illusion of security created security. But right now nobody was watching from above and that told him the thing Vincent had called him in to handle was big and important. This realization juiced Karch's blood a lot better than the twenty-two-ounce cup of 7-Eleven coffee he had gulped down on the drive.

As he cut between the gaming tables and weaved around drunken, all-night gamblers who crossed blindly into his path, Karch kept his eyes on the door behind the pulpit, half expecting someone to come hustling out of security, maybe adjusting his collar or his tie as he took his position. But nobody ever came and Karch finally dropped his eyes when he got to the Euphrates Tower elevator alcove.

The alcove was empty except for one woman who was holding her plastic change cup and waiting. She looked at Karch's severe face and then turned away, putting her free hand over the top of her cup as if guarding its contents. He casually stepped over to the sand jar beneath the call button and brought his foot up onto the edge of it, bending over as if he were about to tie his shoe. He did this so his back was to the woman. Instead of tying his shoe he dipped his finger into the black sand, which had been freshly cleaned of cigarette butts and smoothed. He cut his finger through the sand until it found what he knew would be there. He withdrew the card key and straightened up just as an elevator chimed its arrival.

After following the woman into the elevator, he blew the dust off the card key and used it to engage the PH button after the woman had pushed the six button. Standing next to her Karch could glimpse between her splayed fingers and into her cup. It was about half full of nickels. She was the smallest of the small-timers and either didn't want him to know it or she actually thought there was something suspicious about him. She was about his age, with big hair. He guessed she had come to Las Vegas from somewhere in the south. She stood with her face cast downward but he knew she was keeping an eye on his reflection in the polished wood veneer of the door. Karch knew he had the kind of face that made people wary. His nose and chin were sharply drawn, his skin was always sallow despite a life beneath the desert sun, and his hair was as black as a limousine. These features all took a backseat to his eyes. They were the color of puddle ice and looked just as dead.

Karch reached into his pocket and pulled out his smokes. Holding the four fingers of his right hand together as a blind to the reflection, he shook two cigarettes out, palming one while passing the second to his left hand. He half expected her to protest the very sight of a cigarette but she said nothing. He then expertly performed the ear-to-mouth trick his father had taught him so many years ago. Holding the second cigarette at the end of all four fingers and the thumb of his left hand, he created the illusion of pushing the cigarette into his ear and then using his right hand to pull it out of his mouth and into place between his lips.

He watched her reflection and could tell she had seen the gag. She turned slightly as if she was about to say something but then caught herself. The door opened and she stepped out on six. As she turned to the left to leave the alcove and the elevator doors began to close, Karch called out to her.

'Made you look.'

He then laughed to himself as the doors closed on his vision of the woman turning back toward him.

'Next time take your nickels to Branson,' he said after the elevator began its ascent again.

Karch shook his head. The Cleo had once had such promise. Now it was the destination of the nickel-and-dimers, a place where the carpets were worn thin and the pool was crowded with men wearing sandals and black socks. One more time he wondered what he was doing, how and why he had ever sold out to Vincent Grimaldi.

Ten seconds later he stepped out on the twentieth floor. He stepped into the hallway and found it empty except for a room service cart somebody had shoved into the hallway. It smelled rancid as Karch walked around it and headed down the hallway to the right.

He looked up at the first door he passed and saw it was 2001. He remembered that room from a long time before. It was in that room that he had made his first play to Vincent Grimaldi. It seemed to Karch to have been so long ago and so the memory annoyed him. How far had he come since then? Not far, he knew. Not far at all. Perhaps he, too, was a nickel-and-dimer in a nickel-and-dime palace. His thoughts jumped to the empty pulpit down in the casino and he imagined what the view of the gaming room was like from there.

He came to room 2014 and used the card key to open the door.

As he stepped in he saw Vincent Grimaldi standing at the floor-to-ceiling window of the suite's sitting room. He seemed to be staring out across the city toward the expanse of desert lying before the chocolate-brown mountains that edged the horizon. It was a clear, bright day out there.

Grimaldi apparently had not heard Karch's entry and did not turn around.

Karch came down the entrance hallway and into the suite. He noticed the bedroom doors were closed. The place smelled of old cigars, disinfectant and something else. He tried to place it and then his heart moved up a gear. Burned gunpowder. Maybe Vincent really needed him this time.

'Vincent?'

Grimaldi turned away from the window. He was a short man with a harsh and overtanned, V-shaped face with skin that looked as though it had been stretched too tight across the cheekbones. His iron-gray hair was slicked back perfectly and he wore an impeccable Hugo Boss suit. He always dressed as though the casino and hotel he ran was the Mirage. But he was the mirage. The Cleopatra was second tier, moving toward the third. Its location on the Strip was the only thing stopping that for the moment. But there was no doubt that Grimaldi was the captain of an old river barge in a sea of new luxury liners with names like Bellagio, Mandalay Bay and the Venetian.

'Jack! I didn't hear you. Where you been?'

Karch ignored the question. He looked at his watch. It was 8:10, only forty minutes since he had gotten Grimaldi's page with the 911 emergency code added at the end. Forty minutes wasn't bad, especially in light of Grimaldi's refusal to tell him what the problem was over the phone.

'What's up?'

'What's up is that we have a big fucking problem here.'

He stepped over and held his hand out for the card key Karch still held in his hand. Karch gave him the key and thought about lighting his cigarette but decided to wait.

'You indicated that on the phone, Vincent. Now I'm here. What am I supposed to do, guess what the problem is or are you finally going to tell me?'

'No, Jack, I'll show you. Check it out.'

He pointed to the bedroom door with his chin. It was a typical gesture with Grimaldi, who always employed an economy of physical movement as well as words.

Karch looked at him a moment, awaiting further explanation, but none came. He turned and went to the bedroom door. He opened it and stepped into the room.

The bedroom was dark save for a slice of sunlight that cut through the inch-wide break in the closed curtains. The light cut diagonally across the bed, where the body of an overweight man lay face up. The dead man's right eye was gone, obliterated when a bullet was fired almost point blank through the socket and into his brain. The wood headboard and wall behind the bed were splattered with blood and whitish-gray brain matter. Six inches above the headboard there was a bullet hole in the wall.

Karch came around the front of the bed and looked down, studying the corpse. The dead man was wearing a white T-shirt and a pair of pale blue boxer shorts. Karch saw that a pair of handcuffs had been attached to his right wrist – both cuffs around the same wrist. Also on the bed, a handgun was lying between the dead man's legs. Karch bent down and studied it. It was a Smith & Wesson 9 mm with a satin finish.

Grimaldi came to the bedroom doorway but didn't come in.

'Who found him?' Karch asked, his eyes still on the corpse.

'Me.'

Karch looked over, his eyebrows raised. He had expected the answer to be that a maid had found the body, though it seemed kind of early for that. Still, not the director of casino operations. That was out of left field. Grimaldi picked up on the vibe and offered an explanation.

'I had a seven A.M. breakfast with him. Rather, I was supposed to have one. When he didn't come down, I called. When he didn't answer, I checked. This is what I found. I called you.'

Now things were getting curious, Karch thought.

'Who was he, Vincent?'

'Just a courier. From Miami. Name is – was – Hidalgo, though we had registered him under an alias.'

Karch waited. Grimaldi said nothing else.

'Look, Vincent, you want to take me in and tell me what's going on or am I supposed to bring up Seymour the Psychic from the lounge to guess for me every step of the way?'

Grimaldi blew out his breath. Karch was enjoying the moment. The old man was in a jam and needed him. Karch already knew one fact for sure. He planned to milk this thing, whatever the fuck it was, for all he could get. And if that included finally putting Vincent Grimaldi back on his heels, then Karch would do that in a heartbeat. He thought about the crow's nest downstairs. He could see himself up there. Watching the money. Watching everything.

'Yeah, I'm going to tell you.'

Grimaldi stepped into the room and looked down at the body.

'It's money, Jack. The fat fuck had two and a half million dollars with him. It's not here now and he can't exactly say what happened to it, can he?'

'Two and a half? For what? I assume he didn't bring it to put down on a blackjack table.'

Karch saw a vein high on Grimaldi's temple start to tick. The old man was angry. Karch knew how dangerous he was when he was angry. But he was like a little boy standing at the Christmas tree with a broomstick. He had to see how fragile those glass balls really were.

'He came to make a drop,' Grimaldi said. 'This morning. That's what the meeting was about.'

He gestured toward the body.

'I come up this morning and find this. The fucking mutt brought somebody in here and now the money's gone. We have to get that money back, Jack. It's spoken for, know what I mean? We need to get it quick. We –'

Karch shook his head, took the unlit cigarette from his mouth and cut in.

'Spoken for by who?'

'Jack, some things you don't need to know. You just need to get on this and find out who –'

'Take it easy, Vincent. And good luck with this.'

Karch waved a hand and headed toward the door. He got all the way to the living room and was heading to the suite's front door when Grimaldi caught up with him.

'Okay, okay, hold on, Jack! I'll tell you, okay? I'll tell you the whole thing, you think you need to know.'

Karch stopped. He was still facing the door with Grimaldi behind him. He noticed that the door's flip-over lock was missing. He reached up and touched the unpainted square on the door frame where it had been fastened. There was a grayish, waxy material in the screw holes. He rubbed some of this between his finger and thumb, thinking he had seen it before. He turned back to Grimaldi.

'Okay, Vincent, from the beginning. If you want my help on this you have to tell me everything. Don't leave anything out.'

Grimaldi nodded and pointed to the couch. Karch stepped back into the room and sat down. Grimaldi went back to his position by the room's glass wall. From Karch's angle, he was completely framed in bright blue sky. He was the dark, angry cloud in the middle of that sky. Karch took the unlit cigarette out of his mouth and put it in his coat pocket with the one he had used during the elevator gag.

'All right, this is the story,' Grimaldi said. 'Two weeks ago I got the word from somebody that there was going to be a problem with the transfer. Something came up on the background. What they call an association problem.'

Karch nodded. He wasn't as far inside the loop as Grimaldi, but his job gave him more than a general understanding of what was going on. The Cleopatra Resort and Casino was for sale. A Miami entertainment consortium called the Buena Suerte Group was lined up to buy. The Investigations Unit of the Nevada Gaming Commission had been working on a background inquiry of the buyers for twelve weeks and would soon submit a final report making a recommendation to the commission to approve or disapprove the sale. The commission – an appointed board – almost always followed the investigative branch's lead, making the report the key element in any bid to buy or open a casino in Nevada.

'What happened?' he asked. 'From what I heard, Buena Suerte was gonna come up clean.'

'It doesn't matter what happened. What matters is the money, Jack.'

'Everything matters. I have to know everything. What came up?'

Grimaldi waved his hands in frustration and surrender.

'A name came up, okay? They found a connection between one of the directors and a man named Hector Blanca. Now, you'll ask, who is Hector Blanca. Suffice it to say that he's a silent partner who was supposed to have remained silent. And that's all I'm saying on him.'

'Let me guess, Vincent. La Cuba Nostra?'

Karch said it in an I-told-you-so voice. He and Vincent had talked about the mob hybrid before. Transplanted Mafia soldiers from the northeast teaming with Cuban exiles in Miami to take control of organized crime in South Florida. The word in criminal intelligence circles was that the group had secretly bankrolled a failed gambling referendum in Florida a few years before. It stood to reason that if they couldn't get casinos into Florida, they would look elsewhere to invest their money.

That elsewhere most likely would include Nevada, where you didn't need a referendum approval to set up gambling operations; you just needed to get by the Gaming Commission and the short-term memory of the current city fathers. The fact that Las Vegas was born of a mobster's dream and run for decades by like-minded and associated men was being lost in the community's collective amnesia. Las Vegas had been reborn as the All-American city. It was pirate ships and half-scale Eiffel Towers, waterslides and roller coasters. Families welcome. Mobsters need not apply. The problem was, every time a new subdivision was approved and cut farther into the desert, the backhoes of progress came perilously close to digging up the reminders of the city's true heritage. And some of the sons and grandsons of those forefathers – even some of the ones buried out in the desert – could not let the old place go.

'We're not going to talk about La Cuba Nostra,' Grimaldi said, seemingly putting both an Italian and Cuban accent on the words. 'My ass is on the line here and I don't give two shits about how smart you think you are.'

'Okay, Vincent, then let's talk about your ass being in the crack. What happened?'

Grimaldi turned and gazed out the window as he spoke.

'Like I said, I got wind there was a problem. It was brought to my attention and I was informed that the problem could go away, could be cleaned up, for the right price.'

'Why you?'

'Why me? Because I had the connection. You might not think I'm worth a shit, Jack, but I've been working this city for forty-five years. I was already here a lifetime before your old man got his first gig. I've seen a lot. I know a lot.'

He glanced over his shoulder and looked pointedly at Karch as he said the last sentence. Karch took it as a reminder of what Grimaldi knew about him. Karch looked away and immediately wished he hadn't.

'Okay, Vincent. How much was this little cleaning operation going to cost?'

'Five million. Two and a half up front, the rest after the commission vote.'

'And I guess you stepping in and brokering the deal was going to solidify your position here under the new ownership.'

'Something like that, Jack. It would have solidified yours, too. Anybody with me would be along for the ride. I was going to get kicked up to GM. I would've been able to pick my own man in casino ops, put whoever I wanted up in the nest.'

'What about Hector Blanca? He'd want his own man up there.'

'Doesn't matter. The deal I made gave me the choice.'

Karch got up and joined Grimaldi at the window. They spoke while both looked out across the desert to the mountains beyond.

'So the guy on the bed – Hidalgo – came out here with payment number one and got ripped off. It sounds like their problem, Vincent. Not yours. Not ours.'

Grimaldi responded in an even tone. His words were measured, severe. The histrionics were gone and Karch knew this was when he was most dangerous. Like a dog with a broken tail. You try to pet it and you still might get your hand bitten off.

'It is my problem and that makes it yours,' Grimaldi said. 'I set up the transaction. The second that Hidalgo stepped off the plane at McCarran he and the money were in my care. That's the way Miami looks at it, so it's my ass that is on the line.'

Karch raised his eyebrows.

'You already told Miami about this?'

'I talked to Miami right before I called you. Not an enjoyable call to make. But the picture was made real clear to me. The courier is no great loss. But the money, that's different. They're holding me responsible for it.'

He paused for a moment and when he began again there was a note of desperation and maybe even pleading in his voice. It was a small note but it was there. It was a tone Karch had never heard coming from Vincent Grimaldi in the many years they had known each other.

'I have to get the money back, Jack. The GCIU report goes to the printer on Tuesday. After that it's too late to change. I have to get the money back and make the payment or the sale goes down the toilet. That happens and Miami will be sending people out.'

He used his chin again to point, this time out toward the desert.

'That's where they'll take me. Out with the rest of them who didn't go the distance in this town. Breathing sand.'

Grimaldi shook his head once, a quick, tight back-and-forth.

'I'm sixty-three years old, Jack. Forty-five fucking years in this town and that's what I'll get.'

Karch let a delicious ten seconds slide by before responding.

'We can't let that happen, Vincent. We won't.'

Grimaldi nodded and his mouth turned up into a humorless smile.

'Good old Jack of Spades. I knew I could count on you.'

20

Karch began with the body, studying its position and the pattern of blood spatter on the headboard and wall. The fat man had obviously been sitting upright on the bed when he took the bullet. The shooter had been standing at the foot of the bed.

'A lefty,' he said.

'What?' Grimaldi asked.

'The shooter. He was left-handed. Most likely.'

He stood in the position the shooter would have stood and extended his left arm. He nodded. It was likely that if Hidalgo had been hit in the right eye by a bullet from a gun held by someone facing him, then that person held the gun in his or her left hand.

His eyes traveled up from the body to the headboard and wall. Back at the office he had a couple of books on blood spatter – how to read the meanings of elliptical versus circular blood drops and so on. But he had never gotten past the introductory chapters because the stuff was so deadly boring and rarely usable in his line of work. What was to be read of significance from this tableau? Not much. The guy was alive and then he was dead. That was all.

'Anybody report a shot?' he asked.

'No,' Grimaldi said. 'But I wanted him isolated. So none of the rooms on either side or across were occupied. Also, I don't know if it connects up but there was a fire alarm on this floor last night.'

Karch looked at him.

'About eleven,' Grimaldi said. 'Somebody left a cigarette on a room service cart and parked it in the service alcove, right below a smoke detector.'

Karch nodded at the dead man.

'Was he evacuated? Did he leave his room?'

'Not that we know of. I have somebody pulling together the tapes so we can look at everything.'

Karch nodded but was unsure how the fire alarm could have played into things. He looked at the body again.

'I think what you have here is a half-assed attempt to make this look like a suicide. But –'

'This was no suicide. This was a fucking rip-off.'

'I know, Vincent, I know. Listen to me. I said an *attempt* to make it look that way. A *lousy* attempt at that. Just listen to me before you start going off.'

He decided to discontinue his running commentary. He'd let Grimaldi figure out things for himself. What bothered him most about the scene was the handcuffs. He didn't understand why they weren't removed.

'Vincent, I take it you searched this place top and bottom for the money?'

'Yes, it's gone. The case, too.'

'What about his keys?'

'Keys?'

'Keys.' He pointed to the dead man's wrist with the two cuffs on it. 'The key to the cuffs, where is it?'

'I don't know, Jack. I didn't see any keys. Whoever took the money, took the keys, I guess. But they'll get a surprise.'

'What surprise?'

'The key to the briefcase won't be on there. Fat boy here didn't have it. Mr Bla – uh, his boss didn't want him opening it, maybe going down to the tables with a piece of the cash. So he sent the key to me and I would open the case at the drop meeting this morning. I have the key but no fucking briefcase to open. The case has electronic protection – like a stun gun. Somebody tries to open it without the key, they'll get knocked on their ass good. Ninety thousand volts.'

Karch nodded and took a small notebook and pen from his pocket. He jotted down a note about the key and the briefcase.

'What are you writing, Jack?'

'Just a couple notes, so I can keep things straight.'

'I don't want any of this information getting into the wrong hands.'

Karch turned and looked at Grimaldi. It backed him down.

'I know, Jack. You'll be discreet.'

Karch came around the bed and looked at the watch on the night table. It looked like a Rolex. He hooked the pen through the metal band and lifted it, holding it so that he could look at the wrist plate.

'Whoever it was who did this was smart enough to know this is a phony.'

'Anybody on the con would know that, Jack. They sell those things for fifty bucks on the sidewalk outside of any place on Fremont. Whoever it was was smart enough to know what they wanted was the goddamn money and that was it.'

Karch nodded and put the watch back down. He stepped over to the closet and opened it and looked down at the safe. The door was open and it was empty.

'Tell me about this guy, Vincent. When did he come into town?'

'Three days ago. I wasn't sure when the drop would take place. The guy we were paying was calling the shots on that. We just had to be ready with the cash. Hidalgo came in Monday and we waited.'

Karch squatted on his haunches and closed the door to the safe but not all the way. He studied the combination pad.

'He stay in the room the whole time?'

'No, he spent a lot of time on the floor. I gave him a draw and the fuck started cleaning up on me. Christ, I thought if we didn't get this drop taken care of soon he was going to bankrupt us down there.'

Karch turned and looked up at Grimaldi.

'How much did he win, Vincent?'

'I gave him fifty bees out of the cage on Monday. By last night he had turned that into a hundred K and change. He was doing good. He was tipping hundred-dollar bills around like it was toilet paper.'

Karch looked back at the safe and swung the door open. He looked into its emptiness but was not really seeing anything. He was thinking, brooding on what Grimaldi had just said.

'You see what you did, Vincent? You brought this on yourself.'

'The fuck you talking about?'

'You gave the guy money and he turned it into more money. And he was showing it to the world. This town, that was like putting blood in the water, Vincent. It drew a shark to your fat man.'

'What are you saying, that whoever did this did it for the hundred, not the two and a half million?'

'I'm saying that whoever did this came in for the hundred and then found the rest. Luckiest fucking day of his life.'

'That can't be, Jack. That –'

'Who knew about the money? I mean, that it was here and who had it. Who knew?'

'Only me.'

'What about Miami? Could there have been a leak from there?'

'No, only one person knew.'

'Maybe the courier told somebody.'

'It's unlikely, Jack. He worked directly for the source. If the money was taken he knew they'd look at him.'

'Unless he ended up dead. What about the guy getting the drop?'

'He knew it was here somewhere but he didn't know who had it or where exactly it was. Besides, why steal what we're givin' him?'

'Exactly. So if nobody knew it was here, it goes to prove my point. This was a hot prowler, Vincent. Somebody who picked up on this guy winning a hundred grand and went after it. And he hit the fucking jackpot.'

From his crouched position Karch looked up at the closet. He studied Hidalgo's clothes, all pushed to the side so that the thief could work around the safe. His eyes caught on something on the wall behind the safe. It looked like peeling paint. He moved forward onto his knees and looked behind the safe. He looked closer and saw it was not paint that was peeling, but painted tape. He reached down and grabbed the tab and pulled it up. The tape went along the baseboard of the closet, up alongside the door, over the door frame to the wall over the closet and then out and along the alcove ceiling. It finally ended on the wall above the alcove entrance.

'What the fuck is that?' Grimaldi asked.

'Conducting tape. This was a pro who did this, Vincent. He was watching this guy.'

'You mean cameras?'

Karch nodded and returned to the closet. He scanned the ceiling again and then the walls. He saw the small drill hole on the right-hand wall and found more tape. He pulled it off the wall and it led to the rear of the safe.

'Two cameras. One in the room to watch the mark. The other right here to pick up the combo. This was good.'

'I haven't heard about anybody using cameras since . . . since that last time. Max Freeling.'

Karch looked at Grimaldi.

'I haven't either. But we know that Max didn't do this, don't we?'

'You're right about that.'

Karch left the closet and went back through the suite, his eyes scanning the ceiling and upper walls. He came to the front door and opened it. He squatted down again and studied the locking mechanism.

'What about prints?' Grimaldi said from behind.

'There won't be any.'

He turned the deadbolt and saw the bolt come only halfway out. He closed the door with the bolt extended. He nodded. He admired a job well done. He stood up, closed the door and looked at Grimaldi. Karch couldn't help but smile.

'What's so fucking funny?' Grimaldi demanded.

'Nothing,' Karch said, his smile broadening. 'I just get a rise out of a worthy opponent, that's all. I'm really glad you called me in on this, Vincent. I'm going to enjoy it.'

'Listen, this isn't about you getting a rise. It's about me getting the money back.'

Karch let Grimaldi have the rebuke. It didn't bother him. He could already see how he was going to use this job to his advantage, to get what he had always wanted.

'Vincent, you have a problem.'

'I know that! Why do you think I reached out for you?'

'I mean a problem within a problem. Look at this.'

Karch stepped back so he could show Grimaldi the door's locking mechanism.

'He gaffed the lock. The fat man thought he was locked up tight in here but the deadbolt and the flip-lock were gaffed. So was this Radio Shack piece of shit he added himself.'

Karch jerked the electronic door alarm off the doorknob and tossed it onto the floor.

'But, see, all of this only worked on the in-room protections. The main lock wasn't gaffed. That means –'

'He had a key.'

Karch nodded.

'You're real good, Vincent,' he said in a tone that implied the opposite. 'He had a key. That means he had somebody who got it for him. An insider.'

Grimaldi looked down at the floor and Karch watched as the older man's color deepened again. Karch didn't wait for the wave of anger to subside.

'My guess is our guy also had a key to one of these empty rooms around here so he could set up and watch his cameras and make his move when the time was right.'

'You want to take a look?'

'Oh, yeah.'

The first room they checked was directly across the hall, Suite 2015, and Karch immediately said upon entering that they had found the spot where the thief had waited for the mark to go to sleep.

'How do you know?' Grimaldi asked.

Karch pointed to the table. The magazines, the room service menu and hotel information binder were stacked and pushed to the side along with the bottle of welcome wine.

'This is where he waited.'

Karch looked around the suite but wasn't expecting much. This guy was good and the chances of a mistake were almost nothing. The bedroom looked undisturbed. He poked his head into the bathroom and saw nothing unusual. If the perpetrator had used the toilet he had even put the seat back down when he was finished.

He walked back into the living room, where Grimaldi was standing in the middle of the room with his arms folded. Karch was trying to think of something to say that would twist the knife a little bit but then noticed something beneath the table by the curtains. He stepped over and got down on his knees to crawl under the table.

'What've you got, Jack?'

'I don't know.'

He reached under the curtain and lifted it up. On the floor was a playing card. The ace of hearts. Karch looked at it a moment, considering it. He noticed that two opposite corners had been clipped – an indication it was from a casino souvenir pack. After use in the casino the cards were clipped and then sold in the casino gift shop. The clipping was done to make sure nobody tried to slip one back into play at a casino table.

'What is it?' Grimaldi asked from behind him.

'A card. The ace of hearts.'

Karch suddenly thought of his old man and what he used to say about the ace of hearts. The money card, he called it. Follow the money card, he would say.

'The ace of hearts?' Grimaldi said. 'What do you think it means?'

Karch didn't answer. He reached to the card and picked it up, his thumb and forefinger holding it by the edges. He crawled out from under the table, holding the card out. When he was standing again, he turned his wrist so he could see the top of the card. It had a design of two pink flamingos with their necks entwined and forming the outline of a heart.

'From the Flamingo,' he said.

Grimaldi stared at the card.

'What does it mean?'

Karch shook his shoulders.

'Maybe nothing. But our guy had to have been in here watching the cameras for a while. Maybe he was playing a little solitaire to pass the time.'

'Well, if he dropped the ace of hearts, then he never fucking won.'
'Very perceptive, Vincent.'
Grimaldi exploded.
'Look, Jack, are you going to help me out here or are you going to spend your time playing word games and trying to make me look stupid? Because if that's what you're about, then I'll reach out for somebody else who can do the job without giving me the grief.'
Karch waited a long moment before responding in a calm tone.
'Vincent, you reached out for me because you know there isn't anybody else who can handle this like I can.'
'Then let's stop talking and get it handled. The clock is ticking.'
'All right, Vincent. Whatever you say.'
Karch looked down at the card he still held by the corner. He knew he could call in a favor from Iverson over at Metro and run the card for latent prints. But that would bring Iverson into something that Karch expected was going to get dirty. He decided to keep the idea as a last alternative. He went over to the table and opened the folder containing the hotel information packet. There were envelopes and writing paper inside one of the pockets. He slipped the playing card into an envelope and put it into his inside jacket pocket.
'Prints?' Grimaldi asked.
'Maybe. I'll try a few other things first.'
They went back across the hall to 2014 and took a final look around while they discussed their options. Grimaldi said Miami didn't care what became of the courier and so that left things open. They could back out of the room and let things run their course when the housekeeping maid discovered the body. Or they could bring a laundry cart to the room, put the body in it and take it down the service elevator to the loading dock and a waiting van. Any trace of the courier's stay in the hotel could be wiped off the computers and tapes and his body could then be planted out in the desert after nightfall.
'It will take four guys to lift that sack of shit,' Grimaldi lamented.
'You widen the circle of people who know about this and you widen your exposure,' Karch said.
'But if we let things go, that means Metro comes in, and talk about the hotel getting a black eye. I can't remember the last hotel homicide we had in this town. They'll go after this like Tyson went after Evander's ear.'
'That's true. But maybe that sort of pressure on our guy will be useful. Maybe force him into a mistake.'
'Yeah, and what if Metro Homicide gets to him before you?'
Karch just looked at Grimaldi with an expression that said the idea was absurd.
'You call it, Vincent. We're wasting time. I want to look at the tape downstairs and get on with it.'
Grimaldi nodded.
'Okay, no Metro. I'll have some people come up and take care of things here.'

'Good call, Vincent,' Karch said, but in a way that might make Grimaldi wonder if he really meant it. 'Let's go watch the tape.'

They both backed out of the room then, leaving the dead man behind on the bed. Grimaldi made sure he hooked the DO NOT DISTURB sign on the door handle.

21

On numerous prior occasions Karch had been in Grimaldi's office on the second level of the casino. He held a secret security consulting contract with the Cleopatra – no records, payments in cash – and as such he most often met with Grimaldi in his office, even though the tasks he was given normally had little to do with anything that went on in the casino below. Karch was most often involved in what Grimaldi liked to call ancillary security issues and problems. Karch liked his outside status all right. He knew he would never be the kind of man who could willingly wear a blue blazer with the profile of the Queen of Egypt emblazoned on the breast pocket.

The office was large and opulent, with a desk area, a sitting area and a private bar. The entrance was through the casino's huge security center, where dozens of video techs sat in rows of booths watching the screens of video tubes showing the ever-changing views of the hundreds of cameras focused on the casino floor. This room was dimly lit and never warmer than 65 degrees because of the delicate electronics. Most of the techs wore sweaters beneath their standard blue blazers. In Las Vegas, when you saw somebody wearing a sweater to work in the summer, you knew he worked inside, watching tubes all day.

One wall of Grimaldi's office had windows looking out into the security center. Another wall had windows viewing the casino. And located directly behind Grimaldi's desk was the door leading out to the crow's nest. It could be reached only through Grimaldi's office and he had never once invited Karch out for a view of the casino floor. This was something that bothered Karch and his frustration was compounded because he believed Grimaldi knew.

As they entered the office, Karch noticed a man sitting behind Grimaldi's desk and working the control board of the multiplex video station to the right of the desk.

'What have you got?' Grimaldi said as he turned to lower the blinds on the windows viewing the security center.

'I gotta surprise is what I got,' the man behind the desk said without looking up from the four screens he had active on the video station.

'Tell us.'

The word *us* made the tech look up from the screens. He nodded once to Karch and then cast his eyes back down.

'Well, looks to me like this guy mighta been ripped off by a woman,' he said.

Grimaldi came around the desk and looked over the tech's shoulder at the screens.

'Show us.'

Karch remained on the other side of the desk but could see the screens. He glanced past the two other men and out the glass door that led to the crow's nest. Grimaldi did not bother to introduce the technician to Karch.

For the next five minutes the tech used tapes taken from several overhead cameras to intermittently show Hidalgo's last night in the casino. It was called a video trail. There were enough cameras over the casino floor – any casino floor in Las Vegas – to never lose sight of an individual once he entered the so-called video net. The best techs had the quadrants of the net memorized and with fingers flying across a keyboard could jump from one camera to another to follow a target.

Grimaldi's tech did that now, only it wasn't live action. He had pieced together Hidalgo's video trail from the night before. He showed Hidalgo playing baccarat and blackjack, even a couple of spins on the roulette wheel. Whatever game he was playing, he seemed to do it with a minimum of conversation with fellow players and casino employees. Finally, when the counter showed the time on the tape to be 10:38 P.M. they watched as Hidalgo headed to the VIP desk and retrieved the brushed-aluminum briefcase from the vault. He was met at the desk by a security escort who then walked with him to the elevators.

'Who's the escort?' Karch asked.

'His name's Martin,' Grimaldi said. 'He's a shift supervisor. Been here a couple years, coming over from the Nugget. I had him escorting the fat man all week.'

'We'll have to talk to him.'

'I don't know what it will get you but it will be no problem.'

The tech pointed to a new screen where Hidalgo's trail continued. It showed the fat man and the blue-blazered Martin stepping onto an elevator. Hidalgo took his card key from his pocket and Martin took it and plugged it into the control panel before hitting the penthouse button. Though the tape did not have audio it was clear that the two men were not engaged in conversation.

'And that's the last we see of him,' the tech said.

'No hallway cameras, right?' Karch said.

'Nope. We lose him once he's off the elevator in the penthouse.'

'What about when the fire alarm went off later?' Grimaldi asked. 'Any sign of him then?'

'Nope,' the tech said. 'I checked all elevator and stairwell cams. He didn't evacu –'

'Wait a minute,' Karch suddenly said. 'Go back. Back the elevator tape up.'

The tech looked at Grimaldi, who nodded. He backed the tape up until Karch said he had gone far enough and then replayed it. They watched silently. It was clear Martin said something to Hidalgo, who then reached into his pocket and produced his card key. Martin then used it to engage the penthouse button.

'Vincent, you said Martin's a shift super?'

'Right.'

'Wouldn't he have a key to the penthouse?'

Grimaldi was silent for a moment as he computed what they had just seen on the tape and the meaning of Karch's question.

'Son of a bitch. He used Hidalgo's card when he could've used his own.'

'Because maybe he didn't have his on him.'

'Because maybe he gave it – where's this woman you're talking about?'

The tech hit some memory codes and the tape on one of the screens reversed to a preset point. On the screen was a wide view of the baccarat salon. One table was in use and Hidalgo was the only player. Using a roller ball built into the console the tech moved the image forward a few frames at a time. He pointed to the bottom of the screen, his finger tapping it just below the image of a woman leaning on the railing that separated the salon from the rest of the casino.

'Her,' he said.

'What about her?' Grimaldi asked.

'She's trying not to show it but she's watching him.'

He continued to move the roller and the image moved forward. The three men watched the screen in silence. The woman on the screen appeared to be resting or maybe waiting for someone. She had a small backpack over one shoulder and a black gym bag gripped in one hand. She looked as though perhaps she had just checked in and was waiting for someone, perhaps a husband who had stopped to play a few hands of blackjack before they went up to their room. But twice she glanced into the salon and her eyes seemed to fall directly on Hidalgo. Each time her eyes held for what seemed to be more than a passing glance would call for. It was curious to Karch, but not enough.

'He's the only guy playing,' he said. 'Who else is she going to look at?'

'That's true. But I put her trail together, too.'

He ejected a tape from the console and put another one in. Grimaldi came up closer behind him to look at the screen. Karch put his hands flat on Grimaldi's desk and leaned over for a better view. The tape showed the woman with the two bags entering the casino at 8 P.M. and proceeding to the VIP desk, where she was given an envelope.

'That's got to be the key,' Grimaldi said. 'Martin's fucking key!'

Karch was thinking the same thing but did not say as much. He was also thinking the dark flowing curls that framed – and concealed – the woman's face had to be a wig. He watched as she huddled against a phone in the lobby and probably opened the envelope away from any camera's view. She then turned and started moving toward the casino floor. She moved without hesitation, with a strong purpose. The bags she carried appeared heavy but she held them steady.

After her stop at the baccarat salon, the video trail followed her through the casino and onto an elevator in the Euphrates Tower.

'She was damn good,' the tech said. 'Never looked up once. We've got nothing. That hat and that hair, she might as well been walkin' under an umbrella.'

Karch smiled as he watched. The tech was right. She was good, and already knowing what she had done upstairs, Karch found himself enthralled by the woman on the video screen. She was disguised but he was able to draw a sense of her from the videotape. Young, maybe early thirties, the skin beneath her chin taut, the jawline beneath the brim of the hat set with determination. No earrings, no rings or other jewelry that he could see. No distractions. Nothing but drive toward her goal. Karch wished he could see her eyes because he knew they'd be something to see.

On the screen the woman in the elevator used a card key from her back pocket to engage the penthouse button.

'There's the key all right,' Grimaldi said.

Karch wished he would shut up and just observe but didn't say anything.

'Okay,' the tech said while typing in a new command on the keyboard. 'So she gets off the elevator on twenty. But then we see her two more times.'

'Twice?' Grimaldi said.

'Yes, sir. First time she came back down to meet somebody but they never showed up.'

He pointed at the screen and the video trail continued. The three men watched silently as video snippets showed her moving through the casino to the lounge, picking an empty table and ordering from a waitress. The trail jumped in time twelve minutes and showed the woman sitting alone but with two drinks on the table.

'What the fuck?' Grimaldi said. 'I thought you said nobody showed.'

'Nobody did,' the tech said. 'She ordered the drinks but nobody ever came.'

'Let's just watch, okay?' Karch said, annoyed by their banter.

On the screen the woman casually glanced around herself as if to make sure no one was watching and then picked up the glass in front of her. It looked like a Coke to Karch. The woman reached across the small round table and tapped it on the glass of beer. Karch leaned in closer to the screen and watched her lips as she obviously spoke out loud.

'I think you've tailed the wrong person,' Grimaldi said, his voice rising in frustration. 'This broad's sitting there talking to herself. We don't have the time to be –'

'Wait, sir, check this out. She goes back to the elevators now and goes back up to twenty.'

He fast-forwarded the tape.

'And then we don't see her again until four. She comes back down, and take a look at what she's carrying. She went up originally with two bags and she comes back down with two. But something's different.'

The woman appeared again on the casino floor, moving quickly through the thin crowd of die-hard gamblers. Right away Karch saw that the tech was right. Things were different. She had the backpack strap over one shoulder but the gym bag was gone. Instead she carried a large black canvas bag with two hand straps. The tech hit a key and froze the image. The second bag contained an object that was rectangular, its dimensions clearly showing through the canvas. It was the mark's briefcase.

'That little bitch,' Grimaldi said calmly. 'She's got my money.'

'You follow her out?' Karch asked.

The tech hit a key starting the video again and simply pointed at the screen. The cameras tracked the woman as she made her way completely across the huge casino floor to the VIP desk. From the canvas bag she removed an envelope and left it on the counter without speaking to anyone. She then proceeded to the south exit. It was not the main casino entry and exit point. Karch also knew that it did not lead to a parking lot or drive-up circle. Rather, it led to the sidewalk which took pedestrians to Las Vegas Boulevard.

'She didn't go out the front door, Vincent,' he said.

There was enough urgency in his tone to draw Grimaldi's eyes away from the video console. The older man raised his eyebrows, picking up on the tone but not knowing the significance of it.

'She didn't park here because she didn't want the cameras to see her vehicle,' Karch said. 'So she parked somewhere else and walked in.'

Karch pointed at the screen even though it was now blank.

'The south exit,' he said. 'She was heading to the Flamingo.'

Impressed, Grimaldi nodded.

'Ace of hearts. You have someone there?'

Karch nodded.

'No problem.'

'Then go.'

'Wait a minute, Vincent. What about Martin? We should start with him.'

'I'll take him. You follow the money, Jack. The money's the priority and we're on a fucking clock.'

Karch nodded. He guessed Grimaldi was probably correct in his thinking. He thought about the ace of hearts he'd found upstairs. Follow the money. Follow the money card.

'Well, what are you waiting for?'

Karch broke away from his thoughts and looked at Grimaldi.

'I'm on it.'

He glanced once out the door to the crow's nest and then headed toward the office exit. He stopped at the door.

'Vincent, you might want to send somebody back up to the second room up there to check the AC vents.'

'What for?'

'She went up with two bags, a backpack and a gym bag. She came back down with the backpack and the briefcase inside a black canvas bag. Where's the gym bag?'

Grimaldi paused for a moment while he thought about this. He smiled, impressed that Karch had picked up on the missing bag.

'I'll have it checked. You stay in touch. And remember, Jack of Spades, the clock is ticking.'

Karch shot him with a finger and went out the door.

22

Karch followed the same route out of the Cleopatra that he had watched the woman take on the video screen a few minutes before. As he wound his way around the tables and circumnavigated the idiots who lazily walked into his path, his mind became preoccupied by thoughts of the woman on the video. She had come close to pulling off a perfect caper. One glance too many and too long at the mark while at the baccarat railing. Her only mistake. Otherwise they'd probably still be scratching their heads. Still, he had to admire her. He was looking forward to the moment he would meet her. And he had no doubt that moment would come. She was good but he was better. Their time would certainly come.

He gruffly pushed by a man in shorts who had slowly shuffled into Karch's path while absentmindedly looking up through the glass panels of the atrium.

'Well, pardon *you*,' he protested as Karch went by.

Karch looked back at him without slowing his stride.

'Fuck you, dipshit. Go back to losing your money.'

'Hey!' the man called after him.

Karch stopped and turned back toward the man. The man quickly realized he had overstepped and started shuffling away in the opposite direction. Karch watched him go until the man glanced back and their eyes locked. Karch was smiling, letting the man know he had made him run away like a boy.

Karch followed the River of Nile hallway to the exit the woman had used and soon was on the Strip walking toward the Flamingo, a block away. He realized as he got to the venerable and many times expanded and renovated casino that he needed some cash. He silently chastised himself for not asking Grimaldi for expense funds and thought about going back but knew the delay would probably set Grimaldi off. Instead he looked around inside the Flamingo until he found a cash machine and then withdrew the three-hundred-dollar maximum his account would allow. Usually, Don Cannon charged him five hundred for a trail but the three would have to do. He didn't think Cannon would be a problem. The money came out in hundreds, unlike any machine found outside of a casino. While still standing at the machine, Karch folded the three bills twice so that they could easily be palmed. He creased the bills and put them in the palm of his right hand. He closed it slightly and let it hang naturally at his side. He thought about Michelangelo's hands. The master. He envisioned David's right hand hanging loosely at his side. Or the casual repose of the hands of the figure portraying Dusk at the tomb of Lorenzo de' Medici. Karch's father had gone as a young man to Italy to study the hands of the master. The son didn't have to bother. There was a full-scale replica of Michelangelo's David in the shopping rotunda at Caesar's Palace.

Karch went to the telephone alcove off the lobby area and picked up a house phone. He asked for Don Cannon in security and the call was transferred to an intermediate, who asked who was calling. Karch was then put on hold once more and this time waited more than a minute. He used the time to think about what he would say. Cannon was a shift supervisor in the tube room. Karch had met him on a missing-person case five years earlier and he had been cooperative – for a price – ever since. In a dozen years working the Strip Karch had made connections like Cannon in almost all of the casinos. They were all legitimate except for his relationship with Vincent Grimaldi. But now, one way or the other, he was seeing a way out of Grimaldi's grasp.

A voice barked on the other end of the line.

'Jack Karch!'

'Don? Howzitgoing?'

'Keepin' my powder dry. What can I do you for?'

'I'm working a case and could use a little help from your cameras.'

'You want a little electronic magic, huh? What's the case?'

'Pretty basic. Guy at the DI got ripped off by a hooker. He calls me because he's trying to keep it low profile, if you know what I mean. No coppers, no official record. But the broad took some jewelry – a watch and a ring – that've got sentimental value. You know, inscriptions and bullshit like that. He can't replace them on short notice and if he goes back to Memphis tomorrow without this stuff, he's going to have a hard time explainin' it to the wife.'

'I get the picture. What's it got to do with the Flamingo?'

'I think she parked in your garage – the one fronting Koval. My guy met her at the bar in Bugsy's last night, then they cabbed it to the DI. She ripped him after he passed out. I trailed her through the Desert Inn Casino to the sidewalk and I think she was heading here. This was about four in the A.M. today.'

'You said *here.* You're here now?'

'Downstairs.'

'Why didn't you say so? Come on up.'

He hung up before Karch could say anything else. Karch walked to the elevators and took a ride up to the second floor. As he rode he took a handkerchief out of his back pocket, balled it and stuffed it into the breast pocket of his suit jacket. He pushed it down so that it could not be seen but still served to hold the pocket open about an inch. He then checked his pocket for change and came up with a quarter and a dime. They were both recently minted and very shiny. He bent down and slid the quarter into one shoe and the dime into the other. One at a time he shook his feet to move the coins below the arches. He hoped Cannon wasn't watching him on one of his cameras.

Out of the elevator he went left to the security complex entrance and rang the buzzer to the left of the steel door. There was a two-way speaker mounted on the wall above the buzzer but it remained silent. After five seconds the door buzzed and he went in.

Don Cannon was a big and burly dark-haired man with a full beard and glasses. It was likely he had been hired for his size and what he could do with it when necessary on the casino floor. But over the years he had graduated to inside work, and the only parts of the casino he usually saw these days were on the video screens he and his minions monitored in the so-called tube room. He was waiting for Karch in a small anteroom on the other side of the steel entrance door. They shook hands as they always did and the folded hundred-dollar bills were seamlessly passed from one right hand to the other. As with most hotels on the Strip, it was the Flamingo's policy not to accept any remuneration to itself or its personnel for help given on criminal investigations. However, Karch knew the value of a gratuity and how it would keep that steel door's lock buzzing for him the next time he called.

'I'm a little light today,' Karch said in a low voice. 'I'll have to catch you later on that, if that's okay.'

'No problem. I loaded the four o'clock chip while you were on the way up. Come on back.'

Pocketing the currency as he moved, Cannon led Karch into the tube room, which was not unlike the casino security center at the Cleo. Video techs sat at rows of twelve-screen multiplex consoles, their eyes endlessly moving from screen to screen and using keyboards and joysticks to choose and manipulate camera angles and magnifications. They watched over everything, but most of all the money. It all came down to the money.

Cannon stepped up onto a stage at one end of the room where a lone console was situated so that as shift supervisor he could monitor cameras and video techs at the same time.

'You said she came in from the DI, right? Did she walk?'

Cannon slid into a seat on rollers and then pulled it close to the console. Karch stood behind him.

'Looks like it. A little after four.'

'That's a long walk. Okay, let's see. We'll try the north entrance first.'

His fingers started flailing across the keyboard as he typed in search commands. He continued talking.

'We went digital since I think you were last in here. It's a blast.'

'Great.'

Karch didn't know what going digital meant but it wasn't important to him.

'Okay, here's the door starting at four. I'll put it on double time until you see something.'

He pointed to the large master screen directly in front of him in the console. It was divided into a matrix of twenty-four different camera angles.

He moved the joystick and an arrow moved across the screen to one of the small squares. He hit the enter button and the image on the small square took over the entire screen. The image was from a camera showing an angled overhead shot of a set of automatic glass doors. The image was moving quickly. Cars seen in the distance through the doors sped by and people passing by on the sidewalk seemed to move at a quick trot. Karch stared intently at the screen and at the figures occasionally entering and leaving through the doors.

'There!' he said after nearly three minutes. 'I think that was her. Back it up.'

'All right.'

Cannon moved the digital image until the figure that had gone by so quickly reappeared going backward out the door.

'There.'

The image was frozen and then replayed on slow motion. The automatic doors opened and the woman Karch had watched on the video tubes at the Cleo entered carrying her backpack and the canvas bag containing the briefcase.

'That's her.'

'Not bad-looking for a hooker. Too much hair, though. Wonder what she charges.'

'Five bills minimum, my guy told me.'

Cannon whistled.

'There's your rip-off right there. I don't care what a woman looks like, no piece of ass is worth five bills.'

Karch laughed dutifully.

'She take the guy's luggage, too?'

'Yeah. But he doesn't care so much about that. He just wants that watch and ring.'

'I don't know, she's holding that one bag like it's got Fort Knox jammed into it.'

Karch started to perspire. He had hoped Cannon would run the video trail for him without being too interpretive.

'Well, let's see where she goes,' he said, hoping to get Cannon to stop analyzing what he saw and just move through the video.

It seemed to work. Cannon grew silent and he trailed the woman through the matrix of camera angles until she left the casino building through the rear entrance and entered the eight-story self-parking garage at the rear of the property on Koval Road.

'That's gotta be a wig she's wearing, but even so, she looks new to me,' Cannon finally remarked after five minutes of silence. 'If you want, we can check our hooker bin for her.'

'Hooker bin?'

'That's what we call it. We've got most of the working girls in town on computer file. Might be able to come up with a name if we can match her photo. Trouble is, she hasn't so much as looked up a single time. We don't have a clear shot of her so far.'

And you're not going to get one, Karch thought.

'Well, let's see what she does and then worry about that after,' he said instead.

In the garage the woman took the elevator to the eighth floor. She then walked to a blue unmarked van that was backed into a space in the corner farthest from the elevator. This time of night the upper floors of the garage were nearly empty. There was not another vehicle within twenty spaces of the van.

'No plate,' Cannon said. 'Looks like this girl takes precautions. You sure she's a hooker, Jack? Like I said, she doesn't look all that familiar to me and, besides, mosta these girls use drivers. Especially your five-hundred-an-hour variety.'

Karch didn't answer. He was intently watching the screen. The woman opened the driver's door with a key, then loaded in the bags and climbed in. The lights came on as she started the van. Before putting it in gear the woman reached back and knocked on the partition between the front and the rear cargo area. Karch watched her lips move as she said something. Someone was obviously in the back of the van.

'Don, show that part again, will you?'

'No problem.'

Cannon reversed the digital image and showed the woman knocking on the partition again. He froze it and went through some computer commands in an effort to clean up the picture. He then switched to the roller ball and slowly advanced the recorded image again.

'She said something,' Cannon said. 'I don't . . . it looks like maybe, "How are you doing?" or "How's it going?" Something like that.'

'How's it going back there,' Karch said.

'Damn, Jack, I think you're right. You're good, man. We could use you up here.'

'I'd go stir-crazy inside a week. You going to be able to get a rear shot of the van?'

'As soon as she drives out.'

Cannon went back to the matrix – now displaying only garage cameras – and followed the van down the seven levels until it went out the exit to Koval. As it passed through the exit, the van's rear end was recorded by a ground-level camera focused at the average height of a license plate.

The van's rear plate was missing as well.

'Damn!' Karch cried out, surprised by his own outburst.

'Wait a sec,' Cannon said.

He reversed the image and replayed it in slow motion. He then froze the picture and magnified it. Karch looked at him and then at the screen and then finally understood what he was doing. The van's plates were gone but there was a parking sticker on the left side of the bumper. Cannon expertly moved in on it and expanded it. The larger letters and numbers became almost clear. Karch could see the current year on the sticker and was trying to make out the letters when Cannon whistled.

'What?'

'It looks like HLS to me.'

'Me, too. What's that?'

'That's Hooten Lighting and Supplies. Their logo. You know, the company that makes all of this shit.'

He indicated the console with his hand.

'Okay.'

Karch didn't know what else to say. The discovery was making the cover story he had told Cannon seem more and more of a stretch. For the first time he realized how cold it was in the tube room. He folded his arms across his chest.

'I don't get it,' Cannon said. 'A hooker driving herself in a van from Hooten's. You sure this, uh, client of yours told it to you straight?'

He looked up at Karch, who decided he had to extricate himself from this situation.

'Nope. But that's what I'm going to go find out before I take another step on this thing. If the guy's lying, I'm flying. Thanks for your help, Don. I better get back over there to the DI and talk to this guy.'

'Yeah, it sounds kind of hinky to me. You want to look through the hooker bin anyway? Got some real beauties in there.'

Karch frowned and shook his head.

'Nah, maybe later. Let me talk to this guy first and see what's what. Oh, and I'll catch you later with the rest of what I owe you for the trail.'

Karch nodded at the video console.

'Forget about it. Anyway, looks like I opened more holes for you than I closed. The only thing I want from you is a little sleight of hand. You got something to show me?'

Karch went into his act, feigning that he had been caught off guard by Cannon's request.

'Well . . .'

He patted his pockets for change.

'You got some change? A quarter or something?'

Cannon leaned back in his seat so he could work his hand into his pocket. He finally came up with a palm full of change. Karch pulled the sleeves of his jacket halfway up to his elbows and then chose a recently minted and shiny quarter, taking it off Cannon's palm with his right hand. He then performed a variation on the classic French Drop with an added toss-away vanish devised by J. B. Bobo. It was a sleight-of-hand trick he had been practicing since he was twelve years old. It was one he could do in his sleep. He expertly accomplished it with fluid motions and a practiced ease.

With his right hand palm up and chest high he held the quarter by its edges between his thumb and four fingers, tilting it forward slightly so that Cannon could see its face. He then brought his left hand over the top of the coin as if to take it away. As his left hand closed over the coin he let it drop down into his right palm, completing the fake take.

Karch closed his left fist and held it out toward Cannon. He started manipulating the muscles and balling his fist as if he were pulverizing the coin supposedly held within it to dust. At the same time he moved his right hand in a flat circular motion above his closed left fist. He never took his eyes off his left hand.

'To powder it goes, where it ends up nobody knows.'

He made the circle with his right hand wider and wider until suddenly he snapped his fingers and opened both hands, palms out to Cannon. The coin was gone. Cannon's eyes quickly moved from hand to hand, then a broad smile cracked across his face. It was the usual response. The trick was a double misdirection. The skeptical viewer believes the coin never left the right hand but is baffled when the coin shows up in neither hand.

'Fantastic!' Cannon cried. 'Where'd it go?'

Karch shook his head.

'That's the problem with this one. You never know where that coin's going to turn up. That part I never got a handle on. I guess you can add two bits to what I owe you.'

Cannon laughed loudly.

'You're cool, Jack. How'd you learn that one, your father?'

'Yeah.'

'He still around?'

'Nah, he's gone. Long time ago.'

'And he used to work the Strip, right?'

'Yeah, here and there. In the sixties. One week he opened for Joey Bishop, who opened for Sinatra at the Sands. I have pictures of the three of them.'

'Cool! The Rat Pack. The good old days, huh?'

'Yeah, some of them were good.'

Karch had a vision of seeing his father coming home from the hospital after the incident at Circus, Circus. Both hands bandaged white. It looked like he was holding two softballs. His eyes looked like they were staring at something far, far away.

Karch realized he had lost his smile and looked at Cannon.

'Anyway, I better hit the road and get on this thing. Thanks for the help, Don.'

He offered his hand and Cannon took it.

'Anytime, Jack.'

'I'll find my way out.'

He turned toward the steps and started walking away. But then he stopped and leaned on the railing.

'What the . . . ?'

He raised his left foot and worked the shoe off. Without even glancing at Cannon but knowing he was being watched, he looked inside the shoe and then shook it. Something rattled inside and he turned the shoe upside down, dropping the quarter he had planted earlier into his other hand. He held it up and looked at Cannon. The big man banged a fist on his console and started smiling and shaking his head.

'Son of a gun, I told you,' Karch said. 'Never know where the damn thing'll go.'

He flipped the coin to Cannon, who caught it in his fist.

'I'm saving this one, Jack. It's fucking magic.'

Karch saluted and headed down the steps and out of the tube room. He waited until he was out of the Flamingo and away from the view of Cannon's cameras before reaching into the breast pocket of his suit coat and removing the handkerchief and the quarter he had dropped into it while circling his hand during the trick.

He would get the dime out of his shoe later, when he had time to sit down.

23

Ninety minutes later Karch was standing outside the fenced employee lot of Hooten's Lighting & Supplies with a cell phone in his hand. Parked directly on the other side of the fence was the blue van that had been recorded driving out of the garage at the Flamingo about six hours earlier. Only now there was a license plate attached to the rear bumper. Karch was pacing a little bit, anxious as he waited for a call-back. The small tickle of an adrenaline rush was beginning to caress the back of his skull. He was getting close. To the money, to the woman. He cocked his head back and that seemed to accentuate the trilling up his spine and into his brain.

The phone rang and his thumb was already poised on the button.

'This is Karch.'

'This is Ivy. I got it.'

Ivy was a Metro detective named Iverson who ran plates for Karch for fifty bucks a shot. He'd do other things for other prices, using the power of his badge to generate two incomes. Karch was always circumspect about his requests, even on totally legitimate jobs. He had learned over the years to treat all Metro cops – and Iverson more than others – with the same caution and distance as the prostitutes, pawnbrokers and casino sharps he regularly dealt with on his cases.

Karch tilted his head and hooked the phone in the crook of his neck while he got out his notepad and pen.

'Okay, what've you got?'

'Plate comes back to a Jerome Zander Paltz, forty-seven years of age. Address is three-twelve Mission Street. That's North Las Vegas. I ran him on NCIC for you and he's got a clean ticket. I threw that in for free, by the way.'

Karch had stopped writing after the last name. He knew Jerome Paltz. Or at least he was pretty sure he did. He knew a Jersey Paltz who worked behind the counter at Hooten's. He realized he had always thought the name Jersey referred to where Paltz had come from. He now realized it was apparently a play on his first and middle names.

'Hey, boss, you there?'

Karch came out of his thoughts on Jersey Paltz.

'Yeah. Hey, thanks, Ivy. This clears something up for me.'

'Really? What?'

'Oh, just this thing I'm working on. It's a surveillance outside a construction site. The Venetian. This van's showed up a few times and I was kind of suspicious. But Paltz is on the list of vendors. He works for Hooten's L and S and they're putting in the cameras. So scratch that.'

'What do they have over there, a theft problem?'

'Yeah, construction supplies mostly. This Paltz guy's van isn't marked so I thought I'd check it out.'

'Back to square one, huh? Looking for a wheelbarrow thief.'

Karch guessed Iverson was smiling on the other end of the line.

'You got it. But thanks, man. This'll save me some time.'

'Catch you later.'

Karch closed the phone and looked through the fence at the blue van while he tried to think about his next move. The trace coming back to Paltz put a curve on things.

Finally, he opened the phone again and called information and got the general number for Hooten's Lighting & Supplies. He called and asked for Jersey Paltz, who picked up after a half minute.

'Jerome Paltz?'

There was a pause.

'Yes, who is –'

'Jersey Paltz?'

'Who is this?'

'It's Jack Karch.'

'Oh. What's with the Jerome? Nobody ever –'

'It is your name, right? Jerome Zander Paltz. That's where the Jersey comes from, right?'

'Well, yeah, but nobody ever –'

'I need you to come outside. Right away.'

'What are you talking about?'

'I'm talking about you coming outside right away. I'm waiting for you. Come out through the employee lot. I'm parked on the shoulder. Right on the other side of the fence from your van.'

'Tell me what's going on. I don't –'

'I'll tell you when you get here. Come out now. I can probably still help you but you've got to work with me and come out *right now.*'

Karch closed the phone before Paltz could respond. He then walked over to his car and got in. It was a black Lincoln – a Towncar with the old styling and the big trunk. The windows were tinted an impenetrable black. He liked the car but the tank drained too quickly and he was often mistaken for a limo driver. He adjusted the rearview mirror so he could slouch in the driver's seat and keep an eye on the parking lot entrance thirty yards behind him. He opened his jacket and pulled the Sig Sauer nine out of his holster. He then reached under the seat and up into the springs, feeling around until his fingers closed on the silencer he had taped up there. He tore it loose, snapped it on to the end of the Sig and put the weapon down at his side between his seat and the car door.

After five minutes of waiting Karch saw Jersey Paltz enter the mirror's field of view and start heading toward the Lincoln. He was smoking a fresh cigarette and walked with a deliberate, if not angry, stride. Karch smiled. He was going to have fun with this.

Paltz got into the front passenger seat all blustery and with onion bagel breath.

'This better be good, goddammit. I'm on the fucking clock.'

Karch looked over at him and waited for eye contact before responding.

'I hope so.'

That was all he said. Paltz waited a few moments and then erupted.

'Well, what the fuck do you want?'

'I don't know. What do *you* want? You called me.'

'What are you talking about. You just called me and –'

Karch burst out laughing, which shut Paltz up with confusion. He turned the key and started the car. He quickly dropped it into drive and looked over his left shoulder in preparation for pulling out onto the road. He heard the door locks automatically engage upon the transmission being moved into drive.

'Hey, wait a fucking second here,' Paltz protested. 'I'm on the clock, man. We're not going any –'

He tried to open his door but the auto-lock prevented it. While he started looking around for a button that would disengage it, Karch gunned the engine and pulled out onto the roadway.

'Relax, you can't unlock it while the car's in drive. It's a safety feature. I was thinking, Ted Bundy should've driven a Lincoln.'

'Goddammit,' Paltz said, throwing his hands up in disgust. 'Where are we going?'

'We've got a problem, Jerome,' Karch said calmly.

He turned west on Tropicana. He could see the crests of the mountains rising above the build-up line.

'What are you talking about? We don't have a problem. I haven't talked to you in a year and don't fucking call me that.'

'Jerome Zander Paltz . . . Jerry Z . . . JerZEE. What name do you want on the stone?'

'What stone? Would you just –'

'The stone they put on your fucking grave.'

Paltz was finally silenced. Karch looked over at him and nodded.

'It's that serious, fuckball. They saw your van. Last night. Got it on tape.'

Paltz started shaking his head as if he were trying to shake himself awake from a nightmare.

'I don't know what you're talking about. Where are we going?'

'Some place private. Where we can talk.'

'We're not talking, man. You're talking and I don't know anything about what you're saying.'

'Okay, then, we'll talk when we get there.'

Ten minutes later they were past the industrial warrens and the city sprawl was thinning out as they approached open desert. Karch glanced over at Paltz and saw the man was beginning to get the proper feel for his predicament.

They usually did as the desert started closing in. He reached down for the Sig and brought it up and onto his lap, the muzzle pointing at Paltz's torso.

'Ah, shit,' Paltz said when he saw the gun and fully understood his situation. 'That fucking bitch.'

Karch smiled broadly.

'Who is she?'

'Name's Cassie Black,' Paltz said without delay. 'Fuck her, man. I ain't protecting her.'

Karch squinted his eyes as he tried to think. Cassie Black. The name was vaguely familiar but he couldn't place it at the moment.

'She was the one with Max Freeling six years ago.'

Karch looked sharply at Paltz.

'No lie, man. Don't you remember?'

Karch shook his head. It didn't make sense.

'She was a spotter, a lookout, not the one who went inside.'

'Well, I guess Max must've taught her a thing or two.'

'But they nailed her. She went to High D. For killing him.'

'Manslaughter, Karch. She's out now. She said she's been living in California. In L.A.'

Karch thought about this. He checked his watch. It was three hours since he had met Grimaldi in 2014 and he already had a name and a history. He rolled his shoulders, savoring the excitement building in his chest. He then returned his thoughts to the person and problem at hand.

'You know, Jerome, I thought we had a deal. I thought that anytime something came your way that had *anything* to do with the Cleo, you were going to give me the heads up. And you know I check my messages two, three times a day if I'm not in my office. And it's funny, 'cause I didn't get a call from you this week or last week or anytime that I can remember.'

'Look, man, I didn't know it was going to be the Cleo and I couldn't have called anyway. I was fucking *detained*, man.'

'Detained? In what way were you detained?'

'Tied up in the back of the van.'

Paltz spent the next ten minutes anxiously telling Karch his version of the night before. Karch listened silently and kept a mental list of all the incongruities and conflicts in the story.

'I couldn't have called you,' Paltz said in summation. 'I would have and I was planning on it but she had me in the back of the van all night. Look at this, man.'

He turned and leaned across the seat. Karch raised the gun and Paltz held his hands up, palms out. He then pointed to the corners of his mouth, where there were matching cuts that looked fresh and painful.

'That's from the fucking snap cuff she used to gag me. I'm telling you the truth, man.'

'Sit back.'

Paltz moved back to his side. They drove in silence for a minute while Karch thought about Paltz's story.

'You're not telling me everything. Did she know you snitched them off to me last time?'

'Nope. Nobody knew that except you.'

Karch nodded. There had never been any trial so he had never had to tell his story in public. Only to the cops – and one of the leads was Iverson.

'Who was she working with this time?'

'She was by herself. She just showed up at the counter yesterday and it went from there. I never saw anybody else.'

Still, Paltz's story didn't make complete sense.

'You're not telling me everything. You did something to her. You try to rip her off?'

Paltz didn't say anything and Karch took that as confirmation.

'You did. You saw she was alone and you tried to hijack her. Only she was ready for it and got the drop on *you*. And that's why she couldn't cut you loose until she finished the job.'

'All right, so I did. So fucking what?'

Karch didn't answer. They were well out from the city now. Karch liked it out here, especially in the spring before it got too hot.

'What was she doing in L.A.?' he asked.

'Didn't say and I didn't ask. Look, where are we going? I told you everything I know.'

Karch didn't answer.

'Look, Karch, I know what you're doing. You think I walked out of there without telling anybody exactly who I was going to see out in the lot?'

Karch glanced over at him, a bemused look on his face.

'Yeah, Jersey, that's exactly what I think you did.'

It was hardly a bluff worth calling. Karch knew that the relationship he and Paltz had shared over time dictated that Paltz would tell his fellow countermen that he was stepping out for a smoke, nothing more.

He turned the big Lincoln left on an unmarked road he knew was called Saddle Ranch Road on the county plat books. It was part of a subdivision that had been platted and surveyed three decades before. A few roads had been put in but the plan went bust and no houses were ever built. The city, spreading as quickly as it was, was still a decade or so away from catching up. Then the houses would come. Karch hoped he wouldn't be around for that.

He stopped the car in front of an old and abandoned sales office. The windows and door were long since gone. Bullet holes and graffiti marked every wall inside and out and the floor inside was covered with broken glass and beer cans. The morning sun caught on a silvery spider web that hung in the open doorway. Karch looked past the structure to the Joshua tree growing about ten yards behind it. He had planted it many years before to simply mark a spot. He was always surprised to see how full it had grown in such a desolate place.

He killed the engine and looked at Paltz. The blood seemed to have drained from his passenger's face.

'Look, man, now I've told you everything I fucking know about the bitch and what happened. There's no need for –'

'Get out.'

'What, here?'

'Yeah, out.'

He held the Sig up as a reminder and Paltz tried to open the door. It was still locked. Karch looked on with amusement as his passenger's hands scrabbled over the door, looking for the unlock button. He finally found it and opened the door. He got out of the car and Karch followed him out from his side.

Karch came around the front of the car toward Paltz. He held the Sig at his side.

'What are you going to do?' Paltz asked, holding his hands up in surrender.

Karch ignored the question and looked about their surroundings.

'This place . . . I've been coming out here for years. Since I was a kid. My father used to drive out here at night so we could see the stars. In the winter we'd sit on the hood of the Dodge and the heat from the engine would keep us warm.'

He turned and looked back in the direction of the city.

'Man, at night he could look back at the Strip and pick out the casinos just based on the color and glow of the neon. The Sands, the DI, the Stardust . . . I loved this place then. Now it's just . . . bullshit. Amusement parks and bullshit. No class anymore. Sure, the bent nose bunch ran the place back then but it had class. Now it's just . . .'

He didn't finish. He looked at Paltz as though he had just noticed him for the first time.

'How much did she pay you?'

'Nothing.'

Karch started to advance on him and Paltz blurted out a new response.

'Eight grand. That's it. But that was for the equipment. She didn't cut me in on anything. She just gave me the eight and cut me loose.'

It occurred to Karch that it was odd that Cassie Black had let Paltz go – and had even paid him – after she had not let Hidalgo live. It was a pattern conflict that he would have to think about. Something had happened in that hotel room and there was probably only one person who could tell him what it was.

'Where's the eight grand?'

'In a strongbox in my house. Let's go. I'll show you. I'll give it to you.'

Karch smiled without humor.

'She tell you about the job when she cut you loose?'

'She didn't say jack to me. She just cut me loose and got out of the van. I found the eight grand on the front seat with the keys.'

'What about the briefcase?'

'What briefcase?'

Karch paused for a moment and decided to let it go. He doubted she would have shared knowledge of the briefcase with Paltz. She had probably recognized the case as being electronically trapped and hadn't even opened it at that point anyway.

Karch concluded he had all he was going to get from Paltz – except maybe the eight thousand in his house.

'Come over here,' he said, pointing to the hood of the Lincoln. 'Put your wallet down on the hood. And your keys.'

Paltz did as instructed, standing at the front of the car while Karch stood to the side by the left fender.

'You people stole from the wrong people. And she shot the wrong man.'

Paltz dropped his mouth open but then quickly recovered.

'I don't know what the fuck you're – I didn't steal anything. I –'

'You helped and that makes you just as guilty. You understand that?'

Paltz closed his eyes and when he spoke his voice was a desperate whine.

'I'm sorry. I didn't know. Please, I need a break here.'

Karch looked past him at the surrounding scrub land. His eyes lingered again on the Joshua tree and then moved on. The desert was truly beautiful in its desolation.

'You know why I come out here?'

'Yes.'

Karch almost laughed.

'No, I mean to this place. This specific spot.'

'No.'

'Because thirty years ago when they charted this place and started selling lots to the suckers they had the whole place graded so it would look like it was ready to go, that they'd start building your house as soon as they got your money. It was part of the scam and it worked real well.'

Paltz nodded as though he found the story interesting.

'My old man bought a lot . . .'

'That's why you come out, huh?'

Paltz's conversational tone was forced and desperate. Karch ignored the question.

'Thirty years is a long time. The ground's pretty hard again but you go anywhere else out here and start digging and you got about a foot of top sand and then after that it's like digging through solid rock. People think it's like digging at the beach. But it isn't close. The earth below the top sand hasn't been touched in a couple million years. The fucking shovel bounces off it.'

He looked at Paltz.

'So I like it here. I mean, don't get me wrong, it's still hard work but you got about three feet of earth you can deal with. That's all you really need.'

Karch offered a knowing smile. Paltz suddenly took off as Karch knew he probably would. He ran around the sales office and then past the Joshua tree, attempting to use them as a blind. This also was not new to Karch. He stepped away from the Lincoln and calmly walked out to the left of the office to improve his angle. As he moved he unsnapped the silencer from the Sig because it was no longer needed and would affect his accuracy. He trained on the range with the gun without the silencer.

Paltz was about thirty yards away, moving right to left, his feet kicking up little clouds of sand and dust as he desperately ran in a zig-zag pattern. Karch dropped the silencer into his coat pocket and stopped. He spread his feet, raised the Sig in a standard two-handed range grip and traced Paltz's movement. He aimed carefully and fired once, leading the target by about two feet. He lowered the weapon and watched as Paltz's arms started to windmill and he went down face first into the sand. Karch knew he had hit him in the back, maybe even the spine. He waited for movement and after a few moments he saw Paltz kicking in the sand and rolling over. But it was clear he wasn't getting up.

Karch looked around for the ejected shell and found it in the sand. It was still hot to the touch when he picked it up and put it in his pocket. He went back to the Lincoln and used the key remote to pop the trunk. He took his jacket off and folded it over the bumper, then reached in for his jumpsuit. He stepped into the legs and worked his arms into the sleeves and then pulled the zipper up to his neck. The jumpsuit was baggy and black, chosen for night work.

He then reached in for his shovel and headed over to the spot where Paltz had fallen. There was a bloom of maroon blood at the center of Paltz's back. His face was caked with sand and dirt. Blood was on his lips and teeth. It meant the bullet had ripped through a lung. He was breathing quickly and hoarsely. He wasn't trying to speak.

'All right, that's enough,' Karch said.

He leaned down and tucked the muzzle of the Sig under Paltz's left ear. With his other hand he held the shovel by its neck and positioned the blade so that it would block the blow-back of blood. He fired one shot into Paltz's brain and watched him go still. The shell ejected from the Sig clanked off the shovel and fell into the sand. Karch picked it up and put it in his pocket.

Karch opened the front of the jumpsuit, put the Sig back into his holster and looked up at the sky. He didn't like doing this during the day. It wasn't just being in a black jumpsuit under the desert sun. Sometimes when things backed up at McCarran the airliners were put into low holding patterns out this way.

He started digging anyway, hoping that wouldn't happen and wondering if this would be the time of coincidence, when his spade would strike bone already in the ground.

24

Karch stood in front of the practice mirror adjusting the tie on his fresh suit. It was a Hollyvogue that had belonged to his father, with Art Deco spirals on it. He was wearing it with the two-tone gabardine Hollywood jacket and pleated pants he had picked up at Valentino's in downtown.

His pager sounded and he picked it up off the bureau. He recognized the call-back number as Vincent Grimaldi's. He deleted it, hooked the pager on his belt and finished adjusting his tie. He wasn't going to call Grimaldi back. He planned to drop by in person to inform him of the progress he had made.

When he was done with the tie he went back to the bureau for his guns. He holstered the Sig and snapped the safety strap over it. He then picked up the little .25 popper. It was a Beretta he could fit in his palm. He turned back to the mirror and held his hands loosely at his sides, the .25 hidden in his right hand. He made a few moves and gestures, always sure to keep the pistol hidden from view. David's right hand, he thought. David's right hand.

He then went on to practice the finish, moving his apparently empty hands as if in conversation and then suddenly producing the gun pointed right at himself in the mirror. When he had practiced this enough he put the little gun back into the black silk magician's pocket that he'd had a downtown tailor sew onto the inside rear belt line of his pants – every pair of pants he owned. He then held his hands palms out to the mirror and then brought them together as if in prayer. He bowed his head and backed away from the mirror, end of show.

On his way to the garage Karch stopped in the kitchen and took a mason jar out of one of the cabinets. He took the top off and dropped the two bullet shells from the desert into it with the others. He then held the jar up and looked at it. It was almost half full of shells. He shook the jar and listened to the shells rattle inside. He then put it back in the cabinet and took out a box of Honeycombs cereal. He was famished. He hadn't eaten all day and the physical exertion in the desert had sapped his strength. He started eating the cereal right out of the box, handfuls at a time, careful not to get any crumbs on his clothes.

He stepped into the garage, which had been illegally converted into an office, and sat down behind his desk. He didn't need an office in a commercial building like most private investigators. Most of his work – on the legitimate side – came in from out of state on the phone. His specialty was missing persons cases. He paid the two detectives who ran Metro's missing persons unit five hundred dollars a month to refer clients to him. As a matter of policy, Metro could not act on a routine report of a missing adult until forty-eight hours had elapsed since the time of the report. This practice had originated because most missing people were missing on purpose and often turned up on their own a day or so after supposedly disappearing. In Las Vegas this was most often the case. People came on vacation or for conventions and cut loose in a city designed to knock down inhibitions. They shacked up with strippers and hookers, they lost their money and were too embarrassed to go home, they won lots of money and didn't want to go home. There were endless reasons and that was why the police had a wait-and-see attitude.

However, the forty-eight-hour policy and the reasons behind it did not placate the concerned and sometimes hysterical loved ones of the supposedly missing. That was where Karch and a legion of other private investigators came in. By paying off the cops in the MPU, Karch made sure his name and number were often suggested to people who reported missing persons and didn't want to wait the required forty-eight hours before a search was begun.

The five hundred Karch deposited each month into a bank account the two cops had access to was a bargain. He drew as many as a dozen calls a month on missing persons cases. He charged four hundred dollars a day plus expenses, with a two-day minimum. He often located the supposedly missing person inside an hour with a simple credit card trace but he never told the clients that. He just had them wire payment to his bank account before he revealed their loved one's location. To Karch it was all another form of sleight of hand. Keep things in motion with misdirection. Never reveal what is in your palm.

His office was a shrine to a Las Vegas long gone by. The walls were a collage of photographs of entertainers from the fifties and sixties. There were numerous shots of Frank and Dean and Sammy, some individual and some as a group. There were photos of dancers and framed fight cards.

There were postcards depicting casino resorts that no longer existed. There was a framed collection of gambling chips – one from every casino that opened its doors in the fifties. There was a large blowup photo of the Sands crumbling to the ground after being dynamited to make way for the new era of Las Vegas. Many of the photos were autographed and inscribed, but not to Jack Karch. They were inscribed to 'The Amazing Karch!' – his father.

At center on the wall Karch faced while seated at his desk was the largest frame on any of the walls. It was a blowup photo of the huge neon-gilded headliner sign that had stood outside the Sands. It said

Now Appearing
FRANK SINATRA
JOEY BISHOP
THE AMAZING KARCH!

Karch looked at the photo across from him for a long moment before getting down to work. He had been nine years old when he saw his father's name on the big sign. His father took him with him one night to watch the show from the side of the stage. He was standing there watching his father perform an illusion called The Art of the Cape when he was tapped on the shoulder and looked up to see Frank Sinatra. The man who was the living embodiment of Las Vegas faked a punch off his chin and asked with a smile if he had an exclamation point at the end of his name, too. It was the most indelible memory of his childhood. That and what happened to his father a few years later at Circus, Circus.

Karch looked away from the photo and checked the message machine on the desk. He had three waiting messages. He hit the playback button and picked up a pencil, ready to take notes. The first message was from a woman named Marion Rutter from Atlanta who wanted to hire Karch to look for her husband, Clyde, who hadn't come home from a kitchenware convention in Las Vegas. She was very worried and wanted someone to start looking for Clyde right away. Karch wrote down her name and number but wouldn't be calling back because for the moment he was booked.

The next two messages were both from Vincent Grimaldi. He sounded annoyed. He demanded that Karch check in with him right away.

Karch erased the messages and leaned back in his leather padded desk chair. He grabbed another handful of cereal and studied the two stacks of cash on his desk while he ate. He had gone to Jersey Paltz's apartment after the desert and used the dead man's keys to go in, open the strongbox he found in a closet and take the money. One stack was $8,000 in one-hundred-dollar bills. The other stack was $4,480 in twenties. Karch figured the $8,000 belonged to Grimaldi. Minus the $550 Karch had accumulated so far in expenses – $500 to Cannon for the Flamingo video trail and $50 to Iverson for the plate run. Make it an even $600 to cover gas and other incidentals, he decided. The other stack Karch was going to keep free and clear. It had not been part of the caper at the Cleo. It had apparently been Paltz's own savings.

He put what was his into one of the desk drawers, which he then locked with a key. He took out a preprinted and generic invoice form and wrote out a receipt for the $7,400 he would be returning to Grimaldi. He did not put his name anywhere on the form. When he was finished he folded the money inside the receipt and put it in an envelope he then slid into the inside pocket of his coat.

He sat motionless at the desk for a few moments wondering if he should have deducted more money to cover the trip he knew he would be making to Los Angeles. He finally decided against it and got up and came around the desk to the row of file cabinets beneath the blowup photo of the Sands going down. He unlocked a drawer with a key, looked through the files until he found the one he wanted and then went back to the desk with it.

The file was labeled FREELING, MAX. Karch opened it on the desk and spread the contents out. There were several police reports and handwritten pages of notes. There was also a packet of carefully folded and yellowed newspaper clippings. He opened these and read the one with the largest headline. It had been on the front page of the *Las Vegas Sun* six and a half years before.

'HIGH-ROLLER ROBBER'
PLUNGES TO DEATH

BY DARLENE GUNTER
Sun Staff Writer

A man authorities believe to have been responsible for a string of hotel room burglaries of high rollers at Strip casinos jumped to his death early Wednesday when faced with certain capture in a penthouse suite at the Cleopatra Resort and Casino.

The man's body crashed through the casino's signature atrium ceiling, sending glass showering on players at 4:30 A.M. The body landed on an unused craps table and the incident caused a momentary panic among those in the casino. However, authorities said no one was hurt in the incident other than the man who fell.

Metro police spokesmen said the suspect, identified as 34-year-old Maxwell James Freeling of Las Vegas, fell twenty floors after crashing through the window of a penthouse suite when he was confronted by a Cleopatra security agent who had set up a sting operation to nab him.

It was unclear late Wednesday why Metro police were not involved in the sting operation. Also unclear was why Freeling chose to jump through the window in a fatal effort to avoid capture.

Vincent Grimaldi, the casino's chief of security, was close-lipped about the incident but expressed relief that it occurred during a time when the casino was at its least crowded.

'We were just lucky it happened when it happened,' Grimaldi said. 'There weren't many people in the casino at the time. If it had happened during a high-occupancy period, who knows what could have resulted.'

Grimaldi said the casino would stay open while repairs were made to the atrium ceiling. He said a small portion of the playing area would have to be roped off during the repairs.

After Freeling's death a 26-year-old woman was taken into custody at the hotel and turned over to police officers. She was arrested when she ran to Freeling's body in the casino after his fall. Authorities said that it became obvious by her reactions that she was 'involved' with Freeling in some capacity.

'If she had just split we probably wouldn't have ever known about her,' said Metro detective Stan Knapp. 'But she ran to the guy and gave herself away.'

The woman, whom police declined to identify until charges are filed, was being questioned throughout the day Wednesday at Metro headquarters.

Police said that Freeling is believed to have been the highly skilled thief who struck eleven times in the last seven months at casino hotels on the Strip. In each case, a casino guest was robbed of cash and jewels in his or her hotel room by a thief who entered while they slept.

The thief was dubbed the 'High-Roller Robber' by police because the targets were all 'players' – hotel guests who wagered and won large amounts of cash. The estimated take from the eleven capers was in excess of $300,000, according to police sources.

The thief apparently used several different means of entering the hotel rooms – from air-conditioning vents to gaining room keys from unsuspecting housekeepers and front-desk employees. None of the victims ever saw the thief, who came in after they had gone to sleep. A police source said the thief may have monitored his targets through hidden cameras but would not elaborate.

Karch stopped reading. Because it was the first article on the incident, it had the least information, the writer having woven several paragraphs out of a handful of facts. He went on to the next day's story.

ACCOMPLICE CHARGED IN
'HIGH-ROLLER' DEATH

BY DARLENE GUNTER
Sun Staff Writer

A woman police say was the lookout for the so-called High-Roller Robber was charged Thursday with homicide in his death from a fall from the penthouse of the Cleopatra Resort and Casino.

Cassidy Black, 26, of Las Vegas, was charged under Nevada's felony-homicide law, which holds anyone who takes part in a criminal enterprise responsible for any death that occurs during the commission of the crime.

Although Black was waiting for Max Freeling in the lobby of the Cleopatra when he crashed through a penthouse window twenty stories above, she is still legally responsible for his death, said Clark County District Attorney John Cavallito.

Cavallito said Black, who was also charged with burglary and criminal conspiracy, could face 15 years to life in prison if convicted of the charges. She was being held without bail at the county jail.

'She was just as much a part of this incident and this crime spree as Freeling was,' Cavallito said at a press conference. 'She was a co-conspirator and deserves to be and will be hit with the full weight of the law.'

Freeling's death was ruled an accident and not suicide. He reportedly crashed through one of the windows of the penthouse suite in an effort to avoid capture.

More details on the dramatic events of early Wednesday morning were revealed by Cavallito and police investigators on Thursday.

The so-called High-Roller Robber had struck at Strip resorts eleven times in seven months, prompting the Las Vegas Casino Association to put up a $50,000 reward for the capture and conviction of a suspect.

Police said the thief had allegedly been targeting high rollers who took their winnings in cash with them to their rooms at the end of the day.

On Tuesday a private investigator hoping to claim the reward money contacted officials at the Cleopatra and told them he believed the High-Roller Robber was currently targeting a guest in the hotel and casino.

The investigator, Jack Karch, then agreed to serve as a decoy. When the target gambler, whose name was not released, retired for the evening, a switch was made and it was Karch – disguised as the gambler – who went to the penthouse suite.

Two hours after Karch turned out the lights in the suite and feigned sleep, Freeling entered the room through an air vent he had accessed through the ceiling of the penthouse housekeeping station. As Freeling entered the suite's bedroom he was surprised by Karch, who held him at gunpoint and used a two-way radio to call for help from hotel security agents waiting nearby.

'Before those agents could get to the room, Mr Freeling inexplicably made a run for the window,' Cavallito said. 'He threw his body into it and crashed through and fell.'

Cavallito said there was a small ledge below the window and Freeling may have believed that he could escape on it by moving along the facing of the building to a nearby cable used to lower a window-washing platform down the side of the building.

However, the momentum of Freeling's body going through the glass carried him past the narrow ledge and down. He crashed through the casino's signature atrium window, creating a panic among the few gamblers in the casino at the time. No one else was hurt.

Following Thursday's press conference Cavallito answered few questions, citing the ongoing investigation and prosecution of Black. He refused to reveal how it was that Karch, the private investigator, learned that Freeling was targeting a gambler at the Cleopatra.

Efforts to contact Karch for comment were unsuccessful and messages left on his office answering machine were not returned. As a young child Karch performed on occasion with his father, the now deceased magician known as 'The Amazing Karch!' who was a mainstay at Strip casinos and hotels from the '50s to the early '70s.

The younger Karch was called 'Jack of Spades' because of an illusion in which his father placed him in a locked mail sack in a locked crate and he would disappear and be replaced by a playing card – the Jack of spades.

While Cavallito said Karch has been cleared of any wrongdoing in the death of Freeling, the district attorney did criticize the decision of Karch and Cleopatra officials to set up the sting operation without police involvement.

'We certainly wish that they had contacted the Metro Police Department before going ahead with this,' Cavallito said. 'Maybe then this whole incident could have been avoided.'

Vincent Grimaldi, chief of security at the Cleopatra, declined to comment on Cavallito's criticism.

A spokesman for the Casino Association declined to say whether Karch could claim the reward in light of the death of the suspected thief and arrest of his accomplice.

More details about Freeling were emerging yesterday as well. Authorities said the suspect had twice before been convicted of burglary and had previously spent a total of four years in state prisons. Freeling was said to have grown up in Las Vegas and, like Karch, was the son of a figure of note. Freeling's father was Carson Freeling, who was convicted in 1963 of taking part in a daring armed robbery of the Royale Casino, a caper which many locals believe was inspired by the film *Ocean's Eleven*, starring Frank Sinatra and other members of the so-called Rat Pack.

Maxwell Freeling was three years old at the time of his father's arrest. Carson Freeling died in prison in 1981.

Karch studied the photo that accompanied the story. It was a mug shot of Cassidy Black taken on the day of her arrest. Her long blond hair was messy and her eyes looked red and sore from crying. He remembered that she had refused to say one word to the Metro cops, even through twelve hours of interrogation. She had stood up and Karch admired that.

During the investigation of the Freeling incident, Karch had never met her or even been in the same room with her. It was impossible to confirm that the woman in the photograph was the one he had watched on surveillance videos at the Cleo and the Flamingo but in his gut he knew it was.

He scanned through the remaining few clips until he got to the last story. This one had another photo of Cassidy Black running alongside the story. It showed her in a jailhouse jumpsuit and shackles being led from a courtroom by two bailiffs. There was something about the angle of her jaw and the focus of her eyes upward that he liked. It showed that she still carried her dignity, despite the cuffs and the jumpsuit and the situation she was in.

His eyes moved over to the story and he read it. It was the last story in the saga, the cleanup. It was short and had been buried inside the *Sun*.

HIGH-ROLLER ROBBER

BLACK ENTERS PLEA, GETS PRISON

BY DARLENE GUNTER

Sun Staff Writer

Cassidy Black, one of the so-called High-Roller Robbers, pleaded guilty Monday to charges relating to the crime spree that included the dramatic death of her partner two months ago. She was immediately sentenced to state prison.

In a plea agreement negotiated with the Clark County District Attorney's office, the 26-year-old one-time blackjack dealer pleaded guilty to one count of manslaughter and one count of conspiracy to commit burglary. She was sentenced by Circuit Court judge Barbara Kaylor to serve five to fifteen years in prison.

Black, dressed in a yellow jumpsuit, said little during the courtroom hearing. She spoke the word 'guilty' after each charge was read by Kaylor and then told the judge she fully understood the ramifications of her plea.

Black's attorney, Jack Miller, said the agreement was the best Black could do, considering the overwhelming evidence of her involvement with Maxwell James Freeling in a seven-month crime spree that ended with her arrest and Freeling's plunge from a penthouse window at the Cleopatra Resort and Casino.

'This agreement still leaves her a chance to start over,' Miller said. 'If she keeps her nose clean in prison she can be out in five, six, seven years. She'll still be in her early thirties and that leaves her a lot of time to start over and be productive in society.'

Authorities said the evidence mounted against Black indicated she was Freeling's spotter and lookout on capers in which the hotel suites of high-rolling gamblers were burglarized while they slept.

Karch dropped the clip onto the others without reading it to the end. Cassidy Black's guilty plea had precluded a trial and allowed him to avoid having to testify about what happened in that suite with Freeling. Her conviction also allowed him to claim the reward, though he'd had to get a lawyer to sue the Casino Association for it. After attorney fees and taxes he had walked away with $26,000 in reward money and Grimaldi's leash around his neck. He had allowed himself to become Grimaldi's go-to guy for all the misdeeds and dirty work, the runs out to the desert with the full trunk.

All that is going to change, Karch said to himself. *Soon. Soon.*

Karch carefully refolded the newspaper clippings and closed the file. He then closed the box of cereal and took it back to the kitchen on his way to the front door.

At the front door he picked up the suit bag he had packed earlier and chose a porkpie hat from the rack. His traveling hat. He looked at the inside lining before putting it on. It was chocolate brown, a Mallory, the inside label said, *For Youthful Smartness.* He fitted it on and geeked the brim flat like an old jazz musician would, the way he had once seen Joe Louis wear a porkpie as the greeter at the front door of Caesar's. He stepped out the door into the brilliant white sunlight.

25

As Karch walked through the casino at the Cleo he felt eyes upon him and looked up under the brim of his hat to see Vincent Grimaldi staring back at him from the crow's nest. Grimaldi did not have to gesture for Karch to know he was angry and waiting. Karch looked away and made his way to the elevators, a little more speed in his step.

When he was ushered into Grimaldi's office two minutes later, Karch was met by a large man he knew was Grimaldi's chief in-house thug. Karch couldn't recall his name but remembered it ended in a vowel. It was Rocco or Franco or something close.

'He wants to see me,' Karch said.

'Yes, we've been reaching out to you all morning.'

Karch noted the use of the plural and the condescending smirk on the other man's face as he gestured toward the door that opened onto the walkway to the crow's nest.

As Karch made his way around Grimaldi's desk he saw that it was spread with tools and equipment: an electric drill, a Polaroid camera, a large flashlight and a small tub of earthquake wax. He picked up the drill and saw that it had been wrapped in black rubber sewn together with fishing line.

'We found all of this in the air vent in room –'

'Two-thousand fifteen,' Karch said. 'I know. I told him it would be there.'

He put the drill down and returned the condescending smirk to the man. He then stepped through the door to the walkway. He closed the door behind him, his eyes holding the other man's through the glass.

Grimaldi didn't turn to Karch as he came out. He stood with his hands gripping the railing and stared out at the sea of gamblers below. Karch had never been in the crow's nest before. He looked around and down upon the casino floor with a sense of awe and reverence. He glanced back and saw Grimaldi's thug standing at the glass door watching him. He turned and stepped right next to Grimaldi.

'Vincent.'

'Whereya been, Jack? I've been calling.'

'Sorry, Vincent, I had my hands full.'

'What, changing your suit? Who you supposed to be, Bugsy Siegel or Art Pepper?'

'I'm here, Vincent. What do you want?'

Grimaldi looked at him now for the first time with an expression of warning.

'You know, I wonder if I was right about putting you on lead on this. My ass is on the line and I have no idea what you're doing besides changing clothes and putting on hats. Maybe I should hand this off to Romero. I know he's good to go on it.'

Karch stayed cool. He had a pretty good idea that Grimaldi was only venting.

'If that's what you want, Vincent. But I thought you wanted the money back.'

'I *DO*, goddammit!'

A few gamblers at a craps table below glanced up at Grimaldi's outburst. They were playing at the table where Max Freeling had landed six years before.

Karch decided to stop playing games with Grimaldi.

'Look, Vincent, I've been working the problem, okay? I've made progress. I have the woman's name and I know where she is. I'd already be on my way if you hadn't been calling and paging me.'

Grimaldi turned to him, the excitement clearly showing on his face.

'You've got a name?'

'Yes.' Karch nodded down toward the craps table below. 'You remember the thing with Max Freeling, right? The high diver?'

'Of course.'

'Well, remember the girl they picked up? His lookout?'

'Yeah. She went away, got fifteen, I think.'

'Five to fifteen, Vincent. Must have been a good girl. Because she did the five and got out. It was *her* last night.'

'Bullshit. She was a lookout. You said yourself this morning that this was a pro, somebody who knew exactly what the fuck she was doing.'

'I know. And it's her. Believe me, it's her.'

'Tell me how you know this.'

Karch spent the next ten minutes detailing his tracing of Jersey Paltz and his questioning of the electronics dealer.

'Motherfucker,' Grimaldi said of Paltz. 'I hope you took care of him.'

'Don't worry about him.'

Grimaldi's sharp, dark face cracked into a smile, revealing beautifully white teeth.

'They don't call you Jack of Spades for nothing. The man with a shovel in the trunk.'

Karch let it go. He remembered something and tapped his jacket below the breast pocket.

'I've got the eight K she paid him for the equipment. Minus my expenses. I'll leave it on the desk.'

'That's good, Jack. And guess what, I've got something for you. We've got a name, too.'

Karch looked at him.

'Martin was the insider?'

Grimaldi nodded.

'He acted dumb but we eventually got it out of him. He gave us everything but the girl's name because he didn't know it. So with what you got we have the whole picture.'

'Which is what?'

'The thing was set up by a guy in L.A. named Leo Renfro. He connected with Martin and then he procured the girl for the job. He's the middle man on this thing.'

'How'd he know Martin?'

'He didn't. He was put in touch with Martin.'

'How?'

'That's where it gets dicey. Turns out Martin kept an eye out for Chicago. When he was at the Nugget a few years back he was Joey Marks's ear. When Marks and his crew got taken down by the bureau, things scattered and Martin left the Nugget and started here with a new slate. Of course, I didn't know any of this history when I hired him. Anyway, like I said, he didn't know this guy Renfro. But when he sees Hidalgo raking in the cash at the baccarat table and then going up to his room every night with that handcuff case, he figured there was a nice score to be made. He tipped Chicago and they put him together with this Leo Renfro to set it up.'

Karch was barely listening. The mention of Chicago, of the so-called Outfit's involvement in the caper, was causing blood to pound in his ears. His hands tightened into fists.

'Hey, Jack, you still with me?'

Karch nodded.

'I'm here.'

'Look, I know with what happened with your father and all . . . I just wanted you to see all the cards, you know?'

'Thank you, Vincent. You sure Martin was only working off what he saw the mark win? He didn't know about the two and a half?'

Grimaldi stepped a little closer to him. There was a humorless smile on his face.

'Let's just say that we questioned him closely and extensively on that point. And the answer is he didn't know. Chicago didn't know. It was just a casino score. It was like you said, Jack. I made a mistake giving the guy a draw. He turned it into more money and it drew sharks. Martin and his Chicago people. Everybody involved in this thing works for Chicago.'

Karch just nodded and kept his lips tightly together.

'So if the girl's from L.A. now and Renfro's from L.A., then that's where the money is. You have to get over there and get it before they turn it over to Chicago.'

'They probably already have it by now, Vincent.'

'Maybe, maybe not. She killed the guy in his bed. Maybe they want to check the heat on it before they make any further moves. We have to get over there and be sure. Besides, even if they passed the money on, I want these people dealt with. Due diligence. You know the score.'

Grimaldi looked at his watch.

'But I think we still have a shot at the money. Six hours into this and we've already got the whole story. You get over there and get the money. You have a line on the girl?'

'Not yet. If she came in from L.A. that means she probably jumped parole. I could check to make sure but that would leave an official trail. I don't think you want that yet, Vincent.'

'I don't. So hold that as a last resort. Maybe you should start with Renfro, go from there.'

Karch nodded.

'You have an address for him?'

Grimaldi shook his head.

'We got a cell phone number. The name and number was all Martin had. You'll have to trace it from there. Romero has it on a piece of paper in the office. Also written on there is the name of a guy I know over there in L.A. You need help with anything – tracing the number, anything – you call him and bring him in. There will be no official record with him. He's good people and has a lot of connections he'd be happy to share.'

'All right, Vincent.'

'Now you go grab a plane and you'll be on the ground by three at the latest and –'

'I'm not flying, Vincent. I never fly.'

'Jack, time is of the essence here.'

'Then have your guy in L.A. handle it. I'm driving. I'll be there before five.'

'All right, fine. You drive. Maybe you could make another stop in the desert for me. You know, along the way.'

Karch just looked at him.

'I've still got fat boy and Martin in a laundry basket on the loading dock.'

'It's just sitting down there?'

'I've got Longo down there watching it. Nobody'll get near it.'

Karch shook his head.

'Then have Long-*O* and Romer-*O* take care of it. I'm out of here, Vincent.'

Grimaldi pointed a finger at him.

'All right, Jack, but I want to be kept informed this time. You understand me?'

'Perfectly.'

'Then go get the money, Jack.'

Before heading in from the crow's nest Karch took one last look across the casino. He liked the view from up here. He nodded to himself and walked to the glass door.

26

Cassie Black punched the buzzer on Leo Renfro's door at noon and almost doubled over when the simple action sent a charge of pain up through her sore arm. When Leo opened the door she pushed in past him with the briefcase. He checked the street and then turned back to her as he closed the door. He was holding a gun down at his side. She spoke before he could say a word, and before she saw the gun.

'We've got a big problem, Leo. This thing was – why do you have that out?'

'Not here. Don't talk at the front door. Come back to the office.'

'What, more feng shui bullshit?'

'No, John Gotti. Who the fuck cares? Come on.'

He led her through the house once more to the rear office. He was wearing a white bathrobe and his hair was wet. Cassie assumed he had been swimming laps – which was late for him, unless he needed to do it to relieve stress.

They stepped into the office and Cassie lifted the case with her right arm and banged it down on top of the desk.

'Jesus Christ! Take it easy, would you? I've been going nuts here. Where the fuck you been?'

'Flat on my ass on the living room floor.'

She pointed to the briefcase.

'The fucking thing tried to electrocute me.'

'What?'

'Built-in stun gun. I tried to open it and it was like getting hit by a bolt of lightning. It knocked me out cold, Leo. Three hours. Look at this.'

She leaned forward and used both hands to spread the hair on the top of her scalp apart. There was a surface cut and a swollen bump that looked painful.

'I hit the corner of the table when I went down. I think that knocked me out more than the bolt.'

Leo's look of anger over her lack of communication was immediately replaced with a sincere look of surprise and concern.

'Jesus, you sure you're all right? You better get that checked.'

'I feel like I have that baseball guy Nolan O'Brien's arm.'

'Ryan.'

'Whatever. It feels like it's dead. My elbow joint hurts worse than my head.'

'You've been lying on the floor of your house all this time?'

'Just about. I got blood on my carpet.'

'Jesus. I thought you were dead. I've been going nuts here. I called Vegas and you know what I was told? My guy said something's screwy over there.'

'What are you talking about?'

'The guy disappeared. The mark. It's like he was never there. He's not in the room and his name's off the computer. No record of him at all.'

'Yeah? Well, that's not the worst of it. Take a look.'

She reached for the briefcase's latches but Leo quickly reached for her arms to stop her.

'No, no, don't!'

She shrugged him off.

'It's okay, Leo. I got some heavy-duty rubber gloves – like the ones the guys who work on the power lines use. It took me almost an hour to work the picks with the gloves but then I got it open. I disconnected the battery. The case is safe but not what's in it. Look at this.'

She unlatched the case and opened it. It was lined side to side with stacks of hundred-dollar bills bundled in cellophane and marked with a '50' in thick black ink. She watched as Leo's mouth dropped open and then a look of dismay crossed his face. They both knew that seeing a case full of cash of high denomination was not immediate cause for celebration. It was not the pot of gold at the end of every thief's rainbow. Rather, it was cause for concern and suspicion. Like a trial attorney who never asks a question of a witness that he doesn't already know the answer to, professional thieves never steal blind, taking something they do not know the consequences for stealing. Legal consequences are not the issue. The concern is over consequences of a more serious kind.

It was a good ten seconds before Leo managed to speak.

'Fuck . . .'

'Yeah . . .'

'Fuck . . .'

'I know . . .'

'You count this?'

Cassie nodded.

'I counted the bricks. There are fifty of them. If that fifty on each one means what it looks like it means, then you're looking at two and a half million in cash. He didn't win this money, Leo. He *came* to Vegas with it.'

'Hold on, hold on a minute. Let's think about this for a minute.'

Cassie started unconsciously massaging her sore elbow.

'What is there to think about? They don't pay you at the cashier's cage in fifty-thousand-dollar bricks wrapped in plastic. He didn't win this money in Vegas. Period, Leo. He brought it with him. It's a payoff of some kind. Maybe drugs. Maybe something else. But we took it – I took it – before it was delivered. I mean this guy, the mark, he was just an errand boy. He didn't even have a key to the case on him. He was just going to deliver it and probably didn't even know what was in it himself.'

'He didn't have a key?'

'Leo, have you heard anything I've said? I got knocked on my ass trying to open this with picks. Would I do that if I had the guy's key?'

'Sorry, sorry, I forgot, okay?'

'I took the guy's keys. He had a key that opened the cuffs but none to the briefcase.'

Leo dropped into his chair as Cassie put her backpack on the desk and started digging through it. She took out four rubber-banded stacks of hundreds and put them down.

'This is what he won. A hundred and a quarter. And half of the info you got from the spotter or your partners was for shit.'

She snaked her hand back into the bag. She brought out the wallet she had taken off the bed table in room 2014 and tossed it to him.

'Guy's name isn't Hernandez and he isn't from Texas.'

Leo opened the wallet and looked at the Florida driver's license behind the plastic window.

'Manuel Hidalgo,' he said. 'Miami.'

'He's got business cards in there. He's a lawyer for something called the Buena Suerte Group.'

Leo shook his head in the negative but he did it too quickly. More like he was trying to shake the information off than deny knowledge of it. Cassie didn't say anything at first. She put her palms flat on the desk and leaned down, looking at him with a face that said she saw the move and wanted to know what he knew. Leo glanced out at his pool and Cassie followed his eyes. She could see the hose of the automatic vacuum moving slowly on the surface, the vacuum somewhere down below.

He looked back at her.

'I didn't know a fucking thing about this, Cass, I swear.'

'I believe you about the money, Leo. What about Buena Suerte? Tell me what you know.'

'It's big money. Cubans from Miami.'

'Legit money?'

Leo hiked his shoulders in a gesture that suggested the answer could go either way.

'They're trying to buy the Cleo,' he said.

Cassie dropped heavily into the chair opposite Leo.

'It was a payoff on the license. I stole a fucking payoff.'

'Let's just think about this.'

'You keep saying that, Leo.'

She laid her injured arm across her body.

'Well, what else are we going to do? We have to think this out.'

'Who were these people you did this for? You wouldn't tell me before. But you have to tell me now.'

Leo nodded but then stood up. He went to the sliding door and opened it, then moved out by the pool. He stood at the edge and looked down at the vacuum gliding silently along the bottom. Cassie came up behind him. As he spoke he never took his eyes off the water.

'They're from Vegas by way of Chicago.'

'Chicago. You mean the Outfit, Leo?'

Leo didn't answer but in his silence was the answer.

'How the hell did you get involved with the Outfit, Leo? Tell me.'

Leo started walking along the edge of the pool, his hands deep in the pockets of his robe.

'Look, first of all, I'm smart enough to know not to intentionally get involved with the Outfit, okay? Give me a little fucking credit, okay? I didn't have a choice in the matter.'

'Okay, Leo, I understand. Tell me the story.'

'It started about a year ago. I met these guys. I was at Santa Anita and saw Carl Lennertz over there, you remember him, right?'

Cassie nodded. Lennertz was a scout, always had an eye out for what he called a good book – a score. He sold tips to Leo, usually collecting a flat fee or ten percent of the gross taken out of Leo's end. Cassie had met him once or twice with Leo and Max several years before.

'Well, he was with these two guys and he made the introductions. They were just two guys who hung around the track and were looking to back a move here and there. They said they were venture capitalists.'

'And you just took them at their word.'

A truck with a bad muffler system roared by on the nearby freeway and Leo didn't answer the question until the noise had abated.

'I had no reason to doubt them and they were with Carl and he's good people. Besides, at the time things were drying up and I was scratching bottom. I needed setup money and here were these two guys. So I set up a meeting for later and we got together and I asked them to, you know, back me up on a couple things I had on my desk. They said sure, no problem.'

He stepped to the side of the pool where a surface net at the end of a ten-foot pole was hooked to a fence. He took it down and used it to skim a dead hummingbird out of the pool.

'Poor things, I don't think they can see water or something. They dive right in. This is the third one this week.'

He shook his head.

'Dead hummingbirds are bad luck, you know.'

He flicked the dead bird over the fence into a neighbor's yard. Cassie wondered if maybe the three dead hummingbirds were really just the same one that the neighbor kept throwing back over the fence and into the pool. She didn't say anything. She wanted Leo to get back to the story.

Leo hooked the net back in place on the fence and came back around to Cassie.

'So that's how it started. I took sixty-five bones off them against a hundred when the jobs were paid out. I was thinking six weeks tops. One was diamonds and that's always quick. And the other was a warehouse – Italian furniture. I had somebody lined up in Pennsylvania on that and was probably looking at six weeks tops on the turnaround. My end was going to be about two and I'd owe these guys one. Not bad. Most of the money I needed from them was for the data. The people I was working with had their own equipment.'

He was wandering, telling too many details about the plans and not what happened.

'You can skip all of this, Leo. Just read me the last page.'

'The last page is that both jobs went to shit. The data on the diamonds was bullshit. A rip-off. I paid forty for it and the guy disappeared. And then the furniture turned out to have been made down in Mexicali. It was counterfeit designer stuff and the made-in-Italy tags were as bogus as most of the tits you see in this town. I didn't know it till I got the truck all the way to Philadelphia and my buyer took a look. Shit, what a fucking mess. I just had them abandon the truck on the side of a road in Trenton.'

He paused as if trying to remember some other detail, then waved a hand in a resigned, dismissive gesture.

'And so that was it. I owed these guys a hundred grand and I didn't have it. I explained the situation to them and they were about as sympathetic as a night-court judge to a hooker. But when it was all said and done I thought I had bought some time. Only they just said that and turned right around and sold my fucking paper to another party.'

Cassie nodded. She could finish the story herself now.

'These two new guys come around and say they represent the new holder of the paper now,' Leo said. 'They make it real clear that the new holder is the Outfit without actually having to say it. Know what I mean? They tell me that we have to work out a payment schedule. I ended up paying two grand a week just on the interest. Just to stay afloat. It was killing me. I still owed the hundred but I was never going to get out from under. Never. Until one day they show up with a proposition.'

'What was it?'

'They told me about this job.'

He pointed through the open slider at the briefcase sitting on the desk inside.

'They told me to set it up with their guy in Vegas and that if I did it, then they'd burn my paper and still give me a cut on the caper.'

Leo shook his head. He walked over to the table and chairs near the shallow end and sat down. He reached over to a hand crank on the umbrella pole. He started turning it and the umbrella opened like a flower. Cassie came over and sat down. She cupped her left elbow in her right hand.

'So they obviously knew what was in the case,' she said.

'Maybe.'

'No maybes. They knew. Otherwise, they wouldn't have been so fucking magnanimous with you. When are they coming for it?'

'I don't know. I'm waiting on a call.'

'Did they give you a name?'

'What do you mean?'

'A name, Leo. Whoever bought your paper.'

'Yeah, Turcello. Same name that was on the package at the desk for you.

He's supposedly the guy who picked up the pieces after Joey Marks went down.'

Cassie looked away. She didn't know the name Turcello but she knew who Joey Marks had been. He had been the Outfit's brutal point man in Las Vegas – one in a long line of vicious enforcers. His real name was Joseph Marconi but he was universally known as Joey Marks because of the keepsakes he left on those of his victims he allowed to live. Cassie remembered how she and Max had spent a year living in fear of Marks, who wanted a piece of their action. After she was in High Desert she picked up a newspaper one day and read about how Marks had been killed in his limousine during a bizarre shoot-out with the FBI and police in a bank parking lot in Las Vegas. She had celebrated after reading the story – which in prison amounted to sipping a paper cup of applejack she'd bought with a pack of cigarettes.

She didn't know who Marconi's replacement, Turcello, was but she assumed he had to be just as viciously psychopathic as Marks had been in order to be named to the position.

'And now you've got me in the box with you and these people,' Cassie said. 'Thanks, Leo. Thanks for –'

'No, you're wrong. I protected you. They don't even know about you. I took the job and set it up. Like I told you before, nobody knows everybody in the caper. They don't know you and they never will.'

Leo's promise was not reassuring. Cassie could no longer sit down while it seemed her life was passing in front of her. She got up and walked to the pool's edge and looked down into the calm, clear water. Her left arm hung at her side like a dead weight.

'What are we going to do, Leo? If I have this right, the Chicago mob used us to steal a payoff these Cubans from Miami were making to a third party on the buyout of the Cleo. We're sitting in the middle of what's going to be a war. Do you see that? What do we do?'

Leo got up and came to her. He pulled her into a tight hug and spoke calmly.

'Nobody knows about you. I promise you. Nobody knows about you and nobody ever will. You don't have to worry.'

She pulled away from him.

'Of course, I do, Leo. Come back to reality, would you?'

The tone of her voice silenced Leo. He raised and dropped his hands in a gesture of surrender. He started banging a tight fist against his lips. Cassie paced along the side of the pool. After a long minute she spoke again.

'What do you know about Buena Suerte?'

'Like I said, nothing. But I'll make some calls about it.'

After another long silence, Leo shook his shoulders.

'Maybe we just give the money back and say it was a mistake,' he said. 'We find a go-between who will –'

'Then we have Chicago after us, Leo. This Turcello person. Think, would you? We can't do that.'

'I'll tell them that when you went into the room last night the briefcase wasn't there.'

'I'm sure they're going to believe that. Especially, since the mark has suddenly disappeared.'

Leo flopped back into his seat under the umbrella. A defeated look was overtaking his face. There was a long period of silence while neither looked at each other.

'Sometimes you can steal too much,' Cassie said, more to herself than Leo.

'What?'

'Max used to say that sometimes you can steal too much. We just did.'

Leo pondered the statement in silence. Cassie folded her arms across her chest. When she spoke her voice was resolute and strong. She now looked directly at Leo.

'Let's take the money. All of it. We split it and we run, Leo. One point three and change each. It's more than enough. Fuck Chicago and Miami. We take it all and run.'

Leo was shaking his head before she was finished speaking.

'No way.'

'Leo . . .'

'No fucking way. You think you can run from these people? Where are you going to run? Name a place where it's worth living and they can't find you. No place, that's where. They will hunt you down to the end of the fucking earth just to prove the point. Bring your hands back to Chicago or Miami in a shoe box and put 'em on display at the wise guys' Sunday buffet.'

'I'll take my chances. I've got nothing to lose.'

'Well, I *DO!* I'm set up here. I am dug in and the last thing I want is to spend the rest of my life changing my name every month and holding my Glock behind my back every time I open a fucking door.'

Cassie came over to the table and crouched next to Leo's chair. She held the plastic armrest with both hands and looked up into his eyes but he quickly looked away.

'No, Cass, I can't.'

'Leo, you can take two million and I'll take the rest. It's still more than I'll need. Two days ago I was thinking I'd be lucky to get a couple hundred out of this. You take the two. It's enough for you to –'

He got up and walked away from her. He went back to the edge of the pool. Cassie leaned her forehead against the armrest. She knew she wasn't going to convince him.

'It's not the *money*,' Leo said. 'Aren't you listening to what I'm telling you? It doesn't matter if it's one million or two million. What's the difference if you aren't around to spend it? Let me tell you, there was a guy a few years back. They tracked him all the way to Juneau-fucking-Alaska. Went up there, gutted him like a salmon from the river. I think every couple years they have to make an example. To keep everybody else in line. I don't want to be an example.'

Still crouched like a hiding child, Cassie turned and looked at his back.

'Then what do you want to do? Wait until someone comes *here* and guts you? How is that different from running? At least if we run we have a chance.'

Leo looked down into the pool. The vacuum moved silently along the bottom.

'Fuck . . .' he said.

Something in his tone made Cassie look expectantly at him. She began to think maybe she had convinced him. She waited him out.

'Two days,' he finally said, still looking down into the pool. 'Give me forty-eight hours to see what I can do. I know some people in Miami. Let me make some calls, see what I can find out. And I'll check on things in Vegas and Chicago. Maybe I can talk our way out of this. Yeah, maybe make a deal and even keep a piece of this for ourselves.'

He was nodding to himself, getting himself ready for the biggest negotiation of his life – of their lives. He couldn't see Cassie shaking her head. She didn't believe they had a chance his way. But she stood up and came to his side.

'Leo, you have to understand something. Turcello isn't going to give you a cut of what's in the briefcase. He never was. You call his people and tell him you have it and you'll be saying, "Here I am, guys, come get me." You'll be this year's salmon.'

'No! I tell you I can get us out. I can negotiate with these people. Remember, it's all about money. As long as everybody gets something, we can get out.'

Cassie knew she wasn't going to convince him. She was resigned.

'Okay, Leo, two days. And that's all. After that we cut it up and we go. We take our chances.'

He nodded his agreement.

'Call me tonight. I might know something. Otherwise, do what you do. I can only reach you at the dealership?'

She gave him her cell phone number, telling him not to write it in his book.

'I'm going, Leo. What do we do with the money?'

'The usual. It's still the perfect spot.'

Cassie hesitated. She knew it was best for him to hold the money, but parting with it gave her pause. Then she remembered something that had completely slipped her mind amid the recent developments.

'Hey, did you get my passports?'

'All I can tell you is that I got word they're on their way. I'll check the drop again tonight. If they're not there tonight, they will be tomorrow. Guarantee it.'

'Thanks, Leo.'

Leo nodded. Cassie turned toward the sliding door.

'Wait a minute,' Leo said. 'Let me ask you something, what time was it when you went in the room?'

'What?'

'What time was it when you went in the guy's room last night? You must've looked at your watch.'

She looked at him. She knew what he wanted to know.

'It was five after three.'

'And what, it took five, ten minutes tops to do the job, right?'

'Normally.'

'Normally?'

'He got a phone call, Leo. I was in the closet with the safe. The phone rang and he talked to somebody. I think it was about the payoff. He was going to make it today. Then after he hung up he got up and went into the bathroom.'

'And you snuck out.'

'No. I stayed in the closet.'

'How long?'

'Until he was asleep again. Until I heard him snore. I had to, Leo. It wasn't safe. You weren't there. I couldn't leave until –'

'You went into the void moon, didn't you?'

'It couldn't be helped, Leo, that's what I'm trying to –'

'Oh, Jesus Christ!'

'Leo . . .'

'I told you. I only asked you to do one thing.'

'It couldn't be helped. He got the call – a phone call at three in the morning, Leo. It was just bad luck.'

Leo shook his head as if not listening.

'That's it then,' he said. 'We . . .'

He didn't finish. She closed her eyes.

'I'm sorry, Leo. I really am.'

A buzzing sound near her left ear caught her attention. She looked around and saw a hummingbird suspended in air, its wings a blur.

It darted to the left and then swooped over to the pool, dropping to just a foot above the surface of the calm water. It seemed to be looking down at its reflection on the surface. It then dropped lower until it hit the surface. Its wings fluttered wildly but they were too heavy now for flight. The bird was trapped in the water.

'See what I'm saying,' Leo said. 'Dumb birds.'

He started around the pool to get to the net so he could try to save the tiny creature's life.

27

Just before getting to Los Angeles, Jack Karch pulled off the 10 Freeway at the Ontario airport exit and followed the signs to the long-term parking lot. He cruised up and down five long lanes of parked cars before he came upon a Towncar that was the same make and model as his, and with California plates. He double-parked behind the car and left the engine running while he got out with the battery-powered drill that was among the tools recovered by Grimaldi's thug from the air vent in room 2015.

The drill worked beautifully. Karch had the plates off the front and back of the Towncar in less than a minute. He shoved them under the front seat of his own car and drove toward the exit. He had been in the parking lot so briefly that the cashier at the pay booth told him he had made it under the ten-minute grace period and didn't have to pay a thing. He asked Karch if he had a spare smoke and Karch was happy to oblige.

He had made good time from Vegas, traveling at a steady 100 mph until he hit traffic close to L.A. The last fifty miles took him a frustrating hour to cover. He decided that people in Los Angeles drove the way people walk through casinos: oblivious to the fact that somebody else might be on the road and need to get somewhere. In downtown he branched off the 10 to the 101 and headed northwest toward the San Fernando Valley. Though it had been at least a couple years since the last time, Karch had been to L.A. plenty times enough to know how to get around. When it got down to specific streets and places, he had a Thomas Brothers map book in his briefcase on the seat next to him. It was a few years old but it would do. He was headed to the Valley because the cell phone number Grimaldi had retrieved from Martin as being the contact number for Leo Renfro had an 818 area code and Karch knew that covered the Valley, the city's northern suburban sprawl. It was his assumption that Leo would be found in the confines of his cell phone's area code.

He got off the freeway at the Ventura Boulevard exit and drove until he saw a gas station with a pay phone. He opened his briefcase on the passenger seat and withdrew the folded piece of Cleopatra Resort stationery with the name *Leo Renfro* and the cell phone number written on it. Below the fold was the name of the contact Grimaldi had in L.A. but Karch had no intention of calling the man. Under no circumstances did he plan to allow a perfect stranger – no matter who vouched for him – to have knowledge of his business and activities. That would just be stupid and he wasn't about to turn stupid. The same reasoning prevented Karch from using his law enforcement contacts to run traces on Leo Renfro and Cassie Black. This job had to be done without leaving a trail.

Surprisingly, the pay phone had an intact phone book. Karch pulled it up and started with the white pages on the unlikely chance that Leo Renfro was actually listed. He wasn't. Karch then turned through the commercial business pages until he came to the advertisements for cell phone service providers. Judging by the size and quality of their advertisements, he made a list of the bigger companies and their service numbers. He then used the edge of the shelf under the phone to crack open a roll of quarters he had bought at the change cage at the Cleo and made his first call.

The call was answered by a machine that offered a variety of pathway selections. Karch chose what he wanted and was transferred to billing inquiries, where he was put on hold for two minutes before a human voice picked up.

'Thank you for calling L.A. Cellular, how can I help you?'

'Yes,' Karch said. 'I've been called out of town indefinitely and I want to cancel service on my cell phone account.'

After listening to a sales pitch for out-of-the-area service, the phone representative got down to business.

'Name?'

'Leo Renfro.'

'Account number?'

'I don't have that handy at –'

'Cell phone number?'

'Oh, okay.'

Karch glanced down at the paper and read off the number Martin had provided during his interrogation by Grimaldi.

'One moment, please.'

'Take your time.'

Karch heard the sound of typing on the other end of the line.

'I'm sorry, sir, I'm not showing an account with that name or –'

Karch hung up and immediately dialed the number of the next company on the list. He repeated the story over and over and finally hit the right company on the seventh call. Renfro had his account with a company called SoCal Cellular. When the service operator pulled up the account information on her computer, Karch immediately went in for the final con.

'I'm going to need you to send the final bill to my new address in Phoenix, if you don't mind.'

'Not at all, sir. Let me first set up the close-out screen.'

'Oh, sorry.'

'No problem. It will just take me a second.'

'Take your time.'

Karch let a few seconds go by and then started in again.

'You know, I just realized I'll be back in L.A. at the end of next week for a few days to clear up some things. I may need the phone then. Maybe I should wait and do this after.'

'It's up to you, sir.'

'Uh . . . tell you what, let's wait, then.'

'Okay, sir. Do you want to wait on the address change, too?'

Karch smiled. It always worked best when the victim prompted the con.

'No, let's do – tell you what, maybe I should wait. My mail's being forwarded from my old place anyway. But wait a minute, I forget offhand, which address does the bill go to? My home or office?'

'I don't know, sir. Four thousand Warner Boulevard, number five-twenty. Which is that?'

Karch didn't answer. He was writing the address down on the letterhead.

'Sir?'

'That's the office. So everything is fine. Let's leave it as is and I'll take care of it after next week.'

'Okay. Thank you for calling SoCal Cellular.'

He hung up the phone and went back to the car. He looked up the address in the index of the map book and learned he had been correct. The address was in the 818 area code. But it wasn't Los Angeles. It was Burbank. He started the Lincoln and checked the digital clock on the dash. It was exactly five o'clock. Not bad, he thought. He was getting close.

Fifteen minutes later the Lincoln was at the curb in front of a private mail drop and packaging shop at 4000 Warner Boulevard. He was not too disappointed. It would have been too easy and suspicious if the address he'd conned out of SoCal Cellular had led directly to Leo Renfro's front door.

He checked the business hours marked on the door. The shop closed in forty-five minutes but another sign on the door announced that clients had twenty-four-hour access to their boxes. Karch thought for a while about what to do and decided that Renfro was the type who probably checked his box after hours anyway to avoid becoming familiar to the people who ran the shop. It was in that thought that a plan suddenly sparked in his mind.

Karch entered the shop and saw that it was shaped like an L, with the counter at the end of one branch and the other branch lined with postal boxes. To the left of the door was a counter with a stapler, a tape dispenser and several plastic cups with pens and paper clips and rubber bands in them. Karch saw a man working on something on the floor behind the counter. Above him was a roll-down security fence that allowed for the business side of the shop to be closed and locked while still allowing customers with a key to the front door access to their mailboxes twenty-four hours a day.

Karch glanced to his left and noticed that the postal boxes were the kind with little windows through which holders could just glance in to see if they had mail. He walked into the box alcove and quickly found number 520. He had to bend down to look into it. He could see one envelope lying flat at the bottom of it. He glanced back to the right. There was a mirror positioned in the upper corner over the door that allowed the counterman to see into the mailbox alcove but he was still down behind the counter working on something.

Karch pulled a small penlight from his shirt pocket and turned it on. It lit up the interior of box 520 and he could read the writing on the front of the envelope. It was addressed to Leo Renfro. There was no return address on the upper left corner but there was a set of initials. He leaned closer to the glass to try to read them and realized they were numbers: 773.

Because there was already a piece of mail in the box, Karch thought for a moment about whether he needed to proceed with his plan. He decided to go ahead. His plan, if it worked, would still have the aspect of confusing the target, knocking him for a bit of a loop.

Karch walked around the corner to the counter. Behind it there was a man in his early twenties who was dumping little Styrofoam balls into a large box on the floor behind the counter. He spoke without looking up from his work.

'What can I do for you?'

This sort of impersonal service always annoyed Karch. He saw it all the time in Las Vegas but this time he was pleased because he didn't want the clerk to pay much attention to him.

'I need an envelope.'

'What size?'

'Doesn't matter. Normal size.'

'Number ten?'

The clerk left the box he was filling and walked to the wall at the rear of the service counter area. There were several boxes and envelopes of varying sizes mounted on the wall. Below them was the inventory arranged on shelves according to size. Karch scanned the envelopes and saw the number 10 size.

'Yeah, ten is fine.'

'Padded, unpadded?'

'Uh, padded.'

The clerk grabbed one off the shelf and came to the counter announcing in a high, whiny voice that Karch owed fifty-two cents including tax. Karch paid with exact change.

'Nice hat,' the clerk said.

'Thanks.'

Karch took the envelope to the counter by the door. It occurred to him that the clerk might actually have been making fun of his hat, but he let it go.

With his back shielding the clerk from viewing what he was doing, Karch reached into the pocket of his suit coat and took out the envelope containing the ace of hearts playing card he had found on the floor while searching room 2015 at the Cleo. He took the card out and slid it into the envelope he had just bought, then stapled it closed.

Using the thickest Magic Marker he could find in the plastic cups, he addressed the envelope to Leo Renfro and put down the postal box address and number. In large letters he then wrote DO NOT DELAY! and URGENT! on both sides. On the lines provided for a return address he wrote 773 and on the back he wrote Leo Renfro's cell phone number.

He went back to the service counter and saw the clerk was now taping shut the box on the floor. Again he did not look up. This time he didn't even ask what was wanted. Karch could see the name tag pinned to his shirt said STEPHEN.

'Excuse me, Steve, do you mind putting this into the proper box for me?'

The young man sullenly put down the tape and walked over to the counter. He took the proffered envelope and looked at it as though there was some question as to whether he could accomplish the request.

'I need it to go in there now because this guy always checks his box first thing in the morning.'

The kid finally decided he could handle the assignment and headed behind a partition that apparently led to the mail room.

'And it's *Stephen*,' he called back out to Karch.

Karch stepped away from the counter and went around the corner and down to box 520. He watched through the little glass window as the envelope he had just given the clerk was shoved into the box on top of the other piece of mail waiting for Leo Renfro.

Karch had left the shop before the clerk made his return to the counter. As he walked to his car, he said out loud, 'That'll be fifty-two cents . . . and it's Stephen.'

Once inside the Lincoln he said it again and again, working on the pitch and getting an approximation of the right sullen tone and whine into it. When he had it down close enough he started the car and pulled away from the curb.

To make the call he couldn't use an open pay phone with background traffic noise. He drove around Burbank for ten minutes looking for the proper venue. He finally spotted a restaurant called Bob's Big Boy and parked in the rear lot, backing into a slot next to a Dumpster.

Inside the restaurant he found a pay phone in the alcove leading to the rest rooms. He dropped in coins and called Leo Renfro's cell number. He realized the chance he was taking. Renfro's mailbox was a blind drop. Though it obviously was in his name, there was no way for Karch to know whether the operators of the shop would have Renfro's cell phone number. But his plan had a built-in contingency for that.

The phone at the other end of the line was picked up after two rings but no one said anything.

'Hello?' Karch finally said, his voice the best approximation of a high whine.

'Who's this?'

'Mr Renfro? This is Stephen at Warner Post and Pack It.'

'How'd you get this number?'

'It's on the envelope.'

'What envelope?'

Karch concentrated on his voice.

'That's what I am calling about. You got an envelope today. It's marked urgent and says do not delay. Your phone number is on it. I don't know, I thought I'd call you. We're closing up and since you didn't come in, I thought I should call you in case, you know, you were expecting some –'

'Is there a return address?'

'Yeah – I mean, no. All it says there is seven-seven-three.'

'Okay. Thank you. But do me a favor, don't ever call here again.'

Renfro abruptly hung up. Karch kept the phone to his ear as if giving Renfro the chance to get back on and ask more questions. Finally, he hung up. He thought it had worked. He felt confident. His impression of Renfro from the conversation was that he was a cagey guy. That meant it could be a long night ahead.

Back in the restaurant he went to the counter and ordered two hamburgers well done with ketchup on the side and two black coffees to go. While the order was being prepared he walked out to the parking lot. He got the stolen license plates out of his car and replaced the rear tag of his car with one. The Dumpster provided cover while he worked. He then got in the car, pulled out of the parking slot and pulled right back in forward.

He changed the front plate. Cassie Black's drill made the job a breeze. He decided he was going to keep the drill when the job was finished. The drill and a few other things.

28

One more dread added to an already dreadful day. Cassie sat in the Boxster, the engine idling, at the curb across the street from the house on Lookout Mountain Road. The family had left the curtain behind the big picture window open. She could see in through the living room to the lighted kitchen where the three of them sat at the table eating. She couldn't see it from this angle but Cassie remembered from the open house that the chair where the girl now sat had a phone book on it. She probably thought of herself as too old for a booster chair, yet she needed the extra inches.

She looked away from the window to the sign. A short strip of painted wood had been hooked to the bottom of the realty sign below the name of the Realtor.

IN ESCROW

Cassie had never bought a house before but knew that the new sign meant an offer had been accepted. The place was being sold and the family would move soon. She gripped the wheel tightly. It made her elbow and shoulder throb. She thought about Leo's plan to give the money back. She knew there might not be time for another job – and no job would have the kind of money that had been in that briefcase. She found herself hoping Leo would fail in his efforts. She couldn't help it. She wanted the money now. She wanted to run.

Her cell phone rang. She dug it out of her backpack and answered. It was Leo but he didn't say his name. The connection was horrible. She was surprised he had gotten through to her in the hills at all.

'How you feeling?' he asked.

'The same.'

'Well, you know those . . . you were waiting on? I just got a call. It looks like . . . and I'll pick them up tonight.'

She heard enough to be able to fill in the blanks.

'Good. But they won't do me any good if I don't have the money.'

'. . . ill working on that. I'm reaching . . . Maybe tomorrow I'll know something. One way or anoth –'

'What am I supposed to do in the meantime?'

'I didn't get that.'

'What am I supposed to do in the meantime?' she asked loudly, as if the force of her voice could improve the fragile connection.

'We talked about this, Cass. You go to wor ... your thing. Everything normal until we get this figured ...'

'Whatever. This connection sucks. I want to go.'

She sounded sullen and she didn't care.

'Look, sweetheart, we're almost there. I'm just waiting on –'

'I don't want to give it back, Leo. We're making a mistake. *You* are making a mistake. I have a really bad feeling about this. We need to go. Just *go*. Now!'

Leo was silent for a long time. He didn't even bother reminding her not to say his name. She was thinking that she had lost the connection when he finally spoke.

'Cassie, look,' he said in an overly calm voice. 'I'm getting ... ibes, too. More than I usually get. But we have to ... and cover all the bases. It's the only way to be ...'

Cassie shook her head and glanced over at the realty sign once more.

'Sure, Leo. Whatever you say. Just be sure to call me and let me know when you figure out what to do with my life.'

She flipped the phone closed and turned it off in case Leo tried to call back. As she did it she had a sudden idea of creeping into Leo's house while he slept and getting to the money. She would take only her share, leaving the rest for Leo to do whatever he wanted with. As angry as she was with Leo, the idea filled her with guilt. She pushed the thought aside and looked back at the house.

She saw the husband standing up at the table and looking through the length of the house and out to the street. At her. She saw him put his napkin down and start coming around the table. He was going to come out to her, to see what she was doing in front of his house. She quickly dropped the Boxster into gear and drove off.

29

'Summer Wind' was the song. It always got to Karch. Every time it came up on the *Sinatra's Greatest Hits* CD he had to hit replay and hear it again. They were all good but none could touch 'Summer Wind.' It was the class of the class. Just like Sinatra.

Karch was on the fourth run-through of the CD, watching the front of Warner Post & Pack It from the crowded parking lot of a bar called Presnick's a half block away. It was exactly eleven o'clock when he noticed the brake lights flare on a car going by the shop. It was a black Jeep Cherokee about five years old. It was the second time it had gone slowly by the store. Karch turned the CD down and got ready. He was already wearing his black jumpsuit, though for a different reason this time. The sleeves were decorated with varying lengths of heavy-duty duct tape that he had cut in preparation. He reached into his open briefcase and removed the remote global positioning system receiver along with the cellular link box and antenna as well as the GPS antenna from the foam cushioning. He got the tools he would need ready and got out of the Lincoln after popping the trunk. From the trunk he took the Rollerboy Mechanics Helper – a cushioned creeper board on one-inch wheels – then locked the car and walked quickly across Warner Boulevard.

Warner Post & Pack It was a one-story stand-alone building in a long line of stand-alone buildings, all of which were built to the property line, leaving anywhere from one to three feet of space between buildings. Karch slipped into the opening one storefront down from the mailbox business. It was about twenty inches wide and had primarily been used over time as a trash disposal point by pedestrians. Karch found himself almost knee high in debris – mostly bottles and crumpled bags of fast food. There was also the overpowering smell of urine in the cramped space. His entry into this dark crevice caused some unseen creature to loudly scramble through the debris and go back farther into the darkness.

Karch hung back about three feet from the opening, out of the direct light from the street, and waited. He was sure the Cherokee would come back and that it would be Leo Renfro driving. What Karch had to do next he had done many times before on other cases. But never as fast as he would have to do it this time. He figured he would have less than a minute to complete the installation. There could be no delays or mistakes.

The sound of an approaching car filtered into the hideaway. Karch crouched down and held the Rollerboy up as a shield. Even if Renfro was looking between the buildings, it was unlikely that he would notice Karch unless he completely stopped and shined a light into the darkness.

The car went by slowly and then Karch heard it stop in front of the mail drop business. He slowly moved toward the edge of the building he was leaning against. He glanced around the corner and saw it was indeed the Cherokee, sitting at the curb, still running and with its lights on. Karch pulled himself back into the crevice and waited. He knew he could step out and take Renfro right at that moment. But it was too risky to undertake out in the open and, more important, Renfro wasn't the goal. The money was the priority. To achieve that he needed to follow Renfro to his home, to the place he felt safest. It was there that Karch knew he would find either the money or a line to Cassidy Black.

The Cherokee's engine cut off. Karch braced himself against the wall, ready to move. He felt the hard points of the stucco digging into his back. He bent forward to listen and heard the car's door open and then close. He heard steps moving quickly on the asphalt. He moved forward and looked once more around the corner. He saw a man in his mid forties and of trim build working a key into the front door of Warner Post & Pack It.

Once he had the door open the man looked up the street to the left and then back to the right. Karch ducked behind the corner. When he heard the door close he stepped out and crossed the sidewalk to the Cherokee. Crouching behind the car, he watched through the front window of the business as the man approached the wall of postal boxes. When he bent down in the area where box 520 was located, Karch knew he had his man. It was Leo Renfro.

Karch turned his penlight on and put it in his mouth. He then put the Rollerboy down and lay down on it face up. He grabbed the underside of the bumper and pulled himself completely under the car. He had done an installation on a Cherokee once before and was not anticipating a problem. It was tight quarters and hot; his chest rubbed the greasy undercarriage at several points and he had to keep his face turned to the side to avoid scraping it or even getting it burned on the hot pipes of the exhaust system.

He reached to his legs and removed the satellite receiver and CelluLink transmitter from the right cargo pocket of his jumpsuit. Both were small, square devices that had been lashed together with tape. A small stub antenna for the cellular connection was part of the bundle. The base of the receiver was a heavy-duty magnet. He reached up and attached the devices to the car's undercarriage frame directly below the driver's seat. Though the magnet appeared to hold firm, it was always Karch's practice to supplement to be sure. From his right arm he unwrapped two long pieces of duct tape and used them to lash the devices to the framework, further securing them to the underside of the car.

Using Cassie Black's silent drill he quickly attached the ground wire to the car's carriage pan, using a self-tapping screw. He then rolled to the curb and tried to look up and through the front window of the mail box business. But the angle was bad and he could not see Renfro or gauge how much more time he had.

He quickly pushed back to the middle and pulled down the electrical conduit that ran down the center of the carriage pan. Using an Exacto knife he slit open the plastic casing and quickly pulled out a bundle of wires. He combed through them until he found a red wire, the color indicating it was a full-time carrier of current from the battery to the rear of the car – most likely to a trunk light. The end of the power wire from the GPS receiver had a cut-in connector that he clipped to the red wire and then squeezed down on until he felt it cut through the rubber coating and into the live wire. He looked over at the receiver and saw the faint glow of the red power light beneath the duct tape.

He didn't have time to push the wires back into place. Instead he moved immediately to the last piece of the installation, the GPS antenna. He removed the small disk from his left cargo pocket and started unspooling the wire it was wrapped in. Just as he connected the wire to the receiver he heard the door to the shop open. He quickly turned the penlight around so that the lighted end was inside his mouth. He waited.

The door closed and Karch watched as Renfro's feet started moving around the car to the driver's door. Karch wanted to curse but knew he had to be silent. He continued unspooling the line from the antenna.

As Renfro opened the car door Karch used the sound as cover as he pushed himself down the length of the Cherokee. He was now directly below the rear bumper, the lower half of his body protruding from beneath the car. He reached the antenna up and wrapped the wire around the exhaust pipe just as the car started and he was hit with a blast of hot exhaust.

Karch stifled a cough and quickly brought the disk up and placed it on top of the bumper, where it would be in a direct line with the satellites above. He used the last piece of tape from his sleeve to tape the wire down and hold the antenna to the bumper.

It wasn't a finesse job but it would have to do, given the circumstances of the installation. He knew the GPS antenna would be spotted the first time Renfro looked at the back end of his car. But Karch was gambling that that wouldn't happen this night. What mattered was the next hour, maybe even less.

The Cherokee shuddered as it was put into drive. It started to move away from the curb. Karch let the bumper pass over his face and then quickly rolled off the Rollerboy and pressed himself to the curb. He kept his head down and listened for any hesitation in the Cherokee's engine. There was none. Renfro kept his foot on the gas and drove off. He never looked back. Or if he did, he was checking the road behind him, not the curb.

Karch finally looked up as the Cherokee receded from view. He smiled and got up.

As soon as Karch got to the Lincoln he took the laptop computer out of the briefcase, raised the antenna and booted up the QuikTrak software. With the receiver and the equipment he had just installed on Renfro's car, Karch would be able to track the Cherokee's movements with a global positioning system that took a signal transmitted from the car to a constellation of three satellites miles overhead and then back down. The satellites triangulated the precise location of the car and sent the data by cellular link to the cellular modem in Karch's computer. The QuikTrak software allowed him to follow the car's movements with real-time data displayed on street-level maps on the computer screen, or he could download historical data from the satellite that would show the car's entire movement over a selected time period.

Karch was first interested in making sure the installation had no flaws and he would be able to track the Cherokee by satellite. As a fallback he had committed the car's license plate number to memory and would be able to locate the car through the archaic means of a DMV trace in the morning, a move he hoped to avoid because it would leave an official trail of his activities.

He typed in the receiver code and frequency and waited. After what seemed like an interminable wait during which he could feel beads of sweat pop from his scalp, the lines of a map began to appear on the screen. After the street lines came the words *Los Angeles Region Map*. Then a pulsing red star appeared and began trailing a line. It was the Cherokee. The legend at the bottom of the screen gave the location.

RIVERSIDE DRIVE – WESTBOUND – 23:14:06

Karch smiled. He had him. The installation was successful. He would be able to follow a map right to the treasure. He hoped.

'Fucking A,' he said out loud.

He decided not to follow the Cherokee's real-time movements in his own car at the moment. He figured that it was likely that Leo Renfro had opened the padded envelope in the mail shop or in the car. Either way, the playing card he found inside would be both confusing and threatening. It was Karch's guess – based on Leo Renfro's two drive-bys before finally stopping at Warner Post & Pack It – that his target would take a circuitous route to his next destination in an effort to carefully identify and then lose any surveillance. He typed in a command creating a file for historical data collection beginning immediately. He then closed down the program and put the laptop back into the briefcase.

Just after pulling down the zipper on his jumpsuit and opening the window to get some air, Karch heard a woman's sharp scream from the other side of the parking lot. He turned toward the sound but didn't see anything. He opened the door and got out and looked around. He put a cigarette in his mouth and lit it. He was about to get back into the Lincoln when he heard another shout and saw movement on the other side of a BMW parked about ten slots away.

Karch wasn't wearing his holster with the Sig Sauer. He had taken it off and left it under the front seat before putting on the jumpsuit. Rather than get the weapon now, he peeled off the top half of the jumpsuit and reached behind his back to remove the little .25 from the magician's pocket in his pants. He then tied the arms of the jumpsuit around his waist and went to investigate the screams.

Palming the small black pistol as he casually walked down the row of cars, he got to the BMW and heard the sounds of crying. He saw a couple standing at the front of the car. A young man and woman. The man had the woman bent backward over the front hood. He was leaning on her and kissing her neck while her head constantly rolled back and forth as if trying to get away from the rest of her body.

'Everything all right there?' Karch called.

The man looked over at him.

'We're fine. Why don't you just piss off?'

Karch started moving down the side of the car. The man suddenly stepped away from the woman and turned to Karch. He stood arms and feet wide apart and waiting.

'Why don't you leave her alone?' Karch said. 'It doesn't sound like she –'

'Why don't you fuck yourself? She's fine. She just likes to yell, okay?'

'No, not okay. Maybe you just like to make her yell. Makes you feel like you're in control of things.'

The guy suddenly leaped forward in a charge that Karch was expecting. Like an experienced bullfighter he quickly sidestepped the charging beast and used his hands to redirect his opponent's momentum into the side of a mini-van. The man hit the side door of the van headfirst, causing a dent in the door panel. As he was straightening up and turning around, Karch moved in. He dropped the .25 into place in his hand and brought it up under his opponent's chin, driving the muzzle deep into the soft underside of the jaw.

'You feel that? Feels small, right? It's a twenty-five, just a pop gun really. Very unreliable unless you get in close like this. I cap one off like this, the slug will go right up into your brain and it won't be strong enough to get out. It'll bounce around inside there a few times and cut everything up in there to mush. Probably won't kill you but you'll be wearing a slobber guard and riding a wheel chair the rest of your –'

'Hey, leave him alone,' the girl said from behind him. 'He didn't do anything.'

Karch made the mistake of not watching her.

'Shut up and back away. This guy –'

She grabbed Karch from behind then and he used his left arm to roughly shove her backward while keeping the gun pressed against the man's neck. He heard her hit the BMW hard and then fall to the pavement.

'Johnny!' she cried out.

'See what you did?' Johnny cried out. 'Big man. Look what you did to her. A knight in shining bullshit.'

Karch pulled back from him and stepped backward until he could keep his eyes on Johnny and see the girl as well. She was sitting on the pavement, her legs spread and looking a little dazed. Johnny ran to her and she grabbed him around the neck. She started crying again.

Karch turned and started walking quickly to his car. He was thinking *Why the fuck did I do that? I'm here for one reason only.*

He got into the Lincoln, backed out and drove away. He saw Johnny standing in the lot behind him, watching him go.

Karch pulled to a curb on Magnolia Boulevard, put on the dome light and got the National Law Enforcement Association frequency book out of the glove compartment. He had bought the book from Iverson for $500. It listed every federal, state and local law enforcement agency and the radio transmission frequencies assigned to them. Printed in large letters across the top of every page was 'Law Enforcement Use Only.' Karch had laughed the first time he saw that.

He found the listing for the Burbank Police Department and punched in the three patrol frequencies assigned to the department on the scanner mounted below the dashboard. He then locked in a repeating scan on the three frequencies and waited and listened. If the couple he had just tangled with called in a report, he needed to know about it.

Things seemed quiet in Burbank for a Thursday night. A couple of domestic disputes went out to patrol units and then came a call to the parking lot at Presnick's bar. It had been reported as an assault and threat with a firearm.

'Shit!' Karch yelled loudly.

He banged his fist on the steering wheel. He looked at his watch. It was almost midnight. He knew he wasn't too far from Burbank Airport. He could go there and try to find another set of plates. But it was getting late and he knew he needed to get out of Burbank. He put the car in gear and drove until he reached a residential street. He turned onto the street and drove a block down before stopping. He killed the lights, reached under the seat for the car's proper license plates and got out with the drill. A minute later he got back in with the stolen plates in hand. He shoved them under the seat and put the car in gear. He drove a full block before putting the lights back on.

He drove west and didn't stop again until he was clear of Burbank and well into North Hollywood. He listened to a description of himself being broadcast on the Burbank frequencies and had to smile. The description that went out was fifty pounds too heavy and ten years too old. The rest was so generic it didn't matter. The tag number that went out accurately matched the plates now under his seat but the make of the car was off. It was described as a black Ford LTD. Karch lit a cigarette and tried to relax. Burbank was not going to be a problem.

It was now midnight and Karch thought that enough time had gone by for Leo Renfro to have gotten to wherever he was going. He pulled into the parking lot of a twenty-four-hour supermarket called Ralph's and stopped the car. He had just opened the QuikTrak receiver when his pager went off. He checked the number and saw the page was from Grimaldi. He decided not to call back and even turned the pager off. He didn't want it sounding again at an inopportune time.

The QuikTrak software booted up and Karch typed in a command asking for the historical data file on the movements of the transmitter beneath Leo Renfro's car. A map of northern Los Angeles appeared on the screen with a red line delineating the car's movements. Karch had been right. Renfro had gone on a long and convoluted drive around the Valley, driving in circles and making several U-turns. The computer showed the transmitter to be static for the last twelve minutes. Renfro had stopped. The computer placed the car on Citron Street in Tarzana.

'Here I come, Leo,' Karch said out loud.

He put the Lincoln in drive and nosed it out of the parking lot on his way to Tarzana.

30

The Cherokee was found easily enough. It was parked in a driveway in front of a small house on Citron. As Karch drove by he wondered why Renfro hadn't put it into the garage. He kept driving and continued around the block, looking for anything unusual or suspicious. He then pulled the Lincoln to the curb a half block away from the Cherokee. He worked his arms back into the sleeves of the jumpsuit and zipped up. He got his Sig out of its holster and attached the silencer. Leaving the Lincoln unlocked in case a quick escape was necessary, he headed down the street on foot.

Before approaching the house Karch got down on the pavement next to the Cherokee and reached underneath for his satellite equipment. He pulled it off the pan and jerked the wires free. He then went to the rear of the car to recover the disk antenna and put the equipment in the mailbox at the foot of the driveway. He planned to grab it later on when he headed back to the Lincoln.

Curious about Renfro's decision to park the car in plain sight, he walked to the garage and shined his penlight through one of the small windows on the door. The garage was completely filled with stacks and stacks of champagne cases. He assumed it was a stolen shipment and wondered if it would be worth his time and efforts later to have the shipment removed and sold. He could probably sell it all to Vincent Grimaldi for a nice profit.

He dismissed the idea and focused on the task at hand. He crossed the front of the house and moved down the left side, carefully looking for indications that Renfro had dogs. He wasn't concerned with alarms. People who worked the wrong side of the tracks rarely had alarms. They knew how easy they were to compromise, and they didn't want any kind of security system that could possibly bring the police to their door.

There was a wooden gate halfway down the side of the house. Karch easily scaled it and dropped over. He ran the light over the grass and in the shrub beds running down the side of the house. There were no dog droppings anywhere and no sign of any digging in the plants. He flicked the light off and continued down the side to the backyard. The moon was bright and he didn't need the light.

At the rear corner of the house Karch stepped out and saw the glowing blue surface of a pool. Just as he began moving along the back wall, he heard a sliding door open. He scrambled back to the corner and took a position giving him a view of the rear. A man stepped out through a sliding door and walked to the edge of the pool. It was the man from the mail drop. Renfro. He looked down at the pool and Karch saw an automatic vacuum moving slowly along the bottom. The man then looked up and seemed to be staring at the moon. Karch stepped out from his position and raised his gun.

Because of the background hiss from the nearby freeway Renfro never heard him. Karch put the cold end of the muzzle against the back of his neck. Renfro tensed but that was all. People in his line of work expected sooner or later to feel the cold muzzle of a gun against their neck.

'Nice clear night, eh?' Karch said.

'I was just thinking that,' the man said. 'Are you the ace of hearts?'

'That's me.'

'I looked but I didn't see you.'

'That's because I wasn't there. You're about a decade behind, Leo. I put a satellite bug on your car. I didn't need to follow you.'

'Live and learn.'

'Maybe. Let's go inside and talk. Keep your hands up where I can see them.'

Karch grabbed the back of Renfro's collar with one hand and held the gun against his back with the other. They headed back toward the house.

'Anybody else inside?'

'No, I'm alone.'

'You sure? I find anyone else in there I'll kill them just to make the point.'

'I'm sure you will. There's no one.'

They went in through the open sliding door into an office. Karch saw the desk at one end of the room. One entire wall was covered with more cases of champagne. Karch roughly pushed Renfro toward the front of the desk and let him go. He then reached back and closed the sliding door.

'Stay in front of the desk.'

Leo did as instructed. He kept his hands held up, chest high. Karch came around and went behind the desk. He noticed that sitting on the desk was the padded envelope he had left for Renfro at the mail drop as well as the envelope that had already been in the box. The flaps on both envelopes were torn open. Karch sat down in the chair behind the desk and looked up at Renfro.

'Been a busy man, Leo.'

'Oh, I don't know. Things are kind of slow.'

'Really?' He nodded in the direction of the wall of champagne. 'Looks like you're about to start celebrating something big time.'

'It's an investment.'

Karch picked up the padded envelope and shook it until the ace of hearts dropped out onto the desk. He tossed the envelope over his shoulder and picked up the playing card.

'Ace of hearts. The money card, Leo.'

He put the card into one of the pockets of his jumpsuit. He then picked up the other envelope and looked at it.

'I'm curious. What does the seven-seven-three mean? That some kind of code?'

'Yeah, it's a code. An area code.'

Karch shook his head.

'I should've known. Where?'

'Chicago. It's the new one.'

'Yes, that's right. You work for Chicago.'

'No, that's wrong. I don't work for anybody.'

Karch nodded but the smile on his face indicated he didn't believe Renfro. He picked up the other envelope and shook it. Two passports fell onto the desk. He picked up one and opened it to the photo page. Paper-clipped to one side was an Illinois driver's license and two credit cards. But Karch was more interested in the photo.

'Jane Davis,' he read out loud. 'Funny, that looks like Cassidy Black to me.'

He looked up at Renfro to catch his reaction. For a moment it was there. Surprise, maybe even shock. Karch smiled.

'Yes, I know a little more than you think.'

He picked up the second passport, expecting to find Renfro's picture inside it. Instead, it was a photo of a little girl. The name below the photo was Jodie Davis.

'Well, maybe I don't know everything. Who have we got here?'

Renfro didn't answer.

'Come on, Leo, work with me here. We can't have secrets, you and I.'

'Fuck you. Do what you have to do, but fuck you.'

Karch leaned back in the chair and looked over Renfro as if appraising him.

'You Outfit guys think you're so untouchable.'

'I'm not with the Outfit, but fuck you anyway.'

Karch nodded as if amused by Renfro's protestations.

'Let me tell you a story about the Outfit. Long time ago in Las Vegas there was this magician. He'd been around a long time, worked all the casinos, never really caught on. Always the warm-up, never the headliner. Raisin' a son by himself on the side. Anyway, he had a gig in the Clown Room lounge at Circus, Circus. No big deal. Just a table act for chump change – tips mostly. And so one night he's dealing three-card monte to a table of these three guys and they keep telling him to do it again. You know, "Do it again and I'll get it this time." Only they never got it. They never picked the ace. And it went on and on and it got one of them hotter and hotter. Like he thought this magician was personally makin' a fool of him or something. So skip to the end of the night. The magician punches out and is in the back garage walking to his car. And guess who's waitin' for him but those same three guys from the bar.'

Karch paused but not for effect. The story always got to him at this point. Every time he thought about it or told it, the anger seemed to boil up in his throat like acid.

'And one of them, the boss of these three guys, had a hammer. They didn't say a word. They just grabbed the magician and bent him over the hood of his car. One of them used his tie to gag him. Then one by one the man with the hammer broke every one of the magician's knuckles. At some point he passed out and when they were done they just left him lying on the concrete next to his car. He never worked as a magician again. Couldn't even palm a quarter anymore. Every time he tried, it just dropped on the floor. I used to sit in my bedroom and hear him trying gags in the other room. I'd hear that quarter fall on that wood floor over and over again . . .

'He drove a cab for a living after that. Cancer finally killed him but he was dead long before that.'

Karch looked at Renfro.

'You know who the man with the hammer was?'

Renfro shook his head.

'That was Joey Marks. The Outfit's man in Vegas.'

'Joey Marks is dead,' Renfro said. 'And like I said, I don't work for the Outfit or anybody else.'

Karch stood up and came around the desk.

'I came for the money,' he said quietly. 'You stole from the wrong people and I've come to set it straight. I don't care if you're with Chicago or not. I'm not leaving here without the money.'

'What money? I sell passports. I invest in champagne. I don't steal money from people.'

'Listen to me, Leo. Your spotter's dead. So is your cameraman. You don't want to be like them, do you? So where's the money? Where's Cassie Black?'

Renfro turned so he was facing Karch and his back was to the sliding door. Behind him the pool glowed brightly in the dark. He lowered his chin as if looking inward and coming to a decision. He then nodded slightly to himself and looked back at Karch.

'Fuck you.'

Karch shook his head.

'No, Leo, this time it's fuck you.'

He lowered the barrel of the gun and calmly fired. The bullet blew out Renfro's left knee. It passed cleanly through the bone and tissue, hit the tile floor behind him and bounced up into the sliding glass door. The door shattered into large jagged pieces of glass that crashed down onto the floor and shattered again. Renfro dropped to the floor and grabbed his knee with both hands. His face was a mask of agony.

The breaking glass was more noise than Karch had planned on making. The door was shattered except for one large jagged piece of glass held in the bottom of the frame. He figured the house must have been built before safety glass was required. He looked out into the yard and hoped the freeway noise had covered the sound.

Renfro started gasping and moaning as he rolled over the glass, cutting himself on his arms and back. The floor was quickly becoming slick with blood. Karch stepped over and leaned down over Renfro.

'Give me the money, Leo, and I promise I'll end it quick and painless.'

He waited but got no response. Renfro's face was scarlet. His lips were pulled back, exposing teeth gnashed together.

'Leo? Leo, listen to me. I know you're in a lot of pain but listen to me. If you don't give me the money we're going to be here all night. You think it hurts now? You can't imagine what –'

'Fuck you! I don't have the money.'

Karch nodded.

'Well, at least we're making progress, right? We're now past the "What money?" stage. If you don't have it, then where is it?'

'I gave it to Chicago.'

The answer came too quickly for Karch. He looked closely at Renfro's face and decided he was lying.

'I don't think so, Leo. Where's the girl? Cassie Black, Leo, where is she?'

Renfro didn't respond. Karch stepped back a pace and calmly fired a bullet into his other knee.

Renfro let out a loud scream that was followed by a stream of epithets that dissolved into delirium and moans. He rolled over onto his chest, his elbows tucked in and his face in his hands. His legs were sprawled behind him, twin pools of blood leaking from his knees. Karch looked out the broken door, across the pool, and checked for lights or any indication that the neighbors had taken notice. All he heard was the freeway. He hoped it would keep him covered.

'Okay, okay,' Leo blubbered into his hands. 'I'll tell you. I'll show you.'

'Okay, Leo, that's good. Now we're getting somewhere.'

Renfro raised his head and pushed himself up onto his elbows. He started crawling forward, toward the shattered door, his dead legs dragging behind him and leaving a trail of blood.

'I'll tell you,' he choked out through pain and tears. 'I'll show you.'

'Then talk to me, Leo,' Karch said. 'Where are you going? You can't go anywhere. You can't even walk, for crying out loud. Just tell me where it is.'

Renfro moved another painful foot closer to the door. When he spoke his voice was ragged and was delivered through clenched teeth.

'See . . . you see . . . it was the fucking moon . . . the void moon . . .'

'What are you talking about? Where's the money?'

Karch realized he had gone too far. Renfro was delirious with pain and blood loss. He was quickly becoming useless.

'The void moon,' Renfro said. 'It's the void moon.'

Karch took a step along with him.

'Void moon?' he said. 'What's that mean?'

Renfro stopped moving. He turned his face and looked up at Karch. The tightness had gone out of it. He almost looked relaxed.

'It means anything can happen, motherfucker.'

His voice was strong now. He suddenly raised himself off his elbows onto his hands. He raised himself up to full extension and lurched forward into the sliding door frame. His neck came down on the jagged piece of glass still held in the frame.

Karch realized what he was doing too late.

'No, goddammit!'

He reached down and grabbed Renfro's collar and jerked him up and off the glass. He dropped him to the floor and then grabbed his shoulder and turned him over.

He had acted too late. A deep, wide gash extended across Renfro's neck. He had cut his own throat. Blood was burbling out of the left side where the carotid artery had been severed.

Leo Renfro's eyes were bright as he looked up at Karch. A bloody smile formed on his face. Slowly he reached a hand up and used it to hold his neck together. His voice was a whispered croak.

'You lose.'

Leo dropped the hand and let the blood flow from his neck. He kept the smile on his face and his eyes on Karch.

Karch dropped to his knees and hovered over him.

'You think you beat me? Huh? Huh? You think you won?'

Leo could only answer with his smile. Karch knew it said *Fuck You!* He raised the gun and pressed the muzzle into Renfro's bloody mouth.

'You didn't win.'

He leaned back and turned his face away. He pulled the trigger. The shot blew out the back of Renfro's head and killed him instantly.

Karch pulled the weapon away and studied the dead man's face. His eyes were open and somehow he still had the smile.

'Fuck you. You didn't beat me.'

He leaned back on his heels and looked around himself. He saw a drop of blood spatter on the white instep of one of his two-tone Lite Tread spectator shoes. He used his thumb to wipe it off and then wiped his thumb on Leo's shirt.

He stood up and looked around the office. He sighed loudly. He knew he had a long night of searching ahead. He had to find the money. He had to find Cassie Black.

31

On Friday morning Cassie Black arrived at the dealership at ten and checked with Ray Morales to see what was what. He had taken her calls while she had been out the last few days. Ray said all was quiet but that he had a prospect coming in to test-drive a new Boxster at three. He had just been given a development deal at Warner Brothers that ran into seven figures. Ray had gotten it out of the *Hollywood Reporter* and expected it to be an easy sale. She thanked him for thinking of her with the prospect and was about to head to her office when he stopped her.

'You okay, kid?' he asked.

'Sure, why?'

'I don't know. You don't look like you've been sleeping much lately.'

Cassie brought her right hand up and cupped her left elbow, which still ached from the briefcase jolt.

'I know,' she said. 'Just been thinking about things. Sometimes it keeps me awake.'

'What things?'

'I don't know. Just things. I'll be in my office if you need me.'

She left him then and went to the sanctuary of her tiny office. She dropped her backpack into the foot well of the desk and sat down. She put her elbows up on the blotter and ran her hands through her hair. She felt like screaming I CAN'T DO THIS ANYMORE! But she tried to put her anxieties aside by reminding herself that one way or another her life would be changing very soon.

She picked up the phone to check her voice mail, even though on Tuesday she had left a generic outgoing message saying she would be off work for a few days and referring calls to Ray Morales until she got back. Four messages had been left for her anyway. One was from a body shop reporting a set of customized chrome wheels for a '58 Speedster she had sold were now ready. The second call was from one of Ray's prospects – a producer at Fox – from the week before. He wasn't calling about the car he had test-driven. He was just calling to tell her he had liked her style and wanted to know if she was interested in going with him to a premiere of a friend's picture the following week. Cassie didn't bother writing down the guy's private cell phone number.

'If you liked my style, why didn't you buy the car?' she said into the phone.

The third message was from Leo. There was an agitation in his voice she had not heard before. The message had come in at 12:10 A.M. that morning. She listened to it three times.

'Hey, it's me. What's wrong with your cell phone? I couldn't get through. Anyway, I just got back from my drop. I have those things you wanted but there's something else, something wrong. Somebody got the address somehow and dropped me something there. An ace of hearts from the Flamingo. I don't know what it means but it means something. Call me when you get this. Use all precautions and keep your head down. Oh, and erase this, okay?'

Cassie hit the three button on the phone, erasing Leo's recording before she went on to the fourth message. The last call had come in at seven-thirty that morning and it was a hang-up call. There had been no background noise, just a few seconds of someone breathing and then the hang-up. She wondered if it had been Leo.

She hung up the phone, reached down to the floor and pulled her backpack up onto her lap. She first dug through it until she found her cell phone. It had been turned off. She remembered doing it the night before after hanging up on Leo and deciding she didn't want him calling back.

She turned the phone on now and put it down on the desk. She then continued digging through the bag until she found the box containing the deck of cards she had bought in the gift shop at the Flamingo. She quickly opened it, turned the deck face up and started going through the cards one at a time looking for the ace of hearts. The closer she got to the bottom of the deck the greater the dread was that was building inside her. When she reached the last card without seeing the ace of hearts she cursed out loud and threw the deck across the small office. It hit the Tahiti poster and then cards exploded in all directions, coming down on the floor and the desk.

'Goddammit!'

She buried her face in her palms as she tried to figure out what to do. She snatched up the phone to call Leo but then thought better of it. *Use all precautions.* She thought of using her cell phone but dismissed that, too. She opened the desk drawer and grabbed a handful of change from a tray meant for pens and pencils and got up.

She opened the door and almost walked right into Ray Morales, who had apparently come to see what the commotion was about.

'Excuse me,' she said, making a move to go around him.

Ray looked past her into the office and saw the playing cards all over the place.

'What, you playing fifty-two pickup in there?'

'More like fifty-one.'

'What?'

'I'll be back in a few minutes, Ray. I have to take a walk.'

He silently watched her cross the showroom and go out the glass door.

Cassie walked a block down to the Cinerama Dome, where she knew there was a pay phone out front. She dialed Leo's cell phone number from memory and listened to ten unanswered rings before hanging up. Now questioning everything, she dialed it again in case she had messed up the first time. This time it went twelve rings before she hung up. The dread that had begun to rise in her while she looked through the cards had now gone several notches up the ladder to the level of panic.

She tried to calm herself by trying to think of reasons the call to Leo would go unanswered. The cell phone and Leo were attached like Siamese twins. If the phone had not been turned on, she knew her call would have been diverted to a message. She wouldn't have gotten the continuous ringing. So the phone was on but not being answered. The question was why.

The pool, she suddenly remembered. Leo swam laps in the morning. He'd have taken the phone out to the table next to the pool, but if he was in the middle of his laps he wouldn't hear it, not with the water sloshing around him and the freeway noise as well.

The explanation calmed her a bit. She called Leo's number once more and again it went unanswered. She put the phone back on its hook and decided to go back to the dealership. She would come back and try calling again in a half hour or forty-five minutes. She remembered Leo once told her he swam three miles a day. She had no idea how long that would take but figured that a half hour should be enough time.

Five minutes later she walked back into the dealership showroom and saw Ray and a man who wore a porkpie hat looking at the silver Carrera with the whale tail spoiler. Ray saw her and signaled her over with his fingers.

'Cassie, this is Mr Lankford. He wants to buy a car.'

The customer turned and smiled with embarrassment.

'Well, I want to look at a car. I mean, drive it. Then we'll see.'

He put his hand out.

'Terrill Lankford.'

She took his hand and shook it. His grip was firm, his hand dry as powder.

'Cassie Black.'

She looked at Ray. She didn't want to do this. Her mind wasn't on selling cars.

'Ray, is Billy in yet? Or Aaron? Maybe one of them would be –'

'Meehan's on a test and Curtiss isn't in till twelve. I need you to show Mr Lankford a car.'

Ray's tone indicated he was put out by her flaky behavior and that there was no debate allowed here. She turned her attention to Lankford. He was neat and well dressed in a set of retro clothes that went with the hat. Judging by his pasty complexion she guessed he'd be interested in a coupe. But that was okay because the Boxster didn't come in a coupe. That left only the higher priced Carreras.

'Which model are you interested in?'

Lankford smiled, showing off a perfect set of teeth. Cassie noticed his eyes were sidewalk gray, an unusual combination with the man's jet black hair.

'A new Carrera, I think.'

'Well, I'll get a car ready. If you could give your driver's license and insurance card to Ray, he'll get it copied while I get a car ready.'

Lankford's mouth opened but he didn't say anything.

'You do have proof of insurance, don't you?' Cassie asked.

'Of course, of course.'

'Okay, then let Ray take care of that and I'll get the car. Cab or coupe?'

'Excuse me?'

'Hardtop or cabriolet – convertible?'

'Oh. Well, it's such a nice day, why don't we take the top off?'

'Sounds good to me. We've got one in stock and available. It's arctic silver. That sound good?'

'Great.'

'All right, come on out to the carport when you're done with Ray.'

She pointed to the glass doors at the opposite end of the showroom.

'I'll meet you there,' Lankford said.

While Ray took the prospect into the finance office where the copying machine was, Cassie went into his office and got the key to the silver cab off the board. She then went to her own office and grabbed her wallet out of her backpack. She looked around and saw the playing cards all over the place and realized that if Lankford wanted to make a deal, she'd have to stick him in Ray's office while she cleaned up. There wasn't time now.

She started out of the office and then remembered something. She grabbed her cell phone off her desk and clipped it onto her belt. Just in case Leo calls, she thought to herself.

She headed out to the side lot to the car. She got in, slid her wallet into a CD holder on the dash and then started the engine. She put the windows and top down, checked the fuel level and saw there was a quarter tank, then drove the car up to the showroom door just as Lankford was stepping out.

'Let me drive it until we get out of here,' she called over the sound of the engine that was over-revving as the car warmed up. 'Then you'll take over.'

Lankford smiled and gave her the okay sign and got into the passenger side. She pulled out onto Sunset and then turned north on Vine. At Hollywood Boulevard she took a left and went down to Cahuenga, which she took north toward the hills and Mulholland Drive.

They drove in silence at first. Cassie liked to let the prospects listen to the car, feel its power on the turns, fall in love with it, before there was any talking. She liked to hold back on the sales pitch and the particulars until the customer was behind the wheel. Besides, her thoughts weren't on Lankford and his interest in a $75,000 car. She kept thinking about Leo's call and the anxiety she'd heard in his voice.

The Carrera effortlessly climbed through the Mulholland curves from Cahuenga up to the crest of the Santa Monica Mountains. At the Hollywood overlook she pulled off the road, killed the engine and got out.

'Your turn,' she said, her first words since he had gotten in the car.

She stepped to the railing at the edge and looked down at the shell of the Hollywood Bowl far below. Her eyes moved out from the bowl across Hollywood toward the spires of downtown. The smog was heavy and had a pinkish-orange tint to it. But somehow it didn't look all that bad.

'Nice view,' Lankford said from behind her.

'Sometimes.'

She turned and watched as he got into the driver's seat. She went around and got in the passenger side.

'Why don't you keep going on Mulholland for a little ways. You'll get a good idea of how this handles. We can take Laurel Canyon down to the one-oh-one and take that back to Hollywood. You'll be able to open it up on the freeway a little bit, see how it does.'

'Sounds good.'

He found the ignition on the left side quickly and started the engine. He backed out of the parking slot, then dropped the transmission into first gear and pulled out onto Mulholland. He drove with one hand on the stick shift at all times. Cassie could tell immediately he knew what he was doing.

'I take it you've driven one of these before but I'm going to give you the pitch anyway.'

'That's fine.'

She started listing the attributes of the car, starting with the new water-cooled engine and transmission and moving toward the suspension and brakes. She then moved inside the cockpit and started going over the amenities.

'You've got cruise control, traction control, onboard computer all standard. You've got CD, automatic windows and roof, dual air bags. And down here . . .'

She pointed down between her legs to the front of her seat. Lankford glanced down there but then put his eyes back on the road.

'. . . you have a passenger-side cutoff for the air bag – in case you are traveling with a small child. You have kids, Mr Lankford?'

'Call me Terrill. And no, I don't have kids. You?'

Cassie didn't answer for a moment.

'Not really.'

Lankford smiled.

'Not really? I thought that was a yes or no question for a woman.'

Cassie ignored the statement.

'What do you think of the car . . . Terrill?'

'Very smooth. Very sweet.'

'It is. So what do you do for a living?'

He glanced over at her. The wind was threatening to blow his hat off. He reached up and cranked it down over his forehead.

'I guess you could say I'm a troubleshooter,' he said. 'I'm a business consultant. Have my own company. I take care of things. This and that. I'm a magician, really. I make other people's problems disappear. Why do you ask?'

'Just curious. These cars are expensive. You must be very good at what you do.'

'Oh, I am. I am. And cost is not a problem. I pay cash. Actually, Cassie, I expect to come into a large sum of money soon. Very soon, in fact.'

Cassie looked over at him and felt a sudden shiver of fear. It was instinctive more than intuitive. Lankford pressed the pedal a little harder and the Porsche started moving through the winding curves a little faster. He looked over at her again.

'Cassie. What is that short for? Cassandra?'

'Cassidy.'

'As in Butch? Your parents outlaw fans?'

'As in Neal. As in my father was always on the road. Or so I was told.'

Lankford frowned and hit the pedal a little harder.

'That's really too bad. My father and me, we were close.'

'I'm not complaining about it. You want to slow it down, Mr Lankford? I'd like to get back to the showroom in one piece, if you don't mind.'

Lankford didn't respond at first with his voice or his foot. The car powered through another turn, its tires protesting as they labored to hold the road.

'I said, do you –'

'Yes,' Lankford finally said. 'You do want to get back alive.'

Something about the tone in which Lankford delivered the line revealed that he was not talking about the possibility of a car accident. Cassie looked over at him and shifted in her seat so that her body was pressed against her door.

'Excuse me?'

'I said you want to make sure you get back alive, Cassidy.'

'Okay, pull the car over. I don't know what you think you're –'

Lankford slammed his foot down on the brake pedal and yanked the wheel hard to the left. The Porsche skidded and spun into a 180-degree turn as it stopped. He looked over at her and smiled, then dropped in the gear and popped the clutch out. The car lurched forward and he started speeding through the curves, back in the direction they had come.

'What the hell are you doing?' Cassie yelled. 'Stop the car! Stop the car right now!'

Cassie reached her right hand up and gripped the top of the windshield brace. Her mind was moving as fast as the car as she tried to come up with a plan, an escape.

'Actually, Lankford's not my name,' the man next to her was saying. 'I got it off a book I found on a shelf at Leo Renfro's last night. It's called *Shooters* and I started taking a look at it. I thought it was about a guy in my line of work but it wasn't. But, hell, when your boss came up to me in the showroom and asked my name, it's all I could come up with on short notice, you know. My name is Karch. Jack Karch. And I've come for the money, Cassie Black.'

Through the terror building inside Cassie a thought pressed forward. *Jack Karch,* she thought. *I know that name.*

32

The Porsche was moving wildly through the Mulholland slalom. Jack Karch was going too fast for his skill now and the car was intermittently crossing the yellow line in the middle of the two-lane road and then rebounding by going off the road onto the shoulder. Karch was red-lining the tach but didn't want to take his hand off the wheel to pop the car into a higher gear. The engine roared and whined as the car went through the turns. Cassie gripped the windshield brace with both hands but was being thrown violently back and forth in her seat. Karch screamed over the din of the engine.

'I WANT THE FUCKING MONEY!'

She didn't answer him. She was too busy watching the road uncoiling in front of them and thinking for sure they would go off the shoulder and down the embankment.

'MARTIN IS DEAD! PALTZ IS DEAD! LEO IS DEAD!'

She turned to him at the mention of Leo's name. She felt her heart being pierced. Karch throttled back. He kept the car moving but the engine noise and wind abated.

'They're all dead,' he said. 'But I don't really want or need to hurt you, Cassie Black.'

He smiled and shook his head.

'In fact, I admire you. You do good work and I admire that. But I came for the money and you're going to give it to me. You give me the money and we'll call it square.'

Cassie spoke slowly and sternly.

'I don't know what you are talking about, okay? Please pull the car over.'

A look of sincere disappointment crossed Karch's face and he shook his head.

'I spent all night at Leo's. I tore that place apart. I found a lot of champagne and I found the briefcase I was looking for. But I didn't find what was supposed to be in the briefcase. And I didn't find you until along about dawn when I found you sitting there right in front of me. Leo's cell phone. I hit redial and I got the dealership. I went through the direct extension directory and, lo and behold, I hear the name Cassie Black. I switched over just to hear your voice. "This is Cassie at Hollywood Porsche. I'm not at work for a few days but if you call back and ask for Ray Morales he can handle –" Blah, blah, blah, don't fucking lie to me. I don't like it. I WANT THE MONEY!'

'I SAID PULL THE CAR OVER!'

'Sure.'

Karch suddenly steered the car hard right and they turned violently onto a gravel road that cut through a stand of pine trees. Cassie thought it was a fire road or some kind of public utilities access road. Whatever it was, it was clear Karch was taking them away from other traffic, from potential witnesses.

When they were about two hundred yards down the road, Karch slammed on the brakes and the Porsche skidded to a halt on the gravel. Cassie was thrown forward, her body pressing against her shoulder harness, and then back. She had no sooner recovered from the jarring stop than Karch was leaning across the center console onto her and pressing the long dark barrel of a gun against her face. He brought his free hand up and locked it onto the underside of her jaw.

'Listen to me. Are you listening?'

He was squeezing her jaw and she was unable to speak. She nodded.

'Good. What you need to know is that the people I work for care about one thing at this time. The money. Nothing else. So don't be like your pals Leo or Jersey. It will only get you killed.'

Cassie just stared at him down the length of the gun. She could see it had a silencer attached to it.

'Don't think,' Karch said. 'Just talk.'

He relaxed the pressure slightly so she could speak.

'Okay,' she said. 'Don't hurt me and I'll tell you where it is.'

'You'll do more than that, sweetheart. You'll take me to it.'

'Okay. Whatever you –'

He cut her off by squeezing her neck.

'You get one chance. You understand?'

Cassie nodded. Karch slowly released his grip and took his hand away. He was leaning back toward his seat when he suddenly snapped his fingers and leaned toward her again. He reached up to her face and she flinched, but then his hand went past her face to her ear.

'I looked in your office in the showroom before you showed up. Playing cards all over the place. Like you were looking for something. This what you were looking for?'

He pulled his hand back and seemingly pulled something from her ear. He held it up in front of her face. It was the ace of hearts. He smiled.

'Magic,' he said.

And then it struck her. Magic. The name Karch. She remembered the newspaper stories. Reading them in Metro detention before her arraignment. Jack Karch. He was the one.

He read something in her face.

'You didn't like that, huh? Well, I've got more. After we take care of business I'll show you a real disappearing act.'

He settled behind the wheel, his right arm still stretched across the console and poking the black gun into her ribs.

'Now, we're going to have to work together here, that okay with you? Put it in gear.'

He depressed the clutch pedal and she reached over and moved the shift into the first gear slot. He started the car moving. He turned it around and headed back up the gravel road to Mulholland. After he wound it out he called for second gear and she complied. He started talking again as though they were out for a Sunday drive.

'You know something, I gotta tell you, the way you did this thing, I . . . my hat's off to you. I think, you know, different circumstances . . . you and me, we could've . . . I don't know, done something.'

He took his hand off the wheel and pointed to the gear shift.

'See, we work good together.'

She didn't answer. She knew he was a psychopath, able to talk sincerely about doing things together with a woman he was holding at gunpoint. Cassie knew she had to make a move, to shift things. She knew this man was going to kill her. She would be part of the disappearing act he had promised. She couldn't help but smile sadly at the irony of her situation. She knew she could make the argument that this man had already killed her, six and a half years before.

'What's so funny?'

She looked at him. He had caught her glib smile.

'Nothing. The vagaries of life, I guess. And the coincidences.'

'You mean like fate, bad luck, that sort of thing?'

She casually moved her right arm so that her hand rested between her legs. Karch noticed and pushed the muzzle deeper into her side.

'Like the void moon?'

She turned sharply to look at him.

'Yeah, Leo mentioned something about it last night. Later on when I was looking around I read up on it in one of those books he's got. He was a big believer. Didn't do him any good in the end, did it? Where to?'

They were moving through the grove of pine trees, coming up to Mulholland. Cassie realized this might be her best chance. She took a deep breath and made her move.

'When you get up there you –'

She started raising her left arm as if to point out directions but then snapped her arm straight, knocking the gun away from her mid-section. She then grabbed the wheel with her left hand at the same time her right went down the front of her seat and engaged the air bag kill switch. She yanked the wheel hard right and the car lurched off the gravel road and directly into the trunk of a pine tree. It happened so fast Karch didn't have time to scream or fire his gun.

The driver-side air bag exploded from the steering wheel upon impact with the tree. It slammed Karch back against his headrest.

Cassie's shoulder harness stopped her forward trajectory before she hit the windshield. She was momentarily dazed but knew she had to move. She unfastened the seatbelt and frantically tried to open the door. It wouldn't budge. She didn't try it a second time. She hoisted herself up and jumped out of the car. Immediately, she started running downhill through the trees. She didn't look back at the Porsche.

Karch was more than momentarily dazed by the impact. The air bag hit him like a one-two punch to the chest and jaw. The tiny explosive used to propel it from the steering wheel also singed his face and neck. The impact knocked the gun out of his hand and onto one of the tiny rear seats. As the air bag began to deflate he came out of the daze and slapped it out of his face. He tried to jump up but his seatbelt held him secure. He quickly unfastened it and climbed up with his knees on the seat. He looked in all directions and then finally caught a glimpse of Cassie Black moving quickly away through the trees.

Instinctively he knew he would not catch her. She had a lead and she probably knew where she was going. It was her turf, not his.

'Fuck!'

He looked down into the rear of the car and found the Sig Sauer on the backseat. He reached down and grabbed it and then slipped back into his seat. He turned the key and tried to start the car again. Nothing happened. He turned the key back and forth several times but all he heard was a clicking sound.

'Fuck!'

He tried to open the door but it was jammed closed. The impact from the tree had apparently damaged the car body in such a way that the doors were sealed tight. He started climbing out of the seat again and as he did so he saw the little black wallet that Cassie Black had placed in the CD holder on the dashboard. He reached down for it and opened it. Behind a clear plastic window was a California driver's license. He studied the photo of Cassie Black and then looked at the address. She lived on Selma in Hollywood.

Karch looked off into the woods. Cassie Black was long gone now. Still, standing on the front seat of the Porsche he held the wallet up as though she were in there someplace looking back at him.

'Look what I found,' he called out. 'You didn't win yet, sweetheart!'

He took the silencer off the Sig and fired the gun once into the air, just to let her know he was still coming.

As Cassie sprinted carefully down the hill she began to hear music and used its source as a beacon. Eventually she came out of the woods at a parking lot she recognized as being behind the Hollywood Bowl. She guessed that the Philharmonic must be practicing. She followed the access road down to Highland and then walked down to Sunset.

It took her twenty minutes to get back to the dealership. As she approached she saw two black-and-white police cars parked in the entranceway to the parking lot. There was also an unmarked car with a bubble light on the dashboard parked up on the curb in front of the showroom. Behind it an ambulance was parked but its rear doors were closed.

There were many people standing out on the sidewalk, including most of the dealership's sales and service staff. Cassie walked up to a salesman named

Billy Meehan, who was staring into the showroom with a stricken look on his face.

'Billy, what happened?'

He looked down at her and his eyes grew large.

'Oh, thank God! I thought you were in there with them. Where have you been?'

Cassie hesitated, then decided on a lie that was not technically a lie.

'I was taking a walk. In there with who?'

Meehan put his hands on her shoulders and leaned down into her face as though he was breaking very bad news to her. He was.

'There's been a robbery. Somebody put Ray and Connie down on the floor in her office and shot them both.'

Cassie brought her hands up to her face and stifled a scream.

'They then stole the silver cab. We thought maybe, uh, you were a hostage or something. I'm glad you're okay.'

Cassie just nodded her head. Her history had been a guarded secret with Ray Morales. She realized that if other employees had known about it, they probably would have immediately suggested her as a suspect to the police. Maybe that was what Karch had been counting on.

She felt weak all of a sudden and had to sit down. She practically slid down Meehan's body and sat down on the curb. She tried to understand what had happened and could only conclude that Karch must have shot Ray and Connie because he didn't have a fake driver's license with the name Lankford on it. He knew there was no way he could leave a record with his real name on it. Not with what he had planned to do with her.

'Cassie, you all right?'

'I just can't believe – are they dead?'

'Yeah, both of them. I looked in there before the police came. It wasn't a pretty picture.'

Cassie leaned forward and vomited into the gutter. It was one deep heave that seemed to empty her totally. She wiped her mouth with her hand.

'Cassie!' Meehan cried as he watched. 'I'll go get one of the paramedics.'

'No, don't. I'm fine. I just . . . poor Ray. All he wanted to do was help.'

'What do you mean?'

She realized she had made a mistake giving her thoughts voice.

'I mean he was just a nice guy. Connie, too. They would have given up the keys or the money. Why'd he have to shoot them?'

'I know. It makes no sense. By the way, did you see someone?'

'No, why?'

'I noticed you said "he" when you were talking about it.'

'No, I've been gone. I was just saying it was a he because I just think it probably was. I can't think straight right now.'

'I know what you mean. I can't believe this is happening.'

She sat on the curb with her face in her hands, the guilt of the world weighing down on her. The words *I did this, I did this, I did this* kept running through her head. She knew she had to get away from this place and never look back.

She found her strength and stood up, grabbing Meehan's arm one time to steady herself.

'Are you sure you're okay?' he asked.

'Yes, fine. I'm fine. Thanks, Billy.'

'You should probably let the police know you're okay and you're here.'

'Okay, I will. Actually, could you tell them for me? I'm not sure I want to go in there.'

'Sure, Cassie, I'll go tell them right now.'

Cassie waited a few moments after Meehan walked away, then walked down the sidewalk to the alley that ran behind the dealership. She followed the alley behind the service center to the other side of the dealership and walked into the sales lot. The silver Boxster that Ray had been letting her use was there. She always parked it in the sales lot in case a customer was interested.

The car was unlocked but her key was in her backpack in her office. She opened the door and pulled the front trunk release. She came around and opened the lid and took out the leather-bound owner's manual, then closed the trunk and got into the car. Behind one of the folds of the booklet was a plastic key for the eventual owner to put in a wallet as an emergency backup. She took it out, started the car and drove out of the lot into the alley. She kept a slow, deliberate speed until she had covered two blocks in the alley. She then cut up to Sunset and took a right, in a direction away from the dealership and toward the 101 Freeway.

Tears ran down her cheeks as she drove. What had happened at the dealership changed everything. Leo's death was awful and hurt her deeply. But Leo had been in the circle and knew the risks. Ray Morales and Connie Leto, the finance manager, were innocents. Their deaths signaled the lengths to which Karch was willing to go to recover the money. It meant there were no bounds anymore. To Karch, to her guilt, to anything.

33

Karch watched through the window of the taxi as it went by the Porsche dealership. He didn't care about the assemblage of police and television news vehicles surrounding the glass walls of the showroom. His eyes scanned the numerous people standing on the sidewalks. He was hoping to see Cassie Black but knew he was too late. His cell phone had failed to get a signal up in the hills. He'd had to hike up to Mulholland and then over to the Hollywood overlook, where he'd remembered seeing a pay phone earlier. It took him nearly an hour to cover the ground. Then it was another twenty minutes waiting for the taxi he called for to show up.

The taxi driver said something in very bad English about what had happened at the dealership but Karch paid no attention. The taxi continued another few blocks and turned onto Wilcox. Karch had him stop in front of a Hollywood memorabilia store. He paid and got out. After the taxi took off and had turned back onto Sunset he crossed the street to his Lincoln, which was parked at the curb. On its bumpers were a set of fresh plates he had picked up that morning in a long-term lot at LAX.

Karch got in and fired the car up. But before pulling out of the space he looked up Selma in the map book. He saw he was in luck. He was less than five minutes away.

There were no cars parked in front or on the driveway of the bungalow on Selma where Cassie Black's driver's license said she lived. The house was on a dead end and Karch decided on a direct approach. He pulled right into the driveway and parked. Breaking and entering in daylight was not his idea of a wise move but he had to get into the house to see if Cassie Black had been there yet. He decided the safest way to go was straight in. He pulled into the drive, honked the Lincoln's horn twice and waited. Finally, he killed the engine, got out and went right up the front steps, spinning his key chain on his finger. When he got close to the door he bent over and raised his lock picks. He quickly went to work on the deadbolt, acting as though he were a man having trouble with his keys. He had no idea if he was being watched but he was putting on a good show.

He picked the lock in about forty seconds. He then turned the knob and walked in.

'Hey, Cassie?' he called loudly and for the benefit of any neighbor who might have been watching. 'Come on, I'm waitin' out here!'

He closed the door, pulled out his gun and quickly attached the silencer. He began a quick room-to-room check of the house.

It was empty. He began a second and slower sweep, looking around to try to determine if Cassie Black had been to the house in the time since she had escaped from him up on the hill. The home, though sparely furnished, seemed to be in neat order. He became convinced that she had not been there yet. He sat down on the couch in the living room and thought about what this could mean. Did she already have the money or did she not have the money? Had it been at Leo Renfro's and he had somehow missed it during his all-night search? Worse yet was another possibility that poked through: that Renfro had been telling the truth when he claimed to have already given the money to his Chicago contacts.

Karch felt something lumpy beneath the spot where he was sitting. He moved down the couch and then pulled up the cushion. He picked up a clothes hanger with seven padlocks attached to it. It served to remind him of how formidable Cassidy Black had turned out to be. He decided in that moment that if he found out she had the money and was gone, he would chase her to the ends of the earth. Not for Grimaldi and definitely not for the faceless group that pulled strings from Miami. He would do it for himself.

He left the hanger on the coffee table and got up to start his third sweep of the house. This one would take the longest.

The bedroom was the logical place to start. Karch knew people liked to sleep with the things dear to them close by. The white-walled room was furnished with the basics, a four-poster bed, two bed tables, a bureau and a mirror. A framed poster of a beach scene from Tahiti was taped to a wall. He studied it for a moment and quickly realized it was a duplicate of the poster he had seen in Cassidy Black's office when he had stepped in while looking for her in the showroom. He had been looking at the poster when the manager had stuck his head in and asked if he could help.

Karch stepped over to the wall and studied the poster, wondering if it had any significance for his mission. The woman on the beach did not look like Cassidy Black. He finally decided he would have to worry about it later and turned to the nearby bed table and opened the top drawer.

The drawer contained a stack of *Popular Mechanics* magazines that looked as though they had been bought at a yard sale. They were all in poor condition and were several years old. Still, he flew the pages on every one of them in case there was a note or maybe a hidden address. He found nothing and dropped the last magazine back in the drawer and kicked it closed.

The bottom drawer of the table was empty except for a little net bundle containing cedarwood shavings and dried rosemary. He slammed that drawer closed and came around the bed to the other night table.

Before he opened the drawer he had a feeling he would have good luck here. This table had a lamp on it and the pillow on this side of the bed had an indentation from someone sleeping on it. He knew this was her side of the bed.

Karch sat down on the bed and put his gun down next to his thigh. With both hands he picked up the pillow and brought it to his face. He could smell her. Her hair. He wasn't good at identifying fragrances but he thought he could smell tea leaves, like when you first open a box of tea bags. He wasn't sure about it and put the pillow back down.

He opened the top drawer of the bed table and hit pay dirt. The drawer was crammed with personal items. There were books and hair bands and photograph albums. There was a still camera with a long lens and a video camera as well. Placed on top of everything was a small framed photograph. Karch picked it up and studied it. It showed Cassidy Black sitting on the lap of a man wearing a Hawaiian shirt. She was holding a pinkish-orange drink with a paper umbrella in it. Karch almost didn't recognize her because the smile on her face was so wide and bright.

However, he easily recognized the man in the photo. His was a face Karch would never forget. Max Freeling, the man who had permanently altered Karch's entire life in one moment of time. Karch knew he wouldn't be where he now sat if it had not been for Max Freeling and the decision he had made at the top of that hotel six years before. All these years, he had been under Grimaldi's thumb because of what happened in that room with Max Freeling.

He turned the picture over and hit the frame's glass harshly on the corner of the bed table. He heard the glass crack. He noticed something written on the cardboard backing of the frame. It said,

> I looked up and saw the outline of Tahiti and I realized this was the place I had been looking for all my life.
>
> *W. Somerset Maugham*

Karch turned the frame over and looked at the photo again. A spiderweb crack started on Cassidy Black's face and branched across the photograph. Karch tossed the frame into a wastebasket that was next to the bed table.

From the drawer he removed a thick photo album with a soft brown leather binding. As he opened it he expected to find more photos of Max Freeling but instead got a surprise. The album was full of photographs of a young girl. Almost all of them were taken from a distance – he glanced at the long-range camera in the drawer – and at the same location, a schoolyard.

He leafed through the book and found one picture of the girl dribbling a basketball. Painted on the wall of a building behind the playing area was the name Wonderland School.

He closed the album and pulled out another. It contained more photos of the girl, though these were not taken at the school. They depicted the girl playing in a yard in front of a house. In some she was pulling a wagon or kicking a ball, in others she was going down a sliding board or laughing on a swing. A grouping of photos in the back of the book but not yet placed in plastic windows showed the girl on a trip to Disneyland. One of the shots, again taken from afar, showed her embracing Mickey Mouse.

Karch realized something and reached into his coat pocket. He pulled out the two passports and opened the top one to the ID photo. It was the same girl from the photos in the albums. Jodie Davis, the name said.

Karch put the passports back in his pocket and let the photo album drop to the floor. He was having an epiphany, a moment when seemingly disparate memories and new pieces of information coalesced into a new truth. He now understood something that had tortured him for six years.

An idea started coming together, a plan for getting the money and Cassie Black, all at the same time. He closed the top drawer and opened the bottom. This one was less crowded. There was an electric hair dryer that didn't look as though it was ever used and a few old pieces of mail from inmates at High Desert Correctional Institution for Women. Karch opened one of the letters and saw it was just a howyadoin' from a former cellmate named Letitia Granville. Karch also threw these into the wastebasket and reached back into the drawer and underneath the hair dryer for a manila envelope that was address side down.

He turned it over and saw that it was addressed to Cassidy Black at High Desert Correctional. Whatever was in the envelope was something she had taken with her from prison. He ran his thumb under the return address and saw the preprinted envelope had been sent from Renaissance Investigations of Paradise Road, Las Vegas. Karch was familiar with the agency. It was mid-size, five or six investigators and an equal number of supposed specialties. He competed with them for the referrals from the Metro missing persons unit. Karch opened the envelope and pulled out a well-thumbed investigation summary. He was about to start reading the particulars when he was jarred by the screaming voice of someone in the doorway behind him.

'FREEZEITUPFUCKHEAD!'

Karch dropped the report and held his hands out in front of him. He slowly started to turn his head. What he saw further shocked him. Just inside the doorway of the bedroom was an enormous black woman. She stood in the classic Weaver stance taught at every law enforcement academy in the country. Feet spread, weight equally distributed, both hands up holding and bracing the gun, elbows slightly bent and pointed outward. Around her neck was a chain with a badge on it. She looked like no cop Karch had ever seen, but the 9 mm Beretta pointed at him won the debate.

'Take it easy now,' he said calmly. 'I'm on your side.'

34

Since getting the news at the dealership Cassie Black had felt as though she were under water, in some kind of surrealistic otherworld that had no bearing on her life. Deep down she knew it was an instinctive defense mechanism. It allowed her to continue, to move and do what needed to be done.

She now stood in the backyard of Leo's house staring at the dried blood streaking the jagged piece of glass standing in the bottom frame of the sliding door. Just seeing the glass confirmed what Karch had told her. She knew now that Leo was dead. If she went into the house she would find his body. And whatever way she found it would constitute an image she would never be able to remove from her memory.

She looked down into the pool at the vacuum standing motionless at the bottom. But almost immediately her eyes were drawn back to the door with the jagged glass. She knew she had to go in. Finally, she nodded once to herself and walked up to the door. And immediately she could see his body on the floor of the office. An eighteen-wheeler going by on the freeway behind the property drowned out the awful sighing sound that came involuntarily from her throat. She stepped over the glass and into the house.

Leo's body was sprawled face up to the side of the door. Blood seemed to be everywhere. Despite the horrible tableau the scene created, her eyes were drawn to what unmistakably appeared to be, if not a smile on his face, a look of satisfaction. Cassie crouched next to him and touched his cold cheek.

'Oh, Leo,' she said. 'What did I do?'

The tears started coming again. She tried to pinch them off by tightly closing her eyes and balling her fists.

Finally, when she opened her eyes again, she tried to study the body and the surroundings as maybe a detective would. She wanted to know what had happened. The fact that Karch had come to her and demanded the money meant Leo had stood up. She looked at the bloody drag marks on the tile floor and put it together. Leo had done it. He had gone to the glass. He had done it for her.

'Leo . . .'

She closed her eyes again and leaned her head down to his silent chest. 'I knew we should've run.'

She straightened back up with a new resolve. She would get away. She knew it was a selfish choice but she also knew that if she failed that Leo's noble death would be for nothing. That was Leo's hope in the end. His last prayer. That was what put the smile on his face. She would honor that.

She stood up and looked around the office. It had been completely destroyed by Karch's search. But he had been looking for two and a half million dollars, not for what she looked for now. She stepped over the body to the overturned desk and looked at the debris on the floor. Leo's astrology books and papers and notebooks were scattered about. The contents of the desk drawers had been dumped. Amidst the clutter she saw two envelopes on the floor, both addressed to Leo and with the same odd return address, just the numbers 773. She stooped down and picked them up. Both were empty. One was postmarked two days before in Chicago and then she knew. Karch had found the passports. He had them.

Cassie abruptly stood up and her head hit the red I-Ching coins that dangled from the ceiling and would have been directly over the upright desk. She looked up at them for a moment and then grabbed the desk chair and moved it over. She climbed up on the chair and unhooked the string of coins. She wanted something of Leo's to take with her. If not for luck, then just to remember him by.

As she got down she knew there was no point in going through the rest of the house. Karch had the passports and there was nothing else inside that she had wanted. She walked over to Leo's body and once more looked down on him. She thought of the song she had listened to so many times on the way to Vegas. She hoped there had been an angel to whisper in his ear.

'Good-bye, Leo,' she said.

She carefully stepped over the glass and through the broken slider out to the backyard. She walked to the pool's edge and looked down at the vacuum. Tracing its hose to a coupling in the wall, she walked around to the other side and then got down on her knees and reached into the water. She grabbed the hose and started pulling it up and out onto the pool's concrete skirt. It was heavy work and twice she almost toppled into the water. Eventually, the vacuum head and debris bag came to the surface and she wrestled it onto the concrete.

Water turned the white concrete dark and soaked the knees of her black jeans. She didn't care. She struggled with the collar of the debris bag but then saw the zipper running alongside the bag. She quickly zipped the bag open and spread it. Inside the bag was another bag, a heavy-duty white plastic bag with its mouth tied in a knot. She carefully lifted it out of the vacuum bag and then worked her fingers into the knot. It was too tight and she didn't have the fingernails for the job. She reached into her back pocket for the Swiss Army knife and used it to cut the knot off the bag.

Cassie looked inside. The bricks of hundred-dollar bills were there. Still wrapped in plastic and as dry as the day they were cut at the mint.

She closed the bag and looked across the pool at the broken sliding door. From this angle she could see the tops of Leo's shoes pointing upward. She silently said her thanks to him. He had said to her when he told where the money would be kept that the best hiding place was one in plain sight. He had been right.

Cassie looked down at the water. Her struggling with the vacuum had created a small current. Floating by her on the surface was a dead hummingbird, its tiny wings spread like an angel's.

35

Karch slowly stood up when ordered to by the woman with the gun.

'Who the hell are you?'

He nodded, hoping it would be a gesture taken as a sign of his full cooperation and compliance.

'My name is Jack Karch. I'm a private investigator. My license is in the inside right pocket of my jacket. May I get it out and show it to you?'

'Maybe later. A PI? What do you want with Cassie Black? And take two steps backward and lean against the wall.'

She was slowly coming further into the room. He did as he was told and leaned his shoulders against the wall as he spoke. He saw her eyeing the Sig, which was still on the bed.

'I'm on a case. A hot prowl in Vegas. A hotel room. A high roller was taken off for a lot of money. If you don't mind me asking, who are you?'

The woman was at the bottom of the bed. Keeping her eyes and the aim of her Beretta on Karch, she bent forward and reached her free hand for the gun.

'Agent Thelma Kibble, state parole.'

'Oh, yeah, Kibble. I was going to try to reach you today to talk about Black.'

'Since when does Nevada allow its PIs to run around with silencer-equipped weapons?'

Karch did his best to look surprised.

'Oh, you mean that? That's not mine. I found that in the drawer there. That's Cassie Black's. And you might be careful how you handle it. I think it's evidence.'

'Of what? You said it was a hot prowl.'

'They found the body of her old partner, a man named Jersey Paltz, in the desert. He was shot.'

Kibble looked down at the weapon in her left hand. Karch was about six feet away from her. He decided it was too risky to make a move from that distance.

'Tell you what, Mr Karch, why don't you very slowly open up your jacket for me?'

'Sure.'

Karch slowly opened his jacket, exposing the empty shoulder holster.

'I know what you're going to say,' he said quickly. ' "Empty holster, the Sig must be his." Not true. I have a license to carry a concealed weapon. But it's a Nevada state license. No good in California. If I had a weapon in this holster I would be breaking the law. My weapon is locked in its case in the trunk of my car. If you want to walk out with me I will show it to you.'

'I'm not worried about that. What I'm wondering is why you are here and not the Vegas cops. If there's a murder, why aren't the authorities involved? Why aren't they here?'

'Well, first of all they are involved. But, as you must know, the police are hampered by bureaucracy. I was hired by the Cleopatra Resort and Casino to investigate the room burglary. I have a staff and an expense account. I move faster. The police will be coming here and be in contact with you soon. In fact, I am working very closely with the Metro police. If you wish, I can give you the name and number of a detective who will vouch for me.'

If she bit, he would give her Iverson's number. He could ad lib it. Karch would have to work something out with Iverson later with either a payoff or a bullet. But Kibble didn't bite.

'Even if someone vouched for you it wouldn't explain why you took it upon yourself to break into a suspect's home,' she said.

'I did not break in,' Karch said indignantly. 'The front door was wide open. Look, that's my car parked outside in the driveway. Would I park there if I was breaking in?'

'You seem to have an answer for everything, Mr Karch.'

'As long as they are true. Could you please stop pointing that gun at me now? I think I have sufficiently established who I am and what I'm doing here. Do you want to see my license now?'

Kibble hesitated but then lowered her gun to her side. Karch dropped his hands to his side without her protesting. He had hoped she would actually put the weapon away but nonetheless was pleased by what he saw. He decided to stay on the offensive.

'Now, can I ask *you* what you are doing here?'

Kibble hiked her sizable shoulders.

'I'm doing my job, Mr Karch. Just a routine home call. Checking up on one of my cases.'

'Seems a little too coincidental to me.'

'I had a conversation with her a couple weeks ago that didn't sit well with me. I put her on my list of field checks. Didn't get to it until today.'

'And you came here instead of visiting the dealership?'

'I called the dealership. She had a message on her line saying she wasn't in today. So I came here. Don't ask me any more questions, Mr Karch. I'm asking you the questions.'

'Fine.'

He waved his hands in surrender.

'You said there's a homicide in this? Well, I know Cassie Black probably better than anybody around here and I'll tell you right now there's no way she's involved in a homicide. No way.'

Karch thought of Hidalgo's body lying on the bed in the Cleo's penthouse.

'We'll have to agree to disagree on that, Agent Kibble. The evidence speaks for itself. And after all, remember, we're talking about an ex-con here, one who served time in Nevada on a murder conviction.'

'It was a manslaughter and we both know the circumstances. The law held her responsible for her partner's death but she was twenty stories below when he went out the window. Somebody may have pushed him, but it wasn't her.'

'Is that what she said? That somebody pushed him?'

'It's the way she had it figured. She said the casinos had to make an example of him. He got pushed.'

'That's bullshit, but never mind. How did she get out here?'

'She had her parole transferred. Once she got the job lined up with Ray Morales at the dealership it was a cinch. She had a lawyer petition and the parole transfer was approved. She knew Ray from Vegas when she was a dealer. Ray's an ex-con who made it in the straight life. He wanted to give her a shot at it. He probably also wanted something else but Cassie never complained.'

Karch had thought Morales was an ex-con. When he'd put him down on the floor of the finance office Morales had taken it with a certain dignity you never saw in citizens. The woman was like the rest of them. She started to whimper and was going to shout so he'd had to shoot her first.

'So did you get close to her?' Karch asked. 'Close enough to know what made her blood move?'

'You mean why she started ripping off high rollers in Vegas?'

Karch nodded.

'You ask me, I think it had something to do with her father. A degenerate gambler. I think she thought she was getting back at the casinos or something. I don't know.'

'I don't think you do. You mind if I sit down? I've got a bad back.'

He brought his arms up behind his back as if stretching the muscles. He kept talking the whole time.

'I'm on a pension from Vegas Metro. Partial disability. Wrecked my back chasing down a guy dusted on meth. He picked me up and *threw* me down a flight of stairs . . .'

None of it was true. It was all part of the sleight of hand. As he talked his left hand went under his jacket and picked the .25 out of the silk pocket inside his rear belt line.

'I have never seen that kind of power in a single human being . . . '

He brought his hands forward and clasped them together in an ad-libbed stretching motion during which he transferred the gun to his right hand. He then held it palmed at his side as he groaned and sat down on the bed. Kibble was now about four feet away and still holding her weapon at her side. She held the Sig by the barrel in her other hand and also at her side. Karch knew he had her. But he wanted to get more information from her first.

'Tell me about the kid she and Max Freeling had,' he said.

Kibble appraised him for a moment before answering.

'What kid and what's it got to do with a hot prowl in Las Vegas?'

Karch smiled and shook his head.

'She didn't come here because some guy offered her a job selling cars, Agent Kibble. She came because she and Max had a kid and that kid ended up out here.'

He looked up at her.

'But I think you know that, don't you?'

'I don't know anything about where the child is but, yes, you're right. Cassie was pregnant when she got arrested. Kept it a secret till it showed. By then she had pleaded out and was at High Desert Correctional. The child was born there. She nursed the baby three days and then it was given away. She put it up for adoption.'

Karch nodded. He hadn't known the details but had already figured out the main aspects of the story.

'You got kids, Agent Kibble?'

'Two of them.'

'Three days. That long enough to make a bond? A bond that nobody can break?'

'Three minutes is enough.'

'You know I'm tired –'

He leaped up off the bed and stuck the .25 into the collar of fat that was Kibble's neck.

'– of your sarcastic way of answering me, Agent Kibble. It is –'

He slapped the Beretta out of one of her hands and then reached over and took the Sig Sauer from the other.

'– *really* starting to bug me.'

Kibble froze and her eyes widened.

'What are you doing?' she asked.

'I'm sticking the short barrel of a twenty-five pop gun into your fat neck, Agent Kibble. I'm now going to ask you a few more questions and you're going to leave the bullshit out of your voice when you answer. Am I right about this?'

'Yes,' she whispered. 'Like I said, I got two kids. I'm all they got, so please don't –'

Karch sidestepped her and then pushed her down onto the bed. He put the .25 back into its pocket and pointed the Sig at her. He reached up and made sure the silencer was still properly attached. He waited until her frightened eyes looked up at him before he spoke.

'Well, if you want to see them again, you answer a few questions and without any of that fat lip anymore.'

'Okay, okay. What questions?'

'What else you know about the kid she had? The girl.'

'Nothing. Just the one time she told me about the birth and stuff. That was all she ever mentioned about it.'

'Why'd it come up?'

'I was showing her pictures of my boys and she just mentioned it. It was at the beginning and she had just come out from Nevada. I was trying to get to know her a bit and she seemed like a good girl.'

'What else she say? She didn't say her kid ended up out here?'

'Never mentioned it. She said she told Max she was pregnant on that last night – the night he went out the window.'

'That night?'

'That's what she said. She said it was going to be their last job. She told him she was going to have a baby beforehand and Max got all protective. He wouldn't let her do the hot prowl. So he did it.'

'What are you saying, that she was supposed to be the one who went up into that room?'

'You didn't know that?'

'How could anybody know? Max ended up splattered across a craps table and she never talked. She took a plea instead. Now I fucking know why.'

Karch winced. The pieces of that night were coming together. He thought he understood everything now – six years too late. He turned and stepped away from the bed as if turning from a bad memory. In the mirror over the bureau he saw Kibble's posture stiffen as though she were going to make a move. Then she saw him watching her in the mirror.

'Don't do anything stupid, Agent Kibble. Remember those two kids of yours. What did Cassie Black say about Max trying to fly that night?'

'She wouldn't talk about it, especially with me. There was just this one time that she talked a little bit about it. And she said Max had to have had some help going through that window. That's all.'

'Yeah, well, she was right. But the help came from her, nobody else.'

'What, you were there?'

Karch looked at her a long moment and he could see fear rise in her eyes.

'I'm asking the questions now, remember?'

He paused to allow her to answer but she didn't. Karch raised the aim of the Sig up her wide body, over her face and to the wall behind her until he was pointing at the woman walking on the beach in the poster.

'Tell me about Tahiti.'

'Tahiti?' She looked backward at the poster on the wall. 'Tahiti was a dream.'

'Was?'

'She went there with Max once. Blew the take on one of the jobs and went there for a week.'

Karch looked over at the wastebasket next to the bed table. The photo of Cassie Black and Max and the umbrella drink could be seen over the lip of the can. He knew without a doubt then that it had been taken in Tahiti.

'She thought that was where the baby got . . . you know, conceived,' Kibble said. 'And the plan was for them to go back. After the baby was born. You know, retire from the hot prowl and live on an island or something in Tahiti. Live happily ever after and raise the child.'

'But all that went out the window with Max.'

Kibble nodded.

'They never made it,' she said. 'So Tahiti isn't a place anymore. Not for Cassie. It's a dream. It's all her plans. It's everything she never got with Max.'

Karch paused for a moment before responding. He looked down at the investigation report from Renaissance that was on the floor by Kibble's feet.

'It's almost everything,' he finally said, his eyes still on the report. 'But our Cassie Black has a plan, Agent Kibble. Something tells me she's the type who always has a plan.'

He was totally into his own thoughts. He quickly scanned through his theories and suddenly looked up at Kibble.

'Last question,' he said. 'What do I do with you now?'

36

Cassie pulled to the curb a block from the house on Selma and studied it for any indication that Karch might be there waiting for her. There was nothing obvious; no cars in the driveway, the front door wasn't kicked in. She watched for ten minutes but never picked up a warning vibe. Finally, she drove off to the street running parallel to Selma and one block over. She parked again, then got out and cut between two houses and climbed a fence into her backyard. She left the money locked in the front trunk of the Boxster. Her plan was to not leave the car for very long. She was only going in to get a single photograph, maybe some spare clothing if she wanted to push it. She dug the spare key out of the flowerpot on the back porch and quietly entered the house through the kitchen door.

Karch had been there. The place had not been searched and destroyed like Leo's house. But he had been there. The vibe was there. She could tell. There was something disturbed, something amiss. She stepped into the living room without making a sound and confirmed her instinct when she saw the hanger and seven locks lying on the coffee table. She hadn't worked the locks since before going to Las Vegas. She had not left them out in the open like that. He had.

She stood perfectly still and concentrated on the sounds of the house for almost two minutes. When she heard nothing else she retreated to the kitchen and took the largest knife she had out of a drawer. She carried it at her side as she entered the front hallway and slowly walked into her bedroom.

The first thing she saw was the poster. It hung askew on the wall and slashed across it was a large X that looked to her to have been painted with blood. It was a long moment before she could pull her eyes away from it to take in the rest of the bedroom. This room had been searched. Cassie did not have enough belongings to make the debris all over the floor seem to be much more than a minor mess. But she quickly dropped to the floor and grabbed her two photo albums. The idea that Karch might have handled them and looked in them repulsed her. She put the albums on the bed for taking even though she knew she didn't need them anymore. She then quickly began scanning the floor for the one photo that she did need, that was irreplaceable.

Finally, she saw it in the trash can, the glass over the photo shattered. She grabbed it out of the can and shook the glass out of the frame. The photo appeared to be undamaged and she let out a sigh of relief. It was the only photo ever taken of Max and her together. For five years it had been taped to the wall next to her bed at High Desert. She pulled it from the frame and placed it on top of the two albums on the bed. She looked at her watch and saw it was almost three. She needed to hurry. She grabbed a pillow off the bed and stripped off the case. She then put the albums and the photo of Max into it.

She went to the bureau next and shoved handfuls of underwear and socks into the pillowcase. She had no jewelry other than her Timex and one pair of earrings that she almost never wore – the silver hoops that Max had actually paid for and given her on a birthday.

She next went to the closet to grab extra pairs of jeans and a few shirts. She opened the door with her eyes already angled up toward the string pull of the overhead light. So she didn't see Thelma Kibble until the light was on and she glanced down to see what her foot had just bumped into.

Her parole agent was lying on the floor of the walk-in closet with her back propped against the rear wall, her legs spread wide. Her head was tilted at an odd angle, her mouth was wide open and the front of the large, flowing dress she wore was a crimson mess. A hand came up and stifled a scream in Cassie's mouth. She jerked backward from it and then realized it was her own. The pillowcase dropped from her other hand and thumped on the floor.

The noise prompted Kibble to slowly open her eyes. It almost seemed that in all of that huge body the action of opening her eyes exhausted all her stores of strength. Cassie dropped to her knees between Kibble's outstretched legs.

'Thelma! Thelma, what happened?'

Without waiting for an answer she already knew, Cassie reached up and jerked one of the two dresses she owned off a hanger. She bunched it in her hands and moved in close to Kibble to use it as a compress. She saw a single bullet wound high on Kibble's chest. A tremendous amount of blood had leaked from the wound. So much that Cassie was stunned that Kibble was still alive. She pressed the dress over the wound and looked at Kibble's lips. They were soundlessly working as Kibble attempted to say something.

'Thelma, don't talk, don't talk. Was it Karch? A man named Karch?'

The mouth stopped working for a moment and there was a slight nod.

'Thelma, I am so sorry.'

'– ot me wi' my own gun . . .'

Her voice was no more than a rasp.

'Thelma, don't talk. I'm going to get help. You hang in there and I'll get help. Can you hold this?'

Cassie lifted the woman's left hand and put it over the bunched dress. When she released her hold the hand started to fall away. Cassie reached over to a plastic laundry basket and dragged it over. She overturned it and pulled it in tight against Kibble's side. She raised Kibble's left arm again and propped the elbow on the overturned basket. She then put the left hand back onto the makeshift compress. The weight of Kibble's huge arm kept her hand and the compress in place.

'Hang in there, Thelma,' Cassie ordered. 'There's no phone in the house. I have to go to my car. I'll call for help and be right back. Okay?'

She waited and saw Kibble's jaw start to tremble as she tried to say something.

'Don't answer! Just save your strength. Help will be here soon.'

Cassie started to get up but saw Kibble's mouth still working. She was determined to say something. Cassie leaned in close and turned so her left ear was close.

'He knows . . .'

Cassie waited but there was nothing else. She turned and looked at Kibble.

'He knows? He knows what?'

Kibble's eyes came up to hers and Cassie knew that what she was trying to say was important.

'Karch? He knows what, Thelma?'

She turned and leaned in again.

'Your daughter. He . . . has her picture.'

Cassie sprang back as if punched. She looked at Kibble with fearful and alert eyes. She then looked down at the pillowcase next to her as if it might contain a bomb set to go off at any moment. She grabbed the bag and turned it over, dumping its contents. She grabbed up one of the albums – the one she called the school album – and opened it. The first photo was missing from the clear plastic window. Written across the window in a black marker was a message that froze her heart.

NO COPS
702–881–8787

Without a doubt she knew what the message meant.

'Go . . .'

Cassie looked up from the photo album to Kibble.

'Go now . . . go get her . . .'

Cassie looked at her a long moment and then nodded. She jumped up and ran from the closet, taking the photo album with the phone number in it and leaving everything else behind.

37

From a steady distance of three blocks Karch's Towncar trailed the white Volvo wagon as it left the Wonderland School. As Karch expected, the Volvo didn't go far. It stayed on Lookout Mountain Road until it almost crested the hill and then turned down a driveway next to a 1920's style home set well back from the road. Karch slowed and by the time he was abreast of the house he saw the woman and the little girl with the happy-face backpack heading toward the front door of the house. He went on by and turned around in a driveway a block farther up the street. He went back down the street and parked at the curb across the street from the driveway with the Volvo wagon parked in it. The woman and child were inside now.

Karch noticed the real estate sign on the property and the smaller hook-on sign announcing the property was in escrow. He thought another piece of the story was falling into place. He believed that if he ever got the chance to ask Cassidy Black, she would tell him that everything started with that sign. She saw that sign and put things into motion.

'And here we are,' he said out loud.

He had been doing that a lot lately – the audio commentary when no one was around to hear it but himself. But he wasn't worried about it. It ran in the family. He used to sit in the bedroom and listen to his father in the next room talking to himself in the mirror. He'd do it while running quarters over his knuckles – both hands at once – and practicing coin and card gags. He always said the patter was as important in the art of the sleight as anything you did with your hands. Words could be part of the misdirection as well.

He heard a shout and looked over at the house. The girl had come outside. She had changed and was now wearing denim overalls over a long-sleeved T-shirt. She was kicking a ball with a ladybug design on it around the yard and finding something in the activity to yell about. Karch saw the woman standing just inside the open front door and watching over her. He waited and watched and eventually the woman stepped back into the house and out of sight. She apparently felt confident in the safety and sanctity of the yard.

Karch checked his watch and waited for her to come back to check on the girl. He wanted to get an idea of the time intervals and then he would know how much time he had. While he waited he thought some more about Cassidy Black. He believed he would soon have the high card in the game they were playing. And the last deal would be on his table, not hers.

The woman came back to the door to check on the girl after six minutes. Karch had also been counting the cars during that time. Only three had gone by. Traffic was beyond prediction but he figured, to be safe, he had between two and three minutes from getting out to getting back in.

He picked the Renaissance Investigations report off the seat next to him and checked the name once more. He then got out of the car and crossed the street, checking the surrounding houses for witnesses as he went. There were none that he could see. As far as he was concerned he had the green light. The plan was a go.

The girl looked up from her ball when he got to within a few feet of the picket fence at the front of the property. The fence was a design flourish, not a safety measure. It was barely higher than Karch's knees. If needed he'd be able to reach over and grab her.

The girl didn't say anything. She just stopped her playing and looked at him.

'How do you do?' Karch said. 'You're Jodie Shaw, aren't you?'

The girl looked back at her house and didn't see her mother at the door. She looked back at Karch.

'You are, aren't you?'

She nodded and Karch took the last few steps to the fence. He had his hands in his pockets, a subliminally nonthreatening pose.

'I was hoping so. See, your daddy sent me over from the office to pick you up for the surprise party.'

'What su'prise party?'

Karch took his hands out of his pockets and stepped up to the little fence. He dropped into a baseball catcher's stance so he would be closer to her level. His face was still above the top of the fence. He looked over the girl's head at the front door. No sign of the woman but he knew he was on a clock. He turned his head and looked over both shoulders. No neighbors anywhere. No cars coming. He still had the green.

'The party he's having for your mommy. He doesn't want her to know about it. But it's going to be a lot of fun. With a lot of your friends there and there's even going to be a magic show.'

He reached over the fence to her right ear and seemed to grab a quarter out of thin air. When he had removed his hand from his pocket the quarter had been clipped between his third and fourth finger in the classic Goshman Pinch sleight. The girl looked at the coin and her mouth opened into a surprised smile.

'Hey!'

'And what about this side?'

He pulled another quarter out of her other ear with his other hand. The girl was grinning broadly now.

'How'd you do that?'

'If I told you I'd have to . . . uh, well, you know if you come with me now to see your dad, then I promise he and I will teach you how to do it. What do you say, Jodie? Okay? He's waiting for us, baby.'

'I'm not a baby. And I'm not supposed to go with strangers.'

Karch silently cursed to himself and checked the front door again. Still clear.

'I know you're not a baby. It's just a figure of speech I use, that's all. And the other thing is, I'm not really a stranger. I mean, you and I just met for the first time but I know your daddy and he knows me. Enough for him to pick me to come get you for the party.'

He checked the front door one last time. He knew he was going too long with this. He was way over time. The green light was now red.

'Anyway, your daddy really wants you there at the office so –'

He straightened up and reached over the fence.

'– you can yell "Surprise!" when your mommy gets there.'

He reached under her arms and lifted her up. He knew the key thing was to keep her quiet for thirty feet – from the fence to the car. That was all. After that, it didn't matter. He turned and walked quickly across the street toward the Lincoln.

'Mommy?' the girl said in a timid voice.

'Shhhh, shhhh,' he responded quickly. 'We don't want her to know about this, sweetheart. That would spoil the surprise.'

He got to the car, opened the back door and loaded her in. He then closed it and jumped into the front seat. He had done it, he realized. Grabbed her without incident or detection. He dropped the car into drive and started down Lookout Mountain.

'Is there going to be dancing at this surprise party?' Jodie said from the backseat.

Karch adjusted the rearview mirror so he would be able to watch the girl. The moment he did it he heard a scream in the distance. The windows were up in the Lincoln so the origin of the sound could not be pinpointed. Karch readjusted the rearview mirror and immediately saw the woman from the house run into the street fifty yards behind. Her hands were balled into fists and pressed against her temples as she stared at the retreating Lincoln. He quickly hit the button that turned on the stereo.

He checked the mirror again. The woman was still in the middle of the street screaming but the stereo was covering it in the car. It was Frank Sinatra singing 'That's Life.'

Karch started thinking about the license plates on the Lincoln. He doubted the woman had gotten a read off the back plate but he knew he needed to find a safe place to switch back to the originals. And he wasn't worried about having been seen himself. The windows were tinted too dark for that. He felt good. He was clear.

He remembered the girl had asked a question. He adjusted the mirror again and looked back at her.

'What did you ask?'

'Will there be dancing at the party for my mommy?'

'Sure, baby, plenty of dancing.'

'I'm not a baby.'

'Yeah? Who cares?'

38

The gears of the Boxster whined loudly as Cassie wound them out on the way into Laurel Canyon.

'Nine-one-one emergency, how can I help you?'

She had the phone on speaker.

'Listen to me, you have an officer down. An officer down!'

She gave the address of the house on Selma and the location within where Thelma Kibble could be found. She also described the wound she observed and told the operator to dispatch the ambulance.

'I am doing that by computer while we speak. What is your name, please?'

'Just send the paramedics, would you?'

She disconnected the call and immediately hit redial. At first she got a recording saying all 911 lines were busy but an operator picked up before the recording was completed.

'Nine-one-one emergency, how can I help you?'

At first Cassie thought it might be the same operator.

'Can I help you?'

She decided it wasn't.

'There's a man trying to abduct a little girl. You have to send someone.'

'What is the location, ma'am?'

Cassie looked at the dashboard clock. It was three-fifteen. She knew Jodie Shaw's schedule by heart and that she left Wonderland Elementary every day at three. If Karch hadn't already made his move he would have to do it at the house. She gave the operator the address of the house on Lookout Mountain Road.

'Hurry! Please!'

She disconnected the call. She caught the light at Hollywood and Laurel Canyon Boulevards and sped north into the canyon. She realized that she was probably closer than any LAPD patrol cruiser, unless there happened to be one already in the canyon or at Wonderland Elementary. She had to decide what to do if she got there first.

Traffic slowed as it winnowed to one lane and she found herself caught behind an old LTD that was meandering into the canyon.

'Come on!' she yelled, her hand pressed on the horn. 'Let's go! Let's go!'

She saw the man in the car in front of her looking at her in his mirror. She waved him to the side but he just raised the middle finger of his right hand to her and seemed to intentionally drive even slower. On the next turn she passed him, a dangerous maneuver that made an oncoming car pull off the road. The driver of that car and the man in the LTD serenaded her with long blasts of their horns. Cassie stuck her fist out the window and raised her finger to the LTD. She sped ahead.

She made the turn onto Lookout Mountain and sped up the hill. She slowed as she went by Wonderland Elementary. There were still children in the play yard and the street was crowded with double-parked cars as parents stopped to pick up their children. Cassie picked her way around but didn't bother looking for Jodie. She knew the schedule. She was at home – or already with Karch.

As she made the last curve before the Shaws' house her heart jumped up into her throat. Up ahead was a police car, its lights flashing, parked in the street. Her hope was that it was there in response to her 911 call but her gut said that was impossible. She had made the call just three minutes earlier.

Cassie slowed the Boxster as she got to the house. She saw two police officers, a male and female team, standing on the lawn just inside the picket fence. They were looking at a woman whose face was so contorted and red that it was a moment before Cassie recognized her as Linda Shaw, the woman who had raised her child.

Tears were streaking her face. Her hands were white-knuckled fists held tight against her chest. The female cop was bending down a bit and looking into her face. She had one hand on Linda Shaw's arm in a comforting fashion. The other officer was speaking into a hand-held radio. Cassie knew she was too late.

All at once all three of them looked out into the street and at the Porsche, their attention drawn by the rumbling of the engine as Cassie powered it down.

The two officers checked the car for a few moments and turned their attention back to the woman between them. But Linda Shaw's eyes held on the Boxster. They pierced the windshield and looked right at Cassie Black. The two women had never met before. The adoption transfer had been handled blindly because of Cassie's incarceration and her desire at the time not to meet the people who would take her child.

But in that fleeting moment when their eyes met, Cassie felt something transmitted. They had connected on the cold plane where the worst fears of motherhood are hidden. In Linda Shaw's tortured and wet eyes Cassie saw that there could be no greater love for her daughter.

Cassie was the first to turn her eyes away. She kept the Boxster driving smoothly by. She knew she could take Lookout Mountain up to Sunset Plaza and then back down into the city without having to go by the house again. That was what she would do, she decided.

And then she would go where he wanted her to go. Karch. They would play this out whatever way he wanted.

[illegible] sky was blue-black [illegible]
[illegible] how peaceful [illegible]
[illegible] smooth movement [illegible]
[illegible] resonance. It was [illegible]
[illegible] between [illegible]
[illegible] fighting the horizon [illegible]
[illegible] checked [illegible]
[illegible] time to eat [illegible]
[illegible] getting and [illegible]
[illegible] more [illegible]
[illegible] made Karen [illegible]
[illegible] it all and [illegible]
[illegible] back in [illegible]
[illegible] our holder and [illegible]
[illegible] private office [illegible]
[illegible] picked up [illegible]

[illegible] a backup [illegible]
[illegible] anyway [illegible]

[illegible] from [illegible]
[illegible] the last you had [illegible]
[illegible] trying to get [illegible]
[illegible] know is [illegible]
[illegible] anything [illegible]
[illegible] his head [illegible]
[illegible] the lid [illegible]
[illegible] Vincent [illegible]
[illegible] check [illegible]
[illegible] check [illegible]
[illegible] out here? Hold [illegible]
[illegible] wait [illegible]
[illegible] [illegible]
[illegible] look up. The backup [illegible]
[illegible] was [illegible]

39

The desert sky was blue-black, the air cool and crisp. Karch loved the desert at night. He loved how peaceful it was and the memories it brought him. Even inside a Lincoln moving at ninety miles an hour he appreciated it. The desert was restorative. It was the city that took everything away.

He was halfway between Primm and Las Vegas and the glow of the Strip was lighting the horizon ahead like a distant wildfire. The 15 Freeway was wide open. He checked the dash clock and saw it was almost eight. He decided it was time to call Grimaldi. The old man was probably going nuts anyway, wondering and waiting. He turned the overhead light on and checked the girl once more. She was still lying across the backseat asleep. Just looking at her made Karch yawn. He hadn't slept in over thirty-six hours.

He shook it off and gulped black coffee from a to-go cup. He had bought it all the way back in Barstow and it was cold. He put it back in the dashboard cup holder and got the cell phone out of his jacket. He punched in Grimaldi's private office number and then turned the overhead light off. The call was picked up immediately.

'Yes?'

There was a lot of background noise. People noise, talking and yelling and clapping. Karch knew Grimaldi had picked up the extension in the crow's nest.

'Vincent, I need you to go to your computer.'

'Where the hell you been? I've been paging you since –'

'I've been trying to get your money back. Now can you –'

'All I want to know is if you have it, not that you're *trying* to get it. Trying doesn't mean anything without the other.'

Karch shook his head. He felt like yelling into the phone but knew it would wake up the kid. He kept his voice calm and even.

'It's coming, Vincent. But in order to collect it I'm going to need a little help. Now, can you check a room for me or not?'

'Of course I can check a room. Let me put you on hold while I get someone out here. Hold on.'

Grimaldi didn't wait for a reply. Karch was put on hold as the Lincoln steadily closed in on Las Vegas. After a good five minutes Grimaldi finally picked back up. The background noise was gone. He was in his office now. There was no banter. He got right to the point.

'What's the number?'

'The penthouse. Two-thousand-one. Like the space odyssey.'

'Wait a minute. That's the –'

'I know. Anybody in it?'

'I'm checking . . . No, it's clear tonight.'

'Good, Vincent. Now block it off and reserve it under the name Jane Davis. You got a pen? I'll give you a credit card number.'

Karch took the passports out of his pocket and pulled an American Express card off the paperclip on the Jane Davis identification package. He turned the overhead light on and read Grimaldi the card number.

'Got it,' Grimaldi said. 'What else?'

The tone in Grimaldi's voice made Karch smile. It was so eager. Karch knew he was in control now. The trick would be to maintain it after this was all over. He spent the next ten minutes outlining his plan, looking over his shoulder twice to make sure the girl was still asleep and not listening. While he spoke the Lincoln passed the WELCOME TO LAS VEGAS sign that had adorned the city's outer perimeter for four decades. The neon-edged shapes of the Strip hotels came into view. Grimaldi badgered him during the telling with questions and voiced doubts. By the time he was finished the mood had shifted and he was exasperated.

'You sure this will work?' Grimaldi said.

'It is called synchronicity, Vin-*CENT*,' Karch said angrily. 'Have you ever heard the word? It will all fit together and you will have the money back. That is what you want, isn't it?'

'Yes, Jack, it's what I want.'

'All right then, we're in business. Better get things going. I'm almost there.'

He closed the phone and put it on the seat next to him. He checked the girl again and saw she was still out. He turned the light off just as the phone started to ring. He quickly grabbed it and opened it up before it woke the girl.

'What's wrong now, Vincent? You can't find *synchronicity* in your dictionary?'

'Who is Vincent?'

It was Cassie Black. Karch smiled, realizing he should have known it would not be Grimaldi because he didn't have the number.

'Cassidy Black,' he said quickly, hoping to cover. 'It's about time you checked in. Those were some nice moves you made today. But I think that if maybe we had been on my turf then things might have turned out –'

'Where is she?'

Her voice was a steely wire. Karch paused, his smile still fixed on his face. The moment was delicious. He had control and he was going to win this one.

'She's with me and she's doing fine. And that's exactly how she'll stay as long as you do *exactly* what I tell you to do. Do you understand that?'

'Listen to me, Karch. If that little girl gets hurt in any way . . . then it won't go by, you understand. I will make it my life's work to fuck you up. Do you understand *that?*'

Karch didn't answer for a while. He opened his window a half inch and got out a cigarette. He lit it off the dash lighter.

'Are you there, Karch?'

'Oh, I'm here. I'm just thinking to myself how ironic this is. I mean, I think it's irony – I never was very good in English class. Is it ironic when somebody whose plan it was to abduct a child complains about that very same child being snatched by somebody else first? Is that irony?'

Karch waited for her to answer but nothing came over the line. His smile broadened. He knew he was cutting her right to the bone. And the truth was always the best and sharpest knife to use for such a procedure.

'So tell me something, Cassie Black, what were you doing living in L.A.? Selling cars or watching the girl? And who was it you were going to take to Tahiti with you, seeing that Max can't exactly make the trip?'

He waited but there was only more silence on the open line.

'The way I figure it, I probably got to her maybe a half hour or an hour before you. So save the righteous indignation. I don't buy it.'

He thought maybe he could hear her crying but wasn't sure. He felt some kind of strange closeness to her. Maybe it was from knowing her plan, from knowing what her secret dream was. It felt wonderful to be so intimately knowledgeable of the very thing another being lived for. It was almost like love.

'That's right,' he said quietly. 'I know all about you and your little plan. Keep an eye on the girl and wait out your parole – what did you have, a year or so to go? Then grab her and head off to paradise – Tahiti, the place you and Max had that wonderful, wonderful time so long ago. By the way, I have something of yours – and I don't mean the girl.'

He hooked the phone in the crook of his neck and picked the passports off the seat next to him. He opened one and looked at the photo of the woman he was now talking to on the phone.

'Jane and Jodie Davis,' he said. 'Isn't that nice? Whoever made these up for Leo did a really fine job. Too bad you didn't get the chance to try 'em out.'

Cassie was silent.

Karch kept sticking in needles.

'I guess when that For Sale sign went up you knew you were in trouble. Jodie told me the family was moving to *Pawis*, as she calls it, in a month. I bet that sure as hell shook you up and put a clock on your plan. You went to Leo for a job. And he put you into the Cleo again. Now here we are.'

'What do you want me to do, Karch? I have the money. Let's talk about the money and get this over with.'

'Where are you?'

'Where do you think, L.A.'

'That's bad. I guess that means you didn't get my little message until it was too late for Agent Kibble. Too bad. That'll be a big pair of shoes to fill at the parole office.'

Karch started laughing as he pulled into the exit lane for Tropicana Boulevard. He would be at the Cleo in ten minutes.

'You're sick, you know that, Karch? Thelma Kibble never did anything to you.'

'Honey, let me tell you something. Half the people I take out never did anything to me. Neither did Jodie Shaw – or should I say, Jodie Davis. I don't give a fuck, you understand?'

'You're a psychopath.'

'Exactly. So this is what you do. You listening? You bring that money back to Vegas as fast as you can. I don't care if you are flying or driving, but you get back here to the Cleo with it by midnight tonight. Back to the scene of the crime.'

He checked the dash clock.

'Four hours. That gives you plenty of time. When you get here you call me again and I'll have someone bring you up to me.'

'Karch, you –'

'Shut up! I'm not finished. I better hear from you by midnight or the Shaws will have to go back to High Desert to see if some other convict's got a bun in the oven they want to give away.'

'I didn't *want* to give her away!'

Karch held the phone away from his ear.

'I had no choice! I wasn't going to raise my daughter in a –'

'Yeah, yeah, same difference. You and Max must've thought along the same lines.'

There was silence on the line for a long time.

'What are you talking about? You killed him. I know it was you up there that night.'

'I was up there, but you got the rest wrong, lady. But I gotta tell you I didn't even know for sure what happened until today. Until I found out about the girl.'

He paused and she said nothing.

'You want me to go on?'

He waited again. Finally, in a small voice, she told him to go on.

'See, I was in the bed like I was asleep. I let him go through the room and then go out into the second room, the living room. I then got up, got my gun from under the pillow and went out there. I confronted him. I had the gun and he didn't have shit. What else could he do but get down on the ground like I told him. But he didn't do it. I told him again and he just looked at me. Then he said something that's taken me all this time to figure out. Because, see, I didn't know about the baby, about you and him and what you told him that night before he went up to do the job.'

40

Cassie hated driving through the desert at night. It was like being in a tunnel with no end. What Karch was saying only made it worse. Tears began clouding her vision of the road in the lights of her car. She swallowed and tried to calm her voice.

'What did he say?' she said. 'Tell me what he said.'

She had the call on speaker. Karch's voice came to her out of the dark. Disembodied and carrying a slight echo, it sounded as though he was all around her and even inside her head.

'He said "Not again. Better none, than one in stir." Then he turned and ran right through that window. And I never knew what he meant until I found out from Kibble today what he knew that night. You told him he was a father, that you and him, you know. So he knew right then if he went with me he'd be in jail when that little kid was born and grew up. And that happened to him, remember? He grew up with an old man in stir. And he didn't want that for anybody.'

He stopped talking and Cassie had nothing to say. She wished she could just hang up, pull off the road and walk blindly into the desert night. She wouldn't care what was waiting out there in the darkness.

She believed Karch. She had no reason to but she knew in her heart that he was telling the truth about what Max had said. She realized then that telling him, surprising him with the news that night, had set things into a terrible motion. In her mind she suddenly saw Max's crumpled body on the casino table. She had run to him and cradled his head in her arms. They'd had to pull her away from him.

'So you see,' Karch suddenly said, 'if there's anybody you should blame it's you, not me. You had the kid in your belly and you told him the news. What do you think about that, Cassie Black?'

She didn't answer. She gripped the wheel so tightly her knuckles glowed white in the dim light from the dash gauges. She felt a deep-rooted tremble go through her. It started in her chest and then made her shoulders shake. It moved like a wave down her arms until control of the wheel was in question. Finally, it passed. She tried to put thoughts about Max aside, to be dealt with later. Jodie was the important thing. She had to concentrate on Jodie.

'You know something?' Karch said. 'Now that I understand what happened in that room with Max, the one thing I don't understand is what happened in the room with Hidalgo. I mean, why'd you do it?'

Cassie didn't understand why he asked such an obvious question.

'Why else? The money.'

'But why put the guy down unless you had to and it didn't seem to me that –'

'What are you talking about? Hidalgo? Hidalgo's dead?'

'You should know that better than –'

'No! I don't know what you're talking about!'

'It looked pretty cold-blooded to me. Guy sitting there in bed in his underwear, defenseless, and you pop him like that.'

As he spoke Cassie remembered her last moments in the room. Hidalgo was restless, waking up. She stood at the foot of the bed and raised the gun. She had been ready and willing to do what was necessary. To cross the final line. Had she done it, had she crossed, and then blocked it from her memory? Impossible.

'Karch, listen to me. If he's dead somebody else did it.'

There was a pause and then Karch's voice came back.

'Sure. Whatever you say. It still doesn't change things. You're coming back here with the money and –'

'Karch?'

'What?'

'How do I know you even have her?'

He laughed in a fake way into the phone.

'That's just it. You don't.'

'I need to talk to her. Before I come there, I need to know you have her. And that she's alive. Please, Karch.'

'Oh, well, if you're going to be so polite about it . . .'

She listened. She thought she heard a horn honking and then Karch cursed at someone. She realized he was in a car and guessed it meant that he had pulled over and maybe cut someone off. She heard a rustling sound and then Karch's voice again, but not directed into the phone.

'Wake up, kid,' he said. 'Somebody wants to talk to you. Say hello.'

Cassie heard her daughter's breathing before her voice. Then she spoke one word that went through Cassie's heart like a diamond-tipped drill.

'Mommy?'

Cassie involuntarily drew her breath in and held it. She tried to halt the torrent of tears she knew was waiting to come down. She opened her mouth and tried to respond to the first word her daughter had ever said to her. But before she could form a sound, Karch's rude and gruff laugh loudly filled the inside of the car.

'Out of the mouths of babes, right?' he said. 'The Cleo by midnight, Cinderella, or your pumpkin gets smashed.'

He killed the connection and Cassie was suddenly riding in silence and darkness. In the tunnel.

She thought about calling Karch back but knew that all that was to be said had been said. She gazed out the windshield at the WELCOME TO LAS VEGAS sign as it passed. She had lied to Karch. She was coming in right behind him. It would give her a time advantage – a few hours to get ready – but little else. She had no idea what it was she would be getting ready for.

41

The girl sat up in the backseat of the Lincoln and took in the dazzling lights of the Strip.

'Where are we?' she asked.

'We're almost there.'

'I want my daddy.'

Karch turned the rearview mirror and looked back at her. It sounded like she was going to start crying again. Halfway from L.A. she had started crying and screaming for her mother and father. Karch had had to pull off in Barstow and calm her. Mostly he bribed her with French fries and a Coke. He got her to agree to stop the outburst until they got to the hotel in Las Vegas where her daddy was waiting. The one good thing was that all the crying made her tired and she slept most of the rest of the way.

'Remember our deal. No crying and no outbursts until we get to the hotel room and you see your daddy. Okay?'

'I don't care. I want my daddy.'

'We're almost there,' he said. 'You're going to be with your daddy real soon.'

He smiled, though he knew she would never comprehend the joke.

'Are we in France now?'

'What?'

He checked the mirror and saw her staring out the window to her right, the reflection of neon light playing on her young face. He looked out the windshield to the right and saw what she was looking at. They were passing a half-size Eiffel Tower fronting a casino.

'Could be, kid. Could be.'

After a few more minutes he turned the car into the Cleopatra's entrance and followed the signs that said SELF PARKING to the rear of the property. He drove into the west parking garage as he had told Grimaldi he would. He found a parking slot on the fourth level and then he and the girl took the stairs down to the ground floor. Karch walked quickly, holding the girl by the hand and tugging her along.

An emergency exit door that Karch knew led from the elevator lobby of the Euphrates Tower directly to the parking garage had been left propped open for them with a towel tied around the inside push bar and then looped around the edge of the door and tied to the outside handle. By entering here he would be able to bypass all of the cameras in the casino. He could not allow there to be any video documentation of himself with the girl. Once they were through the door Karch yanked the towel free so that the door closed and locked. He left the towel on the floor.

In the elevator lobby Jodie Shaw stopped and tried to jerk her hand out of Karch's grip. It reminded him of the slightest tug of a throw-back fish on a fishing line. He looked down at her.

'Where's my daddy?'

'We're going up to see him right now. You want to push the button?'

He pointed to the elevator call buttons.

'No, I'm almost six years old. Not three.'

'Oh, okay then.'

Karch pulled her to the panel and pushed the button. He then glanced around and made sure no one was paying attention. He dipped his fingers into the sand jar below the buttons and eventually pulled out the card key Grimaldi had had planted there for him. An elevator opened and Karch pulled the girl into it. He used the card key to engage the penthouse button. Once the door was closed he let go of her hand. He looked up at the camera in the corner. There was no light or other means of determining if it was on or had been shut down per his instructions.

He looked down at the girl and he could tell she was confused and about to start crying again. He squatted down to her level and smiled.

'It's all right, kid. This will all be over in a few hours.'

'I want my mommy and daddy now.'

'You will all be together real soon. I promise. Hey, tell you what, did I show you this?'

He took the pack of cigarettes out of his pocket and shook one out. He then performed the in-the-ear-and-out-the-mouth transfer flawlessly. The girl's eyebrows arched in wonder. He lit the cigarette with a lighter and blew the smoke up over her head.

'That's magic,' he said. 'My daddy taught me that.'

He stood up.

'Or at least the guy who thought he was my daddy.'

The doors opened and he led the girl out into the alcove. They stepped into the hallway and went to the first door to the right. He used the card key to open the door and the girl charged in ahead of him.

'Daddy!'

He watched her look around expectantly and then go through the open double doors leading to the bedroom. Karch closed and locked the door, dropped the card on a little table beneath a mirror in the entranceway and followed her into the bedroom. She was leaning against the bed, her face down on the spread.

'Where's my daddy?'

'I guess we have to wait for him.'

She turned and looked up at him with accusing eyes.

'You told me he was here.'

'Don't worry. He's around somewhere. We just have to wait for him to come back. I'll make some calls to see if I can't find him, okay? In the meantime, this here is the room where you are going to wait. You can get on the bed and go back to sleep or you can watch TV, whatever you want. They have a channel just for cartoons, right? Why don't you check it out?'

He looked at the girl nodding and smiling but she wasn't with the program. She hardly seemed mollified and Karch was just about out of patience. The next move would be to tie the kid up and put her in the shower with a gag in her mouth. He decided to try once more before going to that extreme.

'Tell you what, you hungry? I'll order us up some room service. I'm fucking starved. How about a nice, juicy steak?'

'Gross. And you talk dirty.'

'That I do, that I do. All right, no steak. What would you like instead?'

'Spaghettios.'

'Spaghettios? You sure about that? They got some great cooks down there. You sure you want Spaghettios?'

'Spa-*ghettios*.'

'All right, all right, Spaghettios. Tell you what, you watch the TV in here and I'll go call room service.'

He took the remote off the top of the TV and turned it on. He handed her the remote and walked out of the room. He then remembered something and came back in and disconnected the phone. She watched silently as he left the room with the phone. Just as he closed the double doors she called out from within.

'And a Coke, too.'

He wondered for a moment whether a child that age was allowed to have Coke. He then dismissed the thought because it didn't matter.

'Okay, one Coke coming up.'

Karch took the phone cord and wrapped it around the necks of the two doorknobs. He doubted she would try to make a break but it didn't hurt to be thorough. He then walked over to the little desk and picked up the phone. He dialed Grimaldi's direct line again and the casino director answered immediately.

'You're in.'

'You turned the elevator cams off, right?'

'And the garage. Just like you asked. Routine maintenance. If you stayed clear of the casino then there's no record of you coming in.'

'Okay. What about the stairs?'

'I've got people in every stairwell. And we know she doesn't have a card because Martin got his back. So she can't use the elevators. Just the stairs. You want somebody up there in the penthouse, like in the hallway?'

'No.'

'You sure she's going to come back with the money? Just for the kid?'

'She's coming, Vincent. I guarantee it.'

'With your life, Jack. You understand that?'

Karch didn't answer. Grimaldi was trying to reassert himself but it was too late for that. Karch still had control.

'She says she didn't put Hidalgo down on the bed like that.'

'Who says this?'

'Cassie Black. She says she didn't pop him.'

'Bullshit. What's she going to say? "Things went wrong up there and I did it?" No, they never cop to anything, Jack, you know that.'

Karch thought about this.

'All right,' he finally said. 'I guess you're right.'

'I know I am. So you're all set up there?'

'Yeah – oh wait, one last thing. I need you to call room service and have them send up a steak. Make it bloody rare. And . . .'

He looked toward the doors to the bedroom. The low sound of cartoon gunfire was coming from the room.

'What?'

'And do they have any Spaghettios down there?'

'That canned shit?'

'Kids like it.'

'No, Jack, no fucking Spaghettios. This is a four-star kitchen.'

'Well, then something close to it. And two Cokes, no ice. Tell them to knock on the door and leave it outside. Tell them I don't have to sign for it. Nobody can see me up here, Vincent. You understand?'

'Perfectly. Anything else?'

'That's it. This will all be over by midnight, Vincent. You'll have the money, everything. Miami will get the Cleo, you'll run the show, and Chicago gets fucked.'

'I'll be very grateful, Jack.'

'You bet your ass you will be.'

He hung up. He then took the cell phone out of his pocket and used it to check his messages. There were a couple of new missing persons referrals but nothing else. Karch knew that one way or another his missing persons days were going to end soon.

When he put the phone back into his inside suit pocket he felt something in there and remembered he had taken Leo Renfro's date book. He took it out and opened it. He had only glanced through it before, at the time hoping there would be a clue to the whereabouts of the money or Cassie Black. Instead, he found the calendar pages filled with penciled notes about astrological conditions. It fascinated him that there were people who made life decisions based upon configurations of the stars and the sun and moon. He felt that it was stupid and what happened to Leo sure proved it.

He now paged through the calendar to see what Leo had written about the future he didn't live to see. He started to smile when he got to a particularly large notation penciled into the block denoting the current date.

'Hey, we got a void moon rising tonight,' he said out loud. 'Ten-ten till midnight.'

He thought maybe there was something valid to all of this. After all, he knew the night was going to be bad luck for somebody. He put the date book down and stood up. He stepped to the corner and opened the curtains, revealing the floor-to-ceiling window. He stood back and appraised the view and the glass. He pinpointed the spot where Max Freeling had hit the glass and crashed through.

He looked over at the bedroom doors. He heard the signature *Beep Beep* of a Road Runner cartoon and he knew the coyote was on the case.

42

Cassie analyzed and reanalyzed everything Karch had said during the cell phone-to-cell phone conversation. She was in Vegas now, parked in the Flamingo garage again. She sat with her hands on the wheel even though the car was stopped in a parking slot. She stared at the wall in front of her and analyzed the conversation once more. At one point Karch had mentioned the scene of the crime. He also said that when she called after arriving he would have someone bring her 'up' to him. This meant to Cassie that he was waiting for her in the penthouse of the Cleo. In room 2014 to be exact. The scene of the crime.

But then she overanalyzed things and began to wonder if the clues he had dropped into the phone call had been dropped intentionally. Perhaps Karch knew she had been lying and was on the road just behind him. Perhaps he knew that she would make a move to rescue her daughter. Finally, though, she dismissed this latter possibility. Looking at it from the standpoint of Karch's believing he held all the cards this time, she decided that he had something else in mind when he chose 2014 for their meeting and supposed exchange of money for the girl.

One thing that needed no analyzing was the exchange. Cassie knew as an absolute given that there would be no trade. Whatever Karch had in mind did not include Cassie's leaving Las Vegas with her daughter. She knew that if she went through with this Karch's way that she would be going to her death. Karch was a no-witnesses man. And to him an ex-con hot prowler wasn't worth a second thought. While she was pretty sure that she could and would trade her life for Jodie's, she was also absolutely sure that Karch's no-witnesses ethic would even apply to a five-and-a-half-year-old innocently caught in the crosswinds of her mother's fatal mistakes.

So after all the furious thinking there was no choice. It came down to a given. She had to get back into the Cleopatra and up to the top floor. She then had to get into room 2014 again. Using that resolve as a foundation, she finally hatched a plan from which she hoped at least one person – a child – would come out alive.

Thirty minutes later she was moving through the casino at the Cleopatra with a new wide-brimmed hat on and a determined step in her walk. She carried a matching black gym bag she had also bought at one of the shops at the Flamingo. It contained more cash than was on the entire casino floor at the moment. It also contained the fanny pack with the tools of her trade but no gun. If things worked out as she planned a weapon would not be necessary. If a weapon became necessary she knew she'd already be lost.

She had to assume the stairwells were being watched. It was the only way up without a key. So she ignored them and headed directly to the Euphrates Tower elevator alcove. She pushed the up button.

Before an elevator arrived two couples walked into the alcove, the male half of each pushing the already lit call button. Cassie needed an elevator to herself. When one arrived she stepped back and let the others have it, then pushed the button again. This happened two more times until she started to think she would never get her own elevator. Finally, she decided to take her chances and got on an elevator with a woman carrying a plastic change cup. She waited until the other passenger chose her floor – luckily it was the sixth floor – and then punched the button for the nineteenth floor.

While they rode up Cassie checked her watch. It was ten o'clock. As soon as her fellow passenger stepped off the elevator, Cassie pushed the buttons for the seventeenth and eighteenth floors as well. She then removed her hat and hooked it over the camera in the upper corner. She did it in such a way that the hat was held between her face and the camera until the camera was blocked. Her hope was that when the tampered camera was discovered and investigated it would be written off as a prank.

Cassie slipped her lock picks out of her back pocket and put them in her mouth. She hooked one arm through both straps of the gym bag, then put one foot up on the railing that ran along the side wall of the elevator. She hoisted herself up with her back to the corner and put her other foot on the railing on the rear wall. Braced against the corner she went to work with the picks on the lock on the elevator's overhead door.

The elevator stopped on seventeen and the doors opened. Cassie glanced down and out into the empty alcove and then went back to work on the lock. She was having trouble because of her uncomfortable posture and having to work on tumblers in vertical alignment. The door closed and the elevator made a quick jump to the next floor.

Just as the doors slid open Cassie heard the click of the final tumbler and turned the lock. She pushed the door upward and open, then looked down as she pulled the gym bag off her arm. She saw a man standing in the elevator looking up at her. He was wearing a Hawaiian shirt tucked into beltless pants. Cassie didn't know how much he had seen but she knew there was no valid explanation for what she was doing. His eyes moved from Cassie to the black hat hooked over the camera. The doors started closing behind him but he suddenly shot his arm out and hit the bumper with his hand. The doors opened again.

'I think I'll catch the next one,' he said.

'Thank you,' Cassie said, one of her picks still in her mouth.

She didn't know what else to say. The man stepped out and the doors closed behind him. Cassie shoved the gym bag up through the hatch, which was about two feet square. She then reached her arms up through the opening and braced them on the top of the elevator roof. She pulled herself up and through.

The elevator started moving upward again. Cassie quickly closed the hatch and heard its lock click into place. Dim light came down from the top of the elevator shaft where a single bulb hung from a roofing beam.

Cassie stood up with the gym bag and maintained her balance while waiting for the elevator to stop at the nineteenth floor. When it did, she stepped off the elevator onto an iron crossbeam that separated the elevator shaft from the one next to it. After a few moments, the elevator she had ridden up in began descending, leaving her on a six-inch-wide piece of metal nineteen stories from the ground.

The doors to the penthouse alcove were just across the chasm and up another six feet. She slowly moved along the ironwork until she reached the front wall of the shaft. There was latticework of steel cross struts creating a support cage for the elevator. She began climbing these, finding the going slippery and treacherous because the struts were caked with dust.

When she had reached a point where she was level with the penthouse doors, she gripped one of the struts with one hand and reached across the open chasm to the doors. Once she had a grip on the inside lip of one of the doors, she reached a foot across to the five-inch ledge below the doors. She swung her body across to the ledge. In doing so the gym bag slipped down her arm and was going to drop when she caught one of the straps in her hand. The bag, heavy with bricks of currency and her tools, banged sharply on the thin metal of the elevator doors. The sound echoed loudly down the shaft below her. Cassie froze. She thought the noise must have been just as loud in the alcove and the penthouse hallway.

Karch looked up from Leo Renfro's date book. He had heard a loud banging from somewhere out in the hall. He stood up and pulled the Sig from its holster while his other hand went into his pocket for the silencer. Then he thought better of it. He holstered the weapon and his hand went under his jacket to his rear beltline. He pulled the .25 out and went to the door.

Through the peephole the hallway was empty. He debated whether to investigate the noise or to call Grimaldi. He decided it was better not to wait for someone to be dispatched. He stepped back and grabbed the card key off the entranceway table and opened the door.

In the hallway Karch saw no one. He stood with the .25 palmed in the same hand in which he held the card key. He paused and listened. He heard nothing but the buffered sounds of the elevators from the nearby alcove. He walked that way and stepped into the alcove. Again he stood still and listened.

Cassie gripped the door with taut muscles, her ear pressed to the crack between the panels. She had thought she had heard a door open and close but then there was no other sound. After a minute she decided it was time to move. She released one hand's grip and removed a penlight from her back pocket. She flicked it on and put it in her mouth. She then directed the beam over the door's framework until she saw a spring-activated release lever on the upper left side. She inched her way over to that side of the door. Just as she reached up and put a hand on the lever she felt a strong rush of air from below. She hesitated and looked down, just as the elevator directly below her loomed up out of the darkness and came up to crush her against the door. In a split second she had to decide whether to pull the lever and try to push through the doors or to catch the elevator by stepping back onto its roof as it came up.

The light over one of the elevators went on and there was a soft chiming sound. Karch quickly stepped backward out of the alcove. He looked both ways down the hall and saw the double-push doors leading to the housekeeping station. He quickly stepped over and pushed through the doors.

He held one of the doors open an inch and looked back out into the hallway. He heard the elevator doors open and close. Then a man and woman stepped into the hallway and headed the opposite way from Karch's position. The man looked like he was in his fifties, the woman her twenties. Karch watched as the man reached behind the woman and stuck his hand up the short black dress she was wearing. She giggled and playfully slapped his hand away.

'Wait till we get to your room, sugar,' she said. 'Then you can grab whatever you want.'

He watched until they went into a room down the hall. He then looked around the housekeeping station. On one end there were linen and bathroom supplies locked in a fenced closet. On the other side was a service elevator. Also in the small space was a room service table piled with dirty dishes. It smelled rancid and Karch thought it had been forgotten about all day.

He stepped back into the hallway and went back toward 2001, pausing at the entrance to the elevator alcove but again not hearing or seeing anything that raised his suspicion. He moved on to the door of 2001 and used the card key to go back in.

After thirty seconds the elevator was called to another floor and dropped down the shaft. Cassie stepped off the roof onto the crossbeam and once again worked her way to the door. This time she secured the gym bag when she made the final move to the door ledge. She made it without a sound, then reached up and pulled the spring-release lever. She heard a metallic click and the two panels of the door separated a half inch. She worked her fingers into the crack and then pulled the door panels apart.

She stepped out into the elevator alcove, then turned around and slid the door panels closed until there was a click as they locked back into place.

She quickly moved into the hallway and headed toward 2014, unsure what she was going to do when she got there. But as she passed the door to 2001 she suddenly stopped as she realized something. *Synchronicity.* Karch had said the word when she had called and he thought it was someone named

Vincent on the phone. She had immediately jumped to the conclusion that the Vincent he had referred to was Vincent Grimaldi, director of casino operations. The same Vincent Grimaldi that Hidalgo had referred to. The same Vincent Grimaldi who was chief of security six years earlier. But now who Cassie thought Karch was speaking to seemed less important than what he had actually said. *Synchronicity.* Cassie knew what it meant. It had been in the *Las Vegas Sun*'s crossword puzzle at least a dozen times during the five years she religiously worked it. The aspect of seemingly separate events occurring in conjunction over time: *synchronicity.*

She knew Karch's plan. From suite 2001 a man had fallen to his death almost seven years before. Tonight that man's lover – and their child – would do the same. Karch would take the money. All other things could be laid to blame on Cassie, the distraught mother who shot her co-workers and her parole agent, abducted her daughter and then returned to Las Vegas to end it all as her lover had.

The plan was smart. She knew it would work. But knowing it wrested an advantage to Cassie's side of the board. She leaned forward, her head close to the door. She heard the faint sounds of cartoon mayhem coming from a television inside the suite.

Cassie gently placed a hand against the door and whispered, 'I'm coming, baby. I'm coming.'

43

Karch unwound the telephone wire from around the two doorknobs and looked in on the girl. She was lying on her stomach at the end of the bed, her hands propping up her head as she fought to stay awake and watch cartoons.

'Everything okay in here, kid?'

'Where's my daddy?'

Karch looked at his watch.

'Soon . . . real soon.'

He closed the door and wound the wire back around the knobs.

'More like where's the goddamn food,' he said to himself.

He walked over to the phone and called Grimaldi's number. Again the call was answered immediately.

'Anything?' Karch asked.

'Not on this end.'

'Did you call in that room service order?'

'As soon as we hung up.'

'Vincent, your four-star kitchen isn't worth a shit. I'm fucking starving up here.'

'It's busy down there. But I'll make another call.'

'All right. And let me know the minute somebody has her.'

'Will do.'

'Oh, and Vincent?'

'What, Jack?'

'You better close a few craps tables down there. You don't want anybody getting hit.'

'Jesus! Are you sure it has to be this way? Can't we just –'

'Vincent! Vincent! You don't want questions, right?'

'No, Jack.'

'Then there is no other way. Synchronicity, Vincent. Call the pit chief. Close the tables.'

He hung up and walked over to the window. He banged a fist on it, hoping to get a feel for the tension in the glass. He wondered if he shot the glass out first, to make it easier, if the Metro investigators would be able to tell that. Would they actually gather the glass and examine it? Probably not, he decided. Too much trouble, especially for what looked like an obvious murder-suicide.

He decided the plan would be to shoot the glass out and then immediately drop the bodies. The girl first and then the mother. A classic murder-suicide: distraught mother tosses her daughter, then jumps herself.

In the housekeeping station Cassie moved the room service table into a position directly below one of the panels of the drop ceiling. She then cleared the dirty dishes to one side of the table and climbed onto the other. The table was constructed with large wheels so that it would roll smoothly across the deep carpets in the penthouse suites. This made it unsteady as a platform. Cassie slowly stood up on it and reached to the ceiling. She pushed the panel up and to the side. She then gripped the tracks of the frame that held the panel and tested them against her weight. She was 110 pounds in her clothes, the gym bag another 20 or so. The tracks held secure. She tossed the gym bag up first, then grabbed the frame again and swung her legs up. She climbed into the utility crawl space between the false ceiling and the real one.

The crawl space was no more than four feet top to bottom. It was crowded with electrical conduits, water lines and the fire sprinkler pipes. But what took up the most room was the network of air-handling ducts for the heating and air-conditioning system. Twin return and delivery ducts ran the length of the hallway and branched off in smaller tributary lines that went to vents in each suite on the floor. The main ducts were three feet square and large enough to crawl through easily. The tributary lines were smaller but Cassie knew from experience that the air-return ducts were large enough for her to move through, provided she pushed her equipment bags in front of her. She also knew that if she could make it through, Jodie could as well.

Her plan had serious faults and difficulties. Noise would be a major factor. Any sound in the ventilation tunnels was magnified by the time it got to the room vents. She wasn't as much worried about her entry as she was her exit with Jodie. Keeping a five-and-a-half-year-old quiet in what was going to be a frightening situation would be difficult. She hoped the cartoons were still on the television and could be used as sound cover when they made their escape.

Another problem that Cassie knew for sure was ahead would be the removal of the vent cover once she got to the room where Jodie was being held. The cover would be screwed on from inside the room. The difficulty would be in accessing the screws. Her plan was to use a small pry bar from the gym bag to bend the vent slats. She would then reach out with a screwdriver and remove the screws that held the vent in place. This, she knew, would be laborious and time consuming. If she dropped the screwdriver or even one of the screws the resulting noise could bring Karch right to her.

Its success was predicated on her belief that Karch most likely had Jodie in the bedroom of the suite, while he was in the sitting room. But if she was wrong and Karch was keeping the girl close to him, then Cassie knew her chances of getting a shot at a rescue were infinitesimal.

Despite all of this she pressed on. She carefully moved into the crawl space and slid the panel back into place. Once again she put her penlight into her mouth and directed it along the main air-handling ducts until she found the bolted seam of two conjoining segments. She crawled that way, careful to keep her weight at all times on the framework of the drop ceiling.

Cassie started removing the bolts from the bracket that held the two segments of duct together. The work was difficult. Each of the eight bolts had been spot welded as an apparent security measure. It had been almost seven years since Cassie had been in this same crawl space – when she had set up the job Max then wouldn't let her do – but she still remembered and she knew the spot welds were new. It took all of her strength to break the weld on the first bolt and a half minute to remove it. The process instilled a feeling of panic in her. It was taking too long.

Cassie had just started working on the last bolt when she heard the chime from the service elevator in the housekeeping alcove. She put her wrench down and quickly crawled back to the panel she had climbed up through. She lifted it a crack and looked down just as the elevator opened and a room service waiter pushed a table out onto the landing.

As the elevator closed behind him the waiter slipped a leather check folder out of the inside pocket of his red uniform jacket. He opened it to double-check on his destination. Cassie was three feet above him and could easily read the notations on the check inside the folder.

> #2001
> Leave in hallway.
> – V. Grimaldi

Seeing the note was one more confirmation of Vincent Grimaldi's involvement. It also gave Cassie an idea for a new plan.

The knock on the door startled Karch from his reverie at the window.

'Room service,' a voice called from the hallway.

He turned and stared at the door and waited but there was no second knock or sound. He picked the .25 up off the desk and cautiously approached the door. Before putting his eye to the peephole he put his ear to the jamb and listened. He heard nothing.

He looked out through the convex view of the peephole. He saw a room service table sitting in the hallway. It was covered with a white tablecloth and was set for two. A small vase of cut flowers was placed at the center. He saw no one else in the hallway. He continued to watch and wait, just in case the room service waiter was waiting by the elevator alcove. Karch had no idea what Grimaldi would have instructed and if his instructions would have made the waiter curious.

After thirty seconds he opened the door, looked both ways in the empty hallway, and then down at the table. He realized there were no plates on the table. He lifted the tablecloth and looked underneath. There was a warming oven built in below the table. Satisfied, Karch pulled the table into the suite. The table was difficult to move and he made a mental note to tell Grimaldi the carpets were too thick in the rooms. He kicked the door closed and pushed the cart toward the bedroom doors, putting the .25 down on the entrance table as he went by.

After opening the doors he pushed the cart into the room and beside the bed.

'Come and get it,' he said to the girl.

'I'm not hungry,' she said.

Karch gave her a look and said, 'Suit yourself. I'm starved.'

He flipped up the end of the tablecloth and opened the plate warmer. A blast of warm air greeted him. There were two dishes with aluminum covers sitting on a shelf. He pulled the first plate out and was holding it with both hands when he realized it was burning him. He quickly brought it up and put it down on the table.

'*FFFFFUUUUCCKKKK*, that's hot!'

He shook his hands out and bent down to look under the shelf. There were three cans of Sterno flaming directly below the aluminum shelf where the plate had been.

'Fuckers!'

He looked at the girl to make sure she wasn't finding humor in what had happened. She was just staring at him, a note of fear on her face.

'I know, I talk dirty. I gotta put some water on this.'

As soon as Cassie heard the water running in the bathroom she crawled out from beneath the other end of the room service table. Kneeling on the floor next to the table, she took a quick look around to see if Karch had left a weapon nearby. He hadn't.

'Hey!'

She turned to Jodie and quickly leaned over the bed. She had her ears trained on the sound of the water. The bathroom door was open and she could see Karch's back in a mirror reflection. She knew as soon as the water went off she had to be out of sight.

'Jodie, I'm here to take you away from that man,' she whispered quickly.

'Good, I want –'

Cassie put her finger across the girl's lips.

'Whisper, whisper, so he won't hear. Do you want to go with me?'

The girl was a fast learner. She nodded.

'Okay, then you have to do what I tell you, okay?'

Jodie nodded again.

Karch pulled his hands out of the cold water and looked at them. Both his thumbs and index fingers had red marks. He cursed again. He felt like going down to the hotel kitchen and grabbing whoever was responsible and holding his head down on a hot stove. He went into a short reverie in which he envisioned doing it, then realized the person whose head he was holding over the stove was Vincent Grimaldi. Karch looked at himself in the mirror and smiled. He was sure there was something a shrink could do with that.

He turned the water off and went back out to the bedroom. The girl was now standing at the other end of the table and looking under the tablecloth. Karch came over quickly and, realizing the .25 was in the other room, brought his hand inside his jacket to his Sig. He didn't want to draw it in front of the girl if he could help it.

'What are you looking at?'

'Nothing.'

He pulled her aside and then whipped up the tablecloth, ready with his other hand to pull the Sig. There was nothing underneath on this side.

'Looking for a place to hide, huh?'

'No, just looking.'

Karch grabbed one of the napkins off the top and went back around to the plate warmer. He used the napkin to take the second plate out.

'So let's see what we've got,' he said.

Still using the napkin he removed the cover from the first plate. It contained a New York strip steak in a pool of still sizzling butter next to a pile of mashed potatoes. The steak was rare and bloody juices were mixing with the hot butter.

'Gross,' Jodie said.

'What are you talking about? This is a goddamn thing of beauty. Now let's see what you got.'

He removed the other cover revealing a large bowl of rigatoni with meat sauce.

'That's not Spaghettios.'

'You're right. But what do you care? You're not hungry, remember?'

He walked over to the bed and took the pillowcase off one of the pillows. He folded it to quarter-size and then put it in his open palm. He used the napkin to push the hot steak plate onto the pillowcase and then put a set of utensils into his shirt pocket.

'Tell you what, I'm going to eat out there and leave you with your cartoons in here. Eat, don't eat, I don't care, kid. Doesn't bother me one way or the other.'

'Fine, I won't, then.'

'Good. Just don't burn yourself on that plate.'

He carried his food out to the desk, then went back to the bedroom for his Coke and the salt shaker. After he left he tied the doorknobs again with the phone wire. He then went over to the entrance table and brought the .25 back to the desk. He started sawing through the steak and putting large hot chunks of it into his mouth.

'This is fucking good,' he said with his mouth full.

44

Cassie rolled out from under the bed, put her finger to her lips to remind Jodie to be quiet, and picked up the television remote. She slowly raised the volume so that it would better cover their whispering and any other noises that were made. She then walked around the side of the bed to where Jodie was sitting. Cassie pulled her daughter into a heartfelt embrace but noticed the girl's arms were held down at her waist. Jodie had no idea who this woman was who was hugging her. Cassie pulled back and put her arms on the girl's shoulders and leaned down close to her to whisper.

'Jodie, are you all right?'

'I want my mommy. I want my daddy.'

Cassie had thought about this moment for a long time. Not these circumstances but the moment when she would be close to her daughter and what it was she would say and try to explain.

'Jodie, I'm . . .' she started but didn't finish. In that moment she decided this was not the right time. The child was already confused and scared. 'Jodie, my name is Cassie and I'm going to take you out of here. Did that man hurt you?'

'He made me –'

Cassie quickly put her finger across Jodie's lips to remind her to whisper. The girl then started over.

'He made me go in the car with him. He said he was a magician and that my daddy was having a party here for my mom.'

'Well, he's a liar, Jodie. I am going to get you away from him and out of here. But we have to be very –'

Cassie stopped when she heard a sound from the doors.

Karch unwrapped the telephone line from the knobs and opened the bedroom doors. He stepped in and looked at the girl lying on the bed, her face propped in her hands. He stepped further in and surveyed the room and saw nothing amiss.

'Loud enough for you?' he asked.

'What?'

'I said, "Loud –" '

He stopped when he saw her smile, realizing the joke. He pointed a warning finger at her and stepped over to the curtains. He opened them, revealing another floor-to-ceiling wall of glass. He stepped close enough that he could see his breath on the glass and looked down. He could see through the atrium below to the crowded gaming tables.

'They're all suckers,' he said. 'Nobody beats the house.'

'What?' Jodie said from behind him.

He turned and looked at her. Then his eyes moved to the room service cart and her untouched plate of pasta.

'I said you better eat your dinner, kid. You won't be getting another.'

'I'll eat when my daddy comes.'

'Have it your way.'

He stepped through the door, closed it and this time decided the telephone wire wasn't necessary.

'Where's she gonna go?' he said to himself as he returned to his steak.

After she heard the bedroom doors close Cassie closed her Swiss Army knife and got down off the toilet, where she had been poised to jump and attack if Karch had come in to search the bathroom. She went out to the bedroom and whispered into Jodie's ear that she had done a fantastic job in handling his visit to the room.

'Now, I have to go back into the bathroom, close the door and make a phone call. This time I want you to come with me. This way if he comes back you can say you're going to the bathroom and that he can't come in.'

'I don't have to go to the bathroom.'

'I know, sweetie, but you can tell him that.'

'Okay.'

'Good girl.'

Cassie kissed the top of her head and realized that the last time she had done that had been in the hospital ward at High Desert. A nurse was standing impatiently next to her bed, waiting for the baby with her arms outstretched.

Jodie's hair smelled like Johnson's baby shampoo and for some reason Cassie's identification of it served to remind her of all she had missed. She faltered for a moment while leaning over her child and the bed.

'Are you okay?' Jodie whispered.

Cassie smiled and nodded that she was. She then led the girl to the bathroom and quietly closed and locked the door. She took one of the bath towels off a shelf over the bathtub, put it on the floor and pressed it against the bottom crack of the door.

'My daddy does that when he smokes in the bathroom,' Jodie whispered.

Cassie looked up at her and nodded.

'Mommy doesn't like him to do it because it smells funny.'

Cassie got up and picked Jodie up and sat her on the closed toilet. The black gym bag was on the tank behind her.

'Now if he tries the door or knocks, you tell him he can't come in because you're going to the bathroom. Then flush the toilet and go on out, okay? But remember, before you go out take that towel from the door and throw it into the bathtub so he doesn't see it, all right?'

'Okay.'

'Good girl. You stay here. I'm going to go into the shower stall to make the phone call.'

'Are you calling my daddy?'

Cassie smiled sadly.

'No, baby, not yet.'

'I'm not a baby.'

'I know. I'm sorry.'

'He called me that.'

'Who did?'

'The magician. He said I was a baby.'

'He was wrong. You're a big girl.'

She left her there, grabbed the gym bag and another towel and went into the shower stall. She carefully and quietly closed the door and then got her cell phone out of her pocket and unfolded it. She had a page of blank note paper she had torn from a hotel pad in the bedroom. The toll-free number for the Cleopatra was printed on the bottom. She pulled the towel over her head to further deaden the transmission of sound out to Karch and punched in the number. In a low voice she asked the operator for Vincent Grimaldi. The call was transferred and picked up by someone who was not Grimaldi. He told Cassie that Mr Grimaldi was too busy to take a call at the moment and that he would be happy to take a message.

'He'll want to talk to me.'

'How so, ma'am?'

'Just tell him there are two and a half million reasons to talk to me.'

'Hold, please.'

She waited a nervous minute, wondering how long it would be before Karch checked on Jodie again, saw the bed empty and came to the bathroom door. Finally, another voice came on the line. It was calm and smooth and deep.

'Who is this?'

'Mr Grimaldi? Vincent Grimaldi?'

'Yes, who is this?'

'I just wanted to thank you.'

'For what, I don't know what you're talking about. Two and a half million reasons? What two and a half million reasons?'

'Then I guess Jack hasn't gotten it to you yet.'

This was met with a long silence. Cassie lifted the towel and looked out through the glass door of the shower stall. Jodie was where she had left her. She was rolling the toilet paper into a pile on the tile floor.

'You say Jack Karch has this money?'

Cassie dropped the towel back down. She noted Grimaldi's use of the word *money* for the first time in the conversation. Also the name *Karch.* He was getting hooked in.

'Well, yeah, I gave it to him like we agreed. I was calling just to thank you. He told me it was you who okayed the trade.'

Grimaldi's voice took on an urgent tone now. Cassie was getting juiced because she thought it was working.

'I'm not clear on what you are – could you speak up? I can hardly hear you.'

'I'm sorry. I'm in the car on the cell phone and my daughter's sleeping. I don't want to wake her. Plus out here in the desert, I think I'm losing reception.'

'What exactly did Karch say I okayed? What trade?'

'You know, the trade. My daughter and me for the money. I told him, we didn't know about the payoff or Miami or any of that. We didn't want to be greedy. As soon as we opened the case and saw all that money we knew we'd made a mistake. We wanted to give back the money. I'm just glad we were able to –'

'You're saying Karch has the money now?'

Cassie closed her eyes. She had him.

'Well, I think he was going to bring it down to you. But he had some arrangements to make first, he said. He was on the phone when we left. He was –'

The line went dead. Grimaldi had hung up.

Cassie closed the phone and slid it into her pocket. She dropped the towel and came out of the shower. She went right to Jodie and knelt down in front of her. She started untying the girl's sneakers.

'We're going to go now, Jodie. We have to take these off so we don't make any noise.'

'How come?'

'Because we're going to climb up into the wall and crawl through a tunnel that will take us out to the elevator.'

'I'm afraid of tunnels.'

'You don't have to be afraid, Jodie. I'll be right behind you the whole time. I promise.'

'No, I don't want to do it.'

The girl looked down at her hands, which were in her lap. She looked as if she might be about to start to cry. Cassie reached a finger under her chin and tilted it up.

'Jodie, it's all right. There won't be anything to be afraid of.'

'No . . .'

She shook her head. Cassie didn't know how to budge her. If she threatened her she would only scare her. And she didn't want to lie to her, either.

She leaned forward, her forehead against her daughter's.

'Jodie, I can't stay here. If that man comes back in and finds me he'll take me away. So I have to go. I wish you would go with me because I want you to be with me. But I have to go now.'

She kissed Jodie on the forehead and stood up.

'No, don't leave me,' the girl protested.

'I'm sorry, Jodie, I have to go.'

Cassie picked up the gym bag and went to the bathroom door. She kicked the towel aside and put her hand on the knob. Jodie whispered behind her.

'If I go with you, will I have to see that man again?'

Cassie turned and looked back at her.

'Never again.'

45

The steak was a bloody mess, just the way Karch loved it. He had been so hungry and the piece of meat was so good that he was on the verge of having a religious experience as he worked his way toward the last bite, dipping each chunk that he cut into the mashed potatoes before delivering it to his mouth. Being totally consumed in this process, he was taken by surprise when the door to the suite opened. He looked up, a forkful of meat and potato poised in front of his mouth, and saw a man he remotely recognized entering the sitting room followed by Vincent Grimaldi and then Grimaldi's top thug, Romero. The new man and Romero held guns at their sides.

Karch put the fork down on his plate.

'How's it taste, Jack?' Grimaldi said.

'It's excellent, Vincent. You know, you're a little early.'

'I don't think so. More like a little late.'

Karch frowned and stood up from the desk. He instinctively knew something was wrong and that he was in trouble. He picked up the napkin from the desk and wiped his mouth. He then held his hands down at his sides, the napkin still in his right hand. Very casual. Michelangelo's David.

'She's going to call any minute now,' he said. 'But you don't want to be up here when it all goes –'

'Really?' Grimaldi interrupted. 'A little bird told me she's already been here. Come and gone, as a matter of fact.'

Grimaldi nodded to the man who had led the procession into the suite. 'Check him.'

The man came over to Karch, who raised his arms outstretched. He held the napkin hanging loosely from his right hand. The man held his gun in his left hand and pointed at Karch's gut while his right hand went inside Karch's jacket and pulled the Sig out of its holster. He then patted down the rest of Karch's body, finding the silencer barrel in a coat pocket. His hands went up under his crotch without hesitation and he finished by flipping up the cuffs of his pants looking for an ankle holster. It was a professionally thorough job but not thorough enough. The whole time Karch watched him and tried to place where he had seen him before. When the search was finished the man shoved Karch's Sig under his belt and silently stepped back to the side of Grimaldi.

'What's going on, Vincent?' Karch asked.

'What's going on is you fucked up, Jack. Letting her go like that, it puts a big kink in my plan. I'm going to have to chase her down now.'

'What plan is that?'

After removing the first three, Cassie loosened the last screw of the air-intake vent and carefully pulled the vent forward and pivoted it on the remaining screw. The duct was now open and the vent hung below it. She then looked down from the room service table on which she was standing and signaled Jodie up. The girl climbed onto a chair and stepped up onto the table. Cassie lifted her up, careful not to lose her balance, and pushed her toward the opening into the duct system. Jodie struggled and put one hand out and against the wall, stopping Cassie from pushing her in.

'It will be all right, Jodie,' Cassie whispered. 'Just go in and I'll come in behind you.'

'Noooo,' the girl replied in a small voice.

Cassie pulled her down into a hug and whispered in her ear.

'Remember you told me you weren't a baby, that you were a big girl? Well, this is something a big girl would do. You have to go, Jodie, or I have to leave you here.'

Cassie closed her eyes, the last threat making her feel awful.

The girl didn't say anything. Cassie raised her toward the duct again and this time she climbed in. As she moved into the opening her knees banged on the aluminum siding and Cassie froze. But the stern tones of the voices in the other room continued without interruption. Once Jodie had crawled completely into the vent, Cassie handed her the penlight and told her in a whisper to go farther in. Cassie then hoisted herself up and climbed into the duct, catching her belt pack on the edge of the duct at first. Once in the duct, she unbuckled the tool bag and pushed it through the vent in front of her.

The space was so tightly confining that she could not reach back to pull the vent cover back into its place on the bedroom wall. She urged Jodie forward to the main air-return duct, thinking she would have room to turn around there and then crawl back to pull the vent cover back into place.

But after they were only twelve feet or so into the duct there was a junction where another similar-sized duct joined it. Cassie looked down this branch and could see light and hear voices. She realized it was Karch asking, 'What's going on, Vincent?'

Silently she went past this duct, then backed into it. She then turned and slid herself back in the direction of the bedroom. When she got there she reached down to the vent cover and slid it up the wall and back into its place. She then started backing herself up in the duct.

Karch was rapidly trying to assimilate the situation and figure out what was happening. He then hit upon the only possible explanation.

'She called you, didn't she, Vincent?'

Grimaldi didn't answer, just as he hadn't when Karch had asked him about his so-called plan. Grimaldi just stared with eyes that seemed dark with anger and hatred.

'Look, Vincent, I don't know what she told you, but it's bullshit, okay? She hasn't been here yet and I don't have the money. I'm waiting, Vincent. She's gonna call and I'll get her up here. I'll take the money and she and the kid go out the window. Like I said, synchronicity.'

As he said the last word Karch felt an internal falter. He remembered he had let the word slip when Cassidy Black had called. He wondered if that had been enough. Had he given her enough with that simple slip to read his plan and come up with a counter?

'Look, Vincent, please. Tell me what's happening here.'

Grimaldi's eyes were scanning the suite.

'What's in the bedroom, Jack?'

'Not what. Who. The kid's in the bedroom.'

Grimaldi nodded to the man who had searched Karch and the man went to the bedroom doors. He disappeared inside the room and Karch and Grimaldi just stared at each other while they waited. Romero took two steps to his left. Karch guessed he thought this put him in a better position in case he had to make a move in the room.

'I'm telling you, she's playing you, Vincent,' Karch said. 'She's play –'

He stopped when he saw the man emerge from the bedroom carrying a black gym bag. Its zipper was open and Karch could see into the bag. He saw the face of Benjamin Franklin. Several times. The bag was filled with bricks of hundred-dollar bills. Karch's mouth dropped open. Cassidy Black, he thought. She had somehow made the switch. He started toward the bedroom door but the man with the gym bag and Romero both raised their weapons and told him to hold where he was.

'There was a girl,' he said.

'Sure,' said the man with the bag. 'There ain't now.'

He walked over to Grimaldi and pulled the two handle straps wide, opening the bag and completely exposing several of the plastic-wrapped bricks of cash.

'Vincent, that's not . . .'

He didn't finish. He didn't know what to say and he could see Grimaldi was intent on the money, not him. Grimaldi put his hand into the bag and laid it flat on one of the bricks as if touching the shoulder of a long-lost friend. He then nodded to the man holding the bag.

'Okay, Martin, close it.'

Karch watched the bag being closed and then he looked at the face of the man who held it. Martin? He remembered the videotape. Hidalgo riding the elevator up with his security escort. Martin. Who was supposed to be dead. Martin, whom Grimaldi had asked Karch to bury in the desert.

'Martin?' he said.

He looked from Martin to Grimaldi as it all came to him. It was all a bluff, all part of a more elaborate plan.

'You,' he said to Grimaldi. 'You staged this whole thing. It was all a setup.'

He then looked at Martin, who held the gym bag in his right hand and his weapon in his left. He remembered Hidalgo's body on the bed. The bullet in the right eye, delivered by a gun held in the left.

'And you,' he said to Martin. 'You're the one who hit Hidalgo.'

One side of Martin's mouth turned upward in an approximation of a proud smile.

'It wasn't the girl,' Karch said, looking back at Grimaldi. 'All she did was take the money you wanted her to take.'

When Cassie turned around in the junction she heard intense voices from the sitting room. She didn't wait to listen. She headed toward the main air duct and covered the ground in about ten seconds. She saw the penlight that Jodie was holding and realized the girl was still in the smaller tributary vent and had not moved into the main conduit.

As she got closer she realized why. Jodie had reached a dead end. Metal bars criss-crossed the opening to the main duct. Cassie reached around the girl and out into the larger duct. She felt the end of each bar to determine how they were attached to the wall of duct. She felt the smooth metal weld joints. They could go no further.

'What –' Jodie started to say before Cassie got her hand over her mouth. She gave the silence signal and the girl continued in a whisper. 'What do we do?'

Cassie gripped one of the bars. She shook it and then braced her back against the upper wall of the duct and pushed on the bar with all of her strength. The bar didn't move or show any weakness in its weld points. Cassie shook her head. The operators of the hotel had put bars in the air ducts but hadn't bothered to replace the half gears in the deadbolts. It made no sense to spend money in one area and not the other. That was why hitting this dead end was so surprising and distressing.

'What do we do?' Jodie whispered again.

Cassie looked at her innocent and beautiful face in the shine of the small light. She then looked at the bars and realized something.

'Jodie, you can fit through.'

'What about you?'

'Don't worry about me. You go through. I'll go out and come around and get you.'

'No, I want to go with you.'

'No, you can't. This is the only way. You squeeze through and wait for me to come get you.'

She pushed the girl toward the bars. Jodie reluctantly stuck her head between the bars and into the larger duct, then worked her upper body through. She then pulled her legs into the new space and looked back at Cassie.

'Good girl,' Cassie whispered. 'Now you wait there. I'll come around as soon as I can but I have to wait for those men to leave the room, okay?'

'How long will that be?'

'I don't know, darling. You'll have to wait. Do you know how to tell time?'

'Of course, I'm almost six.'

Cassie took off her watch and handed it through the bars. She showed her the button to press to light the face. She then gave the girl her cell phone and showed her how to open it. Jodie said her daddy had one but never let her play with it.

'If I don't come for you by twelve o'clock you open that phone and call nine-one-one. Do you know how to do that?'

The girl did not immediately answer. Cassie took the cell phone back and showed her what to do.

'You press nine-one-one and then this button – the send button. You tell whoever answers that you are stuck on the top floor of the Cleopatra. Can you remember that?'

'Of course.'

'Where are we?'

'The Cleo-pah-tra. Top floor.'

'Good girl. I'm going to go now and listen for the men to leave. Then I will come around and get you. Come here.'

The girl leaned forward and Cassie leaned her face through the bars and kissed her forehead. She could smell her hair again. She hesitated and then started backing toward the junction, where she would be able to monitor what was happening in the suite.

Cassie saw Jodie wave to her through the bars and had a premonition that she was seeing her daughter for the last time. She waved back and then blew her a kiss.

Grimaldi was beaming as he watched Karch come to an understanding of his scheme.

'I was just like Leo and the girl, a piece you used,' Karch said.

'A piece I used beautifully and that performed beautifully,' Grimaldi responded.

'And Chicago, did they have anything to do with this?'

'That was the beauty of it. I used Chicago and they didn't even know it. But I knew just the mention of the Outfit would get your blood boiling and you'd go off like a loaded gun. Leo Renfro had markers with some people I know. I bought his paper and sent Romero and Longo over to L.A. to let him know there was a new sheriff in town. They told him they were from Chicago, that they worked for Tony Turcello. He bought it and started shitting his pants. Then they gave him a way out: hit Hidalgo on the hot prowl and his debt is clear. He went for it. Just like you went for it, Jack.'

Karch nodded.

'Yeah, I went for it. My job was to follow the trail, wipe out all parties and collect the money.'

'And you did a fine job – all except for letting the girl go. Now she's a loose end but we'll take care of it. This is the important thing.'

He raised the gym bag full of money. Karch tried to keep any physical showing of his anger in check.

'You're making a big fucking mistake, Vincent. I didn't –'

'I don't think so, Jack. I don't think so at all.'

They stared at each other for a long moment, their hatred enough to warm the room.

'So what happens now?' Karch finally asked.

'What happens now is that we still need someone to disappear with the money. Someone Miami can send their people after.'

'And that would be me.'

'You were always a smart man, Jack.'

Karch shook his head. The shortsightedness of Grimaldi's plan was staggering.

'And you always thought small, Vincent. Short range. You should have just gone along with the plan. That bag of money would have been just a drop in the bucket once Miami got the license and got into this place. You sold off the long run for the short end; one bag of money. That was stupid.'

Instead of getting angry, as Karch expected he would, Grimaldi laughed loudly and shook his head as if amused by a child's naïveté.

'You still don't get it, do you, Jack?'

'Get what? Why don't you tell me, Vin-*CENT?*'

'Miami will *never* get the license. Don't you see? There never was going to be a payoff. This is the new Las Vegas, Jack. Miami will never get in here. I set this up from day one. Me, Jack! I called Miami and said they had a problem and it would cost them five million to get it fixed and to get in here. Half up front and half after the license app was approved. They're greedy and they went for it. Just like you.'

Now Karch saw it. A perfect plan. Grimaldi would get away with two and a half million and Miami would forever search for Karch – only he'd never be found because he was about to be escorted out to the desert on a one-way trip. Karch dropped his eyes to the floor. He no longer wanted to look at Grimaldi.

'You know what *your* problem was, Jack?' Grimaldi asked. He was so full of himself and his success that he couldn't help but turn the knife further. 'Your problem was that you thought too *long* range. I know all about you. The looks, the comments behind my back, the bullshit. You wanted to get to me and you thought this was the way. I knew that and I used it, man. I played you like a fucking piano and now the song's over. So fuck you, Jack. Tonight you sleep in the sand. We're gonna take the service elevator down and then we'll use your car – it probably knows its fucking way. You already have the shovel in the trunk, right, Jack of Spades?'

Grimaldi waited for Karch to respond but there was only silence in the room. Grimaldi then delivered his last turn on the knife.

'We'll pick a nice spot for you near your mother.'

Now Karch brought his eyes back to Grimaldi's. The older man nodded.

'Yeah, I know all about it. You and your old man – the favorite spot out there. But here's something I bet you didn't know. I was the one, Jack. I took her away from him. Ten years I was with her behind his back. But she wouldn't leave him because of you. I loved her and then he . . . Tell me, what kind of kid helps his old man bury his mother? You sick fuck. I'm going to enjoy this. Let's go.'

Martin and Romero took two steps back and maintained a safe distance as they escorted Karch out of the suite. As Karch walked his mind grew dark with pain and rage. He concentrated his vision on the man walking in front of him. Vincent Grimaldi. Now Karch knew every last secret.

The four men moved down the hallway until Grimaldi directed them through the push doors into the housekeeping station. Martin hit the button and they waited for the elevator. Karch had his head down and still carried the cloth napkin in his right hand like a flag of surrender. Grimaldi saw it and smiled.

'How was your last supper, Jack?'

Karch looked at him but didn't answer. When the elevator arrived Romero stepped on first to hit the door-open button. He kept the black hole of his gun's muzzle focused on Karch's body the whole time. Grimaldi then stepped on, passing for an instant between Karch and Romero. It was the instant Karch had been waiting for. He raised his right hand toward Martin, who stood to his side. Martin watched the hand holding the napkin come up toward his face.

There was a pop as the .25 hidden in the napkin and Karch's hand was discharged. Martin's head snapped back in the same instant, the bullet catching him in the left eye and entering his brain. At the same moment he was falling lifelessly to the floor of the housekeeping station, Karch was swinging his arm over Grimaldi's shoulder. He fired the first shot at Romero too early. The slug hit the wall of the elevator, a foot to the right of Romero's face.

Romero straightened his shooting arm but hesitated. Grimaldi was in his shot. The delay in his action was all the time Karch needed to correct his own mistake. His second shot hit Romero on the left cheek. The third hit his forehead, snapping his head back. The fourth shot hit the soft underside of Romero's chin and went up into the brain. He dropped to the floor of the elevator without ever getting a shot off.

Karch grabbed Grimaldi by the tie and yanked him to the door of the elevator. Karch had his foot firmly planted against the bumper so the door would not close. He drove the .25 up under Grimaldi's chin so that his face was angled upward while his eyes looked downward and back at Karch.

An evil smile slowly spread across Karch's face.

'So, Vincent, how's the short range looking now?'

'Jack . . . please . . .'

'Be sure to say hello to Mom for me.'

Karch waited for the comeback but there was none.

'You don't know, do you?'

'Know what, Jack?'

'Let me tell you a quick story. About ten years ago the old man got sick. Cancer. It was shot through him and the only way he was going to make it was if he got a bone marrow transplant. I wanted to do it and they took my blood for the match test.'

Karch shook his head.

'No match, Vincent. I told them to do a few other tests and they did. I didn't match because he wasn't my father.'

Karch just stared into Grimaldi's eyes.

'Thanks, Vincent. Back in there you filled in the last part of the story for me.'

'You mean –'

Karch squeezed off two quick shots and watched Grimaldi drop on top of Romero's body. He then looked down at his hand and saw the napkin as well as his fingers and the gun bathed in blood. He felt a tremendous rush move through him. Three against one and he had beaten the odds. He looked around as if hoping someone had seen the magic act he had just performed and would applaud.

And what was more stimulating than the adrenaline blitz of surviving was the release and relief of knowing he was leaving one of life's rooms and going through the door to the next.

He dropped the napkin and reached down and wiped his bloody hand and gun back and forth on Grimaldi's white shirt until they were reasonably clean. He then tucked the gun back into its pocket in his pants and jerked the gym bag out of the dead grip of Grimaldi's right hand.

Karch backed up, grabbed one of Romero's legs and pulled his body out into the elevator's threshold so that the bumper would hit it and the door wouldn't close. He then moved from body to body checking pulses and pulling his Sig Sauer out of the waistband of Martin's pants. He checked the weapon to make sure there was no blood on it and then holstered it. He patted Martin's body until he found and removed the silencer from a front pants pocket.

Finally, he looked around the housekeeping station and saw in the fenced enclosure there was a large laundry basket on wheels. He checked the door but it was locked. He stepped back and shot his leg out, his heel striking the fencing just above the key lock. The door snapped open and inward and he went in for the basket, turning it over first and dumping several stacks of fresh towels onto the floor.

It took almost all of his strength to load all three bodies into the laundry cart. He then used some of the towels to mop up the blood. When he was done he grabbed a blanket off one of the shelves and used it to cover the cart. He pushed it into the fenced enclosure and closed the door.

46

Cassie heard the series of pops that she knew to be gunfire. It sent an electric chill down the muscles of her back.

'Cassie?'

It was Jodie's urgent whisper. Cassie looked toward the reflected glow from the penlight in the duct ahead. Jodie was scared. It was impossible to tell where the shots had come from. She crawled toward the light.

Jodie was huddled by the bars. She put the light on Cassie as she got closer.

'Cassie, I heard loud noises.'

'It's all right, Jodie. It's all right. I'm going to go around now and come get you. You wait right there, okay? You wait for me.'

'No! Don't –'

Cassie had to put her hand over her mouth. When she did it she felt tears on the girl's cheeks.

'It's okay, Jodie. We're almost done. You have to wait here. It's the only way. I will be coming around for you in five minutes. I promise. Look at that watch and see how short five minutes is, okay?'

'Okay,' she said in a small voice. 'I'll be here.'

This time Cassie just reached a hand through the bars that separated them and touched Jodie's cheek. She then started pushing herself backward through the duct toward suite 2001.

When she got to the vent she tapped it with her foot to push it out of its frame. It swung down the wall on the one screw still in place. She climbed out feet first and dropped down to the room service table, carrying her belt bag of tools with her. She took the fact that the table was still in place as a good sign. She went to the television console and was about to turn it off so she could hear better when a voice from behind stopped her.

'Nice move getting in here.'

She turned and Karch was standing in the alcove leading to the bathroom, which was blocked off by the room service table beneath the overhead vent. He held the gym bag down at his side with one hand and a gun pointed at her with the other. She saw the gun had the silencer attached. He pushed the room service table out of his way with a foot and stepped into the room. Cassie backed up against the television, which was showing another Road Runner cartoon.

Karch smiled but there was no warmth or humor in it.

'The Trojan horse,' he said. 'The enemy was inside and they rolled it right in. One of the best magic tricks ever.'

Cassie still didn't say anything. She stood perfectly still and just hoped the television noise was loud enough that Jodie didn't hear this.

'You know those bars you ran into up there in the duct?' Karch asked. 'They were put in after your little spree with Max seven years ago. All the hotels did it. I guess you could say you did your little part to help make Las Vegas what it is today. A safe place for the gambler and his family.'

He smiled again.

'Where's the girl?'

Cassie pointed to the bag in his hand.

'You have the money, Karch. You have me. Let her go.'

Karch frowned as if he was actually considering the suggestion. Then he shook his head.

'Can't do it. I hate loose ends.'

'She's not a loose end. She's not even six years old. What possible danger is she to you?'

Karch ignored the question and wagged the gun at her.

'Let's go into the other room. I like that window better. There's a symmetry to it. That was Max's window.'

Cassie turned and started to move slowly toward the door as she tried to consider options. She decided her only chance was at the door. She had to make a move there, even though he would be expecting it. She gripped the strap of the tool bag tighter and was a few steps from the door when again a voice stopped her. But this one wasn't Karch's.

'Don't you hurt her!'

As Cassie turned she saw that the voice had also caught Karch by surprise. He was instinctively turning, swinging his gun hand up toward the air vent behind him. Cassie's eyes followed the movement and saw Jodie crouched in the air duct, looking down on them.

Cassie acted instinctively, too. She moved toward Karch and swung the tool bag in a wide overhead arc at the same time she yelled to Jodie.

'Jodie, go back!'

The tool bag came down on the back of Karch's head, the steel tools impacting heavily and propelling Karch forward and downward. He fired a shot – which was still quite loud despite the silencer – but the aim was way low and the slug spiderwebbed a mirror in the bathroom alcove.

Cassie moved quickly into him while he was bent over and jerked his suit jacket up and over his head. She then brought her knee up into the tangle of the jacket and felt it connect solidly with Karch's face.

Karch desperately started turning and swinging his arms. A forearm caught Cassie across the side of the face and knocked her away. Karch turned in the direction of the impact and started firing the gun blindly. Stunned by the blow to the face, Cassie was still able to leap onto the bed and roll across it, coming down into a crouch on the floor behind Karch.

Karch continued to fire as he swung his arm right to left. The shots peppered the walls and hit the floor-to-ceiling window twice, causing twin spiderwebs to craze across the glass. He finally was able to straighten up and jerk his jacket back down over his head. He dropped the money bag to do so.

As the jacket came down off his head and his vision cleared, Karch was confused by his location. He was looking out at the Las Vegas night through a wall of shattered glass. There was no sign of Cassidy Black. He realized how vulnerable he was and started to turn just as something solid and hard crashed into the back of his thighs and he was propelled into the glass wall.

The weakened glass gave easily and he crashed through. As he went he let go of the gun and grabbed desperately with both hands for any purchase. His left hand found the curtain and he grabbed on as his upper body went through the glass into the chill night air.

As the glass fell away into the night Karch was momentarily poised on the precipice like a rappeller on a sheer cliff facing. Clinging now with both hands to the golden curtain, his body hung out into the night and was bolstered by his feet on the edge of the window sill.

His weight swung him gently to his left and the curtain started to close. He quickly spread his feet to stabilize himself and the curtain stopped at the halfway mark. He looked back into the room and saw Cassidy Black staring at him, both her hands flat on the room service cart she had hit him with. His eyes dropped to the floor and he saw the money bag and the gun. He reached one hand further up the curtain and started pulling himself back into the room.

With his first pull he heard a popping sound and the curtain gave way a few inches. He froze and waited. Nothing else happened. He looked in at the woman who had put him in this position and their eyes locked. Karch smiled and reached further up the curtain again.

This time the shifting of pressure and weight on the curtain brought a long ripping series of pops as one by one the curtain hooks gave way. The curtain started coming off its attachments and Karch started dropping. He kept his smile, looking at Cassidy Black until the curtain ripped completely free and he was falling through the night.

Karch did not yell. He did not close his eyes. To him his plummet seemed to be in slow motion. Above him he saw the golden curtain waving like a flag. The windows went by, some lighted and some not. Above the building he saw the moon in the blue-black sky.

The void moon, he realized.

His last thought was of the trick. The mail sack and the crate. The secret zipper and the false bottom. How he had to reach up and place the playing card – the Jack of Spades – in the right spot. He remembered how proud his father was. And the applause from the audience.

The clapping was loud and ringing in his ears when he hit the atrium glass. His body crashed through and landed in the empty crow's nest. His eyes were open and there was still a smile on his face.

Glass shattered down on the casino and cries of panic followed. But as the players looked up they saw the gaping hole in the glass and nothing else.

Karch's body could not be seen from below. Then the golden curtain dropped through the shattered atrium like a failed parachute. It seemed to open at the last moment as it glided down into the crow's nest. It draped over Karch's body like a shroud.

A hush settled over the casino and all eyes remained fixed on the gaping, unexplained hole above them. Then out of the blackness of the night sky money came floating down and into the casino. Thousands and thousands of bills came floating in. Hundred-dollar bills. Soon the shouting started again and people began rushing to the money, hands outstretched, jumping and snatching hundred-dollar bills out of the air. A blackjack table was overturned. Men in blue blazers ran into the melee but were overrun by the crowd. Some of them joined in the fight for the money.

Cassie broke open another brick of hundreds and threw the loosened currency out into the night air. The five hundred bills spread apart and started languidly floating down. She heard screams from far below. She looked down and saw that some of the bills were being carried on air currents out to the fountains at the entrance and even over to the Strip. Cars were stopping, horns blasting. People were running into the traffic and the wading pools. People were fighting over the money. She had needed a diversion for an escape. She had one now.

She turned and pushed the room service cart back beneath the open air vent. She climbed up and peered into the darkness.

'Jodie! It's all right. It's me, Cassie. We can go now.'

She waited and then the girl crawled from the shadows of her hiding spot and into the light. Cassie reached her hands in to her and hooked them under her arms. She pulled the girl out and lowered her to the table. She then got down and brought Jodie down. She hugged her for a long moment.

'We have to go now, Jodie.'

'Where's that man?'

'He's gone. He can't hurt us.'

As she turned to lead the girl from the room she saw on the floor two green passports. She picked them up and realized they must have fallen from Karch's jacket when she had pulled it over his head. She opened one and saw her own photo staring back at her. Jane Davis. Clipped to the page was an Illinois driver's license with the same name.

'What's that?' Jodie asked.

'Just some things I dropped.'

She opened the other passport and looked at the photo of Jodie for a long moment. She then closed it and shoved both passports into the back pocket of her jeans. She took Jodie's hand and started leading her out. As she went she bent down and grabbed the gym bag with her other hand. She hadn't kept count but she was pretty sure there were still more than twenty bricks in the bag. More than a million dollars.

She looked at the gun lying on the floor near the open window. She thought about it for a moment but decided to leave it. No guns.

'Let's go,' she said to herself more than Jodie.

As they went through the bedroom Cassie glanced back into the room. In the bullet-fractured mirror she caught a disjointed image from the television. It was Porky Pig doffing his hat. He said, 'Th-th-th-that's all, folks.'

The disorder in the casino was still in full thrust when they came out of the elevator alcove and started making their way toward the exit doors. Cassie picked up Jodie and carried her. They skirted around two men who had wrestled each other to the ground as they fought over a sheaf of bills that had apparently fallen without coming apart.

'What are they doing?' Jodie asked.

'Showing their true hearts,' Cassie answered.

They made it to the exit doors without Cassie seeing a single blue blazer. Cassie turned to push the glass door open with her back because her hands were full with Jodie and the gym bag. She glanced back across the casino, her eyes rising above the melee to the crow's nest. She saw one corner of the gold curtain hanging over the edge. Otherwise it looked empty.

47

Cassie's full focus was on getting to the car and then getting out of Las Vegas. So she and Jodie did not speak until the Boxster was on the freeway heading toward Los Angeles. It was as if Cassie could not take a breath until she was far from the neon glow of the Strip. When she had pushed the Boxster into fifth and set the cruise control at seventy-five, she finally looked over at the little girl belted into the seat next to her.

'Are you okay, Jodie?'

'Yes. Are you?'

'I'm fine.'

'You have a bruise on your cheek where that man hit you. I saw him. That's when I hid in the tunnel.'

'Bruises go away. Are you tired?'

'Nope.'

But Cassie knew she was. She reached across and reclined Jodie's seat to the maximum so that she could sleep. She put the Lucinda Williams CD into the player and put it on low. She was listening to the lyrics and thinking about the choice she had to make at some point on the drive to L.A. when Jodie spoke again.

'I knew you would come for me.'

Cassie looked over at her. The glow from the dashboard revealed her daughter's face looking back at her.

'How did you know?'

'My mommy told me I have a guarding angel watching me. I think it is you.'

Cassie looked back at the road ahead. She felt tears welling in her eyes.

'Guardian angel, baby. *Guardian.*'

'I'm not a baby.'

'I know. I'm sorry.'

They drove in silence for a half minute. Cassie thought about her choice.

'I know,' she repeated.

'How come you're crying?' Jodie asked.

Cassie wiped the tears aside with the heels of her palms. She then tightly gripped the steering wheel and willed herself not to shed another tear in front of the girl.

'Because I'm happy,' she answered.

'About what?'

Cassie looked over at Jodie and smiled.

'Because I'm with you. And because we got away.'

A confused look crossed Jodie's face in the dim light.

'Are you taking me home?'

Cassie nodded slowly.

'Jodie, I'm . . . From now on you're going to be with your mother.'

Jodie fell asleep soon after and dreamed all the way to Los Angeles. Cassie took long looks at her as she slept and thought she saw both Max and herself. She definitely had Max's high forehead. It made her love her all the more.

'I love you, Jane,' she said, using the name she would have given her.

By five the dark tunnel of the desert had turned to a predawn gray and the desolate landscape was overtaken by the gradual buildup of the Los Angeles sprawl. Cassie gulped the last of the cold coffee she had gotten at the window of a twenty-four-hour McDonald's in Barstow. She was on the 10 Freeway heading toward the interchange with the Golden State Freeway, the north-south route which could take her south to Mexico in three hours.

She turned the radio on low and tuned in KFWB, the all-news station that repeated the top stories every twenty minutes. She caught the tail end of a feature report on champagne hoarding for the millennium and then the news anchor broke to a traffic report before starting at the top of the news.

Hers was the first story. She looked over at Jodie to make sure she was still asleep and leaned forward toward the dashboard speaker to hear it better. The anchor had a deep and smooth voice.

> 'This morning authorities were searching for a female ex-convict believed responsible for a one-day crime spree that included two separate shootings and a kidnapping. LAPD spokesmen said Cassidy Black, a thirty-three-year-old woman who served five years in a Nevada prison for a manslaughter conviction, was being sought as the chief suspect in the double murder of two co-workers yesterday morning. The shootings at Hollywood Porsche, where Black had worked as a saleswoman for less than a year, were followed by the shooting in Black's Hollywood home of her parole agent, identified as Thelma Kibble, a forty-two-year-old resident of Hawthorne. Kibble, according to authorities, had gone to Black's home on a routine parolee check and was apparently unaware of the shootings at the dealership earlier. Investigators believe there was a confrontation and Kibble was overpowered and shot once in the chest with her own weapon. Kibble was in critical but stable condition last night at Cedars-Sinai Medical Center. She is expected to recover.'

Cassie leaned forward, closed her eyes and made an audible sigh of relief. Thelma Kibble had made it. She opened her eyes and checked Jodie once more. The girl was still asleep. Cassie focused on the rest of the radio report.

> 'Authorities said Kibble had not yet been interviewed because of her

condition. Late Friday investigators confirmed that Black had also been linked to the abduction of a five-and-a-half-year-old girl from the front yard of her Laurel Canyon home. Authorities said Black is Jodie Shaw's natural mother but gave the girl up for adoption shortly after she was born at High Desert Correctional Institution in Nevada. It was believed that Black abducted the girl in a late-model Lincoln or Chrysler that was black in color with dark-tinted windows. LAPD detectives initially were handling the abduction investigation separately until they learned the missing girl had been adopted and her natural mother was Black. More on this developing story will be available today as the investigation progresses.'

Cassie turned off the radio. She could now see the spires of downtown ahead. She thought about the radio report. The police were following Karch's plan to the letter. She realized that even in death he might succeed.

'Thelma,' she said out loud.

She knew Thelma Kibble was the key. If she made it through she would tell them and the real story would be revealed.

Still, it did not absolve her, she knew. She was guilty. So many deaths. All because of her desires.

She tried to push the thoughts and the guilt away. She knew they would always be near and one day would have to be answered. But for now she had to put them aside.

She reached to her back pocket for the passports. She hit the light over the rearview and opened them side by side on the steering wheel so that her photo was right next to Jodie's. Her eyes fell to the line marked employment. It said Homemaker and she had to smile. Leo's last joke.

She folded the passports closed, one inside the other, and held them against her heart. A sign that announced the Golden State Freeway interchange in two miles went by. Two miles, she thought. Two minutes to decide the future of two lives.

She looked at the gym bag on the floor between Jodie's shoeless feet – her sneakers had been left in the bathroom in the room at the Cleo. The bag contained more money than she had ever conceived of. More than a new start. She knew she could dump the Boxster in South L.A., where it would be picked to a clean skeleton in a day. Take a cab to an auto mall in Orange County and pay cash as Jane Davis. There'd be no connection, no trace. Cross the border and take a flight from Ensenada to Mexico City. From there she could pick the destination.

'The place where the desert is ocean,' she said out loud.

She put the passports back into her pocket and turned off the light. In doing so her hand hit the I-Ching coins she had hung from the mirror. Leo's good luck coins. They swung back and forth and hooked her eyes like a hypnotist's gold watch.

Finally, she pulled her eyes away and looked at her sleeping daughter. Jodie's lips were slightly parted and revealed her small white teeth. Cassie wanted to touch them. She wanted to know every part of her daughter.

She reached over and moved a strand of hair from the girl's face and hooked it behind her ear. It didn't wake her.

Cassie looked back up at the road just as the Porsche approached an overhead sign with arrows pointing out the proper lanes for all traffic heading south.

48

Jodie slowly came awake under Cassie's gentle hand. Her eyes opened and at first seemed concerned as they moved about the car. When they came to Cassie's face the concern was replaced by a look of trust. It was almost imperceptible but it was there and Cassie read it.

'You're home now, Jodie.'

The girl sat up straight and looked out the window. They were driving up Lookout Mountain Road, about to pass Wonderland Elementary.

'Are my mommy and daddy there?'

'They'll be inside waiting for you. I'm sure.'

Cassie reached up and unwound the string of I-Ching coins from the mirror. She handed them to the girl.

'Take these. For good luck.'

The girl took the coins but the concerned look crept back into her eyes.

'Are you coming in to meet my mommy and daddy?'

'I don't think so, sweetheart.'

'Well, where are you going?'

'Away. Someplace far away.'

She waited. All the girl had to say was *Take me with you* and she would change her mind, turn the car around. But those words didn't come and she hadn't expected them.

'But I want you to remember something, Jodie. Even if you can't see me, I'm there. I'll always be watching over you. I promise.'

'Okay.'

'I love you.'

The girl didn't say anything.

'And can you keep a secret?'

'Of course. What is it?'

They were a few blocks from the house now.

'The secret is I have somebody else to help me watch over you. All the time, even though you can't see him.'

'Who is it?'

'His name is Max but you can't see him. He loves you very much, too.'

She looked over and smiled at the girl, remembering her promise to herself not to cry – at least not in front of her.

'So now you have two guarding angels. That's pretty lucky for one girl to have, don't you think?'

'*Guardian* angels. That's what you said.'

'Right. Guardian angels.'

Cassie looked up and saw that they were there. Even though it was not yet five in the morning, the lights were on inside and outside the home. There were no police vehicles at the house. Only the white Volvo was in the driveway. Cassie guessed that the cops figured the last place she would turn up was at Jodie's house. She pulled to a stop next to the curb and kept it running. She immediately reached across and opened the passenger door. She knew she had to do this quickly – not because the cops might be hiding in the house. But because her decision was that close and was that fragile that in another five seconds she knew she might change her mind.

'Give me a hug, Jodie.'

The girl did as instructed and for ten seconds Cassie held her so tight she thought she might be close to hurting her. She then pulled back and held her daughter's face in both hands and kissed both of her cheeks.

'You be a good girl, okay?'

Jodie started to try to pull away.

'I want to see my mommy.'

Cassie nodded and let go. She watched as Jodie climbed down and ran around the picket fence and across the lawn to the well-lighted front door.

'I love you,' she whispered as she watched the girl go.

The front door was unlocked. The girl opened it and went inside. Before the door was closed Cassie heard Jodie's name called out in a piercing scream of relief and joy. Cassie reached across and pulled the passenger door closed. When she straightened back up she looked over at the house and saw Jodie in the arms of the woman the girl thought was her mother. The woman was fully dressed and Cassie knew she had not slept a minute during the night. She cradled Jodie's head in the hollow of her neck, holding her as tightly as Cassie had a few moments before. In the porch light Cassie could see tears streaming down the woman's face. She also saw the woman mouth the words *Thank you* as she looked out at the Porsche.

Cassie nodded, though she knew that in the darkness of the car the gesture probably could not be seen. She put the car into gear, lowered the hand brake and drove away from the curb.

49

She cut up Laurel Canyon to Mulholland and then drove the snaking road east. At a pull-over point overlooking the Valley she watched the sun creep over the mountains to the east and flood the flats below. She put the top down on the Boxster before taking off again. The dawn's air was bone cold but it kept her awake and somehow made her feel good. Where Mulholland dipped down to the Hollywood Freeway she crossed over to the freeway entrance and started heading north.

In her mind she conjured a vision of Max in his Hawaiian shirt on the night in Tahiti when they had made life promises and, in her heart, Cassie knew that their daughter had been conceived. She remembered how they slow-danced barefoot on the beach to music crossing the inlet from the distant lights of a fancy resort. She knew what they had together was inside. All inside. It had always been that way. The place where the desert turned to ocean was the heart. And she would always have that.

By the time she hit the Ventura County line she needed to put on her sunglasses. The air was warming up and whipping her hair around her ears. She knew she had to dump the car and get another. But she couldn't stop. She believed that if she took her foot off the pedal and even slowed down for a moment everything that was behind her would catch up and overtake her. All the death and guilt would come roaring down on her in the road. All she knew was that she had to stay ahead of it.

She just drove.

Acknowledgments

The author gratefully acknowledges the help and efforts of several people during the writing of this book.

Special thanks to Jerry Hooten for his expertise in surveillance equipment and systems and their surreptitious installation. All surveillance technology described in the book actually exists and is available to the public. Any mistakes made herein belong exclusively to the author.

Also thanks for excellent creative input to Bill Gerber and Eric Newman, as well as Bryan Burk, Mark Ross, Courtenay Valenti, Steve Crystal, Linda Connelly and Mary Lavelle.

Thank you to Joel Gotler for his guidance and the title of the book. Also, thanks to Philip Spitzer, Betty Power, Dennis McMillan and Gene Griepentrog, formerly of the California Department of Corrections, Parole and Community Services Division.

The book titled *The New Modern Coin Magic* by J. B. Bobo, published by Magic, Inc., was also a valuable resource to the author.

Thank you to Jane Davis, of See Jane Run, designer and manager of www.michaelconnelly.com, for keeping the web site up to date and interesting.

Lastly, thank you to Michael Pietsch, editor-in-chief at Little, Brown and Company, for another excellent edit.